11 08

MIGUEL DE CERVANTES SAAVEDRA

The Adventures and Misadventures of DON QUIXOTE

An Up-to-Date Translation For Today's Readers

Translated and Carefully Compared
With the 15 Principal English Translations
(from 1612 to 2003)

By

James H. Montgomery

Ne Plus Ultra Publications

ISBN 1-4196-2691-4

To order additional copies, please contact us.
BookSurge, LLC
www.booksurge.com
1-866-308-6235
orders@booksurge.com

Dedicated to Lois,

(My Dulcinea of Toboso)

and to the

Incomparable Miguel de Cervantes

Translator's Note to the Reader

A translator that would write with any force or spirit of an original, must never dwell on the words of an author – John Dryden

A translation is no translation . . . unless it will give you the music of a poem along with the words of it – John Millington Synge

To translate something witty requires a witty translator
– Douglas R. Hofstadter

The present translation is the product of a 21-year labor of love. Twenty-one years is quite a long time to devote to translating any work of literature but, then, this is no ordinary work of literature but the greatest novel ever written according to the Norwegian Book Clubs organization, which in 2002 polled 100 of the world's most celebrated writers from 54 countries. They asked the writers to submit their lists of the greatest works of fiction of all time. *Don Quixote* won the contest hands down; in fact, it garnered over 50 per cent more votes than the work that came in second. But who needs a poll to tell us what people the world over have known and acknowledged for four centuries? In fact, the unique qualities of *Don Quixote* have resulted in its being translated into more languages than any other book, with the single exception of the *Bible*. But despite the novel's acknowledged greatness the fact remains that very few people have actually read the entire novel. And what is equally surprising is that all too many people's knowledge of it is limited to the episode of the windmills, an episode that barely fills two pages! I suspect that a partial explanation for this is the less than satisfactory quality of many of the English translations. With the present one I hope to rekindle interest in this enduring classic in the hopes that readers will discover the magic that has led people like William Faulkner to want to reread it once every year.

Readers will find *Don Quixote* engrossing from beginning to end, due to 1) its all-pervasive irony and humor; 2) its two timeless, universal protagonists, Don Quixote and Sancho Panza, who are among the most lovable characters in world literature; 3) its ability to transport the reader into the society and customs of 17th-century Spain; and 4) Cervantes' captivating literary style which, though simple and straightforward, pushes the limits of the Spanish language with its inventiveness, charm, and playful modes of expression. Then too there are the novel's ingeniously crafted plots and subplots that introduce over 500 characters, all presented so deftly that they emerge as real living human beings. And lastly, there is the wonderfully crafted dialogue, which is among the best ever penned. The challenge for the translator, then, is to bring all these disparate elements across into English. Literally dozens of translators have translated *Don Quixote* into English, beginning in 1612 with Thomas Shelton and ending with Edith Grossman in 2003 and Tom Lathrop in 2006. It is amazing how good the earliest translations were in their attempts at verbal accuracy and fidelity towards the tone and spirit of the Spanish original. But they all possess a certain quaintness imposed upon them by the language of their times. English has changed considerably since the early translators labored and not always for the better. The twentieth century saw six English translations and the twenty-first has already seen three additional ones. The moral here is that we translators intend to keep translating *Don Quixote* until somebody gets it right! Cervantes deserves as much.

The greatest difficulty of all is Cervantes' literary style, which is where many recent English translations have come up short. The style is crucial because it is Cervantes' literary style that lays the foundation for all the other elements in the work, especially for Cervantes' incomparable humor. And, of course, any translation of *Don Quixote* should read as though it has been written in English and is from the pen of a world-famous writer. A literary rendering that settles for anything less is simply not acceptable. Several translators have taken the liberty to make Sancho speak in a less than cultured manner, basing their decision, I suppose, on the fact that in *their* opinion a squire should not speak as eloquently as a knight. But Cervantes derives much of his humor from having Sancho speak in a manner every bit as sophisticated as that of Don Quixote, and this often incongruous speech on the part of the squire accounts for a large portion of the humor. Another major failing of translators is their slavishly literal approach to the Spanish text. A translator's obligation is to convey the *meaning* of the original work rather than to provide a stilted word-for-word translation, for, even though a literal rendering may be easily understood, all too often any humor that was present in the original has vanished. This literalness in rendering idioms and proverbs into English quite often results in English phrases and passages that are unintelligible or stilted.

My first attempt to read *Don Quixote* in the original Spanish was in high school. Later, as a Spanish major in college I came to appreciate its beauty and literary qualities and, as the years passed, read it over and over again in Spanish without any desire on my part to read the novel in English. Finally, out of curiosity I bought a paperback edition in English in early 1986 without bothering to notice whose translation I had bought, inasmuch as I thought all translations would be more or less the same with very little difference among them. I began to read and what a revelation I experienced! I found the English translation to be a tremendous disappointment. While all the characters, ideas, and situations were present, the tone and spirit were very, very different. Where was the enchanting language with its subtlety, irony, wordplay, rhetorical devices, etc.? Where was the humor? I then looked at several other translations and, though some were better than others, I never found any that came close to being satisfying. My disappointment was so great that I told myself I could do a better job than that – after all, how hard could it be to translate this novel? Well, I very quickly found out. I also discovered why the existing translations left so much to be desired. My version for the first few years was no better than the ones I had found so disappointing. However, by continuing to fine-tune my craft and to study the major earlier translations and several modern critical editions of the text, I eventually began to make progress. Finally, in the mid 1990s I found my true literary voice and was soon able to bring across into English the substance and style of the Spanish original that had so captivated me in the first place.

Throughout the years of working on my version I have met with a variety of reactions from my fellow faculty members. Some have considered my efforts to be a bit futile and unpromising at best, others Quixotic at worst, because none of them saw the need to redo what had already been done an endless number of times, a view that is probably shared by the reading public in general. At one institution a professor in the English department even said (facetiously, I have always hoped), 'Hasn't that work already been translated?' – as though any translation would suffice and, hence, would be the definitive one. Unfortunately, this is not the case. When you read a translation of Don Quixote, you are doing just that: reading not the original but *a translation by a particular translator*, and not all translators are created equal. Unfortunately, most English translations do not adequately reproduce the spirit and playfulness of the Spanish original, and no two translations even remotely resemble each other for the simple reason that translating is not a science but an art. Translators are not a *tabula rasa* upon which the original work rewrites itself in the new language; they bring a wide variety of individual qualities to the task at hand. First and foremost, there are their basic personalities and life experiences, which are different for every single person. There is their knowledge of the language, literature, culture, and period of the work being translated, as well as their linguistic and literary skills in the English language. And last but not least, there is the authoritativeness of the text from which the translators are working. Tremendous advances have been made in the last 60 or so years in establishing a reliable Spanish text (or *princeps* edition) with its accompanying linguistic, literary, and cultural apparatus. Surely, in this area modern translators enjoy an enormous advantage over earlier ones. Inasmuch as there can never be a final, definitive translation of *Don Quixote* in English (or in any other language), it is the task of each generation to approximate ever more closely to that elusive ideal. In the present translation I have tried to strike a balance between the worlds of the early 17th century of Cervantes and the 21st century of the present-day reader, a laudable but difficult-to-achieve goal. (If the reader is interested in knowing more about the art and craft of translating, I recommend the fascinating book by Robert Wechsler, *Performing Without a Stage : the Art of Literary Translation*. North Haven, CT : Catbird Press, c1998.) Following are some of the objectives I have set for myself in this new version.

Although *Don Quixote* is universally recognized as one of the most humorous books in world literature, this fact has not always been evident in the various English versions. Its humor, which is present on all levels of the novel, can be savored only if the translator is able to reproduce it in English. Indeed, some translators seem hell-bent on ignoring or downplaying it – or what is just as bad, they concoct their own brand of humor rather than reproducing that of Cervantes. I feel that my translation preserves more of the genuine humor than any previous translation.

I have consistently tried to bring over into English Cervantes' deft and playful use of language, along with his rhetorical devices. Many of his sentences bear the stamp of irony and a tongue-in-cheek perspective and it behooves the translator to reproduce this or he or she will have been unfaithful to Cervantes. Even the best translator is hard pressed to bring across more than 85 to 90 percent of the wordplay of the original. The rest 'remains in the inkwell,' as Cervantes would say.

A number of translations have far too many passages that are awkward, sound translated, or, worse still, are downright unintelligible. I have tried to make my version read as though it were originally written in English and not translated. I have tried to make every sentence read as though the translator was aware of the sentences that preceded and followed it so that the work would possess a coherent style from beginning to end. Some translations read as though each sentence were composed by a different person without regard for what the others were doing.

I am a firm believer in the *mot juste*, that is, finding the correct meaning (or *a* correct meaning) for every word in the text. This contrasts with the practice of a number of translators who appear to choose the first word that comes to mind and then employ that same word every time they encounter the Spanish term, regardless of the context, as though it had a generic equivalent that would fit in every situation.

Any translator worthy of the name will not translate Spanish idioms literally but will seek out their English equivalents. Why, then, will that same translator not treat Spanish proverbs and sayings accordingly? Instead, he or she will translate them with a literalness that often renders them meaningless and incomprehensible in English, making it necessary to resort to footnotes to explain what they *really* mean. I have employed the following strategy: when a literal rendering is understandable and natural sounding in English, I have translated the proverb literally; when this is not the case, I have substituted an equivalent English proverb or, not finding one, have constructed one that has the sound and feel of a *bona fide* proverb conveying the intended meaning of the original.

I have not turned Sancho Panza into a buffoon or a country bumpkin who uses substandard speech. Much of the charm and humor of the *Quixote* arises from the fact that Sancho's manner of speech is every bit as sophisticated as that of Don Quixote, and a considerable amount of the humor derives from the frequent malapropisms that result from his attempts at expressing himself in a manner that is beyond his ability, a source of endless irritation to his master.

I have chosen to retain the Spanish form of all proper names; hence, *Cristóforo* and not *Christopher.* I have kept most place names except when there is a well known modern English equivalent; hence, *Saragossa* instead of *Zaragoza*. In the case of the preposition *de* in people's names I have generally retained the Spanish form but in some cases have converted it to *of*, e. g., *Don Quixote <u>of</u> La Mancha*, rather than *Don Quixote <u>de</u> la Mancha*. The word *señor* I have translated variously as *sir, sire, gentleman, lord, master*, etc., depending upon the context. The same is true with *señora*. To retain the terms *señor* and *señora* in the translated text, as some translators have done, leads to some very peculiar and awkward constructions, plus the uncomfortable situation of continually reminding readers that what they are reading is a translation. The term *hidalgo* has been retained and will be explained in a footnote in the text.

Translator's Note to the Reader

A sizeable problem presents itself with forms of address, viz., 'you.' Mercifully, English long ago gave up class distinctions when people address one another. Not so the Spanish of the Golden Age, which possessed the following forms: *tu* ('thou'), which is the informal 'you;' *vuesa merced* ('your grace'), which is the formal 'you;' and *vos*, a medial form between the two, more formal than *tu* and less formal than *vuesa merced*. All three of these forms (and their slight variations), are pregnant with cultural overtones and present a challenging problem for the translator. I have chosen to render *tu* as 'you,' *vuesa merced* as 'your grace,' and *vos* as 'you' or 'your grace,' depending upon the context in which it occurs. I have reserved 'thou' for poetry in the *Quixote* and for those passages that poke fun at the archaic language found in the older books of chivalry. Don Quixote frequently lapses into this form of speech when amorously addressing his beloved Dulcinea of Toboso or some other lady.

I have retained the Spanish names of monetary units, e.g. '*real* instead of dollar.

Finally, because this translation is aimed at the general reading public, footnotes have been held to a minimum and are designed only to clarify the meaning of the text, never to provide literary interpretations.

James H. Montgomery
Austin, Texas 2006

For any reader interested in a list of the works consulted in the preparation of this translation, please see page 697.

TABLE OF CONTENTS

Table of Contents

Part Two

Table of Contents

[Translation of the title page of the original Spanish edition]

THE INGENIOUS
HIDALGO DON QUI-
XOTE OF LA MANCHA

Composed by Miguel de Cervantes
Saavedra

DEDICATED TO THE DUKE OF BEJAR,
Marquis of Gibraleón, Count of Benalcázar and Baña-
res, Viscount of La Puebla de Alcocer, Lord of
the Towns of Capilla, Curiel, and
Burguillos

In the Year 1605

PRINTING RIGHTS
IN MADRID To Juan de la Cuesta
For Sale at Francisco de Robles, Bookseller to Our Lord the King

[Part One]

Dedication

To the Duke of Béjar, Marquis of Gibraleón and Bañares, Viscount of the Township of Alcocer, Lord of the Towns of Capilla, Curiel, and Burguillos

Confident of the kind reception and homage that your excellency, as a most charitable patron of the fine arts, accords to all types of books, but chiefly to those which, owing to their nobility, do not debase themselves in the service and pay of the masses, I have decided to send forth the *Ingenious Hidalgo Don Quixote of La Mancha* under the umbrella and protection of your illustrious name, and I, with due reverence to one so great, beseech you to welcome him into your gracious protection so that he, though divested of those precious adornments of eloquence and erudition customarily exhibited by works composed in the homes of learned men, may safely and boldly expose himself to the judgement of some who, refusing to confine themselves within the bounds of their ignorance, are given to condemning the works of others with great severity and scant justice. Your excellency, if you in your wisdom will consider my good intentions, I trust that you will not disdain such a meager and humble service.

MIGUEL DE CERVANTES SAAVEDRA

PROLOGUE

Idle reader, you may be assured, without my swearing an oath, that I should like this book, as the child of my intellect, to be the most beautiful, the most elegant, and the most tasteful one imaginable but I have been unable to contravene the law of nature, according to which each thing begets its own likeness. Consequently, what could my sterile, uncultivated wit beget except the story of a lean, shriveled, and fanciful offspring full of various ideas never dreamt of by anyone else, like one begotten in prison, where every lack of comfort has its place and every mournful sound its abode? Leisure, a peaceful site, a pleasant landscape, a serene sky, a murmuring brook, and a carefree soul can go far towards making the most sterile muses turn fecund and bring forth offspring into the world that fill it with wonder and delight.

Occasionally, a father will sire an ugly child devoid of all charm but his paternal love will place a blindfold over his eyes that will make him unable to see its shortcomings, which he will consider qualities of wit and elegance and will describe to his friends as keenness and gracefulness. Though I appear to be the father of Don Quixote, I am only his stepfather and thus refuse to be swept along by the current of custom or to implore you, dearest reader, as others do, virtually with tears in my eyes, to forgive and overlook the defects you may observe in this child of mine, since you are neither a relative nor a friend of his but one whose soul is your own and whose will is as free as the next person's. You are as much a master in your own house as the king is over his taxes, and you know the old saying: 'Beneath my cloak I'll command the king.' [1] Inasmuch as all this exempts and frees you from every consideration and obligation, you are free to express your feelings about this work without fear of being maligned for the unkind things you say or rewarded for the kind ones. I should simply like to present it to you plain and unadorned without the trappings of a prologue or the usual endless list of sonnets, epigrams, and eulogies placed at the beginning of books. I can assure you that, though its composition cost me considerable effort, this was nothing compared to what I expended in writing the preface you are reading, for many times I took up my pen to write and just as

[1] The Spanish saying is: ***Debajo de mi manto, al rey mato*** ['Beneath my cloak, I'll kill the king'] or its variant form: ***Debajo de mi manto, al rey mando*** ['Beneath my cloak, I'll command the king'] The second form of the expression would seem to be the older of the two because of the rhyme ***manto - mando***. A variant of this saying is: ***Delante hago cato, y por detrás, al rey mato*** ['In front of the king I'll obey, but behind him I'll have my way [literally, 'will kill him]'] Here again we have a rhyme: ***cato - mato***. To be sure, the *princeps* edition of 1605 has ***mato*** and not ***mando*** but, whether the former is the word submitted to the printer, we will probably never know. My own feeling is that Cervantes was too finely attuned to language to have intended ***mato***.

many times laid it down, having no idea what to say.

On one occasion, when I was in a thoughtful mood with the paper before me, the pen behind my ear, my elbow on the table, and my head cradled in my hand, pondering what I might say, a genial and perceptive friend of mine unexpectedly entered the room. Finding me thus pensive, he inquired about the cause, and since I had no reason to conceal it, I told him I was mulling over the prologue I was composing for the history of Don Quixote and it had me so out of sorts that I was reluctant to write it, much less to publish the deeds of so noble a knight.

"Because," I said, "how can you expect me not to be concerned about what that ancient lawgiver called the public will say when it sees that, after spending so many years in silent oblivion, I now emerge wearing all my years upon my back with a work as dry as dust, lacking originality, stylistically impoverished, spare in its conceits, devoid of all erudition and doctrine, and lacking quotations in the margins as well as notes at the end of the book, such as I find in other works, regardless of how fanciful or profane – works so full of maxims of Aristotle, Plato, and that whole horde of philosophers that they arouse wonderment in their readers and lull them into believing the authors are well-read, learned, and eloquent men? And when these same authors quote the Holy Scriptures, they are perceived as so many Saint Thomases and other Church fathers, for they are so clever and decorous that in one line they depict a wanton lover and in the very next deliver a devout little sermon that is a delight to hear and a treat to read.

"All this shall be absent from my book because I have nothing to quote in the margins and nothing to explain in the notes and, since I am equally unclear about which authors I am following, I have no idea which ones to place at the front of my book in the usual alphabetical order, beginning with Aristotle and ending with Zeulus or Zeuxis, though the former was a slanderer and the latter a painter. My book shall also forego all sonnets at the beginning, at least, sonnets composed by dukes, marquises, counts, bishops, and celebrated ladies and poets, though I have no doubt that, were I to request them of two or three poet friends of mine, they would provide me with some, and such that they would not be equaled by those composed by more renowned poets in this Spain of ours. In short, my dear friend" – I continued – "I am determined that my lord Don Quixote shall remain buried in the archives of his La Mancha until heaven provides someone who will supply him with everything he lacks, for I find myself incapable of remedying them due to my inadequacies and lack of learning and because I am too lazy and indolent by nature to go about seeking authors to say what I am perfectly capable of saying myself. Out of this arose the confusion and reverie, my friend, in which you found me, and what you have just heard me say is sufficient cause for my distraction."

After listening to this, my friend slapped himself on the forehead and broke into a fit of laughter, at which point he said to me,

"For heaven's sake, my friend, I have just come to the realization that I have been mistaken about you for all the years I have known you, for I have always considered you prudent and judicious in all your actions, but now I see that you are as far from being so as the sky is distant from the earth. How is it possible for matters of so little import and so easily resolved to have the power to paralyze and incapacitate a mind as mature as yours and one so accustomed to overcoming greater difficulties and trampling them underfoot? I assure you that this does not spring from a lack of ability but from an overabundance of laziness as well as poor judgement. Would you care to see if what I am saying is true? If so, listen to me carefully and you shall see more quickly than you can bat an eye how I shall confound all your difficulties and correct all those faults that you say immobilize you and make you hesitate to bring to light the history of your famous Don Quixote, light and mirror of all knight-errantry."

"Say what you have to say," I replied after listening to him speak. "How do you intend to fill the void of my fear or bring order to the chaos of my confusion?"

To which he answered,

"As for the first matter you mentioned, namely, the sonnets, epigrams, and eulogies that you need at the beginning whose authors must be persons of eminence and noble standing, this may be resolved by your taking the trouble to compose them yourself, after which you may baptize them and assign them any names you please, fathering them upon Prester John of the Indies or the Emperor of Trebizond, who, I know for a fact, were famous poets, but even if they were not and there happened to be a few pedants or university graduates who would criticize you behind your back and question your veracity, you need not give it a second thought, for even if they catch you in a lie, they will not cut off the hand with which you wrote it.

"As for the matter of quoting in the margins those books and authors from whom you have taken the maxims and sayings employed in your history, all you need do is to include a few appropriate Latin sayings that you know by heart, or ones that, at best, will not be difficult to locate. For example, if you are making a comparison between freedom and slavery, you can write:

> '*Non bene pro toto libertas venditur auro.*' [2]

And then in the margin you can cite Horace or whoever said it. Should you be discussing the power of death, you can bring in:

> '*Pallida mors aequo pulsat pede pauperum tabernas,*
> *regumque turres.*' [3]

When dealing with the love and friendship that God commands us to extend to our enemies, you can

---

[2] Latin: 'One should not sell his freedom for any amount of gold.'

[3] Latin: 'Death strikes with equal measure the huts of the poor and the palaces of kings.'

come straight to the point with the Holy Scriptures, something you can do with a minimum of research, and you can quote the words of no less a personage than God Himself:

> '*Eco autem dico vobis, diligite inimicos vestros.*' [4]

If you are dealing with the matter of evil thoughts, bring in the Gospel:

> '*De corde exeunt cogitationes malae.*' [5]

If with the inconstancy of friendship, there is Cato, who will lend you his couplet:

> '*Donec eris felix, multos numerabis amicos,*
> *Tempora si fuerint nubila, solus eris.*' [6]

With these and other such bits of Latin you may even be taken for a grammarian, and to be one nowadays is of no small benefit or honor. With regard to adding notes at the end of the book, you may certainly do so, and in the following manner: if you name some giant in your work, make certain it is the giant Goliath, for by this simple act that will cost you nothing you will have an excellent note, because you can write:

> 'The giant Goliath, or Golias, was a Philistine whom
> the shepherd David slew with his mighty sling in the
> Valley of Terebinth, as related in the Book of Kings;'

and then you indicate the chapter in which you found it. Following this, to demonstrate your knowledge of the Humanities and Geography, see to it that the Tagus River is mentioned in your work and you will find yourself with another outstanding note:

> 'The Tagus River, so named by a Spanish king, has its source
> in such-and-such a place and empties into the ocean, bathing

---

4 Latin: 'But I say unto you, love your enemies.' From Matthew 5:44 in the Latin Vulgate Bible.

5 Latin: 'From out of the heart proceed evil thoughts.' Matthew 15:19.

6 Latin: 'So long as you are prosperous, you will have many friends, but when your sky becomes overcast, you will find yourself alone.' *Tristia*, I, 9.

the walls of the famous city of Lisbon, and is reputed to have
golden sand, etc.'

If you are dealing with thieves, I shall tell you the story of Cacus, which I know by heart; if with prostitutes, there is the Bishop of Mondoñedo, who will provide you with Lamia, Laida, and Flora, the note about whom will do you much credit; if with cruelty, Ovid will give you Medea; if with sorceresses and witches, Homer has Calypso, and Virgil Circe; if with valiant commanders, Julius Caesar will lend you himself from his *Commentaries*, and Plutarch will supply you with a thousand Alexanders. When you are dealing with love, even your slight knowledge of the Italian language will enable you to make the acquaintance of León Hebreo, who will satisfy your every need. But if you prefer not to travel abroad, you have Fonseca here at home, whose *Love of God* summarizes everything that you or the most inquisitive person might wish to know on the subject. In short, you need do nothing more than refer to these persons' names or allude to the works I have mentioned and you may leave it to me to provide the annotations and quotations, for I swear by all that is holy I shall fill the margins for you plus two and a half dozen [7] pages at the end of the book.

"Let us now turn to those authors referred to in other books but lacking in yours. The solution to this is quite simple, for you need do nothing more than locate a book that quotes everyone from A to Z, as you have mentioned. You then include that same list in your book, and though the deception may be readily apparent because of the slight need you had in making use of it, it will not matter one whit, and there may even be someone so naive as to believe you have made use of all of it in this simple, uncomplicated work of yours. And even if it should serve no other purpose, at least this long catalogue of authors will lend your work an offhand air of authority. Moreover, there will be no one who will set about to determine whether you have followed all the authors or not, as he will have nothing to gain by doing so, particularly when this book of yours, if I understand correctly, has no need of any of those things you say it lacks, since the entire work is an invective against books of chivalry, which Aristotle never alluded to, Saint Basil never mentioned, and Cicero never heard of. Nor does the faithfulness to truth or the observations of astrology fall within the scope of its outlandish, make-believe world. It is not concerned with geometric figures or with refuting the arguments of those versed in rhetoric. It has no reason to preach to anyone by mixing the human with the divine, a type of fabric in which no decent intellect will clothe itself. It should merely attempt to be true to life in what it describes, for the more realistic your work, the better it will be. And since this work of yours aims only at discrediting the authority and acceptance that books of chivalry enjoy among the world's masses, there is no reason to go about collecting precepts of the Holy Scripture, sententious sayings of philosophers, fables of poets, speeches of orators, or miracles of saints. Rather, by writing in a straightforward manner and using words that are meaningful, appropriate, and

[7] 32 pages, to be exact.

well ordered, strive to make your sentences and clauses pleasant and harmonious, setting forth your intentions to the best of your ability and explaining your concepts without making them obscure or overly involved. Similarly, strive to make your history such that a melancholy reader will be made to smile, a smiling reader will be moved to laughter, an unsophisticated reader will not lose interest, a perceptive reader will marvel at the originality, a serious reader will not hold it in contempt, and a wise reader cannot fail to praise it. In short, keep your sights fixed upon overturning that ill-founded artifice of books of chivalry abhorred by many but praised by so many more, and should you succeed in this, you will have accomplished no small task."

I sat there speechless as I listened to what my friend had to say and his words made such an impression upon me that without questioning them I wholeheartedly accepted them and resolved to let them constitute my prologue, in which you, gentle reader, will discern my friend's keen intellect, my own good fortune in finding so able a counselor at such a time of need, and your good fortune in being given the straightforward and uncomplicated history of Don Quixote of La Mancha, who, in the opinion of all the inhabitants of the district of Campo de Montiel, was the chastest lover and bravest knight seen in those parts for many a year. I have no intention of exaggerating the service I am providing by introducing to you such a noble and honorable knight but I should like you to thank me for allowing you to make the acquaintance of his squire, the famous Sancho Panza, in whom, to my way of thinking, I have concentrated all the squirely qualities that are dispersed throughout that horde of vain books on knight-errantry.

With this, may God grant you health and may He not forget His humble servant. *Vale.*[8]

[8] Latin: 'Farewell'.

FIRST PART
OF
THE INGENIOUS HIDALGO DON QUIXOTE OF LA MANCHA

Chapter One

The character and pursuits of the famous hidalgo [1] Don Quixote of La Mancha

In a village of La Mancha, which I have no intention of naming, there lived not long ago one of those old-fashioned hidalgos who always have a lance in the rack, an ancient buckler, a skinny nag, and a swift greyhound for hunting. A daily stew consisting of more beef than mutton, hash almost every evening, 'grief and sorrows' [2] on Saturdays, lentils on Fridays, and a pigeon or so extra on Sundays consumed three-fourths of his income, with the remainder going for a doublet of broadcloth, velvet breeches with their matching slippers for feast days, and the finest homespun suit, which he sported on weekdays. His household consisted of a housekeeper past forty, a niece not yet twenty, and a servant lad for town and country who did everything from saddling his horse to pruning his trees. Our hidalgo, who was an early riser and fond of hunting, was approaching fifty and had a robust constitution, a lean face, and little flesh on his bones. There are those who would have us believe his family name was Quijada or Quesada (there being some difference of opinion among those authorities writing on the subject), though one might just as easily conclude that his name was Quejana, but since none of this is of the slightest importance to our story, it will suffice if in our narration of it we stray not one iota from the truth.

It should be noted at this point that during his moments of leisure, which amounted to the greater part of the year, the abovementioned hidalgo surrendered himself with such enthusiasm and dedication to reading books of chivalry that he all but neglected the pursuit of hunting and even the

---

[1] ***Hidalgo,*** one of several Spanish words for a nobleman, denotes the lowest class in the hierarchy of nobility. An inherited title, it exempted its possessor from paying taxes but at the same time prohibited him from working for a living. Because it has different meanings in different contexts, I have chosen to retain the Spanish term rather than translate it variously as 'gentleman,' 'nobleman,' 'lord,' etc., as no single translation does it justice in all instances.

[2] In Spanish: ***duelos y quebrantos*** (a popular name for 'eggs and bacon')

administration of his estate. His curiosity and folly increased to the point that he sold off a number of acres of farmland to buy books of chivalry that he could pore over, and carried home as many as he could lay his hands on. Of all those various tomes, he thought none quite so good as those by the famous Feliciano de Silva, for the clarity of his prose and his involved conceits were simply too beautiful for words, particularly in those amorous passages and challenges to duels, such as the following:

> The reason for my reason's being subject to your unreason so
> weakens my reason that, with reason, I protest me of your beauty.'

Or again:

> 'Those divine heavens, which, because of your divine nature,
> fortify you divinely with the stars and make you deserving of
> that desert your greatness deserves.'

As a result of such locutions as these our poor gentleman was slowly losing his wits and would lie awake nights trying to understand them and unravel their meaning, which Aristotle himself could not have unraveled or understood had he been resurrected for just that purpose. He was not entirely satisfied with the wounds Don Belianís inflicted and received, arguing that, regardless of the skill of the surgeons who cared for his wounds, his entire face and body could hardly fail to be covered with scabs and scars. But, for all that, he praised the author for the way he ended his book with his promise of an adventure that would never end and he oftentimes got the urge to take up his pen and finish it himself exactly as it is therein promised, and doubtless would have done so and even been successful at it, had not other greater preoccupations constantly kept him from it. It was his custom to debate with the priest of his village, a learned man and graduate of Sigüenza, [3] as to which had been the superior knight, Palmerín of England or Amadís of Gaul, but Master Nicolás, a barber of his village, said no one could equal the Knight of Phoebus, adding that if anyone could compare with him, it would be Don Galaor, brother of Amadís of Gaul, whose nature allowed him to adapt to any type of situation, since he was not a finicky knight nor as whining as his brother, and in the matter of valor was not one step behind him.

In a word, Don Quixote became so engrossed in his books that he spent all his nights from dusk until dawn and all his days from dawn until dusk poring over them, so that from little sleep and much reading his brain dried up and he finally lost his wits. His mind became so filled with that

[3] To be a graduate of the University of Sigüenza with its low reputation and few students was no great honor.

make-believe world he had encountered in his books – enchantments, disputes, battles, challenges, wounds, amours, broken hearts, adversities, and every sort of impossible nonsense – that it became ingrained in his imagination that all that famous but fanciful fiction [4] that he had read there had actually happened, for in his opinion there was no history on earth that was more factual. He said that the Cid Ruy Díaz had been a very good knight but could not hold a candle to the Knight of the Blazing Sword, who with a single stroke of his blade had cleft asunder two enormous, blustering giants. He looked more kindly upon Bernardo del Carpio, who at Roncesvalles had slain Roland while the latter was under a spell, availing himself of Hercules' stratagem when Hercules strangled Antaeus, son of Earth, in his arms. He had a number of kind things to say about the giant Morgante, who, though springing from that boastful, disrespectful race of giants, was himself affable and well-mannered. But most of all he admired Reinaldos de Montalbán, particularly on those occasions when he would sally forth from his castle to rob anyone he encountered, or on that particular occasion overseas when he stole Mohammed's idol, which was made of solid gold, or so the story goes. And just for the opportunity to administer a fistful of kicks to the behind of that traitor Ganelon, he would have forsaken his housekeeper and his niece as well.

In short, once his wits were no more, he conceived the strangest notion any madman had ever conceived, namely, he deemed it necessary and proper, not only for the increase of his own honor but as a service to his country, to become a knight-errant and to travel throughout the world armed and on horseback in quest of adventures and to perform all those deeds he had seen knights in his books perform: righting all manner of wrongs and exposing himself to battles and dangers whereby, in resolving them, he would win for himself everlasting fame and renown. The poor gentleman imagined himself already crowned emperor of Trebizond at the very least. Swept along thus by these pleasant musings and the uncommon thrill that they afforded him, he hastily set to work to put his plan into operation.

His first act was to clean a suit of armor which had belonged to one of his great-grandfathers and which, now covered with mildew and rust, had been placed ages ago in a corner and forgotten. He cleaned and straightened it as best he could but found it had one major defect, namely, its helmet was not complete, since it lacked a visor. But at this point, his ingenuity coming to the fore, he fashioned a visor from some pasteboard which, when attached to the skull-piece, gave it the appearance of a complete helmet. It should be noted that, in order to test whether it was strong enough to withstand an attack, he drew his sword and gave it a couple of whacks, the first undoing in an instant what it had taken him a week to do, and he was none too pleased with how easily he had demolished it. And so, to insure against this danger, he set to work again and placed some iron strips inside in such a way that he felt satisfied with its strength, but not wishing to put it to the test a second time, he gave it his

---

4 '... famous but fanciful fiction': the Spanish *princeps* edition has: ***sonadas soñadas invenciones*** [***sonadas*** = 'famous'; ***soñadas*** = 'imaginary'; **invenciones** = 'inventions' or 'fiction'] All subsequent editors in Spain have failed to appreciate Cervantes' wordplay and have thus dropped ***sonadas,*** considering it a printing error. Because I have been unable to reproduce the intended effect in English, I have feebly resorted to alliteration.

blessing and dubbed it the finest helmet and visor in existence.

He next went to inspect his nag, who had more cracks in his hooves than a dog has fleas and more blemishes than Gonela's steed, which *tantum pellis et ossa fuit*, [5] but it was his belief that neither Alexander's Bucephalus nor the Cid's Babieca could equal him. Several days passed while he pondered what name to assign him, for, as he said to himself, it would not be proper for the horse of so famous a knight and one so worthy in his own right not to have a name of equal renown. He thus sought to provide him with one that would proclaim what the horse had been prior to belonging to a knight and what he was at the present time, for it was only reasonable that, inasmuch as his master had changed his station in life, the horse should also change *his* name, acquiring one that would be distinguished and high-flown, as befitted the new order and profession he was following. And so, after many names that he devised, altered, threw out, reinstated, threw out again, and refashioned in his mind and imagination, he finally settled upon Rocinante, [6] a name, in his opinion, high-falutin, sonorous, and one signifying what he had been when he was only a nag and what he was now – the first and foremost nag in the world.

Having given his horse a name, and one so to his liking, he set about to confer one upon himself and in this deliberation spent another week, concluding by calling himself Don Quixote, because of which, as already noted, the authors of this most trustworthy history concluded that without a doubt he should be called Quijada and not Quesada as others have maintained. And remembering that the brave Amadís had not been content to call himself simply Amadís but had added the name of his region to make it famous, calling himself Amadís of Gaul, he decided, good knight that he was, to add to his own name that of his native region and to call himself Don Quixote of La Mancha, whereby, in his opinion, he would proclaim aloud his lineage and homeland, thus paying it homage by taking it as his surname.

Once his armor had been cleaned, his helmet fitted with a visor, his nag provided with a name, and himself confirmed, he concluded that all that remained was to single out a lady of whom he might be enamored, for a knight-errant without a lady was a tree without leaves and a body without a soul. And so he said to himself, 'If, owing to my past sins or to my great good fortune, I should encounter some giant along the way, as knights-errant are wont to do, and should defeat him in single combat or split his body down the middle, or simply overcome him and bring him to his knees, would it not be fitting to have some lady whom the giant might seek out and, once finding her, prostrate himself at her feet to proclaim in a voice both humble and subdued, "My lady, I am the giant Caraculiambro, [7] lord of

---

[5] Latin: 'was nothing but skin and bones.'

[6] The Spanish ***rocín*** means 'nag', and ***ante*** (from ***antes***) has two meanings in the present context: 'formerly' and 'foremost'.

[7] ***Caraculiambro***, a made-up word and one of Cervantes' occasional attempts at off-color humor. To a Spanish-speaking reader (or listener) the word would immediately call up ***cara*** ('face') and ***culo*** ('anus').

the isle of Malindrania,[8] who was defeated in hand-to-hand combat by that never-sufficiently-extolled knight Don Quixote of La Mancha, who has ordered me to present myself before your grace, that you may dispose of me according to your will and pleasure.'"

Ah, how pleased our good knight felt after delivering himself of this speech, particularly when he settled upon the one he would designate as his lady. Legend has it that in a village not far from his own there lived a handsome farm girl with whom he had once been in love, though as far as is known, she never became aware of the fact. Her name was Aldonza Lorenzo [9] and he thought it proper to confer upon her the title of lady of his thoughts. And so, searching for a name that would not differ greatly from her own but would incline towards and hint at that of a princess and highborn lady, he concluded by calling her Dulcinea [10] of Toboso – she being a native of Toboso – a name that in his opinion was musical, quaint, and expressive, as were the others he had chosen for himself and all his possessions.

Chapter Two

The ingenious Don Quixote sallies forth for the first time

Having made these preparations, he could hardly wait to proceed with his plan, being pressured by his conviction that the world was in dire need of his presence, such were the grievances he intended to redress, the wrongs to right, the injustices to reprove, the abuses to correct, and the debts to settle. And so, without confiding in a solitary soul or being observed by anyone, early one morning before daybreak (it was one of those scorchers in July) he donned his suit of armor, including his ill-contrived helmet, mounted Rocinante, strapped on his buckler, took up his lance, and through the back gate of a courtyard sallied forth onto the open plain, enormously pleased and even surprised to see how easily he had undertaken his noble venture. But no sooner did he find himself on the open plain than he was assailed by a terrifying thought, so terrifying in fact that it nearly caused him to abandon the barely begun enterprise, for he suddenly remembered that he was not yet a knight and, according to the laws of chivalry, he could not and should not take up arms against any knight whatsoever. And even after becoming one, he would have

---

[8] ***Malindrania***, another made-up word, from ***malandrín*** ('scoundrel')

[9] The name ***Aldonza*** was a common peasant name and was found in a number of popular sayings. It also called to mind the Spanish ***aldea***: 'small22222 village.' Thus, for Don Quixote to have chosen as his ladylove a woman with such an undistinguished name would have provoked considerable laughter in his readers.

[10] From the Spanish ***dulce*** ('sweet')

to wear plain armor – being a novitiate – without any device on his shield until such time that he earned one by his prowess. These thoughts caused him to vacillate in his resolve but, his madness being more persuasive than his arguments, he proposed to have himself knighted by the first knight he encountered, in imitation of a number of knights-errant who had observed this same custom according to all he had read in those books that had such a hold on him. And, as for the plain white armor, he intended at the first opportunity to clean his own so thoroughly that it would be whiter than ermine. With this, he set his mind at ease and continued on his way, giving his horse free rein to follow whichever road he chose, inasmuch as he believed the key to adventure lay in proceeding thus.

While our brand-new adventurer rode along in this fashion, he reasoned with himself as follows: 'Who can doubt that in some future age, when the true history of my deeds comes to light, the sage who records them will write the following when he recounts this my first sally at this early hour: [1] "Scarcely had rubicund Apollo spread the beautiful strands of his golden tresses over the face of the broad, spacious earth, and scarcely had the tiny colorful birds with their harp-like tongues greeted with their dulcet, mellifluous trills the arrival of rosy Dawn, who, abandoning the downy couch of her jealous spouse, revealed herself to mortals along the gates and balconies of the Manchegan horizon, than did the famous knight Don Quixote of La Mancha rouse himself from his idle bed, mount his famous steed, and set out to explore the ancient and renowned plain of Montiel,"' and in truth this is where his horse was wandering. He then went on to exclaim, 'Fortunate the age and fortunate the epoch when these famous deeds of mine shall come to light, worthy of being cast in bronze, sculpted in marble, and painted on canvas as a future memorial. O wise enchanter, whosoever thou art, whose lot it shall be to serve as chronicler of this extraordinary history, I beg thee not to forget my good Rocinante, my constant companion on every road and highway I travel.' Then as though truly smitten, he continued to speak: 'O Princess Dulcinea, mistress of this captive heart, a grievous wrong hast thou done me by dismissing me so cruelly and by obstinately insisting that I not appear in the presence of thy beauty. My lady, pray be mindful of this thy obedient heart, which suffers such anguish for love of thee.'

He rode along stringing out a whole litany of similar absurdities, imitating the style of those he had gleaned from his books and insofar as possible even imitating their language. During all this time, he had traveled so slowly and the sun had risen so quickly and with such intensity that it would have been sufficient to bake his brains if he'd had any. He traveled virtually the entire day without experiencing a single noteworthy adventure, a fact that drove him to despair because he desired right then and there to encounter someone with whom to test the prowess of his mighty arm. Certain authors say the first adventure to come his way was that of Puerto Lápice, while others claim it was that of the windmills, but what I have been able to uncover in this matter and have discovered in the annals of La Mancha is that he traveled the entire day and that, as night approached, he and his nag

[1] In the following passage, as in a number of similar passages farther along, Cervantes pokes fun at the high-flown style found in books of chivalry.

were both so exhausted and famished that he cast his eyes in every direction to see if he could spy a castle or at least a sheepfold where they might retire for the night and relieve their great hunger and other necessities. At that moment he spied not far off the road he was following an inn and it was as though he were seeing a star that was leading him not to the gate of some inn but to the fortress of his salvation, so by quickening his pace he managed to reach the inn just as darkness was closing in.

At the gate there happened to be two young women (also referred to as ladies of the evening) who were traveling to Seville with some muleteers who had stopped at the inn that evening. Now, since everything our adventurer thought, saw, or imagined, assumed the appearance and aspect of those things he had read in his books, the moment he saw the inn, he took it into his head that it was a castle with four turrets and spires of shining silver, the ever-present drawbridge and moat, together with all the other accouterments with which such castles are depicted. He continued to approach the inn – which he fancied a castle – but at a short distance from it drew up on Rocinante's reins, expecting some dwarf to mount the battlements and give a blast on his trumpet to signal that a knight was approaching the castle. But when he discerned that there was some delay and that Rocinante was stepping up his pace to reach the stable, he headed for the gate where he had seen the two dissolute girls, who struck him, however, as two beautiful maidens or two charming ladies taking their ease by the castle gate. It so happened that at this moment in a nearby field a swineherd who was rounding up a drove of hogs (which, without begging anyone's pardon, is what they are called) [2] gave a blast on his horn to round them up, and Don Quixote immediately imagined this to be just what he had desired, namely, that some dwarf was signaling his arrival, and so with rare satisfaction he proceeded towards the inn. The ladies, seeing the approach of a man with lance, buckler, and suit of armor, turned to reenter the inn but Don Quixote, inferring their fear from their flight, raised his pasteboard visor to reveal a parched and dusty face, and in a manner ever so elegant addressed them in a calm voice:

"Flee not, your ladyships, nor fear any impropriety whatsoever, for it ill befits or accords with the order of chivalry, which it is my good fortune to profess to offend anyone, least of all highborn maidens, which your deportment shows your graces to be."

The girls stood staring at him with their eyes darting here and there in an effort to catch a glimpse of his face, which the ill-made visor failed to reveal, but hearing themselves addressed as maidens, a quite unheard-of occurrence in their profession, they could scarcely refrain from laughing, and so uproariously that Don Quixote took offense and said,

"Restraint is becoming in fair damsels, whereas laughter that arises from nothing is absurd in the extreme. If I address your graces thus, it is not my intention to upset you nor to incur your displeasure,

---

[2] The pig or boar was sacred to the goddess-worshiping religions encountered by the Israelites when they occupied the Holy Land, and was subsequently considered unclean by them, a belief that obtained in Spain down to the time of Cervantes and, indeed, even to the present day, especially among the masses. Throughout *Don Quixote* our author pokes fun at the custom of avoiding even the mention of this 'unclean' animal.

for I have no other desire than to be of service to your ladyships."

Our knight's language, which made no sense to the ladies, in conjunction with his woeful appearance, only increased in them their laughter and in him his annoyance, so that matters would have gotten out of hand had the innkeeper not appeared at that moment, a man who, owing to his considerable girth, was quite peaceable. When he saw that ill-contrived figure armed with his mismatched lance, buckler, and corselet, he might very easily have joined the damsels in their expressions of merriment but, fearing such an array of paraphernalia, he thought it best to address him courteously, so he said,

"If, sir knight, your grace seeks lodging other than a bed, since there is none in the inn, all the rest will be found in great abundance."

When Don Quixote observed the humility of the governor of the castle, which is what he fancied the innkeeper and the inn to be, he said,

"For myself, sir castellan, anything at all is sufficient, for

'Arms are my adornments,
Battles my means of rest . . .'"

The innkeeper thought he had called him castellan because he mistook him for one of those good souls from Castile, whereas in actuality he was from Andalusia, San Lúcar Beach[3] to be exact, and was every bit as thieving as Cacus and no less malicious than malice itself; and so he responded in this manner:

"In that case, sir knight, your grace's bed will be hard rocks and your sleep an all-night vigil. Therefore, you may confidently dismount, secure in the knowledge that you will find in this lodge more than enough reasons for getting no sleep in an entire year, much less in a single night."

In saying this, he went over to hold the stirrup for Don Quixote, who dismounted with considerable difficulty and effort, like someone who had not broken his fast during the entire day. The latter told the host to look after his horse, as he was one of the finest specimens that ever ate oats. The host looked him over but did not judge him to be quite as good as Don Quixote had said, in fact, not even half as good. After putting him into the stall, he returned to see what his guest might require and found him being helped out of his armor by the two damsels, who by now had come to accept him. Though they had removed his breastplate and backplate, they were never able to figure out how to disengage his gorget or to remove his ill-fashioned helmet, which was tied on with several green ribbons that would have to be cut because they refused to allow themselves to be untied. Inasmuch as Don Quixote would consent to no such thing, he spent the entire night wearing his helmet, thereby presenting the strangest and drollest sight imaginable. While being undressed, he fancied that these used and abused souls undressing him were two illustrious ladies of the castle, so with great gallantry he said to them,

---

3 A place famous for its criminal elements.

"Never was there a knight
By ladies so well served
As was Don Quixote,
When from his home he rode;
Damsels attended to him,
And princesses to his steed,

or Rocinante, for this, fair ladies, is the name of my steed, and Don Quixote of La Mancha is mine. Though I had preferred not to reveal myself until my exploits performed in your graces' service should do so, the necessity of adapting this old ballad of Lancelot's to the present occasion is responsible for your learning my name so out of season. Still, the time will come when you will command me and I shall obey, and the prowess of my arm shall make manifest my desire to serve your ladyships."

The girls, unaccustomed as they were to hearing such rhetoric, uttered not a word but simply asked him if he would like something to eat.

"I would partake of whatever there is," said Don Quixote, "for according to my understanding, I could do nothing more appropriate."

Since that particular day happened to be a Friday, there was nothing to eat in the entire inn except a few portions of fish called codfish in Castile and Andalusia but troutlet in other parts of Spain. They asked him if he would care for some troutlet, since there was no other fish they could offer him.

"So long as there are a number of troutlets, they may possibly add up to a whole trout," said Don Quixote, "for it is all the same to me whether they give me eight *reals* [4] in change or a single piece-of-eight. And who knows: perhaps these troutlets will be like veal, which is better than beef, or like kid, which is better than goat. But enough talk; bring them quickly, for the burden of bearing arms cannot be sustained unless one's innards have been attended to."

They set him a table near the door for the sake of the fresh air and the host brought him a portion of codfish that had been badly seasoned and worse prepared, together with a piece of bread as black and moldy as his armor. It was quite amusing to see him attempt to eat, for, since he was wearing his helmet and needed both hands for holding up the visor, he was unable to put anything into his mouth and had to have someone else do it for him, which one of the two ladies volunteered to do. Even then it would have been impossible to give him anything to drink had the innkeeper not bored through a reed, placing one end of it in Don Quixote's mouth and pouring wine into the other. All this he patiently endured rather than allow the ribbons on his helmet to be cut. While this was taking place, a hog-gelder arrived at the inn, and no sooner did he arrive than he blew four or five times on a reed pipe, which convinced Don Quixote that he was undoubtedly in some famous castle and was being regaled with music, and that the codfish was trout, the bread white, the prostitutes ladies, and the innkeeper the governor of the castle. Because of all this, he was certain he had made the right

[4] ***Real:*** a silver coin worth one-fourth of a ***peseta,*** the ***peseta*** being the monetary unit of Spain.

decision in undertaking this mission, but the thing that troubled him most was that he had not yet been knighted, for he felt he might not legitimately undertake a single adventure until he had received the order of knighthood.

Chapter Three

The comical manner in which Don Quixote had himself knighted

Troubled by this reflection, he cut short his meager tavernly meal and immediately asked the innkeeper to accompany him to the stable, where he knelt before him, saying,

"Never will I rise from where I am, valiant knight, until your grace has granted me a boon I would request, one whose concession will redound to your everlasting praise and to the benefit of mankind."

The host, seeing his guest at his feet and hearing such talk as this, stared at him in disbelief and did not know what to say or do. After attempting to make Don Quixote rise but, failing to do so, he finally agreed to grant him the boon he sought.

"I should have expected nothing less from your grace's great magnificence," said Don Quixote. "Therefore, I would have you know that the boon I have requested, which you have so generously granted, is that on the morrow you are to dub me a knight, but tonight I shall stand vigil over my armor in the chapel of this castle and, come morning, as I have said, your grace shall perform that which I so fervently desire, that I may travel, as is meet, to the four corners of the earth in quest of adventures on behalf of those in need, for such is the mission of knight-errantry and knights-errant, in whose company I number myself and whose noble aims I share."

The innkeeper, being a bit of a prankster, as we have said, already had an inkling that his guest was not in full possession of his wits and was convinced of it when he heard such talk as this. And so, to amuse himself that night, he resolved to humor Don Quixote by assuring him that he was quite correct in his request and that such a proposal was both natural and appropriate for a knight as illustrious as Don Quixote appeared and his noble bearing showed him to be. As a matter of fact, he himself had followed that honorable profession in his youth, traveling through diverse parts of the world in his quest of adventures, taking particular pains to visit the fisherman's sector of Málaga, the red-light district of Riarán, the thieves' quarter of Seville, the rogues' plaza of Segovia, the alleys and hideouts of Valencia, the prowling grounds of Granada, the waterfront of San Lúcar, the pickpockets' district of Cordova, the gambling houses of Toledo, and sundry other places where he had exercised the celerity of his feet and the dexterity of his hands, committing many wrongs, making off with a number of widows, ruining several maidens, deceiving not a few orphans – in short, making himself known in as many courts and tribunals as there were in the whole of Spain. But he had finally retired to this castle, where he lived off his own possessions and those of others, and where he provided a haven for any and all knights, regardless of their quality or circumstance, simply out of the great affection he bore them and to allow them to share their wealth with him as compensation for his hospitality. He added, however, that there was no chapel in the castle where he could stand vigil over his armor, as it had been torn down to make way for a new one, but he was certain that in an emergency one could stand vigil in any place whatsoever. Tonight Don Quixote could perform the ceremony in one of the castle's courtyards and in the morning, God willing, the requisite ceremonies would be performed, enabling him to be dubbed a knight – and such a knight as the world had never seen.

He asked Don Quixote if he had brought any money with him. The knight informed him that he did not have a cent on him, for he had never read in any of his histories of chivalry that knights carried money with them. To this the host responded that Don Quixote was mistaken, for the mere fact that it was not mentioned in the histories did not mean it was not done, since the authors would have thought it unnecessary to mention anything as obvious and indispensable as money and clean shirts. He might thus rest assured that knights actually kept their pockets lined for whatever emergencies came their way, as confirmed by all the knights with whom those histories were filled and crammed. In like manner they carried shirts with them, as well as small cases filled with unguents to heal any wounds they might receive, for in the fields and plains where they fought and bled there was not always someone at hand to care for them, unless they had some wise enchanter who could aid them by transporting some damsel or dwarf through the air on a cloud carrying a flask of water of such virtue that a single sip of it would instantly cure their wounds and sores, leaving them as though nothing had ever ailed them. But in the event that they themselves had no money, those knights of old considered it acceptable for their squires to come provided with money and other necessary articles, such as lint and ointment for dressing their wounds. In those rare instances when knights lacked squires, they carried everything themselves in rather inconspicuous saddlebags on the haunches of their horses in an effort to disguise them or to make them appear more important than they were, for the custom of using saddlebags was quite frowned upon by knights-errant. Consequently, he would advise him, being unable to command him as he would a godson – which, however, he was about to become – to proceed no further without money or those other provisions already mentioned and he would see how greatly they would benefit him when he least expected it.

Don Quixote promised to comply precisely as he was being advised and it was arranged for him to stand vigil over his armor in a large courtyard situated at one side of the inn. Gathering together all his armor, Don Quixote placed it on top of a trough next to a well; then attaching his buckler and taking up his lance, he began to pace back and forth in front of the trough with an air of dignity, and as he began to pace, night began to fall.

The host informed everyone in the inn of his guest's madness, of the vigil he was engaged in, and of his eagerness to be dubbed a knight. Marveling at such a strange sort of madness, they came outside to observe him but did so from a safe distance. They noticed that at times he would pace back and forth with a look of composure but at other times would lean upon his lance and fix his gaze upon his armor, whence he would not remove it for a considerable length of time. Meanwhile, night had finally arrived but the moon shone so brightly she was able to compete with that other orb that lent her his light, [1] so that everything the novitiate knight did was clearly discernible to everyone. At that moment one of the muleteers lodging at the inn took a notion to water his team, thus requiring him to remove Don Quixote's armor from the trough. No sooner did Don Quixote see him approach than he cried out,

"I say there, rash fellow, whoever you are, how dare you touch the armor of the bravest knight who ever wielded a sword! Think twice about what you are doing, for if you touch that one more time, you shall pay for your insolence with your life."

The muleteer did not concern himself with these words, though he would have been well advised to do so had he been concerned with his health. Instead, he grabbed the armor by the leather straps and flung it some distance away. When Don Quixote saw this, he raised his eyes towards heaven and fixed his thoughts (or so it seemed) upon his lady Dulcinea and said,

"Succor me, my lady, in this first affront with which thine adoring servant must contend. May thy favor and support not fail him now in this his first crisis."

Having said this, together with a number of other things, he threw down his buckler, raised his lance with both hands, and gave the muleteer such a blow on the head that he knocked him to the ground grievously injured and, had he followed it with another such blow, there had been no need of a surgeon to attend him. Having disposed of this matter, he picked up his buckler and resumed his pacing with the same composure as before. A short while later, another muleteer, knowing nothing of what had befallen the first, who still lay on the ground in a daze, approached with the same intention of watering his mules. As he drew near the trough to remove the obstructing armor, Don Quixote, without saying a word or asking anyone's leave, again threw down his buckler and raised his lance. Though the ensuing blow did no harm to his lance, it did considerable harm to the muleteer's head, splitting it open in three places. The noise attracted everyone in the inn, including the innkeeper, and when Don Quixote observed this, he strapped on his buckler, gripped his sword, and said,

"O Mistress of Beauty, strength and support of this faint heart, it is now meet that thou shouldst turn thy sublime attention to this thy captive knight, who stands in readiness for this awesome adventure."

He appeared to gather such fortitude from this speech that, if he had been attacked by every muleteer on earth, he would not have retreated a single step. The wounded men's companions, assessing their situation, began to rain stones on Don Quixote, who attempted to protect himself with his buckler as well as possible but who dared not abandon the trough lest he leave his armor unprotected. The innkeeper shouted at them to leave him alone, having already told them that Don Quixote was mad and for that reason would go free even if he killed everyone there. Don Quixote was also shouting, and even louder, calling them knaves and traitors and saying that the governor of the castle was a good-for-nothing uncouth lout for allowing knights-errant to be treated thus, and were

[1] I.e., the sun.

he already knighted, he would make him pay for his villainy.

"But I take no notice of the likes of you lowly rabble," he said. "Come, attack me and do your worst! You shall see what your insolence and folly earn you!"

He said this with such spirit and bravado that it instilled mortal terror in those who were stoning him. As a result of this and the innkeeper's pleas, they ceased hurling their stones and he in turn allowed them to remove the wounded, at which point he returned to his vigil with the same calm and composure as before. The host, not taking kindly to his guest's pranks, decided to conclude the affair and immediately confer upon him the accursed order of knighthood before any further misfortune could befall them. And so, approaching him, he apologized for the insolent treatment which, unknown to him, Don Quixote had received at the hands of the rabble, who, he pointed out, had been nicely chastised for their insolence. He also repeated that there was no chapel in the castle, nor was one really necessary for what remained to be done, for the crux of the knighting ceremony consisted of being tapped on the neck and shoulder with one's own sword, and this ceremony, according to everything he had read, could be performed in the middle of an open field. Besides, Don Quixote had already satisfied the requirement of standing watch over his armor, since this could be met with only a couple of hours of vigil and he had already put in more than four. Don Quixote naively believed all this and said he was prepared to obey him but asked that it be concluded as quickly as possible, for should he be attacked again once he was knighted, it was his intention not to spare any persons in that entire castle except those the governor might designate, whom he would not harm out of respect for him.

Duly warned and fearing what might happen, the governor produced a book in which he kept the accounts of the hay and barley owed by the muleteers. Accompanied by a boy holding the stub end of a candle and by said maidens, he approached Don Quixote and commanded him to kneel. Then reading from his 'prayer manual' as though he were reciting some devout prayer, he raised his hand midway through the ceremony and gave Don Quixote a smart slap on the neck and a firm blow on the shoulder, both with the knight's sword, during which time he continued to murmur under his breath as though he were praying. Following this, he ordered one of the ladies to gird on Don Quixote's sword, which she did quite coquettishly but cautiously, for it would have required very little to make her burst out laughing at every stage of the ceremony. However, their laughter was held in check by the knight's prowess, which they had just witnessed. As she girded the sword round his waist, the good dame said,

"May God make your grace a most fortunate knight who will be victorious in battle."

Don Quixote asked what her name was so he might know from that moment forward to whom he was indebted for the boon received, as he intended to share with her any honors he should win by the might of his arm. She answered with great humility that she was called La Tolosa [2] and was the daughter of a cobbler and native of Toledo; that she lived among the shops in the Plaza Sancho

---

2 The definite article before the names of the two 'ladies' reveals the nature of their profession.

Bienaya and that wherever she might find herself, she would embrace and serve him as her master. Don Quixote replied that as an expression of her love she was to adopt a title and call herself *Doña* Tolosa, which she promised to do. While the other girl was engaged in buckling on his spurs, he carried on a conversation with her virtually identical to that of the first. He also asked what her name was and was told she was called La Molinera [3] and was the daughter of an honorable miller of Antequera. Don Quixote said she too was to adopt a title and call herself *Doña* Molinera, renewing his offers to serve and favor her.

Once these outlandish ceremonies were concluded, albeit at full tilt, Don Quixote could hardly wait to mount his horse and sally forth in quest of adventures. After embracing his host and saying ever so many quaint things which are too numerous to record, he thanked him for having dubbed him a knight and then strapping the saddle on Rocinante, seated himself on his steed. The innkeeper, in his desire to see him off as soon as possible, answered with no less rhetoric but with much more brevity and, without demanding the cost of his lodging, allowed him to leave, bidding him adieu and good riddance.

Chapter Four

The things that befell our knight when he left the inn

Day was just beginning to dawn as Don Quixote sallied forth from the inn so content, proud, and delighted to see himself knighted that his joy threatened to burst the cinches of his horse, but recalling his host's advice regarding the indispensable provisions he was to carry with him, in particular money and shirts, he decided to return home to provide himself with everything he needed, including a squire. He intended to enlist one of the neighboring farmers, a poor family man who would be perfect to serve as a knight-errant's squire. With this thought in mind, he turned Rocinante towards his village, and his horse, who could virtually smell his stamping ground, began to gallop with such eagerness that his hooves barely grazed the ground. Don Quixote had traveled only a short distance when from a dense forest off to his right he thought he detected some feeble cries like those of someone moaning. No sooner did he hear them than he said to himself,

"I give thanks to heaven for so quickly favoring me by placing opportunities in my path that will enable me to fulfill my obligations to the order of chivalry and to reap the harvest of my noble desires. These cries undoubtedly come from some needy man or woman who requires my favor and assistance."

Tugging at the reins of Rocinante, he turned in the direction from which the cries appeared to come and, after riding a short distance into the wood, saw a mare tied to an oak, and tied to another was

3 'The Miller' or 'The Grinder'.

a lad of about fifteen bare from the waist up and the one who was doing the shouting, and not without cause, for a husky farmer was flogging him with a belt and was accompanying each lash with scoldings and advice, crying out,

"Keep your mouth shut and your eyes open!"

To which the boy replied,

"I won't do it again, master, for the love of God, I won't do it again. I promise to take better care of the flock from now on."

Having observed what was taking place, Don Quixote said in a pique of anger,

"Ungracious knight, it ill becomes your grace to strike a person unable to defend himself. I order you to take up your lance and mount your steed" – for the farmer also had a lance leaning against the oak to which the mare was tied – "and I shall give you to understand that what you are doing is a cowardly act."

The farmer, observing the figure hovering above him clad in armor and brandishing a lance in his face gave himself up for dead and responded with these submissive words:

"Sir knight, this lad I am chastising is one of my servants, whose task is to watch over a flock of sheep I keep in these parts but he's so careless that every day I end up with one less sheep and, because I chastise him for his carelessness, or his knavery, he claims I do it out of stinginess so I won't have to pay him the wages I owe him, but as God is my witness, he is a lying dog!"

"How dare you use such language in my presence, you lowly peasant!" said Don Quixote. "By the sun that shines above us, I have a good mind to run you through with this lance. You shall pay him at once without any more quibbling or I swear to Almighty God that I will put an end to you and annihilate you right here and now, so untie him at once."

The farmer hung his head and without saying a word untied his servant. When Don Quixote asked the latter how much his master owed him, he said he was due nine months wages at seven reals per month. Performing his calculations, Don Quixote found it came to seventy-three *reals*, which he ordered the farmer to pay him on the spot if he valued his life. The frightened serf replied that, by the straits in which he found himself and by the oath he had sworn (having, in fact, sworn no such oath), the sum he owed him did not amount to that much, for one should subtract the money he had given him for three pairs of shoes, plus a *real* for two blood-lettings he had received when ill.

"That is all very well," said Don Quixote, "but let the shoes and blood-lettings be paid for by the lashings you have given him without justification, for if he tore the hide on the shoes you bought him, you have torn the hide on his body; and if the barber has drawn his blood when he was ill, you have drawn it when he was well, so on that score he owes you nothing."

"The problem, sir knight, is that I have no money with me," said the farmer. "Let Andrés come home with me and I'll pay him everything I owe him down to the last *real*."

"Me go home with him?" cried the boy; "not on your life! No, sire, I won't even consider it, for as soon as he has me to himself, he will flay me like another Saint Bartholomew."

"He shall do nothing of the sort," said Don Quixote. "I have only to command him to gain his respect, and provided he gives me his pledge as the knight that he is, he may go free and I shall guarantee the payment."

"I beg your grace to consider what you're saying," said the lad, "for this master of mine is no knight, nor has he ever been admitted to any order of chivalry. He is the wealthy Juan Haldudo of Quintanar."

"That is of no consequence," said Don Quixote, "for even Haldudos [1] may become knights, since each person is the child of his deeds."

"That is certainly true," said Andrés, "but this master of mine – what deeds is he the child of, seeing as how he denies me the wages of my sweat and toil?"

"I am not denying them, brother Andrés," replied the farmer. "Just be so good as to come with me and I swear by all the orders of chivalry on earth to pay you, as I have said, every last *real* all scented and fragrant."

"We can do without the perfume," said Don Quixote, "simply pay him in coin of the realm and I shall be satisfied. And you are to comply as you have sworn to do or I swear by that same oath to hunt you down and punish you, for I shall be sure to ferret you out even if you hide as stealthily as a lizard. And should you care to know who commands this of you so as to be more committed to the task of carrying it out, be advised that I am the valiant Don Quixote of La Mancha, righter of wrongs and injustices. God keep you and may you not forget what you have promised and sworn under penalty of those penalties I have mentioned."

In saying this, he spurred Rocinante and was soon out of sight. The farmer followed him with his eyes and when he saw him enter the forest and disappear, he turned to his servant Andrés and said,

"Come here, my son, I want to pay you what I owe you, as that righter of wrongs has made me promise."

"And paid I shall be," said Andrés. "Your grace would be wise to comply with the command of that wonderful knight – may he live a thousand years! – and, by heavens, if you don't pay me, that knight, who is a brave and noble judge, will return and make good what he's promised to do."

"Of course, I will," said the farmer, "but because I love you so much, I want to increase my debt so as to increase my payment."

And seizing him by the arm, he once again tied him to the oak, where he gave him such a thrashing that he nearly left him for dead.

"Cry out now, Master Andrés," said the farmer, "to your righter of wrongs but you'll see that he won't right this one, which I don't think is finished yet, for I've a good mind to skin you alive as you feared."

But he finally untied him and gave him permission to go find his judge so the pronounced sentence could be carried out. Andrés went away somewhat sulkily, swearing to seek out the valiant Don Quixote and report point by point what had taken place so he could give his master everything he had coming to him, and then some. But despite all that, he went away sobbing while his master remained behind laughing.

Thus did the valiant Don Quixote undo one wrong, being extremely satisfied with what had transpired, for he deemed he had made a most felicitous and auspicious beginning in this chivalry

---

1 ***Haldudo,*** or more precisely ***faldudo,*** means 'full-skirted,' hence Don Quixote's observation that "even Haldudos may become knights."

business. And so, highly pleased and satisfied with himself, he rode along towards his village while softly muttering under his breath,

"Well mayest thou consider thyself more fortunate than any other woman on earth, O Dulcinea of Toboso, fairest of the fair, for it has been thy lot to hold captive and submissive to thy will and pleasure as brave and renowned a knight as is and always shall be Don Quixote of La Mancha, who, as all the world knows, was yesterday ordained a knight and today has righted the greatest wrong and insult ever conceived by injustice or perpetrated by cruelty: today he has wrested the scourge from the grasp of the pitiless adversary who was flogging that delicate child for no reason at all."

Just then, he came to a place where the road branched in four directions and there immediately sprang to mind those crossroads where knights ponder which route they should take. In imitation of them, he sat there motionless for some time and, after thoroughly pondering the situation, relaxed his grip on Rocinante's reins, allowing his nag to follow his own inclination, and to no one's surprise he did what he had done the first time: he chose the road leading back to his stable.

After traveling some two miles, Don Quixote caught sight of a throng of people who, he later learned, were merchants from Toledo on their way to Murcia to purchase silk. There were six of them traveling with their parasols, followed by four servants on horseback and three lackeys on foot. No sooner had Don Quixote caught sight of them than he imagined that here were the makings of a new adventure, and since he imitated as closely as possible all those incidents he had read in his books, here came one ready-made, or so he fancied, for what he intended. And thus, in a display of nobility and bravery he planted himself firmly in the stirrups, tightly gripped his lance, pulled his buckler against his chest, and stationed himself in the middle of the road, where he awaited the arrival of those knights-errant, which is what he judged and believed them to be. When they drew near enough for him to be heard, he raised his voice and in a gesture of arrogance shouted,

"No one shall pass who does not confess that there is no more beautiful maiden upon the face of the earth than the empress of La Mancha, the peerless Dulcinea of Toboso."

The merchants halted at the sound of these words and the sight of the strange figure who uttered them. Sizing him up by his appearance and manner of speaking, they immediately realized he was mad but, wishing to discover in a leisurely fashion where the confession they were being asked to make might lead, one of them who was quite a practical joker and extremely clever said to him,

"Sir knight, we are not acquainted with that noble lady your grace has mentioned. Let us see her and if she is as beautiful as you say, we shall willingly and freely confess the truth of what we are being asked to affirm."

"If I were to show her to you," said Don Quixote, "what virtue would there be in confessing such a manifest truth? The important thing is for you to believe, confess, affirm, swear, and defend without ever having seen her; otherwise, you shall have me to reckon with because of your extraordinary arrogance. So lay on – attack me one at a time as the laws of chivalry demand, or all at once as is the custom and ill-usage among those of your ilk, for here I stand ready and waiting, secure in the knowledge that right is on my side."

"Sir knight," said the merchant, "I beg your grace on behalf of all these nobles here – lest we be forced to burden our conscience by confessing a thing we have never before seen or heard, and one, moreover, so prejudicial to the queens and empresses of Alcarria and Estremadura – to be so kind as to show us some likeness of that lady, be it ever so small as a grain of wheat, for by following the thread, one locates the spool, whereby we shall be satisfied and assured and your grace will be contented and pleased, for I feel so strongly that we are on her side that even if her picture were to show her askew in one eye and oozing vermillion and sulphur from the other, we would say anything in her favor that your grace might wish in an effort to be accommodating."

"Her eye does not ooze, you blasphemous scoundrel," responded Don Quixote in a fit of choler; "I mean it does not ooze what you have said but amber and civet mixed with cotton, nor is she askew in one of her eyes or bent over but straighter than a Guadarrama spindle. You shall pay for the way you have blasphemed such great beauty as that of my lady."

And as he said this, he lowered his lance and charged with such fury and rage at the one who had spoken that, had Lady Luck not caused Rocinante to stumble and fall in the course of his charge, the foolhardy merchant would not have fared too well. As it was, Rocinante did fall and his master went sprawling on the ground. The knight attempted to get to his feet but was unable to do so, such were the encumbrances of his lance, buckler, spurs, and helmet, together with the weight of the ancient armor; and even as he vainly struggled to stand, he kept shouting,

"Flee not, ye cowards! Stand fast, you caitiffs! It is not my fault I am lying here but my horse's."

One of the muleteers who happened to be present was not all that well-intentioned, so when he heard such arrogant taunts coming from the poor soul lying on the ground, he could not refrain from giving him a reply in his ribs. Going over to where he lay, he picked up the lance, broke it into several pieces, and, seizing one of them, began to give our Don Quixote such a pummeling that despite his armor he felt like threshed wheat. The muleteer's masters shouted at him to stop beating him and leave him alone but the servant's blood was so incensed he was unwilling to withdraw from the gambling table before wagering the rest of his anger. Picking up the remaining pieces of the lance, he completely demolished them on the body of the unfortunate knight, who despite that torrent of blows never closed his mouth as he continued to hurl threats at heaven and earth and at those scoundrels, which is what he took them to be.

The servant finally became exhausted and the merchants once again resumed their journey with enough things to talk about to last them the entire trip. When our belabored knight saw himself alone, he made one more attempt to see if he could stand, but if he could not manage it when he was hale and hearty, how could he do so now that he was throttled almost to death? Nevertheless, he considered himself fortunate, for he assumed that this type of misfortune was everyday fare for knights-errant, and the entire fiasco he attributed to the shortcomings of his horse. However, the fact remained that his beaten and battered body would not allow him to rise to his feet.

Chapter Five

The continuation of the narration of our knight's misfortunes

When he finally realized that he could not move a muscle, Don Quixote had the presence of mind to resort to his usual course of action, which was to recall some incident from his books. Accordingly, his madness brought to mind that episode of Valdovinos and the Marquis of Mantua in which the former was left wounded and abandoned by Carloto on the mountainside, a story familiar to children, not unknown to youths, celebrated and even believed by the elderly, and yet no more real than the miracles of Mohammed. This one seemed ready-made for the situation in which he found himself, and so with a demonstration of deep emotion he began to roll about on the ground, feebly murmuring the same things the wounded Knight of the Wood is said to have murmured:

"Where art thou, mistress of my heart,
Unconscious of thy lover's smart?
Ah me! thou know'st not my distress,
Or else art false and pitiless." [1]

and the ballad continued in this manner down to the verses that go:

"O noble Marquis of Mantua,
My lord and my very uncle!"

As luck would have it, when he came to this verse, a farmer chanced to pass by, a neighbor of his from his own village, who was on his way home after delivering a load of wheat to the mill. When he saw the man lying on the ground, he went over to him and asked him who he was and what seemed to be ailing him to make him groan so piteously. Since Don Quixote never doubted for a moment that this man was the Marquis of Mantua, his uncle, he responded by simply continuing to recite the ballad, whereby he gave an account of his misfortune and the love affair between his wife and the

---

1 I have taken all verse translations (with minor modifications) from the extremely popular translation of Charles Jarvis, first published in London in 1742, and republished as recently as 1995 by Barnes & Noble. I have as my precedent the 1818 translation of Mary Smirke, who also appropriated Jarvis' translation of Cervantes' poetry. John Cohen (1950) used the poetry of Thomas Shelton (1612 and 1620). Most translators have provided new translations, though Burton Raffel's (1995) does not employ rhyme. Morton Smith (1908) omitted all the longer poems and many of the shorter ones, which in the opinion of a number of scholars is no great loss.

emperor's son, precisely as it is recounted in the ballad. Astonished to hear such nonsense, the farmer removed Don Quixote's visor, which had been smashed in the pummeling, so he could wipe off his dust-covered face. No sooner did he do so than he recognized him, at which point he exclaimed,

"Sir Quijana (for this was surely his name when he still had his wits about him and had not yet gone from a sedentary hidalgo to a wandering knight), who has gotten your grace into this predicament?"

But Don Quixote responded to everything he was asked by reciting his ballad. When the good man realized this, he removed the breast- and backplates as best he could to see if he was wounded but he was unable to find any wounds or blood. After considerable effort he succeeded in getting him to his feet and seated him on his own jackass, deeming it the more tranquil mount. Picking up the armor and the pieces of the lance, he tied them to Rocinante, whom he led by the reins while leading his jackass by the halter, and then headed towards their village quite disconcerted by the crazy things Don Quixote had uttered. The latter, who was no less disconcerted because of the thrashing and pummeling he had received, was barely able to stay atop the jackass. From time to time he would send forth a sigh that rose to heaven and would cause the farmer to ask him once again what it was that ailed him. It would appear to have been the Devil Himself who was reminding Don Quixote of these stories that were so apropos of the situation, for just at that moment Don Quixote forgot Valdovinos only to recall the Moor Abindarráez when the governor of Antequera, Rodrigo de Narváez, captured him and carried him to the governor's house as his prisoner. And so, when the farmer again asked him how he was and how he felt, he answered with the same words and expressions with which the captive Abindarráez had responded to Rodrigo de Narváez, exactly as he had read the account in Jorge de Montemayor's *Diana*, where it is recorded, and his quotations from the work were so much to the point that the farmer was becoming exasperated at listening to this barrage of absurdities. Inasmuch as he was convinced that his neighbor was indeed mad, he hurried to reach his village to free himself from the anger Don Quixote was causing him with his lengthy harangue. Meanwhile, Don Quixote was saying,

"Sir Rodrigo de Narváez, your grace should understand that this beautiful Jarifa of whom I speak is none other than the fair Dulcinea of Toboso, upon whose behalf I have performed and shall continue to perform the most famous deeds ever witnessed on earth."

To which the farmer replied,

"Pray understand, your grace, that I, alas, am not Don Rodrigo de Narváez nor the Marquis of Mantua but your neighbor Pedro Alonso; nor are you Valdovinos or Abindarráez but the worthy hidalgo Sir Quijana."

"I know perfectly well who I am," said Don Quixote, "and know that I can be not only those I have mentioned but all Twelve Peers of France, and even all Nine Worthies, for the total exploits performed by them as a group or individually shall be surpassed by my own."

While discussing these and related matters, they arrived at their village just as night was falling but the farmer waited for the sky to grow a bit darker so no one would see the battered gentleman who cut such a sorry figure as a rider. When the appropriate hour arrived, he went into the village and up to Don Quixote's house, which he found astir with commotion, for there in the house were the priest and the village barber, who were close friends of Don Quixote, together with the housekeeper, who was saying to them,

"Sir Priest Pero Pérez (which was the priest's name), what does your grace think of my master's misfortune? For three days now we haven't seen hide nor hair of *him*, his horse, the buckler, the lance, or the suit of armor. Wretch that I am, now I can see who the culprit is and I'm as sure of it as of the fact that I was born to die! It's those accursed book's of chivalry he's always reading; they're the ones that have driven him mad. I now remember hearing him say to himself that he would like to become a knight and travel far and wide in quest of adventures. Well, Satan and Barrabas can have those books that have ruined the keenest mind in all La Mancha!"

The niece not only echoed these sentiments but added,

"I would have you know, Master Nicolás (which was the barber's name), that my uncle is in the habit of reading some soulless book of adventure (or misadventure) for two whole days and nights and, once he has finished, will throw it down, grab his sword, and dance about the room slashing at the walls. After he has exhausted himself, he will announce that he has just killed half a dozen giants as tall as towers, adding that the sweat he is sweating is blood from the wounds he has received in the battle. He will then drink a large jug of cold water and become calm, saying the water is a most precious draught supplied him by Esquife, a great enchanter and friend of his. But I'm to blame for everything because I didn't inform your graces of the outrageous things my uncle was doing so the situation might have been remedied before it went as far as it has, for you gentlemen could have burned every last god-forsaken book of his – and, lord knows, he has a bunch that deserve to be burned as though they were heretics."

"I can vouch for that," said the priest, "and upon my word, tomorrow shall not pass before we subject them to an *auto-da-fe* [2] and condemn them to the flames lest they cause those who read them to do what my good friend has probably done."

Since the farmer and Don Quixote were listening to all this, the farmer finally understood his neighbor's illness, at which point he began to cry out,

"Make way for Sir Valdovinos, or rather the Marquis of Mantua, who comes gravely wounded, and the Moorish lord Abindarráez, whom the valiant Rodrigo de Narváez, governor of Antequera, has captured."

At these shouts everyone ran outside, where some recognized their friend, and others their master and uncle, who had not yet dismounted from his jackass, being unable to do so. They ran up to him and embraced him, whereupon he exclaimed,

"Everyone stand back, for I come sorely wounded because of my steed's misstep. Help me to my bed and, if your graces can possibly manage it, summon the wise Urganda, who will treat and care for my wounds."

"Plague take it!" said the housekeeper at this point, "I should have guessed where my master was

---

2 Portuguese ('act of faith'): a public execution of persons condemned to death by the Spanish Inquisition, usually by burning at the stake.

heading with his reading. Master, the bed is waiting and we'll be able to cure your grace without any help from that Urgada. [3] Lord! a thousand curses upon those books of chivalry that have brought your grace to such a pass!"

After carrying him to his bed, they examined him for wounds, and though they were unable to find any, he assured them that his entire body ached from the awful tumble he had taken with his horse Rocinante while fighting ten of the biggest, toughest giants to be found anywhere on earth.

"Good heavens!" cried the priest, "how did giants get into the act? Upon my word, I intend to burn those books tomorrow before the sun goes down."

They put a thousand and one questions to Don Quixote but he merely responded that all he wanted was to be given something to eat and to be allowed to sleep, as those were of the utmost importance to him at the moment. Once his request had been granted, the priest asked the farmer for a full description of how he had found Don Quixote. The farmer described everything, including the outlandish things Don Quixote had said while being brought back home. This made the licentiate [4] all the more anxious to do what he in fact did do the following day, which was to call upon his friend the barber Master Nicolás, who then went with him to Don Quixote's house.

Chapter Six

The grand and exquisite inspection carried out by the priest and the barber in our ingenious hidalgo's library

Because Don Quixote was still asleep, the licentiate asked the niece for the key to the room in which the knight kept his books, inasmuch as these were the authors of all that mischief. She gladly gave it to him and they all went inside, including the housekeeper, where they discovered more than a hundred large volumes all handsomely bound, together with several smaller ones. No sooner did the housekeeper see them than she turned and left the room, only to return a short time later with a bowl of holy water and a bundle of hyssop.

"Take these, sir licentiate," she said, "and sprinkle the room in case there's one of those countless enchanters from his books in here who might cast a spell over us in retaliation for our desire to banish them from the face of the earth."

The priest, who was forced to laugh at the housekeeper's simple faith, ordered the barber to hand him the books one at a time so he could examine their contents, thinking it possible to find some that

3 ***Urgada*** for ***Urganda*** (***urgada***, or, more correctly, ***hurgada***, means 'poked' and has a sexual connotation in the present context).

4 Licentiate: a person with a university degree licensed to practice his or her profession. The priest of the story will have held a Master of Theology degree.

might not deserve burning at the stake.

"No," said the niece, "there's no reason to pardon any of them, for they're all guilty. It will be better to toss them through the window and pile them up in the courtyard, where we can set fire to them. Or we might take them to the stable and build a bonfire out there so the smoke won't bother anyone."

The housekeeper echoed this sentiment, such was the two women's desire to see these innocents put to death, but the priest would not agree to it without at least reading their titles. The first that Master Nicolás placed in his hands was *The Four Books of Amadís of Gaul.*

"There is something mysterious about this one," said the priest, "for according to what I have heard, it was the first book of chivalry published in Spain, all the others having taken their origin and inception from it. Therefore, it seems to me that as the dogmatizer of such an evil sect it should be consigned to the flames without right of pardon."

"I disagree," said the barber, "for I've heard it called the best book of its kind ever written, and since it is unique in its field it should be pardoned."

"True enough," said the priest, "and for that reason its life shall be spared but only for the present. Let me see that one next to it."

"This," said the barber, "is *The Exploits of Esplandián*, lawful son of *Amadís of Gaul*."

"Well," replied the priest, "unfortunately the virtue of the father will be of no avail to the son. Here, madam housekeeper, open the window and throw this one into the courtyard. Let it be the first of the books to fuel our bonfire."

The housekeeper did so with great delight and the good Esplandián went flying into the courtyard, where he patiently awaited the threatening flames.

"Proceed," said the priest.

"This one," said the barber, "is *Amadís of Greece* and it is my understanding that all the books on this side of the room are of the same lineage as Amadís."

"Well, into the courtyard with them all!" said the priest. "To have the opportunity to burn Queen Pintiquiniestra, the shepherd Darinel and his eclogues, together with those diabolically involved conceits of its author, I would burn alongside them the father who bore me if he went about acting like a knight-errant."

"I'm of the same opinion," said the barber.

"Me too," added the niece.

"In that case," said the housekeeper, "give me the books and I'll throw them into the courtyard."

They handed them to her but because there were so many, she spared herself the trouble of using the stairs and simply heaved them through the window.

"What might that hefty tome be?" asked the priest.

"This," replied the barber, "is *Don Olivante de Laura*."

"The author of that book," said the priest, "is the same one who composed *The Flower Garden*, and for the life of me I cannot decide which of the two books is more truthful, or to put it differently, which is less fraudulent. All I can say is that it is headed for the courtyard because of its nonsense and arrogance."

"This next one," said the barber, "is *Florismarte de Hircania.*"

"You mean Sir Florismarte is here?" said the priest. "Upon my word, he shall quickly find himself in the courtyard despite his foreign birth and celebrated adventures, for his dry style and lack of polish give us no alternative. To the courtyard with him, madam housekeeper, as well as that other one."

"With pleasure," replied the housekeeper, as she gleefully carried out his order.

"This one is *Platir the Knight*," said the barber.

"That is an old book," said the priest, "and I find nothing in it worth pardoning. Let him join the others without right of appeal."

Once this was done, they opened another book and saw it was *The Knight of the Cross.*

"Because this book bears such a saintly title, its ignorance might be forgiven, but since they say that 'behind the cross lurks the Devil,' to the flames with it."

Picking up another book, the barber said,

"This is *The Mirror of Chivalry.*"

"I am acquainted with his grace," said the priest. "In this book we have Reinaldos de Montalbán with his friends and companions – bigger crooks than Cacus – as well as the Twelve Peers, and the faithful historian Turpin. Frankly, I am inclined to sentence them to no more than perpetual exile if only because of their contribution to that inspired creation of the famous Mateo Boiardo, from whose work the Christian poet Ludovico Ariosto also wove his fabric.[1] If I find Ariosto here and he is speaking a language other than his own, I shall hold him in contempt, but if he is speaking his native tongue, I shall accord him the greatest respect."

"Well, I have him in Italian," said the barber, "and don't understand him at all."

"It is just as well that you don't," said the priest. "We might pardon the good captain[2] if only he had not brought him to Spain and turned him into a Spaniard, for in doing so he took away many of his native values, just as others do who attempt to translate works of verse into another language. Regardless of how careful they are or how much ability they demonstrate, these will never achieve the heights reached in the language that gave them birth. I shall go so far as to say that this book or any others you find dealing with France are to be saved and stored in a dry well until we are better able to decide what to do with them – with the exception of a certain *Bernardo del Carpio*, who is around here somewhere, and another entitled *Roncesvalles.* As soon as these fall into my hands, they shall be delivered into those of the housekeeper, and from hers into those of the flames without hope of pardon."

The barber nodded his approval to all this, considering it proper and correct, for it was his understanding that the priest was such a good Christian and champion of the truth that he would never utter a falsehood for any reason on earth. Opening another book, he saw it was *Palmerín de Oliva* and next to it was another with the title *Palmerín of England.* When he saw them, the licentiate

---

1 Boiardo's poem was called *Orlando innamorato* and Ariosto's continuation of it was the famous *Orlando Furioso.*

2 A reference to Captain Jerónimo de Urrea, who in 1556 made a shoddy verse translation into Spanish of *Orlando Furioso.*

said,

"Let that *olive* palm be converted into kindling and burned till not even the ashes remain, but this palm of *England* shall be spared and preserved as a unique object. Let another chest be built for it like the one Alexander found among the spoils of Darius, which he set aside to house the works of the poet Homer. This book, my friend, is authoritative for two reasons: first, because it is quite good in and of itself, and second, because it is rumored to have been composed by a wise king of Portugal. All the adventures in the castle of Miraguarda are excellent and quite inventive, and the dialogue is clear in that it always makes each person speak in character, this being done most appropriately and with great understanding. I say then, Master Nicolás, that, subject to your judgement, this book and *Amadís of Gaul* shall be spared the flames, but all the rest, without further inquiry or investigation, shall perish."

"No, my friend," said the barber, "the one I have here is the noted *Don Belianís*."

"Well," replied the priest, "that one with its second, third and fourth parts could use a bit of rhubarb to purge it of its excess choler, and it needs to rid itself of that whole affair of the Castle of Fame, as well as several other more serious incongruities. To that end we shall postpone our judgement while the defense prepares its case and, if these defects are corrected, we shall show it mercy and justice. In the meantime, my friend, keep it in your house but let no one read it."

"Gladly," said the barber.

And not wishing to tire himself further by looking at any more books of chivalry, the priest instructed the housekeeper to take all the oversized volumes and throw them into the courtyard. This was not said to just any person at all but to one who had a greater desire to see them burned than to weave the biggest and finest tapestry in the world; and so, seizing about eight at a time, she began throwing them through the window, but due to her grabbing so many at once, one fell out and landed at the barber's feet, whereupon he felt compelled to read its title, which was *The History of the Famous Knight Tirant lo Blanch*.

"Bless my soul!" cried the priest, "here is Tirant lo Blanch. Let me have it, my friend, for I can attest to the fact that I have found in this book a treasure of happiness and a wealth of entertainment. In it we encounter the valorous knight Quirieleisón de Montalbán, his brother Tomás de Montalbán, the knight Fonseca, the battle between the brave Tirant and the large mastiff, the barbed wit of the maiden Placerdemivida, together with the love affairs and duplicity of the widow Reposada, and the empress herself in love with Hipólito her squire. I tell you, my dear friend, that among those of its genre it is the best book in the entire world, for in it knights eat and sleep, die in their beds, and draw up their wills just before they die, along with other such things that all other books of this genre lack. Considering all this, together with the fact that the one who composed it did not commit all those imbecilities on purpose, I maintain that he deserves to be sent to the galleys – the printer's, that is – for the rest of his life. Take him home and read him and you will see that everything I have said is true."

"I'll do that," said the barber, "but what shall we do with these small books that are left?"

"Those," said the priest, "are surely not works of chivalry but of poetry."

Opening one, he saw it was Jorge de Montemayor's *La Diana* and, believing all the rest to be of the same type, said,

"These do not deserve to be burned like the others, for they will not do as much harm as books of chivalry either at the present time or in the future because they are books of the intellect that will corrupt no one."

"O mercy, sir!" exclaimed the niece, "your grace should have them burned like all the rest, for I wouldn't be the least bit surprised if my uncle, once he's recovered from his illness of chivalry, started reading these books and took it into his head to become a shepherd and go prancing through the woods singing and strumming, or even worse, become a poet, which they say is an incurable disease and quite contagious."

"This young lady knows whereof she speaks," said the priest, "so it will be wise to rid our friend's path of any opportunity to stumble, and since we are beginning with *La Diana*, I feel it should not be burned but should be stripped of everything relating to the enchantress Felicia and the magic potion, along with most of the more learned verse forms. However, it may happily retain its prose and the honor of being foremost among such books."

"This next book," said the barber, "is the second part of the *Diana* by the Salamancan,[3] and following it is one of the same title by Gil Polo."

"Let the one by the Salamancan increase the number of books condemned to the courtyard," replied the priest, "but the one by Gil Polo be preserved as though it were by Apollo himself. But we had better hurry, my friend, and proceed to the next one, for it is beginning to get late."

Opening the next book, the barber said,

"This work is *The Ten Books of the Fortunes of Love,* composed by Antonio de Lofrasso, a Sardinian poet."

"I swear by the orders I have taken," said the priest, "that never since Apollo was Apollo, the muses muses, or poets poets, has such a humorous and outlandish book been written, which in its own genre is the best and most unusual of all those that have seen the light of day. Anyone who has not read it may take my word for it that he does not know what pleasure is. Give it to me, my friend, for I am more pleased to have found it than if I were given a cassock of Florentine brocade."

He laid it aside with great satisfaction and the barber continued, saying,

"These next ones are *The Shepherd of Iberia*, *Nymphs of Henares*, and *Jealousy Unveiled*."

"Well, our only option is to hand them over to the secular arm of the housekeeper and don't ask me why or we shall be here all night."

"This next one is *The Shepherd of Fílida*."

"That fellow is no shepherd," said the priest, "but a most sophisticated courtier. He should be preserved as a precious jewel."

"This large one I have here is entitled *A Bountiful Treasure of Poems*," said the barber.

"If they were not quite so bountiful, they would be more treasured," said the priest. "This book needs to be weeded and cleansed of the numerous vulgarities among its sublimities and it deserves

3 The physician Alonso Pérez.

safekeeping because of the other heroic, elevated works the author has written, and also because he is a friend of mine."

"This one," continued the barber, "is *The Anthology of Poetry* of López Maldonado."

"That author is also a very dear friend of mine," said the priest, "and when he recites the verses himself, everyone listening to him is charmed by the charm of his singing. His eclogues are a bit long but one can never have too much of a good thing, so put it with the chosen ones. But what is that book next to it?"

"*The Galatea*[4] of Miguel de Cervantes," said the barber.

"That Cervantes has been a close friend of mine for many years and I know that he is better versed in misfortune than he is in verses. Though his book has a fair amount of originality, it proposes various things but concludes none; for this, we must wait for the Second Part that he has promised. Maybe when it has been published, it will win the respect the First Part has been denied. While this is being done, though, keep it under house arrest."

"Gladly, my friend," said the barber. "Here come three at one time: *The Araucana* of Alonso de Ercilla, *The Austríada* of Juan Rufo, magistrate of Cordova, and *El Monserrate* of Cristóbal de Virués, a Valencian poet."

"Those three books," said the priest, "constitute the best books of heroic verse ever composed in the Spanish language and they may vie with the most famous ones of Italy. Cherish them as the most precious poetic offerings Spain possesses."

The priest was too weary to peruse any more books, so without inspecting the merchandise he ordered all the rest burned, but the barber had already opened one that was entitled *The Tears of Angélica.*

"I should have shed some myself," said the priest when he heard its title, "had I ordered such a book burned, for its author was one of the celebrated poets of the world, not just of Spain, and his translations of Ovid's fables are absolute marvels."

4 *Primera parte de la Galatea* ['First Part of the Galatea'] published in 1585. A Second Part was promised but never appeared.

Chapter Seven

The second sally of our noble knight Don Quixote of La Mancha

While this was taking place, Don Quixote began to cry out,

"Over here, brave knights! Here is where your graces must demonstrate the might of your valorous arms, for the courtiers are carrying the day in the tourney."

Hurrying to see what the noise and shouting were all about, the priest and the barber called a halt to their inspection of the remaining books, whereby it is believed that *La Carolea* and *The Lion of Spain* went to their fiery deaths without benefit of a hearing, together with *The Exploits of the Emperor*, composed by Luis de Avila, since all these were certainly among the remaining books and would not have received such a severe sentence had they come to the attention of the priest. When they reached Don Quixote, they found him now out of bed, shouting and raving like a maniac. He was as wide awake as if he had never been to sleep and was stabbing and slashing in every direction with his sword. They managed to restrain him and forcibly return him to his bed where, after regaining his composure somewhat, he turned to the priest and said,

"Surely, Sir Archbishop Turpin, it is a great discredit to those of us who call ourselves the Twelve Peers to be resigned, as it were, to permitting the court knights to carry off the victory, seeing that we venturer knights have won the prize on the preceding three days."

"Calm down, my friend," said the priest, "for God will see to it that our luck will change and what is lost today will be regained tomorrow. For the time being, your grace should attend to your health, since you must be extremely tired, if not badly wounded."

"Maybe not wounded," said Don Quixote, "but certainly beaten black and blue, for that whoreson Orlando has given me a thrashing with the limb from an oak, and *that* totally out of envy because he knows I am to be the foil of his endeavors. But I would not call myself Reinaldos de Montalbán if, upon rising from this bed, I did not make him pay for it despite all his incantations. For the present, though, bring me something to eat, which I am certain will be of most benefit to me, and leave the matter of revenge up to me."

Doing as he requested, they brought him some food, after which he fell asleep, leaving them to marvel at his madness. That night the housekeeper set fire to and burned all the books she could find in the house, as well as those in the courtyard. A few that deserved everlasting protection in some archive were probably among those burned, owing to their bad luck and to the laziness of the examiner, thus bearing out the adage that 'Ofttimes the innocent pay for the guilty.'

One of the remedies suggested by the priest and the barber for their friend's malady was to wall up the study containing his books and to plaster over it so that, upon waking, Don Quixote would be unable to find them – perhaps by removing the cause the effect would disappear – and they would tell him an enchanter had carried everything off, study and all. This they hastily did and two days later, Don Quixote rose from his bed and the first thing he did was to pay a visit to his books. When he failed to find his study where he had left it, he wandered from one part of the house to another in search of it. Coming to the spot where the door once stood, he, without saying a word, felt about with his hands while his eyes searched high and low, and after considerable hunting and searching, he asked the housekeeper where the study was that housed his books. The housekeeper, who had been well coached in all her answers, replied,

"What earthly sort of study is your grace looking for? We don't have any study or books in this house, for they were all carried off by the Devil Himself."

"It wasn't the Devil," said the niece, "but an enchanter who arrived on a cloud the night following your grace's departure. After dismounting from the serpent he was riding, he entered the study, where he did who-knows-what inside. A short while later, he went flying out through the roof, leaving the house filled with smoke, and when we decided to see what he had done, we couldn't find the study or a single book. One thing does stick in the housekeeper's and my memory though: at the moment of departing that evil old thing said with a shout that, because of the enmity he secretly bore the owner of these books and study, he had done the damage we would discover inside. He also said he was called Muñatón the Wise."

"He probably said Frestón," replied Don Quixote.

"I don't know whether his name was Frestón or Fritón," said the housekeeper. "All I know is that his name ended in 'tón.'"

"So it does," said Don Quixote, "and that fellow is a shrewd enchanter and a great foe of mine who bears me a terrible grudge because he has discovered through his arts and learning that in the coming years I am to engage a favorite knight of his in head-to-head combat, whom I shall conquer, and he realizes his helplessness to prevent it. For that reason he seeks to cause me all the unpleasantness he can but I can assure him he is wasting his time if he thinks he can contradict or circumvent what heaven has ordained."

"No one would dispute that," said the niece. "Oh, uncle, who gets your grace into these scrapes? Wouldn't it be better to remain quietly at home than to go gallivanting all over the world searching for the impossible and not heeding the fact that 'many who go looking for wool come home fleeced?'"

"My dear niece," replied Don Quixote, "how terribly misinformed you are! Before I would allow myself to be fleeced, I would yank out by the roots the beards of any and all persons who would so much as entertain the thought of touching the tip of a single hair on my head."

The two women were reluctant to comment further, seeing that his anger was mounting. As it turned out, Don Quixote spent two very restful weeks at home, showing no signs of reverting to his madcap behavior, during which time he held the most comical discussions with his companions the priest and the barber. He would assert that knight-errantry was the institution the world was most in need of, and that in him was reborn that chivalresque tradition. At times the priest would disagree with him but at other times was forced to agree, for had he not employed that strategy, there would have been no coming to terms with our knight.

During this period, Don Quixote was wooing one of his neighboring farmers, an honorable man (if such a phrase may be applied to one who is poor) but one quite short on brains. In the end, he talked to him at such great length, used so much persuasion, and promised him so many things that the poor soul decided to go with him to serve as his squire. Among other things, Don Quixote told him he should be glad to come with him because they might possibly have an adventure in which he would win some island quicker than you could bat an eye, and he would make him governor of it. With these and other such promises Sancho Panza (this being the farmer's name) left his wife and children and enlisted as his neighbor's squire.

Don Quixote next set about gathering together some money, and thus, by selling one thing and pawning another but always coming out on the short end of the bargain, he put together a reasonable sum, provided himself with a buckler borrowed from one of his friends, and repaired his broken visor as thoroughly as possible. Next he notified his squire of the day and hour he intended to sally forth so that Sancho might supply himself with whatever he deemed most necessary. He especially urged him to bring some saddlebags and Sancho said he would do so, adding that he also intended to bring an extremely fine jackass he owned, because he was not used to walking. Don Quixote pondered the ass for a moment, doing his best to recall whether any knight-errant had ever brought along a squire traveling jackass-wise, but, as none came to mind, he decided Sancho might bring him but with the stipulation that he would be given a more honorable mount confiscated from the first discourteous knight Don Quixote encountered. The knight provided himself with shirts and other provisions, heeding the advice the innkeeper had given him. After all this was done and attended to, Don Quixote and Sancho Panza – Panza without saying goodbye to his wife or children, and Don Quixote his housekeeper or niece – sallied forth from the village one night unobserved by anyone. They traveled such a great distance that night that they felt certain no one could find them even if they came looking for them. Sancho Panza astride his jackass with his saddlebags and wineskin rode along like some patriarch, eager to see himself set up as governor of the island his master had promised him. Don Quixote was able to follow the same road and route he had followed on his first sally, which led through the plain of Montiel. This time he traveled with much less discomfort than on the previous occasion because the hour was early and the sun's rays struck them at an angle, thereby allowing them to travel refreshed. At that moment Sancho Panza said to his master,

"Sir knight-errant, may I remind your grace not to forget the island you've promised me, for I'll be able to govern it, regardless of how big it is."

To which Don Quixote replied,

"You must understand, Sancho Panza my friend, that it was very much the custom of the knights of old to appoint their squires governors of the islands or kingdoms they conquered, and I am determined that such an esteemed practice shall not fail because of me. Rather, I intend to go them one better, for some of the knights, maybe even the majority, would wait until their squires were old men fed up with years of serving, during which time they had suffered bad days and worse nights, before conferring upon them some title such as that of count or, at the very most, marquis of some valley or province of little or no value. But if you and I manage to survive, it may well be that before six days have passed I shall conquer a kingdom that will also include vassal states subject to it, one of which may be just perfect for making you its king. And don't consider this any great accomplishment, for things and events [1] befall knights in ways never before seen or dreamt of and

1 The Spanish is **cosas y casos,** literally 'things and events.' It is impossible to reproduce this wordplay in English, although two translators have come close: Rutherford (2000) renders this phrase as 'incidents and accidents,' and Grossman (2003) has 'events and eventualities.'

they might easily bring you even more than I have promised."

"That being the case," said Sancho Panza, "if by some miracle I should be made king of those places your grace mentions, my better half Juana Gutiérrez would be nothing less than queen and my children heirs to the throne."

"Can there be any doubt?" asked Don Quixote.

"I have *my* doubts," said Sancho, "for I'm firmly convinced that if God were showering the earth with kingdoms, none would sit well on the head of Mari Gutiérrez. Your grace may as well know she wouldn't be worth two figs as a queen. She'd be somewhat better as a countess, but even there, heaven help her!"

"Put your trust in God, Sancho," said Don Quixote, "for He will provide what is best for her, but at the same time don't set your sights so low you will be content to be anything less than a viceroy."

"I won't, my lord," said Sancho, "especially when I have a master as illustrious as your grace, who will be sure to give me everything that's good for me and that I'll be capable of handling."

Chapter Eight

Our valiant Don Quixote's triumph in the frightful and unprecedented adventure of the windmills, together with other incidents worthy of record

Just then, they spotted thirty or forty windmills scattered across the plain and as soon as Don Quixote saw them, he said to his squire,

"Fate is guiding our affairs better than we could ever have hoped, for you see there before you, brother Sancho, thirty or more colossal giants with whom I intend to do battle and relieve every last one of them of their lives. With the spoils from this adventure we shall take our first step towards enriching ourselves because this is a just war and it is a great service to God to sweep such bad seed from the face of the earth."

"What giants?" asked Sancho Panza.

"Those you see over yonder," said his master, "with those long arms, which on some giants reach up to two leagues in length."

"May your grace observe," replied Sancho, "that those objects are not giants but windmills, and what looks like arms are the vanes the wind drives to turn the millstone."

"It is obvious," said Don Quixote, "that you are not versed in this business of adventures. Those are giants, but if you are so afraid, go off somewhere and say your prayers while I engage them in fierce and unequal combat."

And as he said this, he dug his spurs into Rocinante's flanks, paying no heed to his panic-stricken squire, who was shouting that those objects he was about to attack were windmills and not giants; but so strong was his conviction that they were giants that he failed to hear his squire's shouts or to notice, now that he was quite near, what they were. On the contrary, he rode forward shouting,

"Flee not, ye cowardly, detestable creatures! It is but a single knight who opposes you."

At this moment, the wind increased slightly and the large vanes began to revolve. When Don Quixote saw this, he said,

"Even if ye wave more arms than those of the giant Briareus, ye shall have me to reckon with!"

As he said this, he commended himself heart and soul to his lady Dulcinea, imploring her to assist him at this moment of peril. Then with his buckler shielding his body and his lance in its socket he charged as fast as Rocinante could run, striking at the first mill he encountered. But just as he thrust at the vane with his lance, the wind suddenly gave the vane such a furious turn that it made splinters of the lance and sent him and his horse sprawling on the ground. In an effort to assist him, Sancho rode towards him as fast as his jackass could run and, upon arriving, found him so battered he was unable to move, such had been his fall from Rocinante.

"Heaven help me!" cried Sancho, "didn't I warn your grace to consider what you were doing, since those were only windmills and anyone who couldn't see *that* must have some sort of windmills in his own head?"

"Hold your tongue, my friend," said Don Quixote. "Affairs of war more than all others are subject to continual change. I am more convinced than ever of the truth of this observation when I think that the sage Frestón, who made off with my study and books, has transformed these giants into windmills to rob me of the satisfaction of overcoming them, such is the hatred he bears me; but when all is said and done, his evil arts shall be powerless against the goodness of my sword."

"May God grant that, which He is certainly capable of doing," said Sancho.

After being helped to his feet, Don Quixote once again seated himself on Rocinante, whose back had nearly been dislocated. Then while they discussed the adventure they had just concluded, they set out once again on the road to Puerto Lápice, where Don Quixote said they could hardly fail to meet with numerous and varied adventures because people came to that town from all parts. Nevertheless, riding along with a heavy heart because of the loss of his lance, he said to his squire,

"I remember reading that a Spanish knight named Diego Pérez de Vargas, after breaking his lance in battle, tore a thick limb or branch from an oak tree and with it performed such deeds and thrashed so many Moors on that occasion that he earned the nickname of Thrasher, by which he and his descendants have been known from then until now. I tell you all this because from the first oak that we encounter, I propose to rip off another such limb – and one just as good – and intend to perform such deeds with it that you will consider yourself most fortunate to be privileged to view them and to witness things that will scarcely be believed."

"It is in God's hands," said Sancho, "and I believe everything is just as your grace has described it, but you might sit up a little straighter, for you seem to be listing to one side, which is probably due to your painful fall from the horse."

"That is quite true," said Don Quixote, "and if you do not hear me complain of the pain, it is because knights-errant are not permitted to complain of any wound even if their guts are spilling out through it."

"If that is so," said Sancho, "there is nothing I can say, but God knows how much it would please me if your grace would simply complain when anything is hurting you. I can assure you that, for my part, I am going to complain of the tiniest pain I have, unless that rule of not complaining also applies to squires."

Don Quixote could not keep from laughing at his squire's naiveté and made it clear that Sancho might certainly complain however and whenever he felt the need, willingly or unwillingly, for up until then he had never read anything to the contrary in his books of chivalry. When Sancho reminded him that it was mealtime, his master told him he had no need to eat just then but Sancho might eat whenever he felt like it. No sooner was Sancho given permission than he made himself as comfortable as possible atop his jackass and proceeded to remove from his saddlebags what he had stored inside them. Following along behind his master in this fashion, he rode and ate at his own pace, taking a draught from time to time from his wineskin and with such zest that it would have aroused envy in the most intemperate wine merchant in Málaga. While riding along thus, taking one drink of wine after another, he was unmindful of any promises his master had made him, nor did he consider it laborious but quite restful to be riding about in quest of adventures, however dangerous they might be.

In short, they spent the night among some trees from one of which Don Quixote tore a dead limb to serve him as a make-shift lance, to which he attached the iron tip he had removed from the lance that had gotten broken. He failed to sleep a wink that night from contemplating his lady Dulcinea, thereby imitating what he had read in his books, in which knights were accustomed to spending any number of sleepless nights in the forests and wilds given over to thoughts of their ladies. But this is not the way Sancho Panza spent it, for, having his belly full – and not of chicory water either – he spent the entire night dreaming and, had his master not roused him the following morning, he would not have been awakened either by the sun's rays, which struck him squarely in the face, or by the sounds of the numerous birds greeting the arrival of a new dawn with their joyous chirping. As soon as he got up, he took a swig from his wineskin, which he found somewhat flatter than the night before, a circumstance that grieved his heart, for it seemed to him they were on the wrong road for remedying that situation any time soon. Don Quixote refused to eat breakfast because, as we have already mentioned, he was in the habit of getting nourishment from his savory memories. They resumed their journey to Puerto Lápice and around three in the afternoon were able to make it out. When Don Quixote saw it, he said,

"Here, brother Sancho Panza, we can plunge our arms up to the elbows in this thing called adventure, but remember: even if you should see me facing the most perilous situation in the world, you are not to draw your sword to defend me unless you see that those attacking me are rabble and scoundrels, in which case you may assist me. But if they should be knights, you are by no means allowed or permitted to aid me until you yourself have been knighted."

"Your grace may rest assured," said Sancho, "that I will most strictly observe that point; besides, I am peaceable by nature and averse to butting into other people's rows and disputes. Now, it's true that when it comes to defending my own person, I won't pay a great deal of attention to those laws, since both human and divine ones permit a person to defend himself against anyone who would seek to harm him."

"No one would dispute that," said Don Quixote, "but in the matter of assisting me against knights you are to keep your natural impulses under control."

"I promise to do exactly that," said Sancho, "and I'll observe that precept as faithfully as I do the Sabbath."

While they were engaged in this conversation, there appeared down the road two friars of the Order of Saint Benedict astride two dromedaries, for the two mules they were riding were actually that large. They wore dust masks and carried parasols, and behind them came a coach with four or five men on horseback followed by two muleteers on foot. Traveling in the coach, as they later learned, was a lady from Biscay on her way to Seville to join her husband, who was headed for the Indies to occupy a most prestigious post. The friars were not in her party though they were traveling on the same road. When Don Quixote saw them, he said to his squire,

"Unless I am mistaken this will be the most fabulous adventure ever seen, for those dark forms up ahead must be, and are without a doubt, enchanters transporting some abducted princess in yon coach. Thus, it is imperative that I right this wrong to the best of my ability."

"This will be worse than the windmills," said Sancho. "Pray observe, master, that those are friars of Saint Benedict and the coach probably belongs to someone who's on a journey. Your grace should heed my advice and be careful what you do lest you be deceived by the Devil."

"I have told you before, Sancho," said Don Quixote, "that you have little understanding of this business of adventures. What I am telling you is the truth, as you shall now see."

Having said this, he rode forward and stationed himself in the middle of the road on which the friars were traveling and, when he thought they were close enough to make himself heard, he cried out in a loud voice,

"Ye demons and monsters, release at once those highborn princesses you hold against their will in that coach or prepare to die on the spot as just punishment for your evil deeds!"

The friars drew up on the reins of their mules and sat there astonished not only at Don Quixote's appearance but at his words as well.

"Sir knight," they replied, "we are neither demons nor monsters but two Benedictine monks on a journey, nor do we know if there are any princesses in that coach being held against their will."

"Honeyed words will not mollify me," said Don Quixote. "I already recognize you, you lying scoundrel!"

And without waiting for anyone to respond, he spurred Rocinante, lowered his lance, and attacked the first friar with such fury and daring that, had the friar not let himself slide down from his mule, he would have been knocked to the ground and, contrary to his wishes, badly wounded, if not in fact killed. The second ecclesiastic, observing the way his companion had been treated, slapped the sides of his mountainous mule with his legs and took off across the field faster than the wind itself. When Sancho saw the friar on the ground, he quickly dismounted from his jackass, rushed over to him and began stripping him of his habit. At this moment two of the friars' servants came up and demanded to know why he was removing their master's clothing. Sancho informed them that it now all legitimately belonged to him as spoils of the battle his master Don Quixote had just won. The servants, who were in no mood for jokes, understood none of this talk of battles and spoils and so, when they saw that Don Quixote was now some distance away conversing with the ladies in the coach, they charged at Sancho, knocked him to the ground, and began to kick him and pull the hair from his beard, leaving him prostrate on the ground unconscious, and barely breathing. The friar did not hesitate a moment in remounting his mule, having been intimidated and filled with such dread that all the blood had drained from his face. The instant he saw himself mounted, he took off after his companion, who was waiting for him a safe distance from there hoping to discover how that ambush would end, but being unwilling to wait around for that whole affair to unfold, they resumed their journey and made more signs of the cross than if the Devil had been at their heels. Don Quixote, as we have said, was engaged in conversation with the lady in the coach and was saying,

"Your beauteous ladyship may now dispose of your person as you see fit, for those robbers' arrogance lies there in the dust, laid low by this mighty arm of mine, and lest you be troubled by not knowing your liberator's identity, be advised that my name is Don Quixote of La Mancha, errant and venturer knight and captive of the beautiful and peerless Dulcinea of Toboso. As compensation for the benefits your grace has received at my hands, my only request is that you travel to Toboso and present yourself to that lady on my behalf, informing her of all I did to win your ladyship your freedom."

Everything that Don Quixote had said was overheard by one of the squires accompanying the coach, who happened to be a Biscayan. Seeing that Don Quixote was refusing to let the coach move forward and was even insisting that it return at once to Toboso, the Biscayan lunged at Don Quixote, seized him by his lance, and said to him in poor Spanish and worse Basque,

"Go away, sir, for bad you act. By the God that bred me, if you not leave coach, I kill you as sure as I be here Biscayan!"

Don Quixote understood him perfectly well and with great self-control replied,

"If you were a knight, which you are not, I would already have chastised your foolishness and foolhardiness, you miserable creature!"

To which the Biscayan replied,

"Me not knight? I swear to God you lie big like Christian. If lance you throw down and sword take, you see fast who winner be. Me Biscayan by land, hidalgo by sea, hidalgo by Devil, and you lie if other thing say."

"Now you've gone too far!" said Don Quixote, and throwing down his lance, he drew his sword, slipped the buckler onto his arm, and attacked the Biscayan, being absolutely determined to take his life. When the Biscayan saw the knight rushing at him thus, he would have preferred to dismount from his mule – having no confidence in it, since it was one of those sorry, rented ones – but all he had time to do was to draw his sword. However, it was his good fortune to be next to the coach, from which he was able to snatch a cushion that could serve him as a shield. The next moment found each bearing down upon the other as though they were mortal enemies, while the others tried unsuccessfully to make peace between them. The Biscayan shouted in his poorly constructed sentences that if they did not let him finish the battle, he himself would kill his mistress and anyone else who tried to interfere. The lady in the coach, frightened and shocked by what she saw, made the coachman drive off a short distance, from where she could observe the fierce struggle. In the course of the fray the Biscayan dealt Don Quixote a mighty chop on one of his shoulders, over which he had placed his buckler, and had the blow been delivered without protection, it would have split him down to his waist. When Don Quixote felt the impact of this monstrous blow, he cried out,

"O Dulcinea, mistress of my soul, fairest of the fair, succor this thy knight, who in his quest to repay thy great kindness finds himself in these dire straits!"

To say this, grab his sword, cover himself with his buckler, and attack the Biscayan were but the work of an instant, for he was determined to risk everything on just one blow. When the Biscayan saw Don Quixote rushing at him in this manner, he recognized his courage and resolved to do the same as the knight, and so, standing his ground, he shielded himself with his cushion but was unable to turn his mule one way or the other, for the beast found itself incapable of taking a single step, due in part to sheer exhaustion and in part to his lack of familiarity with such childish activities. Don Quixote, as we have said, had begun his charge at the cautious Biscayan with his sword raised high, determined to cleave him in twain, and the Biscayan sat waiting for him, his sword similarly raised aloft and himself shielded by his cushion. The spectators were all terrified and could hardly wait to witness the outcome of such awesome blows as those that threatened to fall, while the lady in the coach and her retinue of maids made a thousand vows and pledges to all the icons and shrines of Spain for God to deliver their squire and themselves from the great peril confronting them.

But the problem with this whole affair is that at this very time and place the author of our history leaves the battle hanging in midair, offering the feeble excuse that he found nothing more recorded about the exploits of Don Quixote than those already narrated. Still, the second author of our work refused to believe that such a curious history could have been consigned to oblivion or that those persons of intellect in La Mancha had been so lacking in curiosity as to fail to preserve in their archives or registry offices some records bearing upon this famous knight. Because of this, he never despaired of finding the conclusion to this pleasant history, which he did indeed find, being favored by heaven, in the manner that will be described in the second part.

SECOND PART [1]
OF
THE INGENIOUS HIDALGO DON QUIXOTE OF LA MANCHA

Chapter Nine

The conclusion and end of the stupendous battle between the brave Biscayan and the valiant Manchegan

In the first part of our history we left the valorous Biscayan and the famous Don Quixote with their swords drawn and raised, ready to unleash two such furious blows that, should they land squarely, each of the parties would be split open from head to foot like pomegranates. It was at this indecisive moment that our most savory history was halted and truncated, its author failing to inform us where the missing section could be found. This caused me considerable grief, for the pleasure I had experienced in reading such a small portion of it turned into displeasure when I contemplated the difficult road I should have to travel to find the larger portion which in my opinion was missing from this delectable history. I considered it impossible and contrary to normal usage that such a noble knight should fail to have some sage to assume the responsibility of recording his unprecedented achievements, a thing never lacking to any other knights-errant,

'Who go, as people say,
Adventures rare to find;'

for each of them had one or more sages tailor-made, as it were, who not only recorded his every deed but also delineated his most trivial acts and thoughts, however well concealed these might have been; nor could such a noble knight be so unfortunate as to lack what Platir and similar knights had in abundance. And because I could not bring myself to believe that so elegant a history could remain maimed and crippled, I attributed the blame to the malevolence of time, devourer and consumer of all things, which had either hidden or consumed it.

On the other hand, owing to the fact that among his books several modern ones had been found, such as *Jealousy Disabused* and *Nymphs and Shepherds of Henares*, it seemed to me his history

1 Four parts comprised the 1605 publication. In 1614, Alonso Fernández de Avellaneda brought out his continuation of *Don Quixote*, which consisted of parts five, six, and seven. In order to point out the bogus nature of Avellaneda's work, Cervantes dispensed with assigning numbered parts within his own continuation of 1615, calling the later publication the Second Part and referring retrospectively to his 1605 publication as the First Part.

must also be modern and, though possibly not written down, might still be remembered by persons in his village or the surrounding ones. This observation left me confused and eager to learn more of the life and exploits of our famous Spaniard Don Quixote of La Mancha, light and reflection of Manchegan chivalry and the first in our age and these most calamitous times to dedicate himself to the pursuit and practice of chivalry and to the task of righting wrongs, assisting widows, and protecting maidens, including those who rode their palfreys, whip in hand, from hill to hill and valley to valley bearing their maidenhood on their backs, for there have been maidens in times gone by, who, unless violated by some scoundrel, rough-necked peasant, or enormous giant, went to their graves at the age of eighty as pure as the mothers who bore them, notwithstanding the fact that during all those years they never spent a single day under a roof. So in these and a number of other respects I maintain that our brave Don Quixote is deserving of everlasting and wondrous praise, nor should I be denied such consideration myself, by reason of the labor and diligence I expended in ferreting out the conclusion of this pleasant history, though I know all too well that if heaven, circumstances, and fate had not come to my aid, the world would have been left wanting and deprived of the couple of hours of entertainment and pleasure that may be derived from a careful reading of it. Now, my discovery occurred in the following manner.

One day, I was in the Alcaná [2] of Toledo when a lad passed by on his way to sell some manuscripts and parchments to a silk merchant, and since I love to read, even if it is no more than scraps of paper in the streets, I followed my natural inclination and looked at one of the manuscripts the lad was selling, at which point I noticed that some of the characters were Arabic. I recognized what they were but, being unable to read them, began to look about for some Spanish-speaking Moor who could. It was not very difficult to find such an interpreter, for had I sought someone to translate an even better and more venerable tongue, I would have succeeded. In short, fate provided me with one and, when I told him what I wanted and placed the book in his hands, he opened it in the middle and after a brief perusal broke out in laughter. I asked him what had caused him to laugh and he said it was something written in the margin of the book by way of annotation. When I asked him to read me what it said, he, without ceasing to laugh, replied,

"This, as I have said, is what is written in the margin: 'They say that this Dulcinea of Toboso, so frequently referred to in this history, had a better hand than any other woman in all La Mancha at salting pork.'"

When I heard him mention Dulcinea of Toboso, I was astounded and flabbergasted, for it suddenly occurred to me that those portfolios contained the history of Don Quixote. Acting on this assumption I immediately asked him to read the first page, which he did, making an improvised translation from Arabic into Spanish. According to him, it read: *History of Don Quixote of La Mancha, Composed by Cide Hamete Benengeli, Arabic Historian.* I had to be awfully clever to disguise my joy when that title reached my ears, and so, getting the jump on the silk merchant, I bought all the papers and portfolios from the boy for half a *real.* Had the lad been astute and realized how badly I wanted them, he could

2 A market street.

easily have anticipated and received more than six *reals* from the sale. I at once withdrew with the Moor to the cathedral cloister, where I asked him to translate into Spanish all those manuscripts which dealt with Don Quixote and not to add or subtract a thing. When I offered to pay him any amount he wanted, he agreed to fifty pounds of raisins and two bushels of wheat and promised to translate them faithfully and concisely. But to facilitate the transaction and not to allow my lucky find to escape my grasp, I took him to my home, where in slightly more than a month and a half he translated it in its entirety, exactly as it is herein recorded.

In the first portfolio, executed in a most realistic style, was a picture of the battle between Don Quixote and the Biscayan, who were shown in the same pose described in the history: their swords raised, one covered by his buckler and the other by his cushion, with the Biscayan's mule so lifelike it showed from as far away as a musket shot that it was one of those sorry mules for hire. At the Biscayan's feet was a caption that read: *Don Sancho de Azpeitia*, which was undoubtedly his name. At Rocinante's feet was another that read: *Don Quixote*. Rocinante was marvelously depicted: so long and extended, so drawn and thin, so much of his backbone showing, and so obviously consumptive that he clearly demonstrated how advisedly and appropriately he had been given the name Rocinante. Next to him was Sancho Panza holding his jackass by the halter, at whose feet was another caption that read: *Sancho Zancas*. By the way the picture portrayed him, he must have had a large paunch, a short frame, and long shanks, for which reason he was probably given the names 'Panza' and 'Zancas,' [3] the two names by which he is called in different sections of the history. There are other minor details that might be pointed out but they are all insignificant and have no bearing upon the faithful relation of this history. No history is bad, though, so long as it is true.

And yet, if any objection might be raised concerning the truthfulness of this chronicle, it can only be that its author was an Arab, it being a common occurrence for those of that race to be liars. And since they are such enemies of ours, I am more inclined to believe something has been omitted rather than added, for it seems to me that when he could and should have employed his pen in praise of this wonderful knight, he purposely passed over them in silence, an act that is bad enough to contemplate but worse still to carry out, for historians are obliged to be exact, truthful, and impartial, and neither their interests, fears, likes, nor dislikes should make them stray from the path of truth, whose mother is history, rival of time, repository of deeds, witness to the past, example and advisor to the present, and admonition to the future. In this history I feel certain you will find everything as pleasant as you might wish but, if anything good should be lacking, I am convinced it was the fault of that dog of an author rather than a defect in the subject. In short, its second part, according to the translation, began with these words:

With their trenchant swords raised high in anticipation, the two brave, enraged combatants appeared to be defying heaven, earth, and hell, such were their aspect and demeanor. The first to unleash his blow was the incensed Biscayan, which blow was delivered with such force and fury that,

---

3 ***Panza*** means 'paunch' or 'belly'; ***zancas*** 'shanks'. Never again in the entire history is the squire referred to as Sancho Zancas — only as Sancho or Sancho Panza.

had the blade not turned sideways in its trajectory, that single stroke would have been sufficient to put an end to their bitter struggle and to all our knight's adventures. But good fortune, which was preserving him for greater things, caused his adversary's sword to turn sideways so that, despite landing on his left shoulder, it did no more harm than to knock off all the armor on that side of his body and to strip him of a large portion of the visor plus half of an ear, all of which came to the ground with a frightful crash, leaving him badly battered.

But, bless my soul, if only there were someone who could describe the outrage that filled our Manchegan's heart when he saw himself treated in such a manner. Let me simply say that once again he braced himself in his stirrups, gripped his sword even more securely with both hands, and unleashed a furious blow at the Biscayan, hitting him squarely on top of the cushion and hence squarely on top of his head owing to his ineffectual defense. The latter felt as though a mountain had fallen on him and he began to spurt blood from his nostrils, mouth, and ears. He also seemed on the verge of falling from his mule, which he would certainly have done had he not grabbed it round the neck. However, when he pulled his feet from the stirrups and relaxed his grip, the mule, which had been frightened by the terrible blow, took off across the field and after a few bucks and kicks threw its rider to the ground.

Don Quixote had been observing all this quite calmly and, when he saw him fall, he leapt from his horse, ran over to him in great haste, and stuck the point of his sword between the Biscayan's eyes, ordering him to surrender or have his head cut off. The Biscayan was so stunned he was unable to utter a word and would have fared badly, so blinded by rage was Don Quixote, had the ladies in the coach, who until that moment had viewed the battle in dismay, not hurried over to plead with great insistence that he favor them by sparing their squire's life; to which Don Quixote responded with considerable haughtiness and severity:

"Most assuredly, fair ladies, I shall be happy to comply with your graces' request but only on one condition and understanding, namely, that this knight shall promise me to go to the village of Toboso and present himself on my behalf to the peerless Dulcinea, that she may deal with him according to her pleasure."

The frightened, disconsolate ladies, not understanding what Don Quixote was requesting and not asking who Dulcinea was, promised him their squire would do everything demanded of him.

"Well then, on the strength of that promise I shall inflict no further harm upon him, though he certainly has it coming."

Chapter Ten

The amusing conversation between Don Quixote and his squire Sancho Panza [1]

In the meantime, Sancho, who had been somewhat manhandled by the friar's servants, struggled to his feet and, closely observing his master Don Quixote's battle, prayed in his heart that God would make his master victorious and permit him to win some island over which he could appoint him governor, as he had promised. Once the struggle had ended and he saw his master was about to remount Rocinante, he went over to hold his stirrup but, before Don Quixote could mount, Sancho knelt before him, took his hand in his and, kissing it, said,

"Master Don Quixote, I pray your grace will be so kind as to grant me the governorship of the island you've just won in this fierce encounter, for regardless of its size, I feel I'm as qualified to govern it as anyone who ever governed an island."

To this Don Quixote replied,

"Be advised, brother Sancho, that this adventure and others like it are not adventures involving islands but crossroads, from which one comes away with nothing more than a fractured skull or a missing ear. Be patient, my son, for adventures will come by virtue of which I can make you not only a governor but something even better."

Heartily thanking his master, Sancho once again kissed his hand and the hem of his tunic and helped him to mount Rocinante. He himself mounted his jackass and followed along behind his master who, without taking leave of the ladies in the coach or directing any further remarks to them, rode off at full gallop into the nearby forest. Sancho followed as fast as his jackass could trot but Rocinante was traveling so fast Sancho found himself being left behind and was forced to shout to his master to wait for him, which Don Quixote proceeded to do, drawing up on the reins of Rocinante until his panting squire could catch up with him. Sancho said upon arriving,

"Master, I think we would be wise to seek sanctuary in some church, for having seen how poorly that fellow fared with whom your grace was fighting, I wouldn't be surprised if the Holy Brotherhood was notified and we were arrested, and as surely as that happens, we won't get out of prison till hell

---

1 The heading for Chapter 10 in the princeps edition of 1605 was: *Further Things Which Befell Don Quixote and the Biscayan, and the Danger in Which He* [Don Quixote] *Found Himself With a Bunch of Yangüesans*. Since the adventure of the Biscayan was concluded in Chapter 9, and the 'misadventure' of the Yangüesans does not occur until Chapter 15, the heading of the 1738 London edition published by J. and R. Tonson was changed to: *The Discourse Which Don Quixote Held With His Squire, Sancho Panza*. In 1780, in its first edition of the work, the Spanish Academy adopted the present heading and this form has been retained in most subsequent editions, both Spanish and English. There are certain scholars who believe the faulty caption was deliberate on the part of Cervantes in order to create a humorous effect but I am not persuaded.

freezes over."

"Hold your tongue," said Don Quixote "Where have you ever seen or read that a knight-errant was hauled up before a judge, regardless of the number of homicides he had committed."

"I don't know a thing about *hommy sides*," said Sancho, "because I've never seen any in my whole life. All I know is that the Holy Brotherhood has jurisdiction over disputes out in the country and I'm not getting involved in their affairs."

"Well, fret not, my friend," said Don Quixote, "for I shall deliver you from the hands of the Chaldeans, not to mention those of the Brotherhood. But tell me, in all your born days have you ever seen a braver knight than me anywhere in the civilized world? Have you ever read in any history of anyone bolder in his attack, more untiring in sustaining it, more skilled at wounding his adversary, or more accomplished at subduing and humbling him?"

"The truth of the matter," said Sancho, "is that I've never read a history in my whole life for the simple reason that I can't read or write, but I *am* willing to wager that never in all the days of my life have I served a master more foolhardy than your grace, and may God not make you pay for all that foolhardiness in the way I've mentioned. What I ask is that your grace tend to your wound, for you're losing a lot of blood from that ear. I've got some bandages and ointment in my saddlebags."

"We would have no need of that," said Don Quixote, "if I had only remembered to make a flask of Fierabrás' balsam, for a single drop of it would save us both time and medicine."

"What flask and balsam is that?" asked Sancho Panza.

"It is a balsam," said Don Quixote, "whose ingredients I know by heart. Whoever possesses it need not fear death nor even give a thought to dying from a wound. When I make some and give it to you, all you need to do when you see my body severed in half in some battle, as quite often happens, is to deftly and gently pick up the part that has fallen to the ground and, before the blood can congeal, place it on top of the other half that remained in the saddle, making sure that it fits evenly and exactly. Then you are to give me just two sips of the balsam I have described and you will see me become sounder than an apple."

"If that stuff exists," said Sancho, "I hereby renounce the governorship of the promised island and as payment for my many and faithful services want nothing more than for your grace to give me the formula of that most wondrous potion, for as far as I can see, an ounce of it ought to bring in more than two *reals* anywhere and I don't need any more than that to get through this life honorably and comfortably. But would it be too much to ask how much it would cost to make it?"

"For less than three *reals* you could make six quarts," said Don Quixote.

"Merciful heavens!" exclaimed Sancho, "what is your grace waiting for? Pray hurry and make some and teach me the secret."

"Stop your babbling, my friend," said Don Quixote. "I intend to teach you greater secrets and show you greater favors, but for now let us attend to our own bodies, for this ear is paining me more than I should like."

Sancho took some bandages and ointment from the saddlebag but, when Don Quixote noticed that his helmet was smashed, he thought he would go out of his mind. Drawing his sword and lifting his eyes towards heaven, he cried out,

"I swear by the Creator of all things and by the four Sacred Gospels and the Holy Bible, wherein they are described at length, that I shall lead the same life the great Marquis of Mantua led when he swore to avenge the death of his nephew Valdovinos: not to eat at a table, not to lie with his wife, nor any of the other things that escape me but which I herein consider included, until I have taken complete revenge upon the one who has committed this outrage against me."

When he heard this, Sancho said,

"Master Don Quixote, your grace should be advised that if the knight has complied with what he was ordered to do, namely, to present himself to my lady Dulcinea of Toboso, he has already fulfilled his obligation and thus deserves no further punishment unless he commits some further crime."

"You have spoken wisely and to the point," said Don Quixote, "and so I declare null and void that portion of the oath concerned with taking fresh vengeance upon him, but I swear and affirm anew the life I have described until such time that I forcibly take from some knight another helmet just as good as this one. And don't think, Sancho, that I do this rashly – no, I have the perfect person to imitate in this, for the same thing happened down to the smallest detail with Mambrino's helmet, which cost Sacripante so dearly."

"My lord, you should consign such oaths to hell," said Sancho, "for they are most harmful to one's health and a great detriment to one's conscience. But if you won't do so, there is something I would like to know: suppose we don't meet anyone wearing a helmet for a number of days, what will we do? Will your grace keep that oath even if it entails a number of inconveniences and discomforts such as sleeping with our clothes on, spending every night out in the open, or a thousand other penances contained in the oath of that crazy old Marquis of Mantua that you want to revive? I would urge your grace to notice that up and down these roads there are no armed men but only muleteers and oxcart drivers who not only are not wearing helmets but may possibly have never even heard the word in their whole lives."

"That is where you are mistaken," said Don Quixote, "for we shall not be at one of these crossroads more than a couple of hours before we see more men in armor than those who overran Albraca and made off with the fair Angélica."

"If that is the case, so be it," said Sancho, "but may God grant us success and hasten the time when we win this island that's costing me so dearly; then I can die in peace."

"I have already told you, Sancho, not to let that worry you, for if there should be no islands available, there will always be the kingdom of Denmark or that of Sobradisa, which will fit you like the glove on your hand, and since they are on terra firma, you should be even happier. But let us leave this for the proper time; for now, see if you have anything we can eat in those saddlebags of yours, and afterwards we shall seek some castle where we can secure lodging for tonight and make the balsam I spoke of, for I swear to God this ear is killing me."

"I've got an onion and a piece of cheese and who knows how many scraps of bread," said Sancho, "but these aren't fit morsels for such a valiant knight as your grace."

"How poorly you understand," said Don Quixote. "I would have you know, Sancho, that it is the glory of knights-errant to go a month without eating but, when they do eat, it will be whatever they have at hand. This would be evident to you if you had read as many histories as I have; and yet, despite having read quite a number of them, I have never found any mention of knights eating, unless it was by chance or in some sumptuous banquet given in their honor, the rest of the time being fairly lean. Still, it is obvious they could not have gone without eating or performing all their other natural functions, being men like ourselves, nor should it be forgotten that, since they spent most of their lives in the woods and wilds with no one to do their cooking, their ordinary meals consisted of rustic fare like what you are offering me now. Therefore, Sancho my friend, don't be upset by what I find pleasurable and don't try to remake the world or knock knight-errantry off its hinges."

"I hope your grace will forgive me," said Sancho, "but since I don't know how to read or write, as I said earlier, I am not now and never have been acquainted with the rules of the profession of chivalry but from this day forward I promise to stock my saddlebags with every sort of dried fruit for your grace, since you are a knight. However, since I am not one, I'll provide myself with poultry and other more substantial things."

"I am not saying, Sancho, that it is imperative that knights eat only the fruit you speak of but that their ordinary diet should consist of it plus certain herbs that grow wild, which they recognize just as I do."

"It's a good thing to recognize those herbs," said Sancho, "for the way I see it we're going to need that knowledge some day."

As he said this, he removed what he said he had brought with him, and the two of them dined among friends and in good company, but because they were anxious to seek lodging for the night, they quickly finished their sparse, dry meal and hastily remounted in order to reach some village before nightfall. Not only did the sunlight fail them but so did their hope of reaching their destination, and since they found themselves near the huts of some goatherds, they decided to spend the night there. Now, if it was distressing to Sancho not to reach town, it was just as satisfying to his master to sleep under the open sky, for it seemed to him that each time this occurred, he was performing an act that would clearly facilitate his claim to knighthood.

Chapter Eleven

The things that befell Don Quixote in the company of some goatherds

Don Quixote was cordially received by the goatherds, and Sancho, who had made Rocinante and the ass as comfortable as possible, allowed himself to be lured by the odor of sliced goat cooking in a pot over a fire. And though at that very instant he would have liked to see if the goat was ready to be transferred from the pot to his stomach, he did not have to do so, for the goatherds removed it from the fire and, spreading some sheepskins over the ground, swiftly prepared their humble repast. Then in a genuine gesture of goodwill they invited the pair to share in what they had. A half dozen of the members of the sheepfold seated themselves round the skins, having first, in their own rustic fashion, invited Don Quixote to join them, offering him a seat on an upside-down trough they had placed there just for him. Don Quixote took his seat while Sancho remained on his feet to fill his master's cup, which was made from a horn. When Don Quixote saw him still standing, he said to him,

"So that you may see, Sancho, the good that knight-errantry encompasses within itself and how ready the world is to honor and esteem those of us who practice any aspect of it, I would have you sit by my side in the company of these good men and be one with me. Since I am your master and natural lord, I want you to eat from my plate and drink from my cup, for the same may be said of knight-errantry as of love: that it is the leveler of all things."

"I am ever so grateful," replied Sancho, "but your grace should be advised that so long as I have enough to eat, I'll enjoy eating it as much, or more, standing off to myself as I will seated beside an emperor. In fact, to be perfectly frank, everything I eat in my corner without niceties and rituals, even if it's only bread and onions, tastes much better than turkey served at another's table where I have to chew slowly, drink sparingly, wipe my mouth constantly, avoid sneezing and coughing even when I feel the urge, as well as other things which privacy and a lack of restraint allow. Thus, my lord, those honors you would confer upon me as the ministrant and follower of knight-errantry, which I am as your grace's squire, may be exchanged for others I will find more comfortable and useful; and though I acknowledge them as having been duly received, I renounce them from this moment till the end of time."

"Nevertheless, you shall sit down, for 'Whosoever humbleth himself, God doth exalt.'[1]

And seizing him by the arm, he forced Sancho to sit beside him. The goatherds, who understood none of this nonsense about squires and knights-errant, merely ate in silence and stared at their guests, who nimbly and ravenously put away chunks of meat as big as one's fist. Once the meat course was finished, they spread over the sheepskins a large quantity of dried acorns and half a cake of cheese, which could not have been harder had it been made of mortar; nor was the horn idle during all this time, being passed round so often – now full, now empty, like the buckets of a waterwheel – that it easily emptied one of the two wineskins that hung in view. After Don Quixote had thoroughly satisfied his stomach, he took a fistful of acorns in his hand and, studying them closely, raised his voice and launched into the following discourse.

"Happy those centuries and happy that age upon which the ancients bestowed the name of golden, not because gold was acquired without effort in that fortunate age, gold which in our own Iron Age is so much esteemed, but because people living then did not know the meaning of these two words: 'yours' and 'mine.' In that blessed age all things were common property and a person seeking to sustain life had only to raise his hand and reach out towards the oaks that generously beckoned to

1 Luke 14:11.

him with their sweet ripe fruit. The clear springs and flowing rivers offered him their delicious, transparent waters in splendid abundance. In the clefts of rocks and the hollows of trees the industrious, intelligent bees built their republics, unselfishly offering to any hand the fertile harvests of their sweetest of labors. The mighty cork oaks, with no motive beyond that of courtesy, surrendered their wide, light bark, which men had just begun to use to cover their houses – houses that were supported on rough-hewn stakes – the bark being needed only as a defense against the inclement weather. During that epoch the world was filled with peace, friendship, and concord. The curved plow's heavy blade had not yet dared violate the merciful bowels of our first mother, who without compulsion offered from every part of her broad fertile bosom all those things that might satisfy, sustain, and delight her children who possessed her at that time. In those days innocent, lovely maidens could roam totally carefree from valley to valley and hill to hill, their hair in braids, their heads bare, and wearing no more clothes than those necessary to modestly cover what modesty demanded be covered. Their ornaments, unlike these extravagantly priced ones in use today that are made of Tyrian purple and silk fashioned in so many tortuous ways, consisted of only a few green leaves of lily or ivy, interwoven, which they wore with as much pomp and elegance as do our courtesans of today with their rare, exotic creations taught them by idle curiosity. In the days of old the amorous conceits of the heart were adorned with simplicity and plainness in the same manner and fashion in which they were conceived, without searching for some artificial or circuitous way to increase their value. Truth and sincerity were not in league with fraud, deception, and malice. Justice existed on its own terms without the threat of being disturbed or assailed by those seeking favors or having special interests, which so discredits, upsets, and perverts it today. Arbitrary law had still not ingrained itself in the judge's thinking, for at that time there was no need to judge or be judged. Maidens and modesty, as I have said, went wherever they pleased, alone and unattended, without the fear that some lewd or lascivious person might ruin them, and if they lost their virginity, it was due to their own pleasure and choice. But nowadays in these detestable times no maiden is safe even if she is locked up and hidden away in another labyrinth like that of Crete, for even here the amorous plague by its zealous and damnable insistence insinuates itself into her presence either through the air or between the cracks, leading her to ruin despite all precautions. As a result of the increase of malice as the years passed by, the order of chivalry was instituted to safeguard maidens, give shelter to widows, and assist the homeless and those in need. I myself belong to this order, my brother goatherds, and I thank you for the hospitality and cordial reception you have extended to me and my squire, for though according to natural law it is incumbent upon every living soul to show respect to knights-errant, you have received and welcomed us without any knowledge of that obligation. Therefore, with all the goodwill of which I am capable I thank you for that goodwill of yours."

This entire lengthy harangue (which might just as easily have been dispensed with) was delivered by our knight because the acorns they had offered him reminded him of the Golden Age, at which point he felt compelled to make this useless speech to the goatherds, who did not say a word but sat there bewildered, listening to him with their mouths agape. Sancho likewise sat there eating acorns and making frequent visits to the second wineskin they had hung from a cork tree to keep it cool. It took Don Quixote longer to finish his speech than to finish his supper but, when he finally did so, one of the goatherds said,

"Sir knight-errant, so that your grace may state with more justification that we spontaneously and willingly extended to you our hospitality, we would like to provide you with some recreation and entertainment by having a colleague of ours sing for you. This fellow, who should be arriving at any moment, is young, quite intelligent, and very much in love, and not only can he read and write but his fiddle playing leaves nothing to be desired."

The goatherd had no sooner said this than the sound of a fiddle reached their ears and a few moments later they witnessed the arrival of the one who was playing it, a nice-looking youth in his early twenties. His friends asked him if he had already eaten and, when he informed them that he had, the one who served as their spokesman said,

"In that case, Antonio, you might honor us by singing something that will show our honored guest here that in these hills and forests we have someone who knows a thing or two about music. We've told him of your great talent and trust you'll prove us right, so I beg you to take a seat and sing that ballad of your loves composed for you by your uncle the priest, which has been so well received in the village."

"I'll do so with pleasure," said the young man, who, without having to be prodded, seated himself on the trunk of a fallen oak. Then after tuning his fiddle, he began to sing the following song in a most ingratiating manner.

Song of Antonio

"Yes, lovely nymph, thou art my prize;
I boast the conquest of thy heart,
And, yet, thy tongue and sparkling eyes
Have not revealed the latent smart.

Thy wit and sense assure my fate,
In them my love's success I see,
Nor can he be unfortunate
Who does avow his flame for thee.

Yet, sometimes hast thou frowned, alas!
And dealt my hopes a cruel shock;
Then did thy soul seem formed of brass,
Thy snowy bosom formed of rock.

But in the midst of thy disdain,
Thy sharp reproaches, cold delays,

Hope, from behind, to ease my pain,
 The border of her robe displays.

Ah, lovely maid! in equal scale
 Weigh well thy shepherd's truth and love,
Which ne'er but with his breath can fail,
 Which neither frowns nor smiles can move.

If love, as shepherds wont to say,
 Be gentleness and courtesy,
So courteous is Olalia,
 My passion will rewarded be.

And if obsequious duty paid
 The grateful heart can ever move,
Mine, sure, my fair, may well persuade
 A due return, and claim thy love.

For, to seem pleasing in thy sight,
 I dress myself with studious care,
And, in my best apparel dight,
 My Sunday clothes on Monday wear.

And shepherds say I'm not to blame,
 For, spotless dress and spruce attire
Preserve alive love's wanton flame,
 And gently fan the dying fire.

To please my fair, in mazy ring
 I join the dance, and sportive play,
And oft beneath thy window sing,
 When first the cock proclaims the day.

With rapture on each charm I dwell,
 And daily spread thy beauty's fame;
And still my tongue thy praise shall tell,
 Though envy swell, or malice blame.

Teresa of the Berrocal,

When once I praised you, said in spite,
Your mistress you an angel call,
But a mere ape is your delight:

Thanks to the bugle's artful glare,
And all the graces counterfeit;
Thanks to the false and curléd hair,
Which wary Love himself might cheat.

I swore 'twas false, and said she lied;
At that her anger fiercely rose:
I fought the boor who took her side,
And how I fought my fairest knows.

I court thee not, Olalia,
To gratify a loose desire;
My love is chaste, without alloy
Of wanton wish or lustful fire.

The Church hath silken cords that tie
Consenting hearts in mutual bands;
If thou, my fair, its yoke wilt try,
Thy swain its ready captive stands.

If not, by all the saints I swear
On these bleak mountains still to dwell,
Nor ever quit my toilsome care,
But for the cloister and the cell."

With this the goatherd brought his song to a close and though Don Quixote asked him to sing something else, Sancho Panza would not permit it, for he was more in the mood for sleeping than for listening to songs; so he said to his master,

"Your grace would do well to go and settle in where you plan to sleep tonight, for the labor these good men face all day long won't allow them to spend their nights singing."

"I understand what you are saying," said Don Quixote. "It is evident that visits to the wineskin demand compensation in dreams rather than in music."

"Well, it *does* taste good to us all," said Sancho, "for which God be praised!"

"I cannot deny that," said Don Quixote, "but you may go make your own bed wherever you like. It is more seemly for those of my calling to stand vigil than to spend their time sleeping. Still, Sancho, you could do me a great favor by tending to this ear, which is paining me more than need be."

Sancho did as ordered and one of the goatherds inspected the wound. The latter told him not to worry, as he would apply a remedy that would speedily cure him. Then picking some leaves from the rosemary that grew all about, he proceeded to chew them and mix in some salt. This he applied to the ear, which he carefully bandaged while assuring him there would be no need of further medication, and such proved to be the case.

Chapter Twelve

What one of the goatherds told the others who were with Don Quixote

Just then, one of the young men who brought them provisions from the village arrived and said, "I say, fellows, do you know what is happening in the village?"

"How should we know?" said one of the goatherds.

"Well, I am here to tell you," the young man went on, "that this morning that celebrated student-shepherd Grisóstomo died and it's rumored that he died from love of that she-devil of a girl Marcela, daughter of Guillermo the Wealthy, the one who goes about these wilds dressed as a shepherdess."

"You're referring to Marcela," said one of the men.

"She's the one I mean," said the goatherd, "but the strange thing is that in his will he asked to be buried in the countryside as though he were some Moor, and that it be at the base of the precipice where the spring and cork tree are located, for rumor has it - and they say this is exactly what he said – that is where he saw her the first time. He also left other instructions, and such strange ones that the village abbots say they are not to be carried out, nor should they be, for they smack of heathenism; to which his close friend and fellow student Ambrosio, who also went about in shepherd attire, insists that everything is to be carried out down to the smallest detail exactly as Grisóstomo requested. The village is in a state of turmoil over this but, according to what everyone says, everything will eventually be done that Ambrosio and all his shepherd friends desire. Tomorrow, he will be buried with great ceremony in the place I mentioned and I understand it will truly be worth seeing. I for one wouldn't miss it even if I knew it meant staying there overnight."

"We'll all do the same," said one of the goatherds, "but we need to draw lots to see who'll stay and look after the goats."

"A good idea, Pedro," said another of the goatherds, "but it won't be necessary to go to all that trouble because I'll stay. And don't attribute it to generosity or a lack of curiosity on my part but to the broken stick I stuck in my foot the other day, which won't allow me to do any walking."

"All the same, we thank you," said Pedro.

Don Quixote asked Pedro to explain who the dead man and the shepherdess were, and Pedro said that all he knew for certain was that the deceased had been a rich noble from one of the villages in those mountains. He had been a student at Salamanca for a number of years but had eventually returned to his village, where he was considered quite learned and well read. He was said to be especially accomplished in the science of the stars and the motions of the sun and moon in the heavens, for he could predict the exact day of an ellipse of the sun and the moon."

"It is called an 'eclipse,' not 'ellipse,' my friend," said Don Quixote, "when those two great luminaries obscure one another."

But Pedro, taking no notice of such trifles, continued his story, saying,

"He would likewise predict whether the year would be one of plenty or scarciness."

"Scarceness, you mean, or scarcity," said Don Quixote.

"Scarcity or scarciness," replied Pedro, "it all means the same thing. I can state for a fact that his father and friends who believed in him became wealthy by following his advice. He would say, 'This year plant barley rather than wheat;' or, 'This year you can plant peas but not barley; next year there will be an abundant crop of olives but in the three following years there will not be a drop of olive oil.'"

"That science is called astrology," said Don Quixote.

"I don't know what it's called," said Pedro, "but I do know he knew all those things and more. To make a long story short, not many months after his return from Salamanca, he unexpectedly showed up one day dressed as a shepherd with his crook and sheepskin jacket, having discarded the long gown he had worn as a student. At the same time, another very close friend of his by the name of Ambrosio, who had been his fellow student, also took to dressing as a shepherd. I nearly forgot to mention that Grisóstomo, the deceased, was quite skilled at composing verses, so skilled in fact that he wrote Christmas carols for Christmas Eve and plays for Corpus Christi Day, which the young people of our village performed and which everyone said were outstanding. When the villagers saw the two students suddenly turn up as shepherds, they were astonished and could not imagine what had caused them to effect such a strange transformation. It was during this period that Grisóstomo's father died, leaving him heir to a large inheritance: chattel as well as land, no insignificant amount of cattle, and a considerable sum of money. The young man was the absolute owner of all this and truthfully deserved it, for in addition to being charitable, he was a friend to good-hearted people, was an excellent companion, and had the face of an angel. Later, it was learned that he had exchanged his clothing for no other reason than to roam these wilds on the trail of the shepherdess Marcela mentioned earlier by this lad, with whom the poor deceased Grisóstomo had fallen in love. But I would now like to explain, since your grace needs to know this, who this young lady is. It is possible and even quite likely that you will never again hear such a thing in all the days of your life even if you live to be as old as Jerusalem."

"You mean Methuselah," said Don Quixote, unable to tolerate the goatherd's misuse of words.

"Jerusalem is very old," retorted Pedro. "However, sir, if your grace keeps correcting my words at every step of the way, we won't finish in an entire year."

"Forgive me, my friend," said Don Quixote, "but because there is such a difference between Jerusalem and Methuselah, I felt compelled to point it out. On the other hand, you responded quite well, for Jerusalem is even older than Methuselah, so proceed with your story and I promise not to quibble about anything else."

"As I was saying, my esteemed sir, there was a farmer in our village by the name of Guillermo, who was even wealthier than Grisóstomo's father. In addition to his considerable wealth God had blessed him with a daughter whose birth caused the death of her mother, the most respected woman in all these parts. I can just see her now with her face framed by the sun on one cheek and the moon on the other, but most importantly, she worked so actively on behalf of the poor that I am certain her soul must be in the presence of God at this very hour. His grief over the death of such a wonderful wife killed the husband Guillermo, leaving their daughter Marcela, who was wealthy and still a child, in the care of one of her uncles, a priest who holds a benefice in our village. The girl grew to be such a beauty that she reminded all of us of her mother, who was herself extremely beautiful, but it was felt the girl's beauty would surpass even that of her mother, which is in fact what occurred, for when she attained the age of fourteen or fifteen, everyone who saw her gave thanks to God for having made her so beautiful, and most fell hopelessly in love with her. Despite the fact that her uncle, who was extremely cautious, guarded her under lock and key, the fame of her beauty spread far and wide and because of this as well as her personal qualities and great wealth, the men of our village as well as those from many leagues around – and the most eligible ones at that – begged, implored, and pleaded with her uncle to give them her hand in marriage but he, being by all rights a good Christian and wishing to see her married as soon as she came of age, refused to do so without her consent, not that he coveted the gain and profit her inheritance afforded him while she deferred getting married. And I can truthfully say this was expressed in more than one gathering in the village in praise of the good priest, for you should know, sir knight, that in these small villages people talk about anything at all and gossip about everyone, so your grace may be assured, as I certainly am, that a priest must be more pious than pious to have his parishioners speak well of him, particularly in the villages."

"What you say is true," said Don Quixote, "but do continue, for the story is quite good and our worthy Pedro is relating it with a great deal of grace."

"May that of Our Lord not fail me," replied Pedro, "for His is the grace that matters. As for the rest, your lordship should know that the uncle sat down with his niece and went over the individual qualities of each of the many suitors who sought her hand, and asked her to choose a husband based upon her own volition. She always responded that she did not wish to wed just yet, for, being so young, she felt herself incapable of bearing the responsibilities of marriage. As a result of these seemingly justifiable excuses, her uncle abandoned his efforts of persuasion and decided to wait until she was older, when she would be able to choose a companion of her own liking, for he used to say, and quite rightly, that parents should not marry their children against their wishes. But, lo and behold, when it was least expected, the fastidious Marcela showed up one day turned shepherdess and, without the approval of her uncle or anyone else in the village – they, in fact, had all tried to talk her out of it – took to the fields with all the other village shepherdesses to tend her own flock.

"Once she had appeared in public and her beauty was on open display, it is impossible to say precisely how many wealthy youths, both hidalgos and commoners, adopted the attire of Grisóstomo and began roaming these wilds in an effort to pay her court. One of those, as I've said, was our deceased friend, who was reported to have stopped loving and begun idolizing her. But your grace should not suppose that because Marcela has chosen a life so unfettered and free and with so little privacy, if any, that she has therefore given any signs of compromising her honor or virtue. On the contrary, the vigilance with which she watches over her honor is such that of all those who serve and court her not one has ever boasted, or ever will, that she has given him the faintest hope of realizing his desires. She doesn't flee from or shun the conversation of the shepherds but treats them with courtesy and friendliness. However, if just one of them is so bold as to reveal to her his intentions, albeit as pure and spiritual as that of matrimony, she casts them all from her like a catapult. With this type of behavior she is doing more harm in these parts than if the plague were to strike, for her friendliness and beauty captivate the hearts of those who would serve and love her but her disdain and refusal to offer encouragement drive them to the point of taking their own lives. The way matters stand, they have no idea how to respond except to call her cruel and ungrateful, along with similar expressions that clearly delineate the character of her disposition. If your grace were here some day, you would hear these hills and valleys resound with the lamentations of her rejected suitors. Not far from here is a site where there are some two dozen tall beech trees, each of which has the name of Marcela carved into its smooth bark, and on some there is also a crown etched in the same tree, as though her lover were clearly saying that Marcela rightfully deserves to wear it since she is the crowning glory of earthly beauty. Nearby one detects the sighs of a shepherd, in the distance the laments of another; in one direction love songs are heard and in another dirges of despair. Several of the shepherds spend every hour of the night seated at the foot of some oak or bluff bewitched and transported by their thoughts where, without closing their tearful eyes, they are greeted by the sun the following morning. Similarly, there are those who, finding no relief or respite, are seen stretched out at noon on the burning sand in the middle of the hottest days of summer, directing their complaints to the compassionate heavens, while the beautiful Marcela triumphs, carefree and footloose, over this one and that one, over these and over those. Everyone who knows her wonders where her aloofness will end and who will be the lucky fellow to tame such a fiery temperament and possess such a consummate beauty. Since everything I have related is true, as may quite easily be verified, I also tend to believe everything is true that our lad has said about Grisóstomo's death. And so, sir, I would advise your grace not to miss the funeral, for it will be well worth seeing because of Grisóstomo's many friends; besides, it is less than a league from this village to the spot where he asked to be buried."

"I shall give it every consideration," said Don Quixote, "and I thank you for the pleasure you have given me by the narration of such a delectable story."

"Oh," replied the goatherd, "I don't know the half of what happened regarding Marcela's lovers but tomorrow we may meet some shepherd who will tell us the whole story. For the time being, it would be advisable for your grace to sleep indoors because the night air might not be good for your wound, though the medicine I applied to your ear is such that there is no need to worry about any unexpected developments."

Sancho Panza, who had been cursing the goatherd's long-windedness, begged his master, for his sake, to sleep in Pedro's hut. Don Quixote did as advised and spent virtually the entire night contemplating his lady Dulcinea in imitation of Marcela's suitors. Sancho Panza settled himself between Rocinante and his jackass and slept, not like a rejected lover, but like a man who had been kicked and stomped.

Chapter Thirteen

The conclusion of the shepherdess Marcela's story, together with other incidents

No sooner had day begun to appear on the eastern horizon than five of the goatherds rose from their beds and went to rouse Don Quixote to see if it was still his intention to attend the notable funeral of Grisóstomo and, if so, whether he might care to join them. Don Quixote, who could have wished for nothing better, rose and ordered Sancho to saddle the horse and ass at once, which Sancho did with great dispatch, and with equal dispatch they all set out on their journey. They had not traveled a quarter of a league when they came to a spot where two roads crossed and there they saw as many as half a dozen shepherds coming towards them clad in black jackets, their heads wreathed in garlands of cypress and bitter oleander, and each carrying a stout holly staff in his hand. In their company were two riders with handsome physiques appropriately outfitted for the journey, followed by three foot-servants. When the two parties met, they each greeted the other courteously and asked the other's destination. When they learned that they were all going to the funeral, they proceeded to travel along together, at which point one of those on horseback addressed his companion, saying,

"It appears to me, Sir Vivaldo, that we may consider as well employed the time we shall spend in attending this remarkable funeral, and remarkable it must be, judging by the strange things these shepherds have told us about both the dead shepherd and the murderous shepherdess."

"I agree," said Vivaldo, "but it will entail a delay of only one day and I should gladly tarry several days for the opportunity to witness it."

Don Quixote asked them what they had heard about Marcela and Grisóstomo. The traveler explained that early that morning they had come across these shepherds and, seeing them attired in such mournful outfits, had asked them why they were dressed in this manner. One of them then related the entire story, including the unconventionality and beauty of the shepherdess Marcela, the numerous suitors who sought her affection, and the death of Grisóstomo, whose burial they were going to attend; in short, he related everything Pedro had told Don Quixote.

No sooner did this conversation end than a new one began, as the rider named Vivaldo asked Don

Quixote what led him to travel about such a peaceful land in all that armor; to which Don Quixote replied,

"The exercise of my profession will not permit me to dress otherwise. Pleasure, repose, and a life of ease were devised for your delicate courtiers but toil, unrest, and the bearing of arms were devised and designed for none other than those the world calls knights-errant, of whom I am an unworthy member, in fact, the unworthiest of all."

When they heard this, they all concluded that he was mad but in order to discover what form of madness held him in its grip, Vivaldo proceeded to ask him what he meant by knights-errant.

"Have your graces not read," said Don Quixote, "the annals and chronicles of England which deal with the famous exploits of King Arthur, the one we always call Artús in our Spanish ballads? There is an ancient tradition throughout the kingdom of Great Britain to the effect that he did not die but was magically transformed into a raven and will with the passing of time recover his kingdom and scepter, at which time he will resume his rule, for which reason no Englishman from that day to this has ever killed a raven. It was during the reign of this good king that they instituted that famous order of chivalry, the Knights of the Round Table, and when the love affair between Lancelot of the Lake and Guinevere occurred, chronicled there in all its details, with that highly esteemed Lady Quintañona serving as their go-between and confidante, whence arose the ballad that is so well-known and so celebrated here in Spain:

'And ne'er was there a knight
By ladies so well served,
As was good Lancelot,
When he from Britain came,'

followed by that pleasant, ingratiating exposition of his exploits and loves. From that time to this the order of chivalry has passed from one person to another, spreading to numerous and diverse parts of the world. It has included such famous and well-known persons as the brave Amadís of Gaul, all his sons and grandsons down to the fifth generation, the valiant Felixmarte de Hircania, the never-sufficiently-praised Tirant lo Blanch, and virtually in our own time, some of us have seen and conversed with that brave invincible knight Belianís of Greece. This then, gentlemen, is what it means to be a knight-errant and what I have described is the order of chivalry of which I am a member, albeit an unworthy one. I profess the same things the above-mentioned knights professed, for which reason I travel about these out-of-the-way places in quest of adventures in support of the weak and the needy, my heart set upon exposing my life and limb to the most perilous ones fate may send my way."

From these pronouncements the travelers came to the realization that Don Quixote had lost his wits and they understood the nature of the malady that had hold of him, being just as astonished at his madness as was everyone who learned of it for the first time. Since Vivaldo was of a clever and mischievous turn and, because he wished to render as painless as possible the small portion of the trip said to remain between there and the burial site, he resolved to give Don Quixote every opportunity to go forward with his foolishness, so he said,

"It strikes me, sir knight-errant, that your grace is following one of the most austere professions on earth, for in my opinion not even that of the Carthusian monks is as austere."

"As austere maybe," replied Don Quixote, "but not as indispensable to the world, and of this I am absolutely certain. If the truth be told, the soldier who carries out his captain's orders does no less than the captain who issues them. By this I mean that ecclesiastics in complete peace and repose pray to heaven for the earth's well being but we knights and soldiers bring to fruition what they merely pray for, and we defend it by the might of our arms and the edge of our swords, not under a roof but out in the open where we become the target of the unbearable sun of summer and the biting cold of winter. We, therefore, are God's ministers on earth and the instruments through whom His justice is carried out. And just as affairs of war and related matters may be realized only by sweat, dedication, and hard work, it follows that those who practice it undoubtedly have a harder task than those who in carefree peace and repose supplicate God to favor the weak. I do not mean to say, nor has it ever crossed my mind, that the calling of the knight-errant is as noble as that of the cloistered ecclesiastic. It is simply that, judging by my own painful experience, I am forced to conclude that ours is more laborious, more subject to beatings, hunger, and thirst, more wretched, more threadbare, and more lice-ridden, for there is no doubt that the knights of old suffered untold adversities in the course of their lives. If there were some who rose to become emperors by the might of their arms, it undoubtedly cost them a precious amount of blood and sweat, and if those who did rise to such heights had not had magicians and sages to assist them, they would have had their wishes completely disappointed and their hopes dashed."

"I am of the same opinion," said the traveler, "but one thing in particular about knights-errant has never set well with me, namely, that whenever they see themselves about to undertake some great and perilous adventure in which there is a manifest risk of losing their lives, they never remember at that exact moment of undertaking it to commend their souls to God, as every Christian is obliged to do in similar perils. Instead, they commend themselves to their ladies with such zeal and devotion that one would think these were their gods – a practice, I think, that smacks of heathenism."

"Sir," responded Don Quixote, "that is exactly what must be done. Were a knight-errant to do otherwise, he would suffer in the world's esteem, for it is now the custom and usage of chivalry for a knight-errant about to undertake some great feat of arms to imagine his lady at his side, towards whom he tenderly and lovingly turns his eyes as he implores her to favor and succor him at that critical moment, the outcome of which may be very much in doubt. Even if there is no one present to hear him, he is obliged to utter a few words under his breath by which he commends himself to her with all his body and soul, and we have numerous examples of this in the histories, not that one should conclude from this that they fail to commend themselves to God, since they have both the time and opportunity to do so while performing their tasks."

"Nevertheless," said the traveler, "I still have one nagging concern: I have often read that two knights will exchange words and before one knows it, something causes them to become angered, at which point they turn their horses and ride off a short distance in opposite directions and without further ado charge at one another as fast as their horses can run; and in the midst of that charge they commend themselves to their ladies. What usually happens when they meet is that one of them is toppled from his horse, pierced through and through by his adversary's lance, while his opponent has to grab his horse's mane to avoid joining him on the ground. What I fail to understand is how the dead knight had the opportunity to commend himself to God in the course of such an accelerated enterprise. It would have been better if he had taken the words he used during his charge – when commending himself to his lady – and employed them according to his duty and obligation as a Christian, particularly when I consider the fact that not all knights-errant have ladies to whom they may commend themselves, for not all of them are in love."

"That is simply not true!" exclaimed Don Quixote. "I declare it to be an impossibility for knights-errant not to be enamored of some lady, for it is as proper and natural for them to be in love as for the heavens to have stars. Surely a history has never existed in which there was a knight without a lady, but in the event that there might have been some individual knight who lacked one, he would not be considered an authentic knight but an impostor who had made his way into the fortress of said knighthood, not by the front gate, but over the wall like some highwayman or thief."

"Nevertheless," said the traveler, "I seem to have read, if I am not mistaken, that Don Galaor, brother of the brave Amadís of Gaul, never had any particular lady to whom he could commend himself, and yet he was no less esteemed and was considered a most brave and famous knight."

To which our Don Quixote responded,

"Sir, 'One swallow does not a summer make,' especially when I know that this knight was secretly very much in love, and this on top of his natural proclivity to fall in love with every lady who caught his fancy, a habit he was never able to control. In fact, it is well established that he had only one lover whom he made the mistress of his heart, and he commended himself to her frequently and quite secretly because he prided himself on being a secretive knight."

"Well then," said the traveler, "if it is essential that every knight be in love, it may safely be assumed your grace also has a lady, since you are a member of that fraternity, and if you do not pride yourself on being as secretive as Don Galaor, I beg you with all the powers at my disposal and in the name of everyone present, including myself, to inform us of your lady's name, her rank, where she is from, and how beautiful she is, for she would consider herself fortunate to have the entire world know she was loved and served by such a knight as your grace appears to be."

Here Don Quixote heaved a deep sigh and said,

"I cannot affirm or deny whether my sweet adversary is pleased that the world knows that I serve her. I can only say in response to what I have so graciously been asked that her name is Dulcinea; she is from Toboso, a village in La Mancha; her rank is probably that of princess at the very least, since she is my lady and queen; and her beauty is not of this world, for in her are realized all the impossible and chimerical traits of beauty that poets attribute to their ladies: her hair is gold, her brow the Elysian Fields, her eyebrows rainbows, her eyes suns, her cheeks roses, her lips corals, pearls her teeth, alabaster her neck, marble her bosom, her hands ivory, her skin snow, and the parts that modesty hides from human view it is my belief and understanding that they are such that it might be possible, but only with discretion and consideration, to extol them but certainly not to compare them with anyone else's."

"We should like to know from whom she is descended," said Vivaldo.

To which Don Quixote responded,

"She is not descended from the ancient Roman Curtii, Caii, nor Scipios, or the modern Colonnas and Orsini, nor from the Moncadas and Requesens of Catalonia, much less from the Rebellas and Villanovas of Valencia, nor from the Palafoxes, Nuzas, Rocabertís, Corellas, Lunas, Alagones, Urreas, Foces, and Gurreas of Aragon, nor the Cerdas, Manriques, Mendozas, and Guzmanes of Castile, nor the Alencastros, Palhas, and Meneses of Portugal. Rather, she stems from the Tobosos of La Mancha, a lineage which, albeit modern, may be the august progenitor of the most illustrious lines in the coming centuries, and let no one dispute this except on the condition Zervino inscribed at the foot of the trophy of Orlando's arms, which reads:

Let none these arms remove,
'Cept him who dares Orlando's might to prove."

"Though *my* descent is from the Cachopines of Laredo," said the traveler, "I dare not compare it to the Tobosos of La Mancha but, if I may speak frankly, until now such a name has never reached my ears."

"And why has it not reached your grace's ears?" retorted Don Quixote.

All the others were listening quite intently to the discussion between the two, and even the goatherds and shepherds recognized our Don Quixote's excessive lack of wits. Only Sancho Panza believed everything his master had said was true, even though he knew who he was and had known him from birth. But if there was one thing he did have his doubts about, it was the difficulty of believing that business of the lovely Dulcinea of Toboso, for such a name and princess had never come to his attention even though he lived very near Toboso.

While traveling along discussing these matters, they suddenly saw in a gap in the hills as many as twenty shepherds walking towards them, all clad in black woolen jackets and crowned with garlands of yew and cypress as they later learned. Six of them were carrying a bier covered with a variety of flowers and boughs, and when the shepherds saw it, one of them said,

"Those people coming this way are bearing the corpse of Grisóstomo, and the base of that hill is where he asked to be buried."

Accordingly, they hurried to arrive and did so just as those carrying the bier set it down on the ground. Four of them, using sharp pickaxes, began digging a grave beside a massive boulder. After the two different groups courteously greeted one another, Don Quixote and those of his party went to inspect the flower-bedecked bier that bore the corpse dressed in shepherd's attire. He was apparently some thirty years of age and showed even in death that, when alive, he had been the possessor of handsome features and a noble disposition. Strewn about him on the bier were some manuscripts and a number of books, some open, some closed. All those present maintained an astonishing silence, the ones observing and the ones digging the grave, until one of the men who had been carrying the corpse said to his companion,

"Ambrosio, make sure this is the place Grisóstomo designated, since you would like everything he requested in his will to be carried out to the letter."

"This is the place," replied Ambrosio, "because a number of times on this very spot my unfortunate friend told me the story of his misfortune. This is where he said that he first laid eyes upon that mortal enemy of the human race; this is where he first declared to her his intentions, as honorable as they were passionate, and where on the final occasion Marcela gave him to understand that his solicitations were completely in vain. Subsequently, he put an end to that tragedy that was his miserable life and here, to commemorate all his unhappiness, he asked to be buried in the bowels of eternal oblivion."

Then turning to Don Quixote and the travelers, he said,

"This body, gentlemen, which your graces are viewing with such compassion, was the repository of a soul to which heaven imparted an infinite portion of its riches. This is the body of Grisóstomo, who was unrivaled in wit, unequaled in courtesy, unexcelled in gentility, a Phoenix in friendship, unlimited in generosity, solemn but not arrogant, jovial but not vulgar, and finally, first in what it means to be good but second to none in what it means to be unblest. He offered love but received hate; he was adoring but was rejected; he sought favors from a wild beast, importuned a block of marble, chased after the wind, cried out in the wilderness, served at the feet of ingratitude, and was rewarded by being made the spoils of death in the very prime of his life, which was cut short by a shepherdess whom he sought to immortalize so she might live in everyone's memory, as those papers you are perusing would clearly show, had he not ordered me to commit them to the flames as soon as his body was committed to the earth."

"You will be proceeding with more severity and cruelty," said Vivaldo, "than their owner himself, for it is neither fitting nor appropriate to comply with the wishes of one incapable of rational thought. Caesar Augustus would not have considered it appropriate to carry out everything the divine Mantuan [1] stipulated in his will. And so, Sir Ambrosio, though you may be consigning your friend's body to the earth, you must not consign his writings to oblivion, for if he ordered it as one who had been wronged, you must not comply as one who lacks discretion. Rather, by granting life to these papers, you will allow Marcela's cruelty to live forever and serve as an example to all men now living that they are to flee from and avoid similar pitfalls. I now know, as does every person here, the story of your friend, whose love was hopeless, and we understand your friendship and the circumstances surrounding his death, together with the orders he left in his will. From this heart-wrenching story your graces may grasp the enormity of Marcela's cruelty, Grisóstomo's love, the steadfastness of your friendship, and the fate that awaits those who run at full tilt along the path that reckless love places before their eyes. Last night we learned that Grisóstomo had died and was to be buried on this very spot, and so out of curiosity and pity we agreed to change our plans so we could see with our own eyes what had

1 I.e., the poet Virgil.

caused us such grief when we heard of it. As recompense for this grief, together with the desire that arose in us to provide a remedy for it, we beg you, O wise Ambrosio – at least I myself beg you – not to burn those papers but to let me keep some of them."

And without waiting for the shepherd to respond, he grabbed several of those nearest him. Seeing this, Ambroslo said,

"Out of courtesy, sir, I shall consent to your keeping those you have already taken but to imagine that I shall not burn these remaining ones is wishful thinking."

Vivaldo, who was curious to see what was in those papers, opened one of them and saw that its title was 'Song of Despair.' When Ambrosio heard this, he said,

"That is the final poem the unfortunate soul wrote, and so that you may see, sir, the extreme to which his misfortune had brought him, read it aloud for all these people to hear; besides, you will have sufficient time to do so before they finish digging his grave."

"I shall gladly do so," said Vivaldo, and since all those present were of a like mind, they eagerly gathered round him, at which point he in a strong, clear voice read the following poem.

Chapter Fourteen

The verses of despair of the deceased shepherd, together with other unexpected incidents

Grisóstomo's Song

"Since, cruel maid, you force me to complain
From clime to clime the triumphs of your scorn,
Let hell itself inspire my tortured breast
With mournful numbers, and untune my voice;
While the sad pieces of my broken heart
Mix with the doleful accents of my tongue,
At once to tell my griefs and thine exploits.
Hear, then, and listen with attentive ear,
Not to harmonious sounds, but echoing groans,
Fetched from the bottom of my lab'ring breast,
To ease, in spite of thee, my raging smart.

The lion's roar, the howl of midnight wolves,
The scaly serpent's hiss, the raven's croak,
The burst of fighting winds that vex the main,

The widowed owl and turtle's plaintive moan,
With all the din of hell's infernal crew,
From my grieved soul forth issue in one sound,
Leaving all my senses confused and lost.
For ah! no common language can express
The cruel pains that torture my sad heart.

Yet let not Echo bear the mournful sounds
To where old Tagus rolls his golden sands,
Or Betis, crowned with olives, pours his flood.
But here, 'midst rocks and chasms deep,
Or to obscure and silent vales removed,
On shores by human footsteps never trod,
Where the gay sun ne'er lifts his radiant orb,
Or with th'envenomed face of savage beasts
That range the howling wilderness for food,
Will I proclaim the story of my woes;
Poor privilege of grief! while echoes hoarse
Catch the sad tale, and spread it round the world.

Disdain gives death; suspicions, true or false,
O'erturn th'impatient mind; with surer stroke
Fell jealousy destroys; the pangs of absence
No lover can support, nor firmest hope
Can dissipate the dread of cold neglect:
Yet I, strange fate! though jealous, though disdained,
Absent, and sure of cold neglect, still live,
And 'mid the various torments I endure,
No ray of hope e'er darted on my soul,
Nor would I hope: rather in deep despair
Will I sit down, and brooding o'er my griefs,
Vow everlasting absence from her sight.

Can hope and fear at once the soul possess,
Or hope subsist with surer cause of fear?
Shall I, to shut out frightful jealousy,
Close my sad eyes, when ev'ry pang I feel
Presents the hideous phantom to my view?
What wretch so credulous but must embrace

Distrust with open arms, when he beholds
Disdain avowed, suspicions realized,
And truth itself converted to a lie?
O cruel tyrant of the realm of Love,
Fierce Jealousy, arm with a sword this hand,
Or thou, Disdain, a twisted cord bestow.

Let me not blame my fate, but, dying, think
The man most blest who loves, the soul most free
That love has most enthralled; still to my thoughts
Let fancy paint the tyrant of my heart
Beauteous in mind as face, and in myself
Still let me find the source of her disdain;
Content to suffer, since imperial Love
By lover's woes maintains his sovereign state.
With this persuasion, and the fatal noose,
I hasten to the doom her scorn demands,
And, dying, offer up my breathless corpse,
Uncrowned with garlands, to the whistling winds.

And thou, whose unrelenting rigor's force
First drove me to despair, and now to death,
When the sad tale of my untimely fall
Shall reach thine ear, though it deserve a sigh,
Veil not the heaven of those bright eyes in grief,
Nor drop one pitying tear, to tell the world
At length my death has triumphed o'er thy scorn;
But dress thy face in smiles, and celebrate,
With laughter and each circumstance of joy,
The festival of my disastrous end.
Ah! need I bid thee smile? too well I know
My death's thy utmost glory and thy pride.

Come, all ye phantoms of the dark abyss;
Bring, Tantalus, thy unextinguished thirst,
And Sisyphus, thy still returning stone;
Come, Tityus, with the vulture at thy heart,
And thou, Ixion, bring thy giddy wheel;
Nor let the toiling sisters stay behind.

Pour your united griefs into this breast,
And in low murmurs sing sad obsequies
(If a despairing wretch such rites may claim)
O'er my cold limbs, denied a winding-sheet.
And let the triple porter of the shades,
The sister Furies, and Chimeras dire,
With notes of woe the mournful chorus join.
Such funeral pomp alone befits the wretch
By beauty sent untimely to the grave.

And thou, my song, sad child of my despair,
Complain no more; but, since my wretched fate
Improves her happier lot who gave thee birth,
Be all thy sorrows buried in thy tomb."

Grisóstomo's poem made a favorable impression upon his audience, though the one who read it said it was not consistent with what he had heard of Marcela's modesty and goodness, for in it Grisóstomo complained of jealousy, suspicions, and abandonment, all to the discredit of Marcela's good name and reputation. Here Ambrosio responded as the one most intimately acquainted with his friend's innermost thoughts:

"So that you, sir, may be satisfied concerning that doubt, you should know that when the ill-fated Grisóstomo composed that song, he had already chosen to separate himself from Marcela to see if absence might have its customary effect, but since there is nothing that fails to upset a lover separated from his beloved and no fear that does not assail him, Grisóstomo's imagined jealousies and dreaded suspicions were as vexing to him as if they had been real. And thus it was that Marcela's virtue, which was legendary, remained unsullied, for aside from being cruel, a bit arrogant, and quite aloof, there was no fault that even envy itself could find in her."

"That is true," said Vivaldo, but as he was about to read another of the papers he had rescued from the flames, he was restrained by a miraculous vision (or so it seemed) that suddenly appeared before their eyes, for at the top of the precipice at whose base the grave was being dug appeared the shepherdess Marcela, and her beauty surpassed even its reputation. Those who had never until that moment seen her stared at her in silent wonder, while those who were already acquainted with her were no less astonished than the ones who had never before seen her. The moment Ambrosio caught sight of her, he became visibly indignant and cried out,

"O fierce basilisk of these mountains, have you perhaps come to see if your presence will cause the blood to flow from the wounds of this wretch whom your cruelty has deprived of life? Or have you come to boast of your nature's cruel accomplishments, or to look down from those heights like another pitiless Nero upon the smoldering ruins of his Rome, or merely to trample upon this unfortunate corpse, as the ungrateful daughter of Tarquinius trampled upon her father's? Tell us right here why you have come and what it is you seek. And just as I know that Grisóstomo never failed to obey you in life, I shall see to it, now that he is dead, that all those who called themselves his friends shall obey you."

"Ambrosio," replied Marcela, "I have come for none of the reasons you have mentioned. I have returned simply to defend myself and to show how unreasonable those persons are who blame me for their sorrow and for Grisóstomo's death. I hope that everyone present will hear me out, for it will not require a long-drawn-out explanation to persuade sensible persons of the truth. As your graces have observed, heaven made me beautiful and to such a degree that you are compelled to fall in love with me, being powerless to do otherwise, and because of this love, you claim and even demand that I am obligated to love you in return. As a consequence of the native intelligence God has given me, I recognize that what is beautiful is worthy of being loved but I fail to understand why the woman who is loved because of her beauty is obligated to love that person who loves her simply because he does so. Besides, the beautiful woman's lover may himself be ugly and, since everything ugly deserves to be abhorred, it is unreasonable for him to say, 'I love you because you are beautiful, therefore, you must love me despite my ugliness.' Or consider the case in which both persons are equally attractive, it does not follow that their desires will also be equal, for not all types of beauty engender love, because some are pleasing to the eye but do not overpower the heart. If every beautiful person were to triumph over all others and make them fall in love, then everyone's heart would be in a constant state of confusion and would not know which way to turn or what choice to make, and given that there would be an infinite number of beautiful objects, the number of desires would likewise be infinite. But according to what I have heard, true love is indivisible and must be voluntary rather than forced. This being the case, as I believe it is, why would you have me surrender my heart by force, obliging me to do so by the mere fact that you say you love me? Answer me this: if heaven, which made me beautiful, had made me ugly, would I have the right to complain if your graces did not fall in love with me? What is more, you must acknowledge that I did not choose the beauty I possess, which, such as it is, was freely granted me by heaven without my requesting or choosing it. And just as the viper does not deserve to be blamed for the poison with which nature endowed it and by which it can cause death, neither do I deserve to be reproached for being beautiful.

"Beauty in a virtuous woman is like a distant fire or a sharp-edged sword; these will not burn or cut anyone who does not approach too closely. Honor and virtue are adornments of the soul without which the body has no right to appear beautiful even if it is. If purity is one of the virtues that most adorn and embellish the body and soul, why must the woman who is loved for her beauty lose her virtue by acquiescing to the man who, solely to satisfy his lust, strives with all his might and guile to make her lose it? I was born free and, to continue living free, I chose the solitude of these fields. The trees of these hills are my companions and the clear waters of these streams are my mirrors, and with these streams and trees I share my thoughts and beauty. I am a distant fire and a sword set apart. Those whose hearts I have turned with my looks I have dissuaded with my words. If desire thrives upon hope – and I have given none to Grisóstomo or to any other – it is fair to say that his persistence killed him rather than my cruelty. And should the charge be brought against me that his intentions were honorable and I was therefore bound to grant them, I shall simply say that when he revealed to me his noble intention in this very place where his grave is being dug, I told him that mine was to live in perpetual solitude; that the earth alone would enjoy the fruits of my life of seclusion and the spoils of my beauty. Now, if in the face of this clear disavowal on my part he chose to persist against all odds and to sail against the wind, is it any wonder that he drowned in the midst of his confused folly? Had I encouraged him, I would have been false. Had I gratified him, I would have done so against my better judgement. He persisted even though I rebuffed him and he despaired without being despised. I ask your graces whether this is sufficient reason to lay at my feet the blame for his suffering! Let him whom I have deceived complain; let him despair whose hopes I have encouraged; and let him be trustful whom I summon, and him be boastful whom I accept; but let no one call me cruel or murderous whom I have not encouraged, deceived, summoned, or accepted. Until now, heaven has not decreed whom I shall love, and whoever believes I shall fall in love voluntarily is terribly mistaken. Let each of my suitors heed this general admonition because it applies to each one's individual case, and let it be understood from this moment forward that if anyone dies because of me, he does not die as a result of envy or misfortune, for a woman who is not in love with anyone is incapable of inspiring jealousy. Disavowals, therefore, are not to be interpreted as disdain. Let him who calls me a wild beast and a basilisk shun me as a harmful and evil thing; let him who calls me ungrateful not serve me; him who claims he has been slighted not acknowledge me; and him who calls me cruel not follow me. For this wild beast, this basilisk, this ungrateful, cruel, and disdainful woman will not seek, serve, recognize, or follow them in any manner whatsoever. If Grisóstomo was slain by his impatience and foolhardy desire, why will your graces place the blame on my innocent behavior and reserve? If I preserve my innocence in the company of trees, why will that person who would have me keep the company of men strive to make me lose it? As you know, I possess riches of my own and covet no one else's. I have my freedom and abhor the idea of subjecting myself to anyone. I love and hate no one. I do not deceive one person while courting another, nor do I seduce this one and amuse myself at the expense of that one. The innocent conversations I hold with the girls of the village and the tending of my goats constitute my sole recreations. My desires are bounded by these hills and if they ever extend beyond this site, it is to contemplate the beauty of the heavens, steps by which the soul ascends to its former abode."

Once she finished saying this, she turned and without waiting for a reply made her way into the densest part of the nearby forest, leaving everyone present overawed by both her intelligence and her beauty. Several persons who had been wounded by the potent rays from her beautiful eyes acted as if they might follow her, disregarding the frank disabusal they had just heard. When Don Quixote observed this, it struck him that this would be the proper occasion to exercise his chivalry by coming to the aid of a maiden in distress, and so, placing his hand on the hilt of his sword, he said in a voice that was both loud and clear,

"Let no one, regardless of his rank or position, dare follow the beautiful Marcela under pain of my fury and wrath. She has demonstrated with clear and abundant reasons that she bore little or no responsibility for the death of Grisóstomo and that she is far from condescending to the desires of any of her suitors, because of which she deserves to be, not followed and hunted down, but honored and esteemed by every good person on earth, for she shows herself to be the only woman alive with such virtuous intentions."

Whether it was Don Quixote's threats or the fact that Ambrosio reminded them that they should fulfill their obligation to their good friend, none of the shepherds made a move to follow her but finished digging the grave. Then after burning Grisóstomo's papers, they lowered his body into it with no little weeping on the part of all those present. The grave was capped with a heavy stone while the finishing touches were put on a headstone, which Ambrosio said he intended to have inscribed with the following epitaph:

> The body of a wretched swain,
> Killed by a cruel maid's disdain,
>   In this cold bed neglected lies.
> He lived, fond, hapless youth! to prove
> Th'inhuman tyranny of love,
>   Exerted in Marcela's eyes.

Then after scattering a number of flowers and boughs over the grave and offering their condolences to his friend Ambrosio, everyone there bade him farewell, including Vivaldo and his companion. When Don Quixote took leave of his hosts and the travelers, the latter urged him to accompany them to Seville, as it was a convenient place for finding adventures, which were more plentiful there in the streets and round every corner than in any other city. Don Quixote thanked them for their advice and goodwill but told them he was unwilling to go to Seville at this time, nor could he do so until he had rid those hills of the thieves and scoundrels known to infest them. Seeing that he had made up his mind, the travelers were reluctant to press him further, and so, once again bidding him farewell, took their leave and proceeded on their way with no lack of things to talk about: the story of Marcela and Grisóstomo, together with the absurd things said and done by Don Quixote, who was determined to seek out the shepherdess Marcela and place himself completely at her disposal. But things turned out differently from what he anticipated, as we shall discover in the course of this true history, the second part of which hereby draws to a close.

THIRD PART
OF
THE INGENIOUS HIDALGO DON QUIXOTE OF LA MANCHA

Chapter Fifteen

The unfortunate adventure that happened to Don Quixote when *he* happened upon some merciless Yangüesans [1]

The sage Cide Hamete Benengeli relates that as soon as Don Quixote took leave of his hosts and all the persons attending Grisóstomo's burial, he and his squire entered the forest at the same place they had seen the shepherdess Marcela enter. After riding about for more than two hours in all directions in search of her but without success, they finally stopped in a meadow carpeted with fresh grass, alongside which flowed such a cool, inviting brook that one was irresistibly drawn to linger there during the hours of siesta, a siesta that had set in with a vengeance. Don Quixote and Sancho dismounted, allowing the ass and Rocinante to graze unfettered on the abundant grass while they themselves ransacked the saddlebags. Then without ceremony master and servant peaceably and sociably ate what they found inside.

Sancho had not bothered to hobble Rocinante, being convinced the beast was so temperate and free of lust that all the mares in the pastures of Cordova could not induce him to commit a lecherous act, but fate and the Devil, who does not spend all his time sleeping, had seen to it that a herd of Galician mares belonging to some Yangüesan muleteers was grazing in that valley. Among the Yangüesans it was customary for them and their teams to spend the siesta in places providing grass and water, and the spot where Don Quixote happened to be was very much to their liking.

Now, it turned out that Rocinante got the urge to frolic with their ladyships the mares, and the moment he caught their scent, he abandoned his usual behavior and manners and, without asking his owner's permission, broke into a sprightly little trot and went over to communicate his needs to them. But they were apparently more interested in grazing than in any other activity and thus received him with such kicks and bites that within a very short while his cinches broke, his saddle fell off, and he was left as naked as the day he was born. But his greatest regret must have been that when the muleteers saw how their mares were being pestered, they ran up with their staves and gave him such a thrashing that he was knocked to the ground badly mauled. By this time Don Quixote and Sancho, who had observed Rocinante's beating, arrived out of breath, with Don Quixote saying to Sancho,

"The way I see it, Sancho my friend, is that these are not knights but rabble and commoners. I tell

1 Persons from Yanguas, a small village in the province of Soria in Old Castile.

you this so you may legitimately assist me in taking revenge for the outrage inflicted upon Rocinante right before our eyes."

"What the devil kind of revenge are we going to take," asked Sancho, "when there are more than twenty of them and only two of us – maybe only one and a half?"

"I am equal to a hundred," replied Don Quixote.

Then without further discussion, he whipped out his sword and made for the Yangüesans, and Sancho Panza, encouraged and inspired by his master's example, did the same. Don Quixote led off by slashing at one of them, splitting open a leather jacket he wore, as well as a large portion of his shoulder. The Yangüesans, who saw themselves ill-used by only two men whereas there were so many of them, grabbed their staves and, surrounding the two, began to rain blows upon them with great earnestness and vehemence; in fact, the second blow knocked Sancho to the ground, with the same fate befalling Don Quixote, whose skill and courage were of no avail to him. As luck would have it, he came to rest beside Rocinante, who had still not gotten to his feet, thereby demonstrating how furiously sticks can pound when placed in the hands of enraged rustics. Seeing the mischief they had done, the Yangüesans rounded up their team as hastily as they could and proceeded on their way, leaving the two adventurers looking bad and feeling worse. The first to show signs of life was Sancho Panza, who, finding himself at his master's side, said in a voice that was weak and filled with pain,

"Master Don Quixote, oh, Master Don Quixote!"

"What do you want, Sancho my brother?" replied the knight in the same aching, high-pitched tone as Sancho's.

"I would like," said the latter, "if such were possible, for your grace to give me a couple of swallows of that drink of Feo Blas [2] – that is, if you have it here at hand. Perhaps it will be as beneficial for broken bones as it is for wounds."

"Wretch that I am!" said Don Quixote, "if only I had some with me, what more could we ask? But I give you my word as a knight-errant, Sancho Panza, that before two days have passed, unless fortune decrees otherwise, I shall have it in my possession or these hands will not operate the way they should."

"Well," said Sancho Panza, "how many days does your grace think it will take our feet to operate?"

"Speaking for myself," said the belabored knight, "I cannot say how many days that will take but I am to blame for everything, for I should not have raised my sword against men who were not knights-errant like myself. For having transgressed the laws of chivalry, I feel the god of battles has permitted me to be punished in this manner, and because of this, Sancho Panza, it is fitting that you be advised of a matter that I shall now explain to you, since it is of the utmost importance to the well being of us both. Whenever you see that scoundrels such as these have wronged us in some fashion, you are not to wait for me to draw my sword against them, for I shall not do so under any circumstances. Rather, you are to draw your sword and chastise them to your heart's content. Should

---

2 ***Feo Blas*** ('ugly Blas'), Sancho's malapropism for ***Fierabrás*** ('mighty of arm') from the French ***Fier à bras***.

knights come to their defense and support, I shall be prepared to defend you and oppose them with all my might, for you must already have had a thousand indications of how far the valor of my mighty arm extends."

This is how arrogant the poor knight had become by virtue of having defeated the valiant Biscayan, but Sancho did not think so highly of his master's advice as to fail to respond by saying,

"Master, I am a man who is peaceable, meek, and mild, and I can forgive any injury because I have a wife to support and children to rear. Therefore, I hereby advise your grace, since mandates are out of the question, that in no way will I draw my sword against anyone, either peasant or knight, and that from this moment till I find myself in the presence of God I hereby pardon and forgive any and all wrongs I have ever suffered or ever will suffer, which have been, are, or will be at the hands of any person of high or low degree, rich or poor, nobleman or commoner, regardless of his rank or status – without exception, amen."

When his master heard this, he said,

"I wish I had the breath to speak with less effort and the pain in my side would abate so I might make you see, Sancho, how mistaken you are. Look, you poor soul, if the winds of fortune, albeit now so unfavorable, should turn in our direction and swell the sails of our desires so that, barring a sudden shift of the wind, we might safely make port in one of the islands I have promised you, what would become of you if, after I had conquered it, I made you lord of the island? You would make it impossible for me to do so because you are not a knight and have no desire to be one, nor do you have the courage or willpower to avenge your wrongs or to defend your dominion. You should know that in newly conquered kingdoms and provinces the natives are never so lacking in spirit, nor are they such champions of the new lord, as to have any qualms about attempting to change the state of affairs, or, as the saying goes, 'to try their wings.' Therefore, the new administrator must possess understanding for governing, and valor for attacking and defending himself in any given situation."

"In this situation we were just in," said Sancho, "I would have loved to possess that understanding and valor your grace speaks of but I swear upon my word as a poor man that I'm more in the mood for poultices than for discussions; so I beg your grace to see if you can stand up, because if you can, we'll help Rocinante even though he doesn't deserve it, since he was the chief cause of all these beatings. I never would have believed such a thing of Rocinante because I always held him to be a continent person and every bit as peaceable as myself. They're certainly right when they say, 'It takes a lot of living to know what people are really like,' and 'There's nothing in this life that's certain.' Who would have predicted that after the way your grace cut that unfortunate knight-errant to pieces there would follow so closely upon its heels the mighty storm of staves that has fallen on our backs?"

"Your back, Sancho, is probably inured to storms of this sort, but mine, which was reared among fine linens, will clearly feel the pain of this misfortune more keenly. If it were not for the fact that I imagine – what do I mean imagine, since I am certain – that these inconveniences are part and parcel of knight-errantry, I would allow myself to expire on this very spot out of sheer anger."

To which his squire replied,

"Master, since these misfortunes are the harvests of chivalry, tell me whether they occur frequently or only in their appointed seasons, for I'm of the opinion that after two such harvests we won't be fit for a third unless God in His infinite mercy comes to our aid."

"Be advised, Sancho my friend," said Don Quixote, "that the lives of knights-errant are subject to a thousand perils and misadventures and yet they may become kings and emperors at any moment, as experience has shown in the case of many and diverse knights whose histories I know down to the smallest detail. I could tell you now, if my pain would permit, of some who simply by the valor of their arms have risen to those high positions I mentioned, and those very persons, both before and after, saw themselves in various sorts of calamities and miseries. The brave Amadís of Gaul, for example, found himself in the clutches of his mortal enemy Arcalaus the Magician, who, it has been determined, tied him to a column in the court and gave him more than two hundred lashes with his horse's reins. There is even an anonymous author – and quite a respected one at that – who says the Knight of Phoebus was captured in a certain castle by means of a trapdoor that opened beneath his feet, and at the bottom of his fall he found himself in a deep underground pit bound hand and foot, where they administered to him what is called an enema, of ice water and sand. This came close to killing him and, had he not been assisted in that emergency by a sage who was a close friend of his, the poor knight would not have fared very well. And so I shall manage quite well in the company of these good souls, for the indignities they suffered are greater than those we suffer today. Besides, Sancho, I would have you know that wounds inflicted by instruments that one happens to be holding at the time do not constitute an insult to one's honor, as is explicitly stated in the dueling code. If a cobbler strikes someone with the last he is holding in his hand, even though it may be made of birch, the man who was struck cannot claim he was birched.[3] I tell you this lest you think we suffered an indignity simply because we were the object of a pummeling in this fray. The arms the men used were nothing more than their staves and not one of them, as I recall, carried a rapier, sword, or dagger."

"They didn't allow me enough time to observe them that closely," said Sancho, "for no sooner had I taken hold of my trusty sword than they blessed my shoulders with their sticks in such a manner that they caused my eyes to lose their sight and my feet their strength, and they knocked me to the ground where I am now lying and am not so much bothered by the question of whether the staves constituted an affront as I am by the pain from the blows, which is certain to remain impressed in my memory as it is on my back."

"For all that, Panza my brother, I would have you know there is no memory that time will not obliterate and no suffering that death will not soothe."

"Well," replied Panza, "what greater disaster can there possibly be than one whose solution depends upon time to obliterate it and death to soothe it? If only this calamity of ours were of the sort that could be cured with a couple of poultices, it wouldn't be quite so bad, but I've got the feeling that all the poultices in a hospital won't be enough to put us back together."

"That is enough of such talk, Sancho," said Don Quixote. "Try to draw strength from weakness and

---

3 This sentence contains a play on words that no translator, including the present one, has been able to reconstruct satisfactorily. It opposes the word ***palo*** ('wood') with ***apaleado*** ('cudgelled')

I shall do the same; but let us see how Rocinante is, for the way it appears, that poor soul was not the least recipient in this fiasco."

"That's not surprising," replied Sancho, "seeing as how he's such a good knight-errant. What I find astonishing, though, is that my jackass has escaped with no cost to himself, while it has cost us our ribs."

"In adversity fate always leaves a door open to a solution," said Don Quixote. "I mention this because this small beast can compensate for the lack of Rocinante by carrying me from here to some castle where my wounds can be cared for. What is more, I shall not consider it a dishonor to go mounted in this fashion, for I remember reading that good old Silenus, tutor and teacher of the merry god of laughter, made his entrance into the city of the hundred gates in a manner that was very much to his liking: riding a very handsome jackass."

"It's probably true that he was riding," said Sancho, "but there's a big difference between riding and being toted like a sack of garbage."

To which Don Quixote responded,

"Inasmuch as wounds received in battle bestow honor rather than withhold it, Panza my friend, don't argue with me but do as I say. Just stand up the best way you can and place me on your beast in whatever posture you find most pleasing so we can get started before night arrives and overtakes us out in these wilds."

"Well, I've heard your grace say," replied Sancho, "that it's very much in the line of knights-errant to sleep out of doors on some field or plain for the greater part of the year and they even consider themselves quite fortunate."

"That is what they do," said Don Quixote, "when they have no other option or when they are in love, and it is so true that there have been knights who have spent two years atop some precipice exposed day and night to the inclemencies of heaven, all without their ladies' knowledge of it. One of those was Amadís, who, when he went by the name of Beltenebros, withdrew to the Barren Rock for eight months or maybe eight years – I am not certain of the exact figure; the point is that he was doing penance there due to some sort of displeasure the Lady Oriana had caused him. But let us drop the matter, Sancho, and get started before another misfortune befalls the ass the way it did Rocinante."

"That would be the last straw," said Sancho. Then delivering up thirty sighs, sixty wails, and a hundred and twenty curses against the one who had brought him there, he struggled to his feet in the middle of the road but was unable to straighten up, remaining bent over like a Turkish bow. However, by dint of sheer hard work he saddled his jackass, who had been wandering aimlessly about due to the excessive freedom he had enjoyed that day. He next helped Rocinante to his feet, who, had he only had a tongue with which to complain, would surely have outdone Sancho and his master. In the end, Sancho settled Don Quixote onto the ass and then leading Rocinante by the reins and the ass by the halter, headed more or less in the direction in which he felt the king's highway must lie. Fate, which was beginning to improve their lot, brought them, before they had traveled one short league, back to the road on which there appeared an inn, which was soon to be a castle much to Sancho's sorrow and Don Quixote's delight; in Sancho's opinion it was absolutely an inn but in Don Quixote's it was not an inn but a castle. The argument lasted long enough for them to reach the inn but not to settle their dispute, and so with no further attempt to ascertain what it was, Sancho made his entrance through the gate, followed by all his troops.

Chapter Sixteen

The things that befell the ingenious hidalgo in the inn which he fancied to be a castle

When the innkeeper saw Don Quixote draped across the ass's back, he asked Sancho what seemed to be ailing him. Sancho said it was nothing; that he had simply suffered a fall from a crag, which accounted for his ribs' being slightly bruised. Now, the innkeeper had a wife whose disposition was quite different from that normally encountered among women of her trade, for she was charitable by nature and sympathetic to other people's afflictions. She immediately set about caring for their guest Don Quixote and in this endeavor enlisted the aid of her daughter, who was young, unmarried, and quite good-looking. Also serving in the inn was an Asturian girl with a broad face, a head flattened at the back, a stub nose, one eye that was blind, and the other that was less than sound, but her graceful figure more than made up for whatever else she might have lacked, for she was not seven hands tall [1] from head to foot, and her shoulders, which were somewhat stooped, forced her to look at the ground a good deal more than she would have liked. This comely lass assisted the young girl and the two of them prepared a fairly sorry bed for Don Quixote in a garret that showed signs of having served as a hayloft in years gone by. A muleteer who was also lodged in this room had his bed set a little beyond Don Quixote's and though it was made from only the blankets and trappings of his mules, it was quite superior to Don Quixote's, which consisted of only four rough boards laid across two not very level sawhorses, and a mattress so thin it gave every indication of being a quilt. It was also full of lumps which, through the torn places, showed they were tufts of wool but because of their hardness felt more like cobblestones. Its two sheets were made from the kind of leather used for shields, and the blanket was so threadbare you could have counted every thread without missing a stitch, had you cared to do so. Don Quixote stretched out on this miserable bed, whereupon the innkeeper's wife and daughter immediately plastered him from head to foot with poultices while the lamp was held by Maritornes, this being the Asturian maid's name. When the innkeeper's wife noticed during the plastering that Don Quixote was black and blue all along his body, she remarked that it looked more like the results of a beating than a fall.

"It wasn't a beating," said Sancho. "The rocks simply had jagged edges sticking out and each one left its mark." He then added, "Madam, I beg you to save some of those bandages, for someone else

1 About four feet eight inches tall.

is sure to need them; in fact, my back is also slightly sore."

"In that case," replied the innkeeper's wife, "you must have fallen too."

"It wasn't a fall," said Sancho Panza, "but the sudden start I gave when I saw my master fall and it was such that my body aches just as though it had been beaten with a thousand sticks."

"And that may truly be the case," put in the young girl, "for I have often dreamed of falling from a tower and just before reaching the ground, I would wake up to find myself as battered and bruised as if I had actually fallen."

"Ah, but that is the point, my lady," said Sancho Panza, "for without dreaming at all but being wider awake than I am at this very moment I find I have nearly as many bruises as my master."

"What is this gentleman's name?" asked the Asturian Maritornes.

"Don Quixote of La Mancha," said Sancho Panza. "He's a venturer knight and one of the best and hardiest seen for quite some time."

"What is a venturer knight?" asked the lass.

"Are you such a newcomer to the world," replied Sancho Panza, "that you don't know? Be advised, my child, that a venturer knight is a person who may be cudgeled at one moment and made an emperor at the next. Today he may be the most unfortunate creature on earth, and the most needy, but tomorrow he will win the crowns of two or three kingdoms, which he'll award to his squire."

"Well, since you are this gentleman's squire," said the innkeeper's wife, "how is it that you are not in charge of so much as an earldom, or so it would appear?"

"It's still early," replied Sancho, "for we've ridden in quest of adventures for no more than a month and up to now we've not come across any adventure worthy of the name, for there are times when one goes looking for one thing and finds another. The truth is that if my master Don Quixote recovers from his wound – I mean his fall – and I'm not left crippled by mine, I won't swap my chances for the best title in Spain."

Don Quixote, who had been listening closely to all these pleasantries, sat up in bed as erect as possible and took the hostess by the hand, saying,

"Believe me, fair lady, you may consider yourself fortunate to have given your humble servant lodging in your inn, and if I do not praise myself, it is due to the well-known saying that 'Praise of oneself is demeaning.' However, my squire will inform you of who I am. Let me simply say that I shall keep the kindness you have shown me eternally etched in my memory and shall be beholden to you for as long as I live. I only wish to heaven that love did not hold me so submissive and subject to its laws and to the eyes of that beautiful ingrate whose name I scarcely dare to speak; otherwise, my will would be your ladyship's to command."

The innkeeper's wife, her daughter, and that good soul Maritornes were confused as they listened to the knight's words, which they understood as well as if he were speaking Greek, though they clearly recognized that they all had to do with gratitude and compliments. But being unaccustomed to such language, they stared at him in disbelief, for he seemed quite unlike that breed of men they were acquainted with. Then thanking him in their tradesmenlike manner for his kind offers, they left him while the Asturian Maritornes tended to Sancho, who was in need of her help no less than was his master.

The muleteer had arranged with her that, as soon as it was night, they would partake of each other's company, for she had given him her word that once the guests had retired and her masters were asleep, she would seek him out and satisfy his every desire, and it was said of this good lass that she never made promises she did not intend to keep, even if she made them on a mountaintop without a single witness, for she prided herself on being quite an hidalga and did not consider it beneath her to be employed in an inn; after all, she said, it was misfortune and bad luck that had placed her in that situation.

Don Quixote's bed, which was hard, narrow, cramped, and disappointing, was situated first in that star-bedecked stable. Next to it, Sancho had his bed, which consisted solely of a mat of bulrushes and a blanket that more nearly resembled burlap than wool. Beyond these two beds was situated that of the muleteer, constructed, as we have said, from the saddle blankets and other trappings from the two best mules of the dozen he had brought with him, all sleek, well-fed, and first-rate, for he was one of the rich muleteers of Arévalo according to the author of this history, who makes particular mention of this muleteer, since he was well acquainted with him; and there are even those who insist that he may have been a relative of his. Besides, Cide Hamete Benengeli was a historian of great curiosity and precision in all matters, as is quite evident, and he preferred to record every single detail rather than pass over it in silence even when it was trifling and insignificant. He should serve as an example to serious historians who, because of negligence, malice, or ignorance, record incidents so briefly and succinctly that we are barely able to savor them and consequently the most substantial part of their work remains in the inkwell. A thousand blessings upon the author of *Tablante de Ricamonte* and the author of that other book in which the exploits of Count Tomillas are related. What preciseness they employ in all their descriptions! But, as I was saying, once the muleteer had visited his team and given them their second feeding, he stretched out on his makeshift bed and resigned himself to waiting for the most punctual Maritornes. Sancho Panza was already in bed covered with plasters and, though he struggled to go to sleep, the pain in his ribs would not permit it. Don Quixote, because of the pain in his, lay there with his eyes wide open like a rabbit's. Silence pervaded the inn and the only light in the entire building was that provided by a lamp hanging in the middle of the entranceway.

The remarkable silence plus our knight's constant preoccupation with the incidents related on every page of those books responsible for his plight brought to mind one of the strangest delusions imaginable. He fancied he had arrived at a famous castle – for, as we have observed, the inns where he lodged all became castles in his eyes – and the innkeeper's daughter was the daughter of the lord of the castle, who had been captivated by his gentility and, because of her love for him, had promised to steal away from her parents that night to come lie with him for a spell. Inasmuch as he considered this whole fantasy firm and binding, he began to fret and ponder the perilous predicament in which his virtue was about to find itself and he swore in his heart not to be unfaithful to his lady Dulcinea of Toboso even if Queen Guinevere and her lady Quintañona should appear in his presence.

While he was pondering such nonsense, the time and the hour – for him the fatal hour – arrived for the return of the Asturian, who, dressed in her nightgown, her feet bare, and her hair gathered up in a coarse net, cautiously and silently entered the room in which the three men were lodged, but scarcely had she reached the door when Don Quixote sensed her presence. Sitting up in bed despite his poultices and the pain in his ribs, he held out his arms to receive his beautiful maiden. The Asturian, quite cautiously and without saying a word, entered with outstretched arms in search of her lover, whereupon she met those of Don Quixote, who seized her tightly by the wrist, pulled her towards him and made her sit on the bed, during which time she dared not utter a word. He felt of her nightgown, which despite being made of burlap, struck him as being of the finest and sheerest gauze. On her wrists were some glass beads, which he fancied precious Oriental pearls. Her hair, which was strongly reminiscent of a horse's mane, he took to be strands of the most glimmering gold of Arabia, the resplendence of which made the sun pale by comparison. And her breath, which without a doubt reeked of stale, leftover salad, seemed to him a faint aromatic scent issuing from her lips. In short, he conjured up a picture exactly like the one he had read in his books involving that other princess who, overcome by love, paid a visit to the badly wounded knight, together with all the details therein described. And such was the poor hidalgo's blindness that neither the way the good lass felt and smelled nor any of her various other traits were sufficient to enlighten him, though they would have made anyone else vomit who was not a muleteer. On the contrary, because he fancied that he held in his arms the goddess of beauty, he tightened his grip and began to speak in a voice that was soft and loving:

"Most beautiful and exalted lady, I should be pleased to find myself in circumstances in which I might repay the great favor thou hast shown me by allowing me to feast mine eyes upon thine extraordinary beauty, but fate, which never tires of persecuting the good, has seen fit to keep me in this bed where I lie beaten and broken; and though I would willingly satisfy thy desires, it is an impossibility. Moreover, there is an even greater obstacle, namely, the allegiance I have sworn to the peerless Dulcinea of Toboso, sole object of my innermost thoughts. However, were this not an obstacle, I should not be so foolish a knight as to fail to avail myself of this golden opportunity thy generosity is offering me."

Greatly distressed and covered with perspiration at finding herself in the grasp of Don Quixote, as well as not understanding anything he said, Maritornes without uttering a word struggled to free herself from his clutches. Our good muleteer, who had been kept awake by his wicked thoughts, sensed his concubine as soon as she entered the room but decided to listen to everything Don Quixote said, fearing the lass had broken her promise because of another man. Edging ever closer to Don Quixote's bed, he waited quietly to see where those words were leading, words he was unable to fathom. But when he saw the lass struggling to escape while Don Quixote strove to hold her in his grasp, he thought the joke had proceeded far enough, and so, raising his arm aloft, he unleashed such a terrible blow to the enamored knight's emaciated jaws that his whole mouth was bathed in blood. And not being content with that, he climbed on top of his chest where, moving his feet faster than he would if he were trotting, he stomped on his rib cage from one end to the other. The bed, which was rather flimsy because it lacked a firm foundation, could not withstand the added weight of the muleteer and thus fell to the floor with such a crash that it woke the innkeeper. The latter immediately imagined that all this was due to Maritornes' shenanigans, for when he had called her, she had failed to answer. With this thought in mind, he got out of bed, lit his lamp, and hurried to where he had heard the disturbance. Seeing her master approach in such a frightful mood, the servant girl, flustered and scared to death, crawled into bed with Sancho Panza, who was still asleep, and curled herself up into a ball. The innkeeper came in shouting,

"Where are you, you little slut? I'll bet all this ruckus is your doing!"

At this moment Sancho woke and, feeling that lump nearly on top of him and believing he was having a nightmare, began throwing punches in every direction imaginable. There is no telling how many blows he gave Maritornes who, stung by the pain, threw modesty to the wind and gave Sancho so many in return that he became wide awake in spite of himself. When he saw himself manhandled in this fashion and not knowing by whom, he sat bolt upright in bed and pulled Maritornes towards him, at which point the two began the most hard-fought and comical skirmish ever seen. When the muleteer saw by the light of the innkeeper's lamp how his lady was faring, he left Don Quixote and hurried over to lend her the necessary assistance. The innkeeper did the same but for a different reason, for he intended to punish the servant girl, doubtless believing her to be the sole cause of all that harmony. And so, as the saying goes – 'the cat caught the rat, the rat gnawed the rope, the rope bound the stick . . .' – the muleteer punched Sancho, Sancho punched the girl, the girl punched the innkeeper, and everyone was punching so fast and furiously that they scarcely allowed themselves a moment's rest. To crown it all, the innkeeper's lamp went out, leaving everyone in the dark, whereupon they began slugging away so mercilessly and indiscriminately that wherever their fists landed they left their mark.

On this particular night, there happened to be lodging in the inn a member of the so-called Ancient and Holy Brotherhood of Toledo, who, hearing all the noise from the altercation, grabbed his staff of office and the tin box containing his credentials and entered the darkened room, crying out,

"Halt in the name of the law! Halt in the name of the Holy Brotherhood!"

The first person he encountered was the battered Don Quixote, who lay senseless on his back on his collapsed bed. During the process of feeling about, his hand came across Don Quixote's beard, at which point he shouted at him once more,

"The law demands your assistance!"

But perceiving that the one he had grabbed neither moved nor budged, he assumed he was dead and those in the room were his murderers. Driven by this suspicion, he cried out even louder,

"Shut the inn gate and see that no one leaves; a man has been murdered here!"

This came as a surprise to everyone there and each person stopped at whatever stage of the fight he was in when the voice reached his ears. The innkeeper withdrew to his room, the muleteer to his packsaddles, and the girl to her roost; only the unfortunate Don Quixote and Sancho were unable to move from where they were. At this point the officer released Don Quixote's beard and left to look for a light in order to ferret out and apprehend the guilty parties but he was unable to find one, for the innkeeper upon retiring to his quarters had purposely extinguished his lamp. And so the officer had to resort to the hearth, where after considerable time and effort he lit another lamp.

Chapter Seventeen

The continuation of the innumerable ordeals the valiant Don Quixote and his noble squire underwent in the inn, which, much to Don Quixote's sorrow, he fancied a castle

In the meantime Don Quixote had recovered from his swoon and in the same tone of voice with which he had called to his squire in the Valley of the Stakes he began to call to him again:

"Sancho my friend, are you asleep? Are you sleeping, my friend?"

"How can I sleep, confound it!" replied Sancho in total grief and despair. "Unless I'm sadly mistaken, I've been kept company tonight by a horde of demons."

"You are justified in believing that," said Don Quixote, "for either I know very little or this castle is enchanted. You should know . . . but what I am now about to tell you you must give me your word to keep secret till my days on earth are over."

"I give you my word," said Sancho; to which Don Quixote replied,

"I say this because I am loath to cause anyone to lose his honor."

"Let me repeat," said Sancho, "that I promise to keep quiet till your grace's days on earth are over and, God willing, I'll be able to reveal it tomorrow."

"Have I treated you so badly," said Don Quixote, "that you wish to see me dead so soon?"

"It has nothing to do with that," said Sancho; "it's just that I hate to keep secrets too long because I don't want them to spoil from being kept in storage."

"Well, whatever the reason," said Don Quixote, "I feel certain that I may rely upon your love and respect. Therefore, I would have you know that tonight I experienced one of the strangest adventures I ever hope to undergo. To make a long story short, you should know that just now the daughter of the lord of this castle came to me and she is the most elegant, beautiful maiden anywhere in the entire world. How can I describe her personal adornments, her elegant mind, or her other hidden charms, which, to remain loyal to my lady Dulcinea of Toboso, I shall leave intact and unmentioned? I shall simply say that, because heaven was envious of the great riches fate had placed in my hands, or perhaps – and this is more likely – this castle is enchanted, as I have mentioned previously, there emerged at the very moment that I engaged her in tender, loving conversation a hand attached to the arm of some enormous giant, which, without my seeing it or knowing where it came from, unleashed such a blow to my jaws that he left them completely bathed in blood. He then gave me such a thrashing that I am worse off today than when the muleteers, thanks to Rocinante's excesses, treated us so unmercifully, as you no doubt remember. From this I conclude that some enchanted Moor must be guarding the treasure of this damsel's beauty, which is not meant to be mine."

"Or mine either," said Sancho, "because more than four hundred Moors pummeled me in such a manner that, in comparison, the beating with the staves was peaches and cream. But I wish your grace would please tell me what name you give this fine and rare adventure that has left us in this fix, though it was not as bad for your grace, since you got to hold in your arms that incomparable beauty you mentioned. But me, what did I get except the best drubbing I ever expect to receive in my whole life? Woe unto me and the mother who bore me! I am not a knight-errant and never intend to be one but whenever there's bad luck around, I always end up with more than my share!"

"Then you have also been beaten?" said Don Quixote.

"Didn't I just say so, for God's sake?" replied Sancho.

"Fret not, my friend," said Don Quixote, "for I shall now make some of the precious balsam with which we shall both be cured in the twinkling of an eye."

At that moment the officer of the Holy Brotherhood finished lighting his lamp and came in to have a look at the person he assumed was dead. When Sancho saw him enter dressed in his nightgown and sleeping cap with the lamp in his hand and a foreboding look on his face, he said to Don Quixote,

"Master, can this by chance be the enchanted Moor coming back to give us another beating that might have been left in the inkwell?"

"It cannot be the Moor," said Don Quixote, "for enchanted ones never let themselves be seen by anyone."

"They may not let themselves be seen but they certainly let themselves be felt, to which my shoulders can attest."

"So can mine," said Don Quixote, "but that is not sufficient reason to believe the person before us is the enchanted Moor."

When the officer arrived, he found them in quiet conversation, which left him confused, though Don Quixote was still flat on his back and unable to move a muscle due to the pummeling and all the plasters. The officer came up to him and asked,

"How goes it, you poor devil?"

"I would speak with more civility if I were you," said Don Quixote. "Is that any way to address knights-errant in this land, you blockhead?"

The officer, hearing himself maligned by such a miserable-looking man, was unable to tolerate it, so, raising the lamp, which was filled with oil, he brought it down on Don Quixote's head, leaving it badly bruised, and because everything was now enveloped in darkness, the officer proceeded to withdraw.

"Undoubtedly, master," said Sancho Panza, "this is the enchanted Moor who must be saving the treasure for someone else because all he has for us is punches and bangs on the head with lamps."

"That is how it is," answered Don Quixote, "but one should take no notice of these matters of enchantment nor be upset by them, for inasmuch as these beings are invisible and imaginary, we can never lay hands on the person who deserves to be punished however hard we try. Therefore, get up, Sancho, if you are able, and go find the governor of this fortress and see if you can get me some oil, wine, salt, and rosemary so I can prepare the health-giving balsam. To tell the truth, I think I really could use some right now, for I am losing quite a lot of blood from the wound inflicted upon me by this phantom."

Sancho managed to stand up despite his aching bones and made his way through the darkness to where the innkeeper was. Along the way he bumped into the officer, who had been listening in an effort to learn what his adversary was up to.

"Your grace," said Sancho, "whoever you are, pray be so kind and merciful as to give us some rosemary, oil, salt, and wine, which are needed to cure one of the best knights-errant on the face of the earth. He's lying in that bed severely wounded by the enchanted Moor who haunts this inn."

When the officer heard such talk as this, he took him to be a half-wit, but because it was beginning to get light, he opened the door and called to the innkeeper, telling him what the poor devil wanted. The innkeeper provided him with everything he had requested and Sancho carried it to Don Quixote, who was holding his head and complaining of the pain from the lamp, which had done no more harm than to raise two rather puffy welts on his head. And what he thought was blood was actually only sweat pouring down as a result of the turbulent ordeal he had just undergone.

In short, Don Quixote took his simples, from which he made a compound by mixing everything together, and proceeded to boil it until he thought it was done. He then asked for a flask into which to pour it. Since there was none in the inn, he settled for putting it into an empty can of olive oil the innkeeper graciously donated. Then Don Quixote muttered over the can more than forty Our Fathers and as many more Hail Marys and other prayers, accompanying each word with the sign of the cross by way of benediction. Present at all this were Sancho, the innkeeper, and the officer, as the muleteer was now leisurely engaged in tending to his mules. Once this was done, Don Quixote chose to test upon himself the virtue of the precious balsam, which is what he fancied it to be, and thus drank nearly a quart that could not be poured into the can but remained in the brewing pot.

But no sooner had he finished drinking it than he began to retch so violently that nothing was left in his stomach, and due to the anxiety and exertion from the vomiting he broke into a copious sweat, at which point he asked them to put more covers over him and leave him alone. Once they complied with his wishes, he fell asleep and slept for more than three hours. When he awoke, he felt completely renewed and his bruises were so much improved that he considered himself cured and was convinced he had truly hit upon Fierabrás' balsam and that by possessing this remedy, he might fearlessly undertake any sort of confrontation, battle, or contest, however dangerous it might be. Sancho Panza also considered his master's improvement miraculous and begged him to give him what was left in the pot, which was no small amount. With this permission, he picked up the pot with both hands and with great trust and greater enthusiasm raised it to his lips and drank nearly as much as his master. But it turned out that poor Sancho's stomach was not as delicate as Don Quixote's, for rather than vomiting, he was overcome by such nausea and a desire to vomit, accompanied by so much sweating and swooning, that he really and truly believed his final hour had come. Seeing himself thus afflicted and distressed, he cursed the balsam and the scoundrel who had given it to him. When Don Quixote saw him in this state, he said,

"Sancho, I believe all this trouble is due to your not having been dubbed a knight, for I have the feeling this liquor must be of no benefit to those who have not been knighted."

"If your grace knew that," responded Sancho, "why in the name of me and all my kinfolks did you let me try it?"

But at that moment the concoction took effect and the poor squire began to discharge through both channels with such suddenness that the cattail mat on which he was lying and the burlap blanket he had drawn over himself were of no further use to anyone. And he was sweating so profusely from his retching that not only he but everyone present thought his end had truly come. This tempest and ordeal lasted nearly two hours, at the end of which time, unlike his master, he felt so throttled and manhandled that he was unable to stand. Don Quixote, however, felt perfectly well and whole, as we have said, and wished to leave immediately in quest of adventures, since it seemed to him that all the time spent there might be better employed assisting those in need of his favor and support, particularly after all the certainty and confidence he had garnered from his balsam. And so, driven by this desire, he himself placed the saddle on Rocinante and the packsaddle on his squire's beast. After helping Sancho to dress and mount his jackass, he mounted his own horse and, coming to the corner of the inn, grabbed a pike he found there, which he intended to use as a lance. All those in the inn, who numbered more than twenty persons, stood there observing him. The innkeeper's daughter also had her eyes fixed upon him and he, likewise, was unable to take his eyes off her. From time to time he would heave a sigh that seemed wrenched from the depths of his being, which everyone thought must be due to the pain in his side – at least, those thought so who had seen him covered with poultices the night before. As soon as they were both mounted, Don Quixote called to the innkeeper, who was standing at the gate, and said in a voice that was the height of serenity and seriousness,

"Many and great, sir governor, are the kindnesses I have received in this your grace's castle and I shall be indebted to you for all the days of my life. If I may be of service by avenging a possible injustice done your grace by some arrogant knave, I would have you know that my mission is none other than that of aiding those who are weak, avenging those who have been wronged, and punishing acts of treachery. Therefore, kindly search your memory and if you find anything of this nature to entrust to me, you have only to mention it and I give you my word as a knight that you shall be satisfied and repaid to your heart's content."

The innkeeper answered him with the same seriousness:

"Sir knight, I have no need of your grace's help to avenge myself for any wrongs done me, for I know enough to take the appropriate vengeance when I am wronged. All I ask is that you pay the expenses you have incurred tonight in the inn: the straw and barley for your two animals, as well as your supper and beds."

"Then this is an inn?" said Don Quixote.

"And a most honorable one," replied the innkeeper.

"I have been laboring under a misconception until this very moment," said Don Quixote, "for I truly fancied it a castle, and not a bad one at that; but since it turns out to be an inn instead of a castle, what you must do is to forego the payment, for I cannot contravene the practice of knights-errant, who, I know for a fact – having until now read nothing to the contrary – have never paid for lodging or anything else in the inns in which they have stayed, since any and all hospitality they receive is rightfully due them by law as compensation for the intolerable ordeals they suffer in seeking out adventures day and night, in winter and in summer, on foot and on horseback, hungry and thirsty, sweltering and freezing, and exposed to all the inclemencies of heaven and the discomforts of earth."

"That is of little concern to me," replied the innkeeper. "I just want to be paid what I am owed, so let's cut out this business of histories and chivalry. I am not interested in anything except collecting my accounts."

"Then you are a foolish, evil innkeeper," said Don Quixote, and slapping Rocinante with his legs while adjusting his pike to carry it more easily, he rode away from the inn – not that anyone tried to stop him – and traveled a considerable distance without looking back to see whether his squire was following him.

When the innkeeper saw him leave without paying, he went over to Sancho Panza to collect but the latter said that because his master had refused to pay, he would not pay either, for as the squire of a knight-errant, which he was, the same rule and reason applied to him as to his master in the matter of not paying for things in inns and taverns. The innkeeper grew incensed at this and threatened that unless he was paid, he would collect it in a manner Sancho would find painful. To this Sancho responded that under the privilege of chivalry his master had received he would not pay one cent even if it cost him his life, for the ancient and noble tradition of knight-errantry was not about to be undermined by him, nor would those knights' squires yet unborn be able to reproach him for having broken with so honored a privilege.

Now, our beleaguered Sancho's bad luck was such that among the persons in the inn were four woolcarders from Segovia, three needlemakers from the pickpockets' district of Cordova, and two residents from the thieves' quarter of Seville – souls who were not only lighthearted and 'well-intentioned' but mischievous and playful as well. All of them, as though moved and impelled by a single spirit, came over to Sancho and pulled him off his jackass, while one went inside to get the blanket from the host's bed. Throwing Sancho into it, they looked up and saw that the ceiling was somewhat lower than what their task required, at which point they decided to go into the courtyard, where the sky was the limit. Once there, they placed Sancho in the center of the blanket and began tossing him into the air, amusing themselves with him as one might with a dog at Shrovetide. The cries of the poor tossed wretch were so loud they reached the ears of his master, who, stopping to listen closely, believed some new adventure was headed his way until he finally realized that the one doing the shouting was his squire. Pulling up on the reins, he headed back towards the inn at a laborious gallop and arrived to find the gate closed. Circling round the inn in search of a place to enter, he had not gotten as far as the wall surrounding the courtyard when, over the top of it, he could see the sorry diversion they were having with his squire. He saw him rise and fall in the air with such grace and agility that, had he not been angry, I have to believe he would have burst out laughing. He attempted to climb from his horse onto the wall but was so battered and bruised that he could not even dismount, and so from atop his steed he began to hurl such a barrage of taunts and insults at those tossing Sancho that it is impossible to record them word for word. This, however, did not stop them from laughing or tossing Sancho, nor did it cause the airborne Sancho to cease his protests, mixed now with threats, now with pleas, all of which were of little or no avail. But they finally called a halt from sheer exhaustion, at which point they brought him his jackass, helped him to mount it, and threw his jacket over his shoulders. The compassionate Maritornes could see his exhaustion and, thinking it appropriate to lift his spirits with a jug of water, brought him one from the well, since it would be colder. Sancho took it and put it to his lips but stopped short when his master cried out to him,

"Sancho my son, don't drink that water or it will kill you. Do you see what I am holding? Here is the most holy balsam, two drops of which will leave you as fit as a fiddle," and here he held up the can containing the brew. At these shouts Sancho looked at him out of the corner of his eye and shouted even louder,

"Can your grace have forgotten that I am not a knight or do you want me to vomit up the guts left over from last night? You can consign your brew to hell and leave me alone!"

To finish saying this and begin drinking were one and the same action, but because the first swallow showed him it was only water, he refused to proceed, asking Maritornes to bring him some wine, which she did quite willingly and even paid for it with her own money. Indeed, it was said of her that, despite her particular profession, she had about her some faint and distant aura of Christian charity. When Sancho finished drinking, he dug his heels into his jackass and sallied forth through the gate, which had been swung open, delighted to have gotten his way without paying, albeit at the expense of those that usually went his bail: his shoulders. To be sure, the innkeeper kept the saddlebags as payment for what he was owed but Sancho rode away so dazed he did not even notice they were missing. The innkeeper started to barricade the gate as soon as Sancho left but the blanket tossers would not permit it, for they were the sort who would not have given two figs for Don Quixote if he had been one of the actual knights of the Round Table.

Chapter Eighteen

The conversation between Sancho Panza and his master Don Quixote, together with other adventures worthy of record

By the time that Sancho caught up with his master, he was so faint and exhausted that he could scarcely urge his jackass forward. When Don Quixote saw him in this state, he said,

"I finally believe, noble Sancho, that yond castle, or inn, is indeed enchanted, for what could those people be who disported themselves so atrociously at your expense except phantoms and beings from another world? I can confirm this because when I was at the wall surrounding the courtyard, spectator to the scenes of your sad drama, I was unable to climb over it, and since I could not even dismount from Rocinante, I must have been under a spell. I give you my word of honor that, had I been able to dismount and scale the wall, I would have exacted such revenge that those good-for-nothing scoundrels would remember their prank for the rest of their lives, though I knew that in doing so I should contravene the laws of chivalry, which, as I have often said, will not permit a knight to lift a finger against any man who has not been knighted, unless it is a case of great and urgent necessity in defense of his own life and limb."

To which Sancho replied,

"I too would have avenged myself, knight or no knight, but I was unable to do so. However, I'm of the opinion that those who amused themselves at my expense were neither phantoms nor men under a spell, as your grace claims, but men of flesh and blood like ourselves. Moreover, they all had names, which I heard while they were tossing me. One was called Pedro Martínez, another Tenorio Hernández, and I heard the innkeeper referred to as Juan Palomeque, or 'Lefty.' Thus, my lord, your inability to scale the wall or get off your horse may be explained by something other than enchantments. What I make of all this is that these adventures we're riding about in search of are certain to bring us at some time and place so many misadventures that we won't know our right feet from our left. It would be better and wiser for us, according to my limited understanding, to return to our village now that it's harvest time, attend to our affairs, and stop this wandering here, there, and everywhere."

"How little you understand, Sancho," said Don Quixote, "of this business of knight-errantry. Stop your complaining and be patient, for the day will come when you will see with your own eyes how honorable it is to follow in this calling. Just tell me: what greater satisfaction can there ever be, or what pleasure can equal that of being victorious in battle and triumphing over one's enemies? None whatsoever."

"I'll take your grace's word for it," said Sancho, "since I know nothing about such matters. All I know is that for as long as we have been knights-errant, or at least your grace has been, there being no reason to include myself in such distinguished company, we've not been victorious in a single battle unless we count that of the Biscayan, and even there your grace came away with only part of a helmet and half of one ear missing. From that time to this it's been nothing but punches and beatings and more punches and more beatings, with me holding the edge in blanket-tossings involving persons who are not real. And I can't even take revenge on them to savor the heights to which one's pleasure soars when conquering one's enemy, to quote your grace."

"That is what grieves me, Sancho, and what should grieve you," replied Don Quixote, "but from now on I shall keep at hand a sword fashioned with such craftsmanship that whoever has it at his side will be impervious to any sort of enchantment. It may even turn out that fate will provide me with the one belonging to Amadís when he was called the Knight of the Blazing Sword, which was one of the best swords a knight ever possessed, for in addition to its previously mentioned virtue it would cut like a razor and there was no armor that could withstand it, however strong and enchanted that armor might be."

"Well, with my luck," said Sancho, "when that occurs and your grace comes into possession of such a sword, it will be of use and benefit only to those who have been knighted, as in the case of the balsam. But as for us squires, just let us suffer our afflictions the best way we can."

"Fear not, Sancho," said Don Quixote, "for heaven will deal more kindly with you."

The knight and his squire were engaged in this conversation when Don Quixote saw on the road ahead of them a large thick cloud of dust coming their way and, as soon as he saw it, he turned to Sancho and said,

"Today is the day, O Sancho, when we shall see what boon my fortune holds in store for me! This is the day, I say, when the prowess of my arm will be revealed as much as on any other; when I am certain to accomplish deeds that will remain inscribed in the Book of Fame throughout the coming centuries. Do you see that cloud of dust rising over yonder, Sancho? Well, it is all churned up by a vast army of countless and diverse races marching this way."

"In that case," replied Sancho, "there must be two armies, for there's another cloud of dust just like it rising in the opposite direction."

Don Quixote turned to look and saw that such was the case. He was beside himself with joy because he firmly believed that here were two armies about to meet and do battle in the middle of that broad plain, and since his imagination was filled at all hours of the day with those battles, enchantments, adventures, feats of daring, love affairs, and challenges to duels recounted in his books of chivalry, everything he discussed, thought, or did was directed along those lines. As for the clouds of dust he had seen, they were raised by two large flocks of sheep traveling towards each other on the same road, but due to all the dust they could not be made out until they drew near. Don Quixote was so insistent in his assertion that they were armies that Sancho ended up believing it.

"Master," asked Sancho, "what shall we do?"

"Do?" responded Don Quixote; "we shall favor and support the helpless and the needy. Be advised, Sancho, that the army approaching from our front is led and commanded by the great emperor Alifanfarón, lord of the great island of Trapobana. The other approaching from the rear is that of his foe, king of the Garamantas, Pentapolín of the Bare Arm, so called because he always rides into battle with his right sleeve rolled up."

"And why do these two gentlemen hate each other so?" asked Sancho.

"They hate each other," said Don Quixote, "because this Alifanfarón is a raving Moslem and is enamored of Pentapolín's daughter, who is very beautiful, exceedingly charming, and a Christian. Her father refuses to give her in marriage to the pagan king unless he first renounces the faith of his false prophet Mohammed and becomes a Christian."

"By the beard of my chin, Pentapolín is doing the right thing," said Sancho, "and I'll lend him all the help I can."

"And you will thereby be doing your duty," said Don Quixote, "for to participate in such battles as this, it is not necessary to have been dubbed a knight."

"I can certainly understand that," replied Sancho, "but where shall we put this ass so we can find him when the battle is over, since I don't believe it has been the custom up to now to ride into battle on such a mount?"

"That is true," said Don Quixote. "You may simply leave him to his own devices even if he gets lost, for there will be so many horses for us to choose from once we are victorious that even Rocinante runs the risk of being swapped for another. But pay close attention and observe, for I want to give you an account of the most outstanding knights in these two armies. And so that you may have a better view, let us withdraw to that rise over yonder, from where the two armies may be seen."

Accordingly, they situated themselves on a hill from which it would have been possible to see the two flocks that Don Quixote took to be armies, had the rising clouds of dust not blocked and obscured their view. Nevertheless, seeing with the help of his imagination what he could not see in actuality, Don Quixote raised his voice and began to speak:

"Yon knight you see there in the bright yellow armor, bearing on his shield a crowned lion crouching at the feet of a damsel, is the valorous Laurcalco, Lord of the Silver Bridge. That other one with gold flowers on his armor, whose shield displays three silver crowns against an azure background, is the dreaded Micocolembo, Grand Duke of Quirocia. The one to his right with those gigantic limbs is the ever fearless Brandabarbarán de Boliche, Lord of the Three Arabias, who wears a serpent skin as armor and whose shield displays a door that tradition says is one of those Samson tore from the temple when he sought revenge upon his enemies, though it cost him his life. But direct your gaze in the other direction and you will see there in the vanguard, leading the other army, the ever-conquering and never-conquered Timonel de Carcajona, Prince of New Biscay, whose armor is divided into quarters: *azure*, *vert*, *argent*, and *or*, and whose shield bears a golden cat against a tawny background with a motto that reads, 'Miau,' the first letters of the name of his lady, who is said to be the peerless Miaulina, daughter of Duke Alfeñiquén del Algarbe. The one beside him, sitting ponderously on the back of that powerful charger whose armor is as white as snow and whose shield is blank and devoid of any device is a novitiate knight from the land of France named Pierres Papin, Lord of the Baronies of Utrique. The next one, digging his iron spurs into the flanks of that fleet-footed zebra and wearing azure cups for armor, is the powerful Duke of Nerbia, Espartafilardo of the Wood, whose shield bears an asparagus plant with a motto in Castilian that reads: *My fortune goes creeping along.*"

In this manner he went on naming any number of knights from one squadron and then the other, all of whom he conjured up and to each of whom he assigned on the spur of the moment that knight's armor, colors, device, and motto, inasmuch as he was caught up in the imaginary world that was the product of his unheard-of madness; and so without pausing, he went on to say,

"The squadron facing us is made up of people of diverse nations. Here we find those who quaff the fresh waters of the famous Xanthus; those who tread the rugged plains of Massilia; those who pan for the pure, fine gold of Arabia Felix; those who delight in the famous cool banks of the clear Thermodon; those who divest the Pactolus by many and varied means of its golden sand; Numidians, untrustworthy in their promises; Persians, famous archers; Parthians and Medes, who fight while fleeing; Arabs, with their portable houses; Scythians, as cruel as they are fair-skinned; Ethiopians, with their pierced lips; and an infinite number of other nations whose faces I see and recognize but whose names I fail to recall. In that other squadron are those who drink of the crystal waters of the olive-bearing Betis; those who smooth and polish their faces with the liquor of the ever-rich golden Tagus; those who savor the beneficial waters of the divine Genil; those who tread the Tartesian plains with their abundant pastures; those who disport themselves in the Elysian fields of Jerez;

Manchegans, rich and crowned with golden ears of corn; those clad in iron, ancient relics of the Gothic race; those who bathe in the Pisuerga, famous for its gentle current; those who graze their flocks in the pastures along the banks of the winding Guadiana, famed for its hidden course; those who shiver from the cold of the wooded Pyrenees and the snowflakes of the lofty Apennines – in a word, all those contained and enclosed within the whole of Europe."

May God strike me dead if he did not go on naming one province and nation after another, bestowing upon each with astounding rapidity the attributes it possessed, since he was completely absorbed and caught up in the things he had read in his fallacious books. Sancho hung upon his every word while uttering none himself and from time to time looked about to see if he could make out the knights and giants his master named but he was never able to recognize a single one.

"Master," he said, "of all those your grace has mentioned, the Devil can have any man, giant, or knight who is anywhere around here; at least I don't see any! But maybe it's all a matter of enchantments like the phantoms from last night."

"How can you say that?" replied Don Quixote. "Do you not hear the neighing of horses, the blaring of trumpets, and the beating of drums?"

"I don't hear anything," said Sancho, "except the bleating of some ewes and rams."

And such was indeed the case, for the two flocks were now drawing near one another.

"The fear you have, Sancho," said Don Quixote, "prevents you from hearing or seeing correctly, for one of the effects of fear is to cloud the senses and make things appear to be what they are not. But if you are so afraid, go off somewhere to yourself and leave me here, for I alone shall suffice to bring victory to whichever side I decide to support."

Having said this, he placed his lance in its socket, spurred Rocinante, and took off down the slope like a bolt of lightning. Sancho cried out after him, saying,

"Master Don Quixote, please come back, for I swear to God those are rams and ewes your grace is about to attack. Please come back! Oh, woe unto the father who begat me! What madness is this? May you observe that there is not a single giant or knight, and there are no cats or armor, no shields quartered or whole, no cups *azure* or bedeviled! What is your grace doing? Oh, woe is me!"

But Don Quixote was not about to turn back; instead, he rode forward shouting,

"Hallo, you knights who fight and serve under the banner of the valorous emperor Pentapolín of the Bare Arm, if you will all follow me, you shall see how easily I exact vengeance from his enemy Alifanfarón of Trapobana!"

As he said this, he charged into the midst of the squadron of sheep and began spearing them with his lance with great spirit and daring, as though he were truly spearing his mortal enemies. The shepherds and herdsmen riding with the flock shouted at him to stop but, when they saw that their warning was being ignored, they took out their slings and began to pepper his ears with stones as big as one's fist. Don Quixote took no notice of the stones; on the contrary, directing his shouts in every direction, he cried out,

"Where are you, my proud Alifanfarón? Show yourself, for it is but a single knight who wishes to test your might in head-to-head combat and take your life as punishment for the wrong you have done the valorous Pentapolín Garamanta."

At that moment a 'sugar-coated' stone from the stream arrived and struck him in the side, burying two ribs in his chest. Seeing himself thus ill-used, he had no doubt he was dead or at least mortally wounded. Then remembering his liquor, he pulled out the can, put it to his lips, and began pouring the contents into his stomach but, before he could finish drinking as much as he thought necessary, another bonbon arrived and caught him squarely on the hand, smashing the can and knocking out several teeth, as well as severely crushing two of his fingers. Such was the first blow and such the second that they toppled the poor knight from his horse. The shepherds gathered round him and, believing they had slain him, rounded up their flock as quickly as they could, loaded up their dead animals, which amounted to seven or more, and without further investigation departed.

During all this time Sancho stood on the hill observing all his master's outrageous actions while tearing at his beard and cursing the time and place that fortune had ever brought them together. When he saw that Don Quixote lay prostrate on the ground and the shepherds had gone away, he ran down the hill and up to the knight, whom he found looking simply dreadful though he had not lost consciousness.

"Master Don Quixote," said Sancho, "didn't I warn your grace to turn back; that those you were attacking were not armies but flocks of sheep?"

"Now you see, Sancho," said Don Quixote, "how my enemy, that thieving enchanter, can transform things and make them invisible. Be advised that such creatures can make us assume any appearance they choose. The evil one who pursues me was envious of the glory he saw I was about to win in this battle and for that reason transformed the enemy squadrons into flocks of sheep. If you doubt this, I suggest you do something that will be a revelation to you and will show you that what I say is the truth. Mount your jackass and follow them in a furtive manner and you will see that after they have traveled a short distance, they will resume their former shapes and no longer be sheep but will turn back into men, exactly as I first described them to you. But don't leave just yet, for I need your help and assistance. Come here and see how many of my teeth are missing, for it feels as though I have none left in my mouth."

Sancho drew so near he virtually stuck his eyes inside Don Quixote's mouth. This was at the very moment the balsam in Don Quixote's stomach had done its work, and so, just as Sancho came up to peer into his mouth, Don Quixote, faster than a gunshot, vomited up everything he had in his stomach, and every last bit landed on the beard of his compassionate squire.

"Holy Mary!" cried Sancho, "what is happening here? Without a doubt this poor soul is mortally wounded and is spitting up blood."

But after a little more investigation, Sancho noticed by its color, taste, and odor that it was not blood but the balsam he had seen him drink from the can. He was so overcome with revulsion that his own stomach turned inside out and he vomited *his* guts all over his master, leaving them both smelling like roses. Sancho hurried back to his jackass to get something from his saddlebags with which to clean himself and care for his master but, when he found the saddlebags missing, he thought he would go out of his mind. Cursing himself anew, he made up his mind to leave his master and return to his village even if it cost him the wages for the time he had already served, as well as any hopes of governing the island he had been promised.

At this point Don Quixote rose to his feet and, putting his left hand over his mouth to prevent his teeth from falling out, grasped with the other the reins of Rocinante, who had never moved from his master's side (such were his loyalty and training) and went over to his squire, who was leaning across his jackass, his head propped up with his hand and a look on his face of someone extremely troubled. When Don Quixote saw him so obviously distraught, he said,

"I would have you know, Sancho, that no man is greater than another unless he performs greater deeds. All these storms that now beset us are signs that the weather will soon clear and things will begin to improve, for it is impossible for good times or bad to last forever. From this it follows that, inasmuch as bad times have been with us for quite some time, good times must be just around the corner, so don't be upset over misfortunes that happen to me, since you don't share in them."

"Don't share in them!" replied Sancho; "the one who was tossed in a blanket yesterday – was that perhaps someone other than my father's son? And my saddlebags that are missing with all my prized possessions – do they belong to someone other than the same person?"

"Your saddlebags are missing, Sancho?" said Don Quixote.

"Yes, they are missing," answered Sancho.

"In that case we shall have nothing to eat today," said Don Quixote.

"That would be true," said Sancho, "if these meadows didn't contain those herbs you say you can recognize, which unfortunate knights like your grace use for supplying their needs in these situations."

"Nevertheless," responded Don Quixote, "at this moment I would rather have a quarter loaf of bread or a couple of sardine heads than all the herbs described in Dioscorides' *Herbal*, even if it was the one illustrated by Doctor Laguna. But, noble Sancho, mount your jackass and follow me, because God, who is the provider of all things, will not fail us now, particularly when we are so dedicated in His service, for He does not fail the mosquitoes in the air, the worms in the earth, or the tadpoles in the water, and He is so merciful that 'He makes His sun to shine upon the good and the evil alike,' and 'He rains on the just and the unjust;'" to which Sancho replied,

"Your grace would make a better preacher than a knight-errant."

"Knights-errant have always known a smattering of all sorts of things, as they should," replied Don Quixote, "for in the days of old a knight-errant was always prepared to stop and deliver a sermon or discourse in the middle of a royal encampment, as though he were a graduate of the University of Paris. From this we can deduce that the lance has never blunted the pen, nor the pen the lance."

"I suppose what your grace says is true," responded Sancho, "but let's be on our way and find a place to stay tonight, and may it please God to provide us with one where there are no blankets, blanket-tossers, phantoms, or enchanted Moors, for, if there are, the Devil can have the lot of them."

"Direct your prayer to God, my son, and choose whichever road you will, for this time I wish to leave our choice of lodging up to you. But first take your hand and feel about with your finger to see how many teeth and molars are missing from my upper "Four," responded Don Quixote, "not counting my wisdom tooth, and every one whole and quite sound."

"Are you absolutely certain of the number?" asked Sancho.

"I told you: four – maybe even five. In my entire life I have never had a tooth pulled from my mouth, nor has one ever been knocked out or lost to decay or abscess."

"Well, in the part down below," said Sancho, "your grace has only two and a half molars, but up above there's not even half a tooth – nothing in fact, for it's as smooth as the palm of my hand."

"I am truly cursed!" exclaimed Don Quixote when he heard the sad news his squire had given him. "I would sooner have had my arm ripped off, so long as it was not my sword arm. I would have you know, Sancho, that a mouth without molars is like a mill without a millstone, wherefore a molar is more to be treasured than a diamond. But since those of us who follow the rigorous profession of knighthood are subject to all this, mount up, my friend, and lead the way and I shall follow you at whatever pace you set."

Sancho did as commanded and kept to the king's highway, where he thought they might find shelter because that stretch of the road was heavily traveled. But because the pain in Don Quixote's jaw gave him no peace nor any desire to travel at a faster pace, they rode along slowly while Sancho made an effort to amuse and entertain him by speaking of first one thing and then another, one of which was the matter that will be related in the following chapter.

Chapter Nineteen

The judicious conversation that Sancho Panza held with his master, together with the adventure of the corpse, and other memorable happenings

"It seems to me, master," said Sancho, "that all the misadventures we've undergone in the last few days have undoubtedly come about as punishment for the transgression your grace committed against the order of chivalry by failing to carry out your oath of not eating at a table, not lying with the queen, and all those other things you included and swore to abide by until you recovered Malandrino's helmet, or whatever the Moor's name was."

"You are absolutely right, Sancho, but frankly it had slipped my mind, and I can assure you that as a result of your failure to remind me in time you were subjected to that blanket-tossing. However, I shall set things aright, for in the order of chivalry there are ways to correct everything."

"Well, did I by chance take an oath too?" asked Sancho.

"The point is not whether you took an oath," said Don Quixote. "It is sufficient if I understand that as an accomplice you are on very shaky ground. In any case we would do well to provide ourselves with a way out."

"Well, if that's how things stand," said Sancho, "I hope you won't forget this the way you did the oath. The phantoms may take it into their heads to amuse themselves with me once more or even with your grace if they see you're so persistent."

While they were discussing these and other topics, night overtook them midway through their journey, as a result of which they were unable to locate a place to spend the night. Their greatest concern was the fact that they were dying of hunger, for the missing saddlebags left them without provisions or rations, and to put the final touches on their misfortune, they had an adventure that required no contriving whatsoever to give it the appearance of the real thing. Even though this particular night was quite dark, they had continued traveling because Sancho believed they were on the king's highway and could reasonably expect to find an inn a league or two farther down the road. As they rode along in this manner – the night dark, the squire hungry, and the master eager to dine – they saw on the road on which they were traveling a great multitude of lights that looked exactly like moving stars headed in their direction. Sancho was scared to death by the sight and Don Quixote was not a little frightened himself, and so, after one pulled up on the reins of his jackass and the other on those of his horse, they sat there motionless, straining to see what it could be. They saw the lights coming closer and, the closer they came, the larger they appeared. The sight caused Sancho to shake like quicksilver and the hairs on Don Quixote's head to stand on end but, screwing up his courage, the knight said,

"Without a doubt, Sancho, this will be a very great and perilous adventure in which I shall be forced to demonstrate all my valor and strength."

"Heaven help me!" replied Sancho, "if this turns out to be an adventure of phantoms, which is what it looks like, I hope my ribs will be able to stand it."

"It will not matter how many phantoms there are," responded Don Quixote, "for I shall not allow them to touch a thread on your clothing. If they made sport of you the last time, it was because I was unable to scale the courtyard wall but now that we are on open ground, I shall be able to wield my sword as I please."

"If they cast a spell over your grace," replied Sancho, "and paralyze you the way they did the last time, what difference will it make whether we're on open ground or not?"

"Nevertheless, Sancho," said Don Quixote, "I am asking you to be courageous, for experience should show you that I am."

"I'll be brave if it is God's will," replied Sancho.

Moving over to the side of the road, the pair began to observe closely in order to discover what all those moving lights could be. Very soon they made out a large number of figures clad in white surplices and this fearsome sight completely annihilated any courage Sancho might have possessed. His teeth began to chatter like someone undergoing a chill of quartan fever, and the chattering increased when they finally saw what it was. They were able to make out as many as twenty men in white vestments riding horses and carrying blazing torches in their hands, followed by a litter draped in black. These were accompanied by six other men riding mounts caparisoned in black down to their hooves, and, judging by the leisurely pace at which the beasts were traveling, they were mules, not horses. As the men in white rode along, they were murmuring to themselves in hushed and mournful tones. This strange spectacle at such an hour and in such a desolate place was enough to strike terror into the heart of Sancho and even into his master's, which is precisely what happened. Although

Sancho's courage had been annihilated, the opposite occurred with his master, who at this point took it into his head that one of the adventures from his books was about to unfold. He had no doubt the litter was a bier bearing some mortally wounded or lifeless knight whose vengeance was reserved for him alone, and so without further reflection, he fixed his lance in its socket, set himself firmly in the saddle, and with calm and composure planted himself in the middle of the road, where the men in white would be forced to pass. Once he saw them draw near, he raised his voice and cried out,

"Halt, sir knights, or whatever your lordships are. I demand that you tell me who you are, where you are from, what your destination is, and who it is you are carrying on that litter, for by all indications either you have committed some outrage or have been the victims of one yourselves. It is proper and necessary that I be informed so as to punish you for the evil you have committed or to avenge you for the wrong committed against you."

"We are in a hurry," replied one of the men in white, "and, because the inn is some distance away, cannot stop to give your grace such an account."

Then spurring his mule, he started forward. Don Quixote was so greatly piqued at this reply that he seized the mule by the bridle and said,

"Stay right where you are and show a bit more civility by giving me the information I have requested; otherwise, you shall all have me to reckon with."

Because the mule was excitable, when its bridle was seized, it reared up on its hind legs and threw its master over its haunches onto the ground. When the foot servants saw the man in the surplice fall, one of them began to hurl insults at Don Quixote, who, now incensed, hesitated no longer but socketed his lance and charged at the man in mourning, knocking him to the ground severely wounded. When Don Quixote turned in the direction of the others, it was marvelous to observe the speed with which he attacked them and sent them scurrying. Indeed, at that moment it seemed as though Rocinante had sprouted wings, so briskly and proudly did he maneuver. Inasmuch as all the men in white were faint-hearted as well as defenseless, they abandoned the fray in an instant and began running across the field with their torches blazing, looking exactly like maskers cavorting during a night of celebrating and merrymaking. The mourners, however, clad in their cassocks and long skirts, were unable to move, and thus it was that Don Quixote without risk to himself gave them all a good drubbing and drove them from the site very much against their will. They all took him to be, not a man, but a devil from hell who had come to rob them of the corpse they were carrying on the litter. Sancho, who had witnessed all this, was astonished at his master's boldness and said to himself,

"Without a doubt this master of mine is as brave and intrepid as he claims."

A blazing torch lay on the ground next to the man who had been thrown from the mule, and the light from it allowed Don Quixote to see his face. Going up to him, the knight waved the tip of his lance in the man's face, commanding him to submit or be killed; to which the prostrate figure responded,

"I am submissive enough already and am unable to move because of my broken leg. I beg your grace, if you are a Christian, not to kill me or you will be committing a great sacrilege because I am a Master of Arts and have completed my first orders."

"What the devil has brought you here," asked Don Quixote, "if you are a man of the cloth?"

"What, sir?" replied the fallen man: "my ill fortune."

"Well, an even worse fortune awaits you," said Don Quixote, "if you do not satisfy me in all I have asked you."

"It will be easy to satisfy your grace," said the man. "You should know that, though I said I was a Master of Arts, I am only a Bachelor and my name is Alonso López. I am a native of Alcobendas and have come from the city of Baeza with eleven other priests, the ones who fled with the torches. We are headed for the city of Segovia with the corpse borne on this litter. The gentleman died in Baeza and was buried there but we are carrying his bones to his tomb in Segovia, which is his birthplace."

"And who killed him?" asked Don Quixote.

"God Himself by means of a pestilential fever that carried him off," said the bachelor.

"In that case," replied Don Quixote, "Our Lord has saved me the trouble of avenging his death had he been slain by anyone else at all, but since he was slain in that manner, there is nothing I can do except shrug my shoulders and seal my lips, and I should do the same even if He were to slay me. I should inform your reverence that I am a knight from La Mancha named Don Quixote and it is my calling and profession to travel throughout the world righting wrongs and redressing injuries."

"I don't understand that part of righting wrongs," said the bachelor, "for your grace has changed my health from good to bad, leaving me with a broken leg that will never be straight again in all the days of my life; and the injury you have redressed has left me so crippled I shall never be whole again. I had to have the *ill*-fortune to cross paths with a person who goes about in quest of *good* fortune."

"Things do not always turn out the way one anticipates," replied Don Quixote. "The problem, Sir Bachelor Alonso López, lay in your coming at night wearing those surplices, carrying torches, praying, and clad in mourning clothes, for you truly looked like something evil from another world. Thus, I could hardly fail to carry out my obligation to attack you and would have done so even if I had known you were actual demons from hell, which is what I took you to be from the beginning."

"Since this is what my fate has decreed, sir knight-errant, who have caused me such errant sorrow, I beseech your grace to help me out from under this mule, which has my leg pinned between the stirrup and the saddle."

"I might have talked all night," said Don Quixote. "How long were you going to wait before informing me of your concern?"

He then shouted for Sancho to lend a hand but the latter did not bother to respond, as he was engaged in plundering one of the pack mules those gentlemen had been good enough to bring with them, which were well provisioned with things to eat. Sancho fashioned a sack from his coat and, stuffing everything that would fit into this makeshift container, loaded up his jackass and only then did he respond to his master's shouts and assist him in freeing the bachelor pinned beneath the mule. After helping him to remount, Sancho handed him his torch and Don Quixote told the man to catch up with his companions and to implore them on his behalf to forgive him for the injury he could not avoid inflicting. Sancho also added,

"If by chance those gentlemen should like to know who the brave soul was who did them so much mischief, your grace may inform them that he is the famous Don Quixote of La Mancha, otherwise known as the Knight of the Woeful Countenance."

Once the bachelor had ridden away, Don Quixote asked Sancho what had led him to call him the Knight of the Woeful Countenance, particularly at that precise moment.

"I'll tell you why," replied Sancho. "For quite some time now I've been observing your grace by the light from the torch this poor soul was carrying, and to speak quite bluntly, for the last several minutes you have had the most woeful countenance I've recently seen, which must be the result of your weariness from this battle or your missing teeth."

"It is neither of those," said Don Quixote; "rather, the sage who is entrusted with chronicling my deeds must have deemed it appropriate for me to have some title like those the knights of old were wont to adopt, one being called the Knight of the Blazing Sword, another the Knight of the Unicorn, this one the Knight of the Damsels, this other one the Knight of the Phoenix, that one the Knight of the Gryphon, and yet another the Knight of Death, all of whom were known by these names and designations throughout the length and breadth of the land. Therefore, I say that the sage I mentioned has put it into your head and mouth to call me the Knight of the Woeful Countenance, by which name I intend to call myself from this day forward. And so that such a name will be more fitting, I intend at the first opportunity to have a most woeful face painted on my shield."

"There is no need to spend the time and money painting such a face," said Sancho; "all that is required is for your grace to show your own and without any other image or device, anyone seeing you will immediately call you the Knight of the Woeful Countenance. You may trust me, for I speak the truth when I assure you – and this I say half in jest – that hunger and the missing teeth give your grace such a forlorn appearance that the woeful painting may be dispensed with, as I've said."

Don Quixote was amused at Sancho's wit but nevertheless proposed to call himself by this name as soon as he could have his shield painted the way he envisioned it.

[At that moment the bachelor returned and addressed Don Quixote, saying,] [1]

"I forgot to advise you that you are hereby excommunicated for having violently laid hands upon holy things—*Iuxta illud, si quis suadente diabolo ..., et cetera.*" [2]

"I don't understand that Latin," said Don Quixote, "but I am certain I did not touch you with my hands but with my lance, particularly when I had no idea I was harming church property or injuring priests – whom I respect and adore as the Catholic and faithful Christian that I am – but, rather, phantoms and monsters from another world. However, should this turn out to be the case, I am reminded of what happened with Cid Ruy Díaz when he smashed the chair of the royal ambassador in the presence of His Holiness the Pope, for which he was excommunicated, and yet the noble Rodrigo de Vivar conducted himself that day as a most honorable and brave knight."

---

1 This line was added by R. Schevill to explain the sudden reappearance of the bachelor. It does not appear in the earliest editions.

2 The beginning words of a canon of excommunication; the Latin reads: 'Accordingly, if anyone at the urging of the Devil ..., etc.'

When the bachelor heard this, he rode off without saying another word. Don Quixote was curious to see whether the corpse on the litter was actually a skeleton but Sancho would not permit it, saying,

"Master, your grace has emerged from this perilous adventure in much better shape than from any other I've seen, but these men, though defeated and routed, may possibly figure out they've been defeated by a single person and, because of their embarrassment and humiliation over this, may regroup and come looking for us and give us something to think about. Inasmuch as the jackass is ready to travel, the hills are nearby, and we're beset by hunger, we need do nothing more than withdraw at a leisurely pace, for, as the saying goes: 'To the grave with the dead but the living to their bread.'" And so, driving his jackass before him, he begged his master to follow him, and because Don Quixote felt Sancho was right, he did so without further discussion.

After traveling a short distance between two small hills, they found themselves in a spacious, secluded valley, where they dismounted and Sancho unpacked the ass. Then dining on the grass with hunger as their sauce, they ate breakfast, lunch, and supper all at one sitting, satisfying their stomachs on more than one food basket the dead man's clerics (who seldom go unprovided for) had brought with them on the pack mule. But another misfortune befell them, which Sancho considered the worst of all: they had no wine to drink or even water with which to moisten their lips, in addition to which they were dying of thirst. But when Sancho noticed that the meadow they were in was carpeted with fresh grass, he said what will be revealed in the following chapter.

Chapter Twenty

The unprecedented adventure achieved by the valiant Don Quixote of La Mancha with less risk to himself than that ever achieved by any other famous knight on earth

"Master, this grass shows that very near here there must be some stream or spring supplying the moisture for this vegetation, so we would be wise to go on a bit farther, because we're bound to come to a place soon where we can quench this awful thirst, which without a doubt is even more terrible than hunger."

Don Quixote thought this good advice, and so, leading Rocinante by the reins while Sancho led his jackass by the halter, having first loaded it with the supplies left over from the meal, they began to grope their way through the meadow, for the darkness of the night provided no visibility whatsoever. They had not proceeded two hundred paces when their ears perceived a loud noise, as of water cascading from some high massive cliff, the sound of which buoyed their spirits enormously. But when they halted in an effort to discover its source, they heard to their sorrow another sound that put an end to the joy which that of the water had given them, especially Sancho's, since he was by nature cowardly and fainthearted.

They heard something striking the water at regular intervals, together with a certain creaking of iron and chains, as well as the sound of roaring water, all of which would have struck terror into the heart of anyone except Don Quixote. As previously noted, the night was dark and they had ended up among some tall trees whose leaves, when blown by the gentle breeze, made a faint but frightening sound. It thus transpired that the solitude, the locale, the darkness, the sound of the water, and the rustling of the leaves all inspired horror and dread, particularly when the pair noticed that the pounding never ceased, the wind never abated, and morning never arrived, in addition to which they had no idea where they were. But Don Quixote, undaunted as ever, mounted Rocinante, strapped on his buckler, leveled his lance, and said,

"Sancho my friend, I would have you know that I was born by heaven's decree into this iron age of ours to revive the age of gold, commonly known as the Golden Age. I am the one for whom are reserved perils, great accomplishments, and valiant deeds. I am, I say, the one destined to resurrect the Knights of the Round Table, the Twelve Peers of France, and the Nine Worthies – the one who will consign to oblivion the Platires and Tablantes, the Olivantes and Tirantes, the Febos and Belianises, and that whole horde of famous knights-errant of past ages by performing in the present age in which I find myself such prodigious deeds, wonders, and feats of arms that they will eclipse the most brilliant ones performed by all those others. You will observe, my faithful and loyal squire, tonight's darkness, its strange silence, the dull, bewildering sound of these trees, the frightful noise of that water we seek that seems to be rushing headlong down the towering mountains of the moon, and that ceaseless pounding that is paining and vexing our ears, all of which, taken together or separately, is sufficient to instill fear, dread, and terror in the breast of Mars himself, let alone in one not accustomed to such adventures and goings-on. All the things I am describing are spurs and incentives to my courage, which is causing my heart to burst in its breast from my desire to undertake this adventure, however difficult it may prove to be. Therefore, make sure Rocinante's cinches are tight and wait for me here up to three days, at the end of which time if I am not back, you may return to our village. After that, as a favor and service to me, you are to go to Toboso, where you shall inform my incomparable Dulcinea that her captive knight died undertaking tasks that would make him worthy to consider himself hers. And now, Sancho, I bid you farewell."

When Sancho heard these words of his master, he began to sob with the greatest tenderness in the world and said,

"Master, I don't know why your grace wishes to undertake such a frightful adventure as this. Since it's now nighttime and there's no one here who can see us, we could easily change our route and avoid the path of danger even if we got nothing to drink for three whole days, and since there are none who can see us, there are even fewer who can call us cowards. What's more, I once heard a sermon by our village priest, whom your grace knows, in which he stated that whoever goes looking for trouble will surely perish by it. It is unwise to tempt God by undertaking a task that is so outrageous one can escape from it only by some miracle. You should be satisfied with those heaven has already performed when it spared you from being tossed in a blanket as I was, or when you emerged safe and sound after triumphing over all those adversaries accompanying the corpse. If all this fails to move or soften that hard heart of yours, may it be moved by the thought and certainty that no sooner will you have departed from here than I, out of fear, will surrender my soul to the first person who wishes to carry it off. I left my home, forsaking my wife and children, to serve your grace in the belief that I would be better off, not worse, but just as greed causes the sack to tear, so have I been torn because of my hopes, for just when I thought I might achieve that wretched, ill-starred island you have so often promised me, I now see that in exchange and payment for it you would leave me in a place completely isolated from human contact. In the name of the one and only God, dear master, don't do me such an injustice. However, if you are absolutely determined to carry out this deed, may you at least put it off until morning, for according to what I learned of the heavens when I was a shepherd, dawn must be no more than three hours away, since the mouth of the Horn is directly above the Pole Star and it's midnight when the mouth is exactly to the left of it."

"Sancho, how can you see where that line is, or the position of that mouth and nape of the neck you mention, for the night is so shrouded in darkness there is not a star in the entire sky?"

"That's true," said Sancho, "but fear has many eyes and can even see beneath the earth, let alone up in the sky; besides, one can figure out by simple logic that day is just a short while away."

"However short it may be," replied Don Quixote, "it shall never be said of me, now or at any other time, that tears and pleas kept me from fulfilling my duties as a knight. Therefore, Sancho, I am asking you to stop your pleading, for God, who is now granting me the courage to undertake such a frightful and unheard-of adventure, will be certain to watch over my health and console you in your sadness. What you must do is to tighten Rocinante's cinches and wait here while I quickly return either dead or alive."

When Sancho saw his master's firm resolve and how little effect his tears, advice, and pleas were having upon him, he decided to use his ingenuity to make him delay until daylight if possible. Accordingly, while tightening the horse's cinches, he stealthily and without being observed hobbled both of Rocinante's hind legs by using the halter from his jackass. When Don Quixote tried to ride off, he was unable to do so, as his horse could not move forward but could only buck up and down.

When Sancho saw the success of his ploy, he said,

"See there, master: heaven, having been swayed by my tears and prayers, has decreed that Rocinante can't move. If your grace persists in endlessly spurring him, it will only provoke fate, and you will be, as they say, 'flying in the face of destiny.'"

At this point Don Quixote began to despair, for the more he slapped his horse with his legs, the less he was able to make him move. Inasmuch as he had no inkling of the hobbling, he thought it best to rest and wait for daylight to come or for Rocinante to stir, undoubtedly believing all this had its origin in something other than Sancho's ploy, so he said,

"Well, Sancho, since Rocinante is unable to move, I am content to wait for Dawn to smile upon us, though I shall weep from now until the moment she arrives."

"There is no need to weep," replied Sancho, "for I'll entertain your grace by telling stories from now till dawn, unless you would prefer to dismount and catch a few winks on the grass, as knights-errant are wont to do, so as to be more rested when day comes and it's time to undertake this incomparable adventure that's awaiting your grace."

"What do you mean: dismount and catch a few winks?" said Don Quixote. "Do I look like one of those knights who rest in the midst of danger? You go and sleep, since you were born for sleeping, or do whatever you please; I shall do what I deem most consistent with my plan."

"I wish your grace wouldn't get angry," said Sancho, "for I didn't mean anything by what I said."

And going up to him, Sancho placed his left hand on the front pommel and his right on the rear one, leaving himself pressed against his master's left thigh, from where he refused to budge an inch, such was his fear of the alternating sounds produced by the pounding. Don Quixote asked Sancho to tell him an entertaining story as he had promised, and Sancho said he would do so if he could rid himself of the fear caused by those sounds he kept hearing.

"Nevertheless, I'll try to tell a story which, if I'm able to finish telling it without getting mixed up or being interrupted, is a terrific one. Now, I hope your grace is paying attention because I'm ready to begin. Once upon a time . . . but first: 'May the good that is about to be revealed redound to us all, but any ill only to him who goes seeking it.' Your grace should note that the ancients didn't begin their stories just any old way; they began them with a sentence from Cato, the Roman sensor [1] which says, 'Woe betide him who goes looking for misfortune.' Now, since this fits your grace like a glove, you should stay put instead of looking for trouble and we should go back by another route, since no one is forcing us to stay on this one where we're beset by so many terrors."

"Go on with your story," said Don Quixote, "and let me decide which route to take."

"Well, as I was saying," continued Sancho, "in a village of Estremadura there lived a goat shepherd, that is, a man who herded goats, and this goatherd, or shepherd as I'll call him in my story, was named Lope Ruiz; and this Lope Ruiz was in love with a shepherdess named Torralba; and this shepherdess named Torralba was the daughter of a rich cattleman; and this rich cattleman . . . . "

"If that is the way you intend to tell your story, Sancho," said Don Quixote, "saying everything twice, you won't finish in two days. Tell it in a straightforward manner like a man with some sense; otherwise, don't tell it at all."

"The way I'm telling it," replied Sancho, "is the very way they always tell stories where I come from and I don't know any other way to tell it; besides, it's not right for your grace to ask me to institute new customs."

"Then tell it any way you please," said Don Quixote, "and since fate has seen to it that I have no choice but to listen to you, proceed."

"Well then, my dear, beloved master," replied Sancho, "as I was saying, this shepherd was in love with Torralba the shepherdess, a lass who was stockily built, unsociable, somewhat on the masculine side, and graced with a slight mustache. In fact, I can just see her now."

"Then you knew her?" asked Don Quixote.

"I didn't know her myself," said Sancho, "but the person who told me this story said it was so accurate and true that if I told it to anyone else, I could truthfully swear and affirm I had witnessed it all myself. Thus, as the days came and went, the Devil, who never sleeps but goes about creating

---

1 Sancho meant to say 'censor.'

turmoil, saw to it that the love the shepherd felt for the shepherdess turned into hatred and ill will. According to malicious gossip, she had caused him a certain amount of jealousy, for not only had she been unfaithful but had overstepped the bounds of decency. Such was the shepherd's hatred of her from that moment on that, to avoid seeing her, he decided to leave that land and go where he would never lay eyes upon her again. Torralba, who found herself scorned by Lope, then began to love him, though she had never done so before."

"That is the natural disposition of women," said Don Quixote: "to scorn those who love them and to love those who hate them, but do continue, Sancho."

"It came to pass," said Sancho, "that the shepherd put his plan into effect and, driving his goats before him, set out across the plains of Estremadura headed for the kingdom of Portugal. Learning of this, Torralba struck out after him on foot following at a safe distance, her feet bare, a shepherd's staff in her hand, and a knapsack round her neck in which they say she carried part of a mirror, a piece of comb, and a little bottle of makeup for her face, but let her carry whatever she will because I refuse to get involved in trying to find out. I'll simply say, in order to continue my story, that the shepherd arrived with his flock at the Guadiana River, which at that time of the year was so swollen it was virtually overflowing its banks. Along that stretch of the river there was no sign of any boat or person that could carry him and his flock to the other side. He became quite upset at this, seeing that Torralba was drawing nearer and knowing she would cause him considerable grief with her pleas and tears, and so he looked about until he spotted a fisherman with a small boat that could hold only one person and one goat at a time. Nevertheless, he spoke to the fisherman and arranged to have him row him and his three hundred goats to the other bank. The fisherman got into the boat and carried one goat across. He returned and carried across another. Coming back one more time, he carried across still another. Your grace is to keep count of the number of goats the fisherman rows across, for the instant that a single goat is unaccounted for, the story is over and I won't be able to say another word about it. But to continue: since the landing site on the other side was muddy and slippery, the fisherman took quite a while for the round trip. In spite of all this, he returned for another goat, and another, and another . . . "

"Just say," said Don Quixote, "that he rowed them all across. Don't keep him coming and going like this or you won't get them to the other side in a year."

"How many have been carried across so far?" said Sancho.

"How the dickens should I know! " said Don Quixote.

"There! Didn't I tell your grace to keep an exact count? Well, so help me God, the story's over and there's no going on with it now."

"How can that be?" said Don Quixote. "Is it so essential to the story to know exactly how many goats have gone across that if the count is off by just one, you are unable to go on with the story?"

"That's right, under no circumstances," said Sancho, "because the moment I asked you to tell me how many goats had gone across and you said you didn't know, at that very instant everything I still had to say faded from my memory, and I swear it was quite good and entertaining."

"And so the story is finished?" said Don Quixote.

"As finished as my mother is," replied Sancho.

"I have to hand it to you," said Don Quixote, "you have told one of the most novel tales or stories anyone could ever dream up, and the way you have told it and concluded it has never been nor ever will be witnessed in an entire lifetime, though I should have expected nothing less from your fine intellect. Still, it is not surprising, for that interminable pounding has probably confounded your thinking."

"Anything is possible," said Sancho, "but as far as my story is concerned, I can assure your grace there is nothing more to be said, for it ends right where the counting error begins."

"Let it end where it darned well will," said Don Quixote, "but right now let us see if Rocinante can move."

Once again he slapped the horse with his legs and Rocinante once again bucked up and down and then stood motionless, thanks to having been so well fettered. But at that moment, due either to the chill of the approaching morn, or to something laxative that Sancho had eaten, or to something natural, which is more likely, Sancho suddenly got the urge and desire to do what no one else could do for him, but so great was the fear that had penetrated his breast that he dared not move away from his master by so much as the tip of his finger, and yet, to imagine not doing what he had the urge to do was likewise impossible. So what he did for the sake of peace was to release his grip on the rear pommel, which he had been clutching with his right hand, and discreetly and silently to loosen the knot, which was the only thing holding up his breeches. As soon as he loosened it, the breeches fell to his ankles, where they remained like fetters. He then raised his shirt as high as possible and stuck out both buttocks, which were not all that petite. Having done this, which is what he thought must be done in order to rid himself of his terrible affliction and anxiety, he was overcome by an even greater apprehension, for it occurred to him that he might not be able to move his bowels without making some sort of noise. So he began to clench his teeth and hunch up his shoulders while holding his breath as long as he could, but despite all these precautions, his ill luck was such that he finally made a slight noise quite different from the one that had filled him with such dread. Don Quixote heard it and asked,

"What was that rumbling, Sancho?

"I don't know, master," said Sancho, "it must be something new, for adventures and misadventures never come without their fellows."

Once again he resolved to try his luck and it went so well that with no more noise or disturbance than before he found himself free of the burden that had caused him so much discomfort, but because Don Quixote's sense of smell was as acute as his hearing, and because Sancho was standing so close that he was virtually one with him, the vapors rose nearly straight up, a portion of which could hardly fail to reach Don Quixote's nostrils. No sooner did they do so than he came to the rescue by holding his nose between his forefinger and thumb and then said in a somewhat nasal tone,

"It appears to me, Sancho, that you are quite frightened."

"Yes, I am," replied Sancho, "but what has brought this to your grace's attention at this particular moment?"

"Because at this particular moment there is an aroma about you – and not of ambergris either."

"That may well be the case," said Sancho, "but I'm not the one to blame; it's your grace's fault for dragging me out at this inconvenient hour and putting me through these unaccustomed paces."

"Speaking of paces, my friend, pray be so kind as to take three or four back from me," said Don Quixote, still holding his nose, "and from now on be more considerate with your person and what you owe mine. Undoubtedly, my continual conversations with you have bred this contempt."

"I'll wager," said Sancho, "that your grace thinks I've done something with my person that I shouldn't have."

"It only gets worse if you stir it, Sancho my friend," said Don Quixote.

Master and servant spent the night in this and similar discussions but Sancho, seeing that morning was approaching at full speed, very cautiously unfettered Rocinante and tied up his own breeches. When Rocinante found himself free, he seemed to show renewed signs of life and, though not at all frisky by nature, began pawing the ground with his front hooves, for, if he will forgive my saying this, he had no idea how to rear up on his hind legs. When Don Quixote saw that Rocinante was able to move, he took it as a good omen, thinking it meant he was to undertake that fearful adventure. Now that dawn had arrived and everything could be distinctly seen, Don Quixote noticed that he was among some tall trees, chestnuts to be exact, which accounted for the extremely thick shade. He could also hear that the pounding had not ceased but saw no one who could be responsible for it, and so without further delay he applied the spurs to Rocinante. Then turning to take leave of Sancho, he ordered him to wait there for three days at most, as he had already explained, saying that if he had not returned in that time, Sancho could be certain that God had seen fit to end his days in that perilous adventure. He once again reminded Sancho of the message and dispatch he was to carry to Dulcinea on his behalf, adding that regarding the payment for his services Sancho had no need to worry because, before leaving his village, he had drawn up his will in which Sancho would find himself remunerated for everything having to do with his wages, prorated for the time he had served. But if God should bring him through this peril safe, sound, and absolved, the promised island could be considered an absolute certainty. Sancho once again began to sob listening to his master's touching words and was determined not to leave him until the crucial and final episode of that business.

Because of Sancho Panza's tears and his most honorable resolve, the author of our history concluded that he must have been wellborn and, at the very least, a pure-blooded Christian. Don Quixote was quite touched by his squire's distress but not to the point of showing any lack of resolve. Instead, dissimulating as much as possible, he began to ride towards the place from where the sound of the water and the pounding appeared to originate. Sancho followed on foot and, as was his wont, led the ass by the reins, who was his constant companion in good times and bad.

After traveling a considerable distance among the chestnuts and other shade trees, they came to a small meadow at the foot of a lofty cliff over which a mighty torrent of water plunged. At the base of the cliff were several poorly constructed buildings that more nearly resembled ruins than dwellings, and they noticed that from inside them came the noise and uproar of the pounding that never ceased.

Rocinante grew excited at the pounding and sound of the water but was calmed by Don Quixote as he slowly approached the houses. Commending himself heart and soul to his lady, he asked her to favor him in this fearsome circumstance and undertaking; he also commended himself to God, in passing as it were, asking that He not forget him. Sancho, who had never left his side, stretched his neck to peer between Rocinante's legs to see if he could make out what was causing him such consternation and dread. They continued for perhaps another hundred paces and when they rounded a bluff, there appeared – revealed and manifest – the very cause (as there could be no other) of that horrendous and (for them) frightful noise that had kept them bewildered and horrified the entire night. It turned out to be – if you, gentle reader, will not consider it too disappointing or irritating – half a dozen fulling hammers [2] that produced that racket with their methodical pounding.

When Don Quixote saw what it was, he said nothing but grew numb from head to foot. Sancho looked up and saw his master's head hanging down on his chest in a posture of embarrassment. Don Quixote also glanced at Sancho, whose puffed-out cheeks and smirking lips gave every indication of wanting to erupt in laughter, whereupon even Don Quixote's dejection could not keep him from laughing at Sancho's appearance. The moment that Sancho saw his master begin to laugh, he opened the floodgates himself, having to hold his sides to keep from bursting. Four times he collected himself and just as many times broke forth again in laughter as violent as before, which made Don Quixote furious, particularly when he heard Sancho say in imitation of himself,

"'Sancho my friend, I would have you know that I was born by heaven's decree into this Iron Age of ours to resurrect in it the age of gold, or the Golden Age. I am the one for whom are reserved perils, great accomplishments, and valiant deeds . . . '"

In this way he went on repeating all or most of the speech Don Quixote had delivered the first time they had heard the frightful pounding. Seeing Sancho make sport of him, Don Quixote became so ashamed and incensed that he raised his lance and gave him two fierce blows, and such that, had they landed on his head instead of his shoulder, he would have been relieved of paying his wages, unless it had been to his heirs. When Sancho saw that his levity was being taken seriously, he was afraid his master might continue in this same vein, so he said with great humility,

"I beg your grace to control yourself, for I swear I was only joking."

"Well, just because *you* are joking does not mean that I am," replied Don Quixote. "Listen here, sir merrymaker, do you think that if this thing that turned out to be fulling hammers had been some perilous adventure, I would not have possessed the necessary courage to undertake it and see it through? Am I by chance obliged, as the knight that I am, to recognize and distinguish among sounds and know which ones are fulling hammers and which ones are not? What is more, it may just turn out, which happens to be the case, that I have never seen such things in my entire life the way you have, being the lowly peasant that you are, born and bred in their midst. Just turn those six hammers into

---

2 Fulling mills, which are powered by waterwheels, are machines designed to increase the weight and bulk of woolen cloth by pounding it with wooden hammers while the cloth soaks in a wooden trough.

six giants and fling them in my face one at a time, or all at once, and if I don't set them on their backsides, you may make as much fun of me as you like."

"Please, your grace, no more!" replied Sancho, "I admit I've been a bit too lighthearted but I wish you would tell me, now that we're at peace – and may God bring you through every adventure that befalls you as safely and soundly as He has in this one – whether this thing that frightened us so much isn't good for a laugh and worth telling others about? At least I was afraid, though I realize your grace doesn't know the meaning of fear or terror."

"I confess," said Don Quixote, "that what has happened to us is worth laughing at but not worth telling others about, for not everyone is intelligent enough to put things into their proper perspective."

"At least," said Sancho, "your grace knew how to put your lance into its proper perspective, aiming at my head but landing on my shoulder, thanks to God and my ability at leaping aside – but never mind, it will all come out in the wash. There's the proverb that says, 'The one who loves you will cause you to weep.' Furthermore, I've heard that great lords, after they've spoken harshly to their servants, are in the habit of giving them some breeches but I have no idea what they give them after they've thrashed them, unless they do what knights do and give them islands or kingdoms on *terra firma* after they've beaten them."

"The cast of the die," said Don Quixote, "may be such that everything you say will come to pass. Please forgive me for what has just happened, for you are intelligent enough to know that a person's initial reaction is not always under his control. Also, be advised of something else from this moment forward, namely, that you are to abstain and refrain from incessantly talking to me, for in all the books of chivalry I have ever read, which are infinite in number, I have never encountered any squire who talked as much to his master as you do to yours, and quite frankly, I consider it a great failing both on your part and on mine – on yours in that you hold me in such low esteem, and on mine in that I do not command your respect. We read of Gandalín, squire of Amadís of Gaul, who was count of Terra Firma Island, that he always addressed his master cap in hand, his head bowed, and his body bent in the Turkish manner. Or take the case of Gasabal, Don Galaor's squire, who was so reticent that, to convey to us how unexcelled his astonishing silence was, he was referred to by name only once in that history, which is as great as it is truthful. From everything I have said, you must understand, Sancho, that it is necessary to maintain a proper distance between master and servant, lord and underling, knight and squire, and so from this day forward we should treat one another with more respect and take fewer liberties, for, whatever the reason for my annoyance with you, you will always come off second best. The favors and benefits I have promised you will arrive in due time, but even if they do not, your wages at least will not be lost, as I have already explained."

"What your grace has said is all well and good," responded Sancho, "but I would like to know, just in case their due time never gets here and it should be necessary for me to resort to my wages, how much did a knight's squire earn in the good old days, and was he hired by the month or by the day like some bricklayer's helper."

"I do not recall," said Don Quixote, "any squires working for wages – only for favors. If I have mentioned you in the sealed will I left at home, it is out of consideration for what may happen, because I am still not sure how knight-errantry will fare in these most calamitous times of ours and I should not want my soul to suffer in the next world because of some trifle, for I would have you know, Sancho, that in this world there is no more perilous profession than that of venturer knight."

"That's quite true," said Sancho, "since the mere sound of fulling hammers was enough to upset and vex the heart of such a valiant venturer knight as your grace. But rest assured that from this time forth I'll not open my lips to make fun of anything remotely connected with your grace, unless it is to honor you as my master and natural lord."

"In that case," said Don Quixote, "you will prosper upon the face of the earth, for after his parents, one should respect his master as though he were his very own father."

Chapter Twenty-One

The exalted adventure of the acquisition of Mambrino's priceless helmet, together with other incidents that befell our invincible knight

Just then, a light rain began to fall and Sancho suggested that they take shelter in the fulling mill but Don Quixote had developed such a hatred of it because of his painful deception that he refused to go inside under any circumstances. At this point, the road veered to the right and they came to another road like the one they had followed the previous day. They had not traveled very far down this new one when Don Quixote caught sight of a man on horseback wearing something on his head that glistened like gold. No sooner did he see him than he turned to Sancho and said,

"It would seem, Sancho, there is no proverb that is not true, for each is drawn from experience itself, the mother of all knowledge, particularly the one that says, 'If one door closes, another will be opened.' I mention this because, if last night Dame Fortune closed the door on the adventure we were seeking by deceiving us with the fulling hammers, she is now opening up another to an even better and more clear-cut adventure and, if I fail to gain entrance to this one, it will be my own fault, for I shall not be able to place the blame on my scant knowledge of fulling mills or on the darkness of the night. I tell you this because, unless I am mistaken, someone is riding this way wearing Mambrino's helmet upon which I swore the oath, as you no doubt remember."

"I hope your grace will carefully consider what you're saying and especially what you're doing," said Sancho, "for I wouldn't want this to be more fulling hammers that'll end up pounding and beating our brains out."

"You can go to blazes, Sancho," replied Don Quixote; "just what does a helmet have to do with fulling hammers?"

"I don't know," said Sancho, "but I can assure your grace that if I were allowed to talk as much as I once was, I could perhaps provide you with such an explanation that you would realize you're mistaken in what you're saying."

"How can I be mistaken in what I am saying, you traitorous coward? Just tell me that you don't see that knight riding this way on a dapple-gray steed with a gold helmet on his head."

"All I can see and make out," replied Sancho, "is a man riding an ass that's gray like mine and he's wearing something shiny on his head."

"Well, that is Mambrino's helmet," said Don Quixote. "Go off somewhere and leave me here with him and you shall see how I conclude this adventure without wasting a word in idle chatter, and the helmet I have so greatly coveted shall be mine."

"I'll give serious thought to going off somewhere," said Sancho, "but I repeat: may God let it be what your grace says it is and not fulling hammers."

"I have told you, my friend, not to mention or even think of mentioning fulling hammers or I swear to – but I'll not say it – that I will throttle your soul with a hammer of my own."

Sancho remained silent, fearing his master might carry out the vow he had made, the meaning of which was as plain as the nose on his face.

Now, the explanation for the helmet, horse, and knight was as follows. In that vicinity there were two villages, one so small it had neither a barber nor apothecary's shop, both of which services were available in the nearby second village, so that the barber from the larger village also served the smaller one. On this particular day there was a sick man in the small village who required a blood-letting and another who needed a shave, for which reason the barber had been summoned and had brought along a brass basin. As luck would have it, it had begun to rain along the way and because he did not want to get his hat wet, which was probably a new one, he had placed the basin on his head, and since it was spotless it glistened from half a league away – and he was riding a gray ass, just as Sancho had said. This then was the situation that led Don Quixote to believe he was seeing a dapple-gray steed, a knight, and a gold helmet, for everything he saw he made to conform to his deranged and errant ideas of chivalry. The moment that Don Quixote saw the unlucky rider draw near, he lowered his lance and, without exchanging a word with him, charged at him as fast as Rocinante could trot, having every intention of running him through. While bearing down upon him, he shouted in the midst of his furious charge,

"Defend yourself, you cur, or relinquish of your own free will that which so rightfully belongs to me!"

The barber, who saw that phantom bearing down upon him so unexpectedly that he had no time to be afraid, found no other means of escaping the lance thrust than to let himself slide off his jackass, and the moment he hit the ground, he took to his feet more nimbly than a deer and began running across the plain so fast that not even the wind could have overtaken him. The basin lay on the ground, which delighted Don Quixote, who observed that the infidel had acted wisely in imitating the beaver, which, when seeing itself pursued by hunters, will bite and tear off by natural instinct that part of its body it knows the hunters are seeking. He ordered Sancho to pick up the helmet, which Sancho did. Holding it in his hands, the squire said,

"My word! the basin is a good one and worth a *real* if it's worth a cent!" He then handed it to his master, who placed it on his head, turning it one way and another in an effort to make it fit but, failing to accomplish this, he said,

"Undoubtedly the infidel who served as the model by which this helmet was originally forged must have had an enormous head. The worst part, though, is that half of it is missing."

When Sancho heard the basin called a helmet, he could not keep from laughing but, remembering his master's anger, broke it off abruptly.

"What are you laughing at, Sancho?" said Don Quixote.

"I'm laughing at what a huge head that infidel must have had who owned this helmet, which I swear looks just like a barber's basin."

"Do you know what I think, Sancho? I think the wonderful piece we have here from the enchanted helmet must by some strange accident have fallen into the hands of someone who failed to recognize it or appreciate its value and without knowing what he was doing and seeing that it was solid gold must have melted down the other half to increase his profits and from this half made what looks like a barber's basin, as you say. But be that as it may, so long as I recognize it for what it is, its transformation is of little consequence, for I shall have it repaired in the first town that has a blacksmith so it will not be surpassed or even equaled by the one made and wrought by the god of the forge for the god of war. In the meantime I shall make it fit as best I can, for 'Something is better than nothing at all;' besides, it will serve quite well for defending me against a barrage of stones."

"That it will do," said Sancho, "so long as they don't use slings to hurl the stones the way they did in the battle between the two armies when they blessed your grace's molars and broke the can that held that most holy concoction that made me vomit up my guts."

"I am not overly concerned at having lost it," said Don Quixote, "for, as you already know, I have the recipe stamped in my memory."

"So have I," replied Sancho, "and if I should ever make it or try it again in my whole life, may that be my final hour. Besides, I don't intend to get myself into a situation where I'll need it, for I mean to make use of all five of my senses to guard against being wounded or wounding anyone else. As for being tossed in a blanket again, I have no comment, since it's hard to foresee such misfortunes as that. When they arrive, there's nothing to do except hunch up your shoulders, hold your breath, close your eyes, and let yourself go wherever fate and the blanket take you."

"You are a poor Christian, Sancho," said Don Quixote in response to this, "for you never forget a wrong someone has done you. You should know that it is customary for noble and generous hearts to ignore trifles. Did you come away from the tossing with one of your feet lame, or a rib broken, or your head split open, that you cannot forget that joke? Because when one considers the matter carefully, it *was* only a joke and a diversion. If this were not my understanding of it, I would already have returned there and exacted greater revenge than the Greeks did over the rape of Helen, who, if she were living today or my Dulcinea were living back then, might be assured that her beauty would not be as celebrated as it is." And here he heaved a sigh that rose towards heaven, whereupon Sancho said,

"Let it pass as a joke since we can't take revenge in earnest but I know the difference between joking and seriousness. I also know its impression will never be erased from my memory any more than it will be removed from my shoulders. But putting all this aside, will your grace please tell me what we should do with this dapple-gray steed that has been abandoned here by that Martino fellow your grace defeated, which looks an awful lot like a gray jackass. By the way he took to his heels and ran away, he gave no indication of returning for him, and the dapple, if I do say so myself, is quite a good one!"

"It has never been my custom," said Don Quixote, "to plunder those I defeat, nor is it the custom of knights-errant to rob them of their mounts and leave them on foot unless the one who is victorious lost his horse in the battle, in which case it is legitimate to take that of the vanquished knight as something won in lawful combat. Therefore, Sancho, leave this horse, or ass, or whatever you insist upon calling him, for the instant his owner sees us gone, he will return for him."

"God knows I'd like to keep him," replied Sancho, "or at least to exchange him because mine doesn't quite measure up to him. The laws of chivalry are certainly strict when they won't even permit one ass to be swapped for another. I would like to know if I might at least exchange the riding gear."

"I am unsure on that point," responded Don Quixote, "but since the matter is in question, I declare that you may exchange it until I am better informed if you have an extreme need to do so."

"So extreme," said Sancho, "that my need would not be greater if it were for my own person."

Having thus been duly authorized, he performed the *mutatio capparum*[1] and magnificently decked out his jackass, who came out the winner in the exchange. Once this was done, they dined on the spoils they had taken from the pack mule and drank water from the stream of the fulling mill without ever turning their heads to look at it, such was their hatred of it due to the fright it had given them.

Having thus assuaged the master's anger and the squire's disappointment, they mounted their beasts and with no particular route in mind (it being the custom of knights-errant not to choose a predetermined route), proceeded to follow the one dictated by the whims of Rocinante, who commanded the allegiance of his master, not to mention that of the ass, who always followed him wherever he led out of love and companionship. Despite this they returned to the king's highway, where they let chance be their guide. As they rode along, Sancho said to Don Quixote,

"Master, may I have your permission to say what is on my mind? Ever since your grace imposed that harsh restriction of silence on me, more than a few things have gone sour in my stomach and there's now one on the tip of my tongue that I would hate to have go to waste."

"Speak up," said Don Quixote, "but be brief in your speech, for none is pleasing that is too long."

"Well, master," replied Sancho, "I would like to say that for some days now I've been considering how little is gained and won in this wandering about in quest of the adventures your grace is seeking in these out-of-the-way places and crossroads. Even if we're victorious and bring them to a successful conclusion, there's no one to witness them or learn of them and consequently they'll remain eternally silent, much to the detriment of your grace's mission and to what they themselves deserve. So it strikes me that it would be better – unless your grace has a still better idea – for us to go serve an emperor or some other illustrious noble who's at war, in whose service you might demonstrate the fearlessness of your person, your awesome might, and your superior understanding, for, when this

1 Latin: 'exchanging of the hoods.'

was observed by the lord we were serving, he would be sure to reward us, and each according to his merits. Besides, there can't fail to be someone present who will set down your grace's achievements as an everlasting memorial. As for my own I have no comment, since they'll not go beyond squirely limits, though I can say that if it is the custom of knight-errantry to record the deeds of squires, I feel that mine will not be added as mere footnotes."

"Well said, Sancho," replied Don Quixote, "but before a knight can reach that stage, he must travel throughout the land on probation, as it were, in quest of adventures so that by concluding them successfully he will win such fame and renown that when he presents himself at the court of some great monarch, his reputation will have preceded him, and as soon as the boys see him ride through the city gate, they will follow him, gather round him, and begin to shout, 'Come see the Knight of the Sun,' or of the Serpent, or of any other such insignia under which he will have brought off his great achievements. 'Here is the one,' they will say, 'who in hand-to-hand combat defeated the enormous giant Brocabruno the Mighty; the one who freed the Grand Mameluke of Persia from the prolonged enchantment under which he had lain for nine hundred years;' and by word of mouth they will go about proclaiming his exploits. Because of the excitement of the youngsters and the general populace, the king will appear at a window of his royal palace. As soon as he catches sight of the knight, he will recognize him by his armor or by the device on his shield, whereupon he will say perforce, 'Hark! let all the knights of my court come forth to receive the flower of chivalry who is approaching.' At this command they will all come forth, while the king himself will descend the stairs half way, where he will welcome the knight by embracing him and kissing him on the cheek. He will then escort him to the queen's chamber, where the knight will find her with her daughter, the heir apparent, who will be one of the most beautiful and accomplished damsels to be found virtually anywhere in the civilized world. It will transpire that a moment later she will furtively glance at the knight and he at her, each considering the other an object more divine than human. And without knowing how or why, they will be caught up and entangled in an inextricable web of love and their hearts will be filled with trepidation, for they will not know how to communicate to one another their feelings and anxieties. From there they will undoubtedly take him to some richly furnished chamber of the palace where, after removing his armor, they will bring him a rich scarlet cloak to wear, and if he was handsome in his armor, he will be just as handsome or more so in his quilted jacket.

"With the arrival of evening, he will dine with the royal family and will never take his eyes off the maiden but his glances will go undetected by everyone present. She will do the same, exercising the same caution, for, as I have said, she will be a most discreet young lady. The tables will then be cleared, at which point a small unsightly dwarf will suddenly enter the banquet hall accompanied by a beautiful matron lady and two giants. He will have brought a test, or ordeal, devised by some ancient sage, and will announce that whoever successfully undertakes it will be acclaimed the best knight in the world. The king will then order all those present to attempt it but none will be able to accomplish it except the visiting knight, much to the increase of his fame, whereupon the girl will rejoice and consider herself happy and most fortunate to have directed and set her thoughts so high. But best of all, this king, or prince, or whatever he happens to be, will be engaged in a bitter, hard-fought war with someone as powerful as himself. The visiting knight, after a few days at court, will request permission to serve him in the above-mentioned war. The king will very graciously give his consent and the knight will kiss his hand most civilly for the favor extended to him.

That evening, he will take leave of his lady the princess at a garden grating that opens onto her sleeping quarters, through which he will have conversed with her on many other occasions but only in the presence of a handmaiden whom the princess trusts highly and who serves as go-between and all-round confidante. He will sigh, she will swoon, and the handmaiden will send for water because she will be greatly distressed by the approach of day and, for the sake of her lady's honor, would not have them discovered. Finally, the princess will regain her senses and through the grating will hold out her pallid hands to the knight, who will kiss them a thousand times or more, bathing them with his tears. The two will agree upon a method for making known to one another the good and bad experiences they undergo, and the princess will plead with him to stay away no longer than is necessary, which he will swear to do by any number of oaths. Kissing her hands once again, he will take his leave with such regret that he will be on the verge of expiring. Going straight to his chamber, he will throw himself onto his bed but will be unable to sleep due to the painful parting.

He will rise early the following morning to bid farewell to the king, queen, and princess but, upon taking his leave of the royal couple, will be informed that the princess is indisposed and unable to receive visitors. Inasmuch as the knight will believe her grief at their parting is responsible for this, his heart will be pierced and it will require very little to make him openly reveal his sorrow. The handmaiden (and go-between), who will be present, will note all this and report it to her lady, who will receive her with tears in her eyes and will tell her that one of her greatest regrets is not knowing the name of her knight or whether he is descended from a line of monarchs. The handmaiden will assure her that only a serious and regal subject could encompass such breeding, gallantry, and valor as her knight possesses. The anxious girl will be consoled by this or at least will make the effort lest she arouse suspicion in her parents, and two days later will appear in public. The knight, who will have already departed, will fight in the war, defeat the king's enemy, conquer a number of cities, triumph in numerous battles, return to the court, and visit his lady in the customary location, where they will agree that he will ask her father for her hand in marriage as payment for his services. The king will refuse to grant his request because he will not know who the knight is, but despite this the princess will become his wife either by abduction or by some other means and her father will come to consider this most fortunate, for it will have been ascertained that the knight is the son of a valiant king of some kingdom or other which I believe is not located on any map. The father will die, the princess will inherit the throne and, in a word, the knight will become king. Now it will be time for him to bestow favors upon his squire and all those who have assisted him in ascending to such a high position. He will wed his squire to the princess's maid, who without a doubt will have been the go-between in their love affair and will be the daughter of a most illustrious duke."

"All I want is my fair share," said Sancho, "and that's what I'm counting on. Everything down to the smallest detail is bound to come true, because they don't call your grace the Knight of the Woeful Countenance for nothing!"

"You may depend upon it," said Don Quixote, "for in the same way and by the same steps I have related here, knights-errant have risen to become kings and emperors. So all that remains is for us to see which Christian or heathen king is at war and has a beautiful daughter. However, there will be time to consider this, because, as I have said, we must first gain a reputation in some other region that will find its way back to court. And yet, I have still another shortcoming: suppose a king is located who is at war and has a beautiful daughter and I have acquired an incredible reputation throughout the entire universe, I do not see how it can be shown that I come from a line of kings or am at the very least second cousin to an emperor, for the king will refuse to give me his daughter unless he is first fully informed on this point however much my famous exploits may warrant it. Because of this shortcoming I fear I shall lose what my arm has rightfully won. To be sure, I am an hidalgo from a distinguished line with possessions and property whom the courts recognize as a noble, and it may just transpire that the scholar who records my history will delineate my ancestry and forebears in such a way that I shall turn out to be a fifth or sixth generation descendant of a king. You should know, Sancho, that there are two kinds of pedigrees in the world: those persons who trace their descent from princes and monarchs but whom time has diminished little by little until they end in a point, like a pyramid turned upside down, and others who have a humble beginning but continue to rise from one rank to the next until they become grandees. Thus the difference is that some used to be what they no longer are, while others have become what they formerly were not. It may turn out that I belong to the former and, once an investigation is made, it will be found that my origins were grand and famous, and because of this the king who is to be my father-in-law will be content. If not, the princess' love for me will be such that, despite her father, she will accept me as her husband and lord, even if she clearly knows I am the son of a water-carrier. But should she not do so, this is where I abduct her and carry her off to any place I please, for either time or death will put an end to her parents' displeasure."

It was at this point that Sancho said,

"There's something that certain callous individuals say which is very much to the point: 'Don't seek by favors what you can take by force,' though more to the point is this other saying: 'Fleeing for one's life is worth more than good men's prayers.' I bring this up because should his majesty the king, your grace's father-in-law, not deign to surrender my lady the princess, there is nothing to do, as your grace has said, but to abduct her and make our escape. But the problem with this is that, until peace is made and one can tranquilly enjoy the fruits of reigning, the poor squire will be left wondering where his next meal is coming from, unless, of course, the go-between, who will be his wife, accompanies the princess and he shares his misfortunes with her till heaven decrees otherwise, for in my opinion his master may properly award her to him as his wife without further ado."

"No one would dispute that," said Don Quixote.

"Well, if that's the case," replied Sancho, "there's nothing to do except commend ourselves to God and let fortune take whatever course it will."

"And may God grant everything," said Don Quixote, "according to my wishes and your needs, Sancho. Let that person be wretched who thinks he is."

"Yes, let him, in God's name," said Sancho, "for I'm a Christian from way back and that's enough to qualify me to be a count."

"Or more than enough," said Don Quixote, "but even if it is not, it will not matter, for I shall be king and can bestow nobility upon you without your having to buy it or to defer to me in any way. And when I make you a count, hold your head high and let others say what they will, for I give you my word that they shall address you as 'your grace,' however much it may pain them."

"And, by Jove, I will wear my title with credulity!" replied Sancho.

"You mean 'credibility,' not 'credulity,'" said his master.

"Whatever," replied Sancho; "I'm simply saying that I'll know how to adapt myself because – bless my soul! – I was once a beadle of a confraternity, and the beadle's robe was so becoming to me that everyone said that with my bearing I could have been the steward of the confraternity. So what will I look like when I throw a duke's robe across my shoulders or deck myself out in gold and pearls in the manner of some of the foreign counts? I'll bet people will come from a hundred leagues around just to get a glimpse of me."

"You will look fine," said Don Quixote, "but you must trim your beard often, for yours is coarse and unruly and even bare in spots. You will have to shave with a razor every other day or people will see what you are from as far away as a musket shot."

"All I'll have to do," replied Sancho, "is hire me a barber and bring him to my house to live, and if necessary, I'll even have him ride along behind me like the groom of some grandee."

"How do you know, Sancho, that grandees have their grooms ride behind them?"

"I'll explain it to your grace," said Sancho: "some years ago I spent a month at court and while I was there, I saw a man taking a stroll who was a very small grandee and was said to be a noble of some importance. He was followed by a man on horseback who turned every way his master turned, exactly as if he were the man's tail. I asked why that man never rode beside the other man but always behind him, and they explained that he was the groom and it was the custom of nobles to have their grooms follow along behind them. That made such an impression upon me I've never forgotten it."

"And I might add that you are correct," said Don Quixote. "Therefore, you may take your barber with you and, since not all customs arrived together or were invented at the same time, you can be the first count to have his barber trail along behind him; besides, it takes more courage to have one's beard shaved than to have one's horse saddled."

"I'll take care of the barber business," said Sancho, "if your grace will try to become king and make me a count."

"I shall do so," responded Don Quixote and, raising his eyes, he saw what will be related in the following chapter.

Chapter Twenty-Two

The freedom that Don Quixote afforded a number of unfortunate souls, who, much against their will, were being taken to a place where they had no desire to go

Cide Hamete Benengeli, the Arabic historian of La Mancha, relates in this most serious, grandiloquent, meticulous, pleasant, and original history that at the conclusion of the conversation between Don Quixote and his squire Sancho Panza related at the end of chapter twenty-one, Don Quixote raised his eyes and saw coming down the road on which they were traveling some dozen men on foot, all bound by the neck, wearing handcuffs, and strung out like beads on a long iron chain. They were accompanied by two men on horseback carrying wheel-lock muskets and two men on foot carrying javelins and swords. When Sancho saw them, he said,

"Here comes a chain gang of convicts sentenced by the king to forced labor in the galleys."

"What do you mean 'forced'" exclaimed Don Quixote; "is it possible the king would use force against anyone?"

"Not personally," said Sancho, "but these are men who because of their crimes have been sentenced to serve the king forcibly in the galleys."

"In other words," said Don Quixote, "these men, however you put it, are going there by force and not of their own free will."

"That's right," answered Sancho.

"Well, in that case," said his master, "it behooves me to call upon my profession, whose purpose is to oppose force and to aid and abet those who are less fortunate."

"May your grace be advised," said Sancho, "that justice in the person of the king is not committing a wrong against such people as these but is punishing them for their crimes."

Just then, the gang of galley slaves arrived and Don Quixote very courteously asked the men guarding them to be so kind as to inform him of the reason or reasons those men were being marched along in that fashion. One of the guards on horseback responded that they were convicts in His Majesty's service who were bound for the galleys and there was nothing further to be said or for Don Quixote to know.

"Nevertheless," added Don Quixote, "I should like to learn from each of them individually the cause of his misfortune." To these arguments he added others just as respectful in an effort to persuade them to tell him what he wished to know. Finally, the second mounted guard said,

"Though we have with us the registry and certificate of sentence of each of these wretches, this is not the time and place to take them out and read them. However, your grace may approach and question the men themselves and they will inform you if they feel so inclined, which they certainly will because they're the sort who take pride in performing wicked deeds and then boasting of the fact."

With this permission, which he would have taken even if it had not been granted him, Don Quixote approached the chain gang and asked the first man what sins had brought him to such a pass. The man responded that it was due to his having been in love.

"For nothing more than that?" said Don Quixote. "Why, if they can send a man to the galleys just for being in love, I might have been pulling an oar myself for quite some time now."

"It is not the kind of love your grace has in mind," said the galley slave. "I was in love with a basket stuffed with clean clothes, which I clasped so tightly to my bosom that if the law had not taken it from me by force, I would not willingly have parted with it even till now. It was a fragrant act, [1] torture was out of the question, the lawyers put forth their arguments, my back was blessed with a hundred lashes, and for good measure they gave me three years riding the planks, and the matter was settled."

"What is 'riding the planks'?" asked Don Quixote.

"That means going to the galleys," replied the galley slave, who was a lad of about twenty-four and said to be from Piedrahita. Don Quixote put the same question to the second man who, because of his sadness and depression, did not say a word. The first man, however, answered for him, saying,

"This man, sire, finds himself here for being a canary, that is, a musician and a singer."

"How is that?" asked Don Quixote. "People can be sent to the galleys for being musicians and singers?"

"Yes, sire," responded the galley slave, "for there's nothing worse than singing under duress;" to which Don Quixote replied,

"I have always heard that 'singing chases one's cares away.'"

"Here it is the opposite," said the galley slave, "for whoever sings just once will weep for the rest of his life."

"I don't understand," said Don Quixote. One of the guards then explained:

"Sir knight, among these sinners 'to sing under duress' means to confess under the water torture. This poor devil was tortured and confessed his crime: that of being a cattle and horse thief, and for having confessed, he was sentenced to six years in the galleys plus two hundred lashes, which he already wears on his back. He always looks sad and distracted because the rest of the thieves who are still free, as well as those who are here, treat him with abuse and derision and hold him in contempt because he confessed and lacked the courage to say 'no', for they say it is just as easy to say 'no' as it is to say 'yes', and that a criminal has all the luck he will ever need if his life or death hinges on his own tongue rather than on that of witnesses or evidence, and in my opinion they're not far off the mark."

"That is my understanding as well," replied Don Quixote. Proceeding then to the third man, he asked him the same question he had asked the others, and this man in a hasty and most carefree manner answered,

"I'm going to ride those marvelous planks for five years because I was ten ducats short."

"I shall gladly give you twenty," said Don Quixote, "to free you from that burden."

---

1 Word play on 'a flagrant act.'

"That," said the galley slave, "is like a person who is dying of hunger in the middle of the ocean and has money but no place to buy what he needs. I say this because if at the time I'd had those twenty ducats your grace is now offering me, I could have greased the notary's palm and sharpened my attorney's wits to such a point that I would find myself today in Zocodover Plaza [2] in Toledo instead of on this road like a dog on a leash. But God is merciful and I'll be patient, and that's all I've got to say."

Don Quixote went on to the fourth convict, a man with a venerable face and a gray beard that reached down to his waist. When he heard himself asked why he was there, he began to sob and was unable to say a word but the fifth convict served as his tongue, saying,

"This good man is on his way to the galleys for four years, having been paraded through the streets on horseback, together with the usual humiliating ceremonies."

"That sounds to me," said Sancho Panza, "as though he must have been sentenced to a public disgracing."

"Precisely," replied the galley slave, "and the crime for which he was given that punishment was that of being a money broker, or to be more exact, a body broker. What I'm trying to say is that this gentleman is here for being a procurer and for having a hint of sorcery about him."

"If you had just not added that business of sorcery," said Don Quixote, "he would not deserve to be sent to the galleys for simply being a procurer; on the contrary, he would deserve to be in command of the galleys, for the occupation of procuring is no ordinary one but one which demands discretion and is absolutely essential in a well-run state. It should be practiced only by people of good birth and there should be examiners and overseers of it, just as there are for other occupations, with a definite number being appointed and recognized as with brokers on the stock exchange. In this way we might avoid any number of evils that are occasioned by this occupation and profession's being in the hands of idiots and dullards, namely, frivolous women and immature, inexperienced little pages and scoundrels, who on the most demanding occasions in which it necessary to come up with something clever let the opportunity slip through their fingers because they don't know their right hands from their left. I would be happy to continue enumerating the reasons why it would be advisable to choose by election those persons who are to hold such an important office in the republic but this is not the time or place to do so. Some day I shall explain it to someone who can remedy the situation. For now, I shall merely say that the grief I have experienced at seeing this grey head and venerable countenance in such distress for being a procurer has now been removed by the additional fact that he is a sorcerer, though I am convinced there is no sorcery on earth that can compel or force one's volition as some simpletons believe. Our will is free and there is no herb or charm that can force it. What some little old ladies and charlatans customarily do is to concoct a mixture, or poison, which drives men mad, the latter having been led to believe they had the ability to make women fall in love with them; though, as I have said, it is impossible to control a person's will."

"So it is," said the kindly old man. "However, upon my honor, sire, I was never guilty of that

2 A favorite meeting place of crooks.

business of sorcery; that of procuring, though, is a different matter. Still, I never dreamed I was doing anything wrong by it, for my sole purpose was to have everyone enjoy himself and to live in peace and calm without quarrels or disharmony. But this noble intention has not been able to keep me from going to a place from where I never expect to return because of my advanced years and a urinary ailment that won't allow me a moment's peace." And here he began to shed tears as before. Sancho felt such compassion for him that he took a *real* from his shirt and gave it to him in an act of charity.

Don Quixote moved down the line and asked the next person his crime. This man answered with even greater frankness than the previous one:

"I am here because I was too familiar with two female cousins of mine and two others who were not. In the end, I was so familiar with each of them that it resulted in such a complicated set of blood relationships that the Devil himself couldn't figure it out. I was found guilty of everything and, because I lacked friends and money, saw myself about to be hanged. They sentenced me to the galleys for six years and I accepted it, since the punishment was of my own doing, but I am young and if I manage to survive, who knows what I can do? Sir knight, if your grace has anything to give us poor wretches, God will repay you in heaven, and those of us on earth will make certain to pray to God for your health and life, that they may be as good and lengthy as your noble countenance deserves." This man was dressed as a student and, according to one of the guards, was an excellent Latin scholar and a person who would talk your head off besides.

Next came a man of about thirty whose appearance was quite nice despite his being slightly cross-eyed. He was bound differently from the rest, for round his ankle he wore a chain that was so long it wound about his entire body. There were two iron rings round his neck, one attached to the chain and the other to a so-called 'friend-keeper' or 'friend's foot,' from which were suspended two strips of iron reaching to his waist, at the ends of which were two manacles round his wrists secured by a thick padlock. In this way he could neither raise his hands to his mouth nor lower his head to his hands. Don Quixote asked why this man was wearing so many more irons than the others and the guard informed him that he alone had committed more crimes than all the others combined and was so rash and crafty that, even though he was bound in that manner, they still felt uneasy about him and feared he might manage to escape."

"What crimes can he have committed," asked Don Quixote, "if his only punishment is being sent to the galleys?"

"He is sentenced to ten years," replied the guard, "which is equivalent to the death penalty. That's all I'll say except that this fine fellow is the notorious Ginés de Pasamonte, who also goes by the name of Ginesillo the Thief."

"Sir commissary," said the galley slave at this point, "I would go easy there and not get into the matter of names and nicknames. My name is Ginés, not Ginesillo, and I am descended from the Pasamontes, who are not thieves as you imply. Each person should examine himself before calling other people names."

"Speak with less arrogance, you overinflated thief," said the commissary, "unless you want me to shut your mouth, which I'll do much to your sorrow;" to which the galley slave replied,

"It certainly seems that man's fate is dependent upon God's will but some day people will know whether my name is Ginesillo the Thief or something else."

"Well, isn't that what people call you, you scoundrel?" exclaimed the guard."

"They do call me that," said Ginés, "but one day I'll put a stop to it or will yank out all their hair from you know where! Sir knight, if you have anything to give us, do so at once and then be on your way, for all this enquiring into other people's lives is becoming tedious. If you wish to know about mine, I would have you know I am Ginés de Pasamonte, whose life has been written down by these very fingers."

"He's telling the truth," said the commissary, "for he himself has written his life story and it leaves nothing to be desired. It's a story he hocked for two hundred *reals* and left in the jail."

"And I intend to redeem it," said Ginés, "even if it should take two hundred ducats."

"It is that good?" said Don Quixote.

"It is so good," responded Ginés, "that it will be bad news for *Lazarillo de Tormes*[3] and all the others of that ilk that have been, or ever will be, written. What I can tell you is that it deals with things that are true, and they are so marvelous and clever that there is no work of fiction that can equal it."

"And what is the title of your book?" asked Don Quixote.

"*The Life of Ginés de Pasamonte*," replied Ginés.

"Is it finished?"

"How can it be finished when my life is not yet finished? The part that is written extends from my birth up to where I was sent to the galleys the last time."

"Then you have been there before?" said Don Quixote; to which Ginés replied,

"I spent four years there serving God and the king and I know the difference between a biscuit and a whip, but I don't much mind going to the galleys because it will afford me the opportunity to finish my book, for I still have a number of things to say. Moreover, in the Spanish galleys there is more than enough leisure time, though I need very little for what remains to be written, since I already have it memorized."

"You sound talented," said Don Quixote.

"And unfortunate," answered Ginés, "for misfortune always pursues gifted people."

"It also pursues scoundrels," said the commissary.

"Sir commissary," replied Pasamonte, "I have already told you to take it easy. You were not given that staff for the purpose of mistreating us poor souls but of leading and taking us to where His Majesty has ordered; otherwise, for the life of . . . but never mind, I know a certain person whose dirty laundry will be aired one of these days. For now, everyone should shut his mouth and look alive. Let's talk about something else and be on our way, for this diversion has lasted long enough."

The commissary raised his staff to strike Pasamonte in reaction to his threats but Don Quixote jumped between them and begged him not to harm the prisoner, for it was only natural for someone who had his hands so securely bound to be a little free with his tongue. Then turning to everyone in

---

3 One of the most famous picaresque novels, published in 1554.

the chain gang, he said,

"From all you have told me, my dearest brothers, I conclude that even though you are being punished for your sins, the punishments you are about to undergo will not be very pleasurable to you and you go to them quite begrudgingly and very much against your will. Thus, the cause of your perdition and the fact that you have not received the justice you deserved may possibly stem from the lack of courage one of you demonstrated under torture, or to another's lack of money, or to this other one's lack of friends, or finally to the mistaken verdict of the judge. I can picture all this so vividly in my mind that it is telling me – nay, it is persuading and even compelling me to demonstrate through you the purpose for which heaven has placed me upon this earth, making me follow, as I do, the profession of chivalry. I hereby reaffirm the oath I have sworn of coming to the aid of the downtrodden and those in need. But since I know it is a sign of prudence to do that which may be done in the name of good- rather than ill-will, I should like to ask these guards and this commissary to be so kind as to unshackle you and allow you to go in peace, for there will be no lack of others who can serve the king under better circumstances. It strikes me as cruel to make slaves of those whom God and nature have created free, particularly, sir guards, when these poor souls have done nothing against you. Let each person atone for his own sins, for God in heaven will not fail to castigate the evil and reward the good, for which reason it is not right for honorable men to be the executioners of others, since that is no concern of theirs. I request this calmly and humbly so that if you comply, I shall have some reason to thank you, but should you not do so willingly, this lance and this sword, together with the might of my arm, shall see to it that you do so forcibly."

"What delightful folly!" responded the commissary; "what a fine bit of cleverness to come up with at a time like this! This gentleman wants us to release the king's convicts, as though we were authorized to set them free or he could order us to do so. Sir, may you continue on your way with our blessing and straighten up that chamber pot on your head and stop looking for a cat with three legs."

"You are the cat – and the rat and the scoundrel," said Don Quixote, and converting his words into action, he attacked the commissary with such suddenness that before the latter had a chance to defend himself, he was knocked to the ground severely wounded by the lance, and Don Quixote was fortunate in that this was the officer with the musket. The other guards were bewildered and dumbfounded by the sudden turn of events but soon regained their composure. The ones on horseback drew their swords and those on foot seized their javelins and went as a group to attack Don Quixote, who waited for them quite calmly and would have come off badly had the galley slaves, who saw the opportunity being offered them to gain their freedom, not made the effort to break the chain to which they were linked. The revolt was such that the guards – either because they were busy attacking the galley slaves, who were breaking their bonds, or because they were attacking Don Quixote, who was attacking them – did nothing that proved beneficial to themselves. Sancho for his part lent a hand in freeing Ginés de Pasamonte, who was the first to leap onto the field free and unrestrained. The latter attacked the fallen commissary, taking away his sword and musket, whereupon he brandished the sword at one guard and aimed the musket at another but never fired a shot. Not a single guard remained on the field, for they had all taken to their heels, as much from the fear of Pasamonte's musket as from the shower of stones the newly freed galley slaves hurled at them. Sancho was heartsick at this development, for he could just imagine that those running away would report the incident to the Holy Brotherhood, who at the urging of the insistent bells would come searching for the guilty parties, which is what he told his master while at the same time suggesting that they withdraw from there and go into hiding in the hills that lay close by.

"That is all very well," said Don Quixote, "but I know what must be done at this time." He then called out to all the galley slaves, who were rushing about excitedly after stripping the commissary and leaving him in his undergarments, and they gathered round the knight to see what he had to say, at which point he began to address them thus:

"It is the mark of well-bred persons to show their gratitude for benefits received, for one of the sins most offensive to God is that of ingratitude. I say this, gentlemen, because the benefits your graces have received from me have been made manifestly clear to you, in payment for which – and this is my request – I would ask you to take up the chain I removed from your necks and set out at once for the city of Toboso, where you shall present yourselves to my Lady Dulcinea of Toboso and inform her that her knight, He of the Woeful Countenance, commends himself to her. You shall describe to her point by point all the details of this famous adventure up until the moment I gave you your longed-for freedom; once this is done, you may go wherever you please with my blessing."

Ginés de Pasamonte answered for everyone, saying,

"Though we acknowledge your grace as our lord and liberator, your request is completely and totally out of the question, for we cannot travel on the roads in a group but must split up, each of us going our own separate way in an effort to bury ourselves in the bowels of the earth lest we be apprehended by the Holy Brotherhood, who will no doubt come hunting for us. What you could and rightfully should do is to substitute for this service and tribute to the Lady Dulcinea of Toboso a certain number of Hail Marys and Credos, which we shall gladly recite to satisfy your wishes, for this is something that can be performed day or night, while fleeing or resting, in war or in peace. But to imagine that we shall now return to the fleshpots of Egypt, that is, take up our chain and set out on the road to Toboso, is to believe it is already nighttime when in fact it is not yet ten in the morning. To demand such a thing of us is like asking the elm tree to produce pears."

"Confound it!" said Don Quixote, now enraged, "you son of a whore, Don Ginesillo the Creep, or whatever you call yourself, you shall make the trip all by yourself with your tail between your legs, carrying the whole chain on your back."

Pasamonte, who was not at all long-suffering, had become aware that Don Quixote was not in full possession of his wits because of his outrageous act of setting them free, so when he saw himself treated thus, he winked at his companions, who all spread out evenly and started showering Don Quixote with such a barrage of stones that he did not have enough hands to protect himself with his buckler; and poor Rocinante paid no more attention to the spurs than if he had been made of bronze. Sancho crouched behind his jackass, using him to defend himself from the cloud and shower of stones that rained down upon the two of them. Since Don Quixote was unable to shield himself very effectively, there is no telling how many cobblestones left their marks on his body, arriving with such force that they knocked him to the ground. No sooner did he fall than the student was on top of him, at which point he snatched the basin from his head and banged it three of four times on Don Quixote's back and as many more times on the ground, leaving it a shambles. While some of them removed a jacket he wore over his armor and would have removed his stockings as well had his leg armor not prevented it, others stripped Sancho of his coat, leaving him in only his shirt and pants. Then dividing the remainder of the spoils of battle among themselves, they left, each going his own way, for they were more intent on eluding the Holy Brotherhood, whom they feared, than on encumbering themselves with the chain and putting in an appearance before the Lady Dulcinea of Toboso.

The ass, Rocinante, Sancho, and Don Quixote remained there all alone – the ass crestfallen and pensive, twitching his ears from time to time out of fear that the hail of stones that had sorely vexed his ears had still not ceased; Rocinante prostrate beside his master, having been knocked to the ground by another hail of stones; Sancho in nothing but his shirt and pants and terrified of the Holy Brotherhood; and Don Quixote extremely displeased at seeing himself treated so harshly by the very people he had done such a good turn.

Chapter Twenty-Three

The things that befell the famous Don Quixote in the Sierra Morena, which is one of the most unusual adventures related in this true history

Finding himself so thoroughly belabored, Don Quixote said to his squire,

"I have always heard it said, Sancho, that to do peasants a good turn is like pouring water into the sea. If I had heeded your advice, I would have avoided this grief but it is too late now. I shall be satisfied if I have learned a lesson that can serve me in the future."

"Your grace will have learned a lesson from this," said Sancho, "as surely as I'm a Turk, but, since you admit that you might have avoided this adversity if you had listened to me, may you listen to me now and avoid an even greater one. I wish I could make you understand that knight-errantry is of no use against the Holy Brotherhood, for they don't give two figs for all the knights-errant on earth. You should also be advised that I can hear their arrows whizzing past my ears."

"You are a coward by nature, Sancho," said Don Quixote, "but to prevent you from claiming that I am stubborn and never follow your suggestions, I shall heed your advice just this once and put distance between me and the fury that frightens you so, but only on one condition: that you promise never in this life or the next to tell anyone I withdrew or retreated from this peril out of fear but only to accede to your wishes. If you say anything to the contrary, you will be lying, and from this time to that and that time to this I shall give you the lie and shall swear you are lying and will be lying every time you mention it or even think it. So don't say another word, for the mere thought of withdrawing or retreating from any danger, particularly the present one, which does seem to have a hint of peril about it, makes me determined to remain here and wait not only for the Holy Brotherhood, whose name you speak with such dread, but also for the brothers of the twelve tribes of Israel, the seven Maccabees, Castor and Pollux, and all the brothers and brotherhoods of the world."

"Master," responded Sancho, "to withdraw is not to flee, for it is unwise to remain when danger is greater than hope. A wise man will save himself for tomorrow and will not risk everything today. Your grace should understand that I may be coarse and unlettered but I still manage to conduct myself somewhat sensibly. Therefore, you needn't worry about taking my advice but should mount Rocinante if you are able – and if not, I'll assist you – and then follow me, for my brains tell me we have more need of our feet at this moment than of our hands."

Don Quixote remounted without saying a word, and with Sancho leading the way on his jackass, they entered a portion of the Sierra Morena located only a short distance away. Sancho's intention was for them to cross the entire sierra and eventually to emerge at Viso or Almodóvar del Campo but first they would hide in that rugged terrain for the next several days to avoid being discovered should the Holy Brotherhood come hunting for them. He was prompted to do this by having observed that the provisions he had brought on his jackass had come through the episode with the galley slaves unscathed, a circumstance he regarded as miraculous, considering all the things the galley slaves had found and carried off. [1]

[That night they reached the very heart of the Sierra Morena, where Sancho felt they should spend the night and several more days besides, but at least as many as their supplies would provide for, and so they spent the night between two boulders that were surrounded by a number of cork oaks. But fate, which in the opinion of those who have not been enlightened by the True Faith, guides, arranges, and determines all things, ordained that Ginés de Pasamonte, that famous thief and con man who had escaped from the chain gang thanks to Don Quixote's folly, had the presence of mind to hide in

1 The following passage in italics did not appear in the first edition of 1605. The inserted material deals with the theft of Sancho's jackass by Ginés de Pasamonte. In the first edition it was not until Chapter 25 that mention was made of the theft, which had obviously occurred some chapters earlier. While Juan de la Cuesta was still in the process of preparing the second edition (also 1605), he was apparently given the additional material by Cervantes, which he inserted at this point in Chapter 23. However, Cervantes failed to make all the necessary changes in the subsequent text, for Sancho is described several times as still in possession of the ass. In Chapter 4 of the Second Part, which appeared in 1615, Cervantes explains in detail the theft of the ass, and his various references to it in the sequel, whatever the facts of the case, place the blame for all the confusion squarely upon the shoulders of the printer.

There are certain scholars who believe the omission of this passage, as well as the one explaining the reappearance of the ass in Pt. 1, Ch. 30, was deliberate on the part of Cervantes and was done for comic effect, but I fail to see the humor in all this. Cervantes' forays into humor were never so *recherché*. There are even those commentators who go so far as to assert that the interpolated passages were not composed by Cervantes at all. I categorically reject this assertion because said passages display absolutely the same mind set and literary style found in the rest of *Don Quixote*.

these same hills, being driven here by his dread of the Holy Brotherhood, which he justifiably feared. His luck brought both him and his fear to the same spot to which Don Quixote and Sancho Panza's had brought them, and this just after they had fallen asleep but while there was still sufficient light for him to recognize them. Since the wicked are forever ungrateful, and since necessity provides the excuse to take what does not belong to one, and since a present solution assumes more importance than any consideration of the future, Ginés, who was neither grateful nor well-intentioned, resolved to steal Sancho Panza's jackass, passing up Rocinante, a jewel who would be as hard to pawn as he would be to sell. And so while Sancho Panza slept, Ginés made off with the ass and, before the sun rose, was too far away to be overtaken.

When dawn arrived, it brought happiness to the earth but gloom to Sancho Panza when he found his dapple missing. No sooner did he become aware of his loss than he began the saddest and most mournful sobbing ever heard, and it was such that Don Quixote was awakened by his outcries, which included the following:

"O son of my loins, born in my own house, plaything to my children, joy to my wife, envy of my neighbors, ease of my burdens, and last but not least, supplier of half my livelihood, since half of my provisions come from the twenty-six maravedís [2] *you earn each day!"*

Hearing his sobbing and understanding the cause, Don Quixote consoled Sancho with the best arguments he could adduce and begged him to be patient, promising to give him a certificate of exchange guaranteeing him three asses from the five he had left back home. Allowing himself to be consoled by this, Sancho wiped away his tears, choked back his sobs, and thanked Don Quixote for his thoughtfulness.]

The knight rejoiced in his heart as he entered the sierra, judging it to be the perfect place for the adventures he sought. There came to mind all the marvelous ones that had befallen knights-errant in similar out-of-the-way places and hardships, and while riding along contemplating these things, he was so enchanted and transported by them that he could think of nothing else. Sancho too had no other care, now that they appeared to be traveling in a safe area, than that of satisfying his stomach with what remained of the ecclesiastical spoils. *And so he trudged along behind his master loaded with everything his dapple would have carried,*[3] pulling food from a sack and stuffing it into his stomach. So long as he was traveling in this manner, he would not have given a fig for another adventure, but just then, in raising his eyes, he saw his master had stopped and with the tip of his lance was attempting to lift some sort of bulky object lying on the ground. Sancho hurried to catch up to assist him if necessary and, when he arrived, it was just as Don Quixote was lifting a saddlepad

2 *Maravedí*, a relatively worthless coin, 34 of which were equivalent to one *real*.

3 For my translation of this italicized passage, I am following the 3rd edition of 1608. The first two editions read (in translation): "And so, he rode along behind his master, sitting side-saddle on the donkey."

with a valise attached to it, both half rotten, or completely rotten, for in addition to falling to pieces they were so heavy it was necessary for Sancho to help him lift them. When his master ordered him to see what the valise contained, Sancho did so with great haste, for, though the valise was secured by a chain and padlock, it was so rotten and torn one could make out the contents inside, which consisted of four shirts of fine chambray and various other linen articles that were no less exquisite than they were clean. In a small handkerchief he found a sizeable quantity of gold coins and, as soon as he saw them, he said,

"Praised be heaven in all its fullness for finally providing us an adventure worthy of the name!"

Continuing to rummage, he found a small handsomely bound memorandum book. Don Quixote asked to see it, telling Sancho to keep the money and consider it his. Sancho kissed his hand for the favor and then removed all the linens from the valise and put them into the sack containing the rest of the provisions. After observing all this, Don Quixote said,

"It seems to me, Sancho – and it cannot possibly be otherwise – that some traveler passing through this sierra must have lost his way and was waylaid by some scoundrels who probably murdered him and brought him here and buried him in this most remote spot."

"It can't possibly be that," replied Sancho, "for if they had been thieves, they would never have left this money."

"You are right," said Don Quixote, "and that being the case, I cannot imagine what this is all about. But wait, let us see if there is anything written in this book that can put us on the trail of discovering what we wish to know."

Opening it, the first thing he found there, written in a rough draft though quite legible, was a sonnet, which he read aloud so that Sancho could hear it, and the sonnet said the following:

Know'st thou, O Love, the pangs that I sustain,
   Or, cruel, dost thou view those pangs unmoved?
Or has some hidden cause its influence proved,
   By all this sad variety of pain?

Love is a god: then surely he must know,
   And, knowing, pity wretchedness like mine;
From other hands proceeds the fatal blow–
   Is then the deed, unpitying Phyllis, thine?

Ah, no! a form so exquisitely fair
   A soul so merciless can ne'er disclose.
   From heaven's high will, my fate resistless flows,
And I, submissive, must its vengeance bear.
   Nought but a miracle my life can save,
   And snatch its destined victim from the grave.

"Nothing can be learned from these verses," said Sancho, "unless by knowing which little filly they're referring to we can get to the bottom of the matter."

"And which filly are *you* referring to?" asked Don Quixote.

"I thought your grace mentioned a filly there," replied Sancho.

"I said 'Phyllis,' which is undoubtedly the name of the lady about whom the author of this sonnet is complaining, and you may mark my word for it: either he is a reasonably good poet or I know very little about the art."

"Then," said Sancho, "your grace is versed in poetry too?"

"More than you imagine," answered Don Quixote; "you will see this for yourself when you deliver a letter to my lady Dulcinea of Toboso written in verse from beginning to end. I would have you know, Sancho, that all or nearly all knights-errant in former times were both great troubadours and great musicians, for these two abilities – or gifts, to be more exact – are tools-in-trade of lovers-errant, though, to be sure, the verses of the knights of old do exhibit more spirit than skill."

"Continue reading, your grace." said Sancho, "because you may just come across something that will tell us what we want to know."

Don Quixote turned the page and said,

"Here is something in prose that appears to be a letter."

"What sort of letter?" asked Sancho.

"By the way it begins, I think it is simply a love letter."

"Then I wish your grace would read it aloud," said Sancho, "for I like anything dealing with love."

"Gladly," said Don Quixote, and reading it aloud as Sancho had requested, he saw it said the following:

Your false promise and my certain misfortune are sending me to a place from where news of my death will reach your ears before any words of complaint on my part. You cast me aside, O ingrate, for one whose possessions are greater than mine but who himself is not as worthy. If only virtue were highly esteemed, I should envy no one else's possessions, nor should I bemoan my own misfortune. What your beauty has raised up, your actions have torn down, and because of your beauty I believed you were an angel but your actions show you to be a mere woman. I bid you peace, you who have brought me unrest, and may heaven see to it that your infidelities are never revealed to your husband lest you remain repentant for what you have done or I take revenge for something I do not seek.

After reading the letter, Don Quixote said,

"One learns even less from this than from the poem, except that whoever wrote it was a rejected lover."

In leafing through virtually the entire book, he found other verses and letters, some that were legible and some that were not; yet what they all contained were complaints, laments, suspicions, things tasteful and distasteful, favors and rejections, some joyous, others filled with remorse. While Don Quixote went through the book, Sancho went through the valise, leaving no part of it or the saddlepad unsearched, unscrutinized, or uninvestigated, nor was there any seam he failed to undo or any tuft of wool he did not comb through lest he overlook something for lack of diligence and care, such was the greediness awakened in him by the discovery of the coins, which totaled more than a hundred. But despite the fact that he discovered nothing more than what he had already found, he felt this made up for all the ascents in the blanket, the vomiting of the balsam, the beatings with the staves, the punches from the muleteer, the loss of his saddlebags, the theft of his coat, and all the hunger, thirst, and exhaustion he had undergone in the service of his good master, for which reason he considered himself more than handsomely remunerated by the recent favor of being allowed to keep the coins he had found.

The Knight of the Woeful Countenance was still extremely curious to know who the owner of the valise was, having surmised from the sonnet and letter, the gold coins, and the fine shirts that he must be a lover of some consequence whom scorn and ill-treatment by his lady had led down this desperate path. But as there was no one in this harsh, inhospitable place who could tell him anything, his immediate concern was to continue traveling, leaving the choice of routes completely up to Rocinante, who invariably went where the footing was the easiest, for Don Quixote was firmly convinced there must be some rare adventure hidden in these wilds. While riding along to the accompaniment of these thoughts, he saw at the top of a hill that loomed before him a man leaping from crag to crag and from bush to bush with uncommon agility. He appeared to Don Quixote to be half naked and to have a thick black beard with long matted hair. His legs and feet were bare and he was clad in short pants apparently made of brown velvet but so tattered that his skin showed through in a number of places; and his head was bare. Though he had passed by quickly, the Knight of the Woeful Countenance saw and noted all these details but, try as he might, he could not keep up with him because Rocinante's feebleness would not allow him to negotiate such rough terrain, in addition to which he was phlegmatic and too short of stride. Since Don Quixote at once imagined this man to be the owner of the saddlepad and valise, he made up his mind to travel about these hills in search of him even if it should take a year to find him. And so he told Sancho to head round the hill in one direction while he would go in the opposite one. In this way they might possibly come across the man who had so quickly disappeared from sight.

"I can't do that," said Sancho, "for the moment I leave your grace's side, I will be immediately beset by fear, which will overcome me with a thousand sorts of terrors and imaginings. You should thus be forewarned that from this moment forth I'll not budge one inch from your grace's side."

"So be it," said He of the Woeful Countenance; "I am flattered that you should wish to avail yourself of my courage, which will not fail you even if your soul is frightened out of your body; so follow along behind me slowly, or any way you can, and turn your eyes into searchlights. We shall circle round this small ridge and perhaps meet up with that man, who without a doubt is none other than the owner of everything we have found."

To which Sancho responded,

"It would be better not to look for him, for if we find him and he turns out to be the owner of the money, it is obvious I'll have to return it to him. It would suit me better if we didn't go to all this trouble so I could own it with a clear conscience, at least until its real owner appeared by some other less curious and laborious means; and who knows: maybe it will occur after I've already spent the money, in which case the king will free me from all responsibility."

"That is where you are mistaken," said Don Quixote, "for, inasmuch as we have come to suspect who the owner is and virtually have him within our grasp, we are obliged to seek him out and return it to him. Should we not do so, our conviction that he is the one we seek makes us just as guilty as if he were, and so, Sancho my friend, do not let our search for him grieve you but think of the apprehension you will be lifting from me if I find him."

Accordingly, Don Quixote spurred Rocinante, while Sancho followed behind on foot toting the provisions himself, thanks to Ginesillo de Pasamonte. After traveling through a large portion of the mountain, they came across a dead mule lying in a stream complete with saddle and reins but half devoured by dogs and crows. All this further confirmed their suspicion that the one who had fled was the owner of the mule and saddlepad. While they paused to observe this, they heard a whistle similar to that of a shepherd tending his flock, and suddenly to their left appeared a rather large number of goats followed at the top of the hill by the goatherd who was tending them, a man obviously advanced in years. Don Quixote shouted to him to come down and join them. The man shouted back, asking them what had brought them to that place that was seldom, if ever, frequented by anything but goats, wolves, and other wild animals that roamed there. Sancho told him to come down and they would give him a full account of everything. As soon as the man did so, he said to Don Quixote,

"I'll wager that your graces have just found the dead packmule in that hollow, which upon my word of honor has been in that spot for six months. But tell me, have you come across its owner in these parts?"

"We have not come across anyone," said Don Quixote, "just a saddlebag and a small valise, which we found not far from here."

"I found that valise too," replied the goatherd, "but I never dared pick it up or even get close to it because of my fear of having bad luck or of being accused of stealing it. The Devil is sly and places obstacles in man's path that cause him to stumble and fall without having the slightest idea why."

"Those are my sentiments exactly," said Sancho. "I also found it but refused to go within a stone's throw of it. I left it right where I found it because I didn't want to do anything that might sound the alarm."

"I wonder, my good sir," said Don Quixote, "if you could inform me of the owner of those items."

"All I can say," replied the goatherd, "is that about six months ago there arrived at a shepherd's hut some three leagues from here a young man with a pleasing, graceful figure riding the very mule that's lying there dead with the same saddlebag and valise you say you found but did not disturb. He asked us which part of these hills was the most rugged and remote, and we told him it was where we are now, for, in truth, if one were to continue for another half league, he might possibly never find his way out. I'm amazed that you were able to come this far, for there's no road or path leading to this place. But as I was saying, when the young man heard our reply, he turned and rode towards the spot where we had pointed, leaving all of us spellbound by his good looks and astonished by both his request and the speed with which he disappeared into the hills. From that moment on, we did not see him again until several days later when he went up to one of our shepherds on the highway and without saying a word to him started to punch and kick him. He then went over to the ass that was loaded with our provisions and made off with all the bread and cheese it was carrying. Once having done that, he again disappeared into the hills with unusual haste. On learning of this, several of us goatherds spent nearly two days searching for him in the densest part of the sierra and finally found him in the hollow of a huge cork tree, where he had taken shelter. He climbed out with great tranquility, his clothes now torn and his face so disfigured and sunburned that we hardly recognized him, and though his clothes were in tatters, we were able to make out that he was the one we were looking for because of the way he had been described to us. He courteously greeted us and in a few carefully chosen words told us not to be shocked at seeing him in that condition, inasmuch as it was necessary if he was to fulfill a certain penance imposed upon him because of his many sins. We begged him to tell us who he was but were never able to elicit that information. We also asked him to tell us where we might find him whenever he needed food, which he must have in order to survive; that we would bring it to him with all our affection and concern but, if that was not agreeable to him, we begged him at least to approach the shepherds and ask them for it rather than take it by force. He thanked us for our kind offer, begged our forgiveness for his past assaults, and agreed in the future to ask for food in God's name without harming a solitary soul. In answer to the question of where he lived, he said he had no other abode than that afforded him by the place in which he happened to find himself when night overtook him. He concluded his speech with such heartfelt sobs that those of us who had listened to him would have had to be made of stone not to shed a few tears of our own, particularly when we compared what he looked like the first time we saw him and what he looked like now. As I have said, he was a most refined and elegant young man and in his courteous, pleasing speech showed himself to be a highborn, well-bred person. Despite the fact that all of us there were simple country folk, his refinement was so great it impressed itself even upon us. But just as he reached the best part of his story, he suddenly stopped speaking and began staring at the ground, during which time we all stood there in amazed silence waiting to see what might be the outcome of his reverie, for it was pitiful to see him thus. We could tell that some fit of madness had overcome him as he stood there staring at the ground without moving an eyelash, his lips taut, and his eyebrows raised. He soon gave us to understand that our suspicions were correct, for he furiously sprang from the ground where he had hurled himself and attacked the first person he came to with such rage and defiance that, had we not pulled him off, he would have killed the man with his punches and bites, and during all that time he kept shouting, 'You double-crossing Fernando, you shall pay for the wrong you have done me! These hands will rip out that heart of yours in which every form of evil resides, above all, fraud and deceit!' He shouted other things as well, all aimed at vilifying someone named Fernando, whom he charged with treachery and deceit. We managed to separate them with no little effort but he, without saying another word, fled from us and disappeared among these thickets and undergrowth, making it impossible for us to follow him. From all that, we concluded that his madness comes and goes and that someone named Fernando must have done him an evil turn so grievous it had driven him to that extreme. All this has since been confirmed by the numerous times he has come onto the highway, sometimes to beg the shepherds to give him something to eat, at other times to take it from them by force, for when he is suffering an attack of madness, though the shepherds may freely offer him food, he'll not permit it but will snatch it from them in a violent manner. On the other hand, when he has his wits about him, he courteously and politely asks for food in the name of God, while expressing his gratitude and shedding not a few tears. The truth is, gentlemen," continued the goatherd, "that yesterday I and four lads, two of them hired hands and the other two friends of mine, decided to hunt for him until we found him and then, either forcibly or willingly, to take him to the village of Almodóvar, which is eight leagues from here, where he can be cured if his ailment admits of cure. Also, as soon as he returns to his senses, we'll find out who he is and whether he has any kin who can be notified of his affliction. This, gentlemen, is all I can say in regard to what I've been asked. Your graces may rest assured that the owner of the articles you found is the same person you saw running about as agile as he was threadbare," for Don Quixote had already described how he had seen the man go bounding among the boulders.

Don Quixote was dumbfounded by what the goatherd had told him and was more curious than ever to find out who the young man was who was mad, so he decided to do what he had already contemplated doing, namely, to scour the hills for him, leaving no cave or niche uninvestigated until he located him. But his luck turned out better than he had ever imagined or hoped because at that very moment the young man they sought appeared in a gap between the hills and was walking towards them talking to himself. What he was saying could not be understood even when he drew near, much less when he was some distance away. His clothing was just as it had been described but Don Quixote noticed, as he drew nearer, that the tattered jacket he wore bore the scent of amber, whereby he concluded that a person wearing such apparel could not be of humble origin.

When the young man arrived, he greeted them in a hoarse, monotone voice but most courteously, and Don Quixote returned the greeting with no less graciousness. Dismounting from Rocinante, the knight went over with genteel bearing and grace to embrace him, holding him securely in his arms for some time as though he had known him for ages. The other man, whom we shall call the Ragged Knight of the Sorry Countenance (since Don Quixote's is the Woeful one) allowed himself to be embraced and then drew back from him a pace, placing his hands on Don Quixote's shoulders, where he stood eyeing him as though he were trying to decide if he knew him, for he was perhaps no less astonished at seeing the face, figure, and armor of Don Quixote than the latter was at seeing him. Finally, the first to speak following their embrace was the Ragged One, who said what will be related directly.

Chapter Twenty-four

The continuation of the adventure of the Sierra Morena

Our history relates that Don Quixote listened with great interest to the ragged, ill-starred Knight of the Sierra, who continued his story, saying,

"Whoever you are, sir, I am most grateful to your grace for the courtesy you have shown me and wish I might repay you for your thoughtfulness and kind reception but my situation is such that I can show my gratitude only by my desire to do so."

"My desire," replied Don Quixote, "has simply been to serve your grace, and it is such that I had resolved not to abandon these hills until I found you and learned from you whether there was any sort of remedy for your attendant affliction, as demonstrated by your strange behavior, and should it prove necessary, I would ferret you out with all possible diligence. Even if your misfortune were such that it had closed the door on every type of consolation, I was fully prepared to share in your tears and lamentations, for in misfortune it is still comforting to find someone who will commiserate with your suffering. If my good intentions do indeed deserve to be reciprocated by some sort of generosity, I beg you by that bounteous nature you so obviously possess, at the same time entreating you in the name of whatever you most cherish or have ever cherished in this life, to tell me who you are and what circumstances have brought you here to live and die in isolation like a dumb brute, for you are living in a state very far removed from what your dress and appearance show your true nature to be. I hereby vow, sir," added Don Quixote, "by the profession of knight-errantry and the order of chivalry of which I am an unworthy member that if you comply with this request, I shall serve you with all the fervor at my command, thereby either putting an end to your misfortune if there is a solution, or helping you to lament it, as I have said."

When the Knight of the Wood heard Him of the Woeful Countenance speak in such terms, he could only stare at him, and stare at him he did from head to foot. Once he had thoroughly scrutinized him, he said,

"If your grace has some food you could give me, for the love of God may you let me have it. After I have eaten, I shall comply with all your requests out of gratitude for the kind intentions you have expressed here."

At this point, Sancho from his pouch and the goatherd from his sack provided the Ragged One with the wherewithal to satisfy his hunger. He ate the food they gave him like a person transported, and so hastily that he gulped down one mouthful after another, swallowing everything whole rather than chewing it, and while he was eating, neither he nor those in observance said a word. Once he had finished eating, he motioned to them to follow him and led them to a pleasant, verdant meadow situated a short distance beyond a group of boulders, where he stretched out on the grass and the others did the same, and during all this time no one said a word until the Ragged One settled himself in his place and said,

"Gentlemen, if you wish me to describe in only a few words the immensity of my misfortunes, you must promise not to interrupt the thread of my sad story with questions or anything of the sort, for at the point at which you do so, everything that is still to be related shall remain unstated."

These words of the Ragged One reminded Don Quixote of the story his squire had related in which the exact number of goats that had crossed the river could not be determined and the story had remained suspended in midair. But to return to our story: the Ragged One went on to say,

"I make this stipulation because I should like to make my way through the story of my misfortunes quickly, for to recall them serves only to increase my suffering. The fewer questions your graces ask, the sooner I shall finish, though I shall omit nothing of importance in order to comply with your wishes."

Don Quixote promised in the name of everyone present not to interrupt, and with this assurance the goatherd began speaking:

"My name is Cardenio, I come from one of the best cities in Andalusia and, though my ancestry is distinguished and my parents wealthy, my misfortunes have been so great that my parents must have grieved and lamented these misfortunes without being able to alleviate them with their wealth, for the riches of this world are of no avail against adversities from heaven. In that same land lived a creature in whom love had vested all the glory I might ever desire, such was the beauty of Luscinda, a maiden who was noble, wealthy, and more fortunate than I but less faithful than she should have been, considering my honorable intentions. I loved, desired, and adored this Luscinda from my earliest and tenderest years with the innocence and sincerity that her youthful age permitted. Our parents were aware of our feelings but were untroubled by them, for they saw that when we grew older it could only result in our eventual marriage, a fact virtually assured by the equality of our families and wealth. But as our age increased, so did our love, and Luscinda's father reasoned that for the sake of propriety he found himself obliged to deny me entry to their home, thereby closely imitating the parents of Thisbe, whose story is so widely celebrated by the poets. But this denial only added flame to flame and desire to desire, for though it silenced our tongues, it was never able to silence our pens, which, because of their greater freedom, were able to reveal what each of us had in our heart, for the presence of the beloved quite often upsets the most determined intentions and silences the most daring tongue. And heavens! what a bevy of letters I wrote her and what caressing yet chaste answers I received. Oh, the numberless songs I composed and the untold verses of love in which my soul declared and laid bare its feelings, painted its ardent desires, reveled in its memories, and indulged its fancies! Finally, finding myself exhausted and my soul consumed by my desire to see her, I resolved to act and do once and for all what seemed to me most expedient for the attainment of my desired and well-deserved prize – I asked her father for her hand in marriage. He expressed his gratitude for my desire to honor him and said he would be pleased to reciprocate by granting me that jewel of his but, considering the fact that my father was still alive, it was up to *him* to make such a request, for should it not meet with his approval and pleasure, Luscinda was not a woman to be given or taken away by stealth. I thanked him for his kindness, considering him correct in everything he said, for I believed my father would grant his consent once I spoke to him. With this in mind I went to tell my father what I wished to do but when I entered his room, I found him with an open letter in his hand. Before I could say a word, he handed it to me and said, 'By this letter, Cardenio, you will see how eager Duke Ricardo is to favor you.' This Duke Ricardo, gentlemen, as you probably know, is a Spanish grandee whose lands are situated in the best regions of Andalusia. I took the letter and read it and it was so solicitous that even I felt it would be remiss of my father to fail to comply with what was being requested, namely, that I be dispatched at once, for the duke wished me to be, not the servant, but the companion of his eldest son and he would see to it that I was placed in a position commensurate with the esteem in which he held me. I continued to read the letter and, after finishing it, was speechless, particularly when I heard my father say, 'Two days from now, Cardenio, you shall depart in compliance with the duke's wishes, and you may give thanks to God for opening these doors that will enable you to attain everything I am sure you deserve,' and he added other fatherly advice as well.

"As the time for my departure approached, I spoke to Luscinda one evening telling her everything that had occurred. I also discussed it with her father, pleading with him to delay a few days before giving her away in marriage until I learned what Duke Ricardo had in mind for me. He promised to do so and she confirmed it with a thousand vows and swoons. I subsequently arrived at the duke's home and was quite well received, but it was from that moment that envy reared its ugly head, as some of the older servants thought the duke's show of affection for me might work to their own disadvantage. The one most pleased by my arrival was the duke's second son Fernando, a gallant young man, generous, mannerly, and in love, who in a short time was so intent upon making me his friend that he had tongues wagging. Though his older brother was fond of me and treated me with kindness, he did not do so as effusively as Don Fernando. Needless to say, it is impossible to maintain secrets between friends, and since the privileged relationship I enjoyed with Don Fernando ceased, having turned into one of friendship, he revealed to me all his concerns, in particular a love affair that was causing him no little anxiety. He was in love with a girl who was a vassal of his father's but whose parents were quite wealthy. This farm girl was so beautiful, demure, discreet, and pure that everyone who knew her was unable to decide in which of these qualities she most excelled. The beautiful girl and her outstanding virtues had such an effect upon Don Fernando's passion that he decided – in order to achieve his goal, which was that of laying siege to and overcoming her maidenhood – to promise to be her husband, because to have done otherwise would have been to attempt the impossible. Bound by our friendship, I attempted to dissuade and turn him from such a proposal by employing the best reasons I knew and the most eloquent examples I could adduce, but seeing my lack of success, I decided to apprize his father Duke Ricardo of the matter. Don Fernando, however, being the sly, clever soul that he was, suspected that my duty as a loyal servant to my master the duke might compel me to reveal things that would be prejudicial to his honor, and so, in order to divert and deceive me, he said he could think of no better way to forget that beauty who held him so enthralled than to go away for several months, and he proposed that the two of us spend the time away from home at my father's house, doing so under the pretext of going there to examine and purchase some splendid horses in my hometown, which breeds the best ones in the world. Even if his proposal had not been so noble, I would have approved of it as one of the best imaginable, seeing the wonderful opportunity it would afford me to see my Luscinda again. Motivated by this thought and by my own desires, I approved of his idea and proposal, encouraged his plan, and suggested that he undertake it as soon as possible, for absence was having its usual effect upon me despite my firm resolve.

"When he came to tell me this, as I later learned, he had already possessed the girl in the role of husband and was seeking a way to make the fact known without risk to himself, fearing how his father the duke might react when he learned of his foolhardiness. And since love in young people is by and large not love but lust, which has pleasure as its goal, it vanishes the moment the goal is attained and what was thought to be love will recede, since it cannot go beyond the limits set by nature, limits that are not imposed, however, upon true love. But to return to my story: no sooner had Don Fernando seduced the farm girl than his desires were satisfied and his ardor cooled and, whereas in the beginning he had pretended to want to go away to relieve his passion, he now actually wanted to do so to avoid keeping his promise. The duke granted his permission and ordered me to accompany him. We reached my hometown, and my father accorded Don Fernando the kind reception due a person of his rank. I went at once to see Luscinda and my desires were revived, though they had never been dead or even dormant. But to my sorrow I gave an account of them to Don Fernando, feeling that his close friendship with me prevented my keeping secrets from him. I extolled Luscinda's beauty, wit, and intelligence in such a way that my praises awakened in him the desire to see a maiden endowed with such qualities. I complied with his wishes, to my hasty regret, by letting him see her one night by the light of a candle at a window where she and I were in the habit of conversing with one another. He observed her in her nightgown and her beauty was such that it made him forget all those he had seen up till that moment. Speech failed him, he fell into a swoon, as though he were in a trance, and was completely transported by love, as will be seen as this account of my unhappiness unfolds. And as if his desire were not sufficiently inflamed, which he hid from me but revealed to heaven when he was alone, fate saw to it that one day he found a letter from her begging me to ask her father for her hand – a letter so discreet, pure, and endearing that, after reading it, he said Luscinda encompassed within herself all the qualities of beauty and understanding apportioned separately to all other women on earth. As a matter of fact I must now confess that even though I understood how justified Don Fernando was in praising Luscinda, it grieved me to hear such praise from his lips and I began to fear and distrust him, for hardly a moment went by without his attempting to discuss her, and he would broach the subject himself even if it had to be dragged into the conversation, a practice that aroused a certain twinge of jealousy in me but not because I feared any fickleness on the part of Luscinda. Nevertheless, my fortune made me fearful at the very moment that Luscinda was reassuring me. Don Fernando inevitably managed to read the notes I sent to Luscinda as well as those I received from her and he did so under the pretext of admiring our wit and cleverness. When Luscinda, who was quite fond of books of chivalry, happened to ask me for one she might read, I gave her *Amadís of Gaul*. . ."

No sooner did Don Quixote hear him mention this book of chivalry than he said,

"If, sir, your grace had simply mentioned at the outset of your story that her ladyship was fond of books of chivalry, no other extravagant praise would have been necessary to make me appreciate the sublimity of her understanding, for I should not hold her in the same high esteem as your grace if she lacked the taste for such delightful reading. So as far as I am concerned, it is unnecessary to expend further words describing her beauty, worth, and intelligence, for by simply learning of her tastes, I declare her to be the most beautiful, intelligent woman on the face of the earth. I wish your grace had sent along with *Amadís of Gaul* a copy of the fine *Don Rugel of Greece*, for I am sure the lady Luscinda would love Daraida and Garaya, together with the wit of the shepherd Darinel and those admirable bucolic verses sung and performed by him with complete charm, wit, and simplicity. But there may yet come a time when that shortcoming can be rectified, and its correction will take no longer than it takes your grace to accompany me to my village, for there I can show you more than three hundred books that are the sustenance of my soul and the joy of my life, though it is my understanding that I have none left, thanks to the malevolence of some wicked, envious enchanters. I hope you will forgive me for having broken our promise not to interrupt your story but when I heard you speak of chivalry and knights-errant, it was no more in my power to refrain from speaking than it is for the sun's rays to cease providing warmth or the moon's moisture. Therefore, I apologize and beg your grace to proceed with your story, which is what matters most at this moment."

While Don Quixote was saying this, Cardenio's head slumped forward and he showed signs of distraction. Despite the fact that Don Quixote twice asked him to continue his story, he neither looked up nor said a word. Finally, after a long pause he raised his head and said,

"I cannot rid myself of the belief, nor can I be persuaded of anything to the contrary, but anyone who can't see or understand that that scoundrel Master Elisabat lay with Queen Madásima is a blockhead!"

"That is a lie, upon my oath!" shouted Don Quixote in his usual manner. "That is the height of perversity, or should I say rascality! Queen Madásima was a most illustrious lady and it is unthinkable that so lofty a princess would go to bed with a saw-bones. Anyone who believes that is a liar and a scoundrel and I shall show him the error of his ways, mounted or on foot, armed or unarmed, by day or by night, or in whatever manner he prefers."

Cardenio, who had just suffered another attack of his madness, stood there staring at him and was in no mood to proceed with his story, nor would Don Quixote have heard it, so terribly upset was he by Cardenio's comments about Madásima. It was a strange situation, for here was Don Quixote coming to her defense as though she were really and truly his lady, such was the hold his god-forsaken books exerted upon him. But to return to our story: Cardenio, now being mad and having heard himself referred to as a liar and a scoundrel among other such abusive terms, failed to find the joke amusing, and so, picking up a stone that lay within reach, he unleashed such a blow to Don Quixote's chest that the latter was knocked over backwards. When Sancho Panza saw his master treated thus, he lunged at the maniac with his bare fists but the Ragged One, who was ready for him, knocked him down with just one punch and then jumped on top of him, stomping his ribs to his heart's content. And the goatherd, who attempted to defend him, met with the same fate. Having thus subdued and throttled everyone, Cardenio walked away most nonchalantly and disappeared into the hills. Sancho, who was furious at finding himself the innocent victim of this pummeling, sprang to his feet and rushed at the goatherd to take out his wrath on *him*, telling him he was to blame for not warning them of the man's sudden bouts of insanity, for had they known that, they would have been prepared to defend themselves. The goatherd replied that he had already warned them and it was not his fault if Sancho had not listened. Sancho Panza then said something to the goatherd, who said something back to him, and all this bickering resulted in each one's grabbing the other's beard and unleashing a barrage of punches at him, and had Don Quixote not calmed them down, they would have beaten each other to a pulp. Sancho said, while holding onto the goatherd,

"Sir Knight of the Woeful Countenance, since this one is a commoner like myself and not a full-fledged knight, I may with your grace's leave legitimately exact satisfaction from him for the wrong he has done me and fight him hand to hand like an honorable man."

"True," said Don Quixote, "but I know for a fact that *he* is not to blame for what has just happened."

With this observation Don Quixote managed to pacify them and once again asked the goatherd whether it would be possible to locate Cardenio, because he still had a consuming desire to know how the story ended. The goatherd repeated what he had told him the first time: that he did not know where he made his abode but that if Don Quixote were to do much traveling in those parts, he would be certain to come across him and he would be either sane or mad.

Chapter Twenty-Five

The strange things that befell the valiant knight of La Mancha in the Sierra Morena, and his imitation of the penance of Beltenebros

Don Quixote took leave of the goatherd and once again mounted Rocinante, ordering Sancho to mount his jackass and follow him, which Sancho did very begrudgingly. As they gradually made their way into the most rugged part of the mountain, Sancho was dying to talk to his master but waited for him to begin the conversation so as not to disobey his order. However, being unable to tolerate such an extended silence, he said,

"Master Don Quixote, I would like your grace's blessing and permission to leave this place and return home to my wife and children with whom I can at least talk and converse as much as I like. For your grace to ask me to accompany you through all these desolate places day in and day out without saying a word, even when I feel the urge, is like burying me alive. If only animals could talk as they once could in the days of Aesop, it wouldn't be quite so bad, for I could chat with my jackass whenever I felt like it and in that way could endure my sad lot. But it's an arduous task and a virtual impossibility to spend one's life riding about in quest of adventures and then to find nothing but kicks, punches, stonings, and blanket-tossings, on top of which one has to sew up his lips and dare not say what he has in his heart, as though he were mute."

"I understand, Sancho," said Don Quixote, "you are dying to have me remove the prohibition I placed on your tongue. Well, consider it removed and say whatever you will but with the stipulation that the removal shall last no longer than the time we spend traveling about these hills."

"So be it," replied Sancho, "therefore, let me speak fast, for God knows what will happen next. The first thing I'd like to know, now that I'm granted this reprieve, is why your grace made such a fuss over that Queen Magimasa or whatever her name was? Who cares whether that abbot was her lover or not? If your grace had let that pass, not being her judge, I'm sure the maniac would have gone on with his story and we would've been spared the stoning, kicks, and more than half a dozen bangs on the head."

"My word, Sancho," responded Don Quixote, "if you knew, as I do, what an honorable and illustrious lady Queen Madásima was, I feel certain you would agree that I demonstrated a great deal of restraint in not smashing the mouth from which such blasphemies spewed, for it *is* nothing but blasphemy to say or even to think that a queen is the mistress of a saw-bones. The fact of the matter is that Master Elisabat, whom the madman mentioned, was a most prudent man who gave sound advice and served the queen as her tutor and physician, but to imagine that she was his lover is an outrage deserving of the severest punishment. To convince you that Cardenio did not know what he was saying, remember that when he said it he was already out of his mind."

"That is what I'm talking about," said Sancho; "there was no reason to pay attention to the words of a madman, and if good fortune hadn't smiled upon your grace by making the stone hit your chest instead of your head, we'd be in a fine fix, and all because of coming to the defense of that lady of mine, confound her! Moreover, I'll bet Cardenio would've gotten off scot-free for being mad!"

"Regardless of whether the person is sane or insane," said Don Quixote, "a knight-errant is obliged to come to the defense of a woman's honor, whoever she may be, but particularly when she is a queen of such high degree and rank as Queen Madásima, for whom I have a particular fondness because of her noble qualities. In addition to being extremely beautiful, she was also most prudent and long-suffering in the face of her adversities, of which she had her share. The companionship and counsel of Master Elisabat were a great source of aid and comfort to her in enduring her ordeals with prudence and patience, because of which the ignorant, malicious masses have gotten the impression that she was his mistress, but they are lying, I tell you, and anyone who says or thinks such a thing will be lying even if he repeats it two hundred times."

"That's not what I'm saying or even thinking," replied Sancho; "that is their business, so let them make the best of it. Whether they were lovers or not, they will have answered for it to heaven. Why, I'm as innocent as a newborn babe and have no idea what is going on, nor do I care what other people do with their lives. 'If someone makes a purchase and lies about the price, his purse will tell the story.' Moreover, I came into this world with nothing and still have nothing, so I'm neither winning nor losing; but suppose they had been lovers, what business is that of mine? 'Many expect to find birds where there aren't even nests,' and it would be easier to chain the wind than to keep people from gossiping. Why, some people even speak ill of God."

"Heaven have mercy on my soul!" said Don Quixote; "how you do go on with your imbecilities! How did we go from what we were discussing to your endless homilies? If you know what is good for you, Sancho, you will shut your mouth and occupy yourself from now on with caring for your jackass and stop butting into what is none of your business. Try to understand with all five of your senses that everything I do, have done, or ever shall do, is quite reasonable and conforms to the rules of chivalry, which I know better than any other knight who ever professed them."

"Master," said Sancho, "is there another fine rule of chivalry that says we should be wandering about lost in these hills, following no road or path and looking for a madman who, if we find him, may get the urge to finish what he started – not his story but your grace's head and my ribs – and will finish them off once and for all?"

"I am warning you for the last time, Sancho, to be quiet," said Don Quixote. "I would have you know it is not my desire to locate the madman that brings me to these parts so much as it is to undergo an ordeal whereby I shall win eternal fame and renown throughout the civilized world, and it will be such that I shall set the standard by which knights-errant will strive to become perfect and famous."

"Is this ordeal very dangerous?" asked Sancho Panza.

"No," said He of the Woeful Countenance, "though the toss of the die may be unfavorable as well as favorable. But everything will depend upon your diligence."

"My diligence?" said Sancho.

"Yes," replied Don Quixote, "for if you return quickly from where I intend to send you, my penance will end quickly and my glory will just as quickly begin. But since it is unfair to keep you in suspense any longer waiting to see where my words are leading, I would have you know, Sancho, that the famous Amadís of Gaul was one of the most perfect knights-errant who ever lived. I should not have said 'one of:' he was unique, the first, the only one, foremost among all those living during his lifetime. A pox upon Don Belianís and all those who claim to be the equal of Amadís in a single regard, for they are very much deceived, as I can prove. I might likewise point out that when a painter wishes to gain fame in his profession, he strives to imitate the original works of those painters he knows are unique, and this same practice holds for the most important offices and activities that serve to adorn governments. What one must and will do who would gain a reputation for being prudent and long-suffering is to emulate Ulysses, of whose character and works Homer paints us a vivid picture of prudence and suffering. Virgil too showed us in the person of Aeneas the virtue of a dutiful son and the sagacity of a brave and skillful captain, not painting or describing them as they were but as they should have been, so that their virtues would remain examples for future ages. In this same way Amadís was the north star, the morning star, the sun for those valiant, enamored knights, and the person all of us should imitate who do battle under the banner of love and chivalry. And this being the case, Sancho my friend, I find that the knight-errant who most nearly imitates Amadís will come closest to achieving perfection in knight-errantry. One of the ways in which this knight most clearly demonstrated his prudence, worth, bravery, endurance, steadfastness, and love was to withdraw to the Barren Rock to do penance, having been spurned by the Lady Oriana and having changed his name to that of Beltenebros, [1] a name most certainly significant and proper for the life he had chosen of his own free will. Thus it will be easier for me to imitate him in this than in cleaving giants asunder, decapitating serpents, slaying dragons, routing armies, destroying fleets, and breaking spells. And since this site is so well suited to such a purpose, there is no reason to let an opportunity slip through my fingers that is virtually being offered me on a platter."

"In a word," replied Sancho, "what is it your grace intends to do in this god-forsaken place?"

"Have I not already said," replied Don Quixote, "that I intend to imitate Amadís by assuming the guise of one who is desperate, out of his mind, and berserk, while simultaneously imitating the valiant Roland when he discovered in a fountain signs that Angélica the Fair had committed an infamy with Medoro, the grief from which drove him mad? As a consequence he uprooted trees, muddied the waters of the limpid springs, slew shepherds, destroyed livestock, set fire to huts, demolished houses, carried off mares, and did a hundred thousand other unheard-of things worthy of being recorded and never forgotten. But since I have no intention of imitating in every single detail Roland, or Orlando, or Rotolando – he was known by all three of these names – in all the insane things he did, said, and thought, I shall pare them down as far as possible to those I deem most essential. It may turn out that I shall simply be content to imitate Amadís, whose acts of madness consisted, not in doing harm to anyone, but in sobbing and grieving, and yet he gained as much fame as the next knight."

"It seems to me," said Sancho, "that knights who did such things had been provoked and had reason to perform those foolish deeds and penances but what reason does your grace have for going mad? What lady has scorned you, or what indications have you seen that might lead you to believe the lady Dulcinea of Toboso has committed some indiscretion with Moor or Christian?"

"That is the whole point," said Don Quixote, "and therein lies the subtlety of my enterprise, for a knight-errant who goes mad for a reason deserves no praise or thanks. The essential thing is to go mad for no reason at all, to make my lady understand that if I can do such a thing when dry, what can't I do when wet? Besides, I shall have opportunities galore during the long separation I have taken from the lady Dulcinea of Toboso, who shall always be mine. You heard that shepherd Ambrosio say a while back that one who is absent from his beloved is beset by all sorts of ills and fears. Therefore, Sancho, you are wasting your time seeking to dissuade me from performing such a rare, felicitous, and original penance. Mad I am and mad I shall remain until you return with the answer to the letter I intend to intrust to you for my lady Dulcinea. If her answer is what my faithfulness deserves, my madness and penance will come to an end, but if it is the opposite, then I shall truly go mad and, being so, shall feel nothing. Thus, however she responds, I shall be free of the conflict and travail in which you leave me – either delighting in the glad tidings you bring me because of being sane, or being insensible to the ill tidings you bring me by virtue of being mad. But tell me, Sancho, have you taken good care of Mambrino's helmet, which I saw you pick up off the ground when that ungrateful soul tried to destroy it but was unable to do so, thereby demonstrating how finely tempered it is?"

---

1 ***Bel*** (archaic form of ***bello***) 'handsome' + ***tenebros*** (shortened form of **tenebroso**) 'somber'; 'darksome'.

To this, Sancho responded,

"In God's name, Sir Knight of the Woeful Countenance, I can't patiently suffer and abide some of the things your grace says, wherefore I am led to believe that everything you tell me about chivalry – the winning of kingdoms and empires, the awarding of islands, and the bestowing of other gifts and boons – is just so much bluster, falsehood, and humbug. If someone heard your grace call a barber's basin Mambrino's helmet and then not discover the error for a number of days, what might he think except that anyone who says and claims such a thing must be out of his mind? I have the basin in my sack, dents and all, which I'm taking home to have mended so I can shave in it if God will be merciful enough to allow me to rejoin my wife and children some day."

"Look, Sancho," said Don Quixote, "by the One you swore to just then I swear to you that you have the least understanding of any squire who ever lived. Is it possible that in all the time you have spent with me you have not noticed that everything having to do with knight-errantry appears to be fantastical, foolish, or absurd, and that everything is the reverse of what it should be? And not because this is how things really are but because there is a horde of enchanters forever in our midst changing and altering all our enterprises and transforming them as they see fit, according to whether they wish to favor or ruin us, so what looks like a barber's basin to you I fancy Mambrino's helmet, and it may take on the appearance of something entirely different to a third party. It was rare foresight on the part of the sage who favors me to make what is really and truly Mambrino's helmet look like a basin to everyone else. Because it is so valuable, the whole world would be trying to wrest it from me, but now, when they see it is only a barber's basin, they make no effort to take it, as was clearly demonstrated by the one who tried to destroy it and left it on the ground instead of carrying it off, for upon my word, had he recognized it for what it was, he would never have left it there. Take good care of it, my friend, as I have no need of it at the present time. Instead, I must remove all my armor and become as naked as the day I was born, that is, if I am led to base my penance more upon Roland than upon Amadís."

While engaged in this conversation, they arrived at the base of a tall hill that stood alone, as though it had been carved out from all the others that surrounded it. Flowing at its base was a gentle brook and spreading out in all directions was a meadow that was so verdant and luxuriant that it gladdened the eyes of everyone who beheld it; and the site included a number of forest trees and various flowering plants that made it an inviting spot. This is the site the Knight of the Woeful Countenance chose for carrying out his penance. In fact, as soon as it came into view, he began to cry out in a loud voice, as though he were truly mad,

"This is the site, O ye heavens, that I designate and choose for lamenting the ill-fortune in which you yourselves have engulfed me; this is the site where the tears from my eyes shall augment the waters of this tiny stream, and my profound sighs shall continuously rustle the leaves of these untamed trees as a testimony and sign of the grief suffered by my overwrought heart. O ye rustic deities who make your abode in this uninhabited place, whoever you may be, hear the complaints of this ill-starred lover, whom a long absence and imagined jealousies have brought to this desolate place to voice his laments and complain of the hardened heart of that ungrateful beauty who is the epitome of human loveliness. O ye nymphs and dryads whose custom is to inhabit the most inaccessible parts of these hills, may the fleet-footed, lecherous satyrs who love you, though in vain, never disturb your sweet repose, and may you help me lament my misfortune or at least not grow weary of listening to it. O Dulcinea of Toboso, day of my night, glory of my afflictions, pilot of my wanderings, star of my good fortune, may Heaven bless thee in whatever thou wouldst request. Mayest thou consider the place and condition to which thine absence has led me; and mayest thou repay me with the graciousness that my fidelity deserves. O solitary trees, who from this day forth shall keep me company in this solitude, indicate by gently moving your boughs that my presence is not displeasing to you. And thou, my squire, pleasant companion in all my prosperity and adversity, fix in thy memory what thou shalt see me do here, that thou mayest relate and recite it to the one who is completely responsible for all this."

In saying this, he dismounted from Rocinante and in an instant removed the bridle and saddle, giving him a slap on the flanks and saying,

"Thou, O steed, art granted thy freedom by him who has lost his, as accomplished in thy deeds as unfortunate in thy lot! Roam wheresoever thou wilt, for on thy forehead it is written that Astolfo's Hippogriff never equaled thee in speed, nor did the renowned Frontino, who cost Bradamante so dearly."

When he observed this, Sancho said,

"I hope that scoundrel is happy who has spared us the trouble of unpacking the ass! Your grace may mark my word that if the dapple were here, I'd be sure to caress him and say something in his praise but I wouldn't let anyone unpack him, as there'd be no reason to do so. And those legal interrogatories to determine whether one is enamored or forlorn would not apply to him, since his owner was neither one nor the other – and I *was* his owner so long as God was willing. If indeed, Sir Knight of the Woeful Countenance, my departure and your madness are genuine, it will be well for me to saddle Rocinante again to make up for the lack of the ass, as this will save time on my journey there and back. If I make the journey on foot, there's no telling when I'll get back, for to put it bluntly, I'm not very good at walking."

"As far as I am concerned, Sancho," said Don Quixote, "you may do whatever you like, for I think your idea is a good one but I repeat that I would have you stay here for three days before departing, during which time you can witness what I say and do on my lady's behalf, which you may then report to her."

"Well," asked Sancho, "what remains to be seen that I haven't seen already?"

"You certainly are well informed!" said Don Quixote. "Look, I must still rend my garments, scatter my armor about, and butt my head against these rocks, together with other things of like nature that will astound you."

"For the love of God, your grace," said Sancho, "be careful where you do your butting, for you may come to a rock with such a sharp edge that the first butt will bring this whole penance business to a close. But since you are of the opinion that these butts are necessary and this affair can't be carried off without them, and since all this is mere pretense and make-believe anyway, I'm of the opinion that you should be content with butting against water or something soft like cotton. You may leave the rest to me and I'll tell my lady you were butting your head against the edge of a rock that was harder than a diamond."

"I am grateful for your noble intentions, Sancho my friend, but I would have you know that nothing I do is done in jest but in the utmost seriousness; to do otherwise would be to contravene the rules of chivalry, which prohibit our telling a single lie lest we be punished for backsliding. Besides, to do one thing in lieu of another is the same as telling a lie, for which reason my butts must be real, firm, and binding, having nothing about them of sophistry or fantasy. Also, you need to leave me some bandages for treating my wounds, for fate has seen to it that we shall have to make do without the balsam we lost."

"The worst part," said Sancho, "was losing the ass, for we lost the bandages and everything he was carrying. But I beg your grace not to keep thinking of that accursed potion, for just hearing it referred to upsets my soul, not to mention my stomach. I would also ask you to consider as already expired the three days during which I am to witness all the insane things you intend to do, since I already consider them witnessed and duly judged; moreover, I'll describe wonderful things to my lady. Now, however, I kindly beg you to write the letter and send me on my way, for I have a great desire to return to deliver you from this purgatory in which you find yourself."

"'Purgatory' did you say, Sancho?" replied Don Quixote; "it would be more accurate to call it hell or something even worse, if there is such a thing;" to which Sancho replied,

"I've heard it said in Latin that 'for those in hell there's no retention.'"

"I have no idea what you mean by 'retention'," said Don Quixote.

"By 'retention,'" said Sancho, "I mean that whoever is in hell can never escape from it,[2] but your grace's case will be an exception or these legs won't do their job, especially now that I'll be wearing spurs to urge on Rocinante. So just set me down in Toboso in the presence of my lady Dulcinea and I'll tell her such stories of the follies and lunacies – for they're one and the same – that you have performed and continue to perform that she'll become softer than a glove even if I find her more unyielding than a cork tree. With her sweet and honeyed reply I'll magically return through the air to deliver your grace from this purgatory, which has the appearance of hell but isn't, since there is hope of escaping from here, unlike hell, from which, as I've said, there is no hope of escape, not that I believe your grace will dispute this."

"You are quite correct," said the Knight of the Woeful Countenance, "but how shall we go about writing the letter?"

"And the bill of exchange for the asses?" added Sancho.

"It will all be included," said Don Quixote, "but since there is no paper, it will be a good idea to write it on tree leaves or small wax tablets following the custom of the ancients, but these will be as difficult to come by as paper. Ah, I just remembered what will be good or even better to write it on: Cardenio's memorandum book. Later you can see to it that it is copied onto paper in a legible hand in the first

2 Sancho, of course, thought he was saying 'redemption'.

village you come to that has a schoolmaster, or lacking that, any sacristan can copy it for you. But don't have it copied by a notary, for they use a legal script that not even Satan himself could decipher."

"Well, what shall we do about the signature?" asked Sancho.

"Amadís' letters were never signed," replied Don Quixote.

"That may be so," said Sancho, "but the bill of exchange must absolutely be signed; and yet, if it's copied, they'll say the signature is false and I won't get my colts."

"The bill of exchange will be in the same memorandum book and will be signed, and when my niece sees it, she will have no qualms about complying with it. As for the love letter, you are to have it signed: 'Thine until death, the Knight of the Woeful Countenance.' Then it will not matter if it is in someone else's handwriting, for to the best of my recollection Dulcinea cannot read or write and has never seen my handwriting on any of my letters, for my love and hers have always been platonic, extending no further than a modest glance, and even *that* so infrequently that I can safely say that in the dozen years during which I have loved her more than I love these eyes the earth will one day devour I have not seen her half a dozen times. And it may be that on those few occasions she has not noticed my observing her, such is the caution and seclusion with which her father Lorenzo Corchuelo and her mother Aldonza Nogales have reared her."

"Well, well!" said Sancho, "so the daughter of Lorenzo Corchuelo is the lady Dulcinea of Toboso, otherwise known as Aldonza Lorenzo?"

"She is the one," said Don Quixote, "and she it is who deserves to be queen of the entire universe."

"I know her very well," replied Sancho, "and can testify that she can toss the bar as far as the brawniest lad in the whole town, and by Jove, she's a sensible girl, tall and straight, with hair on her chest, and capable of helping out of a jam any knight alive or still unborn who might choose her for his lady. And, damn, what strength she has and what a pair of lungs! I recall that one day she climbed to the top of the bell tower in the village to shout at some lads walking through one of her father's fields that lay fallow and though they were more than half a league away, they heard her as easily as if they had been at the foot of the tower. But the best thing about her is that she's not the least bit prudish; in fact, she's quite the coquette and goes about making fun of everyone and kidding and joking about everything. Therefore, Sir Knight of the Woeful Countenance, I can state without fear of contradiction that not only may your grace go crazy on her behalf but you have a perfect right to hang yourself in despair. Anyone who learned of it would not say you didn't do a perfectly reasonable thing, even if the Devil should end up with your soul. But now I'd like to be on my way so I can see her again, for I haven't seen her in quite some time. She's probably changed because working in the fields exposed to the sun and wind is very hard on a woman's looks. Master Don Quixote, I must confess that until now I've labored under a terrible misconception because I really and truly believed the lady Dulcinea was some princess with whom your grace was in love, or of such rank as to be worthy of the lavish presents you've sent her, like that of the Biscayan or the galley slaves, together with all the others there must have been from the many victories you had already won before I became your squire. But when one considers the matter, what good does it do the lady Aldonza Lorenzo – I mean the lady Dulcinea of Toboso – to make all those persons your grace has conquered and sent to her kneel at her feet, for at the moment of their arrival she may be combing flax or threshing wheat, which will embarrass them and make her laugh at their gifts in derision?"

"I have already told you on a number of earlier occasions, Sancho, that you talk too much and despite the fact that you are a simpleton, your pointed wit often breaks because it is too sharp. But so that you may see how dense you are, compared to me, I would have you listen to a short tale.

"There was once a widow who was young, beautiful, independent, rich, and above all else, a free spirit. She fell in love with a lay brother who was plump and rather large. When his superior learned of it, he spoke to the good widow one day in a brotherly fashion, saying, 'I am astounded, my lady, and not without reason, that a woman of your ladyship's nobility, beauty, and wealth should fall in love with a man as humble, lowly, and dumb as So-and-So, when in this house there are so many masters, graduates, and divinity students from among whom you might have chosen, the way one selects pears, saying, "They're all nice but I'll take this one."' She answered with an air of unconcern, saying, 'My lord, you are greatly mistaken and old-fashioned in your thinking if you believe I made a bad choice in picking this lad, because for what I want from him he knows as much philosophy, perhaps more, than Aristotle himself.' And so, Sancho, for the need that I wish Dulcinea to fulfill, she is every bit as worthy as the most exalted princess on earth, for not all poets who sing the praises of their ladies under names they arbitrarily assign them actually have such mistresses. Do you think that each and every Amaryllis, Phyllis, Sylvia, Diana, Galatea, or Fílida, with which all the books, ballads, barber shops, and theaters are filled, really was a flesh-and-blood lady and a mistress of the person who sings or sang her praises? Certainly not. They only pretend they are real in order to have someone to extol in their verses so people will think they are in love or will consider them manly enough to deserve such love. Therefore, it is sufficient if I imagine and believe the fair Aldonza Lorenzo is beautiful and virtuous. Her ancestry is of little importance because no one is going to investigate her background for the purpose of awarding her an honorary degree, and in my eyes she is the most highborn princess in the world. You should know, Sancho, if you do not already, that there are two principal qualities that cause men to fall in love, namely, great beauty and a good reputation. These two things come together in Dulcinea, for no one can equal her in beauty and few can approach her in reputation. To sum up, I imagine everything to be exactly as I say it is, neither more nor less, and I picture her in my imagination the way I desire her to be, not only in beauty but in nobility. She is greater than Helen and is unsurpassed by Lucretia or any other famous woman of antiquity, whether Greek, Roman, or barbarian. Let each say of her what he will, for if I am reproached by the ignorant, I shall not be chastised by the wise."

"I must admit," replied Sancho, "that your grace is right in every regard and I am a jackass – but why did I mention jackass with my own tongue, since one should never mention rope in the house of one who's been hanged. Just let me have the letter and as soon as I can take my leave, I'll be on my way."

Don Quixote took out the memorandum book and, going off to himself, set about composing the letter in a leisurely manner. Once he had finished, he called to Sancho, saying he would like to read it to him so he could commit it to memory in the event that he should lose it along the way, for with his bad luck anything was possible; to which Sancho replied,

"Please, your grace, write it two or three times in the book and I'll take very good care of it, but to think that I can memorize it is sheer folly. My memory is so bad I sometimes forget my own name. Nevertheless, if you'll read it, I'll be happy to listen to it, and it will no doubt be right on the mark."

"Pay attention then," said Don Quixote, "for this is what it says:

LETTER FROM DON QUIXOTE TO DULCINEA OF TOBOSO

Most high and exalted lady:

He who is suffering pangs of absence, having been sorely wounded to the depths of his being, wishes thee, dearest Dulcinea of Toboso, the good health that he unfortunately lacks. If thy beauty should find me contemptible, if thy great worth favor me not, or if thou art disdainful of my afflictions, I, though inured to suffering, shall be unable to bear my present sorrow, which in addition to being severe is most persevering. My faithful squire Sancho will give thee a full account, O fairest ingrate and beloved foil, of the plight in which I find myself by reason of serving thee. Shouldst thou be pleased to succor me, I am thine; if not, do whatever gives thee the greatest pleasure, for when my life draws to a close, I shall have satisfied thy cruelty and my desires.

Thine until death,
THE KNIGHT OF THE WOEFUL COUNTENANCE

"I swear upon my father's soul," said Sancho after hearing the letter, "that is the most high-falutin thing I've ever heard! And the way your grace expresses to her every darned thing you can think of! And how well it all goes with the signature 'The Knight of the Woeful Countenance.' I can truthfully say that your grace is the Devil incarnate and there's nothing you don't know."

"Everything is necessary," replied Don Quixote, "in my chosen profession."

"Well then," said Sancho, "I hope your grace will kindly draw up the certificate for the three colts on the other side and sign it very clearly so they'll recognize it when they see it."

"Gladly," said Don Quixote. As soon as he finished, he read what he had written and it said the following:

Dear Niece, Upon receipt of this certificate, you are hereby requested to give Sancho Panza, my squire, three of the five young asses I left at home in your care. The three said colts, which have been paid for by others of equal value, I hereby order to be duly delivered upon the presentation of this certificate and his receipt of payment. Drawn up in the heart of the Sierra Morena on the twenty-second day of August of the present year.

"That's really good," said Sancho; "now if your grace will sign it."

"There is no need to sign it," said Don Quixote; "I shall simply add a flourish, which is the same as a signature and will suffice for three asses or even three hundred."

"Your grace's word is good enough for me," replied Sancho, "and with your leave, I'll go saddle Rocinante while you prepare to give me your blessing, and though I intend to depart at once without waiting to see all the absurd things you'll be doing, I'll say I saw you do so many it will leave nothing to be desired."

"Sancho, if this is how it must be, I would at least have you see me strip and perform a dozen or so absurd acts, which I can complete in less than half an hour. After you have seen me perform these with your own eyes, you may safely swear to any others you might wish to add, but I can assure you you will not describe half as many as I intend to perform."

"For the love of God, master, may I not see your grace stripped, for it will cause me considerable grief and I won't be able to keep from weeping. My head is so drained from the sobbing I did last night over my dapple that I'm in no mood to get involved in any more tears. However, if you insist that I witness a few foolish acts, pray perform them dressed and keep them short, choosing those that are most appropriate, especially when none of this is necessary for my sake. As I've already said, it would allow me to return from my trip sooner, which will be with the answer you desire and deserve. But if it is not, the lady Dulcinea had better watch out! If she doesn't give me a reasonable answer, I hereby solemnly swear that I'll extract the proper answer from her if I have to beat and kick it out of her. How can a knight-errant as famous as your grace be allowed to go mad for no reason whatsoever over a . . . but she'd better not make me say it, by God, because I'll say what I darned well please and will shout it from the rooftops regardless of the consequences. I'm pretty good at that sort of thing! I can assure your grace that she doesn't know me very well or she would treat me with a little more respect."

"My word, Sancho!" said Don Quixote, "you would appear to be as crazy as I am."

"I may not be as crazy but I'm a lot madder. Setting that aside, though, what will your grace do for food while I'm away? Will you charge out onto the roads like Cardenio and take it from the shepherds?"

"You need not concern yourself with that," said Don Quixote, "for even if I had food, I would eat nothing more than the herbs and fruits provided me by this meadow and these trees, for the efficacy of my undertaking lies in abstaining from eating and in performing other similar austerities, and the rest is in the hands of God."

"But does your grace know what it is I'm afraid of? That I won't be able to find my way back to this spot where we are because it's so well hidden."

"Then take a close look at everything you see here," said Don Quixote, "and I shall try not to stray from this spot. I shall even take the trouble to climb the tallest peak here so I can spot you when you return, but the surest thing you can do to avoid getting lost is to cut some branches from the broom growing all about, which you can drop at intervals until you are out of the forest. They can serve you as landmarks to help you locate me when you return, in imitation of the thread of Perseus [3] in the labyrinth."

"That's what I'll do," said Sancho Panza, and after cutting a few, he asked his master for his blessing and then took his leave but not without considerable tears on the part of both men. He mounted Rocinante, whom Don Quixote praised highly and asked Sancho to care for as he would his own person. And so, setting out in the direction of the open plain while scattering branches of broom at intervals as his master had advised, Sancho rode off despite Don Quixote's pleas that he watch him perform at least a couple of follies. He had not ridden a hundred paces, however, when he returned and said,

"I must admit, master, that your grace was correct. For me to swear with a clear conscience that I've seen you commit absurdities, I should witness at least one – though your decision to remain here was itself a rather sizeable one."

"Did I not say so?" said Don Quixote. "Wait right here, Sancho, for I can perform them faster than you can recite the Credo," and removing his breeches, he stood there clad in nothing but his shirt. Then without further ado, he leapt into the air, clicking his heels together a couple of times before landing, and then turned two somersaults, thereby revealing certain things which caused Sancho to wheel Rocinante about so as not to have to look at them again. With this, the squire was perfectly happy and satisfied that he could swear his master was mad. And so, we shall allow him to go on his way while we eagerly await his return, which will not be long in coming.

Chapter Twenty-Six

The continuation of the acts of devotion that Don Quixote performed as a lover in the Sierra Morena

Returning to the description of what He of the Woeful Countenance did once he found himself alone, our history relates that Don Quixote, dressed from the waist up and bare from the waist down, concluded his leaps and somersaults and, seeing that Sancho had ridden off without wanting to witness any further absurdities, climbed to the top of a high crag, where he again set about considering what he had considered on so many similar occasions but without ever resolving the issue. He pondered which would be better and more appropriate: to imitate Roland in the outrageous follies he had committed or Amadís in his melancholic ones. And so, addressing himself, he said,

'What is so surprising about Roland's much-vaunted goodness and valor as a knight when, after all, he was enchanted and could not be slain unless he was pierced in the sole of his foot with a large

3 Don Quixote should have said 'Theseus.'

pin, but then he always wore shoes with iron soles seven layers thick. Still, his tricks were of no avail against Bernardo del Carpio, who, being wise to them, strangled him in his arms at Roncesvalles. But setting aside the question of his valor, let us consider the loss of his wits, which he certainly suffered as a result of the evidence he found in the fountain, together with the shepherd's news that Angélica had spent more than a couple of siestas lying with Medoro, a curly-haired little Moor and page to Agramante. Therefore, if he believed his lady had deceived him, he did not react in an excessive manner by going mad, but how can I imitate him in his follies if I do not share the same circumstances? I dare say my Dulcinea of Toboso has never in all the days of her life seen a Moor as he actually looks in his native dress and she is as chaste today as the mother who begat her. I would be doing her a grave injustice if I imagined otherwise and went mad from Roland's type of madness. On the other hand, I see that Amadís of Gaul, without losing his mind or performing any insane acts, achieved as much fame as a lover as anyone. What he did according to his history when he saw himself spurned by his Lady Oriana, who had ordered him not to appear in her presence until it was her pleasure, was simply to withdraw to the Barren Rock in the company of a hermit, where he had his fill of weeping and commending himself to God until heaven came to his rescue at the moment of his greatest sorrow and need. If this is true, which it is, why should I go to the trouble of removing all my clothing or of inflicting suffering upon these trees that have done me no harm? Nor have I any reason to defile the clear waters of these brooks, which are ready to quench my thirst whenever I feel the need. Therefore, long live the memory of Amadís! May he be imitated in every conceivable way by Don Quixote of La Mancha, of whom they will say what they said of the former: that if he did not achieve any great successes, at least he died in the attempt. And though I do not find myself disdained or cast aside by Dulcinea of Toboso, my absence from her, as I have said, is punishment enough. And so, shoulders to the wheel! You deeds of Amadís, refresh yourselves in my memory and show me how to emulate your example. I know, of course, that his principal activity was to pray and commend himself to God, but what can I use for the rosary I need?'

But just then, he thought of a way to provide himself with one. Tearing off a long strip from the bottom of his shirt and tying eleven knots in it, one of which he made larger than the rest, he proceeded to pray a million Hail Marys. His greatest distress arose from his failure to find a hermit to hear his confession and console him. He thus passed the time strolling through the meadow, drawing in the sand and carving on the trees a great number of verses, some praising Dulcinea but all dealing with his remorse. When he was later located, the verses that were both complete and still legible comprised no more than the following:

1

Ye lofty trees, with spreading arms,
  The pride and shelter of the plain;
Ye humbler shrubs and flowery charms,
  Which here in springing glory reign!

If my complaints may pity move,
Hear the sad story of my love!
While with me here you pass your hours,
Should you grow faded with my cares,
I'll bribe you with refreshing showers;
You shall be watered with my tears.
Distant, though present in idea
I mourn my absent Dulcinea
Of Toboso.

2

Love's truest slave, despairing, chose
This lonely wild, this desert plain,
This silent witness of the woes
Which he, though guiltless, must sustain.
Unknowing why these pains he bears,
He groans, he raves, and he despairs.
With lingering fires love racks my soul:
In vain I grieve, in vain lament;
Like tortured fiends I weep, I howl,
And burn, yet never can repent.
Distant, though present in idea
I mourn my absent Dulcinea
Of Toboso.

3

While I through honor's thorny ways
In search of distant glory rove,
Malignant fate my toil repays
With endless woes and hopeless love.
Thus I on barren rocks despair,
And curse my stars, yet bless my fair.
Love, armed with snakes, has left his dart,
And now does like a fairy rave,
And scourge and sting my every part,
And into madness lash his slave.
Distant, though present in idea

I mourn my absent Dulcinea
Of Toboso.

His adding 'Of Toboso' to Dulcinea's name provided no little amusement for those who discovered the above verses because they imagined that Don Quixote must have thought that, had he failed to add 'Of Toboso' each time he mentioned Dulcinea, the verses might not be understood, and such was the case as he later confessed. He composed a number of others but, as we have said, it was impossible to find more than these three stanzas that were both complete and legible. In effect, he spent his time in the following manner: writing verses, sighing, and calling upon the fauns and satyrs of those woods, together with the nymphs of the streams and sorrowful, moist Echo to listen to him and to answer and console him. He also sought out certain herbs with which to sustain himself while Sancho was away, for should Sancho be gone for three weeks instead of three days, the Knight of the Woeful Countenance would be so emaciated that not even his own mother would recognize him. But this will be a good place to leave him occupied with his sighs and verses while we relate what happened to Sancho Panza on his mission.

It transpired that when Sancho came to the king's highway, he set out in search of Toboso, arriving the following day at the inn in which he had suffered the disgraceful blanket-tossing. No sooner did he catch sight of it than he had visions of himself flying through the air, for which reason he refused to go inside, though he had arrived at an hour when he could and should have done so, it being the hour for dining and he having a hearty appetite for something hot, since there had been a number of days recently when cold-cuts were the standard fare. This need forced him to approach the inn, still doubting, however, whether or not he should enter. At that moment, two men emerged from the inn and immediately recognized him, one of whom said to the other,

"Tell me, sir licentiate, isn't the man on that horse Sancho Panza, the one our adventurer's housekeeper said had gone off to serve as her master's squire?"

"So it is," said the licentiate, "and that is Don Quixote's very own horse." They were able to recognize him as easily as they did because they were the priest and the barber from his village who had carried out the inspection of the books and passed sentence on them. Once they had recognized Sancho Panza and Rocinante, they approached him in their desire for news of Don Quixote. The priest addressed him by name, saying,

"Sancho Panza my friend, where is your master?"

Sancho Panza immediately recognized them but, being determined to conceal his master's whereabouts and how he was faring, responded that his master was in a certain place occupied with a certain activity that was most important to him, which, however, he was not at liberty to divulge by all that was holy.

"Come, now, Sancho Panza," replied the barber, "unless you tell us where he is, we may possibly suspect, as indeed we do, that you have robbed and killed him, since you are riding his horse; in fact, either you produce the nag's owner or you shall have us to answer to!"

"There's no need to use threats with me, for I don't go about robbing and killing people. Let each person's life be snuffed out by fate or by God, who made him. My master is in the most rugged part of these hills performing a penance very much to his liking."

Then at full gallop and without stopping he described what Don Quixote was doing and the adventures that had befallen him, adding that he, Sancho, was carrying a letter to the lady Dulcinea of Toboso, who was Lorenzo Corchuelo's daughter, whom Don Quixote was in love with up to his elbows. The two were astonished at what Sancho Panza told them, for despite their knowing the nature of Don Quixote's madness, they were astounded every single time it came to their attention. When they asked Sancho Panza to show them the letter he was carrying to the lady Dulcinea of Toboso, he told them it was written in a memorandum book and it was his master's wish to have it copied onto paper in the first village he came to. The priest asked him to show it to them, explaining that he would copy it himself in a very legible hand. Sancho Panza reached into his shirt to retrieve the little book but could not find it, nor could he have done so were he still searching for it, for Don Quixote still had it, having forgotten to give it to Sancho and Sancho having forgotten to ask him for it. When Sancho discovered it missing, a look of death crept over his face and, after another quick search of his entire body showed the total impossibility of finding it, he immediately grabbed his beard with both hands, yanked out half his whiskers, and then rapidly and without ceasing, punched his face and nose half a dozen times, leaving them completely covered with blood. When the priest and the barber saw this, they asked him what had come over him to make him treat himself so cruelly.

"The only thing that has come over me," said Sancho, "is that in transferring them from one hand to the other I've lost three colts in a single instant, each of which was worth a fortune."

"How is that?" asked the barber.

"I've lost the memorandum book containing the letter for Dulcinea as well as the certificate signed by my master in which he directed his niece to give me three of the four or five colts he has at home," and at this point, he told them of the loss of the dapple.

The priest consoled him, telling him that as soon as they found his master, they would have him renew the order and draw up another bill of exchange on paper, this being the usual practice, for those written in memorandum books were never accepted or acknowledged. Sancho was consoled by this and said that if such was the case, he was not overly concerned about the loss of Dulcinea's letter, and since he virtually knew it by heart, it could be copied whenever and wherever they chose.

"Then tell us what it said, Sancho," said the barber, "and we'll copy it later."

Sancho Panza paused and scratched his head in an effort to recall the letter, standing first on one foot and then the other. He stood gazing at the sky for some time and then at the ground. Finally, after chewing off half of one of his fingernails while keeping them both in suspense, he said after a lengthy pause,

"For God's sake, sir licentiate, the Devil can have what little I remember of the letter, though it did begin with 'Lofty and exhausted lady.'"

"He wouldn't have said 'exhausted,'" responded the barber; "he probably said 'exalted lady.'"

"That's it," said Sancho, "and then, if memory serves me, it continued, if I'm not mistaken, 'He who is aggrieved, short on sleep, and wounded kisses your grace's hand, ungrateful and contemptuous beauty' . . . and I don't remember what he then said about health or sickness, which he was sending her. He went on rambling like this till he came to the end, where he said, 'Thine until death, The

Knight of the Woeful Countenance.'"

Both men took considerable delight in observing Sancho Panza's marvelous memory, which they praised highly, asking him to repeat the letter one or two more times so they too could memorize it and have it transcribed at the proper time. Sancho repeated it three more times and just as many times came up with three thousand more bits of nonsense. In addition to this he told them several things about his master but said not one word about the blanket-tossing which he himself had undergone in this inn that he was refusing to enter. He also told them that as soon as his master received a favorable reply from his lady Dulcinea of Toboso, he would set out to become an emperor or at least a monarch, for this is what the two of them had agreed upon. And this would be quite easy to achieve, considering the valor of Don Quixote's person and the prowess of his arm. Likewise, once he became one or the other, Don Quixote would present him with a wife, for by that time he would probably be a widower, and this wife would be one of the handmaidens of the empress who was heiress to a wealthy and sizeable kingdom on dry land without islands of any kind, shape, or form, for he had lost all interest in them. Sancho related all this while nonchalantly wiping his nose from time to time and it all made so little sense that the two of them once again marveled at the intensity of Don Quixote's madness, which had carried off this poor soul's wits as well. They chose not to trouble themselves to point out his misconception, thinking it preferable to leave his belief untouched, inasmuch as it did no harm to his conscience and would provide them with more enjoyment if he carried on with his nonsense. They advised him to ask God to look after his master's health, for with the passing of time it might just be possible and feasible for him to become an emperor, or at least an archbishop or some similar dignitary; to which Sancho responded,

"Gentlemen, if the wheel of fortune should decree that my master were to take it into his head not to become an emperor but an archbishop, I would like to know here what gifts archbishops-errant are accustomed to bestowing upon their squires."

"They usually give them," replied the priest, "some office that may or may not involve the care of souls, or some sacristy whose fixed income is quite good and whose altar fees usually bring in an equal amount."

"It's probably necessary," said Sancho, "for the squire to be unmarried and know how to assist at mass at the very least, and if that's the case, woe is me, because I'm married and don't know the first letter of the ABCs! What will become of me if my master takes it into his head to become an archbishop instead of an emperor, which is the usual practice of knights-errant?"

"Don't worry, Sancho my friend," said the barber, "we shall beg and advise your master, and even make an issue of conscience of it, to become an emperor rather than an archbishop, which will be much easier for him, since he is obviously more spirited than bookish."

"That's how he has always struck me," said Sancho, "though I can attest to the fact that he's talented at everything. What I intend to do on my part is to ask Our Lord to place him wherever he can best serve and can bestow the most boons upon me."

"Spoken like a wise man," said the priest, "and you will thereby be doing your Christian duty. But what we must now do is to determine how to extricate your master from that useless penance you say he is engaged in. In order to consider how to proceed and to dine at the same time, now that it is suppertime, we would do well to enter this inn."

Sancho told them to go in but he would wait outside and would explain later why he was refusing to enter and why it was in his best interest not to do so, but he did beg them to bring him something hot to eat, as well as some barley for Rocinante. Leaving him there, they entered the inn, with the barber returning a short while later with some food. After the two of them had thoroughly discussed the means of carrying out their plan, the priest hit upon a scheme that would appeal to Don Quixote and would at the same time achieve their goal. Telling the barber what he had come up with, he explained that he proposed to dress himself in the outfit of a damsel-errant, while the barber could impersonate a squire to the best of his ability. They would then go find Don Quixote, and the priest would pretend to be a needy damsel-in-distress who would ask Don Quixote for a boon he could hardly fail to grant as a gallant knight-errant. The boon the priest intended to request was that Don Quixote accompany the damsel to any place she might take him in order to right a wrong an evil knight-errant had done her and she would likewise plead with him not to make her remove her veil or to ask her anything about her affairs until he had settled the score with that wicked knight. He had no doubt that Don Quixote would comply with all such requests made under these terms and in this way they could pry him loose from there and take him home to determine whether there was any sort of remedy for his strange madness.

Chapter Twenty-Seven

How the priest and the barber carried out their plan, together with other matters worth relating in this great history

Not only did the barber approve of the priest's scheme but he considered it so good they set it in motion. They asked the innkeeper's wife to lend them a skirt and some veils, for which they deposited the priest's new cassock as security. The barber fashioned a long beard from a rust-colored oxtail in which the innkeeper kept his comb stuck. When his wife asked why they needed those articles, the priest briefly described Don Quixote's madness and the role their disguise was to play in their scheme to get him to leave the mountains where he happened to be at that time. The innkeeper and his wife realized at once that the madman was none other than the guest with the balsam whose squire had been tossed in the blanket, at which point they told the priest everything that had happened to them, including those things that Sancho had been careful *not* to include. In short, the hostess dressed the priest so fetchingly that it left nothing to be desired. She had him put on a dark-velvet cloth skirt with pleats as wide as one's hand and a bodice of green velvet trimmed with a border of white satin, both of which must have been created ages ago in the days of King Wamba, but the priest refused to wear any adornments on his head, though he did put on a small quilted linen cap he had brought along as a nightcap. He bound his forehead with a black taffeta band and from another devised a mask that covered his face and beard quite effectively. After donning a hat large enough to have served him as a parasol, he tossed his cloak across his shoulders and mounted his mule in side-saddle fashion. Mounting his own mule was the barber, whose beard hung down to his waist and was, as we have said, reddish-white and was made from the tail of a clay-colored ox.

They bade everyone farewell, including the good-hearted Maritornes who, though a sinner, promised to pray a rosary that God might grant them success in that most arduous and Christian enterprise they were undertaking. But scarcely had they left the inn than it occurred to the priest that by wearing such attire he was acting improperly because it was indecent for a priest to dress in such clothing, even if a great deal *did* depend upon it. He explained this to the barber and asked him to exchange outfits with him, since it would be more appropriate for the barber to take the role of the damsel-in-distress, while he would assume that of her squire, thereby preserving his dignity somewhat better. But should the barber be unwilling to do so, he himself was determined to proceed no further in that enterprise even if it meant the Devil's carrying off Don Quixote. Just then, Sancho arrived and, seeing them dressed in those outfits, was unable to hold back his laughter. As it turned out, the barber agreed to all the priest's demands and after making the necessary alterations in their plan, the priest explained the things he was to do and say to Don Quixote to urge and convince him to come with him and abandon that site he had chosen for his useless penance. The barber protested that there was no need to give him instructions, for he would do everything just so, but he preferred not to don the rest of his outfit until they were near the spot where Don Quixote was. Accordingly, he folded up his clothes, the priest adjusted his beard, and they proceeded on their way, being led by Sancho, who rode along relating to them everything that had happened The next day they came to the site where Sancho had scattered the broken branches to aid him in finding the place where he had left Don Quixote. As soon as he recognized it, he informed them that this was where they could enter, advising them to put on their costumes if that was to play a role in liberating Don Quixote, for they had told him earlier that their traveling and dressing in that manner was of the utmost importance for persuading his master to forsake that evil life he had chosen and they warned him not to tell his master who they were or to admit that he knew them. If Don Quixote were to ask, as he was certain to do, whether he had given the letter to Dulcinea, he was to say that he had but, because of her inability to read and write, she had simply told him her answer, saying she was ordering him under penalty of falling from grace to come to her at once, as it was of the utmost importance. By means of this and what they themselves intended to concoct, they felt certain they could persuade him to adopt a better way of life by becoming an emperor or a monarch rather than an archbishop, for which reason Sancho had no need to worry. Sancho listened to all this and fixed it firmly in his memory, heartily thanking them for their efforts to urge his master to become an emperor and not an archbishop, for it was his understanding that emperors were in a better position to bestow boons upon their squires than were archbishops-errant. He also suggested that it would be better for him to go in alone to look for Don Quixote and give him his lady's reply, which should be sufficient to make him forsake that place without their having to go to so much trouble. Since everything Sancho Panza suggested sounded reasonable, they decided to wait there until he returned with news of having located his master.

Sancho made his way into the sierra through a mountain pass, leaving both men in a pleasant ravine watered by a gently flowing stream and refreshingly shaded by the cliffs and the few trees that were there. The day on which they arrived was one of those days in August when the heat was most intense, and it was three in the afternoon, all of which made the site most pleasant and invited them to linger there while Sancho was gone, which they proceeded to do. While the two of them were taking their repose in the shade, they heard the sound of singing that was both melodious and pleasant even though it lacked any sort of musical accompaniment. They found it not a little disconcerting, since this seemed an unlikely place to find a person with such a beautiful voice, particularly when they realized that what he was singing was not the verses of rustic herdsmen but of sophisticated courtiers. (For though the claim is often made that it is possible to encounter shepherds with accomplished voices in the woods and wilds, this is more often an exaggeration on the part of poets than an actual fact.) And the men's opinion was confirmed when they heard the following verses:

"What causes all my grief and pain?
Cruel disdain.
What aggravates my misery?
Accursed jealousy.
How has my soul its patience lost?
By tedious absence crossed.
Alas! no balsam can be found
To heal the grief of such a wound,
When absence, jealousy, and scorn,
Have left me helpless and forlorn.

What in my breast this grief could move?
Neglected love.
What doth my fond desires withstand?
Fate's cruel hand.
And what confirms my misery?
Heaven's fixed decree.
Ah me! my boding fears portend
This strange disease my life will end:
For die I must, when three such foes,
Heav'n, fate, and love, my bliss oppose.

My peace of mind what can restore?
Death's welcome hour.
What gains love's joys most readily?
Fickle inconstancy.

Its pains what med'cine can assuage?
Wild frenzy's rage.
'Tis therefore little wisdom, sure,
For such a grief to seek a cure,
That knows no better remedy
Than frenzy, death, inconstancy."

The hour of the day, the season of the year, the solitude of the site, and the talent of the singer inspired wonder and delight in the two listeners, who breathlessly waited to see if anything further was to be heard. But when they realized the silence was unlikely to be broken, they decided to go in search of the person who possessed such a beautiful voice. But just as they were about to do so, they hesitated when they heard the same voice sing the following sonnet:

"Friendship, thou hast with nimble flight
Exulting gained th'empyrean height,
In Heaven to dwell, while here below
Thy semblance reigns in mimic show!
From thence to earth, at thy behest,
Descends fair peace, celestial guest;
Beneath whose veil of shining hue
Deceit oft lurks, concealed from view.

'Leave, friendship! leave thy heavenly seat,
Or strip thy livery off the cheat.
If still he wears thy borrowed smiles,
And still unwary truth beguiles,
Soon must this dark terrestrial ball
Into its first confusion fall."

The song ended with a profound sigh and the two men anxiously waited to see if anything more might be forthcoming, but when they heard the singing turn into pitiful sighs and sobs, they were determined to learn the identity of the unhappy singer who was as accomplished in his singing as he was pitiful in his laments. They had advanced only a short distance when, rounding a boulder, they saw a man with the same looks and build Sancho Panza had described to them in relating the story of Cardenio. When the man saw them, he registered no surprise but stood motionless, his head resting on his chest in an attitude of someone lost in thought, and other than the first time when they had unexpectedly appeared, he did not raise his eyes to look at them again. The eloquent priest, recognizing him from his description and aware of his affliction, approached and with a few well chosen words pleaded with him to forsake that most wretched existence lest he lose his life there, which would be the greatest tragedy of all. During all this time Cardenio was in complete command of his faculties, being free of those fits of madness that so frequently deprived him of his wits. When he saw everyone in such different attire from what he usually encountered in those wilds, he found it difficult not to evince some slight surprise, particularly when he heard them refer to his affairs as though they were common knowledge, a fact he had deduced from the priest's speech. Accordingly, he said the following:

"I can clearly see, gentlemen, whoever your graces may be, that heaven, which takes pains to aid the good and quite often the wicked, has sent to me, unworthy soul that I am, here in this remote spot so far removed from ordinary human contact, several persons who have sought to persuade me to repair to a better place by setting before me various ingenious arguments as to how unreasonable I am in following a life such as this, but because they do not know, as I do, that in escaping from this misery I shall fall into an even greater one, they probably consider me feeble-minded or, what is worse, totally out of my mind; not that it would be surprising if that were the case, for it is evident to me that the very thought of my misfortune is so intense and so capable of causing my ruin that I am unable to control it and am turning into a stone without feelings or awareness. The truth of this is brought home to me each time I am told or shown evidence of the things I do when these terrible fits come over me. All I can do, besides feel remorse, is to vainly curse my lot and beg forgiveness for my madness, explaining its cause to anyone willing to listen, for, once reasonable people understand the cause, they are not surprised at the effects and, if they are unable to provide me a remedy, at least they do not hold me responsible. On the contrary, their anger at my lack of self control turns to pity for my misfortune. If, gentlemen, your graces have come with the same intention as all the others, before you proceed with your words of advice, I beg you to listen to an account of my hopeless misfortune, for once you have heard it, you may possibly save yourselves the trouble of trying to console me over a grief that admits of no consolation."

Inasmuch as both men had no greater desire than to hear the cause of his grief from his own lips, they asked him to relate it, offering to do his absolute bidding with regard to his cure or his consolation. With this assurance the unhappy gentleman began his heart-rending story virtually in the same manner and with the same words with which he had related it to Don Quixote and the goatherd a few days earlier, when because of Master Elisabat and Don Quixote's compunction for preserving the honor of chivalry, the story was left hanging, as our history has recorded. But now good fortune decreed that the attacks of madness be held in abeyance, affording him sufficient time to finish it. When he came to the incident of the note that Don Fernando had found in his copy of *Amadís of Gaul,* Cardenio said he had it etched in his memory and it read:

Luscinda to Cardenio,

Each day, sir, I discover in you qualities that force and oblige me to hold you in greater esteem, so that if you should wish to release me from this debt without compromising my honor, you may easily do so, for I have a father who knows you and loves me, and who, without imposing his own will upon mine, will comply with any just request you may have, that is, if you hold me in as high esteem as you say you do and I believe.

"I was moved by this note to ask for Luscinda's hand in marriage, as I have already mentioned and, because of the note, Luscinda was, in Don Fernando's opinion, one of the most discreet and wise young ladies of her day. It was this note that instilled in him the desire to destroy me before my own could be realized. I told Don Fernando what had made Luscinda's father vacillate: that he preferred my father to request her hand, but I did not dare tell my father for fear he might not agree to it, and not because he was unaware of her rank, goodness, virtue, and beauty, nor of the fact that she possessed the requisite qualities to ennoble any bloodline in Spain, but because he explained to me that he was reluctant to have me rush into marriage until he saw what Duke Ricardo's plans were regarding me. In short, I explained that I did not dare speak to my father because of this difficulty, together with a number of other matters that made a coward of me but which I could not quite put my finger on; besides, it seemed to me that what I desired might never come to pass. To all this Don Fernando said he would make it his responsibility to speak to my father and persuade *him* to speak to Luscinda's.

"O ambitious Marius! O cruel Catiline! O villainous Sulla! O lying Ganelón! O deceitful Vellido! O vengeful Julián! O greedy Judas! O treacherous, cruel, vengeful, and deceitful one, what disservice had I done you, I who with complete frankness revealed to you the secrets and contents of my heart? How did I offend you? What have I ever said or advised that was not designed to increase your honor and well being? But, alas, why do I complain thus, since it is a fact that when the stars in their courses furiously and violently rain down adversity from the heavens, there is no force on earth that can halt it, nor any human ingenuity that can prevent it? Who would have thought that Don Fernando, an illustrious and intelligent gentleman indebted to me for my services and sufficiently powerful to achieve his amorous desires in any given situation, would debase himself by stealing from me a single ewe I did not yet own? But setting these considerations aside as useless and of no benefit, let me tie up the broken thread of my unfortunate story. I shall simply say that, inasmuch as Don Fernando felt my presence to be an obstacle to the execution of his devious and evil scheme, he decided to dispatch me to his elder brother under the pretext of asking for money with which to pay for six horses. And for the sole purpose of getting rid of me in order to carry out his perverse scheme, he purchased them the very day he offered to speak to my father, telling me he wanted me to go for the money. Could I have foreseen this treachery? Could I ever in my wildest dreams have imagined it? No, of course not; on the contrary, I most willingly offered to leave at once, pleased with the bargain he had struck. That evening I spoke with Luscinda, telling her what I had agreed to do for Don Fernando and assuring her that our honorable and just intentions would have a favorable resolution. She, as unsuspecting of Don Fernando's treachery as I, begged me to hasten my return, for she was convinced that the fulfillment of our desires would be delayed no longer than it would take my father to speak to hers. I cannot explain why but, as soon as she finished saying this, her eyes filled with tears and a lump rose in her throat, making it impossible for her to mention any of the various other things she apparently wished to tell me. I was shocked at this latest development, something I had never before observed in her, for on those occasions when our good fortune and my diligence made it possible, we would converse with each other joyfully and cheerfully without ever burdening our chats with tears, sighs, jealousies, or fears. And because heaven had made her my bride, I went about extolling my good fortune, exaggerating her beauty, and marveling at her courage and intelligence. She reciprocated by praising in me those things that seemed to her – as one in love – worthy of praise and in this way we exchanged a hundred thousand bits of gossip about our neighbors and acquaintances. The greatest familiarity I ever permitted myself was to take, virtually by force, one of her beautiful white hands and press it to my lips, the only action permitted by the narrow railing that separated us. But on the eve of the day preceding my sad departure, she was overcome by tears and sighs as she withdrew, leaving me totally confused and apprehensive at the sight of such sorrowful new signs of pain and grief in her. But to sustain my spirits, I attributed all this to the power of love, which held me in its grip, and to the pain that absence causes in lovers. In the end, I departed sad and concerned, my heart filled with doubts and suspicions but not knowing what it was I doubted or suspected – clear foreshadowings of the unhappy outcome and misfortunes that lay in store for me.

"I reached my destination, delivered the letters to Don Fernando's brother, was well received by him but not well dispatched, for he asked me to remain there for a week much to my displeasure and *that* in a place where his father the duke would not see me, since his brother had written to him asking him to send back a certain sum of money by me without their father's knowledge of it. All this, however, was a fabrication of the false-hearted Don Fernando because his brother had more than enough money to have dispatched me at once. This was the order and command that nearly caused me to disobey him, for I felt I could not possibly endure such an extended absence from Luscinda, particularly when I had left her as dejected as I have described. Despite all this, I obeyed as a good servant, though I could see that to do so would be at the expense of my well being. But on the fourth day following my arrival, a man bearing a letter came in search of me and, when I saw the letter, I recognized the writing on the envelope as Luscinda's. I opened it with fear and apprehension, feeling that something important must have caused her to write to me in my absence because she seldom did so even when I was in town. Before reading the letter, I asked him who had given it to him and how long it had taken him to make the trip. He explained that he had been walking along one of the city streets at the noon hour when a very beautiful lady with tear-filled eyes called out to him from a window and quite hastily said,

"'Good brother, if you are a Christian, as your appearance would suggest, I beg you for the love of God to deliver this letter to the person at the address on the envelope – both of which are well known – and you will thereby be doing a great service to Our Lord. And so that you may have the means to do so, please accept what is tied in this handkerchief.'

"Having said this, she threw down a handkerchief containing a hundred *reals* and this gold ring I am wearing, as well as the letter I gave your grace. Then without waiting for my reply, she withdrew from the window but not before she had seen me pick up the letter and handkerchief and signal that I would do as she requested. Seeing myself so handsomely paid for the trouble I would incur in delivering it to a person as well known as your grace, and moved by that beautiful lady's tears, I resolved to trust no one else but to deliver it myself. It has been sixteen hours since she entrusted it to me and I set out and, as your grace knows, it is eighteen leagues from there to here.' While the handsomely compensated makeshift mailman was telling me this, I was hanging upon his every word and my legs were trembling so much I could barely stand. Finally, opening the letter, I saw that it contained the following:

The promise that Don Fernando made to persuade your father to speak to mine has been kept but more to his own satisfaction than to your benefit. You should know that he has asked for my hand in marriage and my father, persuaded by the advantage he believes Don Fernando to hold over you, has acceded to his wishes with such earnestness that the wedding is set for two days from today and will take place in such secrecy and seclusion that it will be witnessed only by heaven and a few members of our household. You can imagine how I feel, and you should consider whether it is important for you to be present. As to whether I love you or not, the outcome of this affair shall make clear. If it please God, this letter will reach your hands before mine find themselves joined to those of one who so poorly keeps his word.

"This, in brief, was what the letter contained and what made me set out without waiting for an answer or money, for at that moment I understood quite clearly that not the purchase of the horses but that of his pleasure was what had caused Don Fernando to dispatch me to his brother. The loathing I conceived for Don Fernando, together with the fear of losing the jewel I had won through so many years of love and devotion, lent me wings for the journey. The next day, by virtually flying, I reached my village at a time convenient for speaking to Luscinda. Entering the village unobserved, I left the mule I had ridden at the house of the good man who had brought me the letter. Thanks to kind-hearted Fate, I found Luscinda at the grating which had been the constant witness to our love. She recognized me at once and I her, but not as she should have – nor I either for that matter. Yet, who in the world can boast of having penetrated or understood the confused thinking and changeable nature of women? No one, to be sure. When Luscinda saw me, she said,

"'Cardenio, you see me wearing this wedding dress because that traitor Don Fernando and my greedy father are at this very moment waiting for me in the hall, along with several other persons who will witness my death before they witness my marriage. Don't be upset, my love, but try to be present at this sacrifice, for if my arguments are unable to prevent it, I have concealed a dagger on my person that will be capable of frustrating the most determined forces by putting an end to my life and showing you how much I have always loved you and always shall.'

"In my confusion, I hastily replied, fearing I might not have time to do so:

"'My lady, may your deeds bear out your words, and if you carry a dagger to preserve your good name, I have my sword here to defend you or to kill myself should fate prove adverse.'

"I am afraid she did not hear everything I said, for I could hear them calling for her to hurry because the bridegroom was waiting. Thus, the night of my sorrow arrived, the sun of my happiness set, my eyes could no longer see, nor my mind reason. I found myself unable to enter her home or to go anywhere else, but when I considered how essential my presence was for whatever might transpire on that occasion, I gathered as much courage as possible and made my way inside, being by then acquainted with all the entrances and exits. And since a general commotion filled the house, to which the outside world was not privy, no one was aware of my presence. Without being seen, I managed to hide in that very hall behind the fringes of a pair of tapestries of a recessed window, from where

I was able to observe, without being observed, everything that took place in the hall. I wish I could now describe how my heart was pounding as I stood there, what thoughts passed through my mind, and what courses of action I considered, but these were so numerous and extraordinary that it would be both impossible and unseemly to recount them. Suffice it to say that the bridegroom entered the hall dressed in no other clothes than those he ordinarily wore. A first cousin of Luscinda's served as best man and in the entire hall there was no one from outside the family except the servants. A short while later Luscinda appeared from a dressing-room in the company of her mother and two of her maids, beautifully attired and adorned as befitted her rank and beauty, a virtual paragon of courtly dress and manners. Owing to my astonishment and fascination I did not pay particular attention to how she was dressed but I did note the colors, which were crimson and white, and the glistening gems and stones adorning her headpiece and scattered about her dress, all of which were surpassed by the singular beauty of her lovely blond hair, for, compared to the precious stones and the light from the room's four torches, it provided a greater splendor to the eyes. O memory, mortal enemy of my repose, of what benefit is it to remind me of the incomparable beauty of my adorable beloved? Would it not be more to the point, cruel memory, to remind me of how she acted on that occasion so that I, spurred by such a manifest wrong, might attempt, if not to seek my vengeance, at least to end my life? I hope your graces do not find these digressions tiresome, for my sorrows are not of the sort that can or should be briefly and cursorily recounted because I believe each circumstance in them is worthy of a lengthy discourse."

To this the priest replied that, rather than being wearied by his tale, they found the details he was relating most delightful, for not only did they not deserve to be passed over in silence but deserved as much emphasis as the main thread of the story.

"Well, as I was saying," continued Cardenio, "once everyone had gathered in the hall, the parish priest came in and took the pair by the hand to perform the mandatory ceremonies, at which point he said, 'Do you, Doña Luscinda, take Don Fernando to be your lawful husband as required by the Holy Mother Church?' I stuck my entire head and neck outside the tapestries and, with my heart pounding and my ears straining, prepared myself for Luscinda's answer, expecting by her reply either my death sentence or my confirmation of life. Oh, if only I had rushed forth at that moment and cried out, 'Luscinda, my darling Luscinda, think what you are about to do; consider what you owe me; remember that you belong to me and to no one else! Understand that your saying 'I do' and the end of my life will be one and the same act! And you, O treacherous Don Fernando, are robbing me of my glory and putting an end to my life! What is it you want? What are you seeking? Consider that you cannot gain your objective in a Christian manner, for Luscinda is already my wife and I her husband.' Oh, fool that I am, now that I am absent and far from danger, it is easy to see what I should have done but did not! Now that I have allowed myself to be robbed of my dearest possession, I curse the thief upon whom I might have avenged myself had I only possessed as much courage then as I have now to complain! In short, because I was then a coward and a fool, it is no wonder that I now find myself dying, bereft of my senses, and filled with shame and remorse.

"The priest waited for Luscinda's answer but she hesitated quite some time before responding. Just when I believed she would draw the dagger to save her good name or would unleash her tongue to voice some truth or repudiation on my behalf, I heard her whisper in a thin, faint voice, 'I do', and Don Fernando responded with the same words. Once the ring was placed on her finger, the two remained indissolubly linked. The bridegroom was about to embrace his bride when she suddenly placed her hand over her heart and fell swooning into her mother's arms.

"It now remains for me to explain how I felt when, because of the vow I had heard, I saw all my hopes dashed, Luscinda's words and promises proven false, and myself unable to recover in any amount of time the treasure I had lost in that single instant. I was left with no one to turn to, completely forsaken by heaven, and in my opinion loathsome to the earth that had once sustained me, while the air denied me breath for my sighs, and water moisture for my tears; fire alone increased, as I was totally engulfed by the flames of rage and jealousy. Everyone was thrown into confusion by Luscinda's swoon and, when her mother unfastened her bodice to give her air, a sealed note was discovered there, which Don Fernando immediately seized and began to read by the light of one of the torches. As soon as he finished reading it, he collapsed onto a chair and cradled his head in his hand like one lost in thought, but he did not join in the efforts to help revive his bride.

"Seeing everyone in the house in a state of confusion, I seized the opportunity to leave, not caring whether I was detected or not, and determined, should they see me, to commit some act that would show them the just indignation in my breast, such as punishing the false Don Fernando and even the fickle, unconscious traitoress. But fate, which must have been preserving me for even worse ills, if such were possible, ordained that at that moment I was to possess an overabundance of lucidity which, however, I have lacked ever since. And so, refusing to take revenge upon my worst enemies, which would have been easy since I was not even in their thoughts, I resolved to take revenge upon my own person and to inflict upon myself the punishment that they deserved, and perhaps with even more severity than I might have employed had I slain them on the spot. For when punishment is administered quickly, suffering ends quickly, but when it is prolonged through torture, it kills continuously without ever ending life. In short, I ran outside and returned to the house of the man with whom I had left the mule. I ordered him to saddle it and, without saying goodbye, rode away from the city, not daring to look back, like a second Lot. When I found myself alone in the open country enveloped by the night's darkness – the silence inviting me to vent my complaints without regard or fear of being heard or recognized – I unloosed my voice and unleashed my tongue in a stream of invectives against Luscinda and Don Fernando as though I might thereby satisfy the injury they had done me. I called her cruel, ungrateful, false, thankless, but above all avaricious, for my rival's wealth had blinded the eyes of her love and taken her from me, handing her over to one whom fate had treated more liberally and generously. But in the midst of those invectives and oaths I forgave her, saying it was not surprising that a maiden locked away in her parents' house and forever accustomed to obeying them should be willing to acquiesce to their wishes when they offered her for her husband a gentleman who was so distinguished, rich, and genteel; for had she refused to accept him, people would think she had taken leave of her senses or had placed her affection elsewhere, a circumstance that would be most prejudicial to her good name and reputation. I immediately changed my mind, however, reasoning that if only she had acknowledged me as her husband, they would have seen she had not made such a poor choice in selecting me that they could not have forgiven her; besides, before Don Fernando made his offer, they themselves could not have desired, had they been reasonable in their aspirations, anyone better than me for their daughter's husband, and she could certainly have said, before placing herself in the irrevocable position of extending her hand in matrimony, that I had already given her mine. I would then have come forward to confirm whatever she had been able to devise concerning that situation. In short, I concluded that her lack of love and good judgement and her enormous ambition and desire for distinction had made her forget the words with which she had deceived and sustained me in my firm hopes and honorable intentions. Preoccupied with these thoughts, I traveled for the remainder of the night and ended up at dawn in one of these mountain passes, through which I traveled for another three days. Following no particular path or road, I eventually stopped in a meadow somewhere in these hills. There I asked some herdsmen how I might reach the most inaccessible part of these mountains and they pointed in this direction. I at once headed for this spot with the intention of ending my life here but, as soon as I entered these wilds, my mule dropped dead from hunger and exhaustion or, as I am more inclined to believe, in order to rid himself of the useless burden he bore in the form of my person. I found myself on foot, exhausted by the rugged terrain, dying of hunger, and without anyone to come to my aid, not that I even dreamed of seeking such aid. I cannot say how long I lay on the ground in that condition but when I finally rose to my feet, I was no longer hungry. I found myself in the company of some goatherds who most certainly were the ones who had ministered to my needs, for they described how they had found me talking so irrationally that I showed I was clearly out of my mind. Since then I have felt I am not always in command of my wits, which at times are so weak and impaired that I commit a thousand outrageous acts: tearing at my clothing, walking about shouting, cursing my fate, and vainly uttering the name of my dear beloved, with no other object or purpose than that of attempting to end my life by shouting. Once I regain my senses, I find myself so exhausted and worn out that I can scarcely move.

"My most common abode is the hollow of any cork oak capable of sheltering this wretched body. Moved by pity, the herdsmen and goatherds who roam these hills sustain my existence by placing food along the roads or on the rocks where they think I may pass and find it. Though I may have taken leave of my senses at the time, my natural instinct leads me to recognize the food and awakens in me a craving for it, as well as a willingness to accept it. At other times, when they find me in command of my senses, they tell me I charge out onto the highway and take by force what the shepherds are bringing from the village to their sheepfolds, which they would gladly share with me if I would only ask them for it. This is the manner in which I shall live out my miserable, desperate existence until heaven is merciful enough to conduct it to its final destination or will put an end to my memory so I shall no longer remember the beauty and treachery of Luscinda or the wrong done me by Don Fernando. If heaven does this without taking my life, I shall direct my thoughts along a better course. If not, there is absolutely nothing for me to do except pray that it will have mercy upon my soul, for I feel I lack the courage or strength to extricate my body from these wilds into which I have willingly placed it.

"Alas, gentlemen, this is the bitter story of my misfortunes. Tell me if it can possibly be commemorated with less emotion than I have shown. Your graces must not exhaust yourselves trying to persuade or advise me to do what reason tells you would be a proper remedy for my ills, for it will be of no more benefit than the medicine a renowned physician prescribes to a sick man who refuses to take it. I have no desire for health without Luscinda and, since she has seen fit to belong to another while being mine – at least she should have been mine – may I see fit to belong to adversity, though I might have belonged to good fortune. By her fickleness she sought to give permanence to my perdition but I shall try to satisfy her wishes by seeking my death, which will prove to future generations that I lacked what every other wretch has had in abundance, namely, the ability to be consoled by the knowledge that consolation is out of my reach. In me this is a source of greater sorrows and ills, which, I fear, will not cease with my death."

Here Cardenio brought to a close his lengthy discourse and story, which was as forlorn as it was impassioned. But just as the priest was about to offer a few words of consolation, he was stopped short by a voice that reached his ears – one that was heard to say in mournful tones what will be related in the fourth part of this narrative, for at this point the wise and prudent historian Cide Hamete Benengeli brings the third part to a close.

FOURTH PART
OF
THE INGENIOUS HIDALGO DON QUIXOTE OF LA MANCHA

Chapter Twenty-Eight

The novel and delightful adventure that befell the priest and the barber in the same sierra

How happy and how fortunate the times when that most daring knight Don Quixote of La Mancha appeared upon the scene! Because of his most honorable determination to revive and reinstitute on earth the faded and virtually extinct order of knight-errantry, we now enjoy in this age of ours, which is so in need of agreeable entertainments, not only the pleasure of his *bona fide* history but also its tales and interludes, which in their own way are no less enjoyable, ingenious, and authentic than the history itself. The latter, following the thread that has been carded, spun, and wound, relates that just as the priest was preparing to console Cardenio, he was prevented from doing so by a voice that reached his ears and said in mournful tones,

"Oh, God, have I possibly found a site that will provide a secluded sepulcher for the painful burden of this body I bear so much against my will? Indeed, it is if I am not deceived by the solitude promised by these mountains. Since these crags and thickets, alas, will afford me the opportunity to lament my fate and communicate my wretchedness to heaven, how much more agreeable will their company be than that of any living human being, for there is no one from whom I can seek answers for my doubts, relief for my complaints, or remedies for my ills!"

This entire discourse was heard and understood by the priest and all his companions and, believing the speaker was nearby, they rose and went to look for him. They had not gone twenty paces when behind a rock they spotted a young man dressed as a farmer seated at the base of an ash tree. They were unable to see his face at that moment, for his head was bent forward while he bathed his feet in the flowing stream. He was unaware of their presence because of their hushed movements and his total absorption in bathing his feet, which were such that they resembled two pieces of white crystal fashioned from the pebbles of the stream. Marveling at the whiteness of his beautiful feet, they fancied these had not been created to tread upon mere soil or to follow behind the ox plow, as his attire would lead one to believe. Noting that he had not sensed their presence, the priest, who was leading the way, signaled to the other two to crouch down and hide behind a pile of rocks, which they both did because of their eagerness to discover what sort of activity the young man was engaged in. The latter's clothing consisted of grey cloth breeches and leggings, a grey cap, and a double-skirted grey jacket open down both sides and tightly girded round his waist with a white sash; and his leggings were rolled halfway up his legs, giving them the appearance of white alabaster. Once he had finished bathing his beautiful feet, he removed a kerchief from beneath his cap and dried them with it. As he did so, he raised his head and revealed to those observing him such an incomparably beautiful face that Cardenio whispered to the priest,

"Since this person is not Luscinda, he can only be some divine being."

The youth removed his cap and shook his head vigorously, allowing a shock of hair that was the envy of the sun itself to unfold and fall over his shoulders. As soon as they saw it, they realized the one they had taken to be a farm lad was a woman, and an exquisite one at that, in fact, the most beautiful that any of them, including Cardenio, had ever laid eyes upon, had they not already seen and known Luscinda; and Cardenio later affirmed that only Luscinda's beauty could compete with this woman's. Her long blond tresses not only covered her shoulders but enveloped her entire body, and had it not been for her feet, no part of her body would have been visible due to the fullness and length of her hair, for which her hands served as a comb at that moment. If in the stream her feet had the appearance of pieces of crystal, her hands against her hair resembled bits of pressed snow, all of which astonished the three onlookers and piqued their curiosity to learn who she was. For this reason they decided to announce their presence but at the sound they made in standing up the beautiful girl raised her head, pulled back her hair from in front of her eyes, and looked at those who had made the noise. No sooner did she see them than she sprang to her feet and, without waiting to put on her shoes or gather up her hair, quickly grabbed a bundle she had beside her, probably of clothes, and started to run away overcome with confusion and alarm. But she had not taken half a dozen steps before falling to the ground, for her tender feet were unable to withstand the sharp stones. Seeing this, the three of them ran towards her, with the priest being the first to speak:

"Whoever you are, my lady, I beg your grace not to turn and flee, for those you see before you wish only to be of service to you. There is no reason to flee so needlessly, for your feet will not allow it nor will we permit such a thing."

To all this she made no reply because of her astonishment and confusion. When they finally caught up with her, the priest took her by the hand and said,

"What your grace's clothing conceals, your tresses have revealed, clearly demonstrating it was no insignificant matter that caused you to disguise your beauty in such unworthy apparel and to come to such a desolate place as this, where it has been our good fortune to find you, if not to provide a remedy for your ills, at least to offer some advice concerning them. So long as there is life, no ill can be so oppressive to a person beset by sorrow as to keep her from accepting advice offered her with all good intentions. And so, my lady, or lord, or whatever your grace wishes to be, you may put aside the fright our presence has caused you and describe to us your ill or good fortune, for in us, all together or individually, you shall find someone who will commiserate with your unhappiness."

While the priest was saying these things, the disguised girl stood there dumbfounded, looking at everyone without moving her lips or saying a word, just like a country girl who is suddenly shown an object that to her is strange and never before dreamed of. But when the priest proceeded with other counsels designed to achieve the same effect, she broke her silence and, heaving a deep sigh, said,

"Since the solitude of these hills has not been able to conceal me and the loosening of my uncombed hair has failed to allow my tongue to be deceitful, it would be futile for me to continue pretending, because, if your graces were to believe me, it would be more out of courtesy than for any other reason. This being so, gentlemen, allow me to thank your graces for these kind offers which compel me to satisfy you in all your requests, though I fear the narration of my misfortunes may arouse your grief as much as your compassion because you will find no remedy to cure them nor any consolation to help me endure them. But lest the state of my honor remain in doubt in your minds, now that you have discovered that I am a woman and am young, alone, and dressed in this fashion, factors which taken together or separately might undermine any woman's reputation, I shall tell your graces what I should prefer to keep secret if it were in my power."

All this was said without a pause by the beautiful woman and was said with such ease of expression and in so pleasant a voice that they marveled at her intelligence no less than at her beauty. When they renewed their offers and asked her to do as she had promised, she, without further urging and in total innocence, put on her shoes, gathered up her hair, and seated herself comfortably on a boulder with the other three seating themselves at her feet. Then making an effort to fight back the tears that had filled her eyes, she began the story of her life in a voice that was both calm and clear:

"Here in Andalusia there is a town from which a certain duke takes his title, making him one of those persons known as grandees. This gentleman has two sons: the elder, heir to his estate and apparently his good manners, and the younger, heir to I know not what, unless it is the treachery of Vellido or the deception of Ganelón. My parents, who are vassals of this lord, are of humble origin but sufficiently wealthy that, had they been as fortunate in birth as they have been in life, they would have nothing more to desire, nor should I have ever dreamed of finding myself in my present situation. My adversity may possibly spring from their misfortune of not having been nobly born, though they are certainly not so humble as to need to complain of their station in life, nor so lofty as to rid me of the suspicion that my misfortune arises from their low estate. Despite the fact that they are plain, simple farmers, they have no trace of tainted blood but are, as the saying goes, 'dyed-in-the-wool Christians.' However, their wealth and liberality are slowly earning them the status of gentry and even nobility, but the thing they considered their greatest treasure and possession was having me as their daughter. Because they were loving parents and had no other child as heir, I was one of the most pampered daughters parents have ever doted upon. I was the mirror in which they saw themselves, the staff of their old age, and the object towards which all their desires, with due consideration to heaven, were directed, their desires being so noble that mine coincided with theirs completely. And just as I was mistress of their hearts, so was I mistress of everything they owned. At my bidding servants were hired and fired; the itemizing and accounting of all the crops that were planted and harvested passed through my hands: the oil mills, the wine presses, and the inventory of the livestock and beehives; in short, everything a farmer as wealthy as my father might possibly own was my responsibility. I strove so diligently to perform my duties and my father was so very pleased with my dedication that I can assure your graces it would be impossible to exaggerate either of these. The leisure hours that remained after I devoted the necessary time to the head shepherds, overseers, and other laborers were spent in activities as permissible to young ladies as they are necessary, such as those afforded by sewing, embroidery, and even spinning. If I occasionally abandoned these activities to nourish my soul, it was to turn to reading some edifying book of devotion or to playing the harp, for experience has taught me that music mends broken spirits and alleviates those troubles originating in the soul. Such then was the life I led in my parents' home. I have related my story in great detail, not out of ostentation nor to show your graces how wealthy I am, but so that you may observe how undeservedly I have gone from that pleasant state to the unhappy one in which I now find myself.

"The truth is that, because I spent my life immersed in my tasks and in a seclusion comparable to that of a convent, I was never seen, or so I thought, by any persons other than the household servants. When I attended mass, it was at such an early hour and I was so heavily veiled and so well chaperoned by my mother and several maids that my eyes scarcely saw more of the earth than where I trod. Despite all this, the eyes of love, or those of idleness as they might more accurately be called, spotted me, eyes that cannot be rivaled even by those of the lynx. They assumed the form of solicitations by Don Fernando, which is the name of the duke's younger son to whom I have referred."

No sooner had Don Fernando been mentioned by the narrator of the story than Cardenio's face grew flushed and he began to perspire, as he was quite visibly moved. The priest and the barber, who noticed the change, feared he might be suffering a sudden fit of the madness which, they had heard, overcame him from time to time, but Cardenio did nothing more than perspire and sit motionless while staring at the country girl and wondering who she was. She, however, took no notice of Cardenio's condition and proceeded with her story, saying,

"The moment he saw me, as he later confessed, he fell madly in love with me, which his behavior clearly gave me to understand. But to end the story of my misfortunes quickly, which unfortunately have no end, I prefer not to describe the countless attempts Don Fernando made to communicate his feelings to me. He bribed all the members of my household by giving presents and enticements to all my kin; each day was a day of partying and celebrating in our street; at night no one could sleep because of the serenades; and the love letters that fell into my hands by some unknown means never ceased to arrive, all filled with proposals and expressions of love but containing less substance than promises and oaths. Not only did all this fail to mollify me but it hardened me as though he were my mortal enemy. Everything he did to make me yield to his way of thinking had just the opposite effect and not because Don Fernando's gentility was unpleasing to me, nor because he carried his courting to excess, for it gave me an inexplicable thrill to see myself thus loved and esteemed by such an illustrious gentleman. Nor was it displeasing to see my praises on paper, for however homely a woman is, in my opinion she always delights in hearing herself described as beautiful. But arrayed against all this were my purity and the unceasing advice of my parents, who were now fully aware of Don Fernando's intentions because it did not matter to him if everyone learned of them. My parents told me they had staked their honor and reputation upon my virtue and goodness and I should consider the disparity between Don Fernando and myself, whereby I would recognize that his thoughts, though he might claim otherwise, were directed more to his own pleasure than to my well being and that, if I wished to erect a barrier against his unreasonable course of action, they would immediately betroth me to anyone of my choosing: either one of the most eligible bachelors from our village or a person from the surrounding ones, for I might set my sights quite high owing to my parents' considerable wealth and my good name. Armed with these promises and the reality of the situation, I became more resolute and determined never to say a single word to Don Fernando, however faint, that might give him the slightest hope of attaining his desires.

"All this reserve of mine, which he must have interpreted as scorn, was surely the thing that whetted his lustful appetite, this being the name I choose to assign to the passion he felt for me. Had it been of the proper sort, your graces would not now know of it, as there would be no reason for me to discuss it. Finally, Don Fernando learned that my parents were making plans for my betrothal in order to thwart his hopes of possessing me or at least were seeing to it that I had additional guardians to protect me, and it was this bit of news, or suspicion, that was the cause of his subsequent actions. One night, when I was in my chamber in the company of one of my serving maids with the doors shut tight for fear my honor might be imperiled through carelessness, suddenly in the midst of those precautions and in the isolation of that silent confinement I inexplicably found him standing before me. The sight of him so upset me that my eyes could not see nor my tongue speak, nor could I bring myself to cry out for help, not that he would have let me do so. He came up to me at once and took me in his arms, for, as I have said, I was too weak to defend myself owing to my confusion. And then something astounding happened: he began to say the most endearing things to me and, though they were all lies, he had composed them so skillfully that they took on the appearance of truths. The traitor made his tears lend credence to his words and his sighs credence to his intentions. I, poor thing, alone and ill-prepared by my family for such situations as that, began to believe, as incredible as it may seem, all those lies but not to the point that his tears and sighs were capable of moving me to compassion for anything that was less than honorable. After the initial shock had worn off, I slowly began to collect my wits and, summoning up more courage than I ever dreamed possible, said to him,

"'If, sir, I were in the clutches of a ferocious lion, as I presently am in your arms, and I might assure my safety by doing something prejudicial to my honor, it would be as impossible for me to do or say such a thing as it would be to undo the past. You, sir, may have my body locked in your arms but I have my soul bound by my honorable desires, which are entirely different from yours, as you shall see if you attempt to carry out your intentions by force. I may be your vassal but I am not your slave, and the nobility of your blood *does* not and *shall* not give you the right to dishonor or show a lack of respect for the humbleness of mine, for I have as much respect for myself, being a farm girl from the country, as you have for yourself, being a nobleman and a gentleman. Understand that your wealth shall be useless and your strength of no avail, nor will I be deceived by your words or mollified by your sighs and tears. If I should find any of these qualities I have mentioned in the man my parents offer me for my husband, I shall make my will conform to his as well as to theirs. Thus, so long as I guard my honor, albeit at the expense of my pleasure, I shall hand over to him voluntarily, sir, what you now seek by force. I mention all this because it is unthinkable that any person will achieve a single thing who is not my lawful husband.' 'If that,' replied the unfaithful gentleman, 'is all that is troubling you, my fair Dorotea" – which was the name of the unfortunate girl – "observe that I hereby offer you my hand in marriage and call upon heaven, from which nothing can be hidden, as well as upon this image of Our Lady, to serve as witnesses to this truth.'"

When Cardenio heard her say her name was Dorotea, he was visibly shaken once again, having concluded that his first impression had been correct, but as he was unwilling to interrupt the story because of his desire to hear how it would end, though being virtually certain of the outcome already, Cardenio did nothing more than say,

"So, Dorotea is your name, my lady? I have heard of another Dorotea whose misfortunes were somewhat similar to yours. But do continue, for the time will come when I shall tell you things that will astound you as much as they will move you to pity."

Dorotea listened to what Cardenio said while simultaneously observing the strange and shabby manner in which he was dressed. She begged him, if he knew anything of her circumstances, to tell her at once, for if there was one thing that fate had left her intact, it was the courage to endure any disaster that might befall her, though she was certain none could transpire that would be worse than the one she was already undergoing.

"I should not let this opportunity pass," replied Cardenio, "without telling you what I am thinking if I thought it was true, but until now there has been no reason to do so, nor would it be of any interest to you to know it."

"In that case," responded Dorotea, "I shall return to my story.

"Don Fernando picked up an icon that was in my room and designated it as a witness to our betrothal. With the most forceful words and most extraordinary oaths he promised to be my husband but, before he could finish, I asked him to think carefully about what he was doing and to consider how angry his father would be to see him betrothed to a country girl who was also one of his vassals. Nor should he be blinded by my beauty, such as it was, for it was not great enough for him to blame it for his transgression. If he wished to show me some kindness because of his love for me, he should let my destiny follow the course demanded by my station in life, for such unequal marriages are never happy ones, because the joy with which they begin does not long endure. I told him all these things I am repeating here, together with a number of others that I do not recall but they were not sufficient to make him desist in his efforts, just as the person who has no intention of paying for a purchase is never troubled by the terms of the sale. At this point I held a conversation with myself which went as follows: 'I shall certainly not be the first woman to have risen by the path of matrimony from a humble to an elevated status, nor will Don Fernando be the first man whom beauty – or blind lust, which is more likely – has led to marry beneath his station in life. And since I shall be establishing no new custom by doing this, it would be advantageous to accept this honor Fate is offering me, though the way he feels about me may last no longer than it takes him to satisfy his appetite; and yet I would be his wife in the eyes of God. On the other hand, if I attempt to rebuff him in a reproachful manner, I can see he is in such a state that he will resort not to rational means but to force and I shall end up dishonored and unable to prove the falsity of the charge brought against me by those who will not know how blamelessly I have arrived at this situation, for what arguments will suffice to persuade my parents and others that this gentleman entered my chamber without my consent?' In an instant I turned over all these questions and answers in my mind and was particularly moved and inclined to the action that led – to my surprise – to my perdition. This was accomplished by means of Don Fernando's oaths, the witnesses he brought to bear, the tears he shed, and lastly by his good manners and gallantry, which, together with his demonstration of true love, might have conquered the heart of anyone as sheltered and alone as I. I summoned my maid as a witness on earth to join those of heaven, and Don Fernando reiterated and reconfirmed his oaths. To the previous saints he added new ones as witnesses; he called down upon himself a thousand future curses should he fail to keep his promise; once again his eyes filled with tears and his sighs increased as he clasped me more tightly to his bosom, having never, in fact, released me. As a result of all this and the fact that my maid again left the room, I ceased to be a maiden and he turned out to be a traitor and a liar.

"The day following the night of my dishonor did not arrive with the speed which, I am certain, Don Fernando desired, for as soon as lust is satisfied, the greatest pleasure one can experience is to distance himself from the scene where his lust was aroused. I say this because Don Fernando hurriedly fled from me and with the help of my maid, the same one who had brought him there, found himself in the street before the sun came up. When he took leave of me, though with less fervor and passion than on his arrival, he said I might rely upon his word and the sincerity and steadfastness of his promises. To make his oath more binding, he took an expensive ring from his finger and placed it on mine. When he eventually left, I don't recall whether I was happy or sad. One thing I do remember, though, is that I felt confused, troubled, and almost beside myself because of this new development; so much so, in fact, that either I did not feel courageous enough or simply forgot to scold the maid for the treachery she had committed in admitting Don Fernando into my own chamber, for I was still undecided whether what had befallen me had been for good or ill. As Don Fernando was leaving, I told him that, inasmuch as I now belonged to him, he might visit me any night he wished using the same route he had used that first night, until he saw fit to announce our betrothal, but except for the following night, he never again returned, nor did I succeed in seeing him in the street or in church for more than a month. I labored in vain asking for him, though I knew he was in the village and spent most of his days hunting, an activity he was quite fond of. I can assure your graces that those were evil days and tedious hours for me and I began to doubt and even to disbelieve Don Fernando's promises. I can also assure your graces that this was the occasion for my maid's becoming the recipient of the reprimand she had not received earlier for her impertinence. I remember being forced to exercise caution with my tears and countenance lest I give my parents grounds for asking about my unhappiness or for making myself invent lies to tell them. But all this suddenly came to an end and every consideration was disregarded, talk of honor terminated, all patience was lost, and my private thoughts were made public. This occurred several days later when it was rumored about town that in a nearby village Don Fernando had wed an extremely beautiful young lady from a most illustrious family, though not so wealthy as to have aspired to such a noble marriage merely on the basis of her dowry. It was also reported that her name was Luscinda, together with other notable events that took place at the wedding."

Cardenio heard the name Luscinda but his only reaction was to shrug his shoulders, bite his lips, and arch his eyebrows, while several moments later two streams of tears began to trickle down his cheeks. None of this, however, kept Dorotea from proceeding with her story.

"When this sad news reached my ears, instead of my heart's turning to ice, my anger and rage became so great my soul was set afire and I came within a hair of running out into the street to cry aloud, that everyone might learn of the treachery and perfidy committed against me, but my fury was tempered at that moment by the thought of putting into action what I indeed did do that very night. I dressed myself in this outfit lent me by one of my father's servants, a swain of his, which is what the farmers call the young shepherds. I confided in him all my unhappiness and begged him to accompany me to the city where I understood my adversary to be. After reproving me for my audacity and ridiculing my plan, he saw my mind was made up and thus offered to accompany me, in his words, 'to the ends of the earth.' At that very instant, I packed a dress in a linen pillowcase, together with some jewels and money for any needs that might arise. Then in the stillness of the night and without informing my treacherous maid, I set out from home, accompanied by my servant and my countless thoughts and began walking towards the city, borne aloft by my desire to arrive, if not to prevent what had already happened, at least to force Don Fernando to explain to me how he could have been so heartless. I made the trip in two and a half days and, upon entering the city, asked directions to the house of Luscinda's parents. The first person I approached told me more than I had bargained for; he told me not only where they lived but everything that had happened at their daughter's wedding, an event of such notoriety that it had spread from one group to another throughout the town. He told me that on the night that Don Fernando had wed Luscinda, she had feebly murmured 'I do' and was overcome by a sudden swoon. In going over to unfasten her bodice to give her air, Don Fernando found a note written in Luscinda's handwriting stating and declaring that she could not be his wife, since she already belonged to Cardenio, who, according to the man's explanation, was a gentleman of some prominence, and that if she had agreed to be Don Fernando's wife, she had done so in order not to disobey her parents. In short, he said that in the note she expressed her intention of killing herself as soon as the wedding was over, setting forth the reasons for taking her life, all of which was confirmed by a dagger found on her person. When Don Fernando saw this, he assumed Luscinda had slighted him or made a fool of him, at which point he lunged at her before she regained consciousness, intending to stab her with the very dagger they had found on her, and would have done so had her parents and the others present not intervened. It was reported that Don Fernando immediately went away and Luscinda did not recover from her swoon until the following day, at which time she informed her parents that she was actually the bride of Cardenio, as I have mentioned. I also learned from what everyone said that Cardenio had been present at the wedding and when he saw her marriage consummated, a thing he could never have imagined, he left the city a desperate man, having first written a letter in which he declared the wrong Luscinda had done him and his intention of going to a place where no one would ever find him. All this was the topic of conversation throughout the city, where it was on everyone's lips, especially when they learned that Luscinda was missing and was nowhere to be found. Her parents almost went out of their minds, for they had no idea what steps to take in order to locate her. When I learned of this, my hopes were renewed and I considered myself more fortunate for not having found Don Fernando than in finding him married, for it occurred to me that the door to my salvation was not yet sealed off. I persuaded myself that heaven might possibly have prevented the second marriage to make him recognize what he owed the first and to realize that, as a Christian, he should show more concern for his soul than for mortal considerations. I turned all these things over in my mind and, without finding any actual consolation, was able to console myself and even to entertain faint and distant hopes of enduring life, a life I now find hateful.

"When I was unable to locate Don Fernando in the city and had no idea which way to turn, I heard one of the town criers say there was a large reward for anyone who found me, and he gave my age and described the very clothes I was wearing. I heard him say the shepherd who was with me had snatched me from my parents' house, a charge that pained me deeply, for it showed how far my good name had fallen. It was not enough for me to lose my reputation by fleeing but they had to add the name of the man I was with, a person so base and so unworthy of my consideration. The moment I heard the announcement, I fled the city with my servant, who was beginning to show signs of wavering in his fidelity to me. That night we entered a heavily wooded section of these hills driven by our dread of being discovered, but as the saying goes, 'One ill calls forth another,' and since the end of one misfortune is often the beginning of an even greater one, that is what happened to me. When he saw that we were alone, my good servant, who up till then had been faithful and trustworthy, became inflamed more by his own wickedness than by my beauty and attempted to take advantage of the opportunity which in his opinion was being afforded him by that wilderness. With little shame, still less fear of God, and no respect for me he made amorous advances towards me. Hearing me respond with words that were offensive but appropriate to his insolent proposals, he set aside his pleading with which he had at first thought to attain his goal and proceeded to use force. But merciful heaven, which seldom if ever fails to notice or favor honorable intentions, favored mine in such a way that I was able with very little effort and my slight strength to push him over an embankment, where I left him either dead or alive. Then with greater agility than my fright or weariness warranted, I entered these hills with no other plan or thought than of hiding in them to elude my father and those who might come searching for me on his behalf. I don't know how many months I had been here with this intention when I met a herdsman who accepted me as his servant and took me to a village deep within these hills, where I served him as swain during that whole period, attempting at all times to stay in the fields where I could conceal my hair, which has now revealed my secret when I least expected it. All my ingenuity and perseverance were of no avail, for my master made the discovery that I was not a man and the same evil idea subsequently occurred to him that had occurred to my servant. Since fate does not always provide solutions for one's every difficulty, I found no precipice or cliff over which to push my master and do him in like the one I had found for the servant, so I chose as the path of least resistance to abandon him and once again hide in this wilderness rather than test my strength or pleas with him. Let me just say that I again buried myself in these hills in an effort to find a place where, unimpeded, I might implore heaven with my sighs and tears to take pity upon my unhappiness and either to provide me with the ingenuity to rid myself of it or to let me die here in this wilderness without leaving a trace of this poor wretch who, despite her complete innocence, has provided grounds for talk and gossip in both her own town and the surrounding ones."

Chapter Twenty-Nine

The amusing stratagem and plan employed to encourage our enamored knight to abandon the harsh penance he had set for himself

"This, gentlemen, is the true story of my tragedy. Your graces may judge for yourselves whether the sighs and lamentations you have heard and the tears that have issued from these eyes might not have been displayed in still greater profusion. And considering the nature of my misfortune, you can see that any attempt to console me will be futile, since there is no solution. All I ask of your graces – something you may easily and rightfully do – is to advise me where I can spend my life without this fear and dread of being discovered by those searching for me, for though I know my parents' great love for me assures my heartfelt acceptance by them, I am filled with such shame when I think of having to face them – and not in the way they had envisioned – that I think it would be better if I went into permanent exile than to look into their eyes with the thought that they might see in mine something different from the purity they have every right to expect."

After saying this, she remained silent and her countenance clearly reflected the sense of shame she felt in her heart. Those who had listened to her story felt in their own hearts as much pity as wonder at her misfortune. The priest was about to offer some words of consolation when Cardenio took her by the hand and said,

"In a word, my lady, you are the fair Dorotea, only daughter of the wealthy Clenardo."

Dorotea was shocked to hear her father's name mentioned by such an unimposing person (we have already mentioned how shabbily Cardenio was dressed), for which reason she said,

"Who are you, my good man, to know my father's name? If I am not mistaken, I have not mentioned his name up to this point in relating the story of my unhappiness."

"I," said Cardenio, "am that ill-fated person to whom, according to you, Luscinda said she was betrothed. I am the unfortunate Cardenio whom that villainous person responsible for your present circumstance has reduced to this condition in which you now see me: ragged, half clothed, totally deprived of human comforts, and what is worse, half mad, for I am in command of my senses only in those brief intervals heaven is kind enough to grant me. I, Dorotea, am the one who found himself present at the perfidy committed by Don Fernando, and the one who stayed to hear Luscinda say she would be his bride. I am the one who lacked the courage to wait to see how her fainting spell would turn out or what would result from the note found in her bosom, for my heart could not bear to witness so many misfortunes at one time. Having thus lost all patience, I left the house after giving a letter to one of my hosts, which I begged him to place in the hands of Luscinda, and I came to this desolate spot with the intention of ending my life, which from that moment to this I have found as hateful as if it were my mortal enemy. Fate, though, has been unwilling to take away my life, being content instead to take away my reason, possibly to preserve me for the good fortune I have had in meeting your grace. If what you have said is true, as it undoubtedly is, it may just be possible that heaven has a brighter outcome in store for both of us than we imagine. Considering the fact that Luscinda cannot marry Don Fernando, since she belongs to me, as she has so openly confessed, nor can Don Fernando marry *her*, since he belongs to you, we may reasonably hope that heaven will restore to us what is ours, particularly when it is still intact and has not been alienated or destroyed. Inasmuch as we have this consolation, not born of some remote hope or founded upon some wild fancy, I beg you, my lady, to turn your noble thoughts in a different direction and prepare yourself for a better destiny, as I myself intend to do. I give you my word as a gentleman and a Christian that I shall protect you until I see you in possession of Don Fernando. If I fail to persuade him through reason to recognize his obligation to you, I shall exercise the right that is mine by virtue of my position as a gentleman and shall with the proper credentials challenge him to a duel by reason of the unreason he has shown you, not giving any thought to my own grievances, whose requital I shall leave to heaven so I may deal with yours here on earth."

Dorotea was astonished by what Cardenio had said and, not knowing how to thank him for such offers, wanted to embrace his feet and kiss them but Cardenio would not permit it. The licentiate responded for them both by voicing his approval of Cardenio's noble sentiments but above all he begged, advised, and finally persuaded them to accompany him to his village, where they could provide themselves with those things they lacked and where arrangements would be made to search for Don Fernando or to return Dorotea to her parents or to do whatever they deemed most advisable. Cardenio and Dorotea expressed their appreciation and accepted the kindness he was extending to them. The barber, who had stood there dumbfounded and speechless during all this, also put in a few kind words, offering with just as much goodwill as the priest to be of service to them in every way possible. He too gave a brief account of what had brought them there, mentioning Don Quixote's strange behavior and the fact that they were waiting for his squire, who had gone on ahead to search for him. Cardenio recalled, as from a dream, the quarrel he'd had with Don Quixote and described it to the others, though he found himself unable to explain the cause of it.

Just then, they heard shouts and realized the one shouting was Sancho Panza, who had begun to bellow when he failed to find them where he had left them. They went out to meet him so they could ask him about Don Quixote. He described how he had found the knight clad only in his shirt, thin, sallow, famished, and sighing for his lady Dulcinea. He had informed his master that she was ordering him to leave that place and come to Toboso, where she was waiting for him but Don Quixote had replied that he was determined not to appear in the presence of his fair lady until he had performed deeds that would make him worthy of her favors. Sancho added that if this course was followed, Don Quixote ran the risk of not becoming an emperor, which was his duty, or even an archbishop, which was the least he might become. They should therefore consider what could be done to force him to abandon that place. The licentiate told him not to worry because they would persuade him to leave whether he was willing or not. He then explained to Cardenio and Dorotea the plan they had devised for bringing Don Quixote to his senses or at least for returning him to his home. Dorotea suggested that she could play the role of a damsel in distress better than the barber, in addition to which she had clothes with her that would make her look more natural. They could also leave it up to her to figure out everything necessary for carrying out their plan, for she had read a number of books of chivalry and was quite familiar with how damsels in distress asked knights-errant for favors.

"Then nothing more is needed," said the priest, "than to set to work at once. Without a doubt good fortune is on our side, for when it was least expected, a door has been opened for your graces' remedy and what we needed has been provided."

At this point Dorotea drew from her pillowcase a dress with a full skirt made from a fine rich fabric, a bright green mantilla, along with a necklace and other jewels in a small box, with which she quickly adorned herself, creating the illusion of some grand and wealthy lady. She explained that she had brought these and other things from home for any need that might arise but until then there had been no occasion to use them. Everyone was exceedingly impressed by her grace, bearing, and beauty, and agreed that Don Fernando was certainly lacking in intelligence to have cast aside such a beauty. But the one who was most impressed was Sancho Panza, for it seemed to him, and such was indeed the case, that never in all the days of his life had he seen so lovely a creature. He begged and insisted that the priest tell him who this gorgeous soul was and what it was she was seeking in this god-forsaken place; to which the priest replied,

"Brother Sancho, I would have you know that this beautiful lady is no less a personage than the heiress in the direct male line of the great kingdom of Micomicón. She has come in search of your master to request a boon of him, which is to right a wrong she has suffered at the hands of an evil giant, and because of the reputation your master enjoys throughout the known world, this princess has come all the way from Guinea in search of him."

"A lucky search and a lucky find," said Sancho at this point, "and even better than that if my master is fortunate enough to right that wrong and redress that injury by killing that whoreson of a giant you speak of; and kill him he most certainly will if he meets him – unless he's a phantom, for my master is absolutely helpless against phantoms. But, sir licentiate, there is one thing among others that I would like to request so my master won't take it into his head to become an archbishop, which is what I fear, and that is for your grace to advise him to marry this princess at once, for by doing so, it will make it impossible for him to receive the office of archbishop, whereby he can easily achieve his kingdom and I the object of my desires. I've looked into the matter carefully and found by my reckoning that it would not sit well with me for my master to become an archbishop, for I'm useless as far as the Church is concerned because I'm a married man. And for me to go about selling dispensations so the Church will have an income, especially when I've got a wife and children, will be a hopeless task. Therefore, the most important thing is for my master to wed this lady at once, and if I don't refer to her by name, it's because I still don't know who she is."

"Her name," replied the priest, "is Princess Micomicona, which is what one would expect, since her kingdom is Micomicón."

"Of course, one would," replied Sancho, "for I've seen lots of people take their names and titles from the places in which they were born, calling themselves Pedro of Alcalá, Juan of Ubeda, or Diego of Valladolid and the same custom must hold true in Guinea with the queens taking their names from their kingdoms."

"That is undoubtedly true," said the priest, "and as for your master's marrying, I shall do everything in my power to bring it about."

Sancho was as greatly pleased by this as the priest was astonished at Sancho's ingenuousness and his complete accommodation of his master's outlandish ideas into his own imaginary world, for without a doubt he had come to believe that Don Quixote would become an emperor. Once Dorotea had mounted the priest's mule and the barber had attached to his face the beard made from the ox tail, they asked Sancho to lead the way to Don Quixote, warning him not to admit that he knew the licentiate or the barber, for his master's becoming an emperor rested squarely upon his not recognizing them.

The priest and Cardenio refused to accompany them lest Don Quixote be reminded of the quarrel he'd had with Cardenio, and since the priest's presence was not required at this time, they allowed them to ride on ahead and they followed slowly on foot. The priest made certain to tell Dorotea what she was to do; to which she responded that there was no reason to be concerned, for everything would be carried out down to the smallest detail exactly as demanded and described in books of chivalry.

They must have traveled three-quarters of a league before they caught sight of Don Quixote among a maze of rocks, now fully dressed except for his armor. As soon as Dorotea saw him and was informed by Sancho that this was Don Quixote, she applied the whip to her palfrey and was imitated in this by the well-bearded barber. When they arrived, the squire sprang from his mule to lend assistance to Dorotea, who dismounted with a free and easy manner and knelt at Don Quixote's feet. Though he made an effort to have her rise, she remained kneeling and said,

"I will not rise from this spot, O valiant and courageous knight, unless your grace, out of your kindness and generosity, will bestow a boon upon me that will redound to the glory and honor of your person and to the benefit of the most aggrieved and disconsolate damsel the sun has ever shone upon. If, indeed, the valor of your mighty arm matches the fame of your undying reputation, you are duty bound to favor this unfortunate lady who has come from such a far-off land on the trail of your famous name in hopes that you will provide a remedy for her ills."

"I will not say a word, fair lady," replied Don Quixote, "nor will I listen to anything more concerning these affairs until your ladyship rises."

"I will not rise, my lord," replied the grief-stricken lady, "until your grace has graciously granted the boon I seek."

"I shall grant and concede it," said Don Quixote, "so long as its fulfillment does not work to the harm or discredit of my king, my country, or the lady who holds the key to my heart and will."

"It will not be to the discredit or harm of those your grace has mentioned, my good sir," said the sorrowful maiden.

At this moment Sancho Panza drew near his master and whispered into his ear,

"Your grace may safely grant the boon she's asking, which is just a trifle – she only wants you to kill an enormous giant, and the lady making this request is the exalted Princess Micomicona, queen of the great kingdom of Micomicón of Ethiopia."

"Regardless of who she is," said Don Quixote, "I shall do what I am obliged to do and what my conscience dictates in conformity with the oath I have sworn;" and turning to the damsel, he said,

"Arise, fair lady, and I shall grant the boon your ladyship seeks."

"What I have to request, your grace," said the damsel, "is that you in your magnanimity accompany me at once to where I shall take you and that you promise not to undertake any other adventure or pursuit whatever before exacting revenge upon a traitor who, contrary to every human and divine law, has usurped my kingdom."

"I hereby declare that I shall grant it," replied Don Quixote, "so that from this day forward your ladyship may throw off the melancholy that oppresses you and allow your faltering hopes to gather strength and courage, for with the help of God and my trusty arm you shall quickly see yourself restored to your kingdom and seated upon its ancient and mighty throne despite any and all scoundrels who might attempt to contravene it. Therefore, shoulders to the wheel, for they say there is danger in delay."

The damsel-in-distress made a great effort to kiss his hand but he, being the height of courtesy and politeness, would not permit it. Rather, he made her rise and embraced her most gentlemanly and courteously, ordering Sancho to check the cinches on Rocinante and then to help him don his armor. Sancho took down the armor, which had been hanging from a tree like a trophy and, after adjusting the cinches, had his master armed in an instant. Once Don Quixote saw himself in his armor, he said,

"Let us ride forth in the name of God to give assistance to this great lady."

The barber, who was still on his knees, made every effort to hold back his laughter and to make sure his beard did not fall off, for should that happen, they would in all likelihood be unable to go forward with their scheme. Seeing that the boon had been granted and observing the eagerness with which Don Quixote was preparing to carry it out, the barber stood up and took the lady by her other hand, whereupon the two men helped her to mount her mule. Don Quixote then seated himself on Rocinante and the barber settled himself on his own mount, while Sancho was left to travel on foot. Once again the loss of his dapple made itself keenly felt at this time but he bore it all cheerfully now that he felt his master was finally on his way to becoming an emperor, for he was absolutely certain Don Quixote would wed this princess and become, at the very least, king of Micomicón. His only concern was that his kingdom might be in the land of black people and all his vassals would be black but he immediately came up with a solution and said to himself,

"What difference will it make if my vassals *are* black? I can always load them up and carry them off to Spain, where I can sell them and get paid on the spot and with the money I can buy some title or office and live a life of ease for the rest of my days. Why, even in my sleep I'll be clever enough to conduct my business and will be able to sell thirty or even ten thousand vassals quicker than you can say 'scat'! By heavens, I'll sell them on the run, throwing in a kid with every adult or whatever will sell; and no matter how black they are, I'll turn them into silver and gold. So come and get 'em, everyone, you're dealing with a sucker!" With these thoughts he walked along so eager and content that he forgot his ordeal of having to travel on foot.

Cardenio and the priest observed all this from among some bushes but had no idea what to do in order to join them. The priest, however, who was a person of great expediency, came up with an idea for achieving their goal. With some scissors he kept in a carrying case, he hurriedly snipped off Cardenio's beard and had him put on a grey jacket he himself had been wearing, along with a black cape, leaving himself in only his breeches and jerkin. Cardenio's appearance was now so different he would not have recognized himself in a mirror. Though the riders had gotten a head start on those who stayed behind donning their disguises, the latter easily reached the main road first, for the underbrush and treacherous footing did not allow those on horseback to travel as easily as those on foot. They waited at the place where the hills opened onto the plain and, when Don Quixote and his companions emerged, the priest fixed his eyes upon him and showed signs of gradually recognizing him. Finally, after staring at him for quite some time, he walked towards him with outstretched arms and cried out,

"Well, if it isn't the mirror of chivalry, my worthy compatriot Don Quixote of La Mancha, flower and cream of nobility, refuge and balm of the needy, quintessence of knighthood!"

As he said this, he clasped the left knee of Don Quixote. The latter, astride Rocinante and in a state of shock from everything the man had said and done, began to stare at him and finally managed to recognize him. As if bewildered at the sight, he made a great effort to dismount but the priest would not permit it. When Don Quixote saw this, he said,

"Begging your grace's permission, sir licentiate, it is not meet for me to ride while so reverend a person as your grace is forced to walk."

"Under no circumstances, your worthiness, will I consent to that," said the priest. "You shall remain mounted, for in that way you will achieve the greatest feats and adventures ever witnessed in our time. As for myself, unworthy priest that I am, it will be sufficient for me to ride on the haunches of one of the mules of these gentlemen traveling with you if they are agreeable, and I shall fancy myself astride the steed Pegasus, or the zebra or stallion of the famous Moor Muzaraque, who even to this day lies enchanted beneath the large hill of Zulema, which is not far from the famed Complutum."

"I was not aware of all that, sir licentiate," responded Don Quixote, "but I do know that my lady the princess will be pleased, out of consideration for me, to have her squire allow your grace to occupy the saddle of his mule, and he can ride on its haunches if the mule will not mind."

"I am sure it will not," replied the princess. "I also know I shall not have to ask my squire to do so, for he is such a courteous gentleman he would never allow a man of the cloth to walk when he might ride."

"That's right," responded the barber, and dismounting at once, he invited the priest to take the saddle, which the latter did with very little urging. But an unfortunate incident occurred, for as soon as the barber had seated himself on the haunches, the mule, which was in fact a rented one – which is tantamount to saying that he was worthless – raised its hind hooves and unleashed a couple of kicks in the air. Had these made contact with Master Nicolás' chest or head, he would have cursed the day he had set out in quest of Don Quixote. As it was, he was so taken by surprise that he fell from the mule, and his beard, which he had forgotten to grab, fell off. Seeing himself beardless, he had no other recourse than to cover his face with both hands while moaning that several of his teeth had been knocked out. When Don Quixote saw the clump of beard lying at some distance from the fallen squire without a trace of blood or skin on it, he exclaimed,

"My goodness, this is an absolute miracle! His beard has been torn from his face as cleanly as if it had been shaved off."

Seeing the danger that threatened to reveal their scheme, the priest quickly picked up the beard and went over to Master Nicolás, who was lying on the ground still moaning. With one motion he pressed the barber's head against his own chest and muttered certain words over him, which he said were a type of incantation for reattaching beards, as they would all see. Once it was reattached, he drew back and the barber turned out as sound and nicely bearded as before. Don Quixote was so completely astonished at this that he begged the priest to teach him that incantation at his earliest opportunity, for it was his belief that its virtue must extend beyond the mere attaching of beards, since it was obvious that where the beard had been ripped off, the skin should have been torn and bleeding but everything had been made whole again, proving it to be beneficial for more things than simply beards.

"And so it is," said the priest, promising to teach it to him at their first opportunity. They agreed that for the present the priest would ride and the three of them would take turns riding until they reached the inn, which was some two leagues away. Once the three were seated on their mounts – namely, Don Quixote, the princess, and the priest – and the other three were traveling on foot – namely, Cardenio, the barber, and Sancho Panza – Don Quixote said to the damsel,

"My lady, your grace may lead wherever you so desire."

Before she could respond, the licentiate spoke up:

"And towards which kingdom, my lady, do you wish to lead us? Could it possibly be that of Micomicón? That is certainly the one or I know very little about kingdoms."

Being privy to everything, she understood she was to agree and thus replied,

"Yes, my lord, that is the very kingdom I am headed for."

"If that is our destination," said the priest, "we shall pass right through my town and from there your grace will take the road to Cartagena, where you can embark with heaven's blessing and, if there is a favorable wind, a calm sea, and no storms, in slightly less than nine years you will come into sight of the great lagoon of Meona, [1] I mean Meótides, from where it is slightly more than a hundred days journey to your highness' kingdom."

"Your grace is mistaken," she replied, "for it was scarcely two years ago that I embarked, and

1 Spanish: 'urination.'

despite our constant lack of good weather I have been fortunate enough to locate the object of my quest, which is his grace Don Quixote of la Mancha, news of whom reached my ears the moment I set foot in Spain, making me set out in search of him so I might commend myself to his civility and entrust my vindication to the might of his invincible arm."

"Please, no more praise," protested Don Quixote at this point, "I am averse to every sort of adulation, and though what your grace says may be true, such statements are offensive to my undefiled ears. What I can state, my lady, is that whether my arm is mighty or not, whatever might it does possess shall be employed in your ladyship's service until the day I perish. But reserving this for its proper time, I beg his grace the licentiate to tell me what circumstances have brought him to these parts so alone and unattended – not to mention ill-provisioned – that it is simply frightful."

"I shall briefly respond to that, Sir Don Quixote," said the priest. "Your grace probably knows that I and Master Nicolás, our friend and barber, were on our way to Seville to collect a certain sum of money sent to me by a relative of mine who had gone to the Indies a number of years ago, and it amounted to more than sixty thousand *pesos* in bullion, a not insignificant sum. As we were passing through these parts yesterday, we were set upon by four highwaymen who robbed us of everything, including our beards, which they removed so thoroughly that the barber thought it advisable for us to put on false ones. Even this young man" – and here he indicated Cardenio – "has been transformed into a different person. The strange thing, though, is that it is public knowledge throughout this region that those who waylaid us were certain galley slaves who, they say, were set free virtually on this very spot by a man who was so brave that, despite the commissary and the guards, he freed every last one of them. Undoubtedly he must have been out of his mind or else must be as big a scoundrel as any in existence, or a person who has no soul or conscience, for he was willing to set loose the wolf among the sheep, the fox among the hens, and the fly among the honeycombs; he was willing to subvert justice and disobey his king by going against His Majesty's just authority; he was willing, I might add, to deprive the galleys of their manpower and to stir up the Holy Brotherhood, which has been dormant for lo these many years. And lastly, he was willing to commit an act that will cost him his soul and will not save him his body."

Since Sancho had described to the priest and the barber the adventure of the galley slaves, which his master had concluded with so much glory to himself, the priest made a big to-do in referring to it to see what Don Quixote might say or do. The latter's face grew redder with each word but he dared not admit that he had been the liberator of those fine souls.

"Those, then," said the priest, "were the people who robbed us and may God in His infinite mercy forgive the one who kept them from receiving their just punishment."

Chapter Thirty

The ingenuity of the beautiful Dorotea, together with other delightful and entertaining matters

The priest had barely concluded when Sancho said,

"Upon my word, sir licentiate, the one who performed that deed was my master and not because I didn't warn him beforehand to mind what he was doing, being as how it was a sin to set free all those men who were there for being such very great troublemakers."

"You blockhead!" said Don Quixote at this point, "it is not the business or concern of a knight-errant to determine whether those persons he encounters on the highways who are afflicted, oppressed, and in chains are traveling in that wretched manner and condition because of their sins or their bad luck. His only obligation is to aid them as persons in need, focusing upon their suffering rather than their wickedness. I came across a veritable rosary of dejected, hapless souls and did for them what my religion demands of me. Anything beyond that is of no concern to me, and anyone who thinks I erred, except his worthy holiness the honorable licentiate, I maintain does not know much about this business of knight-errantry and is a lying, lowborn son of a whore, and my sword and I will show him the facts of the case."

As he said this, he secured himself in the stirrups and simultaneously clapped his helmet down over his head, for the barber's basin, which according to *his* reckoning was Mambrino's helmet, had been hanging from the front pommel waiting to be repaired for the mistreatment it had suffered at the hands of the galley slaves. By now the intelligent and clever Dorotea was aware of Don Quixote's lack of wits and the fact that everyone was making him the butt of their jokes except Sancho Panza, and since she was a clever, fun-loving woman, she was unwilling to be left out of the fun. When she saw him become angry, she said,

"Sir knight, may your grace remember the boon you have promised me, in conformance with which you may not undertake any other adventure, regardless of its urgency. You must temper your anger, for had the good licentiate known the galley slaves were freed by your invincible arm, he would have sealed his lips and bitten his tongue before saying a disparaging word about your grace."

"That is the absolute truth," said the priest, "and I would even have ripped off half of my mustache."

"I shall seal my lips, your ladyship," replied Don Quixote, "and suppress the justifiable anger that arose in my breast, remaining calm and peaceful until such time that I fulfill the boon I have promised your grace, but in exchange for this request I would have you describe, if it is not too painful to do so, the nature of your distress and the identity and number of persons from whom I am to exact complete and justifiable retribution for your grace's satisfaction."

"I shall gladly do so," responded Dorotea, "if it will not be tiresome for your lordship to listen to my woes and misfortunes."

"It will not, my lady," said Don Quixote; to which Dorotea responded,

"Well then, with that stipulation, may I have your graces' attention."

No sooner had she said this than Cardenio and the barber caught up with her, eager to hear what sort of story the clever Dorotea would devise. Sancho did the same, being as thoroughly deceived by her as was his master. After accommodating herself on the saddle, clearing her throat, and going through some preliminary gestures, she began to speak in the following eloquent manner:

"First of all, good sirs, I would have you know that my name is — " and here she hesitated briefly, having forgotten the name the priest had assigned her, but because he realized the reason for her hesitation, he came to her rescue and said,

"Your highness, it is not surprising that you might be confused and upset at recounting your misfortunes, for these are often of such a nature that they cause those afflicted to lose their memories and even to forget their own names, as they have done in the case of your grace, since you have forgotten you are the Princess Micomicona, lawful heiress to the great kingdom of Micomicón. With this prompting you may easily revive in your sorrowful memory everything you wish to relate."

"That is precisely what happened," said the damsel, "and hereafter I shall not need prompting, for I shall safely reach port with my true story, which is that my father the king, Tinacrio the Wise, who was quite adept at the so-called magic arts, foresaw by means of his science that my mother, Queen Jaramilla by name, was to precede him in death and that shortly thereafter he too would depart this life, leaving me orphaned without a father or mother. But as upsetting as that was, he said he was sorely grieved by the certain knowledge that an enormous giant, lord of a large island that virtually abuts our kingdom, whose name is Pandafilando of the Sullen Look, for it is an established fact that though his eyes are straight and in their proper places, he always looks askew as if he were cross-eyed, and this out of malice to frighten those he looks at – my father learned, I say, that as soon as this giant discovered I was an orphan, he would overrun my kingdom with a large army and would strip it of everything, not leaving a single village in which I could take refuge. I might avoid all that ruin and misery if I were willing to marry him but it was my father's considered opinion that I would never agree to such a one-sided marriage, and in this he spoke the truth, for it has never entered my head to marry that giant or any other, regardless of how enormous he might be. My father also said that once he had departed this life and I saw Pandafilando advancing towards my kingdom, I was to make no attempt to set up a defense, which would be my undoing, but was to let him freely enter my open kingdom if I wished to prevent the death and total destruction of all my good and faithful vassals, as it would be impossible to defend myself against the giant's diabolical might. Instead, I was to gather together a number of my subjects and set out for Spain, where I would find the remedy for my ills in the person of a knight-errant whose fame at that time would extend throughout that kingdom and whose name would be, if I remember correctly, Don Azote or Don Jigote."

"My lady," said Sancho Panza at this point, "he probably said 'Don Quixote,' otherwise known as the Knight of the Woeful Countenance."

"That is what he said," replied Dorotea, "and he added that he would be tall of stature and would have a lean face and a dark mole with some bristle-like hairs in it on his right side below his left shoulder or thereabouts."

When he heard this, Don Quixote said to his squire,

"Come here, Sancho my son, and help me undress. I want to see if I am the knight that wise king designated in his prophecy."

"But why does your grace wish to undress?" asked Dorotea.

"To see if I possess that mole your grace's father mentioned," replied Don Quixote.

"There is no need to undress," said Sancho, "for I know your grace has a mole of that description in the middle of your back, and moles, as we know, are a sign of strength."

"That is sufficient," replied Dorotea, "for among friends one may overlook trifles. Whether it is on your grace's shoulder or in the middle of your back is of slight importance. So long as there *is* a mole, it may be anywhere at all, for it is one and the same flesh. Undoubtedly, my good father was correct in every regard and I was right in commending myself to Sir Don Quixote, who is the very one my father spoke of, for the description of his face matches the great reputation this knight enjoys not only in Spain but in all La Mancha. No sooner had I landed at Osuna than I heard mention of so many of his accomplishments that my heart told me this was the very person I had come in search of."

"How is it that your ladyship landed at Osuna," asked Don Quixote, "when that is not a port city?"

Before Dorotea could respond, the priest stepped in and said,

"The princess probably meant to say that after she landed at Málaga, Osuna was the first place in which she received news of your grace."

"That is what I meant," said Dorotea.

"And that makes sense," replied the priest. "Now, if your majesty will be so kind as to continue."

"There is no need to continue," replied Dorotea; "let me just add that my fortune has taken such a favorable turn by my having located Sir Don Quixote that I already reckon and consider myself queen and mistress of my entire kingdom, for, owing to his courtesy and largesse, he has promised me the boon of accompanying me wherever I wish to take him, which will be nothing less than to bring him face to face with Pandafilando of the Sullen Look, that he may slay him and restore to me what that one has so unjustly usurped. All this will turn out exactly as was prophesied by Tinacrio the Wise, my noble father, who also left a prediction written in Chaldean or Greek characters, which I am unable to read, that if the knight of this prediction should desire to marry me after slitting the giant's throat, I without hesitation should immediately offer myself to him as his lawful wife and grant him possession of my kingdom as well as my person."

"What do you think of that, friend Sancho?" said Don Quixote at this point. "Do you see what is happening? Did I not tell you so? Ask yourself now whether we have a kingdom to rule and a queen to marry!"

"I'll say we do!" replied Sancho, "and may the devil take the rascal who refuses to get married after slitting old Pandahilado's gullet! And the queen is not bad either, if I do say so myself; in fact, the fleas in my bed should be so good!"

As he said this, he leapt into the air a couple of times and clicked his heels together as a sign of his unbridled joy. He then took the reins of Dorotea's mule and brought it to a halt, at which point he knelt before her and asked permission to kiss her hand as a token of his allegiance to her as his queen and mistress. Who among those present could contain their laughter when they saw the master's lunacy and the squire's simplemindedness? As it was, Dorotea held out her hand, promising to make him a grandee in her kingdom the moment heaven saw fit to permit her to regain and enjoy it. Sancho thanked her so effusively that it rekindled everyone's laughter.

"That, gentlemen, is my story," said Dorotea. "I merely wish to add that, of all those in my retinue that I brought from my kingdom, the only one remaining is this full-bearded squire, for the rest were drowned in a fierce storm we experienced in sight of port. He and I miraculously made land by clinging to a pair of planks and the entire direction of my life has been just as miraculous and mysterious, as your graces will have noted. If I have exaggerated anything or stretched the truth more than I should have, it may be blamed upon what the licentiate mentioned at the inception of my story – that continual and extraordinary labors cause a loss of memory in those who undergo them."

"They shall not cause me to lose mine, O exalted and courageous lady," replied Don Quixote, "however many I undergo in your grace's service or however great and unusual they may be! I reaffirm the boon I have promised you and vow to accompany you to the ends of the earth until I see myself face to face with that terrible antagonist of yours, whose proud head I intend, with the help of God and my arm, to chop off with the blade of this . . . I hesitate to say *good* sword, thanks to Ginés de Pasamonte, who made off with mine." This he muttered under his breath and then continued to speak. "Once I have cut it off and placed you in peaceful possession of your kingdom, it shall be your prerogative to dispose of your own person as you see fit, for so long as my memory is active, my will captive, and I bereft of my senses because of that other lady . . . but I shall say no more because it is impossible for me to consider or even to contemplate marriage, though it were with the Phoenix herself."

Sancho was so exasperated by what his master had just said about refusing to wed that he raised his voice in anger and said,

"I swear and affirm, Master Don Quixote, you are out of your mind! How is it possible for your grace to entertain any doubts about marrying a princess as exalted as this one? Do you think fate will offer you one at every turn like the one you're being offered now? Is my Lady Dulcinea more beautiful by chance? No, certainly not – not even half as beautiful. I dare say she doesn't even come up to the heel of the one we have here before us. It'll be a cold day before I get the earldom I'm seeking if your grace goes about grasping for the moon. You should get married at once (or you can go to the devil!) and accept this kingdom that's being offered you just for the asking, and when you become king, you can make me marquis or governor and everything else can go to blazes!"

Don Quixote was unable to tolerate such blasphemies against his lady Dulcinea, and so, raising his pike and without so much as a word to Sancho, he unleashed a couple of blows that knocked him to the ground and had it not been for Dorotea's shouting at him not to strike him again, he would no doubt have taken his life right there. Then after a moment of silence Don Quixote said,

"Do you think, you lowly peasant, that you can insult me whenever you feel like it and I shall simply ignore your offense? Well, don't count on it, you irreparable scoundrel, which is what you are, since you have defamed the peerless Dulcinea. Do you not know, you rube, you errand boy, you rogue, that if it were not for the strength that she infuses in my arm, I would not be able to kill a flea? Tell me, you fox with a viper's tongue, who do you think won this kingdom and cut off the giant's head and made you a marquis – all of which I consider already accomplished and duly acknowledged – if not the courage of Dulcinea utilizing my arm as the instrument of her deeds? She goes into battle through me and conquers through me and I live and breathe and have my being in her. You conniving son of a whore, how can you be so ungrateful? Here you are raised up from the dirt of the earth to be a titled lord and you repay me for such a noble deed by speaking ill of the lady who is responsible for all this!"

Sancho's injury was not so severe that he did not hear everything his master said to him, at which point he sprang to his feet and quickly sought refuge behind Dorotea's palfrey, from where he said to his master,

"I would like to know something, master: if your grace has decided not to marry this great princess, it is obvious the kingdom won't be yours and, if that happens, what favors can you bestow upon me? That is what I'm complaining of. Your grace should marry this queen once and for all, now that we have her here like a gift from heaven and afterwards you can take Dulcinea as your mistress, for there must have been plenty of kings in the world who have had mistresses. Now, as to which one is more beautiful, that's something I'm not getting involved in, though to tell the truth, I think they're both nice even if I've never seen the lady Dulcinea."

"What do you mean you have never seen her, you blasphemous traitor? Did you not just bring me a message from her?"

"I mean," said Sancho, "that I didn't look at her long enough to take special note of her beauty or individual charms, but taking her as a whole, I thought she looked nice."

"Well, I forgive you," replied Don Quixote, "and I hope you will forgive me for becoming so angry at you. One's first impulse is not always under his control."

"So I see," said Sancho, "and in the same way that my desire to speak is always *my* first impulse, I can't keep from saying, if only just once, what is on my mind."

"Still, Sancho, you must mind what you say, for 'You can carry the pitcher to the well one time too many' – but I shall say no more."

"Well," said Sancho, "since God in heaven sees both sides, He will be the judge of which of us is behaving worse – me in not saying the right thing or your grace in not doing the right thing."

"That will do," said Dorotea. "Go to your master, Sancho, kiss his hand and ask his forgiveness, and in the future be more judicious in your praise and condemnation by not speaking ill of that lady of Toboso, whom I do not know but at whose disposal I place myself. Finally, put your trust in God, who will not fail to give you a kingdom in which you can live like a prince."

Sancho approached with his head bowed and asked for his master's hand. Don Quixote held it out with an air of severity and, after Sancho had kissed it, gave him his blessing, asking him to ride ahead with him, as he had several matters of great importance to discuss with him. Sancho did as ordered and, when they were both some distance ahead of the others, Don Quixote said to him,

"Since your return, I have had neither the opportunity nor the time to inquire into the details of your mission or the reply you have brought back. Now that fate has provided us this occasion and opportunity, do not deny me the happiness you can give me with your good news."

"Ask whatever you will," said Sancho, "and I'll try to make it turn out as well as it began but I beg your grace not to be so vindictive in the future."

"Why do you bring that up, Sancho?" asked Don Quixote.

"I bring it up because this beating just now is due more to the quarrel the Devil raised between us the other night than to what I said against my lady Dulcinea, whom I love and revere as a holy relic – which, of course, she's not – just because she's associated with your grace."

"If you know what is good for you, Sancho, you will not bring that up again because I find it upsetting. I have already forgiven you for that and you know what they say: 'A new sin requires a new penance.'" [1]

[*While this was taking place, they saw coming down the road in their direction a man riding an ass, who, once he drew near, appeared to be a gypsy. Sancho, whose heart and soul ached each time he saw a jackass, no sooner saw the man than he recognized him as Ginés de Pasamonte and by following the thread, which was the gypsy, he arrived at the ball of yarn, which was the donkey, for Ginés de Pasamonte was indeed riding Sancho's very own dapple. To avoid being recognized and to be able to sell the donkey, Ginés had dressed himself in the outfit of a gypsy, whose language among others he spoke like a native. As soon as Sancho saw and recognized him, he began to shout,*

"Stop, Ginesillo, you thief! Release my darling, my life, my repose, my jewel – my donkey! Give up what is not yours and get out of here, you thieving pimp!"

There was no need of so many words and insults, for at the first one Ginés jumped off and ran at a trot that more nearly resembled a sprint, disappearing from sight in a flash and leaving everyone far behind. Sancho went up to his dapple and embraced him, saying,

"How have you been, my love, dapple of my eye, my dearest companion?"

And here he kissed and caressed him as though he were actually a person. The donkey remained silent, allowing himself to be kissed and caressed without saying a word. Everyone came over and congratulated Sancho for having found his dapple, Don Quixote in particular, who told him this would not void the certificate for the three colts, for which Sancho expressed his appreciation.]

While the two were engaged in this conversation, the priest told Dorotea she had comported herself most ingeniously not only in her story but in its brevity and the resemblance it bore to those of books of chivalry. She replied that she had often entertained herself by reading them but did not know where the provinces and seaports were and because of that had gropingly come up with Osuna.

"That is what I thought had happened," said the priest, "for which reason I interrupted to say what I did, with the result that everything worked out fine. But is it not amazing to see how easily this woe-begone knight believes all these fabrications and untruths just because they bear the stamp and imprint of the absurdities of his books?"

"It is," replied Cardenio, "and it is so strange and unheard-of that if one wished to invent or fabricate such a thing purely out of his imagination, he would never be ingenious enough to do so."

"There is something else I have noticed," added the priest: "apart from the foolish comments this

---

1 The following passage in italics was omitted from the first edition and appears only from the second edition onwards.

worthy gentleman makes in conjunction with his madness, if one discusses other topics with him, he converses quite rationally and displays a mind that is clear and completely untrammeled. So long as one does not touch upon knight-errantry, no one would judge him to be anything but a man of sound mind."

While they were engaged in this conversation, Don Quixote continued with his own, saying to Sancho,

"Panza my friend, let's let bygones be bygones concerning our disagreements. Tell me, putting aside all anger and bitterness, how, when, and where did you find Dulcinea? How was she occupied and what did she say to you? How did she look when she read my letter? Who copied it for you? along with anything else you might think of that would be worth knowing, inquiring about, or being informed of, without adding or falsifying anything to give me pleasure or omitting anything to deprive me of it."

"To tell the truth, master," said Sancho, "the letter wasn't copied by anyone because I didn't have any letter to copy."

"It is just as you say," said Don Quixote, "for, a couple of days after you left I found the memorandum book in which I had written it and that caused me considerable consternation because I did not know what you would do when you failed to find the letter. I always thought you would return here as soon as you found it missing."

"That's what I would have done," said Sancho, "had I not committed it to memory when your grace read it to me. So I repeated it to a sacristan, who copied it the way I remembered it point by point and he said that of the countless letters of excommunication he had read, never in all the days of his life had he seen or read a letter as fine as your grace's."

"And do you still have it in your memory, Sancho?"

"No, master," replied Sancho, "once I dictated it, I saw it would be of no further benefit, so I promptly forgot it; but if there is one thing I do remember, it is the opening, which said, '*Exhausted Lady*,' I mean, '*Exalted Lady*,' and then the closing: '*Thine until death, The Knight of the Woeful Countenance,*' and between these two parts I threw in more than three hundred expressions of love, tenderness, and endearment."

Chapter Thirty-One

The delightful conversation between Don Quixote and his squire Sancho Panza, together with other incidents

"I find nothing displeasing up to this point," said Don Quixote, "so do continue. When you arrived, what was that vision of loveliness doing? I dare say you found her stringing pearls or embroidering some heraldic device with gold thread for this her captive knight."

"I found her," replied Sancho, "simply winnowing a couple of bushels of wheat in the courtyard of her house."

"Well, rest assured," said Don Quixote, "that the grains from that wheat were pearls, having been touched by her hands. Did you notice, my friend, whether it was white or brown wheat?"

"It was neither one but was red," answered Sancho.

"Well, you may take my word for it," said Don Quixote, "that having been winnowed by her hands, it would have made white bread without question. But do proceed; when you gave her my letter, did she kiss it or clasp it to her bosom? Did she perform some ceremony due such a letter, or what did she do?"

"As I was about to hand it to her," replied Sancho, "she had the sieve in her hands and was chasing after a goodly portion of wheat she had tossed into the air. She said, 'Put the letter on that sack, my friend. I can't read it till I finish sifting everything I've got here.'"

"A wise lady!" said Don Quixote. "That was probably so she could read it slowly and savor it at her leisure. But continue, Sancho; while she was about her task, what topics did she discuss with you? What did she ask you about me, and what did you answer? Hurry and tell me everything and don't leave a drop in the inkwell."

"She didn't ask me anything," replied Sancho, "but I told her how your grace, in order to serve her, was performing your penance bare from the waist up, buried in these hills like some savage, sleeping on the ground, eating your meals without benefit of a tablecloth, not combing your beard, and sobbing and cursing your fate."

"In saying that I was cursing my fate you misspoke," said Don Quixote; "on the contrary, I am grateful and shall remain so all the days of my life for having been worthy to merit the love of so lofty a lady as Dulcinea of Toboso."

"She *is* lofty," said Sancho; "in fact, she's a good handspan taller than me."

"How do you know, Sancho?" asked Don Quixote. "Did you measure yourself against her?"

"I measured her in this manner," replied Sancho: "as I approached to help her load a sack of wheat onto an ass, we drew so close together I noticed she was more than a handspan taller than me."

"And is her stature not matched and adorned by a thousand million graces of the soul?" said Don Quixote. "There is one thing you will not deny, Sancho: when you drew near her, did you not notice a Sabaean aroma, a certain aromatic fragrance, something nice that I can't quite find a name for? – I mean, an aroma or scent like those in the shops of exotic glove makers."

"All I can say," said Sancho, "is that I detected a slightly masculine odor, which must have been due to all her exertion, for she was covered with sweat and looked rather leathery."

"It could not have been that," responded Don Quixote; "you must have had a head cold or, more likely, were probably smelling yourself, for I am well acquainted with the scent of that rose among thorns, that lily of the valley, that pool of amber."

"Anything is possible," said Sancho, "for my own body often gives off the same odor that seemed to be coming from the lady Dulcinea's but that's not surprising, since we are all brothers under the skin."

"Well then," said Don Quixote, "after she finished winnowing the wheat and sent it off to the mill, what did she do when she read the letter?"

"She never read the letter," said Sancho, "because she said she couldn't read or write. Instead, she tore it into tiny pieces, saying she refused to give it to anyone to read lest her secrets become known in the village; that she was satisfied with what I had verbally told her of your grace's love for her and the extraordinary penance you were performing on her behalf. Finally, she asked me to tell you that she kisses your hand and will remain at home more desirous to see you than to write you. She begs and implores you, once you're in receipt of this message, to abandon these wilds, stop doing these crazy things, and set out for Toboso absolutely at once unless some other matter of greater importance should intervene, for she is most anxious to see you. She laughed for quite some time when I told her your grace was called the Knight of the Woeful Countenance. I asked her if the Biscayan from a while back had gone there and she said he had and was quite a decent sort. I also asked her about the galley slaves but she said that up till then she hadn't seen a single one."

"So far, so good," said Don Quixote, "but tell me: what jewel did she bestow upon you when she bid you adieu in payment for the news you had brought her? For it is an ancient and honored custom among knights- and ladies-errant to give their squires, handmaidens, and dwarves who bring them news from their ladies or knights some expensive jewel as a token of their appreciation of the message."

"That may well be true, and if it is, I consider it a worthy custom, but it must be a thing of the past. Today it seems to be the custom to reward them with some bread and cheese, which is what my lady Dulcinea handed me over the courtyard wall when I took my leave of her, and what's more, it was sheep's cheese."

"She is generous in the extreme," said Don Quixote, "and if she did not give you a precious jewel, it must have been that she had none at hand, but any gift is better than none at all. When I see her, everything shall be taken care of; but, Sancho, do you know what astonishes me? It would appear that your trip there and back must have been through the air, for you took only slightly more than three days going and coming from Toboso, which is more than thirty leagues from here. By this, I conclude that the wise necromancer who has assumed responsibility for my affairs and is my friend – and there must be one or I would not be a legitimate knight-errant – that necromancer, I say, must have assisted you on your journey without your sensing it. One of those magicians can snatch a knight-errant from the bed in which he is sleeping and have him wake the next morning over a thousand leagues from where he went to sleep without knowing how it came about. If such were not the case, knights would not be able to aid one another when they are in danger, which they do at every turn, for one may be fighting a dragon in the mountains of Armenia, or a fierce serpent or another knight, where he is getting the worst of the fray and is on the verge of expiring, when suddenly at that most unexpected moment, there appears, riding on a cloud or a chariot of fire, another knight – a friend of his – who a short while earlier found himself in England. This knight will join him in battle and deliver him from the jaws of death and night will find him in his own home dining most leisurely; and usually from one place to the other is a distance of two or three thousand leagues. Since all this is accomplished by the cunning and arts of those wise enchanters who watch over us valiant knights, I have no difficulty believing, Sancho my friend, that you traveled in such a short time from this place to Toboso and back, for as I have said, some friendly sage must have transported you through the air without your being aware of it."

"That's how it must've been," said Sancho, "for Rocinante did run as though he were a gypsy's mount with quicksilver in his ears."

"Not only quicksilver," said Don Quixote, "but a legion of demons besides, for gypsies are people who not only travel huge distances themselves without becoming fatigued but can make anyone they choose do the same. But setting all this aside, what do you think I should do about going to see my lady, as she has bade me do? Even though I find myself obliged to carry out her command, I find it impossible because of the boon I have promised the princess traveling with us, for the code of chivalry demands that I fulfill my duty before attending to my personal concerns. On the one hand I am hounded and harassed by my desire to see my lady, while on the other I am driven by the promise I have made and the fame I shall achieve in this undertaking. What I intend to do is to travel as swiftly as possible to reach the giant's domain, whereupon I shall cut off his head and install the princess peacefully on her throne. Then I shall return to view that light who illumines my senses, to whom I shall offer such an explanation that she will come to consider my delay beneficial because she will see that it all redounds to the increase of her glory and fame, for everything I win in this life by the might of my arm accrues to me from the favors she shows me and from the fact that I am hers."

"Mercy!" exclaimed Sancho, "your grace's brains are in worse shape than I thought. I would like to know, master, whether you intend to make this trip for nothing, allowing such a lucrative and eminent marriage to slip through your fingers whereby you are being offered as a dowry a kingdom that is reliably said to measure more than twenty thousand leagues around, has an abundance of everything necessary for the sustenance of human life, and is larger than Portugal and Castile combined. For the love of God, may you not utter a word but bite your tongue for what you have just said and, if I may say so, get married in the first village that has a priest and, if one is not available, we always have our licentiate here who can perform the ceremony admirably. You should also be advised that I am old enough to give advice, and the advice I am giving your grace fits like a glove, for 'A bird in the hand is worth two in the bush,' and 'Whoever has what is good but chooses what is bad should not count his chickens.'"

"Look, Sancho," said Don Quixote, "if you are advising me to wed after I kill the giant so I shall become king and can grant you favors and give you what I have promised, I assure you that without marrying I shall be able to comply with your wishes quite easily. I shall stipulate before engaging in battle that, once victorious, even if I do not wed, I am to be granted part of the kingdom and shall then give it to whomever I choose; and when they have given it to me, upon whom do you wish me to bestow it if not upon you?"

"That is obvious," said Sancho, "but I hope your grace will choose a part that borders on the sea so that if the living conditions should prove unsatisfactory, I can load up my black subjects and dispose of them in the manner I've indicated. For the present, though, I wish your grace would not go to the trouble of visiting my lady Dulcinea but would go kill the giant so we can finish this business, for there's no doubt in my mind that it will bring us both honor and profit."

"I assure you, Sancho," said Don Quixote, "that you are right on the mark and I shall heed your advice and accompany the princess before going to see Dulcinea. I am also warning you not to discuss anything we have spoken of here with anyone, including those traveling with us, for Dulcinea is so modest she would not want her thoughts made public, nor would it be right for me or anyone acting on my behalf to divulge them."

"Well, if that's the case," replied Sancho, "how is it that your grace makes everyone you overcome by your prowess present himself to my lady Dulcinea, which is tantamount to signing a statement to the effect that you are in love with her and are her suitor? And since it's necessary for those who make the trip to get down on their knees in her presence and announce that they are there on your grace's behalf to show their respect, how is it possible to hide what you both have on your minds?"

"Oh, how foolish and naive you are!" said Don Quixote. "Do you not see, Sancho, that all this redounds to her greater glory? You should know that in this chivalry business it is a great honor for a lady to have in her service a number of knights-errant whose thoughts extend no further than serving her simply because of who she is and with no other expectation of reward for their many noble services than for her to accept them as her knights."

"Speaking of that kind of love," said Sancho, "I've heard priests say we should love Our Lord for Himself alone and not be moved by the hope of salvation or the fear of punishment, though I'd prefer to love and serve Him for what He could do for me."

"You are some kind of peasant!" said Don Quixote. "At times you say such wise things one simply has to believe you have been to school."

"Well, I give your grace my word that I don't even know how to read," replied Sancho.

At that moment Master Nicolás shouted for them to wait for the others, who wanted to stop for a drink at a nearby spring. Don Quixote drew to a halt, which afforded Sancho no little satisfaction, as he was now exhausted from telling so many lies and was afraid his master might catch him in one, for even though he knew Dulcinea was a farm girl from Toboso, he had never seen her in his entire life.

During this interval Cardenio donned the clothes Dorotea had been wearing when they found her and, though they were not very good ones, they were superior to those he had taken off. They dismounted beside the spring, where with the food the priest had brought from the inn they appeased, albeit poorly, the ravenous appetites they all had. While they were thus occupied, a lad chanced to pass by who was traveling on the same road and he began to stare hard at those who were gathered at the spring. A moment later he rushed up to Don Quixote, grabbed him round his leg and began sobbing quite deliberately.

"My lord," said the lad, "doesn't your grace know who I am? If you will look at me closely, you will see that I am Andrés, the servant your grace released from the oak tree to which I was tied."

As soon as Don Quixote recognized him, he took hold of his hand, turned to everyone present, and said,

"So that your graces may see how important it is to have knights-errant in the world to right the wrongs and injustices committed by the evil, insolent men who inhabit it, you should know that several days ago, as I was riding through a forest, I heard the most pitiful shouts and cries, as of someone in pain and distress. Urged on by my duty, I hurried to the spot from where the lamentable cries seemed to come and found this lad tied to a tree. My heart is now gladdened in that he may serve as proof that I shall never permit myself to tell a falsehood. But as I was saying, he was tied to a tree bare from the waist up and a farmer, who I later learned was his master, was flaying him with the reins from one of his mares. When I saw that, I asked him the reason for such a flogging and that churlish individual said he was whipping him because he was his servant and possessed certain careless traits that sprang more from thievery than from stupidity; to which this child cried out, 'He's whipping me only because I'm asking for my wages.' His master replied with some sort of excuses and alibis, which, though heard by me, were not accepted. In short, I made him untie the lad and got the rude fellow to give me his word to take Andrés with him and pay him every last real, all perfumed and scented. Is not every bit of this true, Andrés my son? You no doubt noticed with what authority I demanded it of him and with what humility he promised to do everything I imposed, stipulated, and insisted upon. Speak up without hesitation or fear; tell these gentlemen what happened so they can see and appreciate how beneficial it is, as I have said, to have knights-errant on the highways."

"Everything your grace has said is absolutely true," replied the lad, "but the affair turned out quite differently from what your grace imagines."

"What do you mean quite differently," asked Don Quixote? "did the brute not pay you?"

"Not only did he not pay me," said the boy, "but as soon as your grace left the forest and we were alone, he tied me to the same tree again, where he flogged me so severely I was skinned alive like another St. Bartholomew, and with each stroke that he delivered, he made some joke or insult about having made a fool of your grace; and if I had not been in so much pain, I would've had to laugh myself. In fact, he left me in such pitiful shape that I've been in a hospital all this time recuperating from the injuries I suffered at the hands of that evil peasant, all of which your grace is responsible for. If you had continued on your way and not intervened where you were not wanted – butting into other people's affairs – my master would have been content to give me one or two dozen lashes and would then have turned me loose and paid me everything he owed me, but because you insulted him in such uncalled-for terms and said so many vile things to him, he became filled with rage and, since he couldn't take revenge on your grace, once he saw himself alone with me, he unleashed such a storm on me that I don't think I'll be whole again for as long as I live."

"The harm was done," said Don Quixote, "by my going away, for I should have stayed until you were paid; besides, I should have known perfectly well from long experience that there is no peasant who will keep his word as he has sworn to do if he considers it to his advantage not to do so. But you do remember, Andrés, the oath I swore that, if he did not pay you, I would hunt him down and find him even if he hid in the belly of the whale."

"That's very true," said Andrés, "but it didn't do any good."

"You shall now see whether it will do any good," replied Don Quixote, and in saying this, he rose with great haste and ordered Sancho to bridle Rocinante, who had been grazing while they were having their meal. Dorotea asked him what he intended to do; to which he responded that he intended to go in search of that peasant, despite all the peasants in the world, to punish him for such churlish behavior by making him pay Andrés every last *maravedí*. She reminded him that in compliance with the boon he had promised her he might not engage in any other undertaking before dispensing with hers and, since he knew that better than anyone else, he should curb his passion until he returned from her kingdom.

"That is true," said Don Quixote, "and so it is imperative that Andrés be patient until I return, as your ladyship has pointed out, but I hereby renew my vow and oath not to rest until he is avenged and has received his pay."

"I have no faith in those oaths," said Andrés. "I would rather have the things I need for going to Seville than all the vengeance in the world. Just give me something to eat and wear, if you have anything, and I'll pray for you and all knights-errant, that they may all be as helpful to one another as your grace has been to me."

Sancho drew from his reserve a piece of bread and another of cheese and, giving them to the lad, said,

"Take these, Andrés my son, for we all share in your misfortune."

"And what part do you share in?" asked Andrés.

"This cheese and bread I'm giving you," said Sancho, "for God knows how much I'll miss them. I want you to know, my friend, that we squires who serve knights-errant are subject to extreme hunger and misfortune and even other things that are more easily experienced than talked about."

Andrés snatched his bread and cheese and, seeing that he would receive nothing more, bowed to them and 'hit the road,' as they say. Now it is quite true that as he was leaving, he said to Don Quixote,

"For the love of God, sir knight, if you ever meet me again, though you should see me being torn to pieces, will you please not aid or assist me but leave me to my misery, which won't be as great as what I'll get with your help – and may God curse you and all the other knights-errant who have ever been born into this world."

Don Quixote was about to stand up to chastise him but the lad scampered away so quickly that no one attempted to go after him. Our knight was extremely embarrassed by Andrés' story and everyone present had to make a special effort not to laugh out loud lest he be completely humiliated.

Chapter Thirty-Two

The things that happened in the inn To Don Quixote and all those in his party

Once they had finished their 'fine' meal, they saddled their mounts and the following day, nothing noteworthy having happened to them, reached the inn that was the fear and dread of Sancho Panza, who dared not go inside but neither could he avoid doing so. The innkeeper, his wife and daughter, and Maritornes saw them coming and went out to greet them with a great display of joy but were received by Don Quixote with gravity and solemnity. The knight asked them to provide him with a better bed than they had the previous time and the innkeeper's wife said that if he would pay her better than he had the previous time, she would give him one fit for a prince.

Don Quixote said he would do so and they prepared him one in the same garret as before, where he immediately went to bed, having arrived exhausted in both body and spirit. No sooner was he settled into his room than the innkeeper's wife approached the barber, seized him by his beard, and said,

"By all that is holy, you're not going to use my tail any longer for your beard. You must give it back, for it's shameful the way my husband's thing is always on the floor – his comb, that is – which I used to stick in my fine tail."

The barber, despite all her tugging, refused to release it until the licentiate ordered him to let her have it, since it was no longer needed for continuing the deception. He also said he should end the masquerade, reveal his identity, and tell Don Quixote he had fled to this inn after being robbed by the thieving galley slaves; and should Don Quixote inquire about the princess' squire, they would tell him she had sent him on ahead to inform those of her kingdom that she was on her way and was bringing with her one who would liberate them all. With this, the barber willingly handed the tail to the hostess and also returned all the accessories she had loaned them for rescuing Don Quixote. Everyone in the inn was impressed with Dorotea's beauty and the youthful Cardenio's handsome appearance. When the priest asked the innkeeper to prepare them whatever food there was in the inn, the latter, having hopes of better pay, speedily prepared them an acceptable meal. They allowed Don Quixote to sleep through all this, feeling they should not wake him because at the moment he would benefit more from sleep than from food. While the innkeeper, his wife, daughter, Maritornes, and all the guests dined, they discussed Don Quixote's peculiar madness and the manner in which they had found him. The hostess related what had transpired between him and the muleteer, and after looking round to see if Sancho was present, described the details of the blanket tossing, which they found quite amusing. But when the priest told them the books of chivalry Don Quixote had read had befuddled his senses, the innkeeper said,

"I don't see how that is possible, for to my way of thinking there is truly no better reading on earth. I have two or three books here as well as several manuscripts, and they have provided enjoyment not only for me but for many others as well. Whenever harvest time arrives and the feast days attract a crowd of harvesters, there's always someone among them who can read, and that person will pick up one of these books and more than thirty of us will gather round him, where we'll sit and listen with such fascination that it makes us feel years younger. Speaking for myself, at least, I must admit that when I listen to the furious and frightful blows delivered by those knights, I get the urge to join in and would love to keep listening to them straight through the night."

"I feel just the same way," said the innkeeper's wife, "because the only time I get any rest in my place is when you're all listening to someone read, for then you're so caught up you don't even remember to start a fight."

"That's the truth," said Maritornes, "and I assure you that I too love to listen to such things, which I find awfully nice, especially when they describe one of the ladies standing beneath some orange trees in the arms of her knight, while another lady stands watch panic-stricken and dying of envy. I think all that is simply too beautiful for words."

"And you, young lady, what do you think?" asked the priest, directing himself to the innkeeper's daughter.

"I declare, sir, I don't know. I also listen to those books and though I don't understand them, I can truthfully say I still get a thrill from simply listening. Unlike my father, though, who likes the fighting, I love the lamentations of the knights when they're absent from their ladies. They actually make me cry at times, I feel so sorry for them."

"Then you, young lady, would try to console them," added Dorotea, "if they were weeping for you?"

"I don't know what I would do," replied the girl; "I only know that some of those ladies are so cruel their knights call them vixens and bitches and other indecent names. Good heavens! I don't understand how there can be such inhuman and unfeeling women who, rather than admit an honorable man into their presence, would let him die or go mad. I don't see what good all that prudishness does. If they act like that because they want to remain pure, let them marry the knights because that's all the knights want anyway."

"Hush, child," said her mother, "it sounds as though you know an awful lot about these things and it's not proper for young ladies to know so much or to speak of such matters."

"Since this gentleman asked me a question, I couldn't help but answer him," replied the girl.

"Well then, sir innkeeper," said the priest, "bring us those books. I would like to have a look at them."

"Gladly," said the innkeeper, who went to his room and brought back an old suitcase secured by a small chain. Opening it, he pulled out three large books and several manuscripts written in a very fine hand. The priest saw that the first book he had opened was *Don Cirongilio of Thrace,* the next *Felixmarte de Hircania*, and the last a history of the Great Captain Gonzalo Hernández de Córdoba, which also contained the life of Diego García de Paredes. When the priest read the titles of the first two, he turned to the barber and said,

"We need our friend's housekeeper and niece here."

"No, we don't," replied the barber, "I'm perfectly capable of throwing the books into the courtyard or even into the fireplace, since there's already a roaring fire there."

"What!" shouted the innkeeper, "does your grace intend to burn my books?"

"Only these two," said the priest: "the *Don Cirongilio* and the *Felixmarte*."

"Can my books possibly be so heretical or phlegmatic," said the host, "that you want to burn them?"

"You mean 'schismatic', my friend, not 'phlegmatic,'" put in the barber.

"So I do," replied the innkeeper, "but if there is any your grace would burn, let it be the one about the Great Captain and that Diego García. I would rather have one of my own children burned than either of the other two books."

"My son," said the priest, "*your* two books are false and full of nonsense and absurdities. This one about the Great Captain is a factual history and contains a number of deeds of Gonzalo Hernández de Córdoba, who, because of his numerous and outstanding achievements, was known to everyone as *The Great Captain*, a famous and illustrious name worthy of him alone. This Diego García de Paredes was a renowned gentleman, a native of the city of Trujillo, Estremadura, and a most gallant soldier, who possessed such natural strength that with just one finger he once stopped a mill-wheel that was turning at full speed. On another occasion he stationed himself at the approach to a bridge where, armed only with a broadsword, he prevented an entire army from crossing it. He also performed other feats which he himself relates and describes with all the modesty of a gentleman serving as his own chronicler. Were someone else to record them, someone who was impartial and forthright, his deeds would cast those of all the Hectors, Achilles, and Rolands into oblivion by comparison."

"Oh, come now!" said the innkeeper, "what a thing to marvel at – the stopping of a mill-wheel! For heaven's sake, your grace ought to read what I've read about Felixmarte de Hircania, who with a single stroke cut five giants in two at the waist as if they were made of bean-pods, like the little friar dolls that children make. On another occasion he held off a huge, powerful army numbering more than a million six hundred thousand soldiers, each armed from head to foot, and he routed the whole crew as though they had been a flock of sheep. And what more is there to say about the extremely brave and spirited Don Cirongilio of Thrace? The book that deals with him relates that as he was sailing down a river a fiery serpent rose up from the midst of the waters and, the instant he saw it, he jumped on its back and clasped his hands tightly round its throat. The serpent, finding itself in danger of being choked to death, had no other recourse than to dive to the bottom of the river, thus carrying along the knight, who refused to relax his grip. When they reached the bottom, he found himself surrounded by such handsome palaces and gardens that he was stupefied, at which point the serpent changed into a venerable old man who recounted to him so many marvelous things it left nothing to be desired. But I'll say no more, for if you were to read this, you would go mad with delight. Why, I wouldn't give two figs for the Great Captain or that Diego García you speak of!"

Hearing this, Dorotea whispered to Cardenio,

"Our host doesn't have far to go to be another Don Quixote."

"That is how I feel," replied Cardenio, "for, by all indications, he is convinced everything those books describe happened exactly the way they describe it, and not even the discalced friars could make him believe otherwise."

"Look, my son," said the priest again, "there never was a Felixmarte de Hircania, nor a Don Cirongilio of Thrace, nor any of those other knights mentioned in books of chivalry. They are all the creation and invention of the idle minds that composed them for the purpose you describe of pleasantly whiling away the hours, as your harvesters do when they read them. I give you my solemn oath that such knights never walked upon the face of the earth, nor did such deeds and follies ever take place."

"Your grace doesn't think I'm such a simpleton as to believe that!" responded the innkeeper. "I know how much is two and two and where to scratch when I itch! I advise you not to try to deceive me, for I wasn't born yesterday. To think that you would try to make me believe that everything these wonderful books say is absurd or false, especially when they've been printed by authority of the Royal Council, as though these were men who would allow the printing of so many lies and so many battles and enchantments that they simply make one's head swim!"

"I have already told you, my friend," said the priest, "that this was done to provide entertainment for our idle thoughts. Just as people agree that well-run states should provide chess, ball games, and billiards for the entertainment of some who cannot, ought not, or will not work, there is also agreement that such books shall be printed in the belief that no one will be so ignorant as to consider them real histories. If I were granted permission at this moment and everyone present were to insist upon it, I could expound upon the qualities books of chivalry should possess in order to excel. This might prove beneficial and even pleasurable to some of you but I hope to have the opportunity some day to make my ideas known to a person who will be able to remedy the situation. In the meantime, sir innkeeper, believe what I have told you. Take your books and come to an understanding with their truths and their lies, and may you benefit from this and, God willing, not limp on the same leg as your guest Don Quixote."

"Certainly not," replied the innkeeper, "I'll not be crazy enough to become a knight-errant, for I can clearly see that the same customs don't hold today that were once in fashion when those famous knights were said to have ranged over the earth."

Sancho, who had made his appearance in the middle of this discussion, was confused and upset by the assertion that knights-errant no longer existed and that all books of chivalry were nonsense and make-believe but he firmly resolved to wait to see how this journey of his master's would end, for should it not turn out as happily as he imagined, he was determined to leave him and return to his wife and children to resume his old trade once again. Just as the innkeeper was about to carry away the suitcase containing the books, the priest said to him,

"Hold on. I want to see what those parchments are that are written in such a fine hand."

To oblige him, the host pulled them out and gave them to the priest to read. He saw that there were some eight hand-lettered sheets with a title in large letters at the beginning that read: *The Tale of Unreasonable Curiosity*. After reading three or four lines to himself, the priest said,

"The title of this story is certainly not bad, so I am rather inclined to read the entire story; to which the innkeeper responded,

"Then you may certainly do so, your reverence, for I can assure you that several of my guests who have read it have found it quite entertaining and have begged me to let them keep it. However, I've not been willing to do so because I intend to return it to the person who owns the suitcase containing these books and papers. The owner may possibly come back some day, and even though I'll miss the books, I'll return them to him, for I may be an innkeeper but I'm also a Christian."

"You are absolutely right, my friend," said the priest, "but if I like the story, you must let me have it copied."

"Certainly," replied the innkeeper.

While the two of them were discussing this matter, Cardenio picked up the story and began reading it, and, since his impression of it was the same as the priest's, he begged him to read it aloud so everyone could hear it.

"I would certainly do so," said the priest, "if the time might not be better spent sleeping than reading."

"It will be restful enough for me," said Dorotea, "to pass the time listening to a story, for I have still not calmed down enough to retire, though I ought to do so."

"Well, in that case," replied the priest, "I am willing to read it, if only out of curiosity. Perhaps there will be something in it we shall like."

After Master Nicolás also urged him to read it, as did Sancho, he saw it would please everyone, including himself, so he said,

"Well then, if I may have your graces' kind attention, this is how the story begins."

Chapter Thirty-Three

The Tale of Unreasonable Curiosity

In Florence, a rich and famous city in the Italian province of Tuscany, lived two wealthy, distinguished gentlemen, Anselmo and Lotario, who were such close friends that everyone who knew them referred to them, by way of excellence and epithet, as *the two friends.* Inasmuch as the young men were both bachelors and of the same age and interests, it was only natural that they should develop a mutual friendship. Whereas Anselmo was more inclined to affairs of the heart, Lotario pursued those of the hunt, but whenever the occasion arose, Anselmo would forego his own pleasures to follow those of Lotario and Lotario would relinquish *his* to follow Anselmo's. In this manner, their wills were in such accord that there was no clock in existence that was better concerted.

Anselmo was desperately in love with a distinguished and beautiful young lady of the same city, the daughter of such worthy parents and so worthy in her own right, that he made up his mind – after securing his friend Lotario's approval, without which he never acted – to ask her parents for her hand in marriage. This he did and Lotario was the one who delivered the message and concluded the affair, and so much to the satisfaction of his friend that Anselmo soon saw himself in possession of his beloved. Camila was so pleased at having acquired Anselmo for her husband that she never ceased giving thanks to heaven and to Lotario, by means of whom so much happiness had come her way. During the first few days following the wedding, which are by nature festive ones, Lotario continued to visit the home of his friend Anselmo in an effort to pay his respects, entertain him, and make his life as cheerful as possible, but once the wedding festivities were concluded and the stream of guests and congratulations abated, Lotario became studiously remiss in visiting Anselmo's home, for it seemed to him (as it obviously would to any sensible person) that one's married friends should not be visited as frequently as when they were bachelors, for though a firm and true friendship can and should be beyond suspicion, a married man's honor is apparently so fragile it can be jeopardized even by his own brothers, much less by his friends.

Anselmo noticed Lotario's growing neglect and chided him for it, telling him that, had he known his marriage would deprive him of his friend's regular visits, he would never have wed and if, because of the close relationship the two of them had enjoyed so long as he was a bachelor, they had earned as enviable an epithet as that of *the two friends*, he, Lotario, ought not permit such a distinguished and genial epithet to be sacrificed simply and purely out of his desire to appear circumspect. He thus implored him – if it was proper to employ such a term under the circumstances – to consider himself master of his home once again and to come and go as before, for he could assure him that his wife Camila had no other wants or desires than those he wished her to have; and since she knew how truly fond they were of one another, she was perplexed to see such evasiveness on the part of Lotario.

To these arguments Anselmo produced a number of others designed to persuade Lotario to visit his home as he once had, and the latter responded with such calculated prudence and discretion that Anselmo was satisfied with his friend's noble intentions, whereby they agreed that Lotario would dine with him twice each week in addition to holidays. Though this was agreed upon between the two, Lotario resolved to abide by this agreement no more than he deemed appropriate to the honor of his friend, whose good name he valued even more than he did his own. He maintained, and herein he spoke the truth, that a married man whom heaven had blessed with a beautiful wife should be as much concerned about the friends he brought home as about the women friends his wife conversed with, for those matters that women cannot arrange or conclude in marketplaces, churches, public festivals, or religious functions (opportunities that husbands may not always deny their wives) can be easily arranged in the home of some female friend in whom the wife can confide. Lotario also said a husband needed some friend to warn him whenever he was neglectful in his behavior, for it often happens that the great love a husband has for his wife keeps him from counseling or cautioning her, lest he upset her, to do or abstain from doing certain things that may bring him praise or censure depending upon her actions. Being thus alerted by his friend, he might easily take charge of the situation.

But where is one to find a friend as discreet, loyal, and true as Lotario is seeking? I certainly know of no one unless it is Lotario himself, who with the utmost concern and vigilance watched over his friend's honor and attempted to severely limit and curtail the days agreed upon for his visits lest the idle masses with their roving, malicious eyes consider as inappropriate the visits of a rich young man – a highborn gentleman with those noble qualities he believed himself to possess – in the home of a woman as beautiful as Camila. For even though her goodness and virtue could bridle the most slanderous tongue, he was nevertheless reluctant to cast doubt upon his own good name or that of his friend, for which reason he spent most of the days set aside for his visits occupied and involved in other matters which, he insisted, demanded his attention. Consequently, they spent long stretches of each day in discussion, one airing his complaints and the other offering excuses.

Now, it happened that one day, when the two were strolling in a meadow on the outskirts of the city, Anselmo directed the following remarks to Lotario:

"Lotario, my friend, you may think me incapable of showing sufficient gratitude for the gifts I have received or for the favors God has bestowed upon me in making me the child of such wonderful parents, or for the boons He has lavished upon me – both the so-called gifts of nature and those of fortune – particularly the gift He bestowed upon me when He made you my friend and Camila my very own wife, both gifts that I treasure, if not as much as I should, at least as much as I am able. And yet, with these many blessings, which are all that most men would need to live contented, I am the most forlorn and sullen man upon the face of the earth because for some days now I have been vexed and distressed by a yearning that is so strange and so unlike any other that I am astounded at myself. Whenever I find myself alone, I blame and scold myself in an effort to stifle the desire and conceal it from my own mind but I have no more been able to keep it within myself than if I had expressly set out to announce it to the world. And since it is bound to disclose itself to someone, I prefer it to find lodging in the repository of your breast, feeling confident that by this means and because of the diligence that you, as my true friend, will expend in providing me a solution, I shall speedily see myself free of the anguish it is causing me, and as a result of your concern my happiness will reach the same heights reached by my folly-induced unhappiness."

Lotario was left speechless by Anselmo's words, for he had no idea where such a lengthy, cautionary preamble was leading. And though he turned over in his mind every possible fantasy that might be so profoundly troubling his friend, he was invariably far off the mark in determining the truth. To find a speedy release from the anxiety produced by this uncertainty, he told Anselmo he was committing a grave injustice against their firm friendship by seeking roundabout ways of revealing his innermost thoughts, for he, Anselmo, could certainly expect from him either suggestions for making them bearable or avenues for resolving them.

"You are quite right," said Anselmo, "and with that assurance, Lotario my friend, I can tell you that what is troubling me is whether my wife Camila is as good and perfect as I think she is. I shall be unable to determine the truth of this without subjecting her to a rigorous test that will reveal the purity of her virtue, as fire does that of gold, for I am convinced, my friend, that a woman is good or bad only to the extent to which she has been tempted, and that only she is strong who has not yielded to the promises, gifts, tears, and persistent importunings of her relentless suitors. What gratitude is due a virtuous woman if no one has sought to corrupt her? What is so exemplary about a woman's reserve and modesty if she has not had the opportunity to act without restraint or because she knows she has a husband who, if he catches her in some impropriety, will take her life? Consequently, the woman who is good out of fear or the lack of opportunity I refuse to hold in the same esteem as the one who was pursued and solicited but came away with the crown of victory. And so, because of these and a number of other arguments I could adduce in support of the opinion I hold, I should like my wife Camila to undergo a test: to be distilled and purified by the ordeal of finding herself courted and wooed by someone worthy of her. If she emerges from this battle victorious, as I believe she will, I shall consider my happiness unequaled and shall be able to say that the empty cup of my desires has been filled to overflowing. I can also say in response to the wise man who asked, 'Who can find a virtuous woman?' [1] that I have had the good fortune to find her. Should it turn out contrary to my expectations, my satisfaction at seeing that my opinion was correct will enable me to bear without pain the pain that my most costly experiment may cause me, and since any argument you raise against my plan will be incapable of dissuading me from implementing it, I would have you prepare

1 King Solomon, in Proverbs XXXI, 10.

yourself, dear Lotario, to serve as the instrument for carrying out this whim of mine. I shall provide you with the opportunity to do so and you shall lack nothing I deem necessary for courting a woman who is respectable, honorable, reserved, and above intrigue. I am led to entrust this most arduous task to you because, among other reasons, I can see that if Camila is seduced by you, the seduction will not be carried to its rigorous, final conclusion but, owing to your respect, will only go so far as to establish as an accomplished fact that which we set out to achieve. In this way I shall end up offended only by her willingness, and my disgrace will remain buried in the silence of your bosom where, I am certain, everything pertaining to me will be preserved for as long as you live. If, therefore, you would have me enjoy a life worthy of the name, you must engage at once in this contest of love, not hesitatingly or half-heartedly, but with the earnestness and diligence my plan requires and with the allegiance our friendship warrants."

These were some of the arguments Anselmo put forth to Lotario, who listened so attentively that, aside from the remarks he had already made, as noted, he did not unseal his lips until Anselmo had concluded. When he saw that he had finished his speech, he stood there for some time looking at him as though he were observing something he had never before seen that filled him with wonder and dread. After some time he said,

"I cannot convince myself, Anselmo my friend, that the things you have said to me were not said in jest, for, if I thought they were said in earnest, I would not have allowed you to continue speaking at such length, and, by refusing to listen to you, I could have avoided your long harangue. Thus, I can only conclude that either you don't know me or I don't know you, but that is impossible, for I know you perfectly well, as you do me. The problem, I feel, is that you are not the Anselmo you once were and you probably do not consider me the Lotario I ought to be, for the things you have told me are not what Anselmo my friend would say, and what you are asking is not something that should be demanded of the Lotario you know. True friends are to test and use their friends, as a poet has said, '*usque ad aras*,' [2] meaning that they are not to avail themselves of their friendship in ways inimical to God. Now if this was a pagan's attitude towards friendship, how much stronger should be the feeling of a Christian who knows that his friendship with God must not be sacrificed for the sake of a human one. In the event that the friend should go so far as to lay aside the loyalty he owes heaven in order to honor that due his friend, it must not be for some frivolous or insignificant reason but one involving his friend's honor and life. Therefore, Anselmo, tell me right here which of these two things of yours is threatened, that I should venture to humor you by committing an act as detestable as the one you propose? Neither, of course. Instead, you are asking me, if I understand you, to take away both your honor and your life, thereby taking away mine at the same time, for if I take away your honor, it is obvious that I shall also take away your life, and a man without honor is worse off than one who is dead. If I follow your wishes and serve as the instrument of so much misfortune to yourself, do I not end up devoid of honor and by that same token devoid of life? Heed my advice, Anselmo my friend, and be kind enough not to interrupt me until I have told you everything that has occurred to me

2 Latin: 'as far as the altar,' from Plutarch's *Moralia*.

regarding your plan and what it demands of you, for there will be sufficient time for you to respond and for me to listen."

"With all my heart," said Anselmo, "say whatever you will." Lotario then proceeded to speak.

"My dear Anselmo, it appears to me that you are now demonstrating the same reasoning ability as that of the Moors, who are incapable of being shown the errors of their sect even by citations from the Holy Scriptures, or by arguments involving rational considerations, or by those based upon articles of faith. On the contrary, they must be provided with examples that are palpable, simple, easily understood, demonstrable, and indisputable, including mathematical proofs that cannot be questioned, such as the one that states: 'If from two equal parts equal parts are subtracted, the parts that remain are equal.' And whenever they fail to understand this with words, as they invariably do, one must demonstrate it with his hands and place it before their eyes, and even after all this a person can never persuade them of the truth of our hallowed religion. It will be necessary to employ this same system and method with you, for the notion you have come up with is so misguided and so far removed from anything remotely resembling reason that I feel anyone will be wasting his time who tries to make you comprehend your folly, which at the moment I am loath to call by any other name. Moreover, I am half inclined to leave you to your foolishness as punishment for your unwholesome thoughts but am prevented from employing this harsh measure because of my fondness for you, which will not allow me to abandon you to such a manifest risk to your life. So that you may realize this, tell me, Anselmo: have you not said you would like me to court a respectable woman, seduce one who is honorable, press my intentions upon one who is inviolable, and force myself upon one who is sensible? You have, indeed, told me all this. But if you are already convinced that you have a wife who is respectable, honorable, inviolable, and sensible, what is it you seek? If you believe that after all my assaults she will emerge victorious, as she is certain to do, what greater titles do you intend to bestow upon her than those she already has? And how will she be better then than she is now? Or is it that you doubt that she is as good as you say she is, or that you don't understand what you are requesting? If you feel she is not as good as you say, why do you wish to test her? Why not admit she is bad and deal with her in whatever manner you find most satisfying? But if she is as good as you believe, it is unreasonable to put truth itself to the test, for, once tested, it will turn out just as highly esteemed as before. Everyone would agree that to attempt things that can only do us harm is unreasonable and foolhardy, especially when the attempt is unforced, uncoerced, and, when viewed from a distance, obvious madness. Difficult tasks are to be undertaken on behalf of God or the world, or of both. Those undertaken in the name of God are exemplified by saints who strive to live the life of angels in human bodies. The ones undertaken with respect to the world are exemplified by men willing to endure infinite expanses of water and endless diversities of climes and foreign races to acquire the so-called bounties of fortune. Feats attempted in the name of both God and the world are those of valiant soldiers who no sooner spot a hole in the enemy wall as large as that made by an artillery ball than they cast aside all fear and, without wasting words or acknowledging the obvious danger threatening them, intrepidly hurl themselves into the midst of a thousand deaths that await them, borne aloft on the wings of desire to defend their faith, their nation, and their king. These are things that people normally attempt, and to attempt them is honorable, glorious, and beneficial, albeit fraught with obstacles and perils, but the one you wish to undertake will bring you neither the glory of God, bounteous fortune, nor fame among men, for even if it turns out as you wish, you will not end up any prouder, richer, or more honored than you are now. But if it does not, you will find yourself in the greatest misery imaginable, for you will not benefit at that moment from the knowledge that no one knows the disgrace that has befallen you; the fact that you know it will be enough to haunt and destroy you. As confirmation of this truth, I should like to quote a stanza composed by the famous poet Luis Tansilo at the end of the first part of his *Tears of Saint Peter*, which goes thus:

Shame, grief, remorse, in Peter's breast increase
Soon as the blushing morn his crime betrays:
When most unseen, then most himself he sees,
And with due horror all his soul surveys.

For a great spirit needs no censuring eyes
To wound his soul, when conscious of a fault;
But, self-condemned, and e'en self-punished, lies,
And dreads no witness like upbraiding Thought.

"Thus, you will not avoid your suffering by secrecy; instead, you will weep continual tears – not tears from your eyes but tears from your heart, like those shed by that simple doctor who, our poet tells us, underwent the test of the goblet, to which the cautious Reinaldos wisely declined to submit. Though the episode is poetic fiction, it contains within itself moral precepts worthy of being noted, digested, and emulated. Moreover, with what I am now about to say, you will finally realize the grievous error you seem determined to commit. Tell me, Anselmo: if heaven, or good fortune, had made you lord and rightful owner of an exquisite diamond, the quality and weight of which had been certified by all the lapidaries who examined it, and they were unanimous in their opinion that in weight, quality, and purity it was as fine as any that gem was capable of producing, and you yourself shared that belief, having no knowledge to the contrary, would it be right to take it into your head to subject that diamond to the anvil and hammer and thus by sheer force of brawn and blows to see if it was as hard and as pure as they said? If you carried out your plan and the gem was able to withstand such a foolish test, would it for that reason gain in value or reputation? If on the other hand it shattered, which certainly might occur, would not everything be lost? Of course it would and its owner would be considered a fool. Therefore, Anselmo my friend, accept the fact that Camila is an exquisitely fine diamond not only in your opinion but in that of everyone else, and that it is wrong to expose her to the risk of being broken, for even if she remains intact, she cannot assume a higher value than that she already has. But if she should fail the test, consider here and now what you would do without her and how legitimately you would criticize yourself for having been the cause of both *her* perdition and your own. Understand that there is no jewel on earth as valuable as a pure and honorable woman, especially when a woman's honor consists entirely of the good reputation she enjoys. Since your wife's is an excellent one, why do you wish to place that fact in doubt? Remember, my friend, woman is an imperfect creature and one must not strew her path with obstacles that will cause her to trip and fall but should clear it and remove any and all obstacles so that she may hasten unimpeded and without encumbrances to achieve the perfection she lacks, which consists of being virtuous. Naturalists tell us the ermine is a small creature with the world's whitest fur and that, whenever hunters wish to trap it, they use the following stratagem. Since they know which path it normally follows, they spread mud along that route and then after flushing out the ermine, drive it towards that spot. When the animal comes to the mud, it stops short and allows itself to be captured rather than run through the mud and soil its white fur, which it values more than freedom or life itself. A chaste and virtuous woman is an ermine and her virtue of chastity is whiter and purer than snow. Whoever would have her guard and preserve it should use a method different from that employed with the ermine. He should not place in her path the filth of gifts and the solicitations of importuning suitors, for, more likely than not, she may not possess sufficient virtue and inner strength to enable her by her own efforts to negotiate those obstacles and make her way safely through them. One must remove them from her path and replace them with the ideals of virtue and beauty, which constitute a good reputation. Likewise, a virtuous woman is like a mirror of clear, shining crystal, which is liable to grow dim and cloudy from any breath that contacts it. One should treat a respectable woman the way one does a relic: adore her but touch her not. One should cherish and esteem a good woman the way one does a beautiful garden where roses and other flowers abound: it is sufficient to enjoy their fragrance and beauty from a distance through an iron grating without strolling among them and handling them.

"Finally, I should like to recite some verses I heard in a recent play, which have just come to mind and are apropos of what we are discussing. A wise old man was advising another, the father of a maiden, to watch over her and keep her in seclusion, and among other things, he said the following:

> If woman's glass, why should we try
> Whether she can be broke or no?
> Great hazards in the trial lie,
> Because, perchance, she may be so.
>
> Who that is wise, such brittle ware
> Would careless dash upon the floor,
> Which, broken, nothing can repair,
> Nor solder to its form restore?
>
> In this opinion all are found,
> And reason vouches what I say,
> Whenever Danaës abound,

There golden showers will make their way. [3]

"Everything I have said thus far, dear Anselmo, has dealt with those things concerning you. It is now time for you to listen to my concerns. If they turn out to be lengthy, I beg your indulgence but it is all made necessary by the labyrinth in which you find yourself and from which you wish me to extricate you. You consider me your friend, yet your willingness to strip me of my honor is totally inimical to friendship; and not only *that*—you would have me take away yours as well. That you would take away mine is obvious, for when Camila sees me making advances towards her in the manner you propose, she will certainly consider me a man without honor or scruples, since I shall be committing an act totally contrary to what my allegiance and your friendship demand. You obviously want me to rob you of your honor, for when Camila observes my lack of restraint, she will think I have glimpsed some impropriety in her that has led me to reveal my evil intentions, and once she considers herself dishonored, her own dishonor will fall to you, since you are a part of her. From this arises a situation which is all too common: that of a husband who has an adulterous wife but is unaware of the fact. Though he neither gave his wife cause to become a fallen woman nor had it in his power to prevent his misfortune due to his neglect or lack of caution, those who learn of his wife's wickedness will slander and vilify him with malicious names and will view him with eyes of contempt rather than pity even though they see him in that predicament through no fault of his own but because of the whims of his sinful spouse. Let me explain to you why it is understandable for a sinful woman's husband to be dishonored even if he is unaware of her sinfulness and has given her no reason to stray. I hope you will not find it wearisome to listen to me, inasmuch as it will redound to your benefit in the end.

"When God created our first father in the earthly paradise, the Holy Scriptures say He caused a deep sleep to descend upon Adam and that, while he slept, He removed a rib from Adam's left side from which He formed our mother Eve. When Adam awoke, he beheld her and said, 'This is now bones of my bones and flesh of my flesh.' And God said, 'Therefore shall a man leave his father and his mother and shall cleave unto his wife.' At that very moment the divine sacrament of marriage was instituted and it has such strong bonds that only death can undo it. This miraculous sacrament contains such strength and virtue that it converts two separate persons into a single flesh and goes even farther in the case of a happy marriage where, though there are two souls, there is but a single will. From this it follows that because the wife's flesh is one with her husband's, the stains that attach to her and the faults that she incurs will find lodging in the flesh of her husband, though, as I have said, he may have given her no justification to go astray. For just as a pain in the foot or in any other member of the body is felt throughout the entire body, since they are all of one flesh, and just as the head senses when the ankle is hurt without having caused the injury, so too is the husband a participant in his wife's dishonor because he is one with her. And since honor and dishonor are both born of flesh and blood, and since those of a wayward wife are of this kind, the husband will

3 It is not known from which play this poem comes.

inescapably share in them and will be held in contempt without even being aware of it. My dear Anselmo, consider the danger to which you are exposing yourself by daring to disturb the serenity your good wife enjoys. Ask yourself whether you are willing to stir up the passions that are now at rest in your wife's chaste bosom for the sake of such a vain, unreasonable curiosity. Remember that what you expect to gain from your wager is small, whereas what you may lose will be so great I lack words to describe it. Now, if all I have said is insufficient to turn you from your misguided proposal, you may simply seek some other instrument for your dishonor and misfortune, for I don't intend to be the one even if it costs me your friendship, which would be the greatest loss I could imagine."

The virtuous and wise Lotario remained silent after making these remarks, leaving Anselmo so confused and pensive that he was unable to respond for quite some time. Finally, however, he said,

"Lotario my friend, you have just observed how patiently I have listened to everything you wished to say to me, and in your arguments, examples, and illustrations I have discerned your great wisdom and the limits to which your genuine friendship extends. Similarly, I understand and confess that if I do not subscribe to your way of thinking but follow my own, I am fleeing from good and chasing after evil. This being so, you should understand that I presently suffer from that disease that sometimes afflicts women who have a craving to eat dirt, plaster, charcoal, and even worse things – all revolting enough to contemplate but worse still to eat. Thus, some sort of remedy must be devised if I am to be cured. This may be accomplished quite easily, provided that you, even if in a half-hearted and make-believe way, will begin to pay court to Camila, for she will not be so docile as to see her purity sullied on the first meeting. I shall be satisfied if you will merely begin, for you will have met your obligation to our friendship not only by giving me life but by persuading me not to consider myself dishonored. You are obligated to do this for one simple reason: inasmuch as I am determined to subject my plan to this test, you must not make me reveal my foolish scheme to some other person and thereby jeopardize the honor you would have me preserve. Should Camila not hold you in as high regard as she should while you pursue her, it will be of little or no consequence, for we shall shortly see in her the perfection we expect, and you may then reveal to her the entire truth of our scheme, whereby her respect for you will be just as great as it formerly was. By accepting this venture, you will run so little risk and will afford me so much satisfaction that you cannot refuse to do so, regardless of the number of obstacles you may encounter, for as I have said, if you will simply begin, I shall consider the matter concluded."

Lotario could see Anselmo's firm resolve and could think of no other examples or proofs for dissuading Anselmo from proceeding with his plan, but when he saw him threatening to reveal his evil intentions to someone else, he decided, in order to avoid an even greater evil, to humor him and do as he requested, for he intended to maneuver the affair in such a way that, without upsetting Camila's peace of mind, Anselmo would be satisfied. He thus responded that Anselmo was not to divulge his plan to any other person; that he would undertake that affair and would begin it whenever Anselmo wished. The latter embraced him tenderly and affectionately, thanking him for his offer, as though he had done him a very great favor. It was agreed between the two that they would begin their task the following day. Anselmo would provide the time and place for Lotario to speak to Camila alone, and would also provide him with money and jewels to offer her. Anselmo advised him to write some verses in her praise, which he might use in serenading her but, should he be unwilling to compose them, he would do so himself. Lotario agreed to all this but not with the intentions Anselmo supposed. With this accord, they returned to Anselmo's house, where they found Camila anxiously and worriedly awaiting her husband, for on this particular day he was later than usual in returning.

Lotario returned to his own house, leaving Anselmo as satisfied in his as Lotario was perplexed, for the latter had no idea how to carry out that unreasonable affair. That night, however, he thought of a way to deceive Anselmo without offending his wife. The following day, he went to dine with his friend and was welcomed by Camila, who received him with her usual cordiality, since she was aware of her husband's fondness for him. Once the meal was finished and the table cleared, Anselmo asked Lotario to keep Camila company while he went off to attend to some urgent business, explaining that he would return in an hour and a half. Camila begged him not to go and Lotario offered to accompany him but all to no avail. Rather, Anselmo asked Lotario to remain there and wait for him, as he had some very important business to discuss with him. He also told Camila not to leave Lotario alone while he was away. In fact, he was so adept at feigning the necessity, not to mention the folly, of his going away that no one would have suspected it was anything but genuine. Anselmo departed, leaving Camila and Lotario seated at the table, all the others in the house having gone off to dine. By following his friend's wishes, Lotario found himself on slippery ground, confronted by his adversary who, with nothing more than her beauty, might have vanquished a squadron of armed knights. Therefore, is there any doubt that Lotario had good reason to fear her?

He proceeded to lean on the arm of his chair and rest his head on his hand. Begging Camila's forgiveness for his poor manners, he said he would like to take a short nap while Lotario was away. Camila replied that he would be more comfortable in the drawing room than in the dining room and suggested that he go there to rest but Lotario declined her offer and soon fell asleep, not waking until Anselmo returned. When the latter found Lotario asleep and Camila in her room, he imagined that, due to his lengthy delay in returning, they had both found the opportunity to talk or even to lie together and he could hardly wait for Lotario to awaken so he could take him outside and learn how the affair had gone. Everything turned out as he desired, for Lotario just then awoke and the two of them went outside, whereupon he asked Lotario to describe what had happened. Lotario replied that he had considered it inappropriate to reveal his feelings completely on the first occasion, so he had done nothing more than praise Camila as a beautiful woman, pointing out to her that the sole topic of conversation throughout the city was her beauty and wit. He added that he had thought this a good way to begin his attempt to win her affection and to dispose her favorably towards listening to him the next time. By doing this, he was using the stratagem the Devil uses when He wishes to ensnare someone who keeps a sharp lookout for himself, for though an angel of darkness, He transforms Himself into an angel of light and assumes a benevolent aspect, eventually revealing who He is and achieving His goal, unless, of course, His deception is discovered at the outset. Anselmo was quite pleased with all this and said he would provide the same opportunity every day even if he should not leave home, for he could occupy himself with things round the house that would keep Camila from recognizing his ploy.

As it turned out, a number of days went by during which Lotario never said a word to Camila, whereas he would tell Anselmo he had conversed with her but was unable to get her to show the slightest signs of succumbing to anything dishonorable or of offering the tiniest ray of hope. On the contrary, he said she was threatening to tell her husband unless he banished those evil thoughts from his mind.

"Very well," said Anselmo, "until now Camila has resisted words. We must now see how she will react to deeds. Tomorrow, I shall give you two thousand gold *escudos* that you may offer her or even give her, and two thousand more for you to spend on jewels with which to entice her, for regardless of how virtuous women are, particularly beautiful ones, they usually delight in dressing well and looking elegant. If she resists this temptation, I shall be satisfied and shall trouble you no further."

Lotario replied that inasmuch as he had begun that undertaking, he would see it through, though it was his belief that he would emerge weary and defeated. The next day, he received the four thousand *escudos* and with them four thousand uncertainties, for he had no idea how to continue the deception. Finally, however, he resolved to tell Anselmo Camila was as impervious to gifts and promises as she was to words and that his going forward with the enterprise would simply be a waste of time. But fate, which was guiding things along a different path, saw to it that Anselmo, after leaving Camila and Lotario alone as he had done on previous occasions, hid in one of the rooms, where by spying through a keyhole he was able to see and hear what took place between them. He saw that in more than half an hour Lotario did not so much as say a word to Camila, nor would he have done so had he remained there for a century. He came to the realization that everything his friend had told him of Camila's reactions was nothing but fabrication and falsehood. To see if this was true, he came out of the room and drew Lotario aside, asking him about Camila's state of mind and any new developments that might have occurred. Lotario informed him that he intended to prod her no further in that business, for she always reacted so harshly and gruffly that he lacked the courage to speak to her again.

"Ah, Lotario, Lotario," said Anselmo, "how poorly you repay me for all the confidence I have placed in you! I was just now watching you through this keyhole and did not see you say a word to Camila, whereby I am forced to conclude that you are yet to direct your first words to her. If this is so, as it undoubtedly is, why do you deceive me and why by this ploy do you wish to deprive me of the means of achieving my objective?"

Anselmo said nothing further, for he had already said enough to produce shame and confusion in Lotario. The latter, taking it virtually as a point of honor to have been discovered in a lie, swore to Anselmo that from that moment forward he would make it his business to satisfy him and not to lie again, as Anselmo would see if he were to spy upon him again out of curiosity. He stressed that it would not be necessary to take any special measures, for the one he intended to employ to satisfy him would remove all doubt. Anselmo believed him and, in order to provide him with more secure and less unsettled surroundings, resolved to be absent from his house for a week to go to that of a friend who lived in a village not far from the city. To justify his trip to Camila, he arranged for his friend to send him an urgent message asking him to come to his house. Oh, poor, ill-advised Anselmo! what is it you are doing? What are you plotting and what is it you seek? Consider what you are doing to yourself by plotting your dishonor and seeking your perdition. Your wife Camila is virtuous; she provides you with peace and quiet; no one encroaches upon your happiness; her thoughts extend no farther than the walls of her home; you are her heaven on earth, the object of her wishes, the fruition of her desires, and the model against which she measures her will, making it conform completely to yours and to that of heaven. If, then, the mine of her honor, beauty, purity, and reserve effortlessly affords you all the treasures she possesses and everything you might desire, why will you once more probe the earth in search of undiscovered veins, risking the collapse of the entire structure, which, after all, rests upon the fragile foundation of her natural frailty? Remember that if one goes looking for the impossible, the possible may rightfully be denied him, which a poet has expressed much better when he said:

In death alone I life would find,
And health in racking pain;
Fair honor in a traitor's mind,
Or freedom in a chain.

But since I ask what ne'er can be,
The Fates, alas! decide,
What they would else have granted me
Shall ever be denied. [4]

The next day, Anselmo set out for the village after informing Camila that in his absence Lotario would come to look after the house and to dine with her and that she was to treat him as she would Anselmo himself. Camila, as a discreet and respectable woman, was upset by her husband's order and asked him to remember that it was improper during his absence for anyone to occupy his place at their table; that if he was doing it because of his lack of confidence in her ability to manage their house, he should test her just this once and he would see for himself that she was equal to the most demanding tasks. Anselmo replied that he had made his wishes known and there was nothing for her to do except bow her head and obey. Camila said she would do so though against her will.

Anselmo departed and the following day Lotario arrived at her house, where he was received by Camila with affection and modesty. Refusing, however, to remain alone with him in any room of the house, she always managed to be surrounded by her servants and maids, in particular a maidservant of hers named Leonela, of whom she was quite fond and whom she had brought with her when she had married Anselmo, for as girls the two of them had been brought up together in the home of

4 Francisco Rodríguez Marín suspects that these verses may be from the pen of Cervantes, as they bear some slight resemblance to verses in the third act of his *El Gallardo español.*

Camila's parents. During the first three days Lotario did not speak to her, though the opportunity presented itself as soon as the tables were cleared and the household staff hurried off to eat in accordance with their orders from Camila. Leonela had been instructed to dine prior to Camila and never to leave her side, but Leonela, whose mind was occupied with matters more to her own liking and who needed that particular time and opportunity for indulging her own pastimes, did not always comply with her lady's orders; in fact, she would leave them alone as though she had been expressly ordered to do so. Nevertheless, Camila's air of respectability, the look of seriousness on her face, and the composure of her demeanor were so pronounced that they bridled Lotario's tongue. But the silence imposed upon it by Camila's many virtues proved harmful to them both, for if his tongue was silent, his thoughts roamed freely, as he was afforded the opportunity to contemplate every single perfection of Camila's virtue and beauty, which were sufficient to instill love in a marble statue, much less in a human heart. Lotario sat with his eyes fixed upon her during the time he was supposedly engaging her in conversation and he thought to himself how easy it would be for him to succumb to love. Little by little these thoughts began to mount an attack upon the respect he bore Anselmo, and a thousand times he yearned to flee the city and go where Anselmo would never again see him and where he would never again see Camila, but he was prevented from doing so by the pleasure he derived from looking at her. Struggling with himself, he made an effort to cast aside and ignore the pleasure that led him to fix his eyes upon Camila, and each time that he found himself alone again, he would blame himself for his folly and call himself a poor friend and even a poor Christian. In his soliloquies he would draw comparisons between himself and Anselmo, all of which ended in his contention that Anselmo's foolhardy trust had been greater than his own lack of fidelity, and that if he was thus exonerated in the eyes of God and men for what he was about to do, he did not fear being punished for his wrongdoing.

Eventually, Camila's beauty and virtue, combined with the opportunity the foolish husband had placed in his hands, made a shambles of Lotario's loyalty, and with no other consideration than the object towards which his passion inclined him, he began – at the end of three days after Anselmo's departure, during which time he waged a continual battle to resist his urges – to court Camila with such emotion and such loving expressions that Camila was stunned. She, however, did nothing more than rise from her chair and retire to her room without uttering a word in response. This rebuke, rather than causing Lotario to falter in the way of hope – hope being always engendered by love – had the opposite effect by endearing her to him even more. Camila, on the other hand, who had seen something in Lotario she had never before suspected, was at a loss as to how to proceed. Feeling it would not be safe or proper to let him speak to her again, she resolved to dispatch one of her servants that very night with a letter to Anselmo in which she wrote the following:

Chapter Thirty-Four

The continuation of *The Tale of Unreasonable Curiosity*

Just as they say that it ill befits an army to be without its general, or a castle its castellan, I say it is much more unseemly for a young married woman to be without her husband unless occasioned by the most justifiable circumstances. I find myself so miserable without you and so unable to endure your absence that unless you return soon, I shall be forced to seek temporary shelter in my parents' house, though this would entail my leaving yours unprotected. Also, I think the guard you left me, if indeed he deserves that name, is more concerned with his own pleasure than with anything having to do with you, and since you are a man of discernment, I have nothing more to say, nor is it prudent for me to comment further.

As soon as Anselmo received this letter, he concluded that Lotario had finally begun the undertaking and that Camila must have responded as he had hoped. Overjoyed at this news, he advised Camila by messenger that under no circumstances was she to leave their house, as he would return very shortly. Camila was astonished at Anselmo's reply, which left her more confused than before, for she dared not remain in her own house but dared even less to go to that of her parents. If she remained at home, her virtue would be imperiled, whereas if she left, she would be going against her husband's orders. In the end, she opted for what was (for her) the poorer of the two choices, namely, to remain at home, having made the decision not to flee from Lotario's presence lest she give her servants anything to talk about. She now regretted what she had written her husband, fearing he might think Lotario had observed some moral lapse in her that had led him to forego the respect he owed her, but confident of her own goodness and placing her trust in God and her virtuous intentions, she resolved to respond with silence to everything Lotario might say to her and to say nothing further to her husband to avoid embroiling him in any quarrel or intrigue. She even cast about for some way to exonerate Lotario in the eyes of Anselmo when he would ask her to explain why she had written that letter. Armed with these thoughts, more honorable than appropriate or beneficial, she spent the next day listening to Lotario's arguments. He grew so insistent that Camila's steadfastness began to waver when she looked into his eyes, and her virtue had all it could do to keep from revealing the passion Lotario's tears and pleas had awakened in her bosom. Lotario noted this and was inflamed by what he saw. In a word, he now felt it was time during the interval afforded him by Anselmo's absence to intensify the siege upon this fortress, and so he presumptuously attacked by praising her beauty, for nothing more quickly overcomes or lays waste to the fortified towers of a beautiful woman's vanity than vanity itself issuing from the lips of flattery. In fact, by exercising the utmost diligence, he bored away at the foundation of her fortitude with such an arsenal that even if Camila had been made of solid bronze, she would have come crashing down. Lotario wept, pleaded, promised, flattered, importuned, and dissimulated with such determination and emotion that he overwhelmed Camila's defenses and emerged triumphant over what he had least expected but most desired.

Camila yielded; yes, Anselmo's wife yielded, but is it any wonder when Lotario's friendship could not remain upright? – a clear demonstration that one can overcome the passion of love only by fleeing from it, and that no one should grapple with such a powerful adversary because divine strength is needed to overcome its human one. Leonela learned of her mistress' frailty only because the two unfaithful friends and new-found lovers were unable to conceal it from her. Lotario chose not to reveal to Camila what Anselmo had in mind, nor the fact that he had provided Lotario with the opportunity to reach this stage lest she underestimate his love and assume that he had pressed his attentions upon her, not intentionally, but accidentally and unexpectedly. Several days later, Anselmo returned home but failed to notice what was absent there, namely, the thing that he had treated lightly but cherished most. He went at once to see Lotario, whom he found him at home, and after the two embraced, Anselmo asked Lotario whether he was the bearer of good tidings or ill; to which Lotario responded,

"The news I have for you, Anselmo my friend, is that you possess a wife worthy to serve as the model of perfection for all virtuous women. The words I spoke to her dissolved into thin air, the promises I made were met with scorn, the presents I offered her were rejected, and the tears I pretended to shed were openly scoffed at. In short, just as Camila is the sum of all beauty, so is she the repository of respectability and the sanctuary of decorum, modesty, and every virtue that can make an honorable woman praiseworthy and most fortunate. Take back your *escudos*, my friend, which I still have. I had no need to touch them, for Camila's integrity will not yield to things as base as gifts and promises. Be content, Anselmo, and don't insist upon more tests than those already performed. Inasmuch as you have sailed dry-shod across the sea of doubts and suspicions that can and frequently do arise in circumstances involving women, don't insist upon embarking anew on the high seas of new obstacles or of testing with another pilot the quality and strength of the ship heaven has given you as your lot, that you may sail across the ocean that is this world. Accept the fact that you are now safely in port, moor yourself with the anchors of your wife's love and respect, and let yourself remain there till they come to demand the tribute that no hidalgo on earth is exempt from paying."[1]

Anselmo was delighted by the things Lotario had told him and he believed them as truly as if they had been spoken by some oracle. Nevertheless, he begged Lotario not to abandon the enterprise if only for the sake of curiosity and amusement, though in the future he need not employ such stringent measures as those of the past. He asked only that Lotario write some verses in praise of Camila but under the name of Clori and he would tell her that Lotario was in love with a lady to whom he had assigned that name so he might celebrate her with the decorum demanded by her respectability; but should Lotario be unwilling to take the trouble to compose those verses, he would do so himself.

---

1 I.e. death.

"That will not be necessary," said Lotario, "for the muses are not so hostile that they fail to visit me occasionally during the year. You may tell Camila what you mentioned about my make-believe love affair and I shall compose the verses, and if they are not as good as the subject herself deserves, at least they will be the best I can produce."

This was the agreement reached by *the two friends* – the unreasonable one and the treacherous one. No sooner did Anselmo return to his house than he asked Camila the question he had not asked earlier, an oversight that had astounded her: he asked her to describe the circumstances that had led her to write the letter she had sent him. Camila replied that it had seemed to her that Lotario had been freer with his attentions than when Anselmo was at home, but now that she could see things clearly, she believed it had been her imagination, for Lotario avoided seeing her or being found alone with her. Anselmo told her not to burden her conscience with such suspicions, for he knew that Lotario was in love with one of the leading young ladies of the city, whose praises he sang under the name of Clori; but even if he were not, there was no reason to doubt Lotario's veracity or the profound friendship between them. Had Camila not been forewarned by Lotario that his love for Clori was feigned and that he had purposely told Anselmo of it so he might spend a few moments praising Camila herself, she would undoubtedly have been snared in a hopeless web of jealousy; but having been forewarned she underwent this shocking revelation with calm and a lack of concern.

The following day, while the three of them were seated round the dinner table, Anselmo asked Lotario to recite a poem he had written for his beloved Clori, and since Camila was not acquainted with her, he might say whatever he pleased.

"Even if she knew her," replied Lotario, "I would keep nothing concealed, for when a lover praises his lady's beauty but labels her as cruel, he casts no aspersions on her good name. However, be that as it may, let me simply say that yesterday I composed a sonnet to the ingratitude of my Clori, which goes like this:

In the dead silence of the peaceful night,
When others' cares are hushed in soft repose,
The sad account of my neglected woes
To conscious heaven and Clori I recite.
And when the sun, with his returning light,
Forth from the east his radiant journey goes,
With accents such as sorrow only knows,
My grief to tell, is all my poor delight.
And when bright Phoebus from his starry throne,
Sends rays direct upon the parchéd soil,
Still in the mournful tale I persevere.
Returning night renews my sorrow's toil;
And though from morn to night I weep and moan,
Nor heaven nor Clori my complainings hear."

Camila found the sonnet pleasing enough, whereas Anselmo found it delightful. In his praise of it he said the lady had acted too cruelly in failing to be moved by such clear expressions of sincerity; to which Camila responded,

"Then in everything that lovesick poets say, they speak the truth?"

"They do not speak it as poets," replied Lotario, "but as men in love they are as tongue-tied as they are truthful."

"That is certainly true," said Anselmo in an attempt to lend support and credence to Lotario's ideas, but Camila was as unaware of Anselmo's intent as she was enamored of Lotario. Since all his affairs were a source of delight to her and since she knew the sentiments in the poems were addressed to *her*, the actual Clori, she begged him to recite another sonnet or poem if he knew one.

"I do know one," said Lotario, "but I am afraid it is not as good as the first, or, I should say, it is no worse, but I shall read it and let you be the judge.

Believe me, nymph, I feel th'impending blow,
And glory in the near approach of death;
For, when thou seest my corpse devoid of breath,
My constancy and truth thou sure wilt know.
Welcome to me oblivion's shade obscure!
Welcome the loss of fortune, life, and fame!
But thy loved features, and thy honored name,
Deep graven on my heart, shall still endure.
And these, as sacred relics, will I keep
Till that sad moment when to endless night
My long-tormented soul shall take her flight.
Alas for him who on the darkened deep
Floats idly, sport of the tempestuous tide,
No port to shield him, and no star to guide!

Anselmo also praised this second sonnet as he had the first and in this way went along adding link upon link to the chain with which he was binding himself and ensuring his own dishonor, for the more Lotario dishonored him, the more Anselmo extolled Lotario's honor. Because of this, every step Camila took in her descent into the depths of degradation raised her, in the opinion of her husband, towards the heights of virtue and good repute.

It happened that on one occasion during this period when Camila found herself alone with her maid, she said to her,

"I am ashamed, Leonela my friend, to see how little self-respect I have shown, for I promptly gave Lotario complete possession of my will without making him work long and hard to purchase it. I am afraid he will place too much importance upon my hasty acquiescence without considering all the pressure he exerted to make it impossible for me to resist him."

"Don't let that worry you, my lady," said Leonela. "It is not important, nor is there any reason to value less the gift that is promptly bestowed if what is given is truly good and in itself worthy of esteem. There is even the saying: 'A gift given promptly is a gift given twice.'"

"Yes, but there is that other saying," replied Camila: "'A gift less costly is a gift less esteemed.'"

"That saying does not apply to you," said Leonela, "for love, according to what I have heard, sometimes hurries and sometimes dallies, speeding along with some persons but lingering with others, tempering some but inflaming others, while some it merely wounds but others it kills. In a fleeting second it dashes madly to fulfill its desires but just as abruptly curbs and terminates them. In the morning it lays siege to a fortress and by nightfall has overthrown it, since there is no force capable of resisting it. This being so, why are you frightened and what is it you fear, for the same thing must have occurred to Lotario when love availed itself of my master's absence as the instrument for making you yield? It was absolutely essential to carry out during Anselmo's absence what love had decided upon, before he had time to return, for his sudden appearance would have left the task unfulfilled. Love has no better agent to execute its desires than opportunity, of which it avails itself in all its actions, particularly at the outset. Of all this I am quite certain, more from experience than from hearsay, and some day, my lady, I will explain it to you, for I too am made of flesh and my blood is youthful. What is more, my lady, you didn't yield or surrender yourself until you had glimpsed the depths of Lotario's soul in his tears and sighs and in his words, promises, and gifts, whereby his soul and all his virtues showed you how worthy he was of your love. And this being the case, don't let your imagination be beset by scruples or prudishness but be assured that Lotario admires you as much as you admire him. Be happy and content in the knowledge that, now that you have been ensnared in the web of love, it is one that will hold you fast by its worth and esteem, for Lotario possesses not only the four *S*s [2] that true lovers are said to possess but the entire alphabet. If you doubt this, just listen and you will see that I can recite it by heart. He is, in my view and opinion, *a*miable, *b*rave, *c*ourteous, *d*evoted, *e*legant, *f*aithful, *g*enerous, *h*onorable, *i*llustrious, *l*oyal, *m*anly, *n*oble, *o*bliging, *p*ious, *q*uick-witted, *r*ich – the *S*s I've already mentioned – *t*rustworthy, *v*eracious, *x* doesn't suit him because it is an aspirate, *y* has already been mentioned, and *z*ealous of your honor." [3]

Camila found her maid's ABCs amusing and considered her to be more experienced in matters of love than she admitted. Leonela acknowledged as much, informing Camila that she was having an affair with a young man of noble birth from that very city, a fact that disturbed Camila, for she feared the situation might jeopardize her own honor. She pressed her as to whether her conversing with him had led to more than mere conversation. Leonela answered quite shamelessly and brazenly that it had, for it is an established fact that moral shortcomings on the part of the lady of the house lead to

---

2 ***Sabio*** ('wise'), ***solo*** ('single'), ***solícito*** ('solicitous'), and ***secreto*** ('discreet')

3 In Cervantes' day the letter *i* was used to represent *i, j,* and *y,* hence the omission of the last two from the list. Likewise, *u* was used to represent both *u* and *v. K* and *w* were not then nor now letters of the Spanish alphabet. And the modern letters *ch, ll, ñ,* and *rr* were not recognized as separate letters in Cervantes' day.

shamelessness in her maids, for, when they see their mistress stumble, they no longer care whether they themselves misbehave or their mistress learns of it. Camila could do nothing more than plead with Leonela not to mention her affair to the person she said was her lover and to treat her own concerns with secrecy lest they come to the attention of Anselmo or Lotario. Leonela promised to do so but complied in such a way that she confirmed Camila's fear that, because of her maid, she was destined to lose her good name. The bold and shameless Leonela, seeing that her mistress' conduct was not what it once was, had the audacity to bring her lover into the house, feeling confident that even if her mistress saw him, she would not dare expose him. Mistresses by their errant ways bring this and other difficulties upon themselves because *they* become slaves to their own maids, whose indecencies and wicked acts they are forced to conceal as in Camila's situation. Though the latter noticed on more than one occasion that Leonela was with her lover in a certain room of the house, she not only hesitated to scold her but even provided her a place to hide him so as to remove every possibility that her husband might see him. And yet she was unable to remove all of them, because on one occasion Lotario saw him leaving just as the sun was rising. Not knowing who he was, he at first fancied him to be an apparition, but when he saw him take several steps and then pull the cloak over his face to conceal his identity, he abandoned his first naive idea and hit upon another that would have meant the perdition of everyone, had Camilla not come to the rescue. Lotario believed the man he had seen leaving Anselmo's house at such an improper hour had not come there on Leonela's account – in fact, he was not even aware of Leonela's existence. He simply believed that, just as Camila had been free and easy with him, she had behaved the same way with another. Such are the added encumbrances which the misbehavior of an errant woman brings with it, for she raises doubts about her honor in the very one who solicited and persuaded her to yield to him. He believes she will give herself to others just as easily, and he invariably gives credence to any suspicion of this kind that comes his way. It would appear that Lotario took absolute leave of his senses at that moment and forgot all the advice he had given others, for nothing he did was either proper or reasonable. Because of the blind rage of jealousy gnawing at his heart, Lotario could hardly wait to exact revenge on Camila, though she was innocent of any wrongdoing. In his impatience he hurried off to see Anselmo and, finding him still in bed, said to him,

"I would have you know, Anselmo, that for a number of days now I have been struggling with myself to keep from telling you what I can no longer possibly or rightfully hide from you. Be advised that Camila's fortress has fallen and I am free to dispose of it in any manner I choose. If I have been slow to inform you of this fact, it is because I wanted to see if it was merely a whim on her part or whether she did it to test me to see if my proposals of love to her, which with your permission I have begun, were made in good faith. Moreover, I felt that if she was the person she should have been – the one we both believed her to be – she would by now have given you an account of my solicitations. Having observed, however, that she has been slow to do so, I realize the truth of the promise she made me: that the next time you were away from home she would meet me in the dressing room in which you keep your jewels," and it was true that Camila was in the habit of speaking to him there. "I would not have you rush headlong into committing some vengeful act, for until now the sin has been committed only in her imagination and it is possible that between now and the time it becomes a reality, Camila will alter her intentions and repentance will take their place. Inasmuch as you have always followed my advice wholly or in part, accept a word of advice that I am now about to offer you so that you, with complete confidence and assurance, may satisfy your curiosity concerning the thing that matters most to you. Pretend to go away for two or three days as you have done in the past but arrange to remain hidden in your dressing room, where you can use the tapestries and other articles there to conceal yourself quite comfortably. You will then see with your own eyes, and I with mine, what Camila's intentions are. If they are evil ones, which is possible but by no means certain, you may secretly, cleverly, and discreetly serve as the executioner of your own indignity."

Lotario's comments left Anselmo astonished, bewildered, and dumbfounded, having caught him at a time when he least expected to hear them, for he assumed that Camila had always warded off Lotario's feigned assaults and he was beginning to revel in the glory of her triumph. He remained silent for some time while staring at the floor and not moving an eyelash but he finally said,

"You, Lotario, have acted in the manner I would have expected because of your friendship, and I shall follow your advice completely. Do whatever you will but keep this affair secret, which is what matters most in this unexpected development."

Lotario promised to do so but, after leaving, totally repented of everything he had said, realizing how foolishly he had acted, since he himself might have taken revenge upon Camila but not in such a cruel and dishonorable manner. He cursed his judgement, criticized his hasty decision, and could think of no way to rectify what was already done or to find a reasonable solution to his dilemma. He finally decided to give Camila a full account, and since he had every opportunity to do so, he found her alone that same day. But the moment she saw him, she said,

"You should know, Lotario my friend, that my heart is aching so much it seems to want to burst in my bosom and it will be miraculous if it does not. Leonela's lack of shame has assumed such proportions that every night she receives a lover of hers in this house and is with him till morning at great risk to my good name, because anyone who sees him leave my house at such an improper hour is free to interpret it any way he chooses. What troubles me is that I cannot scold or chastise her because her being witness to our affair has put a muzzle on my mouth, making me keep silent about hers, and I am certain something ill will result from all this."

When Camila began to voice these concerns, Lotario believed it was some ploy to make him think the man he had seen leaving her house was Leonela's lover and not her own, but when he saw her weep, become distraught, and plead for his help, he became convinced it was true and, because he believed her, ended up confused and thoroughly repentant. But despite all this, he told Camila not to worry, as he would arrange to put a stop to Leonela's insolence. He also told her what he had said to Anselmo while engulfed by the turbulent rage of jealousy, as well as the fact that Anselmo had agreed to hide in the dressing room, where he could easily observe how unfaithful she had been. Lotario begged her forgiveness for his folly and asked her to advise him how he might remedy the situation and emerge successfully from the intricate labyrinth into which his poor judgement had placed him.

Camila was appalled to hear what Lotario told her and she quite angrily and judiciously scolded him, criticizing his evil intentions and the ridiculously harmful decision he had made, for despite the fact that a woman's mind, more so than a man's, is by nature capable of both good and evil but often fails her the moment she resorts to reason, Camila immediately came up with a solution to that apparently insoluble situation. She told Lotario to have Anselmo hide the next day where he had indicated and she would turn his presence into profit so that from that moment forth the two of them could enjoy each other's company without fear of detection. Without explaining her plan more fully, she told him that, once Anselmo was hidden, he was to come forth when Leonela summoned him and, regarding anything he was asked, was to answer as though he were unaware of Anselmo's presence. Lotario asked her to explain her plan so he might more safely and advisedly do everything he deemed necessary.

"I assure you," said Camila, "there is nothing more for you to do than to respond to everything I ask you."

Camila refused to explain her intentions in advance, fearing he might not be willing to go along with the idea that she esteemed so highly, or that he might come up with another that was not as good. With this taken care of, Lotario left. The next day, under the pretext of going to his friend's village, Anselmo left the house but came back to hide, being able to do so with ease because Camila and Leonela had made every effort to accommodate him. Once hidden, Anselmo felt the trepidation a person might feel who was waiting to view with his own eyes the exposure of the innermost recesses of his honor, and he saw himself on the verge of losing the greatest treasure he felt he possessed in the person of his beloved Camila. Once they were absolutely certain that Anselmo was hidden, Camila and Leonela entered the dressing room, and as soon as Camila came inside she heaved a deep sigh and said,

"Oh, Leonela my friend, before I set in motion the things I wish to keep secret from you lest you try to stop me, would it not be better for you to take Anselmo's dagger, which I asked you to bring, and plunge it into this vile breast of mine? And yet, don't do any such thing, for why should I bear the punishment for someone else's sin? I would first like to know what it was that Lotario's impudent, disrespectful eyes saw in me to make him dare reveal to me a request as vile as the one he revealed, much to the detriment of his friend and to my dishonor. Go to the window, Leonela, and summon him, for he is undoubtedly in the street waiting to put his devious scheme into effect. However, mine, which is just as cruel as it is honorable, shall be put into effect first."

"Oh, my dear lady," replied the shrewd and complicitous Leonela, "what do you intend to do with that dagger? Surely, you are not thinking of taking your own life or Lotario's? Whichever you choose will cause the loss of your good name and reputation. You would be wiser to disguise your hurt and deny that wicked man the opportunity to enter this house and find us alone. Remember, my lady, that we are poor defenseless women whereas he is a man and a determined one at that. Since he is coming here with that evil proposition and is blinded by passion, it may turn out that before you can carry out your plan, he will do something worse than taking your life. Damn my master Anselmo, who has been willing to give that scoundrel such a free hand in his house! Besides, if you kill him, my lady, as I fear you intend to do, what shall we do with him once he is dead?"

"What, my friend?" responded Camila; "we shall leave him for Anselmo to bury, for it is only fitting for him to have the honor and task of burying his own infamy. Now, go ahead and call him, for each moment that I delay exacting the vengeance demanded by my insult makes me feel I am being disloyal to my husband's honor."

Anselmo listened to all this, and every word that Camila uttered caused him to change his mind, and when he heard her say she had resolved to kill Lotario, he started to come forth and reveal himself to prevent her from performing such a deed but was restrained by his curiosity to see where such a decent, noble resolve might lead, for he intended to leap out at the last moment and thwart her. At that instant, Camila was suddenly overcome by a severe swoon and collapsed onto a nearby bed. When Leonela saw this, she began to weep most bitterly and said,

"Oh, woe is me, that I should be so unfortunate as to witness the death, here in my arms, of the flower of earthly respectability, the crown of virtuous women, the paragon of purity!"

Who could have listened to these and similar utterances without considering her the most loyal and distressed maid on earth and her mistress another persecuted Penelope? It was not long before Camila recovered from her swoon and no sooner did she do so than she said,

"Why don't you hurry, Leonela, and summon the most loyal friend of a friend the sun has ever beheld or the night concealed. Stop hesitating and get started. Run along and be fast about it before the fire of my anger burns itself out during the delay, or the just vengeance I seek dissolves into mere threats and oaths."

"I'm on my way to call him, my lady," said Leonela, "but you must first give me that dagger lest, while I am gone, you commit some act that will make all of us who love you shed tears for the rest of our lives."

"You may be certain, my dear Leonela, that I shall do nothing of the sort. I may seem unrestrained and foolish in your eyes but when it comes to my honor, I shall not follow in the footsteps of that Lucretia who is said to have slain herself without ever having committed any wrong and without first having slain the one who was the source of her disgrace. If I die, I die, but it shall be after exacting revenge and satisfaction from the one who, because of *his* actions rather than any fault of my own, forced me to come to this place to lament his insolence."

Leonela required considerable urging to summon Lotario but she finally left. While she was gone, Camila remained behind as though conversing with herself:

"As God is my witness, would it not have been better to send Lotario away, as I have done on so many earlier occasions, than to risk, as I am now doing, being labeled a sinful and wanton woman, if only for so long as it takes me to show him he is mistaken? Unquestionably it would have been better but I would not be avenged nor my husband's honor vindicated if I had once again let him escape so easily and with so little cost from the situation in which his evil intentions have placed him. Let the traitor pay with his life for what he intended by such lascivious desires, and let the world know, if it should learn of it, that Camila not only kept her allegiance to her husband but avenged him with the one who dared offend him. In the long run, I think it might have been better to give Anselmo an account of this but that is exactly what I tried to do in the letter I sent him in the village. I am convinced that his failure to come to the defense of his honor, which I pointed out to him, must have been because he, out of sheer goodness and trust, could not believe that the bosom of such a close friend of his was capable of harboring any sort of intention that would go against his honor. For many days afterwards I did not believe it myself, nor would I have ever believed it, had his insolence not reached such a point that his open gifts, generous promises, and continual tears made it obvious to me. But to what purpose do I now voice these concerns? Can a steadfast resolve possibly require any sort of counsel? Of course not. Then away with traitors and bring on revenge! Let the false one enter, approach, die, and be done with – then let come what may! Spotless I came to the arms of the man heaven gave me for my own, and spotless will I forsake him. At worst, I shall go away bathed in my own undefiled blood and the impure blood of the falsest friendship the earth has ever witnessed."

While saying this, she paced back and forth in the room with the unsheathed dagger in her hand, taking such halting, irregular steps and making such gestures that she gave every indication of being out of her mind – of being, not a delicate woman, but some desperate ruffian. Anselmo observed all this, shielded by the tapestries behind which he had hidden, and was astonished by everything he saw. He felt that what he had now seen and heard was sufficient to rid him of his worst suspicions and he now hoped Lotario's test would not be carried out for fear of some unexpected and undesirable outcome. But just as he was about to step forward to embrace his wife and thereby reveal his presence and expose his scheme, he stopped short when he saw Leonela return leading Lotario by the hand. As soon as Camila saw him, she took the dagger and drew a long line across the floor in front of her, saying,

"Lotario, listen to what I have to say to you. If you so much as dare cross over this line or even come near it, the instant I see you do so will be the very instant I plunge this dagger I am holding into my breast. But before you say a word in response, I would have you listen to several complaints I wish to air, after which you may make any response you please. The first thing I should like, Lotario, is for you to tell me whether you know Anselmo my husband and what opinion you have of him; secondly, I should like you to tell me whether you know me. Just give me a simple answer without getting flustered or spending a lot of time pondering your answer, for what I am asking is not difficult."

From the very first moment that Camila had asked Lotario to have Anselmo hide, Lotario was intelligent enough to understand what she planned to do and accordingly made his own plan of action coincide with hers so cleverly and appropriately that the two of them lent that falsehood the appearance of the absolute truth. And so in response to Camila he said the following:

"I never dreamed, my fair Camila, that you called me here to ask me questions so far removed from the purpose for which I have come. If you are doing this to delay the arrival of the promised favor, you may just as well delay it even longer, for the closer one comes to obtaining the object of his desires, the more anxious he becomes. But so that you will not be able to claim that I refuse to answer your questions, let me just say that, of course, I know your husband Anselmo. Though we have known each other from our tenderest years, I prefer to leave unstated what you already know of our friendship lest I acknowledge the wrong that love forces me to inflict upon him, love which excuses even greater wrongs. I also know you and have the same regard for you that he does, for were it otherwise, any lesser reward than yours would fail to make me contravene the sacred laws of true friendship, broken and violated by me because of an adversary as powerful as love."

"If you are willing to admit that," cried Camila, "you mortal enemy of every person who deserves to be loved, with what effrontery do you dare appear before the one who you know is the mirror in which Anselmo sees himself, he being the one in whom you ought to see yourself so you would realize how little justification you have for wronging him. But, alas, I now understand what has caused you to hold yourself in so much lower esteem than you should: it must have been some oversight on my part, which I refuse to call an indecency, since it will not have resulted from a deliberate decision on my part but from one of those unintentional acts of carelessness oftentimes committed by women who are not cautious enough to exercise restraint in the presence of every single person. But tell me, you traitor, when did I ever respond to your entreaties with any word or act that might awaken in you a semblance of hope for carrying out your ignoble desires? When were your words of love not harshly and sternly rejected and rebuked by mine? When were your numerous promises and still more numerous gifts either believed or accepted by me? But since I am convinced that no one can long persevere in designs of love unless sustained by some sort of hope, I am willing to blame myself for your impertinence, for some negligent act on my part must have sustained your interest over such a lengthy period. I, therefore, am willing to inflict upon myself the punishment your transgression deserves so that you will understand that, if I can deal with myself in this cruel manner, I cannot possibly fail to do so with you. I have thus decided to summon you as a witness to the sacrifice I intend to make to the tarnished honor of my most honorable husband, wronged by you through the greatest diligence you were capable of, as well as by me because of the feeble precautions I took to avoid situations that might encourage and legitimize your evil thoughts. I shall state again that what I most regret and most desire to remedy with my own hands is my suspicion that some negligence on my part encouraged these outrageous intentions of yours, for if I am punished by some other person, my waywardness will become more widely known. But before I do this, I hope through my act of dying to slay and take with me the one who will finally satisfy my longing for revenge, because to whichever afterlife I go, I shall witness there a punishment meted out by an unbiased justice that will not bow and scrape before the person who has driven me to undertake such desperate measures."

In saying this, she took her unsheathed dagger and with incredible strength and swiftness rushed at Lotario so evidently intent upon burying it in his breast that he was somewhat uncertain whether her actions were real or feigned, and he was forced to avail himself of all his skill and strength to prevent Camila from stabbing him. She effected this surprising trick and sham with great realism, and to lend it the appearance of truth, planned to stain it with her own blood. But when she saw herself incapable of overpowering Lotario, or so she pretended, she cried out,

"Though fate refuses to satisfy my most just intention in every regard, at least it shall not keep me from satisfying it in part."

Struggling to free her dagger hand, which Lotario had seized, she pulled it free and, aiming the dagger at a spot where it would not inflict serious harm, plunged it in just above her left collarbone next to her shoulder and then fell to the floor as though she had fainted. Leonela and Lotario were bewildered and dumbfounded at such a development and they questioned the authenticity of this deed when they saw Camila lying on the floor bathed in her own blood. Lotario, pale and gasping for breath, hurried over to pull out the dagger but, seeing the slight wound, shook off the fright that had gripped him until that moment and once again he marveled at the intelligence, foresight, and great cleverness of the beautiful Camila. And so, to provide *his* expected contribution, he began a long, sad lamentation over Camila's body as though she were dead, directing an endless stream of curses at himself but also at the one who had placed him in that predicament. And since he knew his friend Anselmo was listening, he uttered such lamentations that anyone hearing him might have felt more pity for Lotario than for Camila, even if she were presumed dead. Leonela lifted Camila in her arms and placed her on the bed, imploring Lotario to go for someone to secretly care for Camila's wound. She also asked him how they might explain the wound if Anselmo should return before it healed. Lotario replied that they could say anything they pleased, for he was in no condition to give advice that would be of benefit to anyone. He merely told her to stanch the bleeding, for he was going to where no one would ever find him, and with a great display of pain and sorrow he left the house. As soon as he found himself alone in a place where no one could see him, he made countless signs of the cross, marveling all the while at Camila's ingenuity and Leonela's most realistic performance. He could just imagine Anselmo's conviction that in his wife he possessed a second Portia, and he wished he were with Anselmo so the two of them might celebrate that falsehood and most bogus truth imaginable.

Leonela, as we have said, stanched the flow of blood, which had been barely sufficient to make her ploy believable. Cleansing the wound with a bit of wine and bandaging it in her makeshift manner, she said so many things in Camila's praise while ministering to her that, if they had been preceded by no others, they would have sufficed to convince Anselmo that in Camila he possessed a paragon of virtue. The utterances of Leonela were joined by those of Camila, who accused herself of being cowardly and faint-hearted, for she had been found wanting at the very moment she most needed the strength to take her own life, a life she now found totally abhorrent. She asked her maid whether she should tell her dear husband the whole story but Leonela advised her not to do so, for that would obligate him to seek revenge from Lotario, which he could not do without risk to himself. She added that a good wife should not give her husband any reason to become embroiled in quarrels but should do everything in her power to prevent such situations. Camila said she found her advice quite sound and would follow it, but in any event it would be necessary to explain the cause of the wound, which Anselmo could hardly fail to notice. To this, Leonela replied that she simply could not bring herself to tell a lie even for the purpose of make-believe.

"Then, my dear," said Camila, "how can I do so, since I would not dare invent or persist in a lie even if my life depended upon it. If, in fact, we cannot find a solution for this, it will be better to tell him the plain truth than to let him to catch us in an outright falsehood."

"Don't worry, my lady," replied Leonela, "between now and morning I will think of something to say, and who knows: maybe the wound is located where you can cover it up, or maybe heaven will look kindly upon our intentions, inasmuch as they are just and honorable. Try to compose yourself, my lady, and remain calm, and don't let my master see you frightened like this. The rest you may leave up to me and to God, who never fails those who are well-intentioned."

Anselmo had been a model of attentiveness listening to and watching the tragedy being played out on the death of his honor. The actors had performed with such acute feeling and emotion that they seemed genuinely convinced of what they merely feigned. Anselmo looked forward to night and the chance to slip away from home to pay a visit to his good friend Lotario so they might celebrate the precious pearl he had found in the confirmation of his wife's goodness. The two women made it convenient for him to do so and he availed himself of the opportunity by setting out in search of Lotario. Once he found him, it is impossible to describe the number of times he embraced him, how much he extolled his happiness, or the countless praises he heaped upon Camila. Lotario listened to all this without evincing any signs of happiness, for he could not rid himself of the thought that his friend had been completely deceived and that *he* had been the one who had unjustifiably wronged him. Though Anselmo noticed Lotario's lack of joy, he attributed it to the latter's having abandoned the wounded Camila, as well as to Lotario's belief that he was to blame. And so among other things, he told Lotario not to be concerned about what had happened to Camila, as there was nothing to fear, for the wound was undoubtedly a slight one or the women would not have agreed to hide it from him. Instead, from that time forward, Lotario should take heart and rejoice with him, for, thanks to Lotario's skillful participation, Anselmo saw himself raised to the highest pinnacle of happiness one might aspire to. He suggested that Lotario spend his time composing verses in praise of Camila, thus making her name live for centuries to come. Lotario praised his suggestion and said that he, for his part, would help construct such a worthy edifice.

With this, Anselmo remained the most exquisitely deceived man upon the face of the earth, for he had personally brought home what he believed to be the instrument of his glory but which, in actuality, entailed the total destruction of his reputation. Camila received him with a resentful look on her face but with a smile in her heart. This deception lasted for quite some time but several months later Dame Fortune gave her wheel a turn and the wickedness that until then had been so skillfully concealed became public knowledge and Anselmo's unreasonable curiosity cost him his life.

Chapter Thirty-Five

The fierce and extraordinary battle that Don Quixote waged with some wineskins full of red wine, together with the conclusion of *The Tale of Unreasonable Curiosity*

Very little of the story remained to be read when Sancho in a state of panic and shouting at the top of his lungs ran from the room where Don Quixote had gone to bed.

"Come quick, everyone, and help my master, who's engaged in the most hard fought, determined battle my eyes have ever seen! As God is my witness, he has dealt Princess Micomicona's giant adversary such a blow with his sword that he has lopped off his head as neatly as if it were a turnip."

"What are you talking about, my son?" said the priest, putting down his book; "have you lost your wits, Sancho? How the dickens can that be true when the giant is two thousand leagues from here?"

Just then, they heard a loud disturbance in Don Quixote's room, where he was shouting,

"Stop, thief! Now I've got you, you worthless scoundrel! Your scimitar shall avail you not."

And he seemed to be slashing at the walls with his sword, at which point Sancho said,

"Don't everyone just stand there listening; go in and stop the fight or help my master even if it's no longer necessary, since the giant is undoubtedly dead and is giving an account to God of his past life of wickedness. I saw his blood streaming over the floor and his decapitated head lying to one side, and it was as big as a large wineskin."

"I'll be hanged," said the innkeeper, "if Don Quixote, or Don Beelzebub, hasn't slashed some of the wineskins at the head of his bed that are filled with wine, and the spilled wine must be what this poor soul thinks is blood."

At this point he entered the room with the others right behind him, where they found Don Quixote in the strangest outfit imaginable. He was clad in a shirt so short in front it failed to cover his thighs and was six inches shorter in back. His legs were quite long, skinny, hairy, and not overly clean, and his head was topped by a small greasy red cap that belonged to the innkeeper. Round his left arm he had wrapped the blanket from his bed, which Sancho viewed with some misgivings, the reason for which *he* understood all too well. In his right hand Don Quixote clutched his bare sword with which he was striking in all directions while uttering taunts as though he were actually fighting some giant. But the most amazing thing was that his eyes were closed, for he was asleep and dreaming of doing battle with the giant. So intense was his imagination regarding the adventure he was about to conclude that it led him to believe he had already reached the kingdom of Micomicón and was engaged in battle with his adversary. Accordingly, he had struck the skins so many times with his sword, fancying he was striking the giant, that the entire room was swimming in wine. When the innkeeper saw this, he flew into a rage and rushed at Don Quixote, whom he began to belabor with such a torrent of blows from his fists that, had Cardenio and the priest not pulled him off, he would have put an end to the war with that giant. But despite all this, the poor knight never awoke until the barber brought a large jug of cold water from the well and dowsed his entire body with it. At this point Don Quixote did awaken but not sufficiently to understand what had taken place. Dorotea, seeing how skimpily Don Quixote was dressed, refused to go inside to view the battle between her deliverer and her nemesis. Sancho went about looking for the giant's head in every corner of the room but, when he was unable to locate it, he said,

"I now understand that everything in this house is bewitched. On the previous occasion in this same inn they gave me an awful drubbing without my knowing who it was, for I was never able to see anyone, and now this head is nowhere to be found, even though I saw it cut off with my very own eyes and the blood was pouring from his body like water from a fountain."

"What blood and what fountain are you talking about, you enemy of God and all His saints?" exclaimed the innkeeper. "Can't you see, you scoundrel, that the blood and fountain are nothing more than these wineskins that have been split open, plus the red wine the room is swimming in? I just wish the soul of the person who split them open were swimming in hell!"

"I'm innocent," said Sancho. "All I know is that I'll probably be so unlucky as a result of not finding this head that my earldom will dissolve like salt in water."

Sancho awake was worse than his master asleep, being so thoroughly caught up in the things his master had promised him. The innkeeper was on the verge of despair because of Sancho's indifference and Don Quixote's mischief but he swore it would not turn out the way it had the last time when they got off without paying, nor was Don Quixote about to avail himself of the privileges of his knight-errantry to keep from paying for both of them, including the cost of the patches that would have to be sewn onto the wineskins. The priest was holding Don Quixote's hands and the latter, imagining that he had brought this adventure to a conclusion and was now in the presence of the Princess Micomicona, knelt before the priest and said,

"Exalted and illustrious lady, your highness may live from this day forward safe from any harm this base creature might cause you. I too from this day forward am released from the oath I swore, for thanks to the help of Almighty God and the boon of her in whom I have my life and being, I have carried it off with great success."

When Sancho heard this, he said,

"Didn't I tell you I wasn't drunk after all? My master already has the giant salted away and curing, so God's in His heaven and I've got my earldom!"

Who could have kept from laughing at the absurdity of these two, both master and servant? In fact, everyone present was laughing except the innkeeper, who was cursing himself. Finally, the barber, Cardenio, and the priest were able, after considerable effort, to return Don Quixote to his bed, who, showing signs of complete exhaustion, fell fast asleep. Leaving him in the arms of Morpheus, they went down to the entrance of the inn to console Sancho Panza for not having found the giant's head, though they had more trouble pacifying the innkeeper, who was beside himself with grief at the sudden demise of his wineskins. His wife was also shouting and screaming,

"It was a sad day and an ill-fated hour when this knight-errant entered my establishment. Would that I had never laid eyes on this person who's costing me so dearly. The last time, he went away without paying for a night's lodging and meals for himself and his squire, as well as straw and barley for his horse and ass, saying he was a venturer knight (may God give him an *evil* adventure, along with all the other venturer knights in the world) and, as such, he was not obliged to pay for anything, as was stipulated in the codes of knight-errantry. And now because of him this other gentleman has carried off my tail and brought it back to me with more than half a *real*s damage and most of the hair missing, so it no longer serves the needs of my husband. And then on top of everything, to split my wineskins and spill my wine – I'd like to see his own blood spilled! Well, he's got another thought coming, for I swear upon my mother's soul and my father's bones that they're going to pay me every last *real* or my name isn't what it is and I'm not my father's daughter!"

The enraged hostess voiced these and similar complaints, being assisted in this by her good maid Maritornes. The daughter said nothing but merely smiled from time to time. The priest calmed everyone down by promising to make good all her losses, including the wineskins and the wine, but mainly the damage to her tail, over which she was making such a fuss. Dorotea consoled Sancho Panza, telling him that as soon as it could be verified that his master had decapitated the giant and she saw herself in peaceful possession of her throne, she promised to award him the best earldom in her kingdom. Sancho was consoled by this and assured the princess she could be certain he had seen the giant's head, and if further proof was needed, he had a beard that hung down to his waist; but if it failed to turn up, it was because everything that happened in that inn was under a spell, as he had discovered the previous time he had stayed there. Dorotea said she was of the same opinion and told him not to worry, as everything would turn out to his heart's content. Once everyone had calmed down, the priest expressed his desire to finish reading the story, since so little of it remained. Cardenio, Dorotea, and all the others begged him to finish it, and so, wishing to please everyone and being eager to read it himself, he continued the story, which went as follows:

It turned out that as a result of Anselmo's contentment over Camila's goodness he led a happy and carefree life. Camila deliberately turned a cold shoulder to Lotario so that Anselmo would believe her feelings towards him to be the opposite of those she actually felt. And to lend more credibility to her actions, Lotario asked permission to stop coming to their house, since Camila was visibly distressed each time she saw him. But the deceived Anselmo forbade his doing anything of the sort and thus in a thousand different ways he became the architect of his own dishonor rather than of his happiness, as he believed. Meanwhile, the happiness Leonela experienced at seeing her love affair sanctioned reached such proportions that, disregarding all other considerations, she pursued it with reckless abandon, confident that her mistress would conceal it or even advise her how to manage it without undue fear. Then one night, Anselmo heard footsteps in Leonela's room and decided to go inside to see whose they were, but when he found the door locked, it merely increased his determination to open it. Using all his might, he forced it open just in time to see a man jump through the window into the street. Running over quickly in an attempt to apprehend him or at least to see who he was, he was unable to accomplish either objective because Leonela flung her arms round him and exclaimed,

"Control yourself, my lord, and don't get excited or chase after the one who ran away. It's just an affair of mine; in fact, he's my betrothed."

Anselmo refused to believe her; instead, he drew his dagger and threatened to stab her, ordering her to tell him the truth or be slain. Frightened and not knowing what she was saying, she cried out,

"Don't kill me, master, and I'll tell you things that are more remarkable than you can imagine."

"Tell me at once," exclaimed Anselmo; "if not, you are a dead woman!"

"I can't do so at this moment," said Leonela, "for I'm too upset. Give me until tomorrow, when you shall learn things from me that will astound you; but be assured that the one who fled through my window is a young man from this city who has sworn to be my husband."

Anselmo grew calm at this point and agreed to wait until the suggested time, never suspecting that he might hear anything having to do with Camila, such was his satisfaction and confidence in her goodness. He left the room and locked Leonela inside, assuring her she would not get out until she told him what she had to say. Going directly to see Camila, he related everything that had transpired between him and her maid, including the promise she had made to reveal things of the utmost seriousness and importance. That Camila was upset goes without saying; suffice it to say that she experienced considerable dread when she assumed, as she had every right to do, that Leonela would undoubtedly tell Anselmo everything she knew about Camila's lack of faithfulness, and since she did not have the courage to wait to see whether or not her assumption was correct, she waited until she felt Anselmo was asleep and then that very night gathered up her most valuable jewels and a sum of money and, without being observed by anyone, left the house and went to Lotario's. She told him what had transpired and asked him to put her in a secure place or to help her flee to some place where they would be safe from Anselmo. Camila caused Lotario such consternation that he was unable to say a word in reply and was even less able to decide what to do. He finally agreed to take Camila to a convent in which one of his sisters was prioress. Camila consented to this and Lotario with all the haste demanded by the situation went with her to the convent, where he left her and then abandoned the city without informing anyone of his departure.

With the arrival of dawn, Anselmo got out of bed but did not notice that Camila was not at his side, such was his eagerness to learn what Leonela had to tell him. Hurrying to the room in which he had left her enclosed, he unlocked the door and entered but failed to find Leonela inside. All he found there were some knotted sheets hanging from the window, a clear sign that she had let herself down from her room and run away. Saddened by this, he went back to tell Camila but, when he failed to find her in their bed or any part of the house, he became utterly confused. He asked the household servants where she was but no one could tell him what he wanted to know. Then as he was rushing about in search of Camila, he happened to catch sight of her open jewel cases and noticed that most of her jewels were missing, at which point he finally realized the extent of his disgrace and understood that Leonela was not the cause of his misfortune. And so, sad and grief-stricken, he interrupted his dressing at this point and left the house partially dressed, intent upon informing his friend Lotario of his wretchedness. When he failed to find Lotario, and the latter's servants reported that he had not come home that night but had carried off all his money, Anselmo thought he would go mad. And to put the finishing touches on this whole affair, when he returned home, he found none of his servants or maids but a house that was empty and deserted.

Not knowing what to think, say, or do, he began to show signs of losing his mind. Taking stock of the situation, he saw that in a single instant he had lost his wife, his best friend, his servants, apparently the protection of all-encompassing heaven, and above all his honor, for in Camila's disappearance he beheld his own perdition. Finally, after considerable time had passed, he resolved to go to the village of his friend where he had stayed at the time of contriving this whole ill-founded scheme. After locking his house, he mounted his horse and with flagging spirits started on his way. He had scarcely traveled halfway when he was overcome by his thoughts and was forced to dismount. Tying his horse to a tree, he let himself collapse at the base of its trunk, where he sat mournfully and painfully sighing until it was nearly night, at which time he saw a man riding from the city on horseback. Greeting him, he asked him what news there was in Florence. The man from the city replied,

"The strangest that has come to our attention in quite some time, for it is rumored throughout the city that last night Lotario, the close friend of Anselmo the Wealthy who lives in San Giovanni, carried off Camila, the wife of Anselmo, who is also missing. All this was reported by one of Camila's maids, whom the governor discovered last night climbing down a sheet she had hung from a window in Anselmo's house. I don't know exactly how the affair took place; all I know is that the whole city is shocked by these events, since no one would have expected such a development, considering the intimate friendship between the two, which was said to be so strong they were called *the two friends*."

"Is it known," asked Anselmo, "which way Lotario and Camila were headed?"

"No one has any idea," said the man from the city, "though the Governor has been most thorough in his search for them."

"Well, go with God, good sir," said Anselmo.

"And may He remain with your grace," replied the townsman as he rode off. With this wretched news Anselmo came within a hair of going out of his mind and even of ending his life. Struggling to his feet, he made his way to the house of his friend, who still knew nothing of his misfortune, but when the latter saw him arrive pale, haggard, and worn-out, he realized he had suffered some grievous harm. Anselmo immediately asked to be allowed to go to bed and be given some writing materials. They complied with his wishes and even locked his door as he requested. Once he found himself alone, his mind became so filled with thoughts of his misfortune that he could clearly see that his life was drawing to a close. Deciding to leave an explanation of the cause of his strange demise, he set about writing down his thoughts but, before he could record everything he intended to say, he breathed his last breath and delivered up his soul into the hands of the grief that had arisen as a result of his unreasonable curiosity. The master of the house, observing that the hour was late and there was no sign of his guest, decided to go to his room to see if he was still indisposed. He found him slumped over, half of his body on the bed and the other half across the writing desk over which he had been leaning, with the paper on which he had written unsealed and the pen still in his hand. After calling to him and receiving no reply, the host approached and took hold of his hand and, when he found it cold, he realized Anselmo was dead. Overcome with grief and shock, he immediately called the household staff to witness the tragedy that had befallen Anselmo. Then he read the piece of paper, which was written in Anselmo's own handwriting and contained the following sentiments:

A foolish and unreasonable desire has robbed me of my life. Should the news of my death find its way to Camila, I hope she will understand that I forgive her, since she was not obliged to perform miracles, nor did I have the right to ask her to do so. And since I have been the architect of my own dishonor, there is no reason to----------

This is all Anselmo had written and it was clear that death overtook him before he could finish the sentence. The following day, Anselmo's friend sent word of his demise to the relatives, who had already learned of the tragedy, and to the convent that housed Camila. She came within a hair of accompanying her husband on his involuntary journey – not because of the news of his death but because of the news of her lover's departure. It is reported that, although she now found herself a widow, she was unwilling to leave the convent and even less willing to take the vows of celibacy. A few days later, however, word reached her that Lotario had been killed in a battle that Monsieur de Lautrec had launched against the Great Captain Gonzalo Fernández de Córdoba in the kingdom of Naples, which is where her belatedly repentant lover had gone. When Camila learned of this, she took her vows but shortly thereafter met her death at the unrelenting hands of grief and melancholy. Such, then, was the end that befell them all – an end brought about by a most foolish beginning.

"I find the story quite interesting," said the priest, "but I cannot convince myself that it could actually have taken place. If it is indeed fictitious, then the author did a poor job, for it is impossible to imagine a husband so foolish as to undertake an experiment as costly as Anselmo's. On the other hand, were this an affair between a lover and his mistress, it might be carried off – but between a husband and wife is simply unbelievable. And, yet, as for the way the story is told, I do not find it unpleasing."

Chapter Thirty-Six

Further unusual incidents that took place at the inn

While this was taking place, the innkeeper called out from the inn gate,

"Here comes a fine band of guests. If they'll only stop here, we can all sing *Gaudeamus*."[1]

"And who might they be?" asked Cardenio.

"Four men with lances and shields riding swift chargers and wearing black travelers' masks," said the innkeeper, "and in their party, riding on a large saddle with arms and a back, is a veiled woman dressed in white, along with two lads on foot."

"Are they very near?" asked the priest.

"So near," said the innkeeper, "that they are just now arriving."

When she heard this, Dorotea covered her face and Cardenio went into Don Quixote's room. They scarcely had time to do this when into the courtyard filed all the persons the innkeeper had mentioned. The four horsemen, who were elegant in appearance and manners, dismounted and helped the woman down from her saddle, while one of them took her in his arms and seated her on a chair at the entrance to the room in which Cardenio had hidden. During all this time none of them had removed their masks or spoken a single word but, when the woman took her seat, she heaved

1 Latin: 'Let us rejoice.'

a deep sigh and let her arms fall limp, like someone ill or in a swoon. In the meantime, the foot servants had taken the horses to the stable. Observing all this, the priest in his curiosity to learn the identity of the persons attired in such outfits and enveloped in such silence went outside and asked the servants who they were. One of them replied,

"Goodness, your grace, I can't say who they are; all I know is that they give every indication of being persons of prominence, especially the one who came up and took the lady in his arms. The reason I say this is that they all defer to him and nothing is done except what he orders or says."

"And who is the lady, if I may ask?" said the priest.

"I don't know that either," replied the servant. "I've not seen her face during the entire trip but have heard so many sighs and moans from her that she seems to be giving up the ghost with each one. And yet, it is not surprising that we don't know more than we do, for my companion and I have been in their company for only two days. When we met them on the road, they begged and finally persuaded us to accompany them as far as Andalusia, offering to pay us handsomely if we did so."

"Have you heard any of them referred to by name?" asked the priest.

"No, as a matter of fact," said the servant, "for they all keep so silent while traveling that it is frightening. No sound comes from them except the poor lady's sighs and sobs, which move us all to pity. We feel that wherever she's going, she's going there against her will and, judging by her attire, she is either a nun or is about to become one, which is more likely. Perhaps she is becoming a nun against her wishes, which would certainly explain the unhappiness she seems to be experiencing."

"Anything is possible," replied the priest, who left them and returned to Dorotea. When the latter heard the veiled woman sigh, she was moved by her natural compassion to go over to her and say,

"What is the matter, my lady? Mind you, if it is something we women have experience in remedying, I for my part offer you my services most willingly."

The dejected lady made no reply even when Dorotea repeated her offer, and she remained silent until they were joined by the masked rider whom the servant had said the others obeyed. Addressing Dorotea, he said,

"Your ladyship is wasting your time trying to befriend that woman, for it is not in her nature to show gratitude for any favor extended to her, nor should you try to get her to answer unless you want to hear a stream of lies."

"I have never told a single one," said the woman, who until that moment had remained silent; "on the contrary, because I have always told the truth and have never been given to lying, I now find myself in all this misery, and I intend for you yourself to provide proof of this, for my unadulterated truthfulness will show you to be false and deceitful."

Cardenio heard these words quite clearly and distinctly, as though he were next to the person who had spoken them, because only the door of Don Quixote's room stood between them. As soon as he heard this, he cried out,

"Heaven help me! what is this I hear? What is that voice that has reached my ears?"

At this outcry the lady turned her head thoroughly startled. Unable to see the one who had cried out, she stood up and was about to enter the room when the gentleman noticed this and grabbed her, refusing to allow her to take another step. In all the commotion and confusion the taffeta covering her face fell off, revealing a face of incomparable and unearthly beauty, albeit pale and frightened. And because of her eyes, which darted so searchingly into every corner they were able to make out, she behaved like a person who had lost her mind. Dorotea and all those observing her were filled with great compassion even though they failed to understand the reason why. The gentleman holding her firmly by the shoulders was so thoroughly occupied with this task that he was unable to catch his own mask when it began to fall. Dorotea, who held the lady in her arms, raised her eyes and saw that the person holding her was none other than her husband Don Fernando. No sooner did she recognize him than she let out a long plaintive sigh from the depths of her being and fell backwards in a swoon, and had the barber not been present to catch her in his arms, she would have fallen to the floor. The priest went over to remove her mask to dowse her face with water and the moment he removed it, Don Fernando, who was holding the other woman in his arms, recognized her. He was dumbstruck at the sight of her but still managed to hold on to Luscinda, who was struggling to free herself from his grasp, for she had recognized Cardenio by his sigh, as he had her. Cardenio had also heard the sigh Dorotea had made when she swooned, and believing it to be his Luscinda, burst forth from the room terrified. The first person he saw was Don Fernando holding Luscinda in his arms, and Don Fernando also instantly recognized Cardenio. All three – Luscinda, Cardenio, and Dorotea – stood there dumbfounded and speechless, scarcely realizing what was happening to them. No one said a word as they all gazed at one another – Dorotea at Don Fernando, Don Fernando at Cardenio, Cardenio at Luscinda, and Luscinda at Cardenio. The first to break the silence was Luscinda, who addressed Don Fernando:

"Sir Don Fernando, I beg you by virtue of who you are, if you will do so for no other reason, to permit me to cling to this wall on which I am the ivy; to this protector of mine from whom your importunings, threats, promises, and gifts have been unable to separate me. May you observe that heaven by unusual and, to us, mysterious means has placed my true husband before me and you know only too well from a thousand costly demonstrations that death alone will be sufficient to erase him from my memory. May this open declaration lead you, now that you have no other choice, to turn your love into rage and your desire into disdain and thereby to take my life, for since I shall be forfeiting it in the presence of my dear husband, I shall consider it well disposed of. Perhaps with my death he will be satisfied that I have kept my word to him until the final moment of my life."

In the meantime, Dorotea had regained consciousness and heard what Luscinda said, at which point she finally realized who she was. Seeing that Don Fernando was still holding her in his arms and was not responding to anything she was saying, she summoned up all the courage she could and went over to him, at which point she threw herself at his feet, shedding a copious stream of lovely but pitiful tears. At this point she began to speak:

"My lord, unless the rays of that sun you hold in eclipse in your arms have taken away or darkened those of your eyes, you will notice that kneeling at your feet is the one bereft of happiness – until you deem otherwise – the unfortunate Dorotea. I am that humble farm girl whom you out of your kindness or for your pleasure deigned to raise to the level where she could call herself yours. I am the one who, enclosed within the bounds of purity, lived a life of happiness until at your words of importuning and apparently your just and loving sentiments, opened the gates of her modesty and handed over to you the keys to her freedom, a gift so ill-appreciated by you, as is clearly demonstrated by my having found it necessary to come here where you have discovered me and where I see you as you are. But I would not have you suppose that I have been driven to this place by my dishonor. I have been brought here only by the pain and sorrow of seeing myself abandoned by you. You desired me to be yours and you desired it to such an extent that even though you no longer do so, you cannot possibly cease to be mine. Consider, my lord, that the incomparable love I bear you can serve as compensation for the beauty and nobility of the one for whom you have abandoned me. You cannot belong to the beautiful Luscinda because you are mine, nor she to you, since she belongs to Cardenio. It will be easier for you, if you will but consider it, to confine your desires to loving that woman who adores you rather than seeking the love of that woman who hates you; and since you cultivated my negligence, pleaded with me to surrender my innocence, were not unaware of my station in life, and knew all too well how I succumbed to your every desire, you have no right to seek refuge by pleading deception. Now, if all this is true, which it is, and if you are as truly a Christian as a gentleman, why will you by so many evasions put off making me happy at the end as you did at the beginning? If you will not accept me for what I am, your true and lawful wife, at least allow me to be your slave, for so long as I am possessed by you, I shall consider myself happy and most fortunate. Don't abandon me or expose me to a stream of gossip about my dishonor, and don't condemn my parents to such a terrible old age. They are your faithful vassals and don't deserve such treatment as recompense for the loyal services they have always rendered your family. If you feel you will corrupt your blood by mixing it with mine, remember that there are few, if any, noble pedigrees on earth which have not traveled this same path. Remember too that descent through the woman is not what matters in noble blood lines, particularly when true nobility consists of virtue. If you are lacking in this – denying me what you rightfully owe me - I shall end up ahead of you in the matter of nobility. And lastly, sir, the final thing I shall say to you is that whether you like it or not, I am your wife and as a witness we have your words, which should not and cannot be false, if indeed you esteem that which you find hateful in me. As further witnesses we have the signature you wrote and heaven, which you called upon to be witness to the promises you made me. If all this does not suffice, your own conscience will not fail to scream in silence in the midst of your enjoyment, bringing you back to this truth to dampen your pleasure and joy."

These and similar sentiments were expressed by the sorrowful Dorotea with such emotion and sobbing that Don Fernando's companions, together with everyone present, shed tears as well. Don Fernando listened to her and did not say a word until her speech dissolved into sighs and sobs, for it would have required a heart of bronze to fail to be moved by such a display of grief. Luscinda stood gazing at her and was no less pained by her unhappiness than she was astonished at her great intelligence and beauty, and she would have gone over to her to offer a few words of consolation except that Don Fernando would not permit it, for he still gripped her tightly as he stood there filled with confusion and trepidation. After fixing his gaze upon Dorotea for several moments, he relaxed his grip and allowed Luscinda to go free.

"You win, fair Dorotea," said Don Fernando; "I cannot possibly persist in the face of so many truths at one time."

As soon as Don Fernando released Luscinda, she swooned and was about to collapse to the floor, at which point Cardenio, who had stationed himself behind Don Fernando's back to avoid being recognized, cast aside all fear and, exposing himself to great risk, sprang forward to catch Luscinda in his arms, whereupon he said,

"If heaven in its mercy is now pleased and willing to grant you rest, my loyal, steadfast, beautiful lady, I believe that you may do so nowhere more safely than in these arms which now enfold you, as they did on an earlier occasion when fate decreed that I should call you mine."

At these words Luscinda looked up at Cardenio and gradually managed to recognize him, first by his voice and finally by his appearance. Virtually beside herself with joy and paying no heed to decorum, she flung her arms round his neck and pressed her cheek to his, saying,

"You, my lord, are indeed the true master of this slave of yours, however much a hostile fate may try to prevent it or however many threats may be made on my life, which finds its sustenance in yours."

This presented a strange spectacle for Don Fernando and everyone present, as they were astonished at such an unusual turn of events. Dorotea fancied that the blood had drained from Don Fernando's face and that he was acting as though he might take revenge on Cardenio, for she saw him place his hand on his sword. But as soon as the thought occurred to her, she embraced his knees with unusual haste and began kissing them, at the same time holding them in her grasp to prevent him from moving. Then with her tears flowing freely, she said to him,

"What is it you intend to do, you who are my sole refuge at this unexpected moment? You have your wife at your feet, while the one you desire to be yours is in the arms of her husband. Consider whether it will be fitting or possible for you to rend asunder those persons whom heaven has brought together, or whether it will be seemly for you to raise to your own level the woman who, despite every obstacle and confirmed in truth and fidelity, stands before you bathing the face and breast of her rightful husband with her loving tears. I beg you in the name of God and implore you because of who you are not to allow this honest declaration to increase your anger but to diminish it to the extent that you will calmly and dispassionately allow these two lovers to enjoy whatever time heaven may grant them without further interference on your part, for by doing so you will demonstrate the generosity of your noble breast and the world will see that you are governed more by reason than by lust."

While Dorotea was voicing these sentiments, Cardenio held Luscinda in his arms and never took his eyes off Don Fernando, being determined, should he see him make the slightest move in his direction, to defend himself or to strike back at any and all adversaries even if it cost him his life. But at that moment all of Don Fernando's friends who were present came forward, which included the priest, the barber, and even our worthy Sancho. They all gathered round Don Fernando and pleaded with him to look kindly upon Dorotea's tears, for if everything she said was true, as they sincerely believed, she ought not be denied her most just expectations. They begged him to understand that it was not chance, as it might appear, but divine providence from heaven that had brought them all together in this place where one would have least expected it. He should also be advised, the priest reminded him, that death alone could separate Luscinda and Cardenio, and even if they were split asunder by the blade of some sword, they would consider themselves most fortunate, because in these cases for which there is no solution he would be wise to display a generous heart and to restrain and control himself by allowing these two, of his own free will, to enjoy the benefits heaven was now granting them. He would do well to fix his eyes upon Dorotea's beauty and he would see that few if any women could equal her, much less surpass her, for in addition to her beauty he should consider her humility and the profound love she felt for him. He should especially bear in mind, if he prided himself on being a gentleman and a Christian, that his only recourse was to comply with the promise he had made, for by complying with it, he would fulfill his duty to God and satisfy sensible people, who understand and acknowledge that it is the prerogative of a beautiful woman, even one of humble origin, so long as she is a woman of virtue, to raise herself to be the equal of a noble without the slightest discredit to the man who elevates her and makes her the equal of himself. Moreover, when one is overcome by the powerful impulse of passion, so long as no sin is involved, that person is not to be blamed for succumbing.

In short, they added to these convincing arguments so many others that Don Fernando's noble breast was mollified, being fed, after all, by illustrious blood, and he allowed himself to be persuaded by the truth he could not deny even if he wished to; and the sign by which he showed himself to be won over by all this worthwhile advice was to fall to his knees and embrace Dorotea, at which point he said,

"Arise, my lady, for it is unseemly for the one I hold dear to my heart to be kneeling at my feet. If until now I have given no indication of the way I feel, it may have been ordained by heaven so that by seeing how truly you love me, I would be able to hold you in the esteem you deserve. What I ask is that you not reproach me for my shameless behavior or my extreme thoughtlessness, for the very opportunity and force that has moved me to accept you as mine also compelled me to struggle against being yours. And so that you may recognize this truth, turn and gaze into the eyes of the now contented Luscinda, in which you will find forgiveness for all my sins. Since she has found and attained the one she desired and I have found in you the one meant for me, may she live safe and secure with Cardenio for many happy years and I pray that heaven will permit me to live just as many with my Dorotea."

In saying this, he again embraced her and pressed her cheek to his with such tenderness that he had to make a special effort to keep his tears from providing unequivocal proof of his love and repentance. Luscinda and Cardenio were not as fortunate in restraining theirs, nor were the many others who were present, for they began to shed them in such abundance – some because of their own happiness and some that of others – that it gave the impression that some catastrophe had befallen them all. Even Sancho Panza wept, though he later explained that he did so only after learning that Dorotea was not, as he had believed, the Queen Micomicona, from whom he had expected so many favors. Everyone's amazement and weeping had lasted for quite some time when

Cardenio and Luscinda went to kneel before Don Fernando, thanking him in the most gracious terms for the favors he had shown them. Don Fernando, who was at a loss for words, bade them rise and embraced them with a great display of affection and respect. He then asked Dorotea how she had come to that place so far from home. With brevity and wit she related everything she had told Cardenio earlier, which so pleased Don Fernando and those of his party that they were sorry when her story ended so soon, for Dorotea related her misfortunes in an ingratiating manner. Once she finished, Don Fernando explained what had taken place in the city after he had found the note in Luscinda's bodice in which she declared she was Cardenio's wife and could not, for that reason, be his. He explained that he had intended to kill her and would have done so had he not been thwarted by her parents. He had immediately fled from the house in a state of confusion and despair, determined to avenge himself at a more propitious time. The next day he learned that Luscinda was not at her parents' home and no one could tell him where she had gone; but to make a long story short, at the end of several months he finally discovered that she was in a convent determined to remain there for the rest of her life should she be unable to spend it with Cardenio. When he learned this, he chose these three gentlemen to accompany him and went to the convent, deciding, however, not to speak to her for fear that, once his presence was known, greater precautions might be taken in the convent. And so, waiting for a day when the main gate was left open, he placed two men on guard and with the third man entered the convent in search of Luscinda, whom he found in the cloister conversing with one of the nuns. Snatching her up before she had time to react, he took her to a village where they provided themselves with everything necessary for the trip. All this was accomplished without risk to themselves because the convent was in the country some distance outside the town. He added that as soon as Luscinda found herself in his power, she fell into a swoon and since regaining consciousness had done nothing but sob and sigh and remain perfectly silent. Thus, accompanied by her silence and tears, they had come to this inn, which for him had been tantamount to going to heaven, where every earthly misfortune will be concluded and terminated.

Chapter Thirty-Seven

The continuation of the story of the renowned princess, together with other amusing adventures

Sancho Panza listened to all this with no little pain in his heart, for he could just see his hopes for a title go up in smoke, the Princess Micomicona turn into Dorotea, and the giant become Don Fernando. Meanwhile, his master lay sleeping like a newborn babe, oblivious to all that had happened. Dorotea was unable to convince herself that the good that had befallen her was not a dream, and Cardenio's thoughts ran along similar lines, as did Luscinda's. Don Fernando thanked heaven for the favors it had shown him by rescuing him from that intricate labyrinth in which he had come close to losing both his reputation and his soul. In short, every person in the inn was delighted and pleased at the happy outcome of this convoluted set of circumstances. The priest, wise man that he was, put everything into its proper perspective and congratulated all those present for what they had been fortunate enough to receive, but the one who was most elated and pleased was the innkeeper's wife, for Cardenio and the priest had promised to pay her, with interest, for all the damages she had suffered at the hands of Don Quixote. Only Sancho, as we have said, was distressed, unhappy, and out of sorts; so with a downcast look on his face he went in to see his master, who was just waking up, and he said to him,

"Sir Woeful Countenance, your grace may go on sleeping for as long as you like and you can forget about killing any giant or restoring any kingdom to the princess, for all that is done and taken care of."

"I can certainly believe that," replied Don Quixote, "for I had the most extraordinary and colossal battle with a giant that I ever expect to have in all my livelong days. With a single stroke – swish! – I lopped off his head and so much blood gushed forth it flooded the room as though it were water."

"As though it were wine, your grace might more properly say," replied Sancho, "for I would have you know, if you don't already, that the dead giant is a punctured wineskin and the blood is twenty-five gallons of red wine contained in its belly, and the decapitated head is the bitch who bore me – but to heck with it all!"

"What are you talking about, you idiot?" asked Don Quixote; "are you out of your mind?"

"If your grace will only get up," said Sancho, "you will see the fine mess you have made and what we have to pay for, and you will see the queen turned into an ordinary woman named Dorotea, together with other developments, which, if you can comprehend them, will astonish you."

"Not one of those things would surprise me," said Don Quixote, "for if you remember correctly, the last time we were here I told you that everything taking place here was the work of enchanters and it would not surprise me if the same thing were happening now."

"I might believe all that," said Sancho, "if my blanket tossing were of the same nature but it wasn't; it was real and genuine and I noticed that the innkeeper who is here today had hold of one corner of the blanket and was tossing me into the air with great vim and vigor, laughing heartily all the while he did so. Now, when one starts recognizing people, I'm of the opinion, simpleton and sinner that I am, that there's no enchantment involved but a lot of hard work and bad luck."

"Nevertheless, God will set everything aright," replied Don Quixote. "Hand me my clothes so I can go outside, because I want to see the transformations and all those things that you say have happened."

Sancho gave him his clothes and, while he was dressing, the priest described to Don Fernando and all the others Don Quixote's follies and the strategy they had employed to get him to abandon the Barren Rock, where he had imagined himself to be as a result of his lady's scorn. He likewise recounted nearly all the adventures Sancho had related, which evoked no little surprise and laughter, and they felt what everyone always felt: that it was the strangest sort of madness ever to issue from an addled mind. The priest added that, since the happy turn of events involving Dorotea prevented them from proceeding with their plan, it would be necessary to invent or devise some new scheme for convincing Don Quixote to return home. Cardenio suggested that they continue the one they had already begun, since Luscinda could assume Dorotea's role.

"No," said Don Fernando, "that is not the way to proceed. I want Dorotea to continue with the present plan, so long as this worthy gentleman's village is not far from here, for nothing will give me greater pleasure than to see him cured."

"It is no more than a two-day journey from here," said the priest.

"Well, even if it were farther, I would gladly make the trip for the sake of performing such a noble deed."

At that moment, Don Quixote came out armed and in full regalia, wearing Mambrino's helmet – dents and all – brandishing his shield, and leaning on his tree-bough of a lance. Don Fernando and all the others were taken aback at the knight's strange appearance as they observed his lean, sallow face half a league long, his mismatched assortment of arms, and his grave demeanor, and they remained silent to hear what he had to say. Looking at the beautiful Dorotea, Don Quixote said in a calm, serious voice,

"I have been informed by my squire, fair lady, that you have been humbled and your life destroyed, for from the queen and noble lady you once were you have been transformed into an ordinary maiden. If this was ordered by your father the necromancer king out of fear that I would not afford your ladyship the necessary aid, I maintain that he does not and never did know what life is all about and is poorly versed in histories of chivalry. If he had read and studied them as carefully and leisurely as I, he would have noticed at every turn that other knights of less renown than mine achieved more difficult deeds and considered it no great feat to kill a wisp of a giant, however arrogant he might be. In fact, not very many hours ago I was battling one and— but I shall say no more or you will think me a liar. Time, though, which is the revealer of all things, will make the announcement when we least expect it."

"Your grace was battling two wineskins, not a giant," said the innkeeper at this point. Don Fernando ordered him to keep quiet and not interrupt Don Quixote's speech, whereupon the knight proceeded to speak.

"I say in conclusion, exalted and disinherited lady, that if your father has effected this metamorphosis in your grace's person for the reason I have stated, you need not give it a second thought, for there is no peril on earth that will not give way to my sword, with which I shall in a very few days cast down your enemy's head and place upon your own the crown of your kingdom."

Don Quixote said nothing further, waiting for the princess to respond, and inasmuch as she was aware of Don Fernando's determination to go forward with the deception until Don Quixote was safely in his village, she answered with great seriousness and cunning:

"Valiant Knight of the Woeful Countenance, whoever told your grace that I have been changed and transformed did not speak the truth, for I am the same person today that I was yesterday. To be sure, certain strokes of good fortune have effected a slight change in me and surpass even my wildest dreams but I have not for that reason ceased to be who I formerly was or to have the same determination I have always had to avail myself of the valor of your brave, invincible arm And so I beseech you to be so kind as to return the honor to the father who begot me and to esteem him as a prudent and wise man, for by his arts he discovered such an easy and sure way of healing my woes. Also I am certain, sir, that were it not for your grace, I should never have achieved the happiness I now enjoy, and in this I speak the absolute truth, which most of these gentlemen here can attest to. All that remains is for us to set out tomorrow, since we cannot travel very far today. As for the remainder of the good fortune that I expect, I shall leave it up to God and to your grace's noble breast."

Once the clever Dorotea finished her speech, Don Quixote turned to Sancho and with signs of extreme irritation said,

"I declare, Panza, you are the biggest darned scoundrel in Spain! Tell me, you no-good tramp, did you not just say that this princess had been turned into an ordinary damsel named Dorotea and that the head I understood I had cut off was the bitch who brought you into this world, together with other nonsense, which threw me into the greatest confusion I have ever experienced in all the days of my life? I swear" – and here he directed his eyes towards heaven while simultaneously clenching his teeth – "I've a good mind to make mincemeat out of you, which might put some sense into the skulls of all those lying squires of knights-errant from now till the end of time!"

"I beg your grace to control yourself," said Sancho, "for it may well be that I was mistaken about the transformation of the lady Princess Micomicona but as for the giant's head, or at least the puncturing of the wineskins and the blood's being red wine, I am not mistaken, as God is my witness. The wineskins are split open there at the head of your grace's bed and the wine has turned the room into a lake. If you don't believe me, 'It will all be clear when the eggs are fried,' meaning you will see this when his grace the innkeeper asks you to pay for all the damages. As for that other matter of her ladyship's being the same as she was, I rejoice in my soul, for I have as big a stake in this as the next person."

"I am telling you right here, Sancho," said Don Quixote, "that you are a numbskull, if you will pardon my bluntness – but enough of this!"

"Quite right," said Don Fernando, "let us drop the subject. Inasmuch as her ladyship the princess feels that due to the lateness of the hour we should set out tomorrow, so be it. We can spend the night in pleasant conversation till day arrives, at which time we shall all accompany Sir Don Quixote and witness the valiant and unheard-of feats he is certain to perform in the course of this great enterprise he has taken upon himself."

"I am the one," replied Don Quixote, "who should accompany and serve *your* grace, for I am most grateful for the kindnesses shown me and the esteem in which I am held. I shall strive to be worthy of them or die in the attempt, or do something even worse, if there is such a thing."

Don Quixote and Don Fernando placed themselves at one another's disposal but were interrupted by a traveler who was just then entering the courtyard. From his attire he appeared to be a Christian recently returned from Moorish lands, for he was clad in a blue shirt with short sleeves and no collar, blue linen breeches, and a cap of the same color. He was also wearing date-colored boots and a Moorish cutlass attached to a strap across his chest. Behind him, astride an ass, rode a woman in Moorish dress wearing a veil that covered her head and face, a small brocade cap, and a cloak that enveloped her from her shoulders to her feet. The man possessed a handsome, robust build and was slightly more than forty years old. He had a tan complexion, a long moustache, a well-groomed beard, and showed by his bearing that, if he had been well dressed, he would have been taken for a person of quality and noble birth. He went inside and asked for a room, only to be told there was none available, news that was clearly upsetting to him. Turning to the woman who by her attire appeared to be a Moor, he took her in his arms and helped her to dismount. Luscinda, Dorotea, the innkeeper's wife and daughter, and Maritornes were enraptured by the Moorish woman's strange, exotic costume and they proceeded to gather round her. Dorotea, who was as charming and tactful as she was perceptive, sensed that both the woman and the man had been distressed by the lack of a room, so she said to her,

"I hope your ladyship will not be upset by the lack of facilities here, because it is customary for inns to lack them. Still, if you should care to lodge with us," – and here she indicated Luscinda – "you may find it more acceptable than many of the accommodations you will have encountered in the course of your journey."

The veiled woman made no reply but simply rose from her seat and with her hands crossed over her breast curtsied as a sign of her appreciation. From her silence they concluded that she must be a Moor who did not speak Spanish. The captive, [1] who until now had been occupied with another matter, arrived and noticed that his companion was surrounded by the other women and was making no response to anything she was asked, at which point he said to them,

"Gentle ladies, this damsel barely understands my language and speaks none other than that of her own country, for which reason she has not and is not responding to anything you are asking her."

"We are not asking her anything," said Luscinda, "but are offering her our company for the night and a share of our accommodations, by which we shall make her as comfortable as the facilities permit simply out of our desire to be of service to any foreigner in need, especially when the one we shall be serving is a woman."

"On her behalf and mine," said the captive, "I kiss your ladyships' hands and am most grateful for your extremely generous offer, which under the present circumstances and coming from such persons as your countenances clearly demonstrate is a very great one indeed."

"Tell me, sir," said Dorotea: "Is this lady a Christian or a Moor? Judging by her attire and silence, we suspect her of being what we should prefer her not to be."

"In her dress and appearance she is a Moor but in her soul a devout Christian, which she is most eager to become."

"Then she has not been baptized?" said Luscinda; to which the captive replied,

"There has been no opportunity for that from the time she left Algeria, which is her country and homeland. Until now she has not found herself in imminent danger of death, which would necessitate her being baptized without first having studied the rites prescribed by the Holy Mother Church, but

1 This gentleman relates the story of his life in chapter 39, where it will be made clear why he is referred to as 'captive'.

God will soon see to it that she is baptized with the dignity a person of her rank deserves, which is higher than that indicated by her attire or mine."

This explanation made everyone present curious to learn the identity of the Moor and the captive but no one dared broach the subject at the moment, seeing that it would be better to allow them to rest than to question them about their lives. Dorotea took the damsel by the hand and invited her to sit by her side, at the same time bidding her to remove her veil. The woman looked at the captive as if to ask him what they were saying and what her response should be. He informed her in Arabic that they wanted her to remove her veil and that she should do so. When she removed it, she revealed such a lovely face that Dorotea considered her more beautiful than Luscinda, and Luscinda thought her more beautiful than Dorotea. All those present admitted that if anyone's beauty might rival that of the two ladies, it was the Moorish woman's, and there were even some who awarded her the honor in certain respects. And since it is beauty's right and prerogative to reconcile differences and make itself the object of desire, everyone immediately yielded to their desire to shower the beautiful Moor with affection.

Don Fernando asked the captive the woman's name and was told it was 'Lela Zoraida.' Hearing this and understanding what they had asked her Christian companion, she graciously hastened to respond and with some distress said,

"No, no Zoraida – María, María!" giving them to understand that her name was María, not Zoraida.

These words and the great emotion with which the Moorish woman spoke them made some of those present shed a tear, particularly the women, who by nature are tenderhearted and compassionate. Luscinda embraced her affectionately and said,

"Yes, of course: María, María!"; to which the Moor responded,

"Yes, yes: María; *Zoraida macange*!", which means 'not Zoraida.'

By this time night had arrived and at the behest of Don Fernando's traveling companion, the innkeeper had diligently and carefully prepared the best meal of which he was capable. Once the dinner hour arrived, they all seated themselves at a long table similar to those found in servants' quarters, for there were no round or square ones in the inn. They awarded the seat of honor to Don Quixote, who, after unsuccessfully attempting to refuse it, insisted that the Lady Micomicona sit immediately to his right, since he was her guardian. Luscinda and Zoraida sat next to her, and opposite them Don Fernando and Cardenio, then the captive and the remaining gentlemen, with the priest and the barber sitting alongside the ladies. Thus they all dined in an atmosphere of enjoyment, which increased still further when they saw that Don Quixote had stopped eating, as he was suddenly moved by the same spirit that had led him to speak at such great length on the occasion of his repast with the goatherds. He commenced by saying,

"Truly, ladies and gentlemen, if we will but reflect upon it, great and marvelous are the things witnessed by those who profess the order of knight-errantry, for what living person walking through the door of this castle and seeing us as we are now would judge or imagine us to be the persons we really are? Who would suspect that this lady by my side is the great queen we all know her to be, or that I am that Knight of the Woeful Countenance whose name is upon everyone's lips? Without a doubt this vocation and profession exceeds all others invented by man, for the more perils to which it is exposed, the more highly is it esteemed. Let those persons who maintain that a life of letters is superior to that of arms remove themselves from my presence, for I shall show them, whoever they are, that they know not whereof they speak. The argument that such persons usually adduce and most heavily rely upon is the belief that labors of the mind are greater than those of the body; that arms involve only the body, as if their execution were the work of a drudge requiring nothing more than brute strength; or as if this vocation that we who follow it call arms did not include feats of strength that demand great understanding for their execution; or as if the mind of a soldier responsible for an army or the defense of a city under siege did not need to labor mentally as well as physically. If your graces doubt this, I should like to see mere physical strength succeed in figuring out or discovering the enemy's intentions, plans, strategies, and ambushes, or in preparing for some dreaded eventuality, for all these things are the work of the mind in which the body plays no part whatsoever. Since it goes without saying that arms require intelligence, as do letters, let us see which of these two types of intelligence works harder: that of the student or that of the soldier. This shall be determined by the object and goal towards which each is directed, for that endeavor is more highly esteemed which has the nobler goal as its object. In considering the end and goal of letters, I am not referring to divine studies, whose object is to direct and convey souls to heaven – nothing else being comparable to such an end without end – but to human studies, whose goal is to establish distributive justice, to render unto each what is his, and to understand and ensure that just laws are maintained, certainly a goal that is generous, lofty, and worthy of great praise but not as much as that deserved by arms, whose end and goal is peace, the greatest good to which humans can aspire in this life. The first glad tidings the world and mankind received were those proclaimed by the angels on that night which for us was like day, when they sang from on high, 'Glory to God in the Highest, and peace on earth to men of goodwill.' And the greeting the Master Teacher of heaven and earth taught His disciples and chosen ones to say whenever they entered someone's house was 'Peace be unto this house.' On a number of other occasions He said to them, 'My peace I give unto you.' 'My peace I leave with you'. 'Peace be with you' – a jewel or precious gift, as it were, bestowed by His own hand, without which there can be no well being on earth or in heaven. This peace is the real object of war, for arms and war are one and the same. If we can agree that war has peace as its goal and for that reason is superior to letters, let us next turn to the physical labors of the scholar versus those of the bearer of arms, to see which are greater."

Don Quixote proceeded with his discourse in such fine fettle that he made it impossible for any of those in his audience at that moment to consider him mad; on the contrary, since nearly all of them were gentlemen to whom arms were important, they listened to him with the greatest interest. Don Quixote once more began to hold forth.

"As I was saying, the student's principal hardship is poverty, not that every single student is poor but I wish to cite the most extreme case possible. Having said that he is a victim of poverty, I consider it unnecessary to add anything further about his ill fortune, for the person who is poor lacks everything that is good. The student suffers this poverty in all its manifestations: hunger, cold, lack of clothing, or all of these simultaneously. Still, his poverty is not so great that he does not have something to eat, though his meals may come a little later than usual and may be scraps from a rich man's table, for the student's greatest misfortune is having to beg from door to door. However, he never fails to find some brazier or fireplace, which, though it may not warm him completely, at least tempers the cold; and at the very least he has a roof over his head at night. I shall not go into other particulars such as his lack of shirts and underabundance of shoes, his skimpy and threadbare clothing, or his habit of stuffing himself when he is fortunate enough to be invited to some banquet. By this rugged and difficult route I have described, some students after a series of stumbling, losing their footing, picking themselves up, and falling once again, finally achieve the position they seek. Once this has been attained, there are many we have seen who, having passed through these rocky shoals, this Scylla and Carybdis, as though borne upon the wings of good fortune – we have seen them, I say, ruling and governing from some office, their hunger converted into a satisfied stomach, their cold into a refreshing coolness, their threadbare rags into fine clothes, and their bed of matting into one of fine linen and damask, a reward richly deserved because of their virtues. But when *their* hardships are contrasted and compared to those of the combat soldier, they come in a poor second in every way, as I shall now explain."

Chapter Thirty-Eight

The learned discourse that Don Quixote delivered on arms and letters

Don Quixote went on to say,

"Just as we began with the student's poverty and its constituent parts, let us see if the soldier is any richer. We shall discover that in this matter of poverty there is no one poorer, for he is dependent upon a miserable salary, which he receives belatedly, if at all, or upon what he can plunder with his own hands at considerable risk to his life and conscience. At times his lack of clothing is so great that a slashed jacket must serve him as both uniform and shirt, and when he is exposed to the elements in midwinter, his only protection against the inclement weather is the breath from his mouth, which, issuing from a void, must certainly come out cold according to my experience, albeit contrary to every law of nature. But just let him wait until night arrives, at which time he will find respite from all these hardships in the bed that awaits him, a bed that will never be too narrow unless he himself is to blame, for he can measure off as many feet of ground as he likes and can toss and turn to his heart's content without fear of the sheet's becoming untucked. Following all this, the day and hour arrive for him to receive his degree, the occasion being a day of battle on which he is crowned with a mortar board of lint to help him recover from some gunshot that will have pierced one of his temples or left him maimed in an arm or a leg. However, if it does not turn out thus and heaven in its mercy should see fit to preserve and keep him alive and well, it may indeed transpire that he will be just as poor as before, having to engage in one encounter after another, one battle after another, and emerge victorious from them all before he can begin to prosper. However, such miracles are seldom seen. Tell me, if your graces have ever given it any thought, how many fewer soldiers have been decorated than those who have perished in battle. You will no doubt respond that there is no comparison, for those who have died are simply beyond reckoning, whereas those who have survived and received decorations may be summed up by using a number no more than three digits long. The very opposite is true in the case of students, who by fair means or foul manage to get by. Moreover, even though the soldier's hardships are more numerous, his rewards are far fewer. To this, we may counter that it is easier to reward two thousand scholars than thirty thousand soldiers, for we have the irreconcilable situation in which the former can be rewarded by receiving offices which as a matter of course are reserved for persons of their profession, whereas the latter can be rewarded only by being given what belongs to the very lords they serve, a circumstance that makes my argument even stronger. But since this is a labyrinth from which escape is quite difficult, let us set it aside and turn to the preeminence of arms over letters, a matter that still remains to be resolved, with each side adducing reasons on its own behalf.

"Among those I have mentioned, men of letters claim that without them arms could not be maintained because war is bound by its own laws – laws that come under the jurisdiction of letters and men of letters. To this, military men counter that laws cannot be maintained without them, for by means of arms republics are defended, kingdoms maintained, cities protected, roads made safe, and seas freed of pirates; in short, were it not for them, republics, kingdoms, monarchies, cities, and sea and land routes would be subjected to the rigors and confusion war brings with it for as long as it prevails and is free to make use of its privileges and powers. It is widely acknowledged that whatever is more difficult to achieve is held in higher esteem, which is reasonable and just, because for someone to become eminent in letters requires time, nights of study, hunger, lack of clothing, lightheadedness, upset stomachs, and other things of this nature, only a portion of which I have touched upon. But for someone to become a good soldier by his own resources requires everything required of the student, except that the degree is incomparably greater, for at every step of the way the soldier is in danger of losing his life. What fear of necessity or poverty can beset or harass the student as it does the soldier who, finding himself besieged in some fortress or standing watch on some embankment or cavalier, senses that the enemy are tunneling towards the very spot on which he is standing but he cannot leave his post for any reason whatever to flee the danger which threatens him so close at hand? All he can do is report to his captain what is happening so the latter may counter the attempt with another tunnel while the soldier stands his ground in the dread and expectation of suddenly being propelled heavenward without benefit of wings or of descending into the depths against his will. And if this seems a slight risk, let us see if it can be matched or surpassed by that of two galleys that ram one another with their prows in mid-ocean, where they become locked and bound together, with the sailor having nowhere to stand except two feet of plank on the ramming prow. In addition to this, he sees himself threatened by as many ministers of death as there are pieces of artillery aimed at him from the other ship, which are no farther from his body than the length of a lance. He realizes that at his first careless step he will pay a visit to Neptune's watery abode, but despite this, he, with intrepid spirit and inspired by the honor that beckons to him, will set himself up as a target for all those muskets and will attempt to cross over to the other vessel by that narrow pathway. Now, what is most remarkable is that no sooner will he have fallen into the sea from which he will not be resurrected until the end of the world than another will take his place, and if this one too falls into the sea that awaits him as an enemy, he will be succeeded by another and another without a moment's pause between their deaths. This is the greatest courage and daring to be found in all the perilous situations of war. Ah, how happy were those blessed ages that did not know the frightful fury of these devilish instruments of artillery, the inventor of which, I feel certain, is in hell receiving his just deserts for a diabolical invention that makes it possible for an infamous and cowardly arm to take the life of a valiant gentleman, who, filled with the spirit and determination that excite and stir valiant hearts, suddenly and without knowing how or from where, is struck down by a random bullet fired by someone who perhaps ran away with fright at the flash the accursed instrument made when fired, which in an instant cuts off and ends the mind and life of one who was worthy to enjoy them for countless centuries to come. When I consider this, I am tempted to confess that it grieves my soul that I ever undertook this profession of knight-errantry in an age as detestable as the one in which we now live, for though no terror can arouse fear in me, I am distressed by the thought that powder and lead may rob me of the opportunity to become famous and renowned throughout the civilized world by the might of my arm and the edge of my sword. But let heaven do what it will; I shall be all the more esteemed when I achieve my goals, having faced greater perils than those faced by knights-errant in ages gone by."

Don Quixote indulged in this entire lengthy harangue while the others dined, and he even forgot to taste his food, though Sancho Panza reminded him several times that he ought to eat something, as there would be time later to say everything he wished to say. Those who had been listening to him were suddenly overcome with compassion at seeing a man with apparently such a keen mind and the ability to discourse upon any subject of his choice lose it so completely whenever he touched upon his accursed and nefarious knight-errantry. The priest told him he was quite right in everything he had said on behalf of arms, and that he himself, though a man of letters and a university graduate, shared his views.

When the meal was over and they were seated round the table, the innkeeper's wife, her daughter, and Maritornes prepared Don Quixote's room, in which it had been decided that the women could lodge that night by themselves. Don Fernando begged the captive to recount the story of his life, which could hardly fail to be exotic and enjoyable, as suggested by his arrival with Zoraida. The captive responded that he would gladly honor their request but was simply afraid they would not find the story as enjoyable as he would like; and yet, despite this he would relate it in order to comply with their wishes. The priest and all the others thanked him and once again begged him to relate his story. Finding himself importuned by so many persons, he said entreaties were unnecessary where commands were the order of the day.

"Well then, if I may have your graces' attention, I shall relate a true story that I dare say cannot be equaled by any work of fiction, regardless of how exotic or imaginative it is may be."

After saying this, he asked them to make themselves comfortable and to give him their undivided attention. Once he saw that everyone was attentive and eager to hear what he had to say, he began to narrate the following story in a pleasant and relaxed manner.

Chapter Thirty-Nine

The captive relates the events of his life

"My family, which had its roots in one of the mountain villages of Leon, was more blessed by nature than by fortune. Amid the austerity of that region my father had gained the reputation of being a wealthy man and indeed *would* have been had he been as diligent in guarding his wealth as he was in squandering it. His tendency towards generosity proceeded from the fact that in his youth he had been a soldier and, as we all know, soldiering is the school in which a penurious person becomes generous and a generous one extravagant. If there are any soldiers who are tight-fisted, they are as rare as some seldom encountered freak of nature. My father had exceeded the bounds of generosity and was bordering on extravagance, a condition ill-befitting a married man with children who will inherit his name and position. There were three of us children, all sons and all of an age when we were eligible to choose our careers. Inasmuch as my father recognized his inability, as he put it, 'to turn over a new leaf,' he resolved to rid himself of the instrument and source of his liberality and wastefulness: his property, without which Alexander himself would have appeared miserly. One day, he called all three of us together in his room, where he privately carried on a discussion with us that went something like this: 'My sons, to convince you that I love you, I need do nothing more than recognize and acknowledge you as my children, though your realization that I have no self-control when it comes to preserving your inheritance is sufficient to make you doubt my love; but so that you will understand from this moment forward that I love you like a father and am not trying to ruin you like some stepfather, I intend to do something I have been contemplating for several days now, something I have decided upon after much painful deliberation. You are now of an age to assume adult responsibilities or at least to choose a profession that will bring you honor and profit in your later years. I have decided to divide my estate into four equal parts, giving each of you the portion that is your due and keeping the remaining portion to live on and support myself for however many days heaven sees fit to grant me. When you have each received your portion of the estate, I would ask that you select one of the professions I shall indicate. There is a proverb in this Spain of ours, which in my opinion is absolutely true, as indeed they all are, being succinct sayings culled from a variety of sources and from long experience. The one I have in mind says, "The Church, the sea, or the royal palace," or to state it more clearly, "Whoever would aspire to status and wealth should enter the Church, or go to sea to ply the trade of commerce, or serve the king in his court," for it is said that "Crumbs from a king's table are worth more than favors from a lord's." I mention this because it is my will and desire that one of you follow the life of letters, another that of commerce, and the third that of service to the king in war, since it is difficult to serve him at court; and though war may not bring riches, it brings great distinction and fame. Within a week I shall give you your separate portions in cash and no one's shall be a whit smaller than the others, as my actions shall prove. Tell me, then, whether you are willing to follow my advice and the plan I have proposed,' and he commanded me, as the eldest, to respond. After begging him not to give away his wealth but to spend it however he chose – we being young and strong enough to earn our own fortunes – I finally agreed to comply with his wishes, saying it was my intention to follow the profession of arms, thereby serving both God and my country. The second brother, after making the same proposals, elected to go to the Indies, where he would put his portion of the inheritance to work. The youngest, and to my mind the wisest, said he wished to enter the Church or to return to complete the studies he had begun at Salamanca.

"Once we had reached an accord and chosen our professions, my father embraced each of us and within the short time he had mentioned fulfilled all his promises, giving each of us our share, which to the best of my recollection amounted to three thousand ducats, for an uncle of ours had bought the entire estate and paid cash for it so it would not leave the family. That same day, all three of us bade a fond farewell to our dear father but, because I felt it would be cruel to leave my father with such meager resources at his advanced age, I persuaded him to take back two of my three thousand ducats, for what was left would suffice to provide me comfortably with everything a soldier might need. Each of my brothers, moved by my example, gave him a thousand ducats, so my father was left with four thousand in cash plus the three thousand that was the nominal value of his portion of the estate, which he preferred not to sell but to keep as real property. As I have mentioned, we finally took leave of both him and the above-mentioned uncle and not without considerable sorrow and weeping on the part of everyone there. We were charged with keeping them informed, so long as we could comfortably do so, of all our affairs, whether favorable or unfavorable. After we promised to do this, they embraced us and gave us their blessing. One of us set out for Salamanca, another for Seville, and I for Alicante, where I learned there was a Genoese vessel being loaded with wool for Genoa.

"It has been twenty-two years since I abandoned my father's house and in all those years, despite having written several letters, I have received no news of him or my brothers. What happened to me during this period I shall now briefly describe. I embarked at Alicante, landed at Genoa after a safe voyage, and proceeded from there to Milan, where I equipped myself with weapons and a military uniform, intending to serve my enlistment in the Piedmont. While on my way to Alessandria della Paglia, I received word that the Duke of Alba was on his way to Flanders. Changing my plans, I enlisted with him, served in the campaigns he waged, was present at the deaths of the Counts Egmont and Horn, and rose to ensign under a famous captain from Guadalajara named Diego de Urbina. Shortly after arriving in Flanders, I learned that His Holiness Pope Pius V, whom we all fondly remember, had formed an alliance with Venice and Spain against their common enemy the Turk, whose fleet during that same period had taken the island of Cyprus, which had been in the hands of the Venetians, a lamentable and unfortunate loss.

"It was widely understood that the commander-in-chief of this league was to be His Serene

Highness Don Juan of Austria, the natural brother of our good king Don Felipe. It was disclosed that vast preparations for war were being undertaken, all of which stirred my blood and increased my desire to take part in the anticipated campaign. Though I had been led to believe, and had even been promised, that on the first occasion that presented itself I would be promoted to captain, I decided to abandon everything and go to Italy, which I did. As fate would have it, Don Juan of Austria had just arrived at Genoa and was on his way to Naples to join the Venetian fleet, eventually doing so at Messina. In short, I can happily report that I took part in that most felicitous campaign, having now been promoted to infantry captain, a position of honor due more to my good fortune than to my own merits. But that day which was so glorious for Christendom because, on it, all the nations on earth were relieved of their mistaken belief that the Turks were invincible at sea – that day, I say, when the Ottoman haughtiness and pride were smashed, I alone was unfortunate among all those fortunate souls there because the Christians who died there were more blessed than those who emerged alive and victorious. Instead of some military crown that I might have expected had it been in Roman times, I, on the night following that most famous day, found myself with chains on my feet and shackles on my hands, which occurred in the following manner. After Aluch Ali, king of Algiers, a bold and adventurous corsair, had attacked and defeated the flagship of Malta in which only three brave souls survived – and they severely wounded – the flagship of Giovanni Andrea came alongside to lend support. I and my companions were aboard the latter vessel and I, doing what was expected on such an occasion, jumped aboard the enemy galley. It began to pull away from the one it had grappled with, preventing my soldiers from following me, and I found myself surrounded by my enemies, whom I was unable to fend off because of their huge numbers. They finally overwhelmed me after inflicting numerous wounds, and since Aluch Ali escaped with all his squadron, as your graces have no doubt heard, I ended up his prisoner. I was the only unfortunate soul among so many fortunate ones, and the only prisoner among so many who went free, for fifteen thousand was the number of Christians – all rowers in the Turkish fleet – who gained their longed-for freedom that day.

"I was taken to Constantinople, where the Grand Turk Selim made my master admiral of the sea for having performed his duty in the battle by carrying off, as a sign of his valor, the flag of the Order of Malta. The following year, which was 1572, I found myself at Navarino rowing in the flagship of the three lanterns. [1] I saw and witnessed there the missed opportunity to capture the entire Turkish fleet in that harbor, for all the sailors and Janissaries [2] stationed there were certain they would be attacked in that very harbor and for that reason had gathered together their clothes and *bachmaq*, that is, their footwear, to enable them to make their escape over land without having to fight, such was the fear our fleet had instilled in them. But heaven ordained otherwise, not because of any fault or oversight on the part of our commanding general, but because of the sins of Christendom and because God willingly permits us to be beset by scourges designed to chasten us. As it turned out, Aluch Ali took

1 The customary way of indicating the admiral's ship.

2 Elite Turkish soldiers.

refuge at Modón, an island near Navarino. After putting his men ashore, he fortified the mouth of the harbor and sat tight until Don Juan sailed away. On this voyage the galley called *The Prize* was captured, whose captain was a son of that famous corsair Barbarossa. The galley was captured by the flagship of Naples, the *She-wolf*, commanded by that fire-brand of a fighter, that father-figure to soldiers, that daring and never-defeated captain Don Alvaro de Bazán, Marquis of Santa Cruz. I must not fail to mention what happened to *The Prize* when it became the prize of another galley. Barbarossa's son was so cruel and treated his prisoners so horribly that, when those manning the oars saw that the galley *She-wolf* was well on her way to overtaking them, they all dropped their oars at the same instant and seized their captain, who was standing amidship calling for them to row faster. Then passing him from stern to prow one bench at a time, they tore his flesh with their teeth, so that by the time he had gone slightly past the mainmast, his soul had gone all the way to hell. Such, I say, was the cruelty with which he had treated them and the hatred they bore him. We returned to Constantinople and the following year, 1573, it was learned that Don Juan had captured Tunis and wrested that kingdom from the Turks, placing it in the hands of Muley Hamet and thereby thwarting Muley Hamida, the bravest and cruellest Moor on earth, who had hopes of returning there as ruler. The Grand Turk felt this loss deeply and, availing himself of the sagacity all those of his race possess, made peace with the Venetians, who desired it much more than he. The following year, '74, he attacked both La Goleta and the half-constructed fort near Tunis, which Don Juan had abandoned. During all these crucial events I manned an oar without hope of gaining my freedom; at least, I did not expect to achieve it by being ransomed, for I had made up my mind not to send news of my disgrace to my father.

"At length, both La Goleta and the fort were lost, their marketplaces being overrun by seventy-five thousand mercenary Turkish soldiers and more than four hundred thousand Moors and Arabs from all parts of Africa. This enormous assemblage of people was accompanied by hordes of munitions and war provisions and by so many sappers that they could have buried both La Goleta and the fort with the sand they dug up with only their hands. La Goleta was the first to fall, having until then been considered impregnable. It was not lost through any fault of its defenders, who did everything in their power and duty to defend it, but because experience had shown the ease with which entrenchments could be erected in that desert sand, for whereas one would normally strike water at a depth of two hand spans, the Turks were able to dig down two yards before encountering it. Thus, by using an enormous number of sandbags, they raised the entrenchments so high they overlooked the fortress walls and in this way were able to fire down at them from above, so that no defender could remain there to help in the defense.

"It has generally been felt that our men should not have barricaded themselves in La Goleta but should have stood their ground on the dock but those who make such an assertion do so from too great a distance and with too little experience in matters of this sort, for if La Goleta and the fort housed scarcely seven thousand soldiers, how could such a small number, regardless of their courage, move out into the open and maintain their forces against the huge number of enemy soldiers? And how is it possible for a stronghold to avoid being lost if it receives no reinforcements, particularly when it is surrounded by so many fanatical enemies in their own land? A number of persons were of the opinion, as was I, that heaven had been especially benevolent and generous to Spain by permitting the destruction of that swamp and quagmire of evils, that gluttonous sponge and waster of untold funds squandered there without benefit, serving no other purpose than that of preserving the memory of its capture – that most felicitous one by the invincible Charles V – as though it needed those stone supports to make it eternal, which it is and always shall be. The fort also fell, which the Turks were able to gain only a few inches at a time, for the soldiers defending it fought so bravely and effectively that the number of enemy slain in twenty-two general assaults amounted to more than twenty-five thousand. Not one of the three hundred captured survivors came through unwounded – clear and unmistakable proof of their determination and bravery and of how well they had defended themselves and stood their ground. A small fort or tower that stood in the middle of the lagoon under the command of Don Juan Zanoguera, a famous Valencian gentleman and soldier, agreed to a conditional surrender. Taken prisoner was Don Pedro Puertocarrero, commandant of La Goleta, who did everything in his power to defend his stronghold. He was so heartbroken, though, at having surrendered it that he died of grief on the way to Constantinople, where his captors were taking him. They also captured the fort's commandant, whose name was Gabrio Cervellón, a Milanese gentleman, an excellent engineer, and a most gallant soldier. In these two fortresses many persons of prominence met their deaths, among them one Pagano d'Oria, a knight in the Order of Saint John, who was generous by nature, as demonstrated by his extreme generosity towards his brother Giovanni Andrea d'Oria. What made his death so tragic was his dying at the hands of some Arabs he had trusted once he realized the fort was doomed. They offered to take him disguised as a Moor to Tabarca, a small port or structure belonging to certain Genoese engaged in coral fishing, but these Arabs cut off his head and carried it to the commander of the Turkish fleet, who practiced on them what our Spanish proverb preaches: 'Betrayal may be tolerated but not so the betrayer.' It was later reported that the commander had ordered the men hanged who had brought him the present, since they had failed to deliver the prisoner alive.

"Among the Christians who fell captive at the fort was one by the name of Pedro de Aguilar, who was from some place in Andalusia. He had been second lieutenant in the fort, a soldier of great merit, rare intelligence, and with a special gift for the art of poetry. I mention this because fate brought him to my galley and to my very bench as my master's prisoner. Before we set sail from that port, this gentleman wrote two sonnets in the manner of epitaphs, one on La Goleta and the other on the fort, which I must recite because I know them by heart and believe your graces will find them more pleasurable than sorrowful."

When the captive mentioned the name of Don Pedro de Aguilar, Don Fernando glanced at his comrades and all three of them began to smile. At the mention of the sonnets, one of them said,

"Before you proceed, your grace, I wish you would tell us what became of that Don Pedro de Aguilar you mentioned; to which the captive responded,

"The only thing I know is that after spending two years in Constantinople he fled disguised as an Albanian in the company of a Greek spy. I can't say whether he escaped, though I assume he did, for a year later I saw the Greek in Constantinople but had no chance to ask him how that journey had ended."

"Well, he escaped," said the gentleman, "for that Don Pedro is my brother and at this very moment is in our village healthy, wealthy, married, and the father of three children.'

"Thanks be to God," said the captive, "for all the mercy He has shown him. In my opinion there is no greater happiness on earth than regaining one's lost freedom."

"What is more," added the gentleman, "I know those sonnets that my brother wrote."

"Well then," said the captive, "I would ask your grace to recite them, since you probably know them better than I."

"With pleasure," replied the gentleman; "the one on La Goleta goes like this:

Chapter Forty

A continuation of the captive's tale

"O happy souls, by death at length set free
From the dark prison of mortality,
By glorious deeds, whose memory never dies –
From earth's dim spot exalted to the skies!
What fury stood in every eye confessed!
What generous ardor fired each manly breast!
Whilst slaughtered heaps disdained the sandy shore,
And the tinged ocean blushed with hostile gore.
O'erpowered by numbers, gloriously ye fell:
Death only could such matchless courage quell.
Whilst dying thus, ye triumph o'er your foes –
Its fame the world, its glory heaven, bestows!"

"That is how the one goes that I know," said the captive; to which the gentleman responded, "Well, the one about the fort, as I recall, goes like this:

From 'midst these walls, whose ruins spread around,
And scattered clods that heap th'ensanguined ground,
Three thousand souls of warriors, dead in fight,
To better regions took their happy flight.
Long with unconquered souls they bravely stood
And fearless shed their unavailing blood;
Till, to superior force compelled to yield,

Their lives they quitted in the well-fought field.
This fatal soil has ever been the tomb
Of slaughtered heroes, buried in its womb;
Yet braver bodies did it ne'er sustain,
Nor send more glorious souls the skies to gain."

They agreed that the sonnets were not unpleasing and because the captive was delighted by the news he had received of his comrade, he continued his story, saying,

"Once La Goleta and the fort were overrun, the Turks arranged for the dismantling of La Goleta, the fort being in such shambles there was nothing left to tear down, and in order to accomplish this with a minimum of effort and in the shortest time possible, they mined it in three places. However, they were never able to blow up the part that appeared to be the least resistent – the old walls – whereas everything that had remained standing in the new part built by Il Fratín [1] was easily razed. Finally, the fleet returned to Constantinople triumphant and victorious and a few months later my master Aluch Ali died, or as he was also known, Aluch Ali Fartax, which is Turkish for 'the Mangy Renegade,' [2] and that is exactly what he was. It is the custom among the Turks to assign themselves names based upon some personal defect or virtue, a custom that stems from the fact that among them there are only four surnames and these are reserved for the direct descendants of the Ottoman line, everyone else, as I have said, having a given name and cognomen taken from some defect of his body or virtue of his soul. This Mangy One, who was in bondage to the Grand Turk, had been a galley slave for fourteen years. At the age of thirty-four he had become a Moslem after being slapped in the face by a Turk while rowing, an act that made him so desperate for revenge that he renounced his religion. His valor was so great that, without following the perverted paths and steps by which the majority of the Grand Turk's favorites rose to power, he became king of Algiers and later commander of the navy, the third highest rank in that kingdom. He was a Calabrian by birth and, when it came to ethics, was a man of his word. His slaves, some three thousand in number, were treated quite humanely by him, and at his death these were divided in accordance with the provisions of his will among his many renegades and the Grand Turk, who is also heir to everyone who dies and thereby shares with the natural children the inheritance of the deceased. I was placed in bondage to a Venetian renegade who had been captured by Aluch Ali when he was a cabin boy on a ship. The renegade was so fond of the boy that he became one of his favorite paramours but grew up to be the most cruel renegade the world has ever seen. His name was Hassan Aga and he became not only quite wealthy but even king of Algiers. He took me with him from Constantinople and I was delighted at the prospect of being so close to Spain, not that I intended to write to anyone of my disgraceful situation but to see if my lot in Algiers might be more promising than that in Constantinople, where

1 Italian: 'the little brother,' referring to the Italian engineer Jácome Paleazzo.

2 ***Aluch*** (Arabic: 'renegade'), ***Farfax*** (Turkish: 'mangy'), and ***Ali*** was the Calabrian slavemaster's given name.

I had sought to escape by a thousand different means but always without success. In Algiers I resolved to seek some other means of achieving what I so greatly longed for, since I had never abandoned my desire to be free. While nothing I devised, planned, or attempted ever turned out the way I had hoped, rather than give up, I continued to concoct or devise some new scheme that would sustain me even when it was weak and flimsy. In this way I made my existence bearable while shut up in a house or cell the Turks call a *bagnio*, which is where they confine the Christian prisoners, both those of the king and those belonging to various individuals, as well as those 'of the warehouse,' which is to say, 'prisoners of the municipality.' The latter serve the city in its public works and related activities and find it extremely difficult to obtain their freedom because they are held in common under no particular master and have no person to whom they can turn if someone offers to ransom them. Various individuals of the city, as I have said, are in the habit of putting their prisoners in these *bagnios*, particularly when they are eligible for ransom. There their safety is assured and they are not made to work while waiting for their ransom to arrive. What is more, the king's prisoners who are eligible for ransom are not made to labor with the rest of the rabble unless their ransom is late in arriving, at which point they are forced to write for it more zealously by being made to toil along with the others in collecting wood, which is no easy task.

"I happened to be one of those to be ransomed, for it had been discovered I was a captain. Though I explained that my chances of being ransomed were slight due to my lack of wealth, that did not keep them from putting me in with other candidates who were up for ransom, which included various gentry. I was placed in chains, more as a sign of my eligibility for ransom than for keeping me secure. This is how I spent my life in that *bagnio* with a number of other gentlemen and persons of distinction who had been singled out for ransom. Though hunger and a shortage of clothing were difficult for us at times, almost always in fact, nothing was as hard to endure as seeing and hearing at every hour of the day the unheard-of cruelty that my master inflicted upon the Christians. Each day he had his allotment of victims – hanging one, impaling another, cutting off the ears of still another, and this for so little provocation, if any, that the Turks were sure he did it just for the joy of doing it and because he had taken it upon himself to be the executioner of all mankind. The only one who fared well with him was a soldier by the name of Saavedra, [3] whom he never flogged or had flogged and to whom he never said a harsh word despite the fact that this soldier had committed deeds that will live in the memory of those people for many years to come, and each deed designed to win his freedom. We all feared he might be impaled for his slightest act, let alone for the serious ones, and he himself stood in dread of this more times than one. If it were not for the fact that there is so little time, I might say something here of this soldier's deeds, which would entertain and astound your graces considerably more than my own story. But to continue with mine: overlooking the courtyard outside our prison were some windows in a house of one of the more prominent, wealthy Moors. In keeping with the usual custom among the Moors, the openings were more akin to holes than to windows and were covered by thick, tight-fitting shutters. It happened that one day while I and three of my

3 Cervantes himself, his complete name being Miguel de Cervantes Saavedra.

companions were on our prison terrace trying to amuse ourselves by seeing how far we could jump while wearing our chains – the other Christians having gone off to labor, leaving us there alone – I happened to raise my eyes and saw a rod protruding from between some closed shutters with a handkerchief tied to the end of it. The rod was being waved back and forth as if to signal us to come forward and take it. While we observed this, one of my companions went over and stood beneath the rod to see if it would be released or just what might happen. As soon as he reached the spot, the rod was raised and shaken from side to side as if to say 'no'. The Christian withdrew and the rod was again lowered and underwent the same movements as before. Another of my companions approached but the same thing happened to him that had happened to the first. Finally, the third went over and had the same experience as the first two. When I saw this, I could hardly wait to try my own hand. No sooner did I stand beneath the rod than it fell and landed at my feet there in the *bagnio.* I hurried to remove the handkerchief, which I noticed had a knot in it, and inside the knot I found ten *cianís*, which are gold-plated coins used by the Moors, each of which is equal to ten of our *reals*. That I was thrilled with my find goes without saying. My joy increased as did my amazement when I thought of how such good fortune could have befallen us, myself in particular, for their refusal to release the rod to anyone else was a clear indication that I was the intended recipient of that favor. I took my precious coins, broke the rod in two, and went back to my little terrace and stood there staring at the window. I saw protruding from it a very white hand that opened and closed rapidly. [4] We understood or conjectured from this that there must be some woman living in that house who had performed that kind deed for us, and so, to express our appreciation, we performed salaams in the manner of the Moors: bowing our heads, placing our arms across our chests, and bending at the waist. A few moments later, a small cross made of reeds was held out of the same window and then withdrawn. This sign confirmed our suspicion that some Christian woman must be captive in that house and was the one who had shown us that favor, but the whiteness of her hand and the bracelets on her arms caused us to abandon that idea. We thought she might be some Christian renegade, for masters often take these renegades for their very own wives and even consider themselves fortunate, esteeming them more highly than they do those of their own nation. Even though all our conjectures ended up very far off the mark, our sole pastime from that moment forth was to gaze at and consider as our pole star that window where the star in the form of a rod had appeared. But some two weeks passed without our seeing either it or the hand or, for that matter, any other sign, and though we did our utmost during that period to find out who lived in that house and whether there was some Christian renegade in it, all anyone could ever tell us was that a wealthy, influential Moor lived there by the name of Hadji Murad, formerly the warden of La Pata Prison, an extremely prestigious office in that land. When we least expected to have any more *cianís* come raining down, we suddenly saw the rod appear with another handkerchief attached to it with an even bigger knot in it. This occurred at a time when, like the one before, the *bagnio* was deserted and unoccupied. We performed the same test as before, with each of the same three persons approaching it before I went over, but the

4 Rapidly opening and closing the hand was an affectionate way of saying goodbye.

rod responded to me alone, for when I arrived, it was released. Untying the knot, I found forty Spanish gold *escudos* and a sheet of paper with Arabic writing on it and at the bottom a large drawing of a cross. I kissed the cross, took the *escudos*, and returned to the terrace, where we all performed our salaams. When the hand reappeared, I signaled that I would read the note and the window was closed. We were all mystified but delighted by these events and, since none of us knew Arabic, our desire to know what the note contained was considerable but the most serious problem we faced was finding someone who could read it. I finally decided to confide in a renegade, a native of Murcia, who professed to be a good friend of mine and who had taken a pledge with me to keep secret everything I might entrust to him. Quite often, renegades who intend to return to Christian lands carry with them signed statements from various important captives in which the latter make some sort of effort to testify that such-and-such a renegade is a man of his word, has always treated Christians well, and desires to escape at the first opportunity that presents itself. There are some who collect these testimonials in good faith; others use them in dubious and cunning ways, for if the latter lose their way or are taken prisoner on some Christian soil to which they have gone to plunder, they pull out their testimonials and claim that those papers show the reason they went there – which was to remain in a Christian land – as well as why they sailed there with privateering Turks. By this means they avoid their first punishment and are reconciled with the Church without suffering any harm, but as soon as they see their chance, they return to Barbary to resume their former way of life. There are others who obtain these papers, use them in a well-intentioned manner, and remain on Christian soil. One of the renegades I have mentioned was a friend of mine who had testimonials signed by all my comrades in which we endorsed him insofar as possible. If the Moors had found those papers on him, they would have burned him alive. I learned that he was fluent in Arabic and could speak and write the language with equal ease. Before explaining the matter to him completely, I asked him to read a note I had come across in a corner of my cell. He opened it and spent some time perusing it, murmuring to himself as he translated. I asked him if he understood it and he informed me that he understood it perfectly but that, if I wanted him to make a word-for-word translation, I should provide him with pen and ink so he could do a more accurate job. We immediately gave him what he needed and he set about translating a portion at a time. When he finished, he said,

"'Everything that is here in Spanish is what the Moorish note says and not one letter has been omitted. It should also be noted that whenever it says "Lela Marién," it means "Our Lady the Virgin Mary".'

"We read the note, which said:

When I was a girl, my father had a slave woman who taught me the Christian aç-çalá [5] *and told me many things about Lela Marién. This Christian died and I am certain did not go to the flames but to Allah, for I later saw her twice and she told me to go to the land of the Christians to see Lela Marién, who loves me very much, but I do not know how to accomplish this. I have seen a number of*

5 ***Aç-çalá*** (Arabic: a Moslem prayer)

Christians from this window but none has ever impressed me as being a gentleman except you. I am young and quite rich and have lots of money I can take with me. See if you can devise a way for us to go there, where you shall be my husband if you wish, but even if you do not, I shall not mind, for Lela Marién will provide me with someone to marry. It is I who have written this. Be careful whom you get to read it and don't trust any Moors because they are all deceitful. I am quite concerned about this and hope you will not discuss it with anyone, for if my father finds out, he will throw me down a well and pile rocks on top of it. I shall tie a thread to the end of the rod; tie your answer to it and, if you have no one to answer me in Arabic, let me know by means of gestures, for Lela Marién will enable me to understand you. May She and Allah and this cross I have kissed many times preserve you, which is what the slave woman told me to do.

"I ask you, gentlemen, is it any wonder we were surprised and cheered by the contents of this note? Our reaction was so pronounced the renegade figured out this paper had not been found by accident but had actually been written to one of us. He, therefore, asked us, if what he suspected was true, to take him into our confidence and he would risk his life for our freedom. In saying this, he pulled a metal crucifix from his shirt and tearfully swore by the God represented by that image – in whom he thoroughly and faithfully believed despite his sinfulness and wickedness – to remain loyal to us and to keep secret anything we might reveal to him, for he was convinced and would even go so far as to predict that by means of the woman who had written this note he and the rest of us would gain our freedom and he would be able to fulfill his greatest desire: to be returned to the bosom of the Holy Mother Church from which, like a diseased member, he had been separated and cut off because of his ignorance and sinfulness. He said this while shedding such copious tears of repentance that we all agreed to reveal to him the truth of our situation. We thus gave him a complete account, hiding nothing from him and pointing out the small window where the rod had appeared. Observing it, he noted the position of the house and agreed to make a special effort to learn who lived there. We, likewise, agreed that it would be wise to answer the Moorish woman's note, since we now had the perfect person to accomplish this. I at once began to dictate a response, which the renegade wrote down, and I shall now quote its exact words, for nothing significant that transpired in this case has ever been erased from my memory nor ever shall be so long as I have breath in my body. In effect, the answer that we sent the Moorish woman went as follows:

May you be protected by the true Allah, my lady, and by that blessed Marién, who is the true mother of God and the one who has instilled in your heart the desire to go to some Christian land out of her love for you. Pray to her to enable you in all her mercy to carry out what she has commanded you to do, for she is so good she will certainly do so. On behalf of myself and all my Christian companions, I promise that we shall do for you everything in our power, even to the point of dying. Do not hesitate to write and advise me of what you intend to do, for I shall always answer you. The great Allah has provided us with a Christian captive who speaks and writes your language very well, as you will see from this note. You may therefore, without being afraid, inform us of anything you please. As for your offer to become my wife once you are on Christian soil, I, as a good Christian, promise that you shall be; and be advised that Christians abide by their promises better than Moors. May Allah and Marién keep you and preserve you, my lady.

"After the note was written and sealed, I waited two days for the *bagnio* to be deserted again, at which time I went onto the terrace for my usual stroll to see if the rod might appear, which it very shortly did. Though unable to see who was holding it, as soon as I caught sight of it, I held up the note as if to ask her to attach the thread but down came the rod with the thread already attached and I proceeded to tie on the note. Shortly thereafter, our star reappeared with its white flag of peace: the tiny bundle. When it was released, I retrieved it and found inside the cloth all sorts of gold and silver coins amounting to more than fifty *escudos*. These increased our joy fifty-fold and confirmed our expectation of seeing ourselves free. That same night, our renegade returned to inform us that he had learned that, living in that house, was the very Moor we had heard of, Hadji Murad. He was extremely wealthy and had only one child, a daughter who was heiress to his entire fortune. It was the general consensus in the city that she was the most beautiful woman in all Barbary, and a number of viceroys had come there to seek her hand but she had never been willing to marry. He had also learned that she had once owned a Christian slave who was now dead, all of which squared with the contents of the note.

"We then had a meeting with the renegade to decide what we should do to rescue the Moorish woman and enable all of us to reach some Christian land. We agreed that for the time being we would wait for the next communication from Zoraida, this being the name of the woman who now wishes to be called María. We saw that she, and she alone, would be the one to provide us a way out of our difficulties. Once this accord was reached, the renegade told us not to worry because he would secure our freedom or forfeit his life in the attempt. For four days there were people in the *bagnio*, which meant the rod would be four days late in appearing. When the customary solitude returned to the *bagnio* at the end of the four days, the rod appeared with the handkerchief so swollen it betokened a felicitous birth. The rod and the handkerchief were dropped in my direction and inside I found another note and a hundred gold *escudos* as the sole currency. Because the renegade was present, we gave him the note to read in our cell and he informed us that it said the following:

My lord, I have no idea how to arrange for us to go to Spain, nor has Lela Marién told me how even though I have asked Her. What I can do is to give you lots of gold coins from this window. Take them and ransom yourself and your friends. Then one of you can go to some Christian land, purchase a boat there, and return for the others. You will find me in my father's summer house, which is by the port of Barbazón on the coast, where I shall spend this whole summer with my father and servants. You may come for me there at night without fear and take me to the boat. Remember that you are to be my husband; if you refuse, I shall ask Marién to punish you. If you do not trust anyone else to go for the boat, ransom yourself and you go. I am certain you will be more likely to return than anyone else, since you are a gentleman and a Christian. Try to identify the house and when I see you strolling there, I shall know that the bagnio *is unoccupied and shall give you lots of money. May Allah keep you, my dear lord.*

"Such were the contents of the second note. Once we had all seen it, each of us volunteered to be the person ransomed, promising to go and return most punctually, with me offering to do the same. The renegade was opposed to all this, saying that under no circumstances would he consent to any one person's going free until we could all be freed together, for experience had shown him how poorly freed men keep the promises they make in captivity. There were numerous instances of small groups of influential captives who had used that method, paying the ransom of someone in their group to go to Valencia or Mallorca with enough money to outfit a boat and return for those who had paid his ransom but this individual never returned because his new-found freedom and his fear of losing it again made him oblivious to every obligation in the world.

"To confirm the truth of what he had told us, he gave us a brief account of what had just happened to certain Christian gentlemen during virtually that very period – the strangest thing that ever transpired in those parts, where the most frightening and astonishing things occur at every turn. In short, he said that what we could and should do was to give him the money we planned to use to ransom one of us. He could then buy a boat there in Algiers under the pretext of becoming a merchant trader with Tetuan and other towns along that coast, and once he was the owner, he would devise a plan for getting us out of the *bagnio* and aboard the boat, especially if the Moorish woman provided money for everyone's ransom as she had promised to do. And once we were free men, it would be extremely easy to embark in the middle of the day. The greatest difficulty we faced was the fact that Moors did not permit renegades to buy or own a boat unless it was a large vessel for privateering purposes, for they feared that anyone who bought a boat, particularly if he was Spanish, wanted it for no other purpose than to flee to some Christian land. He, however, might overcome that obstacle by getting a Moor from Tangiers to share in the purchase of the boat as well as in the profits from the merchandise. By using this subterfuge, he would become the boat's owner, and once this was done, any other unfinished business could be considered an accomplished fact. Though my comrades and I thought it preferable to send to Mallorca for a boat, as the Moorish woman had suggested, we dared not argue with him, fearing that if we did not follow his proposal, he might expose our scheme and place our lives in jeopardy by revealing our dealings with Zoraida, for whose sake we would all have given our lives. We therefore decided to place ourselves in the hands of God and those of the renegade, and so we wrote an answer to Zoraida at that very moment, explaining to her that we would do everything she had advised, because it was as good as if it had come from Lela Marién herself. We said it was completely up to her whether to delay that enterprise or to go forward with it immediately, with me once again promising to be her husband. So the first day the *bagnio* was unoccupied, she made use of the rod and handkerchief several times, giving us two thousand gold *escudos* and a note stating that on the following *jumá*, or Friday, she would leave for the summer house with her father but would give us additional money before going there. If this was not sufficient, we were to let her know and she would give us as much as we needed, because her father had so much money he would never miss any of it, in addition to which all the keys were in her custody. We immediately gave the renegade five hundred *escudos* to buy a boat and I used eight hundred to purchase my ransom, giving the money to a Valencian merchant who happened to be in Algiers at the time. He had me released on his word, promising that with the first vessel to arrive from Venice, he would pay my ransom. Had he handed over the money at once, the king might suspect that my ransom money had been in Algiers for some time and the merchant for his own profit had kept the matter secret. Moreover, my master was so suspicious that under no circumstances did I dare produce the money right there on the spot. On the Thursday before the Friday on which the beautiful Zoraida was to go to the summer house, she gave us another thousand *escudos* and advised us of her departure, begging me, if I should be ransomed, to acquaint myself at once with her father's summer house and by all means to look for an opportunity to go there to see her. I responded quite briefly saying I would do exactly that, and I asked her to commend us to Lela Marién with all the prayers the slave woman had taught her. Because I was unwilling to be the only one ransomed, and because there was more than enough money, I decided that my three companions should be ransomed to enable them to leave the *bagnio* so they would not rebel or persuade the Devil to do anything that might harm Zoraida, for though I was able to rid myself of this fear, owing to who they were, I nevertheless refused to jeopardize our operation. Accordingly, I had them ransomed, using the same scheme I had used for myself, whereby I turned all my money over to the merchant so he could safely and confidently go bail for us all, but we never revealed to him our secret plan because of the danger it entailed."

Chapter Forty-One

The captive relates still more of his adventures

"Scarcely two weeks had passed when our renegade purchased an excellent boat that could carry more than thirty persons. To insure his transaction and lend it an air of authenticity, he resolved to sail to Cherchel, a village thirty leagues from Algiers in the direction of Oran, where there was a thriving trade in dried figs. He made this voyage two or three times in the company of the *Tagarino* he had mentioned. In Barbary they call Moors from Aragon *Tagarinos*, and those from Granada *Mudéjares*; in the kingdom of Fez the *Mudéjares* are called *Elches*, these being the ones the king most often employs in war. But to continue: each time that he sailed by in his boat he would drop anchor in a small inlet not two crossbow shots from the summer house where Zoraida was staying. Once stationed there, the renegade and the young Moors manning the oars would quite calculatedly turn to their prayers or would run through a mock rehearsal of what they intended to do in actuality. The renegade went to Zoraida's garden to ask for some fruit, and her father, not recognizing him, permitted him to gather some. Though he was eager to speak to Zoraida, as he later confessed, to tell her he was the one I had assigned to take her to a Christian land where she would find happiness and security, he was never able to do so, for Moorish women never allow themselves to be seen by Moors or Turks unless ordered to do so by their husbands or fathers. They do, however, allow themselves to deal and communicate with Christian slaves even more than is seemly. It would have pained me if he had spoken to her, for it might have been upsetting to her to see her affairs on the lips of a renegade. But God, who had other designs, deprived our renegade of the opportunity to carry out his good intentions. However, since the latter saw that I had now been ransomed and it was safe for him to go and come from Cherchel and to drop anchor at any time or place he pleased – his Tagarino partner being in total agreement with all his suggestions – the only thing that remained was to recruit some Christians to man the oars. He asked me to see which ones I wished to take along besides those who had been ransomed, and to engage them for the following Friday, the day he had designated for our departure. Accordingly, I spoke to a dozen Spaniards who were all worthy oarsmen and among those most able to leave the city. It was no mean feat to find as many as this at that time of the year, for there were twenty vessels out at sea that had carried with them all the men who could row. I would not have found as many as a dozen if these men's master had not decided against going to sea that summer so his galley could be repaired in the drydock. I told them nothing except that the following Friday afternoon they were to leave the city one at a time in a leisurely fashion and head for Hadji Murad's summer house, where they were to wait till I arrived. I gave all of them these instructions individually, warning them that even if they saw other Christians there, they were to say nothing except that I had ordered them to wait there. With this concern taken care of, the only task remaining was the one that mattered most to me: that of informing Zoraida of the status of our plan so she would be prepared and not be startled if we suddenly made an appearance before she thought the boatload of Christians had had time to return. I thus made up my mind to go to the summer house to see if I could speak to her. The day prior to our departure, I went there under the pretext of gathering garden greens, and the first person I met was her father, who asked me in that language employed between Christians and Moors throughout Barbary and even in Constantinople, which is neither Arabic, Spanish, nor that of any other nation but a mixture of several languages, by means of which we all communicate with one another – he asked me, I say, in that mongrel language what I was looking for in his garden and who my owner was. I told him I was a slave of Arnaút Mamí – this because I was certain he was a close friend of his – and that I was looking for some greens for making a salad. In response to this, he asked me whether I was eligible for ransom and, if so, how much my master was asking for me. While we were engaged in all these questions and answers, the beautiful Zoraida, who had already caught sight of me some time earlier, came out of the house into the garden and, since Moorish women are not the least bit prudish about appearing in the presence of Christians – nor do they even try to avoid it, as I have explained – she thought nothing of coming over to her father while he was speaking to me. On the contrary, when her father saw her approach but do so hesitantly, he called out to her to come there at once.

"I would be taxing your graces' patience if I were now to describe the great beauty and gentility or the elegant and rich attire with which my beloved Zoraida regaled my eyes. I shall simply say that there were more pearls suspended from her gorgeous neck, ears, and forehead than there were hairs on her head. Round the ankles of her feet, which she ordinarily kept bare, were two *carcajes* – as foot bracelets or anklets are called in the Moorish language – of pure gold, studded with so many diamonds that she later told me that her father set their value at ten thousand *doblas*[1] and that those she wore on her wrists were worth twice that amount. There were also a number of pearls, all of which were of the finest quality, for the greatest display of pomp and elegance among Moorish women is to adorn themselves with fine pearls. For this reason more pearls are found among the Moors than among all other nations combined. Zoraida's father was reputed to own many of the best ones in Algiers, besides having more than two hundred thousand Spanish *escudos*, all of which belonged to the lady I now call mine. If after everything she had endured she could still make herself look so beautiful with just these few adornments, one can imagine how she must have appeared in happier times, for it is well known that some women's beauty has its days and seasons and is diminished or increased by external factors, but it is just as natural for one's mental and emotional state to enhance or lessen it, though it usually has the latter effect. I can safely say that she arrived at that moment looking extremely beautiful and dressed to perfection; at least, she impressed me as the most beautiful woman I had ever seen, and when I considered this and everything I owed her, it struck me that I had before me a goddess from heaven come down to earth for my pleasure and salvation. When she arrived, her father explained to her in her own language that I was a captive of his friend Arnaút Mamí and had come there to look for salad greens. She joined in the conversation and in that mixture of languages I have described asked me if I was a noble and why I had not been ransomed. I informed her that I was now ransomed and she might be the judge of how much my master valued me from the price he had set, for fifteen hundred *zoltanís*[2] were paid for my freedom. In response to this she said,

"'In truth, if you belonged to my father, I would make certain he did not give you up for twice that amount, for you Christians lie every time you open your mouths, pretending to be poor in hopes of defrauding us Moors.'

"'That may be, my lady,' I said, 'but I can assure you that I have always dealt truthfully with my master because I deal truthfully and always shall with every person on earth.'

"'And when do you leave?' asked Zoraida.

"'Tomorrow actually, for there's a French vessel here that sails tomorrow and I intend to be aboard it.'

"'Wouldn't it be better,' replied Zoraida, 'to wait for some vessel from Spain and sail on it rather than one from France, since the French are not your friends?'

"'No,' I said, 'though if it is true that a vessel from Spain is already on the way, as is reported, I shall wait for it. Still, it's more likely that I shall leave tomorrow, for my desire to see myself in my own land among the people I love is so great it will not permit me to employ any measure that involves a delay,

1 The ***dobla*** was a Spanish gold coin first minted in the Middle Ages and worth about ten *pesetas*.

2 ***Zoltaní***: a solid gold Turkish coin equivalent to approximately fifteen and one half *reals*.

no matter how good it may be.'

"'You are no doubt married in your own country,' said Zoraida, 'which is why you wish to go home, to be with your wife.'

"'I am not married,' I replied, 'but I have promised to wed upon my return.'

"'And is the lady beautiful whom you have promised to wed?' asked Zoraida.

"'She is so beautiful,' I replied, 'that to extol her and to do so truthfully is to say that she very much resembles you.'

"After enjoying a hearty laugh, her father said,

"' *Wa-llah,* [3] Christian, she must be very beautiful if she resembles my daughter, who is the greatest beauty in this entire kingdom. If you doubt what I say, take a close look at her and you will see I am telling the truth.'

"Zoraida's father served as interpreter for most of the things we discussed in the conversation, since he was the most adept at languages. Even though, as I've said, she spoke the mongrel language used there, she communicated her meaning more with gestures than with words. While we were discussing these and other matters, a Moor came running our way shouting that four Turks had scaled the garden wall or hedge and were picking the fruit even though it was not ripe. The old man panicked, as did Zoraida, for the Moors' dread of the Turks is wide-spread and almost instinctive, particularly of the soldiers, who are so insolent and domineering over their Moorish subjects that they treat them worse than if they were their actual slaves. But to continue: Zoraida's father said to her,

"'Daughter, go back to the house and shut yourself inside while I speak to these dogs. As for you, Christian, gather your greens and go in peace and may Allah see you safely to your land.'

"I bowed as he went off to look for the Turks, leaving me alone with Zoraida. She acted as though she would follow her father's orders but no sooner had the latter disappeared among the trees in the garden than she turned to me and said with tears in her eyes,

"'*Amexi,* Christian? *Amexi?*' (meaning 'Are you going away, Christian? Are you going away?)'

"'Yes, my lady,' I replied, 'but never without you. Watch for us this coming *jumá* and don't be alarmed when you see us. You may be assured that we shall go to a Christian land together.'

"I said this in such a way that she understood perfectly well everything discussed between us. Then placing an arm round my neck, she began to walk haltingly towards the house but as luck would have it – which might have been quite disastrous had heaven been differently disposed – while the two of us were walking along in the manner I've described with her arm round my neck, her father, who was now returning after chasing away the Turks, noticed the way we were walking and we realized he had seen us. But Zoraida alertly and wisely refused to remove her arm from my neck; on the contrary, she drew closer to me, rested her head against my chest, and acted as if her legs were about to give way under her, all definite signs that she was feeling faint. At the same time, I made it clear that I was supporting her against my will. Her father hurried over to us and, seeing his daughter in that condition, asked her what was the matter. When she failed to respond, her father said,

---

3 An Arabic oath: 'By Allah!'

"'Undoubtedly, the entrance of those dogs has given her such a start that she has fainted.'

"And removing her from my breast, he braced her against his own, at which point she heaved a sigh and, with her eyes still moist from the tears, turned to me and said,

"'*Amxi*, Christian, *amxi.* (Go away, Christian, go away)'

"To which her father responded,

"'It is not necessary, child, for the Christian to go away. He has done you no harm and the Turks have already left. Don't be upset, for there is nothing that can cause you any harm, because as I've said, the Turks at my request left at the same place they had entered.'

"'They frightened her, sir,' I told her father, 'as you indicated, but since she has told me to go away, I don't wish to upset her. Peace be with you, and with your leave I shall return for the greens should it be necessary, for my master says there are no better ones anywhere for salads.'

"'You may return as often as you like,' replied Hadji Murad. 'My daughter did not speak this way because she was angry at you or at any of the Christians. By saying that you should go away, she meant for the Turks to go away, or that it was now time for you to gather your greens.'

"With this, I immediately took my leave, and Zoraida, looking as though her heart would break, went off with her father. Then under the pretext of gathering greens, I made a leisurely but thorough inspection of the entire garden, taking special note of the entrances and exits, the safety features of the house, and any specific thing that might facilitate our overall operation. This accomplished, I went back to give the renegade and my companions an account of everything that had happened, for I could hardly wait to possess the treasure fate was offering me in the person of the beautiful and ravishing Zoraida. Time went by and the designated day we had waited for with such anticipation finally arrived. By following the plan we had devised after much careful consideration and lengthy discussions, we achieved the desired result, for on the Friday following the day I had spoken to Zoraida in the garden, our renegade anchored the ship as soon as it was dark virtually opposite the place where the most beautiful Zoraida was staying.

"The Christians who were to man the oars had hidden at various places along the beach, all apprehensive as they awaited my arrival and eager to make a charge for the ship lay within view, for they knew nothing of the renegade's plan but thought they were there to win their freedom by force of arms, taking the lives of the Moors aboard ship. Accordingly, as soon as I and my companions appeared, those who had been hiding came out and gathered round us. This was at an hour when the city gates were already closed and there was not a soul to be seen in the entire countryside. Once we had assembled there, we could not decide whether it would be better to go for Zoraida first or to subdue the Moors manning the ship's oars. Before we could settle this question, our renegade returned and asked us why we were hesitating, since the hour had arrived and all his Moors were off guard, most of whom were sleeping, in fact. When we told him what had made us hesitate, he said the most important thing was to overpower the ship first, which could be accomplished with the greatest of ease and without any risk at all, and then we could return for Zoraida. What he said seemed reasonable, so without further delay and with him as our leader, we went down to the ship, where he jumped aboard first, reached for his cutlass, and shouted in the Moorish tongue,

"'Don't any of you move a muscle unless you want to pay with your lives!'

"By this time, nearly all the Christians had come aboard. When the Moors, who were not overly stouthearted, heard their captain address them in that manner, they froze in their tracks and none of them reached for their weapons – not that they had many, or even one for that matter. Without saying a word, they allowed their hands to be bound, which the Christians did very hastily, threatening the Moors that if they made any sort of outcry, they would be put to the sword on the spot. Once this was done, half of our men remained on guard while the others, again led by the self-appointed renegade, went to Hadji Murad's garden. Our good fortune was such that when we arrived at the gate, it opened as easily as if it had never been closed, and thus, quite slowly and silently we reached the house without being observed by anyone.

"The beautiful Zoraida was watching for us from a window and, when she sensed our activity below, inquired in a soft voice if we were *Nizarani*, as though she were asking if we were Christians. When I told her we were and that she should join us, she recognized me and without a moment's hesitation or a word in reply immediately came down, opened the door, and stood before us in all her radiance, so splendidly attired that words fail me with which to extol her. When I saw her, I took her hand and kissed it passionately, with the renegade and my two companions doing the same. The others, misinterpreting the circumstances, did what they had seen us do, which seemed to imply that we were simply giving thanks and acknowledging her as the benefactress of our freedom. The renegade asked her in the Moorish tongue if her father was at home and she informed him that he was but was sleeping.

"'Well, it will be necessary to wake him,' replied the renegade, 'and take him with us, together with anything valuable in this beautiful house.'

"'No,' she said, 'under no circumstance is anyone to lay a hand on my father, for there is nothing valuable in this house except what I am taking, and *it* is worth so much it will be enough to make you all rich and contented. Just be patient and you shall see.'

"She turned to go inside, telling us she would return shortly and asking us to wait there quietly without making a sound. I asked the renegade what had transpired between them, and after he explained it to me, I told him that in all such matters we were to do nothing that did not conform with Zoraida's wishes. Just then, she came back carrying a small chest so full of gold *escudos* she could scarcely lift it. But it was our ill fortune that her father had awakened and heard the noise coming from the garden. When he appeared at the window, he realized that all those below were Christians, at which point he frantically called out in Arabic at the top of his lungs, 'Christians, Christians! Thieves, thieves!' We were all frightened and totally confused by this, but the renegade, seeing the danger we were in and the importance of carrying out that operation before we were discovered, ran up the stairs as fast as he could to reach Hadji Murad, with several of us following closely on his heels. I dared not leave Zoraida unattended after she fainted and collapsed into my arms. As it turned out, those who had gone upstairs acted with such deftness that they returned in an instant with Hadji Murad, his hands bound and a handkerchief stuffed into his mouth. He would not have uttered a word even if he could have, for they had threatened him with death if he did so. When his daughter saw him, she covered her eyes to avoid his gaze. Her father was terrified because he did not realize how willingly she had placed herself in our hands. However, since our feet were our greatest need at the moment, we diligently and hurriedly got aboard ship, where the men who had stayed behind were anxiously waiting, fearing we might have met with some setback.

"The night was barely two hours old when we finally found ourselves aboard ship, at which time we untied the hands of Zoraida's father and removed the handkerchief from his mouth, the renegade warning him once again not to make a sound or he would be killed. When he saw his daughter there, he began a series of painful sighs, particularly when he noticed that I was holding her in a close embrace and she was sitting there quietly without defending herself, protesting, or trying to escape. Despite this, he said nothing for fear that they would carry out the renegade's threat. Zoraida found herself aboard ship in the company of her father and the Moors we had bound and, when she saw we were about to lower the oars into the water, she pleaded with the renegade to beg me to release the Moors and set her father free, for she would rather throw herself into the ocean than have her father there, who had always loved her so dearly and who, because of her, was being held prisoner. The renegade explained to me what she had requested and I agreed that the idea sounded like a good one but he explained that it would not succeed, for if we released them there, they would shout out a call to arms that would rouse the city, causing them to come looking for us in swift frigates that would cut us off so effectively on land and sea that escape would be impossible. What we might do, though, was to set them free on the first Christian soil we came to. We all agreed to this suggestion and even Zoraida was satisfied after she was given an explanation of it along with the arguments that had persuaded us not to follow her suggestion. And so, cheerfully and joyously, all our valiant rowers silently and diligently gripped their oars and we pushed off, commending ourselves to God with all our hearts and setting out for the island of Mallorca, which was the nearest Christian land. However, due to a slight north wind and a rather choppy sea, we were unable to continue our course for Mallorca but were forced to sail towards Oran by hugging the coast. We were not a little concerned that we might be spotted from the village of Sargel, which is situated on that coast some sixty miles from Algiers. At the same time, we feared that along that stretch we might encounter one of those galleys that frequently bring merchandise from Tetuan, though we all assumed, individually and as a group, that if we met some merchant ship, provided it did not belong to a privateer, not only would we not be lost but would have a vessel in which we might more safely complete our voyage. As we sailed along, Zoraida kept her head buried in my hands so she would not have to look at her father, and I could see that she was calling upon Lela Marién to aid us.

"We had probably sailed some thirty miles when it began to grow light and we found ourselves some three bowshots from the shore, which we noticed was deserted and without a soul on it who could see us. Despite this, by sheer force of rowing we gradually began heading out to sea, which by now had become somewhat calmer. After sailing almost two miles, we decided that by taking turns we could eat and row at the same time, since the ship was stocked with provisions. But those who were rowing said this was not the time or place to rest, however briefly. Instead, what might be done by the ones not manning the oars was to feed the rowers while they rowed, for they refused to lay down their oars for any reason whatever. We had just begun to do this when a stiff breeze began blowing from the side, causing us to lay down the oars, run up the sail, and head for Oran, since it was impossible to steer in any other direction. All this we did with the greatest haste and were thus driven by the wind at more than eight miles an hour without a care in the world except that of encountering some privateer. We fed the Moorish oarsmen, and the renegade consoled them by assuring them they were not prisoners but would be set free at the earliest opportunity. This was repeated to Zoraida's father, who said,

"'Oh, Christians, your generosity and good manners would make me expect and believe just the opposite, but – you set me free! – I hope you don't take me for a such a simpleton as even to imagine such a thing! You didn't risk your lives to take away my freedom just to give it back to me in an act of generosity, particularly now that you know who I am and know the profit you will realize. If you are looking to set a price on the deal, I shall offer you right here everything you demand in exchange for me and my dear unfortunate daughter; or if that is unacceptable, for her alone, since she is the greatest and dearest part of my soul!'

"In saying this, he began to sob so bitterly that he filled us all with compassion and caused Zoraida to look in his direction. When she saw her father sobbing, she was so moved that she rose from where she had been kneeling at my feet and went over to embrace him. She pressed her face to his and they both began to weep so tenderly that a number of us onlookers began to do the same, but when her father noticed that she was richly attired and was wearing a large assortment of jewels, he said to her in her own language,

"'What is the meaning of this, child? Last night, before this terrible misfortune occurred in which we now find ourselves, I saw you in your ordinary house clothes, but now, despite the fact that you have had no time to dress and have not received an invitation to any festivities that would require you to dress up and adorn yourself thus, I now see you attired in the best clothes I was able to provide when our fortune was more favorable. Explain to me the meaning of this, for I am more confused and astonished by it than by the very misfortune in which I find myself.'

"Everything the Moor had said to his daughter was explained to us by the renegade. Zoraida did not utter a word in response but, when her father noticed at one side of the vessel the small chest in which she had always kept her jewelry, which he was certain had not been brought to the summer house but had been left in Algiers, he became more confused than ever. He asked her how that chest had fallen into our hands and what it contained. The renegade, without waiting for Zoraida to answer, said in response,

"'Sir, don't bother asking your daughter Zoraida so many questions, for I can provide the answer to just one that will satisfy your grace concerning all the others. I would have you know she is a Christian and the one who has cut through our chains and given us our freedom. She has come here of her own free will, as happy in my estimation at seeing herself in this situation as one who goes from darkness to light, from death to life, from hell to heaven.'

"'Is it true, child, what this one is saying?' asked the Moor.

"'It is,' replied Zoraida.

"'In other words,' said the father, 'you are a Christian and the one who has placed your father in the hands of his enemies?'

"To which Zoraida answered,

"'I am the one who is a Christian but not the one who has placed you in this situation, for my intention has never been to cause you harm but only to do what was good for me.'

"'And what sort of good have you done yourself, child?'

"'That,' said the daughter, 'you must ask Lela Marién, for she can explain it better than I.'

"No sooner had the Moor heard this than with incredible speed he threw himself head first into the sea, where he would no doubt have drowned had his long, cumbersome robe not rendered him fairly buoyant. Zoraida shouted at us to save him, at which point we immediately went to the rescue and, seizing him by his robe, pulled him aboard unconscious and half drowned. Zoraida was so distressed by this she knelt over him and wept uncontrollably, as though he were already dead. We placed him face down, where he coughed up a large amount of water and finally regained consciousness two hours later. Meanwhile, the wind had shifted and we were driven towards land, which we managed to avoid by strenuous rowing; and thanks to our good fortune, we reached a cove that lay alongside a promontory or cape the Moors call the *Cava Rumía*, a name that in our language means 'The Sinful Christian Woman.' Among the Moors, tradition has it that, buried in that spot, is the *Cava*, because of whom Spain was lost. *Cava* in their language means 'sinful woman' and *rumía* 'Christian'. They consider it bad luck to anchor a vessel there even when necessary and never do so otherwise. For us, however, it turned out to be not some shelter of a sinful woman but a safe haven of our salvation, considering how rough the sea was. We posted our lookouts on shore and never took our hands off the oars as we ate what the renegade had provided and with all our hearts we implored God and Our Lady to aid and favor us by letting us achieve a fortunate ending after such a propitious beginning. It was arranged as a result of Zoraida's pleadings to put her father ashore, together with the other Moors who were still bound, for she lacked the courage and was too kind-hearted to endure the sight of her father in bonds and her fellow countrymen being held prisoner. We promised to do this at the moment of our departure, since there was no danger in leaving them in that deserted place. Our prayers, which were not made in vain, were heard by heaven, which then shifted the wind in our favor, inviting us, now that the sea was calm, to resume our interrupted voyage with a joyful heart. Seeing this, we untied the Moors and set them ashore one at a time, an act that dumbfounded them. By now, Zoraida's father had fully regained his senses but, as we were about to put him ashore, he said,

"'Christians, why do you think this wicked female is glad to see you set me free? Do you think it is due to the compassion she feels for me? Certainly not; it is only because she does not want my presence to be an obstacle to her when she decides to carry out her wicked intentions. Don't assume that she has been moved to change her religion because she believes yours is superior to ours but because she knows indecency is more openly tolerated in your land than in ours.'

"And turning to Zoraida while I and another Christian held both his arms to prevent him from doing anything rash, he said to her,

"'O infamous and misguided child! where in your blind folly do you think you are going, subjecting yourself to these dogs, our natural enemies? Cursed be the hour in which I begot you, and cursed be the presents and amusements I provided while rearing you.'

"Feeling that he was unlikely to conclude anytime soon, I hurriedly put him ashore but even from there he continued to shout and spout forth his curses and lamentations, calling upon Mohammed to ask Allah to confound, destroy, and put an end to us. And even after we had gotten under way and could no longer hear his words, we could still observe his actions, which were to tug at his beard, rip out his hair, and roll about on the ground; and just once he managed such a shout that we were able to make out what he said.

"'Come back, my darling daughter, come back to shore and I shall forgive you for everything! Let those men have the money, since it is already theirs but come back and console your dear sad father, who will forsake his life in these barren wastes if you forsake him!'

"When Zoraida heard this, she was so grief-stricken she began to sob and as a consequence was only able to say in response,

"'Father dear, may Allah let Lela Marién, who has been the reason for my becoming a Christian, console you in your unhappiness. Allah knows I could do nothing other than what I have done, nor are these Christians to blame for my decision. Even if I had wanted to remain at home rather than go with them, I would have had no choice because of the haste with which my soul urged me to undertake what seems so good to me but which you, dear father, view as evil.'

"This was said at a time when her father could no longer hear her or be seen by us. While I sought to console Zoraida, we turned our attention to our voyage, which the wind facilitated so greatly that we were assured of seeing ourselves on the shores of Spain by the following dawn. But since good seldom if ever arrives pure and unsullied without the accompaniment of some evil that surprises or upsets it, it was our ill fortune, or perhaps the curses the Moor had directed at his daughter, which are always to be feared regardless of which father utters them. It was our ill fortune – now that night was nearly three hours old and we were traveling far out at sea with our sail fully unfurled and our oars lashed as a result of the propitious wind – to discern by the light of the brightly shining moon a square-rigger with all its sails unfurled, heading slightly into the wind ahead of us, and so close that we had to strike our sail to avoid ramming her, and they too were forced to turn the rudder hard to allow us room to pass. Their crew ran over to the side of their vessel and demanded to know who we were, where we were headed, and where we had come from, but because they had asked us in French, our renegade warned,

"'Don't anyone answer, for these are probably French privateers who plunder everything in sight.'

"As a result of this warning no one said a word but, as we had continued to move slightly past the other vessel, which now lay to leeward, they opened fire with a couple of artillery pieces, both of which apparently employed chain-shot, for one cut our mast in two, toppling it and the sail into the sea. Simultaneously firing another canon, they sent the ball into our boat amidships, putting a hole right through our hull but inflicting no other damage whatever. However, realizing that we were sinking, we all began to cry out for help because we could envision ourselves about to drown. At this point, they hauled in their sails and launched a boat or skiff into which as many as a dozen

Frenchmen climbed armed with harquebuses that were loaded and ready to fire. They pulled alongside our ship, at which point they saw how few of us there were, and since our vessel was sinking, they took us aboard, explaining that our insolent action of not responding to them had been responsible for what had happened to us. Our renegade took Zoraida's jewelcase and threw it overboard when no one was observing him. As it turned out, we boarded the Frenchmen's vessel, and they, after informing themselves of everything they wished to know about us as though we were their mortal enemies, stripped us of all our possessions and even took the *carcajes* Zoraida wore on her ankles. I was not as upset by the thing that upset Zoraida as I was by the fear that they might turn from taking her exquisite and precious jewels to taking that jewel she most valued and esteemed, but the desires of such men never extend beyond money, which in their greed they can never get their fill of. They carried that endeavor to such an extreme that they would have even taken our clothes had they been of benefit to them. Some were of the opinion that they should wrap us in a sail and throw us overboard, because they intended to trade at several ports along the Spanish coast by calling themselves Bretons and would be punished if they had us on board alive, whereby their thievery would be discovered. But the captain, as the one who had plundered my beloved Zoraida, said that he was content with the booty he already had; that it was his intention not to touch at any port in Spain but to sail through the Straits of Gibraltar at night, or whenever possible, and head straight for La Rochelle, the port from which they had set out. They agreed to let us have their ship's skiff and everything necessary for the short trip that remained, which they did the following day as soon as Spain came into view. The sight of this land caused us to forget all our trials and tribulations, as though we had never undergone them, such is the joy of regaining one's lost freedom.

"It was sometime round noon when they put us aboard the boat after giving us two barrels of water and a quantity of sea biscuits. The captain, motivated by some sort of compassion, gave the beautiful Zoraida forty gold *escudos* as she boarded the boat, and refused to allow his sailors to strip her of the very clothes she is now wearing. We boarded the vessel and thanked them for the kindness they had extended to us, demonstrating that we were more appreciative than embittered. They made for the open sea, following a course for the Straits, whereas we set our sights on no other beacon than the land that loomed before us. We began rowing with such fury that by sundown we had traveled far enough to convince ourselves that we would arrive before night was very far advanced. But since there was no moon that night and the sky was dark, together with the fact that we were unacquainted with that general area, we felt it unsafe to attempt to land. Several who did, though, urged us to do so even if the site turned out to be rocky or far from any habitation, for in that way we could allay the fear we rightfully felt that some privateering vessels from Tetuan might be sailing there. Such vessels set out at night from Barbary, appear at dawn along the coasts of Spain, take their usual prisoners, and return in time for the crews to spend the night in their own homes. Among the various conflicting opinions, the one we opted for was that of gradually making for land and, if the calmness of the sea permitted, of going ashore wherever we could. We followed this plan and it must have been shortly before midnight when we arrived at the base of a very steep, ill-formed cliff that was not so close to the shore, though, as to prohibit an easy landing. We ran our boat onto the sand, jumped out, kissed the soil, and shed tears of the utmost joy, giving thanks to Our Lord God for the incomparable kindness He had shown us. We removed what provisions we had in the boat, pulled it onto higher ground, and then climbed a considerable way up the cliff, for despite having arrived, we could not be certain in our hearts or bring ourselves to believe it was Christian soil we were standing on.

"When day finally began to dawn, (and much later than we would have liked), we finished climbing to the top of the cliff, where we hoped to see if there was some settlement in sight or some shepherds' hut, but search as we might, we failed to discover a single settlement, person, road, or path. Despite this, we decided to head inland, feeling we could hardly fail to discover someone who could tell us where we were. But what most distressed me was seeing Zoraida forced to walk on that rough terrain, for though I carried her on my back part of the time, my fatigue was more tiring to her than her being carried was restful. Refusing to let me continue to exert myself on her behalf, she walked alongside me most patiently, radiating happiness as I led her by the hand. We had probably gone slightly less than a quarter of a league when our ears detected the sound of a small bell, a clear indication that there must be a flock nearby. We were all straining to see if someone might appear, when we spied at the foot of a cork tree a young shepherd who leisurely and with great unconcern was whittling on a stick. We called out to him, at which point he raised his head and then scrambled to his feet in a flurry, for we later learned that the first persons to catch his eye were the renegade and Zoraida, and since he saw them in Moorish dress, he imagined the whole of Barbary was descending upon him, at which point he fled into the woods with uncommon agility while crying out for all he was worth,

"'Moors! The Moors have landed, the Moors have landed! To arms, to arms!'

"His shouting left us all confused and undecided as to what course of action to follow, but fearing the shepherd's cries might wake the countryside, at which point the mounted coast guard would immediately come to investigate the problem, we agreed that the renegade should remove his Turkish clothes and put on a *gilecuelco*, or captive's jacket, which one of us gave him on the spot, though it left the donor in only his shirt. Then commending ourselves to God, we took the same road we had seen the shepherd take, expecting the coast guard to swoop down upon us at any moment. Our expectation proved to be well-founded, for no sooner had we emerged from that underbrush onto an open plain – less than two hours having elapsed – than we caught sight of some fifty agile horsemen riding towards us at a leisurely gallop. The moment we saw them, we stood still and waited for them. When they arrived, they found, instead of the Moors they were pursuing, so many poor Christians that they were overcome with confusion. At this point, one of them asked if we were responsible for a shepherd's having sounded the alarm. 'Yes,' I said, and was just about to relate our story, where we came from, and who we were, when one of our Christians recognized the rider who had questioned us and spoke up before I could say anything further.

"'Let us give thanks to God, gentlemen, for having led us to such a wonderful place! If I am not mistaken, the ground beneath our feet is that of Vélez Málaga, unless my years of captivity have erased from my mind the memory that you, sir, who asked us who we were, are Pedro de Bustamante, my very own uncle.'

"No sooner had the Christian captive said this than the rider leapt from his horse and went over to embrace the young man, saying to him,

"'My dear nephew, light of my life and soul, now I recognize you. I was already mourning your death, as were my sister – your mother – and all your family, who are still alive, inasmuch as God has permitted them to live long enough to experience the thrill of seeing you. We had heard you were in Algiers, and judging by the appearance of your clothes and those of all your band, I can see that your escape has been miraculous.'

"As soon as the riders realized we were Christian captives, they each dismounted and offered to carry us on their horses to the city of Vélez Málaga, which was a league and a half away. After we told them where we had left the boat, several of them went back to retrieve it. The others seated us on the haunches of their horses, with Zoraida riding the horse belonging to the Christian's uncle. The whole town came out to greet us, having been informed of our arrival by one of the men who had ridden on ahead. They were not surprised to see captives who had been set free or Moors who had been captured, since everyone along that coast was accustomed to seeing both one and the other, but what did surprise them was Zoraida's beauty, which at that moment and time was at its peak, due as much to her being flushed from traveling as to her joy at now seeing herself on Christian soil without the fear of being recaptured. This had brought such a glow to her cheeks that unless my ardor at that moment deceived me, I venture to say there has never been a more beautiful creature on earth, at least, none that I have ever seen.

"We went directly to the church to offer thanks to God for the blessings we had received. When Zoraida entered, she remarked that there were faces there that resembled that of Lela Marién. We explained that those were images in Her likeness, and the renegade to the best of his ability explained their significance, that she might worship each one as though it were actually the very Lela Marién who had spoken to her. Because she was blessed with a good mind and had a natural gift of understanding, she immediately comprehended everything that was explained to her concerning the images. From there they conducted us to various homes in the town where they gave us lodging. The Christian who had made the trip with us took the renegade, Zoraida, and me to the home of his parents, who were moderately well off in the way of worldly possessions and who lavished as much affection on me as they did on their own son.

"We spent nearly a week in Vélez, at the end of which time the renegade, having informed himself of everything he must do, went to the city of Granada to be readmitted through the instrumentality of the Holy Office to the sacred fold of the Church. Each of the other liberated Christians went his own way – wherever he thought best – leaving Zoraida and me there alone with only the *escudos* the gracious Frenchman had given Zoraida, with which I bought the animal she is riding. Until now I have served her as both father and squire, not as husband. It is our intention to see if my father is alive or if one of my brothers has met with a more felicitous fate than I, but since Fortune has made me Zoraida's companion, I feel I could meet with no other fate, however good, that I would treasure more highly. The patience with which Zoraida has borne the discomforts brought about by poverty, and the desire she obviously has to see herself a Christian are such that I am astonished and compelled to serve her during every moment of my life, though the thrill I feel at knowing that I belong to her and she to me is troubled and dampened by not knowing whether I shall find any place where I can live with her in safety, or whether time and death have wrought such changes in my inheritance and in the lives of my father and brothers that, should they no longer be alive, I shall be unable to find anyone who will acknowledge me.

"I have nothing more to relate, gentlemen, regarding my story. Whether it has been entertaining and unusual, I would have your graces' worthy discernment be the judge. For my part, I can say that even though I would have preferred to relate it with still greater brevity, my fear of testing your graces' patience has led me to omit more than a few incidents."

Chapter Forty-Two

Further incidents that took place at the inn, together with a number of other matters worth knowing

Once he had concluded his story, the captive said nothing further, at which point Don Fernando addressed him:

"Most assuredly, sir captain, the account your grace has given of this strange adventure is as novel and rare as the events themselves. It is totally strange, exotic, and full of incidents that will astonish and amaze anyone who hears it. Indeed, the pleasure we have received from it is so great that we should gladly listen to it all over again, even if tomorrow were to find us still being entertained by this same story."

After Don Fernando expressed these sentiments, he and all the others placed themselves completely at the captive's disposal and did so with expressions of such warmth and sincerity that the captain was convinced of their goodwill. Don Fernando in particular suggested that if the captive would return with him, he would see to it that his brother the marquis would serve as godfather at Zoraida's baptism and would provide him with everything necessary to enable him to return to his hometown with the comforts and dignity his person deserved. The captain graciously thanked him but declined his generous offer.

By now, night had fallen and it was at this time that a coach pulled into the courtyard, accompanied by several men on horseback. When they asked for lodging, the innkeeper's wife informed them that in the entire inn there was not a foot of unoccupied space.

"Even if that is so," said one of the mounted gentlemen, "some arrangement must be made for his honor the judge who has just arrived."

The mention of this official troubled the hostess and she said,

"Sir, the problem is that I have no beds. If his honor has brought one with him, as he is certain to have done, he is welcome to come in and my husband and I will vacate our room to accommodate his grace."

"That will do nicely," said the squire.

But a man had already alighted from the coach whose attire immediately announced the office and position he held, for his long robe with its ruffled sleeves showed him to be a judge, as his servant had said. He had in his company a young lady in traveling attire some sixteen years of age, who was so elegant, graceful, and lovely that the sight of her filled everyone with awe, and had they not already seen Dorotea, Luscinda, and Zoraida, who were lodging at the inn, they would have found it difficult to believe there could be another damsel as beautiful as she. Don Quixote, who was present when the judge and the young lady entered, addressed the judge the moment he saw them.

"Your grace may confidently enter and take your ease in this castle, for though it is austere and lacking in comforts, there is no austerity or inconvenience on earth that will not make room for a man of arms and letters, especially when he has beauty as his guide and escort, as your grace has in the person of this fair maiden, for whom not only would castles fling open their gates and lay themselves bare but boulders would move aside and mountains would split asunder and bow down in an effort to make her feel welcome. May I invite your grace once more to enter this paradise, for here you will find not only stars and suns to accompany that heaven you have brought with you but also both arms and beauty that are unsurpassed."

The judge, who was astonished at Don Quixote's language and no less so at his appearance, was at a loss for words and began to scrutinize him from head to foot. He was equally astonished when he saw Luscinda, Dorotea, and Zoraida there in his presence, for as soon as the ladies had been informed by the innkeeper's wife of the new guests and the young lady's beauty, they had come out to see her and to extend their welcome. Don Fernando, Cardenio, and the priest placed themselves at the judge's disposal in language that was plainer but more appropriate. As it turned out, the judge went inside thoroughly confused, as much by what he had seen as by what he had heard. Meanwhile, the beautiful ladies of the inn were busily engaged in making the equally beautiful newcomer feel at ease. The judge could easily see that all those present were persons of quality but he was bewildered by Don Quixote's figure, countenance, and bearing. Once everyone had exchanged pleasantries and inspected the inn's facilities, they proceeded with what they had already decided upon, namely, that all the women would lodge in the abovementioned garret and the men would remain outside on guard, as it were. The judge was delighted that the young damsel, his daughter, would be lodging with these ladies, which she was more than willing to do. Thus, by utilizing the innkeeper's narrow bed and the mattress the judge had brought with him, they spent a more comfortable night than they might ever have imagined.

From the moment the captive saw the judge, his heart began to pound, for he suspected that this was his brother. He asked one of the judge's servants who the judge was and where he was from. The servant informed him that he was the licentiate Pérez de Viedma, who, he had heard, was from a village in the mountains of Leon. As a result of this revelation and what he himself had observed, he was finally convinced this was the brother who had followed his father's advice and dedicated himself to a life of letters. Beside himself with joy, he called aside Don Fernando, Cardenio, and the priest, telling them what had occurred and assuring them that the judge was his brother. The servant had also told him the gentleman was headed for the Indies to assume the post of judge in the high court of justice in Mexico. Moreover, he had learned that the young lady was the judge's daughter at whose birth the mother had died, and that he had lived quite comfortably off the dowry of the daughter, who continued to live at home. He asked them how he might reveal his identity or discover in advance whether his brother, once he revealed himself, would be ashamed to see how poor he was or would welcome him with open arms.

"That determination may be left up to me," said the priest. "I can only believe, Captain, that your grace will be well received, for the quality and intelligence exhibited by your brother's behavior give no hint of arrogance or ungratefulness or of his inability to put the vicissitudes of fortune into their proper perspective."

"Nevertheless," said the captain, "I should like to make myself known, not all at once, but in a roundabout way."

"I have already told your grace," replied the priest, "that I shall manage it in such a way that everyone will be satisfied."

Supper was now announced and they all seated themselves round the table, except the captive and the ladies, who dined alone in their room. Midway through the meal the priest said,

"Your honor, I had a comrade in Constantinople with the same family name as your grace's, where I was a captive for several years. This comrade of mine was one of the bravest soldiers and captains in the entire Spanish infantry but was as unfortunate as he was courageous and daring."

"And what was this captain's name, my good sir?" said the judge.

"His name," responded the priest, "was Ruy Pérez de Viedma, a native of a village in the mountains of Leon. He related an incident that had occurred between his father and his brothers, and had it not been related by a man as trustworthy as he, I might have taken it for one of the old wives' tales told round the fireplace in wintertime. He said his father had divided his estate among his three sons and had imparted to them certain words of wisdom superior to those of Cato. What I know for a fact is that the son who elected to go to war was so successful within a few years, due to his valor and determination, that with nothing more than his considerable merits he rose to the rank of infantry captain and found himself esteemed and well on his way to becoming field commander. Fortune, however, conspired against him, for whereas he had every right to expect to win her favor, he lost it by losing his freedom in that most glorious expedition in which so many won theirs, the Battle of Lepanto; I lost mine at La Goleta. Afterwards, through a series of separate events we found ourselves comrades in Constantinople. I later learned that he went to Algiers, where he met with one of the strangest adventures ever to occur on earth."

The priest continued his story, relating with the greatest brevity what had happened to the judge's brother and Zoraida, during which time the judge was more attentive than he had been in any court of law until that moment. The priest described events only up to the point where the French plundered the Christians on board the boat, leaving his comrade and the beautiful Moor in a state of direst poverty. He had never been able to discover what became of them: whether they had reached Spain or been carried off to France by the French.

The captain, who had been listening from a short distance away to everything the priest said, was observing the way his brother reacted. When the judge heard the priest reach the end of his story, he heaved a deep sigh and with tear-filled eyes said,

"Oh, sir, if your grace only knew what news you have brought me and how personally it relates to me! I am forced to show its effect upon me by these tears which, despite all my discretion and reserve, are flowing from my eyes. That most valiant captain you mentioned is my eldest brother, who, being stronger and more idealistic than either my younger brother or I, chose the noble and honorable profession of arms, one of the three careers our father placed at our disposal, the account of which your lordship interpreted as an exaggerated tale. I chose a life of letters, where by the grace of God and my own efforts I have attained the position I now enjoy. My younger brother is in Peru and so wealthy that the money he has sent me and my father has more than repaid the portion he took with him, and he has even given my father enough to meet the demands of his natural generosity. In addition, I have been able to pursue my studies with more dignity and have achieved the position in which I now find myself. My father is still alive but worries himself sick for news of his eldest son, continually praying to God that death will not seal his eyes until he has seen his son alive. What I find surprising is that my truly intelligent brother should have been so remiss as to fail to send his father news of himself, either of his travails and sufferings or of his good fortune, for if either his father or any of us had known what had become of him, he need not have waited for the miracle of the rod to be rescued. But what I now find frightening is not knowing whether the French have set him free or slain him to cover up their abduction. All this will force me to continue my journey, not with the contentment with which I undertook it, but with considerable sadness and melancholy. Oh, my dearest brother, if only I knew where you were, I would find you and relieve you of your burdens, even if it meant taking them upon myself. If only someone could take our aged father news that you are alive! Even if you should be in the most inaccessible dungeon of Barbary, you would be rescued from there by his wealth and that of my brother and me! O beautiful and generous Zoraida, who can repay you for the kindness you have shown my brother! Who among us would not wish to be present at your soul's rebirth and your wedding, which would afford all of us such happiness!"

The judge, who expressed these and similar sentiments, was filled with such emotion over the news regarding his brother that everyone listening to him was moved to accompany him in his grief. When the priest saw that his plan had worked as well as he and the captain could possibly desire, he was unwilling to prolong their unhappiness and so, rising from the table, he entered the room of Zoraida, whom he led out by the hand, followed by Luscinda, Dorotea, and the judge's daughter. The captain was anxious to see what the priest would do, at which point the priest took the captive by the hand and led the two of them over to the judge and the other gentlemen and said,

"May your tears cease and your fondest desires be fulfilled, for you see before you your dear brother and dear sister-in-law. The man you see here is Captain Viedma and this woman is the beautiful Moor who showed him so much kindness. The French I mentioned placed them in this destitute condition so that your grace might demonstrate the generosity of your noble breast."

The captain hastened to embrace his brother, who, however, held him at arms' length to view him from a distance. When he finally recognized him, he embraced him so tightly, while shedding so many tears of joy, that most of those present were equally overcome with emotion, and the sentiments the brothers exchanged with one another and the feelings they revealed can scarcely be imagined, let alone recorded. Each briefly gave the other an account of his life and demonstrated there in all its fullness the great affection of two brothers for one another. The judge embraced Zoraida, placing all his possessions at her disposal, and then had his daughter embrace her, whereupon the beautiful Christian and the exquisitely beautiful Moor set everyone to weeping once again. Meanwhile, Don Quixote sat there saying nothing while carefully considering these strange events, all of which he attributed to the chimerical nature of knight-errantry. It was decided that the captain and Zoraida would accompany his brother to Seville and word would be sent to his father that he had been set free and discovered there at the inn so the father might attend Zoraida's baptism and wedding if his health permitted. It was impossible for the judge to interrupt his journey, for he had been notified that within the month a fleet would sail from Seville for New Spain and it would be most inopportune for him to miss the sailing. As it turned out, everyone was pleased and contented at the captain's good fortune and, since the night was nearly two-thirds over, they all agreed to retire and rest during the portion that remained. Don Quixote volunteered to stand watch over the castle lest they be accosted by some giant or no-good scoundrel covetous of the great collection of beauty enclosed within that castle, and all those who were acquainted with him expressed their appreciation. They also informed the judge of Don Quixote's strange disposition, which he found most amusing. Only Sancho Panza was in a state of despair at their delay in retiring for the night but he was the only one to get a good night's sleep stretched out on top of his donkey's saddlebags, which were to cost him so dearly, as we shall discover farther along. Once the ladies were settled into their quarters and the others had accommodated themselves with the least discomfort possible, Don Quixote went outside the inn to serve as sentinel of the castle, as he had promised.

Just before daybreak, there happened to reach the ladies' ears a voice so fine and musical that it made them all perk up their ears, Dorotea in particular, who was already awake and at whose side Doña Clara de Viedma lay sleeping, this being the name of the judge's daughter. No one could imagine who the person was who sang so beautifully, for it was a solo voice unaccompanied by any musical instrument. At times the singing appeared to come from the courtyard, at other times from the stable. While they were listening quite intently during all this uncertainty, Cardenio came to their door and called out,

"Anyone who is not asleep will want to listen to a muleteer's singing, which makes one simply long for a song."

"We are already listening, sir," replied Dorotea.

With this, Cardenio withdrew, and Dorotea, who was listening with all her might, was able to make out the following words of the song he was singing:

Chapter Forty-Three

The narration of the muleteer's enjoyable story, together with other strange events at the inn

"Tossed on a sea of doubts and fears,
Love's helpless mariner, I sail
Where no inviting port appears,
To screen me from the stormy gale.

At distance viewed, a cheering star
Conducts me through the swelling tide;
A brighter luminary far
Than Palinurus e'er descried.

My soul, attracted by its blaze,
Still follows where it points the way,
And, while attentively I gaze,
Considers not how far I stray.

But female pride, reserved and shy,
Like clouds that deepen on the day,
Oft shrouds it from my longing eye,
When most I need the guiding ray.

O lovely star, so pure and bright!
Whose splendor feeds my vital fire,
The moment thou deny'st thy light,
Thy lost adorer will expire."

When the singer reached this point in his song, Dorotea thought it would be unfair not to let Clara hear such a wonderful voice and so, shaking her back and forth until she finally woke her, she said,

"Forgive me, young lady, for waking you but I did so to let you hear the finest voice you have ever heard in your whole life."

Upon waking, Clara was still quite drowsy and did not immediately understand what Dorotea was saying. Seeing this, Dorotea repeated what she had said, at which point Clara too began to listen but, as soon as she had heard a couple verses of the song he was singing, she was overcome by a strange trembling, as though she were suffering a severe attack of quartan fever. Throwing her arms tightly round Dorotea, she cried out,

"Oh, my dear, dear lady, why did you have to wake me? The best thing fate might have done under the present circumstances would have been to stop up my eyes and ears so I could not see or hear this unfortunate musician."

"What are you saying, my child? The one singing is only a mule driver, or so they say."

"On the contrary," responded Clara, "he is lord of several estates, and the absolute dominion he holds over my heart shall last for all eternity unless he chooses to withdraw it."

Dorotea was surprised to hear such eloquence from the girl and, because she deemed it quite superior to the wisdom one might have expected from one so young, she said,

"Doña Clara, I do not understand what you are saying; do be more specific. What is this talk of your heart and estates and this musician whose voice has upset you so? But don't answer just yet, for if I attend to you and your fears, I shall forgo the pleasure of hearing him sing and I should not want that to happen now that he seems ready to sing a song about something else."

"Very well," replied Clara, but in an effort to avoid hearing him, she clapped both hands over her ears, which equally amazed Dorotea, who, listening closely, heard him sing the following song:

"Unconquered hope, thou bane of fear,
And last deserter of the brave,
Thou soothing ease of mortal care,
Thou traveler beyond the grave:
Thou soul of patience, airy food,
Bold warrant of a distant good,
Reviving cordial, kind decoy;
Though fortune frowns and friends depart,
Thou Sylvia flies me, flattering joy,
Nor thou nor love shall leave my doting heart.

No slave, to lazy ease resigned,
E'er triumphed over noble foes:
The monarch Fortune most is kind
To him who bravely dares oppose.
They say Love rates his blessings high,
But who would prize an easy joy?
My scornful fail then I'll pursue,
Though the coy beauty still denies;
I grovel now on earth, 'tis true,
But, raised by her, the humble slave may rise."

Here the song ended and Clara's sobs began, all of which increased Dorotea's desire to learn the cause of such tender singing and mournful weeping, so she again asked Clara to tell her what it was she had wanted to say earlier. At this point, Clara, fearing Luscinda might hear them, pulled Dorotea close to her and, pressing her lips to Dorotea's ear so she could speak safely without being overheard, said to her,

"The one singing, my lady, is the son of an Aragonese gentleman, lord of two villages, whose house is opposite my father's in the capital. Despite the fact that the windows in my father's house are covered by curtains in the winter and blinds in the summer, I have no idea how it happened but this gentleman, who was a student at the time, must have seen me in church or some other place. In any event, he fell in love with me, which he gave me to understand from the windows of his house by so many gestures and tears that I came to believe him and even to love him without knowing what he was proposing. Among the gestures he would make was one of joining both hands together to indicate his desire to marry me, and though I would have been quite happy if that had occurred, I had no one to confide in, since my mother had died and I was alone. And so my only course of action was to raise the curtain or blind a little when both *my* father and his were away from home so that he could see me from head to foot, which used to excite him so greatly that it nearly caused him to take leave of his senses.

"Meanwhile, the day of my father's departure arrived, which the young man learned of but not from me, for I had never had the opportunity to speak to him. He fell ill, I was told, from grief, so that on the day of my father's and my departure I was unable to see him to bid him farewell even with my eyes. After traveling for two days, we were about to enter a village inn a day's journey from here when I saw him standing by a tavern door dressed as a muleteer and so well disguised that were I not carrying a portrait of him in my heart, I could not possibly have recognized him; but recognize him I did, which not only shocked me but gladdened my heart as well. He stole a glance at me, unobserved by my father, from whom he always tries to hide when his path crosses mine either on the road or in the inns where we lodge. Since I know who he is and believe in my heart that he is traveling on foot and enduring all those hardships out of his love for me, I am dying of grief as I follow his every move with my eyes. I have no idea what his intentions are or how he has been able to elude his father, who loves him to an extraordinary degree, since he is his only heir and is worthy of such love, as you will see when you meet him. What is more, everything he sings he composes in his own head, and they say he is an excellent scholar and poet. Each time I see him or hear him sing, I tremble all over and am terrified that my father will recognize him and become aware of our mutual longings. I have never spoken to him a single time and yet I love him so much that I shall not be able to live without him. This, my lady, is all I can tell you about this singer whose voice has given you so much pleasure, for from his voice alone you can clearly see he is not a muleteer, as you have said, but a lord of hearts and villages, as I maintain."

"Say no more, Doña Clara," said Dorotea at this point, kissing her a thousand times; "don't say another word but let us wait for day to arrive. I trust that God will so direct your affairs that such virtuous beginnings will have the happy conclusion they deserve."

"But, dear lady," replied Doña Clara, "what possible conclusion can we expect when his father is so rich and important that he will not even consider me worthy to be his son's maid, much less his wife? And as for my marrying without my father's knowledge of it, I would not do so for anything on earth. I simply wish this young man would go back home and leave me in peace. Perhaps, if he were out of my sight and we could put some distance between him and ourselves, the pain I now feel might be alleviated somewhat, though I dare say that the proposal I have in mind will be of little benefit. I haven't the slightest idea how this has developed or where this love I feel for him has come from, for I am so young and he is just a boy. I actually think we are the same age and I am not even sixteen yet – at least, that is how old my father says I'll be next Michaelmas Day."

Dorotea could not help smiling when she heard Doña Clara speak with such childish innocence, so she said to her,

"Let us get some rest, my lady, during what little remains of the night, for tomorrow is another day and our fortunes will begin to improve or I am not as clever as I think I am."

With this they drifted off to sleep and a deep silence pervaded the inn. The only ones not asleep were the innkeeper's daughter and the maid Maritornes, who, knowing the wayward mentality of Don Quixote, together with the fact that he was standing vigil outside the inn armed and mounted on his horse, decided to play a trick on him or at least to pass the time listening to the outlandish things he might say.

It turned out that in the entire inn there was not a single window overlooking the courtyard except a hole in the hayloft through which the hay was pitched. The two demi-maidens stationed themselves at this opening from which they could see Don Quixote astride his horse as he leaned on his lance and from time to time heaved such profound and painful sighs that he seemed, with each one, to be giving up his very soul. At the same time they heard him say in a soft, pleasing, tender voice,

"O my lady Dulcinea of Toboso, fairest of the fair, be-all and end-all of discretion, repository of elegance, reservoir of purity, and lastly, model of all that is beneficial, virtuous, and delightful in this world, what might thine employment be at this moment? Canst thou perchance be contemplating thy captive knight, who has seen fit to expose himself to such great perils for the sole purpose of serving thee? O luminary of the three aspects, bring me tidings of her! Perhaps because of the envy her beauty inspires in thee, thou art observing her at this very moment strolling along a gallery of one of her sumptuous palaces or leaning over a balcony while pondering how, without compromising her honor or dignity, she might mollify the torment this troubled heart is suffering on her behalf, or what balm she might proffer for my pains, what ease for my cares, and lastly, what life for my death and what reward for my services? And thou, O sun, who must now be hurriedly harnessing thy steeds in thy desire to rise and view my lady, as soon as thou catchest sight of her, I entreat thee to greet her upon my behalf; but when thou greetest her, take care not to plant a kiss upon her brow or I shall be more jealous than thou wert of that fleet-footed ingrate who made thee work up such a sweat chasing across the plains of Thessaly, or along the banks of the Peneus, since I frankly don't recall where thou wert running at that moment consumed with love and jealousy."

Don Quixote had reached this point in his mournful monologue when the hostess' daughter called to him:

"Psst, psst, my lord, will your grace be so kind as to approach!"

At the sound of the voice directed his way, Don Quixote turned his head and saw by the light of the moon, which was then at its brightest, that someone was beckoning to him from the opening which for him was a window complete with its gilded grating, like those found in opulent castles, which is what he fancied this inn to be. At this very moment, he took it into his head that once again, just as on the previous occasion, the beautiful damsel, daughter of this castle's mistress, was overcome by her love of him and was there to press her attentions upon him. With this thought in mind and loath to appear discourteous or ungrateful, he turned Rocinante and approached the opening in the wall, where he no sooner saw the two lasses than he said,

"I regret, fair lady, that thou hast fixed thine amorous thoughts upon one who finds it impossible to reciprocate in the manner thy great worth and gentility deserve, the blame for which thou shouldst not ascribe to this lovelorn knight-errant for whom love has made it impossible to give his heart to anyone except her whom he made the absolute mistress of his soul the instant he laid his eyes upon her. Forgive me, noble lady, return to thy quarters, and refrain from baring thy soul to me lest I appear ungrateful; however, if because of the love thou feelest for me thou shouldst discover in me aught else by which I might satisfy thee – so long as it be not love itself – thou mayest ask it of me and I swear by that sweet absent beloved of mine to grant thy request at this very instant, though thou shouldst demand of me a lock of Medusa's hair, which consisted entirely of snakes, or the very rays of the sun enclosed in a vial."

"My lady is in need of none of those things, sir knight," said Maritornes at this point.

"Then what is it, discreet damsel, that your mistress is in need of?" asked Don Quixote.

"Only one of your grace's beautiful hands," said Maritornes, "in order to assuage the great longing that has brought me to this window at such peril to my honor, for if my noble father should discover me, he would at the very least slice off one of my ears."

"I should like to see him try that!" replied Don Quixote. "He would not dare do any such thing unless he wished to meet with the most disastrous end that any father ever met with for having laid hands upon the delicate person of his enamored daughter."

Maritornes never doubted for a moment that Don Quixote would offer his hand as requested, and so, after going over in her mind what she planned to do, she climbed down from the window and hurried to the stable, where she grabbed the halter belonging to Sancho Panza's jackass and quickly returned to the window just as Don Quixote had stood up on Rocinante's saddle in an effort to reach the window grating, where he fancied the smitten damsel to be. As he held out his hand, he said,

"Take this hand, my lady, or rather this scourge of the evildoers of the world. Take this hand, I say, which has never been touched by another woman's, not even by the hand of her who enjoys complete possession of my body and soul. I offer it not for your grace to kiss but to observe the makeup of its sinews, the thickness of its muscles, and the breadth and ampleness of its veins, from which you may judge the strength of the arm attached to such a hand."

"We shall now see about that," said Maritornes, who tied a knot in the strap, slipped it over his wrist, and then climbed down from the opening, where she tied the other end securely to the bolt of the hayloft door. Feeling the rope bite into his wrist, Don Quixote said,

"It feels as though you are grating rather than caressing my hand. Pray do not abuse it so, for *it* is not the one to blame for the wrong you have suffered because of my steadfastness, nor is it right to vent all your anger upon such a small member. You should remember that one who is loving does not take such cruel revenge."

But nothing said by Don Quixote was heard by either woman, for as soon as Maritornes had bound him, she and her companion had gone away bursting with laughter, leaving him fastened in such a way that he was unable to free himself. He was, as we have said, standing upright on Rocinante with his entire arm thrust through the hole, bound by the wrist to the door bolt and extremely troubled, fearing that if Rocinante were to move in one direction or the other, he would be left hanging by his arm. For this reason, he dared not make the slightest movement, though owing to Rocinante's stoicism and lethargy he had every right to expect him to stand there for an entire century without budging. In the end, Don Quixote realized he was securely bound and the ladies had now left, whereupon he began to imagine that everything transpiring there was due to enchantment, as on the previous occasion when he had been beaten by that enchanted Moor of a muleteer; and he cursed himself to the core for having been so dumb as to venture into this castle a second time, having come off so badly the first time. This, he thought, should serve as a warning to knights-errant that when they have attempted an adventure and failed in its execution, it is a sign that it is reserved not for them but for someone else and that to attempt it a second time will thus be fruitless. Nevertheless, he gave a tug on his arm to see if he could free himself but so securely was he fastened that all his attempts were in vain, though it is true that he tugged quite cautiously lest he cause Rocinante to move. And though he would have liked nothing better than to climb down and seat himself on the saddle, he could do nothing but remain standing or have his hand pulled off.

It was at this moment that he longed for Amadís' sword against which all enchantments were powerless; it was here too that he cursed his fate, exaggerating the tribulations his absence would cost the world during the time he was under the spell, for such without a doubt is how he appraised the situation. It was also at this moment when he once more thought of his beloved Dulcinea of Toboso; when he called to his faithful squire Sancho Panza, who, stretched out on his donkey's packsaddle dead to the world, was oblivious even to the mother who had begotten him; when he called upon the sages Lirgandeo and Alquife to assist him; when he invoked his good friend Urganda to aid him; and lastly, it was here that morning overtook him so desperate and confused that he was bellowing like a bull because he did not expect the coming day to bring relief from his suffering, which he concluded might be everlasting, inasmuch as he fancied himself enchanted. He was led to this conclusion by the fact that Rocinante had not stirred or even moved a muscle, and he was convinced that he and his horse might be forced to go without food, drink, and sleep until the evil influence of the stars should pass or another wise enchanter should remove the spell from him.

But he was quite mistaken in his belief, for as soon as it began to grow light, there arrived at the inn four handsomely attired men on horseback with muskets suspended from their saddlebows. They began to pound vigorously on the inn gate, which was still closed, and when this was observed by Don Quixote from his place of vigil, he cried out in a loud, arrogant voice,

"You knights, or squires, or whatever you are, have no business calling at the gates of this castle, for it is perfectly obvious that at this hour those inside are either still asleep or are not in the habit of opening the fortress till the sun has risen throughout the land. Withdraw for now and wait for daylight to arrive, at which time we shall determine whether or not it will be appropriate to permit you to enter."

"What sort of damned castle or fortress is this," said one of the men, "that we should stand on such ceremony? If you are the innkeeper, order them to open up. We are travelers who only want to feed our horses and be on our way because we are in a hurry."

"Gentlemen, do you think that I look like an innkeeper?" said Don Quixote.

"I don't know what you look like," responded the other person, "but I do know that you are talking nonsense if you call this inn a castle."

"It *is* a castle," replied Don Quixote, "and one of the very best in the whole province, for there are people inside who have held scepters in their hands and worn crowns on their heads."

"It is more likely the other way round," said the traveler, "with scepters on their heads and crowns on their hands; [1] and such may well be the case, since there is probably a company of actors inside who, like others of their profession, quite often carry those crowns and scepters you speak of. But I don't believe that in an inn as small and quiet as this one there can be any lodgers worthy of crowns and scepters."

"You are very poorly informed about the world," said Don Quixote, "if you are ignorant of the most commonplace occurrences in knight-errantry."

The questioner's companions, who were growing weary of his conversation with Don Quixote, resumed pounding on the door so vigorously that it woke the innkeeper and every other person in the inn, at which point the host got out of bed to see who was there.

It so happened that at this moment one of the horses belonging to the four men calling at the inn came over to sniff Rocinante, who, melancholy, sad, and with ears drooping, stood motionless while supporting his elongated master, but since Rocinante was, after all, made of flesh and blood and not of wood as one might be led to believe, he could hardly keep from responding by taking a sniff of the one who had come to pay his respects, and no sooner did he move the tiniest bit than Don Quixote lost his footing and slipped off the saddle, at which point he would have fallen to the ground had he not been bound by his arm. This caused him such pain that he was certain they were either cutting off his hand or ripping off his arm. He was hanging so close to the ground that he could brush it with the tips of his toes, which worked to his disadvantage, for when he felt how close he was to being able to plant his feet firmly on the ground, he struggled and stretched himself that much more in an effort to reach it, just as those poor souls do who are tortured by being suspended just above the floor and proceed to increase their own suffering by desperately trying to stretch themselves in the mistaken belief that with a little more stretching they can reach the floor.

---

1 A reference to the practice of branding criminals on their hands with the sign of a crown.

Chapter Forty-Four

The continuation of the unheard-of incidents at the inn

So loud, in fact, were Don Quixote's screams that the terrified innkeeper opened the gate and came outside to see who was responsible for such shouting, and those outside also went to investigate. Maritornes, who had been awakened by the same screams and suspected what was happening, hurried to the hayloft and, unobserved by anyone, untied the halter that held Don Quixote fast. He immediately fell to the ground in view of the innkeeper and the travelers, who came over to ask what could possibly be making him scream like that. Without saying a word, he removed the cord from his wrist, rose to his feet, and mounted Rocinante. Then strapping on his buckler and placing his lance in its socket, he rode some distance onto the field, at which point he headed back at a trot, shouting as he approached,

"If anyone has the audacity to say that I have rightfully been placed under a spell, I will, by the leave of my lady the Princess Micomicona, contest and challenge him in single combat and will prove him a liar."

The newly arrived travelers were taken aback at Don Quixote's words but the innkeeper put them at ease by explaining that this was Don Quixote, who was not to be taken seriously because he was out of his mind. They then asked the innkeeper if there had come to that inn a lad of about fifteen who was dressed as a muleteer and had such and such features, whereupon they described the very ones Doña Clara's lover possessed. The innkeeper replied that, due to all the people in the inn, he had not noticed the one they were inquiring about. But one of the men who had spotted the coach in which the judge had arrived said,

"He simply must be here because that is the coach they say he is following. It will be a good idea for one of us to guard the door while two others go inside to search for him, and the fourth can make a complete circuit of the inn in case he tries to escape over the courtyard wall."

"That's what we'll do," said one of the other travelers.

While two of them went inside, a third man remained at the gate and the other one proceeded to circle the inn. The innkeeper observed their actions but could not imagine why they were going to so much trouble, though he understood that they were looking for the lad whose description they had given him.

Due to the arrival of day and the ruckus Don Quixote had made, the guests were all awake and out of bed, especially Doña Clara and Dorotea, who had slept quite badly that night: one because of her excitement at having her lover so near and the other because of her desire to see him. Don Quixote noticed that the four travelers were paying no attention to him, nor were they answering his challenge, a circumstance that made him furious and fit to be tied, and had he been able to discover in his code of chivalry that it was lawful for a knight-errant to undertake another adventure after giving his word and oath not to engage in any whatsoever before concluding the one to which he had pledged himself, he would have taken on everyone there and made them answer for it, whether they liked it or not. But feeling it would be neither fitting nor proper to undertake any new enterprise before placing Micomicona upon her throne, he was forced to hold his peace and remain silent while waiting to see where the efforts of those travelers would lead. One of them found the lad he was seeking sleeping beside a muleteer, completely unaware that people were looking for him, much less that they would locate him. The man seized him by the arm and said,

"Sir Don Luis, the clothes you are wearing certainly are most becoming to a person of your quality, and the bed in which I find you goes well with the pampered upbringing your mother gave you."

The young man sleepily rubbed his eyes and stared for several moments at the person who held him in his grasp. When he finally recognized him as one of his father's servants, he gave such a start that he was unable to say a word for quite some time. The servant went on to say,

"There is nothing else for you to do now, Sir Don Luis, except to resign yourself to the trip back home unless you want your father – my master – to make a trip to the next world, which is all that may be expected from the suffering your father has undergone because of your absence."

"But how did my father learn," asked Don Luis, "that I was headed in this direction and was wearing these clothes?"

"A student to whom you told your plans," responded the servant, "was the one who made it known, for he was moved to pity by the grief he saw your father display when he learned his son was missing. As a result, your father dispatched four of us servants to look for you and here we are at your grace's service, more delighted than you can imagine at being able to return so soon and deliver you to the one who loves you so dearly."

"We shall do what I want or what heaven ordains," replied Don Luis.

"What can heaven ordain or your grace possibly want except to agree to return home? Anything else is out of the question."

The entire discussion between the two was overheard by the muleteer at Don Luis' side. Rising to his feet, he went over to explain everything to Don Fernando, Cardenio, and all the others, who were now dressed. Not only did he report that the man addressed the lad as *Don* Luis but told them what they had said to each other, including the fact that the man wanted him to return to his father's house, which he was refusing to do. Because of this, together with what they knew of the fine voice heaven had given him, they were all quite eager to learn more about him and even to come to his aid should force be employed against him, and so they went over to where he was still conversing and arguing with his servant. Just then, Dorotea came out of her room, followed by a completely distraught Doña Clara. Taking Cardenio aside, Dorotea briefly recounted to him the story of the singer and Doña Clara. He likewise explained to her what was taking place regarding the arrival of the servants but he failed to speak softly enough to keep Doña Clara from overhearing him. This threw her into such a state that, had Dorotea not hastened to catch her, she would have collapsed in a faint. Cardenio told Dorotea and Clara to return to their room while he attempted to straighten things out, and they did as he advised.

The four men who had come in search of Don Luis had now returned to the inn and gathered round him, trying to persuade him to return home without a moment's delay in order to console his father. He responded that under no circumstance would he do so before attending to a matter that involved his life, his honor, and his soul. Taking hold of him, they informed him that they could not possibly return without him and would take him back whether he was willing to return or not.

"*That* you shall not do," replied Don Luis, "unless you take me home dead. But regardless of how you take me home, it will be to take me there as one who has departed this life."

By this time all the others in the inn had come forward to listen to the argument, especially Cardenio, Don Fernando and his companions, the judge, the priest, the barber, and Don Quixote, who had finally decided there was no longer any need to guard the castle. Cardenio, who was now acquainted with the lad's story, asked those who wanted to take him away why they wished to do so against the lad's wishes.

"We are led to do this," answered one of the men, "to save the life of his father, which he is in danger of losing because of this gentleman's absence."

To which Don Luis responded,

"There is no reason to discuss my affairs here. I am a free man and shall return if I feel like it; if not, none of you can force me to do so."

"We shall use reason with your grace," said the man, "and if that is not sufficient to make you do so, it will be sufficient to make us do what we came for, in order to fulfill our obligation."

"May we know what is at the bottom of all this?" said the judge.

But the man who recognized him as his neighbor said,

"Your honor, do you not recognize this gentleman, your neighbor's son, who has fled his father's house wearing clothes so unbecoming to one of his rank, as your grace can see?"

After scrutinizing him more closely, the judge finally recognized him, at which point he embraced him and said,

"What childishness is this, Sir Don Luis, and what great necessity has caused your grace to come here in this manner and in an outfit so unbecoming a person of your standing."

The young man's eyes filled with tears and he was unable to say a word. The judge told the four men they could be assured that everything would be resolved. Then taking Don Luis by the arm, he drew him aside and asked him the meaning of his arrival. But while he was posing this question among others, shouts were heard at the entrance to the inn, which were occasioned by the fact that two guests who had spent the night there had seen that everyone was involved in trying to discover what the four men wanted and had thus attempted to leave without paying their bill. But the innkeeper, who watched over his own well being better than he did that of others, had grabbed them as they were going out the gate and had demanded his pay, denouncing their evil intentions with such foul language that he caused them to respond with their fists, whereupon they began to belabor him so mightily that the poor innkeeper was forced to shout for help. The innkeeper's wife and daughter saw that no one was more available to lend assistance than Don Quixote, to whom the daughter said,

"Sir knight, I beg your grace, by that virtue God has vested in you, to help my poor father, for two wicked men are thrashing him as though he were wheat."

To which Don Quixote responded most leisurely and phlegmatically,

"Fair damsel, your request is out of the question at the moment, for I am forbidden to become involved in any other enterprise until I resolve the one for which I have given my word. But what I can do, by way of serving your ladyship, I shall now explain. You are to run and tell your father to hang on in that battle to the best of his ability and under no circumstances to allow himself to be overcome. In the meantime I shall ask Princess Micomicona for permission to aid him in his plight. If she agrees, you may be certain that I shall come to his rescue."

"Heaven help me!" said Maritornes, who happened to be present, "before your grace obtains that permission, my master will already be in the next world."

"If you will permit me to seek that permission," replied Don Quixote, "the moment I have it, his being in the next world will be of little consequence, for I shall rescue him from there even if that world attempts to thwart me, or, at least, I shall wreak such havoc upon those who have sent him there that your ladyship will be more than moderately satisfied."

And without further discussion he went to kneel at the feet of Dorotea, whom he implored in knightly and chivalresque language to be so kind as to give him leave to aid and assist the governor of that castle, who now found himself in the direst straits. The princess graciously granted his request, whereupon he strapped on his buckler, seized his sword, and hurried out to the inn gate, where the two guests were still belaboring the innkeeper most mercilessly. But as soon as Don Quixote arrived, he suddenly hesitated as though he had been struck dumb. Maritornes and the innkeeper's wife asked him why he was standing there instead of aiding their master and husband.

"I am hesitating," said Don Quixote, "because it is unlawful for me to draw my sword against anyone who is not a knight. However, your ladyships might be kind enough to summon my squire Sancho Panza, as it is imperative that this defense and vengeance be left up to him."

This took place at the inn gate, where the punches and jabs were flying fast and furiously, all to the detriment of the innkeeper and to the outrage of Maritornes, the innkeeper's wife, and her daughter, who were exasperated at observing Don Quixote's cowardice and the ill treatment of their master, husband, and father respectively.

But let us take leave of his grace, for there cannot fail to be someone who will come to his aid – and even if there is not, let him patiently abide it for having bitten off more than he can chew. Let us go back some fifty paces to hear how Don Luis responded to the judge when we left them alone. The latter had just asked him why he had made that trip on foot and in such wretched attire, at which point the young man grasped him firmly by the hands, as if to demonstrate that some great burden lay heavy upon his breast, and shedding a stream of tears, he said,

"All I can tell your grace is that from the moment I had the good fortune to see your daughter and my lady Doña Clara, thanks to the will of heaven and the proximity of our houses, from that very instant I made her mistress of my will, and if you, my true lord and father, do not forbid it, I shall make her my wife this very day. Because of her I have abandoned my father's house and donned this outfit to follow her wherever she goes, just as the arrow seeks its target or the sailor his pole star. She knows nothing more of my desires than what little she has been able to divine from afar when she has seen my eyes filled with tears. Your grace is probably already aware of the wealth and nobility of my parents and of the fact that I am their sole heir. If you deem these sufficient qualities to risk making me completely happy, pray accept me now as your son, for if my father for reasons of his own should not be pleased with this happiness I have been able to find, time will be more capable of undoing and altering affairs than my own efforts will be."

In saying this, the enamored youth fell silent and the judge was left bewildered, confused, and astonished by what he had heard, as much by the manner and intelligence with which Don Luis had revealed to him his intentions as by his own inability to deal with so sudden and unexpected a situation. His only response was to plead with him to remain calm and to persuade his servants not to take him away on this particular day so he would have time to consider how everyone might best be served. Don Luis seized him by the hands, kissing and even bathing them with his tears, an act that would have mollified a heart of marble, let alone that of the judge, who, as an intelligent man, had already recognized how advantageous this marriage would be to his daughter; though if it were up to him, he would prefer it to be consummated with the blessing of Don Luis' father, who, he knew, wished to marry his son into a title.

Meanwhile, the guests had made peace with the innkeeper, for, due more to Don Quixote's persuasiveness and reasoning ability than to his threats, they had paid him everything he demanded. Don Luis' servants were waiting for the judge to finish his speech to see what their master would do, when the Devil, who never sleeps, decreed that there should enter the inn at that very moment the barber from whom Don Quixote had taken Mambrino's helmet and Sancho Panza the packsaddle for his jackass, which the latter had exchanged for that of his own. While leading his mount to the stable, the barber had spotted Sancho Panza, who was busy mending part of his packsaddle. The moment he saw it, he recognized it and boldly attacked Sancho, crying out,

"Aha, sir thief, now I've got you! Hand over my basin and my packsaddle and all the other trappings you stole from me!"

Sancho, seeing himself challenged so unexpectedly and hearing himself called so many names, seized his packsaddle with one hand and struck the barber's face with the other, leaving his mouth bloody, but this did not make the barber relax his grip on the packsaddle. Instead, he let out such a howl that all those in the inn hurried to the place from where the noise of the altercation was coming, at which point the barber shouted,

"Help in the name of the king and the law! In addition to taking what belongs to me, this thief and highwayman now wants to kill me!"

"That's not true," said Sancho, "I'm not a highwayman, for my master Don Quixote won these spoils in a fair fight."

Don Quixote, who was now present, was delighted to see how manfully his squire was defending himself and returning the attack. From this moment forth he reckoned him a man of consequence and resolved in his heart to have him knighted on the first occasion that presented itself, feeling the order of chivalry would be well served by him. Among the various things the barber said in the course of their struggle was the following:

"Gentlemen, this packsaddle is mine as surely as I owe my soul to God, for I know it as well as if I had given birth to it; and my jackass, who is there in the stable, will prove that I'm telling the truth. If you don't believe me, try it on him yourselves and if it doesn't fit him like a glove, your graces may label me a scoundrel. Morever, the same day that they stole it, they also stole a brand-new brass basin that had never been used and was worth a whole *escudo*."

At this point Don Quixote could not keep from intervening, and so, stepping in to separate the two, he placed the packsaddle on the ground, where it was to remain on display until the truth could be ascertained. He then said,

"So that your graces may see how clearly and obviously mistaken this good squire is who calls this a basin, which was, is, and always shall be Mambrino's helmet, let me explain that I took it from him in a fair fight, thereby becoming its legitimate and lawful owner! Now, the packsaddle is a matter I shall not get involved in; all I can say about it is that my squire Sancho asked my permission to remove the harness from this vanquished coward's mount in order to outfit his own. I allowed him to do so and he appropriated it but, as to how the harness was changed into a packsaddle, I can offer no explanation other than the usual one: that transformations of this type are a frequent occurrence in the business of knight-errantry. As proof of this, hurry, Sancho my son, and fetch the helmet which this good fellow claims is a basin."

"Good lord, master," said Sancho, "if we have no better proof of our claim than what your grace proposes, this basin will no more be Malino's helmet than the packsaddle will be a harness!"

"Do as I say," said Don Quixote, "for not everything in this castle will be subject to enchantment."

Sancho went for the basin and brought it back. When Don Quixote saw it, he took it in his hands and said,

"Would your graces observe the arrogance with which this peasant calls this a basin rather than a helmet, as I maintain! I swear by the order of chivalry I profess that this helmet is the same one I took from him, to which I have not added or subtracted a thing."

"There is no doubt about it," said Sancho at this point, "for from the time my master won it up to now he has worn it in only one battle, the one in which he freed those men in chains who were destitute of hope, and if it hadn't been for this basin of a helmet, he wouldn't have come off very well at that time, for there was stone-throwing a-plenty in that scrape."

Chapter Forty-Five

The resolution of the controversy surrounding Mambrino's helmet and packsaddle, together with a faithful account of other happenings and adventures

"How," said the barber, "do your graces feel about the claim made by these gentlemen, who still insist upon calling this a helmet instead of a basin?"

"And if anyone says anything to the contrary," replied Don Quixote, "I shall give him to understand that he is lying if he is a knight, and, if a squire, is lying a thousand times over."

Our own barber, who was present during all this and was well acquainted with Don Quixote's temperament, decided to encourage his follies and continue the deception for the amusement of everyone present, so he addressed the second barber, saying,

"Sir barber, or whatever you are, I would have you know that I too belong to your profession, having held a license for more than twenty years, and I have a very sound knowledge of every single instrument of the barber's trade. In my youth I was a soldier, which is neither here nor there, but I do know what a helmet looks like and which part is the headpiece and which the visor, as well as other things having to do with military life, that is, the kinds of weapons soldiers use. So unless someone comes up with a better explanation, since I am always ready to yield to a superior mind, I maintain that the device here before us that this worthy gentleman is holding in his hands not only is not a barber's basin but is as far from being one as white is from black, or truth from falsehood; but even though it's a helmet, it is not a complete one."

"Of course not," said Don Quixote, "for half of it is missing, namely, the beaver."

"So it is," said the priest, who now understood what his friend the barber had in mind, and the same was confirmed by Cardenio, Don Fernando, and his companions. Even the judge, had he not been occupied with Don Luis' affair, would have taken part in the deception but the seriousness of what he had on his mind left him so preoccupied he paid little or no attention to all these subtle distinctions.

"May God help me!" cried the barber who was the object of ridicule, "is it possible for so many honorable souls to claim this is not a basin but a helmet? Something of this nature would confound an entire university, regardless of how learned it was. But never mind, if this basin is actually a helmet, then this packsaddle must also be a horse's harness, as this gentleman claims."

"It looks like a packsaddle to me," said Don Quixote, "but I have already said I am not getting involved in that."

"Whether it is a packsaddle or a harness," said the priest, "rests only in the hands of Sir Don Quixote to say, for all these gentlemen and I defer to him in these matters of knight-errantry."

"Heavens, gentlemen," replied Don Quixote, "so many strange things have befallen me in this castle on the two occasions I have lodged here that I dare not make any pronouncement regarding what is going on, for I am of the opinion that everything we are dealing with is under some sort of enchantment. On the previous occasion, I was sorely vexed by an enchanted Moor who was here, not that his cohorts treated Sancho very well either. Last night, I was left hanging by this arm of mine for nearly two hours without ever knowing how on earth I had come by that misfortune, so for me to pass judgement on such a confusing matter now would be to act rashly. With regard to the claim that this is a basin and not a helmet, I have already given my answer, but in the matter of declaring whether that is a packsaddle or a harness, I dare not make a definitive ruling. I shall simply leave it to your graces' good judgement. Perhaps because you have not been knighted as I have, you may not be affected by the enchantments of this place and your minds will be free to judge all the things in this castle as they really and truly are and not as they appear to me."

"There is no doubt that Sir Don Quixote has spoken most wisely today," said Don Fernando. "The decision in this case is up to us, and so that it may be based upon something more solid, I shall take a secret ballot among these gentlemen but shall disclose the results openly and fully."

For those who were already aware of Don Quixote's temperament, all this was cause for the greatest merriment but for those who were not it seemed the greatest nonsense on earth, particularly for Don Luis' four servants and no less so for Don Luis himself and the other three travelers stopping at the inn who appeared to be officers of the Holy Brotherhood, which in fact they were. But the one who was most in despair was the barber whose basin had turned into Mambrino's helmet right before his eyes and whose packsaddle, he had no doubt whatsoever, was about to turn into the plush trappings of a horse. One and all laughed at the sight of Don Fernando's going from one person to another taking their votes and asking them to whisper in his ear whether they thought the jewel over which there had been so much contention was a packsaddle or a harness. Once he had finished taking the votes of those who knew Don Quixote, he addressed the owner in his normal voice, saying,

"My good man, I am tired of listening to so many opinions, for it is obvious, according to everyone who has given me his answer, that it is simply ludicrous to claim this is an ass' packsaddle and not the harness of a horse – and of a thoroughbred at that. Therefore, you shall abide by our ruling, which is, that despite you and your jackass, this is a harness rather than a packsaddle; moreover, you have presented your evidence and defense very poorly."

"May I never go to heaven if your graces are not mistaken," said the surplus barber. "May my soul as surely appear before God as this appears to me to be a packsaddle and not a harness. However, 'When in Rome – ' but I'll say no more; and I certainly am not drunk because I've not broken my fast today except to sin."

The foolish things the barber said evoked no fewer laughs than had the nonsense of Don Quixote, who said at this point,

"There is nothing further to be done except for each to take what is his and may that which God has given him be blessed by Saint Peter."

Here one of the four servants said,

"Unless this is some kind of intentional joke, I cannot convince myself that men as intelligent as your graces are, or appear to be, can have the audacity to affirm and declare this is not a basin nor that a packsaddle, but since I see this is what you are declaring and affirming, I am forced to believe there must be some mystery involved which accounts for your graces' insistence upon something that flies in the face of truth and experience itself, for I swear to . . ." – and this he said with emphasis – "there is no person now living who can make me believe this is not a barber's basin, nor that the packsaddle of a jackass."

"It may well be that of a *she*-ass," replied the priest.

"That is beside the point," said the servant; "that is not what is under discussion but whether it is a packsaddle or not, as your graces contend."

When he heard this, one of the recently arrived officers who had witnessed the argument and dispute cried out angrily and indignantly,

"That is a packsaddle as surely as my father is my father and anyone who says or has ever said anything to the contrary must be drunk."

"You are a lying, lowborn scoundrel," shouted Don Quixote.

And raising his lance, which he had never put down, he unleashed such a blow to the officer's head that, had he not jumped out of the way, it would have laid him out flat. The lance shattered when it struck the ground, and the other officers, seeing their comrade treated thus, cried out for someone to come to the aid of the Holy Brotherhood. The innkeeper, who belonged to the fraternity, immediately went inside to get his sword and staff of office and then took his place beside his comrades. Meanwhile Don Luis' servants had gathered round him to prevent his escape during the commotion. The barber, seeing the inn turned upside down, once again grabbed his packsaddle, with Sancho doing the same. Don Quixote drew his sword and lunged at the officers. Don Luis shouted at his servants to leave him and go help Don Quixote as well as Cardenio and Don Fernando, who were both in Don Quixote's camp. The priest was shouting, the innkeeper's wife was screaming, her daughter was beside herself, Maritornes was sobbing, Dorotea was perplexed, Luscinda was bewildered, and Doña Clara was all aswoon, and the barber was pounding Sancho and Sancho the barber. Don Luis, whose arm one of his servants had the audacity to grab in an effort to prevent his escape, punched him in the mouth, leaving it bloody. While the judge was attempting to help the servant, Don Fernando had one of the officers on the floor and was kicking him at will from one end of his body to the other; and the innkeeper shouted once more for someone to come to the aid of the Holy Brotherhood, with the result that the whole inn was nothing but sobs, shouts, screams, confusion, fear, consternation, dismay, slashes, punches, beatings, and kicks, with blood everywhere.

But in the midst of this mayhem and labyrinthine confusion Don Quixote took it into his head that he had suddenly been plunged headlong into the discord of Agramante's camp, and so with a voice that thundered throughout the inn, he shouted,

"Let everyone stop, put away his sword, and stay calm! Let him heed these words, I say, if he wishes to continue living!"

When they all stopped at the sound of his mighty voice, he went on to say,

"Did I not tell your lordships that this castle was enchanted and there must be a horde of demons residing here? As confirmation of this, I would have your graces observe with your own eyes how the discord of Agramante's camp has been transferred here, where it has insinuated itself among us.

Observe how yond persons are all fighting for the sword, these for the horse, those others for the eagle, and ourselves for the helmet, for we are all at odds and are fighting one another. If their graces the judge and the priest will kindly serve as King Agramante and King Sobrino respectively, they may be able to establish peace among us. As God is my judge, it is scandalous for so many people of note such as ourselves to slay one another for such frivolous reasons."

The officers, who understood none of Don Quixote's language and who had found themselves manhandled by Don Fernando, Cardenio, and their companions, were in no mood to be appeased. The barber *was*, however, for he had lost both his beard and his packsaddle in the brawl. Sancho, as a good servant, obeyed the slightest command of his master. Don Luis' four servants also restrained themselves, seeing how little they had benefitted from not doing so. Only the innkeeper insisted upon punishing the insolence of that madman for disrupting the inn at every turn. The noise abated for the time being but in Don Quixote's mind the packsaddle would be a harness, the basin a helmet, and the inn a castle until Judgement Day. When they had all finally calmed down and made peace with one another through the persuasiveness of the judge and the priest, Don Luis' servants once again insisted that he immediately return with them. While he was trying to reach an understanding with them, the judge discussed with Don Fernando, Cardenio, and the priest what he might do in this matter, which he then described to them, relating everything Don Luis had told him. It was finally agreed that Don Fernando would reveal his identity to Don Luis' servants and tell them he wanted Don Luis to accompany him to Andalusia, where the latter would be accorded by his brother the marquis the esteem he so richly deserved. From this it was obvious that Don Luis had no intention of returning to the bosom of his father even if they were to tear him to pieces. Once the servants had learned of Don Fernando's rank and Don Luis' intentions, they decided among themselves that three of them would return to inform his father of how matters were proceeding and the fourth would remain with Don Luis as his servant until the others returned for him or until they saw what his father might order them to do. In this way that jumble of conflicts was settled by the authority of Agramante and the prudence of King Sobrino, but when the Foe of Concord and Adversary of Peace saw Himself slighted and duped, understanding how little harvest He had reaped from having thrown everyone into a labyrinth of confusion, He decided to try His hand one more time by resurrecting new disputes and disturbances.

The result was that the officers became calm after learning the rank of those with whom they had been fighting, and they withdrew from the fray, having concluded that, regardless of how things turned out, they would get the worst of the deal. But one of them, the one who had been beaten and kicked by Don Fernando, finally remembered that among the warrants in his possession for the arrest of various criminals was one against Don Quixote, whom the Holy Brotherhood had ordered apprehended for having given the galley slaves their freedom, as Sancho had so rightly feared. Once he remembered, he wanted to see if Don Quixote matched the description he carried, and so, drawing forth a parchment from his doublet, he found the warrant he was looking for and began to read it slowly. Not being a very good reader, he would read a few words at a time and then fix his eyes on Don Quixote to compare the description in his warrant with the features of Don Quixote's face. He found that without a doubt he was the one the warrant described, and no sooner had he satisfied himself than he folded the parchment, took the warrant in his left hand, and grabbed Don Quixote's neck so tightly with his right that it prevented him from breathing. He then cried out,

"Assistance for the Holy Brotherhood! and to show your graces that I am serious, read this warrant, which says this highwayman is to be apprehended."

The priest took the warrant and saw that everything the officer had said was true and that Don Quixote answered to the description there. When the latter saw himself maligned by that oafish scoundrel, his blood began to boil, and with every bone in his body creaking he seized the officer by the throat with both hands as tightly as he could, and if the latter's companions had not come to the rescue, the officer would have given up the ghost before Don Quixote would have given up his prey. The innkeeper, who was obliged to help his fellow officers, immediately came to his aid. The innkeeper's wife, seeing her husband in another round of brawls, once again began to shout for heaven and all those present to help him, being instantly joined in her pleading by her daughter and Maritornes. When Sancho saw what was happening, he said,

"As God is my witness, everything my master says about this castle is true, for it's impossible to get an hour's rest here."

Don Fernando separated the officer and Don Quixote, and to the delight of both, disengaged their hands, for one had seized the other by the coat collar, who in turn had grabbed him by the neck. But this did not stop the officers from demanding their prisoner or asking the others to help them overpower him and deliver him into their jurisdiction, since this was demanded by the king and the Holy Brotherhood, in whose name they again asked for help and assistance in arresting that robber and highwayman. Don Quixote chuckled when he heard these words and said quite calmly,

"Come now, you base, ill-bred commoners, do you call a person a highwayman who gives galley slaves their freedom, sets prisoners free, lends assistance to the downtrodden, raises up the fallen, or administers to the needy? Because of your base, vile minds you wretches do not deserve for heaven to let you share in the benefits that flow from knight-errantry, nor to be shown the sin and ignorance in which you wallow when you fail to respect the image, let alone the presence, of any knight-errant! Come, you thieves masquerading as officers, you highwaymen licensed by the Holy Brotherhood, tell me: who was the ignoramus who signed a warrant for the arrest of a knight such as myself? Who was the one who did not even know that knights-errant are exempt from all court orders, since their sword is their law, their prowess their charter, and their own will their statutes? Who was the simpleton, I say, who did not know that there is no certificate of nobility with as many privileges and immunities as the one a knight-errant acquires the day he is dubbed a knight to devote himself to the arduous profession of chivalry? What knight-errant ever paid taxes when he sold some article or when some royal personage was wed, or when he passed through a tollgate or sailed down a river; or simply because he was the king's vassal? What tailor ever charged him for making his clothes? What governor of a castle ever received him into his castle and then asked him to pay for his stay? What king ever refused to seat him at his table? What damsel ever failed to fall in love with him and yield herself utterly to his will and pleasure? And finally, what knight-errant has there ever been on this earth or ever will be who will not be courageous enough to administer singlehandedly four hundred whacks to four hundred officers of the Brotherhood who dare show themselves in his presence?"

Chapter Forty-Six

The notable adventure of the officers, and the great ferocity of our noble knight Don Quixote

While Don Quixote was saying this, the priest was attempting to convince the officers that the knight had lost his mind, as they could see by his actions and words, for which reason there was no need to press the matter further, for even if they were to arrest him and take him away, he would necessarily be set free because of his insanity. To this the officer with the warrant replied that it was not up to him to judge whether Don Quixote was crazy but to carry out what his superior had ordered him to do. Once he was in custody, they could release him three hundred times for all he cared.

"Nevertheless," said the priest, "you must not take him away just now, nor will he allow himself to be taken away, judging by what I have seen."

In short, the priest managed to talk so much and Don Quixote managed to do so many absurd things that the officers would have had to be crazier than the knight not to recognize this defect of his, so they thought it advisable to allow themselves to be pacified and even to serve as peacemakers between the barber and Sancho Panza, who were still carrying on their dispute in the most bitter fashion. In the end, they, as law officers, acted as mediators and arbitrators in the case and performed so well that both parties were, if not completely happy, at least somewhat satisfied, for which reason they exchanged packsaddles but not cinches and halters. As for Mambrino's helmet, the priest, unknown to Don Quixote, secretly gave the barber eight *reals* for the basin and the barber made out a receipt in which he promised never to claim fraud now and forever after, amen.

Once these two disputes were settled, they being the most important and weighty ones, it remained only for Don Luis' servants to arrange for three of them to return home, while the fourth would stay behind to accompany Don Fernando wherever he might wish to take him. Good luck and better fortune, which had now begun to clear the way and diminish the difficulties in favor of the lovers and the other brave souls in the inn, now saw fit to bring everything to a conclusion and provide a happy ending that resulted in the servants' willingness to do everything Don Luis desired, which made Doña Clara so happy that anyone observing her at that moment could not fail to discern the rejoicing in her heart. And though Zoraida did not fully understand everything she had witnessed, she became alternately happy and sad as she gazed at and examined the faces of each person, particularly that of her Spaniard, upon whom she kept her eyes fixed and her soul suspended. The innkeeper, who could hardly help noticing the generous reparations the priest had made the barber, asked Don

Quixote to pay for the damage to his wineskins and the loss of the wine, vowing that neither Rocinante nor Sancho's jackass would leave the inn until he had been paid every last cent. The priest calmed everyone down and Don Fernando paid the entire bill, though the judge had generously offered to do so. In this way they were all pacified and assuaged and the inn no longer resembled the discordant camp of Agramante, as Don Quixote had observed, but the peace and calm of the days of Octavian. It was the general consensus that they could give thanks for all this to the good intentions and great eloquence of the priest and the incomparable liberality of Don Fernando.

When Don Quixote saw himself free and disencumbered of so many disputes -- those of his squire as well as his own -- he thought it advisable to continue the journey he had already begun and to conclude this great adventure for which he had been called and chosen. With this resolute determination he went to kneel before Dorotea, who, however, would not permit him to say a word until he rose. To comply with her wishes, he stood up and said,

"A well known proverb says, fair lady, that 'Diligence is the mother of good fortune.' Experience has shown that in many serious confrontations the persistence of a negotiator can bring a doubtful concern to a happy conclusion. Nowhere is this more evident than in war, where speed and haste can thwart the plans of the enemy and gain the victory before the latter can prepare a defense. I mention all this, exalted and honorable lady, because it strikes me that our stay in this castle is no longer beneficial but may even be harmful, and this may be brought home to us some day, for who knows whether your grace's adversary the giant has already learned by means of secret, diligent spies that I am destined to destroy him and is employing the time thus afforded him to fortify himself in some impregnable castle or fortress against which my efforts and the might of my indefatigable arm will prove powerless? Therefore, my lady, as I have said, let us foil his plans by leaving at once in quest of good fortune, for to realize your desires you shall have to wait no longer than it takes me to confront your adversary."

At this point, Don Quixote said nothing further but calmly waited for the beautiful princess to respond, who with a queenly air replied in a manner modeled after that of Don Quixote's.

"I am most grateful, sir knight, for your grace's willingness to favor me in my great distress as the knight that you are, upon whose shoulders rests the responsibility for protecting the homeless and the needy; and may God grant the fulfillment of both your desires and mine so you may see that there are women in the world capable of gratitude. As for my departure, let it be at once, for *my* only desire is what you desire, and you may do with me according to your will and pleasure, for she who has already entrusted to you the defense of her person and placed in your hands the restoration of her kingdom will be loath to question anything your wisdom might prescribe."

"By Almighty God," said Don Quixote, "if a lady is willing to humble herself before me in this manner, I refuse to forego the opportunity to raise her up and place her upon her rightful throne. Let us ride forth at once, for it is commonly said that 'there is danger in delay' and this is spurring my desire to be underway. Since heaven has never created, nor hell seen, anyone who can frighten or make a coward of me, saddle up Rocinante, Sancho, prepare your jackass and the queen's palfrey, and let us take our leave of the governor and these gentle folk and set out at this very instant."

Sancho, who was present during all this, shook his head from side to side and said,

"Oh, master, master, there is more hanky-panky in these hamlets than your grace imagines, with my apologies to the present company for having to say this."

"What hanky-panky can there be in this hamlet or any city on earth that can soil my reputation, you peasant?"

"If your grace is going to get mad," replied Sancho, "I'll keep quiet and not say what I'm obliged to say as a faithful squire, nor say what a faithful servant should tell his master."

"Say whatever you will," said Don Quixote, "so long as you don't try to fill me with fear by your words, for if you are afraid, you are only being true to your nature, and if I am not, I am being true to mine."

"Upon my word as a sinner," said Sancho, "that is not what I meant but that I have figured out and know for a fact that this lady who claims to be queen of the mighty kingdom of Micomicón is no more a queen than my mother is, for if she were the person she claims to be, she wouldn't continually go about kissing a certain fellow in this and that hiding place every time people turn their backs."

Dorotea blushed at Sancho's remarks because it was true that her betrothed Don Fernando had on occasion, when they were out of view of the others, collected from her lips a portion of the reward his passion deserved. This had been observed by Sancho, who was struck by the fact that such easy abandon was more becoming a courtesan than the queen of such a mighty kingdom. Accordingly, she was unwilling and unable to say a word to Sancho but allowed him to continue speaking, which he did, saying,

"I say this, master, because after all the traveling we've done over highways and byways, plus the bad nights and worse days we've endured, if the one who's having all the fun in this inn is going to reap the fruits of our labors, there is no reason for me to hurry and saddle Rocinante or put the packsaddle on the ass or get the palfrey ready. It will be better for us to sit tight, eat our meal, and leave each whore to her knitting."

Merciful heavens! you can imagine the rage that swept over Don Quixote when he heard such scandalous language from his squire! You, dear reader, may take my word for it that it was so great that with fire shooting from his eyes and his voice choking he said with a stammer,

"You lowborn scoundrel, how can you be so disrespectful, impudent, ignorant, foul-mouthed, insolent, scandalmongering, and slanderous? How dare you utter such words in the presence of me and these illustrious ladies? How dare you entertain such shameless, insolent thoughts in that warped mind of yours? Get out of my sight, you freak of nature, you repository of lies, you storehouse of deceit, you silo of knavery, you manufacturer of wickedness, you spreader of idiocies, you enemy of the civility due persons of royalty! Away with you and never let me see you again under penalty of my wrath!"

In saying this, he furrowed his brow, sucked in his breath, glared in one direction and then the other, and finally with his right foot kicked the ground with all his might, all of which revealed the rage that was churning inside him. At these words and gestures charged with fury Sancho cringed with terror and would have rejoiced if the earth had opened beneath his feet at that instant and swallowed him whole. He had no idea what to do except to turn and quit the presence of his enraged master, but the wise Dorotea, who was now fully aware of Don Quixote's temperament, said in an attempt to assuage his anger,

"Sir Knight of the Woeful Countenance, may your grace not take umbrage at what your faithful squire has said, for he may have good reason for saying such things. Judging by his good sense and Christian conscience, one would not expect him to bear false witness against anyone. One is thus led to believe, since there can be no other explanation, that in this castle, as your grace has pointed out, everything that happens does so under the influence of enchantment, and thus it may be, I repeat, that due to this diabolical device Sancho actually did see what he claims to have seen, and this has cast doubt upon my virtue."

"I swear by Almighty God," said Don Quixote at this point, "your ladyship has hit the nail on the head, and some illusion was placed before the eyes of poor, unfortunate Sancho, who was made to see what he could not have seen by any means other than that of sorcery, for I am convinced of the goodness and innocence of this good fellow, who would never speak ill of anyone."

"That is undoubtedly the explanation," said Don Fernando, "for which reason, Sir Don Quixote, your grace should pardon him and return him to the bosom of your favor, *sicut erat in principio,* [1] before such illusions caused his mind to become muddled."

Don Quixote replied that he had his forgiveness, and the priest went directly to fetch Sancho, who came in most humbly and fell to his knees as he begged his master for his hand. After extending it and allowing him to kiss it, Don Quixote gave him his blessing and said,

"Sancho my son, you have just seen the truth of what I have often told you about this castle, namely, that everything in it is brought about by means of enchantment."

"That's how I see it," said Sancho, "except that business of the blanket, which was actually brought about by ordinary means."

"You are not to believe such a thing," said Don Quixote, "for if that were the case, I would have avenged you then and would do so even now, but neither then nor now have I ever been able to identify anyone I could punish for your humiliation."

Everyone was curious to learn the nature of that business of the blanket, whereupon the innkeeper related point by point Sancho Panza's attempts at flight, which they found not a little amusing and which Sancho would have found not a little embarrassing had his master not assured him it was all an illusion. Still, Sancho's folly had never reached the point that he failed to believe it was an absolute and simple fact with no deception involved whatsoever: that he had been tossed in a blanket by people of flesh and blood and not by phantoms either dreamed or imagined, as his master believed and affirmed.

Two days had now passed since this illustrious assemblage had gathered at the inn and, because they now felt it was time to depart, they agreed not to put Dorotea and Don Fernando to all the trouble of returning with Don Quixote to his village under the guise of freeing Queen Micomicona but to allow

1 Latin: 'as it was in the beginning.'

the priest and the barber to take him with them, which they wished to do so the priest might deal with his madness back home. What they did then was to arrange for the driver of an oxcart who happened to be passing by the inn to transport him on his cart. A makeshift cage with wooden bars was constructed, which was capable of comfortably enclosing Don Quixote. Then Don Fernando, his companions, Don Luis' servants, and the officers, together with the innkeeper, all under the orders and approval of the priest, covered their faces and donned their disguises, some of one type and some of another so that Don Quixote would think them different people from those he had seen in the inn. This accomplished, they very quietly entered the chamber where Don Quixote lay peacefully sleeping following his recent encounters. Approaching him while he was asleep and totally unaware of what was taking place, they laid firm hold of him and tied his hands and feet so securely that when he woke with a start he was unable to move or do anything more than stare in amazement at the sight of so many strange faces before him. He at once resorted to the imaginary world his warped mind continually conjured up, whereby he concluded that all those figures were phantoms of that enchanted castle and that he was undoubtedly under a spell, since he could neither move nor defend himself. The result was that everything turned out just as the priest had predicted, he being the architect of that scheme. Only Sancho among all those present possessed his usual appearance and judgement, and though he did not have far to go to suffer from the same affliction as his master, he did not fail to recognize who all those disguised figures were but he dared not unseal his lips until he saw where the assault and capture of his master was leading. Don Quixote also remained silent, waiting to see what might be the outcome of his misfortune. At this point they brought forth the cage and enclosed him inside it, nailing up the bars so securely that no amount of tugging could have dislodged them. They then hoisted him onto their shoulders but just as they were leaving the inn, a frightful voice was heard, as frightful as the barber could make it – not the barber with the packsaddle but the other one – and the voice said,

"O Knight of the Woeful Countenance, be not aggrieved by the prison in which you are traveling, for this is necessary to bring to a speedier conclusion the adventure in which your great courage has placed you. This shall be achieved when the raging Manchegan lion couples with the white Tobosan dove, having first subjected their eminent necks to the yoke of matrimony, from whose extraordinary union shall issue forth into the light of day the fierce cubs who will imitate the rampant claws of the valiant father. This shall come to pass before the pursuer of the fleeing nymph can twice pay a visit to the constellations in his swift and natural course. And you, the most noble and obedient squire who ever had a sword at his side, a beard on his face, or a nose that could smell, be not unhappy or disheartened at seeing the flower of knight-errantry transported thus before your very eyes, for shortly, if it please the Creator of the universe, you shall find yourself so exalted and sublime you will not recognize yourself, nor shall the promises your good master has made you prove false. I can assure you on behalf of the wise Mentironiana that your wages shall be paid you, as events will bear me out. Follow the footsteps of the valiant and enchanted knight, for it is fitting that you go where you both shall remain. But since I am permitted to say nothing further, God keep you and I shall return to I know where."

Reaching the end of his prophecy, he modulated his voice with such feeling that even those who were privy to the joke were ready to believe that what they were hearing was real. Don Quixote was consoled by the prophecy he had just heard, having immediately understood its full import. He inferred that he was being promised to see himself united in holy and lawful matrimony with his beloved Dulcinea of Toboso, from whose blessed womb would issue the cubs – his sons – to the everlasting glory of La Mancha. This he believed so completely and firmly that he raised his voice, heaved a deep sigh, and said,

"O sir, whoever you are, who have predicted such great happiness for me, I beseech you on my behalf to ask the wise enchanter charged with my affairs not to permit me to perish in this prison in which I now find myself until I see the fulfillment of promises as delightful and incomparable as these made here. So long as this is done, I shall glory in the miseries of my cell and shall find relief in these chains that bind me, nor shall I consider these canes upon which I am forced to lie an arduous battlefield but a soft bed and auspicious nuptial couch. As for the consolation of my squire Sancho Panza, I trust in his goodness and noble behavior, which will not allow him to abandon me in good times or bad. But should it transpire, either because of his ill fortune or mine, that I should be unable to bestow upon him the island or its equivalent that I have promised him, at least his wages will not be lost, for in my will, which is already drawn up, I have stipulated everything that is to be given him, based not upon his long and faithful service but upon my meager resources."

Sancho Panza bowed his head most respectfully and kissed both of his master's hands, being unable to kiss only one because both hands were tied together. These apparitions then lifted the cage onto their shoulders and placed it on the oxcart.

Chapter Forty-Seven

The strange manner in which Don Quixote of La Mancha became enchanted, together with other notable happenings

When Don Quixote saw himself inside the cage on top of the cart, he said,

"I have read a number of very serious histories of chivalry but never have I read, seen, or heard of enchanted knights being hauled about in this fashion or at the lethargic pace permitted by these slow, sluggish beasts. They are generally transported through the air at astonishing speeds riding on a dark grey cloud or in a fiery chariot or astride a hippogriff or some such beast, but to be carried along thus on an oxcart – heavens! – I scarcely know what to think. Perhaps knight-errantry and incantations these days pursue a different course from that pursued in the days of old, and since I am a knight new to the world and the first to have resurrected the now forgotten profession of venturer knights, it is possible that other types of enchantments have recently been invented, together with other methods for transporting the enchanted. What do you think of that, Sancho my son?"

"I don't know what to think," replied Sancho, "not being as well versed as your grace in the writings of chivalry, but despite that, I would venture to vow and affirm that these apparitions we're surrounded by are not absolutely catholic."

"Catholic! My word, Sancho, how can they be Catholic when they are all demons who have assumed these fanciful forms to come here to place me in this predicament? [1] If you should care to see for yourself, just touch them with your hand and you will see that their bodies are nothing more than air and consist of nothing but appearance."

"For goodness' sake, master," said Sancho, "I've already touched them, and this devil here who's making such a fuss is quite plump and possesses a characteristic quite different from the one I've heard devils possess, for according to all accounts, they invariably reek of sulphur or something equally foul but this one smells of amber from half a league away."

Sancho said this for Don Fernando's benefit, for, being quite the nobleman, he undoubtedly smelled the way Sancho said.

"Don't be surprised at that, Sancho my friend," replied Don Quixote. "I would have you know that devils are quite clever and, despite the fact that they are bearers of odors, they give off none themselves because they are spirits, and even when they do, these cannot be good odors but foul, stinking ones. The reason for this is that, wherever they go, they carry hell about with them and are allowed no sort of relief from their torments, and since good odors are things that delight and please, it is impossible for devils to smell good. Therefore, if you believe this devil you mentioned smells of amber, either you are mistaken or he wants to deceive you into believing he is not a devil."

This entire discussion took place between master and servant, and since Don Fernando and Cardenio were afraid that Sancho might see completely through their ruse, which he was on the verge of doing, they decided to hasten their departure. Calling the innkeeper aside, they ordered him to saddle Rocinante and place the packsaddle on Sancho's jackass, which he did without delay. In the meantime, the priest had arranged for the officers to accompany him to his village, for which he promised them a certain amount of pay each day. Cardenio hung the shield on one side of Rocinante's saddle and the basin on the other, and after motioning to Sancho to mount his jackass and lead Rocinante by the reins, he placed the two officers with the muskets on either side of the cart. But before the cart could begin to move, out of the inn came the innkeeper's wife, her daughter, and Maritornes to bid Don Quixote farewell while pretending to shed tears of sorrow over his misfortune. At this point, he said to them,

"Weep not, noble ladies, for all these misfortunes are commonplace occurrences for those who profess what I profess. Were I not to undergo these disasters, I should not consider myself a famous knight-errant, for such things never befall knights of little renown and repute, nor does anyone on earth remember them. They do befall the valiant ones, who by their virtue and valor instill such envy in princes and other knights that these strive to destroy the righteous by evil means. But regardless

1 Sancho uses the word 'catholic' in its figurative sense of 'to be trusted.' Don Quixote understands the word literally — a reversal of roles for our two protagonists.

of this, virtue is so powerful that, despite all the black arts possessed by their original inventor Zoroaster, it will in and of itself emerge victorious from any predicament and will shine forth in the world, as the sun does in the heavens. I beg your forgiveness, fair ladies, if I have thoughtlessly offended your graces in any way, which I have never willingly or intentionally done to anyone, and may you ask God to deliver me from this prison in which some ill-intentioned enchanter has placed me, for once I see myself free of it, the favors your ladyships have shown me in this castle shall not be erased from my memory but shall be heeded, addressed, and rewarded, as they deserve."

While this exchange was taking place between the ladies of the castle and Don Quixote, the priest and the barber said farewell to Don Fernando and his companions, to the captain and his brother, and to all those contented ladies, particularly Dorotea and Luscinda. They all embraced and promised to keep one another informed of what happened to them, and Don Fernando told the priest where he was to write to let him know how things turned out with Don Quixote, assuring him that nothing would give him greater pleasure than to receive news of this. He added that he himself would keep the priest informed of everything that might be of interest to him: not only his own marriage but Zoraida's baptism, together with Don Luis's affair and Luscinda's return home. The priest promised to comply fully with all his requests, and once again they embraced and renewed their offers to one another. The innkeeper went over to the priest to give him some papers he said he had found in the lining of the case containing *The Tale of Unreasonable Curiosity*, and because its owner had not returned for them, the priest was welcome to take them with him, as they were of no use to him, since he was unable to read. Thanking him, the priest opened the papers and saw that the title on the first sheet was *The Novel of Rinconete and Cortadillo*, [2] which he assumed was another novella, and he surmised that since the one about unreasonable curiosity had been interesting, this one would be as well, because they might both be by the same author. He therefore kept it, intending to read it at his earliest convenience.

Having donned their masks to avoid being recognized by Don Quixote, the priest and the barber mounted their horses and began to ride along behind the cart. The order of the procession was as follows: first came the cart driven by its owner; on either side rode the officers with their muskets, as we have mentioned; Sancho Panza followed astride his jackass, leading Rocinante by the reins; and behind them, riding no faster than the gait of the sluggish oxen would permit, came the priest and the barber riding their powerful mules with their faces covered and themselves displaying an air of seriousness and calm. Don Quixote was sitting in the cage with his hands tied together and his legs stretched out in front of him, leaning against the bars completely silent and resigned, as though he were not a man of flesh and blood but a statue hewn from stone. Everyone rode along ploddingly and silently for some two leagues before coming to a valley, which the oxcart driver indicated as a place where they could let the oxen graze. He mentioned this to the priest but the barber preferred to ride on a bit farther because he knew that on the other side of the hill visible in the distance was a valley

2 A story by Cervantes composed around 1602 and finally published in 1613 as one of the twelve *Novelas ejemplares* ('Exemplary novels')

with better and more abundant grass than the one where the driver wished to stop. So following the barber's suggestion, they started forward once again.

Just then, the priest looked back and saw as many as six or seven men on horseback approaching from the rear, all well dressed and well equipped. These men quickly caught up with them because they were not traveling at the listless, lethargic pace of the oxen but like persons riding canons' mules eager to spend the siesta in the inn, which they could see was less than a league away. The diligent travelers caught up with the lethargic ones and both groups greeted one another courteously. One of the men who had arrived was, in fact, a canon of Toledo and the superior of those in his company. When he saw the orderly procession of the cart, the officers, Sancho, Rocinante, the priest, the barber, and particularly Don Quixote imprisoned in the cage, he could not resist asking why they were transporting the man in that fashion, though he had already been led to believe by the officers' badges that he must be a scurrilous highwayman or some sort of criminal whose punishment involved the Holy Brotherhood. One of the officers he had questioned responded,

"Sir, let the gentleman himself explain why he's being transported in this manner because we actually don't know."

Don Quixote overheard their conversation and said,

"Gentlemen, are your graces by chance versed and knowledgeable in matters of knight-errantry? If so, I shall explain my misfortunes, but if not, there is no reason to take the trouble to do so."

At this point, the priest and the barber, having seen the travelers in conversation with Don Quixote of La Mancha, rode up to answer their questions in such a way that their plan would not be exposed. The canon responded to what Don Quixote had said by saying,

"Verily, brother, I know more about books of chivalry than about the *Dialectics* of Villalpando, so if no more than that is involved, you may tell me whatever you wish."

"So be it," replied Don Quixote, "and this being the case, I would have you know, sir knight, that I find myself in this cage enchanted because of the envy and deception of some evil enchanters, for virtue is more persecuted by the wicked than sought after by the good. Also, I am a knight-errant, and not one of those whom Fame has never thought to immortalize in her account but one who, despite Envy herself and all the magicians ever spawned in Persia, the brahmans of India, or the Gymnosophists of Ethiopia, will inscribe his name in the temple of immortality to serve as an example and model in ages to come, whereby knights-errant will perceive the steps they are to follow if they wish to ascend to the summit and pinnacle of honor in the profession of arms."

"What Sir Don Quixote of La Mancha says is true," said the priest at this point, "for he is traveling in this cart enchanted, not because of any failings or sins on his part, but because of the evil designs of those to whom virtue is irritating and valor annoying. This, sir, is the Knight of the Woeful Countenance, whom you may possibly have heard of at some time or other, whose courageous feats and great deeds will be inscribed in solid bronze and everlasting marble, regardless of how laboriously Envy may work at eclipsing them or Malice at obscuring them."

When the canon heard the prisoner and the man outside the cage speak in such terms, he found it so astonishing he was ready to make the sign of the cross and wondered what he had gotten involved in; nor were those in his company any less astonished. At that moment, Sancho, who had crept close to listen to the conversation, spoke up in an effort to clarify matters.

"Well now, gentlemen, whether or not your graces will be pleased by what I am about to say, the fact of the matter is that my master Don Quixote is no more enchanted than my mother is, for he's in complete command of his faculties: he eats, drinks, and attends to all the necessities everyone else does, the same as he did yesterday before they placed him in the cage, and this being the case, no one is going to make me believe he's enchanted. I've often heard people say that those who are enchanted don't eat, sleep, or speak but unless my master is restrained, he'll talk the ears off a lawyer."

And turning again to the priest, he said,

"O sir priest, sir priest! did your grace think I wouldn't recognize you or wouldn't figure out and guess where these new enchantments were leading? Well, I want you to know that I recognize you, regardless of how many disguises you have put on your face, and I've got you figured out however much you try to camouflage your tricks. After all, virtue cannot exist where envy is rampant, nor generosity where there is scarcity. Plague take it! if it weren't for your reverence, my master would already be married to the Princess Micomicona and I would be a count, which is the least I could expect because of my master's goodness – Him of the Woeful Countenance – and my outstanding service! But I see that what they say in these parts is true: 'The wheel of fortune is busier than a mill wheel,' for, those who yesterday were riding high have today been humbled. I am pained by this because of my wife and children, who had every right to see their father come sailing into port made governor or viceroy of some island or kingdom, but instead, they'll see him come home having been turned into a stableboy. Sir priest, I mention all this only to urge you to think seriously about the mistreatment to which my master is being subjected, and to make sure God will not ask you in the life to come about this prison of my master's lest you be held accountable for all the help and favors my master Don Quixote will be unable to bestow during the time he's held captive."

"What a bunch of gibberish, Sancho!" exclaimed the barber at this point. "Are you a member of the same fraternity as your master? As God is my witness, I am beginning to think you ought to join him in the cage, since you must be under the same spell he is, for his temperament and knight-errantry seem to have rubbed off on you. It was a sad day and an evil hour when you allowed yourself to be seduced by his promises and when that island you so dearly covet took possession of your brain."

"I haven't been seduced by anyone," replied Sancho, "nor am I a man who would allow himself to be seduced even by the king himself. I may be poor but I'm a Christian of long standing and don't owe anything to anyone. If I long for islands, other people long for worse things, for 'Each of us is the child of his deeds,' and since I am a man, I can rise to be pope, much less governor of an island, especially when my master is capable of winning so many he'll need someone to award them to. Sir barber, you should mind what you say, for barbering isn't everything and not all men are alike. I mention this because all of us here know one another, and no one is going to use loaded dice with me; and concerning that matter of my master's enchantment, God can see who's telling the truth, so let's leave it at that. Stirring will only make it worse."

The barber was unwilling to respond to Sancho lest the latter reveal by his ingenuousness what the barber and the priest were trying to keep concealed, for which reason the priest suggested to the canon that they ride on ahead a short distance so he could explain the mystery of the caged man, together with other matters that he would find interesting. The canon agreed and, riding ahead with his servants, paid close attention to everything the priest chose to tell him regarding Don Quixote's character, life, madness, and habits, including a brief explanation of the origin and cause of his derangement and a complete account of his escapades up till the moment he was placed in the cage, and, lastly, the plan they had devised for taking him back home to see if they could discover some cure for his madness. The canon and the servants once again marveled at Don Quixote's strange story and, when it was finished, the canon said,

"Truly, sir priest, I for my part find that these so-called books of chivalry are harmful to the state. Even though I have read the first few pages of virtually every one that was ever written, being driven to this by idleness and poor taste, I have never managed to read a single one through from beginning to end. It strikes me that they are all more or less the same, with no individual one containing anything the others do not, for it seems this type of writing and composition falls under the heading of Milesian fables, absurd tales concerned only with entertaining and not with instructing, just the opposite of moral fables, which entertain and instruct at the same time. And though the principal aim of such books may be to entertain, I fail to see how they can achieve this, since they are full of so much outlandish nonsense. Any enjoyment engendered in the soul comes from the beauty and harmony the soul sees and contemplates in those things the eyes and mind place before it. Anything that contains within itself ugliness and disorder can give us no pleasure whatever. What beauty or what proportion can there be between the parts and the whole – or the whole and the parts – of a book or fable in which a lad of sixteen slashes at a giant as tall as a tower and splits him in two as though he were made of icing? When the authors want to describe a battle to us, having already told us there are a million combatants on the enemy's side, we are asked to believe, whether we wish to or not, that the knight, so long as he is the hero of the book, will necessarily emerge victorious simply by the might of his arm. And what can one say of the ease with which a queen or empress-to-be throws herself into the arms of an unknown knight-errant? What mind, unless it is totally uncivilized and uncultured, can find enjoyment in reading that a tall tower filled with knights is scudding across the sea like some barque with a favoring wind and will spend the night in Lombardy, only to find itself the following morning in the land of Prester John of the Indies or in some other land never discovered by Ptolemy or visited by Marco Polo? If someone were to counter that those who compose such books write them as works of fiction and, as such, are not required to pay attention to details or realism, I might respond that the more true-to-life a work of fiction is, the better it will be; and the more believable it seems, the more satisfying it will be. Plots should not insult the intelligence of those who read them but should be written in such a way that, by making the impossible seem plausible, keeping extremes to a minimum, and holding the reader in suspense, they will surprise, astonish, excite, and entertain, with amazement and enjoyment going hand in hand. These things cannot be achieved by one who avoids verisimilitude or the imitation of nature, wherein lies the perfection of all that is written. I have never seen a single book of chivalry that presents a well-balanced plot with all its necessary members such that the middle agrees with the beginning, or the end with the beginning and the middle. Instead, they are composed of countless members, as though they were intended to form a chimaera or freak rather than a well-proportioned figure. Moreover, their style is harsh, their plots unbelievable, their love interests lascivious, their taste crude, their battles too drawn out, their dialogue absurd, their travels ridiculous, and last but not least, they are devoid of any artistic creativity, because of which they deserve to be banished from the Christian community as a worthless tribe."

Inasmuch as the priest, who had been hanging upon the canon's every word, judged him to be a man of considerable understanding and correctness in all he had said, he informed him that he too held books of chivalry in abhorrence and had therefore burned all of Don Quixote's, which had been quite numerous. He described the inspection he had made of them, indicating which ones he had consigned to the flames and which he had permitted to live. The canon found all this most delightful and added that despite all the disparaging things he had said about such books, there was one thing he did find laudable: the fact that a keen intellect could place itself on display in them, as they afford a broad, spacious arena in which the pen may roam unimpeded when describing shipwrecks, storms, encounters, and battles – now portraying a valiant captain who has all the requisite qualifications: who shows his cleverness at anticipating the enemy's ploys, is most eloquent in encouraging or restraining his troops, is wise in his counsel, quick to convert his decisions into action, and is as courageous in awaiting an assault as in mounting an attack – now portraying a lamentable and tragic event, now a happy and unexpected one; portraying on the one hand a most beautiful lady, virtuous, wise, and modest, and on the other, a Christian knight, brave and courteous; in one instance, an outrageously uncouth braggart, and in another a courteous prince, brave and well thought of, while portraying the goodness and loyalty of the vassals and the largesse and favors of the lords. The author may present himself as an astrologer, an accomplished cosmographer, a musician, or a person knowledgeable in affairs of state; or perhaps he will have occasion to present himself as a necromancer if he so desires. He may portray the wiles of Ulysses, the piety of Aeneas, the bravery of Achilles, the misfortunes of Hector, the treachery of Sinon, the friendship of Euryalus, the generosity of Alexander, the courage of Caesar, the clemency and truthfulness of Trajan, the fidelity of Zopyrus, the prudence of Cato, and finally, all those qualities that can make an illustrious gentleman perfect, now placing them in a single individual, now dispersing them among many. If the author does this with an even style and with imagination and ingenuity, keeping as close to the truth as possible, he cannot fail to produce a fabric woven of varied and beautiful threads, which will exhibit such beauty and perfection that, once completed, it will attain the greatest goal writing can aspire to, namely, instruction and entertainment simultaneously, as I have said. The unbounded freedom of these books provides the author with the opportunity to be heroic, lyrical, tragic, and humorous, together with all those qualities contained within the pleasant and agreeable arts of poetry and oratory, for epics can be written in prose as well as in verse.

Chapter Forty-Eight

The continuation of the canon's discussion of books of chivalry, together with other matters worthy of his intellect

"Sir canon, it is just as your grace has said," responded the priest, "and for that reason those persons who until now have composed books of this type are more open to reproach, for they have heeded neither logic nor the craft and rules by which they might have been guided and made famous in prose, as the two princes of Greek and Latin poetry are in verse."[1]

"I myself," said the canon, "have been rather tempted to write a book of chivalry that observes all the points I have touched upon and, to be quite candid, I confess to having more than a hundred pages already written. To test whether my book measures up to my own estimation of it, I have shared it with persons fond of this type of literature, learned and perceptive men as well as ignorant ones who derive pleasure only from listening to nonsense, and I have had a favorable reaction from them all. But despite this, I have not proceeded with my plan because it strikes me that what I am doing is inappropriate to my profession, in addition to which I find the number of simpletons to be greater than that of intelligent persons, and since it is better to be praised by the few who are wise than ridiculed by the many who are fools, I refuse to subject myself to the muddled judgement of the unappreciative masses, who for the most part are given to reading books of this type. But the main reason I ceased to write or even to contemplate writing was a discussion I held with myself based upon the plays currently being staged, which went like this: 'Since all or most of the plays now in fashion, the fictional as well as the historical ones, are notorious claptrap and things without rhyme or reason but which the masses find tremendously enjoyable, approving of them and considering them good when they are far from being so, and since the playwrights who compose them and the actors who appear in them say this is how they must be because this is what the masses prefer and will accept nothing else, and since those that have a design and a plot developed according to the requirements of art end up pleasing no more than a handful of intelligent persons who understand them, all others being incapable of appreciating their craftsmanship; and since they prefer to earn a living from the many rather than to win the respect of the few, this is the fate my book will suffer even after I have burned the midnight oil trying to observe the principles I have mentioned, and thus all my efforts will come to nought.' Though I have on occasion sought to convince the playwright-managers that they are mistaken in their attitude – that they would attract a wider audience and win more renown by presenting plays that followed the rules rather than these absurd ones – they are so rigid and set in their ways that no amount of proof or evidence will make them change their minds. I remember saying one day to one of those stubborn fellows, 'Do you not remember that a few years

1 I.e. Homer and Virgil.

ago three tragedies were staged in Spain composed by a famous poet of this realm, [2] and they were so good they amazed, astounded, and delighted everyone who saw them: the slow-witted as well as the discriminating, the masses as well as the select few? Those three alone brought in more money for the companies than thirty of the best ones staged since.' 'Undoubtedly,' responded the person in question, 'you must be referring to *Isabella, Phyllis*, and *Alexandra*.' 'Those are the ones I mean,' I replied, 'and I ask you whether they observed the principles of art and, by observing them, whether or not they failed to display their superiority or failed to please anyone. The fault, therefore, resides not with the masses, who demand absurdities, but with those too ignorant to stage anything else. *Ingratitude Avenged* certainly was not nonsense, nor was *Numancia*. [3] *The Merchant Lover* contained no nonsense, nor did *The Fair and Obliging Adversary*, nor any of the others composed by various gifted dramatists, to their own credit and renown and to the benefit of those who produced them.' To these arguments I added others, which in my opinion left him somewhat uncertain but not satisfied or sufficiently convinced to rid himself of his erroneous beliefs."

"Sir canon," said the priest at this point, "your grace has touched upon a matter that has awakened an old complaint of mine with the plays now in favor. This complaint is as great as the one I have with books of chivalry, for though in Tully's opinion a play should be a mirror of human life, a model of behavior, and an image of truth, those staged today are mirrors of nonsense, models of idiocy, and images of lasciviousness, for what greater nonsense can there be regarding this subject than for a babe in swaddling clothes to appear in the first scene of the first act and then in the second to appear as a man with a beard? Is there anything sillier than to portray an aged man who is fearless, or a young man who is a coward, or an eloquent footman, a page who counsels wisely, a king who is a porter, or a princess who serves as a kitchenmaid? And what more can I say about the observance of the unity of place governing the locales in which the events occur except to say that I have seen plays in which the first act opens in Europe, the second follows in Asia, the third in Africa, and should there be a fourth, it takes place in America, so that the action touches all four corners of the earth? If verisimilitude is the chief quality a play should strive for, how is it possible to satisfy even a mediocre intellect by pretending an event takes place in the days of King Pepino or Charlemagne but at the same time the main character is represented as the Emperor Heraclius, who made his way into Jerusalem carrying the cross, where he gained possession of the Holy Sepulcher, like Godfrey of Bouillon, there being an infinite number of years between one and the other? Or consider the practice of basing the play upon something fictitious and then attributing historical facts to it, or mixing in snatches of things that happened to different persons in different eras, and to do so not in a believable way but with obvious errors, which are inexcusable under any circumstances? The worst part is that there are ignoramuses who claim this is the height of perfection and to strive for anything more is simply to chase after chimeras.

---

2 Lupercio Leonardo de Argensola (1559-1613).

3 A play written by Cervantes himself.

"Similarly, when we turn to religious dramas, what a bunch of counterfeit miracles they concoct, together with things that are apocryphal and poorly understood by them, the miracles of one saint being attributed to someone else! Even in secular dramas they have the audacity to perform miracles with no other object or consideration than the fact that they feel it expedient to have such a miracle, or 'effect,' as they call it, so that the ignorant will be intrigued and will attend the theater. All this is prejudicial to truth and detrimental to history and even an embarrassment to the genius of Spain. Foreigners, who observe the unities with great precision, consider us ignorant barbarians when they see the absurd nonsense with which we fill our plays. It is not sufficient justification to claim that the chief aim of well-run governments in allowing plays to be publicly performed is to entertain the masses with decent recreation, thereby temporarily taking their minds off the unwholesome thoughts idleness tends to engender. Inasmuch as this may be achieved with any sort of play, good or bad, there is no need to impose laws or to force those who write or perform plays to construct them in the way they should be constructed, for as I have said, they can achieve their goal through any one of them. To this I would respond that this goal might much more easily be attained in every regard by means of good plays rather than poor ones, for having witnessed an artful, well constructed play, the theatergoer would come away amused by the humor, instructed by the truths, astonished by the turns of events, made wise by the reasoning, forewarned by the deceptions, uplifted by the examples, angered by the vices, and inspired by the virtues, all of which emotions a good play will awaken in the minds of an audience, however dull and unsophisticated that audience may be. Besides, it will be absolutely impossible for a play containing all these elements to fail to please, entertain, delight, and satisfy more than those that lack them, as the majority of those do that are staged nowadays. The poets who write these plays, however, are not to blame, for some of them know perfectly well wherein they err, and know with certainty what they should be doing, but since plays have become a salable commodity, they claim, and rightly so, that the managers would not buy them unless they were of that breed, and so the poet reconciles himself to what is demanded by the impresario who will pay him. The truth of this may be seen in an infinite number of plays by a most felicitous talent of this realm, [4] written with such pomp, grace, elegant verse, fine expression, and serious thought -- in sum, filled with such eloquence and high style – that his fame has spread abroad. But because he has been willing to submit to the wishes of the impresarios, some but not all his plays have achieved that peak of perfection that was their due. Other plays are being written with an utter disregard of what is being done, so that following a performance the actors are forced to flee for their lives out of fear of being punished, as they often have been for having portrayed things injurious to certain monarchs or insulting to certain families. All these difficulties would vanish, together with a number of others I have not mentioned, if in the capital there were an intelligent, discriminating individual who would examine all plays before they were staged, not only in the capital but anywhere in Spain, without whose approval, seal, and signature no magistrate would allow their performance in his jurisdiction. In this way playwrights would be certain to send their plays to the

4 Lope Félix de Vega Carpio (1562-1635)

capital and actors would be able to perform them in safety; those who wrote them would take more care with what they wrote because of their dread of having to submit their works to a rigorous examination by a person knowledgeable in the area. In this way good plays would be created and the objectives would be quite easy to achieve: not only the entertainment of the masses but an appreciation of the genius of Spain, the safety and increased interest of the actors, and the elimination of the need to chastise them. If another person, perhaps even the same one, were commissioned to examine newly composed books of chivalry, some of these would undoubtedly exhibit that perfection your grace speaks of, thereby enriching our language with the charming and inestimable treasure of eloquence and occasioning the eclipse of the older books by the light of these new ones that would be appearing, which would serve as a respectable pastime not only for idle persons but active ones as well, for it is impossible for the bow to be drawn back indefinitely or for frail human nature to sustain itself without some type of legitimate recreation."

The canon and the priest had reached this point in their conversation when the barber caught up with them and announced to the priest,

"This is the place, sir licentiate, where I said we could spend the siesta and the oxen would have an abundance of fresh grass."

"And so it would appear," said the priest. After he explained their plan to the canon, the latter decided to stop there himself, having been enticed by the beautiful valley that unfolded before their eyes. In order to enjoy the view as well as the conversation of the priest, for whom he had developed a particular liking, and to learn of Don Quixote's exploits in more detail, the canon ordered several of his servants to proceed to the inn, which was not far away, and to bring them all something to eat, as he had decided to spend the afternoon siesta in that spot. One of the servants informed him that the pack mule, which by now had probably reached the inn, carried enough provisions to make it unnecessary to get anything at the inn except barley.

"In that case," said the canon, "take all the animals with you and bring back only the pack mule."

While this was taking place, Sancho saw that he could speak to his master without the continual presence of the priest and the barber, whose identity he had grave doubts about, and so, approaching the cage in which his master was sitting, he said to him,

"Master, for the relief of my conscience, I would like to explain what is going on regarding your grace's enchantment. Those two men with their faces covered are our village priest and barber, and I'll bet they've concocted this scheme of hauling you about like this out of sheer envy of the fact that you have surpassed them in performing famous deeds. Now if this can be accepted, it follows that you are not enchanted but have been an unwitting dupe. As proof of this I would like to ask one question, and if you answer the way I think you will, you can put your finger on the deception, whereby you will see that you have not been enchanted but have been confused in your thinking."

"Ask whatever you will, Sancho my son," replied Don Quixote, "and I shall answer you and satisfy you to your heart's content, but when you claim that those men who have kept us company on our journey are the priest and the barber – our acquaintances and fellow townsmen – it may indeed be that they resemble those persons but don't believe for one moment that is who they really and truly are. What you are to believe and understand is that if they resemble them, as you say, it must be that those who have placed me under a spell have assumed their appearance and likeness, because it is easy for enchanters to assume any form they please. These will have assumed that of our friends to lead you to believe what you do in fact believe and to cast you into a labyrinth of suspicions from which you cannot escape even with the thread of Theseus. They have also done this to make me question my own thoughts and make me incapable of determining where my affliction is coming from, for if on the one hand, you tell me I am being accompanied by the barber and the priest from our village but on the other, I find myself in a cage and know in my heart that no force on earth other than a supernatural one would be capable of confining me in a cage, what do you expect me to say or think except that the manner of my enchantment exceeds that of every other knight-errant ever cast under a spell in any of the books I have read? Therefore, you may be assured that they are no more the persons you say they are than I am a Turk. But with regard to what you wish to ask me, go ahead and ask and I shall answer you even if your questioning takes all night."

"May the Blessed Virgin deliver me!" said Sancho, raising his voice; "is it possible that your grace is so hard-headed and short on brains that you can't see that what I'm telling you is the absolute truth and that your imprisonment and misfortunes are due more to skulduggery than to enchantment? But since this is the situation, I would like to prove to you beyond a shadow of a doubt that you are not enchanted. I want to ask one simple question so God will deliver you from this torment and you may see yourself in the arms of my lady Dulcinea when you least expect it."

"Stop begging me for favors," said Don Quixote, "and ask whatever it is you wish to ask. I have already told you I shall answer any question you put to me with the utmost precision."

"That is all I wanted to hear," replied Sancho, "so what I want is for your grace to tell me, without adding or subtracting a thing, but with absolute truthfulness, as one would expect from one who follows the profession of arms, as your grace does, under the title of knight-errant– "

"Let me say once more that I shall speak nothing but the truth," responded Don Quixote. "Simply ask your question, Sancho, for I am fed up with all your testing of the waters and your endless preambles."

"And let me say that I am convinced of my master's goodness and truthfulness, and because it has to do with the subject at hand, I would like to ask, respectfully speaking, whether your grace, during the time you have been caged – or enchanted, as you would say – have felt the urge or need to do number one or number two, as the saying goes."

"I don't understand that business of number one and number two, Sancho. Say what you mean if you want me to give you a straight answer."

"Can your grace possibly not understand the expressions 'number one' and 'number two'? Why, that is the first thing children learn at school. What I mean is this: have you by any chance had the urge to do what no one else can do for you?"

"Ah, now I understand, Sancho. Yes, indeed, I have had the urge a number of times but never more than now, so get me out of my predicament because this isn't the most sanitary spot in town!"

Chapter Forty-Nine

The shrewd conversation that Sancho Panza held with his master Don Quixote

"Aha!" cried Sancho, "now I've caught your grace! That is what I wanted to hear more than anything else on earth. Really, master, can you deny what they say about a person who is despondent: 'I don't know what is the matter with So-and-So; he won't eat, drink, sleep, or make a sensible reply to anything he's asked; he acts just like a person possessed.' From this, people have concluded that those who don't eat, drink, sleep, or perform the bodily functions I've mentioned are indeed bewitched, but not those who have the urge to do what you now have, who drink anything you're given, eat whenever there is food, and answer every question you're asked."

"Everything you say is true, Sancho," replied Don Quixote, "but I have already explained to you that there are many different kinds of enchantments. With the passing of time these have possibly undergone changes, so that nowadays it may be the custom for enchanted persons to do everything I do, which they did not do in former times, so there is no sense arguing about the current customs or drawing any conclusions from them. I know for a fact that I am under a spell and that is enough to assuage my conscience, which would be terribly weighed down if I thought I was not enchanted and had permitted myself to remain idle and cowering in this cage where I am unable to render aid to the countless persons who are needy and destitute and who at this very moment are no doubt in dire need of my aid and assistance."

"Well, despite all that, your grace," replied Sancho, "I maintain that for our greater abundance and satisfaction it would be advisable to see if you can escape from your prison, and I pledge myself and all my strength to help you free yourself from it. You should also see whether you can mount your good Rocinante once again, who also seems to be under a spell, judging by his sad and melancholic gait. Once this is done, let us again try our luck at seeking out adventures, and should things not turn out beneficially, we can always return to the cage, and I give your grace my word as a good and faithful squire to lock myself up in it too if you should be so unfortunate, or I so stupid, as to fail to accomplish what I'm talking about."

"I shall be happy to do as you say, Sancho my brother," replied Don Quixote, "and as soon as you see an opportunity for effecting my release, I shall obey you completely and absolutely but, Sancho, you will see how mistaken you are about the nature of my misfortune."

The knight-errant and the errant squire were engaged in this conversation when they reached the place where the priest, canon, and barber had dismounted and were waiting for them. The driver unyoked the oxen to allow them to roam free in that fresh, verdant spot, the delights of which simply beckoned to one – not an enchanted one such as Don Quixote but one in complete command of his faculties such as his squire. The latter asked the priest if his master might leave his cage for a moment, adding that if he were not to do so, his prison might not remain as sanitary as that required by the sense of decency of a knight of his master's caliber. The priest understood his meaning and said he would gladly do as Sancho requested if Sancho was not afraid his master, once he found himself free, might take to his old ways again and flee to a place where no one could ever find him.

"I'll go bail for his not running away," said Sancho.

"So will I," responded the canon, "particularly if he will promise us as a knight not to go away until he has our consent."

"I hereby promise," said Don Quixote, who had been listening to all this, "and all the more so because one who is enchanted as I am is not free to dispose of his person as he might wish. The one who enchanted him can make it impossible for him to budge for three centuries, and if he should flee, he would be brought back in a trice." Here Don Quixote added that, since this was the case, they might just as well let him out because it would be to everyone's benefit. Should they not do so, he argued, he could not keep from committing some outrage against their sense of smell, unless they kept their distance from him.

The canon took him by the hand – though both hands were tied together – and, after being given his word of honor, set him free, whereupon the knight rejoiced hugely and endlessly at finding himself outside the cage. His first act was to stretch his arms and legs and then to go over to Rocinante, whom he gave a couple of slaps on the haunches, saying,

"O flower and mirror of steeds, I still trust in God and His Blessed Mother that we two shall soon see ourselves as we desire: you with your master on your back and I astride you performing the duties of the profession for which God has placed me upon this earth."

Having said this, Don Quixote, accompanied by Sancho, withdrew to a remote spot, from where he returned some time later much relieved and most eager to carry out whatever his squire might suggest. The canon stared at him, marveling at his strange madness and the fact that so long as he conversed and answered questions, he showed himself to possess a marvelous intellect. It was only when someone mentioned knight-errantry that his foot would slip from the stirrup, as we have observed on other occasions. So after they had all seated themselves on the grass to await the arrival of the pack mule, the canon was moved by compassion to say to Don Quixote,

"Is it possible, my good sir, that the dangerous and idle reading of books of chivalry has had such an effect upon your grace and has twisted your mind to such an extent that you have come to believe you are enchanted, along with other similar things, which is as far from the truth as is falsehood itself? Moreover, how can any human mind possibly let itself be convinced that the earth has ever been witness to that endless procession of Amadises, that horde of famous knights, all those emperors of Trebizond and Felixmartes of Hircania, all those palfreys and damsels-errant, those serpents, monsters, and giants, those unheard-of adventures and enchantments of every conceivable description, those battles and outrageous encounters, that array of costumes, those lovesick princesses, squires made counts, comical dwarves, those love letters and flirtations, those courageous ladies, and lastly, all those ridiculous situations with which books of chivalry abound? Speaking for myself, I can state that whenever I read them, so long as I do not consider the fact that they are nothing but trivialities and untruths, they afford me a certain enjoyment, but the moment I consider what they are, I fling the best one among them against the wall and would toss it into the fire, if there was one at hand. They deserve this punishment for being false and deceptive, for going against everything in the world of nature, for creating new sects and new ways of life, and for providing the opportunity for the ignorant masses to come to believe and accept as the absolute truth all the absurdities they contain. They even go so far as to becloud the minds of intelligent and highborn hidalgos, as is clearly demonstrated by what they have done to your grace, for they have brought you to such a pass that it has been necessary to lock you up in a cage and haul you about on an oxcart, like someone carrying a lion or tiger from place to place to put it on exhibit. Come, Sir Don Quixote, you should attend to your own ills, return to the bosom of common sense, and make use of the abundant amount heaven was kind enough to give you, by employing the gracious talent of your intellect in some other type of books that would redound to the profit of your soul and the increase of your honor! But if you still wish to read books of adventure and chivalry, being driven by your natural inclination, you should read the Book of Judges in the Holy Scriptures, where you will find great truths and deeds that are as authentic as they are courageous. Lusitania had its Viriatus, Rome its Caesar, Carthage its Hannibal, Greece its Alexander, Castile its Count Fernán González, Valencia its Cid, Andalusia its Gonzalo Fernández, Estremadura its Diego García de Paredes, Jerez its Garci Pérez de Vargas, Toledo its Garcilaso, and Seville its Don Manuel de León, the reading of whose brave exploits will entertain, instruct, delight, and astonish the best minds that peruse them. This indeed will be reading matter worthy of your grace's good mind, Sir Don Quixote, from which you will emerge learned in history, passionate about virtue, instructed in goodness, improved in manners, courageous but not foolhardy, unflinching in your daring, and all this to the honor of God, to your own profit, and to the glory of La Mancha, where, I understand, you had your origin and inception."

Don Quixote had been absolutely hanging upon the canon's words and, when he saw that he had finished speaking, he stood there observing him for quite some time and finally said,

"It seems to me, sir hidalgo, that your grace's discourse is aimed at trying to convince me that the world has never seen the likes of knights-errant, that all books of chivalry are false, untrue, dangerous, and useless to the state, and that I have acted badly in reading them, worse in believing them, and worse still in imitating them by taking upon myself the demanding profession of knight-errantry they teach. You also deny the existence of Amadís of Gaul, Amadís of Greece, and all the other knights with whom those books are filled."

"Everything is exactly as your grace has recited it," said the canon at this point; to which Don Quixote responded,

"Your grace has also stated that such books have caused me grievous harm by addling my brain and causing me to be placed in a cage, and that it would be better for me to reform and change my reading habits by perusing more truthful works, which I would also find more entertaining and more instructive."

"That is correct," replied the canon.

"Well, I for my part," said Don Quixote, "find that the one who is mad and bewitched is none other than your grace, for you have ventured to utter all those blasphemies against an institution that is so well received by the world and held to be so real that anyone who would deny it, as you have done, deserves the same punishment you say you give the books you read that make you angry, for to attempt to convince anyone that there never was an Amadís or any of those other venturer knights with whom the histories are overflowing is like trying to persuade him that the sun does not shine, ice is not cold, and the earth does not sustain life. What intellect anywhere could persuade a person that what happened between Princess Floripes and Guy of Burgundy was untrue, as well as the episode of Fierabrás and the bridge at Mantible, which took place in the days of Charlemagne? I swear by all that is holy that it is as true as the fact that it is now day; but if it were not true, then there must never have been a Hector or an Achilles, or a Trojan War, or the Twelve Peers of France, or a King Arthur, who was changed into a raven and has remained so to this very day, when his return to his kingdom is expected momentarily. One might just as well claim that Guarino Mezquino's history is untrue, as well as the quest for the Holy Grail, or that the loves of Tristram and his queen Iseult are apocryphal, along with those of Guinevere and Lancelot, though there are persons who can virtually recall having seen Lady Quintañona, the best wine stewardess Great Britain ever had. Now this last is certainly true, for I remember my grandmother on my father's side saying whenever she saw a matron lady with a stately coiffeur, 'That lady, my son, looks just like Lady Quintañona,' from which I conclude that she must have known her or at least had seen a portrait of her. Similarly, who would question the authenticity of the story of Pierres and the lovely Magalona, since to this day one may view in the King's Armory the very peg with which the brave Pierres steered the wooden horse through the air? It is slightly larger than a wagon tongue and next to it is Babieca's saddle. At Roncesvalles there is Roland's horn, which is the size of a large beam, and because of this, people have concluded that the Twelve Peers existed, as did the Pierres and the Cids and other such knights,

'Who ride, as people say,
In quest of ventures bold.'

I should just like to hear someone claim that the valiant Portuguese Juan de Merlo was not a knight-errant and never went to Burgundy, where he fought in the city of Arras with the Lord of Charny, called Monsieur Pierres, and later in the city of Basle with Monsieur Henri de Remestan, emerging from both encounters victorious and crowned with laurels. Or let them dare deny that the valiant Spaniards Pedro Barba and Gutierre Quixada – from whose lineage I directly trace my descent through the male line – answered the call to battle in Burgundy, where they overcame the sons of the Count of San Polo. I simply challenge them to say that Don Fernando de Guevara never went to Germany in quest of adventures, where he did battle with Messire George, a knight of the House of the Duke of Austria. I defy them to assert that the jousts of Suero de Quiñones at the Pass of Honor were a hoax, as well as the struggles of Mosén Luis de Falces against Gonzalo de Guzmán, a Spanish knight, together with any number of other famous deeds performed by Christian knights from both this and foreign lands, whose deeds were absolutely real and authentic. I maintain that anyone who would deny this is devoid of reason and common sense."

"I cannot deny, Sir Don Quixote, that there is a grain of truth in everything your grace has said, particularly with regard to Spanish knights, and I am likewise willing to concede that the Twelve Peers of France existed but I refuse to believe they did all the things Archbishop Turpin ascribes to them, for the truth of the matter is that they were knights chosen by the kings of France and were called peers because they were all equal in caliber, rank, and courage (or, if not, they should have been), for it was a type of religion such as that practiced today in the Orders of Santiago and Calatrava, whose members, it is assumed, should be and will be knights who are worthy, courageous, and of good pedigree. And just as today we speak of the Knights of St. John and those of Alcántara, in those days they spoke of the Knights of the Twelve Peers, which did not mean, however, that those chosen for that militant order were only twelve in number. As for the Cid, there is no doubt that he existed, nor is there any concerning Bernardo del Carpio, but whether they accomplished all the deeds claimed for them I think there is serious doubt. As for that other matter of Count Pierres' peg, which your grace mentioned and which is next to Babieca's saddle in the King's Armory, I must admit my shortcomings; either I am so ignorant or so shortsighted that despite having seen the saddle, I have never noticed the peg even if it is as large as your grace says it is."

"Well, that is where it is without a doubt," said Don Quixote, "and as further proof, they say it is kept in a leather sheath to prevent it from getting rusty."

"Anything is possible," replied the canon, "but I give your grace my word as a priest that I do not recall ever having seen it. But even if I were to acknowledge its existence, I do not thereby feel obliged to believe the stories of all those Amadises and that horde of knights the histories contain, nor is it reasonable for a man like your grace, who is honorable, talented, and possessed of such a good mind, to accept as true all the absurd things described in those ridiculous books of chivalry."

Chapter Fifty

The learned debate between Don Quixote and the canon, together with other matters

"That is a fine thing to say!" responded Don Quixote. "Those books, which are printed by license of the king and approved by the officials to whom they have been submitted; those books, I say, which are widely read, enjoyed, and celebrated by young and old alike, by rich and poor, by both the educated and the uneducated, by the common people as well as the nobility – in other words, by every type of individual regardless of his rank or quality -- does your grace expect me to believe those books are false, despite the fact that they give every indication of being true? Why, they tell us step by step and day by day what deeds each of those knights performed, in addition to informing us of his father, mother, and relatives, his age, hometown, and the region from which he came. May you bite your tongue and utter no more such blasphemies. If you will only peruse those books, you will see what pleasure they have to offer and you may trust me when

I advise you as to what you as an intelligent man should do in this matter. I should like to ask if there can be anything more delightful than to picture here before our very eyes a vast lake of molten pitch in which a number of snakes, serpents, lizards, and other ferocious, frightful creatures are swimming and darting about, and then to hear a most doleful voice cry out from the center of the lake, 'You, sir knight, who are observing this frightful lake, whoever you may be, if you would attain the treasure that lies hidden beneath these murky waters, demonstrate the valor of your stout heart by plunging into the midst of their seething blackness. If you fail to do so, you will be unworthy to view the awesome marvels contained and enclosed within the seven fairies' seven castles that lie beneath these dark waters.' No sooner will the knight hear the dreadful voice than he will commend himself to God and his lady and, without ridding himself of the weight of his heavy armor, will plunge into the midst of the teeming lake without even reflecting upon his welfare or considering the danger to which he is exposing himself. And without knowing or even wondering what his fate may be, he will find himself in some flowering glade whose beauty cannot be rivaled by the Elysian Fields themselves. The sky here will seem more translucent and the sun will shine with a new kind of clarity. His eyes will also be regaled by a pleasant grove covered with lush shade trees whose verdure gladdens the eyes, while his ears will be regaled by the mellifluous, untutored singing of myriad tiny colorful birds flitting here and there among the thick branches. Here he will discover a tiny brook with its refreshing waters as clear as liquid crystal making its way over the fine sand and small white pebbles, which resemble powdered gold and flawless pearls. In one direction, he will see an ingenious fountain constructed of mottled jasper and smooth marble; in another, a fountain with grotesque ornaments and tiny clam shells intermingled with the white and yellow spiral houses of snails in a confused yet orderly pattern, throughout which are embedded bits of sparkling crystal and mock emeralds that create a work of such variety that art, by imitating nature, will appear here to have surpassed it. And suddenly, looming in the distance, will be a mighty castle or imposing palace with solid gold walls, diamond turrets, and hyacinth gates; in fact, so wondrous will be its composition that though its construction materials consist of nothing less than diamonds, garnets, rubies, pearls, gold, and emeralds, its workmanship will be its most outstanding feature. And after all this has been observed, what can be more glorious than to see a large number of maidens stride forth from the castle, dressed so elegantly that were I to describe them as they are described in the histories, I should never be able to finish the task. At this moment, a maiden who is apparently foremost among them will take the hand of this bold knight who has hurled himself into the seething lake and, without uttering a word, will conduct him into the opulent palace or castle, where she will have him strip as naked as the day he was born and will bathe him in water that is neither too hot nor too cold, after which she will anoint his entire body with fragrant oils and dress him in a shirt of the filmiest gauze, all scented and perfumed, while another maiden will approach and drape over his shoulders a mantel said to be worth, at the very least, a fortune or even more. How astounding it will be, after all this, to see them lead him to another hall, where he will find the dining tables displaying such magnificent settings that he will be left amazed and speechless; and how marvelous to watch them as they pour water over his hands, distilled wholly from amber and fragrant flowers, and then seat him on an ivory chair, at which point all the damsels will wait on him in eerie silence as they bring him a variety of dishes of such delicacy that his palate will be unable to decide which one to select. What a treat it will be to listen to the music being played as he dines without knowing who is singing or where the music is coming from. Once the meal is over and the tables have been cleared, the knight will relax on his chair and perhaps pick his teeth in accordance with the current custom, and then another damsel much more beautiful than all the rest will suddenly enter the hall, seat herself at the knight's side, and proceed to give him an account of that castle, informing him that she is there under a spell, together with other matters that will hold the knight in suspense and astonish everyone who reads his story. But I prefer not to proceed in this matter, for one may deduce from what I have said that to read any passage of any book of chivalry whatsoever will delight and amaze the person who reads it. As I have already mentioned, if your grace will read any of these books, you will see how they will banish any melancholy you might have and will improve your disposition, should it need improving. Speaking for myself, I can state that ever since I have been a knight-errant, I have been brave, polite, liberal, well-mannered, generous, courteous, bold, gentle, patient, and enured to hardships, imprisonments, and enchantments. And though a short while ago I found myself shut up in a cage like some lunatic, I expect by the might of my arm, if heaven is favorable and fortune does not prove adverse, to see myself shortly made ruler of some kingdom, whereby I may display the gratitude and generosity of my breast, for upon my word, sir, a poor man is incapable of demonstrating his generosity to anyone, though he may possess this virtue in the highest degree – and gratitude that goes no deeper than the desire to express it is a thing that is dead, just as faith without works is dead, for which reason I wish that fate would soon afford me the opportunity to become an emperor so I might bare my heart and extend my charity to my friends, particularly to this poor Sancho Panza my squire, who is the best soul on earth. I should like to give him an earldom I promised him a number of days ago, and yet I fear he will lack the ability to govern his realm."

Sancho, who scarcely heard more of his master's remarks than this last one, said to him,

"Master Don Quixote, I beg your grace to make every effort to award me that earldom, for your numerous promises are matched only by my numerous hopes, and I promise I'll not lack the ability to govern it. But should I be found wanting, I've heard there are men in this world who will take a nobleman's estate on a lease, paying him a certain amount each year, while they themselves run the government and the noble leads a life of ease, enjoying the income they give him and not having a care in the world. That's what I'll do and I won't haggle over a thing but will wash my hands of the whole affair and will enjoy my income like a duke. Let *them* worry about all that other business!"

"Brother Sancho," said the canon, "that is acceptable insofar as enjoying the income is concerned but the lord of the jurisdiction must attend to the administration of justice, which is where ability enters the picture, together with good judgement and, above all, the honest desire to do what is right, for if this is lacking at the beginning, things will go wrong from then till the very end. It is for this reason that God helps the simpleminded but well-intentioned person, while withholding His favor from one who is intelligent but ill-intentioned."

"I don't understand all that philosophy," replied Sancho Panza, "but I do know that as soon as I get my hands on the earldom, I'll know how to govern it, for I have a soul the same as the next person and a body just like everyone else, and I'll be as kingly in my domain as any king will be in his. And being so, I'll do whatever I please; and by doing whatever I please, I'll do what I like; and by doing what I like, I'll be content; and when one is content, there is nothing more to be desired; and when there is nothing more to be desired, it's all over. So bring on my earldom and 'So long, I'll be seeing you,' as one blind man said to another."

"That philosophy of yours is not bad, Sancho, but, all that aside, there is much to be said on the matter of governing."

To which Don Quixote replied,

"I have nothing more to add. I am simply guided by the example provided me by the great Amadís of Gaul, who made his squire Count of Terra Firma Island. I may thus make Sancho Panza a count without any pangs of conscience, for he is one of the best squires a knight-errant ever had."

The canon was taken aback by the seemingly sensible nonsense Don Quixote had uttered, together with the way in which he had described the Knight of the Lake and the effect those untrue and labored fabrications of the books he was continually reading had exerted upon him; and last but not least he was astonished at the foolishness of Sancho, who so very earnestly desired to be awarded the earldom his master had promised him. By this time the canon's servants had returned from the inn where they had gone to retrieve the supply mule. Utilizing a carpet and the grass of the meadow as a table, they seated themselves under some shade trees and dined there so the oxcart driver would not lose the advantages of that spot, as already mentioned. While they were dining, they unexpectedly heard a loud noise and the sound of a bell which seemed to come from a nearby thicket. At that very instant a beautiful she-goat whose coat was a maze of black, white, and gray splotches sprang from the thicket, pursued by a goatherd shouting the usual commands to make her stop and return to the fold. The fleeing goat ran up to the people frightened and in a panic, where she paused as if to seek their protection. The goatherd arrived and, taking her by the horns, began to speak to her as though she were capable of speech and understanding:

"Come, my wild, spotted one! My, but you are hobbling about these days! What wolves have frightened you, my child? Won't you tell me, my beauty? What else can it be except that you're a female and are always restless. A plague upon your whims and all those you imitate! Come back, my darling, come back to your fold, where you may not be happy but at least you'll be safer with your companions, for if you who are supposed to be their leader and guide go wandering about aimless and lost, what will become of them?"

All those who heard the goatherd's speech were amused by it, particularly the canon, who said to him,

"Please, brother, for your own sake, calm down and don't be in such a hurry to take this goat back to her fold, for, being a female, as you pointed out, she will follow her natural inclination despite all your attempts to prevent it. At least, have a bite of food and some wine, which will give you time to rid yourself of your anger and the goat time to rest."

To say this and to hold out to him a cold loin of rabbit on the tip of his knife were one and the same action. The goatherd accepted it and, after taking a drink, which had a calming effect upon hin, said,

"I wouldn't want your graces to consider me a simpleton for talking to this animal as though she were human, since what I said to her must have sounded strange indeed. I may be coarse but not to the point of failing to understand how to deal with men and beasts."

"I can certainly believe that," said the priest, "for experience has convinced me that the hills breed men of letters, and shepherds' huts are home to philosophers."

"At least, sir," replied the goatherd, "they are home to men who have the benefit of long experience. And so that your graces may verify in a tangible way what was said by this gentleman" – and here he pointed to the priest – "I shall, with your graces' permission and undivided attention and at the risk of appearing to invite myself without being asked, relate a true story, which will demand only a few minutes of your graces' time."

To this Don Quixote replied,

"Seeing that this affair has a certain aura of chivalry about it, I for my part shall gladly listen to you, my brother, as will all these other gentlemen because of their intelligence and fondness for things which are not only novel and strange but which astonish, delight, and entertain, as I feel your story is certain to do. Therefore, my friend, please begin, as we are all ready to listen."

"Count me out," said Sancho. "I'm going down to that stream with this meat pie, where I intend to stuff myself with enough food to last for three days. I've heard my master Don Quixote say that a knight's squire should eat as much as he can hold whenever the opportunity presents itself because it frequently happens that they accidentally stray into a forest that is so entangled they're unable to find their way out of it for a whole week, and unless one goes in well fed or has his saddlebags well stocked, he may end up, as many do, turned into a mummy."

"You are doing the right thing, Sancho," said Don Quixote. "Go wherever you please and eat as much as you can. I am already satisfied, though, and need only to refresh my spirits, which I shall do by listening to this good man."

"We shall all refresh ours as well," said the canon, who then begged the goatherd to relate his story as he had promised. The goatherd, who was holding the goat by the horns, gave her a couple of pats on the back and said to her,

"Lie down beside me, my speckled one, for there will be time for us to return to our fold."

The goat appeared to understand, for as soon as her owner sat down, she quite calmly stretched out beside him and gazed into his eyes as if to show she was listening to what he said. At this point he began to narrate the following story.

Chapter Fifty-One

What the goatherd told those who were taking Don Quixote home

"Three leagues from this valley there is a village which, though small, is one of the richest in all these parts. One of its citizens was a farmer who was held in the highest regard, and though respect is a natural consequence of being wealthy, he was respected more for his virtue than for the wealth he had amassed. But the thing that made him feel most blessed, in his words, was to possess a daughter of such incomparable beauty, rare intelligence, charm, and virtue that everyone who knew her marveled at the extraordinary qualities with which heaven and nature had endowed her. She was beautiful even as a child and her beauty continued to increase as she grew older, so that by the age of sixteen she was a creature of surpassing beauty. Word of her beauty spread to all the neighboring villages – but why do I limit it just to the neighboring villages when it spread to far-away cities and even into the halls of kings, coming to the attention of all classes of people who came from far and wide to see her as though she were some strange object or some holy relic capable of miracles? Her father watched over her and she watched over herself, for there are no padlocks, bolts, or custodians that can safeguard a maiden better than her own vigilance.

"The father's wealth and the daughter's beauty led many to seek her hand in marriage, both townspeople and outsiders, and yet, as one whose task it was to dispose of such a valuable jewel, he was perplexed and unable to decide which of the countless suitors to entrust her to. I was among the many who had such noble aspirations, as I had been given great hopes of success because her father was acquainted with my family's circumstances: the fact that I was a native of the same town, my blood was pure, I was in the bloom of youth, quite well off materially, and possessed a mind that was no less endowed. Another gentleman from the same town with identical qualifications also sought her hand, which was sufficient to cause her father to vacillate and hold his will in suspension, because it seemed to him that with either of us his daughter would be well situated. To extricate himself from his quandary, he decided to speak to Leandra – this being the name of the wealthy girl responsible for all my misery – having concluded that, since there was no difference between either of us suitors, he would be well advised to allow his beloved daughter to choose according to her preference, a practice well worth imitating by all those parents who have children they wish to marry. I do not for a moment suggest that they let them choose base or evil individuals but that they propose several good ones from among whom their children may make their own choice. I have no idea what Leandra's was. All I know is that her father kept us both at bay by alluding to his daughter's youthful age and to other generalities that neither obligated him nor released us from our obligation. My rival's name is Anselmo and Eugenio is mine so that your graces will know the names of the personages who figure in this tragedy, the ending of which is still pending but which gives every indication of being ill-fated.

"At that particular time there arrived in our village a certain Vicente de la Rosa, son of a poor laborer of the same village. This Vicente had just returned from Italy and various other lands where he had been a soldier. As a lad of about twelve, he had enlisted in the company of a captain who happened to pass through our village and now, twelve years later, he was returning in military dress, resplendent in his multi-colored uniform that displayed a thousand glass trinkets and small steel chains. One day he would sport one pompous outfit and the next day a different one but all flimsy and gaudy, weighing almost nothing and worth even less. Country folks, who are malicious by nature and, if given the opportunity, are the very personification of evil, noticed this and kept an exact account of his various outfits and jewelry. They discovered that he had three two-piece suits of different colors with their accompanying garters and stockings but he combined them in so many different ways that, unless people were keeping track of them, they would swear he had worn more than ten outfits and twenty plumes. I hope your graces will not consider all these comments about his wardrobe irrelevant or superfluous, for they play an important role in my story; but to continue:

"He used to seat himself on a stone bench beneath a large poplar tree in our plaza, where he would keep us in suspense, spellbound by the exploits he recounted. There was no land on the entire globe he had not seen, nor any battle he had not participated in. He had slain more Moors than all those in Morocco and Tunis combined and had engaged in more hand-to-hand combats, so he said, than had Gante, Luna, Diego García de Paredes, and a thousand others he would name, and from every battle had emerged victorious without shedding a single drop of blood. On other occasions, he would show us scars from wounds, which, though we were never able to make them out, led us to believe they were caused by musket shots he had received in various encounters and battles. And lastly, with unheard-of arrogance he would address his equals and acquaintances as though they were his inferiors and would say that his mighty arm was his father, his accomplishments constituted his lineage, and that, being a soldier, he was not inferior to the king himself. In addition to this arrogance he rather fancied himself a musician and was so adept at playing the guitar that there were those who said he could make it sing. However, his talents did not end there, for he was also a poet and out of every bit of nonsense that took place in the village he would compose a ballad a league and a half long.

"This soldier I've depicted here, this Vicente de la Rosa, this boaster, ladies-man, musician, and poet, was seen and observed numerous times by Leandra from a window of her house that commanded a view of the plaza. She fell in love with the brass foil on his uniforms and was enthralled by his ballads, for he gave away twenty copies of each one he composed. The exploits he related about himself reached her ears and, because the Devil must have so decreed, she ultimately fell in love with him even before the presumptuous idea of wooing her had entered his head. And since in affairs of love there is none more easily brought to fruition than that which has the lady's volition on its side, Leandra and Vicente easily reached an understanding. Before any of her suitors came to realize what her intentions were, she had already carried them out by abandoning the home of her beloved father and her dear departed mother. She fled the village in the company of the soldier, who came away from that enterprise with a greater triumph than from all the others he had assigned himself. The episode astounded all those in the village and even those outside it when they learned of it. I was in a state of shock, Anselmo was overwhelmed, Leandra's father was grief-stricken, and her relatives humiliated. Thanks to the cooperation of the law, the officers of the Holy Brotherhood were mobilized and took to the roads, where they searched every inch of the forests. At the end of three days they discovered the fickle Leandra in a mountain cave wearing nothing more than a chemise and no longer having any of the money or precious jewels she had brought with her from home. They returned her to her sorrowing father and questioned her about her disgrace and she voluntarily confessed that Vicente de la Rosa had deceived her and, by promising to be her husband, had persuaded her to abandon her father's house, saying he would take her to the richest and most notorious city in the entire world: Naples. She, ill advised and worse deceived, had believed him and had thus wronged her father, placing herself in Vicente's hands on the very night she had slipped away from home. He had taken her to a forbidding mountain and shut her up in the cave in which they later found her. She related how the soldier, without robbing her of her honor, had taken everything she owned and gone away, leaving her alone in the cave, a fact that caused everyone to marvel once again because it was hard to imagine such self-control on the young man's part. But she affirmed it with such earnestness that it led her distraught father to be consoled and to overlook the valuables that had been stolen from him, inasmuch as Vicente had left his daughter the jewel which, once lost, is beyond hope of recovery. The same day that Leandra appeared, her father deprived us of all sight of her by taking her to a convent near here and shutting her up inside it in the hope that time might disperse part of the ugly criticism to which his daughter had exposed herself. Leandra's tender age served to excuse her indiscretion, at least among those who had nothing to gain or lose by her being virtuous or sinful. And those who were acquainted with her intelligence and keen mind attributed her indiscretion not to ignorance but to wantonness and woman's natural disposition, which by and large tends to be fickle and restless.

"With Leandra shut away, Anselmo's eyes were blinded or at least were left with nothing pleasant to view. Mine were left in darkness, being deprived of the light that might have directed them to something pleasant. With Leandra absent our melancholy increased, our patience diminished, we cursed the soldier's fine clothes and felt contempt for the lack of precaution on the part of Leandra's father. At length, Anselmo and I agreed to leave the village and come to this valley, where he grazes a large number of his own sheep and I tend a sizeable flock of goats that belong to me. We spend our lives in the woods giving vent to our emotions: the two of us together praising or reviling the beautiful Leandra in song, or each separately sighing and communicating his complaints to heaven. In imitation of us a number of Leandra's other suitors have come to these rugged hills to adopt our way of life, and they are so numerous that this valley has been converted into a veritable Arcadia, overrun as it is with shepherds and sheepfolds. There is no spot where the name of the beautiful Leandra is not heard. This person curses her and calls her capricious, fickle, and indecent; this other one condemns her for being wanton and loose; a certain one pardons and absolves her; another condemns and reviles her; still another sings the praises of her beauty; another curses her behavior – in a word, they all scorn her and worship her at the same time and their madness has reached such a pitch that there are those who complain of her disdain, though they have never spoken to her, while others, suffering from the maddening disease of jealousy, bemoan their fate, though she has never given anyone cause for hope because, as I have said, people learned of her transgression before they learned of her preference. There is no hollow among the rocks and no river bank or shady spot beneath a tree that is not occupied by some shepherd shouting his misfortunes to the wind. The name Leandra is shouted back from any place capable of echo: 'Leandra!' resound the hills, 'Leandra!' murmur the brooks, and we are all so captivated and enchanted by Leandra that we hope without hope and are fearful without knowing what it is we fear. Of all these absurd individuals, the one who shows the most and yet the least common sense is my rival Anselmo, who, when he has so many other things he might lament, laments only his absence from her, and accompanying himself on the fiddle, which he plays amazingly well, he expresses his laments in songs whose verses reveal his talents. I follow an easier and surer course, which is to speak ill of women's fickleness, their inconstancy, duplicity, empty promises, broken pledges, and, lastly, their feeble ability to know where to place their affection and desires.

"This, gentlemen, is the explanation for the things I said to this goat upon arriving, for since she is a female, I hold her in contempt, though she is the best one in my entire flock. This is the story I promised to relate and though I have taken quite some time in doing so, I shall not hesitate to place myself at your graces' disposal. My sheepfold is not far from here, and there your graces will find fresh milk, tasty cheese, and various fruits in season that will delight the palate as much as they will the eye."

Chapter Fifty-Two

The fight that Don Quixote had with the goatherd, and the bizarre incident of the penitents, which he brought to a happy conclusion by the sweat of his brow

The goatherd's tale provided enjoyment for everyone in his audience, especially the canon, who, contrary to his usual indifference, noted the manner in which he had related it, for far from being an unlettered goatherd, he gave the impression of being a sophisticated courtier, and he said the priest had spoken correctly in observing that the hills bred men of letters. They all placed themselves at Eugenio's disposal but the one who was most generous in this regard was Don Quixote, who said to him,

"Brother goatherd, I promise you that if I found it within my power to undertake some new adventure, I would set out at this very instant and execute it to your satisfaction, for I would go to the convent where Leandra is doubtless being held against her will. There I would rescue her despite the abbess or anyone else who might try to stop me, and would deliver her to you to deal with as you saw fit, but only so long as you observed the laws of chivalry, which stipulate that no untoward act shall be perpetrated against any maiden. And yet, I trust in Our Lord God that the powers of one evil enchanter will not be great enough to withstand those of another with nobler motives. When that time comes, I promise you my aid and support, an obligation imposed upon me by my profession, which is none other than that of aiding and comforting the helpless and those in need."

The goatherd looked at Don Quixote and, noting his sorry dress and appearance, turned to the barber next to him and said,

"Who, sir, is this man who looks and talks like this?"

"Who else can he be," replied the barber, "except the famous Don Quixote of La Mancha, redressor of injuries, righter of wrongs, protector of maidens, dreaded foe of giants, and perennial champion in battle?"

"That," replied the goatherd, "sounds like what books say about knights-errant who do everything you say this gentleman has done, though as far as I am concerned, either your grace is joking or this gentle soul has bats in his belfry."

"You good-for-nothing scoundrel!" cried Don Quixote at this point, "you are the one with bats in his belfry! I am a lot saner than that whoring bitch who brought you into the world."

And converting his words into action, he grabbed a loaf of bread he had at his side and struck the goatherd squarely across the face with it, and so ferociously that it flattened his nose. The goatherd, who was not amused at seeing himself abused with such earnestness, jumped on top of Don Quixote and without regard for the carpet, tablecloth, and those dining, seized him by the neck with both hands and would no doubt have strangled him had Sancho Panza not rushed up at that instant and grabbed him by the shoulders, throwing him down on top of the table, breaking the plates and cups and overturning everything there. Finding himself free, Don Quixote jumped on top of the bloody goatherd, who had just been kicked by Sancho and was crawling about on his hands and knees in search of a table knife with which to avenge himself in some bloody fashion but he was prevented from doing so by the canon and the priest. And due to the barber's action, the goatherd was able to pin Don Quixote beneath him, whereupon he delivered such a succession of punches to the poor knight's face that it ended up as bloody as his own. The canon and the priest were virtually bursting with laughter, the officers were jumping up and down with delight, and one and all were cheering them on, just as people cheer on dogs that are fighting. Only Sancho Panza was in a state of despair, being unable to free himself from the grasp of one of the canon's servants who prevented him from going to the aid of his master.

In short, while they were all in such a jovial mood, except the two combatants who were clawing and scratching each other, they heard the sound of a trumpet that was so mournful it made them all turn in the direction from which it came, but the one who was most surprised to hear it was Don Quixote, who, finding himself beneath the goatherd quite against his will and more than moderately exhausted, said to him,

"Brother devil – and this is what you must be, since you have had the strength and valor to overcome mine – I beg you to let us call a truce for just one hour, for the doleful sound of that trumpet that has reached our ears would seem to be summoning me to some new adventure."

The goatherd, who by now was tired of punching and being punched, released him on the spot. Don Quixote got to his feet and turned in the direction from which the sound was heard, at which point he suddenly saw a large number of men descending a slope, all clad in white in the manner of penitents.

It so happened that in this particular year the clouds had denied their moisture to the earth, so that throughout all the villages of this region people were resorting to pilgrimages, penances, and rogations as they implored God to open the arms of His mercy and send them rain. To this end the inhabitants of a nearby village were on a pilgrimage to a holy hermitage situated on one of the valley's slopes. Don Quixote observed the penitents' strange attire but it never occurred to him how many previous times he must have seen this same sight. Instead, he fancied that here were the makings of an adventure that he alone, as a knight-errant, was responsible for undertaking. This conjecture was more than confirmed when he fancied that an image they were carrying, which was draped in black, was some noble lady being transported against her will by these wicked, insolent scoundrels. The moment this thought crossed his mind, he hastily went over to Rocinante, who was busy grazing. Removing the halter and buckler from the pommel, he bridled him in an instant and, after calling to Sancho for his sword, mounted Rocinante, strapped on his buckler, and cried out to all those present,

"Now, valiant companions, your graces shall see how necessary it is for the world to possess knights-errant who profess the order of chivalry. Now, I say, your graces shall see by my deliverance of that noble lady being held captive there whether or not knights-errant are to be esteemed."

In saying this, he slapped Rocinante with his legs, since he was not wearing spurs, and took off at a trot (for nowhere in this entire true history do we read that Rocinante ever charged at full speed), and rode forth to meet the penitents. Though the priest, the canon, and the barber attempted to stop him, their efforts were in vain, as were the shouts of Sancho, who cried out,

"Master Don Quixote, where are you going and what demons do you have in that breast of yours to incite you against our Catholic faith? Oh, a pox upon me! May your grace be advised that what you see is a procession of penitents, and the lady borne on that litter is an image of the most blessed and immaculate Virgin. Do consider what you are doing because just this once it may be said that this is not what it appears to be!"

But Sancho's efforts were of no avail, for so determined was his master to overtake the cloaked figures and free the lady in black that he did not hear a single word; even if he had, he would not have turned back had the king himself demanded it. When he finally reached the procession, he drew up on the reins of Rocinante, who by now was more than willing to rest a spell, and cried out to them in a hoarse but emotional voice,

"Your lordships, who probably have covered your faces because of your evil ways, would be wise to heed my words and hear what I have to say."

The first ones to halt were those carrying the image. And inasmuch as one of the four clerics chanting the litany had noted Don Quixote's strange appearance, Rocinante's bare bones, and various other ludicrous attributes of Don Quixote, he said to him in response,

"My good brother, if you have anything you wish to say to us, say it quickly, for these brethren are scourging themselves and cannot stop, nor is it reasonable to expect us to stop and listen to anything at all, unless it is so brief it can be said in a couple of words."

"I can say it in only one," replied Don Quixote, "which is this: you shall, right here and now, release that fair lady whose tears and mournful demeanor clearly show her to be held against her will and you to have committed some outrageous villainy against her. I, who was born into this world to right such wrongs as this, will not allow you to take another step forward until she has been granted the freedom she desires and deserves."

Everyone who heard this speech now realized that Don Quixote must be some kind of madman and they began to laugh quite heartily. This laughter merely added fuel to Don Quixote's anger, and so without saying another word, he drew his sword and made a mad dash in their direction. One of those carrying the litter abandoned his post, leaving his companions to hold it up, and with the forked stick or pole used to support the litter while one of the men rested, he went to engage Don Quixote. Clutching it in his hands, he managed to block a mighty sword stroke that Don Quixote unleashed, which split the stick in two. Wielding the half he was left holding, he gave Don Quixote such a whack on the shoulder of his sword arm that the knight was unable to defend himself against this rustic fury and was knocked to the ground severely injured. When the panting Sancho Panza finally caught up with Don Quixote and saw him prostrate, he shouted at his attacker to stop beating him because he was just a poor enchanted knight who had never harmed anyone in all the days of his life. But the thing that caused the rustic to call a halt was not Sancho's cries but his observation that Don Quixote was not moving any of his limbs. Believing he had killed him, he quickly gathered his robe up to his waist and took off running across the field like a deer.

By this time all those in Don Quixote's company had arrived. When the men in the procession saw them running towards them accompanied by the officers carrying crossbows, they feared things might turn out badly, and so, forming a circle round the image, they raised their hoods and took their scourges in their hands, as the clerics did their candlesticks, and waited for the onslaught, determined to defend themselves and even to mount an attack if possible against their assailants. But fortune was guiding things better than they could ever have imagined, for Sancho did nothing more than throw himself across his master's body and break into the most woeful and comical sobbing on earth, believing his master was dead. The priest was recognized by another priest in the procession and their mutual recognition allayed the fears that had developed in both camps. The first priest gave the second a brief account of who Don Quixote was, at which point he and the whole host of penitents went to see if the poor knight was dead. Here they heard Sancho say with tears in his eyes,

"O flower of chivalry, who have had the course of your well-spent life cut short by the single blow of a stick! You who are the pride of your race, the honor and glory of all La Mancha and even the entire world, which, now that your presence is lacking, will be filled with evildoers who will no longer fear punishment for their evil deeds! You have been more generous than all the Alexanders, for after only eight months of service you have given me the best island that any sea encircles or surrounds! You, O master, who were humble with the proud, and arrogant with the humble; who undertook any perilous adventure and bore any affront; who were in love without ever receiving encouragement; who always strove to do what was right; who were the scourge of the wicked, and the foe of all that was base; and lastly, a knight-errant, which is all that one can say!"

Don Quixote was revived by Sancho's moans and cries and the first thing he said was,

"He who lives separated from thee, my dearest Dulcinea, is subject to greater misfortunes than these. Sancho my friend, help me to mount the enchanted cart, for I am in no condition to ride ponderously on Rocinante because this entire shoulder of mine has been shattered."

"I'll very gladly do so, master," replied Sancho, "but let us return to our village in the company of these gentlemen, who are concerned about your grace's well being. There we can make plans for another sally that will be more profitable to us and will make us more famous."

"You are right, Sancho," said Don Quixote, "for we would do well to let pass the malign influence of the stars which is now prevailing."

The canon, the priest, and the barber told him that, in doing this, he would be doing the right thing. Greatly amused at Sancho Panza's simple faith, they placed Don Quixote on the cart as before, and the procession regrouped and proceeded on its way. The goatherd bade everyone farewell and departed. The officers were not willing to proceed farther and were paid what was owed them by the priest. The canon begged the priest to keep him informed of Don Quixote's progress – whether he recovered from his madness or continued as he was – and after saying this, he took leave of everyone and resumed his journey. In short, they all parted and went their separate ways, leaving behind the priest and the barber, Don Quixote, Sancho Panza, and that good soul Rocinante, who during everything he had witnessed had shown as much fortitude as his master.

The oxcart driver yoked his oxen and settled Don Quixote onto a bundle of hay; then with his customary lethargy he set out on the route the priest had designated, arriving six days later at Don Quixote's village, which they entered at midday. It happened to be a Sunday and all the townspeople were in the plaza through which the knight's cart was forced to pass. When they drew near to see who was in the cart, they were astonished to recognize their fellow villager. One of the boys ran off to notify the housekeeper and the niece that their master and uncle had returned emaciated, sallow-looking, and stretched out on a pile of hay in an oxcart. It was pitiful to hear the cries of both these good ladies and to see them beat their breasts and curse anew those damnable books of chivalry, all of which actions they repeated when they saw Don Quixote come through the gate. At the news of the knight's return, Sancho Panza's wife hurried over, having long since learned that her husband had gone with Don Quixote to serve as his squire. When she saw Sancho, the first thing she asked him was whether the jackass was all right. Sancho said he was in better shape than Don Quixote.

"I thank God," she said, "for all the mercy He has shown me; but tell me, my dear, how have you benefitted from being a squire? What sort of skirt have you brought me? and what about shoes for your children?"

"I have brought none of those things, my dear," answered Sancho, "though I did bring other things of greater value and consequence."

"That makes me very happy," replied his wife. "Show me those things of greater value and consequence, my love; I would like to see them to cheer up my heart, which has been sad and unhappy for lo these many ages you've been away."

"I'll show them to you at home, woman," said Panza; "for the present just be patient. If God will be so good as to allow us to set out once again in quest of adventures, you'll soon see me a count or governor of an island, and not one of those ordinary islands either but the best that can be found."

"May heaven be so disposed, my dearest, for we certainly could use that, but, tell me: what is this about islands? I don't understand any of it."

"'One doesn't cast pearls before swine'" replied Sancho. "You will see in good time, wife, and will be amazed to hear yourself addressed as 'your ladyship' by all your vassals."

"What do you mean, Sancho, by this talk of ladyship, islands, and vassals?" asked Juana Panza, for this was the name of his wife, not because they were related but because in La Mancha it was the custom of wives to take their husbands' surnames.

"Don't be in such a hurry to know everything, Juana. You should be satisfied that I'm telling you the truth, so just stop talking. All I'll say – and this only in passing – is that there is nothing more pleasurable on earth than for an honorable man to serve as squire to a knight-errant and to ride about in quest of adventures. To be sure, most of the adventures encountered don't turn out as well as one might wish, since ninety-nine out of every hundred end up twisted and distorted. I know this from experience because I've been thrashed in some and tossed in a blanket in others, but despite all this, it's a marvelous thing to ride about wondering what will happen next when one is crossing mountains, combing forests, scaling cliffs, visiting castles, lodging in any inns one chooses, and never paying a blessed *maravedí*."

All these matters were discussed by Sancho Panza and his wife Juana Panza while Don Quixote's housekeeper and niece took him inside, undressed him, and tucked him into his ancient bed, where he peered at them blankly, being unable to make out where he was. The priest urged the niece to make every effort to humor her uncle, warning her to stay on the alert lest he try to escape again, and here he related everything they had found it necessary to do to bring him home. At this point the women once more raised their voices to heaven and once again heaped curses upon those books of chivalry, imploring heaven to cast the authors of such make-believe nonsense into the depths of hell. In short, they were confused and at the same time afraid they might find themselves without their master and uncle the first time he showed signs of improvement, and things turned out just as they feared.

But the author of this history, despite having carefully and diligently sought out the facts regarding Don Quixote's third sally, has been unable to discover anything, at least from reliable sources. Tradition alone has preserved in the memories of the people of La Mancha the fact that the third time Don Quixote sallied forth from home he went to Saragossa, where he took part in some famous jousts held in that city and was involved in endeavors worthy of his bravery and keen intellect, but our author was unable to uncover a single detail about his final days and death. In fact, he would have learned nothing at all had good fortune not provided an aged physician who had in his possession a lead box which, according to him, had been discovered in the foundation of an ancient hermitage that was being torn down so another might be erected. In the box were found several parchments containing poems in the Spanish language but written in Gothic characters. These described a number of Don Quixote's exploits and supplied information about Dulcinea of Toboso's beauty, Rocinante's appearance, Sancho Panza's faithfulness, the knight's very own tomb, and various epitaphs and eulogies on his life and habits. The ones that could be read and deciphered are those recorded below by the trustworthy author of this unique history. As recompense for the immense effort he has expended in investigating and searching in all the archives of La Mancha to bring this history to light, the author asks nothing more from his readers than that they accord it the same credence intelligent persons usually accord books of chivalry, which enjoy such esteem in all parts of the world, and with this he will consider himself satisfied and well paid and will be encouraged to seek out further episodes, if not as authentic, at least as inventive and entertaining.

The first words written on the parchment found in the lead box were these:

The Academicians of Argamasilla, a Village
of La Mancha, on the Life and Death of
the Valiant Don Quixote of La Mancha,
Hoc Scripserunt [1]

MONICONGO, ACADEMICIAN OF ARGAMASILLA,
ON THE TOMB OF DON QUIXOTE

La Mancha's thunderbolt of war,
The sharpest wit and loftiest muse,
The arm from which Gaeta far
To Cathay did its force diffuse.
He who, through love and valor's fire,
Outstripped great Amadís's fame,
Bid warlike Galaor retire,
And silenced Belianís' name.

He who, with helmet, sword, and shield,
On Rocinante, steed well known,
Adventures fought in many a field,
Lies underneath this frozen stone.

1 Latin: 'wrote this.'

PANIAGUADO, ACADEMICIAN OF ARGAMASILLA,
IN PRAISE OF DULCINEA OF TOBOSO

She whom you see, the plump and fleshy dame,
With high erected chest and vigorous mien,
Was erst th'enamored knight Don Quixote's flame,
The fair Dulcinea, of Toboso queen.

For her, armed cap-à-pie with sword and shield,
He trod the sabled mountain o'er,
For her traversed Montiel's famous field,
And in her service toils unnumbered bore.
Hard fate! that Death should crop so fine a flower,
And Love o'er such a knight exert his tyrant power!

CAPRICHOSO, A MOST INGENIOUS ACADEMICIAN
OF ARGAMASILLA, IN PRAISE OF
DON QUIXOTE'S HORSE ROCINANTE

On the aspiring adamantine trunk
Of a huge tree, whose root, with slaughter drunk,
Sends forth a scent of war, La Mancha's knight,
Frantic with valor, and returned from fight,
His bloody standard trembling in the air,
Hangs up his glittering armor, beaming fair
With that fine tempered steel whose edge o'erthrows,
Hacks, hews, confounds, and routs opposing foes.
Unheard-of prowess! and unheard-of verse!
But art new strains invents, new glories to rehearse.

If Amadís to Greece does give renown,
Much more her chief does fierce Bell
Prizing La Mancha more than Gaul or Greece,
As Quixote triumphs over Amadís.
Oblivion ne'er shall shroud his glorious name,
Whose very horse stands up to challenge fame,
Illustrious Rocinante, wond'rous steed!

Not with more generous pride or mettled speed
His rider erst Reinaldo's Bayard bore,
Or his mad lord, Orlando's Brilladore.

BURLADOR, THE LITTLE ACADEMICIAN
OF ARGAMASILLA, ON SANCHO PANZA

See Sancho Panza, view him well,
And let this verse his praises tell.
His body was but short, 't is true,
Yet held a soul as large as two.
No guile he knew, like some before him,
But simple as his mother bore him.
This gentle squire on gentle ass
Went gentle Rocinante's pace,
Following his lord from place to place.
To be a count he did aspire,
And reason good for such desire;
But worth, in these ungrateful times,
To envied honor seldom climbs.
Vain mortals! give your wishes o'er,
And trust the flatterer Hope no more,
Whose promises, whate'er they seem,
End in a shadow or a dream.

CACHIDIABLO, ACADEMICIAN OF ARGAMASILLA,
ON THE TOMB OF DON QUIXOTE

Here lies a hapless knight,
Well bruised in many a fray,
Whose courser, Rocinante hight,
Long bore him many a way.

Close by his loving master's side
Lies doltish Sancho Panza,
A trusty squire of courage tried,
And true as ever man saw.

TIQUITOC, ACADEMICIAN OF ARGAMASILLA,
ON THE TOMB OF DULCINEA OF TOBOSO

Dulcinea, plump and fleshy, lies
Beneath this frozen stone,
But since to frightful death a prize,
Reduced to skin and bone.

She of goodly parentage came,
And had the lady in her;
She was the great Quixote's flame,
But only death could win her.

These were the only verses that could be deciphered. The remainder, whose writing was worm-eaten, were entrusted to a scholar so he might make a conjecture as to their meaning. We understand that, inasmuch as he has done so at the expense of a number of sleepless nights and considerable effort, he intends to publish them, and it is hoped that Don Quixote's third sally will be among them.

Forse altri canterá con miglior plettro. [2]

2 Italian: 'Perhaps someone else will sing with a better plectrum [i.e. inspiration]' From *Orlando Furioso*.

[Part Two]

Approbation

By commission and order of the lords of the Council, I have examined the *Second Part of Don Quixote of La Mancha*, by Miguel de Cervantes Saavedra, and it contains nothing against our holy Catholic Faith or moral principles. On the contrary, it contains a great deal of innocent recreation and harmless entertainment – things the ancients deemed appropriate for their republics, since even the Lacedaemonians in their solemnity erected a statue to laughter, and the Thessalians dedicated festivals to it, as Pausanias observes (citing book 2, chapter 10 of Bosio's *De signis Eccle.*) whereby they revived languishing souls and melancholic spirits. Tully takes note of this in the first book of *De legibus*, as does the poet when he says: "*Interpone tuis interdum gaudia curis.*" [1] This is what the author [2] does by mixing the real with the make-believe, the entertaining with the beneficial, and the edifying with the facetious, using the bait of humor to disguise the fishhook of admonishment, while carrying out his right-minded goal of driving out books of chivalry, for by his laudable diligence (and cleverness) he has cleansed these realms of this contagious malady. A work most worthy of his great talent, it is the honor and luster of our nation and the wonder and envy of our neighbors; such, at least, is my opinion. In Madrid, the 17th of March, 1615.

Master Joseph de Valdivielso

Approbation

By commission of Dr. Gutierre de Cetina, vicar-general of this city of Madrid, His Majesty's capital, I have examined this book of Miguel de Cervantes Saavedra, *The Second Part of the Ingenious Knight Don Quixote of La Mancha*, and have found nothing in it unworthy of Christian zeal or inimical to the kind of values needed to set a good example and a moral tone. Quite the contrary, it contains considerable erudition and much that is beneficial, both in its restrained but well-developed argument aimed at extirpating those vain, fallacious books of chivalry, whose contagion has spread far more widely than is warranted, and in its straightforward use of the Spanish language, unadulterated by annoying and studied affectation, a vice justifiably abhorrent to sensible persons. In the matter of correcting vices, which it constantly touches upon by means of its incisive speeches, it so wisely observes the precepts of Christian admonition that whoever is afflicted with the infirmity it endeavors to cure will, before he realizes it, have willingly imbibed its sweet, tasty medicine without hesitation

1 Latin: 'Every now and then mix pleasure with your cares.'

2 I.e. Cervantes.

or the least revulsion, together with the benefits thereof, namely, an abhorrence of his vice, whereby he will find himself both reprimanded and entertained – a most difficult accomplishment.

There have been many who, not knowing how to exercise moderation or to strike a proper balance between what is useful and what is pleasurable, have caused all their hard work to collapse, and since they are unable to imitate Diogenes in philosophy and learning, they audaciously (not to say licentiously and ignorantly) attempt to imitate him in cynicism, resorting to slander or inventing situations that never occurred in order to make the vice they are attacking worthy of their harsh rebuke, thereby possibly revealing ways, hitherto unknown, of practicing that vice, so that they end up not censuring but teaching it. They make themselves odious to those who are well informed; they cause the masses to lose respect for their writings, if such they ever had; and the vices they arrogantly and imprudently sought to correct find themselves more solidly entrenched than ever. Not every abscess lends itself equally to prescriptions or to cauterization; some respond much better to a bland and mild medicine, through the application of which the learned but cautious physician accomplishes his desired cure, a result that is often better than the one achieved through the rigors of the iron.

How very differently have the writings of Miguel de Cervantes been perceived both by our nation and by those abroad! Everyone wishes to visit (as though he were something wondrous) this author whose books have been universally applauded in Spain, France, Italy, Germany, and Flanders, as much for their decorum and propriety as for their even, smooth style. I can truthfully certify that on the twenty-fifth day of February of the present year, 1615, while my master His Eminence Don Bernardo de Sandoval y Rojas, Cardinal Archbishop of Toledo, had gone to meet with the Ambassador of France, who had come to make arrangements with His Eminence regarding the marriages between the royal houses of France and Spain, I and several chaplains of my master the Cardinal were visited by a number of French gentlemen who had arrived in the retinue of the Ambassador. Being not only courteous and intelligent but interested in literature, they wished to know which works of fiction were currently most highly esteemed. When I happened to mention the one I was in the process of censoring, they no sooner heard the name of Miguel de Cervantes than they began to hold forth on the esteem that France and its neighboring countries accorded his works: the *Galatea*, which one of them virtually knew by heart, the *Exemplary Novels*, and the First Part of the present work. So effusive was their praise that I offered to take them to see the author of these works, for which they expressed their utmost appreciation. They questioned me in detail about his age and profession, his station in life, and his material circumstances. I was forced to admit he was old, a soldier, an hidalgo, and poor; to which one of them responded with these precise words: 'How is it that Spain has not made such a person a wealthy man and supported him from the public treasury?' Another of these gentlemen offered the following observation, which he announced quite wryly: 'If it takes poverty to make him write, I pray he will never be wealthy but will, by remaining poor, enrich the rest of us with his works.'

I am aware that this is somewhat lengthy for a censor's statement and that someone will say it verges on flattery. But the truth of what I have succinctly stated will rid the critic of suspicion and me of concern. Besides, no one today flatters a person who lacks the means to grease the palm of the flatterer, for even if he affectionately and jokingly says it in jest, he expects to be repaid in earnest. In Madrid, the twenty-seventh day of February, sixteen hundred and fifteen.

THE LICENTIATE MARQUEZ TORRES

Prologue to the Reader

Good heavens! noble reader – or plebeian one – how eagerly you must be awaiting this prologue, expecting to find it filled with complaints, vituperation, and retaliation against the author of the second *Don Quixote*, that is, the one said to have been begotten in Tordesillas and born in Tarragona, but truly I have no intention of giving you that satisfaction, for though injuries awaken anger in the most humble breasts, that rule shall find an exception in mine. You might perhaps have me call him an ass or a fool or an insolent rogue but no such thought has ever crossed my mind. Let his own transgression provide his punishment. He has made his bed, so let him lie in it, and I'll leave it at that.

What I cannot help resenting, though, is his referring to me as an old man with only one arm, as though it were in my power to make time stand still and pass me by, or as if I had suffered my loss in some tavern rather than in the most glorious encounter the past and present ages have ever seen or future ones shall ever hope to see. [1] If my wounds do not dazzle the eyes of those who see them, at least they will be appreciated and esteemed by those who know where I acquired them, for a soldier slain in battle is more esteemed than one who saves his life by fleeing. I feel this so strongly that if someone were to propose to effect the impossible, I should prefer to have taken part in that prodigious battle than to find myself free of my wounds by virtue of not having participated in it. The wounds a soldier displays on his face and breast are so many stars leading others to strive for that paradise of glory and that desire for justifiable praise. Moreover, it should be noted that an author writes, not with his gray hair, but with his mind, which customarily improves with age. I also resent being called envious and being told the definition of envy, as though I were some ignoramus. The fact of the matter is that there are two kinds of envy and I am acquainted only with the one that is pure, noble, and benevolent. This being the case, I have no reason to harass any priest, particularly one who is also an officer of the Holy Office. If he said this about the person he was apparently referring to, he was completely mistaken, for not only do I adore this person's talent but I marvel at his works

1 The Battle of Lepanto, 1571, in which Cervantes permanently lost the use of his left hand.

as well as his virtuous and unceasing industry. [2] I am truly grateful to this gentleman for saying that though my *Exemplary Novels* are more satirical than exemplary, they are nevertheless good. This they could not be unless they contained a little of everything.

I imagine you must be saying that I am showing great self control and am keeping myself within the bounds of modesty, but I realize one should not heap afflictions upon a man who is himself already afflicted and, indeed, this gentleman's affliction must be considerable, inasmuch as he dares not appear openly in the light of day but hides his name and falsifies the place from which he comes, as though he had committed some crime of high treason. If you, dear reader, should discover who he is, pray tell him on my behalf that I do not consider myself offended, for I am well aware of the nature of the Devil's temptations, one of the greatest of which is to put into a man's head the notion that he is capable of writing a book and getting it published, whereby he will acquire as much fame as money and as much money as fame. As confirmation of this, I would have you tell him the following story in your clever and witty way.

There was once a madman in Seville who came up with the most comical and outrageous idea any madman ever conceived. What he did was to fashion a tube from a reed that was tapered at one end and, whenever he would catch a dog in the street or in some other place, he would hold one of its hind legs down with his own foot, lift the other hind leg in the air with his hand, and insert the tube as far as it would go, at which point he would proceed to blow into it until the dog was as round as a ball. Once having the dog in that shape, he would give it a couple of slaps on the belly and then shout to everyone present – and there was always a crowd – 'Do you good people by chance think it an easy matter to blow up a dog?' Similarly, does your grace by chance think it an easy matter to write a book?

Now if this story should not please him, dear reader, you may tell him this other one, which is also about a madman and a dog.

In Cordova there was another madman who was in the habit of carrying on top of his head a marble slab or some rather heavy stone and, whenever he would come across some unsuspecting dog, he would stand beside it and let the weight drop straight down on top of it. The beleaguered dog would take off yelping and howling and not stop for three blocks. Now it happened that one of the dogs on which he dropped his load belonged to a hat maker who loved his dog dearly. The stone fell, hitting the dog on the head, and the injured dog let out a yelp. When his master saw this, he was furious and, grabbing his measuring rod, took off after the madman and left no bone unbeaten, crying out with each blow that he delivered, 'You thieving cur, hit my hunting dog will you! Couldn't you see, you brute, that he was a hunting dog?' And repeating the phrase 'hunting dog' over and over again, he gave the madman a thorough thrashing.

The latter, having learned his lesson, beat a hasty retreat and did not show his face again in the plaza for more than a month but at the end of that period, he was back to his old tricks again and this

---

2 An allusion to Lope de Vega (1562-1635), Spain's most prolific and best known dramatist. Avellaneda had accused Cervantes of attacking Lope, and of doing so out of envy.

time with even heavier loads. But whenever he would approach a dog, he would eye it from one end to the other and then without daring to drop his load, would say, 'This is a hunting dog, beware!' In fact, all the dogs he came across, whether great Danes or Chihuahuas, were hunting dogs in his eyes, so that never again did he discharge his load. Perhaps it may thus transpire that our historian will not dare open the floodgates of his wit again by writing books, which, when bad, are harder than rocks.

Tell him also that I do not give a hang for his threat to deprive me of my livelihood with his book. To echo the appeal from the famous farce *La Perendenga*: "Long live my lord the prefect and may Christ be with you all,' I answer, 'Long live the great Count of Lemos,' whose well known Christian generosity sustains me against all the buffets of my meager fortune. And long live the supreme liberality of His Eminence of Toledo, Don Bernardo de Sandoval y Rojas, even in the event that there should be no more printing presses in the entire world or that they should publish more books against me than there are letters in the couplets of Mingo Revulgo. These two nobles, without being courted by any sort of adulation or flattery on my part, but simply out of their own benevolence, have taken it upon themselves to favor me and shower me with kindness, whereby I consider myself wealthier and more fortunate than if fate had raised me to these heights by ordinary means. A poor man may possess honor but not so an evil one. Poverty can cloud nobility but cannot obscure it entirely, and since virtue emits a certain light of its own, though it may be forced to endure the obstacles and obstructions of indigence, it ends up being esteemed by lofty, noble spirits and, consequently, being favored. Say nothing more to him, nor do I wish to say more to you than to assure you that this second part of *Don Quixote* I am now offering you is cut by the same craftsman from the same fabric as the first.

In it I give you Don Quixote fully developed and certifiably dead and buried lest anyone raise fresh false accusations against him, since those of the past are sufficient. Likewise, it should be sufficient that an honorable man has given an account of these mad but wise doings without any desire to resurrect them anew, for when there is an overabundance of anything, even if it is good, it tends to lose its appeal, but when there is a scarcity of that same commodity, even if it is not quite so good, it is held in some esteem. I nearly forgot to mention that your grace may expect the *Persiles*, which I am now finishing, as well as the second part of *Galatea*.

Dedication to the Count of Lemos

Some days ago, I sent Your Excellency a copy of my plays [1] that are being published prior to being performed and if I remember correctly, I said that Don Quixote was going about with his spurs on ready to kiss Your Excellency's hand. I can now state that he has donned them

1 *Ocho comedias y ocho entremeses nuevos nunca representados* [Eight plays and eight interludes : new and never before performed], published in 1615.

again and is on his way, and if he arrives safely, it would appear I have performed some small service for Your Excellency, for the urgency has been great that has pressured me from all sides to send him forth to dispel the nausea and disgust caused by another Don Quixote who has masqueraded as the *Second Part* and traversed the entire globe.[2] The one who has shown the most interest in him has been the great Emperor of China, who a month ago sent me a messenger with a letter written in Chinese, asking me, or more correctly, imploring me, to send him *Don Quixote*, as he intended to found a college in which Spanish would be taught, and he wanted the history of Don Quixote to be the work studied. In addition to this, he asked me to come and serve as rector of that college. When I asked the courier if His Majesty had given him anything to help defray my expenses, he said it had not even crossed his mind. "Well, brother," I replied, "you may return to China post haste, or at whatever haste you choose, for my poor health will not permit me to make such a long journey, in addition to which I am ill and a virtual pauper. There are all sorts of emperors and all sorts of monarchs but in Naples I have the great Count of Lemos, who, without a bunch of titles such as that of school rector, sustains and supports me and lavishes more favors upon me than I could ever desire."

With this I dismissed him, and with this I shall take leave of Your Excellency by offering you *The Labors of Persiles and Sigismunda*, a work I shall finish within a few months, *Deo volente*.[3] This will either be the worst or best book ever composed in Spanish, that is, among those aimed at entertaining. But I hasten to add that I regret having said 'the worst,' for in the opinion of my friends it will be as good as any book can possibly be. May this letter find Your Excellency in the best of health. *Persiles* will soon be ready to kiss your hand, as this servant is ready to kiss your grace's feet.[4] From Madrid, the last day of October in the year sixteen hundred and fifteen.

Your Excellency's most devoted servant,

MIGUEL DE CERVANTES SAAVEDRA

---

2 A reference to the continuation of *Don Quixote* published in 1614 in Tarragona by one Alonso Fernández de Avellaneda. Inasmuch as the identity of this author has never been established, the pseudonymous work has been attributed to numerous persons, including several of Spain's most famous authors — even Cervantes himself. In the prologue to his *Don Quixote* Avellaneda treats Cervantes most cruelly, and it is to these attacks that Cervantes alludes in the dedication, prologue, and text of his Second Part of 1615.

3 Latin: "God willing.'

4 Cervantes actually finished the "Dedication" to *Persiles* on April 19, 1616, three days before his death. The work was published in early January of the following year.

Chapter One

The matters that the priest and the barber discussed with Don Quixote regarding his illness

It is related by Cide Hamete Benengeli in the second part of our history, which includes Don Quixote's third sally, that the priest and the barber went almost a month without seeing him so as not to reawaken in him the memory of past events, but they did not for that reason fail to visit his niece and housekeeper, whom they charged with humoring Don Quixote by feeding him things that would be both soothing and good for his heart and brain, because the latter, by simple deduction, was obviously the source of all his troubles. The women assured him they were already doing this and would continue to do so as cheerfully and scrupulously as possible, for they had noticed that at odd moments Don Quixote showed signs of being completely sane. This cheered the two men considerably and they felt they had acted correctly in bringing him home enchanted on the oxcart, as related in the last chapter of the first part of our history, a history as great as it is truthful. They decided to pay him a visit to check on his progress, though they considered any sort of improvement to be virtually impossible, and they made certain not to touch upon any aspect of knight-errantry lest they risk reopening the wound that was still so fresh.

When they finally went to see him, they found him sitting up in bed wearing a green woolen waistcoat and a red Toledo cap, and he was so withered and dried up that his skin looked exactly like a mummy's. The two men were most graciously received by him and, when they inquired about his health, he, in a most rational and cordial manner, gave them a full report, together with an account of himself. In the course of their conversation they turned to discussing what is called statecraft and methods of governing, whereby they corrected one abuse and condemned another, reforming this custom and sending that one into exile, with each of the three men becoming a new law-giver, a modern Lycurgus, a brand-new Solon, and they remade the republic so thoroughly that it gave every indication of having been recast in a forge and totally transformed. Don Quixote discoursed so rationally on every topic introduced that the two examiners were convinced he was completely cured and in full possession of his wits. The niece and the housekeeper, who found themselves present at this discussion, could not thank God sufficiently when they saw their master in such a healthy frame of mind.

But the priest changed the original plan, which was to avoid any mention of chivalry, because he wished to test once and for all whether Don Quixote's sanity was real or imagined, and so, changing the subject, he began to discuss some news that had reached the court. He said, among other things, that it was common knowledge that the Turk was descending with a powerful navy but it was not known what his objective was or where his fury would be unleashed. Because of this fear, the alarm was sounded almost every year, placing all Christendom on the alert and forcing His Majesty to fortify the coasts of Naples and Sicily, as well as the island of Malta. Don Quixote said in response to this,

"His Majesty has acted like a most prudent warrior in readying his dominions in a timely fashion lest the enemy catch him unprepared, but if he were to follow my advice, I would urge His Majesty to take a certain precaution that is undoubtedly far from his thoughts at this particular time."

No sooner did the priest hear this than he said to himself, 'May God watch over you, my poor Don Quixote, for I fear you are about to leap from the lofty peak of your madness into the deep abyss of your naiveté!' The barber, who had the same thought, asked Don Quixote what sort of precaution he was suggesting be taken; perhaps it was such that it might be added to the long list of impractical suggestions commonly given the nobility.

"Mine, Sir Face-scraper," said Don Quixote, "will not be impractical but practical."

"I only meant," said the barber, "that experience has shown that all or nearly all the advice given His Majesty is either impossible, absurd, or harmful to the king and his kingdom."

"Well, mine," said Don Quixote, "is neither impossible nor absurd but the easiest, fairest, quickest, and cleverest a counselor could ever conceive."

"Sir Don Quixote," said the priest, "your grace is waiting a terribly long time to declare it."

"I am loath to reveal it just now," replied Don Quixote, "lest it reach the ears of the council members by daybreak tomorrow, whereby some other person will reap the thanks and reward for my labors."

"Speaking for myself," said the barber, "I swear that from this moment till I find myself in the presence of God I will not divulge to king or rook or any mortal man what your grace may tell me. By the way, this is an oath I learned from the ballad about the priest who in the preface informs the king of the identity of the thief who stole his hundred doubloons and his fleet-footed mule."

"I am not up on my ballads," said Don Quixote, "but I am certain the oath is good by virtue of the fact that I know the worthy barber to be an honest man."

"Even if he were not," said the priest, "I would vouch for him and would guarantee that in regard to the present matter he would be as dumb as a person without a tongue under penalty of paying whatever judgement was decreed."

"And who will vouch for your grace, sir priest?" asked Don Quixote.

"My profession," retorted the priest, "which is to keep secrets."

"For goodness sake!" exclaimed Don Quixote at this point, "all His Majesty has to do is to proclaim publicly that all the knights-errant wandering about Spain are to assemble at the court on a designated day, and even if no more than half a dozen show up, there will probably be one among them who by himself will suffice to destroy the Turk's forces. If I may have your graces' attention, I shall explain.

"Is it any novelty, I might ask, for a solitary knight-errant to route an army of two hundred thousand men as though the lot of them possessed but one throat or were made of icing? Otherwise, how is it that we have so many histories filled with these marvels? And though it would work to my own disadvantage – I shall let others speak for themselves – the famous Don Belianís should be alive today or any of the countless descendants of Amadís of Gaul, for if any one of them were living today to confront the Turk, I would not give a fig for the latter's chances! But God will watch over His people and provide someone who, though not so excellent as the former knights-errant, will at least not be their inferior in determination, and since God understands what I mean, I shall say no more."

"Mercy!" cried the niece at this point, "may I be struck dead if my uncle doesn't want to become a knight-errant again!"

To which Don Quixote responded,

"And a knight-errant I shall die! Let the Turk advance or retreat whenever he pleases and let him do so with all the might at his command – but I say once more that God understands what I mean."

At this point the barber said,

"By your graces' leave I should like to give a brief account of something that took place in Seville, which is so apropos it fairly cries out to be told."

Don Quixote consented and, once the priest and the others gave him their undivided attention, he began to speak.

"In a madhouse in Seville was a man who had been placed there by his relatives because of his insanity. He had a degree in canon law from Osuna but even it had been from Salamanca, he would in the opinion of many have still been mad. After several years of confinement said university graduate convinced himself he was sane and in his right mind, and so, armed with this notion, he wrote to the archbishop, imploring him earnestly but diplomatically to order him released from that wretchedness in which he lived, for by the grace of God he had now recovered his lost wits, adding that his relatives, in order to enjoy his share of the estate, kept him there and, contrary to the facts of the situation, were determined he was to remain crazy for as long as he lived. The archbishop, being persuaded by a number of intelligent, well-composed letters, sent one of his chaplains to ascertain from the house's rector whether the things the licenciate wrote him were true. He was also to speak to the madman and, if in his opinion the man was sane, was to demand his release. The chaplain did accordingly and the rector informed him that the man was still mad; that despite the fact that he oftentimes spoke like a most sensible person, he would suddenly burst forth with a barrage of absurd ideas that were just as numerous and extreme as his earlier ones were rational, a fact the chaplain might verify simply by speaking with him.

When the chaplain said he would like to do so, they led him to the madman's cell, where he conversed with him for an hour or more, during which time not only did the madman never once utter an incoherent or outlandish statement but spoke so rationally the chaplain was forced to consider him sane. Among his numerous charges, the madman said the rector was unsympathetic to him so he would not lose the gifts the madman's relatives sent the rector to encourage him to say he was still mad despite his flashes of lucidity. But the greatest obstacle facing him in his misfortune was his great wealth, for in order to enjoy it, those who were against him used deceit and cast doubt upon the beneficence Our Lord had demonstrated in transforming him from a beast into a man. In short, he spoke in such a way that he made the rector appear suspect, his relatives avaricious and heartless, and himself so rational that the chaplain decided to take him along so the archbishop could see him and place his finger on the pulse of that affair. With this naive faith the worthy chaplain asked the rector to have the licentiate given back the clothes he had been wearing at the time of his arrival. The rector once again begged the chaplain to reconsider what he was doing, for there was no doubt the licenciate was still mad. But since the rector's warnings and advice were totally incapable of dissuading the chaplain from taking him away, the rector obeyed, seeing it was by order of the archbishop. They gave the licenciate his old clothes, which were still decent, and when he saw himself dressed as a sane person, having divested himself of his lunatic's garb, he begged the chaplain in the name of charity to let him say goodbye to his mad companions. The chaplain said he would like to go with him to see the inmates who lived there, so they and several others who were present went upstairs. When the licenciate came to a cage that housed a raving lunatic, who happened to be calm and peaceful at the moment, he said, 'My brother, see if there is anything you would like me to do for you because I am on my way home. God in His infinite goodness and mercy has seen fit to restore my sanity though I am undeserving of it. I am now sane and rational, for when it comes to God's power, nothing is impossible. Place all your trust and hope in Him, for He has restored me to my former state and will do the same for you if you will put your trust in Him. I'll make certain to send you some delicacies to eat, and by all means you must eat them, for I can assure you, as one who has been through the mill, that all our madness proceeds from our stomachs' being empty and our brains' being filled with air. Above all, keep up your spirits, for despondency in adversity weakens one's health and leads to death!' This entire speech by the licenciate was overheard by another madman in a cage opposite that of the first. Getting up from an old mat where he had been lying stark naked, he asked in a loud voice who the man was that was going home sane and cured; to which the licenciate replied, 'Brother, I am the one who is leaving. I no longer have any need to be here and I will be eternally grateful to heaven for having shown me this great favor!' 'Mind what you say, licenciate,' said the madman, 'and don't let the Devil trick you. Abandon your urge to travel, stay calm and peaceful in your own home and you'll spare yourself the trip back.' 'I know I'm cured,' replied the licenciate, 'and there'll be no need to make the rounds again.' 'You cured!' cried the madman; 'we'll see about that – but God be with you. I swear by Jupiter, whose majesty I represent here on earth, that because of the sin Seville is committing today in considering you sane and in releasing you from this house, I will be forced to inflict such punishment on her that it will be remembered from now till the end of time, amen. Don't you know, you insignificant little licenciate, that I can do this, being, as I say, Jupiter the Thunderer, who hold in my hands the fiery thunderbolts with which I can and regularly do threaten to destroy the world? However, I choose to inflict only one punishment on this ignorant city: I will refuse to rain on it or any part of its outlying districts for three whole years, which time is to be reckoned from the exact moment of the day on which this threat is made. You free? You sane? You cured while I am crazy, ill, and locked up? Why, I'd sooner hang myself than even think of raining!'

"Inasmuch as those present were spectators to the madman's shouting and raving, our licenciate turned to the chaplain and, taking him by the hand, said, 'My lord, your grace need not worry or pay any attention to what this lunatic has said, for if he is Jupiter and refuses to rain, I, who am Neptune, father and god of the waters, will rain whenever I feel like it or when there is a need.' To this the chaplain replied, 'Still and all, Sir Neptune, it would not be wise to make Sir Jupiter angry. Your grace shall remain here and some other day, when it is more convenient and we have more time, we shall return for you.' The rector and the others broke into laughter, which caused the chaplain a certain amount of embarrassment. They immediately stripped the licenciate and left him there in his home, and that is the end of my story."

"Is this the story, sir barber," said Don Quixote, "that was so apropos it fairly cried out to be told? O master shaver, master shaver, a man would have to be blind not to see through your story! Can you possibly not know that comparisons between different kinds of wit, different kinds of bravery, beauty, and lineages are always odious and ill-received? I, sir barber, am not Neptune, god of the waters, nor do I seek to make anyone take me for a wise person, which I am not. I simply tire myself out striving to show the world the mistake it is making in not resurrecting that happy age when the order of knight-errantry flourished. This depraved age of ours, however, does not deserve to enjoy such benefits as those enjoyed during the ages when knights-errant took it upon their own shoulders to assume the responsibility of the defense of kingdoms, the protection of maidens, the support of orphans and wards, the chastisement of the haughty, and the reward of the humble. Among the majority of knights who go about nowadays, there is heard the rustle of damask, brocade, and other expensive fabrics, which they wear instead of armored coats of mail. There is no longer any knight who, encased in armor from head to foot, will sleep out in the open exposed to the severity of the heavens or anyone who will try to catch a few winks, as it were, while seated on his horse supporting himself with his lance, as the knights of yore were wont to do. There is no longer a single knight who will leave this forest, ride into these hills or walk along some barren, deserted beach beside the sea, which more often than not will be stormy and tempestuous, upon which he will discover a small boat without mast, sail, oars, or any sort of rigging, and who with intrepid spirit will leap into it and surrender himself to the implacable waves of the ocean deep that will alternately lift him towards the sky and plunge him into the depths. Then bracing himself against the unremitting storm, he will find himself, when he least expects it, three thousand leagues or more from where he embarked, only to leap ashore in some remote, unknown land, where he will undergo adventures worthy of being recorded, not on parchment, but on bronze. Nowadays, sloth triumphs over diligence, idleness over labor, vice over virtue, arrogance over valor, and the theory of battle over its actual practice, all of which existed and flourished only in the Golden Age in the days of knights-errant. Tell me this: who was more upright or more valiant than the famous Amadís of Gaul? Who more clever than Palmerín of England? Who more accommodating and easy-going than Tirant lo Blanc? Who more gallant than Lisuarte de Grecia? Who more wounded or wounding than Don Belianís? Who more intrepid than Perión de Gaula, more death-defying than Felixmarte de Hircania, or more sincere than Esplandián? Who more daring than Don Cirongilio de Tracia? Who more fierce than Rodamonte? Who more prudent than King Sobrino? Who more audacious than Reinaldos? Who more invincible than Roland? Who more gallant and courteous than Ruggiero, whose present descendants are the dukes of Ferrara according to Turpin in his *Cosmographia*? All these knights, sir priest, together with many others I might name, were knights-errant, the light and glory of chivalry. I should love for these or others like them to carry out my proposal, for were they to do so, His Majesty would find himself well served at considerable savings and the Turk would be left tearing his beard.

"Having said this, I wish to remain in my own house, not that the chaplain will be able to tear me away from here; and if Jupiter, as the barber has said, should not rain, I am here and shall rain whenever I feel like it. I mention this so Sir Basin will know that I understand him."

"Truly, Sir Don Quixote," replied the barber, "I didn't mean anything by it. May God strike me dead if my intentions were not honorable, nor should your grace feel resentful."

"Whether I should feel resentful or not," said Don Quixote, "is my business."

"Even though I have scarcely said a word until now," put in the priest, "I should like to rid myself of a nagging doubt that has been gnawing and tugging at my conscience as a result of what Sir Don Quixote has said here."

"Your grace," said Don Quixote, "has my permission for this and other things as well and may thus air your doubts, for it is unpleasant to go about with a troubled conscience."

"Well, with that authorization," said the priest, "I can state, regarding my doubt, that I cannot bring myself to believe by any stretch of the imagination that this horde of knights-errant your grace has mentioned really and truly were flesh-and-blood creatures of this world. I rather consider all this fiction, fabrication, falsehood, and dreams told by men awake, or to be more accurate, by men half asleep."

"That is another error," said Don Quixote, "into which many have fallen who do not believe such knights ever existed. Quite often I have with different persons at different times sought to demonstrate the fallacy of this common misconception. On some occasions I have failed in my attempt but on others have been successful, having placed it upon the shoulders of truth, a truth so certain I can almost attest to having seen Amadís of Gaul with my own eyes. He was a tall, fair-complected man with a black well-groomed beard who wore an expression somewhere between tenderness and severity. A man of few words, he was slow to anger but quick to control himself. And just as I have delineated Amadís, I could if I wished, paint and describe every single knight-errant who ever appeared in a book of chivalry. I am convinced knights-errant were just the way they are described in the histories, so that anyone, by examining the deeds they performed and the temperaments they possessed, may deduce by means of sound reasoning their character, features, and stature."

"My dear Don Quixote," said the barber, "how large does your grace think the giant Morgante to have been?"

"Regarding the subject of giants," said Don Quixote, "opinions vary even as to their very existence but the Holy Scripture, which cannot stray one iota from the truth, shows us that they did exist when it relates the story of that huge Philistine Goliath, who was seven and a half cubits tall, a most prodigious size. [1] Moreover, on the isle of Sicily they have found several shinbones and shoulder blades that are so large their size proves their owners were giants as large as huge towers, and geometry proves it beyond a shadow of a doubt. Despite all this, I am unable to state with certainty how large Morgante was, though my guess is that he was not very tall. I am led to this conclusion by finding in the history that specifically mentions his deeds that he often slept with a roof over his head, and since he was able to find houses into which he could fit, it is obvious his size was not overly large."

"That is true," said the priest, who delighted in listening to him say such outlandish things. He then

---

1 Samuel 17:4 states that Goliath was *six* and a half cubits tall, which would make him between 9 and 11 feet tall.

asked him how he pictured Reinaldos de Montalbán, Don Roland, and the other Twelve Peers of France, who were all knights-errant."

"I dare say," said Don Quixote, "that Reinaldos had a broad face, ruddy complexion, darting and somewhat bulging eyes, was rather haughty and irritable, and was a friend to thieves and outcasts. As for Roland, or Rotolando or Orlando, he being called by each of these names in the histories, I am of the opinion and can affirm that he was of medium height, broad-shouldered, and somewhat bowlegged, he had a swarthy complexion, a blond beard, a hairy body, a menacing look, and was a man of few words, being quite mannerly and well-bred."

"If Roland was no more of a gentleman than your grace has said," replied the priest, "it is no wonder the lovely Lady Angélica scorned him and left him for the gaiety, spirit, and wittiness of the downy-cheeked little Moor to whom she gave herself, for she was wise to fall in love with Medoro's gentleness rather than Roland's roughness."

"Sir priest," said Don Quixote, "that Angélica was giddy, capricious, and dissolute, and left the world as full of her indiscretions as of her fame as a beauty. She cast aside a thousand lords, all men of valor and intelligence, to take to herself a little page with a pretty face who had no more wealth or renown than that bestowed upon him because of his allegiance to his friend. The great poet who extolled her beauty, the renowned Ariosto, either because he dared not, or chose not, to record in verse what happened to the lady following her ignoble surrender, which can not have been very ennobling, concluded his account of her with these lines:

> Another bard may sing in better strain,
> How she Cathaya's scepter did obtain.

This was undoubtedly a kind of prophecy, for poets are also called *vates*, meaning 'diviners'. The truth of this is plain to see, for since then a famous Andalucian poet has mourned and intoned her tears, while another famous and unique Castilian poet has extolled her beauty."

"Tell me, Sir Don Quixote," said the barber at this point, "has there never been a poet who composed a satire about that Lady Angélica among all those who have sung her praises?"

"I sincerely believe," said Don Quixote, "that if Sacripante and Roland had been poets, they would have raked that damsel over the coals, for it is natural and proper for poets who have been scorned and rejected by their ladies, whether real or imagined – in short, by those they designated as the ladies of their thoughts – to seek revenge through satires and lampoons, an act certainly unworthy of generous hearts. But until now there has not come to my attention any verse vilifying the Lady Angélica, who turned the world upside down."

"Astounding!" said the priest.

At that moment they heard loud shouts in the courtyard and, when they realized that they came from the housekeeper and the niece, who had previously withdrawn from the conversation, they all hurried to see what the disturbance could be.

Chapter Two

The remarkable confrontation between Sancho Panza and Don Quixote's housekeeper and niece, together with other amusing incidents

Our history relates that the shouts heard by Don Quixote, the priest, and the barber came from the housekeeper and the niece and were directed at Sancho Panza, who, in an effort to see Don Quixote, was struggling to get past the door they were guarding.

"What does this no-good vagabond want here?" the housekeeper said to the niece. "Go back to your own house, brother, for it was you and no one else who was responsible for tempting my master, luring him away, and dragging him through all those god-forsaken places."

To which Sancho replied,

"You fiend of a housekeeper, the one who was tempted, lured away, and dragged through all those god-forsaken places was not your master but me. He took *me* to all those places and you two have got your facts exactly backwards. He hoodwinked me into leaving my home by promising me an island I'm still waiting for."

"Curse you, Sancho," said the niece, "you can take your stupid island and go hang yourself! What is so great about an island? Is it something you can eat, you pot-bellied glutton?"

"It is not something I can eat," said Sancho, "but something I can govern and rule, and it's better than any number of city councils or court judgeships."

"That may all be true," said the housekeeper, "but you're not coming inside, you big bag of wickedness and evil. Go govern your own house, farm your little patch of land, and stop grasping for islands and such."

The priest and the barber found this exchange among the trio highly amusing but Don Quixote, fearing Sancho might unsew his lips and blurt out a stream of malicious nonsense or touch upon points that might not be wholly to the knight's credit, called out to him while ordering the two women to be quiet and let him enter. Sancho came in, whereupon the priest and the barber took their leave of Don Quixote, about whose health they despaired, for they could see how persistent he was in his insane ideas and how immersed in his ridiculous and woe-begotten knight-errantry; and so the priest said to the barber,

"You will see, my friend, that when we least expect it, our hidalgo will once again fly the coop."

"I have no doubt about it," replied the barber, "but I am not as astounded at the knight's madness as I am at the squire's simplemindedness, for he is so convinced of that business of the island that all the arguments one could muster would never get it out of his head."

"God help them," said the priest, "and let us keep on the alert to see what comes of this bunch of absurdities from such a knight and squire. One would think they were both forged in a single mold, for the master's madness without the servant's imbecility would come absolutely to nought."

"So it seems," said the barber, "and I would give anything to know what they are both up to at this moment."

"I am sure," said the priest, "that the niece or the housekeeper will report it to us later, for their temperament is such that they can hardly fail to eavesdrop."

Meanwhile, Don Quixote had shut himself up in his room with Sancho and, once they were alone, said to him,

"I am deeply grieved, Sancho, that you have said and continue to say that I was the one who took you away from home, when you know that I did not stay at home either. We left our homes together, went forth together, traveled abroad together, and have been exposed to the same lot and destiny. If you were tossed in a blanket on one occasion, I was pummeled on a hundred others, and this is the only advantage I hold over you."

"That's only reasonable," said Sancho, "for according to what your grace has said, misfortunes are more closely associated with knights-errant than with their squires."

"That is where you are wrong, Sancho," said Don Quixote, "for according to that, *quando caput dolet*. . ., etc." [1]

"I don't understand any language but my own," said Sancho.

"I mean," said Don Quixote, "that when one's head aches, every member of his body will ache, and since I am your lord and master, I am your head, and you, as my servant, are a member of my body. Therefore, any affliction I suffer will bring you pain, as yours will me."

"That's the way it ought to be," said Sancho, "but when I was being blanketed as a member of the body, my head was on the other side of the wall watching me sail through the air and not feeling any discomfort in this world. Now, since the members are obliged to bear the pain of the head, the head should be obliged to bear theirs as well."

"Do you mean to say, Sancho," said Don Quixote, "that I felt no pain when they were tossing you? If that is what you are implying, don't say it or even think it, for at that moment I felt more pain in my soul than you did in your entire body. But let us set this aside for the present, since there will be time later to ponder and straighten things out. Tell me, Sancho my friend, what are they saying about me in the village? How am I esteemed by the masses? how by the hidalgos? and how by the knights? What do they say of my valor, my deeds, and my gentility? What do they think of my decision to revive and restore to the world the now forgotten order of chivalry? In short, Sancho, pray tell me what has reached your ears regarding this matter and you are to do so without adding a single thing that is good or removing anything that is bad, for it is the responsibility of loyal vassals to tell their lords the truth in its pure, unadulterated form without letting adulation increase it or vain consideration diminish it. I would have you know, Sancho, that if the bare truth were to reach the ears of the nobility without the trappings of flattery, other times would prevail and past ages would be considered ages of iron rather than our own, which, if I may choose from among the labels currently in use, I would say is the age of gold. Take this advice to heart, Sancho, and give me a true and faithful report of the things I

1 The complete Latin expression is: ***Quando caput dolet, caetara membra dolent,*** meaning: 'When the head aches, the other members will ache as well.'

have asked you which you have news of."

"My lord, I will very gladly do so," said Sancho, "if you promise not to get angry at what I say, since you want me to tell you the bare truth without dressing it in any more clothes than it was wearing when it came to my attention."

"Under no circumstances shall I get angry," said Don Quixote, "so you may speak freely, Sancho, without beating about the bush."

"Well, the first thing I have to say," replied Sancho, "is that the masses consider your grace a raving lunatic and me no less a fool. The hidalgos say you have not been content to remain one of them but have given yourself the title of 'Don' and become a knight, owning a few vines, a couple acres of land, and the clothes on your back. The knights say they wouldn't want the hidalgos to start competing with them, especially those hidalgos who polish their own shoes and darn the toes of their black stockings with colored thread."

"That," said Don Quixote, "does not apply to me. I am always well dressed and my clothes are never patched – torn maybe but never patched, and the tears are due more to my armor than to time."

To which Sancho replied,

"As for your grace's courage, gentility, deeds, and mission, there are differing opinions: some call you crazy but amusing; others, brave but unfortunate; still others, polite but officious; but everyone goes about making so many comments you don't have a healthy bone left in your body and neither do I."

"Look, Sancho," said Don Quixote, "wherever virtue exists to an eminent degree, it is always persecuted. Few if any of the famous personages of the past have escaped calumny at the hands of malice. Julius Caesar, that extremely spirited, wise, and courageous captain, was accused of being ambitious and somewhat unclean both in his clothing and in his personal habits. Alexander, whose exploits won him the epithet 'the Great,' was said to have a certain tendency towards drunkenness. It is related that Hercules, the many-labored one, was lascivious and effeminate. It is also rumored that Don Galaor, Amadís of Gaul's brother, was more than a little quarrelsome and his brother was a cry-baby. So, my dear Sancho, compared to the untold calumnies against those good souls mine will manage quite well so long as they are no worse than those you have mentioned."

"That's the problem, darn it!" said Sancho.

"There is more?" asked Don Quixote.

"We still have the tail to skin," said Sancho. "Everything up to now has been cookies and cream but, if you want to know all the slanderous things being said about you, I'll bring someone here right now who'll tell you everything without omitting a single detail. Last night, Bartolomé Carrasco's son came home from Salamanca, where he has been studying and has just received his bachelor's degree. When I went by to welcome him home, he informed me that your grace's history was already making the rounds in a book called *The Ingenious Hidalgo Don Quixote of La Mancha*, and he says they mention me in it by my very own name, Sancho Panza, along with the lady Dulcinea of Toboso, as well as several things we did when there was no one present except us. I was so shocked at this I made the sign of the cross, asking myself how the historian could have learned of all the things he described."

"I assure you, Sancho," said Don Quixote, "that the author of our history must be some wise enchanter, for nothing they wish to describe is ever hidden from them."

"But," said Sancho, "how can he be an enchanter or wise when the author of the history is called Cide Hamete Berengena, [2] according to the bachelor Carrasco, this being the name of the man I mentioned?"

"That name is Moorish," replied Don Quixote.

"That's probably true," said Sancho, "for I've heard it said that more often than not Moors are very fond of eggplant."

"You must be mistaken, Sancho, about the surname of this *Cide*, which means 'Lord' in Arabic."

"That may be," said Sancho, "but if your grace would like me to bring him here, I can do so in nothing flat."

"That would make me very happy, my friend, for I am so confused by what you have told me that nothing I eat will taste right till I am fully informed on this matter."

"Then I'll go get him," said Sancho.

And leaving his master, he went to find the bachelor, with whom he returned a short time later, whereupon the three of them engaged in a most amusing conversation.

Chapter Three

The amusing conversation between Don Quixote, Sancho Panza, and the bachelor Sansón Carrasco

Don Quixote was more than a little anxious as he waited for the bachelor Carrasco, from whom he expected to hear what had been published about himself, as Sancho had said, but he was not convinced that any such book existed, for the blood of the enemies he had slain was still not dry on the blade of his sword and here they were insisting that his mighty deeds of knighthood were already circulating in print. Despite this, he imagined that by means of enchantment some sage, either friend or foe, was responsible for having them printed – if a friend, to exalt and elevate them above the most distinguished ones of knight-errantry, but if a foe, to humble and place them lower than the basest ones ever recorded of a lowly squire, though he reminded himself that the exploits of squires had never been written down. Still, even if it was true that such a history did exist, inasmuch as it dealt with a knight-errant, it would necessarily be grandiloquent, lofty, illustrious, magnificent, and true. In this way he was able to console himself somewhat but was distressed by the thought that its author was a Moor, a fact he had inferred from the name 'Cide', for no truth whatsoever was to be expected from Moors because they were all liars, falsifiers, and fantasizers. He feared the author had treated his amours with a lack of delicacy that might work to the discredit

2 ***Berengena*** is the Spanish word for 'eggplant'.

and detriment of the virtue of his lady Dulcinea of Toboso. He hoped the author had recorded both his fidelity and the decorum he had always displayed in his disdain of queens, empresses, and maidens of every description, together with his self-control over his natural impulses. Sancho and Carrasco found Don Quixote embroiled and ensnared in these and other such fantasies but were received by him with the utmost graciousness.

The bachelor, who was not very large despite his name Sansón, [1] was about twenty-four years of age, intelligent, and rather crafty, in addition to having a sallow complexion, a round face, a flat nose, and a large mouth – all indications that he was of a mischievous disposition and fond of practical jokes, which he demonstrated when he saw Don Quixote by kneeling at his feet and saying,

"May I kiss your grace's hand, Sir Don Quixote of La Mancha, for I swear by the habit of Saint Peter I am wearing, though having completed only the first four orders, that you are one of the most renowned knights-errant who ever walked or ever shall walk upon the face of the earth. Praised be Cide Hamete Benengeli, who has recorded your grace's history, and doubly praised be the diligent soul who has taken the trouble to have it translated from Arabic into our every-day Castilian for the universal enjoyment of mankind."

Don Quixote made him rise and then said,

"In that case, is it true there is a history of me, and the one who composed it was a Moor and a sage?"

"It is so true, my lord," said Sansón, "that it is my understanding that at this very hour more than twelve thousand copies of the history are in print, which Portugal, Barcelona, and Valencia can attest to, for that is where they have been printed. And there is even a report that it is being printed in Antwerp. My guess is there will be no nation or language on earth that will not have its own translation."

"One of the things," said Don Quixote at this point, "that must be most pleasing to a virtuous and eminent man is to see himself in print in his lifetime and be praised by the masses. I said 'praised', for if the opposite is true, there is no death that can equal it."

"Speaking of a good name and reputation," said the bachelor, "your grace has single-handedly carried off the palm against every other knight-errant. The Moor in his language and the Christian in his have taken great pains to paint us a most life-like picture of your gallantry, your great courage in confronting perils, your patience in adversity and suffering, your ability to bear misfortune as well as pain, and your continence and purity in your platonic loves with my lady Doña Dulcinea of Toboso."

"Never," said Sancho Panza at this point, "have I heard my lady called *Doña* Dulcinea but simply the lady Dulcinea of Toboso. Therefore, on this point the history is already mistaken."

"But that is an objection of little importance," said Carrasco.

"Of course," said Don Quixote, "but tell me, sir bachelor, which of my exploits are most highly praised in this history?"

"On that point," said the bachelor, "there are as many different opinions as there are different tastes. Some prefer the adventure of the windmills, which your grace fancied to be Briareus and

1 Spanish for 'Samson.'

various other giants; others prefer the fulling-mill; another the description of the two armies that later took on the appearance of two flocks of sheep; this other one praises the episode of the corpse being carried to Segovia for burial; another considers the freeing of the galley slaves to be unsurpassed; and still another says none can equal that of the two Benedictine giants and the fight with the valiant Biscayan."

"Tell me, sir bachelor," said Sancho at this point, "does it include the adventure of the Yangüesans, when our good Rocinante got the urge to attempt the impossible?"

"The sage left nothing in the inkwell," replied Sansón; "he reveals every last thing, even the somersaults our noble Sancho performed in the blanket."

"I didn't perform any somersaults in the blanket," retorted Sancho, "but in the air I did, and even more of them than I would have liked."

"The way I see it," said Don Quixote, "there is no history on earth dealing with the human race that does not have its ups and downs, particularly those having to do with knight-errantry, for even they must contain some unsuccessful adventures."

"Nevertheless," said the bachelor, "some who have read the book would be just as pleased if its authors had omitted a few of the endless beatings Don Quixote was administered in the various encounters."

"But that's where the history's authenticity comes in," said Sancho.

"Even so," said Don Quixote, "they might have passed over them in silence out of a sense of fairness, for there is no reason to record actions that neither change nor affect the truth of the history, particularly if they lessen one's respect for the hero of that history. I dare say Aeneas was not nearly so compassionate as Virgil paints him, nor Ulysses half so prudent as Homer describes him."

"That is true," said Sansón, "but it is one thing to write as a poet and quite another to write as a historian. The poet may relate or embellish things, not as they were, but as they should have been, whereas the historian must describe them, not as they should have been, but as they actually were, without adding or subtracting a single thing from the truth."

"Well now," said Sancho, "if that Moorish gentleman sticks to telling the truth, my beatings will surely be found alongside those of my master, for people never took the measure of his grace's back without taking it of my entire body. But there's no reason for me to be surprised at that, for, as my very own master has said, the body's members are to share in the head's suffering."

"You are a sly devil, Sancho," said Don Quixote. "I dare say your memory never fails you when there is something you want to remember."

"Even if I wanted to forget the cudgeling I've received, my bruises wouldn't allow it, they're still so fresh on my ribs."

"That is enough, Sancho," said Don Quixote; "stop interrupting our esteemed bachelor, whom I beg to continue relating what is said of me in this history."

"And of me too," said Sancho, "for they also say I'm one of the pretagonists in it."

"*Pro*tagonists, Sancho my friend, not *pre*tagonists," corrected Sansón.

"So, we have us another word vigilante, do we?" replied Sancho. "If we get started on that, we won't finish in our entire lives."

"May mine be one of sorrow, Sancho," said the bachelor, "if you are not the second most important person in the history. In fact, there are those who would rather listen to you than to the most outstanding person in the whole book, though there are also those who say you were too gullible in believing that business of the island promised you by our lord Don Quixote, who is here present."

"It is never too late," said Don Quixote, "and the older Sancho becomes, what with the experience that age brings, the more skillfully he will be able to govern than he is now."

"For goodness sake, master," said Sancho, "the island I can't govern at my present age I won't be able to govern if I live to be as old as Methuselah. The trouble lies in the fact that the island is waiting for me God knows where – not in the fact that I don't have the brains to govern it."

"Trust in the Lord," said Don Quixote, "and everything will be put aright, perhaps even better than you imagine, for there is not a leaf on a tree that stirs except by God's will."

"That is certainly true," said Sansón, "for if it is God's will, Sancho will have a thousand islands to govern, let alone one."

"I've seen governors in these parts," said Sancho, "who aren't worthy to shine my boots and yet they're addressed as 'your lordship' and are served on plates of silver."

"Those are not governors of islands," said Sansón, "but of other more manageable types of government, for those who govern islands should at least know something in the province of grammar."

"I'm perfectly comfortable in the provinces," replied Sancho, "but I want no part of that Grammar, since I have no idea where it is. However, I'll leave the matter of governing in the hands of God and will trust Him to place me wherever He can make the best use of me. I'll merely say, Sir Bachelor Sansón Carrasco, that I'm infinitely pleased that the author of this history has spoken so highly of me that people are not annoyed by the things he has said; but I assure your grace as a faithful squire that, had he said things about me that were unworthy of a long-time Christian, which I am, the deaf themselves would be able to hear us."

"That would be working miracles," said Sansón.

"Miracles or no miracles," replied Sancho, "let each person mind what he says or writes about others and not put down helter-skelter the first things that come into his head."

"One of the blemishes they find in this history," said the bachelor, "is that its author included in it a novella entitled *The Tale of Unreasonable Curiosity*, and not because it is bad or poorly written but because it does not belong there and has nothing to do with the story of his grace Sir Don Quixote."

"I'll bet," added Sancho, "that that son of a she-dog has turned everything upside down."

"In that case," said Don Quixote, "I can state that the author of my history was no sage but some babbling ignoramus who, gropingly and without any plan, set about writing down come what might, as Orbaneja the painter from Ubeda did, who, when asked what he was painting, would say, 'Whatever it turns out to be.' He might, for example, have been painting a rooster that was so unrecognizable it was necessary to print beside it in capital letters: *THIS IS A ROOSTER*. It will probably be the same with my history, which will need a commentary to be intelligible."

"No it won't," said Sansón, "for there is nothing difficult in it. It is so clear children thumb through its pages, young persons read it, adults understand it, and the elderly sing its praises. In a word, it is taken up so often, read so many times, and studied so thoroughly by all sorts of people that no sooner do they spot some skinny nag than they say, 'There goes Rocinante.' The ones most given to reading it are the pages, for there is no lord's antechamber in which you will not find a copy of *Don Quixote*, and no sooner does one put it down than another picks it up and while this one has his head buried in it, another asks him for it. In short, this history is one of the most pleasurable and least harmful entertainments seen up to the present time because nowhere in the entire book does one find anything resembling an indecent word or a less-than-Catholic thought."

"To write in any other manner," said Don Quixote, "would be to write not truthfully but falsely. Historians who avail themselves of falsehoods should be burned at the stake like those who coin counterfeit money. I have no idea what induced the author to make use of extraneous novellas and tales when there were so many of my affairs to describe. He was undoubtedly following the proverb that says, 'Variety is the spice of life,' for by simply setting forth my thoughts, sighs, tears, good intentions, and endeavors, he could have compiled a volume as large or larger than that containing all the works of Tostado. In fact, sir bachelor, it is my understanding that in order to write histories and books, regardless of their nature, one must be quite discriminating and possess a mature understanding, for to write with wit and humor requires very great talent. The cleverest character in drama is the fool, because anyone who would be taken for a fool must not act like one. History is like something holy in that it must be truthful, for wherever there is truth, there too is God, and yet, there are some who write books and toss them off as though they were fritters."

"There is no book so bad," said the bachelor, "that it does not contain something good."

"Absolutely true," replied Don Quixote, "but it often happens that those who have deservedly won and achieved a great deal of renown by circulating their works in manuscript lose it entirely or see it considerably diminished once their books are in print."

"The reason for that," said Sansón, "is that, because printed books may be perused in a leisurely manner, it is easy to spot their defects. Also the greater the fame of the author who composed them, the greater will be the scrutiny of his works. Thus, writers renowned for their genius, great poets, and illustrious historians are always, or nearly always, envied by those who take a particular delight and pleasure in judging the writings of others, having never given birth to any of their own."

"That is not surprising," said Don Quixote, "for there are many theologians who are unsuited for the pulpit but are excellent when it comes to recognizing the defects and excesses of those who preach."

"All that is true," said Carrasco, "but I wish those critics would be more forgiving and less fastidious and would stop quibbling about the spots on the brilliant sun that is the work they are criticizing, for if *aliquando bonus dormitat Homerus,* [2] they should consider how many hours he stayed awake to make his work shine with as few spots as possible. Besides, it may be that the things they considered unsightly were moles, which often increase the beauty of the faces they adorn. Because of this, I contend that one runs a truly great risk in having a book printed, since it is absolutely impossible to write it in such a way as to satisfy and please everyone who reads it."

2 Latin: 'from time to time the noble Homer dozes.'

"The one that deals with me has probably pleased very few," said Don Quixote.

"Quite the contrary, for just as *stultorum infinitus est numerus,* [3] infinite in number are those who have enjoyed the history in question. Some, though, have accused the author of fraud or having a poor memory, for he forgot to explain who the thief was who stole Sancho's dapple, and it is never explained and even the fact that it was stolen can only be inferred from the context. But a short while later, we see Sancho riding the same ass without its ever having reappeared. They say too that he forgot to say what Sancho did with the hundred *escudos* he found in the valise in the Sierra Morena, which he never again mentions, and there are many who would like to know how he disposed of them or what he spent them on, which is one of the major omissions of the work."

"Sir Sansón," said Sancho, "I am in no mood at this time to do any explaining, for my stomach is so delicate that if I don't settle it down with a couple of swigs of old wine, I'm going to waste away to nothing. I've got some at home, where my better half is waiting for me, and as soon as I've eaten, I'll come back and satisfy your grace and anyone else regarding any questions you might care to put to me – the loss of the ass as well as the disposal of the hundred *escudos.*"

And without waiting for an answer or saying another word, he set out for home. Don Quixote begged and pleaded with the bachelor to stay and do penance at his meager table. The bachelor accepted the invitation and a couple of pigeons were added to the regular fare. Carrasco humored Don Quixote by engaging him in a discussion of knight-errantry, and once the banquet came to an end, they observed the afternoon siesta. Later, when Sancho returned, the foregoing conversation was resumed.

Chapter Four

Sancho Panza addresses the doubts and questions of the bachelor Sansón Carrasco, together with other incidents worth knowing and relating

Sancho returned to Don Quixote's house, where he continued the foregoing conversation, saying,

"In response to Sir Sansón's stated desire to know how, when, and by whom my jackass was stolen, let me just say that on the very night that we entered the Sierra Morena to escape the Holy Brotherhood, following the ill-ventured adventure of the galley slaves and that of the corpse being carried to Segovia, my master and I hid in a grove. With me there on my jackass and my master astride his horse supporting himself with his lance, and both of us battered and exhausted from our recent encounters, we fell asleep as though we were stretched out on a pair of feather beds. I in particular slept so soundly that someone or other had the opportunity to come over and prop me up

3 Latin: 'the number of fools is infinite;' from Ecclesiastes I, 15.

on four stakes, which he placed under the four corners of the saddle so he could remove my jackass from beneath me without my feeling a thing. This he did and I was left sitting there in the saddle."

"That is easy enough to do," said Sansón, "and it is certainly not new, for the same thing happened to Sacripante during the siege of Albraca when, by using the same device, that famous thief known as Brunelo slipped Sacripante's horse out from under him."

"Dawn arrived," continued Sancho, "and no sooner did I stretch my muscles than the stakes gave way and I fell to the ground with a thud. I looked about for my jackass but couldn't find him. Tears gushed from my eyes and I let out such a howl that if the author of our history has failed to record it, I can assure him he has committed a grave oversight. At the end of heaven-knows-how-many days, while traveling with the lady Princess Micomicona, I recognized my jackass and saw that the one riding him, dressed as a gypsy, was Ginés de Pasamonte, that great swindler and hoodlum that my master and I freed from the chain gang."

"That is not where the mistake lies," said Sansón, "but in the fact that before the animal reappears the author says Sancho is riding his very own dapple."

"I don't know how to explain that," said Sancho, "except to say that either the historian made a mistake or it was probably carelessness on the part of the printer."

"That is what happened without a doubt," replied Sansón, "but what became of the hundred *escudos*? Did they simply vanish?"

"I spent them," said Sancho, "on myself, my wife, and my children. This is the reason my wife has tolerated my traveling over highways and byways with his lord Don Quixote, for after such a long absence if I had come home without a cent or without the ass, there would've been the Devil himself to pay. If there is anything else your graces would like to know, here I am personally prepared to answer the king himself but it's nobody's business whether I brought the *escudos* or spent them, for if I got paid for all the beatings I've received on these treks and these were valued at just four *maravedís* apiece, another hundred *escudos* wouldn't pay for half of them. Let each person look into his own heart before becoming judge of what is right and wrong, for each person is the way God made him and oftentimes even worse."

"I shall make certain," said Carrasco, "to remind the author of the history not to forget what our good Sancho has said if he should have it sent back to the presses, which will make it a mite better than it already is."

"Is there anything else that needs correcting in that history, sir bachelor?" asked Don Quixote.

"There must be something but nothing can be as serious as the things already mentioned."

"Does the author by any chance promise us a second part?" asked Don Quixote.

"He does," replied Sansón, "but since he says he has not found it and does not know who has it, we have our doubts as to whether or not it will be published. Because of this, together with the fact that some people say sequels are never very good, while others say that all the things already written about Don Quixote are sufficient, it is feared there may not be a second part. Nevertheless, some who are more Jovian than Saturnine say, 'Give us more Quixoticisms; just let the knight attack and Sancho Panza talk and we'll be satisfied with whatever there is.'"

"And what does the author intend to do?"

"As soon as he is able to locate the history," said Sansón, "which he is looking for with the utmost diligence, he will have it printed without delay, being motivated more by the profit he will derive from it than by any sort of adulation."

To which Sancho said,

"So the author is looking for money and profits? It'll be a miracle if he succeeds, for he'll simply work faster and faster like a tailor on the night before Easter, and works performed in haste never display the perfection they should. Let that Moorish gentleman, or whatever he is, pay careful attention to what he's doing, for my master and I will provide him with such a variety of adventures and experiences that he'll be able to write not only a second part but a hundredth. The good man undoubtedly thinks we don't know what is going on but just let him hold up our feet for shoeing and he'll see which leg we limp on. What I mean is that if my master were to take my advice, we would already be on the plains remedying grievances and righting wrongs in accordance with the usage and custom of good knights-errant."

Sancho had scarcely finished this speech when the neighing of Rocinante reached their ears. Don Quixote interpreted this neighing as a good omen and resolved to sally forth once again in the next three or four days. Declaring his intentions to the bachelor, he asked his advice as to where he might begin his travels. The latter replied that in his opinion he should visit the kingdom of Aragon and the city of Saragossa, where within the next few days some very important jousts would be held during the Festival of St. George in which he could win renown for himself over all the knights of Aragon, which would be tantamount to distinguishing himself over all those on earth. The bachelor praised his decision as being quite brave and honorable but warned him to be extremely careful in his perilous confrontations because his life was not his own but belonged to all those who needed him to assist them in their misfortunes.

"That's the part I detest, Sir Sansón," said Sancho at this point. "My master would as soon lay into a hundred armed men as a gluttonous lad would into half a dozen melons. Hang it all, sir bachelor, there's a time to attack and a time to retreat; it shouldn't always be: 'Charge, in the name of St. James and Spain!' Besides, I've heard it said – and by my master himself I believe, if I'm not mistaken – that between the extremes of cowardice and foolhardiness there is the middle course of bravery, and if this is so, I wouldn't have him withdraw without good reason or attack when all the odds are against him but, above all, I would advise my master that if he intends to take me with him, it must be on the condition that he will do all the fighting and my only obligation will be to look after his person in the areas of hygiene and comfort, for in these respects I'll attend to his every need. But to imagine that I'll draw my sword, even if it's against some lowly, churlish peasant, is to imagine the impossible. I, Sir Sansón, am not seeking to win fame as someone valiant but as the best and most loyal squire who ever served a knight-errant, but if my master Don Quixote, obligated by my many worthy services, should wish to bestow upon me one of the many islands he says he's certain to meet with out there, I'll consider it a great honor. On the other hand, should he not do so, I was born into this world and no born soul should put his trust in anyone except God. Besides, bread may taste just as good to me, or even better, in not governing than in governing. And how do I know that somewhere among those governments the Devil is not waiting to trip me up, whereby I'll fall down and knock out all my teeth? Sancho I was born and Sancho I intend to die. On the other hand, should heaven voluntarily provide me with an island or something similar which I need not solicit and which will be virtually risk-free, I'll not be so foolish as to refuse it, for there's the saying: 'When they offer you a heifer, run and fetch a rope,' and this other one: 'When good fortune comes knocking at your door, invite it in.'"

"Brother Sancho," said Carrasco, "you have spoken like a university professor but, notwithstanding that, trust in God and in Don Quixote, who will provide you with a whole kingdom and not just an island."

"Too much is as bad as too little," replied Sancho, "though I can assure Sir Carrasco that my master would not be putting his kingdom into a sack with a hole in it, for I have felt my own pulse and find myself sound enough to rule kingdoms and govern islands, as I've explained to my master on a number of other occasions."

"Mark you well, Sancho," said Sansón, "a new profession alters one's habits. It may turn out that once you see yourself governor, you will refuse to recognize the mother who bore you."

"That," said Sancho, "may hold true for those who were born on the wrong side of town but not for those whose souls are covered by a two-inch thick layer of Christian orthodoxy, as mine is. Why, just examine my features: do I look like a person who could be ungrateful to anyone?"

"May God make you strong," said Don Quixote, "but we shall learn the answer when the governorship arrives, which, by the way, I think I can see in my mind's eye."

After saying this, he mentioned to the bachelor that if he was a poet, he might favor him by composing a few verses dealing with his intended leave-taking of his lady Dulcinea of Toboso, making sure to begin each line with a letter of her name so that, when all the verses were complete, the first letters of all the lines would read: 'Dulcinea of Toboso.' The bachelor said that despite the fact that he was not one of the famous poets of Spain, who were said to be three and a half in number, he promised to compose such a poem, though he felt its composition would be fraught with difficulty because there were seventeen letters in her name.[1] If he were to use four stanzas of four lines each, there would be one letter left over; or if he used stanzas of five lines each, which are called *décimas* or *redondillas*, there would be three letters too few. Nevertheless, he would try to fit the extra line in somewhere so that the four stanzas would contain the name 'Dulcinea of Toboso.'

"That is how it must be in any case," said Don Quixote, "for if the name is not obvious and clear, there is not a woman in existence who will believe the poem was not composed for her."

They reached an understanding on this as well as on the date of departure, which they set for a week from then. Don Quixote charged the bachelor to keep it secret, especially from the priest, Master Nicolás, his niece, and the housekeeper lest they undermine his honorable and worthwhile resolution. Promising to do so, Carrasco bade them farewell and charged Don Quixote with keeping him informed at his convenience of everything that befell him: the good and the bad alike. With this, they took leave of one another and Sancho went off to gather the provisions they would need for the journey.

---

1 Her Spanish name ***Dulcinea del Toboso*** has 17 letters, which accounts for the bachelor's concern.

Chapter Five

The astute and comical conversation that Sancho Panza held with his wife Teresa Panza, together with other incidents happily worth recording

When the translator of our history comes to write this fifth chapter, he says he considers it apocryphal, for in it Sancho Panza speaks differently from what might be expected from a person of his limited understanding. The author feels it would be impossible for Sancho to make such subtle observations but, because he is loath to leave them untranslated, preferring to comply with the obligations of his profession, he goes on to write:

Sancho returned home in such high spirits that his wife could detect his happiness from the distance of a musket-shot, which led her to ask,

"What are you bringing home, Sancho my love, that has made you so cheerful?"

To which he responded,

"Wife dear, I would be just as content, God willing, if I were not as cheerful as I appear."

"I don't understand you, husband," she replied. "I don't know what you mean by saying you would be just as content, God willing, not to be as cheerful as you appear. I may be stupid but I don't know why anyone would choose not to be happy."

"Look, Teresa," said Sancho, "I'm happy because I've once again decided to serve my master Don Quixote, who intends to set out a third time in quest of adventures and I'm going to accompany him again because of my poverty and the comforting hope I have of finding another hundred *escudos* like those I've already spent, though I'm equally saddened by the thought of having to be separated from you and the children. If God would only see to it to provide me with food while allowing me to remain safely at home rather than dragging me over every conceivable type of terrain – which He could do at very little expense to Himself and by a simple command – it's clear that my happiness would be more resolute and binding, for what little I do have is mingled with the sadness of leaving you. Therefore, I spoke correctly when I said I would be just as content, if it were God's will, not to be as happy as I am."

"Look, Sancho, since you became a member of the fraternity of knights, you speak in such roundabout ways there's no one who can understand you."

"It is sufficient if God understands me, wife," said Sancho, "for He understands all things; but let's drop the subject. By the way, my dear, it's most urgent that you look after the dapple for the next three days to make sure he'll be fit and raring to go; double his feed and be sure to check his packsaddle and harness. Remember that we're not going to some wedding but will be roaming over the entire earth, doing battle with giants and all sorts of horrible monsters that hiss, bellow, roar, and screech; and even all this will be a bed of roses if we don't have to contend with Yangüesans and enchanted Moors."

"I certainly believe, husband," said Teresa, "that squires-errant earn their bread, so I will ask Our Lord to give you a speedy release from such awful ordeals."

"I can tell you, wife," replied Sancho, "that if I didn't think I would see myself governor of an island before long, I would drop dead right here on the spot."

"Don't do that, husband dear," said Teresa. "'Let the hen live even if she has the pip.' You keep on living and let the Devil have all the governments there are on earth. You came from your mother's womb without a government, you've lived till now without one, and when God chooses, you'll go or be carried to your grave without one. Why, there are those who go their whole lives without a government but they don't for that reason cease to exist or to count themselves among the living. 'The best spice on earth is hunger' and since those who are poor never lack for that, they always enjoy what they eat. And remember, Sancho, if by some chance you find yourself in possession of a government, don't forget me and the children. Remember too that Sanchico is now every bit of fifteen and by all rights should be going to school, that is, if his uncle the abbot intends to have him groomed for the Church. Also, your daughter Mari Sancha wouldn't exactly die if we let her get married, for she's showing signs of wanting to have a husband the way you're wanting to be a governor, and when you come right down to it, I'd rather have a daughter who's unhappily married than happily prostituted."

"I give you my word," said Sancho, "that if God should give me a decent government, I would marry Mari Sancha so high above her station no one would approach her without calling her 'your ladyship.'"

"Anything but that, Sancho," replied Teresa; "marry her to her equal, which will be far better. If you raise her from clogs to high-heel shoes, from plain gray skirts to hoop skirts and silk petticoats, from 'Marica' and 'you' to 'Doña So-and-so' and 'your ladyship,' the girl won't know who she is and will do something dumb every time she turns round that will expose the weave of her coarse, crude fabric."

"Don't be silly," said Sancho, "it'll take her no more than two or three years to become accustomed and then nobility and dignity will fit her like a glove, and even if they don't, who cares? So long as she's 'your ladyship,' let come what may."

"Be content with what you are, Sancho," said Teresa, "and don't get above your raising. Remember the proverb that says, 'If your neighbor's son comes to your door, wipe his nose and take him in.' It would be a fine thing indeed to marry our María to some high and mighty gentleman or count who, every time he felt like it, would put her in her place by calling her a peasant and the daughter of clodhoppers and laborers! Not as long as I'm alive, husband! Is this what I've raised my daughter to be? You bring home the money, Sancho, and leave the marrying to me. There's Juan Tocho's son Lope, a solid, sturdy lad we already know, who, I'm sure, has a hankering for the girl. With this lad, who's our equal, the girl will be happily married and we can always keep an eye on him. We'll all be together: parents, children, grandchildren, and sons- and daughters-in-law, and peace and God's blessings will dwell among us; so don't go marrying her into those courts and fancy palaces where they won't understand her and she won't understand herself."

"You brainless ninny," retorted Sancho, "why without rhyme or reason do you now want to keep me from marrying my daughter to someone who'll give me grandchildren who'll be addressed as 'your lordship' and 'your ladyship'? Listen, Teresa, I've always heard my elders say that anyone who doesn't have enough sense to accept good luck when it comes his way doesn't have the right to complain when it passes him by. It wouldn't be wise, now that it's knocking at our door, not to let it in. Why not sail with the favorable wind that's blowing?"

(It is because of this manner of speaking, together with what Sancho says farther along, that the translator of our history says he considers the present chapter apocryphal.) Nevertheless, Sancho went on to say,

"Don't you see, you creature, what a wonderful thing it'll be if I personally land some lucrative governorship that will lift us out of the mud? Just let Mari Sancha marry the person I want her to and you'll see yourself called Doña Teresa and will get to sit in church on carpets and cushions despite the way the noblewomen of the village happen to feel. You stay just the way you are without changing your nature one bit, like a figure in a tapestry – but let's drop the subject because Sanchica is going to be a countess, regardless of how you feel."

"Husband, do you realize what you're saying? With all that, I'm afraid my daughter's becoming a countess will be her undoing. Do whatever you please, though. Make her a duchess or a princess but I can assure you it'll not be with my consent or approval. My dear, I have always believed in equality and can't abide uncalled-for haughtiness. They named me Teresa at my baptism, a plain, unadorned name without the frills, trappings, or frippery of gifts and presents. My father's family name was Cascajo and since I'm your wife, they call me Teresa Panza – whereas by rights they should call me Teresa Cascajo, but 'God proposes and man disposes' – and I'm satisfied with this name without anyone's putting a 'Doña' on top of it that'll make it so heavy I won't be able to carry it. Nor do I want to provide any excuse for people to comment when they see me pass by dressed as a countess or a governor's wife, for they'll immediately say, 'Look at the way pompous Miss Pigsty is acting! Only yesterday she was content to sit at her loom spinning flax or to go to mass with her skirt hoisted over her head instead of a shawl, but today she goes about with her hoopskirt, brooches, and airs as though we didn't know her.' If God will preserve my seven or five senses, or however many I have, I never intend to find myself in such a predicament. You, my pet, may go find yourself a government or an island and give yourself airs to your heart's content. I, however, swear by my mother's soul that my daughter and I are not going to budge one step from our village. 'A respectable woman and a broken leg should both stay at home;' besides, 'Keeping busy is the proper recreation for a virtuous girl.' You go off with your Don Quixote to your adventures and leave us women to our misadventures, for God will improve our lot if we will just behave ourselves. And another thing: I certainly don't know where he came by that 'Don', for neither his parents nor grandparents ever used it."

"I declare," said Sancho, "you've got a demon in that body of yours. Women! What a bunch of nonsense to string together without rhyme or reason! What does Cascajo or brooches or proverbs or this haughtiness have to do with what I'm saying? Listen here, you ignorant ninny, which is what I can call you because you don't understand anything I'm saying and you flee from happiness, if I were to ask my daughter to fling herself off some high tower or go wandering through the world the way the princess Doña Urraca chose to do, you would be justified in not complying with my wishes but, if in less time than it takes to bat an eye I dress her up with a 'Doña' and a 'ladyship' and take her out of the country, placing her on a canopied dais or in a chamber with more velvet cushions than there were Moors in the Almohadas family of Morocco, [1] why do you refuse to give in to my wishes?"

"Do you want to know why, husband?" replied Teresa; "because of the proverb that says, 'You can take the girl out of the country but you can't take the country out of the girl!' and because people hardly give a poor person a second glance but stand and stare at one who's rich. But if this rich person has ever been poor, then here come the gossips, the slanderers, and, worst of all, the backbiters, who are as plentiful in the streets as a swarm of bees."

"Look, Teresa," said Sancho, "and listen to what I have to tell you, the likes of which you may never have heard in all your born days. Nothing I am now about to tell you comes out of my head but is from the sermon our village priest preached this past Lent. He said, if I remember correctly, that objects that our eyes happen to be viewing at the moment are more vivid and fix themselves in our memory better and more indelibly than ones from the past."

(This speech of Sancho's is the second one that leads the translator to claim the present chapter is apocryphal, inasmuch as it exceeds Sancho's capabilities.)

"Because of this," continued Sancho, "when we see some person who is well dressed, attired in expensive clothes, and accompanied by a host of servants, we seem to be uncontrollably compelled to hold him in esteem, though there may come to mind at that very instant some base circumstance in which we once saw this person. But this baseness, which had to do either with his poverty or ancestry, is no longer real, since it is a thing of the past, and the only thing that is real is what is presently before our eyes. Now, this particular person whom fortune has raised from his once lowly position – and these were the exact words the priest used – to the heights of prosperity, so long as he is well-bred, generous, courteous to everyone, and doesn't try to compete with those who are nobles of long standing, you may be certain, Teresa, that no one will remember what he used to be but will respect him for what he is now, except, of course, those who are envious, for from them no good name is ever safe."

"I don't understand you, husband," said Teresa, "but do whatever you please and stop exasperating me with your harangues and subtleties. If you're absolutely dissolute in your decision—"

"You mean *res*olute, woman, not *dis*solute."

"Don't start an argument with me, husband," said Teresa. "I talk the way God wants me to and am not one for using highfalutin language. I suggest that, if you are determined to get a government, you take along our son Sancho and start teaching him how to manage one, since it's proper for sons to inherit and learn their fathers' trades."

"As soon as I get a government," replied Sancho, "I'll send for him by post and will send you some money, which I'm bound to have, since there's always someone at hand ready to lend governors money when they don't have any of their own; and dress him in such a way that he'll not show what he is but will give the appearance of what he's going to be."

"You send the money," said Teresa, "and I'll dress him up so you won't recognize him."

"Then we're agreed after all," said Sancho, "that our daughter will be a countess."

---

1 ***Almohadas,*** Spanish for 'cushions'. The family's name was actually ***Almohades***.

"The day I see her a countess," said Teresa, "will be the day I know I'm laying her away. But I repeat that you may do whatever makes you happy, for we women are born under this burden: to be obedient to our husbands even when they are dunces."

At this point she began to sob fitfully, as though she already saw Sanchica dead and buried. Sancho consoled her by saying that even though he intended to make her a countess, he would delay doing so for as long as possible. With this, their conversation came to an end and Sancho went back to see Don Quixote to make arrangements for their departure.

Chapter Six

The things that took place between Don Quixote and his niece and housekeeper, which is one of the most important chapters in this entire history

While Sancho Panza and his wife Teresa Cascajo were engaged in the above gratuitous conversation, Don Quixote's niece and housekeeper did not stand idly by, for they had begun to infer from a thousand different signs that their uncle and master was about to tear free a third time to take up once again his (to them) accursed knight-errantry. They used every means possible to divert him from such unhealthy thinking but it was as productive as preaching in the wilderness or hammering cold iron. Nevertheless, among a number of things said to him by the housekeeper was the following:

"Really, my lord, if you don't give your feet a rest, stay at home, and stop wandering over hill and valley like a soul in torment, seeking those so-called adventures, which I call misadventures, I'll be forced to make my complaints known to God and the king, that they may provide a remedy."

To which Don Quixote replied,

"Housekeeper, I have no idea how God will respond to your complaints, or His Majesty either for that matter. I simply know that if I were king, I would refuse to respond to the endless number of impractical petitions they receive each day, for one of the biggest chores kings face is having to listen to one and all and then respond to them, so I would not want my problems to add to the king's worries."

To which the housekeeper said,

"Tell us, my lord, are there any knights in His Majesty's court?"

"There are," replied Don Quixote, "and quite a number of them, but that is as it should be, inasmuch as they serve as an adornment of the nobles' grandeur and a manifestation of the king's majesty."

"Well then," said the housekeeper, "mightn't your grace be one of those knights who could serve your king and lord at court without lifting a leg?"

"Look, my dear," said Don Quixote, "not every knight can be a courtier, and not all courtiers can be venturer knights nor should they be, since there is a need of both types in the world. While we may all be knights, there is a huge difference between one and the other, for without leaving their quarters or the court grounds the courtier knights may, by perusing a map, travel completely round the world without spending a cent or suffering from hunger and thirst or heat and cold. But we genuine knights-errant all measure the breadth of the land with our own feet and are exposed to the open air, sun, cold, and all sorts of inclement weather by night and by day, on horseback and on foot. We are acquainted with our enemies not just in paintings but in the very flesh, and whatever the circumstance or peril, we go on the attack without regard for the trivialities and rules of dueling, such as whether one's lance or sword is shorter than his opponent's, whether one is wearing religious relics or has a trick up his sleeve, whether both men are facing equally into the sun, and other ceremonies of this nature that are observed in duels between private individuals, with which you are not acquainted as I am. There is something else you should know: a good knight-errant will not feel the slightest intimidation even if he should see ten giants with their heads not simply touching the clouds but protruding above them, with two monstrous towers serving as their legs, arms that resemble the masts of some broad, powerful ship, and eyes that are each as large as a mill wheel and as fiery as a glass furnace. On the contrary, with a determined look and a fearless heart he will lay into them, overcome and destroy them in an instant, despite the fact that they may be armed with certain marine shells alleged to be harder than diamonds and, in lieu of swords, may be carrying sharp knives of Damascus steel or maces studded with spikes of the same metal, which I have seen on more than one occasion. I mention all this, dear housekeeper, so that you may appreciate the difference that exists among different types of knights. There is no reason for any prince not to esteem more highly this second, or I should say first, type of knight, for according to what we read in their histories, there have been certain individuals among them who have been the salvation of not just one kingdom but of many."

"Oh, my dear lord," said the niece at this point, "your grace should remember that everything you have said about knights-errant is fiction and make-believe. Even if their histories haven't been burned, each and every one of them ought to be made to wear the *sambenito*[1] or some sign that would mark him as evil and a corrupter of morals."

"By the God who sustains me," said Don Quixote, "if you were not my lawful niece - my own sister's daughter - I would chastise you so thoroughly for the blasphemy you have just uttered that it would become known round the world. How is it possible for a youngster who can barely manage a dozens bobbins of lace to have the audacity to open her mouth and criticize histories of knights-errant? What would Sir Amadís say if he heard such a thing? He, to be sure, would most certainly forgive you, for he was the most courteous and unassuming knight of his age, as well as a staunch protector of maidens. But some others might hear you who would not treat you so kindly, for not all of them are courteous and well thought of. There are even some who are arrogant and unmannerly,

1 A sleeveless garment open at the sides and extending to the waist. Known as the 'Insignia of the Inquisition,' it was yellow, had a large red cross on the front and another on the back, and was worn by those who had been tried by the Inquisition and confessed.

and not all those who call themselves knights are one hundred per cent genuine, for some are made of gold and others of alloy. They may all appear to be gentlemen but not every one of them can pass the test of truth. Some lowly individuals simply crave to be seen as gentlemen, whereas a few eminent gentlemen are determined to pass as men of low degree. The former rise by means of their ambition or virtue; the latter sink because of their laziness or vice. We must marshall all our mental faculties to distinguish between one and the other - so similar in name but so different in behavior."

"Lord help me, uncle!" said the niece, "to think that you know so much that, were it necessary in an emergency, you could mount a pulpit or go preaching in the streets. And yet, despite that, you can be so absolutely blind and so manifestly absurd that you're able to make people believe you're a man of action when you're actually old; that you're robust when you're infirm; that you're a righter of wrongs when you're exhausted by age; and, above all, that you're a knight when you're not one, for hidalgos may become knights but not so hidalgos who are poor."

"There is a great deal of truth, niece, in what you say," replied Don Quixote, "and there are things I might tell you about bloodlines that would amaze you but, because I prefer not to introduce the divine into human affairs, I shall not do so. Dear ladies, listen closely to what I am now going to say. There are four types of pedigrees to which everyone on earth may be reduced and they are the following: first, there are those who had a humble beginning but gradually expanded and enlarged it until they achieved absolute greatness. Then there are those who had a lofty beginning and went on preserving it just as it was when they began. There is another group who, though having had a lofty beginning, ended in a point like a pyramid, having squandered and diminished their beginning until it ended in nothingness, like the point of a pyramid, which in comparison with its base or foundation is nothing. And lastly, there are those – and they are the most numerous– who had neither a good beginning nor a reasonable middle, and their end will be the same: undistinguished, like the life course of ordinary individuals. Regarding the first group who came from a humble beginning but ascended to the greatness they still preserve, the Ottoman line may serve as an example, which had its beginning in a humble, lowly shepherd but has now attained the height at which we see it. As for the second group that had its beginning in greatness, which it continues to preserve but not to increase, we have the examples of a number of nobles who inherited it from their ancestors and passed it on to their descendants without increasing or diminishing it, being content to live within the limits of their social class. Of those who had a lofty beginning but ended in a point, there are thousands of examples, for all the Pharaohs and Ptolemies of Egypt, the Caesars of Rome, along with that endless mob (if I may use this term) of nobles, monarchs, lords, Medes, Assyrians, Persians, Greeks, and barbarians – all those lineages and lordships ended in a point of nothingness, both they and those from whom they descended. Today it would be impossible to locate all their descendants but even if one could do so, they would be found in humble and lowly circumstances. Regarding the plebeian group, my only observation is that they merely serve to increase the number of the living, and their accomplishments deserve no praise or memorial. From all I have said, my dear simple souls, I would have you understand that there is great confusion on the subject of bloodlines, and that only those are seen as grand and noble whose owners demonstrate that fact by their virtue, wealth, and generosity. I have singled out virtue, wealth, and generosity because the noble who is unvirtuous will be so in the extreme, and the wealthy person who fails to be generous will be a miserly beggar, because the possessor of wealth is not made happy by having it but by spending it, and not by spending it as he pleases but by knowing how to spend it wisely. A poor gentleman has no means of displaying his gentility except through virtue and by being affable, well bred, courteous, and polite, not by being haughty, arrogant, or slanderous, but above all he must be charitable, for the two *maravedís* he gives with a cheerful heart to a poor person show him to be as generous as the one who gives alms to the accompaniment of bells. Every person who sees him endowed with the above-mentioned virtues, even if he should not know him, will be sure to judge and consider him well bred; and should this not prove to be the case, it would be a miracle, for praise has always been the reward of virtue, and those who are virtuous cannot fail to be praised.

"There are two paths, my children, by which men may attain riches and esteem: that of letters and that of arms. I am better acquainted with the latter than with the former, for, having been born under the influence of the planet Mars, I incline towards arms. I am thus virtually forced to follow its path, and follow it I must despite the opinions of others. It will be useless to waste your efforts trying to dissuade me from striving after what heaven intends, fate ordains, reason demands, and, most of all, what my heart desires. Knowing as I do the countless ordeals that knight-errantry is subject to, I also know the infinite good that it brings to one. I know too that the path of righteousness is quite narrow, whereas the path of iniquity is broad and spacious. I also know that their goals and ends are different, for that of iniquity, which is wide and spacious, ends in death, whereas that of righteousness, which is narrow and arduous, ends in life - not the kind of life that ends but that which is eternal. And as our great Castilian poet [2] has said, I also know that,

Through these rough paths, to gain a glorious name,
We climb the steep ascent that leads to fame;
They miss the road who quit the rugged way,
And in the smoother tracks of pleasure stray."

"Oh, dear me!" said the niece, "my uncle is a poet too! Is there anything he doesn't know or anything he can't accomplish? I'll bet if your grace wanted to be a mason, you could build a house as easily as you could a birdcage."

"I promise you, niece," replied Don Quixote, "that if all my senses were not fixed upon thoughts of chivalry, there is nothing I could not do nor any curio I could not make with my hands, especially birdcages and toothpicks."

At that moment they heard a knock at the door and, when they asked who was there, Sancho Panza answered that it was he. No sooner did the housekeeper hear who it was than she ran and hid to avoid having to face him, such was her loathing of him. The niece let Sancho in and his master Don Quixote went forth to receive him with open arms. The pair enclosed themselves in Don Quixote's room, where they held another conversation that was in no wise inferior to the previous one.

---

2 Garcilaso de la Vega (1506-1536)

Chapter Seven

The matters that Don Quixote discussed with his squire, together with other incidents of note

No sooner did the housekeeper see Sancho Panza enclosed in her master's room than she guessed what they were up to, and fearing that this consultation might cause them to sally forth a third time, she grabbed her cloak and with heart-felt grief and sorrow hurried to look for the bachelor Sansón Carrasco, who she thought might persuade Don Quixote to abandon such a crazy notion, for the bachelor was not only a very persuasive person but a new friend of her master's. Finding him strolling in the courtyard of his house, she fell at his feet perspiring and filled with anxiety. When Carrasco saw her so visibly upset and frightened, he asked her,

"What is this, madam housekeeper? What has come over you? You look as though someone were after your soul."

"It is nothing, my dear Sansón, except that my master is breaking out all over again. This time he's breaking out for sure."

"And where is he breaking out, madam?" asked Sansón. "Has some part of his body burst?"

"The only place he's breaking out," replied the housekeeper, "is through the doorway of his madness; I mean, my dear bachelor, that he wants to go away again – this will be the third time – to roam the earth in quest of what he calls his good fortune. How he can call it that is beyond me because the first time they brought him home beaten to a pulp and draped across a jackass. The second time he came home on an oxcart locked inside a cage convinced he was enchanted. The poor soul was so woebegone and looked so thin and sallow with his eyes sunk deep into his skull that he wouldn't have been recognized by the mother who bore him. In order to restore him to a semblance of his former self, I used more than six hundred eggs, as God and everyone knows, especially my hens, who won't let me tell a lie."

"I can certainly believe that," said the bachelor, "for those hens are so good, plump, and well bred that they would sooner burst than say anything untrue. In short then, madam housekeeper, is there nothing else? Has no other outrageous thing occurred than the one you fear Sir Don Quixote is about to commit?"

"No, your worship," she responded.

"Then don't worry," said the bachelor, "return to your house with my blessing and prepare me something hot for lunch, and on your way home recite the prayer of St. Apolonia if you happen to know it. I shall be along directly and shall show you things that will astonish you."

"My goodness!" said the housekeeper, "your grace says I should recite the prayer of St. Apolonia? That *would* be the appropriate one if my master's trouble were in his teeth but all his trouble is in his head."

"I know what I am saying, madam housekeeper," said Carrasco; "be on your way and don't start an argument with me. You know very well that I have a bachelor's degree from Salamanca, and one can't be more of a bachelor than that."

With this the housekeeper left and the bachelor went at once to look for the priest to discuss a matter that will be related at the proper time. During the time that Don Quixote and Sancho were shut up in their room, they discussed matters that our history precisely and accurately records.

"Master," said Sancho to Don Quixote, "I've reduced my wife into letting me go wherever your grace wishes to take me."

"'*In*duced' you mean," said Don Quixote, "not '*re*duced'."

"On one or two occasions," replied Sancho, "if memory serves me, I have asked your grace not to correct my words so long as you understand what I mean. On the other hand, should you not understand, you may say, 'Sancho,' or 'Sancho you rascal, I don't understand you.' Then if I don't make myself clear, you may correct me, for I'm so tractle that— "

"I don't understand you, Sancho," said Don Quixote at once. "What do you mean by 'tractle'?"

"'Tractle' means this is just the way I am."

"Now I am really confused," said Don Quixote.

"Well, if your grace can't understand me, I don't know how else to say it; that's all I can do, so help me God!"

"Ah, now I understand," said Don Quixote; "you mean that you are so *tractable,* meek, and mild that you will accept whatever I tell you and will abide by whatever I teach you."

"I'll bet anything," said Sancho, "that from the very beginning you understood me and knew what I meant but you wanted to confuse me so you could hear me commit several hundred more blunders."

"Maybe so," replied Don Quixote, "but tell me: what does Teresa have to say?"

"Teresa says that in my dealings with your grace I should watch my step and get any promises put down in writing, for 'The person who cuts the cards should not also deal,' and 'One thing received is worth two things promised.' I also think women's advice is foolish but anyone who doesn't take it is even more foolish."

"And I am of the same opinion," said Don Quixote, "but do go on, dear friend; proceed with your speech, for today you are uttering pearls."

"The fact is," said Sancho, "as your grace well knows, that 'We're all subject to death,' since 'We're here today and gone tomorrow.' 'The lamb goes to slaughter as surely as the ram,' and 'No person can promise himself more hours of life on this earth than God wishes to give him,' for Death has no ears and when she comes knocking at the doors of our existence, she is always in a hurry, and neither pleading, force, scepters, nor miters will be able to fend her off according to what is commonly said in the streets and the pulpits."

"All that is true," said Don Quixote, "but I fail to see what you are leading up to."

"What I am leading up to," said Sancho, "is that your grace should indicate to me a fixed wage I'm to be paid each month I'm in your service, and this wage should be paid me from your estate. I refuse to depend upon favors that may not be sufficient or may be late in arriving, if they arrive at all. With God's help I can make do with what I've got. In short, I would like to know how much I'll be earning, regardless of how much or how little it is, because 'A hen will hatch a single egg,' 'Many littles make a much,' and 'So long as something is earned nothing is lost.' If it should actually happen (which I don't believe for a minute) that your grace would give me the island you've promised me, I'm not so ungrateful or so set in my ways that I won't let the income from such an island be appraised and subtracted from my wages at a perated amount."

"I suppose, Sancho my friend, that an amount can be *pre*rated as well as *pro*rated."

"I understand," said Sancho. "I'll bet I should have said 'prorated' instead of 'prerated,' but that's not important, since your grace understood what I meant."

"And so well," said Don Quixote, "that I have penetrated into your innermost thoughts and know which target you are aiming at with the arrows of your never-ending proverbs. Look, Sancho, I would gladly assign you a wage if I had ever found an example in the histories of knight-errantry that might show me or give me the slightest hint as to how much they were accustomed to earning in a month or a year. I have read most if not all their histories and do not recall having read of a single knight-errant who ever paid his squire a fixed wage. I simply know they all served voluntarily and when they least expected it, if their master's fortune had been favorable, they found themselves rewarded with an island or its equivalent, so at the very least they ended up with a title and something to rule. If because of these and other expectations, Sancho, you should wish to serve me once again, you have my blessing, but to imagine that I shall circumvent the rules and limits of the ancient customs of knight-errantry is to imagine the impossible. Therefore, dear Sancho, go back to your home and make my intentions known to your Teresa and if she is pleased and you are willing to labor with me voluntarily, *bene quidem*;[1] if not, we shall remain good friends as before, for 'If the pigeon-roost does not lack feed, it will not lack pigeons.' Be advised, my son, that 'It is better to hope for something good than to own something bad,' and 'A good complaint is better than bad pay.' I speak in this manner, Sancho, to let you see that I too can rain proverbs in torrents. And finally, I wish to state, and shall do so, that if you are unwilling to come with me without pay and confront the same destiny I confront, may God keep you and make you a saint. Besides, I shall not lack for squires more obedient, more obliging, less a hindrance, and less garrulous than you."

When Sancho saw his master's firm resolve, his sky became overcast and the wings of his soul began to droop, for he had never believed his master would set out without him for all the riches on earth. While he was standing there confused and bewildered, in came Sansón Carrasco and the niece, who were eager to hear how the bachelor would persuade their master not to set out again in quest of adventures. Sansón, the famous jokester, came over and embraced Don Quixote exactly as he had done on the previous occasion; then raising his voice, he said,

"O flower of knight-errantry! O resplendent light of arms! O mirror and credit to the Spanish nation! May it please Almighty God, as is herein stated and stipulated, that any person or persons guilty of impeding or obstructing your grace's third sally be unable to find their way out of the labyrinth of their desires or ever achieve what they most long for;" and addressing the housekeeper, he said,

"Madam housekeeper may just as well stop reciting the prayer of St. Apolonia, for it is the absolute decree of the spheres that our lord Don Quixote return to the execution of his lofty and novel ideas.

---

1 Latin: 'well and good!' (literally 'very well')

I would be greatly burdening my conscience if I encouraged and persuaded this knight to keep the might of his valiant arm and the goodness of his most noble soul confined any longer, for he is thereby depriving the wronged of their rights, orphans of their shelter, maidens of their honor, widows of their consolation, married women of their staff of support, and other matters of this nature that deal with, bear upon, concern, and have to do with the order of knight-errantry. Ah, my dear Don Quixote, so handsome and brave, may your exalted grace sally forth this very day at the latest, and if anything should still be needed for setting this enterprise in motion, here I stand ready to supply it with my person and possessions. And should it be necessary for me to serve your magnificence as squire, I would consider it the greatest honor!"

At this point Don Quixote turned to Sancho and said,

"Did I not tell you, Sancho, that I should never lack for squires? And just see who is offering to be one -- none other than the extraordinary bachelor Sansón Carrasco, perpetual amusement and delight of the campuses of Salamanca, sound of body, agile of limb, no chatterbox, inured to heat and cold, hunger and thirst, and possessed of all the qualities necessary to be a knight's squire. But heaven forbid that I, in order to indulge my fancies, should weaken the pillar of letters, break the receptacle of the sciences, or fell the noble palm of the fair and liberal arts. May this new Sansón remain in his own village, where by honoring it he will also be honoring the grey heads of his venerable parents, for I can be content with any squire whatsoever now that Sancho does not deign to come with me."

"But I do deign," said Sancho, deeply moved and his eyes filled with tears. "It shall never be said of me, my lord, that 'I bite the hand that feeds me.' No, master, I don't come from a bunch of ingrates. Everyone knows, especially those of my village, who the Panzas were, which is who I am descended from. Besides, I have observed and learned from your grace's many good deeds and kind words that you wish to favor me. If I made a big to-do about how much my wages should be, it was only to please my wife, for when she takes it into her head to accomplish something, there is no mallet that can force the hoops down over a barrel the way she can force one to do what she wants. But after all, a man must be a man and a woman a woman, and since I'm a man wherever I happen to be, which I can't deny, I intend to be one in my own house as well, regardless of the consequences. So there's nothing more for you to do than to put your will and codicil in order in such a way that it can't be provoked. And let's get started at once lest the soul of Sir Sansón be made to suffer, for he says his conscience compels him to persuade you to sally forth into the world a third time. I again place myself at your grace's disposal faithfully and justly, as well or even better than all other squires who have served knights-errant in times past or present."

The bachelor was astonished to hear Sancho's manner of speaking, and though he had read the first part of his grace's history, he never believed Sancho could be as delightfully amusing as he was described there; but when he heard him say 'provoked' instead of 'revoked', he believed everything he had read about him and would vouch for his being one of the most notorious simpletons of the age. He also said to himself that two such madmen as this master and servant had never been seen before. In the end, Don Quixote and Sancho embraced and were friends once again. And with the approval and blessing of the great Carrasco, who served as their oracle at this particular time, it was decided that their departure would take place three days thence, during which time they would have the opportunity to make all the preparations necessary for the journey and could acquire a complete helmet, for Don Quixote said he absolutely must have one to take with him. Sansón offered him a helmet, feeling certain a friend of his who owned one would lend it to him. But because of the rust and mold, it was duller than it was bright despite its polished steel. The curses that both the housekeeper and the niece directed at the bachelor were too numerous to record. They tore their hair, scratched their faces, and in the manner of professional mourners of the time lamented their master's departure as though it were his death. The scheme that Sansón had in mind for persuading him to sally forth once more was what our history will explain in due time, and all this was at the urging of the priest and the barber with whom he had discussed it earlier.

In short, during these three days Don Quixote and Sancho provided themselves with everything they deemed necessary. On the third day at dusk, after Sancho had pacified his wife – and Don Quixote his niece and housekeeper – the two of them, unseen by anyone except the bachelor, who insisted upon accompanying them for half a league outside the village, set out on the road to Toboso, Don Quixote astride his good Rocinante and Sancho his ancient dapple. The latter's saddlebags had been provided with every sort of foodstuff, and the purse with money, which Don Quixote gave him for any needs that might arise. Sansón embraced Don Quixote and begged him to keep him informed of his good or ill fortune so he might be cheered by the latter or saddened by the former, as the laws of their friendship demanded, and Don Quixote promised to do so. Sansón then headed back to his village and the other two riders headed for the great city of Toboso.

Chapter Eight

The description of what befell Don Quixote when he went to visit his lady Dulcinea of Toboso

'Praised be almighty Allah!' says Hamete Benengeli as he begins this eighth chapter. 'Praised be Allah!' he repeats three times, saying he has uttered this benediction on seeing that he finally has Don Quixote and Sancho under way, and he assures the readers of this delightful history that starting at this point the exploits of Don Quixote and the witticisms of his squire begin. He asks that they forget the past knight-errantries of the ingenious hidalgo and set their sights on those to come, which are just now beginning on the road to Toboso, the others having begun on the plains of Montiel, and what he asks is very little compared to what he promises.

He goes on to say that no sooner did Sansón depart and Don Quixote and Sancho found themselves alone than Rocinante began to neigh and the dapple to break wind (or sigh), which both of them, knight and squire, interpreted as a good sign and a favorable omen. But if the truth be told, the dapple's brays and 'sighs' were more numerous than the nag's neighs, which led Sancho to conclude that his own fortune was to surpass and outstrip that of his master, basing this upon celestial astrology, which he may have known, though our history does not say. He was simply heard to say every time he tripped or fell that he wished he had never left home because nothing was to be gained from tripping and falling except a scuffed shoe and a broken rib, and though not overly bright he was not far off the mark on this point.

"Sancho my friend," said Don Quixote, "night is fast approaching and it is becoming too dark for us to reach Toboso by daybreak, which is where I intend to go before involving myself in any other adventure. There I shall receive the blessing and loving permission of the peerless Dulcinea, with whose leave I am totally convinced and certain that I shall execute and bring to completion every perilous adventure, for nothing in this life makes knights more courageous than seeing themselves favored by their ladies."

"That is how I feel," said Sancho, "but I believe your grace will have difficulty speaking to her or at least seeing her in a place where you can receive her blessing unless, of course, she tosses it to you over the courtyard wall, which is where I saw her the first time I delivered the letter describing all the follies and absurdities you were performing in the heart of the Sierra Morena."

"Did you fancy that object a courtyard wall, Sancho," said Don Quixote, "where you viewed that never-sufficiently-praised elegance and beauty? It could only have been a gallery, corridor, portico, or whatever it's called, of some luxurious royal palace."

"Maybe so," replied Sancho, "but it looked like a wall to me, unless my memory is faulty."

"Nevertheless, Sancho, that is where we are going," said Don Quixote, "and so long as I see her, it is all the same to me whether it is across walls, windows, chinks, or garden grills, for any ray from her beauteous sun that strikes my eyes will illumine my understanding and fortify my heart so greatly that I shall remain unique and unparalleled in intelligence and bravery."

"Well, truthfully, master," said Sancho, "when I saw that sun of the lady Dulcinea's, it was not bright enough to give off any rays whatsoever, which was probably due to the fact that her grace was winnowing the wheat I mentioned and the huge amount of dust it raised settled round her head like a cloud and obscured it."

"Do you still insist, Sancho, upon saying, imagining, believing, and maintaining that my lady Dulcinea was winnowing wheat, a task and occupation completely out of keeping with what is or should be the activity of eminent persons whose proper endeavors and occupations manifest their superiority from half a league away! You, poor Sancho, have unfortunately forgotten those verses of our poet [1] that paint for us the labors in which those four nymphs were engaged in their crystal houses when they emerged from the beloved Tagus and seated themselves in the verdant meadow to weave those rich fabrics, which our ingenious poet described as being woven and laced with gold, silk, and pearls. That is how my lady must have been engaged when you saw her but, because of the envy some evil enchanter has for all my affairs, he changes and turns all those that afford me pleasure into forms different from those they possess. For this reason, I fear that in this history said to be published about my exploits, if its author has by chance been some sage hostile to me, he will have included certain things rather than others, introducing a thousand falsehoods for every fact and

---

1 Garcilaso de la Vega in his *Egloga* III.

going out of his way to include activities other than those required in the course of a factual history. O envy, you cankerworm of virtues and source of infinite ills! Every vice, Sancho, contains within itself a certain indefinable delight but that of envy contains only unpleasantness, rancor, and rage."

"Those are my thoughts too," said Sancho, "and I imagine that in this story or history about us, which the bachelor Carrasco says he has seen, my honor is probably driven through the streets and alleys like a drove of hogs, but upon my word as an honest man, I have never spoken ill of a single enchanter nor do I have enough possessions to instill envy in anyone. Now, it is quite true that I am a bit sly and display certain signs of roguishness but all this is covered and concealed by the broad cape of my simple nature, always natural and never artificial. And even if I had nothing more than my firm and true belief – which I've always had – in everything the Holy Roman Catholic Church holds to be true, plus the fact that I'm a mortal enemy of all the Jews, historians should take pity upon me and treat me kindly in what they write. But let them say what they will, for naked I was born and naked I remain, so I'm neither losing nor winning. However, so long as I see myself in print and am passed from hand to hand out there in the world, I won't give a fig for what they say about me."

"Sancho," said Don Quixote, "that sounds like what happened to a famous contemporary poet who, having composed a malicious satire against all the ladies of the evening, failed to include in it the name of a particular lady, inasmuch as he was uncertain whether she *was* one or not. When she found herself omitted from the list that included everyone else, she complained to the poet and asked him what he had seen in her to make him fail to include her along with the others, and she insisted that he revise the satire and put her in the revised version or she would show him what was meant by the saying that 'man was born to suffer.' The poet did as requested, stripping her of every last vestige of respect, as a result of which she was satisfied to see herself famous, albeit infamous. Another story very much to the point is the one they tell of the shepherd who set fire to and burned the famous temple of Diana, considered one of the seven wonders of the world, simply to keep his name alive in the coming centuries. Though it was ordered that no one mention him or use his name when writing or speaking in order to deprive him of his desired goal, people learned, nevertheless, that his name was Erostratus. Also apropos of this is what happened in Rome to the great emperor Charles V and a certain gentleman. The emperor was eager to see the famous temple of the Rotunda, which in antiquity was called the Temple of All the Gods but today is more properly called All Saints Temple, being the best preserved building of all those erected by the pagans in Rome and the one that best preserves the reputation of its founders' magnificence and resplendency. Shaped like half an orange, it is vast in size and very bright, though no other light finds its way inside save that admitted by a single window, or rather clerestory, which encircles the dome. As the emperor was gazing down from there at the structure, a Roman gentleman stood at his side explaining the exquisite and subtle qualities of that great architectural achievement. Once they had descended from the clerestory, the Roman said to the emperor, 'A thousand times, Your Majesty, I had the urge to seize you in my arms and throw myself down from that clerestory to gain eternal fame for myself throughout the world.' 'I thank you,' replied the emperor, 'for not carrying out such an evil idea and so that from this moment forth I shall not present you with another opportunity to prove your loyalty, I order you never again to speak to me or to appear in my presence;' and in saying this, he presented him with a handsome gift.

"What I am trying to say, Sancho, is that the desire to achieve fame is extremely powerful. What do you think made Horatius throw himself from the bridge into the depths of the Tiber clad in all his armor? What compelled Mutius to sear his arm and hand? What led Curtius to hurl himself into the deep flaming fissure that appeared in the center of Rome? What made Julius Caesar cross the Rubicon in defiance of all the auguries that had shown themselves unfavorable? Or to turn to more recent examples, what led the valiant Spaniards commanded by Cortés, that paragon of gentility in the New World, to scuttle their ships, thus leaving themselves stranded and cut off? All these, together with various other famous deeds, were, are, and will continue to be the stuff of which fame is forged: fame which mortals desire as their share of immortality and as the reward their famous deeds deserve. However, we Christians, Catholics, and knights-errant should fix our sights upon the life to come, which is eternal in the celestial and ethereal spheres, rather than upon the vanity of fame that may be achieved in this present impermanent existence, for this fame, regardless of how long it lasts, will one day come to an end together with the world itself, the days of which are numbered. And so it is, O Sancho, that our works are not to exceed the limits allotted us by the Christian religion we profess. It is our task to overcome pride by slaying giants, envy by generosity and a good heart, anger by a calm countenance and a peaceful soul, gluttony and sleep by eating sparingly and staying awake at all hours of the night, lust and lasciviousness by remaining faithful to those we have made the mistresses of our thoughts, slothfulness by ranging over all parts of the earth in quest of opportunities that can and will make us, in addition to Christians, famous knights. You see here, Sancho, the means by which one achieves the highest praise a noble reputation brings with it."

"Everything your grace has said up to now," said Sancho, "I've understood very well, but despite that, I would like to absolve a doubt that has just this moment sprung to mind."

"You mean 'resolve', Sancho," said Don Quixote. "You have my permission to state it and I shall answer to the best of my ability."

"I would like to know something, master," continued Sancho: "those Julys and Augusts, I mean those Juliuses and Augustuses [2] and all those other gallant gentlemen your grace has mentioned who are dead – where are they now?"

"Those who were heathens," replied Don Quixote, "are undoubtedly in hell and those who were Christians, if they were good Christians, are either in purgatory or in heaven."

"Very well," said Sancho, "but I would like to know one thing: those tombs containing the bodies of those mighty gentlemen, do they have silver lamps in front of them, and are the walls of their

---

2 The wordplay encountered here is quite clever in Spanish but falls completely flat in English translation. The Spanish text reads: ***esos Julios o Agostos***. The humor stems from the double meaning of the Spanish ***Julios,*** which can mean both 'Juliuses' and 'Julys.' Sancho meant to say, ***esos Julios o Augustos,*** which would mean 'those Juliuses and Augustuses,' but he came up with another of his malapropisms, substituting ***Agostos*** ('Augusts') for ***Augustos,*** thereby retrospectively turning the meaning of **Julios** ('Juliuses') into 'Julys.' The Spanish reader will immediately appreciate the wordplay and the fact that Sancho has simply used the wrong word. It is impossible to reproduce the effect in English, a situation that occurs all too frequently in translating *Don Quixote*.

chapels adorned with crutches, shrouds, locks of hair, or eyes and legs made of wax? and if not, what are they adorned with?"

To which Don Quixote responded,

"The tombs of the heathens were for the most part sumptuous temples. The ashes of Julius Caesar's body were placed at the top of an unusually tall obelisk in Rome, which today is called St. Peter's Needle. The emperor Hadrian had as a tomb a castle as large as a good-size village, which was called Moles Hadriani and today is the Castle of St. Angelo in Rome. Queen Artemisia buried her husband Mausolus in a tomb that was reckoned one of the seven wonders of the world, but none of those tombs nor any number of others possessed by the heathens were adorned with shrouds, offerings, or images to indicate that those buried inside were saints."

"That is what I'm driving at," said Sancho; "I simply want your grace to tell me which is greater: to bring a dead person back to life or to slay a giant."

"The answer is quite simple," replied Don Quixote; "it is greater to bring a dead person back to life."

"Now I've got your grace! The fame, then, of those who raise the dead, make the blind to see and the lame to walk, restore the infirm, have lamps burning in front of their tombs, and chapels filled with worshipers on their knees adoring their relics – *their* fame will be greater in this life and the next than that left behind by all the heathen emperors and knights-errant who ever lived."

"I grant that also," said Don Quixote.

"Well," said Sancho, "this fame, these favors and prerogatives, as they're called, are the property of the bodies and relics of these saints who with the approval and permission of our Holy Mother Church contain lamps, candles, shrouds, crutches, paintings, locks of hair, eyes, and legs, which increase devotion and enhance their Christian fame. Kings carry the bodies and relics of the saints on their shoulders, kiss pieces of their bones, and use them to adorn and embellish their chapels and their most highly prized altars."

"What would you have me conclude, Sancho, from all you have said?" asked Don Quixote.

"I am trying to say," continued Sancho, "that we ought to devote ourselves to becoming saints and we could achieve the good reputation we're seeking in a shorter time. Your grace should remember that only yesterday or the day before – I can refer to it in this manner since it's so recent – they canonized, or beatified, two discalced friars, and the chains that bound and tortured their bodies are now considered objects that bestow good luck upon those who touch or kiss them, and they are more highly venerated, as I've said, than Roland's sword, which is in the armory of our lord the king – may God preserve him. Therefore, master, it is better to be a humble little friar in whatever order one chooses than a courageous knight-errant, for two dozen scourgings carry more weight with God than two thousand lance thrusts, whether they're delivered against giants, monsters, or dragons."

"That is how it is," said Don Quixote, "but we cannot all be friars. Many are the paths by which God leads His chosen to heaven. Chivalry is a religion and there are saintly knights in the land of glory."

"True," said Sancho, "but I've heard it said there are more friars in heaven than knights-errant."

"That," replied Don Quixote, "is because the number of ecclesiastics is greater than that of knights."

"There are an awful lot of knights-errant," said Sancho.

"Yes," said Don Quixote, "but very few who are worthy of the name."

They spent the night and the following day discussing these and similar topics, during which time nothing noteworthy happened to them, a fact that caused Don Quixote no little regret. Finally, at dusk on the following day, the great city of Toboso came into view and the sight of it buoyed the spirits of Don Quixote but dampened those of Sancho, since he did not know which house was Dulcinea's because he had never seen it in his entire life, and neither had his master. The result was that they were greatly agitated, one because of his desire to see her, and the other because he had never seen her, and Sancho could not imagine what he would do if his master ordered him into Toboso. Finally, Don Quixote decided they would enter the city as soon as it was night. While waiting for the appointed hour, they rested in an oak grove near Toboso. Then when the designated hour arrived, they entered the city, where they experienced things that were something to behold.

Chapter Nine

The description of what will herein be seen

It was at the very stroke of midnight, more or less, when Don Quixote and Sancho left the forest and entered Toboso. The town was peaceful and silent and all the inhabitants were asleep, or 'dead to the world,' as the expression goes. The night was somewhat bright whereas Sancho would have been more pleased if it had been completely dark so he could use the darkness as an excuse for his ineptitude. In the entire town there was not a sound to be heard except for the barking dogs, which deafened the ears of Don Quixote and vexed the soul of Sancho. From time to time there was also the braying of asses, the grunting of pigs, and the caterwauling of cats, whose cries were magnified by the silence of the night, all of which the enamored knight took as an evil omen. Despite this, he said to his squire,

"Sancho my son, if you will lead the way to Dulcinea's castle, we may possibly find her awake."

"What castle am I to lead the way to, for goodness sake?" said Sancho. "The place where I saw her ladyship was nothing more than a small house?"

"She must have been sequestered at that moment," said Don Quixote, "in some small hideaway of her royal palace, disporting herself privately with her maidservants, as is the custom and usage among great ladies and princesses."

"Master," said Sancho, "since your grace insists over my objections that my lady Dulcinea's home is a castle, can this possibly be the hour to find it open? Will it be appropriate to bang on the door and wake everyone to get them to let us in, which will only excite and upset everyone? Are we by chance calling at the houses of our mistresses the way men do who keep such women, coming and going at every hour of the night regardless of the lateness of the hour?"

"Whatever we do, let us first find the palace," said Don Quixote. "I shall then instruct you as to what we are to do next. But look over there, Sancho, unless my eyes deceive me, that large object we can see all the way from here must be Dulcinea's palace."

"Well, if your grace will lead the way," said Sancho, "maybe that's what it'll be but, even if I see it with my eyes and touch it with my hands, I'll no more believe such a thing than I'll believe it's now day."

Don Quixote led the way and after proceeding some two hundred paces, arrived at the object that was casting the shadow. When he saw it had a large tower, he realized the building in question was not a palace but the city's main church, whereupon he said,

"We have stumbled across the church, Sancho."

"I can see that," replied Sancho, "and, God willing, we won't stumble across our tombs, for it's not a good sign to go strolling through burial grounds at such an hour, especially when I've told your grace, if I remember correctly, that our lady's house is situated in a dead-end alley."

"May God curse you, you blockhead!" cried Don Quixote. "Where have you ever heard of fortresses or palaces being built in alleys?"

"Master," said Sancho, "each country has its own custom. Maybe here in Toboso it's the custom to construct palaces and other large buildings in alleys. Therefore, I beg you to let me search these streets and side streets, for it may just turn out that on some corner I'll come across that palace – and I hope to find it gnawed to pieces by dogs for having led us on such a merry chase."

"I would have you show more respect, Sancho, when you speak of matters involving my lady. Let us not start arguing or throw away the pail simply because the milk was spilled."

"I'll restrain myself," said Sancho, "but just because I saw our lady's house one single time, how can I abide your grace's insistence that I recognize it on every occasion and find it at midnight when you can't even find it after having seen it thousands of times?"

"You are going to drive me to despair, Sancho," said Don Quixote. "Look here, you heretic, have I not told you a thousand times that I have never in all the days of my life seen the peerless Dulcinea, nor has my foot ever crossed the portals of her palace! I am enamored of her only by hearsay and because of the great reputation she has as a beauty and intellect."

"So the truth is finally out!" replied Sancho. "Well, since your grace has never seen her, I can now state that I haven't either."

"That is impossible," cried Don Quixote, "for at the very least you have already told me you saw her winnowing wheat when you brought me the answer to the letter I sent her."

"Don't rely upon that, master," said Sancho, "for I want you to understand that my seeing her and the answer I brought you were also by hearsay because I'm no more capable of recognizing the lady than of punching the sky."

"Sancho, Sancho," said Don Quixote, "there are times for joking and times when it is in very poor taste. Simply because I say that I have never seen or spoken with the mistress of my soul is no reason for you to say the same thing when you know that just the opposite is true."

While the two of them were discussing these matters, they saw a youth with a pair of mules headed in their direction, and from the noise made by the plow he was dragging on the ground they judged him to be a farm lad who had risen before daybreak to begin his plowing, and such proved to be the case. And as he walked along, he was singing the ballad that goes:

> You Frenchmen got the worst of it
> In that affair at Roncesvalles.

"I'll be hanged, Sancho," said Don Quixote when he heard this, "if we are in for anything good tonight. Do you hear what that farm lad is singing?"

"Of course, I do," replied Sancho, "but what does the affair of Roncesvalles have to do with us? He might just as well be singing the ballad of Calainos for all the difference it would make as to whether our affair turns out well or badly."

At that moment the lad arrived and Don Quixote said to him,

"Can you tell me, my friend – and may God see that you prosper – where the palaces of the peerless princess Doña Dulcinea of Toboso are?"

"Sire," responded the lad, "I am a stranger here and have been in this town only a few days working for a rich farmer in the fields. In that house across the street live the village priest and the sacristan, either or both of whom will be able to give your grace news of that princess lady, for they have a list of all the citizens of Toboso, though I suspect there's no princess in the entire town; there are lots of ladies, of course, and illustrious ones at that, because each one is a queen in her own house."

"Well, my friend," said Don Quixote, "among those will surely be the one I'm inquiring about."

"Maybe so," replied the lad, "but I must be on my way because it's getting light."

And whipping his mules, he left without waiting for further questions. Sancho, seeing his master bewildered and none too cheerful, said to him,

"Master, day is rapidly approaching and we would be well advised not to let the sun find us in the street. It'll be better for us to leave the city so your grace can take cover in one of the groves round here. I'll come back during the day and will search every nook and cranny in this town for my lady's house, castle, or palace, and I'll be a pretty sorry fellow if I fail to find it; but when I do, I'll speak to her grace and inform her of your whereabouts and the fact that you are just waiting for her to say the word and advise you when you may see her without compromising her honor or reputation."

"Sancho," said Don Quixote, "you have uttered a thousand gems of wisdom in those few words, and the advice you have just given me I find most appetizing and shall accept with all my heart; but come, my son, let us look for some place where I can hide. You shall return, as you said, to seek out, gaze upon, and speak with my lady, because of whose discretion and thoughtfulness I expect more than supernatural favors."

Because Sancho was dying to get his master out of town lest he discover the falsity of the reply he had brought him in the Sierra Morena on behalf of Dulcinea, he hastened their departure and they left at once. Two miles outside the village they found a forest or grove where Don Quixote took cover while Sancho returned to the city to speak with Dulcinea, and on this mission he experienced things that call for a new type of consideration and a new kind of faith.

Chapter Ten

The description of Sancho's scheme to enchant the Lady Dulcinea, together with other incidents as comical as they are true

When the author of our great history comes to relate the events of this chapter, he says he would have preferred to pass over them in silence, fearing he might not be believed, for in it Don Quixote's follies are equal to the greatest ones imaginable and even surpass those by a couple of bowshots. But despite these fears and doubts, he finally wrote them down exactly as they occurred without altering the facts by so much as an atom, nor was he the least bit concerned about any objections that might be raised regarding his veracity. He was quite right in following this course of action, for truth, which may be bent but not broken, always rises above falsehood as oil does above water.

And so, proceeding with his history, he says that as soon as Don Quixote took cover in the forest, woods, or oak grove just outside the great Toboso, he ordered Sancho to return to the city and not to appear in his presence again until he had spoken to his lady on his behalf, adding that he was to implore her to allow herself to be visited by her unfortunate knight and to bestow her blessing upon him so he might look forward to a most felicitous outcome in his difficult undertakings and enterprises. Sancho agreed to carry out his command and to bring his master as good an answer as he had brought him the first time.

"Be on your way, my son," said Don Quixote, "and don't get flustered when you find yourself in the presence of the light from that beautiful sun you are about to visit. How fortunate you are over all other squires on earth! Remember to take note of how she receives you: does her face change its hue when you deliver my message to her; does she become agitated and anxious at the mention of my name; is she able to restrain herself on her cushion, should you find her seated in the sumptuous chamber of her authority; or if she is standing, notice whether she shifts her weight from one foot to the other, or repeats her answer to you two or three times, or her voice changes from soft to harsh or from disagreeable to loving; whether she raises her hand to arrange her hair, even if it does not need arranging; in short, my son, observe her every action and gesture, for if you will give me a report of what actually transpires, I shall be able to determine what she keeps hidden in the innermost regions of her heart regarding the love I feel for her. You should know, Sancho, if you do not already, that external gestures and actions between lovers are most reliable messengers for revealing what is transpiring in the interior of their souls. Go, my friend, and may your fortune be superior to mine, and may things turn out better for you than those I fear and expect to experience here in the bitter solitude to which you are abandoning me."

"I'll go and return quickly," said Sancho, "but I hope your grace will shore up what little courage you have left, which is probably no bigger than a hazel nut. You should also heed the well-known saying:

'Stout heart overcomes ill-fortune', and that other one: 'Where there's no smoke there's fire,' and still another: 'When one least expects it, up jumps the hare.' I mention all this because, while we may not have found my lady's palaces or castles last night, now that it's day I hope to find them when I least expect it, and once they are found, your grace may leave the rest up to me."

"Sancho," said Don Quixote, "I certainly hope God will bring me more success in my endeavors than He has you in your proverbs."

At these words, Sancho whipped his dapple and started on his way. Don Quixote remained behind seated on his horse, supporting himself with his stirrups and leaning on his lance, his head filled with doleful, perplexing thoughts. This is where we shall leave him while we accompany Sancho Panza, who rode away with no less confusion and apprehension than the master he was leaving behind. No sooner did Sancho emerge from the forest than he turned and looked back. Seeing that Don Quixote was no longer in view, he got off his jackass, seated himself at the base of a tree, and began to converse with himself in the following manner:

'May we know, brother Sancho, where you are going? Is it to look for some jackass that got lost?' 'Of course not.' 'Then what is it you are looking for?' 'I am merely looking for a princess, that's all, who combines in her person the beauty of the sun and the heavens.' 'And where, Sancho, do you think you'll find such a person?' 'Where? In the great city of Toboso.' 'Good, and on whose behalf are you looking for her?' 'On behalf of the famous knight Don Quixote of La Mancha, that righter of wrongs and provider of food for the thirsty and drink for the hungry.' 'That's all quite noble but do you know where she lives, Sancho?' 'My master says it will be in some royal palace or magnificent castle.' 'And have you by chance ever seen her?' 'Neither I nor my master has ever seen her.' 'Well, don't you think that if the citizens of Toboso knew you were here with the intention of luring away their princesses and upsetting their women, they would have every right to give your ribs an outright drubbing and break every bone in your body?' 'They would be perfectly within their rights but only if they failed to consider that I was under orders and that messengers are not responsible for the contents of their messages.' 'Don't rely upon that, Sancho, for the people of La Mancha are as hot-tempered as they are honorable and they won't put up with nonsense from anyone; and, by Jove, if they suspect something, I promise you you'll have a bad time of it.' 'Get away from me, you sodomite! You don't need to threaten me! You don't think I'm going in search of a cat with three legs just to please someone else, especially when looking for Dulcinea in Toboso will be like looking for a girl named Maria in Ravenna or a student in Salamanca. It's the Devil himself and no one else who has gotten me into this mess!'

Sancho held this dialogue with himself and all he got for his efforts was a continuation of the conversation.

'Well now, "There's a remedy for everything except death," under whose yoke we all must pass, like it or not, at the end of our lives. I've seen a thousand signs that this master of mine is a raving lunatic and I'm not far behind him, and since I follow and serve him, I'm probably a bigger fool than he is if the proverbs are true that say, "Tell me whose company you keep and I'll tell you who you are," and "Birds of a feather flock together." Since he's as crazy as he is and suffers from the type of madness that oftentimes mistakes one thing for another – considering white black and black white, as was evident when he claimed the windmills were giants, the ecclesiastics' mules dromedaries, the flocks of sheep hostile armies, and a number of other things of this nature – it won't be difficult to make him believe the first farm girl I come across in these parts is the lady Dulcinea. And if he doesn't believe me, I'll swear it's true; and if he swears the opposite, I'll swear even harder; and if he keeps swearing, I'll go on swearing and in this way will always have the last word. Perhaps if I persist long enough, I can make him stop sending me on these pathetic errands, especially when he sees what poor responses I bring him. Or perhaps he'll fancy, which he probably will, that one of those evil enchanters who he says oppose him has transformed her appearance to cause him pain and suffering."

At this thought Sancho Panza's soul was soothed and he considered the affair nicely consummated. He passed the time in that spot until the afternoon to convince Don Quixote he'd had time to make the trip to Toboso and back. Things turned out so well for him that, just as he stood up to mount his dapple, he saw coming towards him from Toboso three farm girls riding either male or female asses, the author failing to specify which, though as likely as not they were she-asses, for these are the customary mounts of village women; but since none of this amounts to a hill of beans, there is no need to take the time to enquire into the matter. In short, no sooner did Sancho see the farm girls than he rode like a shot back to his master Don Quixote, whom he found sighing and uttering a thousand amorous lamentations. When Don Quixote saw him, he said,

"What news is there, Sancho my friend? Shall I mark today with a white stone or a black one?"

"Your grace had better have it painted with red ocher," said Sancho, "like those notices on the university walls so that everyone who passes by will be sure to see it."

"Then you are bringing good news," said Don Quixote.

"So good," replied Sancho, "that all your grace has to do is spur Rocinante and ride out of the forest, where you will see the lady Dulcinea of Toboso in the company of two handmaidens, all on their way to see your grace."

"Merciful heavens, Sancho my friend! what are you saying?" said Don Quixote. "Don't try to deceive me or alleviate my most genuine sadness with false hopes."

"What would I gain by deceiving your grace," said Sancho, "especially when you're on the verge of determining the truth for yourself? If you will just spur your horse, you will see our mistress the princess attired and adorned as befits a lady of her stature. She and her maids constitute a veritable picture of golden embers, clusters of pearls, diamonds and rubies, brocades ten layers thick, with their flowing tresses cascading down their backs like so many rays of the sun frolicking in the wind; and last but not least, they're all riding three mottled belfries that are really something to behold."

"'Palfreys' you mean, Sancho."

"Is there all that much difference between belfries and palfreys?" said Sancho. "Well, whatever they're riding, they're the finest-looking ladies one could ever hope to see, especially my lady the Princess Dulcinea, who simply dazzles the senses."

"Let us be off, Sancho my son," replied Don Quixote, "and in appreciation of this news – as unexpected as it is good – I shall award you the best of the spoils from the first adventure I have, or if that is not to your liking, I shall give you the foals my three mares will produce this year, which, as you know, are soon to give birth in the public pasture of our village."

"I'll take the foals," replied Sancho, "since I'm not sure the spoils from the first adventure will be worth very much."

At that moment they emerged from the forest and saw the three village lasses nearby. Don Quixote ran his eyes along the entire length of the road to Toboso but, seeing no one except the three farm girls, was completely mystified, at which point he asked Sancho if he had left them outside the city.

"How outside the city?" replied Sancho. "Can your grace possibly have your eyes in the back of your head not to see those three lasses coming towards us, who are as resplendent as the noonday sun itself?"

"I don't see anyone, Sancho," said Don Quixote, "except three farm girls on three jackasses."

"May God deliver me from the Devil!" said Sancho; "is it possible that three belfries, or whatever they're called, that are as white as driven snow can look like jackasses to your grace? As God is my witness, I would pull out my beard if that were the case!"

"Well, I'm telling you, Sancho my friend," replied Don Quixote, "that they are as truly jackasses, or she-asses, as I am Don Quixote and you are Sancho Panza; at least, that is how they appear to me."

"May your grace bite your tongue and refrain from saying such a thing," said Sancho. "You should wipe the cobwebs from your eyes and go pay your respects to the mistress of your thoughts, who is just now approaching."

In saying this, Sancho rode on ahead to greet the three village lasses. Dismounting from the dapple, he grabbed the halter of one of the girls' jackasses and knelt down on both knees, saying,

"O queen, princess, and duchess of beauty, may your haughtiness and highfalutinness be pleased to welcome unto your bosom yon captive knight who is standing there like a block of marble, totally overcome and unnerved at finding himself in your ladyship's magnificent presence. I am Sancho Panza, his squire, and that is the beleaguered knight Don Quixote of La Mancha, also known as the Knight of the Woeful Countenance."

By this time Don Quixote had knelt beside Sancho and was staring with bulging eyes and blurred vision at the one Sancho was calling lady and queen, but since all he could make out was a village girl, and not a very pretty one at that, she being round-faced and flat-nosed, he was bewildered and astonished and dared not open his mouth. The country girls were equally astonished at the sight of two such dissimilar men on their knees who would not let their companion pass, but the one who had been stopped broke the silence and said in a voice that was gruff and brimming with anger,

"Get the heck out of our way and let us pass. We're in a hurry."

To which Sancho replied,

"O princess and lady of all Toboso, how can your ladyship's magnanimous heart fail to be moved when you see kneeling in your sublimated presence the pillar and support of knight-errantry?"

Hearing this, one of the other two girls said,

"Whoa there, you stubborn ass, I'll scratch your eyes out! Will you just look at the way these high-and-mighty gentlemen think they can have their way with us village girls, as though we can't give as good as we get! Get out of our way and let us pass if you want to remain in one piece!"

"Stand up, Sancho," said Don Quixote at this point. "I now see that fate, not being content with my misery, has blocked every avenue by which any happiness might reach the wretched soul I bear in this body. But thou, O most desirable paragon of virtue, the ultimate in human gentility and sole remedy of this afflicted heart that adores thee, now that the evil enchanter who pursues me has clouded my vision with cataracts and has transformed, just for my eyes and no one else's, the incomparable beauty of thy face and form into that of a poor farm girl – and may also have changed mine into those of some monster to make me abominable in thy sight – mayest thou find it in thy heart to look upon me with tenderness and affection. And observe by the submission and resignation that I manifest before thy distorted beauty the humility with which my soul holds thee in adoration."

"Well, now," retorted the girl, "would you listen to the old man! I just love it when they talk dirty! Be off with you both. Leave us alone and you gentlemen will have our deepest gratitude."

Standing aside to allow her to pass, Sancho was overjoyed at extricating himself from his predicament. No sooner did the village lass who had been assigned the role of Dulcinea see herself free than she jabbed her 'belfry' with a sharpened stick she carried and took off across the field, but when the she-ass felt the point of the stick, which pained it more than usual, it began to buck so wildly it tossed the lady Dulcinea to the ground. Seeing this, Don Quixote hurried over to help her to her feet while Sancho adjusted the cinches of the packsaddle, which had slipped beneath the ass' belly. After the packsaddle was adjusted, Don Quixote was about to raise his enchanted mistress in his arms and place her on the ass when the lady saved him the trouble by standing up unassisted. Then, after taking several steps backwards, she made a dash for the mule, clapped both hands on the ass' haunches, and landed in the saddle more agilely than a falcon, where she sat astride the beast as though she were a man. It was then that Sancho said,

"My goodness, the lady our mistress is quicker than a hawk and could teach the most skilled riders of Cordova and Mexico how to mount a horse. Why, she cleared the rear pommel of the saddle in one leap, and without spurs is making the palfrey run like a zebra, and even her friends aren't one step behind her but are riding like the wind."

And such was the case, for as soon as Dulcinea saw herself mounted, she and the other girls spurred their mounts and took off like a shot without looking back for more than half a league. Don Quixote followed them with his eyes and, when he saw them disappear from sight, turned to Sancho and said,

"Sancho, what do you think of enchanters who detest me to this extent? Just observe how far their ill will and malice extend, for they have done their best to deprive me of the happiness I might have received from seeing my lady as she really is. The fact is that I was born to be an example of wretchedness and to serve as the target and mark at which people take aim and shoot their arrows of adversity. You should also note, Sancho, that these traitors were not content to change and transform my lady Dulcinea but they had to transform her into a figure as lowly and ugly as that of a peasant girl, at the same time taking from her the very essence of noble women, namely, their fragrance and scent, which they always have about them owing to their constant association with flowers and amber. I would have you know, Sancho, that when I drew near Dulcinea to help her onto her palfrey – as you call it, but which in my opinion was a she-ass – I got a whiff of raw garlic that made me dizzy and vexed my soul."

"You scoundrels!" cried Sancho at this point, "you evil, malevolent enchanters, if only I might see you all strung up by the gills like sardines on a stick. You are very learned, very adept, but very great mischief-makers. You should have been content, you scoundrels, to transform my lady's eyes of pearls into ungainly pustules and her hair of finest gold into oxtail bristles – in short, all her lovely features into hideous ones – without tampering with her fragrance, for from it we might at least have discerned what lay hidden beneath that ugly exterior. But, if I do say so myself, I never saw any ugliness – only beauty, which was enhanced and perfected by a mole she had on her right upper lip, like a mustache, sprouting seven or eight blond hairs resembling golden threads, each of which was more than a handspan in length."

To which Don Quixote responded,

"According to the correspondence that moles on the face have to those on the body, Dulcinea must have another mole on the broad portion of her thigh that would be on the same side as the one on her face; but hairs as long as those you mention are awfully long for moles."

"Well, I can assure your grace," replied Sancho, "that on her they looked perfectly natural."

"Of course, my friend," said Don Quixote, "for nature endowed Dulcinea with nothing that is not perfect and well wrought. Therefore, if she had a hundred moles like the one you mention, on *her*they would not be moles but moons and shimmering stars. But tell me, Sancho: the thing that you straightened up that looked like a packsaddle, was it a plain saddle or one with armrests and a back?"

"It was a simple sidesaddle," said Sancho, "covered by a canopy that was worth a fortune it was so sumptuous."

"And to think that I missed seeing all that! I say again and shall repeat a thousand times that I am the most unfortunate man on earth."

The crafty Sancho had all he could do to contain his laughter listening to this nonsense of his master, whom he had so ingeniously deceived. After discussing a variety of topics, they finally remounted their beasts and set out for Saragossa, where they planned to arrive in time to participate in some important festivities held in that city each year, but before they could do so, they experienced things which, because of their variety, importance, and novelty, deserve to be recorded and read, as will be seen in the coming chapters.

Chapter Eleven

The strange adventure that befell the valiant Don Quixote with the cart or wagon of the Parliament of Death

Don Quixote was more than a little dejected as he continued his journey, mulling over the cruel deception the enchanters had employed against him by transforming his lady Dulcinea into a repulsive village girl, and he could think of no course of action that might restore her to her former state. He was so distracted by these thoughts that without realizing it he relaxed his grip on the reins of Rocinante, who, sensing the freedom he was being given, made frequent stops to graze on the abundant grass in those fields; but Sancho Panza brought his master back from his reverie by saying,

"Master, sadness was created for men, not for beasts, but if men dwell upon it too long, they themselves turn into beasts. Your grace should cheer up, return to your senses, and take heart. You should also tighten the reins on Rocinante and exhibit that fortitude that knights-errant are supposed to possess. What the dickens is this all about anyway? Why this despondency, since it's not as though we were in France? The Devil can have all the Dulcineas there are in the world, for the health of a single knight-errant is worth more than all the enchantments and transformations on earth."

"Hold your tongue, Sancho," said Don Quixote none too gently; "be quiet, I say, and stop uttering blasphemies against that enchanted lady, for I alone am responsible for her misery and misfortune. Her unhappy fate is born of the envy those evil ones bear me."

"That's what I think," said Sancho, "for who could look at her now, having seen her as she once was, whose heart would not burst from grief?" To this Don Quixote replied,

"You have every right to say that, Sancho, having viewed her in all her perfection and beauty, since her enchantment did not go so far as to becloud your sight or hide her beauty from you. Against me and my eyes alone was the potency of its venom reserved, but despite that, Sancho, I have noticed one thing: you described her beauty very inaccurately, for if I remember correctly, you said her eyes were like pearls, but eyes that resemble pearls are more like a sea-bream's than a lady's. In my opinion Dulcinea's must be green emeralds surmounted by two rainbows for eyebrows. Take those pearls from her eyes, Sancho, and place them in her mouth, for you undoubtedly confused them by mistaking her eyes for her teeth."

"Anything is possible," said Sancho, "for I was as much taken with her beauty as your grace was with her ugliness. But let's leave all this in the hands of God, for He knows which events will transpire in this vale of tears, in this evil world in which we live where one can hardly find a single thing untouched by evil, fraud, or wickedness. But one thing does have me worried, master, more than all the others: namely, the question of what means are to be employed when your grace conquers some giant or knight and orders him to present himself to the beautiful lady Dulcinea. Where will that poor giant or poor vanquished knight find her? I can just see them now walking about Toboso like a bunch of idiots looking for my lady Dulcinea, and even if they bump into her in the street, they won't recognize her any more than they will my father."

"Perhaps, Sancho," said Don Quixote, "the enchantment will not go so far as to prevent her recognition by the defeated giants and knights who present themselves to her. I shall send one or two of the first ones I vanquish to visit her, commanding them to return and give me an account of what transpired. In this way we shall determine whether they are able to see her or not."

"I must say," said Sancho, "that what your grace has proposed sounds like a good idea, and by that same device we will find out what we would like to know. If it turns out that she's invisible only to your grace, then your misfortune will be greater than hers, but so long as the lady Dulcinea is healthy and contented, we'll make out here and get along as best we can, pursuing our adventures and letting the years follow their own course, for time is the best physician for these ills and even worse ones."

Don Quixote was about to respond to Sancho Panza but was prevented from doing so by a wagon rounding a bend in the road which was carrying the strangest and most diverse cast of characters imaginable. The person handling the mules and serving as driver was an unsightly demon, and the wagon, which lacked both top and sides, was completely exposed to the elements. The first figure to catch Don Quixote's eye was that of Death itself, whose face was that of a human. Seated next to him was an angel with large painted wings, and just beyond him sat an emperor wearing a crown, apparently of gold. At Death's feet was the god known as Cupid, minus the blindfold over his eyes but with his bow, quiver, and arrows. There was also a knight in full armor who wore, not a helmet and visor, but a hat of multicolored plumes, together with several other persons in various costumes and make-up. The sudden appearance of all these people was not a little unsettling to Don Quixote and it struck fear into the heart of Sancho, but the knight immediately rejoiced, fancying he was being offered some new and perilous adventure. And so, fortified by this thought and ready to confront any danger, he stationed himself in the wagon's path and shouted in a loud, threatening voice,

"Driver, coachman, devil, or whatever you happen to be, tell me at once who you are, where you are headed, and who those people are you are transporting on your wagon, which more closely resembles Charon's ferry than a modern-day cart."

Bringing the conveyance to a halt, the Devil calmly responded by saying,

"Sir, we are actors in the company of Angulo el Malo. This morning in a village on the other side of that hill we gave a performance of the play *The Parliament of Death,* this being the eighth day of Corpus Christi, and this afternoon we are going to give another in that other village that can be seen from here. Since there is so little distance between the two and to save ourselves the trouble of changing from our costumes into our everyday clothes, we have come here dressed in the same costumes we wear in the play. That young man there represents Death; the one next to him an angel; the woman, who is the manager's wife, plays the queen; the man beside her a soldier; the next man the emperor; and I play the Devil, one of the principal characters in the play, since I perform the leading roles in this company. If your grace wishes to know anything further about us, you have only to ask and I shall give you a most detailed account, for inasmuch as I am a demon, everything is within my ken."

"Upon my word as a knight-errant," said Don Quixote, "the instant I saw this wagon, I imagined some great adventure was coming my way but I am forced to admit one must actually touch with his hands what his eyes see if he wishes to avoid being deceived. Therefore, go with God, my good people, and give your performance. Also, if there is anything your graces require in which I may be of service, I shall provide it most willingly and graciously, for ever since childhood I have been fond of the stage and as a youth my eyes always bugged out at the sight of a company of actors."

While discussing these matters, they were approached by one of the actors dressed as a jester who was covered with bells and was carrying a stick with three inflated cow bladders tied to the end. The clown came up to Don Quixote and began swinging the stick, striking the ground with the bladders and jumping high into the air, which caused the bells to ring. This evil apparition so startled

Rocinante that despite Don Quixote's efforts to restrain him, he clamped the bit tightly between his teeth and bolted across the field with more agility than that promised by the bones of his carcass. Sancho, suspecting his master was in danger of being thrown off, leapt from his dapple and ran as fast as he could to assist him, but when he reached him, Don Quixote was already on the ground with Rocinante beside him, the latter having fallen to the ground along with his master, the usual result and conclusion of Rocinante's exuberance and daring.

No sooner had Sancho abandoned his mount to go to Don Quixote's aid than the demon who had danced about with the bladders mounted the dapple and began striking him with them. The fright and noise, more than the pain from the blows, made the dapple take off across the field towards the village where they were going to perform their play. Sancho observed his dapple's mad dash and his master lying on the ground and was unable to decide which of the two needs to attend to first. But in the end, as a good squire and servant, his love for his master was stronger than his affection for his jackass, even though he suffered the pangs and tortures of death each time he saw the bladders raised aloft and brought down upon the haunches of his dapple, and he would actually have preferred to have his own eyeballs struck than the tiniest hair on his ass' tail. In the midst of this perplexing dilemma he reached Don Quixote, who was quite a bit more battered than he would have liked. Helping him to mount Rocinante, Sancho said to him,

"Master, the demon has made off with the dapple."

"What demon?" asked Don Quixote.

"The one with the bladders," said Sancho.

"Then I shall rescue him," replied Don Quixote, "even if he locks him up in the deepest, darkest dungeon of hell. Follow me, Sancho, and since the wagon is traveling slowly, I shall make up for the loss of the dapple with one of the mules."

"There's no need to go to all that trouble, master," said Sancho. "You may just as well curb your anger, for it seems the dapple has already been abandoned by the demon and is returning to the fold."

And such was the case, for when the demon and the dapple fell, in imitation of Don Quixote and Rocinante, the demon started to run towards the town and the jackass to return to his master.

"Nevertheless," said Don Quixote, "that demon's lack of consideration compels me to take revenge upon someone in the wagon, even if it is the Emperor himself."

"Your grace should banish such thoughts from your mind," said Sancho, "and accept my advice, which is never to get involved with actors because they lead charmed lives. I once saw one get arrested for two murders and go free without so much as a fine. Be advised that, because they are care-free, fun-loving souls, everyone favors them, aids and abets them, and holds them in esteem, especially when they are members of the king's companies and hold a charter, for all or most of them look like princes in their costumes and make-up."

"Still," said Don Quixote, "I will not allow that actor demon to go about boasting, even if the whole human race takes his side."

In saying this, he headed for the wagon, which by now was approaching the town, and as he rode after them, he shouted,

"Halt! Wait up, you band of care-free merrymakers! I intend to teach you how people are to treat jackasses and other animals which serve as mounts to the squires of knights-errant."

Don Quixote's shouts were so loud they were heard and understood by those in the wagon. Having determined the thrust of the shouter's words, Death immediately leapt from the wagon, followed by the emperor, the demon driver, and the angel – not that the queen or Cupid remained behind – whereupon they all armed themselves with stones and formed a line, waiting to receive Don Quixote with their sharp-edged missiles. Seeing them lined up so menacingly with their arms cocked, ready to unleash a hail of stones, Don Quixote drew up on Rocinante's reins and set himself to pondering how he might attack them with the least risk to himself. While he was hesitating, Sancho came up and, seeing him poised and ready to attack the well-organized squadron, said,

"Master, to attempt such an undertaking would be quite mad. Your grace should stop and reconsider, for there is no defensive armor on earth against stone soup except stuffing oneself inside a bronze bell and sitting tight. You should also consider that it's foolhardy, not brave, for a single man to attack an army that includes Death in its ranks, has emperors fighting in the flesh, and is assisted by good and evil angels. And if this argument is not sufficient to persuade you to stay put, may you be persuaded by the undeniable fact that among all those persons there, who may look like kings, princes, and emperors, there is not a single knight-errant."

"At last, Sancho," said Don Quixote, "you have put your finger on the thing that can and should turn me from my intended course. As I have told you on a number of other occasions, I have no right or obligation to draw my sword against anyone who has not been dubbed a knight. It is up to you, Sancho, to avenge the outrage committed against your dapple, and I shall be right here to shout encouragement and advice."

"Master," said Sancho, "there's no reason for me to take revenge on anyone, for good Christians are supposed to turn the other cheek; moreover, I'll get my jackass to leave his defense up to me, which is to live peaceably for as many days as heaven may grant me life."

"Well, if that is your decision, noble Sancho, wise Sancho, Christian and sincere Sancho, let us leave these phantoms and return to the pursuit of better and more worthwhile adventures, for from what I have seen of this land, there must be no end of fabulous ones here."

He then wheeled Rocinante about, Sancho went to retrieve his dapple, and Death and all his fleeing squadron climbed back into the wagon and continued on their way.

Thus did the frightful adventure of the wagon of Death draw to a happy conclusion thanks to the salutary advice Sancho Panza gave his master, who the following day had another adventure with an enamored knight-errant that was no less astounding than this last one.

Chapter Twelve

The strange adventure that befell the valiant Don Quixote and the bold Knight of the Mirrors

After their encounter with Death, Don Quixote and his squire spent the night among some tall shade trees where, at Sancho's urging, Don Quixote ate some of the food the dapple was carrying. During the meal, Sancho said to the knight,

"Master, how stupid I would have been to have chosen as my reward the spoils from your grace's first adventure instead of the foals from the three mares! When all is said and done, 'A bird in the hand is worth two in the bush."

"Nevertheless, Sancho," said Don Quixote, "if you had let me attack as I intended, the least spoils you would have received would have been the Empress' gold crown and Cupid's painted wings, which I would have taken by force and placed in your hands."

To which Sancho replied,

"Those scepters and crowns of stage emperors are never pure gold but are plated with tin or brass."

"That is true," said Don Quixote, "for it would not be appropriate for theatrical props to be real but make-believe and illusory, as the plays themselves are. Also, Sancho, I would have you dispose yourself favorably towards plays and show them every consideration as well as those who act in them and those who write them, for they are all instrumental in performing a great service to the state by placing a mirror before us at every step of the way wherein we may vividly observe the range of human activities. There is nothing that can more faithfully show us what we are and what we ought to be than a play and its actors. Tell me something: have you not seen some play in which they portray kings, emperors, pontiffs, knights, ladies, and sundry other characters – one actor playing the villain, another the trickster, others the merchant, the soldier, the crafty fool, and still another the inexperienced lover, and once the play is over and the actors remove their costumes, they are all reduced to equals?"

"Of course, I have," replied Sancho.

"Well, the same thing," said Don Quixote, "transpires in the drama and events of this world in which some play the emperors, others the pontiffs, and the rest all the characters that can be represented in a play, but when the end comes, that is, when life has run its course, death strips them of the clothes that made them different and they all end up equals in the grave."

"An excellent comparison," said Sancho, "though not so novel that I haven't heard it many times before, like the one from the game of chess, where each piece during the course of the game plays its particular role but when the game is over, all the pieces are collected, mixed together, and laid away in a bag, which is like people being laid away in the grave."

"Every day, Sancho," said Don Quixote, "you are becoming less simpleminded and more intelligent."

"Of course, I am" replied Sancho, "for some of your grace's intelligence just has to rub off on me. Once a barren, dry piece of land has been fertilized and cultivated, it begins to yield good crops. By this I mean that your conversation has been the fertilizer that has fallen over the barren land of my arid mind, and the cultivation is the time I have spent serving your grace. Because of this, I hope to bear fruit that will be a blessing and will not stray or fall from the paths of good breeding you have brought about in this barren understanding of mine."

Don Quixote was forced to laugh at Sancho's affected speech and believed that everything Sancho had said about his improvement was true, for every so often he spoke in a manner that astonished him, though every time or nearly every time that he tried to flaunt his learning by speaking in a courtly and professorial manner, his reasoning invariably plunged headlong from the summit of his simplemindedness into the abyss of his ignorance. But the area in which he showed himself most elegant and memorable was in his habit of citing proverbs, whether or not they bore any relevance to the matter under discussion, as will have been noted and observed in the course of this history.

A large portion of the night was spent in these and other discussions, after which Sancho felt an urge to go looking for the sandman, as he was wont to say whenever he wanted to go to sleep. But before doing so, he removed the harness from the dapple, allowing him to graze unencumbered on the abundant grass, but he made certain not to remove Rocinante's saddle, for his master had expressly forbidden him to do so during the time they were traveling in the country or sleeping under the open sky, because it was the time-honored custom for knights-errant merely to remove the bridle and drape it over the saddle-bow; but to remove the horse's saddle – never! So Sancho did accordingly, giving Rocinante the same freedom he had given the dapple, for his affection for him and Rocinante was so unparalleled and unwavering that a tradition has been passed down from father to son that the author of this faithful history had composed several chapters specifically about this but had not included them in order to preserve the dignity and decorum due so heroic a history. Still, there were times when he failed to carry out his intention and wrote that as soon as the two beasts found themselves alone, they would begin to nuzzle one another until they were tired and satisfied, at which point Rocinante would lay his neck across the dapple's, letting it project more than half a yard on the other side. They would then stand gazing at the ground for three days or at least for as long as they were left to themselves or until they were driven by hunger to forage for food. I might add that our author reportedly left an account in which he compared their friendship to that of Nisus and Euryalus, and of Pylades and Orestes. If this is true, it is easy to see, to the wonderment of mankind, how binding the friendship of these two peaceful animals was, a friendship that is a consternation to men, who are quite incapable of maintaining their friendship for one another. Because of this we have the sayings: 'A friend in need is a friend indeed,' and 'A true friend is hard to find.' I hope no one will consider the author irresponsible for comparing the friendship of these two animals to that of men, for the latter have been taught many things by beasts and have learned a number of things of importance: for example, from storks the enema, from dogs vomiting and gratitude, from cranes vigilance, from ants foresight, from elephants uprightness, and from horses loyalty.

Sancho finally fell asleep at the foot of a cork tree, while Don Quixote dozed beside a sturdy oak, but very little time had elapsed when the knight was awakened by a noise he heard behind him. Springing to his feet with a start, he directed his eyes and ears towards the spot from where the noise had come, at which point he saw two men on horseback, one of whom was easing himself down from his saddle.

"Dismount, my friend," said this rider to the other man, "and unbridle the horses. This place appears to have more than enough grass for the animals, as well as the silence and solitude my amorous thoughts demand."

His saying this and stretching out on the ground were one and the same action, and the noise made by the armor when his body hit the ground left no doubt in Don Quixote's mind that this person was a knight-errant. Going over to Sancho, who was already asleep, Don Quixote shook him by the arm and with no little effort managed to rouse him, saying softly,

"Brother Sancho, we have an adventure."

"May God make it a good one," said Sancho, "but where, master, is her grace: this Dame Adventure?"

"Where, Sancho?" replied Don Quixote. "Just look behind you and you will see a knight-errant stretched out on the ground who in my opinion cannot be overly happy, for I saw him hurl himself from his horse and slump to the ground in a gesture of despair, and as he fell, even his armor let out a groan."

"And what makes your grace think," said Sancho, "that this is an adventure?"

"I do not claim," said Don Quixote, "that it is a complete one but only the beginning of one, for this is how adventures begin. But listen: he seems to be tuning his lute or guitar and, by the way he is clearing his throat and spitting, he must be preparing to sing something."

"Upon my word, that's it," said Sancho; "he's probably a knight in love."

"There is not a single knight who is not," replied Don Quixote, "but let us listen. If he does sing, we may by following the thread locate the spool of his thoughts, for 'Of the abundance of the heart the mouth speaketh.'" [1]

Sancho was about to respond to his master when he was stopped short by the Knight of the Wood's voice, which was neither very good nor very bad. As they stood listening, they heard him sing the following song:

"Bright authoress of my good or ill,
Prescribe the law I must observe:
My heart, obedient to thy will,
Shall never from its duty swerve.

If you refuse my griefs to know,
The stifled anguish seals my fate;

1 A fusion of two passages from the Bible: Matthew XII, 34 and Luke VI, 45.

But if your ears would drink my woe,
 Love shall himself the tale relate.

Though contraries my heart compose,
 Hard as the diamond's solid frame,
And soft as yielding wax that flows,
 To thee, my fair,'tis all the same.

Take it, for every stamp prepared,
 Imprint what characters you choose,
The faithful tablet, soft or hard,
 The dear impression ne'er shall lose."

With a sigh that seemed wrenched from the depths of his being, the Knight of the Wood brought his song to a close and a moment later said in a voice that was both doleful and sad,

"O most beautiful and most ungrateful woman on earth, how can it be, most serene Casildea of Vandalia, that you will allow this your captive knight to be consumed and unstrung by these continual wanderings and these harsh, cruel ordeals? Is it not sufficient that I have exacted the vow (that you are the most beautiful woman on earth) from all the knights of Navarre, from those of León, Andalusia, Castile, and finally from all the knights of La Mancha?"

"Not so, Sancho," said Don Quixote at this point, "I am from La Mancha and have never made such an admission. I neither could nor would confess anything so prejudicial to my lady's beauty. You can already see, Sancho, that this knight is delirious, but let us listen and perhaps he will make things clear."

"That he will do," replied Sancho, "for he looks like a person who could lament for a month without stopping."

But that is not what happened, for when the Knight of the Wood overheard them discussing him, he proceeded no further with his lamentations but stood up and said in a resounding but courteous voice,

"Who goes there? Identify yourself. Do you count yourself among the blessed or the afflicted?"

"Among the afflicted," said Don Quixote.

"Then step forward," said the Knight of the Wood, "where you shall find yourself in the presence of sadness and affliction itself."

Don Quixote, who heard himself addressed in such a sad but courteous manner, walked over to him, with Sancho right behind him. The mourning knight took Don Quixote by the arm and said,

"Sit down here, sir knight. For me to recognize that your grace is one of those who profess knight-errantry, it is sufficient for me to have found you in this place where you will be accompanied by solitude and the night air – the natural bed and proper lodging place of knights-errant."

To which Don Quixote responded,

"I am a knight and belong to the profession your grace has mentioned, and though sorrow, misfortune, and adversity have taken up lodging in my breast, the compassion I feel for the misfortunes of others has not for that reason deserted it. From what you have just sung I gather that your misfortunes stem from love, or more precisely from your love of that ungrateful beauty you mentioned in your song of lament."

While this was taking place, they peaceably and sociably sat beside one another on the hard ground, as though at the break of day they were not destined to break each other's head open.

"Sir knight, are you perchance in love?" the Knight of the Wood asked Don Quixote.

"Unfortunately I am," replied Don Quixote, "though ills born of well-placed thoughts should be considered blessings rather than misfortunes."

"That is certainly true," said the Knight of the Wood, "so long as being rejected does not upset our reason and understanding, because when there are enough rejections, they have all the earmarks of revenge."

"I was never rejected by my lady," said Don Quixote.

"Certainly not," put in Sancho, who was also present, "for my lady is as meek as a lamb and softer than butter."

"Is this your grace's squire," asked the Knight of the Wood.

"Yes, it is," replied Don Quixote.

"I have never met a squire," said the Knight of the Wood, "who would dare speak while his master was speaking; at least, that is true of mine here, who is as big as his father but who, it shall never be charged, has ever opened his lips while I was speaking."

"My word!" said Sancho, "I have spoken and will continue to speak in the presence of anyone who's as big a – but I'll leave it at that, for stirring will only make it worse."

The Squire of the Wood took Sancho by the arm and said to him,

"Why don't we both go where we can have all the squire talk we please and let these lords and masters of ours have their fill of telling each other the stories of their loves. Without a doubt day will find them still at it and still not through talking."

"Gladly," said Sancho, "and I'll explain to your grace who I am so you can see whether I can hold my own with the most talkative squires around."

With this, the squires went off to themselves, where they took part in a discussion that was just as comical as their masters' was serious.

Chapter Thirteen

The continuation of the adventure of the Knight of the Wood, together with the intelligent, novel, and genial conversation that took place between the two squires

The knights and the squires divided into two groups: the latter to recount the story of their lives and the former that of their loves. Our history, which deals first with the discussion of the servants and then with that of the masters, goes on to say that once the two squires had gone off to themselves, the Squire of the Wood said to Sancho,

"My lord, those of us who serve as squires to knights-errant truly lead laborious lives and earn our bread by the sweat of our brows, which is one of the curses God placed upon our earliest ancestors."

"It may also be said," added Sancho, "that we earn it with our bodies frozen, for who suffers more heat and cold than we miserable squires of knight-errantry? It wouldn't be quite so bad if we got anything to eat, since one's burdens are lighter when there is bread, but it sometimes happens that we go one or two days without breaking our fast except on the wafting breezes."

"All of that can be endured and tolerated," said the Squire of the Wood, "because of our expectation of being rewarded, for unless the knight-errant a squire serves is terribly unfortunate, the latter will sooner or later find himself rewarded with at least the governorship of some handsome island or attractive earldom."

"I," replied Sancho, "have told my master I'll be content to govern an island and he's so noble and generous he's promised me one on quite a number of different occasions."

"I," said He of the Wood, "will be satisfied with a canonry in payment for my services, and my master has already promised me one – and what a one!"

"Your grace's master," [1] said Sancho, "must be one of those knights in the ecclesiastical line to be able to grant his faithful squire that sort of favor. Mine is a mere layman, though I do remember the time some clever but, in my opinion, ill-intentioned persons tried to persuade him to become an archbishop but he chose to be an emperor or nothing. At that moment I was afraid he might take it into his head to enter the Church, since I found myself lacking the necessary qualifications for holding a benefice. I would have your grace know that even though I appear to be a man, I'm a regular beast when it comes to serving the Church."

"But surely your grace is misinformed," said He of the Wood, "for islands aren't always the best places to govern; some are corrupt, others poor, still others depressing. In fact, the most progressive and well organized one carries with it a heavy burden of worries and inconveniences, which the unfortunate soul whose lot it is to occupy it takes upon his shoulders. It would be far better for those of us who labor under this damnable servitude to return to our homes and occupy ourselves there with more leisurely activities such as hunting and fishing, for no squire is so poor he doesn't have a nag,

---

1 It is interesting to note in the following exchange between the two squires that Cervantes humorously has them address each other as 'your grace' instead of 'you', the latter being the appropriate form of address between persons of their humble social class.

a couple of greyhounds, and a fishing pole for passing the time in his village."

"I lack none of those things," said Sancho, "but while it's true that I don't have a nag, I have a jackass who's worth twice as much as my master's horse, and may God spoil my very next Easter if I should trade him, even if they threw in four bushels of barley. Your grace probably doesn't take my dapple's value seriously – dapple, by the way, is the color of my jackass – and as for greyhounds, I will never lack for them, since they are everywhere in my hometown. What is more, hunting is always more enjoyable when it's at someone else's expense."

"Really and truly, sir squire," said He of the Wood, "I am firmly resolved to forsake the antics of these knights and return to my village to bring up my children, for I have three who are like Oriental pearls."

"I have two," said Sancho, "who might be presented to the pope himself, especially the girl, whom I'm grooming to be a countess, God willing, albeit over the protests of her mother."

"And how old is that lady who's being groomed to be a countess?" said He of the Wood.

"Fifteen, give or take a couple of years," said Sancho, "and she's as tall as a lance, fresh as an April morn, and as strong as a porter."

"Those qualities," replied He of the Wood, "qualify her to be not only a countess but a nymph in some sacred grove. That little lady must be some strong bitch!"

To which Sancho responded rather incensed,

"She's not a bitch and neither is her mother and they won't be as long as I'm alive. I would appreciate a little more civility, seeing as how your grace was raised among knights-errant, who are the very picture of courtesy. I don't find such language very appropriate."

"Oh, sir squire," replied He of the Wood, "how poorly versed your grace is in the matter of compliments! Don't you know that when some horseman skillfully spears a bull in the arena, or some person does something extremely well, people are in the habit of shouting, 'That was some bitch of a maneuver!' This expression, which in itself appears to be derogatory, is really one of great praise, and you ought to disown your very own sons and daughters if they don't do things worthy of bringing similar praises to their parents."

"I *will* disown them," said Sancho, "and for that very reason your grace may heap an entire whorehouse on the heads of me, my children, and my wife, for everything they do and say is highly deserving of such praise. And just for the chance to see them again, I will ask God to deliver me from mortal sin, which He can do by delivering me from this perilous vocation of squire I've undertaken for a second time, lured and beguiled by a bag containing a hundred ducats I found one day in the Sierra Morena. The Devil is forever tempting my eyes with a bag full of doubloons in some place or other, and at every step of the way I feel I can touch them with my hands, clasp them to my bosom, and take them home, where I can invest them, collect the interest, and live like a prince. Every time I think of this, all the hardships I suffer with this crackpot master of mine become light and bearable, for I'm sure he's more of a madman than a knight."

"For that reason," said He of the Wood, "they say that 'greed causes the sack to tear.' But, speaking of madmen, there's no bigger one on earth than my master, for he's one of those about whom they say, 'He's so occupied with other people's affairs that he neglects his own.' To help another recover his lost wits, he'll lose his, and he goes about searching for I don't know what, and when he finds it, he'll be sorry."

"Is he by any chance in love?" asked Sancho.

"Yes," said He of the Wood, "with a certain Casildea of Vandalia, the cruelest and most overcooked piece of flesh on earth, [2] but cruelty is not her present problem, for there are even greater deceptions growling in her innards, which will come to light before long." [3]

"There is no road so smooth," said Sancho, "that it doesn't contain some obstacles or pitfalls. In other homes they have troubles but in mine we have them by the pots full. Madness must have more friends and companions than sanity has, and if it's true what people say – that 'Misery loves company' – then I'll be able to console myself here, for your grace is serving a master who's as big a fool as mine."

"A fool but brave," said He of the Wood, "and more villainous than either foolish or brave."

"That's not my master," said Sancho. "I can state that in no way is he a scoundrel. Quite the contrary, he possesses a soul as pure as an angel's and because of that treats everyone kindly, and he doesn't have a malicious bone in his body. A child can convince him it's night in the middle of the day, and because of his innocence I love him with all my heart and soul and can't bring myself to leave him, regardless of how crazy he acts."

"Nevertheless, my lord and brother," said He of the Wood, "'When the blind lead the blind, they all run the risk of falling into the ditch.' It would be better for us to beat a hasty retreat and return to our beloved homes, for 'People who seek adventures are not always pleased with those they find.'"

Sancho had been spitting from time to time and, because his saliva seemed thick and sticky, the charitable Squire of the Wood noticed it and said,

"It would appear our topic of conversation is making our tongues stick to our palates but I've got something hanging from my horse's saddlebow that will be very good for unsticking them."

In saying this, he got up and shortly returned with a large wineskin and a meat pie half a yard long, which is no exaggeration, for it contained such a large white rabbit that, when Sancho felt of it, he took it to be a goat, and not just a young one either. When Sancho saw it, he said,

"Sir, is this what your grace carries on trips?"

"Well, what did your grace expect? Am I by chance a squire of little consequence? I carry better provisions in my saddlebags than a general does on a march."

Sancho began to eat without having to be asked and there in the darkness devoured mouthfuls as big as one's fist, at which point he said,

"Your grace is truly a genuine and bona fide squire, tried and true, magnificent and splendid, as this banquet proves, which may not have appeared here by magic but certainly gives that impression,

---

2 Another play on words. "... the cruelest and most overcooked piece of flesh ... " (Spanish: ***la más cruda y la más asada señora***). ***Cruda*** means both 'cruel' and 'not cooked,' whereas ***más asada*** means 'overcooked.'

3 The implication being that she is pregnant.

unlike poor, unfortunate me, who carry in my saddlebags only a small chunk of cheese that's so hard you could bust open a giant's head with it, and to keep it company I've got several dozen carob beans and an equal number of hazelnuts and walnuts thanks to my master's stinginess and his absolute conviction that knights-errant should sustain themselves on nothing more than dried fruits and herbs of the field."

"Upon my word, brother," replied He of the Wood, "my stomach is not made for golden thistles, wild pears, or roots from the hills. Let our masters have their ideas and rules of chivalry and eat whatever they please but, to be prepared, I always carry my food basket and this dear wineskin hanging from my saddlebow to which I am so devoted and so much in love that hardly a moment goes by that I don't give it a thousand kisses and a thousand hugs."

In saying this, he thrust it into Sancho's hands, who raised it to his lips, squeezed it, and sat gazing at the stars for a quarter of an hour. Once he had finished drinking, he let his head fall to one side, heaved a deep sigh, and said,

"That's some bitch of a wine!"

"There!" said the Squire of the Wood when he heard Sancho's exclamation, "don't you see how you praised this wine by calling it a bitch?"

"I have to admit," said Sancho, "that it's no lack of respect to call a person a bitch when it's understood he's being praised, but will your grace please tell me in the name of everything you hold most dear if this wine is from Ciudad Real?"

"What an excellent wine taster!" replied He of the Wood. "That's exactly where it's from and it's been aged for several years."

"Why tell me that?" said Sancho. "Your grace needn't come to my aid till you see I'm stumped. Isn't it marvelous, sir squire, that I possess such a great and natural instinct for judging wines that by smelling any one of them I can guess its region and pedigree, its flavor and age, the changes it will undergo, and all the other qualities having to do with wine? But there's nothing surprising about this, for I had on my father's side of the family the two most excellent wine tasters seen in La Mancha in many a year, and as proof of this I'll tell you an anecdote about them.

"The two men were once asked to judge a barrel of wine and to give their opinion of its condition, quality, strengths, and weaknesses. One of them tasted it with the tip of his tongue, while the other merely held it up to his nose. The first said the wine savored of iron; the second claimed it savored more of leather. The owner insisted that the barrel was clean and the wine contained no ingredients that could give it the taste of iron or leather. Despite this the two famous wine tasters stuck by what they had said. Time passed, the wine was sold, and when the barrel was cleaned, they found inside it a key on the end of a leather strap. Now, will your grace tell me whether someone who comes from such stock can express his opinion in matters of this type?"

"That's why I maintain," said the Squire of the Wood, "that we should stop this wandering about in quest of adventures, for since we have bread, we should not go looking for cake but should return to our humble homes, where God can find us if He wishes to."

"Until my master reaches Saragossa, I'll serve him," said Sancho, "but after that we shall see."

In the end, the two worthy squires talked and drank so much that it took sleep to tie their tongues and to moderate their thirst even though the latter was impossible to quench. And so both squires, still clutching the nearly empty wineskin and having their mouths full of half-chewed food, fell asleep, where we shall now leave them and relate those matters the Knight of the Wood discussed with Him of the Woeful Countenance.

Chapter Fourteen

The continuation of the adventure of the Knight of the Wood

Among the various topics discussed by Don Quixote and the Knight of the Wood, our history relates that He of the Wood said to Don Quixote,

"In short, sir knight, I would have your grace know that fate, or rather my decision, led to my becoming enamored of the peerless Casildea of Vandalia. I call her peerless because she has no equal either in the loftiness of her stature or in the perfection of her rank and beauty. This same Casildea of whom I speak repaid me for my pure thoughts and wholesome desires by involving me, as his stepmother did Hercules, in sundry and diverse perils, promising me at the end of each that my hopes would be fulfilled at the conclusion of the next, but my ordeals have continued to mount so steadily that they are beyond reckoning and I have no idea which one will finally enable me to realize my noble desires. She once ordered me to confront that famous giantess of Seville known as the Giralda, [1] who is as brave and strong as if she were made of bronze and who, without moving from where she stands, is the most changeable and volatile woman on the face of the earth. I came, I saw, I conquered her and made her stand still and cease revolving, so that for more than a week only the north winds blew. On another occasion, she ordered me to lift those ancient stones of the mighty Bulls of Guisando, an enterprise more appropriate for a porter than a knight. On yet another, she ordered me to descend to the bottom of the cave at Cabra, a frightful and unheard-of undertaking, to bring her a detailed description of the things concealed within those dark depths. And so I stopped the Giralda from revolving, lifted the Bulls of Guisando, descended into the bowels of the cave, thereby revealing what lay hidden in its depths, and yet my hopes are deader than dead and her scornful commands are more alive than ever. As a final task, she recently ordered me to ride through all the provinces of Spain to exact a confession from every knight-errant wandering there that she surpasses in beauty every woman now living and that I am the most valiant and truly enamored knight on earth. To satisfy this request, I have already traversed the greater part of Spain and have vanquished a number of knights who have had the audacity to contradict me. But the accomplishment of which I am proudest and most boastful is having defeated in hand-to-hand combat that most famous knight Don Quixote

1 The 'giantess' is a large bronze statue mounted on a globe, both of which are situated atop a beautiful tower of the Cathedral of Seville, where the statue serves as a revolving weather vane.

of La Mancha, whom I forced to confess that my Casildea is more beautiful than his Dulcinea. As a result of this single victory I consider myself conqueror of every knight on earth, for this same Don Quixote I mention has conquered them all himself; and since I have vanquished him, his glory, fame, and honor have all passed to me, for 'The more famous the conquered, the more esteemed the conqueror!' Thus the countless deeds of the above-mentioned Don Quixote are now in my account and belong to me alone."

Don Quixote was shocked at this assertion by the Knight of the Wood and was just on the verge of calling him a liar, already having the word on the tip of his tongue, when he collected himself as much as possible in hopes of leading him to confess his falsehood with his *own* tongue. And so he calmly said to him,

"Regarding the fact, sir knight, that your grace has vanquished the majority of the knights of Spain and even of the entire world I have no comment, but that you have vanquished Don Quixote of La Mancha I am very much in doubt. It may have been some other person who resembled him, though there are few who do."

"Some other person!" exclaimed He of the Wood; "I swear by the heavens above that I fought with Don Quixote and overcame and vanquished him. He is a tall man with a weather-worn face, long lanky arms and legs, graying hair, a sharp, somewhat curved nose, and a large black drooping mustache. He goes into battle under the name of the Knight of the Woeful Countenance and has as his squire a farmer by the name of Sancho Panza. He manfully strides and commands a famous horse called Rocinante and, lastly, has as the lady of his thoughts a certain Dulcinea of Toboso, formerly known as Aldonza Lorenzo, just as mine is called Casilda and comes from Andalusia, whence her name Casildea of Vandalia. If all this evidence does not suffice to substantiate my claim, here is my sword, which shall make my story credible to incredulity itself."

"Compose yourself, sir knight," said Don Quixote, "and listen to what I have to say. I would have your grace know that this Don Quixote of whom you speak is the best friend I have in this world and is such that I hold him in the same regard as I do my own person. Because of that most detailed and accurate description you have given me, I can only believe he is the very one you have vanquished. On the other hand, it is manifestly and patently impossible that it was he, unless it happened that among the numerous enchanters inimical to him, a certain one, in particular, who pursues him as a matter of course, one of them assumed his appearance and allowed himself to be defeated in an effort to defraud him of the fame his great accomplishments as a knight have earned and acquired for him throughout the known world. As confirmation of this, I would also have you know that no more than two days ago his adversaries, the said enchanters, transformed the beautiful Dulcinea's face and body into a lowly, coarse villager and they have probably transformed Don Quixote in the same manner. Now if all this fails to convince you that I am speaking the truth, you see here before you Don Quixote himself, who will back up his words with his weapons, on foot, on horseback, or in whatever manner you choose."

As he said this, he sprang to his feet, drew his sword, and waited to see what response the Knight of the Wood would make. The latter, in the same calm voice, answered,

"'An earnest buyer doesn't mind putting down a deposit,' Sir Don Quixote. If I was able to defeat your grace when you were transformed, I have every reason to expect to subdue you in the flesh, but since it is not proper for knights to perform their feats of arms in the dark like highwaymen or ruffians, let us wait for day so the sun may be witness to our deeds. Our only stipulation shall be that the loser of our combat is to remain at the disposal of the winner to do whatever he designates, so long as the command may be decently obeyed by a knight."

"I am more than satisfied with the propriety of that stipulation," said Don Quixote.

After agreeing to this, they went to look for their squires, whom they found snoring and lying in the same positions they were in when sleep overtook them. Rousing them, they ordered the squires to prepare the horses because at sunrise the two knights were to engage in a bloody, hard-fought hand-to-hand combat. Sancho was stunned and overwhelmed by this news, fearing for the welfare of his master because of the heroic exploits performed by the Knight of the Wood according to his squire's account. But without saying a word, the two squires left to retrieve their beasts, because by now the three horses and the jackass had caught one another's scent and were huddled together. On the way, the Squire of the Wood said to Sancho,

"Brother squire, your grace should know that it is the custom among combatants in Andalusia for the seconds in a duel not to stand idly by with their arms folded while the principals fight. I say this to advise you that, while our masters are fighting, you and I too must fight and cut each other to shreds."

"That custom, sir squire," said Sancho, "may hold true among the ruffians and hoodlums your grace has mentioned but among the squires of knights-errant such a thing is unthinkable; at least, I have never heard my master mention any such custom, and he knows every last requirement of knight-errantry by heart. But let us say for the sake of argument that there is an expressed ordinance requiring squires to fight while their masters do battle, I will still not abide by it but will pay the fine levied against such pacifist squires as myself, which, I feel certain, will not exceed two pounds of wax. I prefer to pay those two pounds because I know they'll cost me less than what I'll spend on the bandages needed for healing my head, which I can already see split open and divided into halves. And there's one more thing: it is impossible for me to fight because I don't own a sword; in fact, I've never even carried one."

"I have an easy solution for that," said He of the Wood. "I've got a couple of linen sacks that are the same size. Your grace can take one and I'll take the other and we can have a sack fight with equal weapons."

"In that case I'll do so with pleasure," replied Sancho, "for such a fight will serve to dust us off rather than wound us."

"Not exactly," replied the other squire, "for in order to keep the sacks from being too light, we'll fill them with half a dozen nice smooth stones so that each sack will weigh the same. In this way we can give each other a good drubbing without doing any damage or harm."

"Merciful heavens!" said Sancho, "would you look at the sable skins and wads of cotton he's putting into the sack so we won't crack open our skulls and pulverize our bones! Even if they were filled with silk cocoons, I mean to state here that I refuse to fight. Let our masters do the fighting – that is their business – but let us have a drink and go on living, for time will rob us soon enough of our lives without our going about looking for excuses to end them before their harvest season arrives and they fall to the ground of their own accord."

"Nevertheless," said He of the Wood, "we must fight, if it's only for half an hour."

"On the contrary," replied Sancho, "I'll not be so discourteous and ungrateful as to raise any quarrel whatsoever with the person I've eaten and drunk with, especially when I bear him no anger or malice, for who the devil can bring himself to fight without provocation?"

"In that case," said He of the Wood, "I have the perfect solution: before we begin our fight, I'll come over to your grace ever so nicely and will strike you three or four times in the face, which will lay you out at my feet. By this means I will awaken your anger even if it is sleeping as soundly as a dormouse."

"And I'll parry that sword thrust," said Sancho, "with another that's just as good. I'll pick up a stick and before your grace can awaken my anger, I'll throttle you into such a deep sleep you won't wake up unless it's in the next life, where I'm known as a man who won't let his face be ill-used by anyone. Each of us should look out for himself, though the smartest thing we could do would be to leave each other's anger undisturbed, for 'No one knows another man's soul,' and 'One often goes looking for wool but comes home shorn;' and God Himself has extolled peace and denounced quarreling. Also, if a cat that is chased, cornered, and seized turns into a lion, God knows what I will turn into, being a man. Therefore, sir squire, I hereby serve notice that all the harm and mischief resulting from our scrap will be on your grace's head."

"That's all right," said He of the Wood, "for God will bring the dawn and we shall prosper."

By now a thousand varieties of colorful birds had begun chirping in the trees and with their diverse and joyous songs appeared to be welcoming and greeting fresh Aurora, who along the portals and balconies of the eastern horizon was revealing the beauty of her countenance, shaking from her tresses an endless succession of liquid pearls. The foliage, bathing itself in her delicate liquor, likewise appeared to be producing and exuding tiny opaque dewdrops. When dawn arrived, the willows distilled their savory manna, the fountains laughed, the brooks murmured, the woods rejoiced, and the meadows donned their finery, but as soon as daylight allowed things to be seen and distinguished, the first object to catch Sancho Panza's eye was the Squire of the Wood's nose, which was so large it virtually shaded his entire body. In fact, it may be described as being outrageously large, bent in the middle, covered with warts, purplish like an eggplant, and hanging an inch and a half below his mouth. Its size, color, warts, and crooked shape made his face so hideous that when Sancho saw it, his arms and legs began to tremble like an epileptic child's and he vowed in his heart to let himself be slapped two hundred times before awakening the ire of that ogre and fighting him.

Don Quixote looked at his own adversary and found he was already wearing his helmet and had the visor closed, so that his face remained hidden, but he noticed that he had a muscular build in spite of his short stature. Over his armor he wore a surcoat or cassock apparently of the most delicate gold cloth dotted with numerous glittering mirrors in the shape of tiny moons, which gave him an exceedingly gallant and flamboyant appearance. Above his helmet fluttered a large number of green, yellow, and white plumes. His lance, which was leaning against a tree, was thick, quite long, and tipped with an iron point as long as one's hand. Don Quixote observed this, took it all in, and concluded from what he saw that this particular knight must be exceedingly strong, but unlike Sancho Panza he experienced no fear. Instead, with wondrous daring he said to the Knight of the Mirrors,

"Sir knight, if your burning desire to fight has not consumed your courtesy, I beg your grace to raise your visor slightly so I may see whether the nobility of your face matches that of your body."

"Sir knight, whether or not you triumph in this enterprise," replied He of the Mirrors, "there will be more than enough time and opportunity for your grace to observe me. If I do not satisfy your desire at this moment, it is because I feel I shall be doing considerable harm to the beautiful Casildea of Vandalia by delaying for the length of time it will take me to raise my visor instead of making you confess what you already know I am demanding."

"Well, while we are mounting our steeds," said Don Quixote, "you can at least tell me whether I am the same Don Quixote you say you vanquished."

"To that I can say," said He of the Mirrors, "that your grace looks as much like the knight I defeated as one egg looks like another, but since you say you are hounded by enchanters, I dare not affirm whether or not you are the one in question."

"That," replied Don Quixote, "is sufficient to make me believe your grace was tricked. But to show you that you are completely mistaken, bring on the horses, for in less time than it would take you to raise your visor, if God, my lady, and my arm fail me not, I shall get a look at your face and you will see that I am not the Don Quixote you imagine."

With this they broke off their conversation and mounted their horses. Don Quixote turned Rocinante and rode to the spot from where he intended to charge at his adversary, with the Knight of the Mirrors doing the same. But Don Quixote had ridden no more than twenty paces when he heard himself being summoned by Him of the Mirrors. Riding back, they met halfway, whereupon He of the Mirrors said,

"Remember, sir knight, the agreement is that the loser of our battle, as I have already stated, shall remain at the disposal of the winner."

"I am aware of that," replied Don Quixote, "so long as the loser is not required or ordered to do anything that exceeds the bounds of chivalry."

"That is understood," said He of the Mirrors.

Just then, Don Quixote caught sight of the squire's strange nose and was taken aback by the sight no less than Sancho had been, so much so, in fact, that he took him to be some monster or freak of nature never before seen on earth. Sancho, who watched his master ride off in preparation for his charge, refused to be left alone with Big Nose, fearing that with one swipe of that appendage against his own his battle would be over and he would find himself laid out on the ground either from the blow or from fear. He therefore caught up with his master and held on to Rocinante's stirrup strap. When it was finally time for the knight to turn his horse, he said,

"Master, before your grace turns to make your charge, I wish you would help me climb that oak tree, where I will have a view more to my liking – better than on the ground – of the fearless encounter your grace is about to undertake with this knight."

"I rather believe, Sancho," said Don Quixote, "that you wish to have a seat that is high and dry so you may 'view the bulls in safety.'"

"To tell the truth," replied Sancho, "this squire's enormous nose has so overwhelmed me and filled me with dread that I dare not remain alone with him."

"It *is* such," said Don Quixote, "that were I not who I am, I too might be frightened. But come: I shall help you climb to your designated spot."

While Don Quixote stopped to help Sancho climb the cork oak, the Knight of the Mirrors had ridden off as far as he deemed necessary and, believing Don Quixote to have done the same, did not wait for the blare of a trumpet or any other such signal but turned his horse, which was no swifter nor any more presentable than Rocinante, and began his charge towards his opponent at full speed, which in actuality was a half-hearted trot. But when he saw Don Quixote engaged in helping Sancho climb the tree, he drew up on the reins of his horse and brought him to a halt in mid-charge, for which action his horse was exceedingly grateful, being no longer capable of budging. Don Quixote, imagining that his adversary was barreling down upon him, drove his spurs violently into Rocinante's lean flanks and set him moving so fast that, according to our history, this was the only time he was ever known to come close to running, for on every other occasion he had simply galloped at a trot. By dint of this unheard-of fury he reached the spot where the Knight of the Mirrors was digging his spurs into his horse up to their shanks but was powerless to make him budge an inch from where he had brought his charge to a halt. Don Quixote found his foe in this predicament, frustrated by his horse and fumbling with his lance, which, due either to his lack of time or lack of experience, he was unable to place in its socket. Don Quixote took no notice of these difficulties and charged at the Knight of the Mirrors so viciously (and without risk or danger to himself) that he sent the knight hurtling over the flanks of his horse, where he landed on the ground much to his sorrow, and his fall was such that he moved neither hands nor feet and gave every indication of being dead.

No sooner did Sancho see him fall than he climbed down from the cork tree and ran to his master as fast as his legs would carry him. The latter leapt from Rocinante and positioned himself over Him of the Mirrors. Untying the straps on the helmet to see if he was dead – or to give him air should he possibly be alive – he saw . . . oh, I wish I could describe what he saw without producing astonishment, wonder, and consternation in all of you listening to this. He saw – so says our history – the very face, the very figure, the very aspect, the very physiognomy, the very effigy, and the very likeness of the bachelor Sansón Carrasco, and when he saw him, he cried out in a loud voice,

"Come here, Sancho, and look at this! You won't believe what you are about to see! Hurry, my son, and see what magic can do – what sorcerers and enchanters are capable of."

When Sancho arrived, he saw the face of the bachelor Carrasco and began making a thousand signs of the cross over his breast. During all this time no signs of life had come from the fallen knight, whereupon Sancho said to Don Quixote,

"I'm of the opinion, my lord, that you should stick your sword into this person's mouth and drive it home – this person who looks like the bachelor Carrasco but who may or may not be. Perhaps, by slaying him, your grace will slay one of the enchanters who are your enemies."

"That is not bad advice," said Don Quixote, "for when it comes to enemies, the fewer one has the better."

But as he drew his sword to execute Sancho's advice and counsel, the Knight of the Mirrors' squire came running up, now minus the nose that had made him look so hideous, and he began crying out in a loud voice,

"Sir Don Quixote, may your grace carefully consider what you're about to do, for that person prostrate at your feet is your friend the bachelor Sansón Carrasco and I am his squire."

Seeing the squire without his earlier ugliness, Sancho said to him,

"And what about your nose?"

"I have it here in my pocket," said the squire. And reaching into his right-hand pocket, he pulled out a false nose made of varnished pasteboard, as already described. Sancho, after staring at him ever more intently, shouted in amazement,

"Mother of God protect me! Can this be Tomé Cecial, my neighbor and friend?"

"It certainly can be!" replied the now unnosed squire. "I am Tomé Cecial, Sancho Panza my friend and companion. Later, I'll explain the means, tricks, and schemes that brought me here but in the meantime please beg and implore your master and lord not to touch, mistreat, wound, or slay the Knight of the Mirrors there at his feet, for he is without the slightest doubt the rash and ill-advised bachelor Sansón Carrasco, our fellow villager."

At this moment, He of the Mirrors regained consciousness and when Don Quixote saw this, he waved the tip of his bare sword in his face and said,

"You are a dead knight, sir, unless you confess that the peerless Dulcinea of Toboso's beauty excels that of your Casildea of Vandalia. In addition to this, you are to promise me that if you escape with your life from your defeat in this battle, you shall go to the city of Toboso and present yourself to her on my behalf, that she may dispose of you as she sees fit. Should she dismiss you without an assigned task, you shall by that same token return here and seek me out – the trail of my deeds will serve to lead you to me – and give me a report of what transpired between you and her, conditions which, in accordance with those we established before our battle, do not exceed the bounds of knight-errantry."

"I confess," said the prostrate knight, "that the soiled and tattered shoe of the Lady Dulcinea of Toboso is worth more than Casildea's ill-groomed but clean bush, [2] and I promise to present myself to her and then return here, at which time I shall provide a full and detailed account of everything your grace demands."

"You are also to confess and believe," added Don Quixote, "that the knight you defeated was not and could not have been Don Quixote of La Mancha but someone else who resembled him, just as I confess and believe that, though you look like the bachelor Sansón Carrasco, it is not he but someone else who looks like him, whom my adversaries have placed here in his likeness so I shall restrain and moderate the intensity of my wrath and forego the celebration of my glorious victory."

"All this I believe, deem, and confess, as you so believe, deem, and feel," replied the disabled knight, "but I beg your grace to permit me to rise, that is, if the impact from my fall will allow it, for it has left me fairly battered."

---

2 Another of Cervantes' veiled obscenities.

He was helped to his feet by Don Quixote and Tomé Cecial his squire, whom Sancho never ceased to scrutinize. The latter asked the squire several questions, the answers to which gave every indication that he really was Tomé Cecial as he claimed, but the apprehension that had been aroused in Sancho when his master had said the enchanters had transformed the figure of the Knight of the Mirrors into that of the bachelor Carrasco prevented him from believing the reality of what he was observing with his very own eyes. In a word, master and servant remained under this delusion, while the Knight of the Mirrors and his squire, hapless and crestfallen, took leave of Don Quixote and Sancho, intent upon finding some place where they could plaster and strap up the knight's ribs. Don Quixote and Sancho once again resumed their journey to Saragossa, which is where our history will leave them in order to provide an account of the Knight of the Mirrors and his nosesome squire.

Chapter Fifteen

The account and revelation of the identities of the Knight of the Mirrors and his squire

Don Quixote was extremely contented, proud, and puffed up as a result of his victory over such a valiant knight as he imagined Him of the Mirrors to be, because of whose chivalric promise Don Quixote expected to learn whether the enchantment of his lady was still in effect, since it was incumbent upon the defeated knight, under penalty of ceasing to be one, to give an account of everything that transpired between himself and the lady. Now, Don Quixote had one thing in mind but the Knight of the Mirrors had quite another, for at that moment his thoughts were directed only towards finding some place where he could get his ribs plastered, as we have mentioned. And so our history relates that when the bachelor Sansón Carrasco once again advised Don Quixote to resume his abandoned knight-errantry, he did so after consulting with the priest and the barber as to what measures they might employ to induce Don Quixote to stay at home in peace and quiet and not to excite himself with his ill-sought adventures. From this consultation came the decision, by the consent of everyone in general and Carrasco in particular, that they should permit Don Quixote to sally forth once again, since it appeared impossible to restrain him, and that Sansón would take to the road once more as a knight-errant, where he would engage him in battle – there being more than enough reasons for such a provocation – and would then defeat him, a goal that would be easy enough to accomplish. There would also be a pact and agreement that the vanquished knight was to remain at the disposal of the victor. Once Don Quixote was defeated, the bachelor knight would order him to return to his home in the village and remain there for two years or until instructed otherwise, for it was obvious that Don Quixote, once defeated, would undoubtedly comply lest he contravene or come up short of the rules of chivalry, and it might turn out that during this period of seclusion he would abandon his outrageous ideas or they would have the opportunity to seek a suitable cure for his madness.

Carrasco agreed to this and Tomé Cecial, a friend and neighbor of Sancho Panza's and a happy-go-lucky simpleton, offered to serve as his squire. Sansón armed himself in the manner described and Tomé Cecial attached to his real nose the false, make-believe one already mentioned so he would not be recognized by his friend when they met. Setting out at once on the same route taken by Don Quixote, they came close to finding themselves present at the adventure of the wagon of Death but finally caught up with them in the forest where everything occurred that the observant reader will have read. And had it not been for the extraordinary ideas of Don Quixote, who had beguiled himself into believing the bachelor was not the bachelor, Master Sansón would have been forever deprived of receiving his degree of licentiate, for he had not even found nests where he had expected to find birds. Tomé Cecial, seeing how poorly their plans had been rewarded and how badly the enterprise had ended, said to the bachelor,

"Sir Sansón Carrasco, we are certainly getting what we deserve. It is easy enough to come up with an idea and set it in motion but most of the time it is hard to bring it to a successful conclusion. Here is Don Quixote mad and ourselves sane, and yet he comes away healthy and smiling, whereas your grace ends up throttled and dejected. I would like to know who is crazier: the person who is mad because he can't help it or the person who is because he chooses to be."

To which Sansón replied,

"The difference between two such madmen is that the person who is mad by necessity will always be mad, whereas the person who is mad by design can cease to be whenever he so chooses."

"In that case," said Tomé Cecial, "I became mad of my own free will when I decided to become your grace's squire and by that same token I would now like to call a halt to all this and return to my home."

"That is all right for you," said Sansón, "but to think that I shall return to mine before I have given Don Quixote a good thrashing is to think the impossible. Nor shall I be induced to pursue him now by my desire to see him regain his sanity but by my desire for retaliation, for this awful pain in my ribs will not permit me to adopt a more charitable course."

The two continued this discussion until they came to a town where they were fortunate enough to find a bone-setter to tend the hapless Sansón. Tomé Cecial departed and returned home, while Sansón was left to ponder his revenge. Our history will have more to say about him in due time but it now incumbent upon us to accompany Don Quixote in his rejoicing.

Chapter Sixteen

What befell Don Quixote and a perceptive gentleman from La Mancha

Don Quixote continued his journey, displaying the happiness, satisfaction, and pride already mentioned and, as a consequence of his latest victory, fancying himself the most valiant knight-errant of the age. He considered as already accomplished and brought to a felicitous conclusion all the adventures that might befall him from that time forward. Scoffing at enchanters and their enchantments, he overlooked the innumerable beatings he had suffered in the course of his knight-errantry: the stoning that had knocked out half of his teeth, the ingratitude of the galley slaves, the audacity of the Yangüesans and their barrage of staves; and lastly, he said to himself that should he find the means, manner, or method for disenchanting his lady Dulcinea, he would not envy the greatest happiness the most fortunate knight of yore had ever attained or ever would attain. As he rode along completely engrossed in these thoughts, Sancho said to him,

"Isn't it odd, master, that I can still see that outrageous, oversized nose of my neighbor Tomé Cecial?"

"And do you still believe, Sancho, that the Knight of the Mirrors could somehow be the bachelor Carrasco, and his squire your neighbor Tomé Cecial?"

"I don't know what to believe," said Sancho; "all I know is that the description he gave me of my house, wife, and children could have come from none other than Tomé himself, and his face, once the nose was removed, was the same as Tomé Cecial's, which I've seen countless times in my village, since only a wall separates his house from mine; and the sound of his voice was one and the same."

"Let us discuss that," said Don Quixote. "Ask yourself, Sancho: under what circumstances would the bachelor Sansón Carrasco come here as a knight-errant, armed both to attack and defend himself, to do battle with me? Have I by chance ever been his enemy? Have I ever given him cause to hold a grudge against me? Am I his rival or has he taken up the profession of arms, that he should be envious of the fame I have won by them?"

"Well, master," replied Sancho, "what are we to conclude then about this knight, whoever he is, who looks so much like the bachelor Carrasco, and his squire like my neighbor Tomé Cecial? If this is enchantment, as your grace has said, aren't there two other people in the world they could have looked like?"

"It is all trickery and deception," said Don Quixote, "of the malicious magicians who pursue me and who, foreseeing that I was to emerge from the battle victorious, arranged for the vanquished knight to display the face of my friend the bachelor so my friendship with him would interpose itself between him and the edge of my sword and the might of my arm, tempering the justifiable anger in my breast that so the one who tried to take my life by fraud and deception might be spared his. As proof of this, Sancho, you already know from experience, which will not let you lie or be deceitful, how easy it is for enchanters to transform certain faces into others, making the beautiful ugly and the ugly beautiful, for not two days ago you saw with your own eyes the beauty and comeliness of the peerless Dulcinea of Toboso in all her purity and perfection, whereas I, through my clouded vision, saw the ugliness and baseness of a coarse village girl with foul breath. [1] It should come as no surprise that

---

1 My translation above is the generally accepted interpretation of the passage in question but Cervantes' text literally says, "I saw in her the ugliness and baseness of a coarse village girl

(continued...)

the perverse enchanter who dared effect such an evil transformation in her has done the same with Sansón Carrasco and your neighbor in an effort to snatch the glorious victory from my hands. But despite everything, I take comfort in the fact that, when all is said and done, I have defeated my enemy in whatever form he has assumed."

"God will know where the truth lies," said Sancho, but because he knew Dulcinea's transformation had been his own contrivance and deception, his master's extravagant ideas failed to convince him. Still, he was unwilling to respond lest he say something that might expose the deception.

While discussing these matters, they were overtaken by a man traveling in their direction riding a beautiful black and white mare. He was wearing a fine green cloth coat with tawny velvet triangles and a hood of the same material, and his mare, whose trappings were green and mulberry, was outfitted for swift cross-country traveling. The rider wore a Moorish cutlass suspended from a wide green and gold shoulder sash, buskins made with the same care as the sash, and spurs that were not golden but were covered with such a polished, shiny green varnish that they matched the rest of his outfit and looked more authentic than if they had been pure gold. The traveler caught up with them and courteously greeted them but, when he spurred his horse and rode past without stopping, Don Quixote called out to him,

"Gallant sir, if your grace should happen to be traveling in our direction and there is no need to hurry, I should consider it an honor for us to travel together."

"Actually," responded the man on the mare, "I would gladly do so if I did not fear your grace's horse might become excited by my mare's presence."

"Sir," said Sancho at this point, "your grace may safely rein in the mare, for our horse is the most virtuous and well-behaved horse on earth. On occasions similar to this one he has never committed a single indiscretion, and the only time he ever strayed from the fold my master and I paid for it seven times over. Therefore, I repeat that your grace may ride along with us if you wish, for even if the mare were presented to the horse on a platter, I am certain he would show no interest in her."

The traveler drew up on the reins while marveling at the face and figure of Don Quixote, who was riding along without his helmet, which Sancho had hung like a valise from the front pommel of the ass' packsaddle. And if the man in green was staring at Don Quixote, the latter was staring at him even harder because the newcomer struck him as a man of quality. He appeared to be about fifty years of age and his hair was slightly gray, his face aquiline, his expression somewhere between cheerful and somber, and lastly, by his apparel and elegant manner he gave the impression of being a man of virtue. What the man in green thought of Don Quixote was that never in his life had he seen a man who looked or acted like this. He marveled at his lanky horse, his tall stature, his lean, sallow face, his armor, countenance, and bearing – a countenance and appearance not seen in those parts in many a year. Don Quixote noticed how intently the traveler was staring at him and divined what he was thinking from his look of astonishment, and since he was ever gracious and eager to please, *he*

(...continued)
with cataracts in her [or my] eyes and a bad odor in her mouth." If Cervantes intended the interpretation given in my translation, he phrased it rather ineptly.

broached the subject before the man could say a word.

"I am not surprised," said Don Quixote, "that your grace should marvel at my appearance, since it is so novel and so unlike that commonly encountered, but you will no longer be surprised when I tell you, as I shall, that I am one of those knights,

'Who ride, the people say,
In quest of ventures bold.'

I have left my home, mortgaged my estate, abandoned my life of ease, and delivered myself into the arms of Fortune, that she may conduct me wherever she pleases. I have attempted to revive the now defunct practice of knight-errantry and for some time now – tripping here, stumbling there, falling down and picking myself up again – have achieved a sizeable number of my goals: coming to the aid of widows, protecting damsels, and favoring married women, orphans, and wards, the natural and proper function of knights-errant. And so, thanks to my numerous valiant and Christian accomplishments, I am worthy to see myself in print in nearly all or most of the nations on earth. Thirty thousand copies of my history have already been printed and thirty million are in the process unless heaven calls a halt to it. In short, to conclude this matter in just a few words, or only one, let me say that I am Don Quixote of La Mancha, otherwise known as the Knight of the Woeful Countenance, and though it is demeaning for me to praise myself, on occasion I am forced to do so, which is understandable when there is no one else present to praise me. And so, gentle sir, this horse, this lance and buckler, this squire, all these arms taken together, my sallow appearance, and my lean, lanky frame should not henceforth surprise you, now that you have learned who I am and which profession I follow."

After saying this, Don Quixote remained silent and the man in green, by hesitating quite some time before responding, appeared to be searching for the right words to do so. After a long pause, he finally said,

"Sir knight, your grace has succeeded in discerning from my bewilderment what I wished to know but you have not succeeded in removing the astonishment I experienced in seeing you, for though, as you say, my knowledge of who you are should rid me of this, it has not done so. In fact, now that I am aware of it, I am more astounded and bewildered than ever. Is it possible that nowadays there are knights-errant on earth and histories being published about real feats of chivalry? No one can convince me that today there is any person on earth who will befriend widows, protect damsels, honor married women, and aid orphans, nor would I believe such a thing had I not observed it in your grace with my own eyes. Praised be heaven, because that exalted history of chivalry you say has been printed containing events that really occurred will consign to oblivion the never-ending escapades of those fictitious knights-errant with which the world is overrun and which are so harmful to our established customs and a detriment and discredit to genuine histories."

"There is much to be said," replied Don Quixote, "on the issue of whether the histories of knights-errant are real or fictitious."

"Well," replied the man in green, "is there anyone who doubts that such histories are false?"

"I doubt it," retorted Don Quixote, "but let us leave it at that. If our journey continues, I trust in God that I can persuade your grace of your error in following those persons who have convinced themselves that these books are fallacious."

Because of this last statement of Don Quixote's, the traveler was left with the feeling that the knight must be some kind of half-wit, so he waited for him to confirm his suspicion by some further pronouncement. But before they could turn to other matters, Don Quixote asked the man in green to tell him who he was, inasmuch as he had already made the traveler privy to his own life and affairs. To this the man in the green coat answered,

"I, Sir Knight of the Woeful Countenance, am an hidalgo and native of the village in which we shall dine today if it is God's will. I am more than moderately wealthy and my name is Don Diego de Miranda. I spend my life in the company of my wife, children, and friends. My pastimes are hunting and fishing, though I maintain neither falcons nor greyhounds but do have a tame partridge for a decoy and a fearless ferret or two. I have in my possession as many as six dozen books in Spanish or Latin, some of which are historical and some devotional. To this day those of knight-errantry have never crossed the portals of my home. I turn more frequently to the profane than to the devotional ones, so long as they provide virtuous entertainment, possess an enjoyable style, and keep one in awe and suspense by means of ingenuity and originality, though there are very few of this type in Spain. From time to time I dine with my neighbors and friends and often invite them to dine with me, and my offerings are spotless, elegant, and never skimpy. I derive no pleasure from gossip and will allow none in my presence, and I never pry into others' lives, nor am I curious about their affairs. I go to mass every day and share my possessions with the poor without making a display of my good works lest hypocrisy and vanity take up residence in my breast, both enemies that insidiously take possession of the most guarded heart. I strive to make peace among those who are at odds with one another, and, being a devotee of Our Lady, trust always in the infinite compassion of our Lord God."

Sancho was absolutely spellbound by the gentleman's story of his life and activities, considering his life one of goodness and saintliness and thinking that a man who led such a life must be capable of performing miracles. As a consequence, he leapt from his jackass, hurriedly grasped the man by the right stirrup and began kissing his foot over and over again, his heart filled with devotion and his eyes with tears. When the gentleman saw this, he said,

"What are you doing, brother? What is the meaning of these kisses?"

"Please, your worship, permit me these few kisses," said Sancho, "for I believe your grace is the first saint I have ever seen on a charger in all the days of my life."

"I am no saint," objected the gentleman, "but a great sinner. You, my brother, are probably a good man, as demonstrated by your simple faith."

Sancho again took his seat on the packsaddle after eliciting a chuckle from his melancholy master and producing further bewilderment in Don Diego. Don Quixote asked the latter how many children he had, adding that one of the things the ancient philosophers, who lacked a true knowledge of God, considered the highest good was natural and worldly possessions, many friends, and a number of good children.

"I, Sir Don Quixote," replied the gentleman, "have one son but were this not the case, I might perhaps consider myself more fortunate than I do, and not because he is bad but because he is not as good as I should like him to be. He is eighteen and has spent the last six years in Salamanca learning Latin and Greek. When I insisted that he move on to the study of other sciences, I found him so intoxicated by that of poetry (if, indeed, this may be called a science) that it is impossible to make him apply himself to that of law, which is what I should prefer him to study, or to the queen of them all: theology. I should like him to be the crowning glory of his line, for we live in an age in which our monarchs handsomely reward virtuous and capable scholars, for scholarship without virtue is like a pearl on a dung heap. My son will spend the entire day trying to decide whether Homer expressed a certain verse in the *Iliad* well or badly; whether or not Martial was indecent in a certain epigram; or in what sense such-and-such verses of Virgil are to be understood. In short, all his conversations revolve round the books of the poets just mentioned or those of Horace, Persius, Juvenal, and Tibullus, as he has little regard for modern Spanish poets. But for all his lack of affection for Spanish poetry, his mind is presently in a cloud from preparing a gloss on four verses sent him from Salamanca, which I suppose are for some literary competition."

To all this Don Quixote responded,

"Sir, children are part of their parents' very own flesh and, as such, are to be cherished, whether good or bad, just as we cherish our souls which give us life. It is the parents' responsibility to guide them from the time they are small along the paths of virtue, good breeding, and noble Christian ideals so that, when adults, they will be the consolation of their aged parents and the glory of their descendants. I think it unwise to force them to study this or that science, though persuasion can do no harm. And when there is no need to study for the sole purpose of earning a livelihood, the student being fortunate enough for heaven to have given him parents who will provide him with one, I am of the opinion that they should allow him to pursue that science towards which they see him most inclined, and even though that of poetry is less useful than enjoyable, it is not one that will bring dishonor to the person who possesses it.

"Poetry, sir hidalgo, in my opinion is like a tender young maiden: beautiful in every regard, whom many other young maidens – namely, all the other sciences – groom, adorn, and refine, and she is the one who will be served by each of them and from whom they will receive their authority. However, this particular maiden refuses to be mistreated, dragged through the streets, or publicly exposed in the marketplace or in the chambers of palaces. She is the creation of an alchemy of such virtue that whoever knows how to manipulate her can turn her into the purest gold of inestimable value. Whoever would possess her should keep her within reasonable bounds, not permitting her to appear in crude satires or lifeless sonnets. She is not to be sold under any circumstances, unless it be for heroic poetry, doleful tragedies, or light, ingenious comedies. She will not allow herself to be dealt with by clowns or by the ignorant masses, who are incapable of recognizing or appreciating the treasures she encloses within herself. You must not think I am calling only commoners the masses, for any person who is unknowledgeable, whether lord or prince, can and should be included in this category. Thus, whoever possesses Poetry and treats her appropriately in the manner I have described will see his name made famous and held in esteem by all the civilized nations on earth. And based upon what your grace has told me – that your son shows little appreciation for poetry written in Spanish – I have to believe he is mistaken in his attitude, because the great Homer did not write in Latin, being a Greek, nor Virgil in Greek, being a Roman. In other words, all the poets of antiquity wrote in the language they imbibed with their mother's milk and did not go about seeking foreign tongues in which to declare their lofty concepts. This being the case, the same practice should be extended to every nation and one should not disparage the German poet because he writes in his language, nor the Castilian or even the Basque poets who write in theirs. Your son, according to my understanding, does not hold Spanish poetry in disfavor but specifically those poets who write in Spanish and know nothing of other languages or fields of learning which might awaken, embellish, and assist their natural talents. But even in this he may be mistaken, for the widely held opinion that poets are born is certainly true, by which is meant that the natural-born poet emerges from his mother's womb a poet and with this natural, god-given talent composes works without further study or inspiration, proving the truthfulness of the saying: '*Est Deus in nobis*. . ., etc.' [2] But I venture to say that the natural-born poet who avails himself of craftsmanship will be far better and quite superior to the would-be poet who has an acquaintance only with poetics, the reason being that art is not superior to nature; it merely perfects it. Thus, when nature is mixed with art or art with nature, the result will be an absolutely perfect poet. Let me conclude my discourse, sir hidalgo, by urging your grace to let your son go wherever his star may lead him, for, being the good student that he is and having already successfully mounted the first rung of knowledge, which is that of language, he will thereby with the help of his own efforts ascend to the heights of the humanities, which are as becoming to a lay gentleman, whom they adorn, honor, and elevate, as the miter is to the bishop or the robe to the learned lawyer. You should reprimand your son if he composes satires harmful to another's honor, and you should chastise him and tear them up. But if he writes satires in the style of Horace in which he criticizes vices in general, as Horace so eloquently did, you should praise him, for it is licit for the poet to inveigh against envy and to criticize in his verses those who are envious or those guilty of other vices, so long as he does not single out specific individuals, for there are some poets who, for the sake of saying something malicious, would expose themselves to the threat of being exiled to the Isles of Pontus. If the poet is pure in his daily habits, he will likewise be pure in his verses. The pen is the soul's tongue, and the concepts that one records on paper are merely a reflection of those engendered in the soul. Whenever kings and princes see the wondrous science of poetry in the possession of prudent, virtuous, and serious individuals, they honor them, esteem them, exalt and even crown them with the leaves of the tree that lightning never strikes, [3] being a sign, as it were, that those who see their brows honored and adorned with such crowns will not be offended by anyone."

The man in the green coat was so amazed at Don Quixote's reasoning that he was beginning to abandon the idea that the knight was a crackpot. In the middle of the discourse, however, Sancho, who did not find much of this to his liking, had left the road to request some milk from several nearby shepherds who were milking their ewes. Just as the traveler was about to resume the conversation,

---

2 Latin: 'God is within us . . .'

3 The laurel, according to popular belief.

having been enormously pleased with Don Quixote's intelligence and logic, Don Quixote raised his eyes and saw coming towards them a cart flying the king's colors. Fancying this to be some new adventure, he shouted to Sancho to bring him his helmet. Hearing his name called, Sancho left the shepherds, spurred the dapple, and in a flash rode back to his master, who was about to be the recipient of a frightful and bewildering adventure.

Chapter Seventeen

The description of the extremes to which Don Quixote's unheard-of courage could and did extend in the adventure of the lions, which he brought to a happy conclusion

Our history relates that when Don Quixote called out to Sancho to bring him his helmet, Sancho, who was busy buying some curds from the shepherds, became so flustered by his master's urgency that he did not know what to do with them or how to carry them. In order not to lose the curds, having already paid for them, he decided to dump them into his master's helmet. Once this precaution was taken, he returned to see what his master wanted.

"Give me my helmet, Sancho, for either I know very little about adventures or what I see over yonder is one that will require me to arm myself."

The man in the green coat, hearing this, looked about in all directions but discovered nothing more than a cart coming towards them bearing two or three small flags, the sight of which led him to believe the cart must be carrying the king's monies, which he explained to Don Quixote. The latter, though, did not believe him, as he was eternally convinced that everything that befell him must necessarily be adventures and more adventures, and so he said to the hidalgo in response,

"Since being prepared is half the battle, I lose nothing by taking precautions, for experience has taught me that my adversaries are both visible and invisible and I never know when, where, at what moment, or in what guise they will attack me."

Then turning to Sancho, he asked for his helmet, which Sancho was forced to hand him just as it was, having had no opportunity to remove the curds. Don Quixote took it and, not noticing what was inside, clapped it down over his head without a moment's hesitation. When the curds were squeezed and compressed, the whey began to ooze down over Don Quixote's entire face and beard, giving him such a start that he said to his squire,

"What can this be, Sancho? I think either my head is turning to putty and my brain is melting or I am sweating from head to toe. If the latter, it is certainly not from fear, though I have no doubt that the adventure about to befall me will be most frightful. Hand me something with which to clean my face if you have anything, for this copious sweat is blinding my eyes."

Sancho handed him a cloth but said nothing while simultaneously giving thanks to God that his master had not seen through the deception. Don Quixote wiped his face and removed the helmet to see what could be freezing his head. When he saw the white gruel inside the helmet, he raised it to his nose, smelled it, and said,

"By the soul of my lady Dulcinea of Toboso, if it is not curds you have put here, you thoughtless rogue, you traitorous squire!"

To which Sancho responded with the greatest composure and dissimulation,

"If they are curds, your grace may give them to me and I'll eat every last one . . . or let the Devil eat them, since he's probably the one who put them there – so now we know who the brazen culprit is. Would I have the audacity to soil your grace's helmet? Upon my word, master, according to my humble understanding, I must have enchanters pursuing me too as an associate and ally of your grace, and they have probably placed that muck there to turn your patience into anger and make you belabor my ribs, as you are wont to do. Well, this time they've bitten off more than they can chew, for I trust in the good judgement of my master, who will have considered the fact that I don't have curds or milk or anything resembling them. And even if I did, I would put them in my stomach before I'd put them in a helmet."

"Maybe so," said Don Quixote.

The hidalgo watched Don Quixote clean his head, face, beard, and helmet, and was bewildered by it all, especially when Don Quixote again placed the helmet on his head, settled himself firmly in the stirrups and, after checking his sword and taking up his lance, said,

"Well, come what may, this is where I propose to station myself with the courage to take on Satan Himself in person."

In the meantime, the cart bearing the flags arrived and there was no one on it other than the driver astride one of the mules and a man seated at the front of the cart. Don Quixote planted himself in their path and shouted,

"Where are you headed, my brothers? Whose cart is that? What are you carrying on it, and what are those flags?"

To which the driver replied,

"The cart is mine and we're transporting two ferocious caged lions the general of Oran is sending to the court as presents for His Majesty. The flags are our lord the King's and mark the official nature of the cart."

"Are the lions very large?" asked Don Quixote.

"So large," replied the man at the front of the cart, "that none larger or even as large have ever been brought from Africa to Spain. I am the lion keeper and have brought in others but never any like these. There are a male and a female; the male is in this front cage and the female in the one behind. Right now they're hungry because they haven't been fed today, so I beg your grace to stand aside, for we must hurry to where we can get them something to eat."

To which Don Quixote responded with a slight smile,

"Lion cubs against me? Against me, Don Quixote? And at such an hour? Well, by heavens, those gentlemen who have sent them here shall see whether I am a person who fears lions! My good man, since you are the lion keeper, kindly dismount, open those cages, and release those beasts, for in the middle of this field I will show them who Don Quixote of La Mancha is despite all the enchanters who may have sent them here."

"Oh my!" said the hidalgo to himself at this point, "our noble knight is showing his true colors. The curds have obviously softened his skull and ripened his brain."

Here Sancho approached and said,

"Sir, for the love of God, I beg your grace to do something to keep my master Don Quixote from engaging these lions, for if he should do so, they will tear us all to shreds right here."

"Is your master so mad," said the hidalgo, "that you fear and even believe he will engage such ferocious beasts?"

"He's not mad," said Sancho, "just foolhardy."

"I shall see to it that this does not happen," said the hidalgo and, going over to Don Quixote, who was pressing the lion keeper to open the cages, he said,

"Sir Quixote, knights-errant should undertake only those adventures that hold out some prospect of success, not those that are completely hopeless. Bravery that verges on temerity contains more madness than fortitude, and all the more so when these lions have not been sent here to confront your grace, nor do they even dream of such a thing. They have come here as presents for His Majesty and it will not be wise to stop them or interrupt their journey."

"Sir hidalgo," replied Don Quixote, "your grace should go attend to your tame partridge and your fearless ferret and let each person look after his own business. This one is mine and I know whether these magnificent lions are meant for me or not!"

And turning to the lion keeper, he said,

"By all that is holy, sir knave, if you do not open the cages at this very instant, I shall pin you to the cart with this lance."

The driver, seeing the determination of this armed apparition, said to him,

"My lord, I beg your grace in the name of charity to allow me to unyoke the mules and take them and myself to a safe place before the lions are turned loose because, if they kill my mules, I'll be ruined for the rest of my life, since I have no possessions other than this cart and these mules."

"O man of little faith," responded Don Quixote, "get down and unyoke them or do whatever you must. You shall soon see that your efforts were in vain and you might have saved yourself the trouble."

The driver dismounted and quite hurriedly unyoked the mules, while the lion keeper said with a shout,

"I want everyone present to be witness to the fact that I am opening the cages and turning the lions loose under duress and against my will, and that I am protesting to this gentleman that all the harm and damage these lions inflict will fall to his account, including my wages and commission. Gentlemen, your graces should take cover before I open the cages; I'm sure the lions will not harm me."

Once again the hidalgo sought to persuade Don Quixote not to commit such an insane act, since to commit this sort of outrage was to tempt God. Don Quixote replied that he knew what he was doing but the hidalgo responded that he should reconsider, for he was certain Don Quixote was making a mistake.

"Well now, my lord," said the knight, "if your grace is unwilling to be a spectator to what in your opinion will be a disaster, you should spur your gray mare and ride off to a safe spot."

When Sancho heard this, he implored him with tears in his eyes to desist from such an enterprise, compared with which all the others had been cookies and cream: the frightful one with the fulling hammers, that of the windmills, together with any number of other endeavors he had undertaken throughout the course of his life.

"Look, master," said Sancho, "there is no enchantment here or anything of the sort. Through the bars of the cage I saw the claws of a real lion and conclude from this that the lion to which such claws belong must be bigger than a mountain."

"Fear, to be sure," said Don Quixote, "will make you imagine him to be bigger than half the earth. Go off somewhere, Sancho, and leave me here with him, and if I should expire here, you know our standing agreement that you are to visit Dulcinea – but I shall leave it at that."

To these arguments Don Quixote added others, removing all hope that he might desist from carrying out his madcap scheme. The man in the green coat would have liked to oppose him but, seeing himself at a disadvantage in the matter of arms, thought it unwise to take issue with a madman, for this is how Don Quixote now impressed him in every regard. The latter, renewing his threats, once again ordered the lion keeper to hurry, which gave the hidalgo a chance to spur his mare, Sancho his dapple, and the driver his mules, whereby they all sought to distance themselves from the cart as far as possible before the lions were turned loose. Sancho lamented the death of his master, who this time, he was certain, would end up in the clutches of the lion, and he cursed his fate, calling it a dark hour when he had gotten the brilliant idea to reenter the service of his master. He did not, however, for all his tears and lamentations fail to whip his dapple to put distance between himself and the cart. Once the lion keeper saw that those fleeing were now quite some distance removed, he renewed the entreaties and warnings he had already made to Don Quixote, who replied that he heard what he was saying but that he should get on with it and not waste his breath with further warnings and entreaties, because they would all be of little avail.

During the time it took the lion keeper to open the first cage, Don Quixote considered whether it would be better to do battle on foot or on horseback. He finally decided to fight on foot, fearing Rocinante might become frightened at the sight of the lions. Accordingly, he dismounted from his horse, cast aside his lance, strapped on his buckler, and, unsheathing his sword, approached the cart one step at a time with astounding bravery and a valiant heart, at the same time commending himself heart and soul to God and then to his lady Dulcinea.

But it should be noted at this point that when the author of our true history comes to this passage, he exclaims, 'O mighty Don Quixote, fearless beyond measure, mirror in whom is reflected every stout heart on earth, reincarnation of Don Manuel de León, and glory and honor of Spanish knighthood! Where can I find words to describe this most frightful undertaking? With what arguments can I render it believable to future generations? What praises can possibly do you justice, even if they are hyperboles of hyperboles? Here is your grace, on foot, one man, intrepid and magnanimous, possessing only a sword – and it not one of the trenchant ones of Toledo – and a rather unclean, lusterless steel buckler, awaiting the two most ferocious lions the African jungles have ever engendered. May your own deeds sing your praises, O valorous Manchegan. I shall let them speak for themselves, for I lack words with which to extol you.'

Here the author ended his interpolated tribute and proceeded to tie up the threads of the story, stating that when the lion keeper saw that Don Quixote was firm in his resolve and he could not avoid releasing the male lion without risking the wrath of the bold, indignant knight, he flung open the first cage, which contained, as we said, a lion that was extraordinarily large and frighteningly hideous in appearance. But the lion simply turned round in the cage in which he had been lying, reached out with one of his paws, and stretched his entire body. Then opening his mouth, he yawned quite broadly and stuck out some eight inches of tongue with which he cleaned the dust from his eyes and washed his face. This done, he poked his head outside the cage and looked in all directions with his eyes of red-hot coals, the sight of which was enough to strike fear into temerity itself. Don Quixote stared at the lion, expecting him to spring from the cart at once and do battle with him, for the knight had every intention of tearing him to pieces.

This is how far his unheard-of madness had come, but the noble lion, more good-natured than savage and showing no interest in such childish bravado, looked about in all directions, as we said, turned his back, displayed his hindquarters to Don Quixote, and then quite sluggishly and lethargically lay down again in the cage. When Don Quixote saw this, he ordered the lion keeper to prod him with his stick to provoke him into coming outside.

"That I will not do, Sir Knight," said the lion keeper, "for if I provoke him, the first person he will tear to pieces will be yours truly. Your grace should be content with what has already transpired, for nothing more may be demanded in the name of bravery, nor should fate be tempted a second time. The lion has the door open and it is his decision whether to come out or not, and since he has so far failed to do so, he will not come out for the rest of the day. Your grace's great courage has already been demonstrated, for no brave contender, according to my understanding, is obliged to do more than challenge his adversary and wait for him on the field of battle. If the latter fails to appear, it is he who is disgraced, whereas the one who waited for him is awarded the crown of victory."

"That is true," said Don Quixote. "Close the door, my friend, and prepare a statement to the best of your ability about what you have seen me perform here, namely, that you opened the cage door, I waited for the lion, he refused to come out, I continued to wait for him, he still refused to come out and, instead, lay down once again. I have no further obligation and these enchantments can all go to blazes! May God sustain right, truth, and genuine chivalry. Close the door as I requested while I signal to those who have fled so they may learn of this deed from your own lips."

The lion keeper did as ordered and Don Quixote attached to the end of his lance the cloth with which he had cleaned the stream of whey from his face and began waving it at those who were still running away while looking back over their shoulders at every step of the way – and the one leading the pack was the hidalgo. Sancho happened to spot the signal of the white cloth and said,

"I'll be hanged if my master hasn't defeated the wild beasts, for there he is waving to us."

They all called a halt to their flight, at which point they recognized that Don Quixote was the one signaling. Recovering somewhat from their fear, they gradually came forward to where they could distinctly hear the shouts of the knight calling to them. At length, they returned to the cart and once they arrived, Don Quixote said to the driver,

"Come back, brother, and yoke up your mules and continue on your journey. You, Sancho, give him two gold *escudos*: one for him and one for the lion keeper as compensation for the time they have been detained by me."

"That I will do most willingly," said Sancho, "but what has become of the lions? Are they dead or alive?"

At this point, the lion keeper gave a leisurely and detailed account of what had taken place in the contest, exaggerating as only he could the bravery of Don Quixote, at the sight of whom the cowering lion was unwilling to leave the cage and, indeed, dared not do so, though the cage door had remained open for quite some time. And because he had warned the knight that it would be tempting God to provoke the lion into coming outside, which Don Quixote, in fact, had wanted him to do, the knight quite against his wishes and completely against his will had permitted the door to be closed.

"What do you think of that, Sancho?," said Don Quixote. "Are there enchantments anywhere that can stand up against real bravery? Enchanters, to be sure, may take away my good fortune but never my strength or my courage."

Sancho handed over the *escudos,* the driver yoked up the mules, and the lion keeper kissed Don Quixote's hand for the favor extended to them, promising to relate this valorous exploit to the king himself as soon as he saw himself at court.

"Well, if His Majesty should ask who performed this deed, you shall inform him that it was the Knight of the Lions, for from this moment forward I should like the title I have had until now – the Knight of the Woeful Countenance – to be altered, changed, transformed, and turned into this new one. In doing this, I am simply following the ancient practice of knights-errant, who changed their names whenever they felt like it or whenever it suited their purpose to do so."

The cart then proceeded on its way and Don Quixote, Sancho, and the man in the green coat continued on theirs. During all this time Don Diego de Miranda had not spoken a word, being totally engrossed in observing and noting the things said and done by Don Quixote, who in his opinion was a sane man gone mad or a madman bordering on sanity. The first part of the knight's history had not yet come to his attention, for had he already read it, he would have ceased to be bewildered by Don Quixote's words and actions and would now understand the nature of his madness. But since he was not familiar with it, at times he considered him sane and at times mad, for everything he said was sensible, elegant, and well expressed, whereas all his actions were outrageous, reckless, and foolish. He said to himself, 'What greater madness can there be than for a person to put on his helmet filled with curds and then to convince himself that enchanters are causing his brain to melt? Or what greater audacity and stupidity than to pit one's strength against lions?' Don Quixote brought him back from this soliloquy and reverie by saying,

"No doubt, Sir Don Diego de Miranda, your grace takes me for a fool and a madman, not that it would surprise me if you did, since all my actions point in that direction. But despite this, I would have your grace know that I am not as mad or as foolish as I must have appeared, for it is quite fitting, in the middle of a great plaza in view of the king, for a gallant knight to successfully spear a fierce bull with his lance. It is equally fitting for a knight in shining armor at some festive joust to ride through the arena in view of the ladies, and for all those knights in military exercises or related activities to entertain, delight and – if I may say so – bestow honor upon the courts of their princes. But above and beyond all these, it is more fitting and proper for a knight-errant to roam the lonely wastelands, uninhabited regions, forests and mountains in quest of perilous adventures, determined to dispatch them happily and successfully with the sole intention of winning glorious and everlasting fame. It is more seemly, I maintain, for a knight-errant to assist a widow in some out-of-the-way village than for a courtier knight to dally with a maiden in the city. Every knight has his own particular duties. Let the courtier serve the ladies, add luster to his king's court with his livery, give sustenance to the poor from the provisions of his splendid table, arrange jousts, preside over tournaments, and demonstrate that he is noble, generous, magnificent, and, above all, a good Christian, for by so doing, he will fulfill his specific obligations. But let the knight-errant seek out the corners of the earth, penetrate the most intricate labyrinths, undertake the impossible at every turn, resist the burning rays of the midsummer sun on the barren plains and the harsh winter winds and ice, and let him do so without being alarmed by lions, frightened by monsters, or terrified by dragons, for by seeking out these, doing battle with those, and conquering them all, he will fulfill his primary and legitimate obligations. Inasmuch as it has fallen to my lot to count myself among the band of knights-errant, I cannot fail to undertake anything that strikes me as falling within the purview of my duties. Thus the confrontation I just now carried out was my right and obligation, though I recognized it as the height of folly, being well aware as I am of the meaning of valor – a virtue situated between vices at either extreme, namely, cowardice and foolhardiness. Because it is preferable for a valiant person to rise until he reaches the level of rashness than to sink to the level of cowardice. And just as it is easier for the spendthrift to become generous than it is for the miser, so is it easier for the foolhardy person to descend to true bravery than for the coward to rise to that same level. Because in the matter of undertaking adventures, Sir Don Diego, I assure your grace that 'It is better to lose by a card too many than by a card too few,' and it is more seemly to hear: 'Such-and-such a knight is rash and foolhardy' than to hear: 'Such-and-such a knight is cowardly.'"

"I must say, Sir Don Quixote," replied Don Diego, "that everything your grace has said and done squares with reason itself, for I am of the opinion that if the rules and ordinances of knight-errantry should ever be lost, they would be found deposited and filed away in your grace's bosom. But let us hurry, for it is getting late and I should like to reach my village and home, where you may rest up from your recent exertions; and though these may not have been physical exertions, they were spiritual ones, which often lead to weariness of the body."

"Sir Don Diego," replied Don Quixote, "I accept your grace's offer for the great favor and kindness that it is." And spurring their mounts even harder than before, they managed, around two in the afternoon, to reach the village and home of Don Diego, whom Don Quixote designated the Knight of the Green Coat.

Chapter Eighteen

What befell Don Quixote in the castle, or home, of the Knight of the Green Coat, together with other extraordinary matters

Don Quixote found Don Diego de Miranda's home to be spacious in typical village style, with a coat-of-arms in rough stone over the front entrance, a storage area in the courtyard, a cellar by the entryway, and a number of large jars at different locations, which, having been made in Toboso, revived in his mind memories of the enchanted and transformed Dulcinea. Consequently, giving no thought to what he was saying or to the persons who were present, he heaved a sigh and said,

"O pledges, once my comfort and relief,
Though pleasing still, discovered now with grief!

O you Tobosan jars, how you remind me of my dear beloved and my greatest heartache!"

This was overheard by the student poet, Don Diego's son, who had come outside with his mother to welcome him, and both mother and son were taken aback at the sight of the strange figure of Don Quixote, who dismounted from Rocinante and ever so graciously requested permission to kiss her hand, at which point Don Diego said,

"My dear, please make welcome with your customary hospitality Sir Don Quixote of La Mancha, whom you see before you, a knight-errant and the bravest and wisest on earth."

The lady, whose name was Doña Cristina, received him with a great display of affection and warmth and Don Quixote placed himself at her disposal with an embarrassment of discreet, tactful utterances. He expressed virtually the same sentiments towards the student, who, after hearing Don Quixote speak, took him to be a man of intelligence and discernment.

Here the author gives us a detailed description of Don Diego's home, by means of which he allows us to view the home of a wealthy country gentleman but the translator of this history has deemed it preferable to pass over these and similar particulars as not being germane to the principal purpose of the history, the strength of which lies in its adherence to truth rather than in tedious digressions.

They led Don Quixote to a chamber, where Sancho removed his master's armor, leaving him in his Walloon breeches and chamois-skin vest, both soiled by the rust from his armor. He wore a plain, unstarched Van Dyke collar in the student style, half-length boots the color of dates, polished shoes, and a fine sword attached to a seal-skin shoulder strap, for it is widely believed that he had suffered for many years from a kidney ailment; and over all this he sported an expensive gray cloak. Before proceeding further, however, he rinsed his head and face with five or six basins of water – the exact number of basins being in some dispute – with the water remaining the color of whey thanks to Sancho's appetite and his purchase of the infernal curds that had left his master so very white. Decked out thus in all his finery, Don Quixote strode forth with dash and elegance into the adjoining hall, where the student was waiting to entertain him while dinner was being prepared, for owing to the presence of such a distinguished guest, the lady Doña Cristina wished to prove she could play the gracious hostess to her house guests.

While Don Quixote was removing his armor, Don Lorenzo – this being the name of Don Diego's son – had occasion to say to his father,

"Sir, what are we to make of this gentleman your grace has brought home? My mother and I are confused by his appearance, his name, and the claim that he is a knight-errant."

"I don't know what to tell you, my son," said Don Diego; "all I can say is that I have seen him do some of the craziest things in the world but have heard him say such intelligent things that they cancel out and belie his actions. Speak to him yourself and find out how much he knows and in your own clever way determine whether his intelligence or his folly has the upper hand, though frankly I tend to think he is more mad than sane."

At this point Don Lorenzo went off to entertain Don Quixote and, while the pair were discussing various topics, Don Quixote made the following observation to Don Lorenzo:

"Your father Sir Don Diego de Miranda has informed me of your grace's rare abilities and keen intellect but, above all, of the fact that you are a great poet."

"A poet, possibly," replied Don Lorenzo, "but a great one is out of the question. I must admit to being rather fond of poetry and of reading good poets but not to the extent that I may be called great, as my father says."

"I admire your humility," said Don Quixote, "for there is no poet who is not arrogant and does not consider himself the best poet on earth."

"Since there is no rule without an exception," said Don Lorenzo, "there must be one somewhere who is but does not think so."

"There are very few," replied Don Quixote, "but may I ask which verses you are presently working on that have you somewhat anxious and preoccupied according to what your noble father has told me? If it is some gloss, I have a passing acquaintance with the art and would be pleased to hear it. If it is for a literary competition, you should strive to win second place because first is always determined by favoritism or by the person's high rank, whereas second place is determined by actual merit. Thus, third place is really second, and first place by this reckoning will be third in the manner of academic degrees awarded at the universities. Still, the title of first place carries considerable prestige."

"So far," thought Don Lorenzo, "I cannot consider him crazy but we shall see;" then he said,

"It is my understanding that your grace has attended the university, and, if so, what fields have you studied?"

"That of knight-errantry," said Don Quixote, "which is as noble as that of poetry and maybe even a mite better."

"I am not acquainted with that science," said Don Lorenzo, "which until now has not come to my attention."

"It is a science," replied Don Quixote, "that encompasses within itself most if not all the sciences on earth, owing to the fact that whoever professes it must be an expert in jurisprudence and have an acquaintance with the laws of distributive and commutative justice in order to award to each person what is his and is most equitable. He must be a theologian, who can give a clear and precise account of the Christian precepts he professes whenever called upon to do so. He must be a physician, primarily an herbalist, to be able to recognize which herbs in the desolate wastelands possess the virtue of healing wounds, for a knight-errant must not go seeking at every turn someone else to heal him. He must be an astrologer, who can ascertain by the stars how many hours of the night have passed and in what clime or part of the world he happens to be. He must be knowledgeable in mathematics, as he will have need of it at every step of the way. And after I mention that he must be adorned with all the cardinal and theological virtues, permit me to turn to less important matters by saying that he must be as good a swimmer as the merman Nicolás, or Nicolao, is said to have been, and must be able to shoe a horse and repair a saddle and bridle. But to return to the previous matters, he must remain faithful to God and his lady, be pure in his thoughts, true to his word, generous in his actions, valiant in his deeds, long-suffering in his hardships, charitable towards those in need, and, lastly, must uphold the truth even if it costs him his life to defend it. A good knight-errant is constituted of all these qualities, both great and small. Therefore, Sir Don Lorenzo, you may be the judge of whether the science possessed by a knight who must study and profess it is frivolous or whether it can be equaled by any of the most prestigious ones taught in the schools or universities."

"If that is true," said Don Lorenzo, "this science, I must confess, surpasses them all."

"If it is true!" exclaimed Don Quixote.

"What I mean," said Don Lorenzo, "is that I doubt there have ever been, or still are, knights-errant, or that they possessed such an array of virtues."

"What I am about to say I have said many times before," replied Don Quixote. "Most people in the world are of the opinion that knights-errant have never existed, and since I feel that unless heaven by some miracle shows them that they did indeed exist and still do, any attempt to accomplish this will be in vain, as experience has shown me on numerous occasions. But I shall not take the time here to disabuse your grace of the mistaken idea you share with the vast majority of people. What I intend to do is to implore heaven to enlighten you and show you how beneficial and necessary to the world knights-errant were in the days of yore and how useful they would be today if it were still the custom. However, due to people's transgressions at the present time, sloth, idleness, gluttony, and pleasure-seeking rule the day."

"Our guest has given us the slip," said Don Lorenzo to himself at this point, "but despite this, he is an out-and-out madman and I would be quite a fool not to recognize it."

With this they brought their conversation to a close, as they were being summoned to dinner. Don Diego asked his son what he had been able to discover about their guest's wits; to which he answered,

"All the physicians and scribes on earth could not make sense of his incoherent scrawlings. He is intermittently mad with intervals of lucidity."

They went in to dinner and the meal was exactly as Don Diego had described it on the road: spotless, abundant, and tasty, but what pleased Don Quixote most was the wondrous silence that reigned throughout the house, for it reminded him of a Carthusian monastery. Once the table had been cleared, grace said, and water poured over their hands, Don Quixote earnestly begged Don

Lorenzo to recite his verses for the literary competition; to which he responded,

"Lest I appear to be one of those poets who, when asked to recite their verses, decline to do so, or, not being asked, spout them forth, I shall recite my gloss, from which I expect no prize whatsoever. I have composed it solely to exercise my mind."

To which Don Quixote replied,

"A wise man – a friend of mine – was of the opinion that one should not waste his time composing poetic glosses, for according to him the gloss could never approach the original text and more often than not would stray from the intention and purpose expressed by the text being glossed. Besides, the rules for glossing are too restrictive in that they do not permit questions, certain types of phrases, the transformation of verbs into nouns, changes in meaning, or any number of other restrictions and obstacles that bind the hands of the glosser, as your grace no doubt knows."

"The truth, Sir Don Quixote," said Don Lorenzo, "is that I should like to catch your grace committing some mistake but am unable to do so, for you keep slipping through my fingers like an eel."

"I do not understand," said Don Quixote, "what your grace is saying or what you mean by 'slipping through your fingers.'"

"I shall explain later but for now I beg your grace's indulgence while I read the original verses and gloss, which go like this:

The Text

"Could I recall departed joy,
  Though barred the hopes of greater gain,
Or now the future hours employ
  That must succeed my present pain.

The Paraphrase

All fortune's blessings disappear,
  She's fickle as the wind;
And now I find her as severe
  As once I thought her kind.
How soon the fleeting pleasures passed!
How long the lingering sorrows last!
Inconstant goddess, in thy haste,
Do not thy prostrate slave destroy;
  I'd ne'er complain, but bless my fate,
Could I recall departed joy.

Of all thy gifts, I beg but this,

Glut all mankind with more,
Transport them with redoubled bliss,
But only mine restore.
With thought of pleasure once possessed,
I'm now as cursed as I was blessed:
Oh, would the charming hours return,
How pleased I'd live, how free from pain!
I ne'er would pine, I ne'er would mourn,
Though barred the hopes of greater gain.

But oh, the blessing I implore
Not fate itself can give;
Since time elapsed exists no more,
No power can bid it live.
Our days soon vanish into nought,
And have no being but in thought.
Whate'er began must end at last;
In vain we twice would youth enjoy,
In vain would we recall the past,
Or now the future hours employ.

Deceived by hope and racked by fear,
No longer life can please;
I'll then no more its torments bear
Since death so soon can ease.
This hour I'll die–but let me pause–
A rising doubt my courage awes.
Assist, ye powers that rule my fate,
Alarm my thoughts, my rage restrain,
Convince my soul there's yet a state
That must succeed my present pain."

When Don Lorenzo finished reciting his gloss, Don Quixote stood up and took Don Lorenzo's right hand in his own and in a voice that resembled a shout exclaimed,

"By all that is holy in heaven, sir, you are the best poet on the globe and deserve to be crowned with laurel, not by Cyprus or Gaeta, as a poet has said – and may God forgive him – but by the academies of Athens if they still existed, and by those that do exist today in Paris, Bologna, and Salamanca! O excellent youth, I pray to heaven that Phoebus will pierce with his arrows the judges who deprive you of first place, and may the Muses never darken the doorsteps of their houses. I wish you would recite for me, if you would be so kind, one of your learned verse forms, for I should like to make a thorough evaluation of your astounding talents."

Is it any wonder that Don Lorenzo was said to be delighted at hearing himself praised by Don Quixote even if he considered him mad? (O wondrous flattery, how far you extend, and how expansive are the bounds of your ingratiating realm!) Don Lorenzo himself proved the truthfulness of this assertion by acceding to Don Quixote's request and wishes, whereupon he recited the sonnet on the fable or story of Pyramus and Thisbe:

Sonnet

The nymph who Pyramus with love inspired
Pierces the wall, with equal passion fired:
Cupid from distant Cyprus thither flies,
And views the secret breach with laughing eyes.

Here silence, vocal, mutual vows conveys,
And, whisp'ring eloquent, their love betrays.
Though, chained by fear, their voices dare not pass,
Their souls, transmitted through the chink, embrace.

Ah, woeful story of disastrous love!
Ill-fated haste, that did their ruin prove!
One death, one grave unite the faithful pair,
And in one common fame their mem'ries share.

"Praised be God," said Don Quixote after listening to Don Lorenzo's sonnet, "to think that among the infinite number of worn-out poets I have found a consummate one in the person of your grace, as the artistry of this sonnet makes clear to me!"

For four days Don Quixote was splendidly entertained in Don Diego's home, at the end of which period he requested permission to depart, expressing his gratitude for the favors and kindnesses he had received there but adding that because it was unseemly for knights-errant to indulge themselves in excessive idleness and luxury, he wished to fulfill the duties of his office by seeking out adventures, for he had been told they abounded in that land in which he expected to pass the time until the day arrived for the jousts at Saragossa, this being his immediate destination. But first he must enter the Cave of Montesinos, about which so many astounding stories were reported in those parts, both to explore and to search for the origin and actual source of the seven lagoons commonly known as the Lakes of Ruidera. Don Diego and his son commended him for his noble intentions and asked him to take with him anything he might find to his liking in their home or among their possessions, for they would most willingly place themselves at his disposal, being led to do this because of Don Quixote's personal merits and his laudable profession.

The day of departure finally arrived, as joyous for Don Quixote as it was sad and ill-fated for

Sancho Panza, who found himself perfectly at home with the provisions of Don Diego's estate and was reluctant to return to the accustomed hunger of the forests and wilds and the meagerness of his ill-provisioned saddlebags, for which reason he filled and stuffed them with everything he considered most necessary. When it was time to take his leave, Don Quixote said to Don Lorenzo,

"I do not recall whether I have mentioned this previously but if so, I shall say it again: if your grace should desire to take a shortcut in both time and direction in your ascent to the inaccessible summit of the temple of fame, you need do nothing more than abandon the path of poetry, which is rather narrow, and follow the extremely narrow path of knight-errantry, which will suffice to make you an emperor more quickly than you can bat an eye."

With these words Don Quixote brought the defense of his madness to a close but only after adding the following:

"God knows, Don Lorenzo, that I should like to take your grace with me to show you how the humble are to be pardoned and the haughty overthrown and trampled upon, both commonplace activities in the profession I follow, but because this is not feasible owing to your young age and the fact that your exemplary pursuits will not permit it, I shall be content simply to advise you that you will become a famous poet if you allow yourself to be guided more by other people's opinions than by your own, for there are no fathers or mothers who consider their children ugly, this deception being especially true when they are simply creations of the imagination."

Once again both father and son were astonished at the jumble of pronouncements of Don Quixote – now brilliant, now absurd – and at the pluck and persistence he possessed in his single-minded pursuit of his ill-ventured adventures, which he considered the goal and object of all his activities. And so, after they all once again exchanged courtesies and placed themselves at one another's disposal, Don Quixote and Sancho, with the kind permission of the lady of the castle, mounted Rocinante and the dapple and resumed their journey.

Chapter Nineteen

The account of the adventure of the enamored shepherd, together with other truly entertaining incidents

Don Quixote had traveled only a short distance from Don Diego's village when he encountered two men who appeared to be priests or students, and two laborers, all of whom were riding mounts of the long-eared variety. One of the students carried a kind of portmanteau fashioned from a green buckram material, which appeared to contain a piece of white linen and one or two pairs of twilled hose, while the other carried nothing more than two new fencing foils with their buttons attached. The laborers were carrying other articles which showed they were returning from some large town where they had purchased them and were taking them to their village. Both the students and laborers were as astonished at the sight of Don Quixote as everyone was when they saw him for the first time and they were dying to learn who this man was whose appearance was so different from that of ordinary men. Don Quixote greeted them and, after learning that their destination was the same as his own, offered to accompany them but asked them to slacken their pace because their jackasses were traveling faster than his horse. To obligate them to do so, he gave them a brief account of who he was and of his profession of knight-errantry, which accounted for his traveling throughout the world in quest of adventures. He informed them that his real name was Don Quixote of La Mancha but that he went by the name of The Knight of the Lions. For the laborers, all this talk was so much Greek and gibberish but not so for the students, who immediately recognized the debility of Don Quixote's faculties. Nevertheless, they continued to stare at him in respectful astonishment until one of them said to him,

"Sir knight, if your grace is following no particular route, as is the custom of those who seek adventures, you are welcome to ride along with us, whereby you shall witness one of the finest and most lavish weddings ever celebrated in La Mancha or for many leagues around."

Don Quixote asked if the wedding he was extolling was that of some noble; to which the student replied,

"It is simply that of a man and a woman from the country, he being the richest farmer in all these parts and she the most beautiful farmgirl men have ever laid eyes upon. The pomp with which it will be performed is extraordinary and unprecedented and the ceremony will be held in a meadow just outside the bride's village. Everyone has given her the nickname of Quiteria the Beautiful, and the bridegroom is called Camacho the Wealthy. She is eighteen and he is twenty-two and they are simply made for each other, though some busybodies who know everyone's family tree by heart claim the beautiful Quiteria's is superior to that of Camacho. However, no one takes this very seriously nowadays, for wealth is capable of soldering a great many cracks. The fact is that this Camacho is liberal with his money and has taken it into his head to cover the meadow with such a canopy of branches that the sun will have difficulty penetrating it to pay its respects to the grass-covered ground underneath. He has also made provisions for dances, and not just those involving swords, but those with bells, for in his village there are dancers who can shake them and make them ring to perfection. Of the clog dancers I have nothing to add except to say that those he has invited are marvels to behold. But none of the things I have mentioned, nor the many others I have left unmentioned, will make this wedding nearly as memorable as I suspect the rejected Basilio will. This Basilio is a young man from Quiteria's village whose house adjoins that of her parents, which has afforded Love the opportunity to revive on earth the long-forgotten loves of Pyramus and Thisbe. Basilio fell in love with Quiteria at a young and tender age and she returned his affection in a thousand innocent ways, as a result of which the loves of the two children Basilio and Quiteria turned out to provide entertainment for the villagers. As they grew older, Quiteria's father decided to deny Basilio entrance to their home, which the latter had always enjoyed. Likewise, to rid himself of his continual doubts and suspicions, the father arranged for his daughter to marry the wealthy Camacho, thinking it unwise to betroth her to Basilio, who had not been as blessed by fortune as by nature, for if the plain truth be told, he is the most agile young man we know: a great tosser of the bar, an accomplished wrestler, and a great ball player. He can run like a deer, jump higher than a goat, and play ninepins like someone bewitched.

He also sings like a lark, plays the guitar so well he can make it talk, and, above all, he wields a sword as well as the best swordsman around."

"For that one ability alone," said Don Quixote at this point, "that young man would be worthy to wed not only the beautiful Quiteria but Queen Guinevere herself if she were alive today, despite Lancelot or anyone else who might try to prevent it."

"Tell that to my wife!" said Sancho, who till now had been listening but not saying a word. "She thinks one should only marry his equal, being guided by the proverb that says, 'To each sheep its mate.' What I would like is to see that nice Basilio, whom I'm beginning to like more and more, marry that Lady Quiteria, and I hope people who keep lovers from getting married . . . *enjoy* (I almost said the opposite) an eternal life of peace and repose."

"If all those who loved each other were to marry," said Don Quixote, "parents would be deprived of their right to marry their children whenever and to whomever they chose. If it were left up to daughters to select their husbands, a certain one might choose her father's servant, or another a man she saw strolling along the street, gallant and self-assured in her eyes though he might be a boaster and a ruffian, for love and affection easily bind the eyes of judgement so necessary in choosing one's station in life. That of matrimony is the one most susceptible to error, for it requires great care and the personal attention of heaven to be successful. When one wishes to take a long journey, he will before setting out, if he is wise, seek someone to accompany him who is trustworthy and companionable. Why, then, will that person not do the same when he takes a journey that will last till death, particularly when his companion will accompany him in bed and board – everywhere, in fact – as a wife will her husband? One's own wife is not merchandise which, once bought, may be returned or exchanged. Matrimony is a permanent condition that lasts as long as life endures. It is a noose which, once placed round one's neck, turns into the Gordian knot, and unless it is cut by death's sickle, there is no way to untie it. There is much more I might say on this subject were I not prevented by my desire to learn whether the worthy licentiate has anything to add to Basilio's story."

To this the student bachelor, or licentiate, as Don Quixote called him, responded as follows:

"The only thing I need to explain is that from the moment Basilio learned of the beautiful Quiteria's plans to wed Camacho the Wealthy, he has never again been heard to laugh or say a sensible thing. He continually mopes about pensive and melancholy, talking to himself and showing definite signs of having lost his wits. He scarcely sleeps or eats, and what little he does eat consists of fruit. And the little time he sleeps, if indeed he does sleep, he does so out of doors on the hard ground like some wild animal. At one moment he will stare at the sky but at the next will fix his gaze upon the ground with such obsession that he will appear to be a mere statue draped with garments that are blown by the wind. In short, he shows signs of being so hopelessly in love that all of us who know him fear the beautiful Quiteria's 'I do' tomorrow will be his death sentence."

"God will see to it that things go better than that," said Sancho, "for 'God, who is responsible for the hurt, will also provide the cure.' 'No one knows how much time he has left,' and 'From now till morning there are many hours' and in just one, or even in an instant, the house may come tumbling down. I've seen it rain while the sun was shining, both at the same time, and a person may go to bed one night feeling fine and wake up the next morning unable to move. Tell me something: has there by chance ever been anyone who can boast of having driven a nail into the wheel of fortune? Of course not, and between a woman's saying yes and her saying no, I wouldn't venture to insert the point of a pin because it wouldn't fit. Just show me that Quiteria loves Basilio with all her heart and soul and I'll show you a man with a sack full of good luck, for love, I've been told, wears glasses that transform copper into gold, poverty into wealth, and beeswax into amber."

"Curse you, Sancho, where are you going to stop?" exclaimed Don Quixote. "When you start stringing together your sayings and proverbs, no one can abide you except Judas himself – and he can have you for all I care! Tell me, you dumb beast, what do you know of nails, wheels of fortune, or anything else?"

"Well," said Sancho, "if people don't understand me, is it any wonder that what I say sounds like gibberish? That's all right, though; I understand myself and know that I've said very few foolish things among all the ones I've uttered. It's just that your grace is always so plastidious about everything I say or do."

"You mean 'fastidious,'" said Don Quixote, "not 'plastidious,' you confounded language butcher!"

"I wish your grace would stop finding fault with me," replied Sancho. "You know I wasn't brought up at court and haven't studied at Salamanca to know whether I'm adding or dropping letters from my words. For goodness sake, there's certainly no reason to expect a person from Sayago to speak as well as one from Toledo; besides, there are probably some in Toledo who aren't any great shakes at speaking properly."

"That is true," said the licentiate, "for those who grow up in the Tanneries and in Zocodover [1] don't speak as well as those who spend most of the day strolling about cathedral cloisters, and yet they are all from Toledo. Language that is pure, proper, elegant, and clear may be found among discriminating courtiers, even though the latter may have been born in Majalahonda. [2] I say discriminating, for there are many courtiers who are not, and discrimination is the grammar of good speech and is perfected with practice. I, gentlemen, for good or ill, have studied canon law at Salamanca and pride myself on using words that are clear, plain, and meaningful."

"If you did not pride yourself more on wielding your sword than on wielding your tongue," said the other student, "you would be at the head of your class instead of last."

"Look, my bachelor friend," responded the licentiate, "your opinion that swordsmanship is useless is the most erroneous opinion on earth."

"To my way of thinking, it is not an opinion but an established fact," said Corchuelo,[3] "and if you would like me to prove it with an experiment, you have your foils there and the opportunity lies before us. I have a steady hand and a strong arm, which, added to my rather considerable determination, shall make you confess that I know what I am talking about. Dismount, sir, and come at me with all

---

1 The Tanneries and Zocodover, places where criminals gathered.

2 A small town near Madrid.

3 The casual mention of Corchuelo's name assumes that Cervantes had already identified him but, of course, he had not.

your measured steps, your circles, angles, and all your science, and I shall make you see stars in the middle of the day with my unsophisticated and recently acquired swordsmanship, for with the exception of God I place all my trust in this sword that the man is not yet born who can make me turn tail and run, nor is there anyone on earth I cannot force to give ground."

"As for the matter of turning tail, I have nothing to say," replied the skilled swordsman, "though it may turn out that the spot where you take your first step will be the spot where they dig your grave, meaning that this is where you may be slain by the very dexterity you scoff at."

"We shall see about that," said Corchuelo, who dismounted from his jackass with great haste and bruskly snatched one of the foils the licentiate was carrying on his jackass.

"This is not the way to proceed," said Don Quixote at this point. "I shall serve in this duel as both fencing master and judge of this often unresolved question."

Dismounting from Rocinante and taking up his lance, he stationed himself in the middle of the road just as the licentiate advanced with graceful bearing and measured steps towards Corchuelo, who came at him 'spouting fire from his eyes,' as they say. The other two laborers in the group remained mounted on their jackasses, serving as spectators in this deadly drama. The strokes, thrusts, chops, slashes, and hacks that Corchuelo delivered were too numerous to count and fell faster and more thickly than hail. He attacked like an angry lion but was met with a slap on the mouth by the buttoned tip of the licentiate's foil, which stopped him in mid-fury and made him kiss it as though it were a relic, though not with the same devotion with which relics are normally and rightfully kissed. In a word, the licentiate flicked off each of the buttons on the short cassock he was wearing, leaving the lower part of it cut into strips like the tentacles of an octopus. He twice knocked off his hat and so thoroughly exasperated him that Corchuelo in a fit of rage and despair grabbed his foil by the hilt and flung it into the air with all his might. One of the laborers in attendance who was a notary went to retrieve it and afterwards swore it landed nearly three-quarters of a league from there, which testimony served then and now to demonstrate with absolute certainty that brute strength may be overcome by skill. Corchuelo sat down exhausted and Sancho went over to him and said,

"Upon my word, sir bachelor, if your grace will take my advice, you should never again challenge anyone to a duel but should stick to wrestling or tossing the bar, for you are young and strong enough to do those things. I've heard it said that these swordsmen called fencers can stick the point of their sword through the eye of a needle."

"I am satisfied," said Corchuelo, "at having learned my lesson the hard way and having been taught by experience how greatly mistaken I was."

And standing up, he embraced the licentiate and they both remained better friends than before. But, being unwilling to wait for the notary who had gone to retrieve the foil, since it seemed he might be some time in returning, they decided to resume their journey in order to arrive early at Quiteria's village, which is where they all resided.

During the remainder of the trip the licentiate expounded upon the virtues of the sword with such demonstrative arguments and with so many figures and mathematical proofs that he convinced everyone of the value of this science, and Corchuelo was cured of his obstinacy. It was beginning to get dark when they arrived and the sky over the village seemed to be filled with an endless number of glittering stars. At the same time they could hear the soft, muffled sounds of various instruments, such as flutes, tabors, psalteries, recorders, tambourines, and bells. As they drew nearer, they saw a bower of trees that had been manually erected at the entrance to the village. These trees were completely covered with lights and were unaffected by the wind, which at the moment was blowing so faintly it was barely capable of moving the leaves. The musicians were busy entertaining the wedding guests by strolling about the festive grounds in separate groups, some dancing, some singing, and some playing the various instruments mentioned above; in fact, the entire meadow seemed alive and bustling with gaiety and merrymaking. A number of other persons were engaged in erecting platforms from which one could comfortably view the plays and dances to be performed the next day on this spot dedicated to the celebration of the wealthy Camacho's wedding and Basilio's funeral. Don Quixote refused to enter the village even though he was urged to do so by both the laborer and the bachelor, offering as his excuse, and more than a sufficient one in his view, that it was the custom of knights-errant to spend the night in woods and fields rather than in towns, even if it was under roofs of gold. And with this, he left the road and rode ahead a short distance totally against the wishes of Sancho, who was reminded once again of the comfortable lodgings he had enjoyed in Don Diego's castle, or house.

Chapter Twenty

The account of the wedding of Camacho the Wealthy and the incident of Basilio the Poor

"You, dear soul, are more fortunate than all those who inhabit the face of the earth, for without envying or being envied you can sleep with your soul at peace, nor are you pursued by enchanters or beset by enchantments! Sleep on, I say and shall say a hundred times, without doubts about your lady's constancy causing you to keep a ceaseless vigil, or lying awake nights thinking of how you will pay your debts, or wondering what you must do to feed yourself and your needy little family for one more day. You are not vexed by ambition or preoccupied by all the useless pomp of this world, since the limits of your wants extend no farther than the care of your jackass. You have laid the concern for your own person upon my shoulders, a weight and counterweight that nature and custom have ever assigned to us masters. Thus the servant sleeps while the master lies awake wondering how he will support him, favor him, and improve his lot. The anguish of seeing the sky turn to bronze and deny its needed moisture to the earth distresses, not the servant, but the master, who in times of drought and famine is responsible for supporting the servant who was by his side in times of plenty and abundance."

Sancho made no response to all this because he was sound asleep, nor would he have later awakened so abruptly had Don Quixote not roused him with the butt of his lance. Finally, waking up drowsy and sluggish, he looked about in all directions and said,

"If I am not mistaken, there is an odor and aroma coming from yond arbor that's much closer to that of fried bacon than of jonquils or thyme, and upon my word, weddings that begin with such aromas as these can't fail to be sumptuous, excellent ones."

"Hurry up, you walking appetite," said Don Quixote, "let us go watch the ceremonies and see what the rejected Basilio will do."

"Let him do whatever he will," said Sancho; "if only he weren't poor, he'd be marrying Quiteria, for is there any greater folly than not to have a cent to one's name and yet want to marry some great lady? I swear, master, I'm of the opinion that the poor soul should be happy with what he's got and not go chasing after the impossible. I'll bet my right arm that Camacho can cover Basilio with *reals*, and that being the case, which it undoubtedly is, Quiteria would be crazy to throw away all the gifts and jewels Camacho can and must have given her, to choose instead Basilio's ability at tossing the bar and his fencing skills, for a good toss of the bar or an excellent sword flourish won't get you a pint of wine in any tavern whatsoever. Abilities and advantages that can't be sold – Count Dirlos can have them all! But when these qualities fall into the lap of someone who has considerable wealth, well, I would like my own lot to be as hard. A good building can always be erected on a good foundation and the best foundation and base on earth is money."

"For heaven's sake, Sancho," said Don Quixote at this point, "bring your tirade to a close. I am convinced that if you were allowed to go on with those harangues you constantly come up with, you would not have time to eat or sleep but would spend all your time talking."

"If your grace were not so forgetful," replied Sancho, "you would remember the articles of our agreement before we set out this last time, one of which stated that you would let me talk as much as I pleased so long as I said nothing against my neighbor or your grace's authority, and up to now it strikes me that I've not violated that particular article."

"I recall no such article, Sancho," said Don Quixote, "and that being the case, I want you to stop talking and come with me, for the instruments we heard last night are just beginning to resound in the valleys. Undoubtedly, the wedding will be performed in the cool of the morning rather than in the afternoon heat."

Sancho did as his master commanded, placing the saddle on Rocinante and the packsaddle on his dapple and, once mounted, the pair began to make their way into the bower one pace at a time. The first object to catch Sancho's attention was a young ox skewered on the trunk of an elm tree. Feeding the fire over which it was being roasted was a veritable mountain of smoldering logs. Six pots placed round the bonfire had been constructed from molds different from the other pots, for they were rather sizeable earthen jars, each capable of holding a storehouse of meat, and as such, contained entire sheep and enveloped them so completely that these were hidden from view as easily as if they had been doves. There was an endless number of skinned rabbits and plucked chickens hanging from the trees until such time that they could be entombed in the pots. And the fowl and various types of game that had been hung there to cool were likewise infinite in number. Sancho counted more than sixty wineskins that held more than five gallons each, all full of excellent wines, as he later learned. In addition, there were heaping mounds of the whitest bread, like the mountains of wheat commonly seen on threshing floors. The cheeses, which were stacked like open brickwork, formed a wall, and two cauldrons of oil larger than those in a dyer's shop served for frying the foods made from dough, which foods, when done, were removed with two large ladles and then plunged into another cauldron of processed honey that stood next to them. There were more than fifty men and women cooks, all spotless, diligent, and cheerful. Twelve tender suckling pigs had been sewn inside the distended belly of the ox for the purpose of rendering it tender and flavorful. The various kinds of spices appeared to have been bought, not by the pound, but in twenty-five-pound sacks, all of which were visible in a large chest. In short, the provisions for the wedding were rustic but so abundant they could have fed an army.

Sancho looked at it all, took it in, and liked everything he saw. First of all, he was captivated and unnerved by the stewing pots, from which he would gladly have helped himself to a medium-size portion. He was also enticed by the wineskins, but most of all by the contents of the frying pans, if the big-bellied cauldrons could rightly be called that. And thus it was that Sancho, being unable to contain himself any longer, did the only thing in his power, which was to go over to one of the solicitous cooks to ask politely and hungrily if he might soak a piece of bread in one of those pots; to which the cook replied,

"Brother, this is not one of those days over which hunger holds sway, thanks to the wealthy Camacho. You may dismount and see if there isn't a ladle nearby with which to scoop up a hen or two, and may you enjoy them."

"I don't see any," said Sancho.

"Just a moment," replied the cook, "how stupid of me. You must be one of those timid, finicky souls!"

In saying this, he grabbed a pot and plunged it into one of the two cauldrons, scooping up three hens and a couple of geese, whereupon he said,

"Eat up, my friend, and may these skimmings tide you over till the dinner hour arrives."

"I don't have anything to put them in," said Sancho.

"You may keep the ladle and everything," said the cook; "it's all provided by virtue of Camacho's wealth and happiness."

While this was taking place with Sancho, Don Quixote observed as many as a dozen men from the country all clad in their festive holiday outfits ride in from one end of the arbor on a dozen beautiful mares equipped with harnesses that were lavish and showy as well as rustic, with numerous tiny bells across the breast-straps. Riding in perfect formation, they made not one but a number of charges across the meadow, yelling and shouting joyously,

"Long live Camacho and Quiteria – he as rich as she is beautiful, and she the most beautiful woman on earth!"

When Don Quixote heard this, he said to himself,

"These people have obviously not seen my Dulcinea of Toboso, for if they had, they would not be so effusive in their praise of that Quiteria of theirs."

A short while later several different groups of dancers began entering the arbor at various points, among whom was a group of sword dancers composed of some two dozen handsome, high-spirited youths, all attired in white lightweight linen with expensive silk kerchiefs of variously colored embroidery on their heads. One of the men riding the mares asked the group's leader, an agile lad, if any of the dancers had ever injured themselves.

"Until now no one has, thank goodness; all of us are healthy."

And, with this, he began weaving in and out among his companions with such dexterous twists and turns that, though Don Quixote was accustomed to seeing dances of this sort, none had ever impressed him as much as this one. He was equally impressed by another dance composed of lovely young maidens who were apparently between the ages of fourteen and eighteen. They all wore green dresses, and their hair, which they wore partly loose and partly braided, was so golden it could have rivaled the rays of the sun, and their heads were crowned with garlands of jasmine, roses, amaranth, and honeysuckle. They were led by a venerable old man and an elderly matron who were more agile and nimble than their years suggested and they all danced to the sound of a double-reed bagpipe. Despite the innocence of their eyes and faces, the girls showed by their agility that they were the best dancers in the world.

Behind them came another group of skilled dancers performing one of those dances in which the members also speak. The group consisted of eight nymphs who formed two lines. Cupid was at the head of one and Wealth at the head of the other, the former outfitted with wings, bow, arrows, and quiver, while the latter was clad in expensive multicolored silk and gold. The nymphs marching behind the god of love bore white parchments on their backs with their names printed in large letters. The name of the first was *Poetry*, that of the second *Intelligence*, the third *Good Family*, and the fourth *Valor*. In like manner, those who were led by Wealth bore the following names: that of the first *Generosity*, the second *Bounty*, the third *Treasures*, and the fourth *Peaceful Possessions*. They were all preceded by a wooden castle drawn by four savages clad only in ivy and hemp dyed green and all so lifelike that they came close to frightening Sancho. On the front of the castle and each of the sides were the words *Castle of Eternal Vigilance*. The dancers were accompanied by four accomplished musicians playing drums and flutes. Cupid opened the dance and, after executing a pair of dance figures, raised his eyes and shot an arrow at a damsel standing between the castle's turrets, to whom he directed the following:

"I am the god whose power extends
Through the wide ocean, earth, and sky;
To my soft sway all nature bends,
Compelled by beauty to comply.

Fearless I rule in calm and storm;
Indulge my pleasure to the full;
Things deemed impossible perform;
Bestow, resume, ordain, annul."

Having concluded his recitation, he shot an arrow over the castle and took up his former position. Wealth then sprang forward and performed two additional figures, with the drums growing silent as he said,

"My power exceeds the might of love,
For Cupid bows to me alone;
Of all things framed by heaven above,
The most respected, sought, and known.

My name is Wealth; mine aid
But few obtain, though all desire:
Yet shall thy virtue, beauteous maid,
My constant services acquire."

Wealth withdrew and Poetry stepped forward and, after executing several dance steps like the others, turned her eyes towards the damsel and said,

"Let Poetry, whose strain divine
The wondrous power of song displays,
His heart to thee, fair nymph, consign,
Transported in melodious lays.

If haply thou wilt not refuse
To grant my supplicated boon,
Thy fame shall, wafted by the Muse,
Surmount the circle of the moon."

Poetry stepped aside and from Wealth's company came Generosity, who, once her figures were executed, said,

"My name is Liberality,
Alike beneficent and wise,
To shun wild prodigality,
And sordid avarice despise.

Yet, for thy favor lavish grown,
A prodigal I mean to prove–
An honorable vice, I own–
But giving is the test of love."

In similar fashion all the dancers from the two groups stepped forward and then withdrew, each performing her configurations and speaking her verses, some serious, some humorous, though Don

Quixote retained in his memory, which was excellent, only the ones noted. They all proceeded to dance as a group, linking and unlinking their arms with utter grace and abandon. Each time that Love passed before the castle, he would shoot an arrow over it, whereas Wealth would assault the castle with gilded balls, which he smashed against it. Finally, after dancing about for quite some time, Wealth pulled out a fat purse fashioned from the hide of a large striped cat, which appeared to be full of coins, and flung it at the castle, the blow from which caused the boards to fly apart and come crashing down, leaving the damsel exposed and completely defenseless. Wealth, together with those of his faction, approached and, after throwing a long gold chain round her neck, pretended to catch her, subdue her, and make her their prisoner. When Love and his followers saw this, they set to work to release her. The actions were all performed to the accompaniment of the small drums to which they all danced and capered in perfect time. Peace was finally established among the contending parties by the savages, who very hastily rebuilt and reassembled the castle, inside which the damsel once again enclosed herself as before. Here the dance concluded to the enormous satisfaction of the spectators.

Don Quixote asked one of the nymphs who it was that had composed and arranged the dances. She informed him that it was the local priest, who had quite a knack for creations of that sort.

"I dare say," said Don Quixote, "that this bachelor or priest likes Camacho better than he does Basilio and is probably better at satire than at vespers. Just notice how cleverly he has worked the accomplishments of Basilio and the riches of Camacho into the dance!"

Sancho Panza, who had been listening to all this, said,

"Well, I want my gamecock to win, so I'm betting on Camacho."

"In a word, Sancho," said Don Quixote, "it is obvious you are from the country and are one of those who say, 'Long live whoever wins!'"

"I don't know if I'm one of those," replied Sancho, "but I do know that I'll never get skimmings from Basilio's pot like the ones I got from Camacho's."

And he showed him the pot full of geese and hens, at which point he seized one and began eating it with a flair and great gusto, saying,

"Let Basilio and all his talents pick up the bill, for 'A person is worth as much as he's got, and he's got as much as he's worth.' There are only two types of people in the world according to a grandmother of mine: the haves and the have-nots, and she was partial to the haves. Nowadays, master Don Quixote, people are more interested in what a person *has* than in what he *knows*, for an ass covered with gold is more attractive than a horse with only a saddle. Therefore, I say once more that I'll stick with Camacho, for the abundant skimmings of his pots consist of geese, hens, hares, and rabbits, whereas those of Basilio's, if they're ever forthcoming, or even fifthcoming, will consist of cheap wine."

"Have you finished your tirade, Sancho," asked Don Quixote.

"I probably have," said Sancho, "since I can see your grace is losing patience. However, if this element had not entered the picture, I had enough material to last for three days."

To which Don Quixote replied,

"May it please God, Sancho, to let me see you silent just once before I die."

"At the rate we're going," said Sancho, "before your grace dies I'll be pushing up daisies and then I'll probably be so silent I won't say a word till the end of the world or at least till Judgement Day."

"Even if that should occur, Sancho," said Don Quixote, "your silence will never equal all the talking you have done, continue to do, and will undoubtedly do for the rest of your life. Besides, the day of my demise will more likely arrive before yours, so I never expect to see you silent except when you are drinking or sleeping, which is the most I can hope for."

"Upon my word of honor, master," said Sancho, "one can't trust that fleshless specter – Death, that is – for she'll eat the lamb as well as the sheep. I've heard our priest say that she tramples with equal disregard the king's lofty towers and the peasant's lowly hut. That lady possesses more of might than of daintiness and is not the least bit squeamish; she eats anything, is ready for everything, and stuffs her saddlebags with people of all types, ages, and degrees. She's not the kind of reaper who takes a siesta but one who reaps during every hour of the day, felling the green grass with the dry. She never seems to chew but swallows and gulps down everything that is put before her because she has a dog's appetite that can't be satisfied; and though she has no belly, she shows she has dropsy and thirsts after the blood of every living soul, as one might drink a jug of cold water."

"That's enough, Sancho!" exclaimed Don Quixote at this point, "stop while you are ahead and don't risk losing it all. Truly, what you have said of death in your own rustic way is what a good preacher might have said. I assure you, Sancho, that with your common sense and intelligence you could take a pulpit in hand and travel the world over preaching wonders."

"Living a good life makes for a good preacher," said Sancho, "and that is all the theology I know."

"Nor do you need to know more," said Don Quixote, "but what I fail to understand or comprehend is how you know so much, since the fear of God is the beginning of wisdom and you fear a lizard more than you fear Him."

"Master," said Sancho, "you should pass judgement on matters having to do with chivalry and not get involved in other people's fears and bravery, for I have as awesome a fear of God as the next person. But with your grace's permission, I'm going to dig into these skimmings, since all the rest is just idle talk for which we'll be held accountable in the next life."

In saying this, he began a fresh assault on the pot with such enthusiasm that he awakened the appetite of Don Quixote, who doubtless would have joined him had he not been diverted by something that demands our attention in the next chapter.

Chapter Twenty-One

The continuation of Camacho's wedding, together with other enjoyable incidents

While Don Quixote and Sancho were discussing the matters related in the preceding chapter, they heard a great outcry from the men on the mares, who were shouting as they thunderously rode out to greet the approaching bride and bridegroom. The latter, surrounded by a wide assortment of instruments, singers, and dancers, were accompanied by the priest, their numerous relatives, and every notable from the surrounding towns, all dressed in their holiday finery. When Sancho saw the bride, he exclaimed,

"My word, she's not dressed like a farm girl but like some elegant lady of the court! If my eyes don't deceive me, she's wearing an expensive coral necklace instead of the medallions she ought to be wearing, and her green wedding gown is made of thirty-pile velvet! Bless my soul but the trim on her gown isn't white linen either but strips of satin! And just look at her hands: are they adorned with jetstone rings, or what? May I be struck dead if they aren't made of gold – and what gold! – and set with pearls as white as curds, each of which must be worth as much as one of my very own eyes! And, damn, what hair! If it's really her own, I've never seen any in my whole life that was longer or more golden! A look at her figure and bearing reminds me of a palm tree laden with clusters of dates swaying in the breeze, which is exactly what the jewels on her hair and neck look like! I swear by my soul she's a gorgeous lass and every bit worthy of the nuptial couch."

Don Quixote had to laugh at Sancho's rustic praises, thinking that apart from his lady Dulcinea of Toboso he had never seen a more beautiful woman himself. The fair Quiteria looked a bit pale, which most likely was due to the bad night brides always undergo in anticipation of their wedding day. The pair were making their way to a stage situated on one side of the meadow, which was decorated with carpets and floral arrangements and was where the wedding ceremony was to be performed and the dances and improvisations viewed. But just as they reached that spot, they heard loud shouts behind them and a voice that said,

"Don't be in such a hurry, you people who are as inconsiderate as you are hasty!"

At this pronouncement they all turned and saw that the shouts came from a man clad in what appeared to be a black tunic decorated with patches of crimson silk shaped like flames. His head, as soon became apparent, was crowned with a funereal wreath of cypress and in his hand he carried a long staff. As he drew nearer, they were shocked to recognize the gallant Basilio and everyone wondered what his shouts might portend, fearing some evil outcome of his presence at this inopportune moment. He finally arrived exhausted and out of breath and stationed himself in front of the bride and bridegroom, whereupon he drove the staff he was carrying into the ground, which had a steel spike on one end. With his face pale and his eyes fixed upon Quiteria, he addressed her in a voice that was hoarse and trembling:

"You, ungrateful Quiteria, know full well that in accordance with the holy law we both acknowledge that you may not, while I am alive, take another husband. Nor are you unaware that, because of my expectation that time and my efforts would improve my material lot, I have never failed to observe the respect your honor is due. But you, casting aside every obligation you owed my honorable intentions, have chosen to make another person lord of what is mine, a person whose wealth affords him not only a sizeable fortune but the greatest happiness as well. And so that he may enjoy it to the fullest, which is not what I think he deserves but is what heaven has seen fit to grant him, I with my own hands shall remove the obstacle and obstruction that is proving a hindrance to it, by removing myself from between you. Let wealthy Camacho and ungrateful Quiteria live a long and happy life but let poor

Basilio perish, whose poverty has clipped the wings of his happiness and sent him to his grave!"

As he said this, he seized the staff he had driven into the ground and, leaving one half of it embedded in the earth, revealed that it was a sheath for the medium-size rapier concealed inside it. With the part that might be called the hilt planted firmly in the ground, he threw himself onto the exposed steel blade with the greatest determination and nonchalance. The bloody tip and half of the steel blade instantly emerged from his back and the unfortunate wretch fell to the ground bathed in his own blood and transfixed by his own weapon. His friends immediately rushed to his side, horrified at this wretched and lamentable development. Don Quixote dismounted from Rocinante to go to Basilio's aid, and finding that he had not yet expired, held him in his arms. Though there were some who would have pulled out the rapier, the priest who was present felt they should not remove it until he had made his confession, as its removal and his expiration might constitute one and the same act. Basilio partially regained consciousness and in a feeble, pained voice said,

"If you, cruel Quiteria, should consent to give me your hand in marriage in this final unalterable crisis, I might still hope that my foolhardiness would be forgiven, for by means of it I shall obtain the bliss of being yours."

When the priest heard this, he advised him to attend to the salvation of his soul rather than to the pleasures of his body, and to implore God with all his heart to forgive his sins and his desperate act; at which point Basilio replied that under no circumstances would he confess until Quiteria first gave him her hand in marriage, for that happiness would reinvigorate his will and give him the strength to make his confession. When Don Quixote heard the dying man's request, he cried out that what Basilio was asking was perfectly just and reasonable and might, moreover, easily be granted, for the distinguished Camacho would be just as honored by receiving the lady Quiteria in the role of the valorous Basilio's widow as he would by receiving her from her father's own hands.

"The only thing that will transpire here is a simple 'I do,'" said the knight, "which will result in nothing more than its pronouncement, since the sepulchre will provide the nuptial couch for this marriage."

Camacho listened to all this and was thrown into a state of confusion by it, not knowing what to say or do, but the cries of Basilio's friends were so numerous, urging Camacho to allow Quiteria to give him her hand in marriage lest he lose his soul by quitting this life without hope, that he was moved, nay, compelled to say that if Quiteria were willing to do so, it was acceptable to him, since it meant delaying for only a moment the fulfillment of his own desires. They all approached Quiteria, whom they urged – some with pleas, others with tears, and still others with persuasive arguments – to give her hand to the pitiful Basilio, but she, more unyielding than a statue and harder than marble, showed that she was neither able nor willing to say a word and in fact would not have done so had the priest not told her to make up her mind quickly, for Basilio was on the verge of giving up the ghost and there was no time for indecision or vacillation. At this point, the beautiful Quiteria, visibly confused and without saying a word, sadly and sorrowfully went over to Basilio, who lay with his eyes rolled back, his breath coming in short, quick bursts, and the name of Quiteria faintly upon his lips, giving every indication of dying as a heathen rather than as a Christian. Once at his side, Quiteria knelt down and asked for his hand, not with words, but with gestures. Basilio rolled his eyes forward and stared steadfastly at her, saying,

"O Quiteria, you have become compassionate at a time when your compassion will serve as the knife that completely severs my life, for I no longer have the strength to bear the glory you are bestowing upon me by choosing me for your own, nor to hold back the grief that is so rapidly clouding my eyes with the frightening specter of death! What I beg of you, O ominous star of my destiny, is that you not ask for my hand nor give me yours out of a sense of obligation nor in an effort to deceive me once again, but that you confess and freely declare of your own free will that you offer it to your lawful husband, for at a critical moment such as this it would be wrong of you to deceive me or resort to trickery with one who has always dealt so honestly with you."

As he spoke these words, he occasionally fell into a swoon, with everyone present imagining that each fainting spell would carry off his soul. Quiteria, in complete innocence and embarrassment, took Basilio's right hand in her own and said,

"No force shall be strong enough to make me change my mind. Therefore, with all the will at my disposal I offer you my hand as your lawful wife and accept yours if you, indeed, extend it of your own free will and your senses have not been impaired or affected by the calamity brought about by your hasty action."

"I indeed offer it," said Basilio, "not as one disturbed or confused but with the clear understanding that heaven saw fit to give me, and thus do I offer and surrender myself to be your husband."

"And I to be your wife," replied Quiteria, "whether you live for many years or they carry you from my arms to the grave."

"To be as seriously wounded as he is," said Sancho, "this young man is certainly doing a lot of talking. They should make him cut out the courting and attend to his soul, for in my opinion he's more likely to make a speech than he is to give up the ghost."

With Basilio and Quiteria now holding each other's hands, the priest tearfully and tenderly gave them his blessing, asking heaven to permit the new bridegroom's soul to rest in peace. No sooner did the latter receive the blessing than he sprang to his feet with the greatest agility and then ever so nonchalantly removed the rapier for which his body had served as sheath. All those present were flabbergasted and a few of them, more credulous than questioning, began to shout in a loud voice,

"It's a miracle, it's a miracle!" but Basilio replied,

"It's not a miracle but a trick – a trick!"

The priest, bewildered and astounded, went over to examine the wound with both hands and discovered that the sword had passed, not through Basilio's flesh and ribs, but through a hollow steel tube he had fitted round them, first having filled it with blood, which, they later learned, he had prepared in such a way as to prevent it from coagulating. In the end, the priest and Camacho, together with the majority of all those present, understood they had been duped and tricked. The bride showed she was not distressed by the deception; on the contrary, having heard someone say that the marriage, because it was fraudulent, would be invalid, she declared that she was reaffirming it. From this, they all concluded that the affair had been planned with the knowledge and consent of the pair. Camacho and his supporters felt so insulted over this that they let their hands take charge of their vengeance and they all drew their swords and headed in Basilio's direction, in whose defense nearly as many swords were instantly drawn. Don Quixote, moving to the front of the line on his horse, his lance poised and resting on his arm, and his shield protecting his body, made everyone give way before him. Sancho, who never found pleasure or solace in such goings-on, took refuge behind the cauldrons from which he had scooped his tasty skimmings, inasmuch as he considered that spot sacred and one that would be respected. Don Quixote cried out in a loud voice,

"Stop this, gentlemen! stop, I say! It is unjust to take revenge for abuses we all suffer at the hands of love. Your graces should remember that love and war are identical, and just as in war, where it is customary and permissible to employ tricks and stratagems to overcome the enemy, so in contests and rivalries of love is it acceptable to employ tricks and stratagems to achieve the desired result so long as they bring no discredit or dishonor to the loved one. Quiteria was meant for Basilio and Basilio for Quiteria in accordance with heaven's just and favorable decree. Camacho is rich and can purchase his pleasure whenever, wherever, and however he pleases. Basilio has but this single ewe and no one, however powerful, shall take her from him. No man can separate these two whom God has joined together, and anyone who attempts to do so must first pass by the point of this lance."

In saying this, he brandished it so fiercely and deftly that he struck fear into all those who did not know who he was, but so intensely did Quiteria's rejection take hold in Camacho's mind that he banished her from his thoughts in an instant. Accordingly, he acceded to the pleas of the priest, a prudent and well-intentioned man, whose persuasiveness calmed and pacified Camacho and those of his party, in acknowledgment of which they returned their swords to their sheaths, ascribing the blame more to Quiteria's fickleness than to Basilio's trickery. Moreover, Camacho argued that if Quiteria loved Basilio as a maiden, she would have continued to love him once she was married and he should thus give thanks to heaven more for its having taken her from him than for having given her to him.

After Camacho and those of his party were assuaged and pacified, all those in Basilio's became calm, and wealthy Camacho, to demonstrate that he harbored no ill feelings regarding the deception but considered it of no importance, ordered the festivities to proceed as if there were actually to be a wedding. However, Basilio, his wife, and their followers were unwilling to attend and thus set out for Basilio's village. (For, the poor who are virtuous and intelligent also have those who follow, honor, and assist them, just as the rich have those who flatter them and swell their numbers.) They took Don Quixote with them, considering him a courageous and manly person. Only Sancho rode along under a cloud from not being allowed to remain there for Camacho's splendid banquet and festivities, which were to last until nightfall. And so, forlorn and sad, he followed along behind his master, who rode ahead in Basilio's company, and thus did Sancho leave behind the fleshpots of Egypt, even though he carried them with him in his thoughts. And the nearly consumed skimmings that he still had in his pot represented the glory and abundance of the wonderful things he was leaving behind. And so, grief-stricken and despondent, despite the fact that his stomach was full, Sancho slumped forward on his dapple and followed along in the footsteps of Rocinante.

Chapter Twenty-Two

The description of the great adventure of the Cave of Montesinos located in the heart of La Mancha, which Don Quixote brought to a successful conclusion

Many and great were the kindnesses extended to Don Quixote by the bridal pair, who were beholden to him for having championed their cause, and they held his intellect in as high regard as they did his valor, considering him a Cid in the matter of arms and a Cicero in that of oratory. Our noble Sancho regaled himself for three days at the expense of the newlyweds, from whom it was learned that Basilio's feigned suicide attempt had not been contrived with the help of the beautiful Quiteria but was Basilio acting alone, and he had expected from it the very success he achieved. To be sure, he confessed to having imparted his scheme to some of his friends so that at the proper moment they would come to his aid and reinforce his deception.

"One cannot and should not call people deceptive," said Don Quixote, "who set their sights on virtuous ends, and what end can be more noble than the uniting of two lovers, particularly when we remember that the greatest obstacles encountered by love are hunger and continual want? Love is total happiness, rejoicing, and contentment, and all the more so when the lover is in possession of the beloved, against whom necessity and poverty are their open and avowed adversaries."

All this was said with the object of convincing Basilio to cease cultivating those talents of his which, though increasing his fame, brought him no income. Instead, he should by lawful and industrious means attend to the business of accumulating wealth, which never fails to accrue to those who are prudent and diligent. The poor man who is honorable (if, indeed, a poor man may be termed honorable) possesses a treasure when he has a beautiful wife. If she is taken from him, he is stripped of his honor and ruined. And an honorable and beautiful woman whose husband is poor deserves to be crowned with the laurels of victory and the palm leaves of triumph. Beauty, by itself alone, attracts the passions of all those who see and recognize it, just as golden eagles and high-soaring hawks swoop down upon a tasty bait, but if this same beauty is accompanied by need and poverty, it is attacked by ravens, kites, and other birds of prey. The woman who can stand firm against so many assaults certainly deserves to be called the crowning glory of her husband.

"Listen, my good Basilio," said Don Quixote, "a certain wise man was of the opinion that there was only one good woman in the entire world and he suggested that if every husband considered and believed this single good woman was his own wife, his life would be a happy one. I have never married nor have I ever entertained the notion up to the present time; nevertheless, I would venture to offer the following advice to anyone who asked me how to go about selecting the woman he should take as his spouse. First of all, I would advise him to place greater emphasis on her good reputation than on her possessions, for a good woman does not acquire a good reputation merely by being good but by appearing to be good because a woman's honor is soiled more by a lack of caution and restraint in public than by wicked deeds committed in private. If you bring home a good woman, it will be an easy matter to maintain or even to improve her goodness but, should you bring home one who is evil, it will cost you considerable effort to reform her because it is no easy task to go from one extreme to the other. I am not saying it is impossible but I consider it quite difficult."

Sancho, who had been listening to all this, muttered to himself,

"This master of mine, whenever I speak of things of pith and substance, invariably says I could take a pulpit in hand and go forth in the world preaching marvelous sermons. Well, I can say in return that whenever he starts stringing together his maxims and giving advice, he could take not only a pulpit in hand but two on each finger and go preaching in the marketplace and give them everything they want. (You are some kind of knight-errant and there's nothing you don't know!) Why, I used to believe with all my heart that he was knowledgeable only about things having to do with chivalry but there's nothing he doesn't poke at or dip his spoon into."

Because Sancho had muttered this rather loudly, Don Quixote overheard him, at which point he said,

"What are you mumbling, Sancho?"

"I'm not mumbling anything," said Sancho; "I was simply thinking to myself that I wished I had heard what your grace just now said before I ever got married. I'd probably be going about saying, 'Only a married man knows the true meaning of freedom.'"

"Is your Teresa so bad, Sancho?"

"It's not that she's bad," replied Sancho, "it's just that she's not very good; at least, she's not as good as I would like her to be."

"You are wrong, Sancho," said Don Quixote, "to speak ill of your wife, who, after all, is the mother of your children."

"She and I don't owe each other anything," said Sancho. "She also speaks ill of me whenever she feels like it, especially when she gets jealous, and when that happens, Satan himself should try to get along with her."

In short, they spent three days with the bridal pair, where they were regaled and treated like royalty. Don Quixote asked the licentiate – the fencing expert – to provide him with a guide to take him to the Cave of Montesinos, as he was quite eager to penetrate it and see with his own eyes whether all the wonders were true that were reported about it in those parts. The licentiate said he would provide him with a cousin of his who was an excellent scholar and very fond of books of chivalry. This cousin would gladly take him to the mouth of that very cave and show him the Lakes of Ruidera, famous throughout La Mancha and even the whole of Spain. He added that Don Quixote would find him quite delightful and entertaining because he was a young man who knew how to write books that were both salable and worthy of being dedicated to various members of the nobility.

The cousin finally arrived with a pregnant jackass in tow whose saddle was covered with a multicolored piece of carpet or burlap. Sancho saddled Rocinante, put the packsaddle on his dapple, and filled the saddlebags with provisions in addition to the cousin's saddlebags, which were equally well stocked. Then commending themselves to God and bidding everyone farewell, they set out on the road to the famous Cave of Montesinos. Along the way, Don Quixote asked the cousin to describe his profession and the sorts of activities and studies he was engaged in. To this he responded that his profession was that of humanist and his activities and studies involved writing books and getting them published, all of which were quite beneficial to the state and were no less entertaining. One was entitled *The Book of Liveries*, in which he described seven hundred and three liveries, including their colors, mottoes, and devices, from which court knights could pick and select those they might need on some festive or gala occasion without having to go about begging anyone for them or 'beating their heads against a stone wall,' as the expression goes, in order to come up with the right ones suitable for their purposes and desires.

"That is because I provide the jealous, the scorned, the neglected, and the absent with liveries that will suit them; in fact, they will find far more to their liking than those that are not. I also have another book I intend to call *Metamorphoses, or, The Spanish Ovid*, a book remarkably novel in its conception, for in it in imitation of the parodies of Ovid I reveal the origins and sources of the Giralda of Seville, the Angel of the Magdalena, the sewer of Vecinguerra of Cordova, the bulls of Guisando, the Sierra Morena, and the fountains of Leganitos and Lavapiés in Madrid, while not overlooking those of the Piojo, the Golden Sewer, and the Priora, all of which, along with their allegories, metaphors, and permutations, will delight, amaze, and instruct simultaneously. I have another book I call *Supplement to Polydore Virgil*, which deals with the history of inventions and is a work of great erudition and scholarship, because those indispensable matters which Polydore failed to mention I investigate and expound upon in a most elegant fashion. Virgil forgot to tell us who was the first person in history to have a head cold, or the first to use ointments to treat himself for the Gallic disease but I explain them down to the smallest detail and cite more than twenty-five authorities in support of them. Your grace may therefore be the judge of whether I have done a good job and whether such a book will be of benefit to anyone."

Sancho, who had been following the cousin's narration quite closely, said to him,

"May God grant your grace success in publishing your books but can you tell me, which you undoubtedly can, since you know everything: who was the first person to scratch his head? I'm of the opinion it must have been our father Adam."

"Yes, it must have been," said the cousin, "for there is no doubt that Adam had a head with hair on it and, that being the case and he being the first man on earth, he must have scratched himself at some time or other."

"That is what I think," replied Sancho, "but tell me this: who was the first tumbler in the world?"

"Truly, brother," said the cousin, "I can't answer that until I do some research, which I shall do as soon as I return to where I keep my books. I shall give you a satisfactory answer the next time we meet, for surely this will not be the last time."

"Just a moment, sir," said Sancho, "you needn't trouble yourself after all, for I just came up with the answer to my own question. Be advised that the world's first tumbler was Lucifer at the time he was ejected and thrown out of heaven and went tumbling into the fiery abyss."

"You are right, my friend," said the cousin, and Don Quixote added,

"That question and answer did not originate with you, Sancho; you heard someone else say it."

"Your grace can't be serious," said Sancho. "Why, if I were to start asking questions and then answer them, I could keep going from now till morning. In order to ask foolish questions and give absurd answers, I certainly don't need to go about asking my neighbors for help."

"You have spoken more profoundly, Sancho, than you realize," said Don Quixote. "There are some people who expend considerable energy studying and figuring things out which, once studied and figured out, are not the least bit worth understanding or committing to memory."

Such was the manner in which they spent the day, discussing these and other pleasant topics, and that night they took shelter in a small village from where the cousin informed Don Quixote that it was no more than two leagues to the Cave of Montesinos and, if he was serious about entering it, he needed to provide himself with rope to lower himself into its depths. Don Quixote replied that even if he should reach the very bottom, he would make certain to observe where he landed. Accordingly, they bought nearly fifty yards of rope and at two the following afternoon arrived at the cave. Its entrance was spacious and wide but choked with box thorn, wild fig, brambles, and other weeds so thick and entangled that they completely covered the entrance and hid it from view. As soon as they saw it, they all dismounted and the cousin and Sancho tied Don Quixote very securely with the rope. While they were binding and girding him, Sancho said,

"Oh, master, I hope you don't intend to bury yourself alive or get into a situation where you'll look like a bottle hung down a well for cooling. It is certainly no concern or obligation of yours to go exploring in this place that must be worse than a dungeon."

"Stop talking and keep tying," said Don Quixote, "for an undertaking such as this will have been reserved just for me." Here the guide said to him,

"Sir Don Quixote, I beg your grace to be extremely observant and examine with a hundred eyes what is down below. Perhaps there will be something I can put in my book *Transformations*."

"The tambourine," replied Sancho, "is in the hands of one who can play it."

After this exchange, they fastened the rope to Don Quixote, not over his armor but over his doublet, at which point the knight said,

"It was careless of us not to provide ourselves with a small bell I could tie next to me on the rope, for the sound from it would let you know I was alive and still descending, but since that is now impossible, I shall place myself in the hands of God, that He may guide me."

At this point he knelt down and in a muffled voice offered up a prayer to heaven, asking God to assist him and bring him successfully through this seemingly perilous and novel adventure. He then said in his normal voice,

"O mistress of all my actions and endeavors, most illustrious and peerless Dulcinea of Toboso, if it is possible for the prayers and supplications of this thy fortunate lover to reach thine ears, I beg thee in all thine incomparable beauty to hear them, for I ask only that thou not deniest me the favor and support I so desperately need at this moment. I am about to leap, plunge, and sink into the abyss I see before me for the sole purpose of showing the world that if thou grantest me thy favors, there is no impossible task I shall not undertake and accomplish."

And as he said this, he approached the abyss, where he saw the total impossibility of entering or lowering himself into it except by making his way in by brute force; and so, drawing his sword, he began to hack and lay waste to the underbrush growing at the mouth of the cave. The immense racket he made drove out an endless number of huge ravens and crows so swift and concentrated that they knocked Don Quixote to the ground and, had he been as superstitious as he was a good Catholic, he would have taken it as an evil omen and declined to enter such a place. Finally, he stood up when he saw there were no more ravens flying out nor any other nocturnal creatures such as the bats that had flown out with the ravens. Then with the cousin and Sancho feeding him rope, he eased himself down into the depths of the frightful cavern and, as he descended, Sancho gave him his blessing and made a thousand signs of the cross over him, saying,

"May you be guided by God and Our Lady of the Rock of France as well as by the Trinity of Gaeta, O flower and cream of knight-errantry! Down you go, hero of the human race with a heart of steel and arms of bronze! May God guide you, I repeat, and bring you back safe, sound, and unencumbered to the light of this world, which you wish to forsake in order to bury yourself in that darkness you are seeking!"

The cousin offered up virtually the same prayers and supplications. Don Quixote kept shouting for them to feed him more rope, which they reeled out a little at a time, and when they could no longer hear his shouts, which emerged from the cave as if through a pipe, they had already reeled out all fifty yards of rope and felt they should pull him up again, since there was no more rope to feed him. Nevertheless, they waited nearly half an hour, at which time they began to reel in the rope with the greatest of ease and with no resistance whatever, leading them to believe Don Quixote had remained down below. Imagining this to be the case, Sancho wept bitterly as he pulled faster and faster in hopes of proving himself wrong. When, in their opinion, they had hauled in more than forty-five yards, they finally encountered a resistance, which absolutely delighted them. Finally, when they were within a couple of yards of the end, they could distinctly see Don Quixote, to whom Sancho cried out,

"Thank goodness, master, you are safely back! We were afraid you had remained down there as seed for the next generation," but Don Quixote made no response.

Once they had pulled him all the way out, they noticed that his eyes were closed and he gave every indication of being fast asleep. Even after they laid him on the ground and untied him, he still refused to wake up. But they turned, twisted, and shook him so vigorously that he eventually regained consciousness, whereupon he stretched his limbs as though he had just awakened from a most profound sleep. Then peering in every direction like someone terrified, he said,

"My children, may God forgive you for having snatched me from the most pleasant, delectable sights and experiences that any human has ever witnessed. In truth, I have just this moment come to realize that all the pleasures of this life are like so many fleeting shadows, dreams, and fading flowers of the field. O hapless Montesinos! O sorely wounded Durandarte! O luckless Belerma! O tearful Guadiana, and you unfortunate daughters of Ruidera, who display in your waters the tears your lovely eyes have shed!"

The cousin and Sancho listened to what Don Quixote said and his words came forth as though painfully wrenched from the very depths of his being. They begged him to explain what he was saying and to tell them what he had seen in that hellish region.

"'Hellish' say you?" replied Don Quixote, "call it by some other name, for it deserves a better one, as you shall soon see."

He asked for something to eat, as he was extremely hungry. The three of them spread the cousin's sackcloth over the grass, turned to the provisions of the saddlebags and, after seating themselves in such agreeable company, ate both lunch and supper at one sitting. Once they had finished eating, Don Quixote of La Mancha said,

"My children, make yourselves comfortable and pay close attention to what I am about to say."

Chapter Twenty-Three

The astounding things that the extraordinary Don Quixote said he had seen deep within the Cave of Montesinos, the magnitude and impossibility of which lead one to believe that this adventure is apocryphal

It was around four in the afternoon when the cloud-covered sun with its dim light and attenuated rays afforded Don Quixote the opportunity to relate to his illustrious audience, refreshed and in comfort, what he had seen in the Cave of Montesinos, and he began in the following manner:

"On the right side of that dungeon at a depth of twelve to fourteen times a man's height there is a recess or space large enough to accommodate a large cart and its mules. A faint light finds its way there through several cracks or openings that extend all the way to the surface of the earth. I spotted that recess or space just as I was becoming weary and annoyed at finding myself hanging upside down from a rope in that awful darkness with no certain or known destination, so I decided to climb into the recess for a short rest. I called out to you not to feed me any more rope until I gave the command but you must not have heard me. I began hauling in the rope you let out and, forming it into a coil or pile, sat down on top of it lost in thought and wondering what I could do to reach the bottom, for I had no one to help me in my descent. While I sat there confused and preoccupied, suddenly and without any effort on my part I was overcome by a profound sleep; then when I least expected it and without knowing how or why, I awoke to find myself in the midst of the most beautiful, pleasant, and delightful meadow nature could engender or the mind of man conceive. Rubbing my eyes to clear them, I saw I was not dreaming but was actually awake. Nevertheless, I pinched my face and chest to make sure it was really I who was there and not some bodiless, counterfeit phantom. But my sense of touch, my emotions, and the coherent conversation I carried on with myself assured me that at that particular moment I was the very person you see before you now. My eyes immediately beheld a royal, stately palace or castle whose walls and sides appeared to be constructed of clear transparent crystal. Both doors of the massive entranceway swung open and through it, headed in my direction, strode a venerable old man with a snow-white beard reaching down to his waist who was wearing a green satin collegiate hood that covered his shoulders and chest, a black Milan cap, and a cloak of royal purple that trailed along the ground. He was not carrying any kind of weapons but had a rosary in his hands, the beads of which were larger than medium-size nuts, with every tenth bead being the size of an ostrich egg. His bearing, gait, and grave demeanor, taken separately or all together, amazed and astounded me. He came up to me and immediately gave me a hearty embrace, saying,

'For many years now, O valiant knight Don Quixote of La Mancha, we enchanted ones in this god-forsaken place have been waiting to see you in hopes that you will give humanity an account of the things contained and enclosed within the depths of this Cave of Montesinos, an undertaking reserved solely for your invincible heart and stupendous courage. Come with me, most illustrious sir, for I wish to show you the marvels this transparent castle conceals. I am its governor and perpetual chief custodian and am the same Montesinos from whom the cave takes its name.' No sooner did he tell me he was Montesinos than I asked him if it was true what was said up here on earth: that he had extracted the heart of his close friend Durandarte from the middle of his chest with a small dagger and carried it to the Lady Belerma, as Durandarte had requested as he lay dying. He informed me that they were correct in everything they had said except that the dagger was not a dagger, nor even small, but a grooved stiletto sharper than an awl."

At this point Sancho said,

"It must have been the famous stiletto of Ramón de Hoces of Seville."

"I am not sure," said Don Quixote, "but it probably was not that particular knife-maker, for Ramón de Hoces lived only yesterday, whereas the one from Roncesvalles, where this tragedy occurred, lived many years ago; but that is neither here nor there, since it does not overturn or alter the truth and import of the story."

"That is true," added the cousin, "but I hope your grace will continue, for I am listening to you with the greatest fervor in the world."

"Nor am I relating it with any less fervor," said Don Quixote, "but to continue: the venerable Montesinos led me into the crystalline palace, where in an exceedingly cool chamber on the ground floor constructed entirely of alabaster there was a marble sepulchre of the finest craftsmanship, upon which I beheld a knight lying in a recumbent position – not one of those knights of bronze, marble, or jasper usually found on tombs but a knight of actual flesh and blood. His right hand, which was apparently rather hairy and sinewy – a sign of great strength – rested over his heart. Before I could question Montesinos, he noticed I was staring in complete bewilderment at the one on the sepulchre, at which point he said, 'This is my friend Durandarte, flower and mirror of all the brave enamored knights of his age. He is under one of Merlin's spells, that French enchanter who they say was the Devil's own son but who in my opinion was not the Devil's son but someone who 'knew a tad more than the Devil,' as the saying goes. I too am under his spell, as are a number of other men and women here. How or why he has enchanted us no one knows but the reason will emerge as time goes by, and that time is not far off by my reckoning. What surprises me is that I know as surely as I know my own name that Durandarte gave up the ghost in my arms and after his death I cut out his heart with my own hands. It must have weighed every bit of two pounds and, according to naturalists, a person with a large heart is endowed with greater bravery than a person with a small one. This being the case, along with the fact that this knight actually died, how is it that he now moans and sighs from time to time as though he were still alive?' As soon as he finished saying this, the tragic Durandarte cried out in a loud voice, saying,

'O cousin Montesinos, hear
this last request of you:
When once I'm dead and, yes,
My soul's departed too,
With sword or dagger keen,
From out my breast you'll tear
This heart of mine and take
It to Belerma fair.'

"When the venerable Montesinos heard this, he knelt before the afflicted knight and with tears in his eyes said, 'Sir Durandarte, my dearest cousin, I did what you commanded of me on the day of our bitter defeat: I cut out your heart as carefully as I could and removed all trace of it from your chest. After cleaning it with a lace handkerchief, I set out with it on the road to France, having first deposited you in the bosom of the earth while shedding such a stream of tears that I could have bathed my hands and cleansed the blood that covered them from their bloody groping inside your body. As further proof of my concern, my dearest cousin, in the first village I came to after leaving Roncesvalles, I sprinkled salt on your heart to keep it smelling sweet, enabling me to deliver it, if not fresh, at least dried and salted, into the hands of the Lady Belerma, who, together with you, me, Guadiana your squire, the matron Ruidera and her seven daughters and two nieces, as well as many other friends and acquaintances of yours, has been kept under a spell by Merlin the Magician for lo these many years, and though more than five hundred years have elapsed, not one of us has died. The only ones absent are Ruidera and her daughters and nieces, whom Merlin must have taken pity upon because of their weeping, transforming them into lakes known now in the world of the living in the province of La Mancha as the Lakes of Ruidera. These seven belong to the sovereigns of Spain, and the two nieces to the knights of that most holy order known as the Order of Saint John. Your squire Guadiana, likewise lamenting your tragedy, was converted into a river of the same name but, upon rising to the surface of the earth and seeing that other heavenly sun, was so bereaved at the thought of forsaking you that he once again plunged into the bowels of the earth. However, finding it impossible to deviate from his natural course, he surfaces from time to time and displays himself to the eyes of the sun and of humans. These lakes minister to him their waters, and with these and a number of others which flow into his he makes a grand and majestic entrance into Portugal. Still, wherever he goes, he displays his sadness and melancholy, boasting not of breeding in his waters delicate, delicious fish but coarse, tasteless ones quite different from those of the golden Tagus. What I am now about to tell you, my dear cousin, I have told you many times before but, judging by your silence, I assume that either you do not believe me or cannot hear me, and God knows how truly this pains my heart. I now wish to relay some news which, though it may not serve to ease your suffering, will by no means increase it. Be advised that if you will only open your eyes, you will see here before you that great knight about whom the wizard Merlin prophesied so many wondrous things, namely, Don Quixote of La Mancha, who once again and to greater advantage than in past ages has revived in the present one the long-since-forgotten practice of knight-errantry, by means of whom our spells may possibly be lifted, for great deeds are reserved for great men.' 'But if this should not prove true,' replied the afflicted Durandarte in a low, faint voice, 'if this should not prove true, O cousin, be patient and shuffle the cards!' Then turning onto his side, he resumed his customary silence and said nothing further.

"Just then, we heard loud cries and screams, accompanied by the most profound groans and anguished sobs. Turning my head and peering through the crystal walls, I saw in the adjoining chamber a procession of beautiful damsels advancing in two columns, all in mourning attire and wearing white turbans in the Turkish style. At the very end of the columns strode a matron lady, or so her grave appearance suggested, also clad in black with a white veil so long and flowing it brushed the floor as she moved, and she wore a turban twice the size of any of the others. Her eyebrows formed an unbroken line across her forehead, her nose was somewhat flat, her mouth large with bright-red lips, and her teeth, which she occasionally displayed, proved to be scattered and unevenly placed, though they were as white as shelled almonds. She carried a gauze-like cloth in her hands, inside of which, as well as I could make out, was a mummified heart, or so I judged from its dried, shriveled condition. Montesinos informed me that all those in the procession were servants of Durandarte and Belerma, who together with their master and mistress were under a spell, and the woman at the end carrying the heart wrapped in cloth was the Lady Belerma. She marched in that procession with her maids four days of each week, chanting, or to be more exact, intoning dirges over her cousin's body and pitiful heart, and if she appeared to me somewhat uncomely or not as beautiful as she was reputed to be, it was due to the bad nights and worse days she had undergone in that enchantment, a fact I might discern by her sickly complexion and the dark circles beneath her eyes. 'But,' said Montesinos, 'the sallow complexion and circles do not arise from that monthly ailment common to women, for it has been many months or even years since she has experienced it or it has come knocking at her door. Rather, it is from the grief she feels because of what she continually carries in her hands, for she is constantly reminded of her ill-fated lover's tragedy. Were it not for this, she would scarcely be equaled in beauty, grace, and vivacity by the great Dulcinea of Toboso, so greatly celebrated in all these parts and even throughout the world.' 'Careful there, Sir Don Montesinos!' I exclaimed at that point, 'you shall tell your story in the proper manner, since you know that all comparisons are odious, and this being the case, there is no reason to compare one person with anyone else. The incomparable Dulcinea of Toboso is simply who she is and the Lady Belerma is who she is and has always been, so let us leave it at that.' To which he replied, 'Sir Don Quixote, I beg your grace's forgiveness. I confess to having behaved badly, for I misspoke when I said the lady Dulcinea was barely the equal of the Lady Belerma. Had I had the slightest inkling that your grace was her knight, that would have sufficed to make me bite my tongue before comparing her to anything but heaven itself.' This apology from the great Montesinos enabled my soul to recover from the shock it had experienced at hearing my mistress compared to Belerma."

"What amazes me," said Sancho, "is that your grace didn't jump on the old codger and break every bone in his body and yank out every last hair from his beard."

"No, Sancho my friend," replied Don Quixote, "it would not have been proper for me to do that, for we are all obliged to be respectful to our elders even when they are not knights but particularly when they are both knights *and* enchanted. Besides, I can assure you we did not come away owing each other anything after all the give and take that occurred between us."

At this point the cousin said,

"I don't understand, Sir Don Quixote, how in the short time your grace was down below, you saw so many things, talked so much, and arrived at so many answers."

"How long has it been since I descended?" asked Don Quixote.

"A little more than an hour," said Sancho.

"That is impossible," cried Don Quixote, "for while I was there, I experienced nightfall and daybreak three separate times, so by my reckoning I spent three days in that desolate place that human eyes have never beheld."

"What my master says must be the truth," said Sancho, "for inasmuch as everything that has befallen him has been by way of enchantment, perhaps what seems to us an hour seems like three days and three nights down there."

"Probably so," said Don Quixote.

"Well, my lord, has your grace eaten during all this time?" asked the cousin.

"I have not broken my fast with a single bite," replied Don Quixote, "nor have I experienced hunger or even thought of food."

"Do persons who are enchanted eat?" asked the cousin.

"They do not eat," replied Don Quixote, "nor do they have bowel movements, though it is thought that their nails, beards, and hair grow."

"Master," said Sancho, "do those who are enchanted sleep by any chance?"

"Certainly not," replied Don Quixote, "at least during the three days I was among them not one of them ever closed an eye, nor did I."

"Then this is as good a place as any," said Sancho, "for the proverb that says, 'Tell me whose company you keep and I'll tell you who you are.' If your grace associates with enchanted souls who go about fasting and never sleep, is it any wonder that you didn't eat or sleep while you were with them? But if your grace will pardon me, I feel compelled to say that of all the things you have said here, may God take me (I was going to say the Devil) if I believe a solitary one."

"Why not?" asked the cousin. "Is our lord Don Quixote a person who would lie? Why, even if he wished to, he has not had time to fabricate or dream up such a multitude of lies."

"I don't believe that my master is lying," said Sancho.

"If not, what *do* you believe?" said Don Quixote.

"I believe," said Sancho, "that Merlin or those enchanters who cast a spell over that whole mob you say you saw and talked to down there have filled your grace's mind and imagination with that conglomeration of things you've already related, as well as those that remain to be related."

"All that may be true, Sancho," said Don Quixote, "except that it was not that way, for everything I have described I saw with my own eyes and touched with my own hands. Also, what will you say when I tell you here that among the infinitude of wondrous things shown me by Montesinos, which I shall leisurely relate at the proper time during the course of our journey because not all of them belong here, he showed me three country lasses who were gamboling and leaping about like goats in that delightful meadow, and no sooner had I seen them than I recognized one of them as the incomparable Dulcinea of Toboso, and the other two as the same farm girls who were with her when we spoke to them on the outskirts of Toboso? When I asked Montesinos if he knew them, he said he did not but imagined they must be some illustrious enchanted ladies who had appeared in those meadows some days before – not that I should be surprised at that, for there were many other ladies there from ages past and present who had been transformed into various and sundry figures, among whom he had recognized Queen Guinevere and her handmaiden Quintañona, who served wine to Lancelot 'when he from Britain came.'"

When Sancho Panza heard his master say this, he thought he would go crazy or die laughing, for he knew the truth of Dulcinea's feigned enchantment, since he had been her enchanter and the inventor of said testimony. He ended up recognizing beyond a shadow of a doubt that his master was mad and completely out of his mind, so he said to him,

"Dear master, it was a bad time, a worse occasion, and an unlucky day when your grace descended into that other world, and an evil moment when you met Sir Montesinos, who has sent you back to us in this shape. Up here on earth you were perfectly sane with all the senses God gave you, spouting maxims and giving advice at every turn, unlike now when you are giving an account of the most outrageous things imaginable."

"Since I know you, Sancho," said Don Quixote, "I do not take such talk seriously."

"Nor do I that of your grace," replied Sancho, "and you may strike me or slay me for what I've said or am about to say if you don't correct and amend your talk. But would you kindly tell me, now that we're at peace, how and by what means you recognized our lady and mistress? And if you spoke to her, what did you say and what did she answer?"

"I recognized her," said Don Quixote, "by the fact that she was wearing the same clothes she had on the day you showed her to me. I spoke to her but she made no reply whatsoever; instead, she turned her back on me and fled with such haste that not even an arrow from a crossbow could have overtaken her. I wanted to follow her and would have done so had Montesinos not advised me against wasting my efforts in such a futile endeavor, particularly now that the hour was fast approaching when I would have to leave the cave. He also told me that by and by I would be advised of how to break the spell that lay over him, Belerma, Durandarte, and all their companions; but the thing that pained me most about everything I had witnessed and observed there was that, while Montesinos was telling me these things, there came up beside me, without my sensing it, one of the two companions of the happiness-bereft Dulcinea. This lady, her eyes filled with tears and her voice faint and trembling, said to me, 'My mistress Dulcinea of Toboso kisses your grace's hand and implores you to inform her of how you are; and because she is in great need, she also begs you as earnestly as she knows how to be so kind as to lend her half a dozen *reals*, or as many as you have, against this new cotton petticoat I have brought with me, and she promises to repay them with all haste.' I was surprised and amazed at such a request, and turning to Sir Montesinos, I said, 'Is it possible that famous persons who are enchanted can also experience want?' to which he replied, 'Sir Don Quixote, your grace may be assured that this thing called want is to be found everywhere, for it extends to all parts and affects everyone, and not even enchanted persons are exempt. Inasmuch as the lady Dulcinea is requesting those six *reals* and her security is obviously good, your only option is to give them to her, for she undoubtedly finds herself in desperate straits.' 'I shall not accept her security,' I answered, 'nor shall I give her what she requests, for all I have is four *reals*.' These I gave her and they, Sancho, were the ones you let me have the other day for distributing as alms to any poor we might meet along the way. Then I said to her, 'My dear, tell your mistress that her afflictions grieve my soul and I wish I were a Fugger [1] to be able to ease them. I would also have her know that I cannot and will not be consoled so long as I am deprived of the sight of her loveliness and the wit of her conversation, and that I implore her as earnestly as I know how to allow herself to be viewed and visited by this her unfortunate servant and beleaguered knight. You are also to tell her that when she least expects it, she shall receive word that I have taken an oath or vow fashioned after the one taken by the Marquis of Mantua to avenge his nephew Baldovinos, whom he found on the verge of expiring in the heart of the mountains, which oath was not to eat at a table until he avenged him, together with certain other trifling matters that he added. This I shall do, not by resting, but by traveling to the seven corners of the earth with more diligence than that of Prince Dom Pedro of Portugal until I have broken her spell.' 'Your grace owes my mistress all that and more,' replied the damsel, who then grabbed the four *reals* and, instead of curtseying, kicked up her heels and jumped a good two feet into the air."

"Oh, my goodness!" shouted Sancho at this point, "is it possible that there are such things in the world and that enchanters and enchantments have such power over it that they've turned my master's good sense into such pure madness? O master, master, for the love of God, may you consider what you're doing, reclaim your dignity, and refuse to give credence to those follies that have left your mind cracked and impaired!"

"Because you love me, Sancho, you speak to me thus," said Don Quixote, and because you are inexperienced in the ways of the world, everything that is somewhat difficult you consider impossible, but the time will come, as I have said, when I shall give you an account of some of the things I witnessed down below and they will make you believe those I have related here, for their veracity is not open to question or debate."

Chapter Twenty-Four

The account of a thousand trivial matters as irrelevant as they are necessary to the true understanding of this great history

The person who translated this great history from the original – the one written by its first author Cide Hamete Benengeli – says that when he came to the chapter dealing with the Cave of Montesinos, he found the following words written in the margin in Hamete's own

1 The members of this German family were some of the wealthiest financiers and merchants of 15th- and 16th-century Europe.

handwriting.

I cannot persuade or bring myself to believe that the valiant Don Quixote experienced all the things in the preceding chapter exactly as they are described there, the reason being that all the adventures taking place up to this point have been possible and plausible, but as for the one in the cave, I can find no justification whatever for considering it authentic, since it goes so far beyond what is reasonable. And yet, for me to imagine that Don Quixote would lie, he being the most truthful gentleman and most noble knight of his age, is impossible, for he would not tell a lie even if they were piercing his body with arrows. On the contrary, I am of the opinion that he did relate and describe it with all the accompanying details, because he was incapable of fabricating such an assortment of follies in so short a period of time. If, then, this adventure appears apocryphal, it is not I who am to blame. I shall record it without affirming or denying its authenticity and you, dear reader, as a person of discernment, may be the judge, relying upon your own perceptions. I have no further obligations nor am I capable of anything more, though it is an established fact that at the time of his death Don Quixote is said to have retracted it, admitting that he had invented everything because it seemed to him to fit in well with the adventures he had read in his histories.

The translator then goes on to say:

The cousin was shocked at Sancho Panza's boldness and the knight's patience but concluded that the indulgence the latter displayed was born of the happiness he had experienced at seeing his lady Dulcinea of Toboso, even if she was enchanted, for had that not been the case, the words and language Sancho had used would have earned him a well deserved thrashing. And since it struck the cousin that Sancho had acted rather impudently towards his master, he said,

"I, Sir Don Quixote of La Mancha, consider this day to have been exceedingly well spent in your grace's presence because I have benefitted from it in four ways: first, in having made your grace's acquaintance, which I consider a stroke of good fortune; second, in having learned what things are concealed in the Cave of Montesinos, including the metamorphoses of Guadiana and the Lakes of Ruidera, which will be of benefit to me in *The Spanish Ovid* that I have underway; third, in learning the antiquity of playing cards, which were used at least as long ago as the time of the Emperor Charlemagne, a fact that may be inferred from the words you say Durandarte spoke when, at the conclusion of the lengthy conversation between him and Montesinos, he awoke and said, 'Be patient and shuffle the cards.' Now this expression and manner of speaking he cannot have learned except while in France – before falling under a spell – in the days of the above-mentioned Charlemagne. This finding is just the thing for that other book I am compiling called *Inventions in Antiquity: a Supplement to Polydore Virgil.* I believe that in his book he forgot to include the invention of playing cards, which I shall now include because of their great importance, particularly when I can cite an authority as serious and trustworthy as Sir Durandarte. And lastly, in having discovered the actual source of the Guadiana River, until now a mystery to mankind."

"You are quite correct, sir," said Don Quixote, "but I should like to know one thing: if God were to be so kind as to allow your grace to print those books (which I doubt), to whom do you intend to dedicate them?"

"There are lords and grandees in Spain to whom I may dedicate them," replied the cousin.

"But not many," said Don Quixote, "and not because they do not consider them deserving of the honor but because of their unwillingness to accept them and thereby be obligated to compensate the author for his efforts and his act of courtesy. However, one noble who is an acquaintance of mine is capable of making up for the shortcomings of the others, and he possesses such superior qualities that, were I to enumerate them, it would probably arouse envy in the hearts of more than a few generous souls. But let us leave this discussion for a more leisurely occasion and go seek a place to lodge tonight."

"Not far from here," said the cousin," is a hermitage where a hermit has his residence. They say he was once a soldier and word has it that he is a good Christian, quite learned, and charitable as well. Next to the hermitage he has a small house built with his own funds, which, though small, can accommodate guests."

"Does this hermit by any chance keep chickens?" asked Sancho.

"Few hermits are without them," said Don Quixote, "for hermits of today are unlike those of the Egyptian desert who clothed themselves with palm leaves and ate roots from the earth. Let it be understood, though, that just because I speak well of the latter, I do not speak ill of the former. What I am simply trying to say is that penitents of today are not faced with the same rigors and austerities as those of by-gone eras. Still, this does not mean they are not all good men – at least, I consider them so. But even if we were to assume the very worst case possible, a hypocrite who pretends to be good causes less harm than a person who sins openly."

While they were engaged in this discussion, they saw a man walking towards them quite briskly using a stick to goad a mule loaded with lances and halberds. When he caught up with them, he greeted them and continued to walk on by. Don Quixote called out to him,

"Wait up, my good man; you appear to be traveling faster than that mule needs to go."

"I can't stop, sir," said the man, "for the weapons I'm carrying are to be placed in service tomorrow, which is the reason I must absolutely keep traveling, so God keep your grace. But if you wish to know why I'm carrying them, I intend to lodge tonight at the inn down the road from the hermitage. If you are traveling in that direction, you'll find me there, where I shall tell you things that will astound you; but once again, may God keep your grace."

And he prodded his mule so vigorously that Don Quixote had no opportunity to ask him what sorts of marvels he intended to describe to them, but since Don Quixote was rather inquisitive and forever eager to learn something new, he gave the order to leave at once so they could spend the night at the inn rather than stop at the hermitage, which is where the cousin wanted them to stay. Accordingly, they all remounted and headed straight for the inn, which they reached shortly before dusk. Along the way, the cousin asked Don Quixote to stop at the hermitage for a drink. No sooner did Sancho Panza hear this than he turned his dapple in that direction, with Don Quixote and the cousin following suit, but it would seem to have been Sancho's ill luck for the hermit not to be at home, which is what they were told by a female acolyte they found living there. They asked her for some of her best wine but she explained that her master had none; however, should they care for some water that was cheap, she would gladly provide them with some.

"If my thirst were for water," replied Sancho, "there are plenty of wells along the way where I might have quenched it. O for the wedding of Camacho and the abundance of Don Diego's home! How terribly I am going to miss you!"

With this, they left the hermitage and spurred their mounts towards the inn. After traveling a short distance, they overtook a young lad walking ahead of them at a leisurely pace, which allowed them to catch up with him. He was carrying his sword over his shoulder, to which he had tied a bundle or sack containing his clothes, which apparently consisted of breeches or pantaloons, a cloak, and one or two shirts, for all he was wearing was a velvet doublet that was thin and shiny in spots, a shirt with its tail hanging down, silk stockings, and square-toed shoes similar to those worn at court. Some eighteen or nineteen years of age, he had a pleasant countenance, appeared agile of limb, and, as he walked along, was singing satirical ballads to while away the tedium of the journey. Just as they overtook him, he was finishing one that the cousin committed to memory and is said to have gone thus:

For want of wealth to war I go:
But, had I money, 'twould not be so.

The first to address him was Don Quixote, who said,

"Your grace is traveling mighty light, gallant sir. We should like to know where you are headed if you do not mind saying."

To which the young man replied,

"The reason for my traveling so scantily clad is the heat and my poverty, and where I am headed is to war."

"Why poverty?" asked Don Quixote, "the heat is understandable."

"Sir," said the young man, "in this bundle I have some velvet breeches that go with this doublet. However, if I spoil them on the road, I won't be able to show them off in the city and I have no money to buy another pair. For this reason then, as well as to keep cool, I am traveling in this manner until I catch up with several infantry companies that are less than twelve leagues from here. There I shall enlist and not lack for baggage wagons to carry me from there to the place of embarkation, which I'm told will be Cartagena. I much prefer to have the king as my lord and master, whom I may serve in war, rather than some penniless soul at court."

"Are you by chance receiving extra pay?" asked the cousin.

"If," replied the youth, "I had served a Spanish grandee or some other important person, I would certainly be receiving it, for that is what comes of serving good masters. It is not unusual for a household servant to rise to lieutenant or captain or to receive some type of pension, but I, poor wretch, always served some hopeless job-hunter or newcomer who had such a miserably low salary and income that it cost him half of it just to keep his collar starched. It would be considered a miracle if any venturer page ever came close to being fortunate."

"I should like your grace to tell me upon your word of honor," said Don Quixote: "is it possible that in all the years you have served you have never received a uniform?"

"I've been given two," said the page, "but just as they take back the habit from one who leaves a religious order before professing, so too did my masters take back mine, for once their business at court was concluded, they returned to their hometowns and repossessed the uniforms they had given out only for show."

"What incredible *spilorceria*, [1] as the Italians say," replied Don Quixote. "However, you should consider yourself fortunate to have left the court with such noble intentions, for there is nothing else on earth more honorable or profitable than first to serve God and then one's king and natural lord, particularly in the bearing of arms, by means of which one earns, if not as much money, at least more honor than that earned through letters, as I have often said. Despite the fact that letters have left a greater legacy than have arms, military men still hold a certain advantage over men of letters and there is a definite splendor about arms that makes them superior to all others. I hope that what I am now about to say will remain etched in your grace's memory, for you will find it of great benefit and comfort in your labors: namely, that you should avoid thinking of all the unfavorable things that might happen to you, of which the worst of all is death, for so long as it is a noble one, the most noble thing possible is to die. They once asked Julius Caesar, that valiant Roman emperor, which death was best. To this he answered: 'the unexpected one,' that which is sudden and unforeseen; and though he spoke as a heathen and a person alien to a knowledge of the true God, he nevertheless did well in ridding himself of human sentimentality. Let us suppose you are killed in the first engagement or skirmish either by a cannon shot or by being blown to pieces by a mine: what difference will it make? It is simply a matter of dying and that is the end of it. According to Terence, a soldier killed in battle is seen to better advantage than one who saves his life by running away, and the more obedient he is to his captains and to those in command, the greater will be his fame. Remember, my son, that the smell of gunpowder on the soldier is more becoming than civet, and if old age should overtake you in this honorable endeavor, though you may find yourself lame, crippled, or covered with scars, at least it will not overtake you without honor, and such honor that poverty will not diminish it, particularly now that steps are being taken for the maintenance and assistance of soldiers who are old and disabled. It is unjust to treat them the way people do who get rid of their black slaves and set them free when they are old and no longer able to serve, turning them out of their homes ostensibly as free men and women but leaving them slaves to hunger, from which they can free themselves only through death. That is all I care to say for the present, except to invite your grace to ride with me on my horse, where you shall dine with me and then continue your journey in the morning, and may God make it as good as your noble intentions deserve."

The page declined the invitation to ride but did agree to dine with him at the inn. It was at this moment that Sancho was said to have muttered to himself, 'Master, may God in heaven preserve your grace! Is it possible that a man capable of saying so many wonderful things as you have just said is the same man who claims to have been witness to all the outlandish nonsense you've related about

1 Italian: 'extreme stinginess.'

the Cave of Montesinos? Oh well, time will tell.'

They reached the inn just as night was falling, and much to the delight of Sancho he saw his master take it for a real inn and not a castle, as was his wont. After they went inside, Don Quixote asked the innkeeper about the man with the lances and halberds and was informed that he had gone to the stable to tend to his mule. The cousin and Sancho did the same and provided Rocinante with the best stall and best location in the stable.

Chapter Twenty-Five

The account of the braying adventure and the amusing one of the puppeteer, together with the unforgettable divinings of the fortune-telling monkey

Don Quixote was 'fit to be tied,' as the expression goes, waiting to hear an account of the wonders promised by the man hauling the weapons. He went to look for him where the innkeeper had indicated and, when he found him, asked him to describe right then and there the marvels he had promised to relate at a later time in response to the questions Don Quixote had asked him on the road; to which the man replied,

"The account of my wonders must be savored at a leisurely pace and while we are seated. If, my good sir, your grace will allow me to finish feeding my beast, I shall tell you things that will astound you."

"That shall not be an obstacle," said Don Quixote, "for I intend to help you with all your chores."

And acting accordingly, he helped him to put out the barley and to clean the stall, a demonstration of humility that gave the man no option but to tell him most willingly everything he had requested. And so, seating himself on a stone bench with Don Quixote beside him, and the cousin, the page, Sancho Panza, and the innkeeper present as senate and audience, he began to relate the following story:

"I should inform your graces that in a village four and a half leagues from this inn, it transpired that an alderman of the village discovered that one of his jackasses was missing, the result of deception and trickery by a servant girl of his, whose story is too long to relate. Though the alderman employed every means possible to locate the jackass, he was unsuccessful. Some two weeks had elapsed, so the story goes, since the jackass had disappeared, when one day the alderman who was its owner was in the village plaza, at which time another alderman from the same village said to him, 'Congratulate me, my friend, for your jackass has turned up.' 'You have my heartiest thanks,' replied the first man, 'but may we know where it has turned up?' 'In the hills,' replied the finder. 'I saw it this morning without a packsaddle or any semblance of a harness and it was so skinny it was a pitiful sight to behold. I tried to corner it and bring it back but it was so wild and shy that when I approached, it took off at a run and headed for the densest part of the hills. If you would like the two of us to go look for it, let me take this she-ass home and I shall return at once.' 'Your grace will be doing me a great favor,' said the owner of the jackass, 'and I shall try to repay you in kind.' All those acquainted with the facts of this case tell the story just the way I'm telling it, including all these details. But to continue: the two aldermen, together and on foot, set out for the hills but when they came to the spot where they expected to find the jackass, they were unable to locate it there or anywhere in the area despite all their efforts. Observing that it was nowhere to be seen, the alderman who had spotted it said to the other, 'Listen, my friend, I have just come up with an idea that without a doubt will enable us to find this animal even if it is buried in the bowels of the earth, let alone in these hills. It so happens that I am an astoundingly good brayer and if your grace can bray just the tiniest bit, you may consider the matter resolved.' 'What do you mean: "the tiniest bit?,"' said the other. 'I would have your grace know that I won't take a back seat to anyone, not even to a jackass itself.' 'Well, we shall see,' replied the second alderman, 'for my plan is for you to travel round one side of the hill and me the other, whereby we shall completely circle it, and every so often you can stop and bray and I'll do the same and in this way the jackass can't help but hear us and will bray – that is, if it is anywhere on the hill.' To which the jackass' owner replied, 'I must admit, my friend, that the plan is an excellent one and worthy of your grace's superior intellect.' And so, after going their separate ways as they had agreed, it chanced that they both brayed at the same time, as a result of which each, having been deceived by the braying, went looking for the other, believing the jackass had finally turned up. When they saw each other, the one whose jackass was missing said, 'Is it possible, my friend, that it was not my jackass that brayed?' 'It was no one but me,' replied the other man. 'Then I can truthfully say,' said the owner, 'that between your grace and a jackass there is no difference whatsoever – when it comes to braying, that is – for never in my life have I heard or encountered anything more natural.' 'My friend, such praise and acclaim,' said the plan's inventor, 'more properly and fittingly apply to you than to me. Why, your grace could spot two brays to the greatest and most accomplished brayer on earth and still defeat him, for your tone is resonant, your voice sustains its tempo and pitch, and your descending inflections are numerous and sprightly. In a word, I consider myself beaten and award you the palm and banner for this rare talent.' 'I too can state here,' said the owner, 'that I shall hold my head higher from this moment forward, knowing now, at least, that I am good at something. I always suspected I was a good brayer but never dreamed I was as excellent as you say.' 'I can also state,' said the other, 'that the world is replete with rare, unfulfilled talents that are wasted by those who do not know how to make use of them.' 'These talents of ours,' replied the owner, 'will be of no benefit to us unless it is in a situation similar to the one at hand, and even then may it please God to let them serve us.' After saying this, they once again split up and returned to their braying. However, at every turn they were fooled and kept coming back together until they finally agreed upon a different signal by which they could recognize it was they and not the jackass, which was to bray two times, one right after the other. By thus doubling their brays each time they stopped, they made a full circuit of the hill without hearing the jackass answer or even seeing any signs of it.

"But how could the poor unfortunate beast answer if, when they found it, it was on the most isolated part of the hill and had been devoured by wolves? When he saw it, its owner said, 'I wondered why it did not answer; if it had not been dead, it would surely have brayed when it heard us or it would not be a jackass. And yet, now that I have heard your grace bray so charmingly, I consider the efforts I have expended in searching for it well worth the trouble, even though I have found it dead.' '*Your* grace is the one who deserves such praise,' replied the other, 'for "if the abbot sings well, the altar boy will not be far behind."' With this, they returned disconsolate and hoarse to their village, where they described to their friends, neighbors, and acquaintances everything that had happened to them in their search for the jackass, each one exaggerating the talents of the other in the matter of braying, all of which became widely known and spread to all the surrounding villages. However, the Devil, who never sleeps and has a fondness for starting quarrels – spreading discord in every direction, setting gossip a-flying, and making mountains out of molehills – decreed and ordained that the people from the other villages, when seeing someone from ours, would bray as though they were throwing up in our faces the braying of our own aldermen. Even youngsters started doing it, which was tantamount to being delivered into the hands and mouths of all the devils of hell. The braying began to spread from one village to another, so that the natives of the brayers' town were as recognizable and distinguishable as white people are from black. This cruel joke has reached such proportions that on a number of occasions those who are the butt of the joke have banded together and gone forth with weapons to do battle with their tormentors, with neither king, rook, fear, nor shame being able to stop them. I believe that tomorrow, or the day after, those of my village, which is that of the brayers, will take the field against another village two leagues away from ours, one of those most abusive towards us. And so that they will be well prepared, I have brought these recently purchased lances and halberds your graces have seen. These then are the wondrous things I said I would relate. If they don't strike you as such, they're all that I know."

With this the good man brought his speech to a close and just at that moment there appeared at the door of the inn a man clad in stockings, pantaloons, and doublet, all of which were made of chamois.

"Sir innkeeper," he said in a loud voice, "I hope you have a room, for here stands the man with the fortune-telling monkey and the puppet-show about the freeing of Melisendra."

"Bless my soul," exclaimed the innkeeper, "if it isn't Master Pedro! We're in for a wonderful evening."

(Before I forget it, I should mention that this Master Pedro had his left eye and half his cheek covered with a patch of green taffeta, an indication that something was amiss on that side of his face.)

"Master Pedro," the innkeeper went on to say, "your grace is most welcome, but where are the monkey and the puppets? I don't see them."

"They will be arriving shortly," replied the man in chamois; "I simply rode on ahead to find out if there was a room."

"I would take one away from the Duke of Alba himself and give it to Master Pedro," said the innkeeper. "Bring on the monkey and the puppet-show, for there are people in the inn tonight who'll pay to see both it and the talented monkey."

"So be it," said the man with the patch, "and I shall lower the price and consider myself well paid if I simply cover my costs. I'll return now to speed up the cart carrying the monkey and the equipment."

At this point he turned and left the inn. Don Quixote asked the innkeeper who this Master Pedro was and what sort of monkey and puppet-show he was bringing; to which the innkeeper responded,

"This fellow is a famous puppeteer who for some days now has been traveling about the eastern part of La Mancha staging his show about Melisendra, who was freed by the renowned Don Gaiferos, and it's one of the most astounding and well-acted histories seen in this part of the country in many a year. He has also brought along a monkey with the most extraordinary ability ever found in such an animal or imagined by the human race. If the monkey is asked a question, he listens to it carefully and then jumps up onto his master's shoulder, where he whispers the answer in Master Pedro's ear, who then announces it. He has much more to say about past events than future ones, and though he's not always one hundred per cent right, he's right more often than not, which has us all believing he's possessed by the Devil. He collects two *reals* for each question to which the monkey responds, I mean, to which his master responds for him after the monkey has whispered in his ear. For this reason it is thought that Master Pedro is exceedingly rich. He's a *galantuomo* [1] and a *buon compagno,* [2] as they say in Italian, and leads the best life on earth. He can outtalk six men and outdrink twelve, all at the expense of his tongue, his monkey, and his puppet-show."

At that moment Master Pedro returned with the cart carrying the puppet-theater and the monkey. The animal was large and tailless with buttocks as smooth as felt and a face that was not unpleasing. When Don Quixote saw him, he said,

"Sir Fortune-Teller, I hope you will be so kind as to tell us *che pesce pigliamo?*[3] That is, what is in store for us? Here are my two *reals.*"

And he ordered Sancho to give them to Master Pedro, who answered for the monkey, saying,

"Sir, this animal does not answer or provide information about the future, though he does possess some slight knowledge of the past and a bit more of the present."

"I swear to goodness," said Sancho, "I wouldn't pay a solitary cent for anyone to tell me what has already happened to me! Besides, who knows that better than I? Why, for me to pay to be told what I already know would be the height of foolishness, but since his illustrious monkeyship knows about present matters, here are my two *reals*. I'd like to know what my wife Teresa Panza is doing at this very moment and how she's passing the time."

Master Pedro declined to take the money, saying,

"I refuse to accept payment before rendering my services."

He then tapped his left shoulder twice with his right hand and the monkey leapt up, placing his mouth next to his trainer's ear and chattering his teeth rapidly. After performing this action for the duration of a Credo, he jumped to the ground, at which point Master Pedro with the greatest haste fell to his knees in front of Don Quixote and clasped his legs, saying,

"I embrace these legs as I would the twin pillars of Hercules, O illustrious resuscitator of the long-

---

1 'Gallant fellow.'

2 'Boon companion.'

3 Italian: literally, 'What kind of fish are we catching?'

since-consigned-to-oblivion knight-errantry, O never-sufficiently-extolled knight, Don Quixote of La Mancha, encouragement to all who are disheartened, support to all who are tottering, helping-hand to all who are prostrate, and staff of consolation to all who are disconsolate!"

Don Quixote was dumbfounded, Sancho spellbound, the cousin bewildered, the page overwhelmed, the man from the town of brayers stupefied, the innkeeper befuddled – in fact, all who had heard the words of the puppeteer were left speechless, but Master Pedro went on to say,

"And you, O noble Sancho Panza, the best squire of the best knight on earth, be of good cheer, for your good wife Teresa is well. At this very hour she's combing a pound of flax and, as further evidence, has placed an open pitcher beside her containing a generous portion of wine to help her through her chores."

"I can certainly believe that," said Sancho, "for she's one of the fortunate ones. If she just weren't jealous, I wouldn't swap her for the giantess Andandona, who, according to my master, was a woman of excellence and distinction. But this Teresa of mine is one of those who make sure their own lives are comfortable, even if it's at the expense of their heirs."

"I wish to state here," replied Don Quixote at this point, "that a person who reads and travels a lot sees and learns lots of things. I mention this because what amount of persuasion could have convinced me there were monkeys in the world capable of telling fortunes, such as the one I have seen here with my own eyes? For I am the very Don Quixote of La Mancha this noble beast has described, though he has gone a bit far in his praise of me. Still, whatever I am, I give thanks to heaven for endowing me with a tender and compassionate nature, leading me always to do good to every person and ill to none."

"If I had the money," said the page, "I would ask his grace the monkey what's going to happen to me on the pilgrimage I'm making."

Master Pedro, who was no longer kneeling at Don Quixote's feet, said in response,

"I have already said this dear beast does not respond to questions about the future, but if he did, it would not matter that your grace has no money. I would forego all the profits on earth just to be of service to Sir Don Quixote, and since I am duty bound to provide him with some sort of entertainment, I would now like to set up my theater for the enjoyment of everyone in the inn at no charge whatsoever."

When the innkeeper heard this, he was overjoyed and pointed to the spot where the theater could be set up, and this was no sooner said than done. Don Quixote was not totally satisfied with the monkey's activities, for it struck him as inappropriate for a monkey to tell fortunes, whether of the future or of the past. So while Master Pedro prepared the puppet theater, Don Quixote took Sancho aside in a corner of the stable where, without being overheard by anyone, he said to him,

"Look, Sancho, I have given careful consideration to this monkey's strange ability and have concluded that without a doubt this Master Pedro, his trainer, has made a pact with the Devil, either implied or expressed."

"If the pack is pressed and also belongs to the Devil, it must really be a pressed pack," said Sancho, "but what earthly good can it do Master Pedro to have such a pack?"

"You misunderstand me, Sancho; I simply meant to say that he must have entered into some sort of agreement with the Devil to endow the monkey with this talent by which he earns his living, but once he is rich, he will hand over his soul, which is what the Adversary of Mankind seeks. I am led to this conclusion by observing that the monkey deals only with current or past events, these being the extent of the Devil's knowledge, since all his accurate predictions of the future are nothing but lucky guesses, and there are very few of those. To God alone is reserved the ability to foretell the seasons or the seconds of the day, because for Him there is neither past nor future, everything being always in the present. Since this is true, which it is, it is obvious that this monkey is speaking in the manner of the Devil. I am astonished that the Holy Office has not brought charges against him, put the question to him, and wrested from him the name of the one who enables him to tell fortunes. It is evident that this monkey is no astrologer, for neither he nor his master casts or knows how to cast those figures called horoscopes, which are so popular in Spain these days that there is no little old lady, page, or cobbler who does not presume to cast them, as though it were the simplest thing in the world. These people, because of their lies and ignorance, bring into disrepute this truly wondrous science. I know of one lady who asked an astrologer whether a small lap dog of hers would become pregnant and give birth and, if so, how many puppies would be born and what colors they would be. To this our esteemed astrologer replied, after casting his horoscope, that the little dog would become pregnant and give birth to three puppies: one green, one crimson, and one a mixture, provided she was covered between eleven and twelve in the morning – or at night – and provided it took place on a Monday or a Saturday. As it turned out, two days later the dog in question died from overeating but our esteemed horoscope caster gained a reputation in the village of being a consummate astrologer, as most if not all of them do."

"That's all very well," said Sancho, "but I wish your grace would have Master Pedro ask his monkey if what happened to you in the Cave of Montesinos was true, for I'm of the opinion – begging your grace's pardon – that it was all falsehood and fraud, or at best a dream."

"Anything is possible," replied Don Quixote, "but I shall do as you suggest, even though I have certain misgivings I cannot rid myself of."

While they were discussing this, Master Pedro came looking for Don Quixote to announce that the show was now set up and that he was to come and see it, as it was well worth attending. Don Quixote explained his concern and begged him to ask his monkey at once whether certain things that had taken place in the Cave of Montesinos had been dreamed or were real, because in his opinion there was a little of both. Without saying a word, Master Pedro returned with the monkey and sat him down in front of Don Quixote and Sancho.

"Listen, my noble creature," said Master Pedro, "this knight would like to know whether certain things that happened to him in a cave known as Montesinos were real or imagined."

The monkey, being given the usual signal, jumped up onto his master's left shoulder and appeared to whisper something in his ear, at which point Master Pedro said,

"The monkey says some of the things your grace saw and experienced in that cave were false and some were real but this is absolutely all he knows in response to this question. He says, though, that should you care to know more, he will answer any question he is asked this coming Friday but for the present his powers are exhausted and will not return to him until Friday, as he has said."

"Didn't I tell you, master," said Sancho, "that nothing would convince me that all the things you said about the goings-on in that cave were true, not even half of them."

"Time will tell, Sancho," said Don Quixote, "for time, the revealer of all things, never leaves a solitary one it does not expose to the light of day even if it is hidden in the bowels of the earth. But enough of this for now; let us go see Master Pedro's show, for I have the feeling it will include a few novelties."

"A few!" exclaimed Master Pedro; "why, this show of mine includes sixty thousand. My dear Don Quixote, I can promise your grace that it is one of the greatest spectacles in the world today, but *operibus credite, non verbis.* [4] Let us start the show, for it is getting late and we have much to do, much to say, and much to present."

Don Quixote and Sancho accepted his invitation and went to the site where the theater had been set up. The curtains were open and lighted wax candles filled every available space, making everything bright and showy. Once they arrived, Master Pedro climbed inside, as he was the person who manipulated the puppets. A boy, Master Pedro's helper, took his place outside to serve as interpreter and narrator of the puppet show, holding in his hand a rod for pointing to the figures on stage. After all those in the inn were seated in front of the stage, except a few who were obliged to stand, with Don Quixote, Sancho, the page, and the cousin occupying the best seats, the narrator began to relate what one will hear or see who listens to or reads the following chapter.

Chapter Twenty-Six

The continuation of the amusing episode of the puppeteer, and other matters that are truly quite good

'All were silent, Tyrians and Trojans;' [1]

which is to say that all those watching the puppet show were spellbound by the words of the person narrating its wonders, when suddenly the sounds of kettledrums and trumpets were heard inside the puppet stand, along with a number of cannon shots. The tumult lasted for only a short time and the lad again raised his voice, saying,

"This true history your graces are watching is taken word for word from the French chronicles and Spanish ballads that are on everyone's lips, even those of the youngsters in the street. It deals with the freeing by his lordship Don Gaiferos of his wife Melisendra, who was being held captive by the Moors in Spain in the city of Sansueña, the city known today as Saragossa, and I direct your graces'

---

4 Latin: 'Believe my works, not my words,' a paraphrase of John 10:38.

1 From the first verse of Book II of the *Aeneid* in the Spanish translation of Gregorio Hernández de Velasco (1557).

attention to the fact that Don Gaiferos is seen here playing backgammon, exactly as related in the ballad:

"At backgammon Gaiferos plays,
Forgetful of his lady fair.

"The person who has just appeared, wearing a crown and holding a scepter in his hands, is the Emperor Charlemagne, Melisendra's alleged father, who, annoyed at seeing his son-in-law's idleness and lack of concern, has come here to chastise him. Pray note the vehemence and zeal with which he does so, for he would appear to like nothing better than to give him half a dozen whacks on the head with his scepter, and there are those writers who say he did that very thing, and quite thoroughly in fact. After pointing out to Don Gaiferos the risk to which he was exposing his honor by not attempting to free his wife, he is said to have told him,

"I've said enough, now act!'

"May I also direct your graces' attention to the way the emperor turns his back and leaves Don Gaiferos resentful, and how the latter, chafing with anger, flings the board and game pieces from him and hastily calls for his armor, asking Don Roland his cousin to lend him his sword Durindana. But note that Don Roland refuses to do so, offering instead to serve as his companion in the difficult enterprise he is undertaking, but the valiant and angry Don Gaiferos refuses his offer, saying that he alone will suffice to rescue his wife even if she is buried in the bowels of the earth. With this, he goes inside to don his armor and sets out at once. May I now call everyone's attention to that tower, which is presumed to be one of the towers of the fortress of Saragossa, now called the Aljafería. That lady on the tower in Moorish dress is the peerless Melisendra, who has often stood there gazing at the road to France in an effort to console herself over her captivity, fixing her thoughts upon Paris and her husband. We also see a new incident taking place that may possibly have never been seen before. Observe that the Moor, having ever so slowly and stealthily sneaked up behind Melisendra with his finger to his lips, is now kissing her squarely on the mouth. Notice how hurriedly she spits and wipes her mouth on the sleeve of her white blouse, at which point she begins to wail and tear her lovely hair as though it bore the blame for her disgrace. Observe too that stern-looking Moor in the gallery, King Marsilio of Sansueña, who, having witnessed the Moor's insolence, orders him seized, though he is a relative and great favorite of his, so that he can be given two hundred lashes while being paraded through the city streets in the customary manner: preceded by public criers and followed by constables. Now you see them leaving to carry out the sentence almost immediately after the crime's commission, for in Moorish law there are no long, drawn-out legal maneuvers as there are in ours."

"Lad, lad!" cried Don Quixote at this point, "keep your story on a straight path without turning aside or taking detours. To establish the facts of a case, one needs evidence and more evidence."

Master Pedro also shouted from inside the puppet stand,

"Boy, do as this gentleman says and stop adding your own comments. Keep your singing simple and forget counterpoint, which usually breaks down of its own subtleties."

"I'll do as you say," replied the lad, who then continued:

"The figure who has now appeared on horseback wearing a Gascon cape is Don Gaiferos himself. Here too is his wife, who has been avenged for the amorous Moor's insolence and who, appearing to have become calm, has just ascended the watchtower, from where she speaks to her husband, believing him to be just another passer-by. She addresses him by reciting the words of the ballad:

"Sir knight, if you towards France are bound,
Seek out Gaiferos' whereabouts;

which is all I shall quote, for verbosity often breeds contempt. Suffice it to observe that Don Gaiferos has just revealed his identity and that by her elated gestures Melisendra shows she has recognized him. We see her ease herself down from the balcony to take her seat on the haunches of her good husband's horse but, woe of woes, she has caught the hem of her skirt on one of the balcony's iron railings and hangs suspended in mid-air, unable to reach the ground. But here one sees how heaven in its compassion comes to one's aid when it is most needed. Don Gaiferos has just approached and, not caring whether her expensive skirt gets torn, has grabbed her and forcibly set her down on the ground. Then with one heave he hoists her onto the haunches of his horse, making her straddle it like a man. And to keep her from falling off, he orders her to hold tight by throwing her arms round his shoulders and locking her hands across his chest, for the Lady Melisendra is unaccustomed to riding in this style. It should also be noted that the horse's neighs demonstrate how happy he is to be carrying this brave and handsome burden in the persons of his master and mistress. Your graces will also observe how they turn their backs on the city and ride away joyous and rejoicing on the road to Paris. O lovers true, and pair without peer, may you go in peace and have safe passage to your beloved fatherland, and may fate in no way bestrew your joyous path with obstacles! May your friends and relatives see you enjoying peace and tranquility for all the remaining days of your lives, and may these be as long as Nestor's!"

Here Master Pedro raised his voice once again and said,

"Keep it plain, boy, and stop embellishing, for all affectation is bad!" The narrator did not respond but went on to say,

"There was no lack of idle souls to observe everything that took place, nor did they fail to note Melisendra's flight, which they reported to King Marsilio, who immediately sounded the alarm. Notice how quickly this is done, for the city is now filled with the sound of bells tolling in the towers of all the mosques."

"Not so!" shouted Don Quixote at this point. "Master Pedro is quite out of line. Moors do not use bells but kettle drums and a type of flute similar to our hornpipe. This business of bells tolling in Sansueña is an absolute outrage."

When this was heard by Master Pedro, the tolling ceased and he said,

"Sir Don Quixote, I wish your grace would not concern yourself with trivialities or look for perfection where it is not to be found. Are there not a thousand plays staged in these parts on a regular basis that are replete with a thousand improprieties and absurdities, and yet they all enjoy a most successful engagement and are greeted not only by applause but by amazement and all the rest? Continue, boy, and leave the gentlemen to their chatter. So long as I line my pockets, I shall stage more improbabilities than the sun has atoms."

"I can believe that," said Don Quixote.

"I ask," continued the narrator, "that your graces note all the glittering horsemen riding out from the city in pursuit of the two Catholic lovers. And listen to the blare of all the trumpets and horns and the beating of the countless kettledrums and tabors. I fear they may overtake them and bring them back tied to the tail of their own horse, which will be a ghastly sight."

Don Quixote, having observed this horde of Moors and listened to the clamor and uproar, deemed it proper to assist those fleeing, and so, springing to his feet, he cried out,

"Never in all the days of my life will I tolerate in my presence a deception and fraud against so famous a knight and so daring a lover as Don Gaiferos. Halt, you lowborn caitiffs; cease and desist from pursuing him or you shall have me to contend with!"

And suiting his actions to his words, he unsheathed his sword and with one leap landed beside the stage, where with unheard-of rapidity and fury he began to rain blows on the Moorish puppet-folk, striking down some, decapitating others, ruining this one, destroying that one, and among a number of such blows, he delivered one which, had Master Pedro not ducked, squatted down, and drawn himself up, would have lopped off his head with greater ease than if it had been made of marzipan dough. Meanwhile, Master Pedro was shouting,

"Sir Don Quixote, pray stop and realize that those are not real Moors your grace is felling, destroying, and slaying but small pasteboard figures. Oh, woe is me! can't you see you're ruining me and destroying all my property?"

But this did not make Don Quixote cease wielding his two-handed slashes, his back-hand strokes, and his chops, which fell as thick and fast as raindrops. In the end, in less time than one could recite a Credo or two, he leveled the entire puppet theater, making splinters of all the sets and puppets and leaving King Marsilio mortally wounded and Emperor Charlemagne with his crown and head split open. The entire senate of spectators was in a state of shock, the monkey had fled over the roof of the inn, the cousin was frightened, the page was cowering, and even Sancho Panza himself was terrified, for, as he confessed after the storm had passed, never had he seen his master in such a rage and frenzy. Once the general destruction of the puppet theater was complete, Don Quixote regained his composure somewhat and said,

"I wish I had present all those who do not believe, or refuse to believe, that knights-errant are a great benefit to the world. Why, if I had not been here just now, what would have become of the noble Don Gaiferos and the beautiful Melisendra? Undoubtedly, at this very hour those Moorish dogs would already have overtaken them and committed some outrage against them. When all is said and done, may knight-errantry live and flourish above all things upon the face of the earth!"

"Long may it live indeed," murmured Master Pedro weakly at this point, "and may I perish, for I am so unfortunate that I can say with King Rodrigo:

'Yesterday I was lord of Spain,
But now I have no tower left
Which I can call my own!'

Less than half an hour ago – nay, not so much as a minute ago – I saw myself lord of kings and emperors, my stables filled with countless horses, and my coffers and trunks with an inexhaustible supply of fine clothes, but now I find myself desolate and dejected, penniless and destitute. Above all, I have lost my monkey and I swear that my teeth will sweat before I ever get him back, and all because of the ill-considered fury of this illustrious knight who they say protects orphans, rights wrongs, and performs other charitable deeds, but against me alone has the knight's generous nature been found wanting. Praised be heaven in all its glory! He is rightly called the Knight of the Woeful Countenance because I can't countenance the woeful things he has done to all my puppets."

Sancho Panza was moved by Master Pedro's words and said,

"Don't weep and grieve so, Master Pedro, for you're breaking my heart. I would have you know that my master Don Quixote is such a good Catholic and scrupulous Christian that, once he realizes the injustice he has done, he will acknowledge it and insist upon paying you for it, whereby you will remain more than satisfied."

"So long as Sir Don Quixote pays me for a portion of the figures he has *dis*figured, I shall be satisfied and his grace will have assuaged his conscience. There is no salvation for a person who takes what belongs to someone else and refuses to give it back."

"That is true enough," said Don Quixote, "but until now I am not aware that I have anything of yours, Master Pedro."

"How is that?" asked the puppeteer; "what about the rubble lying all over this barren, forsaken ground? By what were they demolished and scattered about if not by the invincible might of your powerful arm? To whom do these corpses belong if not to me? And what did I earn my living by if not by them?"

"Well, I am finally convinced," said Don Quixote at this point, "of what I have believed on a number of other occasions: these enchanters who pursue me do nothing but place forms like these before my eyes only to change and transform them into whatever they please. I can really and truly say to your lordships listening to me that I thought everything that just happened here was actually happening: that Melisendra was Melisendra, Don Gaiferos Don Gaiferos, Marsilio Marsilio, and Charlemagne Charlemagne. For that reason I was overcome by anger and, to fulfill my obligation as a knight-errant, I sought to assist and favor those who were fleeing and, spurred on by this noble motive, did what your graces have just witnessed. If the opposite has occurred, it is not I but these nemeses of mine who are to blame, and though this error has not proceeded from malice, I am willing to sentence myself to pay the costs. Let Master Pedro determine how much he wants for the ruined puppets and I shall gladly pay him for them on the spot in good Castilian currency."

Master Pedro bowed in his direction and said,

"I should have expected nothing less from the extraordinary Christian charity of the valiant Don

Quixote of La Mancha, true aid and support of every vagabond who is needy and destitute. Our worthy innkeeper and the great Sancho shall serve as mediators and appraisers between your grace and myself as to what the ruined figures are worth – or used to be worth."

After the innkeeper and Sancho agreed to this, Master Pedro picked up King Marsilió of Saragossa, whose head was missing, and said,

"One can see the total impossibility of restoring this king to his former state, and so, barring a differing opinion, I feel I should be given four and a half *reals* for his death, end, and demise."

"Proceed," said Don Quixote.

"Well," said Master Pedro, picking up the cleaved Emperor Charlemagne, "it would not be excessive to ask five and a quarter *reals* for this one that is riven from top to bottom."

"That is no trifling amount," said Sancho.

"Nor an excessive one," replied the innkeeper. "Let's split the difference and call it five *reals*."

"Give him the whole five and a quarter," said Don Quixote, "for the total cost of this singular catastrophe will not be determined by a quarter more or less, and I hope Master Pedro will finish quickly, for suppertime is approaching and I am feeling definite hunger pains."

"For this figure," said Master Pedro, "which is the beautiful Melisendra, who is missing her nose and an eye, I ask two *reals* and twelve *maravedís*, which I feel is reasonable."

"The Devil's hand is in it," said Don Quixote, "if Melisendra and her husband have not reached the French border by now, for the horse they were riding appeared to be flying rather than running. So don't try to sell me a cat for a hare by handing me a noseless Melisendra when the real one, if all went well, is now in France with her husband, enjoying herself and not having a care in the world. May God grant each person what is rightfully his, my esteemed Master Pedro, so let us conduct ourselves openly and honestly. Now, go ahead and continue.

Master Pedro, seeing that Don Quixote was beginning to list to the port side and revert to his earlier obsession, was determined not to let him get away, so he said,

"Of course, this is not Melisendra but one of her maidservants! Consequently, if I am given sixty *maravedís* for her, I shall be content and consider myself well paid."

In this same way he proceeded to place prices on the remaining ruined figures, which prices were then arbitrated by the two judges to the satisfaction of both parties, with the total coming to forty and three-quarter *reals*. In addition to this sum, which Sancho immediately took from his purse, Master Pedro requested two *reals* for the trouble of catching his monkey.

"Give it to him, Sancho," said Don Quixote, "not for getting his hands on the monkey but on some wineskin. Right now I would gladly give anyone two hundred *reals* who could tell me with certainty that the lady Doña Melisendra and the lord Don Gaiferos are now in France with their loved ones."

"No one could tell us that better than my monkey," said Master Pedro, "but there is no devil who can catch him now, though I feel his need for food and affection may make him return tonight. However, tomorrow is another day and we shall see."

In short, the tempest of the puppet-show subsided and everyone dined in peace and good fellowship at the expense of Don Quixote, who was the height of generosity. Before the sun rose, the man transporting the lances and halberds left the inn and soon after sunrise the cousin and the page came to bid Don Quixote farewell – the former to return to his village and the latter to continue his journey, to assist in which Don Quixote made him a gift of a dozen *reals*. Master Pedro, loath to get into another verbal exchange with Don Quixote, with whom he was all too well acquainted, rose before dawn, collected the remains of his puppet show, together with his monkey, and likewise rode off to seek his adventures. The innkeeper, who knew nothing at all about Don Quixote, was astonished as much by his outlandish behavior as by his generosity. In the end, Sancho, at his master's request, paid him handsomely. Then taking their leave, the pair left the inn around eight in the morning and proceeded on their journey, which we shall allow them to do while we take this opportunity to deal with other matters pertinent to the narration of this famous history.

Chapter Twenty-Seven

The explanation of who Master Pedro and his monkey were, together with Don Quixote's unfortunate outcome in the braying adventure, which he did not execute as he had wished or expected

Cide Hamete, the chronicler of this great history, begins this chapter with the following words: 'I swear as a good Catholic . . . ' The translator says that Cide Hamete, being a Moor, which he undoubtedly was, simply meant by the oath that, just as a good Catholic who takes an oath swears, or should swear, to tell the truth in whatever he says, he too, as though he were a good Catholic taking an oath, was swearing to tell the truth in everything he would write of Don Quixote, particularly the disclosure of the circumstances surrounding Master Pedro and the fortune-telling monkey that had everyone mystified by his divinations. He says that anyone who has read the first part of this history will surely remember Ginés de Pasamonte, who together with the other galley slaves was set free by Don Quixote in the Sierra Morena, for which noble deed the knight received scant appreciation and less thanks from that malevolent, ill-mannered lot. This Ginés de Pasamonte, whom Don Quixote called Ginesillo the Thief, was the one who stole Sancho Panza's dapple, and since no explanation of the means or occasion of the theft was included in the First Part due to the failure of the printers, many readers were left perplexed and have attributed the printing oversight to the faulty memory of the author. But its explanation is that Ginés stole the donkey while Sancho was seated on him asleep, utilizing the method and scheme Brunelo had employed in removing the horse from beneath Sacripante at the siege of Albraca; and Sancho subsequently recovered him in the manner already described. Because our Ginés feared he might be apprehended by the lawmen who were pursuing him to punish him for his countless crimes and infamous deeds, which were so numerous and of such a nature that he himself compiled an account of them which filled a large volume, he resolved to move to the kingdom of Aragon, where he intended to cover his left eye and take up the profession of puppetry, being quite adept at both it and sleight of hand.

It thus happened that some recently freed Christians from Barbary had sold him the monkey, which he taught to jump onto his shoulder at a given signal and to whisper, or appear to whisper, into his ear. Once this was perfected, Master Pedro, before entering a village with his monkey and puppet show, would gather information in the nearest village, or from anyone at hand, about specific events that had taken place in the first village and about the particular individuals to whom these events had occurred. Then with this fixed firmly in his mind, he would begin by presenting his puppet show, sometimes reenacting one history, sometimes another, but all light-hearted, entertaining, and well known. As soon as the performance was over, he would expound upon the abilities of his monkey, informing his listeners that it could divine anything from the past and present but had no talent for divining the future. For an answer to someone's question, he would charge two *reals*, but for some answers even less, depending upon how he sized up his questioners. Whenever he arrived at some house where he knew specific details about the occupants, though they might choose not to ask him a question in order to avoid paying him, he would signal to his monkey and say it had told him such and such a thing, which always squared neatly with the facts. In this way, he was building an incredible reputation and gaining a following wherever he traveled. On other occasions, he would answer in such a way that his answers covered all possible angles, something he was quite clever at. And since no one urged or pressed him to explain how his monkey was able to tell fortunes, he made monkeys of them all and filled his purse with money.

As soon as he entered the inn, he recognized Don Quixote and Sancho, and because he already knew them, it was easy for him to amaze them as well as all the others who were present. This, however, would have cost him dearly had Don Quixote swung a little lower when he chopped off King Marsilio's head and destroyed all the knights, as described in the preceding chapter. Such, then, is what I felt still needed to be explained regarding Master Pedro and his monkey.

Returning now to Don Quixote of La Mancha, let me add that after leaving the inn, he decided to visit the shores of the river Ebro and the surrounding region before entering the city of Saragossa, for there was more than enough time from then until the jousts to accomplish both objectives. With this plan in mind, he resumed his journey, traveling for two days without encountering anything worthy of record. On the third day, however, just as he reached the top of a hill, he heard the sound of drums, trumpets, and muskets. At first, imagining that a regiment of soldiers was passing his way, he spurred Rocinante and climbed to the top of a hill to observe them. From the summit, he could see at the base of the hill what appeared to be more than two hundred men armed with various types of weapons, to wit, lances, crossbows, halberds, pikes, several muskets, and a number of shields. Riding down the hillside, he advanced towards the squadron until he could clearly see the pennants, distinguish their colors, and make out the devices they displayed, particularly one on a pennant or standard of white satin on which was painted in vivid colors a jackass of the small Sardinian variety, its head raised, its mouth open, and its tongue extended in the stance and act of braying. And surrounding it in large letters were these two verses:

THE BAILIFFS TWAIN
BRAYED NOT IN VAIN.

From this device Don Quixote concluded that this group must be from the town of the brayers, which he explained to Sancho, telling him what was printed on the standard. He added that the one who had given them an account of that event had been mistaken when he said two aldermen had been the ones who had brayed, for according to the verses on the standard, they had been no less than bailiffs; to which Sancho Panza responded,

"Master, one should not attach too much importance to that, for it may well be that the then aldermen, with the passing of time, have come to be bailiffs in their village, because of which they may be referred to by both titles, especially when the question of whether the brayers were bailiffs or aldermen has no bearing on the veracity of the history. The important thing is that they did bray, for a bailiff is just as apt to bray as is an alderman."

In short, it became clear that the town that had been humiliated had come there to do battle with the one that had embarrassed them more than was neighborly and more than they could tolerate. Don Quixote continued to approach, causing Sancho no little anxiety, since he was never fond of finding himself in such situations. Those of the squadron received him into their midst, believing him to be someone who supported their cause. Don Quixote raised his visor and with an easy air and demeanor rode up to the standard displaying the jackass. The most important persons in the army gathered round him to catch a glimpse of him, having been struck with the usual astonishment experienced by everyone who saw him for the first time. Don Quixote, who noticed how intently they were observing him but were not saying a word or asking him anything, resolved to take advantage of the silence, which he himself broke by raising his voice and saying,

"Good sirs, I beseech your lordships as earnestly as I know how not to interrupt a discourse I should like to deliver, unless you find it displeasing or annoying, in which case at the slightest sign from you I shall bridle my tongue and seal my lips."

They all told him to say whatever he would and they would gladly listen to him. Having been granted this permission, Don Quixote resumed his speech and said,

"I, my lords, am a knight-errant whose profession is that of arms and whose mission is that of protecting the helpless and going to the aid of those in need. Several days ago, I learned of your graces' misfortune and the incident that has caused you to take up your weapons at every turn to exact retribution from your enemies. Having turned the matter over in my mind more times than one, I find that, according to the laws of combat, your graces are mistaken in considering yourselves insulted, for an entire town cannot be insulted unless the town as a whole is accused of treachery when it cannot be determined which individual was responsible for committing that treachery. We have an example of this in Don Diego Ordóñez de Lara, who challenged the entire town of Zamora because he did not know that Vellido Dolfos alone had committed the treacherous act of slaying his king. Accordingly, he challenged everyone, and everyone was responsible for answering and taking up the challenge. But his lordship obviously went a bit far and even exceeded what is proper in a challenge, for there was no need to include in it the town's deceased, its waters, its loaves of bread, its unborn, and other trifles mentioned there. But, hang it all, when anger overflows its banks, there is no father, tutor, or restraint whatever that can bridle the tongue. This being the case – that no single person can insult a kingdom, province, city, republic, or entire nation – it is perfectly clear that there is no reason to go forth in response to a challenge involving an insult that does not exist. It would be a fine thing if the inhabitants of the City of the Clocks went about quarreling with everyone who asked them what time it was! Or if those who lived in cities with nicknames such as Pot-boilers, Egg-planters, Whale-hunters, or Soap-makers took umbrage at the names and nicknames on the lips of every young whipper-snapper! It would indeed be ludicrous if all these illustrious towns were to feel insulted and went about spoiling for a fight, however insignificant the provocation, sheathing and unsheathing their swords as if they were pistons! May God never permit such a thing!

"There are four things that can provoke prudent men to draw their swords, and well-run republics to take up arms, thereby imperiling their persons, their lives, and their possessions: first, the defense of the Catholic faith; second, the defense of their lives, which is a human and divine right; third, the defense of their honor, their families, and their possessions; fourth, the defense of their king in a just war; and should we care to add a fifth, which is similar to the second, the defense of their country. To these five main causes we might add several others that are just, reasonable, and sufficient to compel one to take up arms, but anyone who would take up arms over some triviality or something that is more amusing and playful than insulting is completely lacking in common sense, especially when to take unjust revenge (is there any that is just?) flies directly in the face of the divine law we profess, which commands us to be charitable to our enemies and to love those who hate us – a commandment that may appear difficult to obey but is so only for those who possess less of God than of the world, and more of the flesh than of the spirit. For Jesus Christ, who was God and man in one flesh and never told a falsehood and never will, being our lawgiver, said that His yoke was gentle and His burden light. He would not, therefore, give us a command that was impossible to carry out. And so, my good sirs, your graces are obliged by laws divine and human to remain calm and peaceful."

"The Devil take me," said Sancho to himself at this point, "if this master of mine isn't a thelogian;[1] and if he isn't, he's as much like one as one egg is like another."

Don Quixote stopped to catch his breath and, seeing that no one had said a word, was about to continue his speech, and would have done so had wily Sancho not intervened, for when he noticed that his master had paused, he took the floor himself and said,

"My master Don Quixote of La Mancha, who once called himself the Knight of the Woeful Countenance but now calls himself the Knight of the Lions, is a most level-headed gentleman who knows as much Latin and Spanish as a bachelor and conducts himself in a soldier-like manner in everything he involves himself in or gives advice about, having at his fingertips all the laws and ordinances of this thing called combat. So there is nothing for your graces to do except let yourselves be guided by what he says, and you may hold me responsible if things go awry, especially when everyone says it is foolish to become upset over a single bray. I remember that, as a child, I used to bray each and every time I felt the urge and no one ever tried to stop me. I brayed with such charm

1 The Spanish word for 'theologian' is ***teólogo*** but Sancho says ***tólogo***. This malapropism has proven an embarrassment to translators, who have rendered it as 'divine' (one translator), 'parson' (1), 'perfect priest' (2), 'thologister' (1), 'theologue' (1), 'tologian' (3), 'thologian' (3), thelogian (2), 'theorologian' (1), and 'theologian' (1). Even with a 'perfect' translation Cervantes' attempt at humor would be rather feeble.

and naturalness that every jackass in the village would answer me, yet I did not for that reason cease to be a child of my parents, who were extremely honorable people. Even though my ability was the envy of more than a few high-and-mighty individuals in my village, I couldn't have cared less. And to show you that what I am saying is true, I ask your graces' brief indulgence, for this skill is like that of swimming – once it is mastered, it is never forgotten."

Then gripping his nose between his thumb and fingers, he began to bray so lustily that all the surrounding valleys resounded. But one of the men standing next to him, thinking he was making fun of them, raised a long stick he held in his hand and struck him with such force that it knocked Sancho to the ground, being scarcely able to have done otherwise. Don Quixote, seeing Sancho thus ill-used, lowered his lance and charged at the one who had struck him, but there were so many who interposed themselves in his path that he was unable to exact revenge. Instead, finding himself beset by a hail of stones and threatened by a thousand crossbows aimed at him and no lesser number of muskets, he tugged at the reins of Rocinante and rode away from there as fast as Rocinante could gallop, commending himself to God with all his heart that He might deliver him from that peril. And fearing that at any moment a ball might enter his back and emerge from his chest, he took a deep breath every so often just to see if he still could. However, those of the squadron chose not to fire at him, being satisfied to see him run away. Sancho, who had barely regained his senses, was placed on his jackass and allowed to follow his master, not that he was conscious enough to do so. Still, the dapple followed in the tracks of Rocinante, from whom he could not separate himself even for an instant. After Don Quixote had ridden off some distance, he looked back and saw Sancho approaching alone, at which point he stopped and waited for him. Those in the squadron remained there until night and when their adversaries failed to come out to fight, returned to their village cheerful and thankful, and had they only known of the ancient custom of the Greeks, they would have erected a monument on that site.

Chapter Twenty-Eight

Things that Benengeli says the reader will learn if he reads this carefully

'When a brave man flees, it will be because he has detected treachery;' likewise, 'A prudent man will save himself for a better occasion.' These truths were borne out in the case of Don Quixote, who, yielding before the fury of the mob and the hostile intentions of the incensed squadron, took off in a cloud of dust and, without giving a thought to Sancho or the danger to which he was abandoning him, rode off as far as he deemed necessary for his own safety. Sancho came trailing along behind, lying across his donkey in the manner described. When he finally arrived, he had by then regained his senses and, once there, let himself slide off his donkey to land at Rocinante's feet totally battered, bruised, and panic-stricken. Don Quixote dismounted to inspect

Sancho's wounds but, finding him sound from head to foot, said to him with more than a little irritation,

"It was an evil hour when you learned to bray, Sancho! When did you ever find it appropriate to mention rope in the house of one who has been hanged? And to the music of brays what counterpoint might you have expected except a beating? Give thanks to God, Sancho, that they blessed your back with a stick instead of making the sign of the cross on your face with a cutlass."

"I'm in no condition to respond," said Sancho, "for my shoulders can do that for me. Let's just mount and get out of here and I'll call a halt to my braying but never to saying that knights-errant run away and leave their worthy squires to be beaten to a pulp by their enemies."

"One who withdraws does not run away," said Don Quixote, "for I would have you know, Sancho, that valor that is not based upon prudence is known as temerity, and any accomplishments by a foolhardy person are due more to good luck than to courage. I confess, therefore, to having withdrawn but not to having fled, and in this I have imitated a number of brave souls who have saved themselves for a better occasion. The histories are full of examples of this but as these are of no benefit to you, nor are they to my liking, I shall not belabor you with them at the moment.

By now Sancho had mounted, having been assisted by Don Quixote, who then mounted Rocinante, and they slowly rode towards a poplar grove that could be seen about a quarter of a league in the distance, which is where they intended to take cover. From time to time Sancho emitted a painful groan or sigh from the depths of his being and when Don Quixote asked him the cause of such intense discomfort, he said he ached so from the base of his spine to the nape of his neck that it was driving him crazy.

"The cause of that pain," said Don Quixote, "will no doubt be that, because the stick with which they beat you was long and straight, it made contact with your entire back, which is where all the aching parts are, and had it landed on additional parts, you would have even more aches."

"Merciful heavens!" cried Sancho, "your grace has certainly cleared up a great mystery and expressed it in the most elegant manner! For God's sake, O lord and master, was the cause of my pain so well hidden that you felt it necessary to tell me that every last place where the stick landed is where I ache? Now, if my ankles were sore, one might indeed try to figure out why they hurt but it's no great feat to figure out that I'm sore where they beat me. I swear, another person's adversity is certainly easy to bear. Every day it's becoming clearer to me how little I can expect from the company I keep with your grace, for if on this occasion I have been allowed to be beaten, on a hundred others we'll return to the blanket-tossings of old and other childish activities. If this time my back has been the target, next time it will be my eyes. I would be better off – except that I'm a dunce and will never do anything right in my whole life – I would be better off, I say, to go back home to my wife and children to support her and rear them with whatever God saw fit to give me instead of trailing along with your grace down roads that are not worthy of the name, or along highways and byways that lead nowhere, with very little to drink and even less to eat. And what beautiful places to sleep! 'Why, brother squire, just pace off seven feet of earth and, should you desire more, pace off as much as you need, since the decision is in your hands, and stretch out to your heart's content.' I'd like to see the person who first devoted himself to knight-errantry burned to ashes, or at least the first person who wanted to be a squire to all those dumb knights, which is what the knights of old must have been.

Regarding the present ones I have no comment, for seeing as how your grace is one of them, I have respect for them and am aware that your grace knows a bit more than the Devil in everything you think and say."

"I am willing to bet, Sancho," said Don Quixote, "now that you can talk without anyone's stopping you, that there is nothing hurting you in your entire body. Speak up, my son, and say whatever comes to mind, for in exchange for your being completely rid of your pains I shall consider it a treat to abide the irritation you are certain to cause me with your ramblings. If you are so eager to return home to your wife and children, God forbid that I should stand in your way. Since you are carrying my money, figure out how long it has been since this third sally from our village and decide how much you could or should be earning each month, and pay yourself with your own hand."

To which Sancho replied,

"When I served Tomé Carrasco, the bachelor Sansón Carrasco's father, whom your grace knows, I used to earn two ducats each month, not counting meals. I don't know how much I should earn in your service, though I do know that the squire to a knight-errant toils more than the person who serves a farmer, for those of us who serve farmers, regardless of how hard we work during the day and how bad a time we have of it, at night at least we have stew to eat and a bed to sleep in, which is more than I've had since I've served your grace, except for the brief time we spent at the home of Don Diego de Miranda, or the feast I had from the skimmings I took from Camacho's pots, or all the food, drink, and sleep I got at Basilio's. During all the remaining time, I've slept on the hard ground under the open sky exposed to the so-called inclemencies of heaven, while nourishing myself on scraps of cheese, crusts of bread, and drinking water, now from the streams, now from the springs, which we encounter in these out-of-the-way places we visit."

"I confess," said Don Quixote, "that all you say, Sancho, may be true. How much more do you think I should give you than Tomé Carrasco did?"

"By my reckoning," replied Sancho, "if your grace would add two more *reals* each month, I would consider myself well-paid, that is, as far as the wages for my labor are concerned, but in the matter of whether I'm satisfied with the governorship of an island you have promised me on your word of honor, it would be fair to add six more *reals*, which would make a total of thirty."

"Very well," said Don Quixote, "so based upon the salary you have set for yourself, plus the fact that we left our village twenty-five days ago, do your arithmetic, Sancho, and see how much I owe you. You may pay yourself, as I have said, with your own hand."

"My word," exclaimed Sancho, "but your grace is terribly mistaken in your calculations, for concerning the promised island, we should count from the day you promised it to me down to the present hour."

"Well, Sancho, how long has it been since I promised it to you?"

"If I remember correctly," said Sancho, "it must be more than twenty years, give or take a few days."

At this point Don Quixote gave himself a vigorous slap on the forehead and began to laugh most heartily.

"I have hardly been afoot for two months," he said, "during the entire course of these travels, let alone those of the Sierra Morena, and you claim, Sancho, that I promised you the island twenty years ago? I can state right here that you want your wages to consume all my money. If this is how things stand and what it will take to make you happy, I shall give it to you right now – and a lot of good may it do you! For the privilege of seeing myself rid of such a worthless squire, I would be happy to end up a pauper without a cent to my name. But tell me, you perverter of the squirely laws of knight-errantry, where have you ever seen or read that a knight-errant's squire entered into a discussion with his master concerning how much the latter would pay him each month for his services? Set sail, you scoundrel, you good-for-nothing ogre; set sail, I say, on the *mare magnum*[1] of their histories and if you discover that any squire has ever said or thought what you have just said, I want you to nail it to my forehead and give me four chucks under the chin by way of insult. Turn the reins (or the halter) of your jackass and go back to your home, for from this moment on you shall not go one step farther with me. O bread ill-received! O promises ill-bestowed! O squire more bestial than human! Just when I intended to award you a position – and such a position that, despite your wife, they would address you as 'your lordship' – you wish to leave me. Are you going to abandon me just when I had reached the firm and binding decision to make you lord of the best island on earth? Well, as you have said on several occasions, 'Honey is not for the ass' mouth.' You have always been an ass, you are still an ass, and you will be one when your life has run its course, for I am convinced your days will be at an end before you ever come to the realization that you are a dumb brute."

Sancho stood there looking at Don Quixote the entire time he was being reviled by his master and he became so filled with remorse that tears welled up in his eyes, at which point he said in a voice that was feeble and pained,

"Master, I confess that all I lack for being a complete ass is the tail, so if your grace wants to pin one on me, I'll acknowledge it as well deserved and will serve you as a jackass every day for the rest of my life. I beg you to forgive me and take pity upon my lack of years and remember that I don't know much and if I talk a lot, it stems more from infirmity than from malice. Still, 'Whosoever goes astray but returns to the path is commendable in the eyes of God.'"

"It would be a miracle, Sancho, if you failed to sneak one of your little proverbs into the conversation. However, I shall forgive you provided you repent and from this moment forth not show such concern for your own interests but make an effort to screw up your courage, take heart, and bolster yourself for assuming the responsibilities of the things I have promised you, for though they may be slow in coming, they are still possible."

Sancho said he would make certain to do so even if it meant drawing strength from weakness. With this, they made their way into the poplar grove, where Don Quixote settled himself at the foot of an elm and Sancho at the foot of a beech, since these particular trees and others like them have feet but not hands. Sancho spent the night in considerable pain because the beating made itself more keenly felt with the coming of the night air, whereas Don Quixote spent the night given over to his ever-present memories, but despite all this, they finally succumbed to sleep. With the arrival of dawn

---

1 Latin: 'open sea.'

they resumed their journey in quest of the shores of the famous Ebro, where they experienced things that will be related in the following chapter.

Chapter Twenty-Nine

The famous adventure of the enchanted boat

By traveling at their usual (albeit unusual) gait, Don Quixote and Sancho were able, two days after emerging from the poplar grove, to reach the river Ebro, the sight of which delighted Don Quixote because it afforded him a chance to view and contemplate its inviting shores, its transparent waters, its unhurried course, and its myriad liquid crystals, the pleasant sight of which revived in him a thousand tender memories. He specifically turned over in his mind what he had seen in the Cave of Montesinos, for though Master Pedro had told him that some of those things were real and some false, he put more stock in the former than in the latter – just the opposite of Sancho, who considered them all false, pure and simple. While traveling along in this manner, they caught sight of a small boat without oars or any kind rigging tied to a tree trunk at the water's edge. Don Quixote looked about in all directions and, seeing no one, dismounted without further ado and ordered Sancho to do the same and to tie both beasts securely to the trunk of a poplar or willow tree that stood there. Sancho asked him the reason for their sudden dismounting and hitching of the animals; to which Don Quixote responded,

"I would have you know, Sancho, that this boat here before us is plainly and unequivocally summoning me to board it and sail to the assistance of a knight or some other illustrious person in distress who no doubt finds himself in some dire predicament, for this is the custom in books of chivalry and of the enchanters who figure in them. When a knight finds himself in some type of difficulty from which he can be freed only by the hand of another knight, though the two of them may be two or three thousand leagues apart or even farther, he is whisked away on a cloud or is provided a boat he can board, and in less time than it takes him to blink an eye he is transported through the air or over the sea to any place they please, wherever his help is needed. Therefore, dear Sancho, this boat has been placed here for that very purpose, which is as certain as the fact that it is now day. So while it is still light, secure both the dapple and Rocinante and we shall place ourselves in the hands of God, that He may guide us, for I should not hesitate to board it even if discalced friars attempted to dissuade me."

"Since this is how things stand," said Sancho, "and since your grace is determined at every turn to engage in these – I don't know if I should call them idiocies – there's nothing to do but bow my head and obey, heeding the proverb that says, 'Do as your master commands and sup with him at his table.' However, so as not to burden my conscience, I should point out that I think this boat belongs, not to enchanters, but to some fishermen along this river, for this is where they catch the best shad on earth."

While Sancho was saying this, he tied up the animals and with more than a little pain in his heart commended them to the care and protection of the enchanters. Don Quixote told him not to be concerned about leaving the animals unprotected, for whoever would transport him and Sancho to places of such longinquity would take pains to provide for them.

"I don't understand that *longickety*," said Sancho, "never having heard such a word in all the days of my life."

"*Longinquity*," replied Don Quixote, "means 'remoteness' but it is no wonder you don't understand it, since you are not obliged to know Latin like some who presume to know it but do not."

"Now that they're tied up," said Sancho, "what do we do next?"

"What do we do?" said Don Quixote: "why, cross ourselves and weigh anchor, that is, get aboard and cut the mooring line holding this boat."

And leaping aboard, followed by Sancho, he cut the line and the boat began to drift slowly away from the bank. When Sancho saw himself about two yards from shore, he began to tremble, fearing he was doomed, but nothing pained him as much as hearing the dapple bray and seeing Rocinante struggle to free himself, at which point he said to his master,

"The dapple is braying from his grief at being abandoned and Rocinante is trying to untie himself to follow us. O dearest friends, peace be with you and may this madness, once it has been exposed for what it is, bring us back to where you are!"

At that instant, he began to sob so bitterly that Don Quixote became annoyed and angrily said to him,

"What are you afraid of, you sniveling coward? Why are you blubbering, you milk-sop? Who is after you or pursuing you, you chicken-hearted soul? What is it you need now, since you are always in need of something even in the midst of plenty? Are you by chance being forced to walk barefoot across the Scythian Mountains rather than being seated here like an archduke, carried along by the gentle current of this delightful river to where we shall shortly embark upon the open sea? We have probably already embarked upon it and traveled at least seven or eight hundred leagues. If I had an astrolabe with me with which to gauge the height of the pole star, I could tell you how far we have traveled; though, either I know very little or we have already passed, or shall do so shortly, the equinoctial line that cuts and divides the opposite poles into equal distances."

"And when we come to that obnoxious line your grace speaks of," said Sancho, "how far will we have gone?"

"A long way," replied Don Quixote, "for of the three hundred and sixty degrees which this globe of water and land contains, according to the computation of Ptolemy, the greatest cosmographer the world has ever known, we shall have traveled halfway when we reach the line I spoke of."

"Merciful heavens," cried Sancho, "your grace has certainly produced a fine witness to support everything you have said, what with this business of *copulation* and *sodomy* and I don't know what all!"

Don Quixote chuckled at Sancho's misinterpretation of the name and *computation* of the cosmographer *Ptolemy*, and so he said to him,

"You should know, Sancho, that among the Spaniards and all those who sail from Cádiz to the

East Indies, one of the signs they use for recognizing that they have crossed the equinoctial line I mentioned is that the lice die on everyone aboard ship. Not one survives and even if they were worth their weight in gold, not one could be found in the entire vessel. And so, Sancho, you are free to run your hand along your thigh and if you come across a living thing, we shall no longer be in doubt, but if you do not, then we have crossed that line."

"I don't believe a word of that," said Sancho, "but, nevertheless, I'll do what your grace has told me to, though I don't understand why there's any need to perform such an experiment. I can see with my own eyes that we haven't moved five yards from shore or shifted two yards from where the animals are, for *there* are Rocinante and the dapple right where we left them. And by taking our bearings, as I am now doing, I swear by all that's holy that we aren't moving or traveling as fast as a snail."

"Perform the experiment I mentioned, Sancho, and put aside your other cares. You know nothing of colures, lines, parallels, zodiacs, ecliptics, poles, solstices, equinoxes, planets, signs, points, and measures, of which the celestial and terrestrial spheres are composed. If you were acquainted with all these things, or even a portion of them, you would clearly see which parallels we have cut, which signs we have seen, and which constellations we have already left behind or are in the process of leaving behind, and so I say once more: take your hand and start hunting, for I am convinced you are cleaner than a sheet of plain white paper."

Sancho placed his hand on his leg and, after cautiously and hesitantly feeling about behind his left knee, raised his head, looked at his master, and said,

"Either the experiment is faulty or we haven't come as far as your grace says – not by a long shot."

"Well," said Don Quixote, "did you come across something?"

"Several somethings," replied Sancho, who shook his fingers and rinsed his hand in the river. Meanwhile, the boat was leisurely drifting in midstream, being propelled, not by some secret intelligence or hidden enchanter, but by the current itself, which at the moment was calm and gentle. Suddenly, they caught sight of some large watermills situated in the middle of the river and when Don Quixote saw them he cried out to Sancho,

"Do you see that, my friend? There stands the city, castle, or fortress that no doubt confines some imprisoned knight, queen, heir apparent, or maltreated princess, on whose behalf I have been summoned here."

"What blessed city, fortress, or castle is your grace talking about?" said Sancho. "Can't you see that those are watermills out in the river where wheat is ground?"

"Come now, Sancho," said Don Quixote, "they may look like watermills but they are not. I have already told you enchanters change and transform all things from their natural state. I do not mean they actually change them from one thing into another but only appear to do so, as experience has shown in the transformation of Dulcinea, sole refuge of all my hopes."

At that moment, the boat, having made its way into the river current, began to drift somewhat more swiftly than before. When the millers saw the boat coming down the river headed towards the channel that led straight to the water-wheels, several of them quickly ran outside with long poles to intercept it, but since they had come out with flour covering their faces and clothing, they presented an ominous spectacle. At the same time, they were shouting,

"You idiots, what are you doing? Are you so desperate you want to drown yourselves or be torn to pieces by these wheels?"

"Didn't I tell you, Sancho," said Don Quixote at this point, "that we have come to a place where I must demonstrate how far the might of my arm extends? Look at all the good-for-nothing scoundrels who have come out to meet me, and all the ogres confronting me, and look at all the horrible faces they are making. Well, I will show you, you ruffians!"

And standing up in the boat, he began to hurl threats at the millers, shouting in a loud voice,

"You depraved and ill-advised rabble, give back the freedom and free will to the person you hold prisoner in that fortress or prison of yours, be he humble or lofty or of whatever degree. I am Don Quixote of La Mancha, otherwise known as the Knight of the Lions, for whom is reserved by order of almighty heaven the right to bring this adventure to a felicitous conclusion."

In saying this, he drew his sword and began to brandish it at the millers, who, hearing but not understanding that gibberish, braced themselves for stopping the boat with their poles now that it was entering the channel leading to the mill-wheels. Sancho sank to his knees and devoutly begged heaven to deliver him from such a manifest danger, which it did through the skill and speed of the millers, for the latter, by pushing against the boat with their poles, managed to stop it but not so dexterously that they could keep from overturning it and throwing Don Quixote and Sancho into the water. Fortunately for Don Quixote he could swim like a goose, though the weight of his armor twice dragged him to the bottom, and had it not been for the millers, who dove into the water and carried them both out over their heads, their days would have been concluded right then and there. Once they were on land, more drenched than thirsty, Sancho knelt down, clasped both hands together, fixed his eyes upon heaven, and implored God in a long fervent prayer to liberate him from that moment on from the audacious ideas and escapades of his master.

Just then, the two fishermen arrived who owned the boat that been smashed by the mill-wheels, and the moment they saw it in shambles, they ran up to strip Sancho and to demand that Don Quixote pay them for their loss. The latter, with an air of unconcern as though nothing had happened, informed the millers and fishermen that he would very willingly pay for the boat, provided they set free without encumbrance the person or persons they held captive in that castle of theirs.

"What persons or castle are you talking about, you lunatic?" said one of the millers. "Can you possibly want to make off with these people who come to grind wheat in these mills?"

"That does it," said Don Quixote to himself; "to attempt to induce this rabble by entreaties to do anything virtuous is like preaching in the desert. In the present adventure two valiant enchanters have undoubtedly come face to face, one frustrating what the other was attempting, one of them giving me the boat and the other throwing me out of it. God help us all, for this world is nothing but stratagems and schemes, all of which are at odds with one another. Well, I have done everything I can." And continuing to stare at the mills, he raised his voice and cried out once more,

"Friends, whoever you may be, who are imprisoned in that citadel, forgive me but, owing to *my* misfortune and yours, I am unable to relieve you of your affliction, since this adventure is undoubtedly reserved for some other knight."

After saying this, he reached an understanding with the fishermen and paid them fifty *reals* for the boat, which Sancho gave them very begrudgingly, saying,

"With another boat affair like this one, we can throw all our money overboard."

The fishermen and the millers were astonished at the sight of these two figures who looked so different from other men, nor could they imagine where Don Quixote's speeches and questions were leading. Considering them lunatics, they left them there and returned to their mills and their huts, whereas Don Quixote and Sancho returned to their beasts and their bestial existence, and thus ended the adventure of the enchanted boat.

Chapter Thirty

Don Quixote's adventure with a beautiful huntress

Both knight and squire were sufficiently crestfallen and disgruntled as they returned to their animals, Sancho in particular, whose soul was pained at having dipped into the money-supply, for he felt that to diminish it by any amount was like plucking the pupils from his eyes. Without exchanging a word, they finally mounted their beasts and rode away from the famous river, Don Quixote lost in thoughts of his beloved, and Sancho in those of his advancement, which at the moment seemed to him quite out of reach, for despite the fact that he was a simpleton, he was still capable of seeing that most, if not all, of his master's undertakings were mad, and he was seeking a way to tear himself free some day and return to his family without getting involved with his master in explanations and farewells. Fate, however, was beginning to arrange things quite differently from what he feared.

It turned out that on the following day just as the sun was setting and the pair were emerging from a forest, Don Quixote cast his eyes about a verdant meadow, at the far end of which he caught sight of several persons and, once he drew near, he realized that they were falconers. As he continued to approach, he saw an elegant lady in their midst seated on a pure-white palfrey or hackney that was outfitted with green trappings and a silver sidesaddle. The lady herself wore green and was so richly and elegantly attired that she was the picture of elegance itself. Perched on her left hand was a hawk, which indicated to Don Quixote that she was a lady of some prominence and was probably mistress of all those hunters, which turned out to be the case. Turning to Sancho, he said,

"Hurry, my son, and inform that lady with the palfrey and hawk that I, the Knight of the Lions, salute her great beauty and vow that if her highness will grant me leave, I shall kiss her hand and serve her to the extent that my strength permits and her highness commands. But mind how you speak, Sancho, and try not to interlard your message with a bunch of proverbs."

"Look who's talking about interlarding proverbs!" cried Sancho. "Imagine telling me such a thing! Heavens, this isn't the first time in my life I've delivered messages to exalted and distinguished ladies!"

"Except for the one to Dulcinea," said Don Quixote, "I know of no others you have delivered, at least not in my service."

"That's true," replied Sancho, "but 'One who'll pay for his purchase doesn't mind putting down a deposit,' and 'In a house of plenty supper is not long in arriving,' meaning that your grace need not instruct or lecture me at all, for I'm prepared for everything and have a nodding acquaintance with all sorts of things."

"I can believe that, Sancho," said Don Quixote. "Now, go in the name of heaven, and Godspeed."

Sancho rode off at a brisk pace, coaxing the dapple out of his usual gait. Once he was in the presence of the beautiful huntress, he dismounted, knelt before her, and said,

"Fair lady, that knight over yonder, called the Knight of the Lions, is my master and I am his squire, known back home as Sancho Panza. That same Knight of the Lions, who only a short while ago called himself the Knight of the Woeful Countenance, has sent me to beg your loftiness to be so kind as to grant him leave that he may – with your ladyship's permission, approval, and consent – approach and fulfill his wishes, which are none other, according to what he says and I understand, than to be of service to your lovely and sublime ladyship. If your grace will grant him this wish, you will be performing an act that will redound to your ladyship's advantage and will afford him the most signal benefit and contentment."

"Most assuredly, my noble squire," replied the lady, "you have delivered your message with all the elements demanded of such missions. Arise, as it is not meet for a squire of so great a knight as Him of the Woeful Countenance to remain kneeling, for we have already received numerous reports of him. Arise, my friend, and tell your master that I and my husband the duke place ourselves at his disposal and shall be delighted to have him join us at a country estate we have nearby."

Sancho rose to his feet, impressed not only by the noble lady's beauty but also by her good breeding and graciousness, but even more so by her statement that she had heard of his master, the Knight of the Woeful Countenance, and if she had not referred to him as the Knight of the Lions, it was no doubt due to his having assumed that title so recently. The duchess, whose name he still did not know, then addressed him:

"Tell me, brother squire, this master of yours, is he not the one about whom a history has been published called *The Ingenious Hidalgo Don Quixote of La Mancha*, and the one who has a certain Dulcinea of Toboso as the mistress of his soul?"

"He is the very one, my lady," said Sancho, "and that squire of his who's included, or should be included, in the history in question – the one they call Sancho Panza – is none other than yours truly, unless they've altered me in the cradle, that is, in the printing process."

"I find all that delightful," said the duchess. "Go, brother Panza, and tell your master he shall be well received and most welcome at my estate, for nothing will afford me greater pleasure."

With this extremely ingratiating reply, Sancho enthusiastically returned to his master, to whom he related everything the great lady had said, while praising to the heavens in his rustic manner her great beauty, elegance, and graciousness. Don Quixote at once assumed a posture of gallantry in the saddle, braced himself firmly in the stirrups, adjusted his visor, applied the spurs to Rocinante, and then with an air of bravado rode over to kiss the hand of the duchess. While Don Quixote was approaching, she summoned her husband the duke and gave him an account of the contents of the message. The two of them, who had read the first part of our history and thereby understood the scatterbrain nature of Don Quixote, waited with great anticipation and delight, for they were quite eager to make his acquaintance. They proposed to honor him by agreeing with him in everything he said and by treating him like a knight-errant for as many days as he might spend with them, including all the usual ceremonies found in those books of chivalry they had read and were quite fond of.

Just then, Don Quixote rode up with his visor raised and, as he was about to dismount, Sancho jumped down to hold his stirrup but, in dismounting from the dapple, he had the misfortune to tangle one of his feet in a cord on the packsaddle in such a way that he was unable to pull it free and was thus left dangling by his foot with his mouth and chest resting on the ground. Don Quixote, who was unaccustomed to dismounting without having his stirrup held, and believing Sancho had already come over to hold it, threw all his weight onto the stirrup, whereupon he hit the ground, taking Rocinante's saddle with him, which must have been poorly cinched, and not without considerable embarrassment to himself and a great number of invectives that he silently hurled at poor, unfortunate Sancho, whose foot still remained in the stocks. The duke ordered the hunters to assist the knight and squire, which they did by helping the battered Don Quixote to his feet, who limped along as best he could in his eagerness to kneel before the lord and lady. But the duke would not permit it, as he himself dismounted and hurried to embrace Don Quixote, to whom he said,

"I am truly sorry, Sir Knight of the Woeful Countenance, that the first step your grace has taken on my estate has been as painful as the one we have just witnessed but squires in their carelessness often cause even worse things to happen."

"The experience I have had in meeting your lordship," said Don Quixote, "could not possibly be unfortunate, even if my fall had landed me in the deepest abyss, for from there I would have been rescued and raised up by the sight of your grace's glorious countenance. My squire – plague take him! – is better at untying his malicious tongue than at tying and cinching a saddle and making it secure. However, in whatever condition I happen to find myself, whether fallen or risen, on foot or on horseback, I shall always be at the service of your grace and my lady the duchess, your worthy consort and queen of all beauty and courtesy."

"Careful, my dear Don Quixote of La Mancha," said the duke, "whenever my lady Doña Dulcinea of Toboso is present, it is unseemly to praise the beauty of others."

By this time Sancho Panza had freed himself from the cord and, being close by, spoke up before his master could respond.

"There's no denying – in fact, it must be admitted – that my lady Dulcinea of Toboso is extremely beautiful, but 'When one least expects it up jumps the Devil.' I've heard it said that this thing called Mother Nature is like a potter who makes pots from clay; anyone capable of making one beautiful pot can make two, three, or even a hundred. I mention this, for, in faith, my lady the duchess is in no way inferior to my mistress the lady Dulcinea of Toboso."

Don Quixote turned to the duchess and said,

"Your highness may possibly get the impression that no knight-errant ever had a more talkative or ludicrous squire than I, and this will be borne out if you should wish to avail yourself of my services for a few days."

To which the duchess replied,

"I find it most admirable that noble Sancho is humorous, for it is a sign of his intelligence. Wit and humor, Sir Don Quixote, as your grace well knows, do not sit well with dull minds, and since our good Sancho is comical and witty, I shall consider him a wise man from this moment forward."

"And a talkative one," added Don Quixote.

"So much the better," said the duke, "for many witty things cannot be expressed in only a few words. But lest we spend all our time talking, I should like the great Knight of the Woeful Countenance to come—"

"'Knight of the Lions' your highness should say," interrupted Sancho, "for there is no longer a Woeful Countenance."

"'Lions' it is," said the duke. "If his grace the Knight of the Lions will accompany me to a castle of mine that is nearby, he shall be given a reception appropriate to such an illustrious personage, one the duchess and I always extend to every knight who is our guest."

During this interval, Sancho had prepared the saddle and cinched it securely, whereupon Don Quixote mounted Rocinante and the duke a handsome steed; then with the duchess between them they made their way towards the castle. The duchess ordered Sancho to ride next to her, for she delighted in listening to all his clever remarks. Not having to be asked twice, Sancho worked his way in among the three of them, adding a fourth voice to the conversation much to the delight of the duke and duchess, who considered themselves most fortunate to receive in their castle such a knight-errant and such an errant squire.

Chapter Thirty-One

The account of a number of important matters

The joy that Sancho experienced was unsurpassed when he found himself, in his opinion at least, the recipient of the duchess' goodwill, for he imagined he would find in her castle what he had found in the homes of Don Diego and Basilio, and since he was partial to the good life, he seized every opportunity by the scruff of the neck to regale himself whenever and wherever he encountered it.

Our history goes on to relate that before they reached the country estate or castle, the duke rode on ahead to instruct all his servants in the way they were to treat Don Quixote. Accordingly, as soon as the latter arrived at the castle gate in the company of the duchess, two lackeys or grooms came out dressed in ankle-length house robes of the finest crimson satin and, before Don Quixote knew what was happening, they took him in their arms and said to him,

"Your exalted lordship should go help my mistress the duchess dismount."

Don Quixote hurried to do so, eliciting an effusive exchange of civilities between the two, but the duchess in her insistence won out, as she refused to abandon the palfrey except into the arms of the duke, saying she found herself unworthy of imposing such a worthless burden upon so great a knight. At length, the duke came out to help her dismount and they all entered a large courtyard where they were met by two lovely maidens, who draped a large exquisite scarlet cloak over Don Quixote's shoulders. All the galleries surrounding the courtyard were suddenly thronged with the duke and duchess' servants, who shouted,

"Welcome to the flower and cream of knight-errantry!"

Virtually everyone present began to sprinkle flasks of scented water over Don Quixote and his host and hostess, all of which caused the knight to marvel, since this was the first time he had ever completely believed he was a real knight-errant and not a make-believe one, for he now saw himself treated exactly the way the knights of yore were treated in the histories he had read. Sancho abandoned the dapple and stayed close to the duchess as they entered the castle, but feeling pangs of conscience at having left the dapple alone, he approached a solemn-looking duenna [1] who had come outside with the others to welcome the duchess, and he said to her in a subdued tone of voice,

"Doña González, or whatever your grace's name is----- "

"Doña Rodríguez de Grijalba is my name," said the duenna. "What may I do for you, my son?"

To which Sancho replied,

"I would ask your grace to be so kind as to go out to the castle gate, where you will find an ass of mine. Then I wish you would have him put – or put him yourself – in the stable, since the poor thing is rather skittish and won't like being left alone under any circumstances."

"If the master is as bright as his servant," said the duenna, "we are in for it! Run along, my son, and attend to your own jackass. You and the one who brought you here can go to blazes, for we duennas of this household are not in the habit of performing such chores."

"Well," said Sancho, "the fact is that my master, who's a keen observer of knight-errantry, has been heard by me to quote a certain passage of Lancelot that says:

'When he from Britain came,
Ladies attended to him,
And duennas to his steed;'

and when it comes to my jackass, I wouldn't swap him for Sir Lancelot's very own steed."

"My son," replied the duenna, "if you are a jester, keep your witticisms for someone who will appreciate them and pay you for them because you will get nothing from me but a fig."

"And a ripe one, I'm sure," said Sancho, "for if years were points, your grace wouldn't lose a hand by coming up a point shy!"

"Damn you!" cried the duenna, seething with anger, "whether I'm old or not is a matter between

---

1 Duennas (Spanish ***dueñas***) were women employed by ladies of nobility to serve simultaneously as companions, confidantes, chaperons, go-betweens, governesses, and heads of the household maid-servants. They were frequently the object of derision in the literature of Spain's Golden Age and apparently deserved their reputation of being haughty, self-serving, duplicitous, meddling, gossip-mongering, etc.

me and God – not you, you garlic-stuffed knave!"

She shouted this so vehemently that it was overheard by the duchess, who turned and saw the duenna terribly upset and spouting fire from her eyes, at which point the duchess asked her whom she was arguing with.

"I am arguing with this fine fellow," said the duenna. "He told me in all seriousness that he had left a jackass of his at the castle gate and asked me if I would take it to the stable, citing as his precedent something certain damsels did somewhere or other when they attended to Lancelot and duennas attended to his steed; and as the final straw, he called me an old woman."

"I would take that as the greatest insult anyone could possibly pay me," replied the duchess, and addressing Sancho, she said, "Be advised, Sancho my friend, that Doña Rodríguez is quite young and wears that headdress more because of custom and her authority than because of her years."

"May all the years I have left be cursed if I meant anything by it," said Sancho; "I only said it because of the great affection I have for my jackass and because it struck me that I couldn't entrust him to a more charitable person than the lady Doña Rodríguez."

Don Quixote, who had been listening to all this, said,

"Is this the proper place to discuss these matters, Sancho?"

"Master," replied Sancho, "each person must make his needs known wherever he is. I happened to be here when I remembered the dapple. If I had thought of him in the stable, I would have mentioned him there."

At which point the duke said,

"Sancho is quite right and there is absolutely no reason to blame him. The dapple shall be given all the fodder he can eat and Sancho may relax, for the dapple shall be treated as royally as Sancho himself."

Following this discussion, which was to everyone's liking except Don Quixote's, they went upstairs, where they escorted Don Quixote to a chamber furnished with expensive gold brocade fabrics. A half dozen damsels serving as his valets removed his armor, having been instructed and advised by the duke and duchess as to what they were to do and how they were to treat him so he would have no doubt that they considered him a genuine knight-errant.

After his armor was removed, Don Quixote stood there in his tight-fitting breeches and chamois-skin doublet, tall, wrinkled, gangling, with his cheeks completely sunken into his jaws. He presented such a comical portrait that, had the damsels waiting on him not made an effort to conceal their amusement (one of the specific orders the duke and duchess had given them), they would have burst out laughing. They asked if they could help him undress and don his shirt but he would consent to nothing of the sort, saying that modesty in knights-errant was just as becoming as bravery. Instead, he asked them to give the shirt to Sancho, with whom he enclosed himself in a chamber containing a sumptuous bed, where he undressed and put on the shirt. Finding himself alone with Sancho, he said to him,

"Tell me, you fledgling clown and inveterate numbskull, do you consider it proper to insult and show a lack of respect to a duenna as venerable and worthy of respect as this one? Was this the time to remember your dapple? Are these lords and ladies persons who will permit animals to be neglected after they have treated their owners so exquisitely? For the love of God, Sancho, control yourself and don't reveal your true fabric or everyone will realize you are woven of coarse, crude thread. Listen, you sinner, the more honorable and well-bred the servants, the more esteemed is the master, and one of the greatest advantages nobles hold over the rest of mankind is that they are served by men and women as noble as themselves. Don't you see – O wretch that you are and hapless soul that I am – that if they perceive you as a coarse peasant or a ludicrous simpleton, they will think me some charlatan or fraudulent knight? No, Sancho my friend, flee from these pitfalls, for whoever makes the mistake of being a babbler and a jester will, the first time he stumbles, be taken for a pathetic buffoon. Therefore, bridle your tongue and consider and reflect upon your words before they come pouring from your mouth. And bear in mind that we have come to a place from where, by the grace of God and the might of my arm, we shall go forth greatly enriched in both fame and fortune."

Sancho promised most earnestly to seal his lips and bite his tongue before saying anything inappropriate or inconsiderate, as he was being ordered to do; that Don Quixote need not be concerned, for he, Sancho, would not be the one to reveal to people what they were really like.

After dressing, Don Quixote strapped on his shoulder-belt and sword, threw the scarlet cloak over his shoulders, donned a green satin cap the damsels had given him and, decked out in this fashion, strode into the great hall, where he found the maidens arrayed on either side of the room, each holding a receptacle for washing one's hands, which they held out to him amid many curtsies and much ceremony. Then a dozen pages entered with the majordomo and escorted him to the dining-hall, where the duke and duchess were now awaiting him. Taking Don Quixote into their midst, they made their way with pomp and majesty to the adjoining hall in which a lavish table had been prepared with only four place-settings. The duchess and duke came to the door to receive him, accompanied by one of those stern-looking ecclesiastics who lord it over the houses of nobles – ecclesiastics who, not being nobly born themselves, are unable to teach those who *are* how to conduct themselves; who desire the largesse of the grandees to be measured by the narrowness of their own souls, and who, wishing to show those they govern how to be frugal, turn them into misers. Such a one, I maintain, was this stern ecclesiastic who came forth with the duke and duchess to welcome Don Quixote. After an exchange of a thousand courtesies and civilities, they placed Don Quixote between them as they led him to the table. The duke invited Don Quixote to sit at its head, and though he declined to do so, the duke's importunings were such that he was forced to sit there. The ecclesiastic seated himself opposite him, with the duke and duchess sitting on either side. Sancho was witness to all this and was stupefied and overwhelmed at seeing how these nobles were honoring his master. After observing the numerous formalities and civilities that passed between the duke and Don Quixote in an effort to make the latter take his seat at the head of the table, Sancho spoke up:

"If your graces will permit me, I will relate a story of what happened in my hometown regarding this matter of where to sit."

Scarcely had Sancho said this than Don Quixote shuddered, convinced beyond a shadow of a doubt that he was about to blurt out something outrageous. Sancho glanced at him and, sensing what he was thinking, said,

"Master, your grace needn't be afraid that I'll behave in an uncouth manner or say anything that's out of place. I haven't forgotten the advice you just now gave me about speaking politely and not talking too much."

"I don't recall any such advice," said Don Quixote; "say whatever you please so long as you say it quickly."

"Well, what I have to say," replied Sancho, "is so true that my master Don Quixote, who is here present, will not let me tell a lie."

"As far as I am concerned," said Don Quixote, "you may lie as much as you please, Sancho, and I shall not try to stop you. However, do consider what you are about to say."

"I've considered and reconsidered it so much that I'm as safe as the bell-ringer in his tower, as will be evident from my tale."

"It would be wise," said Don Quixote, "for your graces to have this idiot ejected from here because he is bound to say a thousand outrageous things."

"Over the duke's dead body!" exclaimed the duchess. "Sancho is not budging one inch from my side, for I am very fond of him because of his great cleverness."

To which Sancho replied,

"And may all your ladyship's days be clever ones because of the good opinion you have of me, though I am undeserving of it. Now, the story I would like to relate is the following. An invitation was sent out by a nobleman of my town, quite a wealthy and important person, having descended from the Alamos of Medina del Campo and married Doña Mencía de Quiñones, who was the daughter of Don Alonso de Marañón, a knight in the Order of Saint James, who was drowned in the Herradura, because of which there was that dispute in our village years ago in which, according to my understanding, my master Don Quixote was involved and that mischief-maker Tomasillo, son of Balbastro the blacksmith, was wounded. Isn't every word of this true, dear master? Please say it's true so these lords and ladies won't think I'm some babbling liar."

"So far," said the ecclesiastic, "I think you are more of a babbler than a liar but I have no idea what I shall think later on."

"You have brought in so many witnesses and so much evidence," said Don Quixote, "that I cannot help believing you must be telling the truth. Proceed with your story but keep it short, for the one you are telling won't end in two days."

"He shall do nothing of the sort," said the duchess, "if only for my sake. On the contrary, he is to tell it any way he knows how, even if he does not finish in six days, which will be the best days I ever spend in my life."

"As I was saying then, your graces," continued Sancho, "this particular nobleman, whom I know like the palm of my hand, since there's not a bow-shot between my house and his, sent an invitation to a poor but honorable farmer."

"Get on with it, brother," said the cleric at this point, "for with the road you are following you won't finish your story before the next life."

"God permitting, I'll finish it in half that time," replied Sancho; "but to continue: when the farmer in question arrived at the home of this nobleman who had invited him – may his soul rest in peace, seeing as how he's now dead, and by all indications they say he died a peaceful death, though I wasn't there, having at the time gone to Tembleque for the harvest."

"For the sake of your soul, my son," said the ecclesiastic, "you shall quickly return from Tembleque and, without burying the nobleman unless you are looking for another funeral, shall finish your story."

"Well," said Sancho, "it turned out that just as they were both about to be seated at the table – ah, it seems I can see them now just as clearly as----- "

The duke and duchess were enormously amused at the annoyance the good churchman displayed over the delays and interruptions Sancho was making in telling his story, and Don Quixote was consumed with rage and anger.

"Well, as I was saying," continued Sancho, "as the two of them were about to sit down at the table, the farmer pleaded with the nobleman to take the place of honor, and the nobleman pleaded with the farmer to do the same, for in his house one was expected to do as he ordered. The farmer, however, who prided himself on being courteous and well-bred, refused to do so until the nobleman clapped both hands on his shoulders and forcibly sat him down, saying, 'Sit down, you numbskull, for anywhere I sit will be the place of honor for you.' Now that's my story and I really don't think it's out of place at this time."

Don Quixote's face turned a thousand different colors, producing a mottled effect on his olive skin. The duke and duchess disguised their elation so Don Quixote would not be embarrassed now that he had caught Sancho's drift. To change the conversation and to keep Sancho from doing anything else absurd, the duchess asked Don Quixote what news he had received of Dulcinea and whether he had recently sent her any giants or scoundrels as presents, having no doubt vanquished quite a few.

"My lady," said Don Quixote, "though my misfortunes did have a beginning, they will never have an end. I have overcome giants and sent her scoundrels and evildoers but how can they possibly find her when she is enchanted and transformed into the ugliest farm girl imaginable."

"Oh, I don't know," said Sancho, "to me she looked like the most beautiful creature on earth; at least, in agility and jumping ability I'm sure she wouldn't come in second to any tumbler. I swear, my duchess, she can bound onto a donkey with the agility of a cat."

"Have you seen her," asked the duke, "since she has been enchanted?"

"Of course, I've seen her," whispered Sancho. "Who the dickens was the person to come up with this scheme of her being enchanted if not me? Why, she's no more enchanted than my father is!"

The ecclesiastic, having heard this talk of giants, scoundrels, and enchantments, came to the realization that this must be Don Quixote of La Mancha, whose history the duke was forever and again reading, for which he had reprimanded him many times, telling him it was ridiculous to read such absurdities. Once the ecclesiastic was convinced of the correctness of his suspicions, he addressed the duke angrily and said,

"My lord, your excellency will have to answer to Our Lord for what this good man does. I believe this Don Quixote, or Don Simpleton, or whatever his name is, is probably not as cracked as your grace might like him to be, though he is being given every opportunity to go forward with his follies and nonsense."

Then directing his tirade at Don Quixote, he added,

"And you, you poor, unsuspecting soul, who has filled your head with the idea that you are a knight-errant and can conquer giants and apprehend evildoers? Leave here in peace, and Godspeed! Return to your home, rear your children if you have any, and attend to your estate. Also, stop wandering over the face of the earth living on air and making a fool of yourself in the presence of all who know you and all who do not. Where in heaven's name have you discovered that there are or ever have been any knights-errant? Where are there any giants in Spain or monsters in La Mancha, or Dulcineas under a spell, or that whole host of mindless things they say about you?"

Don Quixote sat there transfixed as he listened to the words of this venerable man of the cloth. When he saw that he had finished speaking, he rose to his feet, and with a look of anger and disbelief on his face, and without regard for the respect due the duke and duchess, said– but his reply deserves a chapter of its own.

Chapter Thirty-Two

The response that Don Quixote made to his chastiser, together with other matters, some serious, some amusing

Don Quixote rose to his feet and stood there shaking like a leaf from head to foot but he finally said in a hurried and flustered tone,

"This house I am in, the persons in whose presence I find myself, and the respect I have always had and still have for the office your holiness occupies hold fast and bind the hands of my justifiable indignation. For these reasons and because everyone knows that both men of letters and women defend themselves by the same means, namely, their tongues, I shall by using mine enter into combat on an equal footing with your grace, from whom one might have expected constructive counsel rather than vile abuse, for charitable and well-intentioned chastisement requires other circumstances and demands other types of arguments. To see myself reprimanded so harshly in public completely oversteps the bounds of propriety, since it is more effective when done with gentleness than with harshness. Nor is it right for one lacking all knowledge of the sin being chastised to call the sinner a simpleton and a fool just like that. Among the follies your grace has observed in me, will you kindly tell me which ones you are condemning and railing against and which you are ordering me to return home for so I may attend to my affairs and to my wife and children, without even knowing whether I have a wife or children? Is it simply sufficient to worm one's way by hook or crook into another person's home and lord it over the occupants, or for someone having been reared in the narrow confines of a seminary and having seen no more of the world than that portion contained within twenty or thirty leagues of his district to have the audacity to lay down the law to the order of chivalry and to stand in judgement of knights-errant? Is it somehow a vain undertaking or a waste of time on my part to go ranging over the face of the earth, not in quest of its pleasures, but of the austerities by which the good ascend to the seat of immortality? If I were considered a fool by gentlemen or by those who were magnanimous, generous, and of noble birth, I should consider it an unforgivable insult, but to be labeled a fool by students who have never followed nor trod the paths of chivalry matters to me not one whit, for a knight I am and a knight I shall die if it please the Almighty. Some men tread the broad avenue of haughty ambition; some that of lowly, servile adulation; others that of hypocrisy and deceit; and still others that of the True Faith, whereas I, driven by my guiding star, follow the narrow path of knight-errantry, in the execution of which I am scornful of possessions but not of honor. I have redressed injuries, righted wrongs, punished insolence, conquered giants, and run roughshod over monsters, and I am in love but only because it is a requirement of knight-errantry. Even so, I am not one of those carnal lovers but one whose love is chaste and platonic. My intentions are always directed towards virtuous ends, which are to do good to all and ill to none. My most excellent lord and lady, it is for your graces to say whether a person deserves to be called a fool who understands this and occupies himself in such endeavors and performs such deeds."

"Oh my, but that's good!" said Sancho. "O lord and master, your grace need say nothing more on your behalf, for there is nothing nobler in this world to say, think, or strive for. Besides, when this gentleman claims, as he does, that there are not now and never have been knights-errant on this earth, is it any wonder he is ignorant about everything else he says?"

To which the ecclesiastic replied,

"Brother, are you by chance that Sancho Panza they say was promised an island by his master?"

"I am," replied Sancho, "and I'm as worthy of it as the next person. I'm one of those 'Associate with good men and good men you'll imitate'; one of those 'It's not who you were at birth but whose company you keep now'; and one of those 'Choose a good tree to stand under and you'll receive abundant shade.' I've chosen a good master to stand under, I've traveled in his company for lo these many months and would be such a one myself, God willing. Long live him and long live me! He'll never lack for empires to rule nor I islands to govern."

"Of course not, Sancho my friend," said the duke at this point, "for in the name of his lord Don Quixote I shall make you governor of one of those I hold in reserve, which is by no means an insignificant one."

"Get down on your knees," said Don Quixote, "and kiss his excellency's feet for the favor he has shown you."

Sancho did so but when the ecclesiastic saw this, he rose from the table thoroughly disgusted and said,

"I swear by the habit I am wearing that I am forced to say your excellency is as foolish as these poor souls. Why should they not act crazy if sane people countenance their folly? Your excellency may stay here with them but while they are in this house I shall be in mine, where I shall refrain from criticizing what I can't correct."

And without saying or eating another thing, he excused himself, the pleas of the duke and duchess being of no avail in dissuading him, though the duke's pleas were quite weak due to the enjoyment he had received from the ecclesiastic's unjustified anger. Then after enjoying a hearty laugh, he said to Don Quixote,

"Sir Knight of the Lions, your grace has responded so nobly on your own behalf that no further satisfaction need be sought in this affair, and though it may appear to be an insult, it is nothing of the sort, for ecclesiastics, like women, are incapable of insulting anyone, as you know all too well."

"It is just as your grace says," replied Don Quixote, "because a person who cannot be insulted is incapable of insulting anyone else. Women, children, and ecclesiastics, who are unable to defend themselves even when wronged, cannot be insulted, and between a wrong and an insult there is a wide gulf, as your excellency knows. An insult occurs when a person capable of wronging someone does so and then persists in the action. A wrong may arise from any quarter without there being an insult. Take the example of a man standing in the street minding his own business when ten other men bearing arms come up and give him a thrashing. He draws his sword to do what he must but his attackers rise as one against him and prevent him from carrying out his intention, which is to avenge himself. This individual has certainly been wronged but not insulted, as may be confirmed by another example. A man is standing with his back turned, when a second man comes up and starts beating him. Once he has finished, he does not remain there but runs away, while the first man runs after him but is unable to catch him. The one who was beaten was wronged but not insulted, for an insult must be persisted in. If the one who attacked him, though he may have done so stealthily, had drawn his sword and stood his ground, looking his victim squarely in the eye, the latter would have been wronged and insulted simultaneously – wronged because he had been treacherously attacked and insulted because the one who attacked him compounded the wrong he had done by standing his ground rather than fleeing. So, according to the accursed dueling code, I may have been wronged but I was not insulted, for women and children do not realize what they have done, nor do they have any reason to run away or to stand their ground, just like ministers of religion, for these three classes of persons lack both offensive and defensive weapons. Though predisposed by nature to defend themselves, they are not disposed to offend anyone else. And though I said a moment ago that I may have been wronged, I now say there is no way in which I could have been, for whoever is incapable of receiving an insult is even less capable of insulting anyone else. [1] For these reasons I ought not and do not take umbrage at what that good man said to me. I only wish he had not hurried away so I might make him understand the mistake he committed in thinking and saying that there are not now and never have been knights-errant on this earth. Why, if Amadís or any of his numerous progeny were to hear such a thing, I am sure it would not go well with him."

"I can certainly attest to that," said Sancho. "They would have slit him open from head to foot like a pomegranate or a nice ripe melon – they would be fine ones to tolerate such indignities! Upon my word, I am absolutely convinced that if Reinaldos de Montalbán had heard this pipsqueak make such an assertion, he would have given him such a swat across the mouth that he wouldn't say another

---

1 There are several inconsistencies in Don Quixote's reasoning in the foregoing paragraph, which leads one to believe that either Cervantes was dozing in the manner of Homer or, as Vicente Gaos postulates, was satirizing the sophistry of various commentators writing on the subject.

word for three years. No, just let him start something with them and he'll see how easy it is to escape their clutches."

The Duchess was dying of laughter because of Sancho's remarks and in her opinion felt he was more comical and unbalanced than his master, and there were a number of people at the time who shared her opinion. Finally, Don Quixote regained his composure and the dinner came to an end.

Once the table was cleared, four damsels entered, one with a silver basin, another with a water pitcher also of silver, a third with two very expensive white towels draped over her shoulder, and the fourth, her arms bare up to her elbows, carrying in her white hands (and white they most certainly were) a round bar of Neapolitan soap. The one with the basin stepped forward and tactfully and matter-of-factly stuck it under the chin of Don Quixote, who did not say a word. Though taken by surprise by such a ceremony, he believed that in this land it must be the custom to wash, not one's hands, but one's beard. He therefore thrust his chin forward as far as possible and at that very instant water began to pour from the pitcher and the damsel with the soap began vigorously lathering his beard, producing soapsuds that were every bit as white as snowballs, not only over the obedient knight's beard but his entire face and even his eyes, which he was forced to close. The duke and duchess, who were not privy to any of this, sat there waiting to see where such an elaborate cleansing might lead. When the damsel doing the barbering had him covered with several inches of lather, she pretended to run out of water and sent the damsel holding the basin for some more, convinced his grace Don Quixote would sit there patiently. The girl did so, leaving Don Quixote looking as strange and ludicrous as one could possibly imagine. All those present – and there were quite a few – had their eyes fixed upon him, and when they observed his neck, which was half a yard long, his more than moderately tanned skin, his closed eyes, and his soap-filled beard, it required considerable discretion on their part to contain their laughter, which surprisingly enough they were able to do. The damsels responsible for the charade kept their eyes lowered, not daring to look at their master and mistress, who, overcome with equal degrees of anger and a desire to laugh, did not know which impulse to succumb to – whether to chastise the girls for their impertinence or to reward them for the pleasure they themselves had received from seeing Don Quixote in this condition. At length, the damsel returned with the basin and they finished scrubbing Don Quixote; then the one with the towels wiped and dried him off in a most leisurely fashion, whereupon all four damsels, in their desire to absent themselves, simultaneously bowed low and curtsied in a gesture of deep respect. However, lest Don Quixote become aware of the prank being played on him, the duke called to the damsel holding the basin and said,

"Come bathe me too and make sure you don't run out of water."

The girl, being sufficiently keen-witted, came up and placed the basin under the duke's beard exactly as she had done under Don Quixote's and they hurriedly soaped and bathed him and, after wiping and drying him off, performed their curtsies and left. It was later learned that the duke had threatened that should they fail to wash him as they had Don Quixote, he would chastise them for their audacity, which they wisely atoned for by giving him a good sudsing. Sancho, who was witness to the bathing ceremony, said to himself,

"Saints preserve us! I wonder if it is also the custom in this land to wash the squire's beard as well as the knight's. Goodness knows, mine could stand to be washed, and should they go so far as to shave me with a razor, I would consider it an even greater service."

"What are you saying to yourself, Sancho?" asked the duchess.

"I was just saying," replied Sancho, "that I've heard it said that in the courts of other nobles, once the tables are cleared, they provide water for your hands but not lye soap for your face. That's why it's good to live a long life so as to witness lots of things! On the other hand, there's the saying: 'Whoever lives for many years will suffer many ills,' though to undergo one of these scrubbings is more akin to pleasure than to hardship."

"Fret not, Sancho," said the duchess; "I shall see to it that my ladies bathe you and even put you in the tub if necessary."

"I'll settle for having my beard washed," said Sancho, "for now, at least; as time goes by, who knows how I'll feel?"

"Majordomo," said the duchess, "find out what noble Sancho needs and comply with his every wish."

The majordomo replied that Master Sancho's tiniest whim would be attended to and, with this, he left the room to dine, taking Sancho with him. The duke, duchess, and Don Quixote remained seated, discussing a number of different topics but all bearing upon knight-errantry and the exercise of arms. The duchess begged Don Quixote, who appeared to possess an excellent memory, to describe and delineate the beauty and features of the lady Doña Dulcinea of Toboso, for according to all reports about her beauty, the duchess was convinced she must be the most gorgeous creature on earth or even in the whole of La Mancha. Don Quixote heaved a sigh when he heard what the duchess was ordering him to do, and he said,

"If I could pluck out my heart and place it before your excellency on a platter on this very table, it would spare my tongue the pain of uttering what can scarcely be imagined, for your grace would therein discern her entire likeness. But why should I now set about describing and delineating point by point and feature by feature the beauty of the peerless Dulcinea when that is a task for worthier shoulders than mine – an enterprise that would require the brushes of Parrhasius, Timanthes, and Apelles and the gravers of Lysippus to paint her on canvas and etch her in marble and bronze, together with Ciceronian and Demosthenian rhetoric to sing her praises?"

"What does Demosthenian mean, Sir Don Quixote?" asked the duchess. "That is a word I have never heard in my entire life."

"Demosthenian rhetoric," said Don Quixote, "is the same as saying 'the rhetoric of Demosthenes,' just as Ciceronian means 'of Cicero,' these being the two greatest rhetoricians on earth."

"Quite so," said the duke, "and you, my dear, must have been confused to ask such a question. Nevertheless, Sir Don Quixote, you would greatly favor us by describing her to us, for if it were only a sketch or an outline, she would be certain to come across so vividly that the most beautiful women would envy her."

"I should certainly do so," said Don Quixote, "if the misfortune that recently befell her had not blotted her from my memory, for owing to this misfortune I am more inclined to lament her than to describe her. Your highnesses should know that several days ago, when I went to kiss her hand and seek her blessing, approval, and permission for this third sally, I discovered someone different from the one I had expected: I found her under a spell, transformed from a princess into a peasant wench, from a beautiful woman into a hag, from an angel into a devil, from one who was fragrant smelling into one who stank, from a refined speaker into a coarse one, from a lady of leisure into an acrobat, from light into darkness – in a word, from Dulcinea of Toboso into some peasant from Sayago."

"Heaven help me!" exclaimed the duke at this point, "who can have done the world such an injustice? Who has robbed it of the beauty that delighted it, the elegance that graced it, the chasteness that lent it its good reputation?"

"Who!" replied Don Quixote, "who else but one of the countless malevolent enchanters who persecute me out of envy. Who can it be but that accursed race born into the world to obscure and obliterate the deeds of the good and to engender and perpetuate the deeds of the evil. Enchanters have always persecuted me, they still persecute me, and they will continue to do so until they have buried me and my lofty accomplishments as a knight-errant in the deepest abyss of oblivion. They always hurt and wound me where they know I shall feel it most acutely, because to rob a knight-errant of his lady is to take away the eyes with which he sees, the sun with which he illumines his way, and the sustenance with which he nourishes himself. I have said it many times before and shall repeat it here: a knight-errant without a lady is like a tree without leaves, a building without a foundation, a shadow without a body to cast it."

"There is nothing more to say," said the duchess, "but if, despite this, we can believe the history of Don Quixote that has recently seen the light of day to the general applause of mankind, one must conclude, if my memory serves me, that your grace has never seen the lady Dulcinea and that this particular lady is nothing in the world but an imaginary lady you have engendered and given birth to in your mind, depicting her with all the grace and perfection you might desire."

"Regarding that point, there is much room for debate," said Don Quixote. "God Himself knows whether or not Dulcinea is of this world and whether she is real or imagined. These are not matters that can be completely resolved to one's satisfaction. I neither engendered nor gave birth to my lady, though I contemplate her in a manner befitting a lady who encompasses in her person all the qualities capable of making her famous in every part of the globe: she is beautiful and unblemished, majestic but not haughty, amorous but chaste, appreciative because she is gracious, gracious because she is well-bred, and lastly, exalted by birth, for beauty shines forth and flourishes to a greater degree of perfection in a person from a distinguished line than in one of humble origin."

"So it does," said the duke, "but, Sir Don Quixote, you must grant me permission to say what I am forced to say after reading the history of your adventures. One comes away believing – even if one were to concede that there is a Dulcinea in Toboso or its environs who is as consummately beautiful as you have described her – that in the matter of her distinguished ancestry she is no match for the Orianas, the Alastrajareas, the Madásimas, or any others of that caliber who fill those histories with which you are well acquainted."

"If I may be allowed to respond to that," said Don Quixote: "Dulcinea is the child of her deeds, and virtue ennobles a person's bloodline, for a humble but virtuous person is to be held in higher esteem and consideration than one who is exalted but malevolent, particularly when Dulcinea possesses a trait that may raise her to be a queen with a scepter and crown. For the worthiness of a beautiful and virtuous woman is capable of performing greater miracles and contains within itself greater good fortune."

"I maintain, Sir Don Quixote," said the duchess, "that your grace proceeds in all you say with great caution and, as the saying goes, 'keep your finger on the world's pulse.' I, from this moment forward, shall believe and see to it that everyone in my household believes – even my master the duke if necessary – that there is a Dulcinea of Toboso, that she is alive today, is beautiful, nobly born, and worthy of being served by a knight such as your grace, which is the highest praise I am capable of or can pay her. Nevertheless, I still have one reservation, a certain qualm as it were, concerning Sancho Panza. My misgiving lies in the fact that the history under discussion says Sancho Panza found our lady Dulcinea winnowing a sack of wheat when he delivered a letter on your grace's behalf, and the wheat, by all indications, was red wheat, a point that makes me question her distinguished ancestry."

To which Don Quixote responded,

"My lady, your highness should know that everything or nearly everything that befalls me exceeds what normally befalls other knights-errant, whether these things are directed by the inscrutable will of the fates or by the malicious hand of some envious enchanter. Moreover, it is an established fact that all or most famous knights-errant possess a special gift: one particular knight may be impervious to enchantments; another may have such impenetrable flesh that he cannot be wounded, as in the case of the famous Roland, one of the Twelve Peers of France, about whom it is related that he was incapable of being wounded except in the sole of his left foot, and that the wound must be inflicted with the point of a large pin, any other sort of weapon being of no benefit whatever, which is what happened when Bernardo del Carpio slew him at Roncesvalles. When the latter found himself unable to wound him with his steel sword, he lifted him off the ground in his arms and strangled him, having at that moment remembered the manner in which Hercules had killed Antaeus, that ferocious giant said to be the offspring of Earth. I am forced to conclude from everything I have said that I may possibly possess one of those gifts – not that of being impervious to wounds, for experience has often shown me I have tender skin that is not the least bit impenetrable, nor that of being invulnerable to enchantments, since I have seen myself thrown into a cage in which everyone on earth would have been powerless to enclose me had it not been by means of enchantment. But having since freed myself from there, I should like to believe there will be absolutely no other enchantment that can do me harm. However, when those enchanters see they are powerless over my person with their evil arts, they attack those things I hold most dear, attempting to take away my life by taking away that of Dulcinea, in whom I have my being. Therefore, it is my belief that when my squire delivered my message to her, they transformed her into a peasant girl occupied with an activity as lowly as that of winnowing wheat; but I have already said the wheat was neither wheat nor red but beads of Oriental pearls. As proof of this, when I recently traveled through Toboso, I was unable to locate Dulcinea's palace the day after my squire Sancho had seen her in her original form, which is the most beautiful on this earth, for she appeared to me as a coarse, ugly farm girl who could barely speak rationally, though she is the height of intelligence. And since it stands to reason that I *am* not and never again shall be enchanted, it is she who is enchanted, wronged, changed, altered, and transformed, my adversaries having taken revenge upon the one for whom I shall shed eternal tears until such time that I view her in her pristine state. I mention all this so no one will ascribe undue importance to what Sancho has said about Dulcinea's sifting and winnowing wheat. And since they transformed her for me, is it any wonder that they should also change her for him? Dulcinea is illustrious and highborn, and among the noble lineages found in Toboso, which are numerous, ancient, and very solid ones, a goodly portion of them will surely fall to the peerless Dulcinea, because of whom her village will enjoy fame and renown in the coming centuries, as Troy did because of Helen, and Spain because of La Cava, though Dulcinea's will be more famous and possess better credentials.

"In this same vein, I would have your lordships understand that Sancho Panza is one of the most delightful squires ever to serve a knight-errant. At times he is so shrewdly innocent that trying to decide whether he is naive or cunning affords me no little satisfaction. He has a mischievous side that marks him as a rogue, and a lack of concern that confirms him as an idiot. He doubts everything and, yet, believes anything; and just when I think he is about to plunge headlong into something stupid, he comes up with some brilliant idea that sets him apart. When all is said and done, I would not trade him for any other squire, even if a city were included in the bargain, but at the same time I have my doubts as to whether it will be wise to place him in charge of the government your excellency has given him. On the other hand, I do detect in him a certain aptitude for governing, and with a little adjustment to his thinking, he could manage some government as well as the king does his taxes, particularly when we know from long experience that very little ability or learning is necessary for one to be governor. Why, there are a hundred out there who can barely read and write and yet they govern superbly. The key to success lies in having good intentions and always striving to do what is right, for there will never be a shortage of persons to advise one and indicate the direction he should take, like those governors who are unlettered gentlemen and issue their pronouncements through some assessor. I would advise him not to take bribes but to take what is his, together with other matters I have in my craw, which will emerge in due time for the profit of Sancho and the benefit of the island he is to govern."

The ducal pair and Don Quixote had arrived at this point in their conversation when they heard shouting and a great commotion in the palace. Sancho suddenly ran into the hall in a state of panic, wearing a straining cloth as a bib and being pursued by several young men, or more precisely, ruffians and other menials from the kitchen, one of whom carried a dish trough filled with water which by its filthy color showed it was dishwater. The servant was chasing Sancho, doing his best to catch him so he could stick the trough under his chin, while another urchin was apparently intent upon scrubbing him.

"What is this all about, lads?" asked the duchess; "what is going on? And what is it you are trying to do to this good man? Have you no consideration for a governor-elect?"

To which the scampish barber responded,

"This gentleman refuses to let us give his face the customary bathing despite the fact that my lord the duke and his lordship the knight have allowed us to bathe theirs."

"I am willing," said Sancho quite angrily, "but I'd like it to be with cleaner towels, whiter soap, and less filthy hands. After all, there's not so great a difference between me and my master that they should wash him in water fit for angels and me in that fit for devils. The customs of a country or a noble's palace are good only to the extent that they are not offensive, and this particular custom of bathing is worse than being a penitent. My beard is clean and has no need of this type of freshening up and anyone who attempts to wash me or touch a hair on my head, or rather my chin – with all due respect to your graces – I'll give such a punch that my fist will remain embedded in his skull, for such ceremonies and soapings as these are more akin to ridicule than to consideration for one's guests."

The duchess was overcome with laughter at the sight of Sancho's rage and the tenor of his protests but Don Quixote was not at all pleased to see him ridiculously dressed in the filthy towel and surrounded by so many urchins from the kitchen. And so, bowing low to the duke and duchess as though he were seeking their permission to speak, he addressed the rabble solemnly:

"Hold on there, good sirs, you shall leave the lad and go back to where you came from or to any place you please! My squire is as clean as anyone; besides, those troughs are too narrow for him, being no more serviceable than drinking cups. You shall heed my advice and leave him alone because he and I are not amused by these practical jokes."

Sancho took up the conversation right where his master left off and said,

"Just let them try to play a joke on this country boy and, as sure as it's night, I'll not put up with such nonsense! Let them take their comb, or whatever they please, and curry these whiskers, and if they find anything here that offends their idea of cleanliness, they may shave an X on my head."

At this point, the duchess, who was still laughing, said,

"Sancho Panza is right in everything he has said or ever shall say. He is clean and, as he has said, has no need of bathing. If our customs do not agree with him, he is free to do as he pleases, particularly when you ministers of cleanliness have been overly remiss and careless – dare I say insolent – in employing upon such a personage and such a chin, not basins and pitchers of pure gold and imported towels, but wooden troughs and dishcloths from the kitchen. The truth is that you are evil and ill bred and, being the mischief-makers that you are, cannot help showing the envy you bear squires of knights-errant."

Inasmuch as the roguish servants and even the majordomo, who had come with them, understood the duchess was serious about what she had said, they removed the cloth from Sancho's neck and went away flustered and embarrassed, leaving him there while they withdrew to the kitchen. When he saw himself free from what for him had been a most perilous situation, he went over to the duchess and knelt at her feet, saying,

"From great ladies great bounties are to be expected. The one your grace has bestowed upon me today can be repaid with nothing less than my determination to see myself knighted so I may devote the remainder of my life to serving such an exalted lady. I happen to be a farmer, my name is Sancho Panza, I am a married man with children and serve as a squire; and so, if I may serve in any of these capacities, I will do so in less time than it takes your grace to command me."

"It is easy to see, Sancho," said the duchess, "that you have studied courtesy in the school of courtesy itself, or should I say that you have obviously nursed at the bosom of his lord Don Quixote, who is certainly the height of politeness and a model of behavior. God bless such a master and such a servant – one for being the pole star of knight-errantry and the other the star of squirely fidelity. Arise, Sancho my friend, and I shall reward your good breeding by making my lord the duke grant you as quickly as possible the government he has promised you."

Here their conversation concluded and Don Quixote went off to take a nap during the hours of siesta. The duchess asked Sancho to spend the afternoon with her and her ladies in a refreshingly cool chamber, provided he felt no strong urge to take a nap. Sancho replied that, though it was actually his custom to nap for four or five hours during the summer siesta, he would try with all his might, in order to obey her ladyship and comply with her command, not to sleep a single hour that day; and after saying this, he left. The duke gave additional instructions for the way Don Quixote was to be treated so as not to stray one iota from the manner in which people in the days of yore dealt with knights-errant.

Chapter Thirty-Three

The delightful discussion that the duchess and her handmaidens held with Sancho Panza, which is well worth reading and noting

Our history relates that Sancho kept his promise to forego the siesta and rejoined the duchess as soon as he finished eating. Because she was eager to engage him in conversation, she asked him to sit next to her on a stool, though Sancho out of sheer good breeding preferred to remain standing. The duchess, however, insisted that he sit down as governor but speak as squire, for in both respects he deserved the very throne of the hero Cid Ruy Díaz Campeador. Sancho shrugged his shoulders and obeyed by taking his seat, whereupon all the duchess' maids and duennas gathered round him and maintained absolute silence in their eagerness to hear what he had to say. The duchess, however, was the first to speak, saying,

"Now that we are alone and no one can hear us, I should like his honor the governor to resolve certain doubts of mine that have been raised by the history published about the great Don Quixote, one of which is that, since our noble Sancho never saw Dulcinea – the lady Dulcinea of Toboso, that is – and never gave her the letter from his master Don Quixote because it had been left behind in the Sierra Morena in the memorandum book, how is it that he had the nerve to concoct that answer of hers, as well as that business of her winnowing wheat, all of which was a sham and a fabrication quite detrimental to the good name of the peerless Dulcinea and no less ill-becoming the character of a good and faithful squire?"

In response to these words but without uttering any of his own, Sancho rose from his seat and with hushed steps, his body bent, and his finger resting on his lips, walked the entire length of the hall peering behind the tapestries. Once this was accomplished, he returned to his seat and said,

"Well, my lady, now that I have seen that no one can hear us other than the present company, I will without fear or dread respond to what I have been asked and may be asked later. The first thing I'll say is that I take my master Don Quixote to be an out-and-out madman, though he does say things sometimes that in the opinion of me and everyone who happens to hear him are so wise and directed along such a straight course that Satan himself couldn't express them better. But despite this, I've become thoroughly convinced he's a crackpot, and since this is how I view the situation, I throw caution to the wind and make him believe the most outlandish and ridiculous things, such as that business of the answer to the letter, or the thing that happened some six or seven days ago which has not yet found its way into the history, namely, the question of my lady Dulcinea's enchantment. I've given him to understand that she's enchanted, which is as far-fetched as it is untrue."

The duchess asked him to describe that make-believe enchantment and Sancho related the entire story exactly as it had taken place, which provided his audience with no little enjoyment. Then the duchess, continuing her line of questioning, said,

"From what our good Sancho has told me, there is a certain doubt gnawing at my soul and whispering in my ear, a doubt that says, 'Since Don Quixote of La Mancha is a madman, a simpleton, and a fool, and Sancho Panza his squire is aware of this but continues to follow and serve him, blindly believing his empty promises, it stands to reason that Sancho must be a bigger fool and madman than his master, and this being the case, people will speak ill of you, Madam Duchess, if you give this Sancho Panza an island to govern, for if a person cannot govern himself, how can he govern others?'"

"Goodness, my lady," replied Sancho, "that doubt is exactly what I would have expected and I hope your grace will instruct it to speak freely or any way it pleases, for I realize it's speaking the truth. Why, if I had any sense, I would have left my master days ago, but such has been my fate and ill-fortune that I have no choice but to go with him. He and I are from the same village, I've shared his bread, I love him, and he has shown his appreciation of me by giving me several of his colts, but above all I'm so loyal that nothing will ever come between us except the pick and the shovel. However, if your highness decides I'm not to be given the promised governorship, I came into this world with even less, and who knows: my not receiving it may redound to the benefit of my conscience. I may be dense but I understand the meaning of the proverb: 'Pride goeth before a fall.' Besides, it may turn out that Sancho the squire will get to heaven before Sancho the governor. 'Here they bake just as good bread as in France,' 'At night all cats are black,' and 'It's an unfortunate person who has still not broken his fast by two in the afternoon.' 'One person's stomach is not a hand-span bigger than another's,' because they can both be filled, as the saying goes, with hay and straw. Why, even 'the birds of the field have God as their provider and sustainer,' and 'Four yards of the coarsest wool provide more warmth than four of fine linen.' And 'When we leave this world and are buried beneath the earth, the road of the prince is just as narrow as that of the laborer,' and 'The body of the pope occupies no more ground than that of the sexton,' though one is more exalted than the other; for when we enter the grave, we all draw up and make ourselves fit, or others will make us draw up and fit whether we want to or not – and then it's 'good night.' I say once more that if your ladyship is unwilling to give me the island because I'm dumb, I'm smart enough not to let it worry me in the least. I've heard it said that 'Behind the cross lurks the Devil' and 'All that glitters is not gold.' Moreover, they took the farmer Wamba from his oxen, plows, and yokes to make him king of Spain, whereas they took Rodrigo from his brocades, amusements, and wealth to be devoured by serpents, if the verses of the ancient ballads can be believed."

"If they can be believed!" exclaimed Doña Rodríguez the duenna, who was among those present. "There is a ballad that says they put King Rodrigo alive and kicking into a tomb filled with toads, snakes, and lizards, and two days later the king cried out from inside the tomb in a pained and feeble voice,

'They're eating up my body now,
Especially my sinful parts;'

and judging by this, our gentleman here is perfectly correct in saying he would rather be a farmer than a king if vermin are going to devour him."

The duchess could hardly contain her laughter when she observed her duenna's naiveté, nor did she fail to be astounded by the utterances and proverbs of Sancho, to whom she said,

"Noble Sancho already knows that once a knight has given his word, he will make every effort to keep it even if it costs him his life. The duke, my husband and master, though not a member of the errant variety, is still a knight for all that and will keep his pledge of the promised island in the face of all the envy and malice on earth. So let Sancho be of good cheer, for when he least expects it, he will see himself seated on the throne of his island and domain and will lay claim to his government, which he will not exchange for one made of brocade three layers thick. But I would charge him to exercise great care in governing his vassals, bearing in mind that they are all loyal, highborn subjects."

"As for the matter of governing well," said Sancho, "there is no need to remind me of that, for I am charitable by nature and have compassion for the poor. 'No one should steal bread from the one who kneaded and baked it,' and as God is my witness, no one will dare play with loaded dice when I'm around. 'I'm an old dog and know all the tricks' and can prick up my ears when I have to. No one is going to 'pull the wool over my eyes,' for 'I know where the shoe pinches.' I bring all this up to show that those who are good will have influence and favor with me but those who are evil won't get their foot in the door. It strikes me that in this business of governing the hardest thing is getting started, and it may turn out that after a couple of weeks I'll be so taken with the job I'll know more about it than about work in the fields, which is what I've grown up with."

"You are right, Sancho," said the duchess; "no one comes into this world educated, for bishops are made from men, not from stones. But to return to what we were discussing a moment ago about the lady Dulcinea's enchantment, I consider it an established fact that Sancho's idea of deceiving his master and making him believe the farm girl was Dulcinea – and if his master did not recognize her, it must have been due to her enchantment – was all a fabrication of one of the enchanters who persecute his lord Don Quixote, for I have it on absolutely good authority that the country girl who bounded onto the jackass' back was and is Dulcinea of Toboso and that our good Sancho, believing himself the deceiver, was in fact the deceived, and there is no reason to doubt this any more than those things we have never seen. Master Sancho Panza should know that we too have enchanters here who favor us and keep us informed of all that goes on in the world, purely and simply, without trickery or deception. Sancho may rest assured that the agile farm girl was and is Dulcinea of Toboso, who is as enchanted as she can possibly be, and whom, when we least expect it, we shall see as she actually is. At that time Sancho will be rid of the misconception under which he is laboring."

"All that may actually be true," said Sancho Panza, "wherefore I am inclined to believe what my master told me he witnessed in the Cave of Montesinos, in which he claims to have seen the lady Dulcinea wearing the same clothes I said I had seen her wearing when I enchanted her – which I did simply because I felt like it. But everything must be just the opposite, as your grace says, for it cannot and should not be presumed that I in my feeble mind could come up with such a clever deception on the spur of the moment, nor do I believe my master is crazy enough to allow any persuasiveness as weak and feeble as mine to convince him of anything so completely far-fetched. Still, my lady, it would not be right for your excellency to consider me wicked because of this, for a dullard like myself can't be expected to penetrate the evil minds of those abominable enchanters. I invented all that to avoid a fight with my master Don Quixote, not with the idea of hurting him; and if everything has turned out just the opposite, our hearts will be judged by God, who is in His heaven."

"That is certainly true," said the duchess, "but may we know what Sancho has to say about the Cave of Montesinos? I should like to know."

Sancho Panza then related point by point what has already been described about the adventure in question. After listening to his story, the duchess said,

"From these details it is possible to conclude that since the great Don Quixote says he saw the same farm girl there that Sancho saw on the outskirts of Toboso, she is no doubt Dulcinea; besides, the enchanters in these parts are quite clever and more than a little diligent."

"My thoughts exactly," said Sancho Panza, "and if my lady Dulcinea of Toboso is enchanted, that is her hard luck. I'll not pick a fight with my master's enemies, who must be both evil and plentiful. I swear that the girl I saw was a farm girl and a farm girl is what I judged and believed her to be, but if that was Dulcinea, I shouldn't be held responsible for it or have it laid to my account. Just let them try pinning the blame on me at every turn with 'Sancho said it; Sancho did it; Sancho this and Sancho that,' as if Sancho were some nobody instead of that very Sancho Panza who's now making his way through the world in books, according to what I've been told by Sansón Carrasco, who at least has a bachelor's degree from Salamanca. Such a person never lies except when he feels like it or it's to his advantage, so there's no reason for any person to pick a fight with me. I enjoy a good reputation, and since I've heard my master say that a good name is more valuable than great wealth, let them clap me in that government and they'll witness marvels, for anyone who's been a good squire will be a good governor."

"Everything our noble Sancho has said here," replied the duchess, "is Catonian wisdom, or at least wisdom drawn from the very soul of Michael Verino himself, *florentibus occidit annis.*[1] In other words, as Sancho himself might say, 'Beneath a shabby cloak there's often an elegant toper."

1 Latin: 'who died in the flower of youth.'

"Truthfully, my lady," said Sancho, "I've never drunk out of wickedness – out of thirst maybe – and, since I'm not the least bit hypocritical, I do take a drink when I feel like it or even when I don't, or when they offer me one so as not to appear strait-laced or ill-mannered, for in a toast from a friend, who can be so hard-hearted as not to return the toast? I may like to tip the bottle but I can certainly hold my liquor. Besides, squires of knights-errant almost always drink water because they're forever traveling through woods, forests, meadows, mountains, and crags, where they couldn't get a blessed drop of wine if they were willing to swap one of their eyes for it."

"I am of the same opinion," said the duchess, "but right now Sancho should go rest. Later we shall converse at greater length and make hasty arrangements for them to 'clap him in that government,' to use his phrase."

Once again Sancho kissed the duchess' hand, imploring her to be so kind as to take good care of his dapple because he was the apple of his eye.

"What dapple is that?" asked the duchess.

"My jackass," said Sancho, "but so as not to refer to him by that name, I usually call him my dapple. When I entered this castle, I asked this duenna here to take care of him for me but she got so upset one would've thought I had told her she was ugly or old. It simply must be more appropriate and natural for duennas to feed the animals than to stroll about gracing the halls. Oh my, but there was a noble in my village who really had it in for those ladies!"

"He must have been a peasant," said the duenna Doña Rodríguez; "if he had been a noble from a good family, he would have exalted us to the heavens."

"All right," said the duchess, "that is enough. I want Doña Rodríguez to say no more and Master Panza to remain calm. The care of the dapple may be left in my hands and, since he is Sancho's pride and joy, I shall clasp him to my bosom."

"I'll settle for his being in the stable," said Sancho, "since neither of us is worthy of being clasped to your excellency's bosom for a single second. I would as soon stab myself as consent to that, for though my master says that in the game of politeness it's better to lose by a card too many than by a card too few, in matters of asses and donkeys one should proceed with restraint and moderation."

"Sancho may take him along to his government," said the duchess, "and provide for him as he sees fit, even turning him out to pasture."

"Madam Duchess," said Sancho, "your grace needn't think that's an exaggeration, for I've seen more than a couple of jackasses in government, so for me to take mine along would be nothing new."

Sancho's comments once again made the duchess laugh with delight. After sending him off to rest, she went to give the duke an account of what had transpired between them, at which point the two of them contrived a scheme for playing a joke on Don Quixote that would be first-rate and in a style appropriate to knight-errantry. In fact, they played several on him, all so clever and so made-to-order that they constitute the best episodes contained in this great history.

Chapter Thirty-Four

The account of the instructions set down for removing the encantation from the peerless Dulcinea of Toboso, being one of the most remarkable adventures in this entire history

So pleasurable was the duke and duchess' conversation with Don Quixote and Sancho Panza that they reaffirmed their intention of playing several pranks on them that would have the look and appearance of adventures. Basing their scheme on Don Quixote's experience in the Cave of Montesinos, which he had already described to them, they came up with one that would be memorable. What the duchess found most astounding, though, was Sancho's gullibility, which was so great he had come to accept as an incontrovertible fact that Dulcinea of Toboso was enchanted, when he himself had been the enchanter and deceiver in that affair. And so some six days later, after explaining to their servants everything they were to do, they took Don Quixote and Sancho on a hunting trip with an assemblage of hunters and beaters that would have done justice to an actual king. They provided Don Quixote with a hunting outfit and Sancho with one made from the finest green cloth. Don Quixote refused to wear his, saying that the following day he would be returning to the rigorous pursuit of arms and, therefore, could not encumber himself with wardrobes and other paraphernalia. But Sancho gladly accepted the one offered him, for he intended to sell it at his earliest opportunity.

Once the anticipated day arrived, Don Quixote donned his armor and rode forth to join the hunting party, accompanied by Sancho dressed in his new outfit and mounted on his dapple, whom he refused to relinquish even though they had offered him a horse. The duchess arrived in her most elegant attire and Don Quixote out of sheer politeness and gallantry led her palfrey by the reins over the protests of the duke. At length, they arrived at a grove situated between two rather lofty mountain peaks where, after they had stationed themselves in the blinds located along the paths and the beaters had spread out in different directions, the hunt commenced with such shouting and yelling that it was impossible for them to hear one another, what with the barking hounds and the blaring horns.

The duchess dismounted holding a sharpened spear in her hands and took up her position at a spot where she knew wild boars were likely to pass. The duke and Don Quixote likewise dismounted and took up their places on either side of her. Sancho stationed himself behind everyone else without dismounting from the dapple, whom he dared not leave unprotected lest he suffer some mishap. No sooner had they taken up their positions alongside a number of their servants than a giant boar that had been flushed out by the hounds and the pursuing beaters came towards them gnashing its teeth and spewing foam from its mouth. The instant that Don Quixote saw it, he strapped on his buckler, drew his sword, and went forth to confront it, with the duke doing the same with his spear, but the duchess would have gotten the jump on both of them had the duke not restrained her. Only Sancho, when he saw the fierce animal, abandoned the dapple and began to run as fast as he could towards a tall oak he intended to climb. However, he met with difficulty in doing so, for when he had climbed only halfway up the tree, he grabbed a limb in an attempt to reach the top but, owing to his bad luck and ill-fortune, the limb snapped off and in the course of his fall he became snagged on the stub end of a limb and was left dangling in midair unable to reach the ground. When he found himself in this predicament and saw his green outfit beginning to tear, he had no doubt the wild beast would be able to reach him if it ran in his direction. He thus began to shout and plead for help with such insistence that everyone who could hear him (though he was out of sight) imagined him to be in the jaws of some wild beast. Once the tusked boar had finally been transfixed by the numerous spear points confronting it, Don Quixote turned in the direction of Sancho, whom he had recognized by his shouts. He found him hanging upside down from the tree with the dapple beside him, who had not abandoned him in his adversity. (Cide Hamete says that he seldom saw Sancho without the dapple, or the dapple without Sancho, such were the friendship and loyalty each felt for the other.)

Don Quixote came up and unfastened Sancho, who, once finding himself free and firmly on the ground, looked at his shredded hunting outfit and was heartsick, for he believed that in that garment he had possessed a gold mine. Meanwhile, they had slung the mighty carcass across a mule and, after covering it with rosemary sprigs and myrtle branches, carried it as a token of the victory spoils to a group of large field tents that had been erected in the middle of the forest. There they found the tables set and the meal served in such a grand and sumptuous style that it was easy to discern the quality and magnificence of the person providing it. Sancho showed the duchess the rips in his torn outfit and said to her,

"If this hunt had been for hares or small birds, my coat would definitely not find itself in this sad state. I don't understand what pleasure anyone can derive from lying in wait for an animal which, if it pierces him with one of its tusks, can take his life. I remember hearing them sing an old ballad that said:

> May Fávila's fate be thine,
> And make thee food for bears or swine."

"He was a Gothic king," said Don Quixote, "who was devoured by a bear while on a hunting trip."

"That's what I'm talking about," replied Sancho. "I wish nobles and kings wouldn't expose themselves to this kind of danger for the sake of a pleasure which, to my mind, has no right to be one, since it involves killing an animal that has done no harm to anyone."

"That is where you are mistaken," said the duke, "for the exercise of woodland hunting is more fitting and necessary for kings and nobles than for anyone else. Hunting is an imitation of war in that it involves strategy, planning, and ploys that one must utilize to conquer one's enemy without endangering himself. In it one suffers extreme cold and intolerable heat; leisure and sleep are in short supply; one's strength is increased; the limbs of the practitioner are made supple; and, lastly, it is an exercise that will cause harm to no one but will provide pleasure for many. But best of all, it is not for everyone as other types of hunting are, with the exception of falconry, which is likewise reserved for kings and great lords. And so, Sancho, revise your thinking and when you are governor, devote yourself to hunting and you will find yourself a better man for having done so."

"That is not true," said Sancho, "for a good governor and a broken leg should both stay at home. It would be a fine thing indeed if some weary soul came looking for me on business and I was out hunting! The government wouldn't run at all that way! Upon my word, hunting and recreation are more fitting for men of leisure than for governors. I intend to pass the time playing cards on Easter and bowling on Sundays and holidays because hunting and killing don't go with my character or sit well with my conscience."

"Pray to God, Sancho, that it will turn out thus, for 'There's many a slip twixt the cup and the lip.'"

"Be that as it may," said Sancho, "'An honest man's word is as good as a bond,' and 'God's help is better than rising early;' besides, 'The stomach sustains the legs, not the legs the stomach.' By this I mean that if God helps me and I perform my duties with good intentions, I'll undoubtedly govern superbly. Just let them stick a finger in my mouth and they'll see whether I bite it or not!"

"May God and all the saints curse you, you confounded rascal!" exclaimed Don Quixote. "Will the day never come, as I have often said, when I hear you speak one plain, ordinary sentence without some proverb in it? My lord and lady, I would have nothing to do with this fool, for your excellencies will find your souls ground between, not two, but two thousand proverbs, and if these are ever opportune or timely, may God grant him health – and me too if I am crazy enough to listen to him."

"Sancho Panza's proverbs," said the duchess, "though more numerous than those of the Greek commander, [1] are not for that reason less worthy of esteem owing to the conciseness of their expression. As for myself, I must say I find them more enjoyable than others that may be more appropriate or more timely in their application."

After discussing these and other pleasant matters, they left the tent and entered the forest, where they spent the day visiting various blinds and stations until they were overtaken by night, a night that was not as clear and calm as one might have expected at that season of the year, it being midsummer. However, the accompanying haze was a great aid to the duke and duchess' plan. Thus, as the sky began to grow dark but just before dusk, the entire forest suddenly seemed ablaze in all four directions, at which time there was heard from one direction and another an endless number of trumpets and other instruments of war, as if several cavalry battalions were marching through the forest. The light from the fire and the sound of the martial instruments virtually blinded the eyes and deafened the ears of the participants and, indeed, of everyone in the forest. Next was heard an endless succession of battle-cries in the fashion of Moors when they enter battle: there was the blare of trumpets and clarions, the beating of drums, and the echo of fifes, all simultaneous and so continuous and rapid that anyone in his right mind might have gone mad from the overpowering sound of all those instruments. The duke was dumbfounded, the duchess astonished, Don Quixote surprised, and Sancho Panza was beginning to tremble; in fact, even those who were aware of the

1 Hernán Núñez de Guzmán, who collected some 3000 Spanish proverbs in a work published posthumously in Salamanca in 1555.

cause were frightened. Everyone there remained silent out of fear when suddenly a postilion dressed as a demon passed before them blowing, not a trumpet, but a gigantic hollow horn that emitted a harsh, frightening sound.

"I say there, brother courier," shouted the duke, "who are you, where are you headed, and what warriors are those who, it would appear, are passing through this forest?"

To which the courier answered in a harsh and horrifying voice,

"I am a devil come in quest of Don Quixote of La Mancha, and the approaching throng are members of some half dozen bands of enchanters who are transporting the peerless Dulcinea of Toboso on a triumphal cart. She has come here enchanted, together with the gallant Frenchman Montesinos, who will give Don Quixote instructions for disenchanting his lady."

"If you were a devil," said the duke, "as you claim and your appearance indicates, you would already have recognized this knight you seek, Don Quixote of La Mancha, whom you see here before you."

"I swear by God and my conscience," said the devil, "I was not paying attention, for I had my mind on so many distracting matters I was forgetting the main thing that brought me here."

"Undoubtedly," said Sancho, "this devil must be a good man and a Christian. If he weren't, he wouldn't base his oath upon God and his conscience. I am now convinced that there must be good persons even in hell."

At this point, the devil, without dismounting, directed his gaze at Don Quixote and said,

"To you, O Knight of the Lions (and would that I might see you in their clutches) I have been sent here by the unfortunate but valiant knight Montesinos, who has commanded me to announce on his behalf that you are to wait for him in this very spot where I have found you, as he is bringing with him the one they call Dulcinea of Toboso, that he may tell you what is needed for removing her spell. And since this is all I have come to report, I shall not prolong my stay. May demons such as myself accompany you, and blessed angels this lord and lady."

Having said this, he gave a blast on his giant horn, wheeled about, and left without waiting for anyone to reply. Everyone's amazement was rekindled, Sancho's and Don Quixote's in particular: Sancho's because he saw that, in the face of the truth, they were determined that Dulcinea was to be enchanted, and Don Quixote's because of his failure to assure himself that what had happened in the Cave of Montesinos was real. And while the knight was absorbed in these thoughts, the duke said to him,

"Sir Don Quixote, does your grace intend to wait?"

"Should I not?" replied Don Quixote; "I shall wait here stouthearted and firm even if all hell should rise up against me."

"Well, if I see another devil or hear another horn like the last one," said Sancho, "I'll no more stay here than I'll go to Flanders."

By this time the evening sky was growing darker and a number of lights were beginning to flicker in the forest, just as the dry exhalations of the earth flicker in the heavens, which appear to us to be shooting stars. At the same time a terrifying sound was heard like that made by the massive wheels normally found on oxcarts, the harsh and interminable creaking of which is said to drive away wolves and bears should any be in the immediate vicinity. And if all this furor was not sufficient, the mayhem increased still further when fighting and battles seemed to break out in all four directions of the forest simultaneously. In the distance were heard the terrifying sounds of artillery, over here the uninterrupted volleys of muskets, nearby the shouts of the combatants, and far off the endless Mohammedan battle-cries; in a word, the bugles, horns, clarions, trumpets, drums, cannons, muskets, and, above all, the frightening noise of the carts, produced such a jumble of terrifying sounds that it was necessary for Don Quixote to summon up all his courage to endure it. Sancho's courage, however, came to nought, causing him to collapse in a faint on top of the duchess' skirt, where he was allowed to remain while they brought water with which to dowse his face. Once this was done, he regained his senses just as the cart with the screeching wheels pulled up before them. It was drawn by four lumbering oxen encased in black trappings and bearing blazing wax torches tied to their horns. Atop the cart, on an elevated seat, sat a venerable old man wearing a long black buckram robe with a beard that was whiter than snow and so long it fell below his waist. Because the cart was outfitted with a multitude of lights, it was easy to discern everything on it. The cart was driven by two hideous demons clad in the same black buckram, whose faces were so ugly that when Sancho saw them, he closed his eyes to avoid having to look at them again. Once the cart pulled up alongside them, the aged man rose from his elevated seat and, standing erect, said in a loud voice,

"I am the sage Lirgandeo."

The cart then moved on without another word's being spoken. Behind this cart came another of the same construction bearing another aged man on a throne. Motioning for the cart to stop, he said in a voice that was no less solemn than that of the first man,

"I am the sage Alquife, the great friend of Urganda the Unknown."

And he too moved on. Just then, there arrived a third cart moving at the same pace, but seated on its throne was a man not like the others but husky, robust, and evil looking, who, upon arriving, stood up like the others and said in a voice that was hoarser and more diabolical,

"I am Arcalaus the Enchanter, the mortal enemy of Amadís of Gaul and all his kin."

He too moved on and all three carts drew to a halt a short distance away, at which point the annoying creaking of the wheels ceased. Soon afterwards, there was heard, not another noise, but the sound of soft, melodic music, which delighted Sancho because he took it as a good omen, and so, turning to the duchess from whose side he dared not stray for a single second, he said,

"Madam, where there is music nothing bad can occur."

"Nor where there is brightness and light," said the duchess; to which Sancho responded,

"Yes, but since fire produces light, and bonfires brightness, as we can see by those around us, we may possibly get burned, whereas music is always a sign of merriment and festivities."

"That remains to be seen," said Don Quixote, who had been listening to all this, and herein he spoke the truth, as will be seen in the following chapter.

Chapter Thirty-Five

The continuation of the instructions Don Quixote received for disenchanting Dulcinea, together with other astounding adventures

To the accompaniment of this pleasant music, they saw coming towards them one of those conveyances called triumphal carts. It was drawn by six gray mules with white trappings, each of which was surmounted by a penitent also clad in white and holding a large wax torch. This cart was two or even three times as large as the previous ones and its top and sides held a dozen additional penitents as white as snow and all holding blazing torches in their hands, a sight that inspired wonder and dread alike. Seated on an elevated throne was a nymph wearing a thousand silvery gauze veils that were flecked throughout with glittering gold sequins, giving her attire the appearance, if not of opulence, at least of gaudiness. Her face was covered by a veil of such delicacy and transparency that its texture, rather than prohibiting, permitted one to view the face of a most beautiful maiden, and the numerous lights provided the opportunity for discerning that beauty. She appeared to be no younger than seventeen nor older than nineteen. Next to her sat a figure clad in one of those full-length robes and a black veil that covered his head. When the cart drew alongside their excellencies and Don Quixote, the music produced by the cart's hornpipes, harps, and lutes ceased and at that moment the robed figure stood up, flung open its garment, and removed the veil from its head, revealing in no uncertain terms the figure of Death itself, whose cadaverous and hideous appearance troubled Don Quixote, frightened Sancho, and caused the duke and duchess to exhibit no little uneasiness. Once having risen to its feet, this living Death in a voice that was somnambulant and thick-tongued began to speak in the following manner:

"Merlin am I, misnamed the Devil's son
In lying annals, authorized by time;
Monarch supreme, and great depository
Of magic art and Zoroastric skill;
Rival of envious ages, that would hide
The glorious deeds of errant cavaliers,
Favored by me and my peculiar charge.
Though vile enchanters, still on mischief bent,
To plague mankind their baleful art employ,
Merlin's soft nature, ever prone to good,
His power inclines to bless the human race.

In Hades' chambers, where my busied ghost
Was forming spells and mystic characters,
Dulcinea's voice, peerless Tobosan maid,
With mournful accents reached my pitying ears;

I knew her woe, her metamorphosed form
From high-born beauty in a palace graced,
To the loathéd features of a cottage wench.
With Sympathizing grief I searched through all
The numerous tomes of my detested art,
And in the hollow of this skeleton
My soul enclosing, hither am I come,
To tell the cure of such uncommon ills.

O glory thou of all who case their limbs
In polished steel and fenceful adamant!
Light, beacon, polar star, and glorious guide
Of all who, rising from the lazy down,
Banish ignoble sleep for the rude toil
And hardy exercise of errant arms!
Spain's boasted pride, La Mancha's matchless knight,
Whose valiant deeds outstrip pursuing fame!
Wouldst thou to beauty's pristine state restore
Th'enchanted dame, Sancho, thy faithful squire,
Must to his ample buttocks, bare exposed,
Three thousand and three hundred lashes ply,
Such as may sting and give him smarting pain:
The authors of her change have thus decreed,
And this is Merlin's message from the shades."

"For the love of God!" cried Sancho at this point, "I'd just as soon give myself three slashes with a knife as three blows with a whip, let alone three thousand! The Devil can have that kind of disenchanting! I don't know what my backside has to do with enchantments! For heaven's sake, if Lord Merlin hasn't found some better way to remove the enchantment from the lady Dulcinea of Toboso, she can go to her grave enchanted."

To which Don Quixote said,

"I will take you, you garlic-stuffed hayseed, and tie you to a tree as naked as the day your mother bore you and will give you not three thousand three hundred lashes but six thousand six hundred, which I will impress so indelibly on that hide of yours that rubbing them three thousand three hundred times will not rid you of them. Now, don't say another word to me or I will rip out your heart!"

When Merlin heard this, he said,

"This is not the way to proceed, for the lashes noble Sancho is to receive must be received voluntarily, not forcibly, and at whatever time he chooses. He shall not be given any set time but shall even be permitted, should he wish to reduce in half this irksome business of flogging, to allow himself to be flogged by someone else, though that person may be somewhat heavy-handed."

"I'll not be flogged by myself or by anyone else!" said Sancho. "No one is going to touch me, whether he's heavy-handed or not! Did I somehow bring Dulcinea of Toboso into this world so my rump could pay for the sins of her eyes? My lord and master could and should flog himself on her behalf and undertake anything necessary to remove her spell, for she's his support and prop and he's forever calling her 'my sweet' and 'my darling.' But for me to flog myself – never! This I mathematize."

No sooner had Sancho finished saying this than the sequined nymph seated beside the ghost of Merlin stood up and removed her diaphanous veil, revealing a face that struck everyone as far too beautiful. Then with the mannerisms of a man and a voice that was not overly feminine, she addressed Sancho Panza directly, saying,

"O wretched squire, you callous and hardened soul, you heart of stone, you compassionless creature, if we were ordering you, you thieving scalawag, to hurl yourself from some lofty tower: if you were being asked, you enemy of the human race, to eat a dozen toads, two dozen lizards, and three dozen snakes: if you were being ordered to slay your wife and children with some infidel's razor-sharp scimitar, it would not be surprising for you to be a bit reluctant and unwilling, but to balk at a mere three thousand three hundred lashes – since the puniest child in the orphanage schools receives that many each month – astounds, dumbfounds, and shocks the compassionate hearts of all those who hear it and even those who will learn of it with the passage of time. Cast your eyes, you miserable, hardened caitiff; cast, I say, those lily-livered eyes of yours upon these pupils of mine, which have been compared to radiant stars, and you will observe them weeping floods and torrents of tears that cut furrows and paths through the lovely fields that are these cheeks. May you be moved, you sly, perverse monster, by the fact that I am in the very flower of youth, since I am not yet twenty but am still in my teens, nineteen to be exact, and my youth is fading and wasting away under the exterior of a rustic farm girl. If I do not exhibit that appearance at this moment, it is due to the special favor I have been shown by Lord Merlin here for the sole purpose of softening that heart of yours by means of my beauty, for the tears of a beautiful damsel in distress are capable of turning stones into cotton and wolves into sheep. Flog that hide of yours, you untamed beast; shake off that slothful disposition that inclines you only towards eating and more eating, and set free this smooth flesh, this gentle temperament, this beautiful countenance. If you are not willing to allow yourself to be mollified or dealt with rationally, do so for the sake of that poor knight at your side – your master, that is – whose soul I can see stuck in his throat not six inches from his lips, waiting only for your rigid or yielding reply so as to flee from his body or to remain inside it."

When he heard this, Don Quixote felt of his throat and, turning to the duke, said,

"Good heavens, sir, Dulcinea has spoken the truth; my soul is stuck here in my throat and is the size of the nut on a crossbow."

"What do you say to that, Sancho?" said the duchess.

"I say, my lady, what I've already said: that as for the flogging, I mathematize it."

"You mean 'anathematize,' Sancho," said the duke, "not what you said."

"Please, your excellency," replied Sancho, "I'm in no mood for subtle distinctions or for adding and subtracting letters, because I'm in such a state from thinking of this flogging I'm to be given – or I'm to give myself – that I hardly know what I'm saying or what I'm doing. But I'd like my lady Dulcinea of

Toboso to tell me where she learned to ask for favors, for she comes here asking me to lay open my flesh with a whip and does so by calling me a callous, untamed beast, together with a string of foul names the Devil is welcome to. Does my skin happen to be made of bronze or do I give a fig that she's enchanted? Has she brought me a hamper of clean clothes, shirts, kerchiefs, or socks (which, by the way, I don't wear) to soften me up? No, she has come up with one scurrilous name after another, though she's familiar with the proverbs: 'You can catch more flies with honey than with vinegar,' and 'Kindness is the noblest weapon with which to conquer;' also: 'God is a good worker but He likes to be helped,' and 'One thing owned is better than two things promised.' And my lord and master, who should be patting me on the head and praising me so I'll become putty in his hands, says that if he catches me, he'll tie me to a tree naked and will double the number of lashes I'm due. Besides, these compassionate gentlemen should consider that they're ordering not just a squire to be flogged but a governor, gilding the lily as it were. I wish, confound it, that people would show some civility and learn how to plead and ask for favors, for not all occasions are the same and people are not always in a receptive mood! Here I am overflowing with grief at seeing my torn green coat and they come to ask me to flog myself voluntarily, which I'm as far from doing as of becoming an Indian chief."

"Well, Sancho my friend," said the duke, "the fact is that unless you become softer than a ripe fig, you shall not get your hands on your government. It would be a fine thing indeed for me to send my islanders a cruel governor with a heart of stone who would not be moved by the tears of damsels in distress or the pleas of wise, magisterial, and venerable enchanters and sages! In short, Sancho, either you are to be flogged, even if it is by someone else, or you shall not be governor."

"Sir," replied Sancho, "might I be given a couple of days to consider which I would find more beneficial?"

"Certainly not," said Merlin, "we must decide right here and now what is to become of this business: whether Dulcinea is to return to the Cave of Montesinos in her former state as a farm girl or be transported to the Elysian Fields in her present form, where she will await the completion of the required lashings."

"Listen, noble Sancho," said the duchess, "be of stout heart and show some appreciation for the bread you have received from his lord Don Quixote, whom we should all gratefully serve because of his noble character and lofty ideals of chivalry! Say 'yes,' my son, to this flogging, and everything else can go to blazes. Leave fear to the faint-hearted, for 'Stout heart overcomes misfortune,' as you well know."

Sancho changed the subject by directing himself to Merlin:

"Sir Merlin, will your grace please explain something to me: when that courier devil came here, he gave my master a message from Lord Montesinos ordering him to wait here because he was coming with instructions on how the lady Doña Dulcinea of Toboso was to be disenchanted but up to now we haven't seen Montesinos or anyone who resembles him."

To which Merlin replied,

"That devil, Sancho my friend, is an ignoramus and a consummate scoundrel. I sent him in search of your master, not with a message from Montesinos, but from me, for Montesinos is in his cave waiting for, or rather hoping for, his own disenchantment, the most difficult part of which is yet to come. If he owes you anything or you have some business to settle with him, I shall bring him back and set him down wherever you wish, but for the present, say 'yes' to this penance and rest assured that it will be most beneficial to you: as much for your soul as for your body – for your soul because of the charity with which you will perform it, and for your body because I know you possess such a sanguine disposition that it will do you no harm to have a little blood drawn."

"There certainly are a lot of physicians in this world," said Sancho; "even enchanters want to get in the act. Nevertheless, since everybody tells me so, though I don't see the sense in it, I'll agree to give myself the three thousand three hundred lashes provided I may administer them whenever I wish without any set time or number of days, and I'll try to settle my debt as quickly as possible so the world may enjoy the beauty of the lady Doña Dulcinea of Toboso, who apparently, contrary to everything I have believed, is actually beautiful. Another condition I insist upon is that I not be obliged to draw blood while performing the penance and that even if some of the lashes are more like flicks of the hand, these are to count towards the total. Moreover, if I make a mistake in counting, Lord Merlin, who knows everything, shall be responsible for keeping count and shall advise me if I give myself too many or too few."

"There will be no need to advise you of any excess lashes," said Merlin, "for as soon as the exact number is reached, the lady Dulcinea will at once be freed from her spell and will come in search of noble Sancho out of gratitude and will thank and even reward him for his good deed, so there is no reason to be concerned about too many or too few strokes – and heaven forbid that I should cheat anyone by so much as a hair on his head."

"Well then, I place myself in the hands of the Lord," said Sancho, "and will consent to my ill-fortune, meaning that I'll accept the penance under the conditions set forth."

No sooner had Sancho spoken these last words than the music of the hornpipes resounded and a rash of muskets once more began to fire. Don Quixote grabbed Sancho round the neck and covered his cheeks and forehead with kisses, while the duchess and the duke, together with all those present, displayed signs of extreme satisfaction. The cart now began to move forward and, as the beautiful Dulcinea passed by, she bowed her head to the duke and duchess but made a deep curtsy to Sancho.

By this time, joyful, smiling dawn came on apace, the flowers of the fields raised their heads and stood erect, and the crystalline waters of the brooks murmured among the gray and white pebbles as they made their way, to pay tribute, to the rivers waiting to receive them. The joyful earth, the sunny sky, the pure air, and the unobstructed view, each by itself and all together, gave unequivocal proof that this day, which came treading upon the skirts of dawn, would be calm and bright. The duke and duchess were delighted with the hunt and with having so cleverly and successfully achieved their goal. They returned to their castle, where they intended to proceed with their charade, for as far as they were concerned there was nothing that could have afforded them greater pleasure.

Chapter Thirty-Six

The account of the strange and unimaginable adventure of the duenna in distress, otherwise known as the Countess Trifaldi, together with a letter that Sancho Panza wrote to his wife Teresa Panza

The duke had in his employ a majordomo of a playful and easy-going disposition who was responsible for all the preparations in the preceding adventure: the impersonation of Merlin, the composition of the verses, and the enlisting of a page to impersonate Dulcinea. And now, with the collaboration of his master and mistress he came up with another contrivance that was the strangest and drollest imaginable.

The following day, the duchess asked Sancho if he had begun the flogging ordeal he was to perform for effecting Dulcinea's disenchantment. He said he had and only last night had given himself five lashes. The duchess asked him how he had applied them and he said it had been with his hand.

"That," said the duchess, "is more akin to slapping than to flogging. In my opinion the sage Merlin will not be satisfied with such daintiness. Our noble Sancho must scourge himself with a whip or a rod – something that can be felt – for 'Learning and the rod go hand in hand,' and one will not win the freedom of so great a lady as Dulcinea by such a paltry expenditure. Sancho should remember that works of charity performed feebly and half-heartedly carry no merit and are worthless."

To which Sancho responded,

"If your ladyship will give me a proper whip or switch, I'll flog myself with it so long as it doesn't hurt too much, for I'm advising your grace that I may be from the country but my flesh is more like cotton than hemp, and it doesn't make sense for me to cripple myself for the sake of someone else."

"So be it," said the duchess, "tomorrow I shall give you a whip that will be just right and will accommodate itself to your tender flesh as though it were its own sister."

To which Sancho replied,

"I might inform your highness, mistress of my heart, that I've written a letter to my wife, Teresa Panza, in which I give her an account of everything that has happened to me since I left home. I've got it here in my shirt and all that remains is for me to address it. I would be pleased to have your learnedness read it, as it strikes me as governor-like in its style; that is, it sounds like what a governor ought to write."

"Who dictated it?" said the duchess.

"Who else would have dictated it except yours truly?" replied Sancho.

"And did you write it yourself?" asked the duchess.

"Perish the thought," said Sancho, "I can't read or write – but I can sign my name."

"Let us have a look at it," said the duchess; "I dare say that in it you demonstrate the quality and sufficiency of your wit."

Sancho pulled an unsealed letter from his shirt and gave it to the duchess, who saw that it said the following:

LETTER FROM SANCHO PANZA TO HIS WIFE, TERESA PANZA

They may have given me a public flogging but at least I rode along like a gentleman[1] *-- meaning that if I've got me a good government, it has been at the expense of a handsome flogging. Teresa dear, you won't understand this just now but you'll see what it's all about by and by. I want you to know, Teresa, that I've decided that you are to travel about in a coach, which is the proper thing to do, for to travel in any other manner is to go about on all fours. You are the wife of a governor and I'll be hanged if people are going to talk about you behind your back!*

I am sending you a green hunting outfit my lady the duchess gave me. By altering it, you can make a skirt and bodice for our daughter. From everything I hear in these parts, they say my master Don Quixote is a sane madman and an amusing simpleton and that I'm not far behind him. We were in the Cave of Montesinos and Merlin the Magician settled upon me for disenchanting Dulcinea of Toboso, who is known back home as Aldonza Lorenzo, and thanks to three thousand three hundred lashes – less five – which I'm to give myself, she will end up as disenchanted as the day she was born. Don't say anything about this to anyone, for if you let something of yours be exposed publicly, some will say it's white and others black. A few days from now I'll be leaving for the governorship, which I'm looking forward to because I'm very anxious to earn some money, and I've been told that every new governor has the same desire. As soon as I take the public pulse, I'll advise you as to whether or not you're to come and join me. The dapple is fine and sends you his best regards and I don't intend to give him up even if they make me Grand Turk.

My mistress the duchess sends you a thousand kisses. Send her two thousand in return, for, according to my master, nothing costs less or is worth more than good manners. God has not seen fit to provide me with another valise containing a hundred escudos *like the one from a few days back, but don't worry, Teresa dear, 'He who sounds the alarm is always free from harm,' and 'Everything will come out in the wash' when I'm governor. They tell me that once I give governing a try, I will give my right arm and leg to keep it. If this should happen, it'll cost me dearly, though folks who are maimed and crippled already possess a kind of benefice in the alms they beg for, so in one way or another you'll be wealthy and favored by fortune. May God grant this, which He is certainly capable of doing, and may He preserve me to serve you. From this castle, the 20th day of July, 1614.*

Your husband the governor,
SANCHO PANZA

When the duchess finished reading the letter, she said to Sancho,

"On a couple of points our worthy governor has gone a bit astray: first, in saying or implying that

---

1 Hardly like a gentleman, since he would have been paraded about on a donkey as part of the public humiliation ceremony.

he is being granted this government because of the lashes he is to give himself, when he knows for a fact – a thing he cannot deny – that when my lord the duke promised it to him, lashes were the furthest thing from anyone's thoughts. The other thing is that he clearly shows by this that he is greedy and I should not want things to turn out opposite from what he expects. 'Greed often causes the sack to tear,' and a greedy governor metes out justice that is *un*just."

"I didn't mean all those things, my lady," said Sancho. "If your grace feels this letter doesn't read the way it should, there's nothing I can do except tear it up and write a new one, which may turn out even worse, especially if it's left up to my judgement."

"No, no," said the duchess, "this one is fine and I even want the duke to read it."

After this exchange, they went into the garden in which they planned to dine that day. The duchess showed Sancho's letter to the duke, who found it most amusing. Once the meal was finished and the table cleared, they were entertained for quite some time by Sancho's delightful conversation, when suddenly they heard the plaintive sound of a fife and the harsh, discordant one of a drum. They were all surprised and confused by the martial, doleful music, Don Quixote in particular, who could hardly sit still on his seat from sheer excitement. As for Sancho, one need only add that fear led him to his accustomed refuge: clinging to the skirts of the duchess, for really and truly the sound that was heard was lugubrious and melancholy. While they were all on the edge of their seats, they saw coming towards them through the garden two men in long flowing mourning robes that trailed along the ground. They were beating two large drums also draped in black and at their side marched a fifer whose clothing was pitch-black like the others. Following them came a person with an enormous body wrapped (rather than dressed) in a coal-black robe, the train of which was also unusually long. Over his robe was strapped a broad shoulder band, likewise black, and suspended from this band was an oversized scimitar with a black sheath and sword-guard. His face was covered by a transparent black veil through which one could make out an extremely long beard as white as snow. Marching to the beat of the drums, he moved deliberately and effortlessly. In short, his size, gait, somber attire, and the accompanying music could and did astonish all those in observance. Approaching at the slow, deliberate pace just mentioned, he knelt before the duke, who together with everyone else there had been waiting for him, but the duke refused to allow him to speak until he rose. The prodigious bogeyman complied and, once on his feet, removed the veil from his face to reveal the longest, whitest, fullest, and most horrid beard human eyes have ever gazed upon. Following this, he summoned up from his broad, bulging chest a voice that was deep and resonant and, fixing his eyes upon the duke, he said,

"My most exalted and powerful lord, I am Trifaldín of the White Beard, squire to the Countess Trifaldi, also known as the Duenna in Distress. I have brought your grace a message on her behalf requesting that you kindly grant her leave and permission to approach and reveal to you her plight, which is as novel and astounding as any the most troubled mind on earth could ever conceive. First, however, she wishes to know whether you have in your castle the valiant and invincible knight Don Quixote of La Mancha, in quest of whom she has traveled on foot and without food all the way from the kingdom of Candaya to this your grace's realm, an undertaking that might easily be regarded as a miracle or the product of enchantment. She has remained at the gate of this fortress, or country estate, where she is simply awaiting your grace's consent before coming inside. And this is all I have come to say."

At this point he cleared his throat and with both hands stroked his beard from top to bottom, calmly waiting for the duke to respond, which the latter did by saying,

"For a number of days now, O noble squire Trifaldín of the White Beard, we have been aware of the misfortune of my lady the Countess Trifaldi, who, due to enchanters, is called the Duenna in Distress. You may certainly tell her, O stupendous squire, to come inside, where she will find the valiant Don Quixote of La Mancha, by virtue of whose generous nature she may be assured that she shall receive every sort of support and assistance. You may also tell her on my behalf that, should my assistance be needed, it shall not be found wanting, as I am already obliged to grant it by virtue of my knighthood, for to knights-errant it is second nature to come to the aid of all manner of duennas, particularly those who are widowed, wronged, and in distress, as her ladyship shows herself to be."

When he heard this, Trifaldín knelt down on one knee and then after signaling for the fife and drums to resume, withdrew from the garden to the same sounds and gait with which he had entered it, leaving everyone to marvel at his appearance and bearing. At this point the duke turned to Don Quixote and said,

"When all is said and done, O famous knight, the darkness of malice and ignorance is incapable of covering up or obscuring the light of valor and virtue. I mention this, your worthiness, for you have been in this castle a scant six days and already those who are sad and afflicted are coming in quest of your grace from distant, far-off lands, not by carriage or camel, but on foot and fasting, confident that they will find the solutions to their troubles and afflictions in your mighty arm and great deeds, the fame of which has spread throughout the entire civilized world."

"I only wish, sir duke," said Don Quixote, "that the devout ecclesiastic were here who demonstrated at the table the other day that he held knights-errant in such low regard and esteem so he might see with his own eyes whether the world is in need of this type of knight. He would at least discover for himself that the sorely afflicted and disconsolate, when faced with great difficulties and enormous misfortunes, seek relief not from scholars or village priests, nor from knights who have never ventured beyond the confines of their villages, nor from shiftless courtiers who would rather dig up news they can repeat and gossip about than attempt to perform work or deeds that others can talk and write about. No, solutions to problems, assistance to the needy, protection of maidens, and consolation of widows are all to be found in no nobler sort of persons than knights-errant; and for being one, I give eternal thanks to heaven and consider as well-employed any misfortune or hardship that I may undergo in this most honorable profession. Have this duenna come forward and ask whatever she so desires, and I shall provide her relief by the might of my arm and the fearless resolve of my undaunted spirit."

Chapter Thirty-Seven

The continuation of the famous adventure of the duenna in distress

The duke and duchess were amused and delighted to see how well Don Quixote was responding to their charade but at this point Sancho said,

"I wouldn't want this duenna lady to jeopardize this government I've been promised, for I once heard a silver-tongued apothecary from Toledo say that whenever duennas enter the picture, nothing good can follow. Lord, how that apothecary despised them! Which leads me to ask: if all duennas are nosey and pains in the neck regardless of their quality or rank, what about those who are in distress, the way they say this Countess Three-Skirts [1] or Three-Trains is? And, by the way, where I come from skirts and trains are one and the same."

"Now, that is enough, Sancho my friend," said Don Quixote; "since this duenna has come from such far-off lands in search of me, she can hardly be one of those the apothecary had on his list, especially when this one is a countess. When countesses serve as duennas, it will be to queens and empresses, for in their own homes they enjoy the highest standing and even employ other duennas."

Doña Rodríguez, who happened to be present, said in response to this,

"My lady the duchess has in her employ duennas who could be countesses were fortune so inclined, but 'One must be what the fates decree.' Let no one speak ill of duennas, particularly those who are elderly *and* unmarried; and though I am not one of those myself, it is easy for me to understand that a maiden duenna has an advantage over one who is widowed. And remember: 'He who openly criticizes others may privately criticize you.'"

"That is all well and good," said Sancho, "but there's so much to criticize in duennas, according to my barber, that 'It's better not to stir the rice, even if it gets lumpy.'"

"Squires," said Doña Rodríguez, "have always been our adversaries; they haunt the antechambers and spy on us at every turn, and during those intervals when they are not praying, which is most of the time, they spend their days gossiping about us, disinterring our bones, and interring our good names. Well, they can all go to blazes, for regardless of how much it pains them, we intend to be part of this world and serve in the houses of nobles, though we may starve to death and cover with a black mourning habit these delicate or not-so-delicate hides of ours, just as one covers a trash heap with a canvas on the day of a procession. I dare say that if someone were to ask me and time permitted, I could convince not only everyone here but everyone in the world that there is no virtue that is not embodied in a duenna."

"I believe," said the duchess, "that my good Doña Rodríguez is not only right but very much so, but she should wait for a more appropriate time to defend both herself and duennas in general so as to

1 Sancho has misinterpreted the countess' name **Trifaldi,** believing its Spanish equivalent to be **Tres Faldas** ('Three Skirts').

refute the jaundiced attitude of that evil apothecary and to uproot the one noble Sancho Panza has in his breast."

To which Sancho replied,

"From the first moment that I got a taste of being governor, I lost all interest in being a squire and don't give a fig for all the duennas on earth."

They would have continued the dispute about duennas had they not heard the sounds of a fife and drums, from which they concluded that the Duenna in Distress was approaching. The duchess asked the duke if it would be appropriate to go out to welcome her, inasmuch as the duenna was a countess and a person of quality.

"As for the part of her that's a countess," interrupted Sancho before the duke could respond, "I have no problem with your excellencies' going out to welcome her, but as for the duenna part, I'm of the opinion that you should not move a muscle."

"Who asked you to butt in?" exclaimed Don Quixote.

"Who, master?" replied Sancho. "I'm asking myself, which I'm perfectly capable of doing as a squire who has learned the rules of courtesy in the school of your grace, the most courteous and well-bred knight in this whole area of courtesy. I've heard you declare that in these matters 'As much is lost by a card too many as by a card too few,' and 'A word to the wise is sufficient.'"

"It is just as Sancho says," replied the duke; "we shall see what the countess is like and then decide how much courtesy she is due."

The fife and drums now made their entrance as on the previous occasion and here the author brings this short chapter to a close in order to begin the next, where he will continue the same adventure, as it is one of the most notable in this entire history.

Chapter Thirty-Eight

The duenna in distress gives an account of her misfortunes

Marching along behind the joyless musicians were as many as a dozen duennas who had begun to enter the garden in double file, all wearing sheer white gauze veils and twilled serge mourning habits that were so long only the hems of their robes were visible. Behind them came the Countess Trifaldi, escorted by her squire Trifaldín of the White Beard. She was attired in the finest untufted black baize, which, had it been tufted, would have been covered by tufts as large as good-size Martos chickpeas. The train, or skirt, or whatever one would call it, terminated in three corners and was supported by three pages also dressed in mourning attire. This created a dramatic, geometrical figure with the three acute angles formed by the three corners, and everyone who saw the pointed skirt thought she must have been called the Countess Trifaldi for that reason, as though we were to call her the Countess Three Skirts; and, in fact, Benengeli says this was the case, for her proper title was the Countess Lobuna. [1] She was called this because of the numerous wolves bred in her domain, and had these been foxes instead of wolves, she would have been called the Countess Zorruna, [2] because it was the custom in those parts for lords and ladies to take their titles from the thing or things most abundant in their domains. But this countess, to celebrate the novelty of her skirts, had dropped 'Lobuna' and adopted the name 'Trifaldi'.

The lady and the dozen duennas advanced at a processional pace and their faces were covered by black veils which were not transparent like Trifaldín's but so dense that no feature could be seen through them. As soon as the band of duennas came into view, the duke, duchess, and Don Quixote rose to their feet, as did all those viewing the unhurried procession. The dozen duennas halted and formed a passageway through which the Distressed One came forward, with Trifaldín still holding her by the hand. When the ducal pair and Don Quixote saw this, they advanced some dozen paces to welcome her, at which point she knelt before them and, in a voice that was coarse and rough rather than dainty and delicate, said,

"I would ask your excellencies not to make such a display of courtesy to this your servant, I mean, maid-servant. Distressed as I am, I shall not be able to respond as I should because of the strange and unheard-of affliction that has made off with my wits to some unknown place which must be quite far away, for the more I search for them the more impossible it is to locate them."

"Anyone would be lacking his own wits, my dear countess," said the duke, "who could not discern your ladyship's worth from your appearance, which without further inspection is deserving of the highest degree of courtesy and respect."

And helping her rise, he took her hand and led her to a seat beside the duchess, who likewise received her with the utmost graciousness. Don Quixote was left speechless and Sancho was dying to see the face of La Trifaldi [3] or one of her many duennas but this was not to be until they revealed themselves of their own free will and accord. They all remained silent as they waited to see who would be the first to speak, and it was the Duenna in Distress who did so with these words:

"I am confident, most eminently powerful lord, most eminently beautiful lady, and most eminently wise assemblage, that my most eminent afflictions shall find refuge in your most eminently courageous breasts, a refuge no less placid than generous and compassionate. My afflictions are sufficient to soften diamonds, melt marble, and mollify the steel of the most obdurate hearts on earth, but before these announce themselves to your graces' hearing – so as not to say ears – I should like your lordships to tell me if there is present in this guild, circle, or company, his eminence the most eminently immaculate knight Don Quixote of La Mancha and his most eminent squire Panza."

"That Panza," said Sancho before anyone else could respond, "is present, as well as his eminence

---

1 ***Lobuna***: 'Having to do with wolves.'

2 ***Zorruna***: 'Having to do with foxes.'

3 In Spanish, as in various other Romance languages, the feminine definite article 'la' is often used with the surname alone when referring to actresses, divas, etc.; cf. 'La Garbo,' 'La Callas,' etc.

the most eminent Don Quixote; and so, my most eminently distressed duenna, your eminence may say whatever you eminently please, for we are all most eminently ready and willing to extend to your eminence our most eminent services."

At this point Don Quixote stood up and, directing his remarks to the Duenna in Distress, said,

"My distressed lady, if your ladyship's afflictions entertain any hope of relief by the valor or might of some knight-errant, here are mine, which, though weak and insufficient, shall all be employed in your service. I, madam, am Don Quixote of La Mancha, whose calling is to go to the aid of every person in need. And, this being the case, your grace has no need to solicit our goodwill or to compose preambles but simply to relate your misfortunes plainly and without circumlocutions, for there are persons here who will be able, if not to resolve them, at least to commiserate with them."

When the Duenna in Distress heard this, she gave every indication of wanting to throw herself at Don Quixote's feet and indeed did so in an effort to embrace them, saying,

"I prostrate myself, O invincible knight, before these feet and legs that are the foundations and pillars of knight-errantry! I would kiss these feet, upon whose stride rests and depends the solution to my woes, O valorous knight, whose real accomplishments outstrip and eclipse the fabled ones of the Amadises, the Esplandianes, and the Belianises!"

And turning from Don Quixote to Sancho Panza, she took his hands and said,

"And you, the most loyal squire who ever served a knight-errant in ages past or present, whose goodness is more extensive than the beard of Trifaldín my companion, here present, well may you boast that in serving the great Don Quixote you thereby serve all the knights who ever bore arms upon this earth. I conjure you, by all the goodness and loyalty that bind you, to be my kind intercessor with your master, that he may speedily favor this most humble and unfortunate countess."

To which Sancho replied,

"My lady, whether my goodness is as great and abundant as your squire's beard has very little bearing on the case. I should like my soul bearded and mustachioed when I depart this life, which is what matters most. I care little or nothing for the beards of this world and, without sniveling or begging will importune my master, who, I know, holds me in his affection – and even more so now that he needs my assistance in a certain matter – to favor and assist your ladyship in every way he can. I would have you unburden yourself of your vexations by disclosing them here and you may leave the rest to us, for we will be certain to come to an understanding."

The duke and duchess were bursting with laughter at these proceedings, along with all those present who had their fingers on the pulse of this particular adventure, and among themselves they praised the cunning and acting prowess of La Trifaldi, who returned to her seat and said,

"Serving as sovereign of the famous kingdom of Candaya, which lies between the great Trapobana and the Southern Sea two leagues beyond Cape Camorín, was the queen Doña Maguncia, widow of King Archipiela, her husband and lord, the marriage with whom engendered and produced the princess Antonomasia, heiress to the kingdom. Said princess was reared and brought up under my tutelage and instruction, as I was her mother's most experienced and foremost duenna. The years passed and by the age of fourteen the young Antonomasia achieved such perfection of beauty that nature itself could not have improved upon it in any way. Her mind was anything but immature, for she was as intelligent as she was beautiful, and she was the most beautiful creature on earth, and still is if the envious Fates and hard-hearted Parcae have not severed her life's thread. But such will not be the case nor would heaven permit such an outrage against the world, as would occur if this cluster were prematurely plucked from the fairest vineyard on earth.

"Countless nobles both at home and abroad became enamored of this beauty, whom my torpid tongue has failed to praise as highly as she deserves. Among those nobles, a certain knight of the court dared direct his thoughts towards this heavenly beauty, trusting in his youthfulness and gallantry, his many talents and charms, his quick and brilliant wit. I would have your excellencies know, at the risk of becoming tedious, that he was both a poet and a great dancer; he could make a guitar sing and could build such fine bird-cages that he could have earned a living by that alone had he ever found himself in extreme need. Such a multitude of talents and charms is sufficient to bring down a mountain, much less a fragile maiden! But all his gallantry and cunning and all his charms and abilities would have been of little or no avail in conquering the fortress in my charge had the thieving scoundrel not made use of the stratagem of conquering me first. That depraved scoundrel and vagabond began by seeking to win my goodwill and to wheedle my acquiescence so that I, most treacherous warden, would hand over to him the keys to the fortress I was guarding. To make a long story short, he flattered my intelligence and overcame my resistance with lord knows how many gems and trinkets that he gave me, but what most weakened me and made me come tumbling down were some verses I heard him sing one night from a window that opened onto the narrow street where he stood. If I remember correctly, the verses went as follows:

'The tyrant fair whose beauty sent
 The throbbing mischief to my heart,
The more my anguish to augment,
 Forbids me to reveal the smart.'

I found the love song heavenly and his voice divine, and from that moment to this I am convinced, judging by the misfortunes that have befallen me because of these and similar verses, that poets, as Plato suggested, should be banished from moral and well-run states, at least, the sensual ones who write verses, not like those of the Marquis of Mantua, which entertain and cause women and children to weep, but barbed ones that pierce one's heart like smooth thorns, or strike one like lightning while leaving one's clothing untouched. On another occasion he sang:

'Come, death, with gently-stealing pace,
 And take me unperceived away;
Nor let me see thy wished-for face,
 Lest joy my fleeting life should stay'

"– and other couplets and triplets of this type, which are enchanting when sung and enthralling when read. But what might one expect when they condescend to compose a type of verse in fashion in

Candaya at that time known as *seguidillas*? This is when the soul leaps up, merriment starts cavorting about, the body grows restless, and, finally, all the senses turn to quicksilver, for which reason, my lords and lady, such troubadours justifiably deserve to be banished to some uninhabited isle. The fault, though, lies not with them but with the simpletons who praise them and the silly women who believe them. Had I been the strong duenna I should have been, I would not have been moved by his overworked conceits, nor would I have put stock in such phrases as 'In death I live,' 'I am made hot by the frost,' 'I grow cold in the fire,' 'My despair gives me hope,' 'Though departing, I remain,' along with other impossible conceits of this type with which their writings are laced. But what might one expect when they promise the phoenix of Arabia, the crown of Ariadne, the steeds of the sun, the pearls of the south, the gold of Tibar, and the balm of Panchaia? This is where they allow their pens to range the farthest, since it costs them precious little to promise what they never can nor intend to provide. But why do I stray so far afield? Poor, unfortunate me, what folly or madness leads me to relate the shortcomings of others when there is so much I might voice about my own? Again I say, woe unto me and my lack of happiness! I was seduced, not by the verses, but by my own gullibility. I was mollified, not by the music, but by my own inconstancy. My great ignorance and lack of caution opened the way and cleared the path for the advances of Don Clavijo, which is the name of the gentleman in question. So with me serving as go-between, he found himself more than once in the presence of the deceived Antonomasia – deceived by me, not by him – since he had promised to be her lawful husband, for, sinner that I am, I would never have permitted him to touch the sole of her slippers until he first became her betrothed – no, never! Marriage shall be the end result of any affair in which I become involved. There was only one obstacle that presented itself: the disparity between the two, for Don Clavijo was an ordinary gentleman whereas the princess Antonomasia was, as I have said, heiress to the kingdom. This entanglement remained concealed and undiscovered for a number of days thanks to my shrewd precautions, until I saw that a certain swelling of Antonomasia's stomach would very soon disclose it. Our dread of this made us put our heads together and out of this came the resolution that, before the unwelcome news became public, Don Clavijo would ask Antonomasia to be his wife in the presence of the vicar on the basis of an agreement the princess had made with him to be his wife, skillfully formulated by me and so binding that the strength of Samson could not have broken it. The necessary steps were taken: the vicar read the agreement, heard the lady's confession, which she made in full, and ordered her placed in the custody of a highly respected court bailiff----- "

At this point Sancho interrupted:

"So in Candaya too there are court bailiffs, poets, and *seguidillas*. This leads me to reaffirm my belief that things are the same the world over, but, Lady Trifaldi, your ladyship might go a little faster, for it is late and I am dying to hear the end of this very lengthy story."

"And so I shall," replied the countess.

Chapter Thirty-Nine

La Trifaldi continues her stupendous and memorable story

Every word that Sancho uttered delighted the duchess as much as it drove Don Quixote to despair. He ordered his squire to be quiet and the Distressed One went on with her story, saying,

"Finally, after a barrage of questions and carefully considered answers, the princess being dead-set in her resolve and unwavering in her earlier assertion, the vicar decided in favor of Don Clavijo, entrusting her to him as his lawful wife, which so upset the queen Doña Maguncia, the princess Antonomasia's mother, that before three days had passed we buried her."

"She was no doubt dead," said Sancho.

"Of course, she was dead," replied Trifaldín; "it is not our custom in Candaya to bury live persons, only dead ones."

"Well, there are cases on record, sir squire," said Sancho, "where they've buried a person who has lost consciousness, believing he was dead, and I was thinking that Queen Maguncia had every reason to swoon but not to die. So long as one is alive, a great many problems can be solved; besides, the princess' foolishness wasn't so great she was obliged to take it that hard. Now if that lady had married one of her pages or one of her household servants, which I've been told a number of other women have done, the damage would have been beyond repair, but to have married such a refined and accomplished gentleman as he's been described to us here may obviously have been foolish but it wasn't as serious as people thought, for according to the dictates of my master, who is present and will not let me tell a lie, just as they make bishops from men of letters, they also make kings and emperors from knights, especially when they're errant ones."

"You are right, Sancho," said Don Quixote, "for if a knight-errant has an ounce of good luck, he is quite likely to become the greatest lord on earth. But I wish her distressed ladyship would proceed, for though this story has been pleasant enough so far, it appears the bitter part is yet to come."

"I should say it is!" replied the countess, "and it is so bitter that in comparison lemons are sweet and hemlock tasty. Since the queen was dead and not in a faint, we buried her, but scarcely had we covered her with earth and said our last farewells than - *quis talia fando temperet a lacrymis?* [1] – there appeared above the queen's sepulcher, astride a wooden horse, the giant Malambruno, Maguncia's first cousin, who in addition to being cruel was also an enchanter. Because of his disgust for Antonomasia's boldness, as well as his desire to avenge his cousin's death and to punish Don Clavijo's audacity, he cast a magic spell over them and left them there on that very sepulcher: her turned into a bronze monkey, and him into a fearsome crocodile made of some unknown metal.

1 Latin: 'who, in speaking such things, can hold back his tears?'

Between the two he placed a column also made of metal, which displayed the following inscription engraved in the Syriac tongue but subsequently translated into Candayan and now into Castilian: *These two rash lovers shall not resume their original form until the valiant Manchegan does battle with me in hand-to-hand combat, for the Fates have reserved this unheard-of adventure for his great valor alone.* This accomplished, he drew from his sheath a huge, broad scimitar, and seizing me by the hair, made a gesture as if to slit my gullet or lop my head clean off. I was so terrified my voice stuck in my throat and I was distressed in the extreme. But, despite all that, I made the greatest effort I could and with a voice that was both pitiful and trembling resorted to such pleading that he was persuaded to call a halt to that most severe punishment. Finally, he ordered all the duennas of the palace brought before him, and they are the ones who are here today. After railing against the guilt and character of us duennas, our evil habits and worse intrigues, laying the blame on all of us when I alone was guilty, he said he would not sentence us to death but preferred to punish us with long, drawn-out torments that would bring us a lingering, wretched death. At that very moment and place, just as he finished saying that, we all felt the pores of our faces open, as though someone were pricking them with the points of needles. We immediately felt of our faces and discovered what your graces will now see."

At this point the Distressed One and the other duennas removed the veils they were wearing and revealed faces completely covered with beards, some reddish, some black, some blond, and some a mixture, the sight of which surprised the duke and duchess, dumbfounded Don Quixote and Sancho, and astonished everyone who was present. La Trifaldi then proceeded:

"This is how that scoundrel and evil-minded Malambruno has punished us, covering our soft, smooth faces with these rough bristles. I wish to heaven he had cut off our heads with his huge scimitar instead of hiding our radiant faces beneath this bush. Kind sirs and ladies, when we consider the situation – and what I am about to say I should prefer to say with my eyes flowing like fountains but the oceans they have wept up to this moment, together with the consideration of our misfortune, have left them without moisture and made them as dry as dust, and so I shall relate it without tears. Where, I ask, may a bearded duenna turn? What father or mother will pity her? Who will come to her aid? Even when she has smooth skin and tortures her face with every form of lotion and cosmetic, she can scarcely find anyone to love her, so what will she do when she displays a face that resembles a thicket? O duennas and dearest companions, we were born at an unfortunate time and it was an evil hour when our parents conceived us!"

And as she said this, she seemed on the verge of swooning.

Chapter Forty

Matters relating to and having to do with this adventure and this memorable history

Really and truly, all those who delight in histories like the present one should express their gratitude to the original author Cide Hamete for the diligence he has demonstrated in recording its minutest details, however trivial, leaving out nothing while bringing everything to light. He describes what the characters are thinking, reveals what is in their imagination, elaborates on matters that are implied, clarifies what is doubtful, ties up the loose ends of the story, and, lastly, lays open the very fiber of what one is most curious about. O most renowned author! O fortunate Don Quixote! O famous Dulcinea! And, O comical Sancho Panza! – all together or each separately, may you live countless ages for the delight and general amusement of mankind.

Our history goes on to say that when Sancho saw the Distressed One had fainted, he said,

"I swear upon my word of honor and the lives of all the Panzas who have gone before that never have I seen or heard, nor has my master ever related or even conceived of, such an adventure as this. Malambruno, you giant and enchanter, may a thousand devils *bless* you – I almost said the opposite. Couldn't you have found some other type of punishment to inflict upon these poor souls than to give them beards? Wouldn't it have been better – it certainly would have been more to the point – to cut off the upper portion of their noses, even if it made them wheeze when they spoke, than to grow beards on them? I'll bet they even lack the money to pay someone to shave them."

"That is the truth, sir," said one of the twelve ladies; "we even lack the money to get a trim, so that some of us as an economy measure have resorted to using plasters made of pitch or adhesives. By applying these to our faces and suddenly ripping them off, we are left as smooth and clean as the bottom of a stone mortar, and though in Candaya there are women who go from house to house removing facial hair, plucking eyebrows, and preparing cosmetics, we duennas who serve my lady have always refused to let them in, for most of them reek of go-betweens retired from a life of prostitution. If his lordship Don Quixote does not find a remedy for this, we shall all go to our graves with these beards on our faces."

"I will shave off my own," said Don Quixote, "in the land of the Moors if I fail to provide a solution for your ladyship."

At this moment La Trifaldi regained consciousness and said,

"The sound of that promise has reached my ears in the midst of my swoon and caused me to recover and fully regain my senses. Thus, illustrious knight and indomitable lord, I again implore your grace to convert your gracious promise into deeds."

"It shall not remain unfulfilled because of me," replied Don Quixote. "I would ask my lady what it is I must do, since my courage is more than ready to serve her."

"Actually," said the Distressed One, "if one goes by land, the distance from here to Candaya is five thousand leagues, give or take a couple, but if one travels through the air, as the crow flies, it is three thousand two hundred and twenty-seven. I should also mention that Malambruno told me that as soon as fate provided me with the knight who was to be our liberator, he would send him a mount far better and with fewer defects than those rented ones, for it will be the very wooden horse on which the valiant Pierres made off with the fair Magalona when he abducted her. This horse is guided by a peg on its forehead that serves as a bridle and he flies through the air with such swiftness that you will fancy devils themselves are propelling you. This same horse, according to ancient tradition, was constructed by the wizard Merlin, who lent him to Pierres, a friend of his, upon whom the latter took long journeys and abducted, as already stated, the fair Magalona, transporting her through the air on his haunches and causing all the observers on the ground to gasp in astonishment. But he would lend him to no one except a person he liked or one who would pay him a handsome fee, and from the great Pierres until now we know of no one who has ridden him. Malambruno made off with him by employing his magic and has him in his possession, utilizing him on the journeys he constantly takes to different parts of the world – today he is here, tomorrow in France, the next day in Potosí. But best of all, this particular horse neither eats, sleeps, nor wears out horseshoes, and without benefit of wings moves through the air at such a steady gait that anyone riding him can carry a cup filled with water in his hand without spilling a drop, such is the ease and smoothness with which he strides, for which reason the fair Magalona always delighted in riding him."

At this point Sancho said,

"For restful and smooth riding, I'll take my dapple even if he doesn't travel through the air. On the ground, though, I'll stack him up against any pacer on earth."

After they all enjoyed a round of laughter, the Distressed One continued:

"This same horse (assuming that Malambruno really wishes to put an end to our misfortune) will be in our midst before the night is half an hour old. He indicated that the sign he would give me to let me know I had located the knight I was seeking would be his sending me the horse, wherever that might be, speedily and at my convenience."

"And how many can ride on that horse?" asked Sancho.

To this the Distressed One answered,

"Two persons: one in the saddle and one on the haunches, and usually these two are knight and squire, especially when there is no abducted maiden available."

"I'd like to know, distressed lady," said Sancho, "what name this horse goes by."

"His name," said the Distressed One, "is not that of Bellerophon's horse, which was Pegasus, nor that of Alexander the Great, named Bucephalus, nor that of Orlando Furioso, whose name was Brigliador, nor even Bayard, which was Reinaldos de Montalván's, nor Ruggiero's Frontino, nor Boötes or Perithous, which the Sun's are supposedly called, nor is he named Orelia, which is the horse the unfortunate Rodrigo, last king of the Goths, rode into battle in which he lost both his kingdom and his life."

"I'll wager," said Sancho, "that since he hasn't been given any of the well-known names of those famous horses, he hasn't been given that of my master's Rocinante either, which in the matter of appropriateness exceeds all those others your grace has mentioned."

"That is true," replied the bearded countess, "but his own still suits him, for he is called Clavileño the Swift, [1] a name that is fitting in that he is made of wood, is guided by a peg on his forehead, and travels at a swift gait, and so as far as his name is concerned, he may easily compete with the famous Rocinante."

"I have no quarrel with his name," said Sancho, "but what sort of reins does one use for controlling him?"

"I have already said," replied La Trifaldi, "that by turning the peg in one direction or the other, the person riding him can make him go wherever he wishes: either high in the sky, or virtually skimming and touching the earth, or along a middle course, which is the one a person will seek and adhere to in all well regulated actions."

"I'd like to see him," said Sancho, "but to think that I'll ride him, either on the saddle or on the haunches, is as far-fetched as asking an elm tree to produce pears. What a fine state of affairs! When I can barely stand to ride my dapple – and on a packsaddle softer than silk itself – they now want me to ride on some wooden haunches without even a cushion or pillow! Good lord, I have no intention of being jolted to pieces to help some woman get rid of her beard. Let each duenna get shaved the best way she can because I don't intend to accompany my master on such a long journey. Moreover, I shouldn't serve as the agent for getting these beards shaved, since I'm already the agent for disenchanting my lady Dulcinea."

"Yes, you should, my friend," replied Trifaldi; "in fact, without your presence I understand that nothing will be done."

"Now, just hold on!" exclaimed Sancho, "what do squires have to do with their masters' adventures? Are the masters supposed to receive all the glory for what they accomplish, while we do all the work? My, but wouldn't it be amazing if historians were to write: 'Such-and-such a knight completed such-and-such an adventure with the help of So-and-So, his squire, without whom it would have been impossible for him to complete it.' Instead, they simply write: 'Don Paralipomenón of the Three Stars carried off the adventure of the six monsters,' without so much as a mention of his squire, who was present at every moment, as though he didn't even exist! Well, my lords and ladies, I say once again that my master can travel by himself, and a lot of good may it do him! I'll stay here in the company of my mistress the duchess and it may turn out that when he returns, he'll find the lady Dulcinea's cause tremendously improved, for in my idle and leisure moments I intend to give myself such a barrage of lashes that the hair won't grow back on my body."

"Nevertheless, dear Sancho," said the duchess, "you must accompany him if it is necessary, for those asking you to do so are worthy souls and the faces of these ladies must not remain thickly overgrown because of your unfounded fears, as that would certainly be lamentable."

"Now, hold on again!" said Sancho; "if this were a charitable deed for some cloistered maidens or girls in an orphanage, one might undertake any ordeal, but to undergo such a thing to rid some duennas of their beards, to heck with it! – even if I should see them all with beards, from the oldest to the youngest and from the most demure to the most brazen."

---

1 ***Clavileño*** is derived from ***clavija,*** 'peg' + ***leño,*** 'wood'.

"You certainly have it in for duennas, Sancho my friend," said the duchess. "You are following rather closely in the footsteps of the apothecary from Toledo but I can assure you you are mistaken, for there are those in my employ who might serve as models for duennas. Why, take my Doña Rodríguez, who will not let me say otherwise."

"Your excellency may say whatever you please," replied Rodríguez. "God knows the truth of everything: whether we duennas are good or evil, bearded or hairless; besides, we were begotten by our mothers the same as every other woman, and since God, who brought us into this world, knows the reason why, I shall put my trust in His mercy rather than in someone's beard."

"Well now, Madam Rodríguez, Madam Trifaldi, and distinguished company," said Don Quixote, "I shall rely upon heaven to look kindly upon your graces' afflictions, and when Clavileño arrives and I find myself in Malambruno's presence, Sancho shall do as I command. I wish Clavileño were already here and I saw myself face to face with Malambruno, for I am certain there is no razor that will shave your graces with greater ease than my sword will shave Malambruno's head from his shoulders. 'God may tolerate the wicked but He will not do so forever.'"

"Hear! hear!" said the Distressed One at this point, "may all the stars of the celestial regions look benignly upon your greatness, O valiant knight, and instill in your heart all prosperity and courage for becoming the shield and refuge of the beleaguered and vilified race of duennas, detested by apothecaries, slandered by squires, and swindled by pages. A pox upon the little hussy who in the bloom of youth chooses to be a duenna instead of a nun. Woe unto us poor unfortunate duennas! Even if we were descended through the direct male line from Hector of Troy himself, our mistresses would not hesitate to talk down to us if they thought they would be made queens by doing so. O Malambruno you giant, you may be an enchanter but at least you are steadfast in your promises! Send us the peerless Clavileño now so our misfortunes will cease, for if the hot weather comes and we still have these beards, heaven have mercy upon our sad lot!"

This was said by La Trifaldi with such feeling that it brought tears to the eyes of everyone present and even filled to overflowing those of Sancho, who resolved in his heart to accompany his master to the farthest reaches of the earth if that was what it would take to remove the wool from these venerable faces.

Chapter Forty-One

The arrival of Clavileño and the conclusion of this rather lengthy adventure

By now, night had arrived and with it the agreed-upon time for the famous horse Clavileño to appear, but his failure to do so was beginning to trouble Don Quixote, who felt that because Malambruno was delaying sending him, either he, Don Quixote, was not the knight for whom this adventure was reserved or Malambruno dared not engage him in hand-to-hand combat.

But, lo and behold, four savages suddenly entered the garden, all clad in green ivy and carrying on their shoulders a large wooden horse. After setting it on the ground, one of the savages said,

"Let any knight who is brave enough to mount this contraption do so."

"I'm not mounting it," said Sancho, "for not only am I not brave enough, I'm not a knight."

But the savage proceeded with his speech:

"And his squire, if indeed he has one, shall take his seat on the haunches, and he can trust the valiant Malambruno that no sword, unless it is Malambruno's, shall smite him, nor shall he suffer any other indignity. They need do nothing more than turn the peg on Clavileño's neck and he will carry them through the air to where Malambruno is waiting, but lest the height and altitude of the journey make them dizzy, they are to keep their eyes blindfolded until the horse neighs, which will signal the completion of their journey."

After announcing this, they left Clavileño and made a graceful exit at the same place they had entered the garden. When the Distressed One saw the horse, she said to Don Quixote, virtually with tears in her eyes,

"Valiant knight, Malambruno's promises have come true, the horse has arrived, our beards are growing, and we are all imploring your grace with every whisker on our faces to shave and shear us, for you have only to mount him with your squire to give a propitious beginning to your novel journey."

"That I shall do, your ladyship, most willingly and graciously, without pausing to get a cushion or to don my spurs lest I lose a moment's time, for I have the greatest desire, my lady, to see you and all these duennas clean shaven."

"That I will *not* do," said Sancho, "either graciously or ungraciously or in any other manner; in fact, if this shave can't be performed without my riding on the haunches, my master can jolly well look for another squire to accompany him, and these ladies can look for some other means of making their faces smooth. I'm not some wizard who likes to go flying through the air. What will my islanders think when they learn that their governor has been sailing through the clouds? And another thing: since it's over three thousand leagues from here to Candaya, if the horse gets tired or the giant angry, it'll take us half a dozen years to return and there won't be any isle or island on earth that will know who I am. And so, heeding the familiar sayings: 'There's danger in delay,' and 'When they give you a calf, run and fetch a rope,' I hope these ladies' beards will forgive me but 'Saint Peter is quite content in Rome,' meaning that I'm just fine here in this house where I'm being shown so many kindnesses and from whose owner I expect as great a favor as that of seeing myself governor."

At this point the duke said,

"Sancho my friend, the island I promised you will not move or run away. It has such deep roots reaching down into the bowels of the earth that no amount of tugging can uproot it or move it from where it is. And since you know as well as I that there is no first-rate office that cannot be gained by some sort of bribe – some bigger, some smaller – the one I demand in exchange for this office is that you accompany your master Don Quixote and see this memorable adventure to its conclusion. Whether you return on Clavileño in the brief time his swiftness promises or are forced by adversity to return on foot, traveling from inn to inn like some pilgrim, so long as you do return, you shall find your island where you left it and your islanders as eager to receive you as their governor as they have always been, and my own resolve shall be no different. And so, Master Sancho, doubt not the truth of this, for to do so would be a grievous insult to my desire to serve you."

"No more, your grace," said Sancho, "I'm a simple squire and am incapable of carrying so many kindnesses on my back. Let my master mount and then your graces may blindfold my eyes, commend me to God, and let me know, once we're high up in the sky, whether I may commend myself to Our Lord or invoke the angels to favor me."

To which Trifaldi responded,

"Sancho, you may certainly commend yourself to God or to whomever you please, for Malambruno may be an enchanter but he is a Christian one and performs his enchantments most carefully and sagaciously so as not to offend anyone."

"Well then," said Sancho, "may God and the holy Trinity of Gaeta come to my aid!"

"Never since the unforgettable adventure of the fulling-mill," said Don Quixote, "have I seen Sancho so frightened as now, and were I as superstitious as others, his cowardice would arouse certain misgivings in my heart. But come with me, Sancho, for with the permission of these lords and ladies, I should like a couple of words with you in private."

Leading Sancho over to some trees, he took his squire's hands in his and said,

"You now see, Sancho my brother, the long journey that lies before us, and only God knows when we shall return from it or how much free time and leisure this business will allow us. Therefore, I would have you return to your room now as though you were looking for something you needed for the trip but give yourself quicker than a flash at least five hundred lashes as payment towards the three thousand three hundred you are due; you will have these over with and 'Well begun is half done.'"

"Merciful heavens!" said Sancho, "your grace must be out of your mind! That is like saying: 'You see me with child but bid me be a virgin.' Now that I've got to travel seated on a bare board, you want me to flay my backside. Well, the fact of the matter is that you are terribly mistaken. Let's be on our way and get these duennas shaved and, once we're back, I give your grace my word as an honest man that I'll set about discharging my obligation with such speed that you will be satisfied, and that's all I have to say."

To which Don Quixote responded,

"Well, with that promise, noble Sancho, I shall be content and I believe you will keep it, for despite being a simpleton, you are a veracious man."

"I am not voracious," said Sancho, "I just have a good appetite; but even if I were, I'd keep my word."

With this, they returned to mount Clavileño, but as Don Quixote was about to do so, he said to Sancho,

"Mount, my son, and blindfold yourself; anyone who summons us from such a far-off land will be loath to trick us because of the scant glory that would redound to him for deceiving someone who had trusted him. But even if everything turns out contrary to my belief, the glory we shall win from undertaking this feat shall not be discredited by any kind of evil."

"Let's get started, master," said Sancho. "I've got these ladies' beards and tears etched in my heart and I'll not eat another bite that'll taste right till I see them with their own smooth faces again. But your grace should mount first and blindfold yourself, for if I am to ride on the haunches, it's only logical for the one riding on the saddle to mount first."

"True enough," replied Don Quixote, and removing a kerchief from his pocket, he asked the Distressed One to bind his eyes tightly. But no sooner was the blindfold in place than he removed it and said,

"If I remember correctly, I once read in Virgil of the Palladium of Troy, a wooden horse the Greeks presented to the goddess Pallas that was pregnant with armed soldiers who later laid waste to Troy. It would thus be wise to see what Clavileño has in his belly before proceeding."

"There is no need to do that," said the Distressed One; "I can vouch for him, since I know that Malambruno is not the least bit malicious or treacherous. Sir Don Quixote may mount without reservations and it shall rest upon my head if any harm befalls his grace."

It struck Don Quixote that anything he might say about his safety would imperil his reputation for bravery, and so without further discussion he mounted Clavileño and tested the peg, which he was able to turn with ease. Because there were no stirrups, his legs were left dangling down, making him look exactly like a figure in a scene from some Roman triumph painted or woven on a Flemish tapestry. Sancho, after mounting, begrudgingly and ever so slowly made himself as comfortable as possible on the haunches but, finding them none too soft – quite hard, in fact – asked the duke if he might possibly provide him with some sort of cushion or pillow, even if it was from the couch of his lady the duchess or from the bed of some page, for that horse's haunches felt more like marble than wood. To this La Trifaldi responded that Clavileño would allow no sort of paraphernalia on him, but what he might do was to ride sidesaddle like a woman, which would make the seat feel softer. Sancho did accordingly and, after saying farewell, allowed himself to be blindfolded; but no sooner was the blindfold in place than he removed it, soulfully and tearfully looking at everyone in the garden and asking each of them to assist him at that critical moment with a Paternoster and an Ave Maria, that God might provide someone to say the same prayers for them should they ever find themselves in similar circumstances; to which Don Quixote replied,

"You thief, are they taking you to the gallows, or are you at death's door, that you should resort to such prayers? You fiendish, cowardly creature, you are sitting on the same seat the fair Magalona occupied, from where she was taken, not to be buried in some grave, but to become queen of France, if the chronicles can be trusted? May not I, who shall be riding beside you, sit on the same saddle occupied by the valiant Pierres? Blindfold yourself, you unfeeling animal; cover your eyes and don't let that cowardice of yours issue from your lips – at least, not in my presence."

"Someone blindfold me," said Sancho, "and since no one wants me to be commended or to commend myself to God, is it any wonder I'm afraid there may be a whole host of demons here who will dump us in Peralvillo?" [1]

Once they were both blindfolded and Don Quixote felt himself duly settled, he tested the peg, and

1 A town in south-central Spain where the Holy Brotherhood executed 'criminals'.

the moment he placed his fingers on it all the duennas and bystanders raised their voices and cried out,

"May God be your guide, valiant knight!" "May God be with you, intrepid squire!" "Your graces are now flying through the air, piercing it with greater speed than an arrow!" "Your lordships are beginning to amaze and astonish all of us observing you here on earth!" "Hold tight, valiant Sancho, for you are beginning to totter, and be careful not to fall off or your fall will be worse than that of the foolhardy youth who attempted to drive the chariot of his father the Sun!"

Hearing these shouts, Sancho wrapped his arms round his master and hugged him tightly, saying,

"Master, how can these people say we're traveling so very high when their voices can be clearly heard and seem to be right here beside us?"

"Pay no attention to that, Sancho. Since this whole business of flying is so far out of the ordinary, you will see and hear from a thousand leagues away whatever you want to, and don't squeeze me so hard or you will pull me off. I really cannot understand why you are so upset and frightened, for never in my life have I ridden a mount with a steadier gait. Why, it actually feels as though we are not moving at all. Cast off your fear, my friend, for things are going just as they should and we even have the wind at our backs."

"That's true," said Sancho, "for back here I'm being blown by such a strong breeze it feels as though they are puffing away at me with a thousand bellows."

And such was the case, for several large bellows were blowing air at him, this particular adventure having been so well planned by the duke and duchess and their majordomo that nothing was lacking to make it perfect. When Don Quixote felt the air on himself, he said,

"Beyond all doubt, Sancho, we must already be approaching the second celestial sphere where hail and snow originate. Thunder and lightning originate in the third and if we keep ascending at this rate, we shall soon reach the sphere of fire, but I have no idea how to control this peg to keep from soaring so high we shall get scorched."

At that instant several pieces of burning tow attached to a pole were held near their faces by those on the ground. When Sancho felt the heat, he said,

"May I be struck dead if we've not already reached the sphere of fire or are very near it, for a large part of my beard has been singed. Master, I've a good mind to remove my blindfold to see where we are."

"You shall do nothing of the sort," replied Don Quixote. "Remember the true story of the licentiate Torralba, whom devils transported through the air on a pole while his eyes were closed. Within twelve hours he reached Rome and dismounted at Torre di Nona, one of the city's streets, where he witnessed the overthrow, plunder, and murder of Bourbon, and the next morning was back in Madrid giving an account of everything he had seen. He reported, among other things, that while he was flying through the air, the Devil told him to open his eyes, and when he did so, he saw, or thought he saw, the orb of the moon so close he could have touched it with his hand, but he dared not look down at the earth for fear of fainting. Therefore, Sancho, there is no reason for us to remove our blindfolds, for the one who is responsible for us will watch over us. Perhaps, we shall keep circling higher and higher to descend at a swoop on the kingdom of Candaya, just as the hawk or falcon swoops down on the heron to capture it, however high the latter may soar. And though it may seem that we left the garden only an hour ago, you may rest assured that we have traveled a very great distance."

"I don't know about that," said Sancho; "what I *do* know is that if the lady Magallanes, or Magalona, could resign herself to these haunches, she must have had a pretty tough hide."

This entire conversation between the two stalwarts was overheard by the duke and duchess and those in the garden, all of whom found it delightfully entertaining. But deciding to bring an end to this strange and well concocted adventure, they used several tows to set fire to Clavileño's tail, which was filled with exploding rockets. The horse made an unusual noise as it suddenly lurched forward, throwing Don Quixote and Sancho to the ground half scorched.

By this time, La Trifaldi and the entire band of bearded duennas had vanished from the garden and those who remained behind lay prostrate on the ground as if unconscious. Don Quixote and Sancho, battered and bruised, picked themselves up and, looking about in all directions, were astonished to find themselves in the same garden from which they had departed and to see so many people scattered about the garden. Their wonder increased still further when they saw at one side of the garden a large lance planted in the ground, and attached to it by two green silk cords was a plain white parchment bearing the following words in large gold letters:

The illustrious knight Don Quixote of La Mancha, simply by having made the effort, has completed and brought to fruition the adventure of the Countess Trifaldi (otherwise known as the Duenna in Distress) together with all her retinue. Malambruno considers himself content and satisfied in every regard, for the duennas' chins are once again smooth and hairless and their majesties Don Clavijo and Antonomasia have reverted to their original state; and once the squirely flogging is completed, the white dove shall see herself free of the pestiferous gerfalcons that pursue her and shall find herself in the arms of her beloved suitor, as is so ordained by the wise Merlin, enchanter par excellence.

Reading the inscription on the parchment, Don Quixote clearly understood that it referred to Dulcinea, and so, giving thanks to heaven for allowing him to accomplish at so little risk such a great undertaking as that of restoring the former texture to the faces of those venerable duennas, who were nowhere to be seen, he went over to the duke and duchess, who had still not regained consciousness. Taking the duke by the hand, he said,

"I say, noble sir, take heart; take heart, I say, for we were worried about nothing! The adventure has now been completed without injury to anyone, which is made manifest by the inscription attached to that staff."

The duke, as of someone awakening from a deep sleep, gradually regained his senses, as did the duchess and all the others lying about the garden. This was effected with such a show of wonder and fright that they were virtually able to convince everyone that what they could feign so well by way of make-believe had happened to them in actuality. The duke, after reading the notice with his eyes only half open, walked over to Don Quixote with outstretched arms to embrace him and to assure him that he was the noblest knight any age had ever witnessed. Sancho was walking about looking for the

Distressed One to see how her face looked without a beard and to see if she was as beautiful as her noble disposition promised but they informed him that no sooner had Clavileño fallen to earth in flames than La Trifaldi and her entire band of duennas vanished, their whiskers having already been shaven off. The duchess then asked Sancho how he had fared on that long journey; to which he replied,

"My lady, I felt as though we were flying through the sphere of fire, as my master has said, at which point I got the urge to peek out from under my blindfold. When I asked my master's permission to remove it, he refused my request, but since I possess certain traces of curiosity and a desire to find out what is hindering or obstructing me, I, stealthily and without being observed by anyone, lifted the kerchief a tiny bit next to my nose, whereupon I looked down at the earth. It seemed to me that the whole earth was no bigger than a mustard seed and everyone on it was slightly larger than a hazelnut, which shows how high we must have been traveling at the time."

In response to this, the duchess said,

"Sancho my friend, mind what you say, for it would appear you were unable to see the earth but could see men standing on it. It is obvious that if you thought the earth resembled a mustard seed and each man a hazelnut, then one single man would have covered the entire earth."

"That's true," replied Sancho, "but, by observing one small part of it, I was able to see the entire earth."

"Look, Sancho," said the duchess, "we cannot, by observing a small part of an object, tell what the entire object looks like."

"I'm not an expert on observing," said Sancho; "all I know is that your ladyship should understand that, inasmuch as we were able to fly by enchantment, I was able to see by enchantment the whole earth and everyone on it regardless of where I looked. And if I am not believed on this point, neither will your grace believe that when I peeked out from under the kerchief just below my eyebrows, I saw myself so close to the sky there wasn't a hand's breadth between me and it – and I declare by all that's holy, my lady, it is mighty big. Now, it happened that we were just passing through the region where the Seven Young Goats [2] are and I swear upon God and my soul, having once been a goatherd back home in my youth, that when I saw them I got such an urge to frolic with them for a moment or two that I felt if I did not do so I would burst! There I was not knowing what to do, and so without saying a word to anyone, not even to my master, I quietly and stealthily got off Clavileño and for three quarters of an hour gamboled about with the young goats, who were like young shoots or flowers, and during that entire time Clavileño never took a single step or moved from that spot."

"And while our noble Sancho was passing the time with the goats," said the duke, "how did Sir Don Quixote pass it?" To which the knight responded,

"Since all these things and events are so far out of the ordinary, it is no wonder Sancho might say what he does. As for myself, I can state that I never peeked out from under my blindfold either at the top or the bottom, nor did I observe heaven, earth, or the sands of the ocean. The truth is that I felt I was passing through the sphere of air and was verging on that of fire but, that we went any farther

2 The Pleiades, with its seven stars.

I cannot believe, for the sphere of fire lies between that of the moon and the farthest one of the air, so we could not have reached the region of the sky where the Seven Young Goats are, as Sancho claims, without getting burned. And since we were not burned, Sancho is either lying or is dreaming."

"I am not lying or dreaming," replied Sancho. "If none of your graces believe me, just ask me to describe the goats and you will see whether I'm telling the truth or not."

"Then describe them to us," said the duchess.

"Two of them were green," said Sancho, "two were red, two blue, and one a mixture."

"Those are new types of goats," said the duke, "for in our part of the world such colors are not common, such colors on goats, that is."

"Which is to be expected," replied Sancho, "since there must be a difference between goats in heaven and those on earth."

"Tell me, Sancho," said the duke, "did you see any bucks up there among those goats?"

"No, your lordship," answered Sancho, "for I heard them say that none ever got past the horns of the moon."

They declined to question him further about his journey, sensing that he was in the mood for making the rounds of all the spheres and giving an account of everything that transpired there – and all this without ever having left the garden.

In short, such was the conclusion of the adventure of the Duenna in Distress, which gave the duke and duchess something to laugh at not just on this occasion but for the rest of their lives, and Sancho something to talk about for centuries should he live so long. Don Quixote then went over to Sancho and whispered in his ear,

"Sancho, just as you would have people believe what you saw in the sky, I ask you to believe what I saw in the Cave of Montesinos, and I shall leave it at that."

Chapter Forty-Two

The counsels that Don Quixote gave Sancho Panza before the squire set out to govern his island, together with other carefully considered matters

The duke and duchess were so pleased with the successful and amusing outcome of the Distressed One's adventure that they decided to proceed with their charade, realizing they had the perfect subject for making it believable. And so after outlining the plan and giving instructions to their servants and vassals as to how they were to treat Sancho as governor of his promised island, the duke informed Sancho that the following day – the day after Clavileño's flight – he was to prepare himself to become governor, for his islanders were awaiting him as eagerly as the rains of May. Sancho bowed to the duke and said,

"Ever since descending from the sky and the celestial heights from where I looked down at the earth and saw how tiny it was, my consuming passion to be governor has abated somewhat. After all, what is so marvelous about governing a mustard seed or so noble and glorious about ruling half a dozen men the size of hazelnuts, who, as far as I could make out, were the only ones on earth? Should your grace find it in your heart to give me the tiniest plot in heaven, even if it were no wider than half a league, I would accept it more willingly than the largest island on earth."

"See here, Sancho my friend," said the duke, "it is not within my power to give anyone a plot in heaven, even if it is as small as one's fingernail, for to God alone are reserved such favors and rewards. What I can give you I shall, which is an island tried and true, circular and well-proportioned, and exceedingly fertile and fruitful, where, if you manage skillfully, you will be able, by availing yourself of the riches of this earth, to attain those of heaven."

"Well then," replied Sancho, "bring on that island and I'll strive to be such a governor that I'll get to heaven despite every scoundrel on earth, and this not from any craving on my part to escape from my humble situation or to elevate myself but to sample what it tastes like to be a governor."

"If you once try it, Sancho," said the duke, "you will fall in love with governing, for it is extremely gratifying to command and be obeyed. You may be certain that when your master becomes an emperor, which he will undoubtedly do, since all his affairs point in that direction, he will not let it be wrested from him by fair means or foul and will be grieved and vexed to the depths of his soul for not having been one earlier."

"I suppose, sir," replied Sancho, "that it's good to command, even if it's only a flock of sheep."

"You are a man after my own heart, Sancho," said the duke; "you understand everything and I expect you to be the kind of governor your intellect promises. But setting this aside for now, be advised that tomorrow is the very day you are to set out for the island you will govern. This evening you shall be provided with the appropriate clothes to wear and everything necessary for your journey."

"Let them dress me any way they will," said Sancho, "for, regardless of how I'm dressed, I'll still be Sancho Panza."

"That is certainly true," said the duke, "but one's attire must be in keeping with the dignity of the office in question, since it would be inappropriate for a jurisprudent to dress like a soldier, or a soldier like a priest. You, Sancho, shall go dressed partly as a man of letters and partly as a captain, for the island I am giving you has as great a need of arms as of letters, and of letters as of arms."

"I don't have much in the way of letters," replied Sancho, "because I don't even know the ABCs, but for me to be a good governor, it is sufficient if I remain mindful of the *Christus*;[1] and as for arms, I'll wield those they give me until I drop, and the rest is in the hands of God."

"With such a good memory," said the duke, "Sancho can never go wrong."

At this moment, Don Quixote arrived and after learning what was taking place and how soon Sancho would be leaving for his governorship, he took Sancho by the arm and with the duke's permission led him to his quarters, where he intended to counsel him on how he was to conduct himself in his new position. Once they were in the room, Don Quixote closed the door behind them

---

1 Latin: 'Christ' — a name given to the figure of a cross that preceded the alphabet in spelling books of the age.

and literally forced Sancho to sit down beside him, at which point he addressed him in a subdued tone of voice:

"I shall be eternally grateful to heaven, dear friend, that before I myself have met with any particular success, good fortune has come forth to greet and smile upon you. I, who had based the payment of your services upon my good fortune, find myself only at the beginning of my advancement, whereas you, prematurely and contrary to the laws of natural progression, see your desires already fulfilled. Some who bribe, importune, solicit, rise early, entreat, and implore, never achieve what they strive for, while along comes another who, without knowing the first thing about anything, finds himself in possession of the responsible position many others have striven for. This is where we may properly call forth the proverb that says, 'If a person really tries, he will be rewarded with either good luck or bad.' You, who in my opinion are an absolute simpleton, never rising early or staying up all night, never doing any hard work, and having only the tiniest portion of knight-errantry rub off on you, suddenly out of the blue find yourself governor of an island, as though this were an everyday occurrence. I tell you this, dear Sancho, so you will not attribute the favor you have received to your own merits but will give thanks to heaven, which quietly sets things in order, and to the preeminence the profession of knight-errantry encompasses within itself. With your heart thus disposed to believing what I have told you, lend an ear, my son, to this your Cato, who would counsel you and serve as pilot and polestar to steer you to a safe port and rescue you from this tempestuous sea in which you are about to be engulfed, for offices of great responsibility are nothing but a deep sea of confusion.

"First of all, my son, you must fear God, for the fear of God is the beginning of wisdom, and once wise, you will never go astray. Your second obligation is to fix your sights upon who you are, striving always to know yourself, which is the most difficult knowledge imaginable. By knowing yourself, you will not get puffed up like the toad which tried to make itself as big as the ox, for should you do so, your reflection upon the fact that back home you once raised hogs will be a reminder to you that beauty is only skin deep."

"That is quite true," replied Sancho, "but that was when I was a lad. Later, when I was a youth, I raised geese, not hogs, but I don't see the connection anyway, for not all those who govern are descended from a line of kings."

"Quite true," said Don Quixote, "and because of that, those who are not of noble stock must bring to the serious responsibilities of their position moderation and leniency, which, tempered by wisdom, will deliver them from the malicious slander that no government is free from.

"Be proud, Sancho, of your humble ancestry and never be ashamed to admit that you come from a line of farmers; then when people realize you are not ashamed of it, no one will try to shame you. Pride yourself more upon being a man of humble virtue than an arrogant sinner, for infinite in number are those who have risen from lowly beginnings to the highest pontifical and imperial preeminence, in support of which I could cite so many examples they would tire you.

"Remember, Sancho, if you adopt virtue as your guiding principle and pride yourself on performing good deeds, there is no reason to envy those whose accomplishments consist of being descended from nobles and lords, for one's blood is inherited, whereas virtue is acquired, and virtue by its very nature possesses that which blood lacks. This being so, if some of your relatives should visit you when you are on your island, do not turn them aside or snub them. Instead, welcome them and treat them warmly and charitably, for by so doing you will be pleasing heaven, which takes no pleasure in anyone who scorns what it has created, and you will be fulfilling your obligation to this well-ordered scheme of things. If you should bring your wife with you – and it is unseemly for those who administer governments to remain for any length of time without their wives – instruct her, indoctrinate her, and divest her of her natural crudeness, for all too often everything an intelligent governor has amassed is lost or squandered by his foolish, unsophisticated wife. And if by chance you should become a widower – something that might occur – and by virtue of your office should acquire a better consort, do not choose one who will serve you as a fishing rod and hook or as a solicitor, for I assure you that at the Final Reckoning the judge will be held accountable for everything his wife may have received, at which time he will pay, in death, many times over for all the things he took no responsibility for in life.

"Never be guided by arbitrary law, which finds such great favor among the ignorant who view themselves as quick-witted. Let yourself show more compassion but not more justice for the poor man's tears than for the rich man's testimony, and strive to distill the truth from the rich man's many promises and gifts and the poor man's sobs and pleadings. When leniency can and should be exercised, do not encumber the guilty party with the full severity of the law, for the reputation of a rigid judge is no better than that of a compassionate one. If you should ever bend the staff of justice, let it be not from the weight of gifts but from that of mercy. If it falls to your lot to judge the case of one of your enemies, direct your attention away from your injury and focus upon the facts of the case. Make certain that your own passion does not blind you in the matter of someone else's cause, for the errors you commit there will hardly ever be correctable, and even when they are, it will be at the expense of your credibility and even of your estate.

"If some beautiful woman comes to you to seek justice, turn your eyes from her tears, and your ears from her lamentations, to consider calmly and coolly the substance of her request lest your judgement be engulfed by her tears and your integrity by her sobs. Refrain from verbally abusing the unfortunate man you plan to punish bodily, for the pain from the punishment will suffice without the added verbal abuse. Remember that the culprit who falls under your jurisdiction is a wretched mortal who is subject to all the conditions of our depraved nature and, insofar as you are able to do so without injuring the other party, show him mercy and leniency, for though the attributes of God are all equal, that of compassion is more resplendent in our eyes than even that of justice.

"If you observe these rules and precepts, Sancho, your days will be long, your fame eternal, your honors abundant, your happiness inexpressible, and you can marry your children to whomever you please. They and your grandchildren will have titles to their names, you will live in peace with the approval of the populace, and in the final days of your life, death will come to you gently at a ripe old age and your eyes will be closed by the tender, loving hands of your great-grandchildren.

"The instructions I have given you thus far are those designed to adorn your soul. I shall now give you those which will serve as the adornments of your body."

Chapter Forty-Three

The second set of precepts that Don Quixote gave Sancho Panza

Who could have heard the foregoing discourse by Don Quixote without considering him a person of great lucidity and greater principles? However, as has often been noted in the course of this great history, he was in the habit of talking nonsense only when treating of knight-errantry. When dealing with any other subject, he showed himself to possess such a dispassionate and unfettered mind that at every turn his deeds gave the lie to his judgement and his judgement the lie to his deeds. But with regard to the second set of precepts that he gave Sancho, he showed himself to be quite eloquent, raising his wisdom and folly to new heights. Sancho listened to him totally absorbed, attempting to store all the advice in his memory, like someone who intended to save it and employ it later to bring about a successful birth of his pregnant government. Don Quixote proceeded to say,

"With regard, Sancho, to the way you are to govern your person and your household, my first charge to you is that you keep yourself clean and your fingernails trimmed, not permitting them to grow as some do, whose ignorance has led them to believe that long nails enhance the hands, as though these excrescences and appendages which they avoid cutting – a bizarre and filthy practice – were fingernails, when in fact they are nothing more than the claws of a predatory hawk. Refrain from going about, Sancho, without a belt or with your clothes unkempt, for slovenly dress is a sure indication of a soul in disarray, unless the disorder and slovenliness fall into the category of craftiness, as Julius Caesar's were thought to do. Ascertain in a discreet manner how lucrative your office is and, should it allow you to provide your servants with liveries, give them some that are respectable and practical rather than showy and gaudy, dividing them between your servants and the poor, by which I mean that if you are able to clothe six pages, clothe three of them and three persons who are poor. In this way you will have pages for both heaven and earth. This novel method for distributing clothing, however, is one the vainglorious will never discover.

"Likewise, never eat garlic or onions lest your breath expose your rustic roots. Walk slowly and speak unhurriedly but not so slowly that you appear to be listening to yourself talk, for all affectation is bad. Eat sparingly, particularly at supper, for the well being of the entire body is forged in the foundry of the stomach. Be moderate in your drinking, bearing in mind that he who imbibes wine to excess keeps neither secrets nor promises. Take care, Sancho, not to chew with both cheeks full and not to eructate in the presence of others."

"I don't understand that 'eructate'," said Sancho; to which Don Quixote responded,

"'To eructate,' Sancho, means 'to belch,' this being one of the coarsest words in the language even if it is quite expressive. For this reason, careful speakers have resorted to Latin, saying 'eructate' instead of 'belch', and 'eructation' instead of 'belching'. If some people do not understand these terms, it is of little importance, for in time usage will establish them to the point where they will be readily understood, thus leading to the enrichment of language, over which usage and the masses exercise control."

"Truly, master," replied Sancho, "one piece of advice I intend to bear in mind is that of not belching, which I'm in the habit of doing quite often."

"'Eructate', Sancho, not 'belch'," said Don Quixote.

"From now on I'll always 'eructate'," said Sancho, "and I promise not to forget."

"Also, Sancho, you are not to lard your conversation with that horde of proverbs of yours, for though proverbs are encapsulated knowledge, you so frequently drag them in by the hair of the head that they sound more like nonsense than knowledge."

"The solution to that is in the hands of God," said Sancho. "I know enough proverbs to fill a book and so many crowd into my mouth at one time when I speak that they fight among themselves to see which ones get out, and my tongue launches the first one it encounters even though it may not make sense. But from this moment on I'll be sure to use those appropriate to the high calling of my office, for 'When the cupboard is full, the meals come fast,' and 'The one who cuts the cards should not also deal.' Likewise, 'The person who tolls the alarm is always safe from harm,' and 'It takes brains to know when to give and when to keep.'"

"There you go," said Don Quixote, "rattle on with your endless string of proverbs, since no one can stop you! To correct a stubborn person is like carrying water in a sieve. Here I am telling you to forsake your proverbs and a moment later you have reeled off a whole litany that are as appropriate to what we are discussing as is the man in the moon. Mind you, Sancho, I am not saying there is anything wrong with proverbs that are to the point but to unleash a string of proverbs helter-skelter turns a conversation into something dreary and demeaning; but to continue:

"When you ride horseback, avoid leaning back against the rear pommel or riding with your legs stiff and sticking out from the horse's belly, or sitting so limp you appear to be riding a jackass. Horseback riding turns some men into gentlemen and others into stableboys. Exercise moderation in your sleep, for 'He who rises not with the dawn enjoys not the morn.' Remember, Sancho, that 'Industry is the mother of good fortune,' whereas laziness, its opposite, has never achieved the success good intentions deserve.

"This last bit of advice that I wish to give you, though having nothing to do with improving the body, is one I would have you bear in mind, for I believe it will be of no less benefit to you than those I have given you up to this point: namely, that you are never to get into an argument over family trees; at least, don't compare them to one another, for between those persons being compared one will necessarily be superior and consequently you will be despised by the one you have humbled but unrewarded by the one you have exalted. And lastly, your dress is to consist of full-length breeches, a long coat, and a somewhat longer cloak, but under no circumstances those loose-fitting pantaloons, which are unbecoming to gentlemen and governors alike.

"For the time being, Sancho, this is all the advice that comes to mind but as time goes by, my admonitions will be tailored to the situation, provided you take the trouble to inform me of how you are faring."

"Master," said Sancho, "I can plainly see that all the things your grace has told me are good, hallowed, and beneficial but what good will they do me if I can't remember any of them? Hopefully, that business of not letting my fingernails grow or of getting married again, should the situation present itself, will never be forgotten, but all that other rigamarole and stuff I won't remember any more than I will the clouds of yesteryear. I'll need to have someone write them down and even then, since I can't read or write, I'll give them to my confessor so he can cram them into me or remind me of them as the need arises."

"Heaven help my soul, Sancho!" replied Don Quixote, "how unseemly it is for governors not to be able to read and write! I would have you know, dear Sancho, that a left-handed man or one who cannot read suggests one of two things: either he was the son of exceedingly humble, lowly parents or was so bad and mischievous that he was never able to adopt good habits and moral values. This is a sizeable defect you carry about, for which reason I would have you learn to sign your name at the very least."

"I know how to sign my name," said Sancho, "for when I was a steward in my village, I learned to print a few letters like those big ones on sacks, which, I was told, spelled out my name. Besides, I can always pretend my right hand is crippled and have someone else sign for me, for 'There's a remedy for everything except death.' And since I'll be in command and will wield the stick, I'll do what I please, especially when 'The one whose father is mayor . . . ' [1] And once I'm governor, which is greater than being mayor, just let them try something and they'll be in for a surprise! I'd like to see them try to make a fool of me! 'They may come looking for wool but they'll go home shorn.' 'When God loves someone, He knows which house he's in;' moreover, 'A rich man's follies always pass for wisdom,' and when I'm rich, as I intend to be, and am not only governor but a generous one at that, no defect of mine will be labeled as such. No, 'Cover yourself with honey and you'll not want for flies.' 'You're worth as much as you've got,' a grandmother of mine used to say, and 'There's no getting revenge on a man of means."

"Curse your soul, Sancho!" cried Don Quixote at this point, "you and your proverbs can go to blazes! You have been stringing them together for an hour and twisting my soul on the rack with each one. Mark my word, Sancho, those proverbs will get you hanged some day and because of them your vassals will rise up against you and strip you of your government. But tell me one thing: where does an idiot and simpleton like yourself come up with them and know how to apply them? Why, for me to come up with just one and apply it correctly, I have to sweat and slave like a ditch digger."

"For heaven's sake, my lord and master," said Sancho, "your grace is making a mountain out of a mole hill. Why the dickens should it upset your grace if I make use of my resources, since I have nothing else of value except proverbs and more proverbs? By the way, I've just thought of several others that are simply perfect for the occasion and are sitting there like ducks on a pond, but I won't mention them, for I'm not called Silent Sancho for nothing."

"'Silent Sancho' you are not!" said Don Quixote; "not only are you not good at keeping silent but are bad at it, and persistently so. Despite that, though, I should like to know which proverbs you have

1 The entire proverb is: 'The one whose father is mayor goes to trial with confidence.'

just thought of that are so apropos. As for myself I have been racking my brain, which is a fairly good one, and have not come up with a single one."

"What better proverbs," said Sancho, "than these: 'Never stick your finger between anyone's wisdom teeth;' 'To the question, "Have you stopped beating your wife?" what can one answer?'; and 'Whether the jug hits the stone or the stone the jug, the jug gets the worst of it' – all of which fit here like the glove on your hand. No one should pick a fight with his governor or any person in command, for he'll end up on the short end of the stick, like the person who puts his finger between two wisdom teeth, and even if they're not wisdom teeth, so long as they're grinders, it doesn't matter. Likewise, there's no way to respond to the person who asks if you've stopped beating your wife; and as for the stone's hitting the jug, even a blind man can see through that one. Thus it behooves one who sees a mote in his neighbor's eye to see the beam in his own or it will be labeled a case of 'the pot calling the kettle black.' Your grace is certainly aware that 'A fool knows more in his own house than a wise man does in someone else's.'"

"That is not so, Sancho," said Don Quixote; "a fool knows nothing in his own house or in anyone else's, for no edifice of wisdom can be erected upon a foundation of folly. But let us leave it at that, Sancho, for if you govern badly, the fault will be yours but the shame mine. Still, I take comfort in the fact that I have performed my duty and counseled you with all the earnestness and wisdom of which I am capable, thereby fulfilling my obligation and my vow. May God guide and direct you in your government, Sancho, and may He rid me of the suspicion that you will make a mishmash of the whole island; a circumstance I could prevent by letting the duke know who you are and explaining to him that all that corpulence and pettiness of yours is nothing but a sack full of proverbs and mischief-making."

"Master," said Sancho, "if you think I'm not worthy of this government, I'll renounce it from this moment forward, for the dirt under the fingernails of my soul is more precious to me than my entire body. I can get along on bread and onions as plain ole Sancho as well as on partridges and capons as governor, for 'While we're asleep, we are all equal,' great and small, rich and poor. And if you will simply reflect upon it, you'll see it was your grace alone who thrust me into this business of governing. Why, I know less about governing an island than a buzzard does, and if anyone thinks that as a result of my being governor I'll be carried off by the Devil, I prefer to go to heaven as Sancho than to hell as governor."

"By heavens!" said Don Quixote, "those last words alone make me consider you worthy to be governor of a thousand islands, for you have good natural instincts, without which there is no knowledge worth anything. Commend yourself to God, Sancho, and always remain true to your original intention, by which I mean that you are to make it your unshakable goal and purpose to do the right thing in every situation that confronts you, for heaven always favors good intentions. But let us now go dine, for I think these lords and ladies are waiting on us."

Chapter Forty-Four

How Sancho Panza was taken to his island, together with the strange adventure that befell Don Quixote in the castle

The claim is made that in the original version of this history it actually states that when Cide Hamete came to write the present chapter, his interpreter did not translate it as he had written it, for it was in the manner of a complaint brought by the Moor against himself for having undertaken a history as dry and restricted as this one of Don Quixote, for it seemed to him he would always be discussing Don Quixote and Sancho rather than indulging in more serious and entertaining digressions or episodes. He also added that to have one's mind, hand, and pen forever confined to writing on a single subject and speaking through the mouths of only a few characters was an unbearable task that would not redound to the benefit of its author. And so, to avoid this obstacle, he had employed in the First Part the device of novellas such as that of *The Tale of Unreasonable Curiosity* and *The Captive's Tale*, which, in a sense, stand apart from the history, though the remaining ones recounted there deal with incidents that involved Don Quixote himself and could not therefore be omitted. He was also of the opinion that many persons, finding themselves caught up in the exploits of Don Quixote, what with all the attention that these demand, might give short shrift to the novellas and pass over them in haste or annoyance without appreciating the elegance and craftsmanship they contain, which would be all too apparent had they been published separately rather than linked to the insane doings of Don Quixote and the idiotic ones of Sancho. Consequently, in this Second Part he has refused to introduce any novellas, intrinsic or extraneous, but rather a few episodes that have the appearance of novellas but arise as a natural consequence of the plot itself, and even these in a limited way and with no more words than those necessary to describe them. And because he has bound and restricted himself to the narrow confines of this narrative, while possessing the ability, competency, and knowledge to treat of the entire universe, he asks that his efforts be not despised but praised, and not for what he has written but for what he has chosen not to write.

He then proceeds with the history, saying that when Don Quixote finished dining on the day he gave his counsels to Sancho, he wrote them down for him that afternoon so Sancho could find someone to read them to him. But scarcely had he done so than Sancho misplaced them and they fell into the hands of the duke, who showed them to the duchess and they both marveled once again at Don Quixote's madness and intelligence. And so that evening, in order to proceed with their charade, they sent Sancho and a large train of attendants off to the place which for him was to be an island. Now it happened that the person they put in charge of this was one of the duke's majordomos, a very clever and humorous fellow (since there can be no humor where there is no cleverness), the one who had impersonated the Countess Trifaldi with all the assuredness previously described. Armed with these instructions from his master and mistress as to how he was to conduct himself with

Sancho, he executed their plan to perfection. I should add that when Sancho saw this majordomo, he fancied the latter's face was that of La Trifaldi, so he spoke to Don Quixote and said,

"Master, either the Devil is going to whisk me away from this very spot right here and now or your grace must admit that the face of the duke's majordomo here in our midst is the same as that of the Distressed One."

Don Quixote looked closely at the majordomo and after doing so said to Sancho,

"Since there is no reason for the Devil to carry you off either here or now, I have no idea what you are insinuating. The face of the Distressed One and that of the majordomo are one and the same but the majordomo is not for that reason the Distressed One; if he were, it would pose a very great contradiction and this is not the time or place to undertake such an investigation, as it would require entering a labyrinthine maze. Believe me, my friend, we must pray to Our Lord most earnestly to deliver us both from evil sorcerers and enchanters."

"It is nothing to scoff at, master," said Sancho, "for earlier I heard him talk and it seemed as though the very voice of La Trifaldi was echoing in my ears – but never mind: I'll keep quiet but will make certain to keep on the lookout from this moment on to see if he reveals some other sign that'll confirm or dispel my suspicion."

"That is the thing to do," said Don Quixote, "and you must send me news of everything you discover in this matter and everything that befalls you in your government."

In the company of a large retinue, Sancho finally set out, mounted on a cross-country mule and attired in the manner of a lawyer with his broad brown coat of watered camel skin and matching hunting cap, and, trailing behind him in accordance with the duke's orders, came the dapple sporting brand-new silken trappings and decorations. Sancho turned his head every so often to look at his jackass, in whose company he traveled so contentedly that he would not have changed places with the emperor of Germany. Taking leave of the duke and duchess, he kissed their hands and received the blessings of his master, who bestowed them with tears in his eyes, and Sancho accepted them while struggling to choke back tears of his own.

Gentle reader, let us allow our good Sancho to go in peace and good fortune, for you may expect to be the recipient of a couple bushels of laughter when you learn how he conducted himself in his new position. In the meantime, lend me your attention and you will learn what happened to his master that night, and even if you do not laugh at it, at least you will bare your teeth in a broad grin like a Cheshire cat, for Don Quixote's adventures must necessarily meet with astonishment or laughter.

It is related that no sooner had Sancho departed than Don Quixote became keenly aware of his abandonment and, had it been possible for him to rescind Sancho's commission and take away his government, he would have done so. The duchess recognized his melancholy and asked him the reason for his sadness, saying that if it was due to Sancho's absence, she had in her household squires, duennas, and servant-girls who would wait on him to his heart's content.

"Truthfully, my lady," said Don Quixote, "I do miss Sancho's company but that is not the main reason for my sadness. Of the many kindnesses your highness is offering me I can accept only the goodwill with which the offers are made. As for the others, I beg your highness to allow and permit me within the confines of my room to serve as my own servant."

"Truly, Sir Don Quixote," replied the duchess, "I will not allow that. Your grace shall be served by four servant-girls of mine as lovely as flowers."

"To me," said Don Quixote, "they will not be flowers but thorns that will pierce my heart, for which reason I would as soon admit them to my quarters or do anything of the sort as to see them fly. If your highness insists upon showing me these favors that I do not deserve, pray allow me to deal with them and serve myself in my own room, that I may erect a barrier between my desires and my virtue. I should be loath to break this habit simply because of the generosity your highness is extending to me. In fact, I shall sleep fully clothed rather than allow myself to be undressed by anyone."

"Say no more, Sir Don Quixote; I understand!" said the duchess. "I promise to issue orders that not even a fly is to enter your grace's room, let alone a servant-girl. Far be it from me to cause your lordship's innocence to be compromised, for it strikes me that the most outstanding of your many virtues is that of modesty. You may dress and undress in privacy and in your own fashion, however and whenever you please, and there shall be no one to stand in your way. You will even find in your room the necessary receptacles for the needs of one who sleeps behind a closed door so that no natural necessity will oblige your grace to open it. May the great Dulcinea of Toboso live a thousand years and may her renown spread throughout the world, for she has seen herself worthy to be loved by such a brave and modest knight. And may merciful heaven instill in the heart of our governor Sancho Panza a desire to finish his penance quickly so the world may once again enjoy the beauty of so great a lady."

To this Don Quixote replied,

"Your ladyship has spoken words true to your character, for virtuous ladies are incapable of speaking ill of any other woman. Dulcinea will be more fortunate and renowned on earth for having been praised by your highness than by all the praises the most eloquent men on earth could pay her."

"Well now, Sir Don Quixote," said the duchess, "the dinner hour has arrived and the duke is undoubtedly waiting. Come, sir, let us dine so you may retire early, for the journey your grace made yesterday to Candaya will not have been so short as to have left you without certain bruises."

"I feel none, my lady,' said Don Quixote; "in fact, I shall be so bold as to state that never in my life have I ridden a more comfortable animal or one with a steadier gate than Clavileño's. I cannot imagine what could have possessed Malambruno to make him cast aside such a swift and elegant mount, and to set fire to him no less!"

"Concerning that point," replied the duchess, "one might well imagine that, having repented of the wrongs he had committed against La Trifaldi and her companions, and of the injuries he had probably inflicted as a sorcerer and enchanter, Malambruno meant to destroy all the instruments of his art by setting fire to Clavileño as the principal cause of his unrest in his travels from land to land, because by its ashes and the triumph proclaimed by the placard, the valor of the great Don Quixote of La Mancha has achieved immortality."

Don Quixote again thanked the duchess and after dinner retired to the solitude of his chamber, refusing to allow anyone to accompany or serve him, such was his fear of encountering temptations that might induce or compel him to compromise the standards he observed towards his lady Dulcinea, for the virtue of Amadís, flower and mirror of knights-errant, was ever present in his thoughts. Locking the door behind him, he undressed by the light of two wax candles but, upon removing his stockings – Oh, disaster unworthy of such a personage! – there broke forth, not 'sighs' nor any other indelicacies that might bring discredit to his immaculate upbringing, but some two dozen broken stitches on one of his stockings, which left it looking like a window lattice. Our worthy lord was distressed in the extreme and would have given an ounce of silver to have at hand the tiniest amount of green silk thread; I say green because that was the color of his stockings.

When writing this, Benengeli exclaimed,

"O poverty, dear poverty! I have no idea why that great Cordovan poet [1] was moved to call you a 'holy and unappreciated gift!' Though a Moor, I know perfectly well from my dealings with Christians that saintliness consists of charity, humility, faith, obedience, and poverty. But in spite of all this, I might add that one must be filled with the spirit of God to be content to be poor, unless it is that type of poverty about which one of their greatest saints has said, 'Consider all thy possessions as though thou didst not possess them,' [2] which is known as spiritual poverty. But you poverty of the second type, the one I am addressing here, why do you insist upon assaulting nobles and men of high degree more than other persons? Why do you force them to coat their shoes with pitch or to use an assortment of silken, glass, and horsehair buttons on their clothing? Why must their collars, for the most part, be forever wrinkled rather than pressed with an iron, from which practice we may deduce the antiquity of starch and crimped collars?"

And continuing, he went on to say,

"What a highborn wretch is that person who must give himself airs to maintain his honor, eating his sparse meals indoors and then with his toothpick playing the hypocrite in the street, having eaten nothing that would oblige him to pick his teeth! What a miserable soul, I say, whose honor is so tenuous he suspects someone will detect from a league away the repair work on his shoes, the stain spots on his hat, the loose threads on his cloak, or the hunger in his stomach!"

All these thoughts were aroused in Don Quixote by the broken stitches but he took heart when he saw that Sancho had left him a pair of travel-boots, which he resolved to wear the following day. Finally, he lay down heartsick and beset by his thoughts, due as much to the pain occasioned by Sancho's absence as to the irreparable disaster of his stockings, which he would gladly have darned even with different-colored thread, this being one of the surest signs of wretchedness a noble can display in the course of his ever-present poverty. He snuffed out the candles but, because the night was hot, was unable to fall asleep. Getting out of bed, he cracked a window grating that opened onto a beautiful garden and in doing so heard people conversing as they strolled about the garden, at which point he began to listen in earnest. Those below raised their voices so he would be able to make out their remarks.

---

1 Juan de Mena (1411-1456)

2 A paraphrase of Saint Paul's *First Epistle to the Corinthians* VII, 30, which reads: '... they that buy, as though they possessed not.' The Jerusalem Bible renders this as: ' ... those whose life is buying things should live as though they had nothing of their own.'

"Don't insist that I sing, dear Emerencia, for you know that ever since that stranger entered this castle and I caught sight of him, I can only weep, not sing. Besides, since my lady is not a heavy sleeper but a light one, I should not want her to discover us here for all the money on earth; but even if she remained asleep and did not wake, my singing would be for nought if this new Aeneas who has come to these parts to make a fool of me were to continue sleeping and not wake to hear it."

"Don't let that worry you, Altisidora my friend, for surely the duchess and all the others in the house are asleep, except possibly the lord of your heart, who has awakened your soul. Since I just now heard the window of his room open, he is no doubt awake. Sing, my heart-sick one, in a soft, low voice to the accompaniment of your harp, and if the duchess should happen to hear us, we shall lay the blame on the sultry night."

"That is not the problem, Emerencia dear," replied Altisidora, "but the fact that I should not want my song to reveal my feelings, whereby I may be judged by those unacquainted with love to be a giddy, shameless girl. However, let come what may – better a face of shame than a blemished heart."

Here Don Quixote heard the delicate strains of a harp and was dumbfounded as he listened, for at that moment there came to mind an endless procession of previous adventures similar to this one with windows, gratings, gardens, serenades, flirtations, and swoonings, which he had read in his erstwhile books of chivalry. Immediately imagining that one of the duchess' ladies-in-waiting had become enamored of him, whose modesty forced her to keep her desires secret, he was gripped by the fear of succumbing but vowed in his heart not to allow himself to be seduced. Therefore, commending himself body and soul to his lady Dulcinea of Toboso, he decided to listen to the song and, in order to make them aware of his presence, he faked a sneeze, which delighted the damsels in no small measure, for they desired nothing more than for Don Quixote to hear them. Once Altisidora had tuned and plucked the strings on her harp, she began to sing the following ballad:

"Wake, Sir Knight, now love's invading;
Sleep in Holland sheets no more;
When a nymph is serenading,
'Tis an errant shame to snore.

Hear a damsel, tall and slender,
Moaning in most rueful guise,
With heart almost burned to cinder,
By the sunbeams of thine eyes.

To free damsels from disaster
Is, they say, your daily care:
Can you then deny a plaster
To a wounded virgin here?

Tell me, doughty youth, who cursed thee
  With such humors and ill-luck,
Was't some sullen bear dry-nursed thee,
  Or she-dragon gave thee suck?

Dulcinea, that virago,
  Well may brag of such a Cid,
Now her fame is up, and may go
  From Toledo to Madrid.

Would she but her prize surrender,
  (Judge how on thy face I dote!)
In exchange I'd gladly send her
  My best gown and petticoat.

Happy I, would fortune doom me
  But to have thee near my bed,
Stroke thee, pat thee, currycomb thee,
  And hunt o'er they knightly head.

But I ask too much, sincerely,
  And I doubt I ne'er must do't;
I'd but kiss your tow, but fairly
  Get the length thus of your foot.

How I'd rig thee, and what riches
  Should be heaped upon thy bones!
Caps and socks, and cloaks and britches,
  Matchless pearls and precious stones.

Do not from above, like Nero,
  See me burn and slight my woe,
But to quench my fires, my hero,
  Cast a pitying eye below.

I'm a virgin pullet, truly;
  One more tender ne'er was seen:
A mere chicken fledged but nearly:
  Hang me if I'm yet fifteen.

Wind and limb, all's sound about me;
   My hair dangles to my feet;
I am straight too:– if you doubt me,
   Trust your eyes, come down and see't.

I've a bob nose has no fellow,
   And a sparrow's mouth as rare,
Teeth like bright topazes, yellow;
   Yet I'm deemed a beauty here.

You know what a rare musician
   (If you hearken) courts your choice;
I dare say my disposition
   Is as comely as my voice.

Here the song of the smitten Altisidora ended and the anxiety of the hotly pursued Don Quixote began. The latter heaved a deep sigh and said to himself, 'To think that I am such an unfortunate knight that no damsel can lay eyes upon me without falling hopelessly in love, and that the peerless Dulcinea of Toboso is so devoid of happiness they will not allow her to enjoy my incomparable fidelity in peace! What do you queens want with her? Why do you empresses pursue her? Why do you fourteen- and fifteen-year-old damsels harass her? Allow the poor creature to triumph, enjoy herself, and glory in the good fortune Love meant to give her by conquering my heart and delivering my soul unto her. Pay heed, you love-struck throng: to Dulcinea alone am I as sweet as almond candy; to all others I am as hard as flint. To her I am honey but to you I am gall. To me alone is Dulcinea womanhood in all its beauty, wisdom, purity, elegance, and august birth, whereas the rest of you are ugly, foolish, inconstant, and lowborn. For me to be hers and no one else's, nature has placed me upon this earth. Let Altisidora weep or sing and let Madame despair on whose behalf I was throttled in the enchanted Moor's castle but I will belong to Dulcinea one way or another – chaste, pure, and well-mannered – despite all the powers of sorcery on earth!'

With this he slammed the window shut as though beset by some terrible tragedy and stretched out on his bed in sorrow and despair, where we shall leave him for the present because we are being summoned by the great Sancho Panza, who is about to assume the reins of his famous government.

Chapter Forty-Five

How the great Sancho Panza took possession of his island and the manner in which he began to govern

O perpetual explorer of the antipodes, torch of the world, eye of heaven, gentle rotator of wine-coolers, thou who art known variously as Timbraeus, Phoebus, archer, physician, father of poetry, and inventor of music, who always rise and, contrary to appearances, never set; 'tis thee, O sun! – with whose assistance man begets man – whom I call upon to favor and illumine the darkness of my understanding so that my description of the great Sancho Panza's government will include every single detail, for without thee I feel hesitant, weak, and confused!

I can thus report that Sancho and his entourage arrived at a town of some one thousand inhabitants, which was among the best the duke owned. They informed him that the island was called Cheap-Isle either because of the *town's* name, which was Cheapside, or because the government had been awarded to Sancho at so little cost to himself. When they reached the gates of the town, which was encircled by a wall, they were greeted by a regiment of aldermen and the pealing of bells. There was a general display of joy on the part of all the citizens, who with great pomp and ceremony accompanied Sancho to the main church to offer thanks to God. After several ludicrous ceremonies, they presented him with the keys to the town and installed him as permanent governor of Cheap-Isle. The new governor's dress, bearded face, and squat, rotund figure astounded all those who were not in on the secret, which was no small number, and even those who were. Some time later, they left the church and led him to the tribunal, where they had him take his seat on the judicial bench. The duke's majordomo then said to him,

"It is an ancient custom on this famous island, your governorship, that whoever comes to take possession of it is obliged to answer a question he shall be asked, which question is somewhat difficult and complicated but the answer to which allows the people to take the pulse of their new governor and, by doing so, either to be gladdened or saddened by his arrival."

While the majordomo explained this to Sancho, the latter kept his eyes fixed upon a number of large letters painted on the wall across from where he was seated but, because he did not know how to read, he asked them what was painted on the wall; to which they replied,

"Sir, written and recorded there is the day on which your lordship has taken possession of this island, and the inscription reads: *On this day of this particular month of this particular year his lordship Don Sancho Panza has taken possession of this island and may he enjoy it for many long years to come.*"

"And who are they calling *Don* Sancho Panza?" asked Sancho.

"Why, your lordship," replied the majordomo, "for no other Panza has set foot on this island except the one now seated on this bench."

"Well, understand, brother," said Sancho, "that I do not use 'Don', nor have any of my ancestors used it. I am plain Sancho, my father was plain Sancho, and so was my grandfather, without adding any 'Don' or 'Doña'. I imagine that on this island there must be more 'Dons' than pebbles, which is all I'll say because God understands what I mean. It may turn out that if my government lasts several days, I'll weed out these 'Dons', which due to their abundance must be as offensive as mosquitoes. Let his lord majordomo proceed to the question, which I will answer to the best of my ability, whether it saddens the citizens or not."

But at that moment two men entered the court, one dressed as a farmer and the other as a tailor. The latter, who held a pair of scissors in his hand, said,

"Sir governor, this farmer and I have come before your lordship because this good man entered my shop yesterday, inasmuch as I am – if your graces will forgive my saying this – a licensed tailor, for which I give thanks to God, and he placed a piece of cloth in my hands, saying, 'Sir, will there be enough cloth here to make me a cap?' After examining the cloth, I told him there would be. My guess, which turned out to be correct, was that he must have suspected that I intended to steal part of his cloth, basing his belief on his own malevolence and the low reputation of tailors. He asked me whether I thought there was enough for two, and I, reading his thoughts, said there was. Persisting then in his first churlish notion, he kept adding one cap after another and I kept saying 'yes' until we reached five caps, and now, just moments ago, he came to collect the caps and I gave them to him but he refused to pay me for my handiwork, insisting instead that I give him back his cloth or pay him for it."

"Is all this true, my son?" asked Sancho.

"Yes, your honor," replied the man, "but will your grace please make him show everyone the five caps he made me?"

"Gladly," said the tailor, whereupon he withdrew his hand from beneath his cloak and displayed five caps he had fitted over the tips of his fingers. "Here are the five caps," he said, "which this good man asked me to make and I swear by God and my conscience that not one bit of cloth was left over. I'll even let the work be examined by the trade inspectors."

Everyone present laughed at the flock of hats and the unusual lawsuit. Sancho set himself to pondering for a few moments and finally said,

"It seems to me that what is needed here is not some lengthy deliberation but a speedy decision based upon common sense. Therefore, my decision is that the tailor shall lose his handiwork and the farmer his cloth, the caps shall go to the inmates in the jail, and that is the end of the matter."

If the previous verdict on the cattleman's purse caused all those present to marvel, this one moved them to laughter. [1] In the end, however, the governor's order was carried out. Next to appear before Sancho were two old men, one of whom carried a staff as a walking-cane. The one without a cane spoke up:

"Your honor, several days ago I lent this good man ten gold *escudos* to favor him and to do him a good turn but with the understanding that he was to return them to me whenever I asked for them. A number of days passed without my doing so lest his repaying me place him in greater straits than he was in when I lent him the *escudos;* but when it eventually became clear to me that he was negligent in repaying me, I asked him for them on more than one occasion. Not only has he refused

---

1 An obvious lapse on the part of Cervantes, who, subsequent to writing this sentence changed the order of the two incidents but failed to revise this reference.

to pay me but denies that he owes them, claiming I never lent him any such ten *escudos*, or if I did, he has already repaid them. I have no witnesses to the loan or its return because he has never returned them to me. I beg your grace to place him under oath and if he swears he has returned them, I will forget the matter once and for all."

"What do you say to that, old man?" said Sancho to the man with the cane.

"I confess, your honor," said the old man, "that he did lend them to me and, since he leaves it up to me, I will swear I really and truly returned them to him and paid him back if your grace will hold out your staff of justice."

The governor extended the staff in his direction and, as he did so, the man handed his cane to the other man to hold while he took his oath, as though it were very much in his way. He then placed his hand on the staff's cross, swearing it was true that the other man had lent him those ten *escudos* he was requesting but that he had personally returned them to the other man who, without realizing it, kept asking for them at every turn. When the governor saw this, he asked the lender to respond to what his adversary charged. The man replied that without a doubt his debtor must be telling the truth, for he considered him an honest man and a good Christian; that he must have forgotten how and when his debtor had returned the coins to him, and that from that moment on he would never ask for them again. The debtor then took back his cane and with his head bowed left the court. When Sancho saw him leave in this manner without so much as a 'thank you' and also saw the plaintiff's resignation, he rested his chin on his chest and placed the index finger of his right hand across his eyebrow and the bridge of his nose, assuming the pose of someone deep in thought. Then raising his head, he ordered them to go after the old man with the cane who had just left. They brought him back and when Sancho saw him, he said to him,

"My good man, hand me that cane. I would like to see it."

"Gladly," replied the old man, "here it is, your honor."

And he placed it in Sancho's hand, whereupon the latter gave it to the other man, saying,

"Go with God, sir, for you are now repaid."

"How so, your honor?" said the old man; "is this cane worth ten gold *escudos*?"

"Yes," replied the governor, "if not, I'm the biggest dunce on earth. We'll now see whether I have brains enough to govern an entire kingdom."

And there in the presence of everyone he ordered the cane broken open, and when this was done, they found in the middle of it ten gold *escudos*. Everyone was tremendously impressed and proclaimed their governor a second Solomon. They asked him how he had figured out the ten *escudos* were inside the cane and he said it was from having seen the old man hand his adversary his cane while taking his oath and hearing him swear that he really and truly had given him the *escudos*. And later, when he asked for his cane again after finishing his oath, it suddenly occurred to him that inside the cane was the payment the other person was seeking. (From this, one can see that those who govern, even if they are a bunch of fools, are perhaps guided in their decisions by Providence.) Besides, Sancho had heard his village priest tell of a similar case, adding that as far as his memory was concerned, they would find none better in the whole island if they overlooked the fact that he forgot every last thing he ever tried to remember.

Finally, both old men left: one embarrassed and the other pleased, and all those present stood there astonished and awe-struck. The person recording Sancho's words, deeds, and gestures was never able to determine whether to consider him a fool or to set him down as a wise man. Once this lawsuit was concluded, there came into court a woman tightly clutching a man outfitted as a well-to-do herdsman and she was shouting in a loud voice,

"Justice, your honor, justice! If I don't receive it on earth, I'll seek it in heaven! I swear, my dear esteemed Governor, that this evil man grabbed me in the middle of a field and used my body as though it were a dirty rag, and, alas! took from me what I had been guarding for more than twenty-three years, defending it against Moors and Christians, natives and foreigners. But I, always as unyielding as an oak, have kept myself as pure as a salamander in fire, or wool among the briars, only to have this good man come along now and lay his hands on me, albeit clean ones."

"Even that," said Sancho, "remains to be determined: whether this young fellow has clean hands or not."

And turning to the man, he asked him what he had to say in response to the woman's charges. The man, completely flustered, answered,

"My lords and ladies, I am a poor swineherd who left this village this morning to sell – if you'll pardon the expression – four hogs, which, thanks to taxes and the fact that I was swindled, cost me nearly as much money as I sold them for. As I was returning to my village, I met this fine young thing along the way, and the Devil, who has his finger in every pie, caused us to lie together. I paid her a sufficient amount but she, feeling cheated, grabbed me and has not let go of me up to this very moment. She claims I forced her but I swear upon the oath I'm taking, or intend to take, that she's lying. This is the whole truth down to the last particle."

The governor then asked him if he had any silver coins on him. He said he had some twenty ducats in a leather purse in his shirt. The governor ordered him to take out the purse and give it to the plaintiff just as it was, which he hesitantly did. The woman snatched it and performed a thousand salaams while praying to God for the health and life of the worthy governor, who had such regard for orphans and maidens in need, at which point she hurriedly left the court clutching the purse in both hands but not before first looking inside to see if the coins she was carrying were silver. As soon as she had left, Sancho said to the swineherd, who was overflowing with tears and whose eyes and heart trailed after his purse,

"My good man, go after that woman and retrieve your purse, even if she is unwilling, and bring it back to me."

This was not said to a fool or to one who was deaf, for he took off at once like a bolt and did as commanded, leaving everyone present anxiously waiting to see where that affair might end. Presently, the man and the woman returned clutching and holding onto one another more tightly than before. She had wrapped the purse in her skirt, which she had rolled up from the bottom, and he was struggling to take it from her. This, though, was impossible because of the woman's efforts to defend it.

"In the name of God and all His creatures, sir governor," cried the woman, "I wish your grace would see how shamelessly and audaciously this cruel man has attempted out in the street in the very center of town to take from me the purse your grace ordered him to give me!"

"And did he take it from you?" asked the governor.

"Take it from me!" exclaimed the woman, "I would sooner give up my life than surrender my purse; a fine young thing I would be! It'll take more than this disgusting wretch to have his way with me! Pincers and hammers, mallets and chisels, even the claws of a lion would not be enough to get this out of my clutches! He'll come closer to extracting my soul from my very own body!"

"She's right," said the man; "I admit I'm powerless and beaten, and confess I lack the strength to take it from her. Therefore I'll let her go."

The governor then said to the woman,

"Let me see that purse, my brave, honorable woman."

She handed it to him and the governor returned it to the man, saying to the forceful but unforced woman,

"My good sister, had you shown the same spirit and courage in defending your body that you have shown in defending this purse, or even half as much, the might of Hercules could not have made you yield. Be off with you – and you can go to blazes! Don't stop anywhere on this island or within six leagues of it under penalty of two hundred lashes. Away with you at once, I say, you lying, shameless swindler!"

The woman was struck with fear and went away crestfallen and disgruntled, at which point the governor said to the man,

"My good sir, God speed you to your village with your money, and in the future, if you don't want to lose it, try not to get the urge to lie with anyone."

The man thanked him with all the ineptness of which he was capable and left. Those present were once again overawed by the decisions and verdicts of their new governor, all of which was noted by his chronicler and later communicated to the duke, who was most eagerly awaiting it.

But let us now leave noble Sancho and return to his master, who, having been excited by Altisidora's song, is in urgent need of our attention.

Chapter Forty-Six

The frightful bell and cat scare that Don Quixote received in the course of being wooed by the enamored Altisidora

We left the great Don Quixote preoccupied with those thoughts aroused in him by the song of the enamored damsel Altisidora. He took them to bed with him and like fleas they refused to let him sleep or get a moment's rest, being joined in this by those having to do with his frazzled stockings. But since time is swift and nothing can deter it, the hours passed by at a gallop and dawn arrived before he knew it, at which time he abandoned the soft down and with boundless vigor donned his chamois-skin suit and the traveling boots he wore to conceal his misfortune. Tossing a scarlet cloak across his shoulders, he put on a green velvet cap decorated with silver lace, strapped on a shoulder sash that supported his trusty, sharp-edged sword, took up a large rosary he constantly kept with him, and with great pomp and gravity proceeded to the antechamber, where the duke and duchess, now dressed, were obviously awaiting him. But as he passed along a gallery, Altisidora and another damsel – a friend of hers – were already there purposely lying in wait. The moment Altisidora saw him, she pretended to swoon and her friend caught her in the folds of her skirt, at which point she quickly unlaced her bodice. When Don Quixote observed this, he walked over to them and said,

"I can tell you what those fainting spells proceed from."

"Well, I have no idea," said the friend, "for Altisidora is the healthiest young woman in this whole house and I've never even heard her sigh in all the time I've known her. A pox upon all knights-errant if they are all such ingrates as this! My lord Don Quixote, your grace should go away, for this poor child will never recover her senses so long as you are present."

To which Don Quixote responded,

"My lady, if you will kindly have a lute placed in my chamber tonight, I shall do my best to console the afflicted damsel, for in a blossoming love affair a speedy disavowal is likely to provide an effective remedy."

With this, he withdrew to avoid being recognized by anyone who might see him there. No sooner had he departed than Altisidora recovered from her swoon and said to her companion,

"We must see that the lute is placed there for him, for Don Quixote obviously wishes to provide us with a serenade, which, coming from him, will not be bad."

They immediately went off to give the duchess an account of what had taken place, mentioning the lute Don Quixote had requested. Overjoyed at the idea, the duchess conspired with the duke and her maids to play a trick on him that would be more amusing than dangerous, so with great anticipation they waited for night, which came as quickly as day had arrived. In the meantime, the ducal pair spent the day in pleasant conversation with Don Quixote. Now, this was the same day on which the duchess actually dispatched one of her pages, the one who had impersonated the enchanted Dulcinea in the forest, to Teresa Panza with a letter from her husband Sancho Panza, together with the bundle of clothes the latter was sending her, and she charged him with bringing back a full report of everything that transpired with Teresa. This business having been attended to and the hour of eleven having arrived, Don Quixote returned to his chamber, where he found a *vihuela.* [1] After strumming it, he opened the window and, sensing the presence of people in the garden, ran his fingers up and down the frets of the *vihuela* to tune it as well as possible, cleared his throat and spat, and then in a voice that was raspy but on key sang the following ballad, which he himself had composed that very morning:

1 A musical instrument confined almost entirely to Spain and shaped like a guitar but tuned like a lute.

"Love, with idleness its friend,
O'er a maiden gains its end;
But let business and employment
Fill up ev'ry careful moment;
These an antidote will prove
'Gainst the poisonous arts of love.
Maidens that aspire to marry
In their looks reserve should carry;
Modesty their price should raise,
And be the herald of their praise.
Knights, whom toils of arms employ,
With the free may laugh and toy;
But the modest only choose
When they tie the nuptial noose.
Love that rises with the sun,
With his setting beams is gone:
Love that guest-like visits hearts,
When the banquet's o'er, departs;
And the love that comes today
And tomorrow wings its way,
Leaves no traces on the soul,
Its affections to control.
Where a sovereign beauty reigns,
Fruitless are a rival's pains;
O'er a finished picture who
E'er a second picture drew?
Fair Dulcinea, queen of beauty,
Rules my heart and claims its duty.
Nothing there can take her place;
Naught her image can erase.
Whether fortune smile or frown,
Constancy's the lover's crown;
And its force divine to prove,
Miracles performs in love."

Don Quixote had reached this point in his song, numbering among his listeners the duke and duchess, Altisidora, and virtually every other person in the castle, when all of a sudden, from a balcony directly above his window a rope was lowered, attached to which were more than a hundred cowbells as well as a large sack, out of which leapt a number of cats with tiny bells tied to their tails.

The noise was so great from the bells and the screeching cats that despite the fact that the duke and duchess had been the originators of this joke, they were startled by it all the same, and Don Quixote was scared out of his skin. As luck would have it, two or three of the cats jumped through the window into his chamber and as they darted about, one might have thought a legion of devils had been set loose there. They knocked over the lighted candles in the chamber as they ran about looking for a means of escape. The cord attached to the large cowbells never ceased being jerked up and down, which astonished and bewildered the majority of the people in the castle who were unaware of the underlying facts. Don Quixote sprang to his feet and, drawing his sword, began stabbing at the window and shouting in a loud voice,

"Get out, you evil enchanters! Get out, you conjuring scoundrels, for I am Don Quixote of La Mancha, against whom your evil intentions are powerless and of no avail!"

And turning to the cats as they dashed madly about the chamber, he began unleashing a barrage of sword thrusts. The cats managed to reach the window and jump through it, but one, seeing itself cornered by Don Quixote's endless slashes, leapt at his face and dug its claws and teeth into his nose, the pain from which caused Don Quixote to scream at the top of his lungs. When the duke and duchess heard this, they surmised what had probably happened and hurried as fast as they could to his chamber, which they entered by using a master key. There they saw the poor knight struggling with all his might to pull the cat off his face, and since they had entered carrying lamps, they were able to observe the one-sided battle. The duke rushed over to separate them but Don Quixote said with a shout,

"Don't anyone pull him off! I will go hand to hand with this demon, this sorcerer, this enchanter, and will personally show him who Don Quixote of La Mancha is!"

But the cat, taking no notice of these threats, screeched and held on. Finally, however, the duke yanked it off and flung it through the window. Don Quixote's face was left riddled but his nose had fared the worst of all. He himself was in a state of despair because they had not let him finish the hard-fought battle he had undertaken with that scoundrel of an enchanter. They sent for some oil of hypericum and Altisidora herself placed bandages on all his wounds with her very own snow-white hands and, as she did so, she said to him softly,

"All these misfortunes have befallen you, O hardhearted knight, because of your sin of obduracy and pertinacity. I pray to God that Sancho your squire will forget to flog himself so your most beloved Dulcinea will never escape from her enchantment and you will never enjoy her or share her nuptial bed, at least not while I am alive – because I adore you."

Don Quixote's only response to all this was to heave a deep sigh. Then lying down on his bed, he thanked the duke and duchess for their kindness, not because of his fear of that bell-ringing enchanter of a scoundrel in the guise of a cat, but because he recognized the good intentions with which they had hastened to his aid. Leaving him there to rest, the duke and duchess withdrew, regretting the painful outcome of their joke, for they had never imagined this adventure would turn out so dearly and painfully for Don Quixote. It cost him five days of confinement to his bed, during which time he experienced another adventure more pleasant than the last, an adventure his chronicler chooses not to relate at the present time, preferring to turn his attention to Sancho Panza, who has been conducting himself most diligently and amusingly as governor.

Chapter Forty-Seven

The continuation of the description of how Sancho Panza conducted himself as governor

Our history relates that from the court of justice they led Sancho Panza to a sumptuous palace, where in a great hall a majestic and immaculate meal had been prepared. As soon as Sancho entered the hall, hornpipes began to play and four pages stepped forward with wash basins in which Sancho washed his hands with the utmost solemnity. Once the music ceased, Sancho seated himself at the head of the table, which was the only seat available, there being no other place-setting along its entire length. Stationing himself at Sancho's side was an individual holding a whalebone rod in his hand, who turned out to be a physician. The servants removed the elegant white cloth that covered the plates of fruit and the various other dishes. A person who apparently was a university student said grace and another placed a bib trimmed with lace round Sancho's neck. A fourth person, who functioned as butler, set before him a plate of fruit as the first course, but scarcely had Sancho taken a bite than the man standing beside him tapped the plate with his rod and it was removed with the greatest haste. The butler, however, placed another dish before him, which Sancho was about to sample, but before he could reach out to do so, the rod had already tapped and the page removed it as quickly as he had the fruit dish. When Sancho saw this, he was mystified. Looking round at everyone, he asked whether the meal was to be eaten or was some type of magic trick like 'Now you see it, now you don't;' to which the man holding the rod replied,

"It is to be eaten, your governorship, but only in accordance with the customs and usage of islands where there are governors. I, sir, am a physician and am employed on this island to serve its governor as such. Indeed, I look after his health much better than I do my own, studying day and night to familiarize myself with the governor's constitution in order to treat him when he falls ill. My chief duty is to supervise all his meals and to permit him to eat what I think will be good for him but to remove what I feel will be bad or will harm his stomach. And so I ordered that dish of fruit removed for being too moist and that other plate of food for being too hot and containing too many spices. These only increase one's thirst and a person who drinks to excess puts an end to and consumes the radical moisture that is the basis of life."

"In that case, yond dish of roasted and apparently well-seasoned partridge will do me no harm."

To which the physician answered,

"Your lordship shall never eat that so long as I am alive!"

"And why not?" asked Sancho; to which the physician replied,

"Because our master Hippocrates, pole star and beacon of medicine, has stated in an aphorism of his that '*omnis saturatio mala, perdicem autem pessima,*' which means: 'Every type of surfeit is bad but that of partridge is the worst of all.'"

"If that is true," said Sancho, "I wish the good Doctor would tell me which one among all these dishes on this table will do me the most good and least harm and then let me eat it without tapping it with his rod, for I swear upon my life as governor – and God grant that I may enjoy it! – that I am dying of hunger and to deny me this food, despite the good Doctor and all his advice to the contrary, will be to rob me of my life rather than prolong it."

"Your governorship is correct," replied the physician, "so it is my belief that you should avoid that stewed rabbit because it comes from an animal with fur. That veal, however, were it not baked and marinated, might be tasted, but since it is, it too is out of the question."

"That steaming plate farther down the table," said Sancho, "looks to me like a pot-luck stew, and considering the great variety of things such stews contain, I will surely come across something in it that will be good for me and be tasty as well."

"*Absit*!" [1] said the physician, "may such an evil thought never cross our minds, for there is no worse dish on earth than a stew. Such dishes should be left to canons and university rectors or to peasant weddings but deliver the tables of governors from them, where elegance and refinement shall be the rule! The reason for this is that simple medicines are always more highly esteemed by people everywhere than compound ones because things cannot go wrong with the former but can with the latter by altering the proportion of their ingredients. What I am convinced that you should now eat to conserve your health and fortify yourself is a hundred wafers and thin slices of preserved quince, which will settle your stomach and help your digestion."

When Sancho heard this, he leaned back on his chair and studied the physician from head to foot. Finally, in a serious tone of voice he asked him his name and where he had studied; to which the physician replied,

"My name, your governorship, is Doctor Pedro Recio de Agüero. I am a native of a place called Tirteafuera, which is between Caracuel and Almodóvar del Campo on a road off to the right, and my medical degree is from the University of Osuna."

To which Sancho, brimming with anger, responded,

"Well, the good Doctor Pedro Recio de *Mal* Agüero, native of Tirteafuera, [2] a village on a road off to the right when one is traveling from Caracuel to Almodóvar del Campo, and graduate of Osuna, had better remove himself from my presence! If he doesn't, I swear by the sun in the sky that I'll grab a club and, beginning with him, will use it to drive from this island every last physician, at least, those I consider ignoramuses. Those physicians who are wise, prudent, and intelligent I will hold in esteem and will honor as divine beings. Let me say once again: Pedro Recio had better get out of my sight! If he doesn't, I'll take this chair I'm sitting on and will break it over his head, and should I be brought to trial, I will acquit myself by saying I did God a service by murdering an executioner of the state, an incompetent physician. Now somebody give me something to eat or you can have this government.

1 Latin: 'Away with it!'

2 ***Recio*** means 'demanding'; ***Mal Agüero*** 'Evil Omen;' and ***Tirteafuera*** 'Get out!'

An office that doesn't provide its holder with food isn't worth two hoots in hell."

The physician was shocked to see the governor so enraged and decided to beat a hasty retreat from the hall, but at that very instant a post-horn sounded in the street. The butler, after peering out the window, came back and reported,

"A courier from my master the duke has arrived and is probably bringing an important message."

The courier entered perspiring and apprehensive and pulled from his shirt an envelope, which he placed in the hands of the governor, who placed it in those of the majordomo, ordering him to see who it was addressed to. It read: *Personal delivery for Don Sancho Panza, governor of Cheap-Isle, or for his secretary.* Hearing this, Sancho asked,

"And who among you is my secretary?"

One of those present answered,

"I am, your lordship, because I can read and write and am a Biscayan besides."

"With that last qualification alone," said Sancho, "you might easily be secretary to the emperor himself. Open that envelope and see what it says."

The newly created secretary did as instructed and, after perusing its contents, said it was a matter to be dealt with in private. Sancho ordered the hall cleared, with no one to remain there except the majordomo and the butler. Once the physician and the others had left, the secretary read the letter, which said:

Dear Don Sancho Panza:

It has come to my attention that certain enemies of mine who are also enemies of that island are planning a furious assault upon it but on which night I know not. It will be prudent for your grace to be on the lookout and stay alert lest they catch you unprepared. I have also learned from some trustworthy spies that four persons in disguise have entered your village with the intention of taking your life because they stand in dread of your intellect. You should keep your eyes open, be wary of anyone who comes to speak to you, and not eat anything you are given. I shall not hesitate to come to your aid should you find yourself in adverse circumstances. Meanwhile, you are to do everything one might expect from a person of your understanding. From this village, the sixteenth of August at four in the morning.

Your grace's friend,
THE DUKE

Sancho was dumbfounded and the others pretended to be equally astonished. Turning to the majordomo, he said,

"The first thing to do, and do at once, is to put Doctor Recio in jail, for if anyone is out to kill me, it has to be him; and he intends to do so by a death as slow and horrible as that of starvation."

"Also," said the butler, "it is my opinion that your grace should not eat anything on this table, for it was all provided by some nuns, and there is the saying: 'Behind the cross lurks the Devil.'"

"I don't deny that," replied Sancho, "but for now give me a piece of bread and about four pounds of grapes, since there can't be any poison in them. The truth is, of course, that I can't manage without eating, and if we are expected to be prepared for these battles that are threatening, it is our duty to be well-nourished, seeing as how the guts sustain the heart, not the heart the guts. And you, secretary, reply to my master the duke and inform him that every single thing he has requested will be done. You are also to send my regards to my lady the duchess and tell her that I beg her not to forget to send one of her servants with my letter and bundle to my wife Teresa Panza, as I will consider it a very great favor and will make every effort to serve her to the extent that my strength allows. In the process you may put in a kind word from me to my master Don Quixote of La Mancha so he'll see that I'm grateful to the hand that feeds me. And you, as a faithful secretary and faithful Biscayan, may add anything you wish that happens to be pertinent. But for now, I'd like someone to clear this table and bring me something to eat and I'll take care of all the spies, assassins, and enchanters who may descend upon me and my island."

At this moment a page entered and announced,

"There is a farmer here on business who desires to speak to your grace about a matter he says is of great importance."

"It is very strange," said Sancho, "about these men on business. Are they possibly so stupid they can't see this is not the time of day to come here on business? Are those of us who govern and serve as judges not men of flesh and blood? Are we not to be allowed to rest as long as necessary without being asked to be made of marble? I swear upon God and my conscience that if my government lasts (and I'm not sure it will, the way things look), I'll show more than one man on business what this world is all about. For now, tell the good man to come in but first see to it that he's not one of the spies or my assassin."

"He is not, my lord," said the page, "for he appears to have a heart of gold. I may be dead wrong but he seems as good as they come."

"There is nothing to fear," replied the majordomo, "because we are all here."

"Would it be possible, butler," said Sancho, "now that Doctor Pedro Recio is not present, for me to eat something solid and substantial, even if it is only a piece of bread and an onion?"

"Tonight at dinner," said the butler, "every sort of food that has been lacking shall be provided and your grace will be satisfied and happy."

"May God grant that," said Sancho. Just then, the farmer entered and made quite a favorable impression, for one could see from a thousand leagues away that he was a good man with a heart of gold. The first thing he said was:

"Who among your graces is his lordship the governor?"

"Who do you think it is," replied the secretary, "if not the one seated on the bench?"

"Then I humble myself in his presence," said the farmer and, getting down on his knees, asked to be allowed to kiss the governor's hand. Sancho rejected the request, ordering him to stand and say what he had to say. At this point the farmer stood up and said,

"Your honor, I am a farmer and native of Miguel Turra, a village that is two leagues from Ciudad Real."

"We've got us another Tirteafuera," said Sancho, "but go ahead and speak, my son, for I would have you know I am well acquainted with Miguel Turra, since it's not far from my own town."

"Your honor," continued the farmer, "the fact of the matter is that by the grace of God I find myself married with the consent and blessing of the Holy Roman Catholic Church. I have two sons at the university, the younger studying to be a bachelor and the older a licentiate. I'm a widower, inasmuch as my wife has died, or more precisely, was killed by an incompetent physician who gave her a purgative when she was pregnant. Had God been pleased to allow the child to be born and it had been a boy, I would have had him study medicine so he would not envy his brothers the bachelor and the licentiate."

"And so," said Sancho, "had your wife not died or been killed, you would not now be a widower."

"Certainly not, your honor," replied the farmer.

"Now that we've got that nailed down," said Sancho, "proceed, my son, though the hour is more appropriate for sleeping than for conducting business."

"As I was saying," said the farmer, "this son of mine, who is well on his way to becoming a bachelor, fell in love with a maiden from our town named Clara Perlerino, daughter of Andrés Perlerino, a wealthy farmer. This name of Perlerino doesn't come from any of their ancestors or forebears but from the fact that everyone on that side of the family is paralytic, but so as to make the name more attractive, they call themselves Perlerino, [3] though if the truth be told, the maiden is as beautiful as an Oriental pearl. Viewed from her right side, she is like a flower of the field, but viewed from her left, she's not as beautiful because she's missing her left eye, which she lost to smallpox. And those who are fond of her say the pockmarks on her face, which are numerous and large, are not pockmarks but graves where the hearts of her lovers are buried. She's so neat that in order not to soil her face her nose is turned up, so to speak, giving the impression that it's trying to avoid her mouth, but despite all this, she's quite striking in appearance and has a broad mouth, which, were it not missing ten or twelve teeth, could hold its own or even surpass the most shapely one around. With regard to her lips I have nothing to add, for they're so thin and delicate that if such were the custom, they could be rolled into a skein, but because their hue is different from that normally found in lips, they have the aspect of something wondrous, being flecked with blue, green, and purple. I hope your governorship will forgive me for going into so much detail in describing the qualities of the one who is to be my daughter, for I truly love her and think she's not bad looking."

"Describe her as much as you like," said Sancho, "for I am enjoying the description and, had I already dined, I could ask for no better dessert than your portrait."

"The dessert is yet to be served," replied the farmer; "the moment will come when we shall partake of it but not just yet. I can assure your honor that if I could only describe her elegance and lofty stature, she would be something to behold. This is not possible, though, for she's bent completely double with her knees drawn up against her chin. It's easy to see, despite this, that if she could stand erect, her head would touch the ceiling. Likewise, she would already have held out her hand in

3 A play on words: ***perlático*** 'paralytic'; ***perlerino*** 'pearl-like.'

marriage to my bachelor, except that she's unable to extend it due to paralysis. Still, it demonstrates by its long, ridged fingernails how fine and well-formed it is."

"All right, my son," exclaimed Sancho, "let the record show that you have described her from one extremity to the other. Just what is it you want? And do get to the point without a bunch of detours and side trips."

"What I would like, sir," said the farmer, "is for your grace to favor me by giving me a letter of recommendation to my son's father-in-law asking him to find it in his heart to permit this marriage, since we are not inferior when it comes to gifts of fortune or those of nature. But to speak quite frankly, your honor, my son is possessed and no day goes by that he isn't set upon three or four times by malignant spirits, and because he once fell into the fire, his face is as drawn and wrinkled as a piece of parchment, and his eyes are always watery and runny. Still, he has the disposition of an angel and, were it not for the fact that he beats and pounds himself with his fists, he could be a saint."

"Is there anything else you would like, my good man?" asked Sancho.

"There is one thing," said the farmer, "but I don't dare mention it. Oh – hang it all! – I may as well get it off my chest regardless of the consequences; I mean, my lord, I would be pleased if your grace would give me five or six hundred ducats to help towards my bachelor's dowry, that is, to help them in setting up their household. After all, they ought to live by themselves without being subject to meddling by their in-laws."

"See if there is anything else you would like," said Sancho, "and don't be too bashful or ashamed to mention it."

"I certainly won't," replied the farmer, but scarcely had he said this than the governor stood up, gripped the back of the seat on which he had been sitting, and exclaimed,

"I swear to heaven, Don Bumpkin, you disgusting lout, if you don't get out of here and make yourself scarce, I'll break your head open! You no-good son of a whore, you agent of the Devil, how dare you come here at this hour to ask me for six hundred ducats! Where am I to get them, you scurrilous swine? Why would I give them to you even if I had them, you sly fool? What do I care about Miguel Turra or that whole line of Perlerinos? Get out of my sight or I swear upon the life of my lord the duke that I'll carry out what I've already threatened. You're not from Miguel Turra but are some crafty fox sent here from hell to tempt me! Listen, you fiend, I've been in charge of this government for only a day and a half and you expect me already to have six hundred ducats in my possession!"

The butler motioned to the farmer to leave the hall, which he did with his head bowed low, apparently afraid the governor might convert his anger into deeds, for the scoundrel knew perfectly well how to play his role.

But let us leave Sancho and his anger – may peace reign among the lot of them! – and return to Don Quixote, whom we left with his face bandaged, nursing his feline wounds from which it took him a week to recover. During this time, he experienced what Cide Hamete promises to relate with all the exactitude and veracity he is wont to employ in relating the events of this history, however minuscule they may be.

Chapter Forty-Eight

The things that transpired between Don Quixote and the duchess' duenna Doña Rodríguez, together with other incidents worthy of record and everlasting remembrance

Our sorely belabored Don Quixote was extremely dejected and melancholy, his face bandaged and marked, not by the hand of God, but by the claws of a cat, a commonplace adversity in knight-errantry. For six days he failed to appear in public and on one of these nights as he lay in bed fitfully tossing about, reflecting upon his bad luck and Altisidora's hot pursuit of him, he sensed that someone was attempting to unlock the door of his room. He immediately imagined the love-smitten maiden had come to lay siege to his innocence and place him in the position of betraying the fidelity he owed his lady Dulcinea of Toboso.

"No," he said in a voice loud enough to be heard, fancying everything he was imagining to be real, "the most beautiful woman on earth shall be incapable of making me cease to adore the one I carry stamped and engraved in the interior of my heart and the innermost recesses of my soul. O dearest Dulcinea, whether they have transformed thee into a farm girl reeking of onions or into a nymph of the golden Tagus knitting fabrics of gold and silk, or whether Merlin or Montesinos has thee in his thrall in his own favorite hideaway, thou shalt belong to me wherever thou art and I to thee wherever I am."

The end of this declaration and the opening of the door were one and the same act, whereupon Don Quixote stood up in bed swathed from head to foot in a yellow satin bedspread, his nightcap on his head, his face and mustache covered with bandages – his face because of the scratches, and his mustache to keep it from drooping and losing its shape – and in this attire he presented a picture of the most extraordinary apparition imaginable. He kept his eyes fixed upon the door, as he expected to see the submissive, love-smitten Altisidora make her appearance, but instead, he beheld the figure of a most venerable duenna with a white hemmed veil that was so long it enveloped and enclothed her from head to foot. She held a short flickering candle in her left hand and with her other shielded her face to keep the glare out of her eyes, which were covered by a pair of enormous spectacles. As she quietly and ever so warily entered, Don Quixote peered down from his watchtower from where he took stock of both her attire and silence. And since he believed her to be some witch or sorceress who had come there in that guise to inflict some sort of mischief upon him, he began to make the sign of the cross as rapidly as possible. The apparition continued to approach and, once in the middle of the room, raised its eyes, at which point it observed the frenzy with which Don Quixote was crossing himself; and if he was frightened at the sight of such a figure, the latter was terrified at the sight of him. The moment she saw him, so tall, sallow, and covered by the disfiguring bedspread and bandages, she cried out in a loud voice,

"Goodness, what is this I see?"

Her sudden start caused the candle to fall from her hand. Finding herself in the dark, she turned to leave but due to her fright tripped over her skirt and fell with a heavy thud. Don Quixote, cowering, began to speak:

"I conjure you, O phantom, or whatever you are, to tell me who you are and what it is you desire of me. If you are a soul in torment, tell me and I shall do for you everything my strength permits because I am a Catholic Christian and am committed to providing my service to everyone. To this end, I have taken up the profession of knight-errantry I pursue, the exercise of which extends to doing good even unto souls in purgatory."

When she heard herself conjured, the perplexed duenna deduced Don Quixote's fear from her own, so she whispered in a low mournful voice,

"Sir Don Quixote – if, in fact, you are Don Quixote – I am neither a phantom, an apparition, nor a soul in purgatory, as you probably believe, but Doña Rodríguez, chief duenna to my mistress the duchess and I have come here with one of those needs your grace is accustomed to relieving."

"Tell me, Lady Doña Rodríguez," said Don Quixote, "your grace has not come here by chance to practice some sort of matchmaking? I would have you know I am not available to anyone, thanks to the matchless beauty of my lady Dulcinea of Toboso. To be blunt, my lady, so long as you put aside and refrain from referring to any amorous message, you may withdraw to relight your candle and return here, at which time we shall discuss whatever topics are of most interest to you and most to your liking, except, as I have said, anything suggestive of love."

"I on an errand of love, my lord?" responded the duenna; "your grace does not know me very well. Thank goodness I am not yet so advanced in years as to have recourse to such childishness, for I am as fit as a fiddle and have all my teeth and grinders in my head, except for a few I have lost due to colds, which are so very common in this land of Aragon. If your grace will wait a moment, I shall go relight my candle and return in an instant to bare my burdens to one who can resolve any problem on earth."

And without waiting for a reply, she left the room, where Don Quixote remained calm and pensive waiting for her return. But a thousand doubts immediately descended upon him regarding this new adventure, for it struck him as ill-advised at best to expose himself to the danger of breaking the oath he had sworn to his lady, whereupon he carried on the following conversation with himself: 'Who knows whether the Devil, who is crafty and subtle, may try to deceive me now with a duenna, having been unable to accomplish this with empresses, queens, duchesses, marchionesses, and countesses. I have heard it said on a number of occasions and by a number of wise souls that if He can, He will give you a woman with a nose that is flat rather than aquiline. And who knows whether the quiet and solitude of this occasion will awaken in me desires that are dormant or will make me fall after so many years during which I have not even stumbled? In situations such as this it is wiser to flee than to stand and fight. But I must be out of my mind to be thinking and saying such absurd things! Why, it is out of the question for a lanky, veiled, bespectacled duenna to excite or arouse a lascivious thought in the most depraved soul on earth. Is there a duenna anywhere who has beautiful skin or has ceased to be impertinent, stern, and prudish? Out of my way, you tribe of duennas, who are incapable of providing a single human pleasure! How very clever that lady was who purportedly kept at one end of her drawing-room the busts of two duennas with their spectacles and sewing pillows as though they were engaged in needlework, for those statues served to lend as much authority to that room as actual duennas would have done.' Having said this, he bounded from his bed, determined to close the door to prevent Doña Rodríguez from reentering, but just as he was about to close it, Doña Rodríguez was already headed his way with a lighted wax candle in her hand. When she saw Don Quixote at close range wrapped in his bedspread and wearing his bandages and cap or bonnet, she once again became frightened and took two or three steps backwards.

"Shall I be safe, sir knight?" she asked. "I do not take it as a very virtuous sign for your grace to have gotten out of bed."

"That is precisely what I might ask your ladyship," said Don Quixote, "and so, may I know whether or not I shall be seduced and assaulted?"

"From whom does your grace seek such assurance, sir knight?" inquired the duenna.

"I seek it from your ladyship," replied Don Quixote, "for I am not constituted of marble nor your grace of bronze, nor is it ten in the morning but midnight, or even a little later I imagine, and in a chamber more secluded and secure than the cave must have been in which the treacherous and daring Aeneas possessed the beautiful, compassionate Dido. But if I may have your grace's hand, I demand no further assurance than that of my own continence and reserve and that which your grace's venerable headdress betokens."

In saying this, he kissed his own right hand and took *her* right hand in his, which she held out to him after performing the same ceremony.

(At this point Cide Hamete states parenthetically that to have seen the two of them walk from the door to the bed holding each other's hand, he would have given away the best cloak he owned).

Don Quixote finally climbed into bed and Doña Rodríguez sat on a chair somewhat removed from it, still wearing her spectacles and holding the candle. The knight huddled up in bed and covered himself completely except for his face, which he left exposed. Once the two had regained their composure, the first to break the silence was Don Quixote, who said,

"My Lady Doña Rodríguez, your grace may now unburden yourself and give vent to all that is pent up in your troubled heart and afflicted soul, for I shall listen to it with undefiled ears and shall act upon it with compassion."

"I am sure you will," said the duenna, "for considering your grace's genteel, ingratiating manner, one would expect just such a Christian response. The fact is that, though you see me seated on this chair in the heart of the kingdom of Aragon in the attire of an exhausted, defeated duenna, I am a native of Oviedo, Asturias, and come from a family having connections with many of the best ones in that province. But my ill fortune and the carelessness of my parents, who prematurely fell into poverty for some unknown reason or other, took me to the court of Madrid, where for the sake of peace and to avoid greater misfortunes they arranged for me to serve as seamstress to a certain lady of the nobility, for I would have you know that in the matter of hem stitching and embroidery no one has surpassed me in my entire life. My parents left me in her service and returned to the town in which they lived, from where a few years later they most certainly were called to heaven, having been exceedingly good Catholic Christians. I was left an orphan dependent upon the miserable wages and niggardly benefits customarily doled out to servants of the palace, but around that time without any encouragement from me I became the object of affection of one of the squires there, a man already advanced in years, full-bearded, personable, and who more than anything else considered himself as noble as the king, since he hailed from the mountains. We failed to manage our love affair with the secrecy necessary to keep it from the notice of my mistress, who, to avoid talk, had us married with the approval and blessing of the Holy Roman Catholic Church. From this marriage was born a daughter destined to bring an end to my happiness, if that is what it can be called, and not because I died in the process of delivering her, for the delivery was full term and without incident, but because a short time later my husband died from a certain shock he received, which, if I now had time to recount it, would astonish your grace."

At this point she began to sob softly.

"Sir Don Quixote," she continued, "I beg your indulgence but I can't help myself. Each time I think of my unfortunate husband, it makes me want to cry. It warms my heart to recall the great dignity with which he used to carry my mistress on the haunches of his powerful mule, one as black as jet itself. In those days it was not the custom as it is today for ladies to employ coaches or special saddles but to ride on the haunches of their squires' mules. At the very least I feel compelled to mention this so my dear husband's good breeding and dependability may be observed. On one occasion in Madrid, as he and my mistress were turning into Santiago Street, which is rather narrow, a court magistrate preceded by two bailiffs was just emerging from it. The moment our noble squire saw him, he drew up on the reins of his mule, acting as though he wished to turn and accompany him. My mistress, who was riding on the haunches of my husband's mule, said to him in a low voice, 'What are you doing, you timid soul? Can't you see that I am here?' The magistrate, out of politeness, brought his horse to a halt and said to him, 'I beg your grace to proceed on your way. I am the one who should accompany the Lady Casilda', this being the name of my mistress. My husband, cap in hand, insisted that he accompany the magistrate. When she saw this, my mistress became enraged and pulled out a thick pin or what I think was an engraver's punch and drove it so deep into his ribs that my husband screamed, twisting his body in such a manner that he knocked his mistress to the ground. Two of her lackeys hurried to help her to her feet, as did the magistrate and the bailiffs, at which point the Gate of Guadalajara went wild; that is, the idlers who were there did. My mistress returned home on foot, whereas my husband staggered into a barber's shop, announcing that he had been stabbed clean through the stomach. My husband's act of courtesy became such a topic of discussion in the town that the youngsters began throwing it up to him in the streets. Because of that incident and the fact that he was somewhat nearsighted, my mistress dismissed him, and I am convinced beyond a shadow of a doubt that the worry from it brought about his unfortunate death. I was left a defenseless widow with a daughter on my hands who was increasing in beauty like the foam on the sea. As it turned out, because of my reputation as an excellent seamstress, my mistress the duchess, who had recently married the duke my master, decided to bring me and my daughter with her to this kingdom of Aragon. Here as the days have come and gone, my daughter has blossomed, as have her many accomplishments, which leave nothing to be desired. She sings like a lark, moves like a dream, dances like a person possessed, reads and writes like a schoolmaster, and does addition like a miser. As for her purity I have no comment, since running water is not more pure. And if I remember correctly, by now she must be sixteen years, five months, and three days old, give or take a day. To make a long story short, one of the sons of an extremely wealthy farmer who lived not very far from here in one of the villages of my master the duke fell in love with my daughter. Somehow they got together and he took advantage of her by promising to be her husband but he now refuses to honor his commitment. Though my master the duke knows this – I having complained to him not once but numerous times, pleading with him to order the farm lad in question to marry my daughter – he has turned a deaf ear and will scarcely listen to me. The reason for this is that the seducer's father is so rich, loans the duke so much money, and so frequently goes bail for his bad debts that the duke is reluctant to displease him or cause him any grief. And so, my lord, I hope your grace will take it upon yourself to undo this injury, whether by pleas or by force, for according to what everyone says, your grace was born into this world to right wrongs, redress grievances, and comfort the afflicted. I ask you to picture in your mind my orphaned daughter, her charms and youthfulness, and her many sterling qualities that I have mentioned. I swear upon God and my conscience that of all the attendants who serve my mistress, there is none who can come up to the sole of my daughter's shoe. There is a certain Altisidora, who is considered to be most outgoing and graceful but who, compared to my daughter, cannot come within two leagues of her, for I would remind your grace that 'All that glitters is not gold.' This Altisidora fancies herself prettier than she is and possesses more brazenness than modesty. Besides, she is not very savory, for she has such bad breath no one can stand to be near her for a second. Why, even my mistress the duchess – but I had better hush, for they say that 'walls have ears.'"

"Upon my life, Doña Rodríguez, what is the matter with the duchess?"

"By virtue of that oath," replied the duenna, "I cannot help but respond with complete frankness to what I have been asked. Sir Don Quixote, has your grace noticed my mistress' beauty, her complexion, which, if anything, resembles a smooth, burnished sword, those rosy, white cheeks that resemble the sun and the moon, and the gracefulness with which she walks or rather seems to glide over the ground, creating the unmistakable impression that she radiates health wherever she goes? Well, I would have your grace know that she owes it all first to God and then to the artificial ulcers she has on her legs that drain away all the evil humors with which her body is filled according to the doctors."

"Holy Mother of God!" exclaimed Don Quixote, "can my lady the duchess have possibly resorted to such remedies? I would not have believed such a thing, had I been told it by discalced friars, but inasmuch as the lady Doña Rodríguez has said so, it must be true; but such ulcers in such places surely do not discharge humors but oil of amber. I am finally forced to admit that this practice of inducing ulcers is probably beneficial to one's health."

Scarcely had Don Quixote finished saying this than the door of his chamber burst open with a loud bang. As a result of the unexpected blow, the candle fell from Doña Rodríguez' hand and the room was left 'as dark as a dungeon,' as the saying goes. The poor duenna immediately felt someone seize her by the throat and grip her so tightly that she could not even let out a squeal. The second person quickly and without saying a word raised her petticoats and, using what appeared to be a slipper, began to whack her so furiously that it was a sight to behold. Don Quixote, despite his compassion for her, did not so much as budge from his bed owing to his confusion about what was happening, and thus lay quiet and still, fearing the punching and clubbing might come his way, not that his fear was an idle one, for as soon as they left off spanking the duenna, who did not even dare to moan, the silent-tongued executioners went over to Don Quixote and, unrolling him from his blanket and bedspread, began to pinch him so hard and so relentlessly that he could not refrain from defending himself with his fists – and all this in eerie silence. The battle lasted nearly half an hour, following which the phantoms withdrew. Doña Rodríguez gathered up her petticoats and, lamenting her humiliation, left the room without saying a word to Don Quixote, who, aching from the pinches, remained behind confused and totally immersed in his thoughts, where we shall leave him and his anxiety to learn who the perverse enchanter was who had done him such a turn. This, however, will be related in due time, for not only does Sancho now summon us but the proper balance of the history demands it.

Chapter Forty-Nine

The things that befell Sancho Panza as he made the rounds of his island

We left the great governor angry and out of sorts with that crafty, gloom-depicting farmer, who, having been instructed by the majordomo, and the majordomo by the duke, made sport of Sancho, but the latter held his own with everyone despite being dim-witted, uncultured, and a bit on the plump side, and so, addressing all those present, which included Doctor Pedro Recio, who had returned to the hall as soon as the private matter of the duke's letter had been dealt with, he said,

"I now truly understand that judges and governors should be, or must be, constituted of bronze so as not to be influenced by the appeals of people on business, who at all times and hours of the day want them to drop everything to lend an ear and listen to their problems, come what may. And should the poor judge not do so, either because he can't or because it's not the designated hour for giving them an audience, they immediately curse him, talk about him behind his back, pick his bones clean, and even hold forth on his family tree. You foolish people with your ridiculous business, don't be in such a hurry. Wait for the proper time and occasion to discuss your concerns and don't come at mealtime or bedtime, for judges are made of flesh and blood and must give their bodies what their bodies demand, except me, who never give mine anything to eat, thanks to his lord Doctor Pedro Recio Tirteafuera here in our midst, who's determined to see me die of hunger. If this is living as he claims it is, may God grant such a life to him and all the others of his ilk, that is, all the incompetent doctors, though the good ones deserve palms and laurels."

All those who knew Sancho Panza were amazed to hear him speak so eloquently and they had no idea what to attribute it to, if not to the fact that offices of great responsibility either sharpen or dull the mind. In the end, Doctor Pedro Recio Agüero de Tirteafuera promised to serve him a meal that evening even if it violated all the aphorisms of Hippocrates. With that, Sancho was content and looked forward with great anticipation to the arrival of evening and the dinner hour. And, though time seemed to stand still instead of moving forward, the moment he had so eagerly anticipated finally arrived, at which time they served him some leftover ground beef with onions and boiled calves' feet. He dug into these with greater gusto than if he were being served partridge from Milan, pheasant from Rome, veal from Sorrento, quail from Morón, or goose from Lavajos, and midway through the meal he turned to the physician and said,

"Remember, my dear doctor, from this day forward not to waste your time serving me delicacies or fancy foods. They'll only throw my stomach out of whack, since it's used to goat, beef, bacon, jerky, and turnips and onions. Whenever it's served palace food, it gets queasy and sometimes nauseous. What the butler *may* do is to serve me one of those pot-luck stews, and the more pot-luck it is the better it will taste. He may cram and stuff into it anything he pleases, so long as it's edible, for which I'll be most grateful and will repay him some day. Let's not have anyone try putting anything over on me, for I am who I am and that's that. 'Let's live and let live' and dine in peace and good fellowship, for 'When God brings the dawn, He brings it for everyone.' I intend to govern this island fairly and squarely, taking bribes from no one, and I want every person to keep his eyes open and look out for himself. Everyone should be advised that I may look harmless but anyone who trifles with me is in for a surprise. No, if you try to be nice to people, they'll be sure to take advantage of you!"

"Without a doubt, sir governor," said the butler, "your grace is quite correct in everything you have said and I can assure you in the name of all the citizens of this island that they will serve you with complete diligence, affection, and goodwill, for the easy-going style of governing that you have set forth in these pronouncements gives them no reason to do or consider anything that might redound to your disservice."

"I should think not," responded Sancho, "for they would be very foolish to do or think otherwise. Let me repeat that my food requirements are to be attended to, as well as those of my dapple, which is what really matters most in all this. Later, at the appropriate hour we intend to make our rounds, for it is my intention to rid this island of every kind of filth and all its vagrants, bums, and loafers. I want you all to understand, my friends, that lazy, shiftless people in a republic are as useless as drones in a beehive, which eat all the honey the worker bees have produced. I intend to favor the farmers, preserve the privileges of the nobles, reward the virtuous, but above all, respect religion and the rights of believers. How does all this sound, my friends? Am I talking sense or just making a big to-do about nothing?"

"Sir governor," said the majordomo, "your grace is making so much sense I am amazed to hear a man who is so short on learning – and your grace to my knowledge has none – say such wise things and give such good counsel, so far from what was expected of your intellect by those of us who have come here and those who sent us here, but each day one sees something new in this world: pretense turned into truth and tricksters finding themselves tricked."

Night arrived and the governor dined with the permission of his lordship Doctor Recio. Once the preparations had been made for making the rounds, Sancho went outdoors with the majordomo, the secretary, and the chronicler responsible for recording his deeds, together with enough bailiffs and notaries to have constituted a medium-size squadron. And walking in the middle with his staff of office was Sancho, who was a sight to behold. They had traveled only a few blocks when they heard the sound of clashing swords. Hastening to the spot, they found two lone men fighting, who, when they saw the law approach, stood motionless, at which point one of them cried out,

"Help in the name of God and the king! Is it possible that people can be robbed in the center of this town or assaulted in the middle of the street?"

"Calm down, my good man," said Sancho, "and tell me the cause of this dispute, for I am the governor."

The man's adversary answered,

"Sir governor, I can easily explain. I should inform your grace that this gentleman has just won more than a thousand *reals* in that gambling house across the street, and only God knows how. Inasmuch as I happened to be present, I decided more than one doubtful play in his favor against the better advice of my conscience. He finally got up from the table with his winnings, at which point I expected him to give me at least an *escudo* as a tip, since it is the usual custom to give something to men of quality such as myself who stand by during fair play and foul to back up any unreasonable claims and to prevent fights, but he stuck the money in his purse and walked out of the establishment. Exasperated at this, I followed him and asked him quite courteously to let me have eight *reals* at the very least, for he knows I am an honorable man and have neither profession nor inheritance, my parents having failed to teach me one or to leave me any. But this rascal, who is as big a thief as Cacus and a bigger crook than Andradilla, refused to give me more than four *reals*. Sir governor, can you imagine such shamelessness and lack of conscience! I swear that if your grace had not arrived, I would have made him cough up his winnings and shown him how much is two and two."

"What does your grace have to say to this?" asked Sancho.

The other man replied that everything his adversary had charged was true; that he had refused to give him more than four *reals* because he had given him money on numerous occasions, and because those who expect something for nothing should be civil and accept with a smile what they are given instead of haggling with the winner unless they know for certain that the winner is a cheat and what he has won has been unfairly won. As proof of the fact that he himself was an honest man and not a thief, as the first man contended, there was his refusal to give him anything, for crooks always pay off their confederates.

"So they do," said the majordomo. "Well now, sir governor, in your grace's opinion what shall we do with these men?"

"What we shall do is this," replied Sancho: "you, sir, the winner, whether you are good, bad, or indifferent, are to give your adversary in this altercation a hundred *reals* plus an additional thirty to be turned over to the poor souls in jail. And you, sir, the plaintiff, who have neither profession nor inheritance but wander about this island with nothing to do, are to take those hundred *reals* right now and by tomorrow night be off this island, from which you are banished for ten years, which sentence, if violated, you shall complete in the next life, for I'll hang you from the gallows, or at least I'll order the hangman to do so. And I don't want to hear another word from either of you or you shall feel the weight of my arm."

The one took the money from his purse and the other accepted it, the latter leaving the island and the former returning to his home. The governor stood there and said,

"Either I'm not as capable as I think I am or I'll do away with all these gambling houses, which, it's obvious to me, are quite harmful."

"This one is an exception," said one of the notaries; "your grace must not do away with it, for it is owned by a man of some standing who invariably loses more at cards each year than he takes in. You may demonstrate your authority against the second-rate gambling dens, which are the ones that do the most harm and are the most obnoxious. In the establishments belonging to nobles and reputable men infamous crooks don't dare cheat, and since the vice of gambling has become a common practice, it is better to have it carried on in reputable houses than in those belonging to various tradesmen where some poor devil is snared in the wee hours of the morning and is skinned alive."

"All right, notary," said Sancho, "I can see there are two sides to the question."

At that moment, a constable came up clutching a youth by the arm.

"Sir governor," he said, "this young man was walking in our direction but the moment he caught sight of us, he began to run away as fast as a deer, a sure sign that he must be some sort of lawbreaker. I took off after him and, had he not tripped and fallen, would never have caught him."

"Why were you running away, my good man?" asked Sancho; to which the youth responded,

"Sire, to avoid having to answer all the questions officers ask."

"What is your trade?" inquired Sancho.

"I'm a weaver."

"And what do you weave?"

"Iron tips for lances, if it please your grace."

"Are you trying to be facetious or do you just take pride in pathetic jokes? But never mind. Where were you headed just now?"

"To get some air, sire."

"And where does one get air on this island?"

"Wherever it blows."

"Well, your answers certainly are pointed! You think yourself clever, young man, but be advised that I am the air and am blowing from your stern and am heading you straight to jail. Seize him, I say, and take him to a place where I'll make him sleep tonight without any air!"

"Oh, come now," said the youth, "your grace can no more make me sleep in jail than crown me king!"

"And just why can't I make you sleep in jail?" asked Sancho. "Am I not powerful enough to arrest you and release you whenever and wherever I feel like it?"

"However powerful your grace may be," said the youth, "it will not be enough to make me sleep in jail."

"Oh no?" exclaimed Sancho; "take him right now to where he will see with his own eyes how mistaken he is, regardless of any self-serving consideration the jailer may show him, for I'll fine the jailer two thousand ducats if he lets you set one foot outside the jail."

"All this is laughable," replied the youth; "the fact of the matter is that no man alive can make me sleep in jail."

"Listen here, you demon," said Sancho, "do you have some angel who'll rescue you and remove the shackles I intend to put on you?"

"Look, sir governor," said the youth in a display of wit, "let's discuss this and get to the bottom of the matter. Suppose your grace orders me put in jail, where they shackle and handcuff me, put me in a dungeon, and threaten the jailer with stiff penalties if he allows me to escape. Even with all that, if I lie awake all night without closing my eyes and refuse to sleep, will your grace with all your power and influence be able to make me go to sleep if I refuse?"

"Certainly not," said the secretary, "and the man has a good point."

"Then," replied Sancho, "you would refuse to go to sleep not to contravene my orders but only to exercise your own free will?"

"Yes, sire," said the youth, "I wouldn't think of going against your grace's orders."

"Well, run along," said Sancho, "go sleep in your own house and may God give you pleasant dreams. Far be it from me to deprive you of them but I advise you not to joke with the law in the future or you may run into someone who'll break the joke over your skull."

The youth went his way and the governor continued to make the rounds. A short while later, two constables came up with a man in their custody.

"Sir governor," said one of the men, "this person who appears to be a man is actually a woman – and not a bad-looking one at that – who has dressed herself in men's clothing."

They held two or three lanterns up to her face, the light from which revealed a woman who appeared to be some sixteen years of age or older and whose hair was gathered up inside a gold and green silk net as beautiful as a thousand pearls. Surveying her from head to foot, they saw she was wearing red silk stockings and white taffeta garters trimmed with gold and pearl. Her green and gold pantaloons were obviously expensive, as was her vest, or doublet, which she wore open. Underneath it, she had on an exquisite gold and white jerkin, and her white shoes were a man's. In lieu of a sword, she carried a jewel-studded dagger at her side, and on her fingers wore several very handsome rings. In a word, everyone thought the young lady very beautiful but no one among all the bystanders recognized her, and the citizens of the town said they could not imagine who she was. Those who were aware of the hoax being played on Sancho were the most astonished, for her sudden appearance had not been part of their plan and they were left perplexed and quite curious to see how this situation would resolve itself. Sancho, who was taken with the girl's beauty, asked her who she was, where she was going, and what circumstances had led her to adopt such attire. The young lady, her eyes staring at the ground in innocent embarrassment, replied,

"My lord, I dare not divulge in such a public place what I have felt so necessary to keep secret. One thing I wish understood though: I am no thief or witch but an unfortunate maiden driven by the power of jealousy to flaunt the respect virtue is due."

When the majordomo heard this, he said to Sancho,

"Sir governor, your grace should ask the people to leave so this lady may say what she has to say without so much embarrassment."

The governor did as advised and everyone withdrew except the majordomo, the butler, and the secretary. Once they saw themselves alone, the young lady proceeded with her story:

"I, my lords, am the daughter of Pedro Pérez Mazorca, the wool tax collector of this village, who frequently visits my father's house."

"That makes no sense, my lady," said the majordomo; "I know Pedro Pérez quite well and know he has no child, either male or female. Besides, you say he is your father and then add that he is a frequent visitor in your father's house."

"I had already noticed that," said Sancho.

"Right now, my lords, I am so upset I am not certain what I am saying," answered the damsel. "The fact is that I am the daughter of Diego de la Llana, whom your graces no doubt know."

"Now that makes sense," replied the majordomo; "I know Diego de la Llana and know that he is a wealthy and famous hidalgo who has a son and a daughter. Ever since he became a widower, no one in this town can claim to have seen the face of his daughter, whom he keeps so secluded that not even the sun itself has a chance to see her, but despite that, rumor has it that she is exceedingly fair."

"That is correct," responded the damsel, "because I am that daughter. Whether the rumor of my beauty is true or not, your graces will have been able to determine for yourselves now that you have seen my face."

At this point, she began to sob softly and when the secretary saw this, he drew near the butler and whispered in his ear,

"Undoubtedly, something serious has befallen this poor maiden who, coming from such a good family, finds herself so far from home and in such attire at this late hour."

"There is no doubt about it," said the butler; "moreover, her tears confirm that suspicion."

Sancho comforted her as reassuringly as he could and told her she might without any fear whatsoever tell them what had befallen her; that they would all try as earnestly as they knew how to provide her with a solution and would investigate every possible avenue.

"The fact is, my lords," she replied, "my father has kept me secluded for ten years, the same number of years since the earth received my mother. During all this time, I have seen nothing but the sun in the sky by day and the moon and stars by night, and know nothing of what streets are like, or public plazas and cathedrals, or even men other than my father and a brother of mine and Pedro Pérez the tax collector. And because he is such a frequent visitor in our house, it suddenly entered my head to say that he was my father instead of having to name my real one. This confinement and refusal to allow me to leave the house, even to go to church – mass being said in our house in a most elegant chapel – have caused me much unhappiness for the last several days and weeks. I should like to see the world, at least the town in which I was born, and it strikes me that such a desire does not violate the propriety young ladies of society are expected to observe. Whenever I have heard there was to be a bullfight, jousting contest, or stage play, I have asked my brother, who is a year younger than I, to explain what those things are, in addition to a number of other things I have never seen. He has explained them as well as he could, all of which has merely increased my desire to see them. But to shorten the story of my perdition, I shall simply say that I begged and implored my brother to – oh, if only I had never begged or implored . . . "

And once again she began to sob.

"My lady," said the majordomo, "I wish your grace would try to continue and finish telling us what has happened to you, for your words and tears are keeping us all in suspense."

"I have few things left to say," replied the damsel, "but a good many tears to shed; and yet, what other sort of outcome might I have expected from such misplaced desires?"

The damsel's beauty had taken root in the butler's breast and once again he raised his lantern to look at her. He fancied it was not tears she was shedding but beads of dew from the meadow, and he exaggerated them still further by turning them into pearls from the Orient. He hoped her misfortune was not as great as her tears and sighs indicated. Inasmuch as the governor had become exasperated at the girl's haphazard manner of telling her story, he begged her not to keep them in suspense any longer, as it was late and there was still much of the town to visit. She, between fits of sobbing and half-formed sighs, went on to say,

"My only misfortune is that I begged my brother to dress me as a man in one of his outfits, and to take me out some night to see the whole town when our father was asleep. Finding himself beseeched and importuned by me, he complied with my wishes by dressing me in this outfit and himself in one of mine. His seems to be made just for him and because of his beardless face he has the selfsame appearance of a beautiful young woman. Tonight – it must have been about an hour ago – we left the house and, following our youthful, unrestrained impulses, made a circuit of the entire town, but just as we decided to return home, we saw a large group of people headed our way and my brother said to me, 'Sister dear, this must be the night patrol. Pick up your feet and give them wings. Follow me as fast as you can run, for if they recognize us, it will not go well with us.' Having said this, he turned and I will not say began to run, because he began to fly; but owing to my fear, I fell before taking half a dozen steps, at which point an officer of the law arrived, the one who has brought me here before your graces, where, like a wicked and capricious girl, I find myself humiliated in the presence of all these people."

"In other words, my lady," said Sancho, "your grace has suffered no misfortune whatever nor any attack of jealousy, which, you said at the beginning of your story, drove you from your home."

"Nothing has happened to me, nor was I driven by jealousy but by my desire to see the world, which went no further than seeing the streets of this town."

The truth of what the damsel had said was confirmed by the arrival of two constables who had her brother in custody, one of whom had apprehended him as he fled with his sister. He was attired in a beautiful skirt, a mantle of blue damask and fine gold lace, without any veil or adornment on his head except his own hair, which was so blond and curly that his head appeared to be covered with golden ringlets. The governor, the majordomo, and the butler took him aside so his sister could not hear them and asked him how he came to be dressed in that fashion. He, with no less shame and embarrassment, related the same story as his sister, much to the delight of the smitten butler. The governor then said to them,

"This, my lord and lady, has certainly been a most childish undertaking but it didn't require so many words or so much sighing and sobbing to relate how rash and foolish it was, for your graces might have said, 'We are Don and Doña So-and-So, who left our father's house in these disguises to have some fun, simply out of curiosity and for no other reason,' and the story would be over without all this sighing and sobbing and all the rest of it."

"That is quite true," replied the damsel, "but your graces need to understand that the agitation I experienced was so great it did not allow me to exercise the self-control that was called for."

"No harm has been done," said Sancho, "so let us get started and we'll take your graces home, for your father may not even have missed his children yet. From this time forth, you must not be so childish or so eager to see the world, for 'An honorable woman and a broken leg should both stay at home;' 'A woman or a chicken that strays from home is soon lost;' and 'A woman who's anxious to see is one who's anxious to be seen,' and that's all I have to say."

The young man thanked the governor for his gracious offer to see them home and they set out at once for the residence, which was located only a short distance away. When they arrived, the young man tossed a pebble at a window, and a servant-girl who had been waiting for them came down momentarily and opened the door, at which point the couple went inside. All the others stood there marveling not only at their gentility and good looks but also at their desire to see the world – and *that* at night and without even leaving town, all of which they attributed to their tender years. The butler, who had been pierced through the heart, made up his mind to ask her father for her hand the very next day, feeling confident it would not be denied him, as he was one of the duke's servants. Even Sancho showed signs of wanting to marry the young man to his daughter Sanchica but decided to act upon it at the proper time, having convinced himself that no man could refuse to be the husband of a governor's daughter.

With this, the night's rounds came to an end, as did the government a couple of days later, whereby all of Sancho's plans were toppled and demolished, as we shall shortly see.

Chapter Fifty

The explanation of who the enchanters and tormentors were who spanked the duenna and pinched and scratched Don Quixote, together with what happened to the page when he delivered the letter to Teresa Sancha, Sancho Panza's wife

Cide Hamete, who has meticulously sought out the most minute details of this true history, relates that at the very moment that Doña Rodríguez left her room to go to Don Quixote's quarters, another duenna who roomed with her heard her leave and, since every duenna is fond of sniffing out everything that is going on, followed her so silently that the good Rodríguez never knew what was happening. When she saw her enter Don Quixote's room, the duenna, lest she be found wanting in the practice of gossiping common to all duennas, hurried off to tell her mistress the duchess that Doña Rodríguez had remained in Don Quixote's chamber. The duchess informed the duke and asked him if she and Altisidora might go see what business the duenna had with the knight. The duke gave his permission and the two women crept ever so cautiously and quietly towards the chamber one step at a time, drawing so near, in fact, that they were able to hear everything that was said inside. And when the duchess heard Doña Rodríguez openly discuss the ulcers on her legs, it was more than she or even Altisidora could bear, so both of them, full of rage and intent upon revenge, burst into the chamber and began riddling Don Quixote with pinches and scratches while slapping the duenna in the manner already described, for insults directed at women's beauty or vanity arouse their utmost wrath and kindle their desire for revenge. The duchess informed the duke of all that had happened, which absolutely delighted him. And the duchess, who still had a desire to amuse and disport herself at Don Quixote's expense, dispatched a page to Teresa Panza, Sancho's wife, with the letter from Sancho and another from herself, together with a present in the form of a long coral necklace. This was the same page who had impersonated Dulcinea in the scheme involving her disenchantment but he was not even in the thoughts of Sancho Panza due to the latter's preoccupation with his government.

Here our history relates that the page, who was quite clever, intelligent, and eager to serve the ducal pair, set out for Sancho's village. Just before entering it, he encountered a number of women washing their clothes in a stream and he asked them if they could tell him if there was a woman named Teresa Panza in that village, the wife of a certain Sancho Panza, squire to a knight known as Don Quixote of La Mancha. At this question, a young girl who had been washing her clothes stood up and said,

"That Teresa Panza is my mother, that Sancho is my dear father, and that knight is our very own master."

"Well, young lady," said the page, "come and take me to your mother, for I am bringing her a present and a letter from your very own father."

"I'll do so with all my heart, good sir," replied the girl, who looked to be about fourteen years of age. Handing the clothes she had been washing to one of her companions, the girl did not bother to put anything on her head or feet (her feet being bare and her hair hanging loose) but began to skip along in front of the page's mount.

"Come with me, your grace," said the girl, "our house is just inside the village and my mother is at home worrying herself sick, for she's had no news of my dear father for a number of days."

"Well, I am bringing her some that is so good," replied the page, "she will have to give thanks to God."

Finally, after considerable running, jumping, and skipping, the girl reached the village and, instead of entering her house, called out from the doorway,

"Come outside, Mother, come quick; there's a gentleman here with a letter and other things from my dear father."

In response to these shouts, her mother, Teresa Panza, stepped outside holding a bundle of flax in her hand and wearing a gray bodice, a blouse, and a gray skirt that was so short it looked as though it had been lopped off as public punishment. Though not old, she appeared to be past forty and looked strong, robust, vigorous, but weathered. When she saw her daughter and the mounted page, she said,

"What is this, child? Who is this gentleman?"

"I," replied the page, "am the humble servant of my lady Doña Teresa Panza," and converting his words into action, he sprang from his mount and with great humility knelt at the feet of the lady Teresa, saying,

"My lady Doña Teresa, may I kiss your grace's hand as the sole and legitimate wife of his lord Don Sancho Panza, rightful governor of Cheap-Isle."

"Please, my dear sir, your grace must rise and not kneel like that. I am certainly no court person but a poor farm woman, daughter of a dirt farmer and wife of a squire-errant – never of a governor!"

"Your ladyship," said the page, "you are the most worthy wife of a most eminently worthy governor, and as proof of this, here are a letter and present for your grace."

With this he pulled from his pocket a necklace of coral beads framed by a gold clasp at either end. As he fastened it round her neck, he said,

"This letter is from his lordship the governor, and this other one and the necklace are from my lady the duchess, who has sent me here."

Teresa stood there dazed but no more so than her daughter.

"I'll be hanged, Mother, if our lord and master Don Quixote isn't at the bottom of this. He must have given Father the government or earldom he's promised him so many times."

"So he has," said the page; "it is due to his lord Don Quixote that his lord Sancho is now governor of Cheap-Isle, as will be seen by this letter."

"Good sir, please read it to me," said Teresa. "I may know how to spin but I can't read a word."

"Me either," added Sanchica, "but if your grace will wait here, I'll go get someone to read it, for either the priest himself or the bachelor Sansón Carrasco will gladly come here just to hear news of my father."

"There is no reason to call anyone," said the page. "I may not know how to spin but I do know how to read, and shall do so."

At this point he read the entire letter, which, because it has already been described, will not be repeated here. He then removed the one from the duchess, which read as follows:

My dearest Teresa,

The qualities of goodness and intelligence of your grace's husband Sancho have moved and led me to ask my husband the duke to permit him to govern one of the many islands he owns. I have received word that he is governing like a prince, which pleases me enormously, as it naturally does my lord the duke. For this, I give thanks to heaven that I have not erred in choosing him for a government such as this. I wish I could make the lady Teresa understand how hard it is to find a decent governor anywhere on earth – and may God make me as good a person as Sancho is a governor.

My dear, I am sending your grace a coral necklace with gold clasps. I only wish they were Oriental pearls, but 'One who throws you a bone does not wish you harm.' The time will come when we can meet and converse but God alone knows what the future holds. Commend me to your daughter Sanchica and tell her on my behalf to get herself ready, for I intend to marry her to some prominent person when she least expects it.

They tell me there are large acorns in your village. Please send me a couple of dozen and I shall treasure them for having come from your grace's hands. I wish you would write me at length and advise me of your health and well-being and, if you are in need of anything, you have only to open your mouth and it shall be filled to overflowing. May God keep your grace. From this villa,

With love and affection,
THE DUCHESS

"Oh my!" cried Teresa after listening to the letter; "what a good, plain, humble lady! May I be buried with such a lady rather than with the blue bloods we have in this town, who think that because they're hidalgas the wind shouldn't blow on them. They also put on such airs when they go to church, as though they were veritable queens, and act as if they considered it disgraceful to look at a woman from the country; but here, one sees that this noble lady, and a duchess no less, calls me a friend and treats me as though I were her equal. May I see her equal to the tallest bell tower in La Mancha! As for the acorns, my lord, I'll send her ladyship a peck of some so big that people will come just to see them and marvel at them. For now, Sanchica, see that this gentleman is made comfortable and look after his horse. Then get some eggs from the stable and cut off a big slice of bacon. We'll give him a meal fit for a king, for the good news he has brought us and his nice smile deserve as much. In the meantime, I'll go out and give the neighbor women the news of our good fortune, as well as visit the priest and Master Nicolás the barber, who've always been very close friends of your father."

"I'll do so, Mother," replied Sanchica, "but remember that half of that necklace should be mine; surely, the duchess wouldn't be so silly as to send the whole thing to you."

"The entire necklace is yours, child," said Teresa; "just let me wear it for a few days, for I truly feel it will gladden my heart."

"Your grace will also be gladdened," said the page, "when you see the bundle I have in my portmanteau. It is a suit of the finest material, which the governor wore only once while hunting, and he is sending all of it to the lady Sanchica."

"May he live a thousand years," exclaimed Sanchica, "as well as the person who has brought it – or even two thousand if need be!"

Then leaving the house with the letters in her hand and the coral beads round her neck, Teresa went off drumming on the letters as though they were a tambourine. As luck would have it, she came across the priest and Sansón Carrasco, at which point she did a little dance and said,

"I dare say we aren't poor relations any longer but have got us a nice little government! Just let some highfalutin hidalga mess with me now and I'll show her a thing or two!"

"What is this, Teresa Panza?" said the priest; "what foolishness is this and what papers are those?"

"The only foolishness is that these letters are from a duchess and a governor, and this necklace I'm wearing has the 'Ave Maria' beads of real coral and the 'Our Father' ones of hammered gold – in addition to which I'm a governor's wife."

"No one, Teresa, from God on down knows what you are talking about."

"Your graces may see for yourselves," replied Teresa, and she handed them the letters, which the priest read aloud so Sansón Carrasco could hear what they said. Sansón and the priest looked at each other and were virtually dumbfounded by what they had read. The bachelor asked who had delivered those letters and Teresa said if they would come home with her, they would see the courier, a jewel of a young man who had brought her an additional present worth even more. The priest removed the necklace from her neck and looked at it, first from one angle and then from another, and after assuring himself that it was genuine, began to marvel once more and said,

"I swear by the habit I am wearing that I don't know what to think or say about these letters and presents. On the one hand I can see and feel the quality of these corals but at the same time I read that a duchess is asking to be sent a couple of dozen acorns."

"Figure that out if you can," said Carrasco at this point. "Let us go see the bearer of this letter and get him to explain the contradictions confronting us."

Accompanied by Teresa, they left and found the page sifting barley for his mount and Sanchica slicing some bacon to cook in an omelet for the page's dinner. They were impressed by his bearing and splendid clothes and, after they courteously greeted him and he them, Sansón begged him to give them news of both Don Quixote and Sancho Panza, for though they had read the letters from Sancho and her ladyship the duchess, they were still puzzled and could not imagine what that business of Sancho's government could be, much less the island, since all or most of his majesty's islands were located in the Mediterranean Sea; to which the page said in response,

"That his lord Sancho Panza is governor there is no reason to doubt, but whether he is governing an island or not is something I choose not to get involved in. Suffice it to say that it is a village with more than a thousand inhabitants. Regarding the acorns, I can safely say that my lady the duchess is so humble and circumspect that she did not tell me she was sending me to get acorns from a farm woman but to borrow a comb from a neighbor of hers. I would have your graces know that though the ladies of Aragon are just as highborn as those of Castile, they are not nearly so fastidious and haughty but treat people with less pretentiousness."

While they were engaged in this conversation, Sanchica came skipping up with an apron full of eggs and said to the page,

"Would your grace tell me whether my dear father has possibly been wearing full-length hose since he's been governor?"

"I have not noticed," replied the page, "but he must wear them."

"My goodness," exclaimed Sanchica, "what I wouldn't give to see my father in tights! Isn't it odd that ever since I was born I've always wanted to see my father in long hose?"

"If you live long enough," said the page, "you will see him in other things besides. In fact, if his government lasts at least a couple of months, he's showing signs of wanting to ride about wearing a traveler's mask."

The priest and the barber were quick to see that the page was pulling everyone's leg but the excellence of the necklace and the hunting suit Sancho had sent, Teresa having already shown them the suit, ran counter to all this and they could not keep from laughing at Sanchica's desire, particularly when Teresa added,

"Sir priest, I wish your grace would look about to see if there's anyone going to Madrid or Toledo who might buy me a real genuine hoopskirt that's in style and one of the best available, for really and truly I should be a credit to my husband's government insofar as I can. And even if I find it irksome, I owe it to myself to go to court and show off in a coach like all the other women, for a woman whose husband is governor can easily afford to have one and maintain it."

"And how, Mother!" said Sanchica, "and I wish to heaven it were today instead of in the future even if those who saw me riding beside my worthy mother should say, 'Look at the little tart, daughter of the garlic glutton, all laid back in her coach as if she were the pope himself!' Well, they can walk in the mud so long as I can ride in my coach with my feet off the ground. A pox upon every last scandalmonger on earth! As long as I keep warm, who cares what people say! Am I making any sense, Mother dear?"

"I should say you are, child," replied Teresa; "all this good fortune and an even better one has been prophesied by my noble Sancho, and you will see, child, that it won't stop till I become a countess, for 'Getting started is everything when it comes to being lucky.' I've often heard it said by your noble father, who's as much the father of his proverbs as he is of you, that 'When they bring you a heifer, run and fetch the halter'; 'When they give you a government, accept it'; 'When they offer you an earldom, grab it'; and 'When they throw you a bone, wag your tail like a good little doggie.' Otherwise, just keep sleeping and don't answer when good luck and prosperity come knocking at your door!"

"Well," said Sanchica, "when they see me uppity and putting on airs, what do I care if they say, 'She's too good now to recognize her old friends.'"

When the priest heard this, he said,

"I simply have to believe that all those in the Panza line were born with a sack full of proverbs in their craw because I have never seen any of them who did not lard their every conversation with them, and at all hours of the day."

"That is the truth," said the page, "because his lordship the governor utters them at every turn, many of which completely miss the mark but are entertaining all the same. Besides, my lady the duchess and the duke approve of them highly."

"My lord," said the bachelor, "does your grace still insist that this business of Sancho's government is true and that there is an actual duchess writing to her and sending her presents? Even though we have touched the presents and read the letters, we do not believe them but think this is one of our compatriot Don Quixote's enchantments, for he believes everything is accomplished by means of enchantment. Because of this, I must say I should like to touch and feel your grace to see if you are a messenger of the imagination or a man of flesh and blood."

"Gentlemen," replied the page, "all I know is that I am a real messenger, that his lord Sancho Panza is an actual governor, and that my lord and lady, the duke and duchess, can and have awarded him the government in question; and I have heard reports that this same Sancho Panza has conducted himself most excellently. Whether or not enchantment is involved in this your graces may debate among yourselves. I don't know what else I can do except swear an oath upon the lives of my parents, who are still alive and whom I love with all my heart."

"That may well be the case," said the bachelor, "but *dubitat Augustinus*." [1]

"Let anyone doubt who will," replied the page. "What I have spoken is the truth, and 'Truth always rises above falsehood as oil does above water;' if not, '*Operibus credite et non verbis*,'[2] If one of you will accompany me, you will see with your own eyes what you do not believe with your ears."

"I'm the one who should make that trip," said Sanchica; "your grace can carry me on the haunches of your horse, for I'd love to go see my dear father."

"Governors' daughters should not travel alone," said the page, "but in the company of coaches, litters, and a large number of servants."

"For goodness' sake," said Sanchica, "I can ride just as well on a she-ass as I can in a coach. I hope your grace doesn't think I'm that fussy!"

"Hush, child," replied Teresa, "you don't know what you're saying. Besides, this gentleman is right; 'There's a time and a place for everything:' when it was 'Sancho,' it was 'Sancha,' but once it's 'your governorship,' it'll be 'your ladyship.' I don't know if I'm making myself clear."

"The lady Teresa is making better sense than she realizes," said the page, "but at the moment I need something to eat and shall then be on my way, for I intend to return this evening."

To which the priest replied,

"Your grace is welcome to come and 'do penance' at my table, since the lady Teresa's good intentions are greater than her ability to serve such a fine guest."

The page at first refused but was finally forced to acquiesce for his own good. The priest was delighted to take him home to have a leisurely opportunity to question him about Don Quixote and his activities. The bachelor offered to write a response to Teresa's letters but she was unwilling to have the bachelor become involved in her affairs because she considered him somewhat untrustworthy. She thus gave a roll and a couple of eggs to an altar boy who knew how to write, and he wrote two letters for her: one to her husband and the other to the duchess, both dictated by Teresa out of her own head and by no means the worst ones included in this great history, as we shall see farther along.

Chapter Fifty-One

The course of Sancho Panza's government, together with other truly entertaining incidents

Dawn arrived following the night on which the governor had made his rounds, a night the butler spent lying awake, his thoughts fixed upon the face, elegance, and beauty of the

1 Latin: 'Augustine doubts it.'

2 Latin: 'Believe my deeds and not my words,' John 10:38.

disguised damsel. The majordomo spent what remained of the night by writing to his master and mistress of everything Sancho Panza was saying and doing, for he was as much astounded by Sancho's deeds as by his pronouncements, since his words and actions were a blend of intelligence and folly. Finally, his lordship the governor rose and on the orders of Doctor Pedro Recio was served a dollop of preserves and a few swallows of cold water, which Sancho would gladly have exchanged for a piece of bread and a bunch of grapes, but seeing that it was more a question of necessity than of choice, he let it pass, albeit with pain in his heart and a gnawing in his stomach, for Pedro Recio had convinced him that small amounts of bland food sharpened the mind, this being the most necessary ingredient for persons occupying important positions of command in which there is a greater need of intellectual prowess than of physical strength.

As a result of this sophistry, Sancho suffered such pangs of hunger that he secretly cursed his government and even the one who had given it to him, but despite the preserves and his hunger, he began to hold court that day. With the majordomo and other officials present he was presented the first case, which involved a matter described by an outsider.

"Your honor," said the man, "there is a wide river dividing two districts that belong to the same lord – your grace should pay careful attention because the case is important and rather involved – but to continue: spanning this river is a bridge, at one end of which are a gallows and a type of law court that ordinarily houses four judges who sit in judgement of a law decreed by the owner of the river, bridge, and jurisdiction. This law states that if anyone would cross from one end of the bridge to the other, he must first state under oath where he is going and why. If he tells the truth, he shall be allowed to cross but should he tell a lie, he shall be hanged on the gallows located on the site, without right of reprieve. Though the law and its severe provision are known, many persons go there and, once it is determined that they are telling the truth, are allowed to cross. But one day, they questioned a certain man who declared under oath purely and simply that he would die on those gallows. After deliberating over the oath, the judges said: 'If we allow this man to cross freely, then he has lied in his oath and according to the law must die. If, however, we hang him after he has sworn that he would die on the gallows, he has told the truth and by that same law should go free.' Sir governor, I beg your grace to render your opinion as to how the judges may deal with this man, for as of this very moment they are filled with considerable doubt and indecision, but because they have heard of your grace's keen, exalted intellect, they have sent me on their behalf to beg you to render an opinion in this involved and uncertain case."

To which Sancho responded,

"Those esteemed judges who sent you here might have saved themselves the trouble, for I'm more ignorant than quick-witted. Nevertheless, repeat your story one more time so I can understand it, and who knows: I might even come up with a solution."

After the questioner repeated several more times what he had already stated, Sancho said,

"In my opinion I can clear up this matter in two shakes of a lamb's tail and here is my answer: if this man swears he will die on the gallows and does so, he has sworn truthfully and, according to the law, deserves to go free and be allowed to cross the bridge, but should they not hang him, he has sworn falsely and, according to the same law, deserves to be hanged."

"It is just as your lordship has described it," said the messenger, "and as far as a complete understanding of the case is concerned, there is nothing further to desire or resolve."

"Well, my decision," replied Sancho, "is that they should let that part of the man cross that has told the truth but should hang that part of him that has lied. In this way the provision of the law will be carried out to the letter."

"But, sir governor," said the questioner, "it would be necessary to split the man in two halves: one lying and the other truthful, but if he is split in two, he will necessarily die and nothing will thereby be accomplished that the law demands, for it expressly says that the law is to be complied with."

"Look here, my good sir," said Sancho, "regarding this traveler you speak of, either I am a dunce or there is equal justification for hanging him or letting him live to cross the bridge, for if telling the truth will save him, lying will likewise condemn him, and this being the case, I'm of the opinion you should inform those who have sent you here that, since the reasons for condemning him or absolving him are equally balanced, they should give him free passage, for it is always more laudable to do good than to do ill; and I would put it in writing and sign it with my own name if I knew how to write. I don't base this upon my own ideas but upon a precept that has sprung to mind from among the many my master Don Quixote gave me the night before I left to become governor of this island, which precept says that when justice is in doubt, I should be flexible and choose mercy. God has seen fit for me to remember it at just this moment and it is tailor-made for this situation."

"So it is," replied the majordomo, "and I am convinced that Lycurgus himself, who gave the Lacedaemonians their laws, could not have rendered a better decision than the great Panza has. This will conclude the audience for this morning and I shall issue orders that the lord governor is be served whatever he wishes to eat."

"That's all I'm asking – and no tricks!" said Sancho; "if you will just feed me, you may shower me with cases and suits and I'll resolve them on the spot."

The majordomo kept his word, since he felt it would weigh heavily upon his conscience if such an intelligent governor were starved to death. Besides, he intended to wash his hands of Sancho that evening by carrying out the final trick he had been commissioned to play on him. It turned out that once Sancho had dined that day against all the rules and aphorisms of Doctor Tirteafuera and the table had been cleared, a courier entered with a letter from Don Quixote to the governor. Sancho ordered the secretary to read it to himself and, if it contained nothing of a confidential nature, to read it aloud. The secretary did accordingly and, after perusing it, said,

"It may certainly be read aloud, for what his lord Don Quixote has written to your grace deserves to be stamped and inscribed in letters of gold. It reads as follows:

LETTER FROM DON QUIXOTE OF LA MANCHA TO SANCHO PANZA, GOVERNOR OF CHEAP-ISLE

Just when I expected to receive word of your carelessness and lack of organization, dear Sancho, I was told of your wisdom, for which I give special thanks to heaven, which is capable of raising up the poor from the dunghill and making wise men out of fools. They tell me you are governing as

though you were a man but acting as though you were a dumb beast, so great is the humility in which you hold yourself. I would have you remember, Sancho, that it is often desirable and necessary because of the dignity of one's office to reject the humility in one's own heart, for the style of a person who has been placed in a position of responsibility should be more in keeping with the requirements of the office than with the humility of his own natural constitution.

Dress well, for a stick that is decorated no longer looks like a stick. I am not suggesting that you use trinkets or fancy clothes, or, being a judge, dress like a soldier, but that you wear the type of clothing your office demands, so long as it is clean and tasteful.

To gain the goodwill of the people you are governing, there are two things among others that you must do: first, be civil to everyone, though I have already mentioned this to you on an earlier occasion; and second, provide an abundance of the necessities of life, for nothing is more exasperating to the poor than hunger and want.

Do not enact a great number of laws but those that you do enact make certain they are good ones, and above all see that they are kept and observed, for laws that are not observed may as well not exist. Instead, they give the impression that the lord who had the wisdom and authority to enact them failed to have the courage to see to their enforcement. Laws which threaten but are not enforced end up like the log that became king of the toads – at first, the toads were afraid of it but with the passage of time they became contemptuous of it and ended up climbing all over it.

Be a father to virtue and a stepfather to vice. Be not always severe or always lenient but adopt a middle course between these two extremes, for therein lies the essence of wisdom. Make frequent visits to the jails, butcher shops, and public markets because the presence of the governor in those places is of great importance; it is comforting to the prisoners, who look forward to a speedy release; it is intimidating to the butchers, who at least for a time use accurate weights; and it is frightening to the women vendors for the same reason. Never show yourself to be covetous, womanizing, or gluttonous, even if you happen to be – which I do not believe – for as soon as the populace and those having dealings with you learn of your predilection, they will lay siege to it until they topple you into the depths of perdition. Consider and reconsider, study and restudy the advice and instructions I wrote down for you before you departed for your government, for if you observe them, you will find in them an advance that will see you through all the troubles and difficulties that confront governors at every turn. Write to your lord and lady and show them you are grateful, for ingratitude is the daughter of pride and is one of the greatest sins known. The person who is grateful to those who have befriended him shows he will also be grateful to God, who has bestowed His past and present blessings upon him.

Her ladyship the duchess has dispatched one of her servants with your suit and a present to your wife Teresa Panza and we are expecting a reply momentarily. I have been slightly indisposed due to a certain clawing my nose suffered in a most inopportune manner, but that does not matter, for if there are enchanters who abuse me, there are others who defend me.

Let me know if your majordomo was involved in La Trifaldi's activities as you suspected, and keep me advised of everything that happens to you, the distance between us being such a short one, particularly since I intend very soon to relinquish this life of idleness I am leading, which is not why

I was placed upon this earth.

A certain matter has arisen which, I fear, may put me out of favor with my lord and lady and, though this matters a great deal to me, I cannot avoid it, for in the final analysis I must be true to my profession before doing what pleases the duke and duchess, heeding the familiar saying: 'Amicus Plato, sed magis amica veritas.'[1] *I state this in Latin because I assume that, now that you are governor, you will have learned it. I commend you to God, and may He keep you from needing anyone's pity.*

Your friend,
DON QUIXOTE OF LA MANCHA

Sancho found the letter totally engrossing and it was praised by everyone who heard it as being erudite. Then rising from the table and calling for his secretary, Sancho shut himself up with him in his chamber, where without further delay he decided to send an immediate reply to his master Don Quixote. He instructed the secretary to begin writing and not to add or delete a thing and the latter did as instructed. The response went as follows:

LETTER FROM SANCHO PANZA TO DON QUIXOTE OF LA MANCHA

My involvement with my affairs has been so great that I haven't had a chance to scratch my head or even to cut my fingernails, which are so long only God can remedy the situation. I say this, my dearest master, so your grace will not be worried if up till now I have not sent news of my good or ill fortune in this government, where I am undergoing more hunger than when the two of us used to go traveling in the forests and wilds.

My lord the duke wrote to me the other day warning me that several spies who are out to kill me had landed on this island but so far I haven't discovered a single one other than a certain doctor who has been hired by the village to murder every governor who comes here. He calls himself Doctor Pedro Recio and is a native of Tirteafuera. You can see that his name alone would make me fear death at his hands! This very same doctor says of himself that he doesn't cure illnesses that already exist but prevents them from ever arising. The medicine he uses is diet and more diet till his patient is nothing but skin and bones, as if wasting away were not worse than burning up with fever. In a word, he is starving me to death and I am dying of despair, for whereas I thought I was coming to this government to get something hot to eat and cold to drink and to indulge my body in Holland sheets and feather beds, I've come to do penance as though I were some hermit, and since I'm not doing it voluntarily, I fear that in the end the Devil may carry off my soul.

Up to now I haven't touched a fee or taken a bribe and I can't imagine where this will lead, for they tell me that before any governor ever comes to this island, he is given or lent a large sum of money by the townspeople, which is the normal practice among those becoming governors everywhere, not

---

1 Latin: 'Plato may be a friend but truth is a greater friend.'

just here.

Last night, while making my rounds, I came across a very beautiful young lady dressed as a man, and one of her brothers dressed as a woman. My butler fell in love with the damsel and has made up his mind to have her for his wife, or so he says, and I chose the young man for my son-in-law. Today, we both intend to make our intentions known to the common father of them both, a certain Diego de la Llana, who is an hidalgo *and as pure-blooded a Christian as one might ever hope to find.*

I've been visiting the marketplaces, as your grace advised, where I came across a woman vendor selling fresh hazelnuts. I discovered that in a bushel of fresh nuts she had mixed a bushel of old ones that were empty or rotten. I confiscated the whole batch for the children at the charity school and they'll be able to tell the good ones from the bad. I sentenced her to two weeks banishment from the marketplace and have been told I acted courageously. All I can say is that it's common knowledge that in this town there is no one more notorious than the women vendors, who have no shame, no feelings, and no fear, and I can certainly believe it, based upon what I have seen in other towns.

I'm delighted that my lady the duchess has written to my wife Teresa Panza and sent her the present your grace mentioned, for which I'll be sure to show my appreciation at the proper time. Meanwhile, I hope your grace will kiss her hand on my behalf and tell her she hasn't put her gift into a sack with a hole in it, as she will see by the way I act. I wouldn't want you to have a falling out with my lord and lady, for if you get angry at them, it will clearly be to my disadvantage, and since I've been advised to be grateful, it doesn't make sense for your grace not to be grateful to those who have shown you so many kindnesses and treated you so royally in their castle.

I don't understand that business of the clawing but I suppose it must be one of those evil tricks the malevolent enchanters are always playing on your grace. However, I'll find out when we see each other.

I would like to send you some gift but have no idea what to send, unless it is an enema nozzle, for here on this island they make some very curious ones that are used with bags. Nevertheless, if my job holds out, I'll find something to send even if it's by hook or by crook.

If my wife Teresa Panza writes me, will you please pay the postage and forward the letter to me. I am quite eager to find out how things stand at home with my wife and children.

And so, may God liberate your grace from evil-minded enchanters and deliver me from this government in one piece, which I doubt, because I'm afraid I may give up the ghost, the way I'm being treated by Doctor Pedro Recio.

Your grace's servant,
SANCHO PANZA, THE GOVERNOR

The secretary sealed the letter and gave it to the courier. The perpetrators of Sancho's charade discussed among themselves how they might divest him of his government, whereas Sancho spent the afternoon drawing up various laws relating to the proper governing of the place he took to be an island. He decreed that there was to be no profiteering of goods on the island; that they might import wine from any place they pleased so long as they indicated its place of origin; that the price was to be determined by its quality, popularity, and reputation; and that any person caught adding water or changing its name would pay for it with his life. He reduced the prices on all footwear, primarily on shoes, for he had the feeling their prices were exorbitant. He placed a ceiling on servants' wages, which had been galloping headlong down the road of self-interest. He imposed severe penalties on anyone singing harmful or suggestive songs at any time of the day or night. He decreed that no blind man could sing songs of miracles unless he carried proof of their authenticity, for it seemed to him that most of those sung by the blind were spurious, which worked to the detriment of the authentic ones. He created a bailiff of the poor, not to persecute them but to determine if they really were destitute, for under the guise of faked lameness and phony sores many turn their limbs to thievery and their health to drunkenness. In short, he created so many good laws, still in force in that village to this day, that they are known as *The Constitution of the Great Governor Sancho Panza.*

Chapter Fifty-Two

The description of the adventure of the second distressed or afflicted duenna, otherwise known as Doña Rodríguez

Cide Hamete relates that, once Don Quixote's scratches healed, it struck him that the life he was leading in that castle ran completely counter to his professed order of chivalry, so he resolved to ask the duke and duchess for permission to depart in time for the approaching festival at Saragossa, where he intended to win the suit of armor awarded at such festivals. One day, while he was dining with the ducal pair and was just on the verge of carrying out his resolve to request their permission, lo and behold, at that most inopportune moment there strode through the door into the great hall two women (as was later learned) dressed in black from head to foot. One of them approached and prostrated herself at Don Quixote's feet, pressing her lips to them and moaning so piteously and profoundly that all those in observance were dismayed; and though the duke and duchess believed it was some joke their servants had contrived for playing on Don Quixote, still, when they saw how earnestly the woman was sighing, moaning, and sobbing, they were puzzled and confused until Don Quixote out of compassion helped her to her feet and had her reveal her identity by removing the mantle from her tear-stained face. In doing so, she revealed what no one would ever have imagined, for here was the face of Doña Rodríguez, duenna of that household, and the other mourner was her daughter who had been cruelly seduced by the rich farmer's son. Everyone who knew the duenna was shocked, particularly the duke and duchess, who considered her a harmless dullard and never dreamed she would commit such an outlandish act as this. After some time, Doña Rodríguez turned to the duke and duchess and said,

"Will your excellencies kindly permit me to take this knight aside: a thing that is necessary if I am to extricate myself from a predicament in which I have been placed by a brazen, evil-minded peasant?"

The duke said she had his permission to take Don Quixote as far away as she wished; and so, turning to Don Quixote, she said,

"Several days ago, valiant knight, I gave your grace an account of the outrage and perfidy an evil farmer had inflicted upon my dear, beloved daughter – this unfortunate girl here in our presence – and you promised to return on her behalf to right the injustice she had suffered, but it has just come to my attention that you now wish to leave this castle in quest of whatever good fortune God may hold in store for you. I wish, before you go hurrying off down the road, you would challenge this uncivilized yokel to a duel and force him to marry my daughter in fulfillment of the oath he swore before he lay with her when he promised to be her husband. To expect justice from my master the duke is like looking for pears on an elm tree for the reason I have already explained in private. And so, may Our Lord grant your grace good health and may He not abandon me and my daughter."

Don Quixote responded to these sentiments with gravity and solemnity:

"My good duenna, pray moderate your sobbing, or better yet, desist altogether and spare us your sighing as well. I shall take it upon myself to redress the injury to your daughter, who would have fared much better had she not been so hasty to believe a lover's promises, which for the most part are easy to make but difficult to keep. Therefore, with my master the duke's permission I shall set out at once in quest of that depraved young man, whom I shall locate, challenge, and slay if he is audacious enough to refuse to keep his promise, for the principal concern of my profession is to forgive the humble and to punish the haughty – to come to the aid of the downtrodden and to bring down the mighty."

"There is no need," said the duke, "for your grace to go to the trouble of looking for the peasant against whom this worthy duenna is leveling her accusations, nor is there any need for you to seek my permission to challenge him. I declare him challenged and accept the responsibility of informing him of this challenge and shall see to it that he accepts and answers to it personally in this castle of mine, where I shall afford you both an untrammeled field, observing all the conditions normally and rightfully observed in these affairs, making certain that each of you is treated fairly, this being incumbent upon every noble who provides an unrestricted arena for those doing battle on the premises of his estate."

"Well, with that assurance and your grace's kind permission," replied Don Quixote, "I just this once hereby renounce my nobility and humble and lower myself to the level of the miscreant by making myself his equal, thereby enabling him to do battle with me. I therefore challenge him *in absentia* and defy him by virtue of the evil he has perpetrated upon this poor maiden who, thanks to him, is one no longer. He shall comply with the oath he took to become her lawful husband or shall die on the field of battle."

Then removing one of his gloves, he tossed it to the floor in the middle of the hall, at which point the duke picked it up and announced, as he had already promised, that he was accepting that challenge in the name of his vassal and was setting the date at six days hence and the site as the courtyard of his castle. The weapons would be the usual ones among knights: lance, shield, articulated armor, and all other such accessories but without tricks, deceptions, or charms of any description, with everything to be examined and inspected by the field judges.

"However, before all these things are done," said the duke, "it is imperative that this good duenna and this sinful maid place their appeal for justice in the hands of Don Quixote. Otherwise, nothing shall be done, nor shall said challenge be carried to its proper resolution."

"I hereby do so," replied the duenna.

"And so do I," added the daughter, sobbing fitfully and blushing with shame.

Once this agreement had been reached and the duke had settled to his own satisfaction how he would proceed in this matter, the women in black withdrew and the duchess decreed that from that moment forth these women were not to be treated as servants but as ladies of fortune who had come to her house to seek justice. Accordingly, they were given a private room and treated as strangers, to the consternation of the other servants, who had no idea where the folly and brashness of Doña Rodríguez and her wayward daughter were leading. At that moment, as if to put the finishing touches on the festivities and to bring the meal to a happy conclusion, who should appear in the hall but the page who had delivered the letters and presents to Teresa Panza, wife of the governor Sancho Panza, and his arrival delighted the duke and duchess, inasmuch as they were eager to hear what had transpired on his journey. But when they asked about the matter, the page responded that because he could not divulge it in public or in only a few words, their excellencies should wait until they could all be alone. In the meantime they might amuse themselves with a couple of letters he had brought with him, and here he took them out and placed them in the hands of the duchess. On the outside of one envelope was written: *Letter for My Lady the Duchess So-and-So of I-Don't-Know-Where*, and on the other: *To My Husband Sancho Panza, Governor of Cheap-Isle – may he prosper for more years than me.* The duchess, as the expression goes, was 'champing at the bit' to read her letter and, after opening and perusing it, saw that it could be read aloud for the sake of the duke and all those who were present. The letter read as follows:

LETTER FROM TERESA PANZA TO THE DUCHESS

I was awfully pleased, my lady, by the letter your grace wrote me, which I had looked forward to with all my heart. The coral necklace is very nice and the hunting suit from my husband is no less so. This whole village is delighted that your ladyship has made my husband Sancho governor, though no one here believes it, especially the priest, the barber Master Nicolás, and the bachelor Sansón Carrasco, but that's no skin off my back; so long as the situation is the way it is, they can think whatever they please.

But to tell the truth, if the necklace and suit hadn't shown up, I wouldn't have believed it either because every person in this town thinks my husband is a dumbbell and, since he's never governed anything but a flock of goats, they don't believe he can govern anything else. But may God direct and guide him, for God can see that His children need all the help they can get. I, my dear lady, am determined, with your ladyship's permission, to strike while the iron is hot by coming to court and showing off in a coach, which will make the eyes bug out of a thousand people who already envy me.

I beg your excellency to have my husband send me a sum of money –and let it be a large one – for things are very expensive at court. A loaf of bread costs a real *and meat is thirty* maravedís *a pound, which is scandalous. However, if he doesn't want me to come, he should tell me so in advance because my feet are itching to hit the road. My women friends and neighbors tell me that if my daughter and I go about at court all puffed up and pompous-like, my husband will become known more because of me than I will because of him. This will cause a lot of people to ask, "Who are those ladies in that coach?" and one of my servants will answer, "The wife and daughter of Sancho Panza, governor of Cheap-Isle," and in this way Sancho will get to be known, I'll be admired, and nothing can stand in my way.*

I'm as sorry as I can be but this year there weren't enough acorns to pick. Nevertheless, I am sending your grace about a quarter of a peck I found here and there in the hills. They are the largest ones I could find. I only wish they were the size of ostrich eggs.

I hope your pompousness won't forget to write me. I'll take pains in my answer to report on my health and anything else that might be reported in this village, where I remain beseeching Our Lord to preserve your highness and not to forget me. My daughter Sancha and my son kiss your grace's hand.

And so with more desire to see your ladyship than to write, I am,

Your grace's humble servant,
TERESA PANZA

They were all delighted by Teresa Panza's letter, particularly the duke and duchess. The latter asked Don Quixote if he would consider it appropriate to open the letter that had arrived for the governor, since she felt it must be quite good. Don Quixote agreed to open it but only to please them, and in doing so, he found that it said the following:

LETTER FROM TERESA PANZA TO HER HUSBAND SANCHO PANZA

I received your letter, my dearest Sancho, and give you my word and swear as a good Catholic Christian that I came within a hair of going crazy with delight. Look, husband dear, when I got word that you were a governor, I thought I would drop dead right there out of sheer joy. You know that they say sudden happiness can kill as quickly as great sorrow. Your daughter Sancha wet herself without realizing it from sheer happiness. There I stood with the suit you sent me in front of me, the coral beads round my neck, the letters in my hand, and the bearer of them beside me, but for all that, I thought for certain that everything I saw and touched was a dream, for who would ever have imagined a goatherd could become governor of an island? You already know, my dear, what my mother used to say: "It takes a lot of living to see a lot of things." I mention this because I intend to see a lot of things if I don't die. In fact, I don't intend to stop till I see you a rent or a tax collector, and even though the Devil may carry off people who abuse those offices, those who occupy them always have money in their pockets. My lady the duchess will tell you how eager I am to come to court. Consider the matter carefully and let me know your decision. I'll try to make you proud of me by arriving in a coach.

The priest, the barber, the bachelor, and even the sacristan find it impossible to believe you're a governor and they claim it's all a fraud or some sort of enchantment like all that monkey business of your master Don Quixote. Sansón says he'll come and find you and will shake that government out of your head and Don Quixote's madness out of his skull, but the only thing I do is chuckle and look at my necklace and plan the dress I'm going to make our daughter from your suit.

I sent some acorns to my lady the duchess, which I wish could have been gold ones. Send me some pearl necklaces if they wear them on your island. The news from here is that the Berrueca woman married her daughter to a hack painter who came to this town to do any sort of painting he could get his hands on. The Council commissioned him to paint His Majesty's coat of arms over the entrance to the town hall and he charged two ducats, which they gave him in advance. He worked for a week, at the end of which time he had produced nothing, saying he couldn't bring himself to paint such trifles. He returned the money but in spite of all that got married on the basis of being a skilled craftsman. Actually, he's already laid aside the brush and taken up the hoe, going out into the fields like some gentleman. Pedro Lobo's son has been ordained and has shaved his head in preparation for becoming a priest. Minguilla, Mingo Silbato's granddaughter, found out about it and accused him of having promised to marry her. Idle tongues are claiming she's pregnant by him but he denies it in no uncertain terms.

This year there are no olives and there's not a drop of vinegar to be found in the entire village. A company of soldiers came through here and took three of the young townswomen away with them. I won't say who they are, since they may come back and find someone who'll have them as wives and will accept both their good and their soiled pasts.

Sanchica has been making lace and clears eight maravedís *a day, which she puts in her little bank to help towards her dowry, but now that her father's governor, he can provide her with a dowry without her having to work for it. The fountain in the market square dried up and a bolt of lightning struck the pillory. I wish they would all strike there.*

I'm looking forward to your answer to this letter and to your decision about my coming to court. For now, may God preserve you for more years than He does me, or at least for as many, because I wouldn't want you to be abandoned in this world without me.

Your wife,
TERESA PANZA

The letters were marveled at, laughed at, admired, and applauded, and as if to put icing on the cake, the courier arrived with the letter Sancho had written to Don Quixote, which was likewise read aloud and raised serious misgivings about the governor's stupidity. The duchess went off to ask the page what had transpired in Sancho's village, which he related at considerable length, leaving no particular untouched. He also gave her the acorns and a block of cheese Teresa had sent her, which was so good it surpassed that of Tronchón. The duchess most graciously accepted it and this is where we shall leave her holding it in her hands so we can write *finis* to the government of Sancho Panza, flower and mirror of all those who ever governed an island.

Chapter Fifty-Three

The exasperating end and conclusion that overtook Sancho Panza's government

'To believe that all things in this life will continue forever in the same state is to believe the impossible. On the contrary, it seems that all things go round in circles: spring pursues summer, summer autumn, autumn winter, and winter spring, and in this manner time keeps revolving on this endlessly turning wheel. Human life alone rushes to its completion more swiftly than the wind with no hope of renewal except in the next life, which has no bounds to limit it.' So writes Cide Hamete, the Mohammedan philosopher. Many persons, illumined not by the light of faith but by that of nature, have come to understand the transience and instability of the present life and the permanence of that eternal one that awaits us. Our author has mentioned this here because of the rapidity with which Sancho's government wasted away, broke into pieces, went up in smoke – in a word, ended. On the night of the seventh day of his governorship, Sancho lay in bed surfeited, not with bread and wine, but with judging, giving opinions, and issuing laws and decrees; and just when sleep, despite his hunger, was beginning to lie heavy upon his eyelids, he heard such a clamor of shouting and bell-ringing that he could only imagine the entire island was being turned upside down. Sitting bolt upright in bed, he strained to see if he could make out the cause of such a commotion. Not only did he not discover the cause but to the din of bells and shouts was added that of an endless number of trumpets and drums that filled him with fear and dread and left him more confused than ever. Getting out of bed, he put on a pair of slippers because of the damp floor but did not don a bathrobe or anything resembling one. Going to the door of his chamber, he was just in time to see more than twenty persons running down a corridor carrying lighted torches and unsheathed swords and all shouting at the top of their lungs,

"To arms, to arms, sir governor! An incredible number of enemy soldiers has landed on the island and we're lost if your ingenuity and valor do not come to our rescue!"

In the midst of this racket, frenzy, and furor, they rushed up to Sancho, who was aghast and mesmerized by what he was seeing and hearing, at which point one of them called out to him,

"Your grace must arm yourself at once unless you want yourself and the whole island to perish!"

"What am I to arm myself with?" cried Sancho; "what do I know about weapons or defending anyone? It will be better to leave these matters to my master Don Quixote, who will dispatch them in nothing flat and put them in safe keeping. I, poor soul that I am, know nothing about such complicated goings-on."

"Ah, sir governor," said one of the men, "what squeamishness do we have here? Your grace shall arm yourself with these offensive and defensive weapons we've brought and shall march forth into the plaza to serve as our guide and captain, which you have every right to do as our governor."

"All right," said Sancho, "let someone arm me."

They immediately produced two large shields they had kept in readiness and slipped them over his shirt before he could put on any more clothing. Then pulling his arms through holes they had bored in the shields, they tied him very securely with some cords, leaving him sandwiched in and boarded up as straight as a spindle and unable to bend his knees or take a single step backwards or forwards. At this point they thrust a lance into his hands on which he was forced to lean to keep from falling. Once they had him trussed in this fashion, they told him to start walking in order to lead them and infuse them with courage, for, having him as their Polaris, their beacon, their morning star, they were certain to achieve success in their enterprise.

"How is a poor wretch like myself supposed to walk?" said Sancho. "I can't even bend my knees because of these boards that are riveted to my body. What you will have to do is carry me in your arms and set me down crosswise or upright in the middle of some gate, which I can guard with this lance or my body."

"Come now, sir governor," said another, "it is not boards but fear that is keeping your grace from walking. Stop stalling and shake a leg; it's late and our enemies are growing in number, their shouts are getting louder, and the situation is becoming more perilous."

Because of these pleas and reproaches the poor governor made an attempt to move but managed to fall down with such a crash that he imagined himself broken into pieces. He lay there like a tortoise confined between its shells, like half a side of bacon wedged between two kneading troughs, exactly like a boat capsized upon a beach. But the sight of him on the ground failed to make those practical jokers show him any mercy. On the contrary, they extinguished their torches and returned to shouting out their call to arms with such urgency, while stepping on top of poor Sancho and continually stabbing at his shields, that had he not drawn himself up and pulled in his head between the shields, the poor governor would not have fared very well. Inside this cramped space he was beset by sweating and more sweating and he commended himself to God that He might deliver him from this peril. Several persons tripped over him, others fell down because of him, and there was even one who stood on top of him for some time, from where, as though from a watchtower, he directed the armies while shouting in a loud voice,

"Over here, men, this is where the enemy are pressing hardest! Someone guard this passageway and someone else close that gate! Cut down those ladders! Bring up the cauldrons of pitch, tar, and boiling oil! Barricade the streets with mattresses!"

In other words, he called out most fervently the names of every instrument and contrivance of war used to defend a city under siege. Poor belabored Sancho, who was painfully listening to all this, said to himself,

"Oh, if only the Lord will let this island be conquered once and for all and either let me be killed or be rid of this awful ordeal!"

Heaven heeded his prayer, for just when he least expected it he heard voices cry out,

"Victory, victory, the enemy soldiers have been routed! I say, sir governor, you may stand up, rejoice in our victory, and distribute the spoils taken from the enemy by the valor of your invincible arm."

"Lift me up," said the aching governor in a pained voice.

They helped him to his feet and, once upright, he said,

"You can nail to my forehead all the enemies /defeated. I have no desire to distribute the spoils of the enemy but to beg and implore one of my friends, if indeed I have any, to give me a drink of wine for this dry mouth of mine and to wipe this sweat off my sopping wet body."

After drying him off, they brought him some wine while they untied the shields, at which point Sancho sat down on his bed and passed out from the shock, fright, and exertion. Those who had played the trick on him were now sorry for having carried it thus far, but their anxiety at seeing him pass out was tempered when they later saw him regain consciousness. Asking what time of day it was, he was told it was now dawn. Without responding or saying another word, he began to dress in complete silence while they all watched and wondered why he was dressing so hurriedly. As soon as he finished, he made his way towards the stable one step at a time, for due to his aches and pains he was incapable of taking two at a time. Accompanied by all those who were present, he approached the dapple, at which point he embraced him and planted a conciliatory kiss on his forehead. Then with no lack of tears in his eyes, he said to him,

"Come to me, my friend, my companion, my fellow-sufferer in all my hardships and sorrows. When I kept you company and had no preoccupations other than those occasioned by my concerns for mending your harness and providing your little carcass with nourishment, I was happy at every hour of every day of the year, but since I abandoned you and mounted the towers of ambition and pride, my soul has been beset by a thousand pangs of pain and several thousand of hardship and unrest."

While Sancho was saying these things, he was busy saddling his jackass and not a word was spoken by anyone there. Once the saddle was in place, he painfully and laboriously mounted the dapple and directed the following remarks to the majordomo, the secretary, the butler, Doctor Pedro Recio, and all the others who were present:

"Make way, gentlemen, let me return to my old-time freedom. Let me go back to my former life, that I may rise once again from this present death. I wasn't born to be a governor or to defend cities and islands against those who would attack them. I know more about hoeing and plowing or pruning and layering vineyards than about making laws and defending provinces and kingdoms. 'Saint Peter is quite content in Rome,' by which I mean that each person would do well to follow the trade for which he was born. I look better with a scythe in my hand than with a governor's scepter. I'd rather fill up my stomach with cold soup than be subjected to a stingy, impudent doctor who's starving me to death. I'd prefer to stretch out in the shade of an elm tree in the summer or to wrap myself in an undressed sheepskin jacket in the winter in a state of freedom than to sleep on Holland sheets and dress myself in sables while being subjected to governing. God preserve your excellencies and you may tell my master that naked I was born and naked I remain, so I'm neither winning nor losing. What I'm trying to say is that I came to this government without a cent and that is how I am leaving it – just the opposite of what usually occurs with governors of other islands. So move aside. Let me get myself some poultices, for I'm afraid every one of my ribs is crushed thanks to all my enemies who have trampled on me tonight. "

"Your governorship shall do no such thing," said Doctor Pedro Recio. "I shall give you a potion against falls and beatings that will immediately restore you to your former health and vigor, and as for meals, I promise to make amends by allowing you to eat your fill of anything you might desire."

"You're a little late!" said Sancho; "I'd rather become a Turk than stay here! I'll not be tricked twice. Good lord, I would as soon stay in this government or accept another one, even if it were served to me on a platter, as to fly to heaven without wings. I come from a long line of Panzas who're all stubborn and when we say that something is white, white it'll be even if it's black and everyone else says so. This stable can have those flimsy wings that carried me up into the air so the birds of prey could devour me. Just give me back my good old *terra firma*. I may not end up wearing fancy Cordovan shoes but neither will I want for hempen sandals. 'Each sheep to its own mate,' and 'No one should get above his raising.' Now, let me through because it's getting late."

To which the majordomo replied,

"We shall gladly allow your governorship to depart but it will pain us greatly to lose your grace, for your intelligence and Christian conduct make us desire to have you remain with us. Also, inasmuch as it is common knowledge that every governor is required to make a report on his administration before leaving the place he has governed, you may depart with our blessings once you submit a report covering your ten days of governing."

"No one can demand such a report of me except someone designated by my master the duke, and since I'm on my way to see him, I'll give him a complete report; and because I'm leaving as naked as I am, no further proof should be necessary to demonstrate that I've governed like an angel."

"I must admit the great Sancho is correct," said Doctor Recio. "I am also of the opinion that we should permit him to leave, for the duke will be pleased beyond measure to see him."

They all agreed to this and allowed him to depart, first offering to accompany him and provide him with anything for his person that might make his trip comfortable. Sancho said he desired nothing more than a little barley for his dapple and some bread and cheese for himself, and there would be no need of any better or further provisions, since the trip was such a short one. They all embraced him and he, with tears in his eyes, embraced all those gathered there and then departed, leaving them to marvel not only at what he had said but also at his most resolute and considered determination.

Chapter Fifty-Four

An account of matters relating to this history and to none other

The duke and duchess decided to proceed with the challenge Don Quixote had issued to their vassal for the reason already mentioned, but because the young man was in Flanders, where he had fled to avoid having Doña Rodríguez as his mother-in-law, they arranged to substitute a Gascon lackey named Tosilos, whom they first thoroughly instructed in everything he was expected to do. A couple of days later, the duke informed Don Quixote that four days from then his adversary would arrive and would appear on the field of battle armed as a knight, where he would maintain the damsel was lying through her teeth, or even her entire mouth, if she claimed he had promised to marry her. Don Quixote was extremely pleased with this news and promised to work wonders, considering himself most fortunate to have been given the opportunity to demonstrate to his hosts how far the valor of his mighty arm extended. Brimming with a sense of joy and contentment, he could hardly wait for the four days to pass, which due to his impatience seemed more like four hundred centuries.

But we shall let them pass (as we have let other things pass) while we accompany Sancho, who half joyous and half sad rode along on his dapple to rejoin his master, in whose company he found more pleasure than in governing all the islands on earth.

It transpired that before he had traveled very far from the island, having never, in fact, made the effort to ascertain whether the place he had governed was an island, city, town, or village, he saw coming down the road half a dozen pilgrims carrying staves, who belonged to those bands of foreigners who sing for their alms.

When they arrived, they lined up in a row and, raising their voices in unison, began to sing a song in their own tongue, which Sancho found incomprehensible except for the word 'alms', which they pronounced quite clearly. From this, he understood they were begging for alms in their song, and since Sancho was charitable in the extreme according to Cide Hamete, he took from his saddlebags a wedge of cheese and half a loaf of bread with which he had come provided and gave these to them, indicating by gestures that he had nothing more to give them. They gladly accepted these but called out,

"*Geld! Geld!*" [1]

"I don't understand, good people," said Sancho, "what it is you're asking me."

At this point one of them drew a purse from his shirt and showed it to Sancho, whereby the latter understood they were asking for money. Placing his thumb to his throat and extending his hand upwards, Sancho gave them to understand that he did not have a cent to his name. Then spurring the dapple, he proceeded to ride through their ranks. But as he did so, one of those who had been staring at him quite intently rushed up and threw his arms round his waist, saying to him in a voice that was both loud and very Castilian,

"Bless my soul! can this be who I think it is? Is it possible that I hold in my arms my dear friend and good neighbor Sancho Panza? It must be so, since I'm not dreaming and am not drunk at the moment."

Sancho was surprised to hear himself addressed by name and to find himself embraced by a foreign pilgrim, but even after staring at him with all his might, he was still unable to recognize him. When the pilgrim saw his consternation, he said to him,

"What! is it possible, Sancho Panza my brother, that you don't recognize your neighbor Ricote, the Morisco [2] shopkeeper from your village?"

Sancho stared at him even harder and, gradually fitting the pieces together, finally came to recognize him down to the smallest detail. Without dismounting from the dapple, he threw his arms

---

1 German: 'Money! Money!'

2 The Moriscos were Moors converted to Christianity after the Reconquest of 1609 to 1614.

round Ricote's neck and said,

"Who the devil could recognize you, Ricote, in that clownish outfit you're wearing? Tell me: when did you get so Frenchified, and how do you have the audacity to return to Spain where, if they recognize you and arrest you, things will go rather badly for you?"

"If you don't turn me in, Sancho," replied the pilgrim, "I'm sure that in this outfit there's no one who'll recognize me. But let's leave the road and go off to that grove of trees over yonder, which is where my companions want to rest and eat their meal. There you can join them while they dine, for they're a very peaceful lot, and I'll have the opportunity to tell you what's happened to me since I left our village in compliance with his majesty's proclamation that threatened the hapless souls of my tribe with such severity, as you know."

Sancho did as requested and after Ricote spoke to the other pilgrims, they all headed for the grove that was situated some distance from the main highway. Tossing aside their staves, they removed their hooded cloaks, which left them in their shirts and breeches, all quite nice-looking young men except Ricote, who was already advanced in years. Each carried a knapsack that was apparently well-stocked, at least with those foods that provoke thirst and do so from a distance of two leagues. They stretched out on the ground and, using the grass as their tablecloth, spread out on top of it bread, salt, knives, nuts, wedges of cheese, and ham bones stripped down to the bone, which, if there was nothing left to chew, could at least be sucked. They also produced a black food which they said was called caviar and was made from fish eggs, a food that fairly cried out for a drink of wine; and there was no lack of olives which, though dried and unsalted, were still tasty and appetizing. But the thing that carried off the chiefest honors on that banquet field was a half-dozen wineskins, one of which each pilgrim pulled from his knapsack. Even our good Ricote, who had been transformed from a Morisco into a German or Dutchman, took out his own wineskin, which was as large as the other five combined. They began to eat with the greatest gusto, spearing small portions of the various foods with the tips of their knives and savoring each mouthful in a leisurely fashion. Then all at once, they raised the wineskins into the air and, aiming the mouths of the wineskins at their own, fixed their eyes upon the sky as though they were taking aim at it. They held this pose for quite some time as they tossed their heads from side to side, an act acknowledging the enjoyment they were deriving from emptying the contents of the vessels into their stomachs. Sancho was a spectator to all this and was untroubled by anything he saw; on the contrary, in order to obey the proverb which he knew by heart – 'When in Rome do as the Romans do' – he asked Ricote for the wineskin and took aim along with the others, and with no less enjoyment. Four times the wineskins permitted themselves to be raised aloft but a fifth was impossible, for they were now drier and dustier than a cactus, a circumstance that cast a pall over the gaiety that had reigned until that moment. From time to time, one of them would clasp Sancho's right hand with his own and say: '*Españoli y tudesqui, tuto uno: bon compaño,*[3] and

3 Italian spelled phonetically in Spanish, meaning: 'Spaniards and Germans, we're all one, good fellow.'

Sancho would answer: *'Bon compaño, jura Di!'*[4] and would break into a laugh that lasted an hour, totally unmindful of everything that had befallen him in his government, for while one is eating and drinking, his cares are of slight importance. Finally, the end of the wine marked the beginning of a drowsiness that overtook them all and they fell asleep on top of their very table and tablecloth. Only Ricote and Sancho remained awake, as they had eaten more and drunk less. Ricote then drew Sancho aside, where they seated themselves at the foot of a beech tree, leaving the pilgrims immersed in pleasant slumber, whereupon Ricote, without once lapsing into his Morisco tongue, made the following speech in perfect Castilian.

"You know, of course, Sancho Panza my friend and neighbor, what great fear and terror were struck into all our hearts by the proclamation and edict His Majesty proclaimed against those of my race; at least, it so affected me that even before the appointed time of our enforced expulsion from Spain, it seemed I could already feel the effects of that harsh penalty on myself and my children. Accordingly I arranged, and wisely so in my opinion (like one who knows that by a certain date the house in which he lives will be taken from him and thus provides himself with another into which he can move) to leave my family there in the village in order to seek some place where I might comfortably take them without the haste others had taken in leaving. I and all our elders could clearly see that those proclamations were not mere threats, as some said, but real laws that would be put into effect at their designated time. I was led to this conclusion by learning of the disgustingly absurd schemes my people were planning, which were so absurd I feel it was divine inspiration that moved His Majesty to take such a bold measure – and not because all of us were guilty, for some of us were true confirmed Christians, but we were so few in number we didn't compare with those who were not. Nor would it have been wise to nourish a viper in our midst by keeping the enemy inside the house. In short, we were justly punished by being banished, a mild and moderate punishment in the opinion of some but in ours the most terrible we could have received. Wherever we find ourselves, we shed tears for Spain, for, after all, this is our native land and the place of our birth. Nowhere do we meet with the reception our unfortunate plight deserves. In Barbary and all those parts of Africa where we expected to be accepted, welcomed, and embraced, those are the places where we are most abused and ill-treated. We didn't realize how well off we were until we lost all this, and our desire to return to Spain, which nearly all of us have, is so great that most of those who know the language, as I do – and there are many – return here, leaving their wives and children ill-provided for, so great is the love they feel for this land. I now know the true meaning of the saying that 'the love of one's country is sweet.'

"I left our village, as I said, and went to France, and though we were well received there, I wanted to visit every country I could. I thus proceeded to Italy and then to Germany, where it seems to me one can live with more freedom, since it's citizens aren't overly critical: each person living as he pleases, for in most parts of the country they enjoy freedom of conscience. I arranged for a house in a town near Augsburg and then joined these pilgrims, many of whom make it a practice to come to Spain each year to visit the shrines, which they regard as their Indies and a sure and recognized

4 The same: 'Good fellow, I swear to God.'

source of profit. We travel through most of the country and there's not a single town we pass through in which we don't receive our fill of food and drink and at least a *real* in coins. At the end of our travels we take with us more than a hundred *escudos* saved, which we exchange for gold we can smuggle out of the country hidden in the hollows of our staves or under the patches on our cloaks or by some other means, and this gold we send back to our families despite the guards at the posts and ports of entry who search us. It is my intention, Sancho, to retrieve the treasure I left buried, which I can do without risk, since it's buried outside the village, and to write or go from Valencia to my wife and daughter, who, I know for a fact, are in Algiers. There I'll figure out how to take them to some French port and from there to Germany, where we'll wait to see what God has in store for us. Besides, I know for a fact that Ricota my daughter and Francisca Ricota my wife are good Catholics, and even if I'm not as good a Catholic as they, I'm still more of a Christian than a Moor and continually pray that God will open the eyes of my understanding and show me how I may serve Him. But what has me puzzled is not knowing why my wife and daughter went to Barbary instead of to France, where they might live like Christians."

To which Sancho responded,

"Look, Ricote, the matter probably wasn't in their hands, for they were taken there by Juan Tiopieyo, your wife's brother, and since he's probably a full-fledged Moor, he went to the safest place. I can tell you something else: I think you'll be wasting your time looking for what you buried, for we received word that they confiscated a number of pearls and a large sum of gold coins your brother-in-law and wife were carrying when they were searched."

"That may well be," replied Ricote, "but I am sure, Sancho, that they never touched what I buried, for I didn't let anyone know where it was for fear that some misfortune might occur. Therefore, Sancho, if you wish to come with me and help me retrieve the treasure and hide it, I'll give you two hundred *escudos*, which can help you with your needs, and you know as well as I that you have your share of them."

"I would do so," said Sancho, "but I'm not the least bit greedy. If I were, I wouldn't have given up a position this morning by which I could've lined the walls of my house with gold and within six months time could be eating off plates of silver. For this reason and because I feel I would be committing treason against my king by giving aid to his enemies, I wouldn't go with you if you gave me four hundred *escudos* here in cash instead of the two hundred you merely promise me."

"What position did you give up, Sancho?" asked Ricote.

"I gave up being governor of an island," said Sancho, "and it was such a good one I'll bet there's not another one like it for leagues around."

"And where is this island?" said Ricote.

"Where?" replied Sancho; "a couple of leagues from here and it's called Cheap-Isle."

"Come now, Sancho," said Ricote, "islands are found in the sea. There aren't any islands on dry land."

"Since when!" said Sancho; "I'm telling you, Ricote my friend, that I came from there just this morning and yesterday I was on it governing as pretty as I pleased and whenever I felt like it, but for all that, I left it because the office of governor struck me as being a dangerous one."

"And what did you gain from being governor?" said Ricote.

"I," replied Sancho, "gained the realization that I'm not fit to govern, except maybe a herd of cattle, and that wealth gained in such governments comes at the expense of rest, sleep, and even food, for governors of islands eat sparingly, especially when they have doctors to look after their health."

"I don't understand what you're talking about, Sancho," said Ricote; "everything you're saying sounds like nonsense. Who would ever give you an island to govern? Was there no one else available more qualified to govern than you? But, come, Sancho, be sensible and make up your mind whether you will come with me to retrieve the treasure I left buried – and it's so large it can truthfully be called a treasure – and I'll give you something to live on, as I've said."

"I've already told you, Ricote, that I have no intention of doing that. Just be satisfied that I won't turn you in. Continue on your way with my blessing and let me continue on mine. I know that even lawfully gotten gains may be lost but ill-gotten ones damn both themselves and their owner."

"I don't wish to insist," said Ricote, "but tell me: were you in our village when my wife, daughter, and brother-in-law left it?"

"Yes, I was," replied Sancho, "and I can assure you that your daughter went away looking so beautiful that everyone in the village turned out to see her, and they all agreed she was the most beautiful creature on earth. With tears in her eyes she embraced all her women friends and acquaintances and everyone who had come to see her off, begging them to commend her to God and to Our Lady His mother, and doing so with such feeling that it made me weep, and I'm not given to weeping. I assure you that many would have liked to hide her away or follow her onto the road and abduct her, but the fear of going against the king's edict kept them from doing so. The person most visibly moved was Don Pedro Gregorio, that rich young heir and acquaintance of yours, a person who was said to be passionately in love with her. Ever since she went away, he has never again shown up in our village and we all think he went after her to steal her away, but up to now we've heard nothing."

"I always suspected that gentleman had a liking for my daughter," said Ricote, "but because I trusted in the uprightness of my Ricota, I never let that knowledge bother me. You've probably heard, Sancho, that Moriscas seldom, if ever, have affairs with Christians of long standing, and my daughter, who in my opinion was more concerned with religion than with love, would have paid no attention to the solicitations of that lord and heir."

"May God grant that," said Sancho, "or it will go badly with them both. However, I must be on my way because I want to catch up with my master Don Quixote tonight."

"May God go with you, Sancho my brother. My companions are also beginning to stir and it's time for us to resume our journey."

The two then embraced, Sancho mounted his dapple, Ricote retrieved his staff, and each went his separate way.

Chapter Fifty-Five

The things that befell Sancho along the way, and other matters that leave nothing to be desired

The time that Sancho spent with Ricote prevented him from reaching the duke's castle that day, though he had come within half a league of it before being overtaken by night, a night that was dark and overcast. But because it was summer, he was not overly concerned and proceeded to move off the road to wait for day to arrive. However, his ill luck and worse fortune saw to it that, in seeking the best place to accommodate himself, he and the dapple fell into a deep dark chasm located among a group of ancient ruins. During the course of his descent, he commended himself to God with all his heart, imagining he would continue falling until he reached the very bottom of the abyss, but it turned out otherwise, for the dapple landed after falling no more than three times his own height. And Sancho, who found himself still seated on him, had suffered no harm or injury whatever. Nevertheless, he felt every part of his body and even took a deep breath to see if he was still intact or had been punctured in some place. Once he found that he was perfectly whole and in good shape, he could not give sufficient thanks to Our Lord God for the mercy He had shown him, for the squire had absolutely imagined himself broken into a thousand pieces. Then feeling along the walls of the chasm with his hands to see if he could possibly escape from there without anyone's help, he saw that all the walls were smooth and lacking any place to grip, which grieved him deeply, particularly when he heard his dapple's pitiful groans, a not unsurprising reaction, considering the fact that the latter was not complaining of a mere trifle but of a truly grievous situation.

"Alas," said Sancho Panza at this point, "how many undreamt-of things happen at every turn to those of us who inhabit this miserable world! Who would've thought that a person who only yesterday was firmly enthroned as governor of an island, commanding servants and vassals, would today find himself buried in some chasm without anyone to rescue him or any servant or vassal to come to his aid? My jackass and I will surely starve to death here if we don't die sooner than that: he from his bruises and broken bones and I from my grief. At least, I'll not be as fortunate as my master Don Quixote of La Mancha was when he descended into that enchanted Cave of Montesinos, where he encountered a person who treated him more royally than he was treated at home, as though the bed had been made and the table set just for him. Down in those depths in which he found himself, he saw beautiful visions that delighted the eye, but down here, if I don't miss my guess, I'll see nothing but toads and snakes. Oh, woe is me! Just look at where my follies and fanciful thinking have brought me! And if heaven should deign to allow me to be discovered, they'll haul up my bones from here, bleached, bare, and picked clean, together with those of my worthy dapple. Perhaps that will show people who we were; at least, it will those who have heard that Sancho Panza never abandoned the ass, nor the ass Sancho Panza. I repeat that our miserable fate has not been willing for us – wretches that we are – to die in our own land among our own people where, even if there was no solution for our misfortune, there would at least be someone to grieve over us and close our eyes in the final hour of our sojourn on earth! O comrade and friend, how poorly I've repaid you for your faithful service! May you forgive me and implore fate in the best way you know how to deliver us from this awful predicament in which we find ourselves. Not only do I promise to place a crown of laurel on your head that will make you look like a poet laureate but I'll even double your rations."

Sancho Panza went on bemoaning his fate in this manner, with his donkey listening to him but not saying a single word, such were the anguish and distress in which the poor beast found himself. Finally, after Sancho had spent the entire night complaining and whimpering, day arrived with such clarity and brilliance that he could see the absolute impossibility of climbing out of that pit without someone's assistance, at which point he began to groan and shout to see if anyone could hear him. But all his shouting was so much crying in the wilderness, for there was no one in the vicinity who could hear him, and it was then that he gave himself up for dead. Seeing the dapple lying with his hooves up in the air, Sancho helped him to his feet, though he had trouble keeping him upright. Then taking from his saddlebags (which had suffered the same fate in the tumble) a piece of bread, Sancho gave it to his jackass, who thought it tasted pretty good, and the squire said to him as though he could understand him,

"Any ache is tolerable so long as there is bread to eat."

At that moment, he spotted an opening at one side of the chasm through which a person could squeeze if he stooped down and made himself short enough. Sancho went over to it, crouched down, and crawled through to the other side where he found a large spacious interior that was light enough to be seen because a beam of sunlight that shone through what might be called the ceiling illuminated everything there. He also noticed that it became wider and opened into another broad cavity, and no sooner did he notice this than he returned for his jackass. Using a stone, he began to chip away the earth in the passageway so that within a short time he had dug a hole through which the ass could pass. Then leading him by the halter, he began to walk deeper into the grotto to see if he could find a way out at the other end, at times walking in the dark, at other times without light, but never without fear.

"May Almighty God help me!" he said to himself; "this thing, a misadventure for me, would be an adventure for my master Don Quixote. He would certainly consider these deep dungeons a bed of roses or the palace of Galiana and would expect to emerge from this dark, confining place into some meadow filled with flowers. But for poor, unfortunate me, who am fainthearted and have no one to guide me, each step is accompanied by my fear that I'll encounter a deeper chasm than the previous one which will suddenly open beneath my feet and will swallow me whole. You, Evil, are welcome if you've come alone."

As he walked along to the accompaniment of these thoughts, he surmised that he had gone slightly more than half a league when he came to a light that seemed like daylight coming from some unknown source and promised a way out of that (for him) road to the next world. And this is where Cide Hamete Benengeli chooses to leave him in order to return to the affairs of Don Quixote.

The knight was jubilantly and eagerly looking forward to the day of the battle he was to undertake with the person who had robbed Doña Rodríguez' daughter of her honor, on whose behalf he intended to right the grievous wrong she had suffered. It happened that on this particular morning Don Quixote had gone out to rehearse what he planned to do in the ordeal in which he expected to find himself the following day, and while putting Rocinante through his paces, he rode so close to a crevice that, had he not pulled up sharply on the reins, he could not possibly have avoided falling into it, but he managed to stop in the nick of time. Edging a bit closer, he looked down into the chasm without dismounting and, while peering down into it, heard loud shouts from within. By listening closely, he was able to make out that the one doing the shouting was saying,

"Hallo up there! Is there any Christian who can hear me or some charitable knight who will take pity upon a poor soul buried alive – upon an unfortunate governor stripped of his government?"

It seemed to Don Quixote that he was hearing the voice of Sancho Panza, which surprised and astounded him. Shouting with all his might, Don Quixote called out,

"Who is that down there making all that racket?"

"Who else would be making all this racket," said the voice, "except the belabored Sancho Panza, governor (thanks to his sins and bad luck) of Cheap-Isle and one-time squire to the famous knight Don Quixote of La Mancha?"

When Don Quixote heard this, his amazement increased and his astonishment redoubled, for the thought struck him that Sancho Panza must be dead and his soul was doing penance down there; and so with this thought in mind, he said,

"I, as a Catholic Christian, conjure you by all the powers at my command to tell me who you are. If you are a soul in torment, tell me what you would have me do on your behalf. Inasmuch as my profession is to favor and succor the needy of this world, it shall likewise be to aid and succor the needy in the next who are incapable of helping themselves."

"In that case," replied the voice, "the person speaking to me must be my master Don Quixote of La Mancha, for that very voice belongs to no one else."

"It is I, Don Quixote," said the knight, "and it is my profession to assist and come to the aid of both the living and the dead in their need. For this reason, tell me who you are because I am completely bewildered. If you are my squire Sancho Panza and have died, since you have not been carried off by the Devil and are by the mercy of God in purgatory, our Holy Mother the Roman Catholic Church has sufficient means to intercede for you and deliver you from the torment in which you find yourself, and I shall personally intercede on your behalf insofar as my wealth permits. Therefore, declare yourself, I say, and tell me who you are."

"Confound it!" responded the voice, "Master Don Quixote of La Mancha, I'll swear upon the head of anyone your grace designates that I am your squire Sancho Panza and have never in all the days of my life died. On the contrary, having given up my government for reasons that require more time than this to explain, I fell into this chasm last night where I now find myself, along with my dapple, who'll not let me tell a lie. If further proof is needed, here he is beside me."

And as though this were not sufficient, the ass in some uncanny way seemed to understand what Sancho had said, for he immediately began to bray, and so robustly that the entire cave reverberated.

"An excellent witness!" cried Don Quixote; "I recognize his bray as though he were my own son and I hear your voice, dear Sancho. Wait for me here and I shall return to the duke's nearby castle to get someone to rescue you from this pit you are in – probably because of your sins."

"For the love of God, may your grace do so and do so quickly," said Sancho; "I'm scared to death down here and can't stand being buried alive for another moment."

Don Quixote left and returned to the castle to inform the duke and duchess of what had befallen Sancho. They found it most astonishing, though they understood from the description of the place that he must have fallen into the grotto that had been there from time immemorial, but what they could not understand was how he had relinquished the governorship without their receiving word of his coming. Everyone eventually arrived with ropes and cords and by dint of hard work and a number of hands pulled the dapple and Sancho Panza out of that darkness into the sunlight. A student who saw this observed:

"This is how every bad governor should leave office – the way this pathetic soul is ascending from the depths of the abyss: dying of hunger, pale, and apparently without a cent to his name."

Sancho heard him and responded,

"It was eight or ten days ago, my slanderous fellow, that I assumed the governorship of the island I was given, during which time I never had my stomach satisfied for one hour. During that same period, I was persecuted by physicians, my bones were crushed by my enemies, and I never had the opportunity to take bribes or collect fees. This being the case, I don't, in my opinion, deserve to leave office in this manner. However, 'Man proposes and God disposes,' and 'God knows what is best and most proper for each person.' Besides, 'Circumstances alter cases,' and don't let anyone say he'll never do such-and-such a thing; nor should he 'count his chickens before they're hatched,' and since God understands what I'm saying, which is sufficient, I'll say no more even though I could."

"Don't be angry, Sancho," said Don Quixote, "or be upset by what you hear or there will be no end to the matter. Keep your own conscience clear and let others say what they will. To attempt to tie the tongues of slanderers is like trying to stop the wind from blowing. If a governor leaves office wealthy, they say he has been a thief; if he leaves poor, he has been a know-nothing and a dimwit."

"Well, in my case," said Sancho, "they'll certainly take me for an idiot rather than a thief."

While they were engaged in this conversation surrounded by children and a number of other persons, they arrived at the castle, where the duke and duchess were awaiting Don Quixote and his squire in one of the galleries. Sancho refused to go see the duke before first settling the dapple in the stable, for, as he said, the animal had spent a very bad night in their last lodging-place. Once he had done this, he went upstairs to see his master and mistress, before whom he fell to his knees and said,

"I, my excellencies, at your graces' request and through no merits of my own went to govern your Cheap-Isle, where I entered naked and came out the same way, neither winning nor losing. And whether I've governed well or badly, there are witnesses present who are free to say what they will. I expressed my opinion in questions of law and passed sentence in legal disputes, during all of which time I was dying of hunger thanks to the efforts of Doctor Pedro Recio, a native of Tirteafuera and the insular and gubernatorial physician. Our enemies attacked us one night and, just when our backs were to the wall, the islanders told me they had emerged free and victorious because of the might of my arm – and anyone who believes that will believe anything. In short, during that time I weighed the duties and responsibilities governing brings with it and determined by my reckoning that my back is not capable of bearing them. They're no load for these shoulders nor arrows for my quiver. And so before the government could get rid of me, I chose to get rid of the government. I left the island yesterday just as I found it, with the same streets, houses, and roofs it had when I arrived there. I never asked anyone for a loan or got involved in money-making schemes, and even though I thought of issuing several worthwhile ordinances, I issued none, fearing they wouldn't be observed, since issuing them amounts to as much as not issuing them. After leaving the island, as I said, accompanied only by my dapple, I fell into a chasm, through which I walked till morning and, when day came, I was able to spot a way out but not a very good one, and had heaven not sent me my master Don Quixote, I would've remained there till Doomsday. Therefore, my esteemed duke and duchess, here kneels your excellencies' governor Sancho Panza, who in only ten days of governing has come to the realization that he'll receive nothing for being governor of the entire world, much less of an island. And so with this settled, I kiss your graces' feet and, in imitation of the children's game of hopscotch, am hopping out of the government and into the service of my master Don Quixote, for though I may eat my bread uneasily while serving him, at least I have enough to eat, and so long as my stomach is full, it doesn't matter whether it's with partridge or carrots."

With this, Sancho brought his lengthy speech to a close, during which Don Quixote was constantly in dread that he might blurt out an endless stream of nonsense; but when he heard him finish with so few absurdities, he thanked heaven from the bottom of his heart. The duke embraced Sancho and told him it pained him that Sancho had forsaken the government so abruptly but he would see to it that he was given another position on his estate less burdensome and more profitable. The duchess also embraced him and ordered her servants to take good care of him, for he showed that if his bruises were bad, his treatment had been even worse.

Chapter Fifty-Six

The prodigious and unheard-of battle that took place between Don Quixote of La Mancha and the lackey Tosilos in defense of the daughter of the duenna Doña Rodríguez

The duke and duchess felt no regrets over the joke they had played on Sancho Panza in granting him the government, particularly when their majordomo arrived that same day and gave them a detailed account of virtually everything Sancho had said and done during that period, ending with an embellished description of the assault on the island and Sancho's fright and departure, all of which they found highly amusing. Following this, our history states that the designated day of the battle arrived, the duke having instructed his lackey Tosilos more times than one how to proceed without wounding or killing Don Quixote. He ordered the metal points removed from the lances, explaining to Don Quixote that his Christian ideals in which he prided himself would not permit the battle to be carried out with such risk and peril to their lives; that Don Quixote should be content with being afforded an unrestricted field on his estate, since dueling went against the decree of the Holy Council, which had placed a ban on such contests; nor should he insist upon carrying the struggle to its ultimate conclusion. Don Quixote replied that his excellency might establish any conditions he wished in that affair and he would abide by them completely.

The duke had a viewing stand erected adjacent to the castle facing the grounds on which the field judges, the duennas, and the plaintiffs – both mother and daughter – were to sit. The dreaded day arrived and an endless throng of people from all the surrounding towns and villages had gathered to witness the unique battle, for in that land such a spectacle had never been seen or heard of by anyone living or dead. The first to make his entrance onto the tilting field was the field marshal, who surveyed the field by riding its entire length to assure himself that it contained no trickery or hidden objects that might cause the combatants to stumble or fall. At this point, the duennas entered and took their seats, their veils covering not only their eyes but their bosoms as well, and they evinced no slight emotion when Don Quixote appeared on the field. A moment later, to the accompaniment of a number of trumpets, there appeared at the other end of the field, seated on a powerful steed that made the entire field quake, the great lackey Tosilos, his visor in place and himself rigidly clad in a suit of rugged, shining armor. His broad gray horse left no doubt that it was Frisian by the twenty-five pounds of hair hanging from each fetlock. The valiant combatant had been well rehearsed as to how to conduct himself with the valiant Don Quixote of La Mancha, having been warned not to slay him under any circumstances but to seek to evade the first encounter lest he risk slaying him, which he was certain to do if he met him head on. Tosilos circled the field and, coming to the spot where the duennas were seated, paused for several moments to feast his eyes upon the damsel who was demanding that he marry her. The field marshal summoned Don Quixote, who had now ridden onto the field and with Tosilos present he addressed the duennas, asking them if they would empower Don Quixote of La Mancha to sue for their rights. They assured him they would and, whatever the outcome of that contest, would abide by it and consider it firm and binding. By this time, the duke and duchess had taken their places in a gallery that overlooked the field, every foot of which was surrounded by the multitude of spectators waiting to view this fierce and never-before-witnessed ordeal. The terms of the contest were that if Don Quixote emerged victorious, his adversary must wed Doña Rodríguez' daughter, but should he be defeated, his opponent was relieved of the promise demanded of him and was under no further obligation.

The field marshal divided the sun equally between the two combatants, placing them at the spot where each was to stand. The drums sounded, the trumpets pierced the air, the ground trembled beneath everyone's feet, and the hearts of all the spectators were held in suspension, some hoping for a happy outcome in this undertaking, others fearing an unhappy one. And lastly, Don Quixote, who had commended himself to Our Lord God with all his soul and to the lady Dulcinea of Toboso, awaited the prescribed signal to begin his charge. Our lackey, however, was of an entirely different frame of mind, for he was thinking only of what I shall now explain.

It would appear that while the lackey had been gazing at his fair adversary, he fancied her to be the most beautiful woman he had seen in his entire life, and the little blind boy commonly known as Cupid was not about to miss the opportunity he was being offered of triumphing over the soul of a lackey and adding it to his list of trophies. And so, approaching stealthily and without being observed by anyone, he drove an arrow two yards long into the lackey's left side, splitting his heart in two, which he was able to do in complete safety because Cupid is invisible and is able to come and go at will without having to account to anyone for his actions. Therefore, when the signal to charge was given, our lackey was in a state of transport from contemplating the beauty of the one who had now made herself mistress of his soul. Accordingly, he paid no heed to the sound of the trumpet, quite unlike Don Quixote, who no sooner heard it than he began his charge, riding towards his adversary as fast as Rocinante would permit. When his good squire Sancho saw him begin his charge, he cried out in a loud voice,

"May God be your guide, O flower and cream of knight-errantry! May God give you victory, for you have right on your side!"

Though Tosilos saw Don Quixote bearing down upon him, he did not advance a single step from where he had stationed himself but called out loudly to the field marshal. When the latter came over to see what he wanted, Tosilos said to him,

"Sir, isn't this battle being waged to see whether or not I am to marry this lady?"

"That is correct," was the reply.

"Well," said the lackey, "I have had second thoughts about it and because it would greatly burden my conscience if I went forward with the battle, I hereby wish to state that I consider myself defeated and am willing to marry this lady without further ado."

The field marshal was taken by surprise by what Tosilos said, and though he was one of those who knew the deception underlying the affair, he was unable to think of a single thing to say. Don Quixote drew up in mid-charge when he saw his adversary fail to attack. The duke could not understand why Tosilos had not gone forward with the battle but the field marshal went over to explain what Tosilos had said, which astounded and angered the duke beyond description. While this was taking place, Tosilos rode over to Doña Rodríguez and said in a loud voice,

"I, madam, am willing to marry your daughter but am unwilling to achieve by contests and battles what I can achieve peacefully and without risking death."

The valiant Don Quixote heard this and said,

"Such being the state of affairs, I remain free and absolved of my promise. Let them wed in good faith, and since God Our Lord has given her to him, may Saint Peter bless this marriage."

Meanwhile, the duke had walked down to the castle courtyard, where he approached Tosilos and said,

"Is it true, sir, that you declare yourself defeated and that, driven by your cowardice, you wish to wed this damsel?"

"Yes, master," replied Tosilos.

"And he's doing the right thing," said Sancho Panza at this point, "for if you intend to give something to the rat, give it to the cat and save yourself the trouble."

Tosilos, who was attempting to unstrap his helmet, asked someone to lend a hand, as he was having trouble getting his breath and could no longer stand being confined in that constricting enclosure. It was quickly removed, leaving him with his lackey's face uncovered and exposed. When Doña Rodríguez and her daughter saw him, they raised an outcry, saying,

"It's a trick! It's a trick! They've substituted my master's lackey Tosilos for my real husband! May God and the king punish such deception, not to mention villainy!"

"May your ladyships not be upset," said Don Quixote; "this is neither deception nor villainy, but even if it were, the duke has not been responsible for it but those evil enchanters who dog my footsteps. Those fiends, envious of the glory I achieved in this victory, have transformed the face of your husband into that of this person you say is the duke's lackey. Despite the maliciousness of my enemies you should take my advice and wed him, for he is undoubtedly the very one you desire for your husband."

Listening to this, the duke was about to vent his rage in the form of laughter when he said,

"The things that befall his lord Don Quixote are so extraordinary I might easily believe this lackey of mine is not who I think he is, but let us resort to the following plan: we shall postpone the marriage for a fortnight if your graces agree, and shall lock up this person about whom we have these doubts, during which time he may resume his original appearance. Certainly, the spitefulness the enchanters have for his lord Don Quixote will not last that long, particularly when these frauds and transformations are of so little benefit to them."

"Oh, sir," said Sancho, "these evil-mongers are long since accustomed to transforming everything involving my master into something else. Several days ago, he defeated a knight known as the Knight of the Mirrors, who was physically turned into the bachelor Sansón Carrasco, a native of our village and a close friend of ours. And since they turned my lady Dulcinea of Toboso into a farm girl, I suppose this lackey will have to live and die a lackey for the rest of his life."

To which Rodríguez' daughter responded,

"Whoever this person is who is asking for my hand, I am grateful to him and prefer to be the lawful wife of a lackey than the mistress and plaything of a gentleman – not that the one who has dishonored me *is* a gentleman."

The result of all this talk and activity was that Tosilos was locked up while they waited to see how his transformation would turn out. They all proclaimed Don Quixote the victor but most of the spectators were sad and disappointed to see that the long-awaited combatants had not torn each other to shreds, just as boys are saddened when the person to be hanged does not appear because of a pardon from the prosecutor or the judge. All the people went home, the duke and Don Quixote returned to the castle, Tosilos was locked up, and Doña Rodríguez and her daughter were delighted to see that in one way or another that affair would end in matrimony. And Tosilos himself hoped for nothing less.

Chapter Fifty-Seven

How Don Quixote took leave of the duke and what transpired between him and the clever, uninhibited Altisidora, the duchess' handmaiden

Don Quixote now thought it advisable to abandon his life of idleness in that castle, for he could just imagine the tremendous lack he must be creating by allowing himself to live in idle isolation among the myriad pleasures and delights the lord and lady were bestowing upon him as a knight-errant, and since he suspected that he would be called upon by heaven to give a strict account of that leisure and seclusion, he asked the ducal pair's permission to depart, which they granted, while also displaying genuine signs of regret at seeing him leave. When the duchess gave Sancho Panza the letters from his wife, the squire burst into tears while thinking to himself, 'Who would ever have thought that such great hopes as those aroused in the breast of my wife Teresa Panza by the news of my governorship would be dashed by my now returning to the bedraggled adventures of my master Don Quixote of La Mancha? Still, I'm delighted to see that my Teresa acted in accordance with her true nature by sending the acorns to the duchess, for had she not done so, which I would have regretted, she would have shown herself to be ungrateful. What I find comforting is that no one can call this gift a bribe, for I already had my government when she sent them. Besides, it is only reasonable to show one's appreciation for a gratuity, even one given in jest. The fact is that I came to the government naked, and naked is the way I'm leaving it, so I can say with a clear conscience, which is no small matter: naked I was born and naked I remain, so I'm neither winning nor losing.'

Such were the things Sancho said to himself on the day of departure. That morning Don Quixote made his appearance in the castle courtyard in all his armor, having taken his leave of the duke and duchess the night before. All those in the castle were gathered there and watched him from the galleries, including the duke and duchess, who had come to see him off. Sancho, astride his dapple with its saddlebags, valise, and provisions, was bursting with joy because the duke's majordomo who had impersonated La Trifaldi had, unknown to Don Quixote, given him a small purse containing two hundred gold *escudos* to provide for the necessities of the journey. While they were gazing down at him, as we have said, suddenly from among the duchess' various duennas and handmaidens who had their eyes fixed upon him the uninhibited and prankish Altisidora raised her voice and said to him in the most woeful tones,

"Stay, cruel knight,
Take not thy flight,
Nor spur thy battered jade,
Thy haste restrain,
Draw in the rein
And hear a love-sick maid.
Why dost thou fly?
No snake am I,
That poison those I love.
Gentle I am
As any lamb,
And harmless as a dove.
Thy cruel scorn
Has left forlorn
A nymph whose charms may vie

With theirs who sport
In Cynthia's court,
Though Venus' self were by.
Since, fugitive knight, to no purpose I woo thee,
May Barabbas' fate pursue and undo thee!

Like ravenous kite,
That takes its flight
Soon as't has stole a chicken,
Thou bear'st away
My heart, thy prey,
And leav'st me here to sicken.
Three nightcaps too,
And garters blue,
That did to legs belong
Smooth to the sight,
As marble white,
And, faith, almost as strong.
Two thousand groans,
As many moans,
And sighs enough to fire
Old Priam's town,
And burn it down,
Did it again aspire.
Since, fugitive knight, to no purpose I woo thee,
May Barabbas' fate pursue and undo thee!

May Sancho ne'er
His backside (bare)
Chastise as is his duty;
And thou still want
To disenchant
Dulcinea's injured beauty.
May she, transformed
And still deformed,
Toboso's nymph remain,
In recompense
Of thine offence,
Thy scorn and cold disdain.
When thou dost wield

Thy sword in field,
In combat or in quarrel,
Ill-luck and harms
Attend thine arms,
Instead of fame and laurel.
Since, fugitive knight, to no purpose I woo thee,
May Barabbas' fate pursue and undo thee!

May thy disgrace
Fill ev'ry place,
Thy falsehood ne'er be hid;
But round the world
Be tossed and hurled
From Cádiz to Madrid.
If, brisk and gay,
Thou sit'st to play
At euchre or at chess,
May ne'er spadill [1]
Attend thy will,
Nor luck thy movements bless.
Though thou with care
Thy corns dost pare,
May blood the penknife follow,
May thy gums rage,
And naught assuage
The pain of tooth that's hollow.
Since, fugitive knight, to no purpose I woo thee,
May Barabbas' fate pursue and undo thee!"

While the heartsick Altisidora was bemoaning her fate in the manner just described, Don Quixote stood there with his eyes fixed upon her and, without replying, turned to Sancho and said,

"Sancho my son, I implore you by the souls of all your ancestors to tell me the truth: do you in fact have the three nightcaps and garters mentioned by this lovesick lass?"

To which Sancho replied,

"I do have the three nightcaps but as for the garters, her accusation is totally far-fetched."

The duchess was astonished at Altisidora's brazenness, for she may have considered her bold, carefree, and unrestrained, but not to the point of taking such daring liberties; and because she had not been informed of this prank, her astonishment was all the greater. The duke chose to reinforce

---

1 The highest trump in certain card games (from the Spanish ***espadilla,*** 'little spade')

the clever deception by saying,

"It strikes me as ill-advised, sir knight, considering the friendly reception your grace has been accorded in this castle of mine, that you should dare carry off my maid's three nightcaps, not to mention her garters, this being a sign of ingratitude that does not square with your grace's reputation. Return the garters to her; if not, I shall challenge you to a fight to the death with no fear on my part that scurrilous enchanters will change or transform my face as they did that of my lackey Tosilos, who did battle with your grace."

"God forbid," said Don Quixote, "that I should unsheathe my sword against your lordship's illustrious person, from whom I have received so many kindnesses. The nightcaps I shall return, since Sancho says he has them. The garters, though, are a different matter, for I do not have them and neither does he. If this damsel will only look in those places where she keeps her belongings, she will undoubtedly find them. I, my lord duke, have never been a thief and am determined never to be one for as long as I live if God will hold me in His hand. This damsel, as she herself admits, is talking like a girl in love, which is no fault of mine. I therefore have no reason to ask the forgiveness of anyone, either of her or of your grace, and I would ask you to hold me in higher esteem and once again grant me permission to continue on my way."

"May God grant your grace such great success," said the duchess, "that we shall continually receive favorable reports of your exploits. Go with God, sir knight, for the longer you delay, the more you inflame the bosoms of these damsels whose eyes are fixed upon you. I shall chastise mine in such a way that from this time forth she will not play fast and loose with either her eyes or her words."

"A word is all that I ask of your grace, valiant Don Quixote," said Altisidora at this point. "I wish to beg your forgiveness for claiming that my garters were stolen. I swear upon God and my soul that I am wearing them, having made the same mistake the man did who went looking for his jackass while mounted on its back."

"Didn't I say as much?" replied Sancho; "I'm the last person to try to hide stolen goods! Why, if I had wanted to do such a thing, I had plenty of opportunities as governor."

Don Quixote bowed his head and made obeisance to the duke and duchess and all the bystanders. Then he turned Rocinante and, followed by Sancho astride the dapple, rode forth from the castle, choosing the road that led to Saragossa.

Chapter Fifty-Eight

The description of the adventures that rained so thick and fast upon Don Quixote that they scarcely allowed themselves room to move

When Don Quixote found himself in the open country free and disencumbered of Altisidora's amorous advances, he fancied himself in his element and considered his spirits to be sufficiently revived to return to his pursuit of chivalry, so he turned to Sancho and said,

"Liberty, Sancho, is one of the most precious gifts heaven ever bestowed upon mankind, for it exceeds all the treasures the earth encompasses or the sea conceals. One may and shall risk his life for the sake of liberty, just as he does for the sake of honor. On the other hand, captivity is the greatest evil that can befall a person. I mention this, Sancho, because you clearly witnessed the abundant delights we enjoyed in this castle we are leaving behind, and yet, even while surrounded by those delightful banquets and snow-cooled beverages, I seemed to undergo the severest hunger, for I did not enjoy them as I would have, had they been my own. The obligation to repay benefits and favors received is an obstacle that binds the free spirit. Fortunate is the man to whom God has given a crust of bread for which he is obliged to give thanks to no one but heaven itself!"

"Despite everything your grace has said," replied Sancho, "it is not right for us to fail to show our gratitude for the two hundred gold *escudos* the duke's majordomo gave me in a small purse that I'm carrying next to my heart as a soothing poultice for whatever emergency may arise. We'll not always encounter castles where they'll lavish favors upon us. We may even come across a few inns in which we'll be soundly beaten."

The errant pair, both knight and squire, were engaged in this and similar discussions when, having traveled slightly more than a league, they saw in a verdant meadow a dozen or so men dressed as farmers who were eating their meal while reclining on the cloaks they had spread out beneath them. Nearby, evenly spaced on the ground, were several objects covered by white cloths, like sheets, with some of the objects standing upright and some lying on their sides. Don Quixote reached the spot where the men were having their meal and, after courteously greeting them, asked them what those cloths concealed; to which one of the men replied,

"Sir, beneath these cloths are several sculptures and models that are to be used on a religious float we're constructing in our village. We're keeping them covered so they won't fade, and are carrying them on our shoulders so they won't get broken."

"If you would be so kind," said Don Quixote, "I should like to see them, for images handled with such care must certainly be excellent ones."

"I should say they are," replied one of the men; "their prices will attest to that, for there's not one of them that cost less than fifty ducats. Wait just a moment and your grace will see the truth of this with your own eyes."

And, interrupting his meal, he rose and went over to remove the cover from the first image, which proved to be Saint George on his horse, a serpent twisting at its feet, and the lance piercing its jaw with all the ferocity customarily depicted, and the entire image shone like a blaze of gold. When Don Quixote saw it, he said,

"This was Saint George, defender of maidens and one of the noblest knights-errant the heavenly host ever enlisted. Let me see the next one."

The man uncovered one that appeared to be Saint Martin on horseback dividing his cloak with the beggar. As soon as he saw it, the knight said,

"This gentleman was also a Christian knight who to my way of thinking was more generous than brave, as you can see, Sancho, by the fact that he is sharing his cloak with the beggar, giving him half of it – and this even though it was undoubtedly winter. Otherwise, he would have given him the entire cloak because of his charitable nature."

"It probably wasn't that," said Sancho, "but he was heeding the proverb that says, 'A wise person knows when to give and when to keep.'"

This brought a smile to Don Quixote's face, who then asked them to remove the next cloth, which revealed an image of the patron saint of all Spain on horseback with his blood-stained sword, riding roughshod over Moors and trampling them underfoot. Seeing this representation, Don Quixote said,

"This is a knight indeed and a member of the squadrons of Christ. His name is Saint James the Moorslayer, one of the most valiant saints and knights the world has ever had or heaven has now."

Yet another cloth was removed, revealing what appeared to be Saint Paul as he fell from his horse, including all the attendant details usually shown in portrayals of his conversion, and it was depicted with such vividness that one might have believed Christ was speaking to him and Saint Paul was responding.

"This person," said Don Quixote, "in his time was the greatest foe of our Lord's Church and the greatest defender it will ever have: a knight-errant in life and a saint in death – a tireless laborer in the vineyards of the Lord and missionary to the Gentiles, who had heaven as his school and Jesus Christ Himself as his teacher and master."

Since there were no more images, Don Quixote told the men to cover them and he added the following:

"My brothers, I take it as a good omen to have witnessed what I have seen here, for these saints and knights profess what I profess: the exercise of arms, the difference between them and me being that they were saints who did battle on the divine level, whereas I am a sinner doing battle on the human one. They overcame heaven by force of arms, for 'The kingdom of heaven suffereth violence,' [1] but until now I have no idea what I have overcome through all my efforts. Still, should my Dulcinea of Toboso be freed of those ills from which she suffers and my fortune be improved and my brain set straight, I might just direct my steps along a better path than the one I have been following."

"May God hear that prayer and the Devil turn a deaf ear!" said Sancho at this point.

Astonished as much by Don Quixote's appearance as by his pronouncements but unable to understand half of what he had tried to explain to them, the men finished their meal, hoisted the images onto their shoulders and, taking leave of Don Quixote, continued on their way. Once again Sancho was astonished at Don Quixote's knowledge, as though he were making his acquaintance for the first time, and because it seemed to him that there must be no history on earth his master did not carry about stamped in his memory nor any incident he did not have at his fingertips, he said to him,

"Really, master, if this thing that has just happened to us can be called an adventure, it must be one of the easiest and pleasantest ones to have befallen us in the course of our wanderings. We've come away from it without being beaten or the least bit frightened. We've not laid hands on our swords or graced the ground with our bodies, nor have we undergone hunger. Praised be God, who has finally permitted me to witness such a thing with my own eyes!"

---

1 From the Gospel of Matthew XI, 12.

"Truly spoken, Sancho," said Don Quixote, "but you must remember that not all occasions are the same, nor do they share the same fate. These occurrences that the masses call omens – things which have no basis in any rational cause – are viewed and judged by sensible persons to be mere coincidences. A person of such a superstitious bent may get up one morning and leave his house and, should he meet a friar of the Order of the Blessed Saint Francis, will hurry back home as if he had encountered some griffin. Or if a superstitious person should spill salt while eating, his heart will spill over with remorse, as though nature were obliged to warn him of future misfortunes by things of so little import as that. A wise person and a Christian will not go about scrutinizing every jot and tittle that heaven ordains. When Scipio reached Africa, he tripped as he set foot on land, which his soldiers interpreted as an evil omen. He, however, embraced the earth and exclaimed, 'You can't escape from me, Africa; I've got you securely in these arms!' And so, Sancho, my encounter with these images has been for me a most felicitous circumstance."

"I'm of the same opinion," said Sancho, "but I wish your grace would explain to me why Spaniards, when entering battle, always invoke Saint James the Moorslayer by shouting, 'Saint James, and close Spain!' Is Spain somehow open that it should need closing? If not, what sort of war cry is this?" [2]

"Oh, how terribly naive you are," responded Don Quixote. "Look, Sancho, God has given Spain this mighty Knight of the Red Cross as her own patron saint and protector, particularly in the violent conflicts between Spaniards and Moors, for which reason they invoke and call upon him as their defender in all the battles they undertake, for with their own eyes they have often seen him present overthrowing, trampling, destroying, and slaughtering the armies of Hagar. I could cite as proof of this a number of examples recorded in the genuine histories of Spain."

Changing the subject, Sancho said to Don Quixote,

"I am astounded, master, at the lack of restraint on the part of the duchess' maid Altisidora. She must've been seriously wounded and transfixed by the one called Cupid, who they say is a blind young lad, but even if he's blear-eyed or, more accurately, can't see at all, once he takes aim at someone's heart, however tiny it is, he hits the bulls-eye and pierces it right through the center with his arrows. I've also heard it said that Cupid's arrows become blunted and dulled by a maiden's modesty and decorum but in the case of Altisidora they seem to have become sharp instead of dull."

"Remember, Sancho," said Don Quixote, "that Cupid pays no heed to people's intentions, observes no bounds in his discourse, and resembles Death in that they both assault the king's lofty castle and the shepherd's humble hut. When he takes total possession of a person's soul, his first act is to rid it of fear and modesty, and it was the absence of these that led Altisidora to reveal her passion, thus creating confusion in my breast rather than pity."

"What shameless cruelty on the part of your grace!" cried Sancho, "and what unheard-of ingratitude! Speaking for myself, I can state that the slightest suggestion of love on her part would have made me surrender and become her vassal. Damn! what a heart of marble you've got, what a breast of bronze, what a soul of cement! What's more, I can't imagine what this damsel saw in your

---

2 The correct form is: 'Saint James, and close, Spain!' ['close' in this battle-cry meaning 'charge!']

grace to make her surrender and humble herself like that. What charms or ardor, what elegance or looks, what single thing among these by itself or in combination with all the others caused her to fall in love? To speak quite frankly, I've often paused to peruse your grace from the tip of your toe to the topmost hair of your head and I've seen more things that would inspire fright than love. And since I've heard it said that beauty is the first and foremost quality that causes one to fall in love, I don't know what this poor girl fell in love with, since your grace is totally devoid of all these."

"Be advised, Sancho," said Don Quixote, "that there are two types of beauty: one of the soul, the other of the flesh; that of the soul displays and manifests itself in one's intelligence, wholesomeness, decorum, generosity, and good breeding, qualities that may all be found in an unattractive man. Whenever one's sights are directed towards beauty of this type rather than that of the flesh, love is apt to spring forth spontaneously and to good advantage. I can clearly see, Sancho, that I am not handsome but I also know I am not misshapen, and it is enough for a man not to be deformed to be loved, so long as he possesses the spiritual endowments I have mentioned."

They were engaged in the present conversation as they entered a forest located a short distance off the road. Suddenly, without expecting anything of the sort, Don Quixote found himself ensnared in some nets of green thread that stretched from one group of trees to another. Having no idea what it could be, he said to his squire,

"I do believe, Sancho, that the affair involving these nets must be one of the most novel adventures imaginable. I'll be hanged if the enchanters who persecute me are not seeking to ensnare me in them in order to interrupt our journey as revenge for the restraint I demonstrated towards Altisidora! Well, I hereby advise them that if, instead of green threads, these nets were made of the hardest diamonds or were stronger than the net the jealous god of blacksmiths employed in ensnaring Venus and Mars, I would break them as easily as if they were made of bulrushes or cotton thread."

But just as he was about to proceed to rip the whole contraption apart, he saw standing before him two beautiful shepherdesses who had suddenly appeared from among some trees; at least, they were dressed in shepherdess attire, except that their skirts and jackets were made of fine brocade, that is, their skirts consisted of beautiful petticoats of gold-embroidered silk. They wore their hair loose over their shoulders, which due to its color could have rivaled the rays of the sun itself, and their heads were crowned with garlands interwoven with green laurel and red amaranth. The girls were apparently no younger than fifteen nor older than eighteen. Such a sight surprised Sancho, astonished Don Quixote, made the sun halt in its course to observe them, and suspended all four persons in wondrous silence. At length, one of the young shepherdesses addressed Don Quixote, saying,

"Sir knight, I beg your grace not to proceed with your destruction of these nets, for they have been hung here, not for your harm, but for our pastime, and since I realize you are bound to ask why they were placed here and who we are, I shall provide a brief explanation.

"In a village some two leagues from here reside various prominent nobles, hidalgos, and gentlemen of means, and it was agreed that we and several of our friends and relatives would bring our spouses, children, neighbors, friends, and relatives to amuse ourselves in this spot, which is one of the most pleasant in all these parts. Among ourselves we have formed a new pastoral Arcadia in which the young women dress as shepherdesses and the young men as shepherds. We have studied two eclogues, one by the famous poet Garcilaso and the other by the most excellent Camões in his own Portuguese tongue, neither of which we have as yet performed. We came here yesterday for the first time and erected some field-tents, which is what I think they are called, among these bowers bordering the banks of a bountiful stream that provides moisture for all these meadows. Last night, we strung the nets among these trees to ensnare the unsuspecting birds, which, when startled by our cries, fly into them. If your grace will consent to be our guest, you shall be lavishly and graciously regaled, for while one is here, there is no room for cares or melancholy."

She then remained silent and said nothing further, at which point Don Quixote responded,

"Undoubtedly, most beautiful lady, Actaeon could have been no more surprised or astonished when he unexpectedly spied Diana bathing in the stream than I was when I beheld your grace's beauty. I commend these proposed entertainments and am grateful for the invitation, and if I may be of service to your ladyship, you may rest assured that whatever you command of me shall be obeyed, for my profession demands that I extend my gratitude and benevolence to all classes of society, particularly to that distinguished one represented by your grace's group. Instead of covering this small area, if these nets covered the entire surface of the earth, I should seek out new lands through which to pass so as not to break them. And to afford you some reason for believing this exaggeration of mine, be advised that it is none other than Don Quixote of La Mancha who makes this vow, if, indeed, that name has reached your grace's ears."

"Oh, my dearest friend," said the second shepherdess to the first, "what great good fortune has befallen us! Do you see this gentleman we have in our midst? Well, I would have you know that he is the most valiant, the most enamored, and the most courteous knight in the entire world, unless he is not telling the truth or we have been misled by a published history of his exploits that I have read. I dare say this good man with him is a certain Sancho Panza, his squire, whose witty remarks cannot be equaled by anyone else's."

"That is the truth," said Sancho, "for I am that witty fellow and that same squire your ladyship has mentioned, and this gentleman is my master, the same Don Quixote of La Mancha set forth in that history."

"Oh," said the other girl, "let us ask him to stay, my dear, for our parents and brothers and sisters will be immensely pleased by it. I too have heard all these things about the knight's valor and the squire's wit that you mention. In addition, they say the knight is the most steadfast and faithful lover known, and his ladylove is a certain Dulcinea of Toboso, who has been proclaimed the greatest beauty in of all Spain."

"And rightfully so," replied Don Quixote, "unless your ladyships' matchless beauty should place the matter in doubt. But you must not waste your efforts trying to entice me to stay, for the rigorous obligation of my profession will not permit me to linger in any place whatsoever."

At that moment the four of them were joined by the shepherdesses' brother, whose attire exhibited the same splendor and richness as theirs. They informed him that the persons with them were the valiant Don Quixote of La Mancha and his squire Sancho Panza, with whom he was already acquainted from having read their history. The elegant shepherd placed himself at their disposal and invited them to accompany him to their tents. Don Quixote, out of a sense of obligation, accepted his invitation. Just then, the beaters began to rustle the bushes, whereupon a variety of small birds began to fill the nets, for, having been fooled by their color, the birds fell victim to the very danger from which they were fleeing. More than thirty persons who had gathered in that spot, all extravagantly attired as shepherds and shepherdesses, were immediately informed of the identities of Don Quixote and his squire, which afforded them no little satisfaction because they had made his acquaintance through his history. They eventually arrived at the tents where the spotless tables were provided with rich and abundant food. Homage was paid to Don Quixote by having him occupy the seat of honor, and the others sat there observing him while marveling at his appearance. Finally, after the tables had been cleared, Don Quixote very tranquilly took the floor and said,

"Whereas some contend that among the greatest sins a man can commit is that of pride, I maintain it is that of ingratitude, basing my belief upon the oft-heard saying that 'Hell is full of ingrates.' I have striven insofar as possible to flee from this sin from the first moment I was capable of reason, so if I am unable to repay those persons who have befriended me, at least I offer as a substitute my desire to do so, and when that is not sufficient, I announce it publicly, for anyone who will speak openly of the benefits he has received is a person who would repay them if it were within his means. By and large, those who receive are inferior to those who give, for which reason God is superior to all others, He being the most bountiful of them all. Though the gifts of man cannot compare with those of God or even approach them, gratitude is capable of making up for this lack and shortcoming. I am grateful, therefore, for the kindnesses extended to me here but, being unable to reciprocate in kind, I shall limit myself to the meager resources at my disposal by offering what I can from my limited possessions. And so I hereby announce that for the next two days I shall plant myself in the middle of the king's highway that leads to Saragossa, where I shall proclaim that these two would-be shepherdesses are the most beautiful and gracious damsels on earth, with the single exception of the peerless Dulcinea of Toboso, sole mistress of my thoughts, begging the pardon of everyone present."

When Sancho, who had been hanging upon his every word, heard this, he cried out,

"Can there possibly be anyone on earth who would dare say or affirm that my master is crazy? Sir shepherds, what say your graces? Is there any village priest, however wise and learned, capable of saying what my master has just said? Or is there any knight-errant, however great his reputation for bravery, who would volunteer to do what my master has just offered to do?"

Don Quixote, his face glowing with anger, turned to Sancho and said,

"O Sancho, can there possibly be anyone on the entire globe who would not label you a fool to the core with traces of rascality and maliciousness thrown in? Who asked you to butt into my affairs to determine whether I am wise or foolish? Shut your mouth and don't say another word. Just saddle Rocinante if he is unsaddled, and let us put into action what I have proposed. Inasmuch as I have right on my side, everyone here may consider as already vanquished all those who might attempt to oppose me."

At this point, he bruskly rose from his seat and showed signs of indignation, leaving all those present astounded and wondering whether they should consider him mad or sane. But, finally, after attempting to persuade him not to carry out such an endeavor, they reminded him that his grateful nature was well-known and there was no need of anything further to demonstrate his valiant spirit, since those deeds of his that were related in his history would suffice. Notwithstanding all this, Don Quixote went forward with his plan by mounting Rocinante, attaching his buckler, taking up his lance, and stationing himself in the middle of the highway, which was not far from that verdant meadow. Behind him followed Sancho astride his dapple and those of the pastoral flock, who were curious to see where his arrogant and unheard-of proposal might lead. Once situated in the middle of the road, as already mentioned, Don Quixote pierced the air with the following speech:

"You travelers and wayfarers, knights and squires, and persons walking or riding, who pass along this highway or shall do so in the next two days, be advised that here stands Don Quixote of La Mancha to assert and maintain that the beauty and refinement found among the nymphs residing in these meadows and glens is greater than that possessed by any other woman on earth, save the mistress of my soul, Dulcinea of Toboso. Therefore, let anyone approach who may hold a different opinion, for here I stand ready and waiting for him."

Twice he issued this challenge and twice it went unheeded by any venturer knight, but fate, which was beginning to improve the course of his affairs, ordained that shortly afterwards, what should appear on the highway but a large number of men on horseback, many with lances in their hands, traveling in tight formation and with great haste. The moment Don Quixote's companions saw them, they turned and ran from the road, realizing that if they remained there, some great calamity might befall them all. Only Don Quixote stood his ground with intrepid spirit, while Sancho took refuge behind Rocinante's haunches. The band of lancers arrived and one of those riding in the vanguard began to shout at Don Quixote,

"Get out of the way, you idiot, or these bulls will trample you to death!"

"You curs," shouted Don Quixote, "the bulls do not exist that can frighten me – not even the fiercest ones bred on the banks of the Jarama! So without further reflection, confess, you ruffians, that what I have declared here is the truth; otherwise, you shall have me to reckon with."

The herdsman had no chance to respond nor Don Quixote to get out of the way even if he had wanted to, for the herd of fierce bulls, led by the tame ones, and the host of herdsmen and others taking them to a town where a bullfight was to be held the next day trampled underfoot Don Quixote, Sancho, Rocinante, and the dapple, knocking them all down and sending them sprawling on the ground. Sancho was left battered, Don Quixote frightened, the dapple bruised, and Rocinante not exactly unscathed, but finally they all struggled to their feet and Don Quixote, now stumbling, now falling, ran after the herd as fast as he could, calling out at the top of his lungs,

"Stay where you are and do battle, you scurrilous ruffians. It is but a single knight who challenges you and not one of those who believe in turning the other cheek when they have been wronged!"

This failed to stop the herdsmen from hurrying away, for they took no more notice of his threats than of the clouds of yesteryear. Don Quixote, feeling the frustration of his weariness, anger, and more annoyed than avenged, sat down on the highway where he waited for Sancho, Rocinante, and the dapple to catch up with him. Once they arrived, master and squire remounted and, without returning to take their leave of the feigned or make-believe Arcadia, continued on their way considerably more ashamed than pleased.

Chapter Fifty-Nine

The account of the extraordinary incident that befell Don Quixote, which may certainly qualify as an adventure

Don Quixote and Sancho came to a refreshing grove of trees, in the midst of which they found a clear, limpid stream, which they turned to their advantage by ridding themselves of the dust and weariness they had acquired as a result of the bulls' unsociable behavior. After removing the halter and bridle from the dapple and Rocinante to allow them to roam unrestrained along its banks, the belabored pair, both master and servant, seated themselves on the grass while Sancho dug into the provisions of his saddlebags, taking from them what he liked to call his bread helpers. Availing themselves of the stream, Sancho rinsed his mouth and Don Quixote washed his face, by means of which they revived their flagging spirits. Don Quixote ate nothing out of sheer remorse, whereas Sancho dared not touch the food in front of him out of sheer good breeding, waiting for his master to take the first bite. But when he saw that Don Quixote was forgetting even to raise the bread to his mouth, he did not say a word and, breaking every rule of etiquette, began to fill his stomach with the bread and cheese that were there for the taking.

"Eat up, Sancho my friend," said Don Quixote, "and keep yourself alive, which is more important in your case than in mine. Let me die at the hands of my thoughts and my unrelenting misfortunes, for I, Sancho, was born to live dying and you to die eating. To convince you of the truth of what I say, consider the fact that I have had histories written about me, am renowned for my arms, admired for my gentlemanly behavior, respected by nobles, and courted by damsels, but just when I expected to be crowned in triumph with boughs and laurels deservedly earned by my valiant deeds, this morning I saw myself kicked, trampled, and trod upon by the hooves of lowly, filthy beasts. The thought of this so numbs my teeth, dulls my appetite, paralyzes my hands, and robs me of all desire to eat that I intend to die of starvation, the cruellest death of all."

"In that case," said Sancho, continuing his rapid chewing, "your grace probably doesn't subscribe to the proverb that says, 'Let Marta die but do so with a full stomach.' I, at any rate, don't intend to take my own life but will do what the cobbler does who stretches out the leather with his teeth till he gets it to reach as far as he wants; I'll stretch out my life by eating until it runs the course heaven has allotted it. I wish I could make your grace understand that there is no greater madness than to consider dying from despair as you are doing. You should follow my advice and eat something and then take a short nap on this green grassy canopy, after which you'll awaken and find yourself a bit more invigorated."

Don Quixote did as advised, inasmuch as Sancho's advice struck him as that of a philosopher rather than a fool.

"Dear Sancho," said the knight, "if you will agree to do what I am now going to propose, my mind will be greatly relieved and my cares lightened. While I sleep, heeding your advice, I want you to go off a short distance, expose your flesh to the air, and using Rocinante's reins, give yourself three or four hundred lashes towards the more than three thousand you are to undergo for the disenchantment of Dulcinea. It is a downright shame for that poor soul to remain enchanted because of your thoughtlessness and negligence."

"There are two sides to that question," said Sancho, "but for now let's both get some sleep and later, who knows what will happen? Your grace should understand that for a man to flog himself in cold blood is an arduous thing to do, especially when the lashes fall upon a body that is ill-nourished and poorly fed. My lady Dulcinea needs to be patient, for when she least expects it, she will see me turned into a sieve from the beatings – and 'Where there is life, there is hope.' I mean that I still possess life as well as the desire to carry out what I've promised to do."

Don Quixote thanked him and then ate a bite of food, whereas Sancho ate a mouthful. Following this, they both lay down to sleep, giving free rein to the two inseparable companions and mutual friends, Rocinante and the dapple, to graze at their leisure on the abundant grass growing in that meadow. They awoke rather late in the day, at which time they remounted and resumed their journey in an effort to reach an inn they could see in the distance. I say it was an inn because that is what Don Quixote called it, contrary to his usual habit of calling every inn a castle.

When they arrived, they asked the innkeeper if he had a room and were assured he had one with all the comforts and luxuries a person might hope to find in Saragossa. They dismounted and Sancho carried his provisions to a room to which the innkeeper had given him the key. Afterwards he took the animals to the stable, fed them, and then returned to see what tasks he might be assigned by Don Quixote, whom he found seated on a bench. He gave special thanks to heaven that his master had not fancied the inn a castle. Once the dinner hour arrived, they returned to their room and Sancho asked the innkeeper what he had to offer them. The latter informed them that their stomachs could be their guides; that Sancho might order anything he desired because his inn was stocked with birds of the air, fowl of the earth, and fish of the sea.

"There's no need of all that," said Sancho; "if you'll just roast us a couple of chickens, we'll be satisfied, because my master has a delicate stomach and eats sparingly and I don't eat an awful lot either, since I'm not a glutton."

The innkeeper told him he had no chickens because the hawks had carried them off.

"Well, sir innkeeper," said Sancho, "you may roast us a nice, tender pullet."

"A pullet?" replied the innkeeper; "my word, the fact is that I sent more than fifty to town yesterday to be sold, but except for pullets, you may order whatever you like."

"In that case," said Sancho, "there'll surely be veal or kid."

"There's none in the house just now," replied the host, "since it has all been eaten, but next week there'll be more than enough."

"A lot of good that'll do us," said Sancho. "I'll bet all these shortages will be more than made up for by an overabundance of bacon and eggs."

"Mercy," replied the innkeeper, "my guest certainly has a nerve! I've already told him I don't have any chickens or pullets and yet he expects me to have eggs. I wish he would choose some other delicacy and stop asking for chicken."

"Let's settle this, confound it!" said Sancho; "will you kindly tell me once and for all what you have and stop all this useless talk!"

"What I really and truly have," said the innkeeper, "is two cows' feet that could be calves' feet they're so tender, or two calves' feet that could be cows' feet they're so big. They've been cooked with peas, onions, and bacon and at this very moment are crying out to be eaten."

"I brand them as mine right here," said Sancho, "and nobody had better touch them, because I'll pay more for them than anyone else. I couldn't hope for a tastier treat for myself and I don't care if they are calves' feet, so long as they're as big as cow's feet."

"Nobody will touch them," said the innkeeper, "for my other guests are persons of quality, who have brought their own cooks, butlers, and food."

"Speaking of persons of quality, " said Sancho, "there is none more so than my master, and yet the profession he follows will not allow for provisions or foodstuffs. We simply stretch out in the middle of a meadow and eat our fill of acorns and medlars."

Such was the conversation Sancho carried on with the innkeeper, which he chose not to prolong by answering questions, even though he had just been asked what profession or trade his master plied. Once the supper hour arrived, Don Quixote retired to his room, where the host brought the stew, such as it was, and the knight sat down to eat it very single-mindedly. But it seems that in the room adjoining Don Quixote's, which was separated from it by a thin partition, he heard someone say,

"As a favor to me, Sir Don Jerónimo, while supper is being prepared, let us read another chapter of the second part of *Don Quixote of La Mancha.* [1]

No sooner did Don Quixote hear his name mentioned than he stood up to listen with all his might to what they were saying about him, and he heard the just-referred-to Don Jerónimo say,

"Sir Don Juan, why do you want us to read this nonsense, when anyone who has read the first part of *Don Quixote of La Mancha* could not possibly derive any pleasure from reading the second?"

"Nevertheless," said Don Juan, "we would do well to read it, for no book is so bad it does not contain something good. The thing I find most unsatisfying, though, is that it depicts Don Quixote as no longer being enamored of Dulcinea of Toboso."

When Don Quixote heard this, he was filled with rage and despair and, raising his voice, cried out,

"Whoever says that Don Quixote of La Mancha has forgotten or is capable of forgetting Dulcinea of Toboso shall be made to understand by me in a fair fight that he has strayed very far from the truth, for the peerless Dulcinea of Toboso can never be forgotten, nor can such forgetfulness ever find lodging in Don Quixote's breast. His motto is faithfulness and his mission is to preserve it through moderation and without violence of any kind."

"Who is that speaking to us?" they asked from the next room.

"Who else would it be," said Sancho, "except Don Quixote of La Mancha himself, who will make

1 The reference is to the apocryphal second part which appeared in Tarragona in 1614, under the title *Segundo tomo del ingenioso hidalgo don Quijote de la Mancha, que contiene su tercera salida* (i.e., Second Volume of the Ingenious Hidalgo Don Quixote of La Mancha, Which Contains His Third Sally) The author of this second part purports to be one Alonso Fernández de Avellaneda but his identity has never been determined. What is certain, though, is that he treated Cervantes most cruelly in the prologue to his work.

good on everything he has said or ever will say, for he'll put his money where his mouth is."

Scarcely had Sancho said this when through the door of their room came two gentlemen, or so they appeared, one of whom flung his arms round Don Quixote's neck and said,

"Your grace's appearance leaves no doubt as to your name, and your name can only confirm your appearance. Your grace is without a doubt the real Don Quixote of La Mancha, beacon and north-star of knight-errantry, despite the one who has tried to usurp your name and eclipse your deeds, as claimed by the author of this book I have here."

And he handed him a book his companion had been carrying. Don Quixote took it and, without saying a word, began to leaf through its pages. After a few moments, he returned the book to him and said,

"In the little I have perused, I have found three things in this author that are reprehensible: the first being several statements I read in the prologue; the second being the fact that the language is Aragonese, for at times he omits the definite article. But what proves he is ignorant is the fact that he errs and strays from the truth in the most important aspect of the history: he says my squire Sancho Panza's wife is named Mari Gutiérrez, whereas she is named no such thing but Teresa Panza. Now whoever would err on such a critical point might possibly err on all other aspects of the work."

To which Sancho replied,

"A fine thing for a historian! He must certainly be well acquainted with our affairs if he refers to my wife Teresa Panza as Mari Gutiérrez! Master, I wish your grace would look at the book again and see if I am in it or if my name has been changed."

"From what I have heard," said Don Jerónimo, "you are undoubtedly Sancho Panza, squire to his lord Don Quixote."

"I am," replied Sancho, "and am proud of it."

"Well, you may take my word for it," said the gentleman, "this new author has not treated you with the honesty you deserve. He portrays you as a glutton, a simpleton, and a person devoid of humor – quite different from the Sancho described in the first part of your master's history."

"May God forgive him," said Sancho; "he should leave me in my corner, forget me, and give the castanets to the person who can play them, for 'St. Peter is perfectly content in Rome.'"

The two gentlemen invited Don Quixote to their room to dine with them, being well aware that there was nothing in the inn suitable for a person of his caliber. Don Quixote, who was always gracious, accepted their offer and dined with them while Sancho remained behind undisputed master of the stew. The squire seated himself at the head of the table and was joined by the innkeeper who, no less than Sancho, was fond of his cows' and calves' feet. In the course of the meal Don Jerónimo asked Don Quixote what news he had received of the lady Dulcinea of Toboso: had she wed, borne a child, or become pregnant, or, if she was still a maiden, having preserved her innocence and chastity, was she still in the amorous thoughts of her lord Don Quixote? To which the knight responded,

"Dulcinea is still a maiden, my intentions are more resolute than ever, our relationship is just as unproductive, and her beauty has been transformed into that of a lowly farm girl."

He then proceeded to describe every detail of the lady Dulcinea's enchantment, including what had befallen him in the Cave of Montesinos, together with the conditions the sage Merlin had laid down for her disenchantment, namely, the scourging Sancho was to give himself. The two gentlemen were overjoyed when they heard Don Quixote describe the strange incidents in his history but they were equally astonished at his outlandish antics and his elegant manner of describing them. At one moment they considered him sensible but at the next he would slip back into absurdity, because of which they were unable to decide where to place him on the scale between wisdom and folly. Sancho finished his meal and, leaving the innkeeper at the table three sheets to the wind, returned to the room where he had left his master. Going inside, he said,

"I'll be darned, gentlemen, if the author of that book is trying very hard to make me like him. He may call me a glutton, as your graces have said, but I would hope he doesn't also call me a drunkard."

"He does," replied Don Jerónimo, "but I don't recall his exact words. I do know, however, that they were offensive and untrue as well, based upon what I have observed in the countenance of the noble Sancho here in our presence"

"Your grace may rest assured," said the squire, "that the Sancho and Don Quixote in that history are different persons from the ones who figure in the history composed by Cide Hamete Benengeli in which we are ourselves: my master brave, wise, and in love, and me a simpleton and a wit, not a glutton or a drunkard."

"That is how I see it," said Don Juan, "and if it were possible, they should pass a law prohibiting anyone from presuming to treat of the affairs of the great Don Quixote, unless it is Cide Hamete, his first author – just as Alexander forbade anyone from presuming to paint his portrait except Apelles."

"Let anyone paint me who will," said Don Quixote, "but let him do so fairly, for one is apt to lose patience when insults are heaped upon him."

"No one can insult his lord Don Quixote and expect to get away with it," replied Don Juan, "unless the knight parries the insult with the patience of his buckler, which I am led to believe is a large, strong one."

A considerable portion of the night was spent discussing these and other topics, and though Don Juan was eager for Don Quixote to read more of the book to see what other glosses it contained, the latter could not be prevailed upon, saying he considered it read and was pronouncing it complete folly. Likewise, he did not want its author to be cheered by the thought that he had read it should it possibly come to his attention that Don Quixote had held it in his hands, for if one's thoughts should flee from things that are dull and crude, one's eyes should certainly do so. When they asked him where he intended to go in his travels, he said to Saragossa to participate in the jousts held in that city each year. Don Juan informed him that this new history described how Don Quixote, or whoever the person was, had already gone there to tilt at the ring, an episode that was devoid of originality, weak on chivalric mottoes, quite short on liveries, but rich in foolishness."

"Then for that very reason," said Don Quixote, "I shall not set foot in Saragossa, thereby making manifest to the world the untruthfulness of that new historian and showing people I am not the Don Quixote he speaks of."

"And your grace will be doing the right thing," said Don Jerónimo, "for there are other jousts in Barcelona in which his lord Don Quixote may display his valor."

"That is where I intend to go," replied Don Quixote, "but since it is now bedtime, I beg your permission to retire. However, your graces may count me among your greatest friends and servants."

"And me too," added Sancho; "perhaps I can serve in some capacity."

With this, they took leave of one another, and Don Quixote and Sancho retired to their room, leaving Don Juan and Don Jerónimo to marvel at the marriage the knight had effected between his good sense and his folly, for they absolutely believed that here were the true Don Quixote and Sancho – not the ones described by that Aragonese author.

Don Quixote rose early the next morning and, tapping on the partition of the adjoining room, bade farewell to his hosts. Sancho paid the innkeeper handsomely but advised him in the future to boast less of his inn's accommodations or to provide better ones.

Chapter Sixty

The things that befell Don Quixote on his way to Barcelona

The morning had been cool and the afternoon on which Don Quixote rode forth from the inn gave every indication of being the same. The knight had first informed himself of the most direct route to Barcelona without passing through Saragossa, such was his desire to give the lie to the new historian who was said to have vilified him so mercilessly. As it turned out, nothing of consequence occurred during the next six days but on the seventh, while riding through a forest, he was overtaken by night in a grove of oak or cork trees, for on this point Cide Hamete does not observe his customary precision.

Master and servant dismounted from their beasts and made themselves comfortable at the base of some trees. Sancho, who had actually eaten lunch that day, let himself plunge headlong into the arms of Morpheus but Don Quixote, who was kept awake by his thoughts much more than by his hunger, was unable to close his eyes, as his thoughts kept darting here and there in a thousand different directions. At one moment, he fancied himself in the Cave of Montesinos; at another, he observed Dulcinea – now transformed into a country wench – skip and vault onto her donkey; and at still another, the words of the sage Merlin echoed in his ears, setting forth the terms to be fulfilled and the conditions to be met for Dulcinea's disenchantment. He despaired at the sight of his squire Sancho Panza's lack of backbone and compassion, who, to his knowledge, had given himself a mere five lashes, a disproportionately small number considering the huge number remaining. This left him so disgruntled and angry that he made the following pledge to himself: 'If Alexander the Great could cut the Gordian knot and say that cutting it had the same effect as untying it, and this did not keep him from becoming ruler of all Asia, the very same thing might occur with the disenchanting of Dulcinea if I were to flog Sancho, whether he liked it or not. For if the requirements of this remedy call for Sancho to receive three thousand-plus lashes, what difference will it make whether they are administered by him or by someone else? The essential thing is for him to receive them, regardless of their source.'

With this thought in mind he approached Sancho, having first removed Rocinante's reins, which he gripped in such a way that they served him as a whip, and he began to untie the laces that held up Sancho's breeches, though tradition has it that he had only one set in front. But no sooner did he arrive than Sancho became wide awake and cried out,

"What is this? Who has got his hands on me and is untying my breeches?"

"It is I," said Don Quixote. "I have come to make up for your shortcomings so I may ease my troubled conscience. I am here to flog you, Sancho, and to discharge a portion of the debt to which you are obligated. Dulcinea languishes while you go about unconcerned and I die from longing. Therefore, unfasten your breeches voluntarily because I intend to give you at least two thousand lashes here in this wilderness."

"I beg to differ," said Sancho. "Your grace had better stay right where you are, for if you don't, I swear to God Almighty that even the deaf are going to hear us. The lashes I promised to give myself must be voluntary, not forced, and right now I don't feel like flogging myself. It should be sufficient that I have given your grace my word to lash and flog myself when the mood strikes me."

"We are not leaving it to your discretion," said Don Quixote, "for you are hardhearted and, for a man from the country, tender-skinned."

At this point, he began struggling to untie Sancho's breeches. When Sancho saw this, he sprang to his feet, lunged at his master and grabbed him in an armhold while putting one leg behind the knight's and throwing him down onto his back. Positioning his right knee against Don Quixote's chest, he pinned both arms with his hands so the knight was unable to twist about or even to breathe.

"You traitor!" cried Don Quixote, "have you no respect for your master and natural lord? How dare you do this to the person who feeds you!"

"I don't make or break kings," said Sancho; "I just look out for myself, since I'm my own master. You must promise me to get hold of yourself and stop trying to flog me. If you promise, I'll let you go free and unrestrained; if not,

'Here thou diest, traitor,
Foe of Doña Sancha.'" [1]

Don Quixote promised to do so, swearing upon the life of the object of his affections not to touch a thread on his clothing but to leave it completely up to Sancho to flog himself whenever he pleased. Sancho stood up and walked some distance away, but in going over to another tree, he felt something touch his head. Raising his hands, he could feel a person's feet with shoes and stockings on them. Trembling with fear, he moved to another tree, where the same thing occurred. Sancho screamed for help and Don Quixote came running to see what was terrifying him so. Sancho exclaimed that those trees were full of people's legs and feet. Don Quixote felt of them and immediately sized up the situation.

"You have nothing to fear," he told Sancho, "for these feet and legs which we can feel but not see undoubtedly belong to various outlaws and bandits who have been hanged on these trees. In these

1 Lines from an old Spanish ballad.

parts the law routinely hangs them after apprehending them, and twenty or thirty at a time, which leads me to believe we must be near Barcelona."

And such was the case, exactly as he imagined it, for at the crack of dawn they looked up at the boughs and indeed saw there the bodies of bandits, but by this time it had begun to grow light and if the corpses had frightened them, they were no less distressed by the more than forty live bandits who had unexpectedly surrounded them and ordered them in Catalan to stand still and not move until their captain arrived. Don Quixote found himself unmounted, his horse unbridled, his lance leaning against a tree, and lastly, himself completely defenseless. Accordingly, he thought it best to fold his hands, bow his head, and save himself for a better time and occasion. The bandits came over to frisk the dapple lest they overlook anything in the saddlebags or valise. Sancho considered himself lucky in that the *escudos* from the duke and those he had brought from home were in a money belt he had strapped round his stomach, but despite all this, those good souls would have searched and ferreted out anything that might have been hidden even between his hide and flesh if their captain had not arrived at that moment.

This individual, who appeared to be thirty-four at the oldest, was stern looking, dark complected, of a robust build, and of more than medium height. He had ridden up on a powerful steed and wore a coat of chain mail with four pistols at his sides, which in those parts are called flintlocks. He noticed that his squires (this being the name of those who practice that trade) were in the process of stripping Sancho's possessions and he ordered them to stop their search, which they did at once, thus allowing the stomach pouch to escape. He was amazed to see the lance leaning against the tree, the buckler on the ground, and Don Quixote in his armor lost in thought and exhibiting the saddest and most melancholy face sadness itself could ever devise. Approaching him, he said,

"Don't be so sad, my good man, you haven't fallen into the hands of some cruel Osiris[2] but into those of Roque Guinart,[3] which are more merciful than cruel."

"My remorse," replied Don Quixote, "arises not from my having fallen into your hands, O valiant Roque, whose fame knows no bounds on earth, but from having been so careless as to allow myself to be caught off my horse, since I am obliged by the laws of chivalry to remain ever alert, serving at all times as my own sentinel. I can assure you, O great Roque, that had they found me astride my horse armed with my lance and buckler, they would have found it no easy matter to overpower me, for I am Don Quixote of La Mancha, that same one whose achievements have resonated throughout the world."

It was then that Roque Guinart understood that Don Quixote's illness bordered more on madness than on valor, and though he had heard mention of him on several occasions, he had never considered his deeds genuine, nor could anyone have convinced him that any such humor was to be found in the breast of man. He was quite delighted, therefore, to have come across him so he might

---

2 Guinart mistakenly alludes to Osiris instead of Busiris, an early king of Egypt who, according to Greek legend, practiced human sacrifice.

3 Perot Roca Guinarda was a famous Catalonian outlaw much admired by a great many Spaniards.

consider at close range what he had heard about him from afar; so he said to him,

"Valiant knight, your grace need not be downcast or regard as ill-fated this situation in which you find yourself. It may turn out that by these setbacks your wayward fortune will be directed along a straighter course, for heaven by strange and roundabout ways undreamt of by man oftentimes raises up the fallen and enriches the poor."

Don Quixote was about to thank him when a commotion was heard behind them as of a troop of horses, though it proved to be but a single horse driven at breakneck speed by a youth who looked to be about twenty years of age. He was clad in a green damask jacket and breeches trimmed with gold lace, a hat worn aslant in the Walloon style, tight-fitting polished boots, spurs, a gold dagger and sword, with a small gun in his hand and a pair of pistols at his sides. Roque turned his head in the direction of the sound and saw this handsome figure approaching him.

"I have come in search of you, O valiant Roque," said the figure, "in hopes of finding in you, if not a solution, at least alleviation for my affliction. And lest you be kept in suspense, since we have never met, I shall explain who I am. I am Claudia Jerónima, daughter of Simón Forte, your very good friend and sworn enemy of Clauquel Torrellas, who is *your* enemy as well, since he belongs to your rival band. You are aware that this Torrellas has a son called Vicente Torrellas – at least, that is what he called himself a scant two hours ago – but to keep the story of my misfortune brief, I shall describe in just a few words the anguish this Vicente has caused me. From the first moment he saw me, he began to lavish his attentions upon me, and I, succumbing to his words, fell in love with him unbeknownst to my father, for there is no woman, regardless of how secluded and cautious she is, who cannot find the opportunity to give vent to her desires once her willpower has undergone such a siege. In short, he promised to be my husband and I in turn swore to be his wife but to carry the affair no further than that. I learned yesterday that he had forgone his obligation to me and was going to wed another and that the wedding was to take place this morning, news that unsettled my reason and caused me to lose all patience. And because my father was away from the village, I was forced to wear the present outfit. By urging my horse as hard as I could, I overtook Don Vicente about a league from here where, without pausing to state my complaints or to listen to his excuses, I fired this musket at him, as well as these two pistols for good measure. It is my belief that I buried more than a couple of bullets in his body, opening portals in it through which my honor, bathed by his blood, might escape. I left him there among his servants, none of whom could or dared come to his defense, and I have come in search of you to beg you to take me to France, where I have relatives with whom I can live, and also to beg you to defend my father from Don Vicente's many kinsmen, who may be so bold as to seek some sort of retaliation against him."

Roque, marveling at the beautiful Claudia's elegance, gallantry, handsome figure, as well as everything that had just befallen her, said to her,

"Come, my lady, and let us see if your enemy is dead. We shall then decide what will be the most expedient thing to do on your grace's behalf."

Don Quixote, who had been listening closely to each of Claudia's comments and Roque's answers, said,

"There is no reason for anyone to trouble himself to defend this lady, for I shall take the responsibility upon my own shoulders. If you will return my horse and weapons and wait for me here, I shall seek out that knight and, dead or alive, shall force him to keep the promise he has made to so fair a creature."

"And let no one doubt it," said Sancho, "for my master is quite adept at matchmaking, having only a few days ago forced another man to marry who had likewise failed to keep his word to another maiden. And if it weren't for the fact that the enchanters who pursue my master had transformed the man's actual appearance into that of a lackey, the maiden in question would be a maiden no longer."

Roque, whose thoughts were directed more to the beautiful Claudia's circumstances than to the remarks of the master and servant, failed to hear a word they said. He ordered his squires to return to Sancho everything they had taken from the dapple and to withdraw to the place they were to camp that night, at which point he rode off with Claudia at full speed in search of the wounded or dead Don Vicente. They came to the place where Claudia had found him but they saw nothing there except several fresh blood stains. However, in looking all about, they caught sight of several persons climbing a hill, and surmised, and rightly so, that it must be Don Vicente being carried by his servants to be cared for or to be buried. They hurried to overtake them and, since the men were walking quite slowly, were able to do so with ease. They found Don Vicente being carried by his servants, pleading with them in a weak, exhausted voice to let him die there because the pain from his wounds would not allow him to travel farther.

Claudia and Roque leapt from their horses and went over to him. The servants were frightened by Roque's presence, and Claudia was distraught at the sight of Don Vicente. Half-tenderly and half-sternly she went up to him and took his hands in hers.

"If you had given me these," she said, "according to our agreement, you would not find yourself in this plight."

The wounded gentleman opened his half-closed eyes and, once he recognized Claudia, said,

"I see now, beautiful but mistaken lady, that you are the one who has slain me, a punishment my intentions did not deserve or merit, for never would I or could I wrong you either in thought or in deed."

"Well, is it not true," said Claudia, "that this morning you planned to wed Leonora, the wealthy Balvastro's daughter?"

"Certainly not," replied Don Vicente, "my cruel fortune must have brought you that news so you in your jealousy would take my life. But since I am surrendering it into your hands and arms, I consider my fate a fortunate one. To demonstrate to you the truth of this, take my hand and accept me as your husband if you will. I have no greater satisfaction to offer you for the wrong you think I have committed."

As Claudia gripped his hand tightly in hers, her heart was so heavy she collapsed in a faint against Don Vicente's blood-spattered breast at the very moment that he was seized by a fatal spasm, all of which left Roque confused and uncertain as to what to do. The servants hurried off to find water and, after returning, dowsed the victims' faces with it. Claudia recovered from her swoon but not Don Vicente from his death throe, for his life had come to an end. When Claudia saw this and understood that her dear husband was no longer alive, she pierced the air with her screams, shook heaven with her laments and sobs, tore her hair, scattering it to the wind, and disfigured her face with her own hands, displaying all the grief and emotion one would expect from a soul in torment.

"O cruel, thoughtless woman," she screamed at herself, "how easily you were moved to carry out such an evil notion! O raging powers of jealousy, to what desperate ends you drive those who have given you refuge in their breasts! My dear husband, your fate, which has been so unfortunate as to make you my beloved, is taking you from the nuptial couch to the grave."

So pitiful were Claudia's laments that they brought tears to the eyes of Roque, who was unaccustomed to shedding them regardless of the circumstances, and the servants too were in tears. Claudia swooned at every moment and the entire area took on the appearance of a scene from some tragedy. In the end, Roque Guinart ordered Don Vicente's servants to carry the body to the father's nearby village so Don Vicente could be buried. Claudia told Roque she wished to go away to a convent in which an aunt of hers was abbess, because she intended to spend the rest of her life in the company of a better and more enduring husband. Roque praised her noble proposal and offered to accompany her wherever she desired and to defend her father against Don Vicente's relatives or anyone else on earth who might seek to harm him. On no account would Claudia allow him to accompany her but thanked him for his offer as graciously as she knew how and then tearfully took leave of him. Don Vicente's servants carried his body with them, Roque returned to his comrades, and thus ended the tale of Claudia Jerónima, whose love was so ill-fated – but is it any wonder when the fabric of her lamentable story was woven by those invincible, unforgiving powers of Jealousy?

Roque Guinart found his squires waiting for him in the place where he had ordered them to go, and there in their midst was Don Quixote mounted on Rocinante, delivering a speech in which he was attempting to persuade them to abandon that perilous way of life, perilous to them in body and soul alike. But since the majority were Gascons, a rough and undisciplined lot, Don Quixote's lecture made little or no sense to them. When Roque arrived, he asked Sancho Panza if his men had returned the jewels and possessions they had removed from his dapple. Sancho replied that they had, with the exception of three missing nightcaps that were worth as much as three cities.

"What are you talking about, man?" said one of those present; "I have them and they're not worth three *reals*."

"That is true," said Don Quixote, "but my squire values them as highly as he does because of the one who gave them to me."

Roque Guinart ordered him to return them at once. Then commanding the men to bring forward the clothing, jewels, money, and everything they had plundered since the last distribution, he had his men line up. After making a hasty appraisal and assigning a monetary value to those items that could not be divided, he distributed everything among his companions so prudently and fairly that he did not overlook a single thing or violate any principle of distributive justice. Once this was concluded, and to everyone's satisfaction and contentment, he said to Don Quixote,

"If I did not deal with these men as scrupulously as this, there would be no living with them."

To which Sancho responded,

"According to what I've seen here, justice is such a good thing it's necessary even for thieves to employ it among themselves."

A squire overheard him and, drawing back the butt-end of his gun, would have split Sancho's head open had Roque Guinart not shouted at him to halt. Sancho turned pale and vowed not to unseal his lips during the entire time he was among these people. Just then, there arrived one of the squires who had been stationed as sentinels along the roads to see who was traveling on them and to report to their superior everything that was going on.

"Sir," he said, "not far from here on the road to Barcelona there's a large group of people headed this way."

To which Roque responded,

"Could you see whether they are one of the groups that go around looking for us or the ones we are searching for?"

"They are the ones we are searching for," replied the squire.

"Well, everyone out," shouted Roque; "bring them here at once and don't let anyone escape!"

They did as ordered and Don Quixote, Sancho, and Roque were left there alone, waiting to see whom the squires might bring back. During this interval Roque said to Don Quixote,

"Our way of life must seem strange to his lord Don Quixote: strange adventures, strange experiences, and all dangerous; not that it would surprise me if your grace thought so, for I must actually confess that there is no more unsettled and unpredictable way of life than ours. I was thrust into this life by certain vague desires for revenge, a sentiment that has the power to unsettle the most placid bosom. By nature I am compassionate and well-intentioned but, as I said, the desire to avenge myself for an injustice I suffered so undermines my good intentions that I persevere in this business despite everything I know of it. And since 'deep calleth unto deep' [4] and one sin calls forth another, matters of revenge have become so entangled I have taken upon my shoulders not only my own cause but that of others as well. But even though I find myself in this labyrinth of confusion, God will see to it that I shall not despair of sailing out of it into some safe port."

Don Quixote was astounded to hear Roque express such noble and sensible ideas, for he had thought that among men engaged in such activities as banditry, robbery, and murder no person would be capable of this sort of eloquence.

"Sir Roque," he said at this point, "the first step towards finding a cure is to ascertain the nature of your illness and to be willing to take the medicines the physician prescribes. You are ill and know the nature of your illness, and heaven – or God, to be more precise, who is our physician – will provide medicines that will cure you. However, these usually cure gradually and not all at once in some miraculous way. What is more, wise sinners are more likely to be saved than foolish ones, and since you have demonstrated your wisdom by what you have just said, you need do nothing more than to take heart and wait for your ailing conscience to improve. And should you care to shorten the journey and take a shortcut to your salvation, come with me and I shall teach you to be a knight-errant, whereby you will undergo so many ordeals and misadventures that if these count as penances, you will go to heaven in the twinkling of an eye."

Roque was forced to chuckle at Don Quixote's advice but, changing the subject, he told him of the tragedy that had befallen Claudia Jerónima, which sorely grieved Sancho, who had not failed to be

4 From Psalm 42 of the Bible.

impressed by the girl's beauty and adventurous spirit. At that moment, the squires arrived with their catch, bringing with them two gentlemen on horseback, two pilgrims on foot, and a coach filled with women, accompanied by as many as half a dozen servants – some on horseback, some on foot – as well as two muleteers the gentlemen had in attendance. The squires gathered round them in a circle and both captives and captors remained perfectly silent waiting for the great Roque Guinart to speak. At length, he asked the gentlemen who they were, where they were headed, and how much money they were carrying; to which one of them replied,

"We, sir, are two Spanish infantry captains, our companies are at Naples, we're on our way to embark on four galleys said to be at Barcelona with orders to proceed to Sicily, and we're carrying some two to three hundred *escudos*, because of which, in our opinion, we're traveling rich and contented, for a soldier's usual poverty allows for no greater savings.

Roque asked the pilgrims the same questions he had asked the captains and they informed him that they were to embark for Rome and that between the two of them they had some sixty *reals*. He also wanted to know what persons were traveling in the coach, what their destination was, and how much money they were carrying; to which one of those on horseback replied,

"Traveling in the coach are my lady Doña Guiomar de Quiñones, wife of the regent of the vicarage of Naples, her small daughter, a maid, and a duenna; six of us servants are in her company, and the money we have amounts to six hundred *escudos*."

"Well then," said Roque Guinart, "here we have nine hundred *escudos* and sixty *reals*. My soldiers and I must number about sixty, so see how much that comes to for each man, as I am not very good at numbers."

When the highwaymen heard this, they let out a shout, saying,

"Long live Roque Guinart despite all the hoodlums who seek his downfall!"

The captains were visibly distressed, the regent's wife saddened, and the pilgrims not at all pleased to witness the confiscation of their possessions. Roque kept them all in suspense for quite some time but, being unwilling to prolong their unhappiness, which could be discerned from the distance of a bowshot, he turned to the captains and said,

"Sir captains, your graces shall out of courtesy lend me sixty *escudos* and the wife of the regent eighty to satisfy these men who follow me, for 'Every person must look out for himself.' You may then continue on your way free and unrestrained with a safe-conduct I shall give you so that if you happen to encounter any other bands of mine scattered throughout these parts, you will not be harmed. It is not my intention to wrong soldiers or women, especially women who are illustrious ones."

Profuse and eloquent were the words with which the captains thanked Roque for his courtesy and generosity, which is how they regarded his gesture of permitting them to keep their own money. The lady Doña Guiomar wanted to leap from the coach to kiss the feet and hands of the great Roque but he would not permit such an indignity. Instead, he begged forgiveness for the wrong he had been forced to inflict upon her by complying with the obligations of his evil trade. The regent's wife at once ordered one of her servants to hand over the eighty *escudos* she had been assessed, and the captains had already taken the sixty *escudos* from their purses. The pilgrims were ready to contribute their pittance when Roque told them to put it away. Then turning to his men, he said,

"Each man shall receive two *escudos* with twenty left over. Ten of these shall go to these pilgrims, and the other ten to this good squire so he will speak kindly of this experience."

And ordering his writing materials brought forth, which he always kept with him, Roque wrote them a safe-conduct for the leaders of his bands, and after bidding them farewell, allowed them to go free. Astonished at his noble character, generous disposition, and uncommon behavior, they considered him an Alexander the Great rather than an infamous bandit. One of the squires said in his Gascon-Catalan dialect,

"This captain of ours would make a better friar than a bandit. If he wants to show his generosity in the future, let him do so with his own property, not with ours."

But because the unfortunate squire did not speak softly enough to prevent Roque from overhearing him, the latter drew his sword and almost split open his head.

"This," he said, "is how I punish those who are impudent and loose with their tongues."

They were all so stunned no one dared say a word, such was their respect for his authority. Roque then went off to himself to write a letter to a friend of his in Barcelona. He informed him that he had in his company the famous Don Quixote of La Mancha, that knight-errant about whom there had been so much discussion, and he assured him the knight was the most gracious and knowledgeable man on earth, adding that four days from then, which would be the day of Saint John the Baptist, he would deposit him on the city strand fully armed and mounted on Rocinante his horse, along with his squire Sancho riding an ass. Roque added that he was to notify his friends the Niarros [5] of this so they might avail themselves of the knight's delightful company, but he wanted the rival Cadells to be deprived of this pleasure which, however, would be impossible owing to the fact that Don Quixote's intelligence and folly and his squire Sancho Panza's wit could not fail to provide general enjoyment for every person on earth. He sent this letter by one of his squires, who, after changing his bandit outfit for that of a farmer, left for Barcelona, where he delivered the letter to the person to whom it was addressed.

Chapter Sixty-One

What befell Don Quixote on the outskirts of Barcelona, together with other incidents that are more real than fanciful

Don Quixote spent three days and three nights with Roque but had he remained there for three hundred years, he would never have lacked things to observe or marvel at in that way of life. They would begin the day in one place and eat their meals in another; at times they would find themselves fleeing from something or someone unknown, while at other times they would

5 The Niarros were one of two warring bands in Catalonia, the other being the Cadells; the historical Roca Guinarda belonged to the former.

lie in wait for something or someone equally unknown; and they would sleep standing up only to break their slumber and move to another place. It was a continual ritual of sending out spies, receiving reports from sentinels, and keeping the fuses of their matchlock guns dry, the few that they had, that is, since virtually everyone carried a flintlock gun. Roque would spend the night in different places away from his men in an effort to conceal his whereabouts, for the numerous proclamations issued by the viceroy of Barcelona against his life kept him so uneasy and fearful that he dared not confide in a solitary soul, fearing that his very own men might attempt to murder him or turn him over to the authorities, truly a wretched and wearisome existence.

At length, Roque, Don Quixote, and Sancho set out for Barcelona, together with six of Roque's squires. Following untraveled roads, shortcuts, and secret trails, they arrived at the strand on the night of Saint John's Eve, at which time Roque embraced Don Quixote and Sancho and gave the latter the ten *escudos* he had promised to give him but had not done so until then. After both parties had placed themselves at the other's disposal an untold number of times, Roque took his leave, while Don Quixote remained there on horseback waiting for day to arrive. He had barely begun his vigil when fair Aurora made her appearance along the balconies of the east, bringing joy to the grass and flowers, if not to the ears, though even the latter were simultaneously greeted by the sound of hornpipes, drums, bells, and cries of 'Out of the way! Stand aside!' of the runners who had obviously come from the city. Dawn gave way to the sun, which with a face larger than that of a shield rose slowly above the lowest point on the horizon.

Directing their gaze in all directions, Don Quixote and Sancho caught sight of the sea, which they had never before seen, and it impressed them as being quite a bit wider and more expansive than the Lakes of Ruidera with which they were familiar in La Mancha. Along the beach they saw the galleys with their awnings lowered, boldly displaying all their streamers and pennants, which were fluttering in the wind as they brushed and kissed the water. From the galleys came the sounds of clarions, trumpets, and hornpipes, which filled the air near and far with their dulcet yet warlike tones. As the galleys began to stir, they acted out a sort of skirmish on the calm waters, being imitated in this, as it were, by countless horsemen who came streaming from the city mounted on handsome steeds and sporting showy liveries. The soldiers on the galleys continuously fired their artillery and were answered by those on the walls of the city's forts, while the heavy artillery rent the air with its frightful roar and the galleys' gangway cannons responded. The joyous sea, the cheerful earth, and the clear air – clear except when clouded by artillery smoke – seemed to infuse and instill unexpected joyousness in everyone there, but what Sancho could not understand was how those bobbing, undulating hulks could have so many legs.

At that moment, the livery-clad horsemen amid shouts and war cries came galloping up to where Don Quixote stood aghast and stupefied, and one of them – the one to whom Roque had written – cried out to Don Quixote with a shout,

"Our city welcomes the mirror, beacon, guide, and north star of all knight-errantry in the fullest sense of the word. Welcome, I say, to the valiant Don Quixote of La Mancha – not that false, fictitious, apocryphal one recently foisted upon us in that counterfeit history but the real, true, genuine one described to us by Cide Hamete Benengeli, epitome of historians."

Don Quixote made no reply, nor did the horsemen wait for him to do so as they wheeled their mounts about and, after rejoining their company, began to prance in a circle round the knight, who turned to Sancho and said,

"These men have truly recognized us. I would venture to say they have read our history, as well as the one just published by that Aragonese."

The rider who had addressed Don Quixote rode up to him once more and said,

"Sir Don Quixote, I bid your grace to come with us, for we are all at your lordship's command and are good friends of Roque Guinart."

To which Don Quixote replied,

"If courtesy breeds courtesy, kind sir, then your grace's is the child or close relative of that of the great Roque. Lead me wherever you will, for my desire is none other than to do your bidding, particularly if you should wish to employ me in your service."

The gentleman answered with words that were no less gracious, and so with Don Quixote in their midst they set out for the city to the accompaniment of hornpipes and drums. But just as they were making their entrance, the Wicked One, who is responsible for all things evil, together with two impertinent, mischievous boys (all boys being worse than the Devil Himself) made their way among the crowd. One of the boys lifted the dapple's tail and the other Rocinante's, at which point they each poked several handfuls of briars into the animals' rear ends. As soon as the poor beasts felt these newfangled spurs, they tightened the muscles in their tails, which only increased their discomfort, and began to buck up and down and jump about so vigorously that they threw their riders to the ground. Embarrassed and insulted, Don Quixote hurried to remove the bouquet from the tail of his broken-down nag, and Sancho the one from his dapple's. The men leading the way for Don Quixote would have liked nothing better than to punish the boys for their insolence but it was impossible, as the latter had lost themselves among the thousands who had gathered there.

Don Quixote and Sancho remounted their beasts and, to the accompaniment of the same music and cheers, proceeded to the home of their guide, which was a large and stately one befitting a gentleman of his means. And this is where we shall leave them in accordance with Cide Hamete's wishes.

Chapter Sixty-Two

The adventure of the enchanted head, and other trifles that demand to be related

Don Antonio Moreno was the name of Don Quixote's host, a wealthy, intelligent gentleman who was fond of amusing himself with honorable and well-intentioned entertainments. Once he had Don Quixote in his home, he set about searching for ways to allow his guest's madness to display itself but only those that would not be harmful to him, for jests that cause pain are not jests, and amusements that injure others are not worthy of the name.

The first thing he did was to have Don Quixote remove his armor and don his tight-fitting chamois-skin suit, which we have described earlier, and then to appear on a balcony overlooking one of the city's main streets, where he was viewed by the general public and gawked at by the youngsters as though he were some sort of freak. The riders once again paraded before him sporting their liveries, as though they had worn them just for him and not to enliven the festive occasion. Sancho was ecstatic, for it seemed to him that, without knowing how or why, he had stumbled upon another Camacho's wedding, another home like Don Diego de Miranda's, another castle like the duke's. Several of Don Antonio's friends dined with him that day, honoring Don Quixote and treating him as though he were a knight-errant, with the latter becoming so vain and puffed up he could barely contain himself. Sancho came up with so many witty remarks that the household servants and everyone listening to him hung upon his every word. Once they were seated at the table, Don Antonio said to Sancho,

"We have received word, noble Sancho, that you are quite fond of chicken croquettes and meatballs, so if there are any left over, you may put them in your pocket for a rainy day."[1]

"No, your lordship, that is not quite correct," said Sancho; "I am more given to neatness than to gluttony, and my master, who is here in our presence, can vouch for the fact that we're both in the habit of going a week on a handful of acorns or nuts. Now, it's true that if someone brings me a calf, I'll run and get a rope, meaning that I eat what I'm given and take the times as I find them, but anyone who claims I eat like a pig or am a slovenly eater can be certain he doesn't know what he's talking about, which I would express in very different terms if I didn't see all these venerable faces before me."

"Most assuredly," replied Don Quixote, "the moderation and care with which Sancho eats might well be inscribed and engraved on plates of bronze to serve as an everlasting reminder to future generations. To be sure, when he is hungry, he drinks a bit too much as a result of eating fast and chewing with his mouth full but he is always scrupulously tidy, and during the time he was governor he became such a fastidious eater that he would eat grapes and even pomegranate seeds with a fork."

"What!" exclaimed Don Antonio, "Sancho has been a governor?"

"Yes," said Sancho, "and of a place called Cheap-Isle, where I governed for ten days as pretty as you please but during which time I ceased to be carefree and learned to despise every government on earth. I fled from there and fell into a cave where I gave myself up for dead, but by some miracle I finally escaped from there alive."

Don Quixote related point by point everything that had transpired while Sancho was governor, which delighted everyone present. Once the table was cleared, Don Antonio took Don Quixote by the arm and led him to a secluded chamber in which there were no furnishings except a table apparently of marble, supported by a pedestal of the same material. On the table stood a bust like those of Roman emperors, which appeared to be made of bronze. Don Antonio, accompanied by Don

---

1 A reference to an episode in the apocryphal *Quijote* in which Sancho stuffs these leftover foods into his shirt.

Quixote, paced from one end of the chamber to the other and, after they had circled the table several times, he said to the knight,

"Sir Don Quixote, now that I have assured myself that the door is locked and no one can overhear us, I want to tell your grace of one of the strangest circumstances, or to be more exact, one of the strangest inventions imaginable, but only on condition that you guard what I am about to tell you in the most secret recesses of your bosom."

"I swear to do so," replied Don Quixote, "and shall even place a capstone on top of it for greater security. I would have your grace know, Don Antonio," – for Don Quixote had finally learned his host's name – "that you are speaking to someone who, though he has ears to hear, has a tongue that will not speak. Therefore, your grace may with complete assurance convey to my breast what you have in your own with the certainty that you have cast it into an abyss of silence."

"On the strength of that promise," said Don Antonio, "I expect to make your grace marvel at what you are about to see and hear, as well as to give myself some relief from the frustration I feel at not having anyone with whom to share my secrets, since these are not to be entrusted to just anyone."

Don Quixote was on tenterhooks waiting to see where all these admonitions were leading, when Don Antonio took the knight's hand and passed it over the bronze head, along the length of the table, and down the marble pedestal on which the object rested; he then said,

"This head, Sir Don Quixote, has been designed and constructed by one of the greatest enchanters and magicians the world has ever known. I believe he was Polish by birth and had been a disciple of the famous Escotillo, about whom so many wonders are related. This person was here in my home, where for a fee of one thousand *escudos* he fashioned this head which has the power and ability to answer any question spoken into its ear. This same individual proceeded to get his bearings, sketch various figures, observe the heavenly bodies, note the celestial coordinates, and finally to produce the perfection we shall view tomorrow, for on Fridays the head is mute, and since today is Friday, we must wait until tomorrow. In the meantime, your grace may prepare any questions you might like to ask it, for I can state from experience that the head responds truthfully to any question put to it."

Don Quixote was astonished at the virtues and abilities of the head but was rather inclined to doubt Don Antonio. However, in view of the fact that he would soon be able to put it to the test, he thought it advisable to show his gratitude for Don Antonio's willingness to reveal so great a secret to him. They left the chamber, which Don Antonio locked, and returned to the hall where the other gentlemen were waiting, during which time Sancho had been describing to them the adventures and incidents that had befallen his master.

That afternoon, they took Don Quixote on an outing, not in his armor but in street clothes consisting of a tawny-colored cassock, which in such weather could have made ice itself perspire, and they arranged for their servants to entertain Sancho to prevent his leaving the house. Instead of Rocinante, Don Quixote rode a large mule with a steady gait and handsome trappings. They helped him to don his cassock, to the back of which, unknown to him, they had sewn a parchment printed in large letters: *THIS IS DON QUIXOTE OF LA MANCHA*. As they began their stroll, the placard attracted the attention of everyone who saw it, and the knight was amazed to discover that everyone recognized him and could call him by name. Turning to Don Antonio, who was riding at his side, he said,

"Great are the privileges that knight-errantry encompasses within itself, for it brings to him who professes it fame and renown from all corners of the earth. If, Sir Don Antonio, your grace doubts this, just notice that even the youngsters of this city who have never before seen me know who I am."

"So they do, Sir Don Quixote," replied Don Antonio, "for just as fire cannot be hidden or enclosed, neither can virtue fail to be recognized; and virtue achieved through the profession of arms flourishes and stands out above all others."

It then chanced that as Don Quixote was riding along to the above-mentioned applause, a Castilian who had read the inscription on his back cried out,

"Damn my soul if it isn't Don Quixote of La Mancha! How have you managed to come this far without getting yourself killed by the countless beatings you carry on your back? You're mad, you know, and if you were simply mad in private and kept your madness to yourself, it wouldn't be quite so bad, but you have the ability to drive everyone mad or insane who has any dealings with you or comes into contact with you. If you don't believe me, just look at those gentlemen you've got with you. Go back home, you madman, and look after your estate and your wife and children and forsake those mindless activities that are eating away your brain and skimming off the choicest layers of your mind."

"Brother," said Don Antonio, "be off with you and refrain from giving advice to anyone who does not seek it. His lord Don Quixote of La Mancha is quite sane and the rest of us here are not exactly fools. No, virtue is to be honored wherever it is found. May you be hounded by bad luck, sir, and not go meddling where you are not wanted."

"By heavens, your grace is right," said the Castilian; "to give advice to this gentleman is like shouting into the wind. Despite all that, it pains me greatly that the good sense this crackpot is said to display in all other matters should go down the drain of his knight-errantry. May the bad luck you mentioned haunt me and all my descendants if from this day forward, though I should live to be older than Methuselah, I ever give advice to anyone, even if asked."

The advice-giver then departed and the tour continued but so great was the laughter of the boys and all the people when they read the sign that Don Antonio was forced to remove it, which he accomplished by pretending to be removing something else. Night arrived and they returned home, where several ladies had gathered for an evening of dancing, for Don Antonio's wife, a delightful, beautiful, and intelligent lady of some prominence, had invited a number of her women friends to honor her guest and be entertained by his unheard-of harebrained ideas, and a number of them had attended. Following a splendid dinner a dance was held, which began around ten in the evening. Present among the ladies were two of a mischievous and playful turn who, though behaving quite properly, were somewhat unrestrained when it came to playing harmless jokes. These two created such a flurry in coaxing Don Quixote onto the dance floor that they exhausted him in body and spirit alike. Don Quixote was a sight to behold: tall, skinny, sallow, squeezed into his clothes, ungainly, but, above all, not the least bit graceful. These courtesans flirted with him on the sly and he rebuffed them in like manner, but seeing himself hard-pressed by their flirtatious remarks, he cried out,

"*Fugite, partes adversae*! [2] Leave me in peace, you unwelcome thoughts! Keep your desires within bounds, ladies, for the one who is my mistress, the peerless Dulcinea of Toboso, will allow none but hers to subdue and enslave me."

As he said this, he sat down on the floor in the middle of the room battered and bruised from his arduous exercise. Don Antonio had him carried bodily to his bed and the first person to take hold of him was Sancho, who said,

"Hang it all, master, your grace picked a fine time to go dancing! Do you think every brave man is a dancer or every knight-errant can frolic and gambol about? I can assure your grace that if you think so, you are sadly mistaken. Why, there are men who would rather slay a dragon than trip the light fantastic. If you were to do a country dance, I could supply what you lack, for I can clog with the best of them, but I don't know a thing about these ballroom dances."

This and other such talk by Sancho evoked laughter from everyone in the ballroom. He then dumped his master onto the bed and covered him up so he could sweat off any chill he might have contracted from dancing. The following day Don Antonio thought it appropriate to perform the experiment with the enchanted head, and so with Don Quixote, Sancho, and two other friends present, together with the two ladies who were spending the night with Don Antonio's wife – those who had exhausted Don Quixote with their dancing – he locked himself up in the room containing the head. He described to them the abilities it possessed, swore them to secrecy, and informed them that this was the first time the virtues of this head were being tested; that with the exception of Don Antonio's two friends, no one else knew the secret behind the enchantment. He added that, had he not earlier revealed it to these two friends of his, even they would experience the same astonishment as everyone else there, for the skill and care with which it had been constructed was so great no other reaction was conceivable.

The first to approach the head was Don Antonio himself, who spoke into its ear in a low voice but not so low he could not be heard by everyone present.

"Tell me," he said, "by calling upon that power you possess within yourself, what am I thinking at this very moment?"

The head, without moving its lips, made the following reply in a clear, distinct voice that was understood by everyone:

"I make no pronouncements about what people are thinking."

When they heard this, they were all astonished, especially when they saw there was no one in the room near the table who could have answered in that manner.

"How many of us are here?" asked Don Antonio as his second question. The head answered in the same subdued tone as before,

"There are you and your wife, two friends of yours, and two friends of hers, a famous knight called Don Quixote of La Mancha, and a squire of his by the name of Sancho Panza."

This indeed was renewed cause for astonishment, and this is where the hair on everyone's head surely stood on end from sheer fright. Then moving away from the head, Don Antonio said,

---

2 Latin: 'Flee, you adversaries!' — an ecclesiastical expression used in exorcisms.

"This is sufficient to prove I was not deceived by the one who sold you to me, O wise head, who speak, answer, and provoke wonder! Let someone else approach and ask it anything at all."

Since most women are impatient and inquisitive, the first to step forward was one of the two friends of Don Antonio's wife, who asked the following question:

"Tell me, head, what may I do to be very beautiful?"

To which the head responded,

"Be very pure."

"I have nothing more to ask," said the questioner. Her companion then went up and said,

"I should like to know, head, whether my husband loves me or not."

And it responded,

"Observe how he treats you and you will have your answer."

The married woman withdrew and said,

"For such an answer there was no need to ask a question, for it goes without saying that actions reveal the sentiments of the person performing them."

Next, one of Don Antonio's two friends approached and asked,

"Who am I?"

"You know who you are," was the reply.

"That is not what I am asking," said the gentleman; "I should like you to tell me if you know me."

"Of course, I know you," it answered, "you are Don Pedro Noriz."

"I need hear nothing further, for this is sufficient to convince me that you, O head, know everything."

As he stepped back, the other friend went up and said,

"Tell me, head, what would my eldest son and heir like to see happen?"

"I have already explained," said the head, "that I do not speculate about what people are thinking but I can assure you that what your son would like to see is you in your grave."

"That is true," said the gentleman, "and it is as plain as the nose on his face!"

Inasmuch as he had nothing more to ask, Don Antonio's wife approached and said,

"I have no idea what to ask you, head. I should simply like to know if I shall enjoy many years with my dear husband."

"Yes, indeed," answered the head, "for his health and moderation in all things promise him many years of life, which a good many people cut short by their intemperance."

Next, Don Quixote approached and said,

"Tell me, you who answer any question, did I actually experience or merely dream what happened to me in the Cave of Montesinos? Will Sancho finish giving himself all the lashes? And will Dulcinea's disenchantment ever be effected?"

"As for the cave," responded the head, "there is a great deal to be said, since it contains some things that are true and some that are not. Sancho's lashes will proceed slowly and Dulcinea's disenchantment will take place in due time."

"I need hear nothing more," said Don Quixote; "the moment I see Dulcinea disenchanted, I shall consider every happiness I ever hope to attain as already accomplished at one fell swoop."

The last questioner was Sancho, who asked the following:

"Is there any chance, head, that I'll have another government? Will I ever escape from this toilsome life of squire? And will I ever see my wife and children again?"

To which the head responded,

"You will govern in your own house if you will simply return to your home, where you will also see your wife and children. Likewise, by ceasing to serve, you will thereby cease to be a squire."

"My goodness, what an answer!" said Sancho; "I could've told myself that. For brevity, Pero Grulla [3] the prophet couldn't beat that."

"You dunce," said Don Quixote, "what kind of answer did you expect? Is it not sufficient if the answers this head gives correspond to what it is asked?"

"It is," replied Sancho, "but I wish it had expanded on its answer a bit and told me more than it did."

With this, the question-and-answer session came to an end but there was no end to the amazement they all experienced with the exception of Don Antonio's two friends who were privy to the situation. At this point Cide Hamete Benengeli saw fit to explain all this lest he keep everyone in suspense believing this particular head contained within itself some magical and extraordinary mystery. He thus explained that Don Antonio, to imitate another head he had seen in Madrid devised by a toolmaker, arranged for this one to be built in his home to amuse himself and all those not in on the secret. The apparatus was constructed as follows: the top of the table, which was wooden, had been painted and varnished to give it the appearance of marble, and the pedestal on which it rested was made of the same material, with four eagle's claws flaring out at the foot for greater stability. The head, which resembled a bust or figure of a Roman emperor, was bronze-colored, completely hollow, and fitted so precisely into the top of the table that no sign of a joint was visible. The table's central support was also hollow, as were the figure's chest and neck, and all this was connected to another room situated directly beneath the room containing the head. Through these cavities in the pedestal, table, chest, and neck ran a tin tube that was so well fitted it went undetected by everyone. In the room below, the person who was to answer stood with his mouth against this same tube, so that in the manner of an ear-trumpet the sound traveled from the lower room to the upper, and from the upper to the lower, and with such well articulated clarity that it was impossible to detect the trickery. A nephew of Don Antonio's, a bright and clever student, was the one who acted as spokesman for the head, having been instructed by his uncle as to which persons would accompany him that day to the room containing the head. It was, therefore, easy for him to respond to the first questions quickly and precisely. The subsequent questions he answered by conjecture and, being quite intelligent, did so quite cleverly. Cide Hamete adds that this marvelous contraption lasted some eleven or twelve days but that, because news spread throughout the city that Don Antonio had in his house an enchanted head that could answer any question it was asked, he was afraid news of this might reach the ears of the ever-attentive sentinels of our Faith, so he explained the situation to the inquisitors, who ordered him to cease using it and to dismantle it so the ignorant masses would not be shocked. And

3 A legendary character who was famous for prophesying things that were ridiculously obvious.

yet, in the opinion of Don Quixote and Sancho Panza the head was still enchanted and capable of responding, albeit more satisfactorily for Don Quixote than for Sancho.

The gentlemen of the city, to please Don Antonio and to entertain Don Quixote while affording him the opportunity to display his follies, made arrangements for a tilting at the ring six days from that date, which was not held due to reasons that will be explained below. Meanwhile, Don Quixote fancied taking a leisurely tour of the city on foot but fearing that, if he did so on horseback, he might be harassed by the boys; and so he and Sancho set out with two servants Don Antonio had provided them. It happened that as they were walking down a certain street, Don Quixote looked up and saw above a doorway a sign with very large letters that read: *BOOKS PRINTED HERE*. He was delighted at this, for never before had he been inside a print shop and he was quite curious to learn what one was like. Going inside with all his retinue, he observed persons in various parts of the shop casting and setting type, proofreading, and revising – in other words, the entire process that is found in a large print shop. Don Quixote went up to one of the cases and asked what was being done there. The workman gave him a full account, all of which he found fascinating. Moving on to another case, he asked the man at that one what he was doing and the workman answered,

"Sir, this gentleman," and here he pointed to a nice- but rather stern-looking man, "has translated an Italian book into our Spanish tongue, for which I myself am setting the type so it can go to the printer."

"What is the book's title?" asked Don Quixote; to which the translator answered,

"Sir, in Italian the book is called *Le Bagattelle*."

"And what does *Le Bagattelle* mean in our language?" asked Don Quixote.

"*Le Bagattelle*," replied the translator, "is what we would call *Trifles* in our language, but despite the book's humble name, it contains and encompasses much that is fine and substantial."

"I possess some slight knowledge of Italian," said Don Quixote, "and pride myself upon being able to recite a few stanzas of Ariosto. So tell me, good sir – and I ask this not because I wish to test your grace's powers of observation but only out of curiosity – have you ever come across the word *pignatta* in your reading?"

"Yes, many times," replied the translator.

"And how do you translate it?" asked Don Quixote.

"How else would one translate it," said the translator, "except as *pot*?"

"My word!" said Don Quixote, "your grace is quite accomplished in the Italian language! I would make a sizeable wager that where the Italian says *piace*, you say *pleases*, and where it says *piu*, *su*, and *giú*, you say *more*, *above*, and *below*."

"Of course, I do," said the translator, "for those are their proper equivalents."

"I would also hazard a guess," said Don Quixote, "that your grace has received no recognition from the world, which is forever reluctant to reward the best minds and the most praiseworthy labors. Oh, the many talents that remain undiscovered out there and the many neglected intellects and unappreciated skills! However, it strikes me that translating from one language into another, provided it is not from those queenly ones, Greek and Latin, is like looking at the reverse side of a Flemish tapestry, for, though its design can be made out, it is covered with threads that obscure it, wherefore it lacks the smooth texture of the front side. Translating from less complicated languages does not argue for either intelligence or literary ability, any more than transcribing or copying one document from another does. However, I do not mean to suggest that the task of translating is not a laudable one, for a man may occupy himself in worse ways and with less benefit to himself. I would exclude from this observation two famous translators: the first, Doctor Cristóbal de Figueroa with his *Pastor Fido*, and the other, Don Juan de Jáuregui with his *Aminta*, two works that happily leave one in doubt as to which is the translation and which the original. But I should like to know if this book is being printed at your grace's expense or whether the printing rights have already been sold to some bookseller."

"I am printing it at my own expense," said the translator, "and I expect to earn at least a thousand ducats from this first printing, which will consist of two thousand copies that can be sold at six *reals* apiece, and faster than you can shake a stick."

"Your grace really is wet behind the ears," said Don Quixote; "you obviously do not know the ins and outs of printers and how they conspire with one another. I can assure your grace that when you see yourself weighed down with two thousand copies of your book, you will think your back so belabored it will be frightening, particularly if the book is somewhat out of the ordinary or is not the least bit racy."

"So what!" said the translator, "would your grace have me give it to a bookseller who would pay me three *maravedís* for the privilege and feel he was doing me a favor at that? I don't print my books to win fame in this world, since I am already known by virtue of my own works. What I seek is profit, for without that a good reputation is not worth a cent."

"May God look kindly upon your grace," replied Don Quixote.

And moving on to the next case, he saw them correcting a proof sheet for a book with the title *Light of the Soul*. When he saw it, he said,

"Books such as these, though there are many in this genre, are the kinds that are simply begging to be printed, for the world is full of sinners these days and there is an endless need of light for so many unenlightened souls."

Proceeding to the next case, he saw them correcting another book. Asking its title, he was told it was *The Second Part of the Ingenious Hidalgo Don Quixote of La Mancha*, composed by What's-His-Name, a native of Tordesillas.

"I have heard of that book," said Don Quixote, "but truthfully and in good conscience I assumed it had already been burned to ashes because of its impertinence, but the author's Saint Martin's Day [4] will arrive, as it does for every pig. Fictional histories are good and enjoyable to the extent that they approximate the truth, or appear to do so, just as true histories are good to the degree that they are authentic."

In saying this, he left the print shop evincing a slight sign of disgust. On that same day, Don Antonio arranged for him to be taken to see the galleys docked offshore, which delighted Sancho because they were something he had never seen. Don Antonio informed the commander of the

4 The day on which pigs are traditionally slaughtered in Spain.

galleys that during the afternoon he would show the galleys to his guest, the famous Don Quixote of La Mancha, about whom the commander and all the citizens of the city were now aware. And everything the knight experienced on board will be related in the following chapter.

Chapter Sixty-Three

The indignity that Sancho Panza suffered in his visit to the galleys, and the novel adventure of the beautiful Morisca woman

As profound as Don Quixote's thoughts were concerning the enchanted head's response, not one of them saw through the deception because they were all focused upon Dulcinea's promised disenchantment, which Don Quixote regarded as certain. Revisiting the matter time and time again, he felt an inner glow because of his conviction that he would soon witness its fulfillment. Sancho, for all his loathing of being governor, as already noted, still longed for one more chance to give orders and be obeyed, such are the evil consequences of governing, even when carried out in a make-believe manner.

Finally, that afternoon the host Don Antonio Moreno, together with his two friends and Don Quixote and Sancho, paid a visit to the galleys. The commander welcomed the news of their visit, for it would allow him to see both Don Quixote and Sancho in person. No sooner did they arrive at the waterfront than the ships' awnings were lowered, the hornpipes began to sound, and a skiff outfitted with handsome carpets and crimson velvet cushions was lowered into the water. When Don Quixote stepped aboard the skiff, the flagship fired its midship canon and the other galleys followed suit. Later, as Don Quixote boarded the flagship by the starboard ladder, the entire crew greeted him with three rounds of hurrahs, as is customary when a dignitary boards a galley. The admiral – this being the title we shall assign him – who was a gentleman of note from Valencia, extended his hand to Don Quixote and embraced him, saying,

"I shall mark this day with a white pebble, for it is one of the best days I ever hope to spend in my entire life, what with meeting his lordship Don Quixote of La Mancha. This day's marker shall forever remind us that he epitomizes and encompasses within himself all that is laudable in knight-errantry."

Don Quixote responded in a manner that was no less gracious, for he was overjoyed at seeing himself treated in such a princely fashion. They all mounted the poop deck, which was quite handsomely decorated, and seated themselves on the benches along its periphery. The boatswain walked onto the gangway and with his whistle gave the signal for the crew to strip to the waist, which they did in an instant. Seeing so many bare bodies, Sancho was flabbergasted, and when he saw them hoist the awnings with such speed, he could only conclude that a horde of demons was at work there. But all this was bread and honey compared to what I shall now describe.

Sancho was seated on the aft-beam of the poop deck next to the sternmost rower on the starboard side when this oarsman, who had previously been given his instructions, grabbed Sancho and lifted him in his arms. Then the whole crew, already alerted and on their feet, began passing him forward along the starboard side, tumbling him over and over in their arms from bench to bench and so rapidly that poor Sancho's eyes glazed over, for he undoubtedly believed he was in the clutches of devils from hell. They never ceased their labor until they had passed him back down the port side and returned him to the poop deck, where the poor soul sat down, battered, panting, perspiring, and unable to imagine what had just befallen him. Don Quixote, who had witnessed Sancho's wingless flight, asked the admiral if such ceremonies were always performed with persons boarding galleys for the first time, for if they were, he had no intention of being initiated or of undergoing such treatment, and he swore to God that if anyone laid a hand on him to send him flying, he would kick him to kingdom come, and as he said this, he rose to his feet and clutched his sword.

At that instant, they lowered the awnings and let the lateen-yard fall to the deck with such a mighty thud that Sancho feared the sky was coming loose from its hinges and was about to fall on his head, at which point he bent forward terror-stricken and stuck his head between his legs; nor did Don Quixote exhibit any more composure, for he too began to tremble as he sat there hunched over, his face as white as a sheet. The crew hoisted the lateen-yard with the same speed and clamor with which they had lowered it, and all this without saying a word, as though they had neither voices nor breath. The boatswain gave the signal to weigh anchor and, leaping to the middle of the gangway, began to lash the backs of the crew with his *kurbash*, or bullwhip, whereupon the ship gradually put out to sea. When Sancho saw so many red feet (which is what he took the oars to be) moving in unison, he said to himself,

"These are real enchantments, unlike those my master is always mentioning, but what have these poor wretches done to deserve such a flogging? And how does this single man who keeps blowing his whistle have the audacity to flog so many men? If you ask me, this is hell or at least purgatory."

Don Quixote, who had noticed how closely Sancho was observing all the proceedings, said to him,

"Ah, Sancho my friend, how quickly and at how little cost to yourself might you, if you would, strip to the waist and take your seat among these good souls and by doing so effect Dulcinea's disenchantment, for with the pain and suffering of all these men, you would hardly feel your own. Besides, Merlin the Magician might allow each of these lashes to count as ten towards the total you are to give yourself, since they are being applied with a firm hand."

The admiral was about to inquire about these lashes and Dulcinea's disenchantment, when one of the sailors cried out,

"The lookout on Montjuich has signaled there's a vessel with oars off the coast to the west."

When he heard this, the admiral leapt onto the gangway and shouted,

"Ho, lads, don't let her get away. It must be a brigantine of pirates from Algiers the lookout is signaling us about."

The other three galleys pulled alongside the flagship to receive their orders. The admiral ordered two of them out to sea while he and the remaining one would hug the coast, thereby preventing the vessel from escaping. The convicts stepped up their rowing, propelling the galleys so furiously that they appeared to be flying. The two that had put out to sea, after traveling some two miles, spotted the vessel, which they judged to have upwards of fourteen or fifteen banks of oarsmen, and this later proved to be the case. As soon as the vessel caught sight of the galleys, it took flight, hoping and fully expecting to escape because of its speed, but it miscalculated, for the flagship was among the fastest craft plying the seas. The flagship steadily gained on the brigantine, and the latter's crew could clearly see that escape was impossible, because of which the Moorish commander wanted them to drop their oars and surrender lest they anger our galleys' captain. But fate, which was guiding things along a different course, saw to it that just as the flagship drew close enough for those aboard the other vessel to hear the flagship's crew calling for them to surrender, two *Toraquis*, that is, two Turks – and both drunk – who were among the fourteen men on board, fired their muskets, killing two of our sailors stationed on the gunwales. When the admiral saw this, he swore not to spare the life of a single prisoner, but as he bore down on the vessel, it eluded him by passing beneath the flagship's oars. The galley ran by it some distance and those aboard the brigantine, seeing themselves lost, ran up the sails while the galley was returning, and once again, using both sails and oars, made a run for it. But their diligence did them less good than their audacity did them harm, for once the flagship overtook them after slightly more than half a mile, it grappled onto the brigantine with its oars and took everyone alive. Just then, the other two galleys arrived and all four returned to shore with their prize, where a vast number of people were eagerly waiting to see the booty they had brought. The admiral cast anchor near the spot on the shore where he saw the city's viceroy standing. He had the skiff launched to bring him aboard and ordered the lateen-yard lowered so they could immediately hang the captain and the rest of the Turks he had captured on the brigantine: some three dozen men, all brave souls and most of them Turkish musketeers. The admiral asked who was captain of the brigantine and was informed in Spanish by one of the captives who turned out to be a Spanish renegade:

"Sir, this young man here is our captain."

And he pointed to one of the most handsome, gallant youths anyone could imagine, a lad apparently not yet twenty years of age.

"Tell me, you ill-advised cur," shouted the admiral, "what led you to murder my sailors when you could see the total impossibility of escape? Is that the kind of respect you show flagship captains? Don't you know that foolhardiness is not bravery? Hope, when the outcome is doubtful, should make men bold but not desperate."

The captain was about to respond but the admiral could not wait for his answer at that moment, as he went to receive the viceroy, who was just boarding the galley, together with several of his servants and a group of townspeople.

"Hunting has been good, admiral!" said the viceroy.

"Your grace may judge how good," replied the admiral, "by the trophies you shall soon see hanging from this yardarm."

"How so?" asked the viceroy.

"Because," said the admiral, "they, against every law, right, and custom, killed two of the best sailors on these galleys, and I have sworn to hang every last man I have captured, this young man in particular, who is the brigantine's captain."

Here he indicated the one who already had ropes round his hands and a noose about his neck, waiting to be hanged. When the viceroy looked at him and saw how handsome, gallant, and submissive he was, the youth's good looks immediately served as a letter of recommendation and the viceroy was seized by a desire to spare him.

"Tell me, captain," he said to him, "are you a Turk by birth, a Moor, or a renegade?"

To which the youth responded, and in Castilian no less,

"I am neither a Moor nor a renegade, nor was I born a Turk."

"Then what are you?" asked the viceroy.

"A Christian woman," said the youth.

"A woman and a Christian? - and in this attire and in these circumstances? This is simply too astounding to be believable."

"I beg your graces to suspend my execution," pleaded the youth, "long enough for me to relate the story of my life, which will not greatly delay your vengeance."

Whose heart could be so hard as to fail to be mollified by these words, at least to hear what the grief-stricken young woman wished to relate? The admiral told her to say whatever she would but not to expect a reprieve for her blatant crime. Having been granted this permission, the young lady began the following account:

"I was born of Moorish parents in that nation which is more unfortunate than wise and upon which a sea of woes has recently descended. In the course of my parents' misfortunes I was taken to Barbary by an uncle and aunt of mine over my protests that I was a Christian, which in fact I am, and not one of those phony, public ones but a genuine Catholic. I was wasting my breath in saying that to those charged with our wicked expulsion, and even to my aunt and uncle, who refused to believe it. They all simply considered it a lie and a ruse on my part to remain in the land of my birth. Thus, it was more by coercion than by my own free will that I was taken away by them. My mother was a Christian, my father was wise and Christlike in every regard, and I imbibed the Catholic faith through my mother's milk. I was brought up to have proper manners and neither in my speech nor my behavior did I ever, in my opinion, show the slightest sign of being a *Morisca*. And along with these virtues, which is what I consider them, my beauty, if indeed I possess any, continued to increase, but as great as my caution and seclusion were, they were not great enough to hide me from the eyes of a young gentleman by the name of Don Gaspar Gregorio, eldest son and heir of a gentleman whose estate is next to ours. To explain how he happened to see me, how we managed to speak to one another, how he fell hopelessly in love with me, and how I was able to keep my honor intact, would require more time than this, particularly now that I feel the cord threatening to tighten itself round my neck. I shall merely add that Don Gregorio insisted upon accompanying me in our exile. We mingled with those *Moriscos* who had arrived from other lands because he knew the language quite well, and he struck up a friendship on the journey with the aunt and uncle who had taken me with them. As soon as my wise, farsighted father heard the first proclamation of our banishment, he abandoned the village and went to seek a foreign land that would accept us. He left behind a great many pearls and precious stones he had buried, together with a sum of money in *cruzados*[1] and gold doubloons, and I alone know where he hid them. He forbade me under any circumstances to touch the treasure he

1 ***Cruzado***: an old Castilian coin.

was leaving behind, even if we should be expelled before he returned. I obeyed his order and in the company of this same aunt and uncle, as well as other relatives and neighbors, went to Barbary, settling in the city of Algiers, which was like settling in hell itself. The king was informed of my beauty, and rumor apprized him of my wealth, which in a way was fortunate for me. He summoned me before him and asked which part of Spain I was from and what money and jewels I had brought. I told him the name of the village, adding that there were jewels and money buried there that could easily be reclaimed if I were to return for them myself. I told him all this, fearing he might be blinded by my beauty rather than by his greed.

While we were discussing this, he was informed that one of the most gallant and handsome young men imaginable was traveling with me. I immediately realized they were referring to Don Gaspar Gregorio, whose good looks cannot be exaggerated. I was alarmed when I thought of the risk Don Gregorio faced, for among those barbarous Turks a good-looking boy or young man is more highly prized and esteemed than a woman, regardless of how beautiful she is. The king immediately ordered the young man brought before him and asked me if what they said of him was true; to which, as if instructed by heaven, I replied that it was, but I explained that he was not a man but a woman like myself and I begged him to let me dress 'her' in her normal attire so her beauty might be fully appreciated and she might appear before him with less embarrassment. He gave me his permission to do so, saying that the next day we would discuss the preparations necessary for my return to Spain to retrieve the hidden treasure. I spoke with Don Gaspar and warned him of the risk he ran if he let them see he was a man. I then dressed him as a Moorish woman and that same afternoon presented 'her' to the king, who, upon seeing her, was struck with awe and proposed to keep her and make a present of her to the Grand Turk. But to avoid the risk she might run in his seraglio and to suppress his own temptations, he ordered her placed in the home of some high-ranking Moorish ladies who would watch over and care for her, and Don Gregorio was taken there at once. What the two of us felt – and I cannot deny that I love him – must be left to the imagination of any lovers who have ever been separated. The king arranged for me to return to Spain on this brigantine in the hands of the two native Turks who have murdered these sailors. This Spanish renegade" – and here she pointed to the one who had been the first to speak – "also came with me, and he, I know for a fact, is secretly a Christian and would much prefer to remain in Spain than to return to Barbary. The rest of the brigantine's crew are Moors and Turks who serve no other purpose than to row. The two Turks, both greedy and insolent, failed to follow the plan they had agreed to of setting me and this renegade ashore on the first Spanish soil we came to, dressed in the Christian clothing we had come provided with. They decided, instead, to sweep the coast and engage in plundering, fearing that if they put us ashore at once, we might reveal the presence of their brigantine and they would be captured if there happened to be galleys along this coast. Last night, we came to this beach and, because we were unaware of these four galleys, were discovered and have suffered the fate your graces have seen. To make a long story short, Don Gregorio finds himself surrounded by women, dressed in women's clothing, and manifestly in danger of losing his life, and I am here with my hands tied and fearing, or I should say, desiring death, since I am now weary of living. This, gentlemen, is the end of my lamentable story, as true as it is unfortunate. What I beg of you is that I be allowed to die a Christian, for, as I have said, I have been guilty of none of the things in which those of my race have engaged."

Here she fell silent, her eyes brimming with tears, as were those of everyone present. The viceroy, tenderly, compassionately, and without saying a word, went over to the Moorish woman and removed the cord that bound her beautiful hands. While the Christian *Morisca* had been relating the tale of her wanderings, an elderly pilgrim who had boarded the galley at the same time as the viceroy kept his eyes fixed upon her, and no sooner had the *Morisca* finished speaking than he threw himself at her feet and embraced them, crying out in a voice punctuated by a thousand sobs and sighs,

"O Ana Félix, my poor unfortunate daughter! I am your father, Ricote. I have come back in search of you because I can't live without the person who is my very soul."

At these words, Sancho opened his eyes and raised his head, which he had kept lowered while reflecting upon the disgraceful way he had been passed from hand to hand. When he looked at the pilgrim, he recognized him as the same Ricote he had met on the day he had relinquished his governorship, and he was convinced that she was indeed Ricote's daughter. Once her hands were untied, she embraced her father and mingled her tears with his, at which point, her father said to the admiral and the viceroy,

"This, gentlemen, is my daughter, happier in name than in circumstance, her name being Ana Félix. [2] Ricote is her family name and she is as famed for her beauty as for my wealth. I left my native country to seek some foreign land that would receive us and give us shelter. Finding it in Germany, I returned in this pilgrim's habit in the company of some Germans in order to retrieve my daughter and dig up the many riches I had buried. I failed to find my daughter but did find the treasure, which I have brought with me, and now by the strange circuitous route your graces have witnessed, I have found the greatest treasure of them all, namely, my beloved daughter. If our slight guilt and both her tears and mine can, by appealing to the goodness of your laws, open the gates of mercy, may you employ it with us, for not once did we intend to offend you, nor have we ever shared the objectives of our compatriots who have been justifiably expelled."

At this point, Sancho said,

"I am well acquainted with Ricote and know it's true when he says Ana Félix is his daughter, but as for that other rigamarole about his goings and comings and his good or bad motives I won't commit myself."

All those present were amazed at this strange turn of events, at which point the admiral said,

"Fair Ana Félix, each one of your tears will prevent me from keeping my oath. May your grace enjoy life for as many years as heaven has allotted you, but these insolent, audacious souls who committed this crime shall pay with their lives."

He immediately gave the order to hang from the yardarm both of the Turks who had murdered his two sailors but the viceroy earnestly begged him not to hang them, for theirs had been acts of folly rather than daring. The admiral acceded to the viceroy's request, for vengeance is difficult to carry out once the passions have cooled, and they immediately set to work to devise a plan for rescuing Don Gaspar Gregorio from the perilous situation in which he found himself. For this, Ricote offered

---

2 From Latin ***Felix***: 'happy'.

more than two thousand ducats that he had in pearls and jewels. Several schemes were discussed but none was as good as that suggested by the Spanish renegade we have mentioned, who offered to return to Algiers in a small boat with some half-dozen banks of Christian rowers, since he knew how and where he could land, besides knowing the very house in which Don Gaspar would be found. The admiral and the viceroy had reservations about the renegade's sincerity and whether they should entrust to him the Christians who were to man the oars but Ana Félix vouched for him, and Ricote her father said he would pay the ransom of the Christians if they were taken prisoner.

Once this plan was agreed to, the viceroy went ashore and Don Antonio Moreno took the *Morisca* and her father to his own home. Inasmuch as he had been charged by the viceroy to treat them with the utmost hospitality and kindness, he placed everything in his home at their disposal, such were the benevolence and charity the beautiful Ana Félix had inspired in his breast.

Chapter Sixty-Four

The description of the adventure that caused Don Quixote greater distress than any other that had yet befallen him

Don Antonio Moreno's wife, so says the history, was delighted to have Ana Félix in her home and she gave her a warm reception, being charmed as much by her beauty as by her intelligence, for the *Morisca* excelled equally in both areas; and everyone in the city, as though summoned by the pealing of bells, flocked to see her. Don Quixote complained to Don Antonio that the plan they had agreed upon for freeing Don Gregorio was not a good one because its risks outweighed its advantages; that it would be better to send him, Don Quixote, to Barbary with his horse and armor, where he would rescue Don Gregorio in defiance of the entire Moorish race, exactly as Don Gaiferos had rescued his wife Melisendra.

"Your grace should remember," said Sancho when he heard this, "that the lord Don Gaiferos rescued his wife on dry land and carried her to France on dry land, but in our case, if we succeed in rescuing Don Gregorio, we have no way of bringing him to Spain, since the sea lies in between."

"There is a remedy for everything except death," replied Don Quixote; "as soon as some ship docks there, we shall board it in spite of anyone who tries to stop us."

"The way your grace paints everything," said Sancho, "it all sounds so simple but 'There's many a slip twixt the cup and the lip.' I'll put my money on the renegade, who strikes me as being good-hearted and a man of his word."

Don Antonio replied that, should the renegade not succeed in his attempt, they would opt for the expediency of sending the great Don Quixote to Barbary. Two days later, the renegade put out to sea in a swift boat with six oars to a side, all manned by a crew of unexcelled valor, and two days after that the galleys set out in an easterly direction. The admiral asked the viceroy to keep him informed of everything involving Ana Félix, including the freeing of Don Gregorio, and the viceroy agreed to comply with his wishes in every regard.

One morning, when Don Quixote had gone out for a ride on the beach clad in all his armor – for as he was wont to say, 'Those were his adornments, and battles his means of rest,' and never for a moment was he without them – he saw riding towards him a knight similarly armed from head to foot with a radiant moon painted on his shield. Once this person came close enough to make himself heard, he called out to Don Quixote:

"Illustrious knight and never-sufficiently-extolled Don Quixote of La Mancha, I am the Knight of the White Moon, whose incredible deeds have undoubtedly brought me to your grace's attention. I have come here to do battle with you to test the might of your arm, my object being to make you recognize and acknowledge that my lady, who shall remain nameless, is incomparably more beautiful than your Dulcinea of Toboso. If you openly and tacitly acknowledge this fact, you will avoid your death and will spare me the trouble of having to slay you. But, should you choose to fight and I emerge victorious, I seek no other satisfaction than for you to lay aside your arms, abstain from seeking adventures, and retire to your village for the span of one year where, without laying a hand on your sword, you shall abide in tranquility and beneficial repose, since this is necessary for the betterment of your estate and the salvation of your soul. However, should you defeat me, my life shall be yours to command. My armor and horse shall become your spoils and the glory of my accomplishments shall pass to your grace. Choose whichever you will and give me your answer at once, for I have set aside this entire day for dealing with this matter."

Don Quixote was surprised and shocked, as much by the Knight of the White Moon's arrogance as by the reason he had offered for challenging him, and so with a serene but stern look, he said to him,

"Sir Knight of the White Moon, whose deeds have *not* come to my attention until now, I shall wager that your grace has never seen the illustrious Dulcinea, for if you had, I am convinced you would not make such a claim, for the sight of her would have proven to you that there never has been, nor ever shall be, any beauty comparable to hers. Consequently, without calling you a liar but simply suggesting that you do not know what you are talking about, I shall accept your challenge on the conditions you have set forth – and right at this very moment so that the day you have set aside will not be lost. The only condition I do not accept is the one whereby your glorious deeds pass to me, for I have no idea what they are or what they are like. I shall be content with my own, such as they are. Therefore, choose whichever end of the field you like and I shall take the other, and may Saint Peter bless him whom God favors."

By now, people from the city had learned of the Knight of the White Moon's presence and had reported it to the viceroy, together with the fact that he was conversing with Don Quixote. The viceroy, believing this was some new adventure concocted by Don Antonio Moreno or some gentleman from the city, immediately went down to the strand with Don Antonio and several other gentlemen and arrived just as Don Quixote was spurring Rocinante to pace off as much of the field as necessary. The viceroy, seeing that both men were about to turn and begin their charge, stepped in between them and asked them to explain their reason for suddenly doing battle. The Knight of the White Moon replied that it was a question of whose lady was more beautiful, and he briefly related what he had told Don Quixote, including the conditions both parties had agreed to. The viceroy approached Don

Antonio and asked him in a low voice if he knew who this Knight of the White Moon was and if this was some joke they intended to play on Don Quixote. Don Antonio said he did not know the gentleman nor could he say whether his challenge was genuine or not. This reply left the viceroy in a quandary as to whether to permit the contest to proceed, but finding it hard to believe that it was anything but a joke, he retired from the field and said,

"Sir knights, since it appears that the only options are an admission from Don Quixote or a fight to the death, and since his lord Don Quixote has any number of reasons for not making such an admission and his grace the Knight of the White Moon has just as many of his own, your graces, with God's blessing, may have at it."

The Knight of the White Moon courteously and tactfully thanked the viceroy for granting his permission, as did Don Quixote, who, commending himself to heaven with all his soul as well as to Dulcinea, as was his wont before entering any impending combat, began pacing off a bit more ground when he observed his adversary doing the same. Then without the blare of a single trumpet or instrument of war to signal the beginning of their charge, they both wheeled their mounts about at the same moment. Because the Knight of the White Moon had the fleeter horse, he covered two-thirds of the distance between them, where without touching his adversary with his lance, having obviously hoisted it on purpose, he collided with Don Quixote so violently that he sent him and Rocinante crashing perilously to the ground. The knight at once dismounted and stood over Don Quixote, at which point he poised the lance over his visor and said,

"Consider yourself defeated, sir knight, and even a dead man unless you acknowledge the conditions of our combat."

Don Quixote, battered, dazed, and unable to raise his visor, said in a week, feeble voice, as though speaking from inside a tomb,

"Dulcinea of Toboso is the most beautiful woman in the world and I am the most unfortunate knight on earth, and it is a shame that my feebleness cannot substantiate this truth. Drive home your lance, sir knight, and take away my life, since you have already taken away my honor!"

"*That* I most certainly will not do," said the Knight of the White Moon; "rather, long live, I say, the fame of the lady Dulcinea's beauty in all its fullness! I shall simply be content if the great Don Quixote will retire to his village for a year or until instructed otherwise, as we agreed before entering this contest."

All this was heard by the viceroy and Don Antonio together with the others who were present, and Don Quixote was heard to say that so long as he was not asked to perform any act prejudicial to Dulcinea, he would comply with all the other stipulations as the true and conscientious knight that he was. This acknowledgment having been made, He of the White Moon turned his horse, made obeisance to the viceroy with a nod of his head, and rode back to the city at a canter.

The viceroy ordered Don Antonio to follow him and to find out by any means possible who he was. They helped Don Quixote to his feet and uncovered his face, which they found pale and bathed in perspiration. Rocinante, due to his outright mauling, was still unable to move, and Sancho, who was thoroughly sad and downcast, had no idea what to say or do, for it struck him that this whole affair was simply a dream and that all this tomfoolery was witchcraft pure and simple. He saw his master defeated and forbidden to take up arms for a whole year and he could just see the light of his master's glorious deeds darkened and his own hopes, based upon recent promises, swept away, as smoke is swept away by the wind. He was afraid Rocinante might be left crippled and his master's bones knocked out of joint, which would not be entirely bad if some sense had also been knocked into his head. Finally, Don Quixote was carried to the city on a sedan-chair provided by the viceroy. The latter returned there himself with the fervent desire to learn the identity of the Knight of the White Moon, who had left Don Quixote in such pitiful shape.

Chapter Sixty-Five

The account of the Knight of the White Moon and the freeing of Don Gregorio, together with other matters

Don Antonio followed the Knight of the White Moon, as did a number of boys who not only followed him but pestered him until he was cornered in one of the city's inns, which Don Antonio also entered in his eagerness to learn the knight's identity. A squire came out to welcome the knight and to help him remove his armor, after which he led him to one of the rooms on the ground floor, still being followed by Don Antonio, who was champing at the bit to discover who the knight was. When He of the White Moon noticed the gentleman following him, he said,

"I have no doubt, sir, why your grace has come, and since you are curious to know who I am and there is no reason for me to deny you this, I shall, while my servant is removing my armor, relate my story without omitting a single significant detail. Be advised that I am the bachelor Sansón Carrasco from the same village as Don Quixote of La Mancha, whose hare-brained capers cause all of us who know him to pity him, and I number myself among those who pity him the most. And because I became convinced that his road back to health depended upon returning him to his village, where he might relax in his own house, I came up with a scheme for getting him to return there. Consequently, some three months ago, I took to the road as a knight-errant under the name of the Knight of the Mirrors, intending to engage him in battle and, without harming him, to defeat him. Moreover, I intended to establish as a condition of our battle that the loser was to remain at the disposal of the victor, and what I proposed to demand of him, inasmuch as I considered him already defeated, was that he return to his village and not abandon it for one entire year, during which time he might possibly be cured. But fate arranged things differently, for he defeated me and unseated me from my horse, because of which my plan ended in failure. He returned to his peregrinations and I returned home defeated, humiliated, and injured by my fall, which had been an especially severe one, but I did not for that reason lose my desire to seek him out and defeat him, as you have witnessed today. And since he is absolutely scrupulous about observing the rules of knight-errantry, he will undoubtedly observe the one I have given him and will keep his word. This, sir, is the entire affair in a nutshell and I have nothing more to add. I beg your grace not to reveal my identity nor to divulge to Don Quixote who I am so my good intentions will bear fruit and this gentleman of such enormous intellect will come to his senses and forsake this chivalry nonsense."

"My dear sir," said Don Antonio, "may God forgive your grace for the wrong you are doing the entire world by seeking to restore to his senses the most delightful madman on earth. Do you not see that the good resulting from Don Quixote's cure will never equal the pleasure he imparts through his outrageous behavior? It is my opinion that every ounce of the worthy bachelor's ingenuity will be incapable of returning to his senses a man who is hopelessly mad. If it were not being uncharitable, I would say that Don Quixote should never be cured, for with his recovery we shall lose not only his witty remarks but those of Sancho Panza as well, either of whom is capable of cheering up melancholy itself. Because of all this, I shall seal my lips and say nothing to him to see if he confirms my suspicions that the worthy Carrasco's efforts will come to nought."

The bachelor replied that, inasmuch as this undertaking was proceeding nicely in every regard, he expected a favorable outcome. Don Antonio agreed to comply with all the bachelor's wishes and the latter, who had already strapped his armor onto the back of a mule, said goodbye and, remounting the horse he had ridden into battle, left the city that very day and returned to his home, during which journey he experienced nothing worth relating in this most faithful history. Don Antonio described to the viceroy everything Carrasco had told him, which afforded the viceroy scant joy because Don Quixote's confinement would restrict the enjoyment that might reasonably be expected by all those who had heard of his follies.

For six days, Don Quixote remained in bed, weak, morose, brooding, out of sorts, and endlessly reenacting in his mind the unfortunate adventure that had ended in his defeat. Sancho, in an effort to console him, said (among other things),

"Dear master, you should hold your head high and be of good cheer if you can, and give thanks to heaven that in being knocked to the ground you didn't end up with a broken rib. And since 'One must accept the good with the bad,' and 'Everyone suffers disappointment at some time or other,' you should thumb your nose at the doctors, for they are not needed to cure what your grace is suffering from. Let us go back to our homes and stop this wandering about seeking adventures in places and lands we don't even recognize. Besides, when all is said and done, I am the one who has lost the most, though your grace is the one in the worst shape. I, who have given up all desire to be a governor, have not lost my desire to be a count but this will never come to pass if you fail to become king as a result of abandoning your profession of chivalry; and if that happens, there go my hopes up in smoke."

"Just hush, Sancho," said Don Quixote, "for you know that my withdrawal and seclusion are to last no more than a year, at which time I shall resume my honorable endeavors and there will be no lack of kingdoms for me to conquer or some earldom for me to bestow upon you."

"I hope God is listening and the Devil is not," replied Sancho, "for I've always heard that 'A good hope is better than a bad possession.'"

While they were thus occupied, Don Antonio entered with a look of delight on his face and said,

"Great news, Sir Don Quixote! Don Gregorio and the renegade who went to rescue him have just landed. What do I mean 'landed'? – they are already at Don Antonio's house and will arrive here at any moment."

Don Quixote was somewhat cheered by this and said,

"I must truthfully admit that I would be more pleased if it had turned out just the opposite; then I would have been obliged to travel to Barbary, where by the might of my arm I could have freed not only Don Gregorio but every last Christian captive in that land. But, alas! why am I saying these things? Am I not the one who was defeated? the one who was toppled? Am I not the one who cannot bear arms for an entire year? What good are my promises now? What do I have to boast of, since it will be more seemly for me to ply the spinning-wheel than the sword?"

"That's enough such talk, master," said Sancho, "'Better a hen with the pip than no hen at all!' Besides, 'You win some and lose some.' In this business there's no use trying to make sense of these encounters and pummelings, for a person who falls down today may pick himself up tomorrow, unless he's determined to stay in bed; I mean, unless he loses heart instead of gathering renewed strength for new encounters. Your grace should get up right now and go welcome Don Gregorio, who is probably already in the house, judging by the big to-do I hear everyone making."

And such was the case, for as soon as Don Gregorio and the renegade had given the viceroy an account of their trip there and back, Don Gregorio in his desire to see Ana Félix had gone to Don Antonio's with the renegade. Though Don Antonio had been wearing women's clothes when they brought him from Algiers, he had exchanged them on the boat for the clothes of a captive who had fled with him. But regardless of his attire, he would have readily been taken for a person worthy to be esteemed, served, and envied because he was exceedingly handsome and looked to be seventeen or eighteen years of age. Ricote and his daughter went forth to welcome him: Ricote tearfully and his daughter modestly and shyly, and all those present were particularly taken with Don Gregorio and Ana Félix' handsome appearance. No embraces were exchanged, for where there is true love, displays of familiarity may be dispensed with. It was silence that spoke for the two lovers, while their eyes served as tongues for revealing their joyous and wholesome sentiments. The renegade recounted the ingenious means he had employed in rescuing Don Gregorio, and the latter described the dangers and difficulties in which he had found himself among the women with whom he had resided, and he did this not with a protracted speech but with a few well-chosen words, demonstrating an advanced wisdom for his years. In the end, Ricote paid and liberally compensated the renegade and those who had manned the oars. The renegade was subsequently duly examined and reinstated into the Church, thereby making a rotten limb sound and respectable again through penance and contrition.

Two days later, the viceroy discussed with Don Antonio what might be done to enable Ana Félix and her father to remain in Spain, since they felt there could be no objection if such a Christian daughter and a seemingly well-intentioned father were to remain there. Don Antonio offered to negotiate this in the capital, where he was already headed on other business, explaining that by means of favors and bribes many difficult things could be accomplished at court.

"Nothing can be expected from favors and bribes," said Ricote, who was present during this exchange, "for neither pleas, promises, gifts, nor appeals for sympathy will have any effect on the great Don Bernardino de Velasco, Count of Salazar, to whom His Majesty has entrusted our expulsion. It may be true that he tempers justice with mercy but because he views the body politic of our nation as contaminated and corrupt, he employs the cautery that burns rather than the salve that soothes. And so by prudence, sagacity, diligence, and the fear that he inspires, he on his own strong shoulders has carried the weight of this great enterprise to its logical conclusion, and none of our ingenuity, scheming, pleading, or guile has been able to dazzle this Argus' eyes, which he keeps continually on the alert lest one of us remain behind or escape his notice to sprout forth with the passing of time like a hidden root bearing poisonous fruit in a Spain finally purified and freed from the fear in which our vast numbers held her. What a heroic solution by the great Phillip the Third, and what unheard-of prudence to entrust it to the said Bernardino de Velasco!"

"All the same," said Don Antonio, "once I am at court, I shall do everything in my power, and heaven may do whatever *it* deems most fitting. Don Gregorio shall accompany me and console his parents for the anxiety his absence will have caused them. Ana Félix shall stay with my wife in our home or in a convent, and I feel certain his lordship the viceroy will be pleased to have the good Ricote reside with him until we see how my negotiations turn out."

The viceroy agreed to everything that was proposed but Don Gregorio, aware of what was transpiring, said that under no circumstances could he, or would he, abandon Doña Ana Félix. But since he had his heart set on seeing his parents, together with devising some way to return for her, he agreed to the proposed plan and Ana Félix stayed with Don Antonio's wife and Ricote in the home of the viceroy.

The day of Don Antonio's departure arrived, as did that of Don Quixote and Sancho's two days later, for the knight's fall would not permit him to take to the road any sooner. Don Gregorio's leave-taking of Ana Félix was accompanied by all manner of tears, sobs, swoons, and sighs. Ricote offered Don Gregorio a thousand *escudos* but he would accept only five – and these he *borrowed* from Don Antonio, promising to repay them at the court. With this, as we have said, the two of them departed, as did Don Quixote and Sancho a short time later: Don Quixote not in his armor but in traveling clothes and unarmed, and Sancho Panza on foot, because the dapple was carrying the armor.

Chapter Sixty-Six

An account of what will be seen by him who reads this or heard by him who has it read to him

As they left Barcelona, Don Quixote turned to view the spot where he had fallen and he said, "Here is where Troy stood! Here is where my ill fortune – not my cowardice – deprived me of my hard-won glory; where Fate mischievously wrought her fickleness against me; where my deeds were eclipsed; and, lastly, where my happiness fell, never to rise again!"

When Sancho heard this, he said,

"Dear master, stout hearts should exhibit fortitude in adversity as well as joy in prosperity. I base this upon my own experience, for if I was happy when I was governor, I am not unhappy now that I'm a squire and am traveling on foot. I've heard it said that this thing called Fortune is a woman who is besotted, capricious, and above all blind, for which reason she can't see what it is she's doing or who it is she's raising up or knocking down."

"You are waxing most philosophical, Sancho," said Don Quixote, "and are saying some very wise things. I cannot imagine who is teaching you all this. What I can tell you is that there is no such thing on earth as fate, nor do occurrences here, whether good or bad, happen by chance but by the special providence of heaven, whence comes the saying that 'Each person is the forger of his own destiny.' I have been the forger of mine but not with the necessary prudence, and consequently all my presumptions have ended in one disaster after another. I should have guessed that Rocinante's decrepitude could not withstand the awesome might of the Knight of the White Moon's steed. Nevertheless, I accepted the challenge and did everything in my power. I was toppled from my horse and, though humiliated, did not forfeit my honor by failing to keep my promise. When I was a bold and valiant knight, I backed up my intentions with my hands and my actions, but now that I am a lackluster squire, I shall validate my words by keeping the promise I have made. So start walking, dear friend, and let us keep the year of the novitiate in our own land, for by means of this confinement we shall gain renewed strength to return to the exercise of arms, which shall never be forsaken by me."

"Master," said Sancho, "traveling on foot is not such a pleasurable activity that it makes or encourages me to want to go on long journeys. Let's hang up your grace's armor on some tree and leave it there as a substitute for a hanged man, for once I'm seated on the dapple's back with my feet swinging in the air, we can take as many trips as your grace wishes, however long they may be. But if you think I'm going to take long trips on foot, you've got another thought coming."

"An excellent idea, Sancho," said Don Quixote; "let us hang up my armor as a trophy and beneath or around it we shall carve on the trees what was inscribed on the trophy of Orlando's armor:

> Let none these arms remove,
> Save him who dares Orlando's might to prove."

"That suits me just fine," replied Sancho, "and if it weren't for the lack Rocinante's absence would cause us on the road, it would be appropriate to leave him hanging there too."

"Well," said Don Quixote, "neither he nor the armor is going to be hung up lest people say this is how I reward noble service!"

"Your grace is absolutely right," said Sancho, "for in the opinion of the wise, 'One shouldn't blame the packsaddle for the shortcomings of the ass,' and since your grace is to blame for this situation, you should chastise yourself and not vent your anger on your battered and bloody armor, or on Rocinante's meekness, or on my tender feet, which you seem determined to make travel more than is reasonable."

They spent the entire day and the next four as well discussing these and other matters, during which time nothing occurred that might interfere with their journey, but on the sixth day, as they were entering a village, they came across a number of people at the door of an inn who, because it was a holiday, had gathered there to enjoy themselves. As Don Quixote approached, one of the laborers cried out,

"Here come two gentlemen who are not acquainted with the parties involved, so one of them can decide what should be done about our wager."

"I shall be glad to decide it and with complete fairness," said Don Quixote, "if I manage to understand the problem."

"Well, here is the situation, good sir," said the laborer: "a man from this village is so fat he weighs two hundred seventy-five pounds and he has challenged to a foot race a neighbor of his who weighs no more than a hundred twenty-five pounds. The terms say they're to run a hundred paces bearing the same total weight. When the neighbor asked the challenger how the weights might be made equal, he answered that the challenged man, who weighs a hundred twenty-five pounds, should carry a hundred fifty pounds of iron on his back, by means of which the weight of the lighter man will equal that of the fat one."

"Not so fast!" said Sancho at this point before Don Quixote could respond; "it is my job to decide these questions and to pass judgement in all such legal disputes, for it was only a few days ago that I gave up my position as governor and judge, as everyone knows."

"Sancho my friend," said Don Quixote, "you may respond with my blessing, for I am so upset and my mind is so confused I am not fit to feed a cat."

Having received permission, Sancho addressed the numerous laborers gathered round him who were standing there with their mouths open as they waited for the pronouncement from his own:

"My brothers, what the fat man is asking is unreasonable and lacks even a hint of fairness, for if what they say is true – that the person challenged may choose the weapons – it is stupid for him to choose ones that will prevent or keep him from being victorious. So it is my judgement that the fat man – the challenger – should prune, pare, peel, shear, crop, and lop off a hundred fifty pounds of flesh from any part of his body that he prefers or thinks best. In this way, by reducing his weight to a hundred twenty-five pounds, he will be equal to his opponent's weight and they can thus run an even race."

"By heavens!" said one of the laborers who heard Sancho's pronouncement, "this gentleman has spoken like a saint and passed judgement like a canon, but you can be certain the fat man will be reluctant to part with an ounce of his flesh, let alone a hundred and fifty pounds!"

"The best thing is for them not to race at all," said another, "so the small man won't be worn out carrying the weight or the fat man won't be stripped of his flesh. Let us spend half the wager on wine and take these gentlemen to a tavern where they serve some of the very best, and if there are problems, you may hold me responsible."

"I am most grateful to you gentlemen," said Don Quixote, "but I cannot stop even for an instant. Such an apparent lack of courtesy on my part stems from melancholic thoughts and circumstances that force me to travel at this less than leisurely pace."

And here, he spurred Rocinante and rode on ahead, leaving everyone astonished who had viewed his strange appearance and observed the wisdom of his servant, which is what they took Sancho to be. One of the other laborers then said,

"If the servant is this wise, what must the master be like! I'll bet that if they go to Salamanca to study, they'll be court bailiffs in a trice. After all, there's nothing to it except study and more study, plus having influential friends and good luck; then when one least expects it, he'll find himself with a staff in his hand and a miter on his head."

That night was spent by master and servant in the middle of a field under the stars. The next morning, when they resumed their journey, they saw a man walking towards them with a knapsack round his neck and a javelin or pike in his hand – the very picture of a foot-courier. As he drew near Don Quixote, he quickened his pace and, half running, went up to the knight and embraced him by the right thigh, being unable to reach any higher. Then with obvious delight he said to him,

"Oh, my lord Don Quixote of La Mancha, how greatly my master the duke's heart will rejoice when he learns that your grace is returning to his castle, which is where he and my mistress the duchess are staying!"

"I do not recognize you, my friend," replied Don Quixote, "and shall never know who you are unless you tell me."

"I, Sir Don Quixote," said the courier, "am Tosilos, lackey to my master the duke, the one who refused to fight your grace for the hand of Doña Rodríguez' daughter."

"Bless my soul!" said Don Quixote, "can you possibly be the one whom my enemies, the enchanters, transformed into that lackey you claim to be, to rob me of the honor of that battle?"

"Don't say that, good sir," said the messenger; "there was no enchantment whatever, nor was anyone's appearance changed. I was the same lackey entering the lists that I was coming out. I hoped to marry the girl without fighting, having been quite taken with her looks, but my hopes turned out just the opposite, for no sooner did your grace leave our castle than the duke had me soundly beaten with a rod for disobeying the orders he had given me before I entered the contest. The result of all this is that the girl is now a nun, Doña Rodríguez has gone back to Castile, and I'm on my way to Barcelona to give the viceroy a packet of letters my master is sending him. If you would like a drink of some pure but warm wine, I've got a gourd here filled with the best there is, along with I-don't-know-how-many slices of Tronchón cheese that will serve to arouse and awaken your grace's thirst if it should happen to be sleeping."

"I accept that invitation," said Sancho, "and we can dispense with the rest of the formalities. Let the worthy Tosilos start pouring and all the enchanters in the Indies can go to blazes."

"Without a doubt, Sancho," said Don Quixote, "you are the biggest glutton in the entire world and the most ignorant man on earth if you are still not convinced that this courier is enchanted and this Tosilos a fake. You stay here with him and gorge yourself. I shall ride on ahead at a leisurely pace and you can catch up with me."

After enjoying a hearty laugh, the lackey uncorked his gourd and took the cheese from his knapsack, together with what remained of a loaf of bread. He and Sancho then seated themselves on the grass where they peacefully and sociably dispatched and consumed the contents of the knapsack, and with such hearty appetites that they even licked the letters, since these smelled of cheese. At this point, Tosilos said to Sancho,

"Without a doubt, Sancho my friend, that master of yours is not playing with a full deck."

"What do you mean: 'not playing with a full deck?' His deck is as full as the next person's, and if follies were cards, his deck would be overflowing. I myself can see all this quite clearly but when I tell *him* so, it does no good whatsoever, especially now that he's sunk into the deepest depression from having been vanquished by the Knight of the White Moon?"

Tosilos asked him to describe what had befallen Don Quixote but Sancho said it would be impolite to keep his master waiting; however, should they chance to meet again, there would be time enough to do so. At this point, Sancho stood up and, brushing the dust from his jacket and the crumbs from his whiskers, said goodbye to him. Then tugging at his jackass, he left Tosilos and caught up with his master, who was waiting for him in the shade of a tree.

Chapter Sixty-Seven

Don Quixote's resolve to become a shepherd and to follow the pastoral life during the year of his promised confinement, together with other truly delightful incidents

If Don Quixote was plagued by a number of thoughts *before* being toppled from his horse, he was plagued by even more after his fall, and so, while waiting in the shade of a tree, as we said, his thoughts like flies round honey kept swarming about him and stinging him: some having to do with the disenchanting of Dulcinea and others with the life he was to lead during his forced retirement. Sancho caught up with him and began to praise the generous nature of the lackey Tosilos.

"Alas, Sancho," said Don Quixote, "is it possible that you still believe this individual is an actual lackey? You seem to forget that you have seen Dulcinea changed and transformed into a farm girl and the Knight of the Mirrors into the bachelor Carrasco, both the works of those enchanters who persecute me. But tell me: did you ask that person you call Tosilos how God has dealt with Altisidora? Has she wept over my absence or already cast from her mind those thoughts of love that tormented her so in my presence?"

"My thoughts," replied Sancho, "were not such that I had occasion to ask foolish questions. My goodness, master, is your grace presently in any condition to inquire into the thoughts of others, particularly amorous ones?"

"Look, Sancho," said Don Quixote, "there is a wide gulf between deeds performed in the name of love and those of gratitude. There may be a knight somewhere who is not in love but I can state with absolute certainty that there cannot be one who is ungrateful. Altisidora was apparently in love with me because she gave me three nightcaps, wept at my departure, and with shameless disregard publicly cursed, criticized, and called me names, all signs that she actually adored me, for anger between lovers often ends in name-calling. I could not promise her hope or grant her treasures, for those few I have are pledged to Dulcinea, and any treasures that knights possess are, like those of fairies, illusory and unreal. All I can grant Altisidora are my memories of her, that is, without adversely affecting those I have of Dulcinea, whom you are doing a grave injustice by your delay in scourging yourself and chastising that flesh of yours, which would rather preserve itself for the worms than to rescue my poor lady – and the wolves can devour it for all I care!"

"Master," said Sancho, "if the truth be told, I can't convince myself that flogging my backside can possibly disenchant a person under a spell. Why, that's like saying, 'If your head hurts, rub some salve on your knee.' At least, I'm willing to bet that in all the histories your grace has read dealing with knight-errantry you have never seen a single soul disenchanted by flogging. But be that as it may, I'll give myself a few lashes when the mood strikes me and I'm able to chastise myself in comfort."

"May God grant that," replied Don Quixote, "and may heaven grant you the grace to realize your obligation to aid my lady, who is yours as well, since you are my squire."

As they were traveling along discussing these topics, they came to the exact spot where they had been trampled by the bulls. When Don Quixote recognized it, he said to Sancho,

"This is the meadow where we came across the elegant shepherdesses and gallant shepherds who were intent upon reviving and re-enacting a pastoral Arcadia, a proposal as novel as it is clever. If such a re-creation appeals to you, Sancho, I would have us convert ourselves into shepherds, if only during the time of my confinement. I shall buy some sheep and everything else necessary to the pastoral avocation. Calling myself the shepherd Quixotiz and you the shepherd Pancino, we shall roam the hills, forests, and glades singing, intoning dirges, and quaffing the crystalline liquids of the springs, limpid streams, and bounteous rivers. The oaks will provide us the sweet fruits from their abundant stores, the trunks of the hard cork trees a seat, the willows shade, the roses perfume, the broad meadows carpets dyed a thousand colors, the clean, clear atmosphere air to breathe, the moon and stars light to overcome the night's darkness, the act of singing pleasure, that of weeping joy, Apollo verses, and love conceits, whereby we shall gain fame and immortality not only in the present age but in those to come."

"By heavens," said Sancho, "that sort of life suits me to a T or even some other letter. What's more, the bachelor Sansón Carrasco and Master Nicolás will no sooner see all this than they will want to follow along and become shepherds like us but, God willing, the priest won't take it into his head to join the sheepfold too, he's such a jolly, fun-loving fellow."

"You are absolutely right," replied Don Quixote, "and if the bachelor joins the pastoral brotherhood, as he is certain to do, he is free to call himself the shepherd Sansonino or Carrascón, and Nicolás the barber may call himself Miculoso, just as old Boscán called himself Nemoroso. I don't know what name to assign the priest, unless it is a name derived from his office, such as the shepherd Curiambro. [1] And we shall be able to pick, as one does pears, the names of the shepherdesses who will be our lovers. But since that of my lady is as fitting for a shepherdess as for a princess, there will be no need to trouble myself looking for one that will suit her better. You, Sancho, may assign your lady any name you please."

"I don't intend to assign her any but Teresona," [2] said Sancho, "which will go well with her ampleness and her own name Teresa. Moreover, when I celebrate her in my verses, I can reveal my

1 Derived from ***cura,*** the Spanish word for 'priest'.

2 The ***ona*** suffix of Teresona connotes large size.

honorable desires, since I'm not one to go looking for greener pastures. It'll be best for the priest not to have a shepherdess in order to set a good example; however, if the bachelor wants one, his life is his own business."

"Bless my soul!" said Don Quixote, "what a life we shall lead, Sancho my friend! How our ears will be regaled by the delightful music of flutes, Zamoran bagpipes, tabors, timbrels, and fiddles! And how wonderful the *albogues* will sound with these different types of music! Virtually every pastoral instrument will be present."

"What are *albogues*?" asked Sancho; "that is something I've never heard of or seen in my entire life."

"*Albogues*," said Don Quixote, "are clappers in the shape of brass candlesticks, and when struck together on their hollow or concave sides, they produce a sound which, though not very mellifluous or harmonious, is not unpleasing and goes well with the rustic nature of the bagpipe and tabor. This word *albogue* is Moorish, as are all those in our language that begin with *al*, such as albacore, algebra, Alhambra, alcohol, alfalfa, albatross, and alchemy, together with a few others of this sort. There are only three in our language that are Moorish and also end in *í*, these being *borceguí*, *zaquizamí*, and *maravedí*.[3] *Alhelí* and *alfaquí*,[4] by their initial *al* and their final *í*, show that they are Arabic. I simply mention this in passing, having been reminded of it when I used the word *albogues*. We shall be assisted in this venture by the fact that I am a poet of sorts, as you know, and the bachelor Sansón Carrasco is also one, and a consummate one at that. I shall not comment on the priest but would wager that he has a touch of the poet in him, and I have no doubt that Master Nicolás has, for most if not all barbers are guitar players and ballad singers. I shall lament my separation; you may sing your praises as the constant lover; the shepherd Carrascón may lament the fact that he has been spurned; and the priest Curiambro may do whatever he pleases. In this way everything will proceed as planned and will leave nothing to be desired."

To which Sancho responded,

"I, master, am so unlucky that I'm afraid the day will never come when I see myself part of such a venture. Ah, but once I'm a shepherd, what polished spoons I'll make and what great fried bread crumbs and whipped cream, along with garlands and pastoral knickknacks! These may not win me the reputation of being wise but they can't fail to win me one of being clever. My daughter Sanchica will bring our meals to the sheepfold – but hold on! she's nice looking and some of those shepherds are more malicious than innocent. I wouldn't want her 'to go looking for wool but come home shorn.' And since lovemaking and unwholesome desires are as common in the country as in the city, and in shepherds' huts as in royal palaces, I say, 'Take away the opportunity and mischief-making will take care of itself,' for 'If the eyes see not, the heart suffers not,' and 'Fleeing from danger is worth more than pleading with one's assailant.'"

"No more proverbs, Sancho," said Don Quixote, "for any one of those you have mentioned will

---

3 ***Borceguí***: 'high shoe'; ***zaquizamí***: 'garret'; and ***maravedí***: a Spanish coin of varying value.

4 '***Alhelí***: 'gilleyflower', and ***alfaquí***: 'an expounder of the Koran.'

suffice to express what you are thinking. How many times must I tell you not to be so extravagant with your sayings but to exercise a little restraint in citing them? Trying to teach you anything is like 'preaching in the wilderness' or 'pouring water on a duck's back.'"

"It strikes me," said Sancho, "that your grace is like the proverbial pot that called the kettle black. You are forever criticizing me for using proverbs and you then unload them yourself two at a time."

"Listen, Sancho," said Don Quixote, "I bring in proverbs that are appropriate, and when I cite them, they fit like the ring on your finger, but you drag them in by the hair of the head and leave them to fend for themselves. If my memory is correct, I have explained to you on several occasions that sayings or proverbs are short maxims drawn from experience and observation by our learned forefathers, but a proverb that is inappropriately used is nonsense rather than a maxim. However, since night is approaching, let us drop the subject and find a place off the highway where we can spend the night, for God alone knows what tomorrow will bring."

After retiring to a secluded spot, they dined belatedly and badly, very much to the disappointment of Sancho, who had visions of those hardships encountered by knights-errant in the hills and forests, though abundance did manifest itself in castles and homes, as in the case of Don Diego de Miranda, Don Antonio Moreno, and the wedding of the wealthy Camacho. But since Sancho felt that neither day nor night could last forever, he spent the night sleeping, whereas his master spent it wide awake.

Chapter Sixty-Eight

The porcine adventure that befell Don Quixote

The night was rather dark despite the fact that the moon was in the sky, for it occupied a part of it that was not visible, because from time to time the lady Diana pays a visit to the antipodes, thereby leaving the hills in darkness and the valleys in shadows. Don Quixote succumbed to the requirements of nature by sleeping the first few hours of the night but was unable to fall asleep a second time – just the opposite of Sancho, who was unable to fall asleep a second time because his first sleep lasted all night long. Herein he displayed his placid constitution and virtual lack of worries. Don Quixote's worries, however, kept him so wide awake that he roused Sancho and said to him,

"I am astounded, Sancho, at your carefree disposition. I have to believe you are made of marble or hardened bronze and have no room in that body of yours for any sort of feelings or emotions. I lie awake while you sleep; I weep while you sing; I swoon from fasting while you lie there listless and lethargic from stuffing yourself. Faithful servants should help bear their masters' suffering and share in their sorrows if only for the sake of appearance. Note the calmness of the night and the solitude of this place, both of which are inviting us to interrupt our sleep with some sort of vigil, so get up for heaven's sake and go off to some nearby place where daringly and courageously you can oblige me by giving yourself three or four hundred lashes as payment towards Dulcinea's disenchantment, which is what I beg and implore of you. However, I have no desire to come to blows with you again, knowing as I do how handy you are with your fists. Once you have finished, we shall spend the remainder of the night baring our hearts in song: I of my absence and you of your constancy, whereby we shall embark upon the pastoral life we are to lead in our village."

"Master," replied Sancho, "I am not some ecclesiastic who can rise in the middle of his sleep and scourge himself, and I'm even less convinced that one can go from the painful extreme of scourging to the opposite one of singing. Your grace should let me sleep and not press me with this business of flogging myself or I'll be forced to take an oath never to touch a hair on my jacket, let alone one on my body."

"Oh, what a hardened soul! What a compassionless squire! How ill-bestowed and ill-received are the bread and other favors I have given you and intend to give you in the future! Thanks to me you have seen yourself a governor, and because of me you have hopes of becoming a count at any moment or of acquiring some other equivalent title whose fulfillment will take no longer than it takes this year to pass, for *post tenebras spero lucem*."[1]

"Whatever that means," said Sancho; "all I know is that while I'm sleeping, I have no fears, hopes, travails, or joys. Praised be the person who invented sleep – the mantle that shrouds every human thought, the food that banishes hunger, the drink that quenches thirst, the fire that brings warmth, the coolness that tempers ardor, the common coin that allows things to be bought and sold, and lastly, the weight and balance that make the shepherd equal to the king, and the fool equal to the wise man. There is only one drawback to sleep according to what I've heard: the fact that it resembles death in that there is very little difference between a person who is sleeping and one who is dead."

"Sancho," said Don Quixote, "never have I heard you speak with such eloquence before. Because of this, I must admit the truthfulness of the proverb you are always quoting: 'It's not who you are that matters but whose company you keep.'"

"Plague take it, master," replied Sancho, "I'm not the one who's now spewing forth proverbs; they're also spilling from your grace's mouth faster than from mine – and in droves! But there's probably this difference between yours and mine: yours come out at the right time and mine don't, but they're all proverbs just the same."

While they were engaged in this discussion, they suddenly heard a harsh, deafening roar that resounded throughout the surrounding valleys. Don Quixote sprang to his feet and placed his hand on his sword. Sancho crouched beneath the dapple, placing the stack of armor on one side and the packsaddle on the other, for he was as much shaken by fear as Don Quixote was excited. The noise gradually became louder as it drew nearer the frightened pair – at least one was frightened, for the other's valor was well known. It turned out that several men were driving more than six hundred hogs to be sold at a fair and were on their way even at this early hour. The noise they created was so loud, what with all the snorting and grunting, that it deafened the ears of Don Quixote and Sancho, who had no idea what it could possibly be. The grunting herd, which was spread over a wide area, arrived in

1 Latin: "after the darkness I expect the light' (from Job 17:12 in the Vulgate Bible). This was also the motto of the printer Juan de la Cuesta, who brought out the first edition of *Don Quixote* in 1605 (Part I) and 1615 (Part II).

a mad rush and with total disregard for Don Quixote and Sancho's dignity trampled them beneath their hooves, demolishing Sancho's defenses and not only knocking down Don Quixote but dragging along Rocinante for good measure. The massive herd, their grunting, and the speed with which the filthy animals had arrived created pandemonium, leaving the packsaddle and armor strewn across the field, together with the dapple, Rocinante, Sancho, and Don Quixote. Sancho struggled to his feet and asked his master for his sword, saying he would like to slay half a dozen of those gentlemen and their disrespectful hogs, for he had finally recognized what they were. Don Quixote said to him,

"Let them go, my friend; this affront is punishment for my sin, for it is only just that heaven should chastise a vanquished knight-errant by having him devoured by wolves, stung by wasps, and trampled by hogs."

To which Sancho responded,

"Then heaven must also be in the habit of chastising the squires of you defeated knights by having us stung by flies, bitten by lice, and ravaged by hunger. If we squires were sons of the knights we serve or were close relatives of theirs, it wouldn't be surprising for their sins to spill over onto us down to the fourth generation but what do Panzas have to do with Quixotes? Oh well, let's lie down again and get some sleep in what little remains of the night, for 'God will bring the dawn and we shall prosper.'"

"You go and sleep, Sancho," said Don Quixote, "for you were born to sleep. I, who was born to stay awake, shall in the interval between now and dawn give free rein to my thoughts by venting them in a little madrigal which, unknown to you, I composed in my head last night."

"It strikes me," said Sancho, "that thoughts that give rise to the composition of verses can't be very gloomy ones. Your grace is welcome to versify as much as you like but I'm going to get as much sleep as I can."

Then appropriating all the ground he needed, Sancho huddled up and fell fast asleep, undisturbed by finances, debts, or any other sort of worry. Don Quixote, leaning against the trunk of a beech or cork tree (Cide Hamete Benengeli does not specify which type it was) sang the following song to the accompaniment of his own sighs:

"O love, when, sick of heartfelt grief,
I sigh and drag thy cruel chain,
To death I fly, the sure relief
Of those who groan in lingering pain.

"But, coming to the fatal gates,
The port in this my sea of woe,
The joy I feel now life creates,
And bids my spirits brisker flow.

"Thus, dying every hour I live,
And living I resign my breath:

Strange power of love, that thus can give
A dying life and living death!"

Each of these verses was accompanied by a great deal of sighing and no little weeping, exactly like one whose heart had been pierced to the core by his painful defeat and Dulcinea's absence. In the meantime, dawn had arrived and the sun directed its rays at the eyes of Sancho, who awoke and shook off his drowsiness by stretching and shaking his sluggish limbs. After viewing the havoc the hogs had wrought upon his provisions, he cursed the herd and certain other persons besides. At length, the pair resumed their journey and late that afternoon saw coming towards them as many as ten men on horseback and four or five on foot. Don Quixote's heart began to beat faster and Sancho's to skip a beat, for the persons approaching carried lances and shields and were fully prepared for battle. Don Quixote turned to Sancho and said,

"If I could resort to my arms, Sancho, and my hands were not shackled by my promise, I would consider this onslaught about to descend upon us as nothing but peaches and cream but it may turn out to be something other than what we fear."

Just then, the men on horseback rode up with their lances raised and their lips sealed and proceeded to surround Don Quixote while pointing their lances at his back and chest in a menacing manner. One of those on foot placed a finger to his lips as a sign that Don Quixote was to remain silent, while he seized Rocinante's bridle and lead him from the highway. Those on foot drove Sancho and the dapple before them, maintaining an eerie silence as they followed in the footsteps of the one leading Don Quixote. The latter attempted two or three times to ask where they were taking him and what their intentions were but no sooner would he open his mouth than they threatened to close it with the tips of their lances. The same occurred to Sancho, for the instant he showed signs of wishing to speak, one of those on foot would poke him with a goad and even did the same thing to the dapple, as though he had something he wished to say. Night arrived, the pace was accelerated, and the two prisoners' dread increased, particularly when they heard the names the men called them from time to time:

"Move along, you *anchorites*!"

"Keep quiet, you *barbarians*!"

"Now you'll pay, you *cannibals*!"

"No complaining, you *Scythians*! Don't even open your eyes, you murderous Polyphemuses and blood-thirsty lions!" together with other similar epithets with which they tormented the ears of the wretched master and servant. Sancho rode along saying to himself: 'Who are you calling *Ammorites*? We're not *Bulgarians* or *animals*, and we're certainly not *sissies*! Those names don't sit well with me at all! It's an ill wind that's blowing this grain. All these woes have descended upon us at one fell swoop but, God willing, everything that this ill-ventured adventure is threatening us with has already occurred."

Don Quixote rode along spellbound, unable to determine, despite racking his brain, what those scurrilous epithets could portend, from which he concluded that nothing good was to be expected but much ill to be feared. Finally, about an hour past sundown, they came to a castle, which Don Quixote clearly recognized as the duke's, where they had been guests a short time before.

"Good heavens!" he said when he recognized the mansion, "what can this mean? This house is undoubtedly the height of courtesy and graciousness but for those of us who have been defeated things are going from bad to worse."

They entered the castle's main courtyard, which was decorated and furnished in a manner that added to their astonishment and redoubled their fears, as we shall see in the following chapter.

Chapter Sixty-Nine

The strangest and most novel adventure to befall Don Quixote in the entire course of this great history

The men on horseback dismounted and with the help of those on foot bodily picked up Sancho and Don Quixote and whisked them into a courtyard that was encircled by a hundred blazing torches in their holders, together with more than five hundred lamps lining the galleries of the courtyard, all burning so brightly that despite the rather dark night the absence of daylight went unnoticed. In the middle of the courtyard was a bier rising some six feet above the ground and completely covered by an enormous canopy of black velvet, round the tiered sides of which blazed white wax candles in more than a hundred silver candelabra. Atop the bier reposed the corpse of such a beautiful young woman that her beauty made death itself appear beautiful. Her head, which rested on a brocade pillow, was crowned with a garland of fragrant flowers and her hands were folded across her bosom clutching a yellow palm frond in triumph. At one side of the courtyard a stage had been erected on which two individuals were seated who because of their crowns and scepters appeared to be kings, either real or feigned. Situated on one side of the stage at the head of some steps were two additional seats on which Don Quixote and Sancho were forced to sit by those who had brought them there as captives – and all this in absolute silence, for both of them had been given to understand by means of gestures that they too were to remain silent, though they would have complied without being so instructed, for their astonishment at what they were seeing had tied their tongues in knots. Just then, there mounted the stage, in the company of a sizeable retinue, two prominent personages whom Don Quixote immediately recognized as the duke and duchess, his hosts. They took their seats on two ornate chairs next to the pair who appeared to be kings. What person could fail to be astounded at all this, Don Quixote in particular, inasmuch as he had recognized the corpse on the bier as that of the beautiful Altisidora? When the duke and duchess mounted the stage, Don Quixote and Sancho rose and bowed low to them, and the ducal pair returned the honor with a slight nod of the head.

At that moment, an official crossed the stage and went up to Sancho, over whose shoulders he placed a robe of black buckram decorated from top to bottom with fiery flames. Removing Sancho's cap, he placed a cone-shaped hat on his head similar to those the Holy Office forces penitents to wear, whispering into Sancho's ear that unless he kept his lips sealed, he would be gagged or even put to death. Sancho inspected his outfit from head to foot and found himself ablaze with flames, but because he was not being burned, he never gave them a second thought. After removing his penitent's hat and finding it covered with devils, he replaced it on his head and said to himself, 'Everything is all right so long as the flames don't burn me and the devils don't carry me off.' Don Quixote glanced at Sancho, and though fear had paralyzed his senses, he could not keep from chuckling at his appearance. Just then, there began to arise, apparently from beneath the bier, the soft, pleasing sound of flutes, which had a soothing, ingratiating effect due to their not having to compete with a single human voice, for here even silence maintained silence over itself. Suddenly, beside the pillow of the presumed cadaver appeared a handsome youth in Roman dress, who to the accompaniment of a harp, which he himself played, sang the following two stanzas in a clear, velvety voice:

"Till heaven in pity to the weeping world,
Shall give Altisidora back to day,
By Quixote's scorn to realms of Pluto hurled,
Her every charm to cruel death a prey;
While duennas throw their gorgeous robes away,
To mourn a nymph by cold disdain betrayed;
To the complaining lyre's enchanting lay,
I'll sing the praises of this hapless maid
In sweeter notes than Thracian Orpheus ever played.

"Nor shall my numbers with my life expire,
Or this world's light confine the boundless song:
To thee, bright maid, in death I'll touch the lyre,
And to my soul the theme shall still belong.
When, freed from clay, the flitting ghosts among,
My spirit glides the Stygian shores around,
Though the cold hand of death has sealed my tongue,
Thy praise th'infernal caverns shall rebound,
And Lethe's sluggish waves move slower to the sound."

"No more," interjected one of the two would-be kings; "no more, divine singer! It would be an endless task to recount here the death and charms of the peerless Altisidora, who is not dead, as the uninformed believe, but still lives by virtue of the voice of fame and the penance that Sancho here in our midst is to undergo to restore her to the light of this world. Therefore, O Radamanthus, who sit in judgement with me in the gloomy caverns of Dis, because you know everything the inscrutable fates have decreed for restoring this damsel to her former state, speak and declare it at once so the happiness we look forward to through her transformation shall not be delayed."

No sooner was this said by Minos, fellow judge of Radamanthus, than Radamanthus himself rose from his seat and said,

"I say, all you household ministers, high and low, great and small, step forward one at a time and mark the face of Sancho with a couple of dozen slaps, his arms with a dozen pinches, and his thighs with half a dozen pin-pricks, for upon this ceremony does Altisidora's well-being depend!"

When Sancho Panza heard this, he broke his silence and said,

"I swear to goodness, I'd sooner become a Moor than let someone slap me or lay a hand on my face! Bless my soul, what does fiddling with my face have to do with the resurrection of this damsel? 'Give a person an inch and he'll take a mile!' They enchanted Dulcinea and now they want to flog me to break her spell. Altisidora dies from some illness God chose to give her and they want to bring her back to life by slapping my face, jabbing my body with pins, and pinching my arms till they're black and blue. Well, you can play your tricks on someone else because this old dog wasn't born yesterday!"

"Then you shall die," cried Radamanthus in a loud voice; "relent, you tiger! show some humility, you haughty Nimrod, and accept your suffering without complaining. You are not being asked to do the impossible, so don't start making this ordeal more rigorous than it is. Slapped you shall be, pricked you shall find yourself, and mightily shall you howl from the pinches! I say there, ministers, do as I have commanded or upon the word of an honest man you shall see why you were brought into this world!"

At that instant, as many as half a dozen duennas came marching into the courtyard in single file, four of whom wore spectacles and all of whom kept their right hands raised, thereby exposing some four inches of wrist to make their hands appear longer in keeping with the current fashion. Sancho had no sooner seen them than he began bellowing like a bull, saying,

"I may let people lay their hands on me but let myself be touched by duennas – never! Let cats scratch my face as they did my master's in this very castle, or let my body be pierced by the points of sharp daggers, or the flesh be torn from my arms with red-hot pincers and I'll bear it all patiently, doing whatever your graces wish, but let myself be touched by duennas – why, I'll never consent to such a thing even if the Devil makes off with my soul."

Don Quixote also broke his silence, saying to Sancho,

"Be patient, my son; oblige these gentlemen and give thanks to heaven for having placed such powers in your body that through its martyrdom you are able to release enchanted persons from their enchantments and even to raise the dead."

The duennas had now drawn near Sancho, who, feeling more mollified and resigned, seated himself firmly on his chair and stuck out his face and chin for the first duenna, who planted a very solid slap there and then made a deep curtsy to him.

"Fewer formalities and less cosmetics, madam duenna," said Sancho, "for I swear by all that's holy, your hands reek of vinegar water!"

In the end, all the duennas slapped him and a number of the household staff pinched him but he refused to submit to being jabbed with pins. Instead, leaping from his chair in obvious indignation, he grabbed a blazing torch that was nearby and took off after the duennas and all his tormentors, shouting,

"Get out, you ministers of hell! I am not made of bronze that would make me impervious to such outrageous tortures."

Just then, Altisidora, who must have been exhausted from lying on her back for so long, turned onto her side, and when this was observed by the people assembled there, they shouted in one voice as it were,

"Altisidora is alive! She's alive!"

Radamanthus ordered Sancho to control his rage now that he had accomplished his goal. When Don Quixote saw Altisidora stir, he went over to Sancho and knelt before him, saying,

"I beg you here and now, not as my squire but as the son of my loins, to give yourself some of the lashes you are obliged to receive if Dulcinea is to be disenchanted! Now, I say, is the time when your powers are at their peak and are capable of effecting the beneficence expected of you!"

To which Sancho responded,

"That is more like heaping insult onto injury than honey onto pancakes. All I've got to do after these pinches, slaps, and pin-pricks is to give myself a good flogging! Well, your graces may as well take a big rock, tie it round my neck, and throw me down a well, and this I won't mind one bit if I'm to be the scapegoat for curing other people's ailments. You had better leave me alone or I swear to God I'll run amuck – and damn the consequences!"

By now, Altisidora had sat up on the bier when suddenly hornpipes and flutes began to play and the voices of everyone present shouted,

"Long live Altisidora! Long may she live!"

The duke and duchess and the kings Minos and Radamanthus rose from their seats and, together with Don Quixote and Sancho, went as a group to receive Altisidora and to help her down from the bier. The latter, pretending to be faint, curtsied to the duke and duchess and the two kings but, looking at Don Quixote out of the corner of her eye, she said,

"May God forgive you, O hardhearted knight, because your cruelty condemned me to that other world where I spent what seemed to me a thousand years. But to you, O squire, the most compassionate on earth, I am grateful for the life I now possess. From this day forward, Sancho my friend, consider yourself the proud owner of six chemises I shall give you, from which you can make six shirts for yourself, and if they are not all in perfect condition, at least they are clean."

Removing his conical hat, Sancho knelt at Altisidora's feet and kissed her hand in appreciation of the gift. The duke ordered the hat and flame-covered robe taken from Sancho and his own cap and jacket returned to him, but Sancho begged to be permitted to keep the robe and hat, which he wished to take home to his village as a memento of that unparalleled adventure. The duchess said he might certainly do so, as he already knew what great affection she bore him. The duke ordered all those present to vacate the courtyard and retire to their chambers, while Don Quixote and Sancho were taken to those with which they were already familiar.

Chapter Seventy

Which follows the sixty-ninth and deals with matters indispensable for understanding this history

That night, Sancho slept in a trundle bed in the same room as Don Quixote, a circumstance he would have gladly avoided had it been possible, for he knew perfectly well that his master would not let him sleep, what with all the questions and answers, and he was in no mood for a lengthy discussion because the pain from his recent martyrdom still made itself felt and would not allow his tongue full play. Besides, he would have felt more at ease sleeping by himself in a rude hut than with someone else in these sumptuous quarters. His fears proved to be correct and his suspicions so well-founded that no sooner did his master climb into bed than he said,

"Sancho, what do you make of everything that has happened tonight? Great and mighty is the power of love scorned, for with your own eyes you have seen Altisidora slain – not by someone else's arrows, sword, instrument of war, or deadly poison – but by the thought of the severity and scorn I have always adopted in my dealings with her."

"She's welcome to give up the ghost whenever and wherever she pleases so long as she leaves me alone," said Sancho, "for I've neither sought her affection nor scorned her love. At the same time, I don't understand how the well-being of Altisidora, a damsel more fickle than sensible, can, as I've said before, have anything to do with the martyrdom of Sancho Panza, but I've finally come to the clear and unmistakable realization that enchanters and enchantments do exist – and may God liberate me from them, since I don't know how to myself. All the same, I wish your grace would stop asking me questions and let me go to sleep unless you want me to hurl myself headfirst through the window."

"Go to sleep, Sancho my friend," said Don Quixote, "that is, if you can after all the pinpricks, pinches, and slaps you have received."

"No pain," replied Sancho, "was as insulting as the slaps, if only because they were administered by duennas, confound their souls! But I beg your grace one more time to let me go to sleep, for sleep is the balm for the adversities of all our waking hours."

"So be it," said Don Quixote, "and may God watch over you."

The two of them proceeded to fall asleep, during which interval Cide Hamete, the author of this great history, decided to give a detailed account of the circumstances that had led the duke and duchess to devise the elaborate charade described in the last chapter. He explains that, because the bachelor Sansón Carrasco had never forgotten that as the Knight of the Mirrors he had been defeated and toppled from his horse by Don Quixote, which defeat and fall had wrecked and undone all his plans, he had resolved to try his hand again, hoping for a better outcome than on the previous occasion. And so, after learning of the whereabouts of Don Quixote from the page who had delivered the letter and present to Teresa Panza, Sancho's wife, he provided himself with a different horse and armor and painted a white moon on his shield. Loading the armor onto a mule, which was led by a peasant instead of Tomé Cecial his long-time squire lest he be recognized by Sancho or Don Quixote, he went to the duke's castle, where the duke informed him of the exact route Don Quixote had taken in his eagerness to be present at the jousts of Saragossa. He likewise described the jokes they had played on Don Quixote, including the procedure for breaking Dulcinea's spell at the expense of Sancho's backside. And lastly, he gave an account of the joke Sancho had played on his master in making him believe Dulcinea was enchanted and transformed into a farm girl, adding that his wife the duchess had convinced Sancho it was he himself who was misinformed, because Dulcinea really was enchanted. The bachelor was not a little amazed and amused when he considered Sancho's shrewdness and naiveté and Don Quixote's utter madness. The duke asked the bachelor to return to the castle to report how everything turned out in the event that he located the knight, whether he should defeat him or not, and the bachelor promised to do so and rode away in search of Don Quixote. When he failed to find him in Saragossa, he continued his search, and what transpired subsequently has already been described. Returning to the duke's castle, he related everything, including the terms of the battle and the fact that Don Quixote as a good knight-errant was headed back home in keeping with his promise to remain in his village for a year, during which time, according to the bachelor, he might possibly be cured of his madness. This was the consideration that had led the bachelor to undergo those transformations, for he felt it was a pity for a gentleman with as good a mind as Don Quixote's to be mad. With this, he took leave of the duke and returned to his village to wait for Don Quixote, who was traveling along behind him. Such, then, was the situation that gave the duke the opportunity to play his prank, for he took delight in anything involving Sancho or Don Quixote.

Utilizing a number of his servants, some on foot, others on horseback, he placed lookouts on every road surrounding the castle, both near and far – anywhere, in fact, that he thought Don Quixote might be traveling – and instructed them, should they locate him, to bring him to the castle, whether he was willing to come or not. When they eventually did locate him, they sent word of Don Quixote's approach to the duke, who, being already prepared for everything he intended to do, gave the order to light the torches and lamps round the courtyard and to place Altisidora on the bier, together with all the other arrangements that have previously been described – and the entire affair was so realistic and well designed that there was very little difference between it and the real thing. Cide Hamete adds that he himself was convinced that the perpetrators of the joke were as mad as their victims, for the duke and duchess had come within a hair of making fools of themselves by playing tricks on this pair of fools. Meanwhile, the two fools – one of whom was sleeping soundly while the other lay awake encumbered by his unbridled thoughts – were overtaken by day as well as by the desire to rise, for lying in bed had never been to Don Quixote's liking either as conqueror or as conquered.

Inasmuch as Altisidora (who in Don Quixote's opinion had returned from death to life) wished to humor her master and mistress, she entered Don Quixote's room crowned with the same garland she had worn on the bier and dressed in a white taffeta tunic laced throughout with gold flowers. Her hair fell loosely over her shoulders and she carried an exquisite black cane. Don Quixote, confused and troubled by her presence, drew up into a ball and virtually covered himself with the sheets and quilts of the bed, completely tongue-tied and unable to extend even the simplest greeting. Altisidora seated herself on a chair at the head of the bed and, heaving a deep sigh, said to him in a weak, tearful tone of voice,

"When reputable women and reserved maidens show a disregard for their honor and allow their tongues to defy every propriety by revealing the innermost secrets of their hearts, they do so because they find themselves in some desperate situation. I, Sir Don Quixote of La Mancha, am one of those, having been wooed and conquered by love, but despite this I have remained chaste and long-suffering, and to such an extent that my silence caused my heart to break and I lost my life, slain by the thought of how harshly you had treated me, you hard-hearted knight, 'more obdurate than marble to my plaints;' [1] and for two days I lay dead, or was so judged by everyone who saw me. Had it not been for Love, who took pity upon me and made my resurrection dependent upon the martyrdom of this noble squire, I might still be in that other world."

"Love," said Sancho, "might just as easily have made it dependent upon that of my jackass, for which I would now be most grateful! But I would like to ask, my lady – and may heaven provide you with a more tenderhearted lover than my master – what did your grace see in that other world? What is it like in hell, since that must be the destination of anyone who dies without hope?"

"To tell the truth," replied Altisidora, "I must not have died completely, for I never went all the way to hell. Had I done so, I could never have gotten out again even if I had tried. The fact is that I got as far as the gate, where I saw a dozen or so devils playing tennis, all wearing breeches, doublets, Walloon collars trimmed with Flemish lace, ruffles of the same material serving as cuffs, with four inches of wrist exposed to make their hands appear longer as they gripped their flaming raquets. The most astonishing thing was that, instead of balls, they were using what appeared to be books filled with hot air and padding, which was a strange and astonishing sight but which did not surprise me so much as the way the players were conducting themselves, for whereas it is normal for winners to be happy and losers sad, everyone in that game was grumbling, protesting, and cursing."

"That's not surprising," said Sancho, "for devils, whether competing or not, can never be satisfied, win or lose."

"That must be true," said Altisidora, "but there is something else that surprises me – I mean, that surprised me then – which was that after the first serve no ball remained intact or was fit to be served again. In this way they used up so many books, both old and new, that it was a sight to behold. One of the books, a brand-new one with a beautiful binding, was given such a whack that its insides were ripped out and its pages scattered. 'See what book that is,' said one of the devils; to which another devil replied, 'It is the *Second Part of the History of Don Quixote of La Mancha*, composed not by Cide Hamete, its original author, but by an Aragonese who claims to be a native of Tordesillas.' 'Well, take it away from here,' said the first devil, 'and cast it into the depths of hell where I won't have to see it again.' 'Is it that bad?' asked the second devil. 'It is so bad,' replied the first, 'that were I purposely to set out to write a worse one, I could not do so.' At this point they resumed their game of knocking the books back and forth but, because I had heard the name of Don Quixote, whom I love and adore, I made an effort to fix that apparition in my mind."

"Without a doubt," said Don Quixote, "it must have been an apparition, for I am the only Don Quixote on earth, and that book, which is being passed from hand to hand, never remains very long

1 A verse from the first eclogue of the Spanish poet Garcilaso de la Vega (1503-1536)

in any one, for everyone gives it the boot. I have never been angered by hearing that I am made to wander about in it like some specter in darkest hell or here on earth in the bright sunlight, for I am not the one described in that book. By the way, if it should turn out to be good, accurate, and true, it will enjoy centuries of life, but if it is bad, the journey from its cradle to its grave will be a very short one."

Altisidora was about to resume her complaints about Don Quixote when the latter said to her,

"My lady, I have stated a number of times that it grieves me that your grace ever fixed your thoughts upon me, for mine can respond only by being grateful, not by reciprocating. I was born for Dulcinea of Toboso, and the fates (if such beings exist) have designated me for her. To imagine that any other beauty can occupy the place she holds in my heart is to imagine the impossible. This disavowal should be sufficient to make your grace return to what is proper and fitting for one of your modesty, for no man can be compelled to do the impossible."

When Altisidora heard this, she became visibly angered and upset and said to him,

"By the life of Our Lord, Don Blockhead, you shriveled-up clodhopper, you are more stubborn and unyielding than some rustic who is asked to do something when he has already made up his mind to do something else. If I come after you, I'll scratch your eyes out! Do you actually believe, you loser, you human punching-bag, that I died because of you? Why, everything you have seen tonight has been a sham. I am not the sort of woman who would abide dirt under her fingernail for a jackass like yourself, much less die for him!"

"I can certainly believe that," said Sancho, "for the idea that people die because of love is absurd. They may say they do, but actually die – why, only a fool would believe that!"

While they were discussing this, the musician-poet turned singer who had sung the two stanzas recorded earlier made his entrance and, bowing low to Don Quixote, said,

"Sir knight, your grace may count me among your staunchest adherents because for quite some time now I have been an admirer of yours, due as much to your reputation as to your deeds."

To which Don Quixote responded,

"I wish your grace would tell me who you are so I might respond with the courtesy you deserve."

The young man replied that he was the musician and eulogizer of the previous night.

"Most assuredly," said Don Quixote, "your grace possesses an excellent voice but your song did not strike me as very appropriate, for what do Garcilaso's verses have to do with the death of this lady?"

"Your grace should not be surprised at that," replied the musician, "for among the unshorn poets of our time it is common practice for each to write whatever he chooses and to plagiarize whomever he pleases, whether it accomplishes his intentions or not. Nowadays, there is nothing written or sung, however absurd it may be, that is not ascribed to poetic license."

Don Quixote was about to respond but was prevented from doing so by the duke and duchess, who had come to pay their respects. They enjoyed a long pleasant conversation, in the course of which Sancho said so many clever, mischievous things that the duke and duchess once again marveled at his naiveté and shrewdness. Don Quixote then asked for permission to depart that very day because for vanquished knights like himself it was more fitting to live in a pigsty than in a royal palace. They graciously granted his request and the duchess asked if Altisidora was still in his good graces; to which he responded,

"I would have your ladyship understand that all this damsel's problems stem from idleness, the remedy for which is continual and honest labor. She has just informed me that lace is worn in hell and since she obviously knows how to make it, it should never be out of her hands, for once these are occupied with the bobbins, her mind will not dwell on thoughts or images of love. Such, then, is the truth of the situation and such is my conviction and my advice."

"And mine too," added Sancho, "for I've never in my entire life seen a lace maker who died because of love. Damsels who are kept busy spend more time finishing their tasks than worrying about their loves. For myself, I can safely say that when I'm hoeing, I never give a thought to my better half, that is, my Teresa Panza, whom I love more than the nose on my face."

"What you have said is quite true," said the duchess, "and from this time forth I shall keep my Altisidora occupied with some type of needlework, which she does extremely well."

"My lady," replied Altisidora, "there is no need to adopt such a measure, for the mere thought of how cruelly I was treated by this forlorn scoundrel will blot him from my memory without any outside help. Therefore, with your excellencies' permission I prefer to leave this room now so my eyes will not have to look at his . . . not woeful countenance but ugly, disgusting features."

"That sounds to me," said the duke, "like the old adage that says, 'Whoever starts hurling insults is ready to forgive.'"

Altisidora, pretending to wipe away her tears with a handkerchief, curtsied to her master and mistress and left the room, at which point Sancho said,

"I bequeath to you, poor damsel – I bequeath to you, I say, hard luck, for you have had the misfortune to deal with a soul that's as dry as dust and a heart that's made of stone. I assure you that, had your dealings been with me, this rooster would be crowing a different tune!"

Once the conversation ended, Don Quixote dressed, dined with the duke and duchess, and departed that very afternoon.

Chapter Seventy-One

What befell Don Quixote and his squire Sancho Panza on the way to their village

The defeated and exhausted Don Quixote rode along quite dejected in one regard but quite happy in another, his sadness arising from his defeat, his happiness from reflecting upon Sancho's powers as they had been demonstrated in his restoring Altisidora to life, though Don Quixote had some difficulty convincing himself that the love-smitten damsel had actually been dead. Sancho was not at all happy as he rode along, being saddened by the fact that Altisidora had not given him the chemises, as she had promised. After endlessly turning this over in his mind, he said to Don Quixote,

"Truly, master, I am the unluckiest physician on earth, for there are doctors who kill the patients they are treating but still demand to be paid for their efforts, when in fact they've done nothing more than write a few simple prescriptions for medicines that aren't even prepared by them but by an apothecary – so we have another patient swindled. But in my case, after restoring someone else to health at the expense of slaps, pinches, pinpricks, and loss of blood, I'm not given a cent. Well, I swear by the Almighty that if they stick me with another sick person, they'll have to grease my palm before I treat him, for each person must look out for himself. I refuse to believe heaven has given me this power just so I can share it with others for a mere pittance."

"You are right, dear Sancho," said Don Quixote; "Altisidora behaved quite badly in not giving you the promised chemises, and though your powers were bestowed gratis without requiring any study on your part, to have one's body tormented is worse than any amount of studying. For myself, I assure you that, had you sought payment for the lashes needed to break Dulcinea's spell, I would have given you a handsome one, except that I am not certain how effective the treatment will prove if I pay you, and I would not want the compensation to interfere with the medicine. On the other hand, I feel that nothing will be lost by simply trying it, so decide how much you want, Sancho, and start flogging yourself at once. Then pay yourself in cash with your own hand, since you are carrying all my money."

Sancho's eyes and ears snapped to attention at this offer and he resolved in his heart to lash himself most cheerfully.

"Very well, master," he said, "I am willing to place myself at your disposal for any purpose you desire so long as it benefits me, which I'm forced to do out of love for my wife and children. However, I'd like to know how much your grace will give me for each stroke."

To which Don Quixote responded,

"If I were to pay you, Sancho, based upon the nature and importance of the cure, the treasury of Venice and the mines of Potosí would not be sufficient to pay you. See how much of my money you are carrying and decide upon a price for each stroke."

"There are," said Sancho, "three thousand three hundred and some lashes and, since I've already given myself all of five, that leaves the rest of them. Letting those five make up for the odd strokes, let us take the three thousand three hundred, which at a quarter *real* each – and I refuse to accept less even if everybody on earth insists upon it – comes to three thousand three hundred quarter *reals*. Now, since three thousand quarter *reals* are equal to fifteen hundred half *reals*, which are equal to seven hundred fifty *reals*, and since the three hundred are equal to a hundred fifty half *reals*, which are equal to seventy-five *reals* – these added to the seven hundred fifty make a total of eight hundred twenty-five *reals*. I'll skim these off the top of the sum I'm carrying for your grace and will return home rich and contented though thoroughly thrashed; and yet 'Nothing ventured– ' but I'll say no more."

"O kind Sancho, blessed Sancho!" cried Don Quixote, "Dulcinea and I shall be absolutely beholden to you for as long as heaven grants us life! If she returns to her former state, which she cannot fail to do, her *mis*fortune will have been a stroke of *good* fortune and my defeat a most felicitous triumph. Decide, Sancho, when you wish to begin your discipline and if you are quick about it, I shall give you an extra hundred *reals*."

"When?" replied Sancho: "why, tonight without fail. And I hope your grace will arrange to spend the night out of doors under the open sky, in which case I'll lay open my flesh."

Night finally arrived, a night Don Quixote had looked forward to with the greatest anticipation imaginable, though it seemed to him that the wheels on Apollo's chariot must have broken, for the day seemed longer than usual: just as with lovers, who are never objective about matters involving their passion. At last, they made their way into a pleasant grove of trees situated a short distance off the road, where they abandoned Rocinante's saddle and the dapple's packsaddle and stretched out on the grass to dine on Sancho's provisions. After the meal, Sancho fashioned a strong flexible whip from the dapple's rope halter and walked over to some beech trees some twenty paces from his master. Don Quixote, seeing him move with such daring and determination, called out to him,

"Take care, my friend, not to cut yourself to pieces and be sure to allow some time between each series of strokes. Also, take care not to hurry the affair so much that you will run out of breath halfway through it. I mean, don't lash yourself so severely that you will give up the ghost before you reach the desired number. And so that you will not lose by a card too many or a card too few, I shall be here with my rosary keeping count of the strokes you give yourself, and may heaven smile upon you to the extent that your noble intentions deserve."

"'An honest debtor doesn't mind putting down a deposit,'" said Sancho. "I intend to apply the lashes in such a way that without killing myself they'll still smart, which must be the ingredient that makes this miracle work."

Sancho then stripped to the waist, picked up the rope, and began to flail himself while Don Quixote kept count of the strokes. The squire had probably given himself six or eight when it struck him that the ordeal was a bit harsh and the remuneration quite small, and so, pausing for a moment, he shouted to his master that he was calling off the agreement because each of those strokes was worth half a *real*, not a fourth.

"If you will proceed, dear Sancho, and not lose heart," said Don Quixote, "I shall double the stakes."

"In that case," replied Sancho, "the matter is in the hands of God, so let the strokes rain forth!"

But the sly rascal stopped beating his back and began beating the trees, emitting from time to time such groans that one would have thought his soul was being wrenched from his body with each stroke. Don Quixote's soul was so compassionate that he feared Sancho's life might come to an end and as a result of Sancho's lack of precaution he himself might not achieve what he longed for, so he called out to Sancho,

"For the sake of your life, my friend, let this business rest right where it is, for this medicine impresses me as being awfully strong and it would be wise to take it a little at a time; after all, 'Rome wasn't built in a day.' If I have counted correctly, you have already given yourself more than a thousand lashes and that is enough for now. For if you will pardon my indelicacy, 'The ass will bear a full load but not an *over*load.'"

"Oh no, master," said Sancho, "it shall never be said of me that I make promises I don't keep. I would appreciate it if your grace would go off a short distance and let me give myself at least a thousand more lashes, for with a couple of sessions like this one we'll soon have this business finished and even have something left over."

"Well," replied Don Quixote, "since you are in such a good mood, go ahead and lash yourself, and may heaven help you! Meanwhile I shall be over here."

Sancho returned to his task with such fervor that he had soon knocked the bark off several trees, such was the severity with which he lashed himself. And once, raising his voice while unleashing a mighty blow against a beech tree, he cried out,

"Death to Samson and all his companions!"

Don Quixote immediately came running at the sound of Sancho's pained voice and the terrible crack of the whip. Seizing the twisted halter that served as Sancho's scourge, he said,

"Heaven forbid that you should lose your life just to please me, Sancho my friend. Inasmuch as you are needed to support your wife and children, Dulcinea will have to wait for a more auspicious occasion. Meanwhile, I shall be content in the knowledge that help is not far away and shall wait for you to regain your strength so this business may be concluded to everyone's satisfaction."

"Well, master," said Sancho, "if that's what your grace prefers, so be it, but pray throw your cloak over my shoulders, for I'm sweating and wouldn't want to catch cold, which is the risk we fledgling penitents run."

Doing accordingly, Don Quixote removed his cloak and placed it over Sancho, who then slept until awakened by the sun, at which time they resumed their journey. They eventually reached a village some three leagues down the road, where they dismounted at an inn, for, amazingly enough, this is what Don Quixote fancied it to be and not some castle with its deep moat, turrets, portcullises, and drawbridge, for ever since his defeat he had viewed everything more rationally, as we shall now see.

He was given a room on the ground floor which, following the village custom, had dilapidated cloth murals on the walls instead of leather draperies. On one of them was a painting by a pathetic artist depicting the rape of Helen at the point at which the daring intruder steals her away from Menelaus. On another was a scene from the story of the beautiful Dido and Aeneas, showing her standing atop a lofty tower waving half a sheet to the fugitive intruder as he flees at sea in a frigate or brigantine. Don Quixote noticed that in both pictures Helen never seemed very reluctant to leave because she was slyly and furtively smiling, but Dido showed that her eyes were shedding tears the size of walnuts. When Don Quixote saw this, he said,

"Those two ladies were extremely unfortunate not to have been born in this age, and I the most unfortunate person of all not to have been born in theirs. I would have confronted those gentlemen and Troy would not have been burned, nor Carthage destroyed, for both of those calamities could have been avoided simply by my slaying Paris."

"I'll wager," said Sancho, "that before long there won't be a café, inn, tavern, or barber shop that fails to have a painting depicting our exploits but I hope they're painted by a better hand than that of the artist who painted these."

"You are right, Sancho," said Don Quixote; "this painter is like Orbaneja, a painter from Ubeda, who, whenever he was asked what he was painting, would answer: 'Whatever it turns out to be.' And if he happened to have painted a rooster, he would print beneath it: *This is a rooster* so people would not think it was a fox. Thus, it seems to me that the painter or author – for they are one and the same – who brought out the new history of Don Quixote that has recently appeared must be one of those, for he painted (or wrote) 'whatever it turned out to be.' Or perhaps, he is like the poet Mauleón, who was present at the court a few years ago and would give an instant answer to any question put to him. On one occasion, when someone asked him the meaning of *Memento mori*, he replied: 'The Moor's memento.' [1] But setting this aside, tell me, Sancho, whether you intend to have another bout tonight and whether you wish it to be indoors or out in the open."

"My goodness, master," replied Sancho, "for what I intend, it makes no difference whether I'm in a house or out in an open field. On second thought, I'd like it to be among some trees, for they go hand in hand with my ordeal and help me bear up under it to an astonishing degree."

"No," said Don Quixote, "this is not the way to proceed, dear friend. So that you may recover your strength, we shall postpone it until we reach our village, where at the very latest we shall arrive day after tomorrow."

Sancho said Don Quixote might do whatever he pleased but he wished to conclude this business quickly while he was in the mood and still had the stomach for it, for 'To delay is to go looking for trouble,' 'God helps those who help themselves,' 'It's better to have than to wish,' and 'A bird in the hand is worth two in the bush.'

"No more proverbs, Sancho, for the love of God!" cried Don Quixote; "it would appear that you have returned to your old habits again. Speak simply, plainly, and in a straightforward manner, as I have urged you on numerous occasions, and you will see how greatly your blessings will be multiplied."

"I don't understand this bad habit of mine," said Sancho; "I can't utter a sensible thing without adding a proverb, or come up with a proverb that doesn't seem sensible, but I'll mend my ways if I possibly can."

---

1 Latin: 'Remember that you shall die.' Cervantes' text actually has ***Deum de deo,*** a phrase from the Latin version of the Nicene Creed. But because this phrase is simply not translatable into English in a way that does justice to the wordplay, I have substituted another famous Latin saying, ***Memento mori***. When Mauleón was asked the meaning of **Deum de Deo** [Latin: 'God from God'], he answered, ***Dé donde diere*** [Spanish: 'Let him hit where he will']. Mauleón's reply makes some sense in Spanish even though it is not Cervantes at his cleverest, but there is no English translation that provides a play on words for ***Deum de Deo,*** as witnessed by the various efforts of the 15 translators I have studied.

Shelton:	'***Dé donde diere***' [left untranslated]
Motteux:	'Hab-nab at a venture'
Jarvis:	'Wherever it hits'
Smollett:	'Wherever it may hit'
Smirke:	'**Dé donde diere**' [left untranslated]
Duffield:	'Down where it is done'
Ormsby:	'**Dé donde diere**' [left untranslated]
Watt:	'Let him give where he will give' or 'Let him hit where he may hit'
Smith:	'Let him hit where he will'
Putnam:	'**Dé donde diere**' [left untranslated]
Cohen:	'Do as you like'
Starkie:	'Let him give when he will'
Raffel:	'Let him hit me anywhere he can'
Rutherford:	'They'll underpay you'
Grossman:	'Dim down the drummer'

And with this, their conversation came to an end, at least for the time being.

Chapter Seventy-Two

How Don Quixote and Sancho reached their village

Don Quixote and Sancho spent the entire day in the village inn waiting for night to arrive so that one of the two could finish the task of disciplining himself out in the open and the other could see this accomplished and with it the fulfillment of his dreams. Just then, there arrived at the inn a traveler on horseback, accompanied by several servants, one of whom addressed the man who appeared to be their master:

"Don Alvaro Tarfe, this will be a good place to take your siesta, for the inn appears to be clean and cool."

When Don Quixote heard this, he said to his squire,

"Listen, Sancho, as I was thumbing through that book containing the second part of my history, I seem to remember coming across the name Don Alvaro Tarfe."

"That's certainly possible," said Sancho, "but we should let him dismount and afterwards we can question him about it."

The gentleman dismounted and the innkeeper's wife gave him a room on the ground floor opposite Don Quixote's, furnished with painted wall hangings similar to those in Don Quixote's room. The newly arrived gentleman changed into his summer clothes and went out into the front courtyard, where it was cool and uncrowded. When he encountered Don Quixote pacing back and forth, he said,

"Where, my good sir, is your grace headed?"

To which Don Quixote responded,

"To a village near here, which is my hometown. And where might your grace be headed?"

"I, sir," said the gentleman, "am on my way to Granada, which is my native region."

"And a fine region it is!" said Don Quixote, "but will your grace please tell me your name just as a courtesy, for I feel that knowing it will be of greater importance to me than I can possibly explain."

"My name is Don Alvaro Tarfe," said the guest; to which Don Quixote replied,

"I am absolutely convinced your grace must be the same Don Alvaro Tarfe who figures in *The Second Part of the History of Don Quixote of La Mancha,* recently printed and published by a modern-day author."

"I am that very person," said the gentleman, "and that particular Don Quixote, the protagonist of that history, is a very close friend of mine. I am the one who got him to leave his village or at least persuaded him to take part in some jousts held in Saragossa, the city to which I was traveling. The truth of the matter is that I showed him a number of kindnesses and was the one who kept the executioner from giving him a flogging because of his undue rashness."[1]

"I wonder, Sir Don Alvaro, if you would tell me whether I bear any resemblance to that particular Don Quixote you have mentioned."

"Certainly not," replied the guest, "none whatsoever."

"And did that Don Quixote," asked our own, "have a squire with him named Sancho Panza?"

"He did," replied Don Alvaro, "and though the squire had a reputation for being quite humorous, I never heard him say anything that was the least bit funny."

"I can certainly believe that," said Sancho, "for not everyone is cut out to be funny. In fact, gentle sir, that Sancho your grace mentions must be a tremendous scoundrel, dullard, and fraud all rolled into one, for I am the real Sancho Panza and have more funny things to say than you can shake a stick at. If your grace doesn't believe me, you may see for yourself by tagging along with me for at least a year, during which time you'll hear them pop out of me at every turn, and they're so good and so plentiful that quite often, without knowing what I'm saying, I make everyone laugh who's within earshot. Now, the real Don Quixote of La Mancha, the famous, valiant, wise and lovelorn one, the righter of wrongs, guardian of minors and orphans, protector of widows, stealer of hearts, and the one who has as his solitary mistress the incomparable Dulcinea of Toboso, is this gentleman here, who happens to be my master. Any other Don Quixote and any other Sancho Panza whatsoever are a fraud and a figment of the imagination."

"By all that is holy, I can believe that," said Don Alvaro, "for you, my friend, have said more amusing things in the few words you have spoken than that other Sancho Panza did in all the things I ever heard him utter, and he uttered a bunch of them! He was more of a glutton than a wit and more moronic than humorous. I have not the slightest doubt that those enchanters who have persecuted the good Don Quixote have sought to persecute me with the bad one. I can't explain it but I would swear I left Don Quixote shut up in the Nuncium Asylum in Toledo undergoing treatment, and now another Don Quixote turns up, albeit quite different from mine."

"I," said Don Quixote, "do not know whether or not I am good but I do know I am not the bad one. To prove this, my lord Don Alvaro Tarfe, I would have your grace know that I have never been to Saragossa in all the days of my life. On the contrary, when I was informed that the fraudulent Don Quixote had participated in the jousts of that city, I chose not to go there in order to demonstrate the falsity of his claim, so I went straight to Barcelona, that repository of gentility, refuge of wayfarers, asylum of the poor, homeland of the brave, avenger of the wronged, and home of harmonious and lasting friendship, a city unique in its setting and beauty. And despite the fact that not everything that happened to me there was very pleasurable – actually, it was quite painful – I consider it all worthwhile simply for the opportunity to have seen that city. In a word, Don Alvaro Tarfe, I am Don Quixote of La Mancha, the very one who is on everyone's lips – not that pathetic soul who has attempted to usurp my name and cover himself with honor by appropriating my ideas. I appeal to your grace's sense of duty as a gentleman to be so kind as to issue a statement before the magistrate of

1 The following paragraphs contain several references to incidents and characters in Avellaneda's *Don Quixote* which would have been familiar to many readers.

this village to the effect that never until this moment have you seen me in your entire life and that I am not the Don Quixote who appears in the Second Part, nor is Sancho Panza the one whose acquaintance you made."

"I shall do so with all my heart," said Don Alvaro, "even if it shocks everyone to see two Don Quixotes and two Sanchos at the same time, as similar in name as they are dissimilar in behavior. And once again, I state and affirm that I never saw what I saw and never experienced what I experienced."

"Undoubtedly, sir," said Sancho, "your grace must be under a spell like my lady Dulcinea of Toboso. I only wish your grace's disenchantment depended upon my giving myself another three thousand and some lashes, as I am doing on her behalf, for I would do so without any payment whatsoever."

"I don't understand that business of lashes," said Don Alvaro.

Sancho said it was a long story but he would explain it to him if they happened to be traveling in the same direction. Just then, dinner was announced and Don Quixote and Don Alvaro dined together. As luck would have it, the village magistrate entered the inn with a notary, before whom Don Quixote, in order to safeguard his rights, asked Don Alvaro Tarfe, the gentleman here present, to declare by means of a petition and in the presence of his grace that he had not known Don Quixote of La Mancha, also here present; that the latter was not the one making the rounds in a book entitled *The Second Part of Don Quixote of La Mancha*, composed by a certain Avellaneda, native of Tordesillas. In the end, the magistrate drew up the legal petition, which was stated with all the formalities required in such cases. Don Quixote and Sancho were delighted at this, as if such a statement were so very important to them or as if their words and deeds did not clearly demonstrate the difference between the two Don Quixotes and two Sanchos. Don Alvaro and Don Quixote engaged in a number of pleasantries in which the great Manchegan displayed his intellect, and to such an extent that Don Alvaro Tarfe understood how mistaken he had been, for he became convinced that he himself was enchanted, since he had touched with his own hands two such contradictory Don Quixotes.

Once evening arrived, they all left the village and traveled about half a league, where they came to a fork in the road: one way leading to Don Quixote's village and the other the one Don Alvaro was to take. During this short interval, Don Quixote had related his disgraceful defeat and Dulcinea's enchantment, together with the measures required for undoing it, all of which renewed Don Alvaro's amazement. The latter embraced Don Quixote and Sancho and then proceeded on his way, as did Don Quixote on his. The Manchegan spent the night among some trees to afford Sancho the opportunity to carry out his penance, which he did in the same fashion as on the previous night – more to the detriment of the bark on the trees than to the skin on his back – and he took such great care with the blows that they would not have scared away a fly had one been sitting on his back. The unsuspecting Don Quixote did not miss a stroke in his counting and found that, by including those of the previous night, they came to three thousand twenty-nine.

The sun seemed to have risen early to witness the atonement, and with the arrival of its rays the pair resumed their journey. They discussed Don Alvaro's delusion and agreed how beneficial it had been to have him make his statement before the magistrate and to do so with such authority. They traveled all day and all night without experiencing anything worthy of description, unless we note that during the night Sancho finished his task, a deed that left Don Quixote contented beyond measure. The latter looked forward to daybreak to see whether he would come across his now disenchanted mistress Dulcinea somewhere along the way. Consequently, upon resuming his journey, he went up to every woman he met to see if she was Dulcinea of Toboso, believing implicitly that Merlin's promises could not fail to come true. Occupied by these thoughts and longings, they rode to the top of a hill from where they could see their village. When Sancho saw it, he fell to his knees and exclaimed,

"Open your eyes, my beloved homeland, and behold your son Sancho Panza come back to you – if not very rich, very nicely flogged. Open your arms and receive your other son Don Quixote, who, if he comes defeated at the hands of another, comes victorious over himself, and this, he has told me, is the greatest victory anyone can strive for. I've also got money now and, though I may have been given a good flogging, at least I conducted myself like a gentleman."

"Stop all that foolish babbling," said Don Quixote; "let us start off on the right foot when we enter our village, where we shall give free rein to our ideas and draw up plans for the pastoral life we intend to lead."

And with this, they rode down the hill and headed towards their village.

Chapter Seventy-Three

The omens that Don Quixote encountered upon entering his village, together with other incidents that embellish and validate this great history

On the outskirts of town, so says Cide Hamete, Don Quixote saw two boys quarreling on the village threshing floor, one of whom was shouting at the other,

"Don't waste your efforts, Periquillo, because you can say goodbye to the thing you love."

When Don Quixote heard this, he said to Sancho,

"My friend, did you hear what that boy shouted: 'You can say goodbye to the thing you love.'"

"Even if I did," replied Sancho, "what difference does it make what the boy said?"

"What difference does it make?" exclaimed Don Quixote; "don't you see that if it applies to my situation, it means I shall never see Dulcinea again?"

Sancho was about to respond but was prevented from doing so by the sight of a hare scurrying across the field pursued by a number of greyhounds and hunters. The frightened animal ran over to them and crouched at the dapple's feet. Without danger to himself Sancho picked it up and handed it to Don Quixote, who was muttering to himself,

"*Malum signum, malum signum!*[1] A hare is fleeing, greyhounds are chasing it, and Dulcinea is nowhere to be seen!"

"Your grace is an odd one," said Sancho. "Let us suppose this hare is Dulcinea of Toboso and those greyhounds chasing it are the wicked enchanters who transformed her into a farm girl. She flees, I pick her up and hand her to your grace and you take her in your arms and caress her – how is that a bad sign and what evil omen can it portend?"

The two boys who had been quarreling came over to see the hare, whereupon Sancho asked them what they were arguing about. The one who had said, 'You can say goodbye to the thing you love," replied that he had taken a cricket cage from the other boy and never intended to give it back to him for as long as he lived. Sancho took a *real* from his purse and gave it to the boy in exchange for the cage, which he then placed in Don Quixote's hands, saying,

"Here, master, are the omens broken and destroyed, and according to the way I see it, simpleton that I am, they have no more influence over our affairs than do the clouds of yesteryear. In fact, if I remember correctly, I've heard our village priest say that sensible Christians should pay no attention to such foolishness. And even you yourself recently told me the same thing, having convinced me that every last Christian who believes in omens is foolish. Since there is no need to make a big to-do over this, let's be on our way and head for our village."

When the hunters arrived and asked for their hare, Don Quixote gave it to them and he and Sancho then continued on their way. At the entrance to their village they came across the priest and the bachelor Carrasco, who were saying their prayers in a small meadow. Here it should be explained that Sancho, as a make-shift measure, had covered his dapple and its bundle of armor with the flame-emblazoned buckram robe he had been forced to wear in the duke's castle the night Altisidora had returned to life. He had also placed the conical hat on the ass' head, which transformed him into the most novel jackass the world has ever seen. The two men were immediately recognized by the priest and the bachelor, who approached them with open arms, whereupon Don Quixote dismounted and gave them a hearty embrace. The boys, who were as sharp-eyed as lynxes, spotted the ass' hat and ran over to have a look at him.

"Come here, fellows," shouted several of the boys, "and you'll see Sancho Panza's jackass dressed fit to kill and Don Quixote's nag skinnier than the day he was born."

And thus, surrounded by the boys and accompanied by the priest and the barber, they finally made their way into the village and proceeded to Don Quixote's house, where they found Don Quixote's niece and housekeeper standing at the door, having received word that the pair were on their way home. The news had also reached Teresa Panza, Sancho's wife, who, her hair uncombed and herself only partially dressed, had grabbed her daughter Sanchica by the hand and come out to meet her husband. When she saw him decked out differently from what she considered proper for a governor, she said,

"Is this any way to come home, husband dear? You move as though you are footsore from a lot of walking and you look more like something misgoverned than someone who has governed."

1 Latin: 'An evil omen, an evil omen!'

"Just hush up, Teresa," said Sancho; "things aren't as bad as they appear. Once we're home I'll tell you things that will astonish you. The important thing is that I'm bringing home money, all of which I earned by my wits and without harming anyone."

"So long as you bring home money, husband dear," replied Teresa, "I don't care how it was earned; and regardless of the way you earned it, I'm sure you didn't use any method that hasn't been used before."

Sanchica hugged her father and asked him if he had brought her a present, saying she had looked forward to his return more than to the rains of May. With Sancho's wife holding one of his hands and his daughter hugging him round the waist with one arm and tugging at the dapple with the other, they walked back to their house, leaving Don Quixote in the company of the priest and bachelor and in the grips of his niece and housekeeper.

Without regard for time or season, Don Quixote drew the priest and bachelor aside and described to them his defeat and the obligation he was under not to leave his village for one year, which commitment he intended to observe to the letter of the law without straying one iota from it, exactly like a knight-errant bound by the exigencies and rules of knight-errantry. He said he was considering becoming a shepherd and spending the next year in the solitude of the fields, where he would while away the time by giving free rein to his amorous thoughts and engaging in virtuous pastoral activities, and he begged them to accompany him in this if they had nothing better to do and were not prevented from doing so by more pressing matters. He added that he would buy enough sheep and cattle for them to merit the name of shepherds, informing them that the most important part of that enterprise had already been attended to, for he had assigned them names that would suit them to a T. When the priest asked him what these were, Don Quixote said he would call himself the shepherd Quixotiz, the bachelor might call himself the shepherd Carrascón, the priest the shepherd Curiambro, and Sancho Panza the shepherd Pancino. Both men were astounded at Don Quixote's new-found madness but in an effort to prevent him from again forsaking his village for his knight-errantry and, because they entertained the hope that he might be cured in the course of that year, they agreed to his new project and endorsed his insane idea as a wise one, offering to serve as his companions in that enterprise.

"Also," said Sansón Carrasco, "as everyone knows, I am quite a renowned poet and shall compose verses at every turn, either pastoral or courtly or whatever I deem most appropriate, so we shall be entertained as we wander about these out-of-the-way places. But what is most needed, my lords, is for each of us to select the name of the shepherdess he intends to celebrate in his verses, and to leave no tree, however hard its bark, uncarved or uninscribed with her name, which is the customary practice among love-struck shepherds."

"That is perfect," replied Don Quixote, "though I am exempt from having to seek the name of a fictitious shepherdess because I already have the incomparable Dulcinea of Toboso, glory of these banks, adornment of these meadows, repository of beauty, model of gracefulness – in sum, a person to whom every sort of praise is fitting, however extravagant it may be."

"Quite true," said the priest, "but the rest of us shall look about for some accommodating shepherdesses who will make good companions even if they are not overly enthusiastic."

To this Sansón Carrasco added,

"And should it be necessary, we shall give them names that can be found in any number of books: Fílida, Amarilis, Diana, Flérida, Galatea, or Belisarda. And since these are for sale in the marketplace, we can buy some and keep them for ourselves. If my particular lady, or rather shepherdess, happens to be named Ana, I shall sing her praises under the name of Anarda; if Francisca, I shall call her Francenia; if Lucía, Luscinda; and in this way everything will be worked out. And should Sancho Panza join our fraternity, he may celebrate his wife Teresa Panza under the name of Teresaina."

Don Quixote laughed at the mention of this name, and the priest could not say enough in praise of his virtuous and honorable resolution, offering once more to keep him company for as much time as he could spare away from his demanding duties. At this point, they took leave of him, advising and urging him to look after his health and to indulge himself in those things that would be good for him.

But as luck would have it, the niece and the housekeeper overheard the men's conversation and the moment the priest and the bachelor left, both women went inside with Don Quixote, where the niece said,

"What is this, uncle dear? Just when we thought your grace was going to stay at home and lead a quiet, honorable life, it now seems you intend to get involved in some new entanglements to become a quaint little shepherd and go gallivanting over hill and dale. Well, the truth is that 'The barley stalk is already too hard to make a whistle.'"

To which the housekeeper added,

"And will your grace be able to stand the hot summer afternoons, the cold winter nights, and the howling wolves out in the wilds? Of course not, for that is a job and task for robust individuals seasoned and reared for such a calling virtually from the day they were in diapers and swaddling clothes, and if one must choose between two evils, being a knight-errant is better than being a shepherd. I wish, master, you would give this some thought and accept my advice, for I'm not offering it with a stomach full of bread and wine but one that's been fasting, and with fifty years of experience besides. You should stay at home, look after your property, go to confession regularly, and be a friend to the poor, and if any ill should befall you, may it rest upon my head."

"Hush, my children," said Don Quixote, "I know what is best for me. But for now, help me to my bed, for I am not at all well. Still, you may rest assured that whether as a knight-errant today or an errant shepherd tomorrow, I will never fail to minister to your needs, as you shall see by my actions."

The dutiful children (which the housekeeper and niece unquestionably were) helped him to his bed, where they brought him something to eat and lavished as much attention upon him as possible.

Chapter Seventy-Four

How Don Quixote became ill, drew up his will, and then died

Inasmuch as things human are not everlasting, being in constant decline from the moment of their inception until their eventual end – people's lives in particular – and since Don Quixote's enjoyed no special dispensation from heaven to halt its course, the end and close came when he least expected it, due either to his despondency at seeing himself defeated or to the will of heaven, which ordained it. He was taken with a fever that confined him to his bed for six days, during which time he received frequent visits from his friends the priest, the bachelor, the barber, and his faithful squire Sancho Panza, who never left his bedside. They all used every means at their disposal to cheer him up, believing his present condition resulted from his grief at seeing himself defeated and his disappointment at failing to find Dulcinea disenchanted and liberated as he had expected. The bachelor urged him to take heart and abandon his bed so he could begin his pastoral undertaking, for which he himself had already composed an eclogue that would put to shame those composed by Sannazaro, [1] and for which he had already purchased with his own money two famous dogs to guard the flock, one named Barcino and the other Butrón, both of which he had bought from a herdsman from Quintanar. But none of this was sufficient to rid Don Quixote of his depression.

His friends sent for a physician, who took his pulse and was saddened by what he found, saying that, for what it was worth, Don Quixote should attend to the welfare of his soul because that of his body was in peril. Don Quixote received this with his soul at ease, which is not the way it was received by his housekeeper, niece, and squire, who began to sob fitfully as if they were already in the presence of his corpse. In the physician's opinion it was melancholy and despondency that were killing him. When Don Quixote asked to be left alone, saying he wished to get some sleep, they complied with his request and he slept for more than six hours 'at one sitting,' as the expression goes – so long, in fact, that the housekeeper and niece feared he might never wake again; but wake he did at the end of the stated time, whereupon he cried out,

"Praised be Almighty God, who has shown me so much kindness! Indeed, His compassion is limitless, a compassion the sins of man cannot diminish or restrict."

The niece listened to everything her uncle said and, because it sounded more rational than his usual pronouncements, at least during his present illness, she asked,

"My lord, what is your grace referring to? Has something new taken place? What 'compassion' and what 'sins of man' are you talking about?"

"The compassion, my dear niece," replied Don Quixote, "is that which God is showing me at this very instant, for my sins do not keep Him from bestowing it upon me. My mind is now clear and untrammeled, having shaken off the murky veils of ignorance cast over it by my lamentable and constant reading of those detestable books of chivalry. I now recognize how absurd and fraudulent they are, but my greatest regret is that this realization has come so late that it leaves me no time to make amends by reading other types of books that would enlighten my soul. I have the feeling, niece, that I am about to die and should like to do so in a way that will not portray my life as having been so bad I shall be remembered as a madman. I may have been mad but I am loath to have my death confirm the fact. And so, my dear, send for my good friends the priest, the bachelor Sansón Carrasco, and Master Nicolás the barber, for I wish to confess my sins and draw up my will."

The niece, however, was spared the task of doing so because the three men were just making their

---

1 Jacopo Sannazaro (1458-1530), author of the famous Renaissance pastoral novel *La Arcadia*.

entrance. When Don Quixote saw them, he said,

"Congratulate me, good sirs, I am no longer Don Quixote of La Mancha but Alonso Quijano, whose deeds have won him the name of 'Good.' I am now the foe of Amadís of Gaul and his whole horde of descendants and find all those profane histories of knight-errantry abominable. I now recognize my folly and the risk I ran in reading them because now by the grace of God, having learned from my own mistakes, I view them with disgust."

When the three of them heard this, they had no doubt that some new madness had taken hold of him, at which point Sansón said,

"Sir Don Quixote, now that we have received word that the lady Dulcinea is no longer enchanted, how can your grace say such a thing? Why this wish to become a hermit just when we are on the verge of becoming shepherds to spend our lives singing like so many princes? May you cease such talk, return to your senses, and face reality."

"Well, gentlemen," said Don Quixote, "that reality, which until now has been harmful to me, will with the help of heaven work to my advantage after my death. And since I feel I am dying all too quickly, stop trying to shield me from the truth and bring me a priest to hear my confession and a notary to draw up my will. At such crucial times as this, a man must not take his soul lightly, so I beseech your graces to send for the notary while his worship the priest is hearing my confession."

Glancing at one another, they were astonished by what Don Quixote had said and, despite their reservations, tended to believe him. One of the signs leading them to feel he was dying was the ease with which he had passed from madness to sanity, for besides those things already mentioned, he added so many new ones, as rational and well expressed as they were devout, that they removed all doubt and convinced his friends that his mind was sound. The priest had everyone leave the room while he remained with Don Quixote to hear his confession. The bachelor went for the notary and returned a short time later with both him and Sancho Panza, the squire having now been advised by the bachelor of his master's condition. When Sancho found the niece and the housekeeper in tears, he began to pout and let his own eyes overflow. Once the confession was completed, the priest emerged from the room and said,

"Alonso Quijano the Good is truly dying and is just as truly sound of mind. We may now safely go inside so he can make out his will."

This announcement had such a terrible effect upon the housekeeper, the niece, and Sancho Panza, his faithful squire, that they unleashed a thousand sighs from the depths of their being, together with all the tears that had welled up in their eyes. For, in truth, as we have stated at various times, whether the knight was merely Alonso Quijano the Good or Don Quixote of La Mancha, he always possessed such a kindly disposition and gentle manner that he was beloved not only by those of his household but by everyone who knew him. The notary entered along with the others and, once the will's preliminary paragraph had been drawn up and Don Quixote had commended his soul to God, together with all the other religious formalities required under such circumstances, the knight stated, when they came to the matter of bequests,

"Item: Albeit that Sancho Panza, whom I made my squire in a moment of madness, has some moneys of mine as a result of certain accounts, debits, and credits between him and me, no claim shall be made against him nor any payment demanded of him. If anything remains after he is paid what I owe him – which will be precious little – the remainder shall be his, and may it benefit him greatly. Also, just as I was responsible for awarding him the governorship of an island when I was mad, I would hereby award him that of a kingdom now that I am sane, for his simple wit and trusting nature deserve as much." Then turning to Sancho, he said,

"Forgive me, dear friend, for providing you the opportunity to appear as mad as I by causing you to share the same misconception I held: namely, that there have been and still are knights-errant in the world."

"Please, dear master," said Sancho tearfully, "I don't want your grace to die but to take my advice and live for a thousand years. The most insane thing a person can do in this life is to *allow* himself to die – to be slain by no one but to be done in by the hands of melancholy. You must not lie there helpless but rise from your bed so we can go forth into the countryside dressed as shepherds, as we agreed to do. Perhaps behind some bush we'll discover the lady Dulcinea disenchanted and a sight to behold. If you are dying from the grief of seeing yourself defeated, you may place the blame on me and say you were unseated from Rocinante by my failure to tighten the cinches properly, especially when you must have noticed in your books of chivalry that it is a common occurrence for knights to be toppled from their mounts by other knights. Besides, 'He who is defeated today may be victorious tomorrow.'"

"Quite right," said Sansón, "there is much truth in what our noble Sancho has said."

"Easy there, gentlemen," said Don Quixote, "what is done is done and it is too late to relive the past. I once was mad but now am sane. I used to be Don Quixote of la Mancha but am now, as I have said, Alonso Quijano the Good, and I pray that my heartfelt repentance will restore me to my former level of esteem. But now I should like his grace the notary to proceed.

"Item: I bequeath all my household possessions to Antonia Quijana my niece, here present, the choicest items among them, however, to be deducted for satisfying the bequests I shall make. I ask that the top priority be given to paying the wages of my housekeeper for all the time she has served me, plus twenty ducats for a dress. And I appoint as my executors their graces the priest and the bachelor Sansón Carrasco, who are here present.

"Item: It is my desire that if my niece Antonia Quijana wishes to wed, it shall be to a man about whom it has been determined that he has not the slightest acquaintance with books of chivalry. Should it be determined that he knows anything about them and, if despite this my niece insists upon marrying him and does so, she shall forego everything I have bequeathed her, which shall then be distributed among charitable causes as my executors see fit.

"Item: I beg these said gentlemen, my executors, that if they discover the identity of the author purported to have written the history circulating under the title of *Second Part of the Exploits of Don Quixote of La Mancha*, to beg him on my behalf and as earnestly as they know how, to forgive me for having unintentionally provided him with the excuse to write as many outlandish absurdities as the ones he has written. I depart this life with a troubled conscience for having provided him the basis for writing them."

With this, Don Quixote ended his will and, feeling a sudden faintness, fell back on his bed, which alarmed all those who were present and made them hasten to his side. Don Quixote lived for three days from the time he made out his will, during which time he frequently lapsed into unconsciousness. The house was thrown into a state of turmoil but despite this the niece continued to have her snacks, the housekeeper her toddies, and Sancho Panza to maintain his high spirits, for the prospect of coming into an inheritance weakens or obliterates in the heirs the memory of the grief the deceased person has occasioned.

Finally, Don Quixote's life came to an end after he had received all the sacraments and had expressed in no uncertain terms his utter contempt for books of chivalry. The notary, who was present, remarked that never in his life had he read in any book of chivalry of a knight-errant dying in his bed as peacefully and devoutly as Don Quixote, who amid all the tears and lamentations of those present gave up the ghost, which is to say, he died. When the priest observed this, he asked the notary to draft a certificate testifying that Alonso Quijano the Good, commonly known as Don Quixote of La Mancha, had passed from this present life and was, in fact, certifiably dead. He was requesting such a statement to remove the possibility that some author other than Cide Hamete Benengeli might falsely resurrect him and bring out an endless number of books about his exploits.

Such, then, was the end of the ingenious hidalgo of La Mancha, whose place of birth Cide Hamete chose not to locate precisely so as to allow the various villages and towns of La Mancha to vie among themselves for the right to adopt him and claim him as their native son, just as the seven cities of Greece had done in the case of Homer. Cide Hamete chose not to record the lamentations of Sancho, the niece, and the housekeeper, or the new epitaphs on his tomb, with the exception of the following one by Sansón Carrasco:

Here lies the valiant cavalier
Who never had a sense of fear:
So high his matchless courage rose,
He reckoned death among his vanquished foes.

Wrongs to redress, his sword he drew,
And many a caitiff giant slew;
His days of life, though madness-stained,
In death his senses he regained.

At this point the most sagacious Cide Hamete addressed his pen, stating,

"I cannot say, O dearest quill, whether your point is sharp or blunted but here is where you shall remain, hanging from this rack by this slender wire, where you shall abide for countless ages unless some presumptuous, ill-intentioned historians take you down and profane you. But before they lay hands on you, you are to warn them by stating as clearly as you know how:

Beware, beware, you worthless oafs!
Let no one touch this enterprise,

As 'tis reserved for me alone.

"For me alone was Don Quixote born and I for him, he being a man of action and I a man of letters. Together we are as one, notwithstanding that impostor of a writer from Tordesillas who once made so bold, and may do so again, as to take up his coarse, ill-trimmed ostrich quill to describe the deeds of my valiant knight, though these were not a fit burden for his shoulders nor a proper subject for his dull wit. If you should ever meet him, you are to advise him to allow these weary and rotted bones to remain in the grave undefiled, and not to attempt, contrary to every funerary law, to carry him off to Old Castile, making him abandon the grave in which he really and truly lies, stretched out to his full length and powerless to sally forth again a third time; because to make a mockery of all those knights-errant who have sallied forth countless times, two sallies are sufficient – sallies so much to the delight and approval of all who have come to learn of them both here at home and abroad. By so doing, you will be complying with your Christian duty and will be giving good counsel to him who wished you ill, and I shall be content and proud to have been the first to enjoy the full fruits of his writings, as he would have wished, for my sole desire has been to instill in mankind an abhorrence of the false and absurd stories in books of chivalry, which are surely already tottering and headed for total collapse, thanks to those of my genuine Don Quixote.

Vale. [1]

Appendix: The Principal Works Consulted in the Preparation of This Translation

CRITICAL EDITIONS OF DON QUIXOTE

1781 Don Quixote de la Mancha / Miguel de Cervantes Saavedra ; edición de John Bowle ; prefacio de Eduardo Urbina ; introducción de Daniel Heisenberg. [Edición facsímil]. Newark, Del. : Juan de la Cuesta, 2006.

6 v. in 3. (31, 540, viii, 572, 592 p.) : ill. ; 23 cm. (Hispanic monographs – Juan de la Cuesta. Serie: Documentación cervantina ; no. 23)

Facsimile reprint of: Historia del famoso caballero don Quixote de la Mancha / por Miguel de Cervantes Saavedra ; con anotaciones, índices, y varias lecciones / por Juan Bowle. En seis tomos. London : Se hallarán en las Librerías de B. White, P. Elmsley, T. y T. Payne, y J. Robson, 1781.

Vols. 2-6 have imprint: Salisbury : En la Imprenta de Eduardo Easton, 1781.

Vol. 5 has title: Anotaciones a la Historia de don Quixote de la Mancha.

Vol. 6 has title: Indices de nombres propios, de palabras más notables, y varias lecciones, en entrambos partes de la Historia de don Quixote de la Mancha.

1 Latin: 'Farewell'.

1833 *El ingenioso hidalgo don Quijote de la Mancha* / Miguel de Cervantes Saavedra. Edición IV Centenario : adornada con 356 grabados de Gustavo Doré / enteramente comentada por Clemencín, y precedida de un estudio crítico de Luis Astrana Marín ; más un índice resumen de los ilustradores y comentadores del Quijote por Justo García Morales. Madrid : Ediciones Castilla, [1947?]
cviii, 2008 p. : ill. ; 19 cm.

1947 *El ingenioso hidalgo don Quijote de la Mancha* / de Miguel de Cervantes Saavedra. Nueva edición crítica, con el comento refundido y mejorado y más de mil notas nueva / dispuesta por Francisco Rodríguez Marín. Madrid : Ediciones Atlas, 1947-1949.
10 v. : ill. ; 22 cm.
First ed.: Madrid : Tipografía de la Revista de Archivos, Bibliotecas, y Museos, 1917. 4 v.

1950 *Don Quijote de la Mancha* / Miguel de Cervantes Saavedra ; texto y notas de Martín de Riquer. 3a. ed., con anotación ampliada y un índice onomástico y de situaciones. Paris : Librairie des Editions Espagnoles, 1955.
1143 p. : 1 fold. map ; 19 cm.

1987 *El ingenioso hidalgo don Quijote de La Mancha* / Miguel de Cervantes Saavedra ; edición crítica y comentario de Vicente Gaos ; [llevada a cabo por Agustín del Campo]. Madrid : Editorial Gredos, 1987.
3 v. ; 26 cm. (Biblioteca románica hispánica ; IV, Textos ; 18)
Contents: v. 1-2. Texto – v. 3. Apéndices, gramática, bibliografía, e índices.

1998 *Don Quijote de la Mancha* / Miguel de Cervantes ; edición del Instituto Cervantes ; dirigida por Francisco Rico. 2a ed. corregida. Barcelona : Editorial Crítica, c1998.
2 v. (cclxxxvi, 1247, 1294 p.) : ill., facsims., 21 cm. + 1 CD-ROM (4 3/4 cm.) + Guía de uso (44 p. ; 20 cm.)
Vol. [1] is in the series: (Biblioteca clásica ; 50)
Vol. [2] called: Volumen complementario.

2004 *Don Quijote de la Mancha* / Miguel de Cervantes ; [edición y notas de Francisco Rico]. Edición del IV Centenario. Madrid] : Real Academia Española, 2004.
ci, 1249 p. : facsims. ; 21 cm.
Differs from the 1998 ed. by including a different set of essays, footnotes, and bibliography.
"Glosario": (p. 1157-1235)

ENGLISH TRANSLATIONS

1612-20 (Thomas Shelton)

The history of Don Quixote of The Mancha / translated from the Spanish of Miguel de Cervantes by Thomas Shelton ; with a new preface by F.J. Harvey Darton, and illustrated with two portraits, eighteen plates, and facsimiles. London : Privately printed for the Navarre Society Limited, 1923.
2 v. : ill. ; 23 cm.
Original title: The history of the valorous and wittie knight-errant Don Quixote of The Mancha.
Includes 156 footnotes.

1700-03 (P.A. Motteux, revised by J. Ozell in 1719)

Don Quixote / Miguel de Cervantes Saavedra; translated by P.A. Motteux ; introduction and notes by Stephen Boyd. [Complete and unabridged]. Hertfordshire : Wordsworth Editions Limited, 2000.
xvi, 765 p. ; 20 cm. (Wordsworth classics)
Original title: The history of the renowned Don Quixote de la Mancha.
Includes 258 original footnotes and 105 notes by the editor.

1742 (Charles Jarvis)

Don Quixote de la Mancha / Miguel de Cervantes Saavedra ; translated by Charles Jarvis ; edited, with an introd., by E.C. Riley. Oxford, New York : Oxford University Press, 1992.
xxii, 1087 p. ; 19 cm. (The world's classics)
Includes 578 endnotes.

1755 (Tobias Smollett)

The adventures of Don Quixote de La Mancha / by Miguel de Cervantes ; translated by Tobias Smollett ; with an introd. by Carlos Fuentes. New York : Farrar, Straus, Giroux, 1986.
xxxi, 846 p. : ill. ; 23 cm.
Original title: The history and adventures of the renowned Don Quixote.
Includes 189 footnotes.

(The following entry is a modern revision)

2004 (Tobias Smollett/Carole Slade)

Don Quixote / Miguel de Cervantes ; translated by Tobias Smollett ; revised by Carole Slate ; with an introduction and notes by Carole Slate ; illustrations by Gustave Doré. New York : Barnes & Noble Classics, c2004.
xxvi, 902 p. : ill. ; 21 cm.

1818 (Mary Smirke)

Don Quixote de la Mancha / translated from the Spanish of Miguel de Cervantes Saavedra [by Mary Smirke] ; embellished with engravings from pictures painted by Robert Smirke. [1st ed.] London : Printed for T. Cadell and W. Davies, 1818.
4 v. : 50 plates ; 24 cm.
Virtually a cribbing of the Charles Jarvis translation with a few minor changes and additions by the 'translator.'
The name of the translator, who refers to herself as the editor, does not appear in the publication.
Includes 135 footnotes.

1881 (A.J. Duffield)

The ingenious knight Don Quixote de la Mancha / composed by Miguel de Cervantes Saavedra ; a new translation from the originals of 1605 and 1608 [sic] by Alexander James Duffield, with some of the notes of the Reverend John Bowle, Juan Antonio Pellicer, Don Diego Clemencín, and other commentators. [1st ed.]. London : C. Kegan Paul, 1881.
3 v. ; 24 cm.
Includes 357 endnotes.

1885 (John Ormsby)

Don Quixote, the Ingenious Gentleman of La Mancha / by Miguel de Cervantes Saavedra ; the translation by John Ormsby, with a new introduction by Irwin Edman ; and the illustrations by Edy Legrand. New York : Heritage Press, c1950.
682 p., [48] leaves of plates : ill. ; 29 cm.
Original title: The ingenious gentleman, Don Quixote of La Mancha.
Includes 828 endnotes.

(The following entry is a modern revision)

1981 (John Ormsby/Joseph R. Jones and Kenneth Douglas)

Don Quixote : the Ormsby translation revised, back-grounds, and sources criticism / edited by Joseph R. Jones and Kenneth Douglas. New York : W.W. Norton, 1981.
xiii, 1003 p. ; 22 cm. (A Norton critical edition)
At head of title: Miguel de Cervantes.
Includes 411 footnotes on the Don Quixote text.

1888 (Henry Edward Watts)

The ingenious gentleman Don Quixote of La Mancha / by Miguel de Cervantes Saavedra ; done into English by Henry Edward Watts. New ed., with notes, original and selected. London : Adam and Charles Black, 1895.
5 v. ; 22 cm.
Original title: The ingenious gentleman Don Quixote of La Mancha.
Contents: v. 1-4, Don Quixote – v. 5, The life of Cervantes.
Set lacks vol. 5.
Includes 2043 footnotes.

1908 (Robinson Smith)

The visionary gentleman Don Quijote de La Mancha / by Miguel de Cervantes Saavedra ; translated into English by Robinson Smith. 3d ed., complete with a life of Cervantes, notes, and appendices. New York : Hispanic Society of America, 1932.
2 v. ; 24 cm.
Original title: That imaginative gentleman Don Quixote de la Mancha.
Includes 1182 endnotes.

1949 (Samuel Putnam)

The ingenious gentleman Don Quixote de La Mancha / Miguel de Cervantes Saavedra : a new translation from the Spanish ... by Samuel Putnam. New edition. New York : Viking Press, 1958.
xxx, 1043 p. ; 24 cm.
Original title: The ingenious gentleman Don Quixote de La Mancha.
Includes 1652 endnotes.

1950 (J.M. Cohen)

The adventures of Don Quixote / by Miguel de Cervantes Saavedra ; translated by J.M. Cohen. [1st ed.]. Harmondsworth, Eng. : Penguin Books, 1950.
940 p. ; 20 cm. (Penguin classics)
Includes five footnotes.

1964 (Walter Starkie)

Don Quixote of La Mancha / Miguel de Cervantes Saavedra ; translated and with an introd. by Walter Starkie. [1st ed.]. New York : New American Library, 1964.
1052 p. ; 18 cm. (Signet classics)
Includes 357 footnotes.

1995 (Burton Raffel)

The history of that ingenious gentleman Don Quijote de la Mancha / Miguel de Cervantes Saavedra ; translated from the Spanish by Burton Raffel ; introd. by Diana de Armas Wilson. [1st ed.]. New York : W.W. Norton, 1995.
xviii, 733 p. ; 24 cm.
Includes 232 footnotes and numerous bracketed notes in the text itself.

2000 (John Rutherford)

The ingenious hidalgo Don Quijote de la Mancha / Miguel de Cervantes Saavedra ; translated by John Rutherford. [1st ed.]. NY : Penguin Books, 2001, c2000.
xl, 1023 p. ; 20 cm.
Includes 737 footnotes.

2003 (Edith Grossman)

Don Quixote : a new translation / by Edith Grossman ; introduction by Harold Bloom. [1st ed.] New York : ecc, 2003.
xxxv, 940 p. ; 24 cm.
Includes 666 footnotes

2006 Tom Lathrop has just published a translation of *Don Quixote* but it arrived too late to be incorporated into my work.

TRANSLATIONS IN OTHER LANGUAGES

French: (1836)
L'ingénieux hidalgo Don Quichotte de la Manche / Cervantès ; (1836) [traduction de Louis Viardot avec préface, bibliographie et notes par Maurice Bardon]. Paris : Editions Garniers Frères, c1961.
xxxii, 1089 p., [8] p. of plates : ill. ; 19 cm.

German: *(1799)*
Leben und Taten des scharfsinnigen Edlen Don Quixote von La Mancha / Miguel de Cervantes Saavedra ; mit Zeichnungen von Gerhart Kraaz in der Übertragung von Ludwig Tieck ; Geleitwort von Heinrich Heine. [Gütersloh?] : Bertelsmann-Lesering, c1961.
1055 p. : ill. ; 25 cm.

Italian: (1818) *Don Chisciotte della Mancha* / Michele Cervantes di Saavedra ; illustrazioni de Gustave Doré. Ginevra : Edizioni Ferni, c1975.
2 v. (372, 410 p.) : ill. ; 23 cm.
Translated by Bartolomeo Gamba.

Portuguese (1876) *O engenhoso fidalgo Dom Quixote de la Mancha* / Miguel de Cervantes ; [tradução dos Viscondes de Castilho e de Azevedo]. Mem Martins [Portugal] : Publicações Europa-America, c2004.
842 p. ; 22 cm. (Clássicos ; 74)
Translated by Antonio Feliciano de Castilho (1800-1875) and Francisco Lopes de Azevedo Velho da Fonseca, conde de Azevedo (1809-1876)

LINGUISTIC STUDIES OF DON QUIXOTE

1949 Hatzfeld, Helmut. El "Quijote" como obra de arte del lenguaje. 2a ed. refundida y aumentada. Madrid : Consejo Superior de Investigaciones Científicas, Instituto Miguel de Cervantes, [1966], 1972 printing.
vi, 371 p. ; 25 cm. (Revista de filología española. Anejo ; 83)
Includes bibliography (p. [366]-368) and author index.

1971 Rosenblat, Ángel. La lengua del "Quijote". Madrid : Editorial Gredos, c1971.
380 p. ; 20 cm. (Biblioteca románica hispánica. II, Estudios y ensayos ; 158)
Includes bibliography (p. [365]-367) and index.

216220

Made in the USA